Agatha Christie is known throughout the world as the Queen of Crime. Her books have sold over a billion copies in English with another billion in foreign languages. She is the most widely published author of all time and in any language, outsold only by the Bible and Shakespeare. She is the author of 80 crime novels and short story collections, 19 plays, and six novels written under the name of Mary Westmacott.

Agatha Christie's first novel, *The Mysterious Affair at Styles*, was written towards the end of the First World War, in which she served as a VAD. In it she created Hercule Poirot, the little Belgian detective who was destined to become the most popular detective in crime fiction since Sherlock Holmes. It was eventually published by The Bodley Head in 1920.

In 1926, after averaging a book a year, Agatha Christie wrote her masterpiece. *The Murder of Roger Ackroyd* was the first of her books to be published by Collins and marked the beginning of an author-publisher relationship which lasted for 50 years and well over 70 books. *The Murder of Roger Ackroyd* was also the first of Agatha Christie's books to be dramatized – under the name *Alibi* – and to have a successful run in London's West End. *The Mousetrap*, her most famous play of all, opened in 1952 and is the longest-running play in history.

Agatha Christie was made a Dame in 1971. She died in 1976, since when a number of books have been published posthumously: the bestselling novel *Sleeping Murder* appeared later that year, followed by her autobiography and the short story collections *Miss Marple's Final Cases*, *Problem at Pollensa Bay* and *While the Light Lasts*. In 1998 *Black Coffee* was the first of her plays to be novelized by another author, Charles Osborne.

THE AGATHA CHRISTIE COLLECTION

Agatha Christie

SEVEN DEADLY SINS

·

THE ABC MURDERS

·

A MURDER IS ANNOUNCED

·

SPARKLING CYANIDE

·

EVIL UNDER THE SUN

·

AT BERTRAM'S HOTEL

·

ENDLESS NIGHT

·

FIVE LITTLE PIGS

·

HarperCollins*Publishers*

HarperCollins*Publishers*
77–85 Fulham Palace Road,
Hammersmith, London W6 8JB
www.harpercollins.co.uk

This edition first published 2004
1 3 5 7 9 8 6 4 2

ISBN 0 00 717114 5

Typeset in Plantin Light and Gill Sans by
Palimpsest Book Production Limited,
Polmont, Stirlingshire

Printed and bound in Great Britain by
Clays Ltd, St Ives plc

CONTENTS

I don't know if I am the only one to have observed that the work of my grandmother, Agatha Christie, has become identified in this twenty-first century as a record of the period in which she was writing. Her many books are indeed a piece of history, looked back at with nostalgia by those of us who are old enough to remember the times, and with curiosity and fascination by those too young to recall the six decades in question – the 1920s to the 1970s – during which her books were written and published. And, of course, television provides a very vivid portrayal of those years, which then become fixed in viewers' minds. To me, it is interesting and rather reassuring that, in a time of such fundamental change in our society as we are living through today, a body of work as truly British and traditional as my grandmother's remains so enduringly popular.

Seven Deadly Sins, however, reminds us that my grandmother, despite the cosy façade, wrote about the grisly subject of murder and actually cared very much about the circumstances, motives and emotions that came before and after the wicked deed. She believed very strongly in the existence of good and evil, and in particular in the very powerful – at times almost uncontrollable – influence that evil can have on people. I think it is the compulsion of reading about or watching very believable characters becoming caught up in the web spun by evil, and how the otherwise tranquil surroundings in which people live and work can be irretrievably ruptured by evil, that is at least as persuasive a reason why Agatha Christie's books remain so popular as is people's nostalgia for the past.

This impressive collection, possibly the chunkiest Agatha Christie omnibus ever published, contains seven of her very best novels. They are certainly seven of my favourites (particularly *Endless Night* and *Five Little Pigs* – in my opinion two little-known masterpieces), which is a pleasing coincidence because I had no input in the final choice! The Seven Deadly Sins are Pride, Envy, Sloth, Lust, Gluttony, Avarice and Wrath, apparently determined by the sixth-century Pope, Gregory the Great. Commit a Deadly Sin and you would end up in Hell! The books in this collection have been carefully chosen so that the plot of each one represents one of the Deadly Sins, although when you have read them you may agree with me that many of the stories include a whole number of Sins!

I believe my grandmother would have thoroughly approved of this selection. Deadly 'Motives for Murder' notwithstanding, it provides seven classic examples of her talents as a skilful weaver of mysteries, as well as demonstrating her great insight and sympathy for human nature. I hope you enjoy them.

Mathew Prichard
June 2004

PRIDE

•

THE ABC MURDERS

To James Watts
One of my most sympathetic readers

BY CAPTAIN ARTHUR HASTINGS, O.B.E.

In this narrative of mine I have departed from my usual practice of relating only those incidents and scenes at which I myself was present. Certain chapters, therefore, are written in the third person.

I wish to assure my readers that I can vouch for the occurrences related in these chapters. If I have taken a certain poetic licence in describing the thoughts and feelings of various persons, it is because I believe I have set them down with a reasonable amount of accuracy. I may add that they have been 'vetted' by my friend Hercule Poirot himself.

In conclusion, I will say that if I have described at too great length some of the secondary personal relationships which arose as a consequence of this strange series of crimes, it is because the human and personal elements can never be ignored. Hercule Poirot once taught me in a very dramatic manner that romance can be a by-product of crime.

As to the solving of the A B C mystery, I can only say that in my opinion Poirot showed real genius in the way he tackled a problem entirely unlike any which had previously come his way.

CHAPTER I

THE LETTER

It was in June of 1935 that I came home from my ranch in South America for a stay of about six months. It had been a difficult time for us out there. Like everyone else, we had suffered from world depression. I had various affairs to see to in England that I felt could only be successful if a personal touch was introduced. My wife remained to manage the ranch.

I need hardly say that one of my first actions on reaching England was to look up my old friend, Hercule Poirot.

I found him installed in one of the newest type of service flats in London. I accused him (and he admitted the fact) of having chosen this particular building entirely on account of its strictly geometrical appearance and proportions.

'But yes, my friend, it is of a most pleasing symmetry, do you not find it so?'

I said that I thought there could be too much squareness and, alluding to an old joke, I asked if in this super-modern hostelry they managed to induce hens to lay square eggs.

Poirot laughed heartily.

'Ah, you remember that? Alas! no – science has not yet induced the hens to conform to modern tastes, they still lay eggs of different sizes and colours!'

I examined my old friend with an affectionate eye. He was looking wonderfully well – hardly a day older than when I had last seen him.

'You're looking in fine fettle, Poirot,' I said. 'You've hardly aged at all. In fact, if it were possible, I should say that you had fewer grey hairs than when I saw you last.'

Poirot beamed on me.

'And why is that not possible? It is quite true.'

'Do you mean your hair is turning from grey to black instead of from black to grey?'

'Precisely.'

'But surely that's a scientific impossibility!'

'Not at all.'

'But that's very extraordinary. It seems against nature.'

'As usual, Hastings, you have the beautiful and unsuspicious mind. Years do not change that in you! You perceive a fact and mention the solution of it in the same breath without noticing that you are doing so!'

I stared at him, puzzled.

Without a word he walked into his bedroom and returned with a bottle in his hand which he handed to me.

I took it, for the moment uncomprehending.

It bore the words:

Revivit. – To bring back the natural tone of the hair. *Revivit* is *not* a dye. In five shades, Ash, Chestnut, Titian, Brown, Black.

'Poirot,' I cried. 'You have dyed your hair!'

'Ah, the comprehension comes to you!'

'So *that's* why your hair looks so much blacker than it did last time I was back.'

'Exactly.'

'Dear me,' I said, recovering from the shock. 'I suppose next time I come home I shall find you wearing false moustaches – or are you doing so now?'

Poirot winced. His moustaches had always been his sensitive point. He was inordinately proud of them. My words touched him on the raw.

'No, no, indeed, *mon ami*. That day, I pray the good God, is still far off. The false moustache! *Quelle horreur!*'

He tugged at them vigorously to assure me of their genuine character.

'Well, they are very luxuriant still,' I said.

'*N'est-ce pas?* Never, in the whole of London, have I seen a pair of moustaches to equal mine.'

A good job too, I thought privately. But I would not for the world have hurt Poirot's feelings by saying so.

Instead I asked if he still practised his profession on occasion.

'I know,' I said, 'that you actually retired years ago –'

'*C'est vrai*. To grow the vegetable marrows! And immediately a murder occurs – and I send the vegetable marrows to promenade themselves to the devil. And since then – I know very well what you will say – I am like the prima donna who makes positively the farewell performance! That farewell performance, it repeats itself an indefinite number of times!'

I laughed.

'In truth, it has been very like that. Each time I say: this is the end. But no, something else arises! And I will admit it, my friend, the retirement I care for it not at all. If the little grey cells are not exercised, they grow the rust.'

'I see,' I said. 'You exercise them in moderation.'

'Precisely. I pick and choose. For Hercule Poirot nowadays only the cream of crime.'

'Has there been much cream about?'

'*Pas mal*. Not long ago I had a narrow escape.'

'Of failure?'

'No, no.' Poirot looked shocked. 'But I – *I, Hercule Poirot*, was nearly exterminated.'

I whistled.

'An enterprising murderer!'

'Not so much enterprising as careless,' said Poirot. 'Precisely that – careless. But let us not talk of it. You know, Hastings, in many ways I regard you as my mascot.'

'Indeed?' I said. 'In what ways?'

Poirot did not answer my question directly. He went on:

'As soon as I heard you were coming over I said to myself: something will arise. As in former days we will hunt together, we two. But if so it must be no common affair. It must be something' – he waved his hands excitedly – 'something *recherché* – delicate – *fine* . . .' He gave the last untranslatable word its full flavour.

'Upon my word, Poirot,' I said. 'Anyone would think you were ordering a dinner at the Ritz.'

'Whereas one cannot command a crime to order? Very true.' He sighed. 'But I believe in luck – in destiny, if you will. It is your destiny to stand beside me and prevent me from committing the unforgivable error.'

'What do you call the unforgivable error?'

'Overlooking the obvious.'

I turned this over in my mind without quite seeing the point.

'Well,' I said presently, smiling, 'has this super crime turned up yet?'

'*Pas encore.* At least – that is –'

He paused. A frown of perplexity creased his forehead. His hands automatically straightened an object or two that I had inadvertently pushed awry.

'I am not sure,' he said slowly.

There was something so odd about his tone that I looked at him in surprise.

The frown still lingered.

Suddenly with a brief decisive nod of the head he crossed the room to a desk near the window. Its contents, I need hardly say, were all neatly docketed and pigeon-holed so that he was able at once to lay his hand upon the paper he wanted.

He came slowly across to me, an open letter in his hand. He read it through himself, then passed it to me.

'Tell me, *mon ami*,' he said. 'What do you make of this?'

I took it from him with some interest.

It was written on thickish white notepaper in printed characters:

Mr Hercule Poirot, – You fancy yourself, don't you, at solving mysteries that are too difficult for our poor thick-headed British police? Let us see, Mr Clever Poirot, just how clever you can be. Perhaps you'll find this nut too hard to crack. Look out for Andover, on the 21st of the month.

   Yours, etc.,

   A B C.

I glanced at the envelope. That also was printed.

'Postmarked WC1,' said Poirot as I turned my attention to the postmark. 'Well, what is your opinion?'

I shrugged my shoulders as I handed it back to him.

'Some madman or other, I suppose.'

'That is all you have to say?'

'Well – doesn't it sound like a madman to you?'

'Yes, my friend, it does.'

His tone was grave. I looked at him curiously.

'You take this very seriously, Poirot.'

'A madman, *mon ami,* is to be taken seriously. A madman is a very dangerous thing.'

'Yes, of course, that is true . . . I hadn't considered that point . . . But what I meant was, it sounds more like a rather idiotic kind of hoax. Perhaps some convivial idiot who had had one over the eight.'

'*Comment?* Nine? Nine what?'

'Nothing – just an expression. I meant a fellow who was tight. No, damn it, a fellow who had had a spot too much to drink.'

'*Merci,* Hastings – the expression "tight" I *am* acquainted with it. As you say, there may be nothing more to it than that . . .'

'But you think there is?' I asked, struck by the dissatisfaction of his tone.

Poirot shook his head doubtfully, but he did not speak.

'What have you done about it?' I inquired.

'What can one do? I showed it to Japp. He was of the same opinion as you – a stupid hoax – that was the expression he used. They get these things every day at Scotland Yard. I, too, have had my share . . .'

'But you take this one seriously?'

Poirot replied slowly.

'There is something about that letter, Hastings, that I do not like . . .'

In spite of myself, his tone impressed me.

'You think – what?'

He shook his head, and picking up the letter, put it away again in the desk.

'If you really take it seriously, can't you do something?' I asked.

'As always, the man of action! But what is there to do? The county police have seen the letter but they, too, do not take it seriously. There are no fingerprints on it. There are no local clues as to the possible writer.'

'In fact there is only your own instinct?'

'Not instinct, Hastings. Instinct is a bad word. It is my *knowledge* – my *experience* – that tells me that something about that letter is wrong –'

He gesticulated as words failed him, then shook his head again.

'I may be making the mountain out of the anthill. In any case there is nothing to be done but wait.'

'Well, the 21st is Friday. If a whacking great robbery takes place near Andover then –'

'Ah, what a comfort that would be –!'

'*A comfort?*' I stared. The word seemed to be a very extraordinary one to use.

'A robbery may be a *thrill* but it can hardly be a comfort!' I protested. Poirot shook his head energetically.

'You are in error, my friend. You do not understand my meaning. A robbery would be a relief since it would dispossess my mind of the fear of something else.'

'Of what?'

'*Murder*,' said Hercule Poirot.

<hr>

CHAPTER 2

NOT FROM CAPTAIN HASTINGS' PERSONAL NARRATIVE

Mr Alexander Bonaparte Cust rose from his seat and peered near-sightedly round the shabby bedroom. His back was stiff from sitting in a cramped position and as he stretched himself to his full height an onlooker would have realized that he was, in reality, quite a tall man. His stoop and his near-sighted peering gave a delusive impression.

Going to a well-worn overcoat hanging on the back of the door, he took from the pocket a packet of cheap cigarettes and some matches. He lit a cigarette and then returned to the table at which he had been sitting. He picked up a railway guide and consulted it, then he returned to the consideration of a typewritten list of names. With a pen, he made a tick against one of the first names on the list.

It was Thursday, June 20th.

CHAPTER 3

ANDOVER

I had been impressed at the time by Poirot's forebodings about the anonymous letter he had received, but I must admit that the matter had passed from my mind when the 21st actually arrived and the first reminder of it came with a visit paid to my friend by Chief Inspector Japp of Scotland Yard. The CID inspector had been known to us for many years and he gave me a hearty welcome.

'Well, I never,' he exclaimed. 'If it isn't Captain Hastings back from the wilds of the what do you call it! Quite like old days seeing you here with Monsieur Poirot. You're looking well, too. Just a little bit thin on top, eh? Well, that's what we're all coming to. I'm the same.'

I winced slightly. I was under the impression that owing to the careful way I brushed my hair across the top of my head the thinness referred to by Japp was quite unnoticeable. However, Japp had never been remarkable for tact where I was concerned, so I put a good face upon it and agreed that we were none of us getting any younger.

'Except Monsieur Poirot here,' said Japp. 'Quite a good advertisement for a hair tonic, he'd be. Face fungus sprouting finer than ever. Coming out into the limelight, too, in his old age. Mixed up in all the celebrated cases of the day. Train mysteries, air mysteries, high society deaths – oh, he's here, there and everywhere. Never been so celebrated as since he retired.'

'I have already told Hastings that I am like the prima donna who makes always one more appearance,' said Poirot, smiling.

'I shouldn't wonder if you ended by detecting your own death,' said Japp, laughing heartily. 'That's an idea, that is. Ought to be put in a book.'

'It will be Hastings who will have to do that,' said Poirot, twinkling at me.

'Ha ha! That would be a joke, that would,' laughed Japp.

I failed to see why the idea was so extremely amusing, and in any case I thought the joke was in poor taste. Poirot, poor old chap, is getting on. Jokes about his approaching demise can hardly be agreeable to him.

Perhaps my manner showed my feelings, for Japp changed the subject.

'Have you heard about Monsieur Poirot's anonymous letter?'

'I showed it to Hastings the other day,' said my friend.

'Of course,' I exclaimed. 'It had quite slipped my memory. Let me see, what was the date mentioned?'

'The 21st,' said Japp. 'That's what I dropped in about. Yesterday was the 21st and just out of curiosity I rang up Andover last night. It was a hoax all right. Nothing doing. One broken shop window – kid throwing stones – and a couple of drunk and disorderlies. So just for once our Belgian friend was barking up the wrong tree.'

'I am relieved, I must confess,' acknowledged Poirot.

'You'd quite got the wind up about it, hadn't you?' said Japp affectionately. 'Bless you, we get dozens of letters like that coming in every day! People with nothing better to do and a bit weak in the top storey sit down and write 'em. They don't mean any harm! Just a kind of excitement.'

'I have indeed been foolish to take the matter so seriously,' said Poirot. 'It is the nest of the horse that I put my nose into there.'

'You're mixing up mares and wasps,' said Japp.

'*Pardon?*'

'Just a couple of proverbs. Well, I must be off. Got a little business in the next street to see to – receiving stolen jewellery. I thought I'd just drop in on my way and put your mind at rest. Pity to let those grey cells function unnecessarily.'

With which words and a hearty laugh, Japp departed.

'He does not change much, the good Japp, eh?' asked Poirot.

'He looks much older,' I said. 'Getting as grey as a badger,' I added vindictively.

Poirot coughed and said:

'You know, Hastings, there is a little device – my hairdresser is a man of great ingenuity – one attaches it to the scalp and brushes one's own hair over it – it is not a wig, you comprehend – but –'

'Poirot,' I roared. 'Once and for all I will have nothing to do with the beastly inventions of your confounded hairdresser. What's the matter with the top of my head?'

'Nothing – nothing at all.'

'It's not as though I were going *bald*.'

'Of course not! Of course not!'

'The hot summers out there naturally cause the hair to fall out a bit. I shall take back a really good hair tonic.'

'*Précisément.*'

'And, anyway, what business is it of Japp's? He always was an offensive kind of devil. And no sense of humour. The kind of man who laughs when a chair is pulled away just as a man is about to sit down.'

'A great many people would laugh at that.'

'It's utterly senseless.'

'From the point of view of the man about to sit, certainly it is.'

'Well,' I said, slightly recovering my temper. (I admit that I am touchy about the thinness of my hair.) 'I'm sorry that anonymous letter business came to nothing.'

'I have indeed been in the wrong over that. About that letter, there was, I thought, the odour of the fish. Instead a mere stupidity. Alas, I grow old and suspicious like the blind watch-dog who growls when there is nothing there.'

'If I'm going to co-operate with you, we must look about for some other "creamy" crime,' I said with a laugh.

'You remember your remark of the other day? If you could order a crime as one orders a dinner, what would you choose?'

I fell in with his humour.

'Let me see now. Let's review the menu. Robbery? Forgery? No, I think not. Rather too vegetarian. It must be murder – red-blooded murder – with trimmings, of course.'

'Naturally. The *hors d'oeuvres.*'

'Who shall the victim be – man or woman? Man, I think. Some big-wig. American millionaire. Prime Minister. Newspaper proprietor. Scene of the crime – well, what's wrong with the good old library? Nothing like it for atmosphere. As for the weapon – well, it might be a curiously twisted dagger – or some blunt instrument – a carved stone idol –'

Poirot sighed.

'Or, of course,' I said, 'there's poison – but that's always so technical. Or a revolver shot echoing in the night. Then there must be a beautiful girl or two –'

'With auburn hair,' murmured my friend.

'Your same old joke. One of the beautiful girls, of course, must be unjustly suspected – and there's some misunderstanding between her and the young man. And then, of course, there must be some other suspects – an older woman – dark, dangerous type – and some friend or rival of the dead man's – and a quiet secretary – dark horse – and a hearty man with a bluff manner – and a couple of discharged servants or gamekeepers or somethings – and a damn fool of a detective rather like Japp – and well – that's about all.'

'That is your idea of the cream, eh?'

'I gather you don't agree.'

Poirot looked at me sadly.

'You have made there a very pretty résumé of nearly all the detective stories that have ever been written.'

'Well,' I said. 'What would *you* order?'

Poirot closed his eyes and leaned back in his chair. His voice came purringly from between his lips.

'A very simple crime. A crime with no complications. A crime of quiet domestic life . . . very unimpassioned – very *intime*.'

'How can a crime be *intime*?'

'Supposing,' murmured Poirot, 'that four people sit down to play bridge and one, the odd man out, sits in a chair by the fire. At the end of the evening the man by the fire is found dead. One of the four, while he is dummy, has gone over and killed him, and intent on the play of the hand, the other three have not noticed. Ah, there would be a crime for you! *Which of the four was it?*'

'Well,' I said. 'I can't see *any* excitement in that!'

Poirot threw me a glance of reproof.

'No, because there are no curiously twisted daggers, no blackmail, no emerald that is the stolen eye of a god, no untraceable Eastern poisons. You have the melodramatic soul, Hastings. You would like, not one murder, but a series of murders.'

'I admit,' I said, 'that a second murder in a book often cheers things up. If the murder happens in the first chapter, and you have to follow up everybody's alibi until the last page but one – well, it does get a bit tedious.'

The telephone rang and Poirot rose to answer.

''*Allô*,' he said. ''*Allô*. Yes, it is Hercule Poirot speaking.'

He listened for a minute or two and then I saw his face change.

His own side of the conversation was short and disjointed.

'*Mais oui* . . .'

'Yes, of course . . .'

'But yes, we will come . . .'

'Naturally . . .'

'It may be as you say . . .'

'Yes, I will bring it. *A tout à l'heure* then.'

He replaced the receiver and came across the room to me.

'That was Japp speaking, Hastings.'

'Yes?'

'He had just got back to the Yard. There was a message from Andover . . .'

'Andover?' I cried excitedly.

Poirot said slowly:

'An old woman of the name of Ascher who keeps a little tobacco and newspaper shop has been found murdered.'

I think I felt ever so slightly damped. My interest, quickened by the sound of Andover, suffered a faint check. I had expected something fantastic – out of the way! The murder of an old woman who kept a little tobacco shop seemed, somehow, sordid and uninteresting.

Poirot continued in the same slow, grave voice:

'The Andover police believe they can put their hand on the man who did it –'

I felt a second throb of disappointment.

'It seems the woman was on bad terms with her husband. He drinks and is by way of being rather a nasty customer. He's threatened to take her life more than once.

'Nevertheless,' continued Poirot, 'in view of what has happened, the police there would like to have another look at the anonymous letter I received. I have said that you and I will go down to Andover at once.'

My spirits revived a little. After all, sordid as this crime seemed to be, it was a *crime*, and it was a long time since I had had any association with crime and criminals.

I hardly listened to the next words Poirot said. But they were to come back to me with significance later.

'This is the beginning,' said Hercule Poirot.

CHAPTER 4

MRS ASCHER

We were received at Andover by Inspector Glen, a tall fair-haired man with a pleasant smile.

For the sake of conciseness I think I had better give a brief résumé of the bare facts of the case.

The crime was discovered by Police Constable Dover at 1 am on the morning of the 22nd. When on his round he tried the door of the shop and found it unfastened, he entered and at first thought the place was empty. Directing his torch over the counter, however, he caught sight of the huddled-up body of the old woman. When the police surgeon arrived on the spot it was elicited that the woman had been struck down by a heavy blow on the back of the head, probably while she was reaching down a packet of cigarettes from the shelf behind the counter. Death must have occurred about nine to seven hours previously.

'But we've been able to get it down a bit nearer than that,' explained the inspector. 'We've found a man who went in and bought some tobacco at 5.30. And a second man went in and found the shop empty, as he thought, at five minutes past six. That puts the time at between 5.30 and 6.05. So far I haven't been able to find anyone who saw this man Ascher in the neighbourhood, but, of course, it's early as yet. He was in the Three Crowns at nine o'clock pretty far gone in drink. When we get hold of him he'll be detained on suspicion.'

'Not a very desirable character, inspector?' asked Poirot.

'Unpleasant bit of goods.'

'He didn't live with his wife?'

'No, they separated some years ago. Ascher's a German. He was a waiter at one time, but he took to drink and gradually became unemployable. His wife went into service for a bit. Her last place was as cook-housekeeper to an old lady, Miss Rose. She allowed her husband so much out of her wages to keep himself, but he was always getting drunk and coming round and making scenes at the places where she was employed. That's why she took the post with Miss Rose at The Grange. It's three miles out of Andover, dead in the country. He couldn't get at her there so well. When Miss Rose died, she left Mrs Ascher a small legacy, and the woman started this tobacco and newsagent business – quite a tiny place – just cheap cigarettes and a few newspapers – that sort of thing. She just about managed to keep going. Ascher used to come round and abuse her now and again and she used to give him a bit to get rid of him. She allowed him fifteen shillings a week regular.'

'Had they any children?' asked Poirot.

'No. There's a niece. She's in service near Overton. Very superior, steady young woman.'

'And you say this man Ascher used to threaten his wife?'

'That's right. He was a terror when he was in drink – cursing and swearing that he'd bash her head in. She had a hard time, did Mrs Ascher.'

'What age of woman was she?'

'Close on sixty – respectable and hard-working.'

Poirot said gravely:

'It is your opinion, inspector, that this man Ascher committed the crime?'

The inspector coughed cautiously.

'It's a bit early to say that, Mr Poirot, but I'd like to hear Franz Ascher's own account of how he spent yesterday evening. If he can give a satisfactory account of himself, well and good – if not –'

His pause was a pregnant one.

'Nothing was missing from the shop?'

'Nothing. Money in the till quite undisturbed. No signs of robbery.'

'You think that this man Ascher came into the shop drunk, started abusing his wife and finally struck her down?'

'It seems the most likely solution. But I must confess, sir, I'd like to have another look at that very odd letter you received. I was wondering if it was just possible that it came from this man Ascher.'

Poirot handed over the letter and the inspector read it with a frown.

'It doesn't read like Ascher,' he said at last. 'I doubt if Ascher would use the term "our" British police – not unless he was trying to be extra cunning – and I doubt if he's got the wits for that. Then the man's a wreck – all to pieces. His hand's too shaky to print letters clearly like this. It's good-quality notepaper and ink, too. It's odd that the letter should mention the 21st of the month. Of course it *might* be coincidence.'

'That is possible – yes.'

'But I don't like this kind of coincidence, Mr Poirot. It's a bit too pat.'

He was silent for a minute or two – a frown creasing his forehead.

'A B C. Who the devil could A B C be? We'll see if Mary Drower (that's the niece) can give us any help. It's an odd business. But for this letter I'd have put my money on Franz Ascher for a certainty.'

'Do you know anything of Mrs Ascher's past?'

'She's a Hampshire woman. Went into service as a girl up in London – that's where she met Ascher and married him. Things must have been difficult for them during the war. She actually left him for good in 1922. They were in London then. She came back here to get away from him, but he got wind of where she was and followed her down here, pestering her for money –' A constable came in. 'Yes, Briggs, what is it?'

'It's the man Ascher, sir. We've brought him in.'

'Right. Bring him in here. Where was he?'

'Hiding in a truck on the railway siding.'

'He was, was he? Bring him along.'

Franz Ascher was indeed a miserable and unprepossessing specimen. He was blubbering and cringing and blustering alternately. His bleary eyes moved shiftily from one face to another.

'What do you want with me? I have not done nothing. It is a shame and a scandal to bring me here! You are swine, how dare you?' His manner changed suddenly. 'No, no, I do not mean that – you would not hurt a poor old man – not be hard on him. Everyone is hard on poor old Franz. Poor old Franz.'

Mr Ascher started to weep.

'That'll do, Ascher,' said the inspector. 'Pull yourself together. I'm not charging you with anything – yet. And you're not bound to make a statement unless you like. On the other hand, if you're *not* concerned in the murder of your wife –'

Ascher interrupted him – his voice rising to a scream.

'I did not kill her! I did not kill her! It is all lies! You are goddamned English pigs – all against me. I never kill her – never.'

'You threatened to often enough, Ascher.'

'No, no. You do not understand. That was just a joke – a good joke between me and Alice. She understood.'

'Funny kind of joke! Do you care to say where you were yesterday evening, Ascher?'

'Yes, yes – I tell you everything. I did not go near Alice. I am with friends – good friends. We are at the Seven Stars – and then we are at the Red Dog –'

He hurried on, his words stumbling over each other.

'Dick Willows – he was with me – and old Curdie – and George – and Platt and lots of the boys. I tell you I do not never go near Alice. *Ach Gott*, it is the truth I am telling you.'

His voice rose to a scream. The inspector nodded to his underling.

'Take him away. Detained on suspicion.'

'I don't know what to think,' he said as the unpleasant, shaking old man with the malevolent, mouthing jaw was removed. 'If it wasn't for the letter, I'd say he did it.'

'What about the men he mentions?'

'A bad crowd – not one of them would stick at perjury. I've no doubt he *was* with them the greater part of the evening. A lot depends on whether anyone saw him near the shop between half-past five and six.'

Poirot shook his head thoughtfully.

'You are sure nothing was taken from the shop?'

The inspector shrugged his shoulders.

'That depends. A packet or two of cigarettes might have been taken – but you'd hardly commit murder for that.'

'And there was nothing – how shall I put it – introduced into the shop? Nothing that was odd there – incongruous?'

'There was a railway guide,' said the inspector.

'A railway guide?'

'Yes. It was open and turned face downward on the counter. Looked as though someone had been looking up the trains from Andover. Either the old woman or a customer.'

'Did she sell that type of thing?'

The inspector shook his head.

'She sold penny time-tables. This was a big one – kind of thing only Smith's or a big stationer would keep.'

A light came into Poirot's eyes. He leant forward.

A light came into the inspector's eye also.

'A railway guide, you say. A Bradshaw – *or an A B C?*'

'By the lord,' he said. 'It *was* an A B C.'

CHAPTER 5

MARY DROWER

I think that I can date my interest in the case from that first mention of the A B C railway guide. Up till then I had not been able to raise much enthusiasm. This sordid murder of an old woman in a back-street shop was so like the usual type of crime reported in the newspapers that it failed to strike a significant note. In my own mind I had put down the anonymous letter with its mention of the 21st as a mere coincidence. Mrs Ascher, I felt reasonably sure, had been the victim of her drunken brute of a husband. But now the mention of the railway guide (so familiarly known by its abbreviation of A B C, listing as it did all railway stations in their alphabetical order) sent a quiver of excitement through me. Surely – surely this could not be a second coincidence?

The sordid crime took on a new aspect.

Who was the mysterious individual who had killed Mrs Ascher and left an A B C railway guide behind him?

When we left the police station our first visit was to the mortuary to see the body of the dead woman. A strange feeling came over me as I gazed down on that wrinkled old face with the scanty grey hair drawn back tightly from the temples. It looked so peaceful, so incredibly remote from violence.

'Never knew who or what struck her,' observed the sergeant. 'That's what Dr Kerr says. I'm glad it was that way, poor old soul. A decent woman she was.'

'She must have been beautiful once,' said Poirot.

'Really?' I murmured incredulously.

'But yes, look at the line of the jaw, the bones, the moulding of the head.'

He sighed as he replaced the sheet and we left the mortuary.

Our next move was a brief interview with the police surgeon.

Dr Kerr was a competent-looking middle-aged man. He spoke briskly and with decision.

'The weapon wasn't found,' he said. 'Impossible to say what it may have been. A weighted stick, a club, a form of sandbag – any of those would fit the case.'

'Would much force be needed to strike such a blow?'

The doctor shot a keen glance at Poirot.

'Meaning, I suppose, could a shaky old man of seventy do it? Oh, yes, it's perfectly possible – given sufficient weight in the head of the weapon, quite a feeble person could achieve the desired result.'

'Then the murderer could just as well be a woman as a man?'

The suggestion took the doctor somewhat aback.

'A woman, eh? Well, I confess it never occurred to me to connect a woman with this type of crime. But of course it's possible – perfectly possible. Only, psychologically speaking, I shouldn't say this was a woman's crime.'

Poirot nodded his head in eager agreement.

'Perfectly, perfectly. On the face of it, highly improbable. But one must take all possibilities into account. The body was lying – how?'

The doctor gave us a careful description of the position of the victim. It was his opinion that she had been standing with her back to the counter (and therefore to her assailant) when the blow had been struck. She had slipped down in a heap behind the counter quite out of sight of anyone entering the shop casually.

When we had thanked Dr Kerr and taken our leave, Poirot said:

'You perceive, Hastings, that we have already one further point in favour of Ascher's innocence. If he had been abusing his wife and threatening her, she would have been *facing* him over the counter. Instead she had her *back* to her assailant – obviously she is reaching down tobacco or cigarettes for a *customer*.'

I gave a little shiver.

'Pretty gruesome.'

Poirot shook his head gravely.

'*Pauvre femme,*' he murmured.

Then he glanced at his watch.

'Overton is not, I think, many miles from here. Shall we run over there and have an interview with the niece of the dead woman?'

'Surely you will go first to the shop where the crime took place?'

'I prefer to do that later. I have a reason.'

He did not explain further, and a few minutes later we were driving on the London road in the direction of Overton.

The address which the inspector had given us was that of a good-sized house about a mile on the London side of the village.

Our ring at the bell was answered by a pretty dark-haired girl whose eyes were red with recent weeping.

Poirot said gently:

'Ah! I think it is you who are Miss Mary Drower, the parlourmaid here?'

'Yes, sir, that's right. I'm Mary, sir.'

'Then perhaps I can talk to you for a few minutes if your mistress will not object. It is about your aunt, Mrs Ascher.'

'The mistress is out, sir. She wouldn't mind, I'm sure, if you came in here.'

She opened the door of a small morning-room. We entered and Poirot, seating himself on a chair by the window, looked up keenly into the girl's face.

'You have heard of your aunt's death, of course?'

The girl nodded, tears coming once more into her eyes.

'This morning, sir. The police came over. Oh! it's terrible! Poor auntie! Such a hard life as she'd had, too. And now this – it's too awful.'

'The police did not suggest your returning to Andover?'

'They said I must come to the inquest – that's on Monday, sir. But I've nowhere to go there – I couldn't fancy being over the shop – now – and what with the housemaid being away, I didn't want to put the mistress out more than may be.'

'You were fond of your aunt, Mary?' said Poirot gently.

'Indeed I was, sir. Very good she's been to me always, auntie has. I went to her in London when I was eleven years old, after mother died. I started in service when I was sixteen, but I usually went along to auntie's on my day out. A lot of trouble she went through with that German fellow. "My old devil," she used to call him. He'd never let her be in peace anywhere. Sponging, cadging old beast.'

The girl spoke with vehemence.

'Your aunt never thought of freeing herself by legal means from this persecution?'

'Well, you see, he was her husband, sir, you couldn't get away from that.'

The girl spoke simply but with finality.

'Tell me, Mary, he threatened her, did he not?'

'Oh, yes, sir, it was awful the things he used to say. That he'd cut her throat, and such like. Cursing and swearing too – both in German and in English. And yet auntie says he was a fine handsome figure of a man when she married him. It's dreadful to think, sir, what people come to.'

'Yes, indeed. And so, I suppose, Mary, having actually heard these threats, you were not so very surprised when you learnt what had happened?'

'Oh, but I was, sir. You see, sir, I never thought for one moment that he meant it. I thought it was just nasty talk and nothing more to it. And it isn't as though auntie was afraid of him. Why, I've seen him slink away like a dog with its tail between its legs when she turned on him. *He* was afraid of *her* if you like.'

'And yet she gave him money?'

'Well, he was her husband, you see, sir.'

'Yes, so you said before.' He paused for a minute or two. Then he said: 'Suppose that, after all, he did *not* kill her.'

'Didn't kill her?'

She stared.

'That is what I said. Supposing someone else killed her . . . Have you any idea who that someone else could be?'

She stared at him with even more amazement.

'I've no idea, sir. It doesn't seem likely, though, does it?'

'There was no one your aunt was afraid of?'

Mary shook her head.

'Auntie wasn't afraid of people. She'd a sharp tongue and she'd stand up to anybody.'

'You never heard her mention anyone who had a grudge against her?'

'No, indeed, sir.'

'Did she ever get anonymous letters?'

'What kind of letters did you say, sir?'

'Letters that weren't signed – or only signed by something like A B C.' He watched her narrowly, but plainly she was at a loss. She shook her head wonderingly.

'Has your aunt any relations except you?'

'Not now, sir. One of ten she was, but only three lived to grow up. My Uncle Tom was killed in the war, and my Uncle Harry went to South America and no one's heard of him since, and mother's dead, of course, so there's only me.'

'Had your aunt any savings? Any money put by?'

'She'd a little in the Savings Bank, sir – enough to bury her proper, that's what she always said. Otherwise she didn't more than just make ends meet – what with her old devil and all.'

Poirot nodded thoughtfully. He said – perhaps more to himself than to her:

'At present one is in the dark – there is no direction – if things get clearer –' He got up. 'If I want you at any time, Mary, I will write to you here.'

'As a matter of fact, sir, I'm giving in my notice. I don't like the country. I stayed here because I fancied it was a comfort to auntie to have me near by. But now' – again the tears rose in her eyes – 'there's no reason I should stay, and so I'll go back to London. It's gayer for a girl there.'

'I wish that, when you do go, you would give me your address. Here is my card.'

He handed it to her. She looked at it with a puzzled frown.

'Then you're not – anything to do with the police, sir?'

'I am a private detective.'

She stood there looking at him for some moments in silence.

She said at last:

'Is there anything – queer going on, sir?'

'Yes, my child. There is – something queer going on. Later you may be able to help me.'

'I – I'll do anything, sir. It – it wasn't *right*, sir, auntie being killed.'

A strange way of putting it – but deeply moving.

A few seconds later we were driving back to Andover.

CHAPTER 6

THE SCENE OF THE CRIME

The street in which the tragedy had occurred was a turning off the main street. Mrs Ascher's shop was situated about half-way down it on the right-hand side.

As we turned into the street Poirot glanced at his watch and I realized why he had delayed his visit to the scene of the crime until now. It was just on half-past five. He had wished to reproduce yesterday's atmosphere as closely as possible.

But if that had been his purpose it was defeated. Certainly at this moment the road bore very little likeness to its appearance on the previous evening. There were a certain number of small shops interspersed between private houses of the poorer class. I judged that ordinarily there would be a fair number of people passing up and down – mostly people of the poorer classes, with a good sprinkling of children playing on the pavements and in the road.

At this moment there was a solid mass of people standing staring at one particular house or shop and it took little perspicuity to guess which that was. What we saw was a mass of average human beings looking with intense interest at the spot where another human being had been done to death.

As we drew nearer this proved to be indeed the case. In front of a small dingy-looking shop with its shutters now closed stood a harassed-looking young policeman who was stolidly adjuring the crowd to 'pass along there.' By the help of a colleague, displacements took place – a certain number of people grudgingly sighed and betook themselves to their ordinary vocations, and almost immediately other persons came along and took up their stand to gaze their fill on the spot where murder had been committed.

Poirot stopped a little distance from the main body of the crowd. From where we stood the legend painted over the door could be read plainly enough. Poirot repeated it under his breath.

'A. Ascher. *Oui, c'est peut-être là –*'

He broke off.

'Come, let us go inside, Hastings.'

I was only too ready.

We made our way through the crowd and accosted the young policeman. Poirot produced the credentials which the inspector had given him. The constable nodded, and unlocked the door to let us pass within. We did so and entered to the intense interest of the lookers-on.

Inside it was very dark owing to the shutters being closed. The constable found and switched on the electric light. The bulb was a low-powered one so that the interior was still dimly lit.

I looked about me.

A dingy little place. A few cheap magazines strewn about, and yesterday's newspapers – all with a day's dust on them. Behind the counter a row of shelves reaching to the ceiling and packed with tobacco and packets of cigarettes. There were also a couple of jars of peppermint humbugs and barley sugar. A commonplace little shop, one of many thousand such others.

The constable in his slow Hampshire voice was explaining the *mise en scène*.

'Down in a heap behind the counter, that's where she was. Doctor says as how she never knew what hit her. Must have been reaching up to one of the shelves.'

'There was nothing in her hand?'

'No, sir, but there was a packet of Player's down beside her.'

Poirot nodded. His eyes swept round the small space observing – noting.

'And the railway guide was – where?'

'Here, sir.' The constable pointed out the spot on the counter. 'It was open at the right page for Andover and lying face down. Seems as though he must have been looking up the trains to London. If so, it mightn't have been an Andover man at all. But then, of course, the railway guide might have belonged to someone else what had nothing to do with the murder at all, but just forgot it here.'

'Fingerprints?' I suggested.

The man shook his head.

'The whole place was examined straight away, sir. There weren't none.'

'Not on the counter itself?' asked Poirot.

'A long sight too many, sir! All confused and jumbled up.'

'Any of Ascher's among them?'

'Too soon to say, sir.'

Poirot nodded, then asked if the dead woman lived over the shop.

'Yes, sir, you go through that door at the back, sir. You'll excuse me not coming with you, but I've got to stay –'

Poirot passed through the door in question and I followed him. Behind the shop was a microscopic sort of parlour and kitchen combined – it was neat and clean but very dreary looking and scantily furnished. On the mantelpiece were a few photographs. I went up and looked at them and Poirot joined me.

The photographs were three in all. One was a cheap portrait of the girl we had been with that afternoon, Mary Drower. She was obviously wearing her best clothes and had the self-conscious, wooden smile on her face that so often disfigures the expression in posed photography, and makes a snapshot preferable.

The second was a more expensive type of picture – an artistically blurred reproduction of an elderly woman with white hair. A high fur collar stood up round the neck.

I guessed that this was probably the Miss Rose who had left Mrs Ascher the small legacy which had enabled her to start in business.

The third photograph was a very old one, now faded and yellow. It represented a young man and woman in somewhat old-fashioned clothes standing arm in arm. The man had a button-hole and there was an air of bygone festivity about the whole pose.

'Probably a wedding picture,' said Poirot. 'Regard, Hastings, did I not tell you that she had been a beautiful woman?'

He was right. Disfigured by old-fashioned hairdressing and weird clothes, there was no disguising the handsomeness of the girl in the picture with her clear-cut features and spirited bearing. I looked closely at the second figure. It was almost impossible to recognize the seedy Ascher in this smart young man with the military bearing.

I recalled the leering drunken old man, and the toil-worn face of the dead woman – and I shivered a little at the remorselessness of time . . .

From the parlour a stair led to two upstairs rooms. One was empty and unfurnished, the other had evidently been the dead woman's bedroom. After being searched by the police it had been left as it was. A couple of old worn blankets on the bed – a little stock of well-darned underwear in a drawer – cookery recipes in another – a paper-backed novel entitled *The Green Oasis* – a pair of new stockings – pathetic in their cheap shininess – a couple of china ornaments – a Dresden shepherd much broken, and a blue and yellow spotted dog – a black raincoat and a woolly jumper hanging on pegs – such were the worldly possessions of the late Alice Ascher.

If there had been any personal papers, the police had taken them.

'*Pauvre femme,*' murmured Poirot. 'Come, Hastings, there is nothing for us here.'

When we were once more in the street, he hesitated for a minute or two, then crossed the road. Almost exactly opposite Mrs Ascher's was a greengrocer's shop – of the type that has most of its stock outside rather than inside.

In a low voice Poirot gave me certain instructions. Then he himself entered the shop. After waiting a minute or two I followed him in. He was at the moment negotiating for a lettuce. I myself bought a pound of strawberries.

Poirot was talking animatedly to the stout lady who was serving him.

'It was just opposite you, was it not, that this murder occurred? What an affair! What a sensation it must have caused you!'

The stout lady was obviously tired of talking about the murder. She must have had a long day of it. She observed:

'It would be as well if some of that gaping crowd cleared off. What is there to look at, I'd like to know?'

'It must have been very different last night,' said Poirot. 'Possibly you even observed the murderer enter the shop – a tall, fair man with a beard, was he not? A Russian, so I have heard.'

'What's that?' The woman looked up sharply. 'A Russian did it, you say?'

'I understand that the police have arrested him.'

'Did you ever know?' The woman was excited, voluble. 'A foreigner.'

'*Mais oui.* I thought perhaps you might have noticed him last night?'

'Well, I don't get much chance of noticing, and that's a fact. The evening's our busy time and there's always a fair few passing along and getting home after their work. A tall, fair man with a beard – no, I can't say I saw anyone of that description anywhere about.'

I broke in on my cue.

'Excuse me, sir,' I said to Poirot. 'I think you have been misinformed. A short *dark* man I was told.'

An interested discussion intervened in which the stout lady, her lank husband and a hoarse-voiced shop-boy all participated. No less than four short dark men had been observed, and the hoarse boy had seen a tall fair one, 'but he hadn't got no beard,' he added regretfully.

Finally, our purchases made, we left the establishment, leaving our falsehoods uncorrected.

'And what was the point of all that, Poirot?' I demanded somewhat reproachfully.

'*Parbleu*, I wanted to estimate the chances of a stranger being noticed entering the shop opposite.'

'Couldn't you simply have asked – without all that tissue of lies?'

'No, *mon ami*. If I had "simply asked", as you put it, I should have got no answer at all to my questions. You yourself are English and yet you do not seem to appreciate the quality of the English reaction to a direct question. It is invariably one of suspicion and the natural result is reticence. If I had asked those people for information they would have shut up like oysters. But by making a statement (and a somewhat out of the way and preposterous one) and by your contradiction of it, tongues are immediately loosened. We know also that

that particular time was a "busy time" – that is, that everyone would be intent on their own concerns and that there would be a fair number of people passing along the pavements. Our murderer chose his time well, Hastings.'

He paused and then added on a deep note of reproach:

'Is it that you have not in any degree the common sense, Hastings? I say to you: "Make a purchase *quelconque*" – and you deliberately choose the strawberries! Already they commence to creep through their bag and endanger your good suit.'

With some dismay, I perceived that this was indeed the case.

I hastily presented the strawberries to a small boy who seemed highly astonished and faintly suspicious.

Poirot added the lettuce, thus setting the seal on the child's bewilderment.

He continued to drive the moral home.

'At a cheap greengrocer's – *not* strawberries. A strawberry, unless fresh picked, is bound to exude juice. A banana – some apples – even a cabbage – but *strawberries* –'

'It was the first thing I thought of,' I explained by way of excuse.

'That is unworthy of your imagination,' returned Poirot sternly.

He paused on the sidewalk.

The house and shop on the right of Mrs Ascher's was empty. A 'To Let' sign appeared in the windows. On the other side was a house with somewhat grimy muslin curtains.

To this house Poirot betook himself and, there being no bell, executed a series of sharp flourishes with the knocker.

The door was opened after some delay by a very dirty child with a nose that needed attention.

'Good evening,' said Poirot. 'Is your mother within?'

'Ay?' said the child.

It stared at us with disfavour and deep suspicion.

'Your mother,' said Poirot.

This took some twelve seconds to sink in, then the child turned and, bawling up the stairs 'Mum, you're wanted,' retreated to some fastness in the dim interior.

A sharp-faced woman looked over the balusters and began to descend.

'No good you wasting your time –' she began, but Poirot interrupted her.

He took off his hat and bowed magnificently.

'Good evening, madame. I am on the staff of the *Evening Flicker*. I want to persuade you to accept a fee of five pounds and let us have an article on your late neighbour, Mrs Ascher.'

The irate words arrested on her lips, the woman came down the stairs smoothing her hair and hitching at her skirt.

'Come inside, please – on the left there. Won't you sit down, sir.'

The tiny room was heavily over-crowded with a massive pseudo-Jacobean suite, but we managed to squeeze ourselves in and on to a hard-seated sofa.

'You must excuse me,' the woman was saying. 'I am sure I'm sorry I spoke so sharp just now, but you'd hardly believe the worry one has to put up with – fellows coming along selling this, that and the other – vacuum cleaners, stockings, lavender bags and such-like foolery – and all so plausible and civil spoken. Got your name, too, pat they have. It's Mrs Fowler this, that and the other.'

Seizing adroitly on the name, Poirot said:

'Well, Mrs Fowler, I hope you're going to do what I ask.'

'I don't know, I'm sure.' The five pounds hung alluringly before Mrs Fowler's eyes. 'I *knew* Mrs Ascher, of course, but as to *writing* anything.'

Hastily Poirot reassured her. No labour on her part was required. He would elicit the facts from her and the interview would be written up.

Thus encouraged, Mrs Fowler plunged willingly into reminiscence, conjecture and hearsay.

Kept herself to herself, Mrs Ascher had. Not what you'd call really *friendly*, but there, she'd had a lot of trouble, poor soul, everyone knew that. And by rights Franz Ascher ought to have been locked up years ago. Not that Mrs Ascher had been afraid of him – real tartar she could be when roused! Give as good as she got any day. But there it was – the pitcher could go to the well once too often. Again and again, she, Mrs Fowler, had said to her: 'One of these days that man will do for you. Mark my words.' And he had done, hadn't he? And there had she, Mrs Fowler, been right next door and never heard a sound.

In a pause Poirot managed to insert a question.

Had Mrs Ascher ever received any peculiar letters – letters without a proper signature – just something like A B C?

Regretfully, Mrs Fowler returned a negative answer.

'I know the kind of thing you mean – anonymous letters they call them – mostly full of words you'd blush to say out loud. Well, I don't know, I'm sure, if Franz Ascher ever took to writing those. Mrs Ascher never let on to me if he did. What's that? A railway guide, an A B C? No, I never saw such a thing about – and I'm sure if Mrs Ascher had been sent one I'd have heard about it. I declare you could have knocked me down with a feather when I heard about this whole business. It was my girl Edie what came to me. "Mum," she says, "there's ever so many policemen next door." Gave me quite a turn, it did. "Well," I said, when I heard about it, "it does show that she ought never to have been alone in the house – that niece of hers ought to have been with her. A man in drink can be like a ravening wolf," I said, "and in my opinion a wild beast is neither more nor less than what that old devil of a husband of hers is. I've warned her," I said, "many times and now my words have come true. He'll do for you," I said. And he has done for her! You can't rightly estimate what a man will do when he's in drink and this murder's a proof of it.'

She wound up with a deep gasp.

'Nobody saw this man Ascher go into the shop, I believe?' said Poirot.

Mrs Fowler sniffed scornfully.

'Naturally he wasn't going to show himself,' she said.

How Mr Ascher had got there without showing himself she did not deign to explain.

She agreed that there was no back way into the house and that Ascher was quite well known by sight in the district.

'But he didn't want to swing for it and he kept himself well hid.'

Poirot kept the conversational ball rolling some little time longer, but when it seemed certain that Mrs Fowler had told all that she knew not once but many times over, he terminated the interview, first paying out the promised sum.

'Rather a dear five pounds' worth, Poirot,' I ventured to remark when we were once more in the street.

'So far, yes.'

'You think she knows more than she has told?'

'My friend, we are in the peculiar position of *not knowing what questions to ask*. We are like little children playing *cache-cache* in the dark. We stretch out our hands and grope about. Mrs Fowler has told us all that she *thinks* she knows – and has thrown in several conjectures for good measure! In the future, however, her evidence may be useful. It is for the future that I have invested that sum of five pounds.'

I did not quite understand the point, but at this moment we ran into Inspector Glen.

CHAPTER 7

MR PARTRIDGE AND MR RIDDELL

Inspector Glen was looking rather gloomy. He had, I gathered, spent the afternoon trying to get a complete list of persons who had been noticed entering the tobacco shop.

'And nobody has seen anyone?' Poirot inquired.

'Oh, yes, they have. Three tall men with furtive expressions – four short men with black moustaches – two beards – three fat men – all strangers – and all, if I'm to believe witnesses, with sinister expressions! I wonder somebody didn't see a gang of masked men with revolvers while they were about it!'

Poirot smiled sympathetically.

'Does anybody claim to have seen the man Ascher?'

'No, they don't. And that's another point in his favour. I've just told the Chief Constable that I think this is a job for Scotland Yard. I don't believe it's a local crime.'

Poirot said gravely:

'I agree with you.'

The inspector said:

'You know, Monsieur Poirot, it's a nasty business – a nasty business . . . I don't like it . . .'

We had two more interviews before returning to London.

The first was with Mr James Partridge. Mr Partridge was the last person known to have seen Mrs Ascher alive. He had made a purchase from her at 5.30.

Mr Partridge was a small man, a bank clerk by profession. He wore pince-nez, was very dry and spare-looking and extremely precise in all his utterances. He lived in a small house as neat and trim as himself.

'Mr – er – Poirot,' he said, glancing at the card my friend had handed to him. 'From Inspector Glen? What can I do for you, Mr Poirot?'

'I understand, Mr Partridge, that you were the last person to see Mrs Ascher alive.'

Mr Partridge placed his finger-tips together and looked at Poirot as though he were a doubtful cheque.

'That is a very debatable point, Mr Poirot,' he said. 'Many people may have made purchases from Mrs Ascher after I did so.'

'If so, they have not come forward to say so.'

Mr Partridge coughed.

'Some people, Mr Poirot, have no sense of public duty.'

He looked at us owlishly through his spectacles.

'Exceedingly true,' murmured Poirot. 'You, I understand, went to the police of your own accord?'

'Certainly I did. As soon as I heard of the shocking occurrence I perceived that my statement might be helpful and came forward accordingly.'

'A very proper spirit,' said Poirot solemnly. 'Perhaps you will be so kind as to repeat your story to me.'

'By all means. I was returning to this house and at 5.30 precisely —'

'Pardon, how was it that you knew the time so accurately?'

Mr Partridge looked a little annoyed at being interrupted.

'The church clock chimed. I looked at my watch and found I was a minute slow. That was just before I entered Mrs Ascher's shop.'

'Were you in the habit of making purchases there?'

'Fairly frequently. It was on my way home. About once or twice a week I was in the habit of purchasing two ounces of John Cotton mild.'

'Did you know Mrs Ascher at all? Anything of her circumstances or her history?'

'Nothing whatever. Beyond my purchase and an occasional remark as to the state of the weather, I had never spoken to her.'

'Did you know she had a drunken husband who was in the habit of threatening her life?'

'No, I knew nothing whatever about her.'

'You knew her by sight, however. Did anything about her appearance strike you as unusual yesterday evening? Did she appear flurried or put out in any way?'

Mr Partridge considered.

'As far as I noticed, she seemed exactly as usual,' he said.

Poirot rose.

'Thank you, Mr Partridge, for answering these questions. Have you, by any chance, an A B C in the house? I want to look up my return train to London.'

'On the shelf just behind you,' said Mr Partridge.

On the shelf in question were an A B C, a Bradshaw, the Stock Exchange Year Book, Kelly's Directory, a Who's Who and a local directory.

Poirot took down the A B C, pretended to look up a train, then thanked Mr Partridge and took his leave.

Our next interview was with Mr Albert Riddell and was of a highly different character. Mr Albert Riddell was a platelayer and our conversation took place to the accompaniment of the clattering of plates and dishes by Mr Riddell's obviously nervous wife, the growling of Mr Riddell's dog and the undisguised hostility of Mr Riddell himself.

He was a big clumsy giant of a man with a broad face and small suspicious eyes. He was in the act of eating meat-pie, washed down by exceedingly black tea. He peered at us angrily over the rim of his cup.

'Told all I've got to tell once, haven't I?' he growled. 'What's it to do with me, anyway? Told it to the blarsted police, I 'ave, and now I've got to spit it all out again to a couple of blarsted foreigners.'

Poirot gave a quick, amused glance in my direction and then said:

'In truth I sympathize with you, but what will you? It is a question of murder, is it not? One has to be very, very careful.'

'Best tell the gentleman what he wants, Bert,' said the woman nervously.

'You shut your blarsted mouth,' roared the giant.

'You did not, I think, go to the police of your own accord.' Poirot slipped the remark in neatly.

'Why the hell should I? It were no business of mine.'

'A matter of opinion,' said Poirot indifferently. 'There has been a murder – the police want to know who has been in the shop – I myself think it would have – what shall I say? – looked more natural if you had come forward.'

'I've got my work to do. Don't say I shouldn't have come forward in my own time –'

'But as it was, the police were given your name as that of a person seen to go into Mrs Ascher's and they had to come to you. Were they satisfied with your account?'

'Why shouldn't they be?' demanded Bert truculently.

Poirot merely shrugged his shoulders.

'What are you getting at, mister? Nobody's got anything against me? Everyone knows who did the old girl in, that b – of a husband of hers.'

'But he was not in the street that evening and you were.'

'Trying to fasten it on me, are you? Well, you won't succeed. What reason had I got to do a thing like that? Think I wanted to pinch a tin of her bloody tobacco? Think I'm a bloody homicidal maniac as they call it? Think I –?'

He rose threateningly from his seat. His wife bleated out:

'Bert, Bert – don't say such things. Bert – they'll think –'

'Calm yourself, monsieur,' said Poirot. 'I demand only your account of your visit. That you refuse it seems to me – what shall we say – a little odd?'

'Who said I refused anything?' Mr Riddell sank back again into his seat. 'I don't mind.'

'It was six o'clock when you entered the shop?'

'That's right – a minute or two after, as a matter of fact. Wanted a packet of Gold Flake. I pushed open the door –'

'It was closed, then?'

'That's right. I thought shop was shut, maybe. But it wasn't. I went in, there wasn't anyone about. I hammered on the counter and waited a bit. Nobody came, so I went out again. That's all, and you can put it in your pipe and smoke it.'

'You didn't see the body fallen down behind the counter?'

'No, no more would you have done – unless you was looking for it, maybe.'

'Was there a railway guide lying about?'

'Yes, there was – face downwards. It crossed my mind like that the old woman might have had to go off sudden by train and forgot to lock shop up.'

'Perhaps you picked up the railway guide or moved it along the counter?'

'Didn't touch the b – thing. I did just what I said.'

'And you did not see anyone leaving the shop before you yourself got there?'

'Didn't see any such thing. What I say is, why pitch on me –?'

Poirot rose.

'Nobody is pitching upon you – yet. *Bonsoir*, monsieur.'

He left the man with his mouth open and I followed him.

In the street he consulted his watch.

'With great haste, my friend, we might manage to catch the 7.2. Let us despatch ourselves quickly.'

CHAPTER 8
THE SECOND LETTER

'Well?' I demanded eagerly.

We were seated in a first-class carriage which we had to ourselves. The train, an express, had just drawn out of Andover.

'The crime,' said Poirot, 'was committed by a man of medium height with red hair and a cast in the left eye. He limps slightly on the right foot and has a mole just below the shoulder-blade.'

'Poirot?' I cried.

For the moment I was completely taken in. Then the twinkle in my friend's eye undeceived me.

'Poirot!' I said again, this time in reproach.

'*Mon ami*, what will you? You fix upon me a look of doglike devotion and demand of me a pronouncement à la Sherlock Holmes! Now for the truth – *I do not know what the murderer looks like, nor where he lives, nor how to set hands upon him.*'

'If only he had left some clue,' I murmured.

'Yes, the clue – it is always the clue that attracts you. Alas that he did not smoke the cigarette and leave the ash, and then step in it with a shoe that has nails of a curious pattern. No – he is not so obliging. But at least, my friend, you have the *railway guide*. The A B C, that is a clue for you!'

'Do you think he left it by mistake then?'

'Of course not. He left it on purpose. The fingerprints tell us that.'

'But there weren't any on it.'

'That is what I mean. What was yesterday evening? A warm June night. Does a man stroll about on such an evening in *gloves*? Such a man would certainly have attracted attention. Therefore since there are no fingerprints on the A B C, it must have been carefully wiped. An innocent man would have left prints – a guilty man would not. So our murderer left it there for a purpose – but for all that it is none the less a clue. That A B C was bought by someone – it was carried by someone – there is a possibility there.'

'You think we may learn something that way?'

'Frankly, Hastings, I am not particularly hopeful. This man, this unknown X, obviously prides himself on his abilities. He is not likely to blaze a trail that can be followed straight away.'

'So that really the ABC isn't helpful at all.'

'Not in the sense you mean.'

'In any sense?'

Poirot did not answer at once. Then he said slowly:

'The answer to that is yes. We are confronted here by an unknown personage. He is in the dark and seeks to remain in the dark. But in the very nature of things *he cannot help throwing light upon himself*. In one sense we know nothing about him – in another sense we know already a good deal. I see his figure dimly taking shape – a man who prints clearly and well – who buys good-quality paper – who is at great needs to express his personality. I see him as a child possibly ignored and passed over – I see him growing up with an inward sense of inferiority – warring with a sense of injustice . . . I see that inner urge – to assert himself – to focus attention on himself ever becoming stronger, and events, circumstances – crushing it down – heaping, perhaps, more humiliations on him. And inwardly the match is set to the powder train . . .'

'That's all pure conjecture,' I objected. 'It doesn't give you any practical help.'

'You prefer the match end, the cigarette ash, the nailed boots! You always have. But at least we can ask ourselves some practical questions. Why the A B C? Why Mrs Ascher? Why Andover?'

'The woman's past life seems simple enough,' I mused. 'The interviews with those two men were disappointing. They couldn't tell us anything more than we knew already.'

'To tell the truth, I did not expect much in that line. But we could not neglect two possible candidates for the murder.'

'Surely you don't think –'

'There is at least a possibility that the murderer lives in or near Andover. That is a possible answer to our question: "Why Andover?" Well, here were two men known to have been in the shop at the requisite time of day. Either of them *might* be the murderer. And there is nothing as yet to show that one or other of them is *not* the murderer.'

'That great hulking brute, Riddell, perhaps,' I admitted.

'Oh, I am inclined to acquit Riddell off-hand. He was nervous, blustering, obviously uneasy –'

'But surely that just shows –'

'A nature diametrically opposed to that which penned the A B C letter. Conceit and self-confidence are the characteristics that we must look for.'

'Someone who throws his weight about?'

'Possibly. But some people, under a nervous and self-effacing manner, conceal a great deal of vanity and self-satisfaction.'

'You don't think that little Mr Partridge –'

'He is more *le type*. One cannot say more than that. He acts as the writer of the letter would act – goes at once to the police – pushes himself to the fore – enjoys his position.'

'Do you really think –?'

'No, Hastings. Personally I believe that the murderer came from outside Andover, but we must neglect no avenue of research. And although I say "he" all the time, we must not exclude the possibility of a woman being concerned.'

'Surely not!'

'The method of attack is that of a man, I agree. But anonymous letters are written by women rather than by men. We must bear that in mind.'

I was silent for a few minutes, then I said:

'What do we do next?'

'My energetic Hastings,' Poirot said and smiled at me.

'No, but what do we do?'

'Nothing.'

'Nothing?' My disappointment rang out clearly.

'Am I the magician? The sorcerer? What would you have me do?'

Turning the matter over in my mind I found it difficult to give an answer. Nevertheless I felt convinced that something ought to be done and that we should not allow the grass to grow under our feet.

I said:

'There is the A B C – and the notepaper and envelope –'

'Naturally everything is being done in that line. The police have all the means at their disposal for that kind of inquiry. If anything is to be discovered on those lines have no fear but that they will discover it.'

With that I was forced to rest content.

In the days that followed I found Poirot curiously disinclined to discuss the case. When I tried to reopen the subject he waved it aside with an impatient hand.

In my own mind I was afraid that I fathomed his motive. Over the murder of Mrs Ascher, Poirot had sustained a defeat. A B C had challenged him – and A B C had won. My friend, accustomed to an unbroken line of successes, was sensitive to his failure – so much so that he could not even endure discussion of the subject. It was, perhaps, a sign of pettiness in so great a man, but even the most sober of us is liable to have his head turned by success. In Poirot's case the head-turning process had been going on for years. Small wonder if its effects became noticeable at long last.

Understanding, I respected my friend's weakness and I made no further reference to the case. I read in the paper the account of the inquest. It was very brief, no mention was made of the A B C letter, and a verdict was returned of murder by some person or persons unknown. The crime attracted very little attention in the press. It had no popular or spectacular features. The murder of an old woman in a side street was soon passed over in the press for more thrilling topics.

Truth to tell, the affair was fading from my mind also, partly, I think, because I disliked to think of Poirot as being in any way associated with a failure, when on July 25th it was suddenly revived.

I had not seen Poirot for a couple of days as I had been away in Yorkshire for the weekend. I arrived back on Monday afternoon and the letter came by the six o'clock post. I remember the sudden, sharp intake of breath that Poirot gave as he slit open that particular envelope.

'It has come,' he said.

I stared at him – not understanding.

'What has come?'

'The second chapter of the A B C business.'

For a minute I looked at him uncomprehendingly. The matter had really passed from my memory.

'Read,' said Poirot and passed me over the letter.

As before, it was printed on good-quality paper.

Dear Mr Poirot, – Well, what about it? First game to me, I think. The Andover business went with a swing, didn't it?

But the fun's only just beginning. Let me draw your attention to Bexhill-on-Sea. Date, the 25th inst.

What a merry time we are having! Yours, etc.,

A B C.

'Good God, Poirot,' I cried. 'Does this mean that this fiend is going to attempt another crime?'

'Naturally, Hastings. What else did you expect? Did you think that the Andover business was an isolated case? Do you not remember my saying: "This is the beginning"?'

'But this is horrible!'

'Yes, it is horrible.'

'We're up against a homicidal maniac.'

'Yes.'

His quietness was more impressive than any heroics could have been. I handed back the letter with a shudder.

The following morning saw us at a conference of powers. The Chief Constable of Sussex, the Assistant Commissioner of the CID, Inspector Glen from Andover, Superintendent Carter of the Sussex police, Japp and a younger inspector called Crome, and Dr Thompson, the famous alienist, were all assembled together. The postmark on this letter was Hampstead, but in Poirot's opinion little importance could be attached to this fact.

The matter was discussed fully. Dr Thompson was a pleasant middle-aged man who, in spite of his learning, contented himself with homely language, avoiding the technicalities of his profession.

'There's no doubt,' said the Assistant Commissioner, 'that the two letters are in the same hand. Both were written by the same person.'

'And we can fairly assume that that person was responsible for the Andover murder.'

'Quite. We've now got definite warning of a second crime scheduled to take place on the 25th – the day after tomorrow – at Bexhill. What steps can be taken?'

The Sussex Chief Constable looked at his superintendent.

'Well, Carter, what about it?'

The superintendent shook his head gravely.

'It's difficult, sir. There's not the least clue towards whom the victim may be. Speaking fair and square, what steps *can* we take?'

'A suggestion,' murmured Poirot.

Their faces turned to him.

'I think it possible that the surname of the intended victim will begin with the letter B.'

'That would be something,' said the superintendent doubtfully.

'An alphabetical complex,' said Dr Thompson thoughtfully.

'I suggest it as a possibility – no more. It came into my mind when I saw the name Ascher clearly written over the shop door of the unfortunate woman who was murdered last month. When I got the letter naming Bexhill it occurred to me as a possibility that the victim as well as the place might be selected by an alphabetical system.'

'It's possible,' said the doctor. 'On the other hand, it may be that the name Ascher was a coincidence – that the victim this time, no matter what her name is, will again be an old woman who keeps a shop. We're dealing, remember, with a madman. So far he hasn't given us any clue as to motive.'

'Has a madman any motive, sir?' asked the superintendent sceptically.

'Of course he has, man. A deadly logic is one of the special characteristics of acute mania. A man may believe himself divinely appointed to kill clergymen – or doctors – or old women in tobacco shops – and there's always some perfectly coherent reason behind it. We mustn't let the alphabetical business run away with us. Bexhill succeeding to Andover *may* be a mere coincidence.'

'We can at least take certain precautions, Carter, and make a special note of the B's, especially small shopkeepers, and keep a watch on all small tobacconists and newsagents looked after by a single person. I don't think there's anything more we can do than that. Naturally, keep tabs on all strangers as far as possible.'

The superintendent uttered a groan.

'With the schools breaking up and the holidays beginning? People are fairly flooding into the place this week.'

'We must do what we can,' the Chief Constable said sharply.

Inspector Glen spoke in his turn.

'I'll have a watch kept on anyone connected with the Ascher business. Those two witnesses, Partridge and Riddell, and of course Ascher himself. If they show any sign of leaving Andover they'll be followed.'

The conference broke up after a few more suggestions and a little desultory conversation.

'Poirot,' I said as we walked along by the river. 'Surely this crime can be prevented?'

He turned a haggard face to me.

'The sanity of a city full of men against the insanity of one man? I fear, Hastings – I very much fear. Remember the long-continued successes of Jack the Ripper.'

'It's horrible,' I said.

'Madness, Hastings, is a terrible thing . . . *I am afraid . . . I am very much afraid . . .*'

CHAPTER 9

THE BEXHILL-ON-SEA MURDER

I still remember my awakening on the morning of the 25th of July. It must have been about seven-thirty.

Poirot was standing by my bedside gently shaking me by the shoulder. One glance at his face brought me from semi-consciousness into the full possession of my faculties.

'What is it?' I demanded, sitting up rapidly.

His answer came quite simply, but a wealth of emotion lay behind the three words he uttered.

'*It has happened.*'

'What?' I cried. 'You mean – but *today* is the 25th.'

'It took place last night – or rather in the early hours of this morning.'

As I sprang from bed and made a rapid toilet, he recounted briefly what he had just learnt over the telephone.

'The body of a young girl has been found on the beach at Bexhill. She has been identified as Elizabeth Barnard, a waitress in one of the cafés, who lived with her parents in a little recently built bungalow. Medical evidence gave the time of death as between 11.30 and 1 am.'

'They're quite sure that this is *the* crime?' I asked, as I hastily lathered my face.

'*An ABC open at the trains to Bexhill was found actually under the body.*'

I shivered.

'This is horrible!'

'*Faites attention,* Hastings. I do not want a second tragedy in my rooms!'

I wiped the blood from my chin rather ruefully.

'What is our plan of campaign?' I asked.

'The car will call for us in a few moments' time. I will bring you a cup of coffee here so that there will be no delay in starting.'

Twenty minutes later we were in a fast police car crossing the Thames on our way out of London.

With us was Inspector Crome, who had been present at the conference the other day, and who was officially in charge of the case.

Crome was a very different type of officer from Japp. A much younger man, he was the silent, superior type. Well educated and well read, he was, for my taste, several shades too pleased with himself. He had lately gained kudos over a series of child murders, having patiently tracked down the criminal who was now in Broadmoor.

He was obviously a suitable person to undertake the present case, but I thought that he was just a little too aware of the fact himself. His manner to Poirot was a shade patronizing. He deferred to him as a younger man to an older one – in a rather self-conscious, 'public school' way.

'I've had a good long talk with Dr Thompson,' he said. 'He's very interested in the "chain" or "series" type of murder. It's the product of a particular distorted type of mentality. As a layman one can't, of course, appreciate the finer points as they present themselves to a medical point of view.' He coughed. 'As a matter of fact – my last case – I don't know whether you read about it – the Mabel Homer case, the Muswell Hill schoolgirl, you know – that man Capper was extraordinary. Amazingly difficult to pin the crime on to him – it was his third, too! Looked as sane as you or I. But there are various tests – verbal traps, you know – quite modern, of course, there was nothing of that kind in your day. Once you can induce a man to give himself away, you've got him! He knows that you know and his nerve goes. He starts giving himself away right and left.'

'Even in my day that happened sometimes,' said Poirot.

Inspector Crome looked at him and murmured conversationally:
'Oh, yes?'

There was silence between us for some time. As we passed New Cross Station, Crome said:

'If there's anything you want to ask me about the case, pray do so.'

'You have not, I presume, a description of the dead girl?'

'She was twenty-three years of age, engaged as a waitress at the Ginger Cat café –'

'*Pas ça.* I wondered – if she were pretty?'

'As to that I've no information,' said Inspector Crome with a hint of withdrawal. His manner said: 'Really – these foreigners! All the same!'

A faint look of amusement came into Poirot's eyes.

'It does not seem to you important, that? Yet, *pour une femme*, it is of the first importance. Often it decides her destiny!'

Another silence fell.

It was not until we were nearing Sevenoaks that Poirot opened the conversation again.

'Were you informed, by any chance, how and with what the girl was strangled?'

Inspector Crome replied briefly.

'Strangled with her own belt – a thick, knitted affair, I gather.'

Poirot's eyes opened very wide.

'Aha,' he said. 'At last we have a piece of information that is very definite. That tells one something, does it not?'

'I haven't seen it yet,' said Inspector Crome coldly.

I felt impatient with the man's caution and lack of imagination.

'It gives us the hallmark of the murderer,' I said. 'The girl's own belt. It shows the particular beastliness of his mind!'

Poirot shot me a glance I could not fathom. On the face of it it conveyed humorous impatience. I thought that perhaps it was a warning not to be too outspoken in front of the inspector.

I relapsed into silence.

At Bexhill we were greeted by Superintendent Carter. He had with him a pleasant-faced, intelligent-looking young inspector called Kelsey. The latter was detailed to work in with Crome over the case.

'You'll want to make your own inquiries, Crome,' said the superintendent. 'So I'll just give you the main heads of the matter and then you can get busy right away.'

'Thank you, sir,' said Crome.

'We've broken the news to her father and mother,' said the superintendent. 'Terrible shock to them, of course. I left them to recover a bit before questioning them, so you can start from the beginning there.'

'There are other members of the family – yes?' asked Poirot.

'There's a sister – a typist in London. She's been communicated with. And there's a young man – in fact, the girl was supposed to be out with him last night, I gather.'

'Any help from the A B C guide?' asked Crome.

'It's there,' the superintendent nodded towards the table. 'No fingerprints. Open at the page for Bexhill. A new copy, I should say – doesn't seem to have been opened much. Not bought anywhere round here. I've tried all the likely stationers.'

'Who discovered the body, sir?'

'One of these fresh-air, early-morning colonels. Colonel Jerome. He was out with his dog about 6 am. Went along the front in the direction of Cooden, and down on to the beach. Dog went off and sniffed at something. Colonel called it. Dog didn't come. Colonel had a look and thought something queer was up. Went over and looked. Behaved very properly. Didn't touch her at all and rang us up immediately.'

'And the time of death was round about midnight last night?'

'Between midnight and 1 am – that's pretty certain. Our homicidal joker is a man of his word. If he says the 25th, it is the 25th – though it may have been only by a few minutes.'

Crome nodded.

'Yes, that's his mentality all right. There's nothing else? Nobody saw anything helpful?'

'Not as far as we know. But it's early yet. Everyone who saw a girl in white walking with a man last night will be along to tell us about it soon, and as I imagine there were about four or five hundred girls in white walking with young men last night, it ought to be a nice business.'

'Well, sir, I'd better get down to it,' said Crome. 'There's the café and there's the girl's home. I'd better go to both of them. Kelsey can come with me.'

'And Mr Poirot?' asked the superintendent.

'I will accompany you,' said Poirot to Crome with a little bow.

Crome, I thought, looked slightly annoyed. Kelsey, who had not seen Poirot before, grinned broadly.

It was an unfortunate circumstance that the first time people saw my friend they were always disposed to consider him as a joke of the first water.

'What about this belt she was strangled with?' asked Crome. 'Mr Poirot is inclined to think it's a valuable clue. I expect he'd like to see it.'

'*Du tout*,' said Poirot quickly. 'You misunderstood me.'

'You'll get nothing from that,' said Carter. 'It wasn't a leather belt – might have got fingerprints if it had been. Just a thick sort of knitted silk – ideal for the purpose.'

I gave a shiver.

'Well,' said Crome, 'we'd better be getting along.'

We set out forthwith.

Our first visit was to the Ginger Cat. Situated on the sea front, this was the usual type of small tearoom. It had little tables covered with orange-checked cloths and basket-work chairs of exceeding discomfort with orange cushions on them. It was the kind of place that specialized in morning coffee, five different kinds of teas (Devonshire, Farmhouse, Fruit, Carlton and Plain), and a few sparing lunch dishes for females such as scrambled eggs and shrimps and macaroni au gratin.

The morning coffees were just getting under way. The manageress ushered us hastily into a very untidy back sanctum.

'Miss – eh – Merrion?' inquired Crome.

Miss Merrion bleated out in a high, distressed-gentlewoman voice:

'That is my name. This is a most distressing business. Most distressing. How it will affect our business I really cannot *think*!'

Miss Merrion was a very thin woman of forty with wispy orange hair (indeed she was astonishingly like a ginger cat herself). She played nervously with various fichus and frills that were part of her official costume.

'You'll have a boom,' said Inspector Kelsey encouragingly. 'You'll see! You won't be able to serve teas fast enough!'

'Disgusting,' said Miss Merrion. 'Truly disgusting. It makes one despair of human nature.'

But her eyes brightened nevertheless.

'What can you tell me about the dead girl, Miss Merrion?'

'Nothing,' said Miss Merrion positively. 'Absolutely nothing!'

'How long had she been working here?'

'This was the second summer.'

'You were satisfied with her?'

'She was a good waitress – quick and obliging.'

'She was pretty, yes?' inquired Poirot.

Miss Merrion, in her turn, gave him an 'Oh, these foreigners' look.

'She was a nice, clean-looking girl,' she said distantly.

'What time did she go off duty last night?' asked Crome.

'Eight o'clock. We close at eight. We do not serve dinners. There is no demand for them. Scrambled eggs and tea (Poirot shuddered) people come in for up to seven o'clock and sometimes after, but our rush is over by 6.30.'

'Did she mention to you how she proposed to spend her evening?'

'Certainly not,' said Miss Merrion emphatically. 'We were not on those terms.'

'No one came in and called for her? Anything like that?'

'No.'

'Did she seem quite her ordinary self? Not excited or depressed?'

'Really I could not say,' said Miss Merrion aloofly.

'How many waitresses do you employ?'

'Two normally, and an extra two after the 20th July until the end of August.'

'But Elizabeth Barnard was not one of the extras?'

'Miss Barnard was one of the regulars.'

'What about the other one?'

'Miss Higley? She is a very nice young lady.'

'Were she and Miss Barnard friends?'

'Really I could not say.'

'Perhaps we'd better have a word with her.'

'Now?'

'If you please.'

'I will send her to you,' said Miss Merrion, rising. 'Please keep her as short a time as possible. This is the morning coffee rush hour.'

The feline and gingery Miss Merrion left the room.

'Very refined,' remarked Inspector Kelsey. He mimicked the lady's mincing tone. '*Really I could not say.*'

A plump girl, slightly out of breath, with dark hair, rosy cheeks and dark eyes goggling with excitement, bounced in.

'Miss Merrion sent me,' she announced breathlessly.

'Miss Higley?'

'Yes, that's me.'

'You knew Elizabeth Barnard?'

'Oh, yes, I knew Betty. Isn't it *awful*? It's just too awful! I can't believe it's true. I've been saying to the girls all the morning I just *can't* believe it! "You know, girls," I said, "it just doesn't seem *real*. Betty! I mean, Betty Barnard, who's been here all along, *murdered*! I just can't believe it," I said. Five or six times I've pinched myself just to see if I wouldn't wake up. Betty murdered . . . It's – well, you know what I mean – it doesn't seem *real*.'

'You knew the dead girl well?' asked Crome.

'Well, she's worked here longer than I have. I only came this March. She was here last year. She was rather quiet, if you know what I mean. She wasn't one to joke or laugh a lot. I don't mean that she was exactly *quiet* – she'd plenty of fun in her and all that – but she didn't – well, she was quiet and she wasn't quiet, if you know what I mean.'

I will say for Inspector Crome that he was exceedingly patient. As a witness the buxom Miss Higley was persistently maddening. Every statement she made was repeated and qualified half a dozen times. The net result was meagre in the extreme.

She had not been on terms of intimacy with the dead girl. Elizabeth Barnard, it could be guessed, had considered herself a cut above Miss Higley. She had been friendly in working hours, but the girls had not seen much of her out of them. Elizabeth Barnard had had a 'friend' who worked at the estate agents near the station. Court & Brunskill. No, he wasn't Mr Court nor Mr Brunskill. He was a clerk there. She didn't know his name. But she knew him by sight well. Good-looking – oh, very good-looking, and always so nicely dressed. Clearly, there was a tinge of jealousy in Miss Higley's heart.

In the end it boiled down to this. Elizabeth Barnard had not confided in anyone in the café as to her plans for the evening, but in Miss Higley's opinion she had been going to meet her 'friend'. She had had on a new white dress, 'ever so sweet with one of the new necks.'

We had a word with each of the other two girls but with no further results. Betty Barnard had not said anything as to her plans and no one had noticed her in Bexhill during the course of the evening.

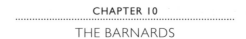

CHAPTER 10

THE BARNARDS

Elizabeth Barnard's parents lived in a minute bungalow, one of fifty or so recently run up by a speculative builder on the confines of the town. The name of it was Llandudno. Mr Barnard, a stout, bewildered-looking man of fifty-five or so, had noticed our approach and was standing waiting in the doorway.

'Come in, gentlemen,' he said.

Inspector Kelsey took the initiative.

'This is Inspector Crome of Scotland Yard, sir,' he said. 'He's come down to help us over this business.'

'Scotland Yard?' said Mr Barnard hopefully. 'That's good. This murdering villain's got to be laid by the heels. My poor little girl –' His face was distorted by a spasm of grief.

'And this is Mr Hercule Poirot, also from London, and er –'

'Captain Hastings,' said Poirot.

'Pleased to meet you, gentlemen,' said Mr Barnard mechanically. 'Come into the snuggery. I don't know that my poor wife's up to seeing you. All broken up, she is.'

However, by the time that we were ensconced in the living-room of the bungalow, Mrs Barnard had made her appearance. She had evidently been crying bitterly, her eyes were reddened and she walked with the uncertain gait of a person who had had a great shock.

'Why, mother, that's fine,' said Mr Barnard. 'You're sure you're all right – eh?'

He patted her shoulder and drew her down into a chair.

'The superintendent was very kind,' said Mr Barnard. 'After he'd broken the news to us, he said he'd leave any questions till later when we'd got over the first shock.'

'It is too cruel. Oh, it is too cruel,' cried Mrs Barnard tearfully. 'The cruellest thing that ever was, it is.'

Her voice had a faintly sing-song intonation that I thought for a moment was foreign till I remembered the name on the gate and realized that the 'effer wass' of her speech was in reality proof of her Welsh origin.

'It's very painful, madam, I know,' said Inspector Crome. 'And we've every sympathy for you, but we want to know all the facts we can so as to get to work as quick as possible.'

'That's sense, that is,' said Mr Barnard, nodding approval.

'Your daughter was twenty-three, I understand. She lived here with you and worked at the Ginger Cat café, is that right?'

'That's it.'

'This is a new place, isn't it? Where did you live before?'

'I was in the ironmongery business in Kennington. Retired two years ago. Always meant to live near the sea.'

'You have two daughters?'

'Yes. My elder daughter works in an office in London.'

'Weren't you alarmed when your daughter didn't come home last night?'

'We didn't know she hadn't,' said Mrs Barnard tearfully. 'Dad and I always go to bed early. Nine o'clock's our time. We never knew Betty hadn't come home till the police officer came and said – and said –'

She broke down.

'Was your daughter in the habit of – er – returning home late?'

'You know what girls are nowadays, inspector,' said Barnard. 'Independent, that's what they are. These summer evenings they're not going to rush home. All the same, Betty was usually in by eleven.'

'How did she get in? Was the door open?'

'Left the key under the mat – that's what we always did.'

'There is some rumour, I believe, that your daughter was engaged to be married?'

'They don't put it as formally as that nowadays,' said Mr Barnard.

'Donald Fraser his name is, and I liked him. I liked him very much,' said Mrs Barnard. 'Poor fellow, it'll be trouble for him – this news. Does he know yet, I wonder?'

'He works in Court & Brunskill's, I understand?'

'Yes, they're the estate agents.'

'Was he in the habit of meeting your daughter most evenings after her work?'

'Not every evening. Once or twice a week would be nearer.'

'Do you know if she was going to meet him yesterday?'

'She didn't say. Betty never said much about what she was doing or where she was going. But she was a good girl, Betty was. Oh, I can't believe –'

Mrs Barnard started sobbing again.

'Pull yourself together, old lady. Try to hold up, mother,' urged her husband. 'We've got to get to the bottom of this.'

'I'm sure Donald would never – would never –' sobbed Mrs Barnard.

'Now just you pull yourself together,' repeated Mr Barnard.

'I wish to God I could give you some help – but the plain fact is I know nothing – nothing at all that can help you to find the dastardly scoundrel who did this. Betty was just a merry, happy girl – with a decent young fellow that she was – well, we'd have called it walking out with in my young days. Why anyone should want to murder her simply beats me – it doesn't make sense.'

'You're very near the truth there, Mr Barnard,' said Crome. 'I tell you what I'd like to do – have a look over Miss Barnard's room. There may be something – letters – or a diary.'

'Look over it and welcome,' said Mr Barnard, rising.

He led the way. Crome followed him, then Poirot, then Kelsey, and I brought up the rear.

I stopped for a minute to retie my shoelaces, and as I did so a taxi drew up outside and a girl jumped out of it. She paid the driver and hurried up the path to the house, carrying a small suitcase. As she entered the door she saw me and stopped dead.

There was something so arresting in her pose that it intrigued me.

'Who are you?' she said.

I came down a few steps. I felt embarrassed as to how exactly to reply. Should I give my name? Or mention that I had come here with the police? The girl, however, gave me no time to make a decision.

'Oh, well,' she said, 'I can guess.'

She pulled off the little white woollen cap she was wearing and threw it on the ground. I could see her better now as she turned a little so that the light fell on her.

My first impression was of the Dutch dolls that my sisters used to play with in my childhood. Her hair was black and cut in a straight bob and a bang across the forehead. Her cheek-bones were high and her whole figure had a queer modern angularity that was not, somehow, unattractive. She was not good-looking – plain rather – but there was an intensity about her, a forcefulness that made her a person quite impossible to overlook.

'You are Miss Barnard?' I asked.

'I am Megan Barnard. You belong to the police, I suppose?'

'Well,' I said. 'Not exactly –'

She interrupted me.

'I don't think I've got anything to say to you. My sister was a nice bright girl with no men friends. Good morning.'

She gave me a short laugh as she spoke and regarded me challengingly.

'That's the correct phrase, I believe?' she said.

'I'm not a reporter, if that's what you're getting at.'

'Well, what are you?' She looked around. 'Where's mum and dad?'

'Your father is showing the police your sister's bedroom. Your mother's in there. She's very upset.'

The girl seemed to make a decision.

'Come in here,' she said.

She pulled open a door and passed through. I followed her and found myself in a small, neat kitchen.

I was about to shut the door behind me – but found an unexpected resistance. The next moment Poirot had slipped quietly into the room and shut the door behind him.

'Mademoiselle Barnard?' he said with a quick bow.

'This is M. Hercule Poirot,' I said.

Megan Barnard gave him a quick, appraising glance.

'I've heard of you,' she said. 'You're the fashionable private sleuth, aren't you?'

'Not a pretty description – but it suffices,' said Poirot.

The girl sat down on the edge of the kitchen table. She felt in her bag for a cigarette. She placed it between her lips, lighted it, and then said in between two puffs of smoke:

'Somehow, I don't see what M. Hercule Poirot is doing in our humble little crime.'

'Mademoiselle,' said Poirot. 'What you do not see and what I do not see would probably fill a volume. But all that is of no practical importance. What *is* of practical importance is something that will not be easy to find.'

'What's that?'

'Death, mademoiselle, unfortunately creates a *prejudice*. A prejudice in favour of the deceased. I heard what you said just now to my friend Hastings. "A nice bright girl with no men friends." You said that in mockery of the newspapers. And it is very true – when a young girl is dead, that is the kind of thing that is said. She was bright. She was happy. She was sweet-tempered. She had not a care in the world. She had no undesirable acquaintances. There is a great charity always to the dead. Do you know what I should like this minute? I should like to find someone who knew Elizabeth Barnard *and who does not know she is dead*! Then, perhaps, I should hear what is useful to me – the truth.'

Megan Barnard looked at him for a few minutes in silence whilst she smoked. Then, at last, she spoke. Her words made me jump.

'Betty,' she said, 'was an unmitigated little ass!'

CHAPTER 11

MEGAN BARNARD

As I said, Megan Barnard's words, and still more the crisp businesslike tone in which they were uttered, made me jump.

Poirot, however, merely bowed his head gravely.

'*A la bonne heure*,' he said. 'You are intelligent, mademoiselle.'

Megan Barnard said, still in the same detached tone:

'I was extremely fond of Betty. But my fondness didn't blind me from seeing exactly the kind of silly little fool she was – and even telling her so upon occasions! Sisters are like that.'

'And did she pay any attention to your advice?'

'Probably not,' said Megan cynically.

'Will you, mademoiselle, be precise.'

The girl hesitated for a minute or two.

Poirot said with a slight smile:

'I will help you. I heard what you said to Hastings. That your sister was a bright, happy girl with no men friends. It was – *un peu* – the *opposite* that was true, was it not?'

Megan said slowly:

'There wasn't any harm in Betty. I want you to understand that. She'd always go straight. She's not the weekending kind. Nothing of that sort. But she liked being taken out and dancing and – oh, cheap flattery and compliments and all that sort of thing.'

'And she was pretty – yes?'

This question, the third time I had heard it, met this time with a practical response.

Megan slipped off the table, went to her suitcase, snapped it open and extracted something which she handed to Poirot.

In a leather frame was a head and shoulders of a fair-haired, smiling girl. Her hair had evidently recently been permed, it stood out from her head in a mass of rather frizzy curls. The smile was arch and artificial. It was certainly not a face that you could call beautiful, but it had an obvious and cheap prettiness.

Poirot handed it back, saying:

'You and she do not resemble each other, mademoiselle.'

'Oh! I'm the plain one of the family. I've always known that.' She seemed to brush aside the fact as unimportant.

'In what way exactly do you consider your sister was behaving foolishly? Do you mean, perhaps, in relation to Mr Donald Fraser?'

'That's it, exactly. Don's a very quiet sort of person – but he – well, naturally he'd resent certain things – and then –'

'And then what, mademoiselle?'

His eyes were on her very steadily.

It may have been my fancy but it seemed to me that she hesitated a second before answering.

'I was afraid that he might – chuck her altogether. And that would have been a pity. He's a very steady and hard-working man and would have made her a good husband.'

Poirot continued to gaze at her. She did not flush under his glance but returned it with one of her own equally steady and with something else in it – something that reminded me of her first defiant, disdainful manner.

'So it is like that,' he said at last. 'We do not speak the truth any longer.'

She shrugged her shoulders and turned towards the door.

'Well,' she said. 'I've done what I could to help you.'

Poirot's voice arrested her.

'Wait, mademoiselle. I have something to tell you. Come back.'

Rather unwillingly, I thought, she obeyed.

Somewhat to my surprise, Poirot plunged into the whole story of the A B C letters, the murder of Andover, and the railway guide found by the bodies.

He had no reason to complain of any lack of interest on her part. Her lips parted, her eyes gleaming, she hung on his words.

'Is this all true, M. Poirot?'

'Yes, it is true.'

'You really mean that my sister was killed by some horrible homicidal maniac?'

'Precisely.'

She drew a deep breath.

'Oh! Betty – Betty – how – how *ghastly*!'

'You see, mademoiselle, that the information for which I ask you can give freely without wondering whether or not it will hurt anyone.'

'Yes, I see that now.'

'Then let us continue our conversation. I have formed the idea that this Donald Fraser has, perhaps, a violent and jealous temper, is that right?'

Megan Barnard said quietly:

'I'm trusting you now, M. Poirot. I'm going to give you the absolute truth. Don is, as I say, a very quiet person – a bottled-up person, if you know what I mean. He can't always express what he feels in words. But underneath it all he minds things terribly. And he's got a jealous nature. He was always jealous of Betty. He was devoted to her – and of course she was very fond of him, but it wasn't in Betty to be fond of one person and not notice anybody else. She wasn't made that way. She'd got a – well, an eye for any nice-looking man who'd pass the time of day with her. And of course, working in the Ginger Cat, she was always running up against men – especially in the summer holidays. She was always very pat with her tongue and if they chaffed her she'd chaff back again. And then perhaps she'd meet them and go to the pictures or something like that. Nothing serious – never anything of that kind – but she just liked her fun. She used to say that as she'd got to settle down with Don one day she might as well have her fun now while she could.'

Megan paused and Poirot said:

'I understand. Continue.'

'It was just that attitude of mind of hers that Don couldn't understand. If she was really keen on him he couldn't see why she wanted to go out with other people. And once or twice they had flaming big rows about it.'

'M. Don, he was no longer quiet?'

'It's like all those quiet people, when they do lose their tempers they lose them with a vengeance. Don was so violent that Betty was frightened.'

'When was this?'

'There was one row nearly a year ago and another – a worse one – just over a month ago. I was home for the weekend – and I got them to patch it up again, and it was then I tried to knock a little sense into Betty – told her she was a little fool. All she would say was that there hadn't been any harm in it. Well, that was true enough, but all the same she was riding for a fall. You see, after the row a year ago, she'd got into the habit of telling a few useful lies on the principle that what the mind doesn't know the heart doesn't grieve over. This last flare-up came because she'd told Don she was going to Hastings to see a girl pal – and he found out that she'd really been over to Eastbourne with some man. He was a married man, as it happened, and he'd been a bit secretive about the business anyway – and so that made it worse. They had an awful scene – Betty saying that she wasn't married to him yet and she had a right to go about with whom she pleased and Don all white and shaking and saying that one day – one day –'

'Yes?'

'He'd commit murder –' said Megan in a lowered voice.

She stopped and stared at Poirot.

He nodded his head gravely several times.

'And so, naturally, you were afraid . . .'

'I didn't think he'd actually done it – not for a minute! But I was afraid it might be brought up – the quarrel and all that he'd said – several people knew about it.'

Again Poirot nodded his head gravely.

'Just so. And I may say, mademoiselle, that but for the egoistical vanity of a killer, that is just what would have happened. If Donald Fraser escapes suspicion, it will be thanks to A B C's maniacal boasting.'

He was silent for a minute or two, then he said:

'Do you know if your sister met this married man, or any other man, lately?'

Megan shook her head.

'I don't know. I've been away, you see.'

'But what do you think?'

'She mayn't have met that particular man again. He'd probably sheer off if he thought there was a chance of a row, but it wouldn't surprise me if Betty had – well, been telling Don a few lies again. You see, she did so enjoy dancing and the pictures, and of course, Don couldn't afford to take her all the time.'

'If so, is she likely to have confided in anyone? The girl at the café, for instance?'

'I don't think that's likely. Betty couldn't bear the Higley girl. She thought her common. And the others would be new. Betty wasn't the confiding sort anyway.'

An electric bell trilled sharply above the girl's head.

She went to the window and leaned out. She drew back her head sharply.

'It's Don . . .'

'Bring him in here,' said Poirot quickly. 'I would like a word with him before our good inspector takes him in hand.'

Like a flash Megan Barnard was out of the kitchen, and a couple of seconds later she was back again leading Donald Fraser by the hand.

CHAPTER 12

DONALD FRASER

I felt sorry at once for the young man. His white haggard face and bewildered eyes showed how great a shock he had had.

He was a well-made, fine-looking young fellow, standing close on six foot, not good-looking, but with a pleasant, freckled face, high cheek-bones and flaming red hair.

'What's this, Megan?' he said. 'Why in here? For God's sake, tell me – I've only just heard – Betty . . .'

His voice trailed away.

Poirot pushed forward a chair and he sank down on it.

My friend then extracted a small flask from his pocket, poured some of its contents into a convenient cup which was hanging on the dresser and said:

'Drink some of this, Mr Fraser. It will do you good.'

The young man obeyed. The brandy brought a little colour back into his face. He sat up straighter and turned once more to the girl. His manner was quite quiet and self-controlled.

'It's true, I suppose?' he said. 'Betty is – dead – killed?'

'It's true, Don.'

He said as though mechanically:

'Have you just come down from London?'

'Yes. Dad phoned me.'

'By the 9.30, I suppose?' said Donald Fraser.

His mind, shrinking from reality, ran for safety along these unimportant details.

'Yes.'

There was silence for a minute or two, then Fraser said:

'The police? Are they doing anything?'

'They're upstairs now. Looking through Betty's things, I suppose.'

'They've no idea who –? They don't know –?'

He stopped.

He had all a sensitive, shy person's dislike of putting violent facts into words.

Poirot moved forward a little and asked a question. He spoke in a businesslike, matter-of-fact voice as though what he asked was an unimportant detail.

'Did Miss Barnard tell you where she was going last night?'

Fraser replied to the question. He seemed to be speaking mechanically:

'She told me she was going with a girl friend to St Leonards.'

'Did you believe her?'

'I –' Suddenly the automaton came to life. 'What the devil do you mean?'

His face then, menacing, convulsed by sudden passion, made me understand that a girl might well be afraid of rousing his anger.

Poirot said crisply:

'Betty Barnard was killed by a homicidal murderer. Only by speaking the exact truth can you help us to get on his track.'

His glance for a minute turned to Megan.

'That's right, Don,' she said. 'It isn't a time for considering one's own feelings or anyone else's. You've got to come clean.'

Donald Fraser looked suspiciously at Poirot.

'Who are you? You don't belong to the police?'

'I am better than the police,' said Poirot. He said it without conscious arrogance. It was, to him, a simple statement of fact.

'Tell him,' said Megan.

Donald Fraser capitulated.

'I – wasn't sure,' he said. 'I believed her when she said it. Never thought of doing anything else. Afterwards – perhaps it was something in her manner. I – I, well, I began to wonder.'

'Yes?' said Poirot.

He had sat down opposite Donald Fraser. His eyes, fixed on the other man's, seemed to be exercising a mesmeric spell.

'I was ashamed of myself for being so suspicious. But – but I *was* suspicious . . . I thought of going to the front and watching her when she left the café. I actually went there. Then I felt I couldn't do that. Betty would see me and she'd be angry. She'd realize at once that I was watching her.'

'What did you do?'

'I went over to St Leonards. Got over there by eight o'clock. Then I watched the buses – to see if she were in them . . . But there was no sign of her . . .'

'And then?'

'I – I lost my head rather. I was convinced she was with some man. I thought it probable he had taken her in his car to Hastings. I went on there – looked in hotels and restaurants, hung round cinemas – went on the pier. All damn foolishness. Even if she was there I was unlikely to find her, and anyway, there were heaps of other places he might have taken her to instead of Hastings.'

He stopped. Precise as his tone had remained, I caught an undertone of that blind, bewildering misery and anger that had possessed him at the time he described.

'In the end I gave it up – came back.'

'At what time?'

'I don't know. I walked. It must have been midnight or after when I got home.'

'Then –'

The kitchen door opened.

'Oh, there you are,' said Inspector Kelsey.

Inspector Crome pushed past him, shot a glance at Poirot and a glance at the two strangers.

'Miss Megan Barnard and Mr Donald Fraser,' said Poirot, introducing them.

'This is Inspector Crome from London,' he explained.

Turning to the inspector, he said:

'While you pursued your investigations upstairs I have been conversing with Miss Barnard and Mr Fraser, endeavouring if I could to find something that will throw light upon the matter.'

'Oh, yes?' said Inspector Crome, his thoughts not upon Poirot but upon the two newcomers.

Poirot retreated to the hall. Inspector Kelsey said kindly as he passed: 'Get anything?'

But his attention was distracted by his colleague and he did not wait for a reply.

I joined Poirot in the hall.

'Did anything strike you, Poirot?' I inquired.

'Only the amazing magnanimity of the murderer, Hastings.'

I had not the courage to say that I had not the least idea what he meant.

CHAPTER 13

A CONFERENCE

Conferences!

Much of my memories of the A B C case seem to be of conferences.

Conferences at Scotland Yard. At Poirot's rooms. Official conferences. Unofficial conferences.

This particular conference was to decide whether or not the facts relative to the anonymous letters should or should not be made public in the press.

The Bexhill murder had attracted much more attention than the Andover one.

It had, of course, far more elements of popularity. To begin with the victim was a young and good-looking girl. Also, it had taken place at a popular seaside resort.

All the details of the crime were reported fully and rehashed daily in thin disguises. The A B C railway guide came in for its share of attention.

The favourite theory was that it had been bought locally by the murderer and that it was a valuable clue to his identity. It also seemed to show that he had come to the place by train and was intending to leave for London.

The railway guide had not figured at all in the meagre accounts of the Andover murder, so there seemed at present little likelihood of the two crimes being connected in the public eye.

'We've got to decide upon a policy,' said the Assistant Commissioner. 'The thing is – which way will give us the best results? Shall we give the public the facts – enlist their co-operation – after all, it'll be the co-operation of several million people, looking out for a madman –'

'He won't look like a madman,' interjected Dr Thompson.

'– looking out for sales of A B C's – and so on. Against that I suppose there's the advantage of working in the dark – not letting our man know what we're up to, but then there's the fact that *he knows very well that we know*. He's drawn attention to himself deliberately by his letters. Eh, Crome, what's your opinion?'

'I look at it this way, sir. If you make it public, *you're playing A B C's game*. That's what he wants – publicity – notoriety. That's what he's out after. I'm right, aren't I, doctor? He wants to make a splash.'

Thompson nodded.

The Assistant Commissioner said thoughtfully:

'So you're for balking him. Refusing him the publicity he's hankering after. What about you, M. Poirot?'

Poirot did not speak for a minute. When he did it was with an air of choosing his words carefully.

'It is difficult for me, Sir Lionel,' he said. 'I am, as you might say, an interested party. The challenge was sent to me. If I say "Suppress that fact – do not make it public," may it not be thought that it is my vanity that speaks? That I am afraid for my reputation? It is difficult! To speak out – to tell all – that has its advantages. It is, at least, a warning . . . On the other hand, I am as convinced as Inspector Crome *that it is what the murderer wants us to do.*'

'H'm!' said the Assistant Commissioner, rubbing his chin. He looked across at Dr Thompson. 'Suppose we refuse our lunatic the satisfaction of the publicity he craves. What's he likely to do?'

'Commit another crime,' said the doctor promptly. 'Force your hand.'

'And if we splash the thing about in headlines. Then what's his reaction?'

'Same answer. One way you *feed* his megalomania, the other you *balk* it. The result's the same. Another crime.'

'What do you say, M. Poirot?'

'I agree with Dr Thompson.'

'A cleft stick – eh? How many crimes do you think this – lunatic has in mind?'

Dr Thompson looked across at Poirot.

'Looks like A to Z,' he said cheerfully.

'Of course,' he went on, 'he won't get there. Not nearly. You'll have him by the heels long before that. Interesting to know how he'd have dealt with the letter X.' He recalled himself guiltily from this purely enjoyable speculation. 'But you'll have him long before that. G or H, let's say.'

The Assistant Commissioner struck the table with his fist.

'My God, are you telling me we're going to have five more murders?'

'It won't be as much as that, sir,' said Inspector Crome. 'Trust me.'

He spoke with confidence.

'Which letter of the alphabet do you place it at, inspector?' asked Poirot.

There was a slight ironic note in his voice. Crome, I thought, looked at him with a tinge of dislike adulterating the usual calm superiority.

'Might get him next time, M. Poirot. At any rate, I'd guarantee to get him by the time he gets to F.'

He turned to the Assistant Commissioner.

'I think I've got the psychology of the case fairly clear. Dr Thompson will correct me if I'm wrong. I take it that every time A B C brings a crime off, his self-confidence increases about a hundred per cent. Every time he feels "I'm clever – they can't catch me!" he becomes so over-weeningly confident that he also becomes careless. He exaggerates his own cleverness and everyone else's stupidity. Very soon he'd be hardly bothering to take any precautions at all. That's right, isn't it, doctor?'

Thompson nodded.

'That's usually the case. In non-medical terms it couldn't have been put better. You know something about such things, M. Poirot. Don't you agree?'

I don't think that Crome liked Thompson's appeal to Poirot. He considered that he and he only was the expert on this subject.

'It is as Inspector Crome says,' agreed Poirot.

'Paranoia,' murmured the doctor.

Poirot turned to Crome.

'Are there any material facts of interest in the Bexhill case?'

'Nothing very definite. A waiter at the Splendide at Eastbourne recognizes the dead girl's photograph as that of a young woman who dined there on the evening of the 24th in company with a middle-aged man in spectacles. It's also been recognized at a roadhouse place called the Scarlet Runner half-way between Bexhill and London. They say she was there about 9 pm on the 24th with a man who looked like a naval officer. They can't both be right, but either of them's probable. Of course, there's a host of other identifications, but most of them not good for much. We haven't been able to trace the A B C.'

'Well, you seem to be doing all that can be done, Crome,' said the Assistant Commissioner. 'What do you say, M. Poirot? Does any line of inquiry suggest itself to you?'

Poirot said slowly:

'It seems to me that there is one very important clue – the discovery of the motive.'

'Isn't that pretty obvious? An alphabetical complex. Isn't that what you called it, doctor?'

'Ça, oui,' said Poirot. 'There is an alphabetical complex. But why an alphabetical complex? A madman in particular has always a very strong reason for the crimes he commits.'

'Come, come, M. Poirot,' said Crome. 'Look at Stoneman in 1929. He ended by trying to do away with anyone who annoyed him in the slightest degree.'

Poirot turned to him.

'Quite so. But if you are a sufficiently great and important person, it is necessary that you should be spared small annoyances. If a fly settles on your forehead again and again, maddening you by its tickling – what do you do? You endeavour to kill that fly. You have no qualms about it. *You* are important – the fly is not. You kill the fly and the annoyance ceases. Your action appears to you sane and justifiable. Another reason for killing a fly is if you have a strong passion for hygiene. The fly is a potential source of danger to the community – the fly must go. So works the mind of the mentally deranged criminal. But consider now this case – *if the victims are alphabetically selected, then they are not being removed because they are a source of annoyance to the murderer personally.* It would be too much of a coincidence to combine the two.'

'That's a point,' said Dr Thompson. 'I remember a case where a woman's husband was condemned to death. She started killing the members of the jury one by one. Quite a time before the crimes were connected up. They seemed entirely haphazard. But as M. Poirot says, there isn't such a thing as a murderer who commits crimes at *random*. Either he removes people who stand (however insignificantly) in his path, or else he kills by *conviction*. He removes clergymen, or policemen, or prostitutes because he firmly believes that they *should* be removed. That doesn't apply here either as far as I can see. Mrs Ascher and Betty Barnard cannot be linked as members of the same class. Of course, it's possible that there is a sex complex. Both victims have been women. We can tell better, of course, after the next crime –'

'For God's sake, Thompson, don't speak so glibly of the next crime,' said Sir Lionel irritably. 'We're going to do all we can to prevent another crime.'

Dr Thompson held his peace and blew his nose with some violence.

'Have it your own way,' the noise seemed to say. 'If you won't face facts –'

The Assistant Commissioner turned to Poirot.

'I see what you're driving at, but I'm not quite clear yet.'

'I ask myself,' said Poirot, 'what passes exactly in the mind of the murderer? He kills, it would seem from his letters, *pour le sport* – to amuse himself. Can that really be true? And even if it is true, on what principle does he select his victims *apart from the merely alphabetical one*? If he kills merely to amuse himself he would not advertise the fact, since, otherwise, he could kill with impunity. But no, he seeks, as we all agree, to make the splash in the public eye – to assert his personality. In what way has his personality been suppressed that one can connect with the two victims he has so far selected? A final suggestion: Is his motive direct personal hatred of *me*, of Hercule Poirot? Does he challenge me in public because I have (unknown to myself) vanquished him somewhere in the course of my career? Or is his animosity impersonal – directed against a *foreigner*? And if so, what again has led to that? What injury has he suffered at a foreigner's hand?'

'All very suggestive questions,' said Dr Thompson.

Inspector Crome cleared his throat.

'Oh, yes? A little unanswerable at present, perhaps.'

'Nevertheless, my friend,' said Poirot, looking straight at him, '*it is there, in those questions, that the solution lies*. If we knew the exact reason – fantastic, perhaps, to us – but logical to him – of *why* our madman commits these crimes, we should know, perhaps, who the next victim is likely to be.'

Crome shook his head.

'He selects them haphazard – that's my opinion.'

'The magnanimous murderer,' said Poirot.

'What's that you say?'

'I said – the magnanimous murderer! Franz Ascher would have been arrested for the murder of his wife – Donald Fraser might have been arrested for the murder of Betty Barnard – if it had not been for the warning letters of A B C. Is he, then, so soft-hearted that he cannot bear others to suffer for something they did not do?'

'I've known stranger things happen,' said Dr Thompson. 'I've known men who've killed half a dozen victims all broken up because one of their victims didn't die instantaneously and suffered pain. All the same, I don't think that that is our fellow's reason. He wants the credit of these crimes for his own honour and glory. That's the explanation that fits best.'

'We've come to no decision about the publicity business,' said the Assistant Commissioner.

'If I may make a suggestion, sir,' said Crome. 'Why not wait till the receipt of the next letter? Make it public then – special editions, etc. It will make a bit of a panic in the particular town named, but it will put everyone whose name begins with C on their guard, and it'll put A B C on his mettle. He'll be determined to succeed. And that's when we'll get him.'

How little we knew what the future held.

CHAPTER 14

THE THIRD LETTER

I well remember the arrival of A B C's third letter.

I may say that all precautions had been taken so that when A B C resumed his campaign there should be no unnecessary delays. A young sergeant from Scotland Yard was attached to the house and if Poirot and I were out it was his duty to open anything that came so as to be able to communicate with headquarters without loss of time.

As the days succeeded each other we had all grown more and more on edge. Inspector Crome's aloof and superior manner grew more and more aloof and superior as one by one his more hopeful clues petered out. The vague descriptions of men said to have been seen with Betty Barnard proved useless. Various cars noticed in the vicinity of Bexhill and Cooden were either accounted for or could not be traced. The investigation of purchases of A B C railway guides caused inconvenience and trouble to heaps of innocent people.

As for ourselves, each time the postman's familiar rat-tat sounded on the door, our hearts beat faster with apprehension. At least that was true for me, and I cannot but believe that Poirot experienced the same sensation.

He was, I knew, deeply unhappy over the case. He refused to leave London, preferring to be on the spot in case of emergency. In those hot dog days even his moustaches drooped – neglected for once by their owner.

It was on a Friday that A B C's third letter came. The evening post arrived about ten o'clock.

When we heard the familiar step and the brisk rat-tat, I rose and went along to the box. There were four or five letters, I remember. The last one I looked at was addressed in printed characters.

'Poirot,' I cried . . . My voice died away.

'It has come? Open it, Hastings. Quickly. Every moment may be needed. We must make our plans.'

I tore open the letter (Poirot for once did not reproach me with untidiness) and extracted the printed sheet.

'Read it,' said Poirot.

I read aloud:

> *Poor Mr Poirot, – Not so good at these little criminal matters as you thought yourself, are you? Rather past your prime, perhaps? Let us see if you can do any better this time. This time it's an easy one. Churston on the 30th. Do try and do something about it! It's a bit dull having it* all *my own way, you know!*
> *Good hunting. Ever yours,*
> *A B C.*

'Churston,' I said, jumping to our own copy of an A B C. 'Let's see where it is.'

'Hastings,' Poirot's voice came sharply and interrupted me. 'When was that letter written? Is there a date on it?'

I glanced at the letter in my hand.

'Written on the 27th,' I announced.

'Did I hear you aright, Hastings? Did he give the date of the murder as the *30th*?'

'That's right. Let me see, that's –'

'*Bon Dieu*, Hastings – do you not realize? *Today is the 30th.*'

His eloquent hand pointed to the calendar on the wall. I caught up the daily paper to confirm it.

'But why – how –' I stammered.

Poirot caught up the torn envelope from the floor. Something unusual about the address had registered itself vaguely in my brain, but I had been too anxious to get at the contents of the letter to pay more than fleeting attention to it.

Poirot was at the time living in Whitehaven Mansions. The address ran: *M. Hercule Poirot, Whitehorse Mansions*, across the corner was scrawled: '*Not known at Whitehorse Mansions, EC1, nor at Whitehorse Court – try Whitehaven Mansions.*'

'*Mon Dieu!*' murmured Poirot. 'Does even chance aid this madman? *Vite – vite* – we must get on to Scotland Yard.'

A minute or two later we were speaking to Crome over the wire. For once the self-controlled inspector did not reply 'Oh, yes?' Instead a quickly stifled curse came to his lips. He heard what we had to say, then rang off in order to get a trunk connection to Churston as rapidly as possible.

'*C'est trop tard,*' murmured Poirot.

'You can't be sure of that,' I argued, though without any great hope.

He glanced at the clock.

'Twenty minutes past ten? An hour and forty minutes to go. Is it likely that A B C will have held his hand so long?'

I opened the railway guide I had previously taken from its shelf.

'Churston, Devon,' I read, 'from Paddington 204¾ miles. Population 656. It sounds a fairly small place. Surely our man will be bound to be noticed there.'

'Even so, another life will have been taken,' murmured Poirot. 'What are the trains? I imagine train will be quicker than car.'

'There's a midnight train – sleeping car to Newton Abbot – gets there 6.8 am, and then Churston at 7.15.'

'That is from Paddington?'

'Paddington, yes.'

'We will take that, Hastings.'

'You'll hardly have time to get news before we start.'

'If we receive bad news tonight or tomorrow morning does it matter which?'

'There's something in that.'

I put a few things together in a suitcase while Poirot once more rang up Scotland Yard.

A few minutes later he came into the bedroom and demanded:

'*Mais qu'est-ce que vous faites là?*'

'I was packing for you. I thought it would save time.'

'*Vous éprouvez trop d'émotion, Hastings.* It affects your hands and your wits. Is that a way to fold a coat? And regard what you have done to my pyjamas. If the hairwash breaks what will befall them?'

'Good heavens, Poirot,' I cried, 'this is a matter of life and death. What does it matter what happens to our clothes?'

'You have no sense of proportion, Hastings. We cannot catch a train earlier than the time that it leaves, and to ruin one's clothes will not be the least helpful in preventing a murder.'

Taking his suitcase from me firmly, he took the packing into his own hands.

He explained that we were to take the letter and envelope to Paddington with us. Someone from Scotland Yard would meet us there.

When we arrived on the platform the first person we saw was Inspector Crome.

He answered Poirot's look of inquiry.

'No news as yet. All men available are on the look-out. All persons whose name begins with C are being warned by phone when possible. There's just a chance. Where's the letter?'

Poirot gave it to him.

He examined it, swearing softly under his breath.

'Of all the damned luck. The stars in their courses fight for the fellow.'

'You don't think,' I suggested, 'that it was done on purpose?'

Crome shook his head.

'No. He's got his rules – crazy rules – and abides by them. Fair warning. He makes a point of that. That's where his boastfulness comes in. I wonder now – I'd almost bet the chap drinks White Horse whisky.'

'*Ah, c'est ingénieux, ça!*' said Poirot, driven to admiration in spite of himself. 'He prints the letter and the bottle is in front of him.'

'That's the way of it,' said Crome. 'We've all of us done much the same thing one time or another, unconsciously copied something that's just under the eye. He started off White and went on horse instead of haven . . .'

The inspector, we found, was also travelling by the train.

'Even if by some unbelievable luck nothing happened, Churston is the place to be. Our murderer is there, or has been there today. One of my men is on the phone here up to the last minute in case anything comes through.'

Just as the train was leaving the station we saw a man running down the platform. He reached the inspector's window and called up something.

As the train drew out of the station Poirot and I hurried along the corridor and tapped on the door of the inspector's sleeper.

'You have news – yes?' demanded Poirot.

Crome said quietly:

'It's about as bad as it can be. Sir Carmichael Clarke has been found with his head bashed in.'

Sir Carmichael Clarke, although his name was not very well known to the general public, was a man of some eminence. He had been in his time a very well-known throat specialist. Retiring from his profession very comfortably off, he had been able to indulge what had been one of the chief passions of his life – a collection of Chinese pottery and porcelain. A few years later, inheriting a considerable fortune from an elderly uncle, he had been able to indulge his passion to the full, and he was now the possessor of one of the best-known collections of Chinese art. He was married but had no children and lived in a house he had built for himself near the Devon coast, only coming to London on rare occasions such as when some important sale was on.

It did not require much reflection to realize that his death, following that of the young and pretty Betty Barnard, would provide the best newspaper sensation for years. The fact that it was August and that the papers were hard up for subject matter would make matters worse.

'*Eh bien*,' said Poirot. 'It is possible that publicity may do what private efforts have failed to do. The whole country now will be looking for A B C.'

'Unfortunately,' I said, 'that's what he wants.'

'True. But it may, all the same, be his undoing. Gratified by success, he may become careless . . . That is what I hope – that he may be drunk with his own cleverness.'

'How odd all this is, Poirot,' I exclaimed, struck suddenly by an idea. 'Do you know, this is the first crime of this kind that you and I have worked on together? All our murders have been – well, private murders, so to speak.'

'You are quite right, my friend. Always, up to now, it has fallen to our lot to work from the *inside*. It has been the history of the *victim* that was important. The important points have been: "Who benefited by the death? What opportunities had those round him to commit the crime?" It has always been the "*crime intime*". Here, for the first time in our association, it is cold-blooded, impersonal murder. Murder from the *outside*.'

I shivered.

'It's rather horrible . . .'

'Yes. I felt from the first, when I read the original letter, that there was something wrong – misshapen . . .'

He made an impatient gesture.

'One must not give way to the nerves . . . *This is no worse than any ordinary crime . . .*'

'It is . . . It is . . .'

'Is it worse to take the life or lives of strangers than to take the life of someone near and dear to you – someone who trusts and believes in you, perhaps?'

'It's worse because it's *mad . . .*'

'No, Hastings. It is not *worse*. It is only more *difficult*.'

'No, no, I do not agree with you. It's infinitely more frightening.'

Hercule Poirot said thoughtfully:

'It should be easier to discover because it is mad. A crime committed by someone shrewd and sane would be far more complicated. Here, if one could but hit on the *idea* . . . This alphabetical business, it has discrepancies. If I could once see the *idea* – then everything would be clear and simple . . .'

He sighed and shook his head.

'These crimes must not go on. Soon, soon, I must see the truth . . . Go, Hastings. Get some sleep. There will be much to do tomorrow.'

CHAPTER 15

SIR CARMICHAEL CLARKE

Churston, lying as it does between Brixham on the one side and Paignton and Torquay on the other, occupies a position about half-way round the curve of Torbay. Until about ten years ago it was merely a golf links and below the links a green sweep of countryside dropping down to the sea with only a farmhouse or two in the way of human occupation. But of late years there had been big building developments between Churston and Paignton and the coastline is now dotted with small houses and bungalows, new roads, etc.

Sir Carmichael Clarke had purchased a site of some two acres commanding an uninterrupted view of the sea. The house he had built was of modern design – a white rectangle that was not unpleasing to the eye. Apart from two big galleries that housed his collection it was not a large house.

Our arrival there took place about 8 am. A local police officer had met us at the station and had put us *au courant* of the situation.

Sir Carmichael Clarke, it seemed, had been in the habit of taking a stroll after dinner every evening. When the police rang up – at some time after eleven – it was ascertained that he had not returned. Since his stroll usually followed the same course, it was not long before a search-party discovered his body. Death was due to a crashing blow with some heavy instrument on the back of the head. *An open A B C had been placed face downwards on the dead body.*

We arrived at Combeside (as the house was called) at about eight o'clock. The door was opened by an elderly butler whose shaking hands and disturbed face showed how much the tragedy had affected him.

'Good morning, Deveril,' said the police officer.

'Good morning, Mr Wells.'

'These are the gentlemen from London, Deveril.'

'This way, gentlemen.' He ushered us into a long dining-room where breakfast was laid. 'I'll get Mr Franklin.'

A minute or two later a big fair-haired man with a sunburnt face entered the room.

This was Franklin Clarke, the dead man's only brother.

He had the resolute competent manner of a man accustomed to meeting with emergencies.

'Good morning, gentlemen.'

Inspector Wells made the introductions.

'This is Inspector Crome of the CID, Mr Hercule Poirot and – er – Captain Hayter.'

'Hastings,' I corrected coldly.

Franklin Clarke shook hands with each of us in turn and in each case the handshake was accompanied by a piercing look.

'Let me offer you some breakfast,' he said. 'We can discuss the position as we eat.'

There were no dissentient voices and we were soon doing justice to excellent eggs and bacon and coffee.

'Now for it,' said Franklin Clarke. 'Inspector Wells gave me a rough idea of the position last night – though I may say it seemed one of the wildest tales I have ever heard. Am I really to believe, Inspector Crome, that my poor brother is the victim of a homicidal maniac, that this is the third murder that has occurred and that *in each case an A B C railway guide has been deposited beside the body*?'

'That is substantially the position, Mr Clarke.'

'But *why*? What earthly benefit can accrue from such a crime – even in the most diseased imagination?'

Poirot nodded his head in approval.

'You go straight to the point, Mr Franklin,' he said.

'It's not much good looking for motives at this stage, Mr Clarke,' said Inspector Crome. 'That's a matter for an alienist – though I may say that I've had a certain experience of criminal lunacy and that the motives are usually grossly inadequate. There is a desire to assert one's personality, to make a splash in the public eye – in fact, to be a somebody instead of a nonentity.'

'Is that true, M. Poirot?'

Clarke seemed incredulous. His appeal to the older man was not too well received by Inspector Crome, who frowned.

'Absolutely true,' replied my friend.

'At any rate such a man cannot escape detection long,' said Clarke thoughtfully.

'*Vous croyez?* Ah, but they are cunning – *ces gens là!* And you must remember *such a type has usually all the outer signs of insignificance* – he belongs to the class of person who is usually passed over and ignored or even laughed at!'

'Will you let me have a few facts, please, Mr Clarke,' said Crome, breaking in on the conversation.

'Certainly.'

'Your brother, I take it, was in his usual health and spirits yesterday? He received no unexpected letters? Nothing to upset him?'

'No. I should say he was quite his usual self.'

'Not upset and worried in any way.'

'Excuse me, inspector. I didn't say that. To be upset and worried was my poor brother's normal condition.'

'Why was that?'

'You may not know that my sister-in-law, Lady Clarke, is in very bad health. Frankly, between ourselves, she is suffering from an incurable cancer, and cannot live very much longer. Her illness has preyed terribly on my brother's mind. I myself returned from the East not long ago and I was shocked at the change in him.'

Poirot interpolated a question.

'Supposing, Mr Clarke, that your brother had been found shot at the foot of a cliff – or shot with a revolver beside him. What would have been your first thought?'

'Quite frankly, I should have jumped to the conclusion that it was suicide,' said Clarke.

'*Encore!*' said Poirot.

'What is that?'

'A fact that repeats itself. It is of no matter.'

'Anyway, it *wasn't* suicide,' said Crome with a touch of curtness. 'Now I believe, Mr Clarke, that it was your brother's habit to go for a stroll every evening?'

'Quite right. He always did.'

'Every night?'

'Well, not if it was pouring with rain, naturally.'

'And everyone in the house knew of this habit?'

'Of course.'

'And outside?'

'I don't quite know what you mean by outside. The gardener may have been aware of it or not, I don't know.'

'And in the village?'

'Strictly speaking, we haven't got a village. There's a post office and cottages at Churston Ferrers – but there's no village or shops.'

'I suppose a stranger hanging round the place would be fairly easily noticed?'

'On the contrary. In August all this part of the world is a seething mass of strangers. They come over every day from Brixham and Torquay and Paignton in cars and buses and on foot. Broadsands, which is down there (he pointed), is a very popular beach and so is Elbury Cove – it's a well-known beauty spot and people come there and picnic. I wish they didn't! You've no idea how beautiful and peaceful this part of the world is in June and the beginning of July.'

'So you don't think a stranger would be noticed?'

'Not unless he looked – well, off his head.'

'This man doesn't look off his head,' said Crome with certainty. 'You see what I'm getting at, Mr Clarke. This man must have been spying out the land beforehand and discovered your brother's habit of taking an evening stroll. I suppose, by the way, that no strange man came up to the house and asked to see Sir Carmichael yesterday?'

'Not that I know of – but we'll ask Deveril.'

He rang the bell and put the question to the butler.

'No, sir, no one came to see Sir Carmichael. And I didn't notice anyone hanging about the house either. No more did the maids, because I've asked them.'

The butler waited a moment, then inquired: 'Is that all, sir?'

'Yes, Deveril, you can go.'

The butler withdrew, drawing back in the doorway to let a young woman pass.

Franklin Clarke rose as she came in.

'This is Miss Grey, gentlemen. My brother's secretary.'

My attention was caught at once by the girl's extraordinary Scandinavian fairness. She had the almost colourless ash hair – light-grey eyes – and transparent glowing pallor that one finds amongst Norwegians and Swedes. She looked about twenty-seven and seemed to be as efficient as she was decorative.

'Can I help you in any way?' she asked as she sat down.

Clarke brought her a cup of coffee, but she refused any food.

'Did you deal with Sir Carmichael's correspondence?' asked Crome.

'Yes, all of it.'

'I suppose he never received a letter or letters signed A B C?'

'A B C?' She shook her head. 'No, I'm sure he didn't.'

'He didn't mention having seen anyone hanging about during his evening walks lately?'

'No. He never mentioned anything of the kind.'

'And you yourself have noticed no strangers?'

'Not exactly hanging about. Of course, there are a lot of people what you might call *wandering* about at this time of year. One often meets people strolling with an aimless look across the golf links or down the lanes to the sea. In the same way, practically everyone one sees this time of year is a stranger.'

Poirot nodded thoughtfully.

Inspector Crome asked to be taken over the ground of Sir Carmichael's nightly walk. Franklin Clarke led the way through the french window, and Miss Grey accompanied us.

She and I were a little behind the others.

'All this must have been a terrible shock to you all,' I said.

'It seems quite unbelievable. I had gone to bed last night when the police rang up. I heard voices downstairs and at last I came out and asked what was the matter. Deveril and Mr Clarke were just setting out with lanterns.'

'What time did Sir Carmichael usually come back from his walk?'

'About a quarter to ten. He used to let himself in by the side door and then sometimes he went straight to bed, sometimes to the gallery where his collections were. That is why, unless the police had rung up, he would probably not have been missed till they went to call him this morning.'

'It must have been a terrible shock to his wife?'

'Lady Clarke is kept under morphia a good deal. I think she is in too dazed a condition to appreciate what goes on round her.'

We had come out through a garden gate on to the golf links. Crossing a corner of them, we passed over a stile into a steep, winding lane.

'This leads down to Elbury Cove,' explained Franklin Clarke. 'But two years ago they made a new road leading from the main road to Broadsands and on to Elbury, so that now this lane is practically deserted.'

We went on down the lane. At the foot of it a path led between brambles and bracken down to the sea. Suddenly we came out on a grassy ridge overlooking the sea and a beach of glistening white stones. All round dark green trees ran down to the sea. It was an enchanting spot – white, deep green – and sapphire blue.

'How beautiful!' I exclaimed.

Clarke turned to me eagerly.

'Isn't it? Why people want to go abroad to the Riviera when they've got this! I've wandered all over the world in my time and, honest to God, I've never seen anything as beautiful.'

Then, as though ashamed of his eagerness, he said in a more matter-of-fact tone:

'This was my brother's evening walk. He came as far as here, then back up the path, and turning to the right instead of the left, went past the farm and across the fields back to the house.'

We proceeded on our way till we came to a spot near the hedge, half-way across the field where the body had been found.

Crome nodded.

'Easy enough. The man stood here in the shadow. Your brother would have noticed nothing till the blow fell.'

The girl at my side gave a quick shiver.

Franklin Clarke said:

'Hold up, Thora. It's pretty beastly, but it's no use shirking facts.'

Thora Grey – the name suited her.

We went back to the house where the body had been taken after being photographed.

As we mounted the wide staircase the doctor came out of a room, black bag in hand.

'Anything to tell us, doctor?' inquired Clarke.

The doctor shook his head.

'Perfectly simple case. I'll keep the technicalities for the inquest. Anyway, he didn't suffer. Death must have been instantaneous.'

He moved away.

'I'll just go in and see Lady Clarke.'

A hospital nurse came out of a room farther along the corridor and the doctor joined her.

We went into the room out of which the doctor had come.

I came out again rather quickly. Thora Grey was still standing at the head of the stairs.

There was a queer scared expression on her face.

'Miss Grey –' I stopped. 'Is anything the matter?'

She looked at me.

'I was thinking,' she said, 'about D.'

'About D?' I stared at her stupidly.

'Yes. The next murder. Something must be done. It's got to be stopped.'

Clarke came out of the room behind me.

He said:

'What's got to be stopped, Thora?'

'These awful murders.'

'Yes.' His jaw thrust itself out aggressively. 'I want to talk to M. Poirot some time . . . Is Crome any good?' He shot the words out unexpectedly.

I replied that he was supposed to be a very clever officer.

My voice was perhaps not as enthusiastic as it might have been.

'He's got a damned offensive manner,' said Clarke. 'Looks as though he knows everything – and what *does* he know? Nothing at all as far as I can make out.'

He was silent for a minute or two. Then he said:

'M. Poirot's the man for my money. I've got a plan. But we'll talk of that later.'

He went along the passage and tapped at the same door as the doctor had entered.

I hesitated a moment. The girl was staring in front of her.

'What are you thinking of, Miss Grey?'

She turned her eyes towards me.

'I'm wondering *where he is now* . . . the murderer, I mean. It's not twelve hours yet since it happened . . . Oh! aren't there any *real* clairvoyants who could see where he is now and what he is doing . . .'

'The police are searching –' I began.

My commonplace words broke the spell. Thora Grey pulled herself together.

'Yes,' she said. 'Of course.'

In her turn she descended the staircase. I stood there a moment longer conning her words over in my mind.

A B C . . .

Where was he now . . . ?

CHAPTER 16

NOT FROM CAPTAIN HASTINGS' PERSONAL NARRATIVE

Mr Alexander Bonaparte Cust came out with the rest of the audience from the Torquay Palladium, where he had been seeing and hearing that highly emotional film, *Not a Sparrow* . . .

He blinked a little as he came out into the afternoon sunshine and peered round him in that lost-dog fashion that was characteristic of him.

He murmured to himself: 'It's an idea . . .'

Newsboys passed along crying out:

'Latest . . . Homicidal Maniac at Churston . . .'

They carried placards on which was written:

CHURSTON MURDER. LATEST.

Mr Cust fumbled in his pocket, found a coin, and bought a paper. He did not open it at once.

Entering the Princess Gardens, he slowly made his way to a shelter facing Torquay harbour. He sat down and opened the paper.

There were big headlines:

SIR CARMICHAEL CLARKE MURDERED.
TERRIBLE TRAGEDY AT CHURSTON.
WORK OF A HOMICIDAL MANIAC.

And below them:

Only a month ago England was shocked and startled by the murder of a young girl, Elizabeth Barnard, at Bexhill. It may be remembered that an A B C railway guide figured in the case. An A B C was also found by the dead body of Sir Carmichael Clarke, and the police incline to the belief that both crimes were committed by the same

*person. Can it be possible that a homicidal murderer is going the
round of our seaside resorts? . . .*

A young man in flannel trousers and a bright blue Aertex shirt who was
sitting beside Mr Cust remarked:

'Nasty business – eh?'

Mr Cust jumped.

'Oh, very – very –'

His hands, the young man noticed, were trembling so that he could
hardly hold the paper.

'You never know with lunatics,' said the young man chattily. 'They
don't always look barmy, you know. Often they seem just the same as
you or me . . .'

'I suppose they do,' said Mr Cust.

'It's a fact. Sometimes it's the war what unhinged them – never been
right since.'

'I – I expect you're right.'

'I don't hold with wars,' said the young man.

His companion turned on him.

'I don't hold with plague and sleeping sickness and famine and cancer . . .
but they happen all the same!'

'War's preventable,' said the young man with assurance.

Mr Cust laughed. He laughed for some time.

The young man was slightly alarmed.

'He's a bit batty himself,' he thought.

Aloud he said:

'Sorry, sir, I expect you were in the war.'

'I was,' said Mr Cust. 'It – it – unsettled me. My head's never been
right since. It aches, you know. Aches terribly.'

'Oh! I'm sorry about that,' said the young man awkwardly.

'Sometimes I hardly know what I'm doing . . .'

'Really? Well, I must be getting along,' said the young man and removed
himself hurriedly. He knew what people were once they began to talk about
their health.

Mr Cust remained with his paper.

He read and reread . . .

People passed to and fro in front of him.

Most of them were talking of the murder . . .

'Awful . . . do you think it was anything to do with the Chinese? Wasn't
the waitress in a Chinese café . . .'

'Actually on the golf links . . .'

'I heard it was on the beach . . .'

'– but, darling, we took our tea to Elbury only *yesterday* . . .'

'– police are sure to get him . . .'

'– say he may be arrested any minute now . . .'

'– quite likely he's in Torquay . . . that other woman was who murdered the what do you call 'ems . . .'

Mr Cust folded up the paper very neatly and laid it on the seat. Then he rose and walked sedately along towards the town.

Girls passed him, girls in white and pink and blue, in summery frocks and pyjamas and shorts. They laughed and giggled. Their eyes appraised the men they passed.

Not once did their eyes linger for a second on Mr Cust . . .

He sat down at a little table and ordered tea and Devonshire cream . . .

CHAPTER 17

MARKING TIME

With the murder of Sir Carmichael Clarke the A B C mystery leaped into the fullest prominence.

The newspapers were full of nothing else. All sorts of 'clues' were reported to have been discovered. Arrests were announced to be imminent. There were photographs of every person or place remotely connected with the murder. There were interviews with anyone who would give interviews. There were questions asked in Parliament.

The Andover murder was now bracketed with the other two.

It was the belief of Scotland Yard that the fullest publicity was the best chance of laying the murderer by the heels. The population of Great Britain turned itself into an army of amateur sleuths.

The *Daily Flicker* had the grand inspiration of using the caption:

HE MAY BE IN *YOUR* TOWN!

Poirot, of course, was in the thick of things. The letters sent to him were published and facsimiled. He was abused wholesale for not having prevented the crimes and defended on the ground that he was on the point of naming the murderer.

Reporters incessantly badgered him for interviews.

What M. Poirot Says Today.

Which was usually followed by a half-column of imbecilities.

M. Poirot Takes Grave View of Situation.
  M. Poirot on the Eve of Success.
  Captain Hastings, the great friend of M. Poirot, told our Special Representative . . .

'Poirot,' I would cry. 'Pray believe me. I never said anything of the kind.'
My friend would reply kindly:
'I know, Hastings – I know. The spoken word and the written – there is an astonishing gulf between them. There is a way of turning sentences that completely reverses the original meaning.'
'I wouldn't like you to think I'd said –'
'But do not worry yourself. All this is of no importance. These imbecilities, even, may help.'
'How?'
'*Eh bien,*' said Poirot grimly. 'If our madman reads what I am supposed to have said to the *Daily Blague* today, he will lose all respect for me as an opponent!'
 I am, perhaps, giving the impression that nothing practical was being done in the way of investigations. On the contrary, Scotland Yard and the local police of the various counties were indefatigable in following up the smallest clues.
Hotels, people who kept lodgings, boarding-houses – all those within a wide radius of the crimes were questioned minutely.
Hundreds of stories from imaginative people who had 'seen a man looking very queer and rolling his eyes', or 'noticed a man with a sinister face slinking along', were sifted to the last detail. No information, even of the vaguest character, was neglected. Trains, buses, trams, railway porters, conductors, bookstalls, stationers – there was an indefatigable round of questions and verifications.
At least a score of people were detained and questioned until they could satisfy the police as to their movements on the night in question.
The net result was not entirely a blank. Certain statements were borne in mind and noted down as of possible value, but without further evidence they led nowhere.
If Crome and his colleagues were indefatigable, Poirot seemed to me strangely supine. We argued now and again.

'But what is it that you would have me do, my friend? The routine inquiries, the police make them better than I do. Always – always you want me to run about like the dog.'

'Instead of which you sit at home like – like –'

'A sensible man! My force, Hastings, is in my *brain*, not in my *feet*! All the time, whilst I seem to you idle, I am reflecting.'

'Reflecting?' I cried. 'Is this a time for reflection?'

'Yes, a thousand times yes.'

'But what can you possibly gain by reflection? You know the facts of the three cases by heart.'

'It is not the facts I reflect upon – but the mind of the murderer.'

'The mind of a madman!'

'Precisely. And therefore not to be arrived at in a minute. *When I know what the murderer is like, I shall be able to find out who he is.* And all the time I learn more. After the Andover crime, what did we know about the murderer? Next to nothing at all. After the Bexhill crime? A little more. After the Churston murder? More still. I begin to see – not what *you* would like to see – the outlines of *a face and form* but the outlines of a *mind*. A mind that moves and works in certain definite directions. After the next crime –'

'Poirot!'

My friend looked at me dispassionately.

'But, yes, Hastings, I think it is almost certain there will be another. A lot depends on *la chance*. So far our *inconnu* has been lucky. This time the luck may turn against him. But in any case, after another crime, we shall know infinitely more. Crime is terribly revealing. Try and vary your methods as you will, your tastes, your habits, your attitude of mind, and your soul is revealed by your actions. There are confusing indications – sometimes it is as though there were two intelligences at work – but soon the outline will clear itself, *I shall know*.'

'Who it is?'

'No, Hastings, I shall not know his name and address! I shall know *what kind of a man he is* . . .'

'And then? . . .'

'*Et alors, je vais à la pêche*.'

As I looked rather bewildered, he went on:

'You comprehend, Hastings, an expert fisherman knows exactly what flies to offer to what fish. I shall offer the right kind of fly.'

'And then?'

'And then? And then? You are as bad as the superior Crome with his eternal "Oh, yes?" *Eh bien*, and then he will take the bait and the hook and we will reel in the line . . .'

'In the meantime people are dying right and left.'

'Three people. And there are, what is it – about 120 – road deaths every week?'

'That is entirely different.'

'It is probably exactly the same to those who die. For the others, the relations, the friends – yes, there is a difference, but one thing at least rejoices me in this case.'

'By all means let us hear anything in the nature of rejoicing.'

'*Inutile* to be so sarcastic. It rejoices me that there is here no shadow of guilt to distress the innocent.'

'Isn't this worse?'

'No, no, a thousand times no! There is nothing so terrible as to live in an atmosphere of suspicion – to see eyes watching you and the love in them changing to fear – nothing so terrible as to suspect those near and dear to you – It is poisonous – a miasma. No, the poisoning of life for the innocent, that, at least, we cannot lay at A B C's door.'

'You'll soon be making excuses for the man!' I said bitterly.

'Why not? He may believe himself fully justified. We may, perhaps, end by having sympathy with his point of view.'

'Really, Poirot!'

'Alas! I have shocked you. First my inertia – and then my views.'

I shook my head without replying.

'All the same,' said Poirot after a minute or two. 'I have one project that will please you – since it is active and not passive. Also, it will entail a lot of conversation and practically no thought.'

I did not quite like his tone.

'What is it?' I asked cautiously.

'The extraction from the friends, relations and servants of the victims of all they know.'

'Do you suspect them of keeping things back, then?'

'Not intentionally. But telling everything you know always implies *selection*. If I were to say to you, recount me your day yesterday, you would perhaps reply: "I rose at nine, I breakfasted at half-past, I had eggs and bacon and coffee, I went to my club, etc." You would not include: "I tore my nail and had to cut it. I rang for shaving water. I spilt a little coffee on the tablecloth. I brushed my hat and put it on." One cannot tell *everything*. Therefore one *selects*. At the time of a murder people select what *they* think is important. But quite frequently they think wrong!'

'And how is one to get at the right things?'

'Simply, as I said just now, by conversation. By talking! By discussing a certain happening, or a certain person, or a certain day, over and over again, extra details are bound to arise.'

'What kind of details?'

'Naturally that I do not know or I should not want to find out. But enough time has passed now for ordinary things to reassume their value. It is against all mathematical laws that in three cases of murder there is no single fact nor sentence with a bearing on the case. Some trivial happening, some trivial remark there *must* be which would be a pointer! It is looking for the needle in the haystack, I grant – *but in the haystack there is a needle* – of that I am convinced!'

It seemed to me extremely vague and hazy.

'You do not see it? Your wits are not so sharp as those of a mere servant girl.'

He tossed me over a letter. It was neatly written in a sloping board-school hand.

'Dear Sir, – I hope you will forgive the liberty I take in writing to you. I have been thinking a lot since these awful two murders like poor auntie's. It seems as though we're all in the same boat, as it were. I saw the young lady's picture in the paper, the young lady, I mean, that is the sister of the young lady that was killed at Bexhill. I made so bold as to write to her and tell her I was coming to London to get a place and asked if I could come to her or her mother as I said two heads might be better than one and I would not want much wages, but only to find out who this awful fiend is and perhaps we might get at it better if we could say what we knew something might come of it.

'The young lady wrote very nicely and said as how she worked in an office and lived in a hostel, but she suggested I might write to you and she said she'd been thinking something of the same kind as I had. And she said we were in the same trouble and we ought to stand together. So I am writing, sir, to say I am coming to London and this is my address.

'Hoping I am not troubling you, Yours respectfully,
'Mary Drower.'

'Mary Drower,' said Poirot, 'is a very intelligent girl.'

He picked up another letter.

'Read this.'

It was a line from Franklin Clarke, saying that he was coming to London and would call upon Poirot the following day if not inconvenient.

'Do not despair, *mon ami*,' said Poirot. 'Action is about to begin.'

CHAPTER 18

POIROT MAKES A SPEECH

Franklin Clarke arrived at three o'clock on the following afternoon and came straight to the point without beating about the bush.

'M. Poirot,' he said, 'I'm not satisfied.'

'No, Mr Clarke?'

'I've no doubt that Crome is a very efficient officer, but, frankly, he puts my back up. That air of his of knowing best! I hinted something of what I had in mind to your friend here when he was down at Churston, but I've had all my brother's affairs to settle up and I haven't been free until now. My idea is, M. Poirot, that we oughtn't to let the grass grow under our feet –'

'Just what Hastings is always saying!'

'– but go right ahead. We've got to get ready for the next crime.'

'So you think there will be a next crime?'

'Don't you?'

'Certainly.'

'Very well, then. I want to get organized.'

'Tell me your idea exactly?'

'I propose, M. Poirot, a kind of special legion – to work under your orders – composed of the friends and relatives of the murdered people.'

'*Une bonne idée.*'

'I'm glad you approve. By putting our heads together I feel we might get at something. Also, when the next warning comes, by being on the spot, one of us might – I don't say it's probable – but we might recognize some person as having been near the scene of a previous crime.'

'I see your idea, and I approve, but you must remember, Mr Clarke, the relations and friends of the other victims are hardly in your sphere of life. They are employed persons and though they might be given a short vacation –'

Franklin Clarke interrupted.

'That's just it. I'm the only person in a position to foot the bill. Not that I'm particularly well off myself, but my brother died a rich man and it will eventually come to me. I propose, as I say, to enrol a special legion, the members to be paid for their services at the same rate as they get habitually, with, of course, the additional expenses.'

'Who do you propose should form this legion?'

'I've been into that. As a matter of fact, I wrote to Miss Megan Barnard – indeed, this is partly her idea. I suggest myself, Miss Barnard, Mr Donald Fraser, who was engaged to the dead girl. Then there is a niece of the Andover woman – Miss Barnard knows her address. I don't think the husband would be of any use to us – I hear he's usually drunk. I also think the Barnards – the father and mother – are a bit old for active campaigning.'

'Nobody else?'

'Well – er – Miss Grey.'

He flushed slightly as he spoke the name.

'Oh! Miss Grey?'

Nobody in the world could put a gentle nuance of irony into a couple of words better than Poirot. About thirty-five years fell away from Franklin Clarke. He looked suddenly like a shy schoolboy.

'Yes. You see, Miss Grey was with my brother for over two years. She knows the countryside and the people round, and everything. I've been away for a year and a half.'

Poirot took pity on him and turned the conversation.

'You have been in the East? In China?'

'Yes. I had a kind of roving commission to purchase things for my brother.'

'Very interesting it must have been. *Eh bien*, Mr Clarke, I approve very highly of your idea. I was saying to Hastings only yesterday that a *rapprochement* of the people concerned was needed. It is necessary to pool reminiscences, to compare notes – *enfin* to talk the thing over – to talk – to talk – and again to talk. Out of some innocent phrase may come enlightenment.'

A few days later the 'Special Legion' met at Poirot's rooms.

As they sat round looking obediently towards Poirot, who had his place, like the chairman at a board meeting, at the head of the table, I myself passed them, as it were, in review, confirming or revising my first impressions of them.

The three girls were all of them striking-looking – the extraordinary fair beauty of Thora Grey, the dark intensity of Megan Barnard, with her strange Red Indian immobility of face – Mary Drower, neatly dressed in a black coat and skirt, with her pretty, intelligent face. Of the two men, Franklin Clarke, big, bronzed and talkative, Donald Fraser, self-contained and quiet, made an interesting contrast to each other.

Poirot, unable, of course, to resist the occasion, made a little speech.

'Mesdames and messieurs, you know what we are here for. The police are doing their utmost to track down the criminal. I, too, in my different way. But it seems to me a reunion of those who have a personal interest in the matter – and also, I may say, a personal knowledge of the victims – might have results that an outside investigation cannot pretend to attain.

'Here we have three murders – an old woman, a young girl, an elderly man. Only one thing links these three people together – *the fact that the same person killed them.* That means that *the same person was present in three different localities* and was seen necessarily by a large number of people. That he is a madman in an advanced stage of mania goes without saying. That his appearance and behaviour give no suggestion of such a fact is equally certain. This person – and though I say *he*, remember it may be a man or a woman – has all the devilish cunning of insanity. He has succeeded so far in covering his traces completely. The police have certain vague indications but nothing upon which they can act.

'Nevertheless, there must exist indications which are not vague but certain. To take one particular point – this assassin, he did not arrive at Bexhill at midnight and find conveniently on the beach a young lady whose name began with B –'

'Must we go into that?'

It was Donald Fraser who spoke – the words wrung from him, it seemed, by some inner anguish.

'It is necessary to go into everything, monsieur,' said Poirot, turning to him. 'You are here, not to save your feelings by refusing to think of details, but if necessary to harrow them by going into the matter *au fond.* As I say, it was not *chance* that provided A B C with a victim in Betty Barnard. There must have been deliberate selection on his part – and therefore premeditation. That is to say, he must have reconnoitred the ground *beforehand.* There were facts of which he had informed himself – the best hour for the committing of the crime at Andover – the *mise en scène* at Bexhill – the habits of Sir Carmichael Clarke at Churston. Me, for one, I refuse to believe that there is *no* indication – no slightest hint – that might help to establish his identity.

'I make the assumption that one – or possibly *all* of you – *knows something that they do not know they know.*

'Sooner or later, by reason of your association with one another, something will come to light, will take on a significance as yet undreamed of. It is like the jig-saw puzzle – each of you may have *a piece apparently without meaning, but which when reunited may show a definite portion of the picture as a whole.*'

'Words!' said Megan Barnard.

'Eh?' Poirot looked at her inquiringly.

'What you've been saying. It's just words. It doesn't mean anything.'

She spoke with that kind of desperate intensity that I had come to associate with her personality.

'Words, mademoiselle, are only the outer clothing of ideas.'

'Well, I think it's sense,' said Mary Drower. 'I do really, miss. It's often when you're talking over things that you seem to see your way clear. Your mind gets made up for you sometimes without your knowing how it's happened. Talking leads to a lot of things one way and another.'

'If "least said is soonest mended", it's the converse we want here,' said Franklin Clarke.

'What do you say, Mr Fraser?'

'I rather doubt the practical applicability of what you say, M. Poirot.'

'What do you think, Thora?' asked Clarke.

'I think the principle of talking things over is always sound.'

'Suppose,' suggested Poirot, 'that you all go over your own remembrances of the time preceding the murder. Perhaps you'll start, Mr Clarke.'

'Let me see, on the morning of the day Car was killed I went off sailing. Caught eight mackerel. Lovely out there on the bay. Lunch at home. Irish stew, I remember. Slept in the hammock. Tea. Wrote some letters, missed the post, and drove into Paignton to post them. Then dinner and – I'm not ashamed to say it – reread a book of E. Nesbit's that I used to love as a kid. Then the telephone rang –'

'No further. Now reflect, Mr Clarke, did you meet anyone on your way down to the sea in the morning?'

'Lots of people.'

'Can you remember anything about them?'

'Not a damned thing now.'

'Sure?'

'Well – let's see – I remember a remarkably fat woman – she wore a striped silk dress and I wondered why – had a couple of kids with her – two young men with a fox terrier on the beach throwing stones for it

– Oh, yes, a girl with yellow hair squeaking as she bathed – funny how things come back – like a photograph developing.'

'You are a good subject. Now later in the day – the garden – going to the post –'

'The gardener watering . . . Going to the post? Nearly ran down a bicyclist – silly woman wobbling and shouting to a friend. That's all, I'm afraid.'

Poirot turned to Thora Grey.

'Miss Grey?'

Thora Grey replied in her clear, positive voice:

'I did correspondence with Sir Carmichael in the morning – saw the housekeeper. I wrote letters and did needlework in the afternoon, I fancy. It is difficult to remember. It was quite an ordinary day. I went to bed early.'

Rather to my surprise, Poirot asked no further. He said:

'Miss Barnard – can you bring back your remembrances of the last time you saw your sister?'

'It would be about a fortnight before her death. I was down for Saturday and Sunday. It was fine weather. We went to Hastings to the swimming pool.'

'What did you talk about most of the time?'

'I gave her a piece of my mind,' said Megan.

'And what else? She conversed of what?'

The girl frowned in an effort of memory.

'She talked about being hard up – of a hat and a couple of summer frocks she'd just bought. And a little of Don . . . She also said she disliked Milly Higley – that's the girl at the café – and we laughed about the Merrion woman who keeps the café . . . I don't remember anything else . . .'

'She didn't mention any man – forgive me, Mr Fraser – she might be meeting?'

'She wouldn't to me,' said Megan dryly.

Poirot turned to the red-haired young man with the square jaw.

'Mr Fraser – I want you to cast your mind back. You went, you said, to the café on the fatal evening. Your first intention was to wait there and watch for Betty Barnard to come out. Can you remember anyone at all whom you noticed whilst you were waiting there?'

'There were a large number of people walking along the front. I can't remember any of them.'

'Excuse me, but are you trying? However preoccupied the mind may be, the eye notices mechanically – unintelligently but accurately . . .'

The young man repeated doggedly:

'I don't remember anybody.'

Poirot sighed and turned to Mary Drower.

'I suppose you got letters from your aunt?'

'Oh, yes, sir.'

'When was the last?'

Mary thought a minute.

'Two days before the murder, sir.'

'What did it say?'

'She said the old devil had been round and that she'd sent him off with a flea in the ear – excuse the expression, sir – said she expected me over on the Wednesday – that's my day out, sir – and she said we'd go to the pictures. It was going to be my birthday, sir.'

Something – the thought of the little festivity perhaps – suddenly brought the tears to Mary's eyes. She gulped down a sob. Then apologized for it.

'You must forgive me, sir. I don't want to be silly. Crying's no good. It was just the thought of her – and me – looking forward to our treat. It upset me somehow, sir.'

'I know just what you feel like,' said Franklin Clarke. 'It's always the little things that get one – and especially anything like a treat or a present – something jolly and natural. I remember seeing a woman run over once. She'd just bought some new shoes. I saw her lying there – and the burst parcel with the ridiculous little high-heeled slippers peeping out – it gave me a turn – they looked so pathetic.'

Megan said with a sudden eager warmth:

'That's true – that's awfully true. The same thing happened after Betty – died. Mum had bought some stockings for her as a present – bought them the very day it happened. Poor mum, she was all broken up. I found her crying over them. She kept saying: "I bought them for Betty – I bought them for Betty – and she never even saw them."'

Her own voice quivered a little. She leaned forward, looking straight at Franklin Clarke. There was between them a sudden sympathy – a fraternity in trouble.

'I know,' he said. 'I know exactly. Those are just the sort of things that are hell to remember.'

Donald Fraser stirred uneasily.

Thora Grey diverted the conversation.

'Aren't we going to make any plans – for the future?' she asked.

'Of course.' Franklin Clarke resumed his ordinary manner. 'I think that when the moment comes – that is, when the fourth letter arrives – we ought to join forces. Until then, perhaps we might each try our luck on our own. I don't know whether there are any points M. Poirot thinks might repay investigation?'

'I could make some suggestions,' said Poirot.

'Good. I'll take them down.' He produced a notebook. 'Go ahead, M. Poirot. A –?'

'I consider it just possible that the waitress, Milly Higley, might know something useful.'

'A – Milly Higley,' wrote down Franklin Clarke.

'I suggest two methods of approach. You, Miss Barnard, might try what I call the offensive approach.'

'I suppose you think that suits my style?' said Megan dryly.

'Pick a quarrel with the girl – say you knew she never liked your sister – and that your sister had told you all about *her*. If I do not err, that will provoke a flood of recrimination. She will tell you just what she thought of your sister! Some useful fact may emerge.'

'And the second method?'

'May I suggest, Mr Fraser, that you should show signs of interest in the girl?'

'Is that necessary?'

'No, it is not necessary. It is just a possible line of exploration.'

'Shall I try my hand?' asked Franklin. 'I've – er – a pretty wide experience, M. Poirot. Let me see what I can do with the young lady.'

'You've got your own part of the world to attend to,' said Thora Grey rather sharply.

Franklin's face fell just a little.

'Yes,' he said. 'I have.'

'*Tout de même*, I do not think there is much you can do down there for the present,' said Poirot. 'Mademoiselle Grey now, she is far more fitted –'

Thora Grey interrupted him.

'But you see, M. Poirot, I have left Devon for good.'

'Ah? I did not understand.'

'Miss Grey very kindly stayed on to help me clear up things,' said Franklin. 'But naturally she prefers a post in London.'

Poirot directed a sharp glance from one to the other.

'How is Lady Clarke?' he demanded.

I was admiring the faint colour in Thora Grey's cheeks and almost missed Clarke's reply.

'Pretty bad. By the way, M. Poirot, I wonder if you could see your way to running down to Devon and paying her a visit? She expressed a desire to see you before I left. Of course, she often can't see people for a couple of days at a time, but if you would risk that – at my expense, of course.'

'Certainly, Mr Clarke. Shall we say the day after tomorrow?'

'Good. I'll let nurse know and she'll arrange the dope accordingly.'

'For you, my child,' said Poirot, turning to Mary, 'I think you might perhaps do good work in Andover. Try the children.'

'The children?'

'Yes. Children will not chat readily to outsiders. But you are known in the street where your aunt lived. There were a good many children playing about. They may have noticed who went in and out of your aunt's shop.'

'What about Miss Grey and myself?' asked Clarke. 'That is, if I'm not to go to Bexhill.'

'M. Poirot,' said Thora Grey, 'what was the postmark on the third letter?'

'Putney, mademoiselle.'

She said thoughtfully: 'SW15, Putney, that is right, is it not?'

'For a wonder, the newspapers printed it correctly.'

'That seems to point to A B C being a Londoner.'

'On the face of it, yes.'

'One ought to be able to draw him,' said Clarke. 'M. Poirot, how would it be if I inserted an advertisement – something after these lines: *A B C. Urgent, H P close on your track. A hundred for my silence. X Y Z.* Nothing quite so crude as that – but you see the idea. It might draw him.'

'It is a possibility – yes.'

'Might induce him to try and have a shot at me.'

'I think it's very dangerous and silly,' said Thora Grey sharply.

'What about it, M. Poirot?'

'It can do no harm to try. I think myself that A B C will be too cunning to reply.' Poirot smiled a little. 'I see, Mr Clarke, that you are – if I may say so without being offensive – still a boy at heart.'

Franklin Clarke looked a little abashed.

'Well,' he said, consulting his notebook. 'We're making a start.

'A – Miss Barnard and Milly Higley.

B – Mr Fraser and Miss Higley.

C – Children in Andover.

D – Advertisement.

'I don't feel any of it is much good, but it will be something to do whilst waiting.'

He got up and a few minutes later the meeting had dispersed.

CHAPTER 19

BY WAY OF SWEDEN

Poirot returned to his seat and sat humming a little tune to himself.

'Unfortunate that she is so intelligent,' he murmured.

'Who?'

'Megan Barnard. Mademoiselle Megan. "Words," she snaps out. At once she perceives that what I am saying means nothing at all. Everybody else was taken in.'

'I thought it sounded very plausible.'

'Plausible, yes. It was just that she perceived.'

'Didn't you mean what you said, then?'

'What I said could have been comprised into one short sentence. Instead I repeated myself *ad lib* without anyone but Mademoiselle Megan being aware of the fact.'

'But why?'

'*Eh bien* – to get things going! To imbue everyone with the impression that there was work to be done! To start – shall we say – the conversations!'

'Don't you think any of these lines will lead to anything?'

'Oh, it is always possible.'

He chuckled.

'In the midst of tragedy we start the comedy. It is so, is it not?'

'What *do* you mean?'

'The human drama, Hastings! Reflect a little minute. Here are three sets of human beings brought together by a common tragedy. Immediately a second drama commences – *tout à fait à part*. Do you remember my first case in England? Oh, so many years ago now. I brought together two people who loved one another – by the simple method of having one of them arrested for murder! Nothing less would have done it! In the midst of death we are in life, Hastings . . . Murder, I have often noticed, is a great matchmaker.'

'Really, Poirot,' I cried scandalized. 'I'm sure none of those people was thinking of anything but –'

'Oh! my dear friend. And what about yourself?'

'I?'

'*Mais oui*, as they departed, did you not come back from the door humming a tune?'

'One may do that without being callous.'

'Certainly, but that tune told me your thoughts.'

'Indeed?'

'Yes. To hum a tune is extremely dangerous. It reveals the subconscious mind. The tune you hummed dates, I think, from the days of the war. *Comme ça*,' Poirot sang in an abominable falsetto voice:

'*Some of the time I love a brunette,*
Some of the time I love a blonde
(Who comes from Eden by way of Sweden).

'What could be more revealing? *Mais je crois que la blonde l'emporte sur la brunette!*'

'Really, Poirot,' I cried, blushing slightly.

'*C'est tout naturel*. Did you observe how Franklin Clarke was suddenly at one and in sympathy with Mademoiselle Megan? How he leaned forward and looked at her? And did you also notice how very much annoyed Mademoiselle Thora Grey was about it? And Mr Donald Fraser, he –'

'Poirot,' I said. 'Your mind is incurably sentimental.'

'That is the last thing my mind is. You are the sentimental one, Hastings.'

I was about to argue the point hotly, but at that moment the door opened.

To my astonishment it was Thora Grey who entered.

'Forgive me for coming back,' she said composedly. 'But there was something that I think I would like to tell you, M. Poirot.'

'Certainly, mademoiselle. Sit down, will you not?'

She took a seat and hesitated for just a minute as though choosing her words.

'It is just this, M. Poirot. Mr Clarke very generously gave you to understand just now that I had left Combeside by my own wish. He is a very kind and loyal person. But as a matter of fact, it is not quite like that. I was quite prepared to stay on – there is any amount of work to be done in connection with the collections. It was Lady Clarke who wished me to leave! I can make allowances. She is a very ill woman, and her brain is somewhat muddled with the drugs they give her. It makes her suspicious and fanciful. She took an unreasoning dislike to me and insisted that I should leave the house.'

I could not but admire the girl's courage. She did not attempt to gloss over facts, as so many might have been tempted to do, but went straight to the point with an admirable candour. My heart went out to her in admiration and sympathy.

'I call it splendid of you to come and tell us this,' I said.

'It's always better to have the truth,' she said with a little smile. 'I don't want to shelter behind Mr Clarke's chivalry. He is a very chivalrous man.'

There was a warm glow in her words. She evidently admired Franklin Clarke enormously.

'You have been very honest, mademoiselle,' said Poirot.

'It is rather a blow to me,' said Thora ruefully. 'I had no idea Lady Clarke disliked me so much. In fact, I always thought she was rather fond of me.' She made a wry face. 'One lives and learns.'

She rose.

'That is all I came to say. Goodbye.'

I accompanied her downstairs.

'I call that very sporting of her,' I said as I returned to the room. 'She has courage, that girl.'

'And calculation.'

'What do you mean – calculation?'

'I mean that she has the power of looking ahead.'

I looked at him doubtfully.

'She really is a lovely girl,' I said.

'And wears very lovely clothes. That crêpe marocain and the silver fox collar – *dernier cri.*'

'You're a man milliner, Poirot. I never notice what people have on.'

'You should join a nudist colony.'

As I was about to make an indignant rejoinder, he said, with a sudden change of subject:

'Do you know, Hastings, I cannot rid my mind of the impression that already, in our conversations this afternoon, something was said that was significant. It is odd – I cannot pin down exactly what it was . . . Just an impression that passed through my mind . . . *That reminds me of something I have already heard or seen or noted . . .*'

'Something at Churston?'

'No – not at Churston . . . Before that . . . No matter, presently it will come to me . . .'

He looked at me (perhaps I had not been attending very closely), laughed and began once more to hum.

'She is an angel, is she not? From Eden, by way of Sweden . . .'

'Poirot,' I said. 'Go to the devil!'

CHAPTER 20

LADY CLARKE

There was an air of deep and settled melancholy over Combeside when we saw it again for the second time. This may, perhaps, have been partly due to the weather – it was a moist September day with a hint of autumn in the air, and partly, no doubt, it was the semi-shut-up state of the house. The downstairs rooms were closed and shuttered, and the small room into which we were shown smelt damp and airless.

A capable-looking hospital nurse came to us there pulling down her starched cuffs.

'M. Poirot?' she said briskly. 'I am Nurse Capstick. I got Mr Clarke's letter saying you were coming.'

Poirot inquired after Lady Clarke's health.

'Not at all bad really, all things considered.'

'All things considered,' I presumed, meant considering she was under sentence of death.

'One can't hope for much improvement, of course, but some new treatment has made things a little easier for her. Dr Logan is quite pleased with her condition.'

'But it is true, is it not, that she can never recover?'

'Oh, we never actually *say* that,' said Nurse Capstick, a little shocked by this plain speaking.

'I suppose her husband's death was a terrible shock to her?'

'Well, M. Poirot, if you understand what I mean, it wasn't as much of a shock as it would have been to anyone in full possession of her health and faculties. Things are *dimmed* for Lady Clarke in her condition.'

'Pardon my asking, but was she deeply attached to her husband and he to her?'

'Oh, yes, they were a very happy couple. He was very worried and upset about her, poor man. It's always worse for a doctor, you know. They can't buoy themselves up with false hopes. I'm afraid it preyed on his mind very much to begin with.'

'To begin with? Not so much afterwards?'

'One gets used to everything, doesn't one? And then Sir Carmichael had his collection. A hobby is a great consolation to a man. He used to run up to sales occasionally, and then he and Miss Grey were busy recataloguing and rearranging the museum on a new system.'

'Oh, yes – Miss Grey. She has left, has she not?'

'Yes – I'm very sorry about it – but ladies do take these fancies sometimes when they're not well. And there's no arguing with them. It's better to give in. Miss Grey was very sensible about it.'

'Had Lady Clarke always disliked her?'

'No – that is to say, not *disliked*. As a matter of fact, I think she rather liked her to begin with. But there, I mustn't keep you gossiping. My patient will be wondering what has become of us.'

She led us upstairs to a room on the first floor. What had at one time been a bedroom had been turned into a cheerful-looking sitting-room.

Lady Clarke was sitting in a big armchair near the window. She was painfully thin, and her face had the grey, haggard look of one who suffers much pain. She had a slightly faraway, dreamy look, and I noticed that the pupils of her eyes were mere pin-points.

'This is M. Poirot whom you wanted to see,' said Nurse Capstick in her high, cheerful voice.

'Oh, yes, M. Poirot,' said Lady Clarke vaguely.

She extended her hand.

'My friend Captain Hastings, Lady Clarke.'

'How do you do? So good of you both to come.'

We sat down as her vague gesture directed. There was a silence. Lady Clarke seemed to have lapsed into a dream.

Presently with a slight effort she roused herself.

'It was about Car, wasn't it? About Car's death. Oh, yes.'

She sighed, but still in a faraway manner, shaking her head.

'We never thought it would be that way round . . . I was so sure I should be the first to go . . .' She mused a minute or two. 'Car was very strong – wonderful for his age. He was never ill. He was nearly sixty – but he seemed more like fifty . . . Yes, very strong . . .'

She relapsed again into her dream. Poirot, who was well acquainted with the effects of certain drugs and of how they give their taker the impression of endless time, said nothing.

Lady Clarke said suddenly:

'Yes – it was good of you to come. I told Franklin. He said he wouldn't forget to tell you. I hope Franklin isn't going to be foolish . . . he's so easily taken in, in spite of having knocked about the world so much. Men are like that . . . They remain boys . . . Franklin, in particular.'

'He has an impulsive nature,' said Poirot.

'Yes – yes . . . And very chivalrous. Men are so foolish that way. Even Car –' Her voice tailed off.

She shook her head with a febrile impatience.

'Everything's so dim . . . One's body is a nuisance, M. Poirot, especially when it gets the upper hand. One is conscious of nothing else – whether the pain will hold off or not – nothing else seems to matter.'

'I know, Lady Clarke. It is one of the tragedies of this life.'

'It makes me so stupid. I cannot even remember what it was I wanted to say to you.'

'Was it something about your husband's death?'

'Car's death? Yes, perhaps . . . Mad, poor creature – the murderer, I mean. It's all the noise and the speed nowadays – people can't stand it. I've always been sorry for mad people – their heads must feel so queer. And then, being shut up – it must be so terrible. But what else can one do? If they kill people . . .' She shook her head – gently pained. 'You haven't caught him yet?' she asked.

'No, not yet.'

'He must have been hanging round here that day.'

'There were so many strangers about, Lady Clarke. It is the holiday season.'

'Yes – I forgot . . . But they keep down by the beaches, they don't come up near the house.'

'No stranger came to the house that day.'

'Who says so?' demanded Lady Clarke, with a sudden vigour.

Poirot looked slightly taken aback.

'The servants,' he said. 'Miss Grey.'

Lady Clarke said very distinctly:

'That girl is a liar!'

I started on my chair. Poirot threw me a glance.

Lady Clarke was going on, speaking now rather feverishly.

'I didn't like her. I never liked her. Car thought all the world of her. Used to go on about her being an orphan and alone in the world. What's wrong with being an orphan? Sometimes it's a blessing in disguise. You might have a good-for-nothing father and a mother who drank – then you would have something to complain about. Said she was so brave and such a good worker. I dare say she did her work well! I don't know where all this bravery came in!'

'Now don't excite yourself, dear,' said Nurse Capstick, intervening. 'We mustn't have you getting tired.'

'I soon sent her packing! Franklin had the impertinence to suggest that she might be a comfort to me. Comfort to me indeed! The sooner I saw the last of her the better – that's what I said! Franklin's a fool! I didn't want him getting mixed up with her. He's a boy! No sense! "I'll give her three months' salary, if you like," I said. "But out she goes. I don't want her in the house a day longer." There's one thing about being ill – men can't argue with you. He did what I said and she went. Went like a martyr, I expect – with more sweetness and bravery!'

'Now, dear, don't get so excited. It's bad for you.'

Lady Clarke waved Nurse Capstick away.

'You were as much of a fool about her as anyone else.'

'Oh! Lady Clarke, you mustn't say that. I did think Miss Grey a very nice girl – so romantic-looking, like someone out of a novel.'

'I've no patience with the lot of you,' said Lady Clarke feebly.

'Well, she's gone now, my dear. Gone right away.'

Lady Clarke shook her head with feeble impatience but she did not answer.

Poirot said:

'Why did you say that Miss Grey was a liar?'

'Because she is. She told you no strangers came to the house, didn't she?'

'Yes.'

'Very well, then. I saw her – with my own eyes – out of this window – talking to a perfectly strange man on the front doorstep.'

'When was this?'

'In the morning of the day Car died – about eleven o'clock.'

'What did this man look like?'

'An ordinary sort of man. Nothing special.'

'A gentleman – or a tradesman?'

'Not a tradesman. A shabby sort of person. I can't remember.'

A sudden quiver of pain shot across her face.

'Please – you must go now – I'm a little tired – Nurse.'

We obeyed the cue and took our departure.

'That's an extraordinary story,' I said to Poirot as we journeyed back to London. 'About Miss Grey and a strange man.'

'You see, Hastings? It is, as I tell you: *there is always something to be found out.*'

'Why did the girl lie about it and say she had seen no one?'

'I can think of seven separate reasons – one of them an extremely simple one.'

'Is that a snub?' I asked.

'It is, perhaps, an invitation to use your ingenuity. But there is no need for us to perturb ourselves. The easiest way to answer the question is to ask her.'

'And suppose she tells us another lie.'

'That would indeed be interesting – and highly suggestive.'

'It is monstrous to suppose that a girl like that could be in league with a madman.'

'Precisely – so I do not suppose it.'

I thought for some minutes longer.

'A good-looking girl has a hard time of it,' I said at last with a sigh.

'*Du tout*. Disabuse your mind of that idea.'

'It's true,' I insisted, 'everyone's hand is against her simply because she is good-looking.'

'You speak the *bêtises*, my friend. Whose hand was against her at Combeside? Sir Carmichael's? Franklin's? Nurse Capstick's?'

'Lady Clarke was down on her, all right.'

'*Mon ami*, you are full of charitable feeling towards beautiful young girls. Me, I feel charitable to sick old ladies. It may be that Lady Clarke was the clear-sighted one – and that her husband, Mr Franklin Clarke and Nurse Capstick were all as blind as bats – and Captain Hastings.'

'You've got a grudge against that girl, Poirot.'

To my surprise his eyes twinkled suddenly.

'Perhaps it is that I like to mount you on your romantic high horse, Hastings. You are always the true knight – ready to come to the rescue of damsels in distress – good-looking damsels, *bien entendu*.'

'How ridiculous you are, Poirot,' I said, unable to keep from laughing.

'Ah, well, one cannot be tragic all the time. More and more I interest myself in the human developments that arise out of this tragedy. It is three dramas of family life that we have there. First there is Andover – the whole tragic life of Mrs Ascher, her struggles, her support of her German husband, the devotion of her niece. That alone would make a novel. Then you have Bexhill – the happy, easy-going father and mother, the two daughters so widely differing from each other – the pretty fluffy fool, and the intense, strong-willed Megan with her clear intelligence and her ruthless passion for truth. And the other figure – the self-controlled young Scotsman with his passionate jealousy and his worship of the dead girl. Finally you have the Churston household – the dying wife, and the husband absorbed in his collections, but with a growing tenderness and sympathy for the beautiful girl who helps him so sympathetically, and then the younger brother, vigorous, attractive, interesting, with a romantic glamour about him from his long travels.

'Realize, Hastings, that in the ordinary course of events *those three separate dramas would never have touched each other.* They would have pursued their course uninfluenced by each other. The permutations and combinations of life, Hastings – I never cease to be fascinated by them.'

'This is Paddington,' was the only answer I made.

It was time, I felt, that someone pricked the bubble.

On our arrival at Whitehaven Mansions we were told that a gentleman was waiting to see Poirot.

I expected it to be Franklin, or perhaps Japp, but to my astonishment it turned out to be none other than Donald Fraser.

He seemed very embarrassed and his inarticulateness was more notice-able than ever.

Poirot did not press him to come to the point of his visit, but instead suggested sandwiches and a glass of wine.

Until these made their appearance he monopolized the conversation, explaining where we had been, and speaking with kindliness and feeling of the invalid woman.

Not until we had finished the sandwiches and sipped the wine did he give the conversation a personal turn.

'You have come from Bexhill, Mr Fraser?'

'Yes.'

'Any success with Milly Higley?'

'Milly Higley? Milly Higley?' Fraser repeated the name wonderingly. 'Oh, that girl! No, I haven't done anything there yet. It's –'

He stopped. His hands twisted themselves together nervously.

'I don't know why I've come to you,' he burst out.

'I know,' said Poirot.

'You can't. How can you?'

'You have come to me because there is something that you must tell to someone. You were quite right. I am the proper person. Speak!'

Poirot's air of assurance had its effect. Fraser looked at him with a queer air of grateful obedience.

'You think so?'

'*Parbleu,* I am sure of it.'

'M. Poirot, do you know anything about dreams?'

It was the last thing I had expected him to say.

Poirot, however, seemed in no wise surprised.

'I do,' he replied. 'You have been dreaming –?'

'Yes. I suppose you'll say it's only natural that I should – should dream about – It. But it isn't an ordinary dream.'

'No?'

'No.

'I've dreamed it now three nights running, sir . . . I think I'm going mad . . .'

'Tell me –'

The man's face was livid. His eyes were staring out of his head. As a matter of fact, he *looked* mad.

'It's always the same. I'm on the beach. Looking for Betty. She's lost – only lost, you understand. I've got to find her. I've got to give her her belt. I'm carrying it in my hand. And then –'

'Yes?'

'The dream changes . . . I'm not looking any more. She's there in front of me – sitting on the beach. She doesn't see me coming – It's – oh, I can't –'

'Go on.'

Poirot's voice was authoritative – firm.

'I come up behind her . . . she doesn't hear me . . . I slip the belt round her neck and pull – oh – pull . . .'

The agony in his voice was frightful . . . I gripped the arms of my chair . . . The thing was too real.

'She's choking . . . she's dead . . . I've strangled her – and then her head falls back and I see her face . . . and it's *Megan* – not Betty!'

He leant back white and shaking. Poirot poured out another glass of wine and passed it over to him.

'What's the meaning of it, M. Poirot? Why does it come to me? Every night . . . ?'

'Drink up your wine,' ordered Poirot.

The young man did so, then he asked in a calmer voice:

'What does it mean? I – I didn't kill her, did I?'

What Poirot answered I do not know, for at that minute I heard the postman's knock and automatically I left the room.

What I took out of the letter-box banished all my interest in Donald Fraser's extraordinary revelations.

I raced back into the sitting-room.

'Poirot,' I cried. 'It's come. The fourth letter.'

He sprang up, seized it from me, caught up his paper-knife and slit it open. He spread it out on the table.

The three of us read it together.

Still no success? Fie! Fie! What are you and the police doing? Well, well, isn't this fun? And where shall we go next for honey?

Poor Mr Poirot. I'm quite sorry for you.

If at first you don't succeed, try, try, try again.

We've a long way to go still.

Tipperary? No – that comes farther on. Letter T.

The next little incident will take place at Doncaster on September 11th.

So long.

A B C.

CHAPTER 21

DESCRIPTION OF A MURDERER

It was at this moment, I think, that what Poirot called the human element began to fade out of the picture again. It was as though, the mind being unable to stand unadulterated horror, we had had an interval of normal human interests.

We had, one and all, felt the impossibility of doing anything until the fourth letter should come revealing the projected scene of the D murder. That atmosphere of waiting had brought a release of tension.

But now, with the printed words jeering from the white stiff paper, the hunt was up once more.

Inspector Crome had come round from the Yard, and while he was still there, Franklin Clarke and Megan Barnard came in.

The girl explained that she, too, had come up from Bexhill.

'I wanted to ask Mr Clarke something.'

She seemed rather anxious to excuse and explain her procedure. I just noted the fact without attaching much importance to it.

The letter naturally filled my mind to the exclusion of all else.

Crome was not, I think, any too pleased to see the various participants in the drama. He became extremely official and non-committal.

'I'll take this with me, M. Poirot. If you care to take a copy of it –'

'No, no, it is not necessary.'

'What are your plans, inspector?' asked Clarke.

'Fairly comprehensive ones, Mr Clarke.'

'This time we've got to get him,' said Clarke. 'I may tell you, inspector, that we've formed an association of our own to deal with the matter. A legion of interested parties.'

Inspector Crome said in his best manner:

'Oh, yes?'

'I gather you don't think much of amateurs, inspector?'

'You've hardly the same resources at your command, have you, Mr Clarke?'

'We've got a personal axe to grind – and that's something.'

'Oh, yes?'

'I fancy your own task isn't going to be too easy, inspector. In fact, I rather fancy old A B C has done you again.'

Crome, I noticed, could often be goaded into speech when other methods would have failed.

'I don't fancy the public will have much to criticize in our arrangements this time,' he said. 'The fool has given us ample warning. The 11th isn't till Wednesday of next week. That gives ample time for a publicity campaign in the press. Doncaster will be thoroughly warned. Every soul whose name begins with a D will be on his or her guard – that's so much to the good. Also, we'll draft police into the town on a fairly large scale. That's already been arranged for by consent of all the Chief Constables in England. The whole of Doncaster, police and civilians, will be out to catch one man – and with reasonable luck, we ought to get him!'

Clarke said quietly:

'It's easy to see you're not a sporting man, inspector.'

Crome stared at him.

'What do you mean, Mr Clarke?'

'Man alive, don't you realize that on *next Wednesday the St Leger is being run at Doncaster*?'

The inspector's jaw dropped. For the life of him he could not bring out the familiar 'Oh, yes?' Instead he said:

'That's true. Yes, that complicates matters . . .'

'A B C is no fool, even if he *is* a madman.'

We were all silent for a minute or two, taking in the situation. The crowds on the race-course – the passionate, sport-loving English public – the endless complications.

Poirot murmured:

'*C'est ingénieux. Tout de même c'est bien imaginé, ça.*'

'It's my belief,' said Clarke, 'that the murder will take place on the race-course – perhaps actually while the Leger is being run.'

For the moment his sporting instincts took a momentary pleasure in the thought . . .

Inspector Crome rose, taking the letter with him.

'The St Leger is a complication,' he allowed. 'It's unfortunate.'

He went out. We heard a murmur of voices in the hallway. A minute later Thora Grey entered.

She said anxiously:

'The inspector told me there is another letter. Where this time?'

It was raining outside. Thora Grey was wearing a black coat and skirt and furs. A little black hat just perched itself on the side of her golden head.

It was to Franklin Clarke that she spoke and she came right up to him and, with a hand on his arm, waited for his answer.

'Doncaster – and on the day of the St Leger.'

We settled down to a discussion. It went without saying that we all intended to be present, but the race-meeting undoubtedly complicated the plans we had made tentatively beforehand.

A feeling of discouragement swept over me. What could this little band of six people do, after all, however strong their personal interest in the matter might be? There would be innumerable police, keen-eyed and alert, watching all likely spots. What could six more pairs of eyes do?

As though in answer to my thought, Poirot raised his voice. He spoke rather like a schoolmaster or a priest.

'*Mes enfants*,' he said. 'We must not disperse the strength. We must approach this matter with method and order in our thoughts. We must look within and not without for the truth. We must say to ourselves – each one of us – what do *I* know about the murderer? And so we must build up a composite picture of the man we are going to seek.'

'We know nothing about him,' sighed Thora Grey helplessly.

'No, no, mademoiselle. That is not true. Each one of us knows something about him – *if we only knew what it is we know. I am convinced that the knowledge is there* if we could only get at it.'

Clarke shook his head.

'We don't know anything – whether he's old or young, fair or dark! None of us has ever seen him or spoken to him! We've gone over everything we all know again and again.'

'Not everything! For instance, Miss Grey here told us that she did not see or speak to any stranger on the day that Sir Carmichael Clarke was murdered.'

Thora Grey nodded.

'That's quite right.'

'Is it? *Lady Clarke told us, mademoiselle, that from her window she saw you standing on the front doorstep talking to a man.*'

'She saw *me* talking to a strange man?' The girl seemed genuinely astonished. Surely that pure, limpid look could not be anything but genuine.

She shook her head.

'Lady Clarke must have made a mistake. I never – Oh!'

The exclamation came suddenly – jerked out of her. A crimson wave flooded her cheeks.

'I remember now! How stupid! I'd forgotten all about it. But it wasn't important. Just one of those men who come round selling stockings – you know, ex-army people. They're very persistent. I had to get rid of him. I was just crossing the hall when he came to the door. He spoke to me instead of ringing but he was quite a harmless sort of person. I suppose that's why I forgot about him.'

Poirot was swaying to and fro, his hands clasped to his head. He was muttering to himself with such vehemence that nobody else said anything, but stared at him instead.

'Stockings,' he was murmuring. 'Stockings . . . stockings . . . stockings . . . *ça vient* . . . stockings . . . stockings . . . it is the *motif – yes* . . . three months ago . . . and the other day . . . and now. *Bon Dieu,* I have it!'

He sat upright and fixed me with an imperious eye.

'You remember, Hastings? Andover. The shop. We go upstairs. The bedroom. On a chair. *A pair of new silk stockings.* And now I know what it was that roused my attention two days ago. It was you, mademoiselle –' He turned on Megan. 'You spoke of your mother who wept *because she had bought your sister some new stockings on the very day of the murder . . .*'

He looked round on us all.

'You see? *It is the same motif* three times repeated. That cannot be coincidence. When mademoiselle spoke I had the feeling that what she said linked up with something. I know now with what. The words spoken by Mrs Ascher's next-door neighbour, Mrs Fowler. About people who were always trying to *sell* you things – and she mentioned stockings. Tell me, mademoiselle, it is true, is it not, that your mother bought those stockings, not at a shop, but from someone who came to the door?'

'Yes – yes – she did . . . I remember now. She said something about being sorry for these wretched men who go round and try to get orders.'

'But what's the connection?' cried Franklin. 'That a man came selling stockings proves nothing!'

'I tell you, my friends, it *cannot* be coincidence. Three crimes – and every time a man selling stockings and spying out the land.'

He wheeled round on Thora.

'*A vous la parole!* Describe this man.'

She looked at him blankly.

'I can't . . . I don't know how . . . He had glasses, I think – and a shabby overcoat . . .'

'*Mieux que ça, mademoiselle.*'

'He stooped . . . I don't know. I hardly looked at him. He wasn't the sort of man you'd notice . . .'

Poirot said gravely:

'You are quite right, mademoiselle. The whole secret of the murders lies there in your description of the murderer – for without a doubt he *was* the murderer! "*He wasn't the sort of man you'd notice.*" Yes – there is no doubt about it . . . You have described the murderer!'

CHAPTER 22

*NOT FROM CAPTAIN HASTINGS'
PERSONAL NARRATIVE*

Mr Alexander Bonaparte Cust sat very still. His breakfast lay cold and untasted on his plate. A newspaper was propped up against the teapot and it was this newspaper that Mr Cust was reading with avid interest.

Suddenly he got up, paced to and fro for a minute, then sank back into a chair by the window. He buried his head in his hands with a stifled groan.

He did not hear the sound of the opening door. His landlady, Mrs Marbury, stood in the doorway.

'I was wondering, Mr Cust, if you'd fancy a nice – why, whatever is it? Aren't you feeling well?'

Mr Cust raised his head from his hands.

'Nothing. It's nothing at all, Mrs Marbury. I'm not – feeling very well this morning.'

Mrs Marbury inspected the breakfast tray.

'So I see. You haven't touched your breakfast. Is it your head troubling you again?'

'No. At least, yes . . . I – I just feel a bit out of sorts.'

'Well, I'm sorry, I'm sure. You'll not be going away today, then?'

Mr Cust sprang up abruptly.

'No, no. I have to go. It's business. Important. Very important.'

His hands were shaking. Seeing him so agitated, Mrs Marbury tried to soothe him.

'Well, if you must – you must. Going far this time?'

'No. I'm going to' – he hesitated for a minute or two – 'Cheltenham.'

There was something so peculiar about the tentative way he said the word that Mrs Marbury looked at him in surprise.

'Cheltenham's a nice place,' she said conversationally. 'I went there from Bristol one year. The shops are ever so nice.'

'I suppose so – yes.'

Mrs Marbury stooped rather stiffly – for stooping did not suit her figure – to pick up the paper that was lying crumpled on the floor.

'Nothing but this murdering business in the papers nowadays,' she said as she glanced at the headlines before putting it back on the table. 'Gives me the creeps, it does. I don't read it. It's like Jack the Ripper all over again.'

Mr Cust's lips moved, but no sound came from them.

'Doncaster – that's the place he's going to do his next murder,' said Mrs Marbury. 'And tomorrow! Fairly makes your flesh creep, doesn't it? If I lived in Doncaster and my name began with a D, I'd take the first train away, that I would. I'd run no risks. What did you say, Mr Cust?'

'Nothing, Mrs Marbury – nothing.'

'It's the races and all. No doubt he thinks he'll get his opportunity there. Hundreds of police, they say, they're drafting in and – Why, Mr Cust, you *do* look bad. Hadn't you better have a little drop of something? Really, now, you oughtn't to go travelling today.'

Mr Cust drew himself up.

'It is necessary, Mrs Marbury. I have always been punctual in my – engagements. People must have – must have confidence in you! When I have undertaken to do a thing, I carry it through. It is the only way to get on in – in – business.'

'But if you're ill?'

'I am not ill, Mrs Marbury. Just a little worried over – various personal matters. I slept badly. I am really quite all right.'

His manner was so firm that Mrs Marbury gathered up the breakfast things and reluctantly left the room.

Mr Cust dragged out a suitcase from under the bed and began to pack. Pyjamas, sponge-bag, spare collar, leather slippers. Then unlocking a cupboard, he transferred a dozen or so flattish cardboard boxes about ten inches by seven from a shelf to the suitcase.

He just glanced at the railway guide on the table and then left the room, suitcase in hand.

Setting it down in the hall, he put on his hat and overcoat. As he did so he sighed deeply, so deeply that the girl who came out from a room at the side looked at him in concern.

'Anything the matter, Mr Cust?'

'Nothing, Miss Lily.'

'You were sighing so!'

Mr Cust said abruptly:

'Are you at all subject to premonitions, Miss Lily? To presentiments?'

'Well, I don't know that I am, really . . . Of course, there are days when you just feel everything's going wrong, and days when you feel everything's going right.'

'Quite,' said Mr Cust.

He sighed again.

'Well, goodbye, Miss Lily. Goodbye. I'm sure you've been very kind to me always here.'

'Well, don't say goodbye as though you were going away for ever,' laughed Lily.

'No, no, of course not.'

'See you Friday,' laughed the girl. 'Where are you going this time? Seaside again.'

'No, no – er – Cheltenham.'

'Well, that's nice, too. But not quite as nice as Torquay. That must have been lovely. I want to go there for my holiday next year. By the way, you must have been quite near where the murder was – the A B C murder. It happened while you were down there, didn't it?'

'Er – yes. But Churston's six or seven miles away.'

'All the same, it must have been exciting! Why, you may have passed the murderer in the street! You may have been quite near to him!'

'Yes, I may, of course,' said Mr Cust with such a ghastly and contorted smile that Lily Marbury noticed it.

'Oh, Mr Cust, you *don't* look well.'

'I'm quite all right, quite all right. Goodbye, Miss Marbury.'

He fumbled to raise his hat, caught up his suitcase and fairly hastened out of the front door.

'Funny old thing,' said Lily Marbury indulgently. 'Looks half batty to my mind.'

Inspector Crome said to his subordinate:

'Get me out a list of all stocking manufacturing firms and circularize them. I want a list of all their agents — you know, fellows who sell on commission and tout for orders.'

'This the A B C case, sir?'

'Yes. One of Mr Hercule Poirot's ideas.' The inspector's tone was disdainful. 'Probably nothing in it, but it doesn't do to neglect any chance, however faint.'

'Right, sir. Mr Poirot's done some good stuff in his time, but I think he's a bit gaga now, sir.'

'He's a mountebank,' said Inspector Crome. 'Always posing. Takes in some people. It doesn't take in *me*. Now then, about the arrangement for Doncaster . . .'

Tom Hartigan said to Lily Marbury:

'Saw your old dugout this morning.'

'Who? Mr Cust?'

'Cust it was. At Euston. Looking like a lost hen, as usual. I think the fellow's half loony. He needs someone to look after him. First he dropped his paper and then he dropped his ticket. I picked that up — he hadn't the faintest idea he'd lost it. Thanked me in an agitated sort of manner, but I don't think he recognized me.'

'Oh, well,' said Lily. 'He's only seen you passing in the hall, and not very often at that.'

They danced once round the floor.

'You dance something beautiful,' said Tom.

'Go on,' said Lily and wriggled yet a little closer.

They danced round again.

'Did you say Euston or Paddington?' asked Lily abruptly. 'Where you saw old Cust, I mean?'

'Euston.'

'Are you sure?'

'Of course I'm sure. What do you think?'

'Funny. I thought you went to Cheltenham from Paddington.'

'So you do. But old Cust wasn't going to Cheltenham. He was going to Doncaster.'

'Cheltenham.'

'Doncaster. I know, my girl! After all, I picked up his ticket, didn't I?'

'Well, he told *me* he was going to Cheltenham. I'm sure he did.'

'Oh, you've got it wrong. He was going to Doncaster all right. Some people have all the luck. I've got a bit on Firefly for the Leger and I'd love to see it run.'

'I shouldn't think Mr Cust went to race-meetings, he doesn't look the kind. Oh, Tom, I hope he won't get murdered. It's Doncaster the A B C murder's going to be.'

'Cust'll be all right. His name doesn't begin with a D.'

'He might have been murdered last time. He was down near Churston at Torquay when the last murder happened.'

'Was he? That's a bit of a coincidence, isn't it?'

He laughed.

'He wasn't at Bexhill the time before, was he?'

Lily crinkled her brows.

'He was away . . . Yes, I remember he was away . . . because he forgot his bathing-dress. Mother was mending it for him. And she said: "There – Mr Cust went away yesterday without his bathing-dress after all," and I said: "Oh, never mind the old bathing-dress – there's been the most awful murder," I said, "a girl strangled at Bexhill."'

'Well, if he wanted his bathing-dress, he must have been going to the seaside. I say, Lily' – his face crinkled up with amusement. 'What price your old dugout being the murderer himself?'

'Poor Mr Cust? He wouldn't hurt a fly,' laughed Lily.

They danced on happily – in their conscious minds nothing but the pleasure of being together.

In their unconscious minds something stirred . . .

CHAPTER 23

SEPTEMBER 11TH. DONCASTER

Doncaster!

I shall, I think, remember that 11th of September all my life.

Indeed, whenever I see a mention of the St Leger my mind flies automatically not to horse-racing but to murder.

When I recall my own sensations, the thing that stands out most is a sickening sense of insufficiency. We were here – on the spot – Poirot, myself, Clarke, Fraser, Megan Barnard, Thora Grey and Mary Drower, and in the last resort *what could any of us do*?

We were building on a forlorn hope – on the chance of recognizing amongst a crowd of thousands of people a face or figure imperfectly seen on an occasion one, two or three months back.

The odds were in reality greater than that. Of us all, the only person likely to make such a recognition was Thora Grey.

Some of her serenity had broken down under the strain. Her calm, efficient manner was gone. She sat twisting her hands together, almost weeping, appealing incoherently to Poirot.

'I never really looked at him . . . Why didn't I? What a fool I was. You're depending on me, all of you . . . and I shall let you down. Because even if I did see him again I mightn't recognize him. I've got a bad memory for faces.'

Poirot, whatever he might say to me, and however harshly he might seem to criticize the girl, showed nothing but kindness now. His manner was tender in the extreme. It struck me that Poirot was no more indifferent to beauty in distress than I was.

He patted her shoulder kindly.

'Now then, *petite*, not the hysteria. We cannot have that. If you should see this man you would recognize him.'

'How do you know?'

'Oh, a great many reasons – for one, because the red succeeds the black.'

'What do you mean, Poirot?' I cried.

'I speak the language of the tables. At roulette there may be a long run on the black – but in the end *red must turn up*. It is the mathematical laws of chance.'

'You mean that luck turns?'

'Exactly, Hastings. And that is where the gambler (and the murderer, who is, after all, only a supreme kind of gambler since what he risks is not his money but his life) often lacks intelligent anticipation. Because he *has* won he thinks he will *continue* to win! He does not leave the tables in good time with his pocket full. So in crime the murderer who is successful *cannot conceive the possibility of not being successful*! He takes to *himself* all the credit for a successful performance – but I tell you, my friends, however carefully planned, no crime can be successful without luck!'

'Isn't that going rather far?' demurred Franklin Clarke.

Poirot waved his hands excitedly.

'No, no. It is an even chance, if you like, but it *must* be in your favour. Consider! It might have happened that someone enters Mrs Ascher's shop just as the murderer is leaving. That person might have thought of looking behind the counter, have seen the dead woman – and either laid hands on the murderer straight away or else been able to give such an accurate description of him to the police that he would have been arrested forthwith.'

'Yes, of course, that's possible,' admitted Clarke. 'What it comes to is that a murderer's got to take a chance.'

'Precisely. A murderer is always a gambler. And, like many gamblers, a murderer often does not know when to stop. With each crime his opinion of his own abilities is strengthened. His sense of proportion is warped. He does not say "I have been clever *and lucky*!" No, he says only "I have been clever!" And his opinion of his cleverness grows and then, *mes amis*, the ball spins, and the run of colour is over – it drops into a new number and the croupier calls out *"Rouge."*'

'You think that will happen in this case?' asked Megan, drawing her brows together in a frown.

'It *must* happen sooner or later! So far *the luck has been with the criminal* – sooner or later it must turn and be with us. I believe that it *has* turned! The clue of the stockings is the beginning. Now, instead of everything going *right* for him, everything will go *wrong* for him! And he, too, will begin to make mistakes . . .'

'I will say you're heartening,' said Franklin Clarke. 'We all need a bit of comfort. I've had a paralysing feeling of helplessness ever since I woke up.'

'It seems to me highly problematical that we can accomplish anything of practical value,' said Donald Fraser.

Megan rapped out:

'Don't be a defeatist, Don.'

Mary Drower, flushing up a little, said:

'What I say is, you never know. That wicked fiend's in this place, and so are we – and after all, you do run up against people in the funniest way sometimes.'

I fumed:

'If only we could do something more.'

'You must remember, Hastings, that the police are doing everything reasonably possible. Special constables have been enrolled. The good

Inspector Crome may have the irritating manner, but he is a very able police officer, and Colonel Anderson, the Chief Constable, is a man of action. They have taken the fullest measures for watching and patrolling the town and the race-course. There will be plain-clothes men everywhere. There is also the press campaign. The public is fully warned.'

Donald Fraser shook his head.

'He'll never attempt it, I'm thinking,' he said more hopefully. 'The man would just be mad!'

'Unfortunately,' said Clarke dryly, 'he is mad! What do you think, M. Poirot? Will he give it up or will he try to carry it through?'

'In my opinion the strength of his obsession is such that he *must* attempt to carry out his promise! Not to do so would be to admit failure, and that his insane egoism would never allow. That, I may say, is also Dr Thompson's opinion. Our hope is that he may be caught in the attempt.'

Donald shook his head again.

'He'll be very cunning.'

Poirot glanced at his watch. We took the hint. It had been agreed that we were to make an all-day session of it, patrolling as many streets as possible in the morning, and later, stationing ourselves at various likely points on the race-course.

I say 'we'. Of course, in my own case such a patrol was of little avail since I was never likely to have set eyes on A B C. However, as the idea was to separate so as to cover as wide an area as possible I had suggested that I should act as escort to one of the ladies.

Poirot had agreed – I am afraid with somewhat of a twinkle in his eye.

The girls went off to get their hats on. Donald Fraser was standing by the window looking out, apparently lost in thought.

Franklin Clarke glanced over at him, then evidently deciding that the other was too abstracted to count as a listener, he lowered his voice a little and addressed Poirot.

'Look here, M. Poirot. You went down to Churston, I know, and saw my sister-in-law. Did she say – or hint – I mean – did she suggest at all –?'

He stopped, embarrassed.

Poirot answered with a face of blank innocence that aroused my strongest suspicions.

'*Comment?* Did your sister-in-law say, hint, or suggest – what?'

Franklin Clarke got rather red.

'Perhaps you think this isn't a time for butting in with personal things –'

'*Du tout!*'

'But I feel I'd like to get things quite straight.'

'An admirable course.'

This time I think Clarke began to suspect Poirot's bland face of concealing some inner amusement. He ploughed on rather heavily.

'My sister-in-law's an awfully nice woman – I've been very fond of her always – but of course she's been ill some time – and in that kind of illness – being given drugs and all that – one tends to – well, to *fancy* things about people!'

'Ah?'

By now there was no mistaking the twinkle in Poirot's eye.

But Franklin Clarke, absorbed in his diplomatic task, was past noticing it.

'It's about Thora – Miss Grey,' he said.

'Oh, it is of Miss Grey you speak?' Poirot's tone held innocent surprise.

'Yes. Lady Clarke got certain ideas in her head. You see, Thora – Miss Grey is well, rather a good-looking girl –'

'Perhaps – yes,' conceded Poirot.

'And women, even the best of them, are a bit catty about other women. Of course, Thora was invaluable to my brother – he always said she was the best secretary he ever had – and he was very fond of her, too. But it was all perfectly straight and above-board. I mean, Thora isn't the sort of girl –'

'No?' said Poirot helpfully.

'But my sister-in-law got it into her head to be – well – jealous, I suppose. Not that she ever showed anything. But after Car's death, when there was a question of Miss Grey staying on – well, Charlotte cut up rough. Of course, it's partly the illness and the morphia and all that – Nurse Capstick says so – she says we mustn't blame Charlotte for getting these ideas into her head –'

He paused.

'Yes?'

'What I want you to understand, M. Poirot, is that there isn't anything in it at all. It's just a sick woman's imaginings. Look here' – he fumbled in his pocket – 'here's a letter I received from my brother when I was in the Malay States. I'd like you to read it because it shows exactly what terms they were on.'

Poirot took it. Franklin came over beside him and with a pointing finger read some of the extracts out loud.

'— things go on here much as usual. Charlotte is moderately free from pain. I wish one could say more. You may remember Thora Grey? She is a dear girl and a greater comfort to me than I can tell you. I should not have known what to do through this bad time but for her. Her sympathy and interest are unfailing. She has an exquisite taste and flair for beautiful things and shares my passion for Chinese art. I was indeed lucky to find her. No daughter could be a closer or more sympathetic companion. Her life had been a difficult and not always a happy one, but I am glad to feel that here she has a home and true affection.

'You see,' said Franklin, '*that's* how my brother felt to her. He thought of her like a daughter. What I feel so unfair is the fact that the moment my brother is dead, his wife practically turns her out of the house! Women really are devils, M. Poirot.'

'Your sister-in-law is ill and in pain, remember.'

'I know. That's what I keep saying to myself. One mustn't judge her. All the same, I thought I'd show you this. I don't want you to get a false impression of Thora from anything Lady Clarke may have said.'

Poirot returned the letter.

'I can assure you,' he said, smiling, 'that I never permit myself to get false impressions from anything anyone tells me. I form my own judgments.'

'Well,' said Clarke, stowing away the letter. 'I'm glad I showed it to you anyway. Here come the girls. We'd better be off.'

As we left the room, Poirot called me back.

'You are determined to accompany the expedition, Hastings?'

'Oh, yes. I shouldn't be happy staying here inactive.'

'There is activity of mind as well as body, Hastings.'

'Well, you're better at it than I am,' I said.

'You are incontestably right, Hastings. Am I correct in supposing that you intend to be a cavalier to one of the ladies?'

'That was the idea.'

'And which lady did you propose to honour with your company?'

'Well – I – er – hadn't considered yet.'

'What about Miss Barnard?'

'She's rather the independent type,' I demurred.

'Miss Grey?'

'Yes. She's better.'

'I find you, Hastings, singularly though transparently dishonest! All along you had made up your mind to spend the day with your blonde angel!'

'Oh, really, Poirot!'

'I am sorry to upset your plans, but I must request you to give your escort elsewhere.'

'Oh, all right. I think you've got a weakness for that Dutch doll of a girl.'

'The person you are to escort is Mary Drower – and I must request you not to leave her.'

'But, Poirot, why?'

'Because, my dear friend, her name begins with a D. We must take no chances.'

I saw the justice of his remark. At first it seemed far-fetched, but then I realized that if A B C had a fanatical hatred of Poirot, he might very well be keeping himself informed of Poirot's movements. And in that case the elimination of Mary Drower might strike him as a very pat fourth stroke.

I promised to be faithful to my trust.

I went out leaving Poirot sitting in a chair near the window.

In front of him was a little roulette wheel. He spun it as I went out of the door and called after me:

'*Rouge* – that is a good omen, Hastings. The luck, it turns!'

CHAPTER 24

NOT FROM CAPTAIN HASTINGS' PERSONAL NARRATIVE

Below his breath Mr Leadbetter uttered a grunt of impatience as his next-door neighbour got up and stumbled clumsily past him, dropping his hat over the seat in front, and leaning over to retrieve it.

All this at the culminating moment of *Not a Sparrow*, that all-star, thrilling drama of pathos and beauty that Mr Leadbetter had been looking forward to seeing for a whole week.

The golden-haired heroine, played by Katherine Royal (in Mr Leadbetter's opinion the leading film actress in the world), was just giving vent to a hoarse cry of indignation:

'Never. I would sooner starve. But I shan't starve. Remember those words: *not a sparrow falls –*'

Mr Leadbetter moved his head irritably from right to left. People! Why on earth people couldn't wait till the *end* of a film . . . And to leave at this soul-stirring moment.

Ah, that was better. The annoying gentleman had passed on and out. Mr Leadbetter had a full view of the screen and of Katherine Royal standing by the window in the Van Schreiner Mansion in New York.

And now she was boarding the train – the child in her arms . . . What curious trains they had in America – not at all like English trains.

Ah, there was Steve again in his shack in the mountains . . .

The film pursued its course to its emotional and semi-religious end.

Mr Leadbetter breathed a sigh of satisfaction as the lights went up.

He rose slowly to his feet, blinking a little.

He never left the cinema very quickly. It always took him a moment or two to return to the prosaic reality of everyday life.

He glanced round. Not many people this afternoon – naturally. They were all at the races. Mr Leadbetter did not approve of racing nor of playing cards nor of drinking nor of smoking. This left him more energy to enjoy going to the pictures.

Everyone was hurrying towards the exit. Mr Leadbetter prepared to follow suit. The man in the seat in front of him was asleep – slumped down in his chair. Mr Leadbetter felt indignant to think that anyone could sleep with such a drama as *Not a Sparrow* going on.

An irate gentleman was saying to the sleeping man whose legs were stretched out blocking the way:

'Excuse *me*, sir.'

Mr Leadbetter reached the exit. He looked back.

There seemed to be some sort of commotion. A commissionaire . . . a little knot of people . . . Perhaps that man in front of him was dead drunk and not asleep . . .

He hesitated and then passed out – and in so doing missed the sensation of the day – a greater sensation even than Not Half winning the St Leger at 85 to 1.

The commissionaire was saying:

'Believe you're right, sir . . . He's ill . . . Why – what's the matter, sir?'

The other had drawn away his hand with an exclamation and was examining a red sticky smear.

'Blood . . .'

The commissionaire gave a stifled exclamation.

He had caught sight of the corner of something yellow projecting from under the seat.

'Gor blimey!' he said. '*It's a b – A B C.*'

CHAPTER 25

NOT FROM CAPTAIN HASTINGS' PERSONAL NARRATIVE

Mr Cust came out of the Regal Cinema and looked up at the sky.

A beautiful evening . . . A really beautiful evening . . .

A quotation from Browning came into his head.

'God's in His heaven. All's right with the world.'

He had always been fond of that quotation.

Only there were times, very often, when he had felt it wasn't true . . .

He trotted along the street smiling to himself until he came to the Black Swan where he was staying.

He climbed the stairs to his bedroom, a stuffy little room on the second floor, giving over a paved inner court and garage.

As he entered the room his smile faded suddenly. There was a stain on his sleeve near the cuff. He touched it tentatively – wet and red – blood . . .

His hand dipped into his pocket and brought out something – a long slender knife. The blade of that, too, was sticky and red . . .

Mr Cust sat there a long time.

Once his eyes shot round the room like those of a hunted animal.

His tongue passed feverishly over his lips . . .

'It isn't my fault,' said Mr Cust.

He sounded as though he were arguing with somebody – a schoolboy pleading to his headmaster.

He passed his tongue over his lips again . . .

Again, tentatively, he felt his coat sleeve.

His eyes crossed the room to the wash-basin.

A minute later he was pouring out water from the old-fashioned jug into the basin. Removing his coat, he rinsed the sleeve, carefully squeezing it out . . .

Ugh! The water was red now . . .

A tap on the door.

He stood there frozen into immobility – staring.

The door opened. A plump young woman – jug in hand.

'Oh, excuse me, sir. Your hot water, sir.'

He managed to speak then.

'Thank you . . . I've washed in cold . . .'

Why had he said that? Immediately her eyes went to the basin.

He said frenziedly: 'I – I've cut my hand . . .'

There was a pause – yes, surely a very long pause – before she said: 'Yes, sir.'

She went out, shutting the door.

Mr Cust stood as though turned to stone.

He listened.

It had come – at last . . .

Were there voices – exclamations – feet mounting the stairs?

He could hear nothing but the beating of his own heart . . .

Then, suddenly, from frozen immobility he leaped into activity.

He slipped on his coat, tiptoed to the door and opened it. No noises as yet except the familiar murmur arising from the bar. He crept down the stairs . . .

Still no one. That was luck. He paused at the foot of the stairs. Which way now?

He made up his mind, darted quickly along a passage and out by the door that gave into the yard. A couple of chauffeurs were there tinkering with cars and discussing winners and losers.

Mr Cust hurried across the yard and out into the street.

Round the first corner to the right – then to the left – right again . . .

Dare he risk the station?

Yes – there would be crowds there – special trains – if luck were on his side he would do it all right . . .

If only luck were with him . . .

CHAPTER 26

*NOT FROM CAPTAIN HASTINGS'
PERSONAL NARRATIVE*

Inspector Crome was listening to the excited utterances of Mr Leadbetter.

'I assure you, inspector, my heart misses a beat when I think of it. He must actually have been sitting beside me all through the programme!'

Inspector Crome, completely indifferent to the behaviour of Mr Leadbetter's heart, said:

'Just let me have it quite clear? This man went out towards the close of the big picture –'

'*Not a Sparrow* – Katherine Royal,' murmured Mr Leadbetter automatically.

'He passed you and in doing so stumbled –'

'He *pretended* to stumble, I see it now. Then he leaned over the seat in front to pick up his hat. He must have stabbed the poor fellow then.'

'You didn't hear anything? A cry? Or a groan?'

Mr Leadbetter had heard nothing but the loud, hoarse accents of Katherine Royal, but in the vividness of his imagination he invented a groan.

Inspector Crome took the groan at its face value and bade him proceed.

'And then he went out –'

'Can you describe him?'

'He was a very big man. Six foot at least. A giant.'

'Fair or dark?'

'I – well – I'm not exactly sure. I think he was bald. A sinister-looking fellow.'

'He didn't limp, did he?' asked Inspector Crome.

'Yes – yes, now you come to speak of it I think he did limp. Very dark, he might have been some kind of half-caste.'

'Was he in his seat the last time the lights came up?'

'No. He came in after the big picture began.'

Inspector Crome nodded, handed Mr Leadbetter a statement to sign and got rid of him.

'That's about as bad a witness as you'll find,' he remarked pessimistically. 'He'd say anything with a little leading. It's perfectly clear that he hasn't the faintest idea what our man looks like. Let's have the commissionaire back.'

The commissionaire, very stiff and military, came in and stood to attention, his eyes fixed on Colonel Anderson.

'Now, then, Jameson, let's hear your story.'

Jameson saluted.

'Yessir. Close of the performance, sir. I was told there was a gentleman taken ill, sir. Gentleman was in the two and fourpennies, slumped down in his seat like. Other gentlemen standing around. Gentleman looked bad to me, sir. One of the gentlemen standing by put his hand to the ill gentleman's coat and drew my attention. Blood, sir. It was clear the gentleman was dead – stabbed, sir. My attention was drawn to an A B C railway guide, sir, under the seat. Wishing to act correctly, I did not touch same, but reported to the police immediately that a tragedy had occurred.'

'Very good. Jameson, you acted very properly.'

'Thank you, sir.'

'Did you notice a man leaving the two and fourpennies about five minutes earlier?'

'There were several, sir.'

'Could you describe them?'

'Afraid not, sir. One was Mr Geoffrey Parnell. And there was a young fellow, Sam Baker, with his young lady. I didn't notice anybody else particular.'

'A pity. That'll do, Jameson.'

'Yessir.'

The commissionaire saluted and departed.

'The medical details we've got,' said Colonel Anderson. 'We'd better have the fellow that found him next.'

A police constable came in and saluted.

'Mr Hercule Poirot's here, sir, and another gentleman.'

Inspector Crome frowned.

'Oh, well,' he said. 'Better have 'em in, I suppose.'

CHAPTER 27

THE DONCASTER MURDER

Coming in hard on Poirot's heels, I just caught the fag end of Inspector Crome's remark.

Both he and the Chief Constable were looking worried and depressed.

Colonel Anderson greeted us with a nod of the head.

'Glad you've come, M. Poirot,' he said politely. I think he guessed that Crome's remark might have reached our ears. 'We've got it in the neck again, you see.'

'Another A B C murder?'

'Yes. Damned audacious bit of work. Man leaned over and stabbed the fellow in the back.'

'Stabbed this time?'

'Yes, varies his methods a bit, doesn't he? Biff on the head, strangled, now a knife. Versatile devil – what? Here are the medical details if you care to see 'em.'

He shoved a paper towards Poirot. 'A B C down on the floor between the dead man's feet,' he added.

'Has the dead man been identified?' asked Poirot.

'Yes. A B C's slipped up for once – if that's any satisfaction to us. Deceased's a man called Earlsfield – George Earlsfield. Barber by profession.'

'Curious,' commented Poirot.

'May have skipped a letter,' suggested the colonel.

My friend shook his head doubtfully.

'Shall we have in the next witness?' asked Crome. 'He's anxious to get home.'

'Yes, yes – let's get on.'

A middle-aged gentleman strongly resembling the frog footman in *Alice in Wonderland* was led in. He was highly excited and his voice was shrill with emotion.

'Most shocking experience I have ever known,' he squeaked. 'I have a weak heart, sir – a very weak heart, it might have been the death of me.'

'Your name, please,' said the inspector.

'Downes. Roger Emmanuel Downes.'

'Profession?'

'I am a master at Highfield School for boys.'

'Now, Mr Downes, will you tell us in your own words what happened.'

'I can tell you that very shortly, gentlemen. At the close of the performance I rose from my seat. The seat on my left was empty but in the one beyond a man was sitting, apparently asleep. I was unable to pass him to get out as his legs were stuck out in front of him. I asked him to allow me to pass. As he did not move I repeated my request in – a – er – slightly louder tone. He still made no response. I then took him by the shoulder to waken him. His body slumped down further and I became aware that he was either unconscious or seriously ill. I called out: "This gentleman is taken ill. Fetch the commissionaire." The commissionaire came. As I took my hand from the man's shoulder I found it was wet and red . . . I can assure you, gentlemen, the shock was terrific! Anything might have happened! For years I have suffered from cardiac weakness –'

Colonel Anderson was looking at Mr Downes with a very curious expression.

'You can consider that you're a lucky man, Mr Downes.'

'I do, sir. Not even a palpitation!'

'You don't quite take my meaning, Mr Downes. You were sitting two seats away, you say?'

'Actually I was sitting at first in the next seat to the murdered man – then I moved along so as to be behind an empty seat.'

'You're about the same height and build as the dead man, aren't you, and you were wearing a woollen scarf round your neck just as he was?'

'I fail to see –' began Mr Downes stiffly.

'I'm telling you, man,' said Colonel Anderson, 'just where your luck came in. Somehow or other, when the murderer followed you in, he got confused. *He picked on the wrong back.* I'll eat my hat, Mr Downes, if that knife wasn't meant for you!'

However well Mr Downes' heart had stood former tests, it was unable to stand up to this one. He sank on a chair, gasped, and turned purple in the face.

'Water,' he gasped. 'Water . . .'

A glass was brought him. He sipped it whilst his complexion gradually returned to the normal.

'Me?' he said. 'Why me?'

'It looks like it,' said Crome. 'In fact, it's the only explanation.'

'You mean that this man – this – this fiend incarnate – this bloodthirsty madman has been following *me* about waiting for an opportunity?'

'I should say that was the way of it.'

'But in heaven's name, why *me*?' demanded the outraged school-master.

Inspector Crome struggled with the temptation to reply: 'Why not?' and said instead: 'I'm afraid it's no good expecting a lunatic to have reasons for what he does.'

'God bless my soul,' said Mr Downes, sobered into whispering.

He got up. He looked suddenly old and shaken.

'If you don't want me any more, gentlemen, I think I'll go home. I – I don't feel very well.'

'That's quite all right, Mr Downes. I'll send a constable with you – just to see you're all right.'

'Oh, no – no, thank you. That's not necessary.'

'Might as well,' said Colonel Anderson gruffly.

His eyes slid sideways, asking an imperceptible question of the inspector. The latter gave an equally imperceptible nod.

Mr Downes went out shakily.

'Just as well he didn't tumble to it,' said Colonel Anderson. 'There'll be a couple of them – eh?'

'Yes, sir. Your Inspector Rice has made arrangements. The house will be watched.'

'You think,' said Poirot, 'that when A B C finds out his mistake he might try again?'

Anderson nodded.

'It's a possibility,' he said. 'Seems a methodical sort of chap, A B C. It will upset him if things don't go according to programme.'

Poirot nodded thoughtfully.

'Wish we could get a description of the fellow,' said Colonel Anderson irritably. 'We're as much in the dark as ever.'

'It may come,' said Poirot.

'Think so? Well, it's possible. Damn it all, hasn't anyone got eyes in their head?'

'Have patience,' said Poirot.

'You seem very confident, M. Poirot. Got any reason for this optimism?'

'Yes, Colonel Anderson. Up to now, the murderer has not made a mistake. He is bound to make one soon.'

'If that's all you've got to go on,' began the Chief Constable with a snort, but he was interrupted.

'Mr Ball of the Black Swan is here with a young woman, sir. He reckons he's got summat to say might help you.'

'Bring them along. Bring them along. We can do with anything helpful.'

Mr Ball of the Black Swan was a large, slow-thinking, heavily moving man. He exhaled a strong odour of beer. With him was a plump young woman with round eyes clearly in a state of high excitement.

'Hope I'm not intruding or wasting valuable time,' said Mr Ball in a slow, thick voice. 'But this wench, Mary here, reckons she's got something to tell as you ought to know.'

Mary giggled in a half-hearted way.

'Well, my girl, what is it?' said Anderson. 'What's your name?'

'Mary, sir, Mary Stroud.'

'Well, Mary, out with it.'

Mary turned her round eyes on her master.

'It's her business to take up hot water to the gents' bedrooms,' said Mr Ball, coming to the rescue. 'About half a dozen gentlemen we'd got staying. Some for the races and some just commercials.'

'Yes, yes,' said Anderson impatiently.

'Get on, lass,' said Mr Ball. 'Tell your tale. Nowt to be afraid of.'

Mary gasped, groaned and plunged in a breathless voice into her narrative.

'I knocked on door and there wasn't no answer, otherwise I wouldn't have gone in leastways not unless the gentleman had said "Come in," and as he didn't say nothing I went in and he was there washing his hands.'

She paused and breathed deeply.

'Go on, my girl,' said Anderson.

Mary looked sideways at her master and as though receiving inspiration from his slow nod, plunged on again.

'"It's your hot water, sir," I said, "and I did knock," but "Oh," he says, "I've washed in cold," he said, and so, naturally, I looks in basin, and oh! God help me, sir, *it were all red!*'

'Red?' said Anderson sharply.

Ball struck in.

'The lass told me that he had his coat off and that he was holding the sleeve of it, and it was all wet – that's right, eh, lass?'

'Yes, sir, that's right, sir.'

She plunged on:

'And his face, sir, it looked queer, mortal queer it looked. Gave me quite a turn.'

'When was this?' asked Anderson sharply.

'About a quarter after five, so near as I can reckon.'

'Over three hours ago,' snapped Anderson. 'Why didn't you come at once?'

'Didn't hear about it at once,' said Ball. 'Not till news came along as there'd been another murder done. And then the lass she screams out as it might have been blood in the basin, and I asks her what she means, and she tells me. Well, it doesn't sound right to me and I went upstairs myself. Nobody in the room. I asks a few questions and one of the lads in courtyard says he saw a fellow sneaking out that way and by his description it was the right one. So I says to the missus as Mary here had best go to police. She doesn't like the idea, Mary doesn't, and I says I'll come along with her.'

Inspector Crome drew a sheet of paper towards him.

'Describe this man,' he said. 'As quick as you can. There's no time to be lost.'

'Medium-sized he were,' said Mary. 'And stooped and wore glasses.'

'His clothes?'

'A dark suit and a Homburg hat. Rather shabby-looking.'

She could add little to this description.

Inspector Crome did not insist unduly. The telephone wires were soon busy, but neither the inspector nor the Chief Constable were over-optimistic.

Crome elicited the fact that the man, when seen sneaking across the yard, had had no bag or suitcase.

'There's a chance there,' he said.

Two men were despatched to the Black Swan.

Mr Ball, swelling with pride and importance, and Mary, somewhat tearful, accompanied them.

The sergeant returned about ten minutes later.

'I've brought the register, sir,' he said. 'Here's the signature.'

We crowded round. The writing was small and cramped – not easy to read.

'A. B. Case – or is it Cash?' said the Chief Constable.

'A B C,' said Crome significantly.

'What about luggage?' asked Anderson.

'One good-sized suitcase, sir, full of small cardboard boxes.'

'Boxes? What was in 'em?'

'Stockings, sir. Silk stockings.'

Crome turned to Poirot.

'Congratulations,' he said. 'Your hunch was right.'

CHAPTER 28

NOT FROM CAPTAIN HASTINGS' PERSONAL NARRATIVE

Inspector Crome was in his office at Scotland Yard.

The telephone on his desk gave a discreet buzz and he picked it up.

'Jacobs speaking, sir. There's a young fellow come in with a story that I think you ought to hear.'

Inspector Crome sighed. On an average twenty people a day turned up with so-called important information about the A B C case. Some of them were harmless lunatics, some of them were well-meaning persons who genuinely believed that their information was of value. It was the duty of Sergeant Jacobs to act as a human sieve – retaining the grosser matter and passing on the residue to his superior.

'Very well, Jacobs,' said Crome. 'Send him along.'

A few minutes later there was a tap on the inspector's door and Sergeant Jacobs appeared, ushering in a tall, moderately good-looking young man.

'This is Mr Tom Hartigan, sir. He's got something to tell us which may have a possible bearing on the A B C case.'

The inspector rose pleasantly and shook hands.

'Good morning, Mr Hartigan. Sit down, won't you? Smoke? Have a cigarette?'

Tom Hartigan sat down awkwardly and looked with some awe at what he called in his own mind 'One of the big-wigs.' The appearance of the inspector vaguely disappointed him. He looked quite an ordinary person!

'Now then,' said Crome. 'You've got something to tell us that you think may have a bearing on the case. Fire ahead.'

Tom began nervously.

'Of course it may be nothing at all. It's just an idea of mine. I may be wasting your time.'

Again Inspector Crome sighed imperceptibly. The amount of time he had to waste in reassuring people!

'We're the best judge of that. Let's have the facts, Mr Hartigan.'

'Well, it's like this, sir. I've got a young lady, you see, and her mother lets rooms. Up Camden Town way. Their second-floor back has been let for over a year to a man called Cust.'

'Cust – eh?'

'That's right, sir. A sort of middle-aged bloke what's rather vague and soft – and come down in the world a bit, I should say. Sort of creature who wouldn't hurt a fly you'd say – and I'd never of dreamed of anything being wrong if it hadn't been for something rather odd.'

In a somewhat confused manner and repeating himself once or twice, Tom described his encounter with Mr Cust at Euston Station and the incident of the dropped ticket.

'You see, sir, look at it how you will, it's funny like. Lily – that's my young lady, sir – she was quite positive that it was Cheltenham he said, and her mother says the same – says she remembers distinct talking about it the morning he went off. Of course, I didn't pay much attention to it at the time. Lily – my young lady – said as how she hoped he wouldn't cop it from this A B C fellow going to Doncaster – and then she says it's rather a coincidence because he was down Churston way at the time of the last crime. Laughing like, I asks her whether he was at Bexhill the time before, and she says she don't know where he was, but he was away at the seaside – that she does know. And then I said to her it would be odd if he was the A B C himself and she said poor Mr Cust wouldn't hurt a fly – and that was all at the time. We didn't think no more about it. At least, in a sort of way I did, sir, underneath like. I began wondering about this Cust fellow and thinking that, after all, harmless as he seemed, he might be a bit batty.'

Tom took a breath and then went on. Inspector Crome was listening intently now.

'And then after the Doncaster murder, sir, it was in all the papers that information was wanted as to the whereabouts of a certain A B Case or Cash, and it gave a description that fitted well enough. First evening off I had, I went round to Lily's and asked her what her Mr Cust's initials were. She couldn't remember at first, but her mother did. Said they were A B right enough. Then we got down to it and tried to figure out if Cust had been away at the time of the first murder at Andover. Well, as you know, sir, it isn't too easy to remember things three months back. We had a job of it, but we got it fixed down in the end, because Mrs Marbury had a brother come from Canada to see her on June 21st. He arrived unexpected like and she wanted to give him a bed, and Lily suggested that as Mr Cust was away Bert Smith might have his bed. But Mrs Marbury wouldn't agree, because she said it wasn't acting right by her lodger, and she always liked to act fair and square. But we fixed the date all right because of Bert Smith's ship docking at Southampton that day.'

Inspector Crome had listened very attentively, jotting down an occasional note.

'That's all?' he asked.

'That's all, sir. I hope you don't think I'm making a lot of nothing.'

Tom flushed slightly.

'Not at all. You were quite right to come here. Of course, it's very slight evidence – these dates may be mere coincidence and the likeness of the name, too. But it certainly warrants my having an interview with your Mr Cust. Is he at home now?'

'Yes, sir.'

'When did he return?'

'The evening of the Doncaster murder, sir.'

'What's he been doing since?'

'He's stayed in mostly, sir. And he's been looking very queer, Mrs Marbury says. He buys a lot of newspapers – goes out early and gets the morning ones, and then after dark he goes out and gets the evening ones. Mrs Marbury says he talks a lot to himself, too. She thinks he's getting queerer.'

'What is this Mrs Marbury's address?'

Tom gave it to him.

'Thank you. I shall probably be calling round in the course of the day. I need hardly tell you to be careful of your manner if you come across this Cust.'

He rose and shook hands.

'You may be quite satisfied you did the right thing in coming to us. Good morning, Mr Hartigan.'

'Well, sir?' asked Jacobs, re-entering the room a few minutes later. 'Think it's the goods?'

'It's promising,' said Inspector Crome. 'That is, if the facts are as the boy stated them. We've had no luck with the stocking manufacturers yet. It was time we got hold of something. By the way, give me that file of the Churston case.'

He spent some minutes looking for what he wanted.

'Ah, here it is. It's amongst the statements made to the Torquay police. Young man of the name of Hill. Deposes he was leaving the Torquay Palladium after the film *Not a Sparrow* and noticed a man behaving queerly. He was talking to himself. Hill heard him say "That's an idea." *Not a Sparrow* – that's the film that was on at the Regal in Doncaster?'

'Yes, sir.'

'There may be something in that. Nothing to it at the time – but it's possible that the idea of the *modus operandi* for his next crime occurred to our man then. We've got Hill's name and address, I see. His description of the man is vague but it links up well enough with the descriptions of Mary Stroud and this Tom Hartigan . . .'

He nodded thoughtfully.

'We're getting warm,' said Inspector Crome – rather inaccurately, for he himself was always slightly chilly.

'Any instructions, sir?'

'Put on a couple of men to watch this Camden Town address, but I don't want our bird frightened. I must have a word with the AC. Then I think it would be as well if Cust was brought along here and asked if he'd like to make a statement. It sounds as though he's quite ready to get rattled.'

Outside Tom Hartigan had rejoined Lily Marbury who was waiting for him on the Embankment.

'All right, Tom?'

Tom nodded.

'I saw Inspector Crome himself. The one who's in charge of the case.'

'What's he like?'

'A bit quiet and lah-di-dah – not my idea of a detective.'

'That's Lord Trenchard's new kind,' said Lily with respect. 'Some of them are ever so grand. Well, what did he say?'

Tom gave her a brief résumé of the interview.

'So they think as it really was him?'

'They think it might be. Anyway, they'll come along and ask him a question or two.'

'Poor Mr Cust.'

'It's no good saying poor Mr Cust, my girl. If he's A B C, he's committed four terrible murders.'

Lily sighed and shook her head.

'It does seem awful,' she observed.

'Well, now you're going to come and have a bite of lunch, my girl. Just you think that if we're right I expect my name will be in the papers!'

'Oh, Tom, will it?'

'Rather. And yours, too. *And* your mother's. And I dare say you'll have your picture in it, too.'

'Oh, Tom.' Lily squeezed his arm in an ecstasy.

'And in the meantime what do you say to a bite at the Corner House?'

Lily squeezed tighter.

'Come on then!'

'All right – half a minute. I must just telephone from the station.'

'Who to?'

'A girl I was going to meet.'

She slipped across the road, and rejoined him three minutes later, looking rather flushed.

'Now then, Tom.'

She slipped her arm in his.

'Tell me more about Scotland Yard. You didn't see the other one there?'

'What other one?'

'The Belgian gentleman. The one that A B C writes to always.'

'No. He wasn't there.'

'Well, tell me all about it. What happened when you got inside? Who did you speak to and what did you say?'

Mr Cust put the receiver back very gently on the hook.

He turned to where Mrs Marbury was standing in the doorway of the room, clearly devoured with curiosity.

'Not often you have a telephone call, Mr Cust?'

'No – er – no, Mrs Marbury. It isn't.'

'Not bad news, I trust?'

'No – no.' How persistent the woman was. His eyes caught the legend on the newspaper he was carrying.

Births – Marriages – Deaths . . .

'My sister's just had a little boy,' he blurted out.

He – who had never had a sister!

'Oh, dear! Now – well, that *is* nice, I am sure. ("And never once mentioned a sister all these years," was her inward thought. "If that isn't just like a man!") I was surprised, I'll tell you, when the lady asked to speak to Mr Cust. Just at first I fancied it was my Lily's voice – something like hers, it was – but haughtier if you know what I mean – sort of high up in the air. Well, Mr Cust, my congratulations, I'm sure. Is it the first one, or have you other little nephews and nieces?'

'It's the only one,' said Mr Cust. 'The only one I've ever had or likely to have, and – er – I think I must go off at once. They – they want me to come. I – I think I can just catch a train if I hurry.'

'Will you be away long, Mr Cust?' called Mrs Marbury as he ran up the stairs.

'Oh, no – two or three days – that's all.'

He disappeared into his bedroom. Mrs Marbury retired into the kitchen, thinking sentimentally of 'the dear little mite'.

Her conscience gave her a sudden twinge.

Last night Tom and Lily and all the hunting back over dates! Trying to make out that Mr Cust was that dreadful monster, A B C. Just because of his initials and because of a few coincidences.

'I don't suppose they meant it seriously,' she thought comfortably. 'And now I hope they'll be ashamed of themselves.'

In some obscure way that she could not have explained, Mr Cust's statement that his sister had had a baby had effectually removed any doubts Mrs Marbury might have had of her lodger's *bona fides*.

'I hope she didn't have too hard a time of it, poor dear,' thought Mrs Marbury, testing an iron against her cheek before beginning to iron out Lily's silk slip.

Her mind ran comfortably on a well-worn obstetric track.

Mr Cust came quietly down the stairs, a bag in his hand. His eyes rested a minute on the telephone.

That brief conversation re-echoed in his brain.

'Is that you, Mr Cust? I thought you might like to know there's an inspector from Scotland Yard may be coming to see you . . .'

What had he said? He couldn't remember.

'Thank you – thank you, my dear . . . very kind of you . . .'

Something like that.

Why had she telephoned to him? Could she possibly have guessed? Or did she just want to make sure he would stay in for the inspector's visit?

But how did she know the inspector was coming?

And her voice – she'd disguised her voice from her mother . . .

It looked – it looked – as though she *knew* . . .

But surely if she knew, she wouldn't . . .

She might, though. Women were very queer. Unexpectedly cruel and unexpectedly kind. He'd seen Lily once letting a mouse out of a mouse-trap.

A kind girl . . .

A kind, pretty girl . . .

He paused by the hall stand with its load of umbrellas and coats.

Should he . . . ?

A slight noise from the kitchen decided him . . .

No, there wasn't time . . .

Mrs Marbury might come out . . .

He opened the front door, passed through and closed it behind him . . .

Where . . . ?

CHAPTER 29

AT SCOTLAND YARD

Conference again.

The Assistant Commissioner, Inspector Crome, Poirot and myself.

The AC was saying:

'A good tip that of yours, M. Poirot, about checking a large sale of stockings.'

Poirot spread out his hands.

'It was indicated. This man could not be a regular agent. He sold outright instead of touting for orders.'

'Got everything clear so far, inspector?'

'I think so, sir.' Crome consulted a file. 'Shall I run over the position to date?'

'Yes, please.'

'I've checked up with Churston, Paignton and Torquay. Got a list of people where he went and offered stockings. I must say he did the thing thoroughly. Stayed at the Pitt, small hotel near Torre Station. Returned to the hotel at 10.30 on the night of the murder. Could have taken a train from Churston at 9.57, getting to Torre at 10.20. No one answering to his description noticed on train or at station, but that Friday was Dartmouth Regatta and the trains back from Kingswear were pretty full.

'Bexhill much the same. Stayed at the Globe under his own name. Offered stockings to about a dozen addresses, including Mrs Barnard and including the Ginger Cat. Left hotel early in the evening. Arrived back in London about 11.30 the following morning. As to Andover, same procedure. Stayed at the Feathers. Offered stockings to Mrs Fowler, next door to Mrs Ascher, and to half a dozen other people in the street. The pair Mrs Ascher had I got from the niece (name of Drower) – they're identical with Cust's supply.'

'So far, good,' said the AC.

'Acting on information received,' said the inspector, 'I went to the address given me by Hartigan, but found that Cust had left the house about half an hour previously. He received a telephone message, I'm told. First time such a thing had happened to him, so his landlady told me.'

'An accomplice?' suggested the Assistant Commissioner.

'Hardly,' said Poirot. 'It is odd that – unless –'

We all looked at him inquiringly as he paused.

He shook his head, however, and the inspector proceeded.

'I made a thorough search of the room he had occupied. That search puts the matter beyond doubt. I found a block of notepaper similar to that on which the letters were written, a large quantity of hosiery and – at the back of the cupboard where the hosiery was stored – a parcel much the same shape and size but which turned out to contain – not hosiery – *but eight new A B C railway guides!*'

'Proof positive,' said the Assistant Commissioner.

'I've found something else, too,' said the inspector – his voice becoming suddenly almost human with triumph. 'Only found it this morning, sir. Not had time to report yet. There was no sign of the knife in his room –'

'It would be the act of an imbecile to bring that back with him,' remarked Poirot.

'After all, he's not a reasonable human being,' remarked the inspector. 'Anyway, it occurred to me that he might just possibly have brought it back to the house and then realized the danger of hiding it (as M. Poirot points out) in his room, and have looked about elsewhere. What place in the house would he be likely to select? I got it straight away. *The hall stand* – no one ever moves a hall stand. With a lot of trouble I got it moved out from the wall – and there it was!'

'The knife?'

'The knife. Not a doubt of it. The dried blood's still on it.'

'Good work, Crome,' said the AC approvingly. 'We only need one thing more now.'

'What's that?'

'The man himself.'

'We'll get him, sir. Never fear.'

The inspector's tone was confident.

'What do you say, M. Poirot?'

Poirot started out of a reverie.

'I beg your pardon?'

'We were saying that it was only a matter of time before we got our man. Do you agree?'

'Oh, that – yes. Without a doubt.'

His tone was so abstracted that the others looked at him curiously.

'Is there anything worrying you, M. Poirot?'

'There is something that worries me very much. It is the *why*? The *motive.*'

'But, my dear fellow, the man's crazy,' said the Assistant Commissioner impatiently.

'I understand what M. Poirot means,' said Crome, coming graciously to the rescue. 'He's quite right. There's got to be some definite obsession. I think we'll find the root of the matter in an intensified inferiority complex. There may be a persecution mania, too, and if so he may possibly associate M. Poirot with it. He may have the delusion that M. Poirot is a detective employed on purpose to hunt him down.'

'H'm,' said the AC. 'That's the jargon that's talked nowadays. In my day if a man was mad he was mad and we didn't look about for scientific terms to soften it down. I suppose a thoroughly up-to-date doctor would suggest putting a man like A B C in a nursing home, telling him what a fine fellow he was for forty-five days on end and then letting him out as a responsible member of society.'

Poirot smiled but did not answer.

The conference broke up.

'Well,' said the Assistant Commissioner. 'As you say, Crome, pulling him in is only a matter of time.'

'We'd have had him before now,' said the inspector, 'if he wasn't so ordinary-looking. We've worried enough perfectly inoffensive citizens as it is.'

'I wonder where he is at this minute,' said the Assistant Commissioner.

CHAPTER 30

*NOT FROM CAPTAIN HASTINGS'
PERSONAL NARRATIVE*

Mr Cust stood by a greengrocer's shop.

He stared across the road.

Yes, that was it.

Mrs Ascher. Newsagent and Tobacconist . . .

In the empty window was a sign.

To Let.

Empty . . .

Lifeless . . .

'Excuse me, sir.'

The greengrocer's wife, trying to get at some lemons.

He apologized, moved to one side.

Slowly he shuffled away – back towards the main street of the town . . .

It was difficult – very difficult – now that he hadn't any money left . . .

Not having had anything to eat all day made one feel very queer and light-headed . . .

He looked at a poster outside a newsagent's shop.

The A B C Case. Murderer Still at Large. Interviews with M. Hercule Poirot.

Mr Cust said to himself:

'Hercule Poirot. I wonder if *he* knows . . .'

He walked on again.

It wouldn't do to stand staring at that poster . . .

He thought:

'I can't go on much longer . . .'

Foot in front of foot . . . what an odd thing walking was . . .

Foot in front of foot – ridiculous.

Highly ridiculous . . .

But man was a ridiculous animal anyway . . .

And he, Alexander Bonaparte Cust, was particularly ridiculous.

He had always been . . .

People had always laughed at him . . .

He couldn't blame them . . .

Where was he going? He didn't know. He'd come to the end. He no longer looked anywhere but at his feet.

Foot in front of foot.

He looked up. Lights in front of him. And letters . . .

Police Station.

'That's funny,' said Mr Cust. He gave a little giggle.

Then he stepped inside. Suddenly, as he did so, he swayed and fell forward.

CHAPTER 31

HERCULE POIROT ASKS QUESTIONS

It was a clear November day. Dr Thompson and Chief Inspector Japp had come round to acquaint Poirot with the result of the police court proceedings in the case of Rex *v.* Alexander Bonaparte Cust.

Poirot himself had had a slight bronchial chill which had prevented his attending. Fortunately he had not insisted on having my company.

'Committed for trial,' said Japp. 'So that's that.'

'Isn't it unusual?' I asked, 'for a defence to be offered at this stage? I thought prisoners always reserved their defence.'

'It's the usual course,' said Japp. 'I suppose young Lucas thought he might rush it through. He's a trier, I will say. Insanity's the only defence possible.'

Poirot shrugged his shoulders.

'With insanity there can be no acquittal. Imprisonment during His Majesty's pleasure is hardly preferable to death.'

'I suppose Lucas thought there was a chance,' said Japp. 'With a first-class alibi for the Bexhill murder, the whole case might be weakened. I don't think he realized how strong our case is. Anyway, Lucas goes in for originality. He's a young man, and he wants to hit the public eye.'

Poirot turned to Thompson.

'What's your opinion, doctor?'

'Of Cust? Upon my soul, I don't know what to say. He's playing the sane man remarkably well. He's an epileptic, of course.'

'What an amazing dénouement that was,' I said.

'His falling into the Andover police station in a fit? Yes – it was a fitting dramatic curtain to the drama. A B C has always timed his effects well.'

'Is it possible to commit a crime and be unaware of it?' I asked. 'His denials seem to have a ring of truth in them.'

Dr Thompson smiled a little.

'You mustn't be taken in by that theatrical "I swear by God" pose. It's my opinion *that Cust knows perfectly well he committed the murders.*'

'When they're as fervent as that they usually do,' said Crome.

'As to your question,' went on Thompson, 'it's perfectly possible for an epileptic subject in a state of somnambulism to commit an action and be entirely unaware of having done so. But it is the general opinion that such an action must "not be contrary to the will of the person in the waking state".'

He went on discussing the matter, speaking of *grand mal* and *petit mal* and, to tell the truth, confusing me hopelessly as is often the case when a learned person holds forth on his own subject.

'However, I'm against the theory that Cust committed these crimes without knowing he'd done them. You might put that theory forward if it weren't for the letters. The letters knock the theory on the head. They show premeditation and a careful planning of the crime.'

'And of the letters we have still no explanation,' said Poirot.

'That interests you?'

'Naturally – since they were written to me. And on the subject of the letters Cust is persistently dumb. Until I get at the reason for those letters being written to me, I shall not feel that the case is solved.'

'Yes – I can understand that from your point of view. There doesn't seem to be any reason to believe that the man ever came up against you in any way?'

'None whatever.'

'I might make a suggestion. Your name!'

'My name?'

'Yes. Cust is saddled – apparently by the whim of his mother (Oedipus complex there, I shouldn't wonder!) – with two extremely bombastic Christian names: Alexander and Bonaparte. You see the implications? Alexander – the popularly supposed undefeatable who sighed for more worlds to conquer. Bonaparte – the great Emperor of the French. He wants an adversary – an adversary, one might say, in his class. Well – there you are – Hercules the strong.'

'Your words are very suggestive, doctor. They foster ideas . . .'

'Oh, it's only a suggestion. Well, I must be off.'

Dr Thompson went out. Japp remained.

'Does this alibi worry you?' Poirot asked.

'It does a little,' admitted the inspector. 'Mind you, I don't believe in it, because I know it isn't true. But it is going to be the deuce to break it. This man Strange is a tough character.'

'Describe him to me.'

'He's a man of forty. A tough, confident, self-opinionated mining engineer. It's my opinion that it was he who insisted on his evidence being taken now. He wants to get off to Chile. He hoped the thing might be settled out of hand.'

'He's one of the most positive people I've ever seen,' I said.

'The type of man who would not like to admit he was mistaken,' said Poirot thoughtfully.

'He sticks to his story and he's not one to be heckled. He swears by all that's blue that he picked up Cust in the Whitecross Hotel at Eastbourne on the evening of July 24th. He was lonely and wanted someone to talk to. As far as I can see, Cust made an ideal listener. He didn't interrupt! After dinner he and Cust played dominoes. It appears Strange was a whale on dominoes and to his surprise Cust was pretty hot stuff too. Queer game, dominoes. People go mad about it. They'll play for hours. That's what Strange and Cust did apparently. Cust wanted to go to bed but Strange wouldn't hear of it – swore they'd keep it up until midnight at least. And that's what they did do. They separated at ten minutes past midnight. And if Cust was in the Whitecross Hotel at Eastbourne at ten minutes past midnight on the morning of the 25th he couldn't very well be strangling Betty Barnard on the beach at Bexhill between midnight and one o'clock.'

'The problem certainly seems insuperable,' said Poirot thoughtfully. 'Decidedly, it gives one to think.'

'It's given Crome something to think about,' said Japp.

'This man Strange is very positive?'

'Yes. He's an obstinate devil. And it's difficult to see just where the flaw is. Supposing Strange is making a mistake and the man wasn't Cust – why on earth should he *say* his name is Cust? And the writing in the hotel register is his all right. You can't say he's an accomplice – homicidal lunatics don't have accomplices! Did the girl die later? The doctor was quite firm in his evidence, and anyway it would take some time for Cust to get out of the hotel at Eastbourne without being seen and get over to Bexhill – about fourteen miles away –'

'It is a problem – yes,' said Poirot.

'Of course, strictly speaking, it oughtn't to matter. We've got Cust on the Doncaster murder – the blood-stained coat, the knife – not a loophole there. You couldn't bounce any jury into acquitting him. But it spoils a pretty case. He did the Doncaster murder. He did the Churston murder. He did the Andover murder. Then, by hell, he *must* have done the Bexhill murder. But I don't see how!'

He shook his head and got up.

'Now's your chance, M. Poirot,' he said. 'Crome's in a fog. Exert those cellular arrangements of yours I used to hear so much about. Show us the way he did it.'

Japp departed.

'What about it, Poirot?' I said. 'Are the little grey cells equal to the task?'

Poirot answered my question by another.

'Tell me, Hastings, do you consider the case ended?'

'Well – yes, practically speaking. We've got the man. And we've got most of the evidence. It's only the trimmings that are needed.'

Poirot shook his head.

'The case is ended! The case! The case is the *man*, Hastings. Until we know all about the man, the mystery is as deep as ever. It is not victory because we have put him in the dock!'

'We know a fair amount about him.'

'We know nothing at all! We know where he was born. We know he fought in the war and received a slight wound in the head and that he was discharged from the army owing to epilepsy. We know that he lodged with Mrs Marbury for nearly two years. We know that he was quiet and retiring – the sort of man that nobody notices. We know that he invented and carried out an intensely clever scheme of systemized murder. We know that he made certain incredibly stupid blunders. We know that he killed without pity and quite ruthlessly. We know, too, that he was kindly enough not to let blame rest on any other person for the crimes he committed. If he wanted to kill unmolested – how easy to let other persons suffer for his crimes. Do you not see, Hastings, that the man is a mass of contradictions? Stupid and cunning, ruthless and magnanimous – *and that there must be some dominating factor that reconciles his two natures.*'

'Of course, if you treat him like a psychological study,' I began.

'What else has this case been since the beginning? All along I have been groping my way – trying *to get to know the murderer*. And now I realize, Hastings, *that I do not know him at all!* I am at sea.'

'The lust for power –' I began.

'Yes – that might explain a good deal . . . But it does not satisfy me. There are things I want to know. *Why* did he commit these murders? *Why* did he choose those particular people –?'

'Alphabetically –' I began.

'Was Betty Barnard the only person in Bexhill whose name began with a B? Betty Barnard – I had an idea there . . . It ought to be true – it must be true. But if so –'

He was silent for some time. I did not like to interrupt him.

As a matter of fact, I believe I fell asleep.

I woke to find Poirot's hand on my shoulder.

'*Mon cher Hastings,*' he said affectionately. 'My good genius.'

I was quite confused by this sudden mark of esteem.

'It is true,' Poirot insisted. 'Always – always – you help me – you bring me luck. You inspire me.'

'How have I inspired you this time?' I asked.

'While I was asking myself certain questions I remembered a remark of yours – a remark absolutely shimmering in its clear vision. Did I not say to you once that you had a genius for stating the obvious. It is the obvious that I have neglected.'

'What is this brilliant remark of mine?' I asked.

'It makes everything as clear as crystal. I see the answers to all my questions. The reason for Mrs Ascher (that, it is true, I glimpsed long ago), the reason for Sir Carmichael Clarke, the reason for the Doncaster murder, and finally and supremely important, *the reason for Hercule Poirot.*'

'Could you kindly explain?' I asked.

'Not at the moment. I require first a little more information. That I can get from our Special Legion. And then – then, *when I have got the answer to a certain question, I will go and see A B C.* We will be face to face at last – A B C and Hercule Poirot – the adversaries.'

'And then?' I asked.

'And then,' said Poirot. 'We will talk! *Je vous assure,* Hastings – there is nothing so dangerous *for anyone who has something to hide* as conversation! Speech, so a wise old Frenchman said to me once, is an invention of man's to prevent him from thinking. It is also an infallible means of discovering that which he wishes to hide. A human being, Hastings, cannot resist the opportunity to reveal himself and express his personality which conversation gives him. Every time he will give himself away.'

'What do you expect Cust to tell you?'

Hercule Poirot smiled.

'A lie,' he said. 'And by it, I shall know the truth!'

CHAPTER 32

AND CATCH A FOX

During the next few days Poirot was very busy. He made mysterious absences, talked very little, frowned to himself, and consistently refused to satisfy my natural curiosity as to the brilliance I had, according to him, displayed in the past.

I was not invited to accompany him on his mysterious comings and goings – a fact which I somewhat resented.

Towards the end of the week, however, he announced his intention of paying a visit to Bexhill and neighbourhood and suggested that I should come with him. Needless to say, I accepted with alacrity.

The invitation, I discovered, was not extended to me alone. The members of our Special Legion were also invited.

They were as intrigued by Poirot as I was. Nevertheless, by the end of the day, I had at any rate an idea as to the direction in which Poirot's thoughts were tending.

He first visited Mr and Mrs Barnard and got an exact account from her as to the hour at which Mr Cust had called on her and exactly what he had said. He then went to the hotel at which Cust had put up and extracted a minute description of that gentleman's departure. As far as I could judge, no new facts were elicited by his questions but he himself seemed quite satisfied.

Next he went to the beach – to the place where Betty Barnard's body had been discovered. Here he walked round in circles for some minutes studying the shingle attentively. I could see little point in this, since the tide covered the spot twice a day.

However I have learnt by this time that Poirot's actions are usually dictated by an idea – however meaningless they may seem.

He then walked from the beach to the nearest point at which a car could have been parked. From there again he went to the place where the Eastbourne buses waited before leaving Bexhill.

Finally he took us all to the Ginger Cat café, where we had a somewhat stale tea served by the plump waitress, Milly Higley.

Her he complimented in a flowing Gallic style on the shape of her ankles.

'The legs of the English – always they are too thin! But you, mademoiselle, have the perfect leg. It has shape – it has an ankle!'

Milly Higley giggled a good deal and told him not to go on so. She knew what French gentlemen were like.

Poirot did not trouble to contradict her mistake as to his nationality. He merely ogled her in such a way that I was startled and almost shocked.

'*Voilà*,' said Poirot, 'I have finished in Bexhill. Presently I go to Eastbourne. One little inquiry there – that is all. Unnecessary for you all to accompany me. In the meantime come back to the hotel and let us have a cocktail. That Carlton tea, it was abominable!'

As we were sipping our cocktails Franklin Clarke said curiously:

'I suppose we can guess what you are after? You're out to break that alibi. But I can't see what you're so pleased about. You haven't got a new fact of any kind.'

'No – that is true.'

'Well, then?'

'Patience. Everything arranges itself, given time.'

'You seem quite pleased with yourself anyway.'

'Nothing so far has contradicted my little idea – that is why.'

His face grew serious.

'My friend Hastings told me once that he had, as a young man, played a game called The Truth. It was a game where everyone in turn was asked three questions – two of which must be answered truthfully. The third one could be barred. The questions, naturally, were of the most indiscreet kind. But to begin with everyone had to swear that they would indeed speak the truth, and nothing but the truth.'

He paused.

'Well?' said Megan.

'*Eh bien* – me, I want to play that game. Only it is not necessary to have three questions. One will be enough. One question to each of you.'

'Of course,' said Clarke impatiently. 'We'll answer anything.'

'Ah, but I want it to be more serious than that. Do you all swear to speak the truth?'

He was so solemn about it that the others, puzzled, became solemn themselves. They all swore as he demanded.

'*Bon*,' said Poirot briskly. 'Let us begin –'

'I'm ready,' said Thora Grey.

'Ah, but ladies first – this time it would not be the politeness. We will start elsewhere.'

He turned to Franklin Clarke.

'What, *mon cher M. Clarke*, did you think of the hats the ladies wore at Ascot this year?'

Franklin Clarke stared at him.

'Is this a joke?'

'Certainly not.'

'Is that seriously your question?'

'It is.'

Clarke began to grin.

'Well, M. Poirot, I didn't actually go to Ascot, but from what I could see of them driving in cars, women's hats for Ascot were an even bigger joke than the hats they wear ordinarily.'

'Fantastic?'

'Quite fantastic.'

Poirot smiled and turned to Donald Fraser.

'When did you take your holiday this year, monsieur?'

It was Fraser's turn to stare.

'My holiday? The first two weeks in August.'

His face quivered suddenly. I guessed that the question had brought the loss of the girl he loved back to him.

Poirot, however, did not seem to pay much attention to the reply. He turned to Thora Grey and I heard the slight difference in his voice. It had tightened up. His question came sharp and clear.

'Mademoiselle, in the event of Lady Clarke's death, would you have married Sir Carmichael if he had asked you?'

The girl sprang up.

'How dare you ask me such a question. It's – it's insulting!'

'Perhaps. But you have sworn to speak the truth. *Eh bien* – Yes or no?'

'Sir Carmichael was wonderfully kind to me. He treated me almost like a daughter. And that's how I felt to him – just affectionate and grateful.'

'Pardon me, but that is not answering Yes or No, mademoiselle.'

She hesitated.

'The answer, of course, is no!'

He made no comment.

'Thank you, mademoiselle.'

He turned to Megan Barnard. The girl's face was very pale. She was breathing hard as though braced up for an ordeal.

Poirot's voice came out like the crack of a whiplash.

'Mademoiselle, what do you hope will be the result of my investigations? Do you want me to find out the truth – or not?'

Her head went back proudly. I was fairly sure of her answer. Megan, I knew, had a fanatical passion for truth.

Her answer came clearly – and it stupefied me.

'No!'

We all jumped. Poirot leant forward studying her face.

'Mademoiselle Megan,' he said, 'you may not want the truth but – *ma foi* – you can speak it!'

He turned towards the door, then, recollecting, went to Mary Drower.

'Tell me, *mon enfant*, have you a young man?'

Mary, who had been looking apprehensive, looked startled and blushed.

'Oh, Mr Poirot. I – I – well, I'm not sure.'

He smiled.

'*Alors c'est bien, mon enfant.*'

He looked round for me.

'Come, Hastings, we must start for Eastbourne.'

The car was waiting and soon we were driving along the coast road that leads through Pevensey to Eastbourne.

'Is it any use asking you anything, Poirot?'

'Not at this moment. Draw your own conclusions as to what I am doing.'

I relapsed into silence.

Poirot, who seemed pleased with himself, hummed a little tune. As we passed through Pevensey he suggested that we stop and have a look over the castle.

As we were returning towards the car, we paused a moment to watch a ring of children – Brownies, I guessed, by their get-up – who were singing a ditty in shrill, untuneful voices . . .

'What is it that they say, Hastings? I cannot catch the words.'

I listened – till I caught one refrain.

'*– And catch a fox*
And put him in a box
And never let him go.'

'And catch a fox and put him in a box and never let him go!' repeated Poirot.

His face had gone suddenly grave and stern.

'It is very terrible that, Hastings.' He was silent a minute. 'You hunt the fox here?'

'I don't. I've never been able to afford to hunt. And I don't think there's much hunting in this part of the world.'

'I meant in England generally. A strange sport. The waiting at the covert side – then they sound the tally-ho, do they not? – and the run begins – across the country – over the hedges and ditches – and the fox he runs – and sometimes he doubles back – but the dogs –'

'Hounds!'

'– hounds are on his trail, and at last they catch him and he dies – quickly and horribly.'

'I suppose it does sound cruel, but really –'

'The fox enjoys it? Do not say *les bêtises*, my friend. *Tout de même* – it is better that – the quick, cruel death – than what those children were singing . . .

'To be shut away – in a box – for ever . . . No, it is not good, that.'

He shook his head. Then he said, with a change of tone:

'Tomorrow, I am to visit the man Cust,' and he added to the chauffeur:

'Back to London.'

'Aren't you going to Eastbourne?' I cried.

'What need? I know – quite enough for my purpose.'

CHAPTER 33

ALEXANDER BONAPARTE CUST

I was not present at the interview that took place between Poirot and that strange man – Alexander Bonaparte Cust. Owing to his association with the police and the peculiar circumstances of the case, Poirot had no difficulty in obtaining a Home Office order – but that order did not extend to me, and in any case it was essential, from Poirot's point of view, that that interview should be absolutely private – the two men face to face.

He has given me, however, such a detailed account of what passed between them that I set it down with as much confidence on paper as though I had actually been present.

Mr Cust seemed to have shrunk. His stoop was more apparent. His fingers plucked vaguely at his coat.

For some time, I gather, Poirot did not speak.

He sat and looked at the man opposite him.

The atmosphere became restful – soothing – full of infinite leisure . . .

It must have been a dramatic moment – this meeting of the two adversaries in the long drama. In Poirot's place I should have felt the dramatic thrill.

Poirot, however, is nothing if not matter-of-fact. He was absorbed in producing a certain effect upon the man opposite him.

At last he said gently:

'Do you know who I am?'

The other shook his head.

'No – no – I can't say I do. Unless you are Mr Lucas's – what do they call it? – junior. Or perhaps you come from Mr Maynard?'

(Maynard & Cole were the defending solicitors.)

His tone was polite but not very interested. He seemed absorbed in some inner abstraction.

'I am Hercule Poirot . . .'

Poirot said the words very gently . . . and watched for the effect.

Mr Cust raised his head a little.

'Oh, yes?'

He said it as naturally as Inspector Crome might have said it – but without the superciliousness.

Then, a minute later, he repeated his remark.

'Oh, yes?' he said, and this time his tone was different – it held an awakened interest. He raised his head and looked at Poirot.

Hercule Poirot met his gaze and nodded his own head gently once or twice.

'Yes,' he said. 'I am the man to whom you wrote the letters.'

At once the contact was broken. Mr Cust dropped his eyes and spoke irritably and fretfully.

'I never wrote to you. Those letters weren't written by me. I've said so again and again.'

'I know,' said Poirot. 'But if you did not write them, who did?'

'An enemy. I must have an enemy. They are all against me. The police – everyone – all against me. It's a gigantic conspiracy.'

Poirot did not reply.

Mr Cust said:

'Everyone's hand has been against me – always.'

'Even when you were a child?'

Mr Cust seemed to consider.

'No – no – not exactly then. My mother was very fond of me. But she was ambitious – terribly ambitious. That's why she gave me those ridiculous names. She had some absurd idea that I'd cut a figure in the world. She was always urging me to assert myself – talking about will-power . . . saying anyone could be master of his fate . . . she said I could do anything!'

He was silent for a minute.

'She was quite wrong, of course. I realized that myself quite soon. I wasn't the sort of person to get on in life. I was always doing foolish things – making myself look ridiculous. And I was timid – afraid of people. I had a bad time at school – the boys found out my Christian names – they used to tease me about them . . . I did very badly at school – in games and work and everything.'

He shook his head.

'Just as well poor mother died. She'd have been disappointed . . . Even when I was at the Commercial College I was stupid – it took me longer to learn typing and shorthand than anyone else. And yet I didn't *feel* stupid – if you know what I mean.'

He cast a sudden appealing look at the other man.

'I know what you mean,' said Poirot. 'Go on.'

'It was just the feeling that everybody else *thought* me stupid. Very paralysing. It was the same thing later in the office.'

'And later still in the war?' prompted Poirot.

Mr Cust's face lightened up suddenly.

'You know,' he said, 'I enjoyed the war. What I had of it, that was. I felt, for the first time, a man like anybody else. We were all in the same box. I was as good as anyone else.'

His smile faded.

'And then I got that wound on the head. Very slight. But they found out I had fits . . . I'd always known, of course, that there were times when I hadn't been quite sure what I was doing. Lapses, you know. And of course, once or twice I'd fallen down. But I don't really think they ought to have discharged me for that. No, I don't think it was right.'

'And afterwards?' asked Poirot.

'I got a place as a clerk. Of course there was good money to be got just then. And I didn't do so badly after the war. Of course, a smaller salary . . . And – I didn't seem to get on. I was always being passed over for promotion. I wasn't go-ahead enough. It grew very difficult – really very difficult . . . Especially when the slump came. To tell you the truth, I'd got hardly enough to keep body and soul together (and you've got to look presentable as a clerk) when I got the offer of this stocking job. A salary and commission!'

Poirot said gently:

'But you are aware, are you not, that the firm whom you say employed you deny the fact?'

Mr Cust got excited again.

'That's because they're in the conspiracy – they must be in the conspiracy.'

He went on:

'I've got written evidence – written evidence. I've got their letters to me, giving me instructions as to what places to go to and a list of people to call on.'

'Not *written* evidence exactly – *typewritten* evidence.'

'It's the same thing. Naturally a big firm of wholesale manufacturers typewrite their letters.'

'Don't you know, Mr Cust, that a typewriter can be identified? All those letters were typed by one particular machine.'

'What of it?'

'And that machine was your own – the one found in your room.'

'It was sent me by the firm at the beginning of my job.'

'Yes, but these letters were received *afterwards*. So it looks, does it not, as though *you typed them yourself and posted them to yourself?*'

'No, no! It's all part of the plot against me!'

He added suddenly:

'Besides, their letters *would* be written on the same kind of machine.'

'The same *kind*, but not the same actual machine.'

Mr Cust repeated obstinately:

'It's a plot!'

'And the A B C's that were found in the cupboard?'

'I know nothing about them. I thought they were all stockings.'

'Why did you tick off the name of Mrs Ascher in that first list of people in Andover?'

'Because I decided to start with her. One must begin somewhere.'

'Yes, that is true. *One must begin somewhere.*'

'I don't mean that!' said Mr Cust. 'I don't mean what you mean!'

'*But you know what I meant?*'

Mr Cust said nothing. He was trembling.

'I didn't do it!' he said. 'I'm perfectly innocent! It's all a mistake. Why, look at that second crime – that Bexhill one. I was playing dominoes at Eastbourne. You've got to admit that!'

His voice was triumphant.

'Yes,' said Poirot. His voice was meditative – silky. 'But it's so easy, isn't it, to make a mistake of one day? And if you're an obstinate, positive man, like Mr Strange, you'll never consider the possibility of having been mistaken. What you've said you'll stick to . . . He's that kind of man. And the hotel register – it's very easy to put down the wrong date when you're signing it – probably no one will notice it at the time.'

'I was playing dominoes that evening!'

'You play dominoes very well, I believe.'

Mr Cust was a little flurried by this.

'I – I – well, I believe I do.'

'It is a very absorbing game, is it not, with a lot of skill in it?'

'Oh, there's a lot of play in it – a lot of play! We used to play a lot in the city, in the lunch hour. You'd be surprised the way total strangers come together over a game of dominoes.'

He chuckled.

'I remember one man – I've never forgotten him because of something he told me – we just got talking over a cup of coffee, and we started dominoes. Well, I felt after twenty minutes that I'd known that man all my life.'

'What was it that he told you?' asked Poirot.

Mr Cust's face clouded over.

'It gave me a turn – a nasty turn. Talking of your fate being written in your hand, he was. And he showed me his hand and the lines that showed he'd have two near escapes of being drowned – and he had had two near escapes. And then he looked at mine and he told me some amazing things. Said I was going to be one of the most celebrated men in England before I died. Said the whole country would be talking about me. But he said – he said . . .'

Mr Cust broke down – faltered . . .

'Yes?'

Poirot's gaze held a quiet magnetism. Mr Cust looked at him, looked away, then back again like a fascinated rabbit.

'He said – he said – that it looked as though I might die a violent death – and he laughed and said: "Almost looks as though you might die on the scaffold," and then he laughed and said that was only his joke . . .'

He was silent suddenly. His eyes left Poirot's face – they ran from side to side . . .

'My head – I suffer very badly with my head . . . the headaches are something cruel sometimes. And then there are times when I don't know – when I don't know . . .'

He broke down.

Poirot leant forward. He spoke very quietly but with great assurance.

'*But you do know, don't you,*' he said, '*that you committed the murders?*'

Mr Cust looked up. His glance was quite simple and direct. All resistance had left him. He looked strangely at peace.

'Yes,' he said, 'I know.'

'But – I am right, am I not? – *you don't know why you did them?*'

Mr Cust shook his head.

'No,' he said. 'I don't.'

CHAPTER 34

POIROT EXPLAINS

We were sitting in a state of tense attention to listen to Poirot's final explanation of the case.

'All along,' he said, 'I have been worried over the *why* of this case. Hastings said to me the other day that the case was ended. I replied to him that the case was the *man*! The mystery was *not the mystery of the murders*, but the *mystery of A B C*. Why did he find it necessary to commit these murders? Why did he select *me* as his adversary?

'It is no answer to say that the man was mentally unhinged. To say a man does mad things because he is mad is merely unintelligent and stupid. A madman is as logical and reasoned in his actions as a sane man – *given his peculiar biased point of view.* For example, if a man insists on going out and squatting about in nothing but a loin cloth his conduct seems eccentric in the extreme. But once you know *that the man himself is firmly convinced that he is Mahatma Gandhi*, then his conduct becomes perfectly reasonable and logical.

'What was necessary in this case was to imagine a mind so constituted *that it was logical and reasonable to commit four or more murders* and to announce them beforehand by letters written to Hercule Poirot.

'My friend Hastings will tell you that from the moment I received the first letter I was upset and disturbed. It seemed to me at once that there was something very wrong about the letter.'

'You were quite right,' said Franklin Clarke dryly.

'Yes. But there, at the very start, I made a grave error. I permitted my feeling – my very strong feeling about the letter – to remain a mere impression. I treated it as though it had been an intuition. In a well-balanced, reasoning mind there is no such thing as an intuition – an inspired guess! You *can* guess, of course – and a guess is either right or wrong. If it is right you call it an intuition. If it is wrong you usually do not speak of it again. But what is often called an intuition is really *an impression based on logical deduction or experience.* When an expert feels that there is something wrong about a picture or a piece of furniture or the signature on a cheque he is really basing that feeling on a host of small signs and details. He has no need to go into them minutely – his experience obviates that – the net result is *the definite impression that something is wrong.* But it is not a *guess,* it is an impression based on *experience.*

'*Eh bien,* I admit that I did not regard that first letter in the way I should. It just made me extremely uneasy. The police regarded it as a hoax. I myself took it seriously. I was convinced that a murder would take place in Andover as stated. As you know, a murder *did* take place.

'There was no means at that point, as I well realized, of knowing who the *person* was who had done the deed. The only course open to me was to try and understand just what kind of a person had done it.

'I had certain indications. The letter – the manner of the crime – the person murdered. What I had to discover was: the motive of the crime, the motive of the letter.'

'Publicity,' suggested Clarke.

'Surely an inferiority complex covers that,' added Thora Grey.

'That was, of course, the obvious line to take. But why *me? Why Hercule Poirot?* Greater publicity could be ensured by sending the letters to Scotland Yard. More again by sending them to a newspaper. A newspaper might not print the first letter, but by the time the second crime took place, A B C could have been assured of all the publicity the press could give. Why, then, Hercule Poirot? Was it for some *personal* reason? There was, discernible in the letter, a slight anti-foreign bias – but not enough to explain the matter to my satisfaction.

'Then the second letter arrived – and was followed by the murder of Betty Barnard at Bexhill. It became clear now (what I had already suspected) that the murders were to proceed on an alphabetical plan, but the fact, which seemed final to most people, left the main question unaltered to my mind. Why did A B C *need* to commit these murders?'

Megan Barnard stirred in her chair.

'Isn't there such a thing as – as a blood lust?' she said.

Poirot turned to her.

'You are quite right, mademoiselle. There *is* such a thing. The lust to kill. But that did not quite fit the facts of the case. A homicidal maniac who desires to kill usually desires to kill *as many victims as possible*. It is a recurring *craving*. The great idea of such a killer is to *hide his tracks* – not to *advertise* them. When we consider the four victims selected – or at any rate three of them (for I know very little of Mr Downes or Mr Earlsfield), we realize that *if he had chosen*, the murderer could have done away with them without incurring any suspicion. Franz Ascher, Donald Fraser or Megan Barnard, possibly Mr Clarke – those are the people the police would have suspected even if they had been unable to get direct proof. An unknown homicidal murderer would not have been thought of! Why, then, did the murderer feel it necessary to call attention to himself? Was it the necessity of leaving on each body a copy of an A B C railway guide? Was *that* the compulsion? Was there some complex connected *with the railway guide*?

'I found it quite inconceivable at this point *to enter into the mind of the murderer*. Surely it could not be magnanimity? A horror of responsibility for the crime being fastened on an innocent person?

'Although I could not answer the main question, certain things I did feel I was learning about the murderer.'

'Such as?' asked Fraser.

'To begin with – that he had a tabular mind. His crimes were listed by alphabetical progression – that was obviously important to him. On the other hand, he had no particular taste in victims – Mrs Ascher, Betty Barnard, Sir Carmichael Clarke, they all differed widely from each other. There was no sex complex – no particular age complex, and that seemed to me to be a very curious fact. If a man kills indiscriminately it is usually because he removes anyone who stands in his way or annoys him. *But the alphabetical progression showed that such was not the case here.* The other type of killer usually selects *a particular type of victim* – nearly always of the opposite sex. There was something haphazard about the procedure of A B C that seemed to me to be at war with the alphabetical selection.

'One slight inference I permitted myself to make. The choice of the A B C suggested to me what I may call a *railway-minded man*. This is more common in men than women. Small boys love trains better than small girls do. It might be the sign, too, of an in some ways undeveloped mind. The "boy" motif still predominated.

'The death of Betty Barnard and the manner of it gave me certain other indications. The manner of her death was particularly suggestive. (Forgive me, Mr Fraser.) To begin with, she was strangled with her own belt –

therefore she must almost certainly have been killed by someone with whom she was on friendly or affectionate terms. When I learnt something of her character a picture grew up in my mind.

'Betty Barnard was a flirt. She liked attention from a personable male. Therefore A B C, to persuade her to come out with him, must have had a certain amount of attraction – of *le sex appeal*! He must be able, as you English say, to "get off". He must be capable of the click! I visualize the scene on the beach thus: the man admires her belt. She takes it off, he passes it playfully round her neck – says, perhaps, "I shall strangle you." It is all very playful. She giggles – and he pulls –'

Donald Fraser sprang up. He was livid.

'M. Poirot – for God's sake.'

Poirot made a gesture.

'It is finished. I say no more. It is over. We pass to the next murder, that of Sir Carmichael Clarke. Here the murderer goes back to his first method – the blow on the head. The same alphabetical complex – but one fact worries me a little. To be consistent the murderer should have chosen his towns in some definite sequence.

'If Andover is the 155th name under A, then the B crime should be the 155th also – or it should be the 156th and the C the 157th. Here again the towns seemed to be chosen in rather too *haphazard* a fashion.'

'Isn't that because you're rather biased on that subject, Poirot?' I suggested. 'You yourself are normally methodical and orderly. It's almost a disease with you.'

'No, it is *not* a disease! *Quelle idée!* But I admit that I may be over-stressing that point. *Passons!*

'The Churston crime gave me very little extra help. We were unlucky over it, since the letter announcing it went astray, hence no preparations could be made.

'But by the time the D crime was announced, a very formidable system of defence had been evolved. It must have been obvious that A B C could not much longer hope to get away with his crimes.

'Moreover, it was at this point that the clue of the stockings came into my hand. It was perfectly clear that the presence of an individual selling stockings on and near the scene of each crime could not be a coincidence. Hence the stocking-seller must be the murderer. I may say that his description, as given me by Miss Grey, did not quite correspond with my own picture of the man who strangled Betty Barnard.

'I will pass over the next stages quickly. A fourth murder was committed – the murder of a man named George Earlsfield – it was supposed in mistake for a man named Downes, who was something of the same build and who was sitting near him in the cinema.

'*And now at last comes the turn of the tide.* Events play against A B C instead of into his hands. He is marked down – hunted – and at last arrested.

'The case, as Hastings says, is ended!

'True enough as far as the public is concerned. The man is in prison and will eventually, no doubt, go to Broadmoor. There will be no more murders. Exit! Finis! R.I.P.

'*But not for me!* I know nothing – nothing at all! Neither the *why* nor the *wherefore*.

'And there is one small vexing fact. The man Cust has an alibi for the night of the Bexhill crime.'

'That's been worrying me all along,' said Franklin Clarke.

'Yes. It worried me. For the alibi, it has the air of being *genuine*. But it cannot be genuine unless – and now we come to two very interesting speculations.

'Supposing, my friends, that while Cust committed *three* of the crimes – the A, C, and D crimes – *he did not commit the B crime.*'

'M. Poirot. It isn't –'

Poirot silenced Megan Barnard with a look.

'Be quiet, mademoiselle. I am for the truth, I am! I have done with lies. Supposing, I say, *that A B C did not commit the second crime.* It took place, remember, in the early hours of the 25th – the day he had arrived for the crime. Supposing someone had forestalled him? What in those circumstances would he do? Commit a *second* murder, or lie low and *accept the first as a kind of macabre present?*'

'M. Poirot!' said Megan. 'That's a fantastic thought! All the crimes *must* have been committed by the same person!'

He took no notice of her and went steadily on:

'Such a hypothesis had the merit of explaining one fact – *the discrepancy between the personality of Alexander Bonaparte Cust* (who could never have made the click with any girl) *and the personality of Betty Barnard's murderer.* And it has been known, before now, that would-be murderers *have* taken advantage of the crimes committed by other people. Not all the crimes of Jack the Ripper were committed by Jack the Ripper, for instance. So far, so good.

'But then I came up against a definite difficulty.

'Up to the time of the Barnard murder, *no facts about the A B C murders had been made public.* The Andover murder had created little interest. The incident of the open railway guide had not even been mentioned in the press. It therefore followed that whoever killed Betty Barnard *must have had access to facts known only to certain persons* – myself, the police, and certain relations and neighbours of Mrs Ascher.

'That line of research seemed to lead me up against a blank wall.'

The faces that looked at him were blank too. Blank and puzzled.

Donald Fraser said thoughtfully:

'The police, after all, are human beings. And they're good-looking men –'

He stopped, looking at Poirot inquiringly.

Poirot shook his head gently.

'No – it is simpler than that. I told you that there was a second speculation.

'Supposing that Cust was *not* responsible for the killing of Betty Barnard? Supposing that *someone else* killed her. Could that someone else have been responsible *for the other murders too?*'

'But that doesn't make sense!' cried Clarke.

'Doesn't it? I did then *what I ought to have done at first*. I examined the letters I had received from a totally different point of view. I had felt from the beginning that there was something wrong with them – just as a picture expert knows a picture is wrong . . .

'I had assumed, without pausing to consider, that what was wrong with them was the fact that they were written by a madman.

'Now I examined them again – and this time I came to a totally different conclusion. What was wrong with them was *the fact that they were written by a sane man!*'

'What?' I cried.

'But yes – just that precisely! They were wrong as a picture is wrong – *because they were a fake!* They pretended to be the letters of a madman – of a homicidal lunatic, but in reality they were nothing of the kind.'

'It doesn't make sense,' Franklin Clarke repeated.

'*Mais si!* One must reason – reflect. What would be the object of writing such letters? To focus attention on the writer, to call attention to the murders! *En vérité*, it did not seem to make sense at first sight. And then I saw light. It was to focus attention on several murders – on a *group* of murders . . . Is it not your great Shakespeare who has said "You cannot see the trees for the wood."'

I did not correct Poirot's literary reminiscences. I was trying to see his point. A glimmer came to me. He went on:

'When do you notice a pin least? When it is in a pin-cushion! When do you notice an individual murder least? When it is one of *a series of related murders*.

'I had to deal with an intensely clever, resourceful murderer – reckless, daring and a thorough gambler. *Not* Mr Cust! He could never have committed these murders! No, I had to deal with a very different stamp of man – a man with a boyish temperament (witness the schoolboy-like letters and the railway guide), an attractive man to women, and a man with a ruthless disregard for human life, a man who was necessarily a prominent person in *one* of the crimes!

'Consider when a man or woman is killed, what are the questions that the police ask? Opportunity. Where everybody was at the time of the crime? Motive. Who benefited by the deceased's death? If the motive and the opportunity are fairly obvious, what is a would-be murderer to do? Fake an alibi – that is, manipulate *time* in some way? But that is always a hazardous proceeding. Our murderer thought of a more fantastic defence. Create a *homicidal* murderer!

'I had now only to review the various crimes and find the possible guilty person. The Andover crime? The most likely suspect for that was Franz Ascher, but I could not imagine Ascher inventing and carrying out such an elaborate scheme, nor could I see him planning a premeditated murder. The Bexhill crime? Donald Fraser was a possibility. He had brains and ability, and a methodical turn of mind. But his motive for killing his sweetheart could only be jealousy – and jealousy does not tend to premeditation. Also I learned that he had his holidays *early* in August, which rendered it unlikely he had anything to do with the Churston crime. We come to the Churston crime next – and at once we are on infinitely more promising ground.

'Sir Carmichael Clarke was an immensely wealthy man. Who inherits his money? His wife, who is dying, has a life interest in it, and it then goes to *his brother Franklin*.'

Poirot turned slowly round till his eyes met those of Franklin Clarke.

'I was quite sure then. The man I had known a long time in my secret mind *was the same as the man whom I had known as a person. A B C and Franklin Clarke were one and the same!* The daring adventurous character, the roving life, the partiality for England that had showed itself, very faintly, in the jeer at foreigners. The attractive free and easy manner – nothing easier for him than to pick up a girl in a café. The methodical tabular mind – he made a list here one day, ticked off over the headings A B C – and finally, the boyish mind – mentioned by Lady Clarke and even shown by his taste in fiction – I have ascertained that there is a book in the

library called *The Railway Children* by E. Nesbit. I had no further doubt
in my own mind – A B C, the man who wrote the letters and committed
the crimes, was *Franklin Clarke*.'

Clarke suddenly burst out laughing.

'Very ingenious! And what about our friend Cust, caught red-handed?
What about the blood on his coat? And the knife he hid in his lodgings?
He may deny he committed the crimes –'

Poirot interrupted.

'You are quite wrong. He admits the fact.'

'What?' Clarke looked really startled.

'Oh, yes,' said Poirot gently. 'I had no sooner spoken to him than I was
aware that Cust *believed himself to be guilty*.'

'And even that didn't satisfy M. Poirot?' said Clarke.

'No. Because as soon as I saw him *I also knew that he could not be guilty*!
He has neither the nerve nor the daring – nor, I may add, the *brains* to
plan! All along I have been aware of the dual personality of the murderer.
Now I see wherein it consisted. Two people were involved – the real
murderer, cunning, resourceful and daring – and the *pseudo* murderer,
stupid, vacillating and suggestible.

'Suggestible – it is in that word that the mystery of Mr Cust consists! It
was not enough for you, Mr Clarke, to devise this plan of a *series* to distract
attention from a *single* crime. You had also to have a stalking horse.

'I think the idea first originated in your mind as the result of a chance
encounter in a city coffee den with this odd personality with his bombastic
Christian names. You were at that time turning over in your mind various
plans for the murder of your brother.'

'Really? And why?'

'Because you were seriously alarmed for the future. I do not know
whether you realize it, Mr Clarke, but you played into my hands when
you showed me a certain letter written to you by your brother. In it he
displayed very clearly his affection and absorption in Miss Thora Grey.
His regard may have been a paternal one – or he may have preferred to
think it so. Nevertheless, there was a very real danger that on the death of
your sister-in-law he might, in his loneliness, turn to this beautiful girl for
sympathy and comfort and it might end – as so often happens with elderly
men – in his marrying her. Your fear was increased by your knowledge of
Miss Grey. You are, I fancy, an excellent, if somewhat cynical judge of
character. You judged, whether correctly or not, that Miss Grey was a type
of young woman "on the make". You had no doubt that she would jump
at the chance of becoming Lady Clarke. Your brother was an extremely

healthy and vigorous man. There might be children and your chance of inheriting your brother's wealth would vanish.

'You have been, I fancy, in essence a disappointed man all your life. You have been the rolling stone – and you have gathered very little moss. You were bitterly jealous of your brother's wealth.

'I repeat then that, turning over various schemes in your mind, your meeting with Mr Cust gave you an idea. His bombastic Christian names, his account of his epileptic seizures and of his headaches, his whole shrinking and insignificant personality, struck you as fitting him for the tool you wanted. The whole alphabetical plan sprang into your mind – Cust's initials – the fact that your brother's name began with a C and that he lived at Churston were the nucleus of the scheme. You even went so far as to hint to Cust at his possible end – though you could hardly hope that that suggestion would bear the rich fruit that it did!

'Your arrangements were excellent. In Cust's name you wrote for a large consignment of hosiery to be sent to him. You yourself sent a number of A B C's looking like a similar parcel. You wrote to him – a typed letter purporting to be from the same firm offering him a good salary and commission. Your plans were so well laid beforehand that you typed all the letters that were sent subsequently, *and then presented him with the machine on which they had been typed.*

'You had now to look about for two victims whose names began with A and B respectively and who lived at places also beginning with those same letters.

'You hit on Andover as quite a likely spot and your preliminary reconnaissance there led you to select Mrs Ascher's shop as the scene of the first crime. Her name was written clearly over the door, and you found by experiment that she was usually alone in the shop. Her murder needed nerve, daring and reasonable luck.

'For the letter B you had to vary your tactics. Lonely women in shops might conceivably have been warned. I should imagine that you frequented a few cafés and teashops, laughing and joking with the girls there and finding out whose name began with the right letter and who would be suitable for your purpose.

'In Betty Barnard you found just the type of girl you were looking for. You took her out once or twice, explaining to her that you were a married man, and that outings must therefore take place in a somewhat hole-and-corner manner.

'Then, your preliminary plans completed, you set to work! You sent the Andover list to Cust, directing him to go there on a certain date, and you sent off the first A B C letter to me.

'On the appointed day you went to Andover – and killed Mrs Ascher – without anything occurring to damage your plans.

'Murder No. 1 was successfully accomplished.

'For the second murder, you took the precaution of committing it, in reality, *the day before*. I am fairly certain that Betty Barnard was killed well before midnight on the 24th July.

'We now come to murder No. 3 – the important – in fact, the *real* murder from your point of view.

'And here a full meed of praise is due to Hastings, who made a simple and obvious remark to which no attention was paid.

'*He suggested that the third letter went astray intentionally!*

'And he was right! . . .

'In that one simple fact lies the answer to the question that has puzzled me so all along. Why were the letters addressed in the first place to Hercule Poirot, a private detective, and not to the police?

'Erroneously I imagined some personal reason.

'Not at all! The letters were sent to me because the essence of your plan was that one of them *should be wrongly addressed and go astray* – but you cannot arrange for a letter addressed to the Criminal Investigation Department of Scotland Yard to go astray! It is necessary to have a *private* address. You chose me as a fairly well-known person, and a person who was sure to take the letters to the police – and also, in your rather insular mind, you enjoyed scoring off a foreigner.

'You addressed your envelope very cleverly – Whitehaven – Whitehorse – quite a natural slip. Only Hastings was sufficiently perspicacious to disregard subtleties and go straight for the obvious!

'Of course the letter was *meant* to go astray! The police were to be set on the trail *only when the murder was safely over*. Your brother's nightly walk provided you with the opportunity. And so successfully had the A B C terror taken hold on the public mind that the possibility of your guilt never occurred to anyone.

'After the death of your brother, of course, your object was accomplished. You had no wish to commit any more murders. On the other hand, if the murders stopped without reason, a suspicion of the truth might come to someone.

'Your stalking horse, Mr Cust, had so successfully lived up to his role of the invisible – because insignificant – man, that so far no one had noticed that the same person had been seen in the vicinity of the three murders! To your annoyance, even his visit to Combeside had not been mentioned. The matter had passed completely out of Miss Grey's head.

'Always daring, you decided that one more murder must take place but this time the trail must be well blazed.

'You selected Doncaster for the scene of operations.

'Your plan was very simple. You yourself would be on the scene in the nature of things. Mr Cust would be ordered to Doncaster by his firm. Your plan was to follow him round and trust to opportunity. Everything fell out well. Mr Cust went to a cinema. That was simplicity itself. You sat a few seats away from him. When he got up to go, you did the same. You pretended to stumble, leaned over and stabbed a dozing man in the row in front, slid the A B C on to his knees and managed to collide heavily with Mr Cust in the darkened doorway, wiping the knife on his sleeve and slipping it into his pocket.

'You were not in the least at pains to choose a victim whose name began with D. Anyone would do! You assumed – and quite rightly – that it would be considered to be a *mistake*. There was sure to be someone whose name began with D not far off in the audience. It would be assumed that he had been intended to be the victim.

'And now, my friends, let us consider the matter from the point of view of the false A B C – from the point of view of Mr Cust.

'The Andover crime means nothing to him. He is shocked and surprised by the Bexhill crime – why, he himself was there about the time! Then comes the Churston crime and the headlines in the newspapers. An A B C crime at Andover when he was there, an A B C crime at Bexhill, and now another close by . . . Three crimes *and he has been at the scene of each of them*. Persons suffering from epilepsy often have blanks when they cannot remember what they have done . . . Remember that Cust was a nervous, highly neurotic subject and extremely suggestible.

'Then he receives the order to go to Doncaster.

'Doncaster! And the next A B C crime is to be in Doncaster. He must have felt as though it was fate. He loses his nerve, fancies his landlady is looking at him suspiciously, and tells her he is going to Cheltenham.

'He goes to Doncaster because it is his duty. In the afternoon he goes to a cinema. Possibly he dozes off for a minute or two.

'Imagine his feelings when on his return to his inn he discovers *that there is blood on his coat sleeve and a blood-stained knife in his pocket.* All his vague forebodings leap into certainty.

'*He – he himself – is the killer!* He remembers his headaches – his lapses of memory. He is quite sure of the truth – *he, Alexander Bonaparte Cust, is a homicidal lunatic.*

'His conduct after that is the conduct of a hunted animal. He gets back to his lodgings in London. He is safe there – known. They think he has been in Cheltenham. He has the knife with him still – a thoroughly stupid thing to do, of course. He hides it behind the hall stand.

'Then, one day, he is warned that the police are coming. It is the end! They *know*!

'The hunted animal does his last run . . .

'I don't know why he went to Andover – a morbid desire, I think, to go and look at the place where the crime was committed – the crime *he* committed though he can remember nothing about it . . .

'He has no money left – he is worn out . . . his feet lead him of his own accord to the police station.

'But even a cornered beast will fight. Mr Cust fully believes that he did the murders but he sticks strongly to his plea of innocence. And he holds with desperation to that alibi for the second murder. At least that cannot be laid to his door.

'As I say, when I saw him, I knew at once that he was *not* the murderer and that my name *meant* nothing to *him*. I knew, too, that he *thought* himself the murderer!

'After he had confessed his guilt to me, I knew more strongly than ever that my own theory was right.'

'Your theory,' said Franklin Clarke, 'is absurd!'

Poirot shook his head.

'No, Mr Clarke. You were safe enough *so long as no one suspected you.* Once you *were* suspected proofs were easy to obtain.'

'Proofs?'

'Yes. I found the stick that you used in the Andover and Churston murders in a cupboard at Combeside. An ordinary stick with a thick knob handle. A section of wood had been removed and melted lead poured in. Your photograph was picked out from half a dozen others by two people who saw you leaving the cinema when you were supposed to be on the race-course at Doncaster. You were identified at Bexhill the other day by Milly Higley and a girl from the Scarlet Runner Roadhouse, where you took Betty Barnard to dine on the fatal evening. And finally – most damning of all – you *overlooked a most elementary precaution.* You left a fingerprint on Cust's typewriter – the typewriter that, if you are innocent, you *could never have handled.*'

Clarke sat quite still for a minute, then he said:

'*Rouge, impair, manque!* – you win, M. Poirot! But it was worth trying!'

With an incredibly rapid motion he whipped out a small automatic from his pocket and held it to his head.

I gave a cry and involuntarily flinched as I waited for the report.

But no report came – the hammer clicked harmlessly.

Clarke stared at it in astonishment and uttered an oath.

'No, Mr Clarke,' said Poirot. 'You may have noticed I had a new manservant today – a friend of mine – an expert sneak thief. He removed your pistol from your pocket, unloaded it, and returned it, all without you being aware of the fact.'

'You unutterable little jackanapes of a foreigner!' cried Clarke, purple with rage.

'Yes, yes, that is how you feel. No, Mr Clarke, no easy death for you. You told Mr Cust that you had had near escapes from drowning. You know what that means – that you were born for another fate.'

'You –'

Words failed him. His face was livid. His fists clenched menacingly.

Two detectives from Scotland Yard emerged from the next room. One of them was Crome. He advanced and uttered his time-honoured formula: 'I warn you that anything you say may be used as evidence.'

'He has said quite enough,' said Poirot, and he added to Clarke: 'You are very full of an insular superiority, but for myself I consider your crime not an English crime at all – not above-board – not *sporting* –'

CHAPTER 35

FINALE

I am sorry to relate that as the door closed behind Franklin Clarke I laughed hysterically.

Poirot looked at me in mild surprise.

'It's because you told him his crime was not sporting,' I gasped.

'It was quite true. It was abominable – not so much the murder of his brother – but the cruelty that condemned an unfortunate man to a living death. *To catch a fox and put him in a box and never let him go!* That is not *le sport*!'

Megan Barnard gave a deep sigh.

'I can't believe it – I can't. Is it true?'

'Yes, mademoiselle. The nightmare is over.'

She looked at him and her colour deepened.

Poirot turned to Fraser.

'Mademoiselle Megan, all along, was haunted by a fear that it was you who had committed the second crime.'

Donald Fraser said quietly:

'I fancied so myself at one time.'

'Because of your dream?' He drew a little nearer to the young man and dropped his voice confidentially. 'Your dream has a very natural explanation. It is that you find that already the image of one sister fades in your memory and that its place is taken by the other sister. Mademoiselle Megan replaces her sister in your heart, but since you cannot bear to think of yourself being unfaithful so soon to the dead, you strive to stifle the thought, to kill it! That is the explanation of the dream.'

Fraser's eyes went towards Megan.

'Do not be afraid to forget,' said Poirot gently. 'She was not so well worth remembering. In Mademoiselle Megan you have one in a hundred – *un coeur magnifique!*'

Donald Fraser's eyes lit up.

'I believe you are right.'

We all crowded round Poirot asking questions, elucidating this point and that.

'Those questions, Poirot? That you asked of everybody. Was there any point in them?'

'Some of them were *simplement une blague*. But I learnt one thing that I wanted to know – *that Franklin Clarke was in London when the first letter was posted* – and also I wanted to see his face when I asked my question of Mademoiselle Thora. He was off his guard. I saw all the malice and anger in his eyes.'

'You hardly spared my feelings,' said Thora Grey.

'I do not fancy you returned me a truthful answer, mademoiselle,' said Poirot dryly. 'And now your second expectation is disappointed. Franklin Clarke will not inherit his brother's money.'

She flung up her head.

'Is there any need for me to stay here and be insulted?'

'None whatever,' said Poirot and held the door open politely for her.

'That fingerprint clinched things, Poirot,' I said thoughtfully. 'He went all to pieces when you mentioned that.'

'Yes, they are useful – fingerprints.'

He added thoughtfully:

'I put that in to please you, my friend.'

'But, Poirot,' I cried, 'wasn't it *true*?'

'Not in the least, *mon ami*,' said Hercule Poirot.

I must mention a visit we had from Mr Alexander Bonaparte Cust a few days later. After wringing Poirot's hand and endeavouring very incoherently and unsuccessfully to thank him, Mr Cust drew himself up and said:

'Do you know, a newspaper has actually offered me a hundred pounds – *a hundred pounds* – for a brief account of my life and history – I – I really don't know what to do about it.'

'I should not accept a hundred,' said Poirot. 'Be firm. Say five hundred is your price. And do not confine yourself to one newspaper.'

'Do you really think – that I might –'

'You must realize,' said Poirot, smiling, 'that you are a very famous man. Practically the most famous man in England today.'

Mr Cust drew himself up still further. A beam of delight irradiated his face.

'Do you know, I believe you're right! Famous! In all the papers. I shall take your advice, M. Poirot. The money will be most agreeable – most agreeable. I shall have a little holiday . . . And then I want to give a nice wedding present to Lily Marbury – a dear girl – really a dear girl, M. Poirot.'

Poirot patted him encouragingly on the shoulder.

'You are quite right. Enjoy yourself. And – just a little word – what about a visit to an oculist? Those headaches, it is probably that you want new glasses.'

'You think that it may have been that all the time?'

'I do.'

Mr Cust shook him warmly by the hand.

'You're a very great man, M. Poirot.'

Poirot, as usual, did not disdain the compliment. He did not even succeed in looking modest.

When Mr Cust had strutted importantly out, my old friend smiled across at me.

'So, Hastings – we went hunting once more, did we not? *Vive le sport.*'

ENVY

•

A MURDER IS ANNOUNCED

To Ralph and Anne Newman
at whose house I first tasted
'Delicious Death!'

CHAPTER I

A MURDER IS ANNOUNCED

Between 7.30 and 8.30 every morning except Sundays, Johnnie Butt made the round of the village of Chipping Cleghorn on his bicycle, whistling vociferously through his teeth, and alighting at each house or cottage to shove through the letterbox such morning papers as had been ordered by the occupants of the house in question from Mr Totman, stationer, of the High Street. Thus, at Colonel and Mrs Easterbrook's he delivered *The Times* and the *Daily Graphic*; at Mrs Swettenham's he left *The Times* and the *Daily Worker*; at Miss Hinchcliffe and Miss Murgatroyd's he left the *Daily Telegraph* and the *New Chronicle*; at Miss Blacklock's he left the *Telegraph*, *The Times* and the *Daily Mail*.

At all these houses, and indeed at practically every house in Chipping Cleghorn, he delivered every Friday a copy of the *North Benham News and Chipping Cleghorn Gazette*, known locally simply as '*the Gazette*'.

Thus, on Friday mornings, after a hurried glance at the headlines in the daily paper

(International situation critical! U.N.O. meets today! Bloodhounds seek blonde typist's killer! Three collieries idle. Twenty-three die of food poisoning in Seaside Hotel, etc.)

most of the inhabitants of Chipping Cleghorn eagerly opened the *Gazette* and plunged into the local news. After a cursory glance at Correspondence (in which the passionate hates and feuds of rural life found full play) nine out of ten subscribers then turned to the PERSONAL column. Here were grouped together higgledy-piggledy articles for Sale or Wanted, frenzied appeals for Domestic Help, innumerable insertions regarding dogs, announcements concerning poultry and garden equipment; and various other items of an interesting nature to those living in the small community of Chipping Cleghorn.

This particular Friday, October 29th – was no exception to the rule –

*   *   *

Mrs Swettenham, pushing back the pretty little grey curls from her forehead, opened *The Times*, looked with a lacklustre eye at the left-hand centre page, decided that, as usual, if there *was* any exciting news *The Times* had succeeded in camouflaging it in an impeccable manner; took a look at the Births, Marriages and Deaths, particularly the latter; then, her duty done, she put aside *The Times* and eagerly seized the *Chipping Cleghorn Gazette*.

When her son Edmund entered the room a moment later, she was already deep in the Personal Column.

'Good morning, dear,' said Mrs Swettenham. 'The Smedleys are selling their Daimler. 1935 – that's rather a long time ago, isn't it?'

Her son grunted, poured himself out a cup of coffee, helped himself to a couple of kippers, sat down at the table and opened the *Daily Worker* which he propped up against the toast rack.

'*Bull mastiff puppies*,' read out Mrs Swettenham. 'I really don't know how people manage to feed big dogs nowadays – I really *don't* . . . H'm, Selina Lawrence is advertising for a cook again. I could tell her it's just a waste of time advertising in these days. She hasn't put her address, only a box number – that's *quite* fatal – I could have told her so – servants simply insist on knowing where they are going. They like a good address . . . *False teeth* – I can't think why false teeth are so popular. *Best prices paid . . . Beautiful bulbs. Our special selection*. They sound rather cheap . . . Here's a girl wants an "*Interesting post – Would travel*." I dare say! Who wouldn't? . . . *Dachshunds* . . . I've never really cared for dachshunds myself – I don't mean because they're *German*, because we've got over all that – I just don't care for them, that's all. – Yes, Mrs Finch?'

The door had opened to admit the head and torso of a grim-looking female in an aged velvet beret.

'Good morning, Mum,' said Mrs Finch. 'Can I clear?'

'Not yet. We haven't finished,' said Mrs Swettenham. 'Not quite finished,' she added ingratiatingly.

Casting a look at Edmund and his paper, Mrs Finch sniffed, and withdrew.

'I've only just begun,' said Edmund, just as his mother remarked:

'I do wish you wouldn't read that horrid paper, Edmund. Mrs Finch doesn't like it *at all*.'

'I don't see what my political views have to do with Mrs Finch.'

'And it isn't,' pursued Mrs Swettenham, 'as though you *were* a worker. You don't do any work at all.'

'That's not in the least true,' said Edmund indignantly. 'I'm writing a book.'

'I meant *real* work,' said Mrs Swettenham. 'And Mrs Finch does matter. If she takes a dislike to us and won't come, who else could we get?'

'Advertise in the *Gazette*,' said Edmund, grinning.

'I've just told you that's no use. Oh dear me, nowadays unless one has an old Nannie in the family, who will go into the kitchen and do everything, one is simply *sunk*.'

'Well, why haven't we an old Nannie? How remiss of you not to have provided me with one. What were you thinking about?'

'You had an *ayah*, dear.'

'No foresight,' murmured Edmund.

Mrs Swettenham was once more deep in the Personal Column.

'*Second hand Motor Mower for sale*. Now I wonder . . . Goodness, what a *price*! . . . More dachshunds . . . "*Do write* or *communicate desperate Woggles*." What silly nicknames people have . . . *Cocker Spaniels* . . . Do you remember darling Susie, Edmund? She really was *human*. Understood every word you said to her . . . *Sheraton sideboard for sale. Genuine family antique. Mrs Lucas, Dayas Hall* . . . What a liar that woman is! Sheraton indeed . . . !'

Mrs Swettenham sniffed and then continued her reading:

'*All a mistake, darling. Undying love. Friday as usual. – J* . . . I suppose they've had a lovers' quarrel – or do you think it's a code for burglars? . . . *More dachshunds*! Really, I do think people have gone a little crazy about breeding dachshunds. I mean, there *are* other dogs. Your Uncle Simon used to breed Manchester Terriers. Such graceful little things. I do like dogs with *legs* . . . *Lady going abroad will sell her navy two piece suiting* . . . no measurements or price given . . . *A marriage is announced* – no, a *murder*. *What? Well*, I never! Edmund, *Edmund*, listen to this . . .

'*A murder is announced and will take place on Friday, October 29th, at Little Paddocks at 6.30 p.m. Friends please accept this, the only intimation.*

'What an extraordinary thing! *Edmund!*'

'What's that?' Edmund looked up from his newspaper.

'Friday, October 29th . . . Why, that's *today*.'

'Let me see.' Her son took the paper from her.

'But what does it mean?' Mrs Swettenham asked with lively curiosity.

Edmund Swettenham rubbed his nose doubtfully.

'Some sort of party, I suppose. The Murder Game – that kind of thing.'

'Oh,' said Mrs Swettenham doubtfully. 'It seems a very odd way of doing it. Just sticking it in the advertisements like that. Not at all like Letitia Blacklock who always seems to me such a sensible woman.'

'Probably got up by the bright young things she has in the house.'

'It's very short notice. Today. Do you think we're just supposed to go?'

'It says "Friends, please accept this, the only intimation,"' her son pointed out.

'Well, I think these new-fangled ways of giving invitations are very tiresome,' said Mrs Swettenham decidedly.

'All right, Mother, you needn't go.'

'No,' agreed Mrs Swettenham.

There was a pause.

'Do you really *want* that last piece of toast, Edmund?'

'I should have thought my being properly nourished mattered more than letting that old hag clear the table.'

'Sh, dear, she'll *hear* you . . . Edmund, what happens at a Murder Game?'

'I don't know, exactly . . . They pin pieces of paper upon you, or something . . . No, I think you draw them out of a hat. And somebody's the victim and somebody else is a detective – and then they turn the lights out and somebody taps you on the shoulder and then you scream and lie down and sham dead.'

'It sounds quite exciting.'

'Probably a beastly bore. I'm not going.'

'Nonsense, Edmund,' said Mrs Swettenham resolutely. '*I'm* going and *you're* coming with me. That's *settled*!'

'Archie,' said Mrs Easterbrook to her husband, 'listen to *this*.'

Colonel Easterbrook paid no attention, because he was already snorting with impatience over an article in *The Times*.

'Trouble with these fellows is,' he said, 'that none of them knows the first thing about India! Not the first thing!'

'I know, dear, I know.'

'If they did, they wouldn't write such piffle.'

'Yes, I know. Archie, do listen.

'A murder is announced and will take place on Friday, October 29th (that's today), *at Little Paddocks at 6.30 p.m. Friends please accept this, the only intimation.'*

She paused triumphantly. Colonel Easterbrook looked at her indulgently but without much interest.

'Murder Game,' he said.

'Oh.'

'That's all it is. Mind you,' he unbent a little, 'it can be very good fun if it's well done. But it needs good organizing by someone who knows the ropes. You draw lots. One person's the murderer, nobody knows who. Lights out. Murderer chooses his victim. The victim has to count twenty before he screams. Then the person who's chosen to be the detective takes charge. Questions everybody. Where they were, what they were doing, tries to trip the real fellow up. Yes, it's a good game – if the detective – er – knows something about police work.'

'Like you, Archie. You had all those interesting cases to try in your district.'

Colonel Easterbrook smiled indulgently and gave his moustache a complacent twirl.

'Yes, Laura,' he said. 'I dare say I could give them a hint or two.'

And he straightened his shoulders.

'Miss Blacklock ought to have asked you to help her in getting the thing up.'

The Colonel snorted.

'Oh, well, she's got that young cub staying with her. Expect this is his idea. Nephew or something. Funny idea, though, sticking it in the paper.'

'It was in the Personal Column. We might never have seen it. I suppose it *is* an invitation, Archie?'

'Funny kind of invitation. I can tell you one thing. They can count *me* out.'

'Oh, Archie,' Mrs Easterbrook's voice rose in a shrill wail.

'Short notice. For all they know I might be busy.'

'But you're not, are you, darling?' Mrs Easterbrook lowered her voice persuasively. 'And I do think, Archie, that you really *ought* to go – just to help poor Miss Blacklock out. I'm sure she's counting on you to make the thing a success. I mean, you know so much about police work and procedure. The whole thing will fall flat if you don't go and help to make it a success. After all, one must be *neighbourly.*'

Mrs Easterbrook put her synthetic blonde head on one side and opened her blue eyes very wide.

'Of course, if you put it like that, Laura . . .' Colonel Easterbrook twirled his grey moustache again, importantly, and looked with indulgence on his fluffy little wife. Mrs Easterbrook was at least thirty years younger than her husband.

'If you put it like *that*, Laura,' he said.

'I really do think it's your *duty*, Archie,' said Mrs Easterbrook solemnly.

The *Chipping Cleghorn Gazette* had also been delivered at Boulders, the picturesque three cottages knocked into one inhabited by Miss Hinchcliffe and Miss Murgatroyd.

'Hinch?'

'What is it, Murgatroyd?'

'Where are you?'

'Henhouse.'

'Oh.'

Padding gingerly through the long wet grass, Miss Amy Murgatroyd approached her friend. The latter, attired in corduroy slacks and battle-dress tunic, was conscientiously stirring in handfuls of balancer meal to a repellently steaming basin full of cooked potato peelings and cabbage stumps.

She turned her head with its short man-like crop and weather-beaten countenance toward her friend.

Miss Murgatroyd, who was fat and amiable, wore a checked tweed skirt and a shapeless pullover of brilliant royal blue. Her curly bird's nest of grey hair was in a good deal of disorder and she was slightly out of breath.

'In the *Gazette*,' she panted. 'Just listen – what can it *mean*?

'A murder is announced . . . and will take place on Friday, October 29th, at Little Paddocks at 6.30 p.m. Friends please accept this, the only intimation.'

She paused, breathless, as she finished reading, and awaited some authoritative pronouncement.

'Daft,' said Miss Hinchcliffe.

'Yes, but what do you think it *means*?'

'Means a drink, anyway,' said Miss Hinchcliffe.

'You think it's a sort of invitation?'

'We'll find out what it means when we get there,' said Miss Hinchcliffe. 'Bad sherry, I expect. You'd better get off the grass, Murgatroyd. You've got your bedroom slippers on still. They're soaked.'

'Oh, dear.' Miss Murgatroyd looked down ruefully at her feet. 'How many eggs today?'

'Seven. That damned hen's still broody. I must get her into the coop.'

'It's a funny way of putting it, don't you think?' Amy Murgatroyd asked, reverting to the notice in the *Gazette*. Her voice was slightly wistful.

But her friend was made of sterner and more single-minded stuff. She was intent on dealing with recalcitrant poultry and no announcement in a paper, however enigmatic, could deflect her.

She squelched heavily through the mud and pounced upon a speckled hen. There was a loud and indignant squawking.

'Give me ducks every time,' said Miss Hinchcliffe. '*Far* less trouble . . .'

'Oo, scrumptious!' said Mrs Harmon across the breakfast table to her husband, the Rev. Julian Harmon, 'there's going to be a murder at Miss Blacklock's.'

'A murder?' said her husband, slightly surprised. 'When?'

'This afternoon . . . at least, this evening. 6.30. Oh, bad luck, darling, you've got your preparations for confirmation then. It *is* a shame. And you do so love murders!'

'I don't really know what you're talking about, Bunch.'

Mrs Harmon, the roundness of whose form and face had early led to the soubriquet of 'Bunch' being substituted for her baptismal name of Diana, handed the *Gazette* across the table.

'There. All among the second-hand pianos, and the old teeth.'

'What a very extraordinary announcement.'

'Isn't it?' said Bunch happily. 'You wouldn't think that Miss Blacklock cared about murders and games and things, would you? I suppose it's the young Simmonses put her up to it – though I should have thought Julia Simmons would find murders rather crude. Still, there it is, and I do think, darling, it's a *shame* you can't be there. Anyway, I'll go and tell you all about it, though it's rather wasted on me, because I don't really like games that happen in the dark. They frighten me, and I *do* hope I shan't have to be the one who's murdered. If someone suddenly puts a hand on my shoulder and whispers, "You're dead," I know my heart will give such a big bump that perhaps it really *might* kill me! Do you think that's likely?'

'No, Bunch. I think you're going to live to be an old, old woman – with me.'

'And die on the same day and be buried in the same grave. That would be lovely.'

Bunch beamed from ear to ear at this agreeable prospect.

'You seem very happy, Bunch?' said her husband, smiling.

'Who'd *not* be happy if they were me?' demanded Bunch, rather confusedly. 'With you and Susan and Edward, and all of you fond of me and not caring if I'm stupid . . . And the sun shining! And this lovely big house to live in!'

The Rev. Julian Harmon looked round the big bare dining-room and assented doubtfully.

'Some people would think it was the last straw to have to live in this great rambling draughty place.'

'Well, I like big rooms. All the nice smells from outside can get in and stay there. And you can be untidy and leave things about and they don't clutter you.'

'No labour-saving devices or central heating? It means a lot of work for you, Bunch.'

'Oh, Julian, it doesn't. I get up at half-past six and light the boiler and rush around like a steam engine, and by eight it's all done. And I keep it nice, don't I? With beeswax and polish and big jars of Autumn leaves. It's not really harder to keep a big house clean than a small one. You go round with mops and things much quicker, because your behind isn't always bumping into things like it is in a small room. And I like sleeping in a big cold room – it's so cosy to snuggle down with just the tip of your nose telling you what it's like up above. And whatever size of house you live in, you peel the same amount of potatoes and wash up the same amount of plates and all that. Think how nice it is for Edward and Susan to have a big empty room to play in where they can have railways and dolls' tea-parties all over the floor and never have to put them away? And then it's nice to have extra bits of the house that you can let people have to live in. Jimmy Symes and Johnnie Finch – they'd have had to live with their in-laws otherwise. And you know, Julian, it isn't nice living with your in-laws. You're devoted to Mother, but you wouldn't really have liked to start our married life living with her and Father. And I shouldn't have liked it, either. I'd have gone on feeling like a little girl.'

Julian smiled at her.

'You're rather like a little girl still, Bunch.'

Julian Harmon himself had clearly been a model designed by Nature for the age of sixty. He was still about twenty-five years short of achieving Nature's purpose.

'I know I'm stupid –'

'You're not stupid, Bunch. You're very clever.'

'No, I'm not. I'm not a bit intellectual. Though I do try . . . And I really love it when you talk to me about books and history and things. I think perhaps it wasn't an awfully good idea to read aloud Gibbon to me in the evenings, because if it's been a cold wind out, and it's nice and hot by the fire, there's something about Gibbon that does, rather, make you go to sleep.'

Julian laughed.

'But I do love listening to you, Julian. Tell me the story again about the old vicar who preached about Ahasuerus.'

'You know that by heart, Bunch.'

'Just tell it me again. *Please.*'

Her husband complied.

'It was old Scrymgour. Somebody looked into his church one day. He was leaning out of the pulpit and preaching fervently to a couple of old charwomen. He was shaking his finger at them and saying, "Aha! I know what you are thinking. *You* think that the Great Ahasuerus of the First Lesson was Artaxerxes the Second. But he *wasn't!*" And then with enormous triumph, "He was Artaxerxes the *Third.*"'

It had never struck Julian Harmon as a particularly funny story himself, but it never failed to amuse Bunch.

Her clear laugh floated out.

'The old pet!' she exclaimed. 'I think you'll be exactly like that some day, Julian.'

Julian looked rather uneasy.

'I know,' he said with humility. 'I do feel very strongly that I can't always get the proper simple approach.'

'I shouldn't worry,' said Bunch, rising and beginning to pile the breakfast plates on a tray. 'Mrs Butt told me yesterday that Butt, who never went to church and used to be practically the local atheist, comes every Sunday now on purpose to hear you preach.'

She went on, with a very fair imitation of Mrs Butt's super-refined voice:

'"And Butt was saying only the other day, Madam, to Mr Timkins from Little Worsdale, that we'd got real *culture* here in Chipping Cleghorn. *Not* like Mr Goss, at Little Worsdale, who talks to the congregation as though they were children who hadn't had any education. Real culture,

Butt said, that's what *we've* got. Our Vicar's a highly educated gentleman – Oxford, not Milchester, and he gives us the full benefit of his education. All about the Romans and the Greeks he knows, and the Babylonians and the Assyrians, too. And even the Vicarage cat, Butt says, is called after an Assyrian king!" So there's glory for you,' finished Bunch triumphantly. 'Goodness, I must get on with things or I shall never get done. Come along, Tiglath Pileser, you shall have the herring bones.'

Opening the door and holding it dexterously ajar with her foot, she shot through with the loaded tray, singing in a loud and not particularly tuneful voice, her own version of a sporting song.

'It's a fine murdering day, (sang Bunch)
And as balmy as May
And the sleuths from the village are gone.'

A rattle of crockery being dumped in the sink drowned the next lines, but as the Rev. Julian Harmon left the house, he heard the final triumphant assertion:

'And we'll all go a'murdering today!'

CHAPTER 2

BREAKFAST AT LITTLE PADDOCKS

At Little Paddocks also, breakfast was in progress.

Miss Blacklock, a woman of sixty odd, the owner of the house, sat at the head of the table. She wore country tweeds – and with them, rather incongruously, a choker necklace of large false pearls. She was reading Lane Norcott in the *Daily Mail*. Julia Simmons was languidly glancing through the *Telegraph*. Patrick Simmons was checking up on the crossword in *The Times*. Miss Dora Bunner was giving her attention wholeheartedly to the local weekly paper.

Miss Blacklock gave a subdued chuckle, Patrick muttered: '*Adherent* – not *adhesive* – that's where I went wrong.'

Suddenly a loud cluck, like a startled hen, came from Miss Bunner.

'Letty – *Letty* – have you seen this? Whatever *can* it mean?'

'What's the matter, Dora?'

'The most extraordinary advertisement. It says Little Paddocks quite distinctly. But whatever can it *mean*?'

'If you'd let me see, Dora dear –'

Miss Bunner obediently surrendered the paper into Miss Blacklock's outstretched hand, pointing to the item with a tremulous forefinger.

'Just look, Letty.'

Miss Blacklock looked. Her eyebrows went up. She threw a quick scrutinizing glance round the table. Then she read the advertisement out loud.

'A murder is announced and will take place on Friday, October 29th, at Little Paddocks at 6.30 p.m. Friends please accept this, the only intimation.'

Then she said sharply: 'Patrick, is this your idea?'

Her eyes rested searchingly on the handsome devil-may-care face of the young man at the other end of the table.

Patrick Simmons' disclaimer came quickly.

'No, indeed, Aunt Letty. Whatever put that idea into your head? Why should I know anything about it?'

'I wouldn't put it past you,' said Miss Blacklock grimly. 'I thought it might be your idea of a joke.'

'A joke? Nothing of the kind.'

'And you, Julia?'

Julia, looking bored, said: 'Of course not.'

Miss Bunner murmured: 'Do you think Mrs Haymes –' and looked at an empty place where someone had breakfasted earlier.

'Oh, I don't think our Phillipa would try and be funny,' said Patrick. 'She's a serious girl, she is.'

'But what's the idea, anyway?' said Julia, yawning. 'What does it mean?'

Miss Blacklock said slowly, 'I suppose – it's some silly sort of hoax.'

'But why?' Dora Bunner exclaimed. 'What's the point of it? It seems a very stupid sort of joke. And in very bad taste.'

Her flabby cheeks quivered indignantly, and her short-sighted eyes sparkled with indignation.

Miss Blacklock smiled at her.

'Don't work yourself up over it, Bunny,' she said. 'It's just somebody's idea of humour, but I wish I knew whose.'

'It says today,' pointed out Miss Bunner. 'Today at 6.30 p.m. What do you think is going to happen?'

'*Death!*' said Patrick in sepulchral tones. 'Delicious death.'

'Be quiet, Patrick,' said Miss Blacklock as Miss Bunner gave a little yelp.

'I only meant the special cake that Mitzi makes,' said Patrick apologetically. 'You know we *always* call it delicious death.'

Miss Blacklock smiled a little absent-mindedly.

Miss Bunner persisted: 'But Letty, what do you really think –?'

Her friend cut across the words with reassuring cheerfulness.

'I know one thing that will happen at 6.30,' she said dryly. 'We'll have half the village up here, agog with curiosity. I'd better make sure we've got some sherry in the house.'

'You *are* worried, aren't you, Lotty?'

Miss Blacklock started. She had been sitting at her writing-table, absent-mindedly drawing little fishes on the blotting paper. She looked up into the anxious face of her old friend.

She was not quite sure what to say to Dora Bunner. Bunny, she knew, mustn't be worried or upset. She was silent for a moment or two, thinking.

She and Dora Bunner had been at school together. Dora then had been a pretty, fair-haired, blue-eyed rather stupid girl. Her being stupid hadn't mattered, because her gaiety and high spirits and her prettiness had made her an agreeable companion. She ought, her friend thought, to have married some nice Army officer, or a country solicitor. She had so many good qualities – affection, devotion, loyalty. But life had been unkind to Dora Bunner. She had had to earn her living. She had been painstaking but never competent at anything she undertook.

The two friends had lost sight of each other. But six months ago a letter had come to Miss Blacklock, a rambling, pathetic letter. Dora's health had given way. She was living in one room, trying to subsist on her old age pension. She endeavoured to do needlework, but her fingers were stiff with rheumatism. She mentioned their schooldays – since then life had driven them apart – but could – possibly – her old friend help?

Miss Blacklock had responded impulsively. Poor Dora, poor pretty silly fluffy Dora. She had swooped down upon Dora, had carried her off, had installed her at Little Paddocks with the comforting fiction that 'the housework is getting too much for me. I need someone to help me run the house.' It was not for long – the doctor had told her that – but sometimes she found poor old Dora a sad trial. She muddled everything, upset the temperamental foreign 'help', miscounted the laundry, lost bills and letters – and sometimes reduced the competent Miss Blacklock to an agony of exasperation. Poor old muddle-headed Dora, so loyal, so anxious to help, so pleased and proud to think she was of assistance – and, alas, so completely unreliable.

She said sharply:

'Don't, Dora. You know I asked you –'

'Oh,' Miss Bunner looked guilty. 'I know. I forgot. But – but you *are*, aren't you?'

'Worried? No. At least,' she added truthfully, 'not exactly. You mean about that silly notice in the *Gazette*?'

'Yes – even if it's a joke, it seems to me it's a – a spiteful sort of joke.'

'Spiteful?'

'Yes. It seems to me there's *spite* there somewhere. I mean – it's not a *nice* kind of joke.'

Miss Blacklock looked at her friend. The mild eyes, the long obstinate mouth, the slightly upturned nose. Poor Dora, so maddening, so muddle-headed, so devoted and such a problem. A dear fussy old idiot and yet, in a queer way, with an instinctive sense of value.

'I think you're right, Dora,' said Miss Blacklock. 'It's not a nice joke.'

'I don't like it at all,' said Dora Bunner with unsuspected vigour. 'It frightens me.' She added, suddenly: 'And it frightens *you*, Letitia.'

'Nonsense,' said Miss Blacklock with spirit.

'It's *dangerous*. I'm sure it is. Like those people who send you bombs done up in parcels.'

'My dear, it's just some silly idiot trying to be funny.'

'But it *isn't* funny.'

It wasn't really very funny . . . Miss Blacklock's face betrayed her thoughts, and Dora cried triumphantly, 'You see. You think so, too!'

'But Dora, my dear –'

She broke off. Through the door there surged a tempestuous young woman with a well-developed bosom heaving under a tight jersey. She had on a dirndl skirt of a bright colour and had greasy dark plaits wound round and round her head. Her eyes were dark and flashing.

She said gustily:

'I can speak to you, yes, please, no?'

Miss Blacklock sighed.

'Of course, Mitzi, what is it?'

Sometimes she thought it would be preferable to do the entire work of the house as well as the cooking rather than be bothered with the eternal nerve storms of her refugee 'lady help'.

'I tell you at once – it is in order, I hope? I give you my notices and I go – I go at *once*!'

'For what reason? Has somebody upset you?'

'Yes, I am upset,' said Mitzi dramatically. 'I do not wish to die! Already in Europe I escape. My family they all die – they are all killed – my mother, my little brother, my so sweet little niece – all, all they are killed. But me I run away – I hide. I get to England. I work. I do work that never – never would I do in my own country – I –'

'I know all that,' said Miss Blacklock crisply. It was, indeed, a constant refrain on Mitzi's lips. 'But why do you want to leave *now*?'

'Because again they come to kill me!'

'Who do?'

'My enemies. The Nazis! Or perhaps this time it is the Bolsheviks. They find out I am here. They come to kill me. I have read it – yes – it is in the newspaper!'

'Oh, you mean in the *Gazette*?'

'*Here*, it is written *here*.' Mitzi produced the *Gazette* from where she had been holding it behind her back. 'See – here it says a *murder*. At Little Paddocks. That is here, is it not? This evening at 6.30. Ah! I do not wait to be murdered – *no*.'

'But why should this apply to *you*? It's – we think it is a joke.'

'A *joke*? It is not a joke to murder someone.'

'No, of course not. But my dear child, if anyone wanted to murder you, they wouldn't advertise the fact in the paper, would they?'

'You do not think they would?' Mitzi seemed a little shaken. 'You think, perhaps, they do not mean to murder anyone at all? Perhaps it is *you* they mean to murder, Miss Blacklock.'

'I certainly can't believe anyone wants to murder me,' said Miss Blacklock lightly. 'And really, Mitzi, I don't see why anyone should want to murder you. After all, why should they?'

'Because they are bad peoples . . . Very bad peoples. I tell you, my mother, my little brother, my so sweet niece . . .'

'Yes, yes.' Miss Blacklock stemmed the flow, adroitly. 'But I cannot really believe *anyone* wants to murder you, Mitzi. Of course, if you want to go off like this at a moment's notice, I can't possibly stop you. But I think you will be very silly if you do.'

She added firmly, as Mitzi looked doubtful:

'We'll have that beef the butcher sent stewed for lunch. It looks very tough.'

'I make you a goulash, a special goulash.'

'If you prefer to call it that, certainly. And perhaps you could use up that rather hard bit of cheese in making some cheese straws. I think some people may come in this evening for drinks.'

'This evening? What do you mean, this evening?'

'At half-past six.'

'But that is the time in the paper? Who should come then? *Why* should they come?'

'They're coming to the funeral,' said Miss Blacklock with a twinkle. 'That'll do now, Mitzi. I'm busy. Shut the door after you,' she added firmly.

'And that's settled *her* for the moment,' she said as the door closed behind a puzzled-looking Mitzi.

'You are so efficient, Letty,' said Miss Bunner admiringly.

CHAPTER 3

AT 6.30 P.M.

'Well, here we are, all set,' said Miss Blacklock. She looked round the double drawing-room with an appraising eye. The rose-patterned chintzes – the two bowls of bronze chrysanthemums, the small vase of violets and the silver cigarette-box on a table by the wall, the tray of drinks on the centre table.

Little Paddocks was a medium-sized house built in the early Victorian style. It had a long shallow veranda and green shuttered windows. The long, narrow drawing-room which lost a good deal of light owing to the veranda roof had originally had double doors at one end leading into a small room with a bay window. A former generation had removed the double doors and replaced them with portieres of velvet. Miss Blacklock had dispensed with the portieres so that the two rooms had become definitely one. There was a fireplace each end, but neither fire was lit although a gentle warmth pervaded the room.

'You've had the central heating lit,' said Patrick.

Miss Blacklock nodded.

'It's been so misty and damp lately. The whole house felt clammy. I got Evans to light it before he went.'

'The precious precious coke?' said Patrick mockingly.

'As you say, the precious coke. But otherwise there would have been the even more precious coal. You know the Fuel Office won't even let us have the little bit that's due to us each week – not unless we can say definitely that we haven't got any other means of cooking.'

'I suppose there was once heaps of coke and coal for everybody?' said Julia with the interest of one hearing about an unknown country.

'Yes, and cheap, too.'

'And anyone could go and buy as much as they wanted, without filling in anything, and there wasn't any shortage? There was lots of it there?'

'All kinds and qualities – and *not* all stones and slates like what we get nowadays.'

'It must have been a wonderful world,' said Julia, with awe in her voice.

Miss Blacklock smiled. 'Looking back on it, *I* certainly think so. But then I'm an old woman. It's natural for me to prefer my own times. But you young things oughtn't to think so.'

'I needn't have had a job then,' said Julia. 'I could just have stayed at home and done the flowers, and written notes . . . Why did one write notes and who were they to?'

'All the people that you now ring up on the telephone,' said Miss Blacklock with a twinkle. 'I don't believe you even know *how* to write, Julia.'

'Not in the style of that delicious "Complete Letter Writer" I found the other day. Heavenly! It told you the correct way of refusing a proposal of marriage from a widower.'

'I doubt if you would have enjoyed staying at home as much as you think,' said Miss Blacklock. 'There were duties, you know.' Her voice was dry. 'However, I don't really know much about it. Bunny and I,' she smiled affectionately at Dora Bunner, 'went into the labour market early.'

'Oh, we did, we did *indeed*,' agreed Miss Bunner. 'Those naughty, naughty children. I'll never forget them. Of course, Letty was clever. She was a business woman, secretary to a big financier.'

The door opened and Phillipa Haymes came in. She was tall and fair and placid-looking. She looked round the room in surprise.

'Hallo,' she said. 'Is it a party? Nobody told me.'

'Of course,' cried Patrick. 'Our Phillipa doesn't know. The only woman in Chipping Cleghorn who doesn't, I bet.'

Phillipa looked at him inquiringly.

'Here you behold,' said Patrick dramatically, waving a hand, 'the scene of a murder!'

Phillipa Haymes looked faintly puzzled.

'Here,' Patrick indicated the two big bowls of chrysanthemums, 'are the funeral wreaths and these dishes of cheese straws and olives represent the funeral baked meats.'

Phillipa looked inquiringly at Miss Blacklock.

'Is it a joke?' she asked. 'I'm always terribly stupid at seeing jokes.'

'It's a very nasty joke,' said Dora Bunner with energy. 'I don't like it at all.'

'Show her the advertisement,' said Miss Blacklock. 'I *must* go and shut up the ducks. It's dark. They'll be in by now.'

'Let me do it,' said Phillipa.

'Certainly not, my dear. You've finished your day's work.'

'I'll do it, Aunt Letty,' offered Patrick.

'No, you won't,' said Miss Blacklock with energy. 'Last time you didn't latch the door properly.'

'I'll do it, Letty dear,' cried Miss Bunner. 'Indeed, I should love to. I'll just slip on my galoshes – and now where did I put my cardigan?'

But Miss Blacklock, with a smile, had already left the room.

'It's no good, Bunny,' said Patrick. 'Aunt Letty's so efficient that she can never bear anybody else to do things for her. She really much prefers to do everything herself.'

'She loves it,' said Julia.

'I didn't notice you making any offers of assistance,' said her brother.

Julia smiled lazily.

'You've just said Aunt Letty likes to do things herself,' she pointed out. 'Besides,' she held out a well-shaped leg in a sheer stocking, 'I've got my best stockings on.'

'Death in silk stockings!' declaimed Patrick.

'Not silk – nylons, you idiot.'

'That's not nearly such a good title.'

'Won't somebody please tell me,' cried Phillipa plaintively, 'why there is all this insistence on death?'

Everybody tried to tell her at once – nobody could find the *Gazette* to show her because Mitzi had taken it into the kitchen.

Miss Blacklock returned a few minutes later.

'There,' she said briskly, '*that's* done.' She glanced at the clock. 'Twenty-past six. Somebody ought to be here soon – unless I'm entirely wrong in my estimate of my neighbours.'

'I don't see why anybody should come,' said Phillipa, looking bewildered.

'Don't you, dear? . . . I dare say you wouldn't. But most people are rather more inquisitive than you are.'

'Phillipa's attitude to life is that she just isn't interested,' said Julia, rather nastily.

Phillipa did not reply.

Miss Blacklock was glancing round the room. Mitzi had put the sherry and three dishes containing olives, cheese straws and some little fancy pastries on the table in the middle of the room.

'You might move that tray – or the whole table if you like – round the corner into the bay window in the other room, Patrick, if you don't mind. After all, I am *not* giving a party! *I* haven't asked anyone. And I don't intend to make it obvious that I expect people to turn up.'

'You wish, Aunt Letty, to disguise your intelligent anticipation?'

'Very nicely put, Patrick. Thank you, my dear boy.'

'Now we can all give a lovely performance of a quiet evening at home,' said Julia, 'and be quite surprised when somebody drops in.'

Miss Blacklock had picked up the sherry bottle. She stood holding it uncertainly in her hand.

Patrick reassured her.

'There's quite half a bottle there. It ought to be enough.'

'Oh, yes – yes . . .' She hesitated. Then, with a slight flush, she said:

'Patrick, would you mind . . . there's a new bottle in the cupboard in the pantry . . . Bring it and a corkscrew. I – we – might as well have a new bottle. This – this has been opened some time.'

Patrick went on his errand without a word. He returned with the new bottle and drew the cork. He looked up curiously at Miss Blacklock as he placed it on the tray.

'Taking this seriously, aren't you, darling?' he asked gently.

'Oh,' cried Dora Bunner, shocked. 'Surely, Letty, you can't imagine –'

'Hush,' said Miss Blacklock quickly. 'That's the bell. You see, my intelligent anticipation is being justified.'

Mitzi opened the door of the drawing-room and admitted Colonel and Mrs Easterbrook. She had her own methods of announcing people.

'Here is Colonel and Mrs Easterbrook to see you,' she said conversationally.

Colonel Easterbrook was very bluff and breezy to cover some slight embarrassment.

'Hope you don't mind us dropping in,' he said. (A subdued gurgle came from Julia.) 'Happened to be passing this way – eh what? Quite a mild evening. Notice you've got your central heating on. We haven't started ours yet.'

'Aren't your chrysanthemums *lovely?*' gushed Mrs Easterbrook. '*Such* beauties!'

'They're rather scraggy, really,' said Julia.

Mrs Easterbrook greeted Phillipa Haymes with a little extra cordiality to show that she *quite* understood that Phillipa was not really an agricultural labourer.

'How is Mrs Lucas' garden getting on?' she asked. 'Do you think it will ever be straight again? Completely neglected all through the war – and then only that dreadful old man Ashe who simply did nothing but sweep up a few leaves and put in a few cabbage plants.'

'It's yielding to treatment,' said Phillipa. 'But it will take a little time.'

Mitzi opened the door again and said:

'Here are the ladies from Boulders.'

''Evening,' said Miss Hinchcliffe, striding over and taking Miss Blacklock's hand in her formidable grip. 'I said to Murgatroyd: "Let's just drop in at Little Paddocks!" I wanted to ask you how your ducks are laying.'

'The evenings do draw in so quickly now, don't they?' said Miss Murgatroyd to Patrick in a rather fluttery way. 'What *lovely* chrysanthemums!'

'Scraggy!' said Julia.

'Why can't you be co-operative?' murmured Patrick to her in a reproachful aside.

'You've got your central heating on,' said Miss Hinchcliffe. She said it accusingly. 'Very early.'

'The house gets so damp this time of year,' said Miss Blacklock.

Patrick signalled with his eyebrows: 'Sherry yet?' and Miss Blacklock signalled back: 'Not yet.'

She said to Colonel Easterbrook:

'Are you getting any bulbs from Holland this year?'

The door again opened and Mrs Swettenham came in rather guiltily, followed by a scowling and uncomfortable Edmund.

'Here we are!' said Mrs Swettenham gaily, gazing round her with frank curiosity. Then, feeling suddenly uncomfortable, she went on: 'I just thought I'd pop in and ask you if by any chance you wanted a kitten, Miss Blacklock? Our cat is just –'

'About to be brought to bed of the progeny of a ginger tom,' said Edmund. 'The result will, I think, be frightful. Don't say you haven't been warned!'

'She's a very good mouser,' said Mrs Swettenham hastily. And added: 'What *lovely* chrysanthemums!'

'You've got your central heating on, haven't you?' asked Edmund, with an air of originality.

'Aren't people just like gramophone records?' murmured Julia.

'I don't like the news,' said Colonel Easterbrook to Patrick, buttonholing him fiercely. 'I don't like it at all. If you ask me, war's inevitable – absolutely inevitable.'

'I never pay any attention to news,' said Patrick.

Once more the door opened and Mrs Harmon came in.

Her battered felt hat was stuck on the back of her head in a vague attempt to be fashionable and she had put on a rather limp frilly blouse instead of her usual pullover.

'Hallo, Miss Blacklock,' she exclaimed, beaming all over her round face. 'I'm not too late, am I? When does the murder begin?'

There was an audible series of gasps. Julia gave an approving little giggle, Patrick crinkled up his face and Miss Blacklock smiled at her latest guest.

'Julian is just frantic with rage that he can't be here,' said Mrs Harmon. 'He *adores* murders. That's really why he preached such a good sermon last Sunday – I suppose I oughtn't to say it was a good sermon as he's my husband – but it really was good, didn't you think? – so much better than his usual sermons. But as I was saying it was all because of *Death Does the Hat Trick*. Have you read it? The girl at Boots' kept it for me specially. It's simply *baffling*. You keep thinking you know – and then the whole thing switches round – and there are a lovely lot of murders, four or five of them. Well, I left it in the study when Julian was shutting himself up there to do his sermon, and he just picked it up and simply *could not* put it down! And consequently he had to write his sermon in a frightful hurry and had to just put down what he wanted to say very simply – without any scholarly twists and bits and learned references – and naturally it was heaps better. Oh, dear, I'm talking too much. But do tell me, when is the murder going to begin?'

Miss Blacklock looked at the clock on the mantelpiece.

'If it's going to begin,' she said cheerfully, 'it ought to begin soon. It's just a minute to the half hour. In the meantime, have a glass of sherry.'

Patrick moved with alacrity through the archway. Miss Blacklock went to the table by the archway where the cigarette-box was.

'I'd love some sherry,' said Mrs Harmon. 'But what do you mean by *if*?'

'Well,' said Miss Blacklock, 'I'm as much in the dark as you are. I don't know what –'

She stopped and turned her head as the little clock on the mantelpiece began to chime. It had a sweet silvery bell-like tone. Everybody was silent and nobody moved. They all stared at the clock.

It chimed a quarter – and then the half. As the last note died away all the lights went out.

Delighted gasps and feminine squeaks of appreciation were heard in the darkness. 'It's beginning,' cried Mrs Harmon in an ecstasy. Dora Bunner's voice cried out plaintively, 'Oh, I don't like it!' Other voices said, 'How terribly, terribly frightening!' 'It gives me the creeps.' 'Archie, where are you?' 'What do I have to *do*?' 'Oh dear – did I step on your foot? I'm so sorry.'

Then, with a crash, the door swung open. A powerful flashlight played rapidly round the room. A man's hoarse nasal voice, reminiscent to all of pleasant afternoons at the cinema, directed the company crisply to:

'Stick 'em up!

'Stick 'em up, I tell you!' the voice barked.

Delightedly, hands were raised willingly above heads.

'Isn't it wonderful?' breathed a female voice. 'I'm *so* thrilled.'

And then, unexpectedly, a revolver spoke. It spoke twice. The ping of two bullets shattered the complacency of the room. Suddenly the game was no longer a game. Somebody screamed . . .

The figure in the doorway whirled suddenly round, it seemed to hesitate, a third shot rang out, it crumpled and then it crashed to the ground. The flashlight dropped and went out.

There was darkness once again. And gently, with a little Victorian protesting moan, the drawing-room door, as was its habit when not propped open, swung gently to and latched with a click.

* * *

Inside the drawing-room there was pandemonium. Various voices spoke at once. 'Lights.' 'Can't you find the switch?' 'Who's got a lighter?' 'Oh, I don't like it, I don't *like* it.' 'But those shots were *real!*' 'It was a *real* revolver he had.' 'Was it a burglar?' 'Oh, Archie, I want to get out of here.' 'Please, has somebody got a lighter?'

And then, almost at the same moment, two lighters clicked and burned with small steady flames.

Everybody blinked and peered at each other. Startled face looked into startled face. Against the wall by the archway Miss Blacklock stood with her hand up to her face. The light was too dim to show more than that something dark was trickling over her fingers.

Colonel Easterbrook cleared his throat and rose to the occasion.

'Try the switches, Swettenham,' he ordered.

Edmund, near the door, obediently jerked the switch up and down.

'Off at the main, or a fuse,' said the Colonel. 'Who's making that awful row?'

A female voice had been screaming steadily from somewhere beyond the closed door. It rose now in pitch and with it came the sound of fists hammering on a door.

Dora Bunner, who had been sobbing quietly, called out:

'It's Mitzi. Somebody's murdering Mitzi . . .'

Patrick muttered: 'No such luck.'

Miss Blacklock said: 'We must get candles. Patrick, will you –?'

The Colonel was already opening the door. He and Edmund, their lighters flickering, stepped into the hall. They almost stumbled over a recumbent figure there.

'Seems to have knocked him out,' said the Colonel. 'Where's that woman making that hellish noise?'

'In the dining-room,' said Edmund.

The dining-room was just across the hall. Someone was beating on the panels and howling and screaming.

'She's locked in,' said Edmund, stooping down. He turned the key and Mitzi came out like a bounding tiger.

The dining-room light was still on. Silhouetted against it Mitzi presented a picture of insane terror and continued to scream. A touch of comedy was introduced by the fact that she had been engaged in cleaning silver and was still holding a chamois leather and a large fish slice.

'Be quiet, Mitzi,' said Miss Blacklock.

'Stop it,' said Edmund, and as Mitzi showed no disposition to stop screaming, he leaned forward and gave her a sharp slap on the cheek. Mitzi gasped and hiccuped into silence.

'Get some candles,' said Miss Blacklock. 'In the kitchen cupboard. Patrick, you know where the fusebox is?'

'The passage behind the scullery? Right, I'll see what I can do.'

Miss Blacklock had moved forward into the light thrown from the dining-room and Dora Bunner gave a sobbing gasp. Mitzi let out another full-blooded scream.

'The blood, the *blood*!' she gasped. 'You are shot – Miss Blacklock, you bleed to death.'

'Don't be so stupid,' snapped Miss Blacklock. 'I'm hardly hurt at all. It just grazed my ear.'

'But Aunt Letty,' said Julia, 'the blood.'

And indeed Miss Blacklock's white blouse and pearls and her hands were a horrifyingly gory sight.

'Ears always bleed,' said Miss Blacklock. 'I remember fainting in the hairdresser's when I was a child. The man had only just snipped my ear. There seemed to be a basin of blood at once. But we *must* have some light.'

'I get the candles,' said Mitzi.

Julia went with her and they returned with several candles stuck into saucers.

'Now let's have a look at our malefactor,' said the Colonel. 'Hold the candles down low, will you, Swettenham? As many as you can.'

'I'll come the other side,' said Phillipa.

With a steady hand she took a couple of saucers. Colonel Easterbrook knelt down.

The recumbent figure was draped in a roughly made black cloak with a hood to it. There was a black mask over the face and he wore black cotton gloves. The hood had slipped back disclosing a ruffled fair head.

Colonel Easterbrook turned him over, felt the pulse, the heart . . . then drew away his fingers with an exclamation of distaste, looking down on them. They were sticky and red.

'Shot himself,' he said.

'Is he badly hurt?' asked Miss Blacklock.

'H'm. I'm afraid he's dead . . . May have been suicide – or he may have tripped himself up with that cloak thing and the revolver went off as he fell. If I could see better –'

At that moment, as though by magic, the lights came on again.

With a queer feeling of unreality those inhabitants of Chipping Cleghorn

186 • AGATHA CHRISTIE

who stood in the hall of Little Paddocks realized that they stood in the presence of violent and sudden death. Colonel Easterbrook's hand was stained red. Blood was still trickling down Miss Blacklock's neck over her blouse and coat and the grotesquely sprawled figure of the intruder lay at their feet . . .

Patrick, coming from the dining-room, said, 'It seemed to be just one fuse gone . . .' He stopped.

Colonel Easterbrook tugged at the small black mask.

'Better see who the fellow is,' he said. 'Though I don't suppose it's anyone we know . . .'

He detached the mask. Necks were craned forward. Mitzi hiccuped and gasped, but the others were very quiet.

'He's quite young,' said Mrs Harmon with a note of pity in her voice.

And suddenly Dora Bunner cried out excitedly:

'Letty, Letty, it's the young man from the Spa Hotel in Medenham Wells. The one who came out here and wanted you to give him money to get back to Switzerland and you refused. I suppose the whole thing was just a pretext – to spy out the house . . . Oh, dear – he might easily have killed you . . .'

Miss Blacklock, in command of the situation, said incisively:

'Phillipa, take Bunny into the dining-room and give her a half-glass of brandy. Julia dear, just run up to the bathroom and bring me the sticking plaster out of the bathroom cupboard – it's so messy bleeding like a pig. Patrick, will you ring up the police at once?'

<hr>

CHAPTER 4

THE ROYAL SPA HOTEL

George Rydesdale, Chief Constable of Middleshire, was a quiet man. Of medium height, with shrewd eyes under rather bushy brows, he was in the habit of listening rather than talking. Then, in his unemotional voice, he would give a brief order – and the order was obeyed.

He was listening now to Detective-Inspector Dermot Craddock. Craddock was now officially in charge of the case. Rydesdale had recalled him last night from Liverpool where he had been sent to make certain inquiries in connection with another case. Rydesdale had a good opinion of Craddock. He not only had brains and imagination, he had also, which Rydesdale appreciated even more, the self-discipline to go slow, to check and examine each fact, and to keep an open mind until the very end of a case.

'Constable Legg took the call, sir,' Craddock was saying. 'He seems to have acted very well, with promptitude and presence of mind. And it can't have been easy. About a dozen people all trying to talk at once, including one of those Mittel Europas who go off at the deep end at the mere sight of a policeman. Made sure she was going to be locked up, and fairly screamed the place down.'

'Deceased has been identified?'

'Yes, sir. Rudi Scherz. Swiss nationality. Employed at the Royal Spa Hotel, Medenham Wells, as a receptionist. If you agree, sir, I thought I'd take the Royal Spa Hotel first, and go out to Chipping Cleghorn afterwards. Sergeant Fletcher is out there now. He'll see the bus people and then go on to the house.'

Rydesdale nodded approval.

The door opened, and the Chief Constable looked up.

'Come in, Henry,' he said. 'We've got something here that's a little out of the ordinary.'

Sir Henry Clithering, ex-Commissioner of Scotland Yard, came in with slightly raised eyebrows. He was a tall, distinguished-looking elderly man.

'It may appeal to even your blasé palate,' went on Rydesdale.

'I was never blasé,' said Sir Henry indignantly.

'The latest idea,' said Rydesdale, 'is to advertise one's murders beforehand. Show Sir Henry that advertisement, Craddock.'

'The *North Benham News and Chipping Cleghorn Gazette*,' said Sir Henry. 'Quite a mouthful.' He read the half inch of print indicated by Craddock's finger. 'H'm, yes, somewhat unusual.'

'Any line on who inserted this advertisement?' asked Rydesdale.

'By the description, sir, it was handed in by Rudi Scherz himself – on Wednesday.'

'Nobody questioned it? The person who accepted it didn't think it odd?'

'The adenoidal blonde who receives the advertisements is quite incapable of thinking, I should say, sir. She just counted the words and took the money.'

'What was the idea?' asked Sir Henry.

'Get a lot of the locals curious,' suggested Rydesdale. 'Get them all together at a particular place at a particular time, then hold them up and relieve them of their spare cash and valuables. As an idea, it's not without originality.'

'What sort of a place is Chipping Cleghorn?' asked Sir Henry.

'A large sprawling picturesque village. Butcher, baker, grocer, quite a good antique shop – two tea-shops. Self-consciously a beauty spot. Caters for the motoring tourist. Also highly residential. Cottages formerly lived in by agricultural labourers now converted and lived in by elderly spinsters and retired couples. A certain amount of building done round about in Victorian times.'

'I know,' said Sir Henry. 'Nice old Pussies and retired Colonels. Yes, if they noticed that advertisement they'd all come sniffing round at 6.30 to see what was up. Lord, I wish I had my own particular old Pussy here. Wouldn't she like to get her nice ladylike teeth into this. Right up her street it would be.'

'Who's your own particular Pussy, Henry? An aunt?'

'No,' Sir Henry sighed. 'She's no relation.' He said reverently: 'She's just the finest detective God ever made. Natural genius cultivated in a suitable soil.'

He turned upon Craddock.

'Don't you despise the old Pussies in this village of yours, my boy,' he said. 'In case this turns out to be a high-powered mystery, which I don't suppose for a moment it will, remember that an elderly unmarried woman who knits and gardens is streets ahead of any detective sergeant. She can tell you what might have happened and what ought to have happened and even what actually *did* happen! And she can tell you *why* it happened!'

'I'll bear that in mind, sir,' said Detective-Inspector Craddock in his most formal manner, and nobody would have guessed that Dermot Eric Craddock was actually Sir Henry's godson and was on easy and intimate terms with his godfather.

Rydesdale gave a quick outline of the case to his friend.

'They'd all turn up at 6.30, I grant you that,' he said. 'But would that Swiss fellow know they would? And another thing, would they be likely to have much loot on them to be worth the taking?'

'A couple of old-fashioned brooches, a string of seed pearls – a little loose change, perhaps a note or two – not more,' said Sir Henry, thoughtfully. 'Did this Miss Blacklock keep much money in the house?'

'She says not, sir. Five pounds odd, I understand.'

'Mere chicken feed,' said Rydesdale.

'What you're getting at,' said Sir Henry, 'is that this fellow liked to play-act – it wasn't the loot, it was the fun of playing and acting the hold-up. Cinema stuff? Eh? It's quite possible. How did he manage to shoot himself?'

Rydesdale drew a paper towards him.

'Preliminary medical report. The revolver was discharged at close range – singeing . . . h'm . . . nothing to show whether accident or suicide. Could have been done deliberately, or he could have tripped and fallen and the revolver which he was holding close to him could have gone off . . . Probably the latter.' He looked at Craddock. 'You'll have to question the witnesses very carefully and make them say exactly what they saw.'

Detective-Inspector Craddock said sadly: 'They'll all have seen something different.'

'It's always interested me,' said Sir Henry, 'what people do see at a moment of intense excitement and nervous strain. What they do see and, even more interesting, what they don't see.'

'Where's the report on the revolver?'

'Foreign make – (fairly common on the Continent) – Scherz did not hold a permit for it – and did not declare it on coming into England.'

'Bad lad,' said Sir Henry.

'Unsatisfactory character all round. Well, Craddock, go and see what you can find out about him at the Royal Spa Hotel.'

At the Royal Spa Hotel, Inspector Craddock was taken straight to the Manager's office.

The Manager, Mr Rowlandson, a tall florid man with a hearty manner, greeted Inspector Craddock with expansive geniality.

'Glad to help you in any way we can, Inspector,' he said. 'Really a most surprising business. I'd never have credited it – never. Scherz seemed a very ordinary, pleasant young chap – not at all my idea of a hold-up man.'

'How long has he been with you, Mr Rowlandson?'

'I was looking that up just before you came. A little over three months. Quite good credentials, the usual permits, etc.'

'And you found him satisfactory?'

Without seeming to do so, Craddock marked the infinitesimal pause before Rowlandson replied.

'Quite satisfactory.'

Craddock made use of a technique he had found efficacious before now.

'No, no, Mr Rowlandson,' he said, gently shaking his head. 'That's not really quite the case, is it?'

'We-ll –' The Manager seemed slightly taken aback.

'Come now, there was something wrong. What was it?'

'That's just it. I don't know.'

'But you *thought* there was something wrong?'

'Well – yes – I did . . . But I've nothing really to go upon. I shouldn't like my conjectures to be written down and quoted against me.'

Craddock smiled pleasantly.

'I know just what you mean. You needn't worry. But I've got to get some idea of what this fellow, Scherz, was like. You suspected him of – what?'

Rowlandson said, rather reluctantly:

'Well, there was trouble, once or twice, about the bills. Items charged that oughtn't to have been there.'

'You mean you suspected that he charged up certain items which didn't appear in the hotel records, and that he pocketed the difference when the bill was paid?'

'Something like that . . . Put it at the best, there was gross carelessness on his part. Once or twice quite a big sum was involved. Frankly, I got our accountant to go over his books suspecting that he was – well, a wrong 'un, but though there were various mistakes and a good deal of slipshod method, the actual cash was quite correct. So I came to the conclusion that I must be mistaken.'

'Supposing you hadn't been wrong? Supposing Scherz had been helping himself to various small sums here and there, he could have covered himself, I suppose, by making good the money?'

'Yes, if he *had* the money. But people who help themselves to "small sums" as you put it – are usually hard up for those sums and spend them offhand.'

'So, if he wanted money to replace missing sums, he would have had to get money – by a hold-up or other means?'

'Yes. I wonder if this is his first attempt . . .'

'Might be. It was certainly a very amateurish one. Is there anyone else he could have got money from? Any women in his life?'

'One of the waitresses in the Grill. Her name's Myrna Harris.'

'I'd better have a talk with her.'

Myrna Harris was a pretty girl with a glorious head of red hair and a pert nose.

She was alarmed and wary, and deeply conscious of the indignity of being interviewed by the police.

'I don't know a thing about it, sir. Not a thing,' she protested. 'If I'd known what he was like I'd never have gone out with Rudi at all. Naturally, seeing as he worked in Reception here, I thought he was all right. Naturally I did. What I say is the hotel ought to be more careful when they employ people – especially foreigners. Because you never know where you are with foreigners. I suppose he might have been in with one of these gangs you read about?'

'We think,' said Craddock, 'that he was working quite on his own.'

'Fancy – and him so quiet and respectable. You'd never think. Though there have been things missed – now I come to think of it. A diamond brooch – and a little gold locket, I believe. But I never dreamed that it could have been Rudi.'

'I'm sure you didn't,' said Craddock. 'Anyone might have been taken in. You knew him fairly well?'

'I don't know that I'd say *well*.'

'But you were friendly?'

'Oh, we were friendly – that's all, just friendly. Nothing serious at all. I'm always on my guard with foreigners, anyway. They've often got a way with them, but you never know, do you? Some of those Poles during the war! And even some of the Americans! Never let on they're married men until it's too late. Rudi talked big and all that – but I always took it with a grain of salt.'

Craddock seized on the phrase.

'Talked big, did he? That's very interesting, Miss Harris. I can see you're going to be a lot of help to us. In what way did he talk big?'

'Well, about how rich his people were in Switzerland – and how important. But that didn't go with his being as short of money as he was. He always said that because of the money regulation he couldn't get money from Switzerland over here. That might be, I suppose, but his things weren't expensive. His clothes, I mean. They weren't really class. I think, too, that a lot of the stories he used to tell me were so much hot air. About climbing in the Alps, and saving people's lives on the edge of a glacier. Why, he turned quite giddy just going along the edge of Boulter's Gorge. Alps, indeed!'

'You went out with him a good deal?'

'Yes – well – yes, I did. He had awfully good manners and he knew how to – to look after a girl. The best seats at the pictures always. And even flowers he'd buy me, sometimes. And he was just a lovely dancer – lovely.'

'Did he mention this Miss Blacklock to you at all?'

'She comes in and lunches here sometimes, doesn't she? And she's stayed here once. No, I don't think Rudi ever mentioned her. I didn't know he knew her.'

'Did he mention Chipping Cleghorn?'

He thought a faintly wary look came into Myrna Harris's eyes but he couldn't be sure.

'I don't think so . . . I think he did once ask about buses – what time they went – but I can't remember if that was Chipping Cleghorn or somewhere else. It wasn't just lately.'

He couldn't get more out of her. Rudi Scherz had seemed just as usual. She hadn't seen him the evening before. She'd no idea – no idea *at all* – she stressed the point, that Rudi Scherz was a crook.

And probably, Craddock thought, that was quite true.

CHAPTER 5

MISS BLACKLOCK AND MISS BUNNER

Little Paddocks was very much as Detective-Inspector Craddock had imagined it to be. He noted ducks and chickens and what had been until lately an attractive herbaceous border and in which a few late Michaelmas daisies showed a last dying splash of purple beauty. The lawn and the paths showed signs of neglect.

Summing up, Detective-Inspector Craddock thought: 'Probably not much money to spend on gardeners – fond of flowers and a good eye for planning and massing a border. House needs painting. Most houses do, nowadays. Pleasant little property.'

As Craddock's car stopped before the front door, Sergeant Fletcher came round the side of the house. Sergeant Fletcher looked like a guardsman, with an erect military bearing, and was able to impart several different meanings to the one monosyllable: 'Sir.'

'So there you are, Fletcher.'

'Sir,' said Sergeant Fletcher.

'Anything to report?'

'We've finished going over the house, sir. Scherz doesn't seem to have left any fingerprints anywhere. He wore gloves, of course. No signs of any of the doors or windows being forced to effect an entrance. He seems to have come out from Medenham on the bus, arriving here at six o'clock. Side door of the house was locked at 5.30, I understand. Looks as though he must have walked in through the front door. Miss Blacklock states that that door isn't usually locked until the house is shut up for the night. The maid, on the other hand, states that the front door was locked all the afternoon – but she'd say anything. Very temperamental you'll find her. Mittel Europa refugee of some kind.'

'Difficult, is she?'

'Sir!' said Sergeant Fletcher, with intense feeling.

Craddock smiled.

Fletcher resumed his report.

'Lighting system is quite in order everywhere. We haven't spotted yet how he operated the lights. It was just the one circuit went. Drawing-room and hall. Of course, nowadays the wall brackets and lamps wouldn't all be on one fuse – but this is an old-fashioned installation and wiring. Don't see how he could have tampered with the fusebox because it's out by the scullery and he'd have had to go through the kitchen, so the maid would have seen him.'

'Unless she was in it with him?'

'That's very possible. Both foreigners – and I wouldn't trust her a yard – not a yard.'

Craddock noticed two enormous frightened black eyes peering out of a window by the front door. The face, flattened against the pane, was hardly visible.

'That her there?'

'That's right, sir.'

The face disappeared.

Craddock rang the front-door bell.

After a long wait the door was opened by a good-looking young woman with chestnut hair and a bored expression.

'Detective-Inspector Craddock,' said Craddock.

The young woman gave him a cool stare out of very attractive hazel eyes and said:

'Come in. Miss Blacklock is expecting you.'

The hall, Craddock noted, was long and narrow and seemed almost incredibly full of doors.

The young woman threw open a door on the left, and said: 'Inspector Craddock, Aunt Letty. Mitzi wouldn't go to the door. She's shut herself up in the kitchen and she's making the most marvellous moaning noises. I shouldn't think we'll get *any* lunch.'

She added in an explanatory manner to Craddock: 'She doesn't like the police,' and withdrew, shutting the door behind her.

Craddock advanced to meet the owner of Little Paddocks.

He saw a tall active-looking woman of about sixty. Her grey hair had a slight natural wave and made a distinguished setting for an intelligent, resolute face. She had keen grey eyes and a square determined chin. There was a surgical dressing on her left ear. She wore no make-up and was plainly dressed in a well-cut tweed coat and skirt and pullover. Round the neck of the latter she wore, rather unexpectedly, a set of old-fashioned cameos – a Victorian touch which seemed to hint at a sentimental streak not otherwise apparent.

Close beside her, with an eager round face and untidy hair escaping from a hair net, was a woman of about the same age whom Craddock had no difficulty in recognizing as the 'Dora Bunner – companion' of Constable Legg's notes – to which the latter had added an off-the-record commentary of 'Scatty!'

Miss Blacklock spoke in a pleasant well-bred voice.

'Good morning, Inspector Craddock. This is my friend, Miss Bunner, who helps me run the house. Won't you sit down? You won't smoke, I suppose?'

'Not on duty, I'm afraid, Miss Blacklock.'

'What a shame!'

Craddock's eyes took in the room with a quick, practised glance. Typical Victorian double drawing-room. Two long windows in this room, built-out bay window in the other . . . chairs . . . sofa . . . centre table with a big bowl of chrysanthemums – another bowl in window – all fresh and pleasant without much originality. The only incongruous note was a small silver vase with dead violets in it on a table near the archway into the further room. Since he could not imagine Miss Blacklock tolerating dead flowers in a room, he imagined it to be the only indication that something out of the way had occurred to distract the routine of a well-run household.

He said:

'I take it, Miss Blacklock, that this is the room in which the – incident occurred?'

'Yes.'

'And you should have seen it last night,' Miss Bunner exclaimed. 'Such a *mess*. Two little tables knocked over, and the leg off one – people barging about in the dark – and someone put down a lighted cigarette and burnt one of the best bits of furniture. People – young people especially – are so careless about these things . . . Luckily none of the china got broken –'

Miss Blacklock interrupted gently but firmly:

'Dora, all these things, vexatious as they may be, are only trifles.

It will be best, I think, if we just answer Inspector Craddock's questions.'

'Thank you, Miss Blacklock. I shall come to what happened last night, presently. First of all I want you to tell me when you first saw the dead man – Rudi Scherz.'

'Rudi Scherz?' Miss Blacklock looked slightly surprised. 'Is that his name? Somehow, I thought . . . Oh, well, it doesn't matter. My first encounter with him was when I was in Medenham Spa for a day's shopping about – let me see, about three weeks ago. We – Miss Bunner and I – were having lunch at the Royal Spa Hotel. As we were just leaving after lunch, I heard my name spoken. It was this young man. He said: "It is Miss Blacklock, is it not?" And went on to say that perhaps I did not remember him, but that he was the son of the proprietor of the Hotel des Alpes at Montreux where my sister and I had stayed for nearly a year during the war.'

'The Hotel des Alpes, Montreux,' noted Craddock. 'And did you remember him, Miss Blacklock?'

'No, I didn't. Actually I had no recollection of ever having seen him before. These boys at hotel reception desks all look exactly alike. We had had a very pleasant time at Montreux and the proprietor there had been extremely obliging, so I tried to be as civil as possible and said I hoped he was enjoying being in England, and he said, yes, that his father had sent him over for six months to learn the hotel business. It all seemed quite natural.'

'And your next encounter?'

'About – yes, it must have been ten days ago, he suddenly turned up here. I was very surprised to see him. He apologized for troubling me, but said I was the only person he knew in England. He told me that he urgently needed money to return to Switzerland as his mother was dangerously ill.'

'But Letty didn't give it to him,' Miss Bunner put in breathlessly.

'It was a thoroughly fishy story,' said Miss Blacklock, with vigour. 'I made up my mind that he was definitely a wrong 'un. That story about wanting the money to return to Switzerland was *nonsense*. His father could easily have wired for arrangements to have been made in this country. These hotel people are all in with each other. I suspected that he'd been embezzling money or something of that kind.' She paused and said dryly: 'In case you think I'm hardhearted, I was secretary for many years to a big financier and one becomes wary about appeals for money. I know simply all the hard-luck stories there are.

'The only thing that did surprise me,' she added thoughtfully, 'was that he gave in so easily. He went away at once without any more argument. It's as though he had never expected to get the money.'

'Do you think now, looking back on it, that his coming was really by way of a pretext to spy out the land?'

Miss Blacklock nodded her head vigorously.

'That's exactly what I do think – now. He made certain remarks as I let him out – about the rooms. He said, "You have a very nice dining-room" (which of course it isn't – it's a horrid dark little room) just as an excuse to look inside. And then he sprang forward and unfastened the front door, said, "Let me." I think now he wanted to have a look at the fastening. Actually, like most people round here, we never lock the front door until it gets dark. *Anyone* could walk in.'

'And the side door? There is a side door to the garden, I understand?'

'Yes. I went out through it to shut up the ducks not long before the people arrived.'

'Was it locked when you went out?'

Miss Blacklock frowned.

'I can't remember . . . I think so. I certainly locked it when I came in.'

'That would be about quarter-past six?'

'Somewhere about then.'

'And the front door?'

'That's not usually locked until later.'

'Then Scherz could have walked in quite easily that way. Or he could have slipped in whilst you were out shutting up the ducks. He'd already spied out the lie of the land and had probably noted various places of concealment – cupboards, etc. Yes, that all seems quite clear.'

'I beg your pardon, it isn't at all clear,' said Miss Blacklock. 'Why on earth should anyone take all that elaborate trouble to come and burgle this house and stage that silly sort of hold-up?'

'Do you keep much money in the house, Miss Blacklock?'

'About five pounds in that desk there, and perhaps a pound or two in my purse.'

'Jewellery?'

'A couple of rings and brooches, and the cameos I'm wearing. You must agree with me, Inspector, that the whole thing's absurd.'

'It wasn't burglary at all,' cried Miss Bunner. 'I've told you so, Letty, all along. It was *revenge*! Because you wouldn't give him that money! He deliberately shot at you – twice.'

'Ah,' said Craddock. 'We'll come now to last night. What happened exactly, Miss Blacklock? Tell me in your own words as nearly as you can remember.'

Miss Blacklock reflected a moment.

'The clock struck,' she said. 'The one on the mantelpiece. I remember saying that if anything were going to happen it would have to happen soon. And then the clock struck. We all listened to it without saying anything. It chimes, you know. It chimed the two quarters and then, quite suddenly, the lights went out.'

'What lights were on?'

'The wall brackets in here and the further room. The standard lamp and the two small reading lamps weren't on.'

'Was there a flash first, or a noise when the lights went out?'

'I don't think so.'

'I'm sure there *was* a flash,' said Dora Bunner. '*And* a cracking noise. Dangerous!'

'And then, Miss Blacklock?'

'The door opened –'

'Which door? There are two in the room.'

'Oh, this door in here. The one in the other room doesn't open. It's a dummy. The door opened and there he was – a masked man with a revolver. It just seemed too fantastic for words, but of course at the time I just thought it was a silly joke. He said something – I forget what –'

'Hands up or I shoot!' supplied Miss Bunner, dramatically.

'Something like that,' said Miss Blacklock, rather doubtfully.

'And you all put your hands up?'

'Oh, *yes*,' said Miss Bunner. 'We all did. I mean, it was *part* of it.'

'*I* didn't,' said Miss Blacklock crisply. 'It seemed so utterly silly. And I was annoyed by the whole thing.'

'And then?'

'The flashlight was right in my eyes. It dazzled me. And then, quite incredibly, I heard a bullet whizz past me and hit the wall by my head. Somebody shrieked and then I felt a burning pain in my ear and heard the second report.'

'It was *terrifying*,' put in Miss Bunner.

'And what happened next, Miss Blacklock?'

'It's difficult to say – I was so staggered by the pain and the surprise. The – the figure turned away and seemed to stumble and then there was another shot and his torch went out and everybody began pushing and calling out. All banging into each other.'

'Where were you standing, Miss Blacklock?'

'She was over by the table. She'd got that vase of violets in her hand,' said Miss Bunner breathlessly.

'I was over here.' Miss Blacklock went over to the small table by the archway. 'Actually it was the cigarette-box I'd got in my hand.'

Inspector Craddock examined the wall behind her. The two bullet holes showed plainly. The bullets themselves had been extracted and had been sent for comparison with the revolver.

He said quietly:

'You had a very near escape, Miss Blacklock.'

'He *did* shoot at her,' said Miss Bunner. 'Deliberately *at* her! I saw him. He turned the flash round on everybody until he found her and then he held it right at her and just fired at *her*. He meant to kill *you*, Letty.'

'Dora dear, you've just got that into your head from mulling the whole thing over and over.'

'He shot at *you*,' repeated Dora stubbornly. 'He meant to shoot you and when he'd missed, he shot himself. I'm *certain* that's the way it was!'

'I don't think he meant to shoot himself for a minute,' said Miss Blacklock. 'He wasn't the kind of man who shoots himself.'

'You tell me, Miss Blacklock, that until the revolver was fired you thought the whole business was a joke?'

'Naturally. What else could I think it was?'

'Who do you think was the author of this joke?'

'You thought Patrick had done it at first,' Dora Bunner reminded her.

'Patrick?' asked the Inspector sharply.

'My young cousin, Patrick Simmons,' Miss Blacklock continued sharply, annoyed with her friend. 'It did occur to me when I saw this advertisement that it might be some attempt at humour on his part, but he denied it absolutely.'

'And then you were worried, Letty,' said Miss Bunner. 'You *were* worried, although you pretended not to be. And you were quite right to be worried. It said a murder is announced – and it *was* announced – *your* murder! And if the man hadn't missed, you *would* have been murdered. And then where should we all be?'

Dora Bunner was trembling as she spoke. Her face was puckered up and she looked as though she were going to cry.

Miss Blacklock patted her on the shoulder.

'It's all right, Dora dear – don't get excited. It's so bad for you. Everything's quite all right. We've had a nasty experience, but it's over now.' She added, 'You must pull yourself together for my sake, Dora. I rely on you, you know, to keep the house going. Isn't it the day for the laundry to come?'

'Oh, dear me, Letty, how *fortunate* you reminded me! I wonder if they'll return that missing pillowcase. I must make a note in the book about it. I'll go and see to it at once.'

'And take those violets away,' said Miss Blacklock. 'There's nothing I hate more than dead flowers.'

'What a pity. I picked them fresh yesterday. They haven't lasted at all – oh, dear, I must have forgotten to put any water in the vase. Fancy that! I'm always forgetting things. Now I must go and see about the laundry. They might be here any moment.'

She bustled away, looking quite happy again.

'She's not very strong,' said Miss Blacklock, 'and excitements are bad for her. Is there anything more you want to know, Inspector?'

'I just want to know exactly how many people make up your household here and something about them.'

'Yes, well in addition to myself and Dora Bunner, I have two young cousins living here at present, Patrick and Julia Simmons.'

'Cousins? Not a nephew and niece?'

'No. They call me Aunt Letty, but actually they are distant cousins. Their mother was my second cousin.'

'Have they always made their home with you?'

'Oh, dear no, only for the last two months. They lived in the South of France before the war. Patrick went into the Navy and Julia, I believe, was in one of the Ministries. She was at Llandudno. When the war was over their mother wrote and asked me if they could possibly come to me as paying guests – Julia is training as a dispenser in Milchester General Hospital, Patrick is studying for an engineering degree at Milchester University. Milchester, as you know, is only fifty minutes by bus, and I was very glad to have them here. This house is really too large for me. They pay a small sum for board and lodging and it all works out very well.' She added with a smile, 'I like having somebody young about the place.'

'Then there is a Mrs Haymes, I believe?'

'Yes. She works as an assistant gardener at Dayas Hall, Mrs Lucas's place. The cottage there is occupied by the old gardener and his wife and Mrs Lucas asked if I could billet her here. She's a very nice girl. Her husband was killed in Italy, and she has a boy of eight who is at a prep school and whom I have arranged to have here in the holidays.'

'And by way of domestic help?'

'A jobbing gardener comes in on Tuesdays and Fridays. A Mrs Huggins from the village comes up five mornings a week and I have a foreign refugee with a most unpronounceable name as a kind of lady cook help. You will find Mitzi rather difficult, I'm afraid. She has a kind of persecution mania.'

Craddock nodded. He was conscious in his own mind of yet another of Constable Legg's invaluable commentaries. Having appended the word 'Scatty' to Dora Bunner, and 'All right' to Letitia Blacklock, he had embellished Mitzi's record with the one word 'Liar'.

As though she had read his mind Miss Blacklock said:

'Please don't be too prejudiced against the poor thing because she's a liar. I do really believe that, like so many liars, there is a real substratum of truth behind her lies. I mean that though, to take an instance, her atrocity stories have grown and grown until every kind of unpleasant story that has ever appeared in print has happened to her or her relations personally, she did have a bad shock initially and did see one, at least, of her relations killed. I think a lot of these displaced persons feel, perhaps justly, that their claim to our notice and sympathy lies in their atrocity value and so they exaggerate and invent.'

She added: 'Quite frankly, Mitzi is a maddening person. She exasperates and infuriates us all, she is suspicious and sulky, is perpetually having "feelings" and thinking herself insulted. But in spite of it all, I really am sorry for her.' She smiled. 'And also, when she wants to, she can cook very nicely.'

'I'll try not to ruffle her more than I can help,' said Craddock soothingly. 'Was that Miss Julia Simmons who opened the door to me?'

'Yes. Would you like to see her now? Patrick has gone out. Phillipa Haymes you will find working at Dayas Hall.'

'Thank you, Miss Blacklock. I'd like to see Miss Simmons now if I may.'

CHAPTER 6

JULIA, MITZI AND PATRICK

Julia, when she came into the room, and sat down in the chair vacated by Letitia Blacklock, had an air of composure that Craddock for some reason found annoying. She fixed a limpid gaze on him and waited for his questions.

Miss Blacklock had tactfully left the room.

'Please tell me about last night, Miss Simmons.'

'Last night?' murmured Julia with a blank stare. 'Oh, we all slept like logs. Reaction, I suppose.'

'I mean last night from six o'clock onwards.'

'Oh, I see. Well, a lot of tiresome people came –'

'They were?'

She gave him another limpid stare.

'Don't you know all this already?'

'I'm asking the questions, Miss Simmons,' said Craddock pleasantly.

'My mistake. I always find repetitions so dreary. Apparently you don't . . . Well, there was Colonel and Mrs Easterbrook, Miss Hinchcliffe and Miss Murgatroyd, Mrs Swettenham and Edmund Swettenham, and Mrs Harmon, the Vicar's wife. They arrived in that order. And if you want to know what they said – they all said the same thing in turn. "I see you've got your central heating on" and "What *lovely* chrysanthemums!"'

Craddock bit his lip. The mimicry was good.

'The exception was Mrs Harmon. She's rather a pet. She came in with her hat falling off and her shoelaces untied and she asked straight out when the murder was going to happen. It embarrassed everybody because they'd all been pretending they'd dropped in by chance. Aunt Letty said in her dry way that it was due to happen quite soon. And then that clock chimed and just as it finished, the lights went out, the door was flung open and a masked figure said, "Stick 'em up, guys," or something like that. It was exactly like a bad film. Really quite ridiculous. And then he fired two shots at Aunt Letty and suddenly it wasn't ridiculous any more.'

'Where was everybody when this happened?'

'When the lights went out? Well, just standing about, you know. Mrs Harmon was sitting on the sofa – Hinch (that's Miss Hinchcliffe) had taken up a manly stance in front of the fireplace.'

'You were all in this room, or the far room?'

'Mostly, I think, in this room. Patrick had gone into the other to get the sherry. I think Colonel Easterbrook went after him, but I don't really know. We were – well – as I said, just standing about.'

'Where were you yourself?'

'I think I was over by the window. Aunt Letty went to get the cigarettes.'

'On that table by the archway?'

'Yes – and then the lights went out and the bad film started.'

'The man had a powerful torch. What did he do with it?'

202 • AGATHA CHRISTIE

'Well, he shone it on us. Horribly dazzling. It just made you blink.'

'I want you to answer this very carefully, Miss Simmons. Did he hold the torch steady, or did he move it about?'

Julia considered. Her manner was now definitely less weary.

'He moved it,' she said slowly. 'Like a spotlight in a dance hall. It was full in my eyes and then it went on round the room and then the shots came. Two shots.'

'And then?'

'He whirled round – and Mitzi began to scream like a siren from somewhere and his torch went out and there was another shot. And then the door closed (it does, you know, slowly, with a whining noise – quite uncanny) and there we were all in the dark, not knowing what to do, and poor Bunny squealing like a rabbit and Mitzi going all out across the hall.'

'Would it be your opinion that the man shot himself deliberately, or do you think he stumbled and the revolver went off accidentally?'

'I haven't the faintest idea. The whole thing was so stagey. Actually I thought it was still some silly joke – until I saw the blood from Letty's ear. But even if you were actually going to fire a revolver to make the thing more real, you'd be careful to fire it well above someone's head, wouldn't you?'

'You would indeed. Do you think he could see clearly who he was firing at? I mean, was Miss Blacklock clearly outlined in the light of the torch?'

'I've no idea. I wasn't looking at her. I was looking at the man.'

'What I'm getting at is – do you think the man was deliberately aiming at her – at her in particular, I mean?'

Julia seemed a little startled by the idea.

'You mean deliberately picking on Aunt Letty? Oh, I shouldn't think so . . . After all, if he wanted to take a pot shot at Aunt Letty, there would be heaps of more suitable opportunities. There would be no point in collecting all the friends and neighbours just to make it more difficult. He could have shot her from behind a hedge in the good old Irish fashion any day of the week, and probably got away with it.'

And that, thought Craddock, was a very complete reply to Dora Bunner's suggestion of a deliberate attack on Letitia Blacklock.

He said with a sigh, 'Thank you, Miss Simmons. I'd better go and see Mitzi now.'

'Mind her fingernails,' warned Julia. 'She's a tartar!'

★   ★   ★

Craddock, with Fletcher in attendance, found Mitzi in the kitchen. She was rolling pastry and looked up suspiciously as he entered.

Her black hair hung over her eyes; she looked sullen, and the purple jumper and brilliant green skirt she wore were not becoming to her pasty complexion.

'What do you come in my kitchen for, Mr Policeman? You are police, yes? Always, always there is persecution – ah! I should be used to it by now. They say it is different here in England, but no, it is just the same. You come to torture me, yes, to make me say things, but I shall say *nothing*. You will tear off my fingernails, and put lighted matches on my skin – oh, yes, and worse than that. But I will not speak, do you hear? I shall say nothing – nothing at all. And you will send me away to a concentration camp, and I shall not care.'

Craddock looked at her thoughtfully, selecting what was likely to be the best method of attack. Finally he sighed and said:

'O.K., then, get your hat and coat.'

'What is that you say?' Mitzi looked startled.

'Get your hat and coat and come along. I haven't got my nail-pulling apparatus and the rest of the bag of tricks with me. We keep all that down at the station. Got the handcuffs handy, Fletcher?'

'Sir!' said Sergeant Fletcher with appreciation.

'But I do not want to come,' screeched Mitzi, backing away from him.

'Then you'll answer civil questions civilly. If you like, you can have a solicitor present.'

'A lawyer? I do not like a lawyer. I do not want a lawyer.'

She put the rolling pin down, dusted her hands on a cloth and sat down.

'What do you want to know?' she asked sulkily.

'I want your account of what happened here last night.'

'You know very well what happened.'

'I want your account of it.'

'I tried to go away. Did she tell you that? When I saw that in the paper saying about murder. I wanted to go away. She would not let me. She is very hard – not at all sympathetic. She made me stay. But *I* knew – *I* knew what would happen. *I* knew I should be murdered.'

'Well, you weren't murdered, were you?'

'No,' admitted Mitzi grudgingly.

'Come now, tell me what happened.'

'I was nervous. Oh, I was nervous. All that evening. I hear things. People moving about. Once I think someone is in the hall moving stealthily – but it is only that Mrs Haymes coming in through the side door (so as not to dirty the front steps, *she* says. Much *she* cares!). She is a Nazi herself, that one, with her fair hair and her blue eyes, so superior and looking at me and thinking that I – I am only dirt –'

'Never mind Mrs Haymes.'

'Who does she think *she* is? Has she had expensive university education like I have? Has she a degree in Economics? No, she is just a paid labourer. She digs and mows grass and is paid so much every Saturday. Who is she to call herself a lady?'

'Never mind Mrs Haymes, I said. Go on.'

'I take the sherry and the glasses, and the little pastries that I have made so nice into the drawing-room. Then the bell rings and I answer the door. Again and again I answer the door. It is degrading – but I do it. And then I go back into the pantry and I start to polish the silver, and I think it will be very handy, that, because if someone comes to kill me, I have there close at hand the big carving knife, all sharp.'

'Very foresighted of you.'

'And then, suddenly – I hear shots. I think: "It has come – it is happening." I run through the dining-room (the other door – it will not open). I stand a moment to listen and then there comes another shot and a big thud, out there in the hall, and I turn the door handle, but it is locked outside. I am shut in there like a rat in a trap. And I go mad with fear. I scream and I scream and I beat upon the door. And at last – at last – they turn the key and let me out. And then I bring candles, many many candles – and the lights go on, and I see blood – blood! Ach, Gott in Himmel, the blood! It is not the first time I have seen blood. My little brother – I see him killed before my eyes – I see blood in the street – people shot, dying – I –'

'Yes,' said Inspector Craddock. 'Thank you very much.'

'And now,' said Mitzi dramatically, 'you can arrest me and take me to prison!'

'Not today,' said Inspector Craddock.

As Craddock and Fletcher went through the hall to the front door it was flung open and a tall handsome young man almost collided with them.

'Sleuths as I live,' cried the young man.

'Mr Patrick Simmons?'

'Quite right, Inspector. You're the Inspector, aren't you, and the other's the Sergeant?'

'You are quite right, Mr Simmons. Can I have a word with you, please?'

'I am innocent, Inspector. I swear I am innocent.'

'Now then, Mr Simmons, don't play the fool. I've a good many other people to see and I don't want to waste time. What's this room? Can we go in here?'

'It's the so-called study – but nobody studies.'

'I was told that you were studying?' said Craddock.

'I found I couldn't concentrate on mathematics, so I came home.'

In a businesslike manner Inspector Craddock demanded full name, age, details of war service.

'And now, Mr Simmons, will you describe what happened last night?'

'We killed the fatted calf, Inspector. That is, Mitzi set her hand to making savoury pastries, Aunt Letty opened a new bottle of sherry –'

Craddock interrupted.

'A new bottle? Was there an old one?'

'Yes. Half full. But Aunt Letty didn't seem to fancy it.'

'Was she nervous, then?'

'Oh, not really. She's extremely sensible. It was old Bunny, I think, who had put the wind up her – prophesying disaster all day.'

'Miss Bunner was definitely apprehensive, then?'

'Oh, yes, she enjoyed herself thoroughly.'

'She took the advertisement seriously?'

'It scared her into fits.'

'Miss Blacklock seems to have thought, when she first read that advertisement, that you had had something to do with it. Why was that?'

'Ah, sure, I get blamed for everything round here!'

'You *didn't* have anything to do with it, did you, Mr Simmons?'

'Me? Never in the world.'

'Had you ever seen or spoken to this Rudi Scherz?'

'Never seen him in my life.'

'It was the kind of joke you might have played, though?'

'Who's been telling you that? Just because I once made Bunny an apple pie bed – and sent Mitzi a postcard saying the Gestapo was on her track –'

'Just give me your account of what happened.'

'I'd just gone into the small drawing-room to fetch the drinks when, Hey Presto, the lights went out. I turned round and there's a fellow standing in the doorway saying, "Stick your hands up," and everybody gasping and squealing, and just when I'm thinking – can I rush him? he starts firing a revolver and then crash down he goes and his torch goes out and we're in the dark again, and Colonel Easterbrook starts shouting orders in his barrack-room voice. "Lights," he says, and will my lighter go on? No, it won't as is the way of those cussed inventions.'

'Did it seem to you that the intruder was definitely aiming at Miss Blacklock?'

'Ah, how could I tell? I should say he just loosed off his revolver for the fun of the thing – and then found, maybe, he'd gone too far.'

'And shot himself?'

'It could be. When I saw the face of him, he looked like the kind of little pasty thief who might easily lose his nerve.'

'And you're sure you had never seen him before?'

'Never.'

'Thank you, Mr Simmons. I shall want to interview the other people who were here last night. Which would be the best order in which to take them?'

'Well, our Phillipa – Mrs Haymes – works at Dayas Hall. The gates of it are nearly opposite this gate. After that, the Swettenhams are the nearest. Anyone will tell you.'

CHAPTER 7

AMONG THOSE PRESENT

Dayas Hall had certainly suffered during the war years. Couch grass grew enthusiastically over what had once been an asparagus bed, as evidenced by a few waving tufts of asparagus foliage. Grounsel, bindweed and other garden pests showed every sign of vigorous growth.

A portion of the kitchen garden bore evidence of having been reduced to discipline and here Craddock found a sour-looking old man leaning pensively on a spade.

'It's Mrs 'Aymes you want? I couldn't say where you'd find 'er. 'As 'er own ideas, she 'as, about what she'll do. Not one to take advice. I could show her – show 'er willing – but what's the good, won't listen these young ladies won't! Think they know everything because they've put on breeches and gone for a ride on a tractor. But it's *gardening* that's needed here. And that isn't learned in a day. *Gardening*, that's what this place needs.'

'It looks as though it does,' said Craddock.

The old man chose to take this remark as an aspersion.

'Now look here, mister, what do you suppose I can do with a place this size? Three men and a boy, that's what it used to 'ave. And that's what it wants. There's not many men could put in the work on it that I do. 'Ere sometimes I am till eight o'clock at night. Eight o'clock.'

'What do you work by? An oil lamp?'

'Naterally I don't mean this time o' year. Naterally. *Summer* evenings I'm talking about.'

'Oh,' said Craddock. 'I'd better go and look for Mrs Haymes.'

The rustic displayed some interest.

'What are you wanting 'er for? Police, aren't you? She been in trouble, or is it the do there was up to Little Paddocks? Masked men bursting in and holding up a roomful of people with a revolver. An' that sort of thing wouldn't 'ave 'appened afore the war. Deserters, that's what it is. Desperate men roaming the countryside. Why don't the military round 'em up?'

'I've no idea,' said Craddock. 'I suppose this hold-up caused a lot of talk?'

'That it did. What's us coming to? That's what Ned Barker said. Comes of going to the pictures so much, he said. But Tom Riley he says it comes of letting these furriners run about loose. And depend on it, he says, that girl as cooks up there for Miss Blacklock and 'as such a nasty temper – *she's* in it, he said. She's a communist or worse, he says, and we don't like that sort 'ere. And Marlene, who's behind the bar, you understand, she will 'ave it that there must be something very valuable up at Miss Blacklock's. Not that you'd think it, she says, for I'm sure Miss Blacklock goes about as plain as plain, except for them great rows of false pearls she wears. And then she says – Supposin' as them pearls is *real*, and Florrie (what's old Bellamy's daughter) *she* says, "Nonsense," she says – "*noovo ar* – that's what they are – costume jewellery," she says. Costume jewellery – that's a fine way of labelling a string of false pearls. Roman pearls, the gentry used to call 'em once – and Parisian diamonds – my wife was a lady's maid and I know. But what does it all mean – just glass! I suppose it's "costume jewellery" that young Miss Simmons wears – gold ivy leaves and dogs and such like. 'Tisn't often you see a real bit of gold nowadays – even wedding rings they make of this grey plattinghum stuff. Shabby, I call it – for all that it costs the earth.'

Old Ashe paused for breath and then continued:

'"Miss Blacklock don't keep much money in the 'ouse, that I do know," says Jim Huggins, speaking up. He should know, for it's 'is wife as goes up and does for 'em at Little Paddocks, and she's a woman as knows most of what's going on. Nosey, if you take me.'

'Did he say what Mrs Huggins' view was?'

'That Mitzi's mixed up in it, that's what she thinks. Awful temper she 'as, and the airs she gives herself! Called Mrs Huggins a working woman to her face the other morning.'

Craddock stood a moment, checking over in his orderly mind the substance of the old gardener's remarks. It gave him a good cross-section of rural opinion in Chipping Cleghorn, but he didn't think there was anything to help him in his task. He turned away and the old man called after him grudgingly:

'Maybe you'd find her in the apple orchard. She's younger than I am for getting the apples down.'

And sure enough in the apple orchard Craddock found Phillipa Haymes. His first view was a pair of nice legs encased in breeches sliding easily down the trunk of a tree. Then Phillipa, her face flushed, her fair hair ruffled by the branches, stood looking at him in a startled fashion.

'Make a good Rosalind,' Craddock thought automatically, for Detective-Inspector Craddock was a Shakespeare enthusiast and had played the part of the melancholy Jaques with great success in a performance of *As You Like it* for the Police Orphanage.

A moment later he amended his views. Phillipa Haymes was too wooden for Rosalind, her fairness and her impassivity were intensely English, but English of the twentieth rather than of the sixteenth century. Well-bred, unemotional English, without a spark of mischief.

'Good morning, Mrs Haymes. I'm sorry if I startled you. I'm Detective-Inspector Craddock of the Middleshire Police. I wanted to have a word with you.'

'About last night?'

'Yes.'

'Will it take long? Shall we –?'

She looked about her rather doubtfully.

Craddock indicated a fallen tree trunk.

'Rather informal,' he said pleasantly, 'but I don't want to interrupt your work longer than necessary.'

'Thank you.'

'It's just for the record. You came in from work at what time last night?'

'At about half-past five. I'd stayed about twenty minutes later in order to finish some watering in the greenhouse.'

'You came in by which door?'

'The side door. One cuts across by the ducks and the hen-house from the drive. It saves you going round, and besides it avoids dirtying up the front porch. I'm in rather a mucky state sometimes.'

'You always come in that way?'

'Yes.'

'The door was unlocked?'

'Yes. During the summer it's usually wide open. This time of the year it's shut but not locked. We all go out and in a good deal that way. I locked it when I came in.'

'Do you always do that?'

'I've been doing it for the last week. You see, it gets dark at six. Miss Blacklock goes out to shut up the ducks and the hens sometimes in the evening, but she very often goes out through the kitchen door.'

'And you are quite sure you did lock the side door this time?'

'I really am quite sure about that.'

'Quite so, Mrs Haymes. And what did you do when you came in?'

'Kicked off my muddy footwear and went upstairs and had a bath and changed. Then I came down and found that a kind of party was in progress. I hadn't known anything about this funny advertisement until then.'

'Now please describe just what occurred when the hold-up happened.'

'Well, the lights went out suddenly –'

'Where were you?'

'By the mantelpiece. I was searching for my lighter which I thought I had put down there. The lights went out – and everybody giggled. Then the door was flung open and this man shone a torch on us and flourished a revolver and told us to put our hands up.'

'Which you proceeded to do?'

'Well, I didn't actually. I thought it was just fun, and I was tired and I didn't think I needed really to put them up.'

'In fact, you were bored by the whole thing?'

'I was, rather. And then the revolver went off. The shots sounded deafening and I was really frightened. The torch went whirling round and dropped and went out, and then Mitzi started screaming. It was just like a pig being killed.'

'Did you find the torch very dazzling?'

'No, not particularly. It was quite a strong one, though. It lit up Miss

Bunner for a moment and she looked quite like a turnip ghost – you know, all white and staring with her mouth open and her eyes starting out of her head.'

'The man moved the torch?'

'Oh, yes, he played it all round the room.'

'As though he were looking for someone?'

'Not particularly, I should say.'

'And after that, Mrs Haymes?'

Phillipa Haymes frowned.

'Oh, it was all a terrible muddle and confusion. Edmund Swettenham and Patrick Simmons switched on their lighters and they went out into the hall and we followed, and someone opened the dining-room door – the lights hadn't fused there – and Edmund Swettenham gave Mitzi a terrific slap on the cheek and brought her out of her screaming fit, and after that it wasn't so bad.'

'You saw the body of the dead man?'

'Yes.'

'Was he known to you? Had you ever seen him before?'

'Never.'

'Have you any opinion as to whether his death was accidental, or do you think he shot himself deliberately?'

'I haven't the faintest idea.'

'You didn't see him when he came to the house previously?'

'No. I believe it was in the middle of the morning and I shouldn't have been there. I'm out all day.'

'Thank you, Mrs Haymes. One thing more. You haven't any valuable jewellery? Rings, bracelets, anything of that kind?'

Phillipa shook her head.

'My engagement ring – a couple of brooches.'

'And as far as you know, there was nothing of particular value in the house?'

'No. I mean there is some quite nice silver – but nothing out of the ordinary.'

'Thank you, Mrs Haymes.'

As Craddock retraced his steps through the kitchen garden he came face to face with a large red-faced lady, carefully corseted.

'Good morning,' she said belligerently. 'What do you want here?'

'Mrs Lucas? I am Detective-Inspector Craddock.'

'Oh, that's who you are? I beg your pardon. I don't like strangers forcing their way into my garden wasting the gardeners' time. But I quite understand you have to do your duty.'

'Quite so.'

'May I ask if we are to expect a repetition of that outrage last night at Miss Blacklock's? Is it a gang?'

'We are satisfied, Mrs Lucas, that it was *not* the work of a gang.'

'There are far too many robberies nowadays. The police are getting slack.' Craddock did not reply. 'I suppose you've been talking to Phillipa Haymes?'

'I wanted her account as an eye-witness.'

'You couldn't have waited until one o'clock, I suppose? After all, it would be fairer to question her in *her* time, rather than in *mine* . . .'

'I'm anxious to get back to headquarters.'

'Not that one expects consideration nowadays. Or a decent day's work. On duty late, half an hour's pottering. A break for elevenses at ten o'clock. No work done at all the moment the rain starts. When you want the lawn mown there's always something wrong with the mower. And off duty five or ten minutes before the proper time.'

'I understood from Mrs Haymes that she left here at twenty minutes past five yesterday instead of five o'clock.'

'Oh, I dare say she did. Give her her due, Mrs Haymes is quite keen on her work, though there have been days when I have come out here and not been able to find her anywhere. She is a lady by birth, of course, and one feels it's one's duty to do something for these poor young war widows. Not that it isn't very inconvenient. Those long school holidays and the arrangement is that she has extra time off then. I told her that there are really excellent camps nowadays where children can be sent and where they have a delightful time and enjoy it far more than wandering about with their parents. They need practically not come home at all in the summer holidays.'

'But Mrs Haymes didn't take kindly to that idea?'

'She's as obstinate as a mule, that girl. Just the time of year when I want the tennis court mowed and marked nearly every day. Old Ashe gets the lines crooked. But *my* convenience is never considered!'

'I presume Mrs Haymes takes a smaller salary than is usual?'

'Naturally. What else could she expect?'

'Nothing, I'm sure,' said Craddock. 'Good morning, Mrs Lucas.'

★   ★   ★

'It was dreadful,' said Mrs Swettenham happily. 'Quite – quite – dreadful, and what I say is that they ought to be far more careful what advertisements they accept at the *Gazette* office. At the time, when I read it, I thought it was very odd. I said so, didn't I, Edmund?'

'Do you remember just what you were doing when the lights went out, Mrs Swettenham?' asked the Inspector.

'How that reminds me of my old Nannie! *Where was Moses when the light went out?* The answer, of course, was "In the Dark." Just like us yesterday evening. All standing about and wondering what was going to happen. And then, you know, the *thrill* when it suddenly went pitch black. And the door opening – just a dim figure standing there with a revolver and that blinding light and a menacing voice saying "Your money or your life!" Oh, I've never enjoyed anything so much. And then a minute later, of course, it was all *dreadful. Real* bullets, just *whistling* past our ears! It must have been just like the Commandos in the war.'

'Whereabouts were you standing or sitting at the time, Mrs Swettenham?'

'Now let me see, where was I? Who was I talking to, Edmund?'

'I really haven't the least idea, Mother.'

'Was it Miss Hinchcliffe I was asking about giving the hens cod liver oil in the cold weather? Or was it Mrs Harmon – no, she'd only just arrived. I think I was just saying to Colonel Easterbrook that I thought it was really very dangerous to have an atom research station in England. It ought to be on some lonely island in case the radio activity gets loose.'

'You don't remember if you were sitting or standing?'

'Does it really matter, Inspector? I was somewhere over by the window or near the mantelpiece, because I know I was *quite* near the clock when it struck. Such a thrilling moment! Waiting to see if anything might be going to happen.'

'You describe the light from the torch as blinding. Was it turned full on to you?'

'It was right in my eyes. I couldn't see a thing.'

'Did the man hold it still, or did he move it about, from person to person?'

'Oh, I don't really know. Which did he do, Edmund?'

'It moved rather slowly over us all, so as to see what we were all doing, I suppose, in case we should try and rush him.'

'And where exactly in the room were *you*, Mr Swettenham?'

'I'd been talking to Julia Simmons. We were both standing up in the middle of the room – the long room.'

'Was everyone in that room, or was there anyone in the far room?'

'Phillipa Haymes had moved in there, I think. She was over by that far mantelpiece. I think she was looking for something.'

'Have you any idea as to whether the third shot was suicide or an accident?'

'I've no idea at all. The man seemed to swerve round very suddenly and then crumple up and fall – but it was all very confused. You must realize that you couldn't really see anything. And then that refugee girl started yelling the place down.'

'I understand it was you who unlocked the dining-room door and let her out?'

'Yes.'

'The door was definitely locked on the outside?'

Edmund looked at him curiously.

'Certainly it was. Why, you don't imagine –?'

'I just like to get my facts quite clear. Thank you, Mr Swettenham.'

Inspector Craddock was forced to spend quite a long time with Colonel and Mrs Easterbrook. He had to listen to a long disquisition on the psychological aspect of the case.

'The psychological approach – that's the only thing nowadays,' the Colonel told him. 'You've got to understand your criminal. Now the whole set-up here is quite plain to a man who's had the wide experience that I have. Why does this fellow put that advert in? Psychology. He wants to advertise himself – to focus attention on himself. He's been passed over, perhaps despised as a foreigner by the other employees at the Spa Hotel. A girl has turned him down, perhaps. He wants to rivet her attention on him. Who is the idol of the cinema nowadays – the gangster – the tough guy? Very well, he will be a tough guy. Robbery with violence. A mask? A revolver? But he wants an audience – he must have an audience. So he arranges for an audience. And then, at the supreme moment, his part runs away with him – he's more than a burglar. He's a killer. He shoots – blindly –'

Inspector Craddock caught gladly at a word:

'You say "blindly", Colonel Easterbrook. You didn't think that he was firing deliberately at one particular object – at Miss Blacklock, that is to say?'

'No, no. He just loosed off, as I say, blindly. And that's what brought him to himself. The bullet hit someone – actually it was only a graze, but he didn't know that. He comes to himself with a bang. All this –

this make-believe he's been indulging in – is *real*. He's shot at someone – perhaps killed someone . . . It's all up with him. And so in blind panic he turns the revolver on himself.'

Colonel Easterbrook paused, cleared his throat appreciatively and said in a satisfied voice, 'Plain as a pikestaff, that's what it is, plain as a pikestaff.'

'It really is wonderful,' said Mrs Easterbrook, 'the way you know exactly what happened, Archie.'

Her voice was warm with admiration.

Inspector Craddock thought it was wonderful, too, but he was not quite so warmly appreciative.

'Exactly where were you in the room, Colonel Easterbrook, when the actual shooting business took place?'

'I was standing with my wife – near a centre table with some flowers on it.'

'I caught hold of your arm, didn't I, Archie, when it happened? I was simply scared to death. I just had to hold on to you.'

'Poor little kitten,' said the Colonel playfully.

The Inspector ran Miss Hinchcliffe to earth by a pigsty.

'Nice creatures, pigs,' said Miss Hinchcliffe, scratching a wrinkled pink back. 'Coming on well, isn't he? Good bacon round about Christmas time. Well, what do you want to see me about? I told your people last night I hadn't the least idea who the man was. Never seen him anywhere in the neighbourhood snooping about or anything of that sort. Our Mrs Mopp says he came from one of the big hotels in Medenham Wells. Why didn't he hold up someone there if he wanted to? Get a much better haul.'

That was undeniable – Craddock proceeded with his inquiries.

'Where were you exactly when the incident took place?'

'Incident! Reminds me of my A.R.P. days. Saw some incidents then, I can tell you. Where was I when the shooting started? That what you want to know?'

'Yes.'

'Leaning up against the mantelpiece hoping to God someone would offer me a drink soon,' replied Miss Hinchcliffe promptly.

'Do you think that the shots were fired blindly, or aimed carefully at one particular person?'

'You mean aimed at Letty Blacklock? How the devil should I know? Damned hard to sort out what your impressions really were or what really happened after it's all over. All I know is the lights went out, and that torch went whirling round dazzling us all, and then the shots were fired and I thought to myself, "If that damned young fool Patrick Simmons is playing his jokes with a loaded revolver somebody will get hurt."'

'You thought it was Patrick Simmons?'

'Well, it seemed likely. Edmund Swettenham is intellectual and writes books and doesn't care for horseplay, and old Colonel Easterbrook wouldn't think that sort of thing funny. But Patrick's a wild boy. However, I apologize to him for the idea.'

'Did your friend think it might be Patrick Simmons?'

'Murgatroyd? You'd better talk to her yourself. Not that you'll get any sense out of her. She's down the orchard. I'll yell for her if you like.'

Miss Hinchcliffe raised her stentorian voice in a powerful bellow:

'Hi-youp, Murgatroyd . . .'

'Coming . . .' floated back a thin cry.

'Hurry up – Polieece,' bellowed Miss Hinchcliffe.

Miss Murgatroyd arrived at a brisk trot very much out of breath. Her skirt was down at the hem and her hair was escaping from an inadequate hair net. Her round, good-natured face beamed.

'Is it Scotland Yard?' she asked breathlessly. 'I'd no idea. Or I wouldn't have left the house.'

'We haven't called in Scotland Yard yet, Miss Murgatroyd. I'm Inspector Craddock from Milchester.'

'Well, that's very nice, I'm sure,' said Miss Murgatroyd vaguely. 'Have you found any clues?'

'Where were you at the time of the crime, that's what he wants to know, Murgatroyd?' said Miss Hinchcliffe. She winked at Craddock.

'Oh, dear,' gasped Miss Murgatroyd. 'Of course. I ought to have been prepared. *Alibis*, of course. Now, let me see, I was just with everybody else.'

'You weren't with me,' said Miss Hinchcliffe.

'Oh, dear, Hinch, wasn't I? No, of course, I'd been admiring the chrysanthemums. Very poor specimens, really. And then it all happened – only I didn't really know it had happened – I mean I didn't know that anything like that had happened. I didn't imagine for a moment that it was a real revolver – and all so awkward in the dark, and that dreadful screaming. I got it all wrong, you know. I thought *she* was being murdered – I mean the refugee girl. I thought she was having her throat cut across the hall somewhere. I didn't know it was *him* – I mean, I didn't even know there was a man. It was really just a voice, you know, saying, "Put them up, please."'

'"Stick 'em up!"' Miss Hinchcliffe corrected. 'And no suggestion of "please" about it.'

'It's so terrible to think that until that girl started screaming I was actually enjoying myself. Only being in the dark was very awkward and I got a knock on my corn. Agony, it was. Is there anything more you want to know, Inspector?'

'No,' said Inspector Craddock, eyeing Miss Murgatroyd speculatively. 'I don't really think there is.'

Her friend gave a short bark of laughter.

'He's got you taped, Murgatroyd.'

'I'm sure, Hinch,' said Miss Murgatroyd, 'that I'm only too willing to say anything I can.'

'He doesn't want that,' said Miss Hinchcliffe.

She looked at the Inspector. 'If you're doing this geographically I suppose you'll go to the Vicarage next. You might get something there. Mrs Harmon looks as vague as they make them – but I sometimes think she's got brains. Anyway, she's got something.'

As they watched the Inspector and Sergeant Fletcher stalk away, Amy Murgatroyd said breathlessly:

'Oh, Hinch, was I very awful? I do get so flustered!'

'Not at all,' Miss Hinchcliffe smiled. 'On the whole, I should say you did very well.'

Inspector Craddock looked round the big shabby room with a sense of pleasure. It reminded him a little of his own Cumberland home. Faded chintz, big shabby chairs, flowers and books strewn about, and a spaniel in a basket. Mrs Harmon, too, with her distraught air, and her general disarray and her eager face he found sympathetic.

But she said at once, frankly, 'I shan't be any help to you. Because I shut my eyes. I hate being dazzled. And then there were shots and I screwed them up tighter than ever. And I did wish, oh, I did wish, that it had been a *quiet* murder. I don't like bangs.'

'So you didn't see anything.' The Inspector smiled at her. 'But you heard –?'

'Oh, my goodness, yes, there was plenty to *hear*. Doors opening and shutting, and people saying silly things and gasping and old Mitzi screaming like a steam engine – and poor Bunny squealing like a trapped rabbit. And everyone pushing and falling over everyone else. However, when there really didn't seem to be any more bangs coming, I opened my eyes. Everyone was out in the hall then, with candles. And then the lights came on and suddenly it was all as usual – I don't mean really as usual, but we were ourselves again, not just – people in the dark. People in the dark are quite different, aren't they?'

'I think I know what you mean, Mrs Harmon.'

Mrs Harmon smiled at him.

'And there he was,' she said. 'A rather weaselly-looking foreigner – all pink and surprised-looking – lying there dead – with a revolver beside him. It didn't – oh, it didn't seem to make *sense*, somehow.'

It did not make sense to the Inspector, either.

The whole business worried him.

CHAPTER 8

ENTER MISS MARPLE

Craddock laid the typed transcript of the various interviews before the Chief Constable. The latter had just finished reading the wire received from the Swiss Police.

'So he had a police record all right,' said Rydesdale. 'H'm – very much as one thought.'

'Yes, sir.'

'Jewellery . . . h'm, yes . . . falsified entries . . . yes . . . cheque . . . Definitely a dishonest fellow.'

'Yes, sir – in a small way.'

'Quite so. And small things lead to large things.'

'I wonder, sir.'

The Chief Constable looked up.

'Worried, Craddock?'

'Yes, sir.'

'Why? It's a straightforward story. Or isn't it? Let's see what all these people you've been talking to have to say.'

He drew the report towards him and read it through rapidly.

'The usual thing – plenty of inconsistencies and contradictions. Different people's accounts of a few moments of stress never agree. But the main picture seems clear enough.'

'I know, sir – but it's an unsatisfactory picture. If you know what I mean – it's the wrong picture.'

'Well, let's take the facts. Rudi Scherz took the 5.20 bus from Medenham to Chipping Cleghorn arriving there at six o'clock. Evidence of conductor and two passengers. From the bus stop he walked away in the direction of Little Paddocks. He got into the house with no particular difficulty – probably through the front door. He held up the company with a revolver, he fired two shots, one of which slightly wounded Miss Blacklock, then he killed himself with a third shot, whether accidentally or deliberately there is not sufficient evidence to show. The reasons *why* he did all this are profoundly unsatisfactory, I agree. But *why* isn't really a question we are called upon to answer. A Coroner's jury may bring it in suicide – or accidental death. Whichever verdict it is, it's the same as far as we're concerned. We can write finis.'

'You mean we can always fall back upon Colonel Easterbrook's psychology,' said Craddock gloomily.

Rydesdale smiled.

'After all, the Colonel's probably had a good deal of experience,' he said. 'I'm pretty sick of the psychological jargon that's used so glibly about everything nowadays – but we can't really rule it out.'

'I still feel the picture's all wrong, sir.'

'Any reason to believe that somebody in the set-up at Chipping Cleghorn is lying to you?'

Craddock hesitated.

'I think the foreign girl knows more than she lets on. But that may be just prejudice on my part.'

'You think she might possibly have been in it with this fellow? Let him into the house? Put him up to it?'

'Something of the kind. I wouldn't put it past her. But that surely indicates that there really was something valuable, money or jewellery, in the house, and that doesn't seem to have been the case. Miss Blacklock negatived it quite decidedly. So did the others. That leaves us with the proposition that there was something valuable in the house that nobody knew about –'

'Quite a best-seller plot.'

'I agree it's ridiculous, sir. The only other point is Miss Bunner's certainty that it was a definite attempt by Scherz to murder Miss Blacklock.'

'Well, from what you say – and from her statement, this Miss Bunner –'

'Oh, I agree, sir,' Craddock put in quickly, 'she's an utterly unreliable witness. Highly suggestible. Anyone could put a thing into her head – but the interesting thing is that this is quite her own theory – no one *has* suggested it to her. Everybody else negatives it. For once she's *not* swimming with the tide. It definitely *is* her own impression.'

'And why should Rudi Scherz want to kill Miss Blacklock?'

'There you are, sir. I don't know. Miss Blacklock doesn't know – unless she's a much better liar than I think she is. Nobody knows. So presumably it isn't true.'

He sighed.

'Cheer up, Craddock,' said the Chief Constable. 'I'm taking you off to lunch with Sir Henry and myself. The best that the Royal Spa Hotel in Medenham Wells can provide.'

'Thank you, sir.' Craddock looked slightly surprised.

'You see, we received a letter –' He broke off as Sir Henry Clithering entered the room. 'Ah, there you are, Henry.'

Sir Henry, informal this time, said, 'Morning, Dermot.'

'I've got something for you, Henry,' said the Chief Constable.

'What's that?'

'Authentic letter from an old Pussy. Staying at the Royal Spa Hotel. Something she thinks we might like to know in connection with this Chipping Cleghorn business.'

'The old Pussies,' said Sir Henry triumphantly. 'What did I tell you? They hear everything. They see everything. And, unlike the famous adage, they speak all evil. What's this particular one got hold of?'

Rydesdale consulted the letter.

'Writes just like my old grandmother,' he complained. 'Spiky. Like a spider in the ink bottle, and all underlined. A good deal about how she hopes it won't be taking up our valuable time, but might possibly be of some slight assistance, etc., etc. What's her name? Jane – something – Murple – no, Marple, Jane Marple.'

'Ye Gods and Little Fishes,' said Sir Henry, 'can it be? George, it's my own particular, one and only, four-starred Pussy. The super Pussy of all old Pussies. And she has managed somehow to be at Medenham Wells, instead of peacefully at home in St Mary Mead, just at the right time to be mixed up in a murder. Once more a murder is announced – for the benefit and enjoyment of Miss Marple.'

'Well, Henry,' said Rydesdale sardonically, 'I'll be glad to see your paragon. Come on! We'll lunch at the Royal Spa and we'll interview the lady. Craddock, here, is looking highly sceptical.'

'Not at all, sir,' said Craddock politely.

He thought to himself that sometimes his godfather carried things a bit far.

★   ★   ★

Miss Jane Marple was very nearly, if not quite, as Craddock had pictured her. She was far more benignant than he had imagined and a good deal older. She seemed indeed very old. She had snow-white hair and a pink crinkled face and very soft innocent blue eyes, and she was heavily enmeshed in fleecy wool. Wool round her shoulders in the form of a lacy cape and wool that she was knitting and which turned out to be a baby's shawl.

She was all incoherent delight and pleasure at seeing Sir Henry, and became quite flustered when introduced to the Chief Constable and Detective-Inspector Craddock.

'But really, Sir Henry, how fortunate . . . how very fortunate. So long since I have seen you . . . Yes, my rheumatism. Very bad of late. Of course I couldn't have afforded this hotel (really fantastic what they charge nowadays) but Raymond – my nephew, Raymond West, you may remember him –'

'Everyone knows *his* name.'

'Yes, the dear boy has been so successful with his clever books – he prides himself upon never writing about anything pleasant. The dear boy insisted on paying all my expenses. And his dear wife is making a name for herself too, as an artist. Mostly jugs of dying flowers and broken combs on window-sills. I never dare tell her, but I still admire Blair Leighton and Alma Tadema. Oh, but I'm chattering. And the Chief Constable himself – indeed I never expected – so afraid I shall be taking up his time –'

'Completely ga-ga,' thought the disgusted Detective-Inspector Craddock.

'Come into the Manager's private room,' said Rydesdale. 'We can talk better there.'

When Miss Marple had been disentangled from her wool, and her spare knitting pins collected, she accompanied them, fluttering and protesting, to Mr Rowlandson's comfortable sitting-room.

'Now, Miss Marple, let's hear what you have to tell us,' said the Chief Constable.

Miss Marple came to the point with unexpected brevity.

'It was a cheque,' she said. 'He altered it.'

'He?'

'The young man at the desk here, the one who is supposed to have staged that hold-up and shot himself.'

'He altered a cheque, you say?'

Miss Marple nodded.

'Yes. I have it here.' She extracted it from her bag and laid it on the table. 'It came this morning with my others from the Bank. You can see, it was for seven pounds, and he altered it to seventeen. A stroke in front of the 7, and *teen* added after the word seven with a nice artistic little blot just blurring the whole word. Really very nicely done. A certain amount of *practice*, I should say. It's the same ink, because I wrote the cheque actually at the desk. I should think he'd done it quite often before, wouldn't you?'

'He picked the wrong person to do it to, this time,' remarked Sir Henry.

Miss Marple nodded agreement.

'Yes. I'm afraid he would never have gone very far in crime. I was quite the wrong person. Some busy young married woman, or some girl having a love affair – that's the kind who write cheques for all sorts of different sums and don't really look through their passbooks carefully. But an old woman who has to be careful of the pennies, and who has formed habits – that's quite the wrong person to choose. Seventeen pounds is a sum I *never* write a cheque for. Twenty pounds, a round sum, for the monthly wages and books. And as for my personal expenditure, I usually cash seven – it used to be five, but everything has gone up so.'

'And perhaps he reminded you of someone?' prompted Sir Henry, mischief in his eye.

Miss Marple smiled and shook her head at him.

'You are very naughty, Sir Henry. As a matter of fact he *did*. Fred Tyler, at the fish shop. Always slipped an extra 1 in the shillings column. Eating so much fish as we do nowadays, it made a long bill, and lots of people never added it up. Just ten shillings in his pocket every time, not much but enough to get himself a few neckties and take Jessie Spragge (the girl in the draper's) to the pictures. Cut a splash, that's what these young fellows want to do. Well, the very first week I was here, there was a mistake in my bill. I pointed it out to the young man and he apologized very nicely and looked very much upset, but I thought to myself then: "You've got a shifty eye, young man."

'What I mean by a shifty eye,' continued Miss Marple, 'is the kind that looks very straight at you and never looks away or blinks.'

Craddock gave a sudden movement of appreciation. He thought to himself 'Jim Kelly to the life,' remembering a notorious swindler he had helped to put behind bars not long ago.

'Rudi Scherz was a thoroughly unsatisfactory character,' said Rydesdale. 'He's got a police record in Switzerland, we find.'

'Made the place too hot for him, I suppose, and came over here with forged papers?' said Miss Marple.

'Exactly,' said Rydesdale.

'He was going about with the little red-haired waitress from the dining-room,' said Miss Marple. 'Fortunately I don't think her heart's affected at all. She just liked to have someone a bit "different", and he used to give her flowers and chocolates which the English boys don't do much. Has she told you all she knows?' she asked, turning suddenly to Craddock. 'Or not quite all yet?'

'I'm not absolutely sure,' said Craddock cautiously.

'I think there's a little to come,' said Miss Marple. 'She's looking very worried. Brought me kippers instead of herrings this morning, and forgot the milk jug. Usually she's an excellent waitress. Yes, she's worried. Afraid she might have to give evidence or something like that. But I expect' – her candid blue eyes swept over the manly proportions and handsome face of Detective-Inspector Craddock with truly feminine Victorian appreciation – 'that *you* will be able to persuade her to tell you all she knows.'

Detective-Inspector Craddock blushed and Sir Henry chuckled.

'It might be important,' said Miss Marple. 'He may have told her who it was.'

Rydesdale stared at her.

'Who what was?'

'I express myself so badly. Who it was who put him up to it, I mean.'

'So you think someone put him up to it?'

Miss Marple's eyes widened in surprise.

'Oh, but surely – I mean . . . Here's a personable young man – who filches a little bit here and a little bit there – alters a small cheque, perhaps helps himself to a small piece of jewellery if it's left lying around, or takes a little money from the till – all sorts of small petty thefts. Keeps himself going in ready money so that he can dress well, and take a girl about – all that sort of thing. And then suddenly he goes off, with a revolver, and holds up a room full of people, and shoots at someone. He'd *never* have done a thing like that – not for a moment! He wasn't that kind of person. It doesn't make *sense*.'

Craddock drew in his breath sharply. That was what Letitia Blacklock had said. What the Vicar's wife had said. What he himself felt with increasing force. *It didn't make sense.* And now Sir Henry's old Pussy was saying it, too, with complete certainty in her fluting old lady's voice.

'Perhaps you'll tell us, Miss Marple,' he said, and his voice was suddenly aggressive, 'what did happen, then?'

She turned on him in surprise.

'But how should I know what happened? There was an account in the paper – but it says so little. One can make conjectures, of course, but one has no accurate information.'

'George,' said Sir Henry, 'would it be very unorthodox if Miss Marple were allowed to read the notes of the interviews Craddock had with these people at Chipping Cleghorn?'

'It may be unorthodox,' said Rydesdale, 'but I've not got where I am by being orthodox. She can read them. I'd be curious to hear what she has to say.'

Miss Marple was all embarrassment.

'I'm afraid you've been listening to Sir Henry. Sir Henry is always too kind. He thinks too much of any little observations I may have made in the past. Really, I have no gifts – no gifts at all – except perhaps a certain knowledge of human nature. People, I find, are apt to be far too trustful. I'm afraid that I have a tendency always to believe the *worst*. Not a nice trait. But so often justified by subsequent events.'

'Read these,' said Rydesdale, thrusting the typewritten sheets upon her. 'They won't take you long. After all, these people are your kind – you must know a lot of people like them. You may be able to spot something that we haven't. The case is just going to be closed. Let's have an amateur's opinion on it before we shut up the files. I don't mind telling you that Craddock here isn't satisfied. He says, like you, that it doesn't make sense.'

There was silence whilst Miss Marple read. She put the typewritten sheets down at last.

'It's very interesting,' she said with a sigh. 'All the different things that people say – and think. The things they see – or think that they see. And all so complex, nearly all so trivial and if one thing isn't trivial, it's so hard to spot which one – like a needle in a haystack.'

Craddock felt a twinge of disappointment. Just for a moment or two, he wondered if Sir Henry might be right about this funny old lady. She might have put her finger on something – old people were often very sharp. He'd never, for instance, been able to conceal anything from his own great aunt Emma. She had finally told him that his nose twitched when he was about to tell a lie.

But just a few fluffy generalities, that was all that Sir Henry's famous Miss Marple could produce. He felt annoyed with her and said rather curtly:

'The truth of the matter is that the facts are indisputable. Whatever conflicting details these people give, they all saw one thing. They saw a masked man with a revolver and a torch open the door and hold them up, and whether they think he said "Stick 'em up" or "Your money or your life," or whatever phrase is associated with a hold-up in their minds, they *saw* him.'

'But surely,' said Miss Marple gently. 'They couldn't – actually – have seen anything at all . . .'

Craddock caught his breath. She'd got it! She was sharp, after all. He was testing her by that speech of his, but she hadn't fallen for it. It didn't actually make any difference to the facts, or to what happened, but she'd realized, as he'd realized, that those people who had seen a masked man holding them up couldn't really have *seen* him at all.

'If I understand rightly,' Miss Marple had a pink flush on her cheeks, her eyes were bright and pleased as a child's, 'there wasn't any light in the hall outside – and not on the landing upstairs either?'

'That's right,' said Craddock.

'And so, if a man stood in the doorway and flashed a powerful torch into the room, *nobody could see anything but the torch*, could they?'

'No, they couldn't. I tried it out.'

'And so when some of them say they saw a masked man, etc., they are really, though they don't realize it, recapitulating from what they saw *afterwards* – when the lights came on. So it really all fits in very well, doesn't it, on the assumption that Rudi Scherz was the – I think, "fall guy" is the expression I mean?'

Rydesdale stared at her in such surprise that she grew pinker still.

'I may have got the term wrong,' she murmured. 'I am not very clever about Americanisms – and I understand they change very quickly. I got it from one of Mr Dashiel Hammett's stories. (I understand from my nephew Raymond that he is considered at the top of the tree in what is called the "tough" style of literature.) A *"fall guy"*, if I understand it rightly, means someone who will be blamed for a crime really committed by someone else. This Rudi Scherz seems to me exactly the right type for that. Rather stupid really, you know, but full of cupidity and probably extremely credulous.'

Rydesdale said, smiling tolerantly:

'Are you suggesting that he was persuaded by someone to go out and take pot shots at a room full of people? Rather a tall order.'

'I think he was told that it was a *joke*,' said Miss Marple. 'He was paid for doing it, of course. Paid, that is, to put an advertisement in the newspaper, to go out and spy out the household premises, and then, on the night in question, he was to go there, assume a mask and a black cloak and throw open a door, brandishing a torch, and cry "Hands up!"'

'And fire off a revolver?'

'No, no,' said Miss Marple. 'He never had a revolver.'

'But everyone says –' began Rydesdale, and stopped.

'Exactly,' said Miss Marple. 'Nobody could possibly have *seen* a revolver even if he had one. And I don't think he had. I think that after he'd called "Hands up" somebody came up quietly behind him in the darkness and fired those two shots over his shoulder. It frightened him to death. He swung round and as he did so, that other person shot him and then let the revolver drop beside him . . .'

The three men looked at her. Sir Henry said softly:

'It's a possible theory.'

'But who is Mr X who came up in the darkness?' asked the Chief Constable.

Miss Marple coughed.

'You'll have to find out from Miss Blacklock who wanted to kill her.'

Good for old Dora Bunner, thought Craddock. Instinct against intelligence every time.

'So you think it was a deliberate attempt on Miss Blacklock's life,' asked Rydesdale.

'It certainly has that appearance,' said Miss Marple. 'Though there are one or two difficulties. But what I was really wondering about was whether there mightn't be a short cut. I've no doubt that whoever arranged this with Rudi Scherz took pains to tell him to keep his mouth shut, but if he talked to anybody it would probably be to that girl, Myrna Harris. And he may – he just may – have dropped some hint as to the kind of person who'd suggested the whole thing.'

'I'll see her now,' said Craddock, rising.

Miss Marple nodded.

'Yes, do, Inspector Craddock. I'll feel happier when you have. Because once she's told you anything she knows she'll be much safer.'

'Safer? . . . Yes, I see.'

He left the room. The Chief Constable said doubtfully, but tactfully:

'Well, Miss Marple, you've certainly given us something to think about.'

'I'm sorry about it, I am really,' said Myrna Harris. 'It's ever so nice of you not to be ratty about it. But you see Mum's the sort of person who fusses like anything. And it did look as though I'd – what's the phrase? – been an accessory before the fact' (the words ran glibly off her tongue).

'I mean, I was afraid you'd never take my word for it that I only thought it was just a bit of fun.'

Inspector Craddock repeated the reassuring phrase with which he had broken down Myrna's resistance.

'I will. I'll tell you *all* about it. But you will keep me out of it if you can because of Mum? It all started with Rudi breaking a date with me. We were going to the pictures that evening and then he said he wouldn't be able to come and I was a bit standoffish with him about it – because after all, it had been his idea and I don't fancy being stood up by a foreigner. And he said it wasn't his fault, and I said that was a likely story, and then he said he'd got a bit of a lark on that night – and that he wasn't going to be out of pocket by it and how would I fancy a wrist-watch? So I said, what do you mean by a lark? And he said not to tell anyone, but there was to be a party somewhere and he was to stage a sham hold-up. Then he showed me the advertisement he'd put in and I had to laugh. He was a bit scornful about it all. Said it was kid's stuff, really – but that was just like the English. They never really grew up – and of course, I said what did he mean by talking like that about Us – and we had a bit of an argument, but we made it up. Only you can understand, can't you, sir, that when I read all about it, and it hadn't been a joke at all and Rudi had shot someone and then shot himself – why, I didn't know *what* to do. I thought if I said I knew about it beforehand, it would look as though I were in on the whole thing. But it really did seem like a joke when he told me about it. I'd have sworn he meant it that way. I didn't even know he'd got a revolver. He never said anything about taking a revolver with him.'

Craddock comforted her and then asked the most important question.

'Who did he say it was who had arranged this party?'

But there he drew a blank.

'He never said who it was that was getting him to do it. I suppose nobody was, really. It was all his own doing.'

'He didn't mention a name? Did he say he – or she?'

'He didn't say anything except that it was going to be a scream. "I shall laugh to see all their faces." That's what he said.'

He hadn't had long to laugh, Craddock thought.

'It's only a theory,' said Rydesdale as they drove back to Medenham. 'Nothing to support it, nothing at all. Put it down as old maid's vapourings and let it go, eh?'

'I'd rather not do that, sir.'

'It's all very improbable. A mysterious X appearing suddenly in the darkness behind our Swiss friend. Where did he come from? Who was he? Where had he been?'

'He could have come in through the side door,' said Craddock, 'just as Scherz came. Or,' he added slowly, 'he could have come from the kitchen.'

'*She* could have come from the kitchen, you mean?'

'Yes, sir, it's a possibility. I've not been satisfied about that girl all along. She strikes me as a nasty bit of goods. All that screaming and hysterics – it could have been put on. She could have worked on this young fellow, let him in at the right moment, rigged the whole thing, shot him, bolted back into the dining-room, caught up her bit of silver and her chamois and started her screaming act.'

'Against that we have the fact that – er – what's his name – oh, yes, Edmund Swettenham, definitely says the key was turned on the outside of the door, and that he turned it to release her. Any other door into that part of the house?'

'Yes, there's a door to the back stairs and kitchen just under the stairs, but it seems the handle came off three weeks ago and nobody's come to put it on yet. In the meantime you can't open the door. I'm bound to say that story seems correct. The spindle and the two handles were on a shelf outside the door in the hall and they were thickly coated with dust, but of course a professional would have ways of opening that door all right.'

'Better look up the girl's record. See if her papers are in order. But it seems to me the whole thing is very theoretical.'

Again the Chief Constable looked inquiringly at his subordinate. Craddock replied quietly:

'I know, sir, and of course if you think the case ought to be closed, it must be. But I'd appreciate it if I could work on it for just a little longer.'

Rather to his surprise the Chief Constable said quietly and approvingly: 'Good lad.'

'There's the revolver to work on. If this theory is correct, it wasn't Scherz's revolver and certainly nobody so far has been able to say that Scherz ever had a revolver.'

'It's a German make.'

'I know, sir. But this country's absolutely full of Continental makes of guns. All the Americans brought them back and so did our chaps. You can't go by that.'

'True enough. Any other lines of inquiry?'

'There's got to be a motive. If there's anything in this theory at all, it means that last Friday's business wasn't a mere joke, and wasn't an ordinary hold-up, it was a cold-blooded attempt at murder. *Somebody tried to murder Miss Blacklock.* Now *why*? It seems to me that if anyone knows the answer to that it must be Miss Blacklock herself.'

'I understand she rather poured cold water on that idea?'

'She poured cold water on the idea that *Rudi Scherz* wanted to murder her. And she was quite right. And there's another thing, sir.'

'Yes?'

'Somebody might try again.'

'That would certainly prove the truth of the theory,' said the Chief Constable dryly. 'By the way, look after Miss Marple, won't you?'

'Miss Marple? Why?'

'I gather she is taking up residence at the Vicarage in Chipping Cleghorn and coming into Medenham Wells twice a week for her treatments. It seems that Mrs What'shername is the daughter of an old friend of Miss Marple's. Good sporting instincts, that old bean. Oh, well, I suppose she hasn't much excitement in her life and sniffing round after possible murderers gives her a kick.'

'I wish she wasn't coming,' said Craddock seriously.

'Going to get under your feet?'

'Not that, sir, but she's a nice old thing. I shouldn't like anything to happen to her . . . always supposing, I mean, that there's anything *in* this theory.'

CHAPTER 9

CONCERNING A DOOR

'I'm sorry to bother you again, Miss Blacklock –'

'Oh, it doesn't matter. I suppose, as the inquest was adjourned for a week, you're hoping to get more evidence?'

Detective-Inspector Craddock nodded.

'To begin with, Miss Blacklock, Rudi Scherz was not the son of the proprietor of the Hotel des Alpes at Montreux. He seems to have started his career as an orderly in a hospital at Berne. A good many of the patients missed small pieces of jewellery. Under another name he was a waiter at one of the small winter sports places. His speciality there was making out duplicate bills in the restaurant with items on one that didn't appear on the other. The difference, of course, went into his pocket. After that he was in a department store in Zürich. There losses from shoplifting were rather above the average whilst he was with them. It seems likely that the shoplifting wasn't entirely due to customers.'

'He was a picker up of unconsidered trifles, in fact?' said Miss Blacklock dryly. 'Then I was right in thinking that I had not seen him before?'

'You were quite right – no doubt you were pointed out to him at the Royal Spa Hotel and he pretended to recognize you. The Swiss police had begun to make his own country rather too hot for him, and he came over here with a very nice set of forged papers and took a job at the Royal Spa.'

'Quite a good hunting ground,' said Miss Blacklock dryly. 'It's extremely expensive and very well-off people stay there. Some of them are careless about their bills, I expect.'

'Yes,' said Craddock. 'There were prospects of a satisfactory harvest.'

Miss Blacklock was frowning.

'I see all that,' she said. 'But why come to Chipping Cleghorn? What does he think we've got here that could possibly be better than the rich Royal Spa Hotel?'

'You stick to your statement that there's nothing of especial value in the house?'

'Of course there isn't. *I* should know. I can assure you, Inspector, we've not got an unrecognized Rembrandt or anything like that.'

'Then it looks, doesn't it, as though your friend Miss Bunner was right? He came here to attack *you*.'

('There, Letty, what did I tell you!'

'Oh, nonsense, Bunny.')

'But is it nonsense?' said Craddock. 'I think, you know, that it's true.'

Miss Blacklock stared very hard at him.

'Now, let's get this straight. You really believe that this young man came out here – having previously arranged by means of an advertisement that half the village would turn up agog at that particular time –'

'But he mayn't have meant *that* to happen,' interrupted Miss Bunner eagerly. 'It may have been just a horrid sort of warning – to *you*, Letty – that's how I read it at the time – "*A murder is announced*" – I felt in my bones that it was sinister – if it had all gone as planned he would have shot you and got away – and how would anyone have ever known who it was?'

'That's true enough,' said Miss Blacklock. 'But –'

'I knew that advertisement wasn't a joke, Letty. I said so. And look at Mitzi – *she* was frightened, too!'

'Ah,' said Craddock, 'Mitzi. I'd like to know rather more about that young woman.'

'Her permit and papers are quite in order.'

'I don't doubt that,' said Craddock dryly. 'Scherz's papers appeared to be quite correct, too.'

'But why should this Rudi Scherz want to murder me? That's what you don't attempt to explain, Inspector Craddock.'

'There may have been someone behind Scherz,' said Craddock slowly. 'Have you thought of that?'

He used the words metaphorically though it flashed across his mind that if Miss Marple's theory was correct, the words would also be true in a literal sense. In any case they made little impression on Miss Blacklock, who still looked sceptical.

'The point remains the same,' she said. 'Why on earth should anyone want to murder *me*?'

'It's the answer to that that I want *you* to give me, Miss Blacklock.'

'Well, I can't! That's flat. I've no enemies. As far as I'm aware I've always lived on perfectly good terms with my neighbours. I don't know any guilty secrets about anyone. The whole idea is ridiculous! And if what you're hinting is that Mitzi has something to do with this, that's absurd, too. As Miss Bunner has just told you she was frightened to death when she saw that advertisement in the *Gazette*. She actually wanted to pack up and leave the house then and there.'

'That may have been a clever move on her part. She may have known you'd press her to stay.'

'Of course, if you've made up your mind about it, you'll find an answer to everything. But I can assure you that if Mitzi had taken an unreasoning dislike to me, she might conceivably poison my food, but I'm sure she wouldn't go in for all this elaborate rigmarole.

'The whole idea's absurd. I believe you police have got an anti-foreigner complex. Mitzi may be a liar but she's *not* a cold-blooded murderer. Go and bully her if you must. But when she's departed in a whirl of indignation, or shut herself up howling in her room, I've a good mind to make *you* cook the dinner. Mrs Harmon is bringing some old lady who is staying with her to tea this afternoon and I wanted Mitzi to make some little cakes – but I suppose you'll upset her completely. Can't you *possibly* go and suspect somebody else?'

*　*　*

Craddock went out to the kitchen. He asked Mitzi questions that he had asked her before and received the same answers.

Yes, she had locked the front door soon after four o'clock. No, she did not always do so, but that afternoon she had been nervous because of 'that dreadful advertisement'. It was no good locking the side door because Miss Blacklock and Miss Bunner went out that way to shut up the ducks and feed the chickens and Mrs Haymes usually came in that way from work.

'Mrs Haymes says she locked the door when she came in at 5.30.'

'Ah, and you believe her – oh, yes, you believe her . . .'

'Do you think we shouldn't believe her?'

'What does it matter what I think? You will not believe *me*.'

'Supposing you give us a chance. You think Mrs Haymes didn't lock that door?'

'I thinking she was very careful not to lock it.'

'What do you mean by that?' asked Craddock.

'That young man, he does not work alone. No, he knows *where* to come, he knows that *when* he comes a door will be left open for him – oh, very conveniently open!'

'What are you trying to say?'

'What is the use of what I say? You will not listen. You say I am a poor refugee girl who tells lies. You say that a fair-haired English lady, oh, no, *she* does not tell lies – she is so British – so honest. So you believe her and not me. But I could tell you. Oh, yes, I could tell you!'

She banged down a saucepan on the stove.

Craddock was in two minds whether to take notice of what might be only a stream of spite.

'We note everything we are told,' he said.

'I shall not tell you anything at all. Why should I? You are all alike. You persecute and despise poor refugees. If I say to you that when, a week before, that young man come to ask Miss Blacklock for money and she sends him away, as you say, with a flea in the ear – if I tell you that after that I hear him talking with Mrs Haymes – yes, out there in the summerhouse – all you say is that I make it up!'

And so you probably are making it up, thought Craddock. But he said aloud:

'You couldn't hear what was said out in the summerhouse.'

'There you are wrong,' screamed Mitzi triumphantly. 'I go out to get nettles – it makes very nice vegetables, nettles. They do not think so, but I cook it and not tell them. And I hear them talking in there. He say to her "But where can I hide?" And she say "I will show you" – and then she say, "At a quarter-past six," and I think, "Ach so! That is how you behave, my fine lady! After you come back from work, you go out to meet a man. You bring him into the house." Miss Blacklock, I think, she will not like that. She will turn you out. I will watch, I think, and listen and then I will tell Miss Blacklock. But I understand now I was wrong. It was not love she planned with him, it was to rob and to murder. But you will say I make all this up. Wicked Mitzi, you will say. I will take her to prison.'

Craddock wondered. She might be making it up. But possibly she might not. He asked cautiously:

'You are sure it was this Rudi Scherz she was talking to?'

'Of course I am sure. He just leave and I see him go from the drive across to the summerhouse. And presently,' said Mitzi defiantly, 'I go out to see if there are any nice young green nettles.'

Would there, the Inspector wondered, be any nice young green nettles in October? But he appreciated that Mitzi had had to produce a hurried reason for what had undoubtedly been nothing more than plain snooping.

'You didn't hear any more than what you have told me?'

Mitzi looked aggrieved.

'That Miss Bunner, the one with the long nose, she call and call me. Mitzi! Mitzi! So I have to go. Oh, she is irritating. Always interfering. Says she will teach me to cook. *Her* cooking! It tastes, yes, everything she does, of water, water, *water*!'

'Why didn't you tell me this the other day?' asked Craddock sternly.

'Because I did not remember – I did not think . . . Only afterwards do I say to myself, it was planned then – planned with *her*.'

'You are quite sure it was Mrs Haymes?'

'Oh, yes, I am sure. Oh, yes, I am very sure. She is a thief, that Mrs Haymes. A thief and the associate of thieves. What she gets for working in the garden, it is not enough for such a fine lady, no. She has to rob Miss Blacklock who has been kind to her. Oh, she is bad, bad, bad, that one!'

'Supposing,' said the Inspector, watching her closely, 'that someone was to say that *you* had been seen talking to Rudi Scherz?'

The suggestion had less effect than he had hoped for. Mitzi merely snorted and tossed her head.

'If anyone say they see me talking to him, that is lies, lies, lies, lies,' she said contemptuously. 'To tell lies about anyone, that is easy, but in England you have to prove them true. Miss Blacklock tells me that, and it is true, is it not? I do not speak with murderers and thieves. And no English policeman shall say I do. And how can I do cooking for lunch if you are here, talk, talk, talk? Go out of my kitchens, please. I want now to make a very careful sauce.'

Craddock went obediently. He was a little shaken in his suspicions of Mitzi. Her story about Phillipa Haymes had been told with great conviction. Mitzi might be a liar (he thought she was), but he fancied that there might be some substratum of truth in this particular tale. He resolved to speak to Phillipa on the subject. She had seemed to him when he questioned her a quiet, well-bred young woman. He had had no suspicion of her.

Crossing the hall, in his abstraction, he tried to open the wrong door. Miss Bunner, descending the staircase, hastily put him right.

'Not that door,' she said. 'It doesn't open. The next one to the left. Very confusing, isn't it? So many doors.'

'There are a good many,' said Craddock, looking up and down the narrow hall.

Miss Bunner amiably enumerated them for him.

'First the door to the cloakroom, and then the cloaks cupboard door and then the dining-room – that's on that side. And on this side, the dummy door that you were trying to get through and then there's the drawing-room door proper, and then the china cupboard and the door of the little flower room, and at the end the side door. Most confusing. Especially these two being so near together. I've often tried the wrong one by mistake. We used to have the hall table against it, as a matter of fact, but then we moved it along against the wall there.'

Craddock had noted, almost mechanically, a thin line horizontally across the panels of the door he had been trying to open. He realized now it was the mark where the table had been. Something stirred vaguely in his mind as he asked, 'Moved? How long ago?'

In questioning Dora Bunner there was fortunately no need to give a reason for any question. Any query on any subject seemed perfectly natural to the garrulous Miss Bunner who delighted in the giving of information, however trivial.

'Now let me see, really quite recently – ten days or a fortnight ago.'

'Why was it moved?'

'I really can't remember. Something to do with the flowers. I think Phillipa did a big vase – she arranges flowers quite beautifully – all autumn colouring and twigs and branches, and it was so big it caught your hair as you went past, and so Phillipa said, "Why not move the table along and anyway the flowers would look much better against the bare wall than against the panels of the door." Only we had to take down Wellington at Waterloo. Not a print I'm really very fond of. We put it under the stairs.'

'It's not really a dummy, then?' Craddock asked, looking at the door.

'Oh, no, it's a *real* door, if that's what you mean. It's the door of the small drawing-room, but when the rooms were thrown into one, one didn't need two doors, so this one was fastened up.'

'Fastened up?' Craddock tried it again, gently. 'You mean it's nailed up? Or just locked?'

'Oh, locked, I think, and bolted too.'

He saw the bolt at the top and tried it. The bolt slid back easily – too easily . . .

'When was it last open?' he asked Miss Bunner.

'Oh, years and years ago, I imagine. It's never been opened since I've been here, I know that.'

'You don't know where the key is?'

'There are a lot of keys in the hall drawer. It's probably among those.'

Craddock followed her and looked at a rusty assortment of old keys pushed far back in the drawer. He scanned them and selected one that looked different from the rest and went back to the door. The key fitted and turned easily. He pushed and the door slid open noiselessly.

'Oh, do be careful,' cried Miss Bunner. 'There may be something resting against it inside. We never open it.'

'Don't you?' said the Inspector.

His face now was grim. He said with emphasis:

'This door's been opened quite recently, Miss Bunner. The lock's been oiled and the hinges.'

She stared at him, her foolish face agape.

'But who could have done that?' she asked.

'That's what I mean to find out,' said Craddock grimly. He thought – 'X from outside? No – X was here – in this house – X was in the drawing-room that night . . .'

CHAPTER 10

....

PIP AND EMMA

Miss Blacklock listened to him this time with more attention. She was an intelligent woman, as he had known, and she grasped the implications of what he had to tell her.

'Yes,' she said quietly. 'That does alter things . . . No one had any right to meddle with that door. Nobody *has* meddled with it to my knowledge.'

'You see what it means,' the Inspector urged. 'When the lights went out, *anybody in this room the other night* could have slipped out of that door, come up behind Rudi Scherz and fired at you.'

'Without being seen or heard or noticed?'

'Without being seen or heard or noticed. Remember when the lights went out people moved, exclaimed, bumped into each other. And after that all that could be seen was the blinding light of the electric torch.'

Miss Blacklock said slowly, 'And you believe that one of those people – one of my nice commonplace neighbours – slipped out and tried to murder me? *Me?* But *why?* For goodness' sake, *why?*'

'I've a feeling that you *must* know the answer to that question, Miss Blacklock.'

'But I don't, Inspector. I can assure you, I don't.'

'Well, let's make a start. Who gets your money if you were to die?'

Miss Blacklock said rather reluctantly:

'Patrick and Julia. I've left the furniture in this house and a small annuity to Bunny. Really, I've not much to leave. I had holdings in German and Italian securities which became worthless, and what with taxation, and the lower percentages that are now paid on invested capital, I can assure you I'm not worth murdering – I put most of my money into an annuity about a year ago.'

'Still, you *have* some income, Miss Blacklock, and your nephew and niece would come into it.'

'And so Patrick and Julia would plan to murder me? I simply don't believe it. They're not desperately hard up or anything like that.'

'Do you know that for a fact?'

'No. I suppose I only know it from what they've told me . . . But I really refuse to suspect them. *Some* day I *might* be worth murdering, but not now.'

'What do you mean by some day you might be worth murdering, Miss Blacklock?' Inspector Craddock pounced on the statement.

'Simply that one day – possibly quite soon – I *may* be a very rich woman.'

'That sounds interesting. Will you explain?'

'Certainly. You may not know it, but for more than twenty years I was secretary to and closely associated with Randall Goedler.'

Craddock was interested. Randall Goedler had been a big name in the world of finance. His daring speculations and the rather theatrical publicity with which he surrounded himself had made him a personality not quickly forgotten. He had died, if Craddock remembered rightly, in 1937 or 1938.

'He's rather before your time, I expect,' said Miss Blacklock. 'But you've probably heard of him.'

'Oh, yes. He was a millionaire, wasn't he?'

'Oh, several times over – though his finances fluctuated. He always risked most of what he made on some new *coup*.'

She spoke with a certain animation, her eyes brightened by memory.

'Anyway he died a very rich man. He had no children. He left his fortune in trust for his wife during her lifetime and after death to me absolutely.'

A vague memory stirred in the Inspector's mind.

IMMENSE FORTUNE TO COME TO FAITHFUL SECRETARY

– something of that kind.

'For the last twelve years or so,' said Miss Blacklock with a slight twinkle, '*I've* had an excellent motive for murdering Mrs Goedler – but that doesn't help you, does it?'

'Did – excuse me for asking this – did Mrs Goedler resent her husband's disposition of his fortune?'

Miss Blacklock was now looking frankly amused.

'You needn't be so very discreet. What you really mean is, was I Randall Goedler's mistress? No, I wasn't. I don't think Randall ever gave me a sentimental thought, and I certainly didn't give him one. He was in love with Belle (his wife), and remained in love with her until he died. I think in all probability it was gratitude on his part that prompted his making his will. You see, Inspector, in the very early days, when Randall was still on an insecure footing, he came very near to disaster. It was a question of just a few thousands of actual cash. It was a big *coup*, and a very exciting one; daring, as all his schemes were; but he just hadn't got that little bit of cash to tide him over. I came to the rescue. I had a little money of my own. I believed in Randall. I sold every penny I had out and gave it to him. It did the trick. A week later he was an immensely wealthy man.

'After that, he treated me more or less as a junior partner. Oh! they were exciting days.' She sighed. 'I enjoyed it all thoroughly. Then my father died, and my only sister was left a hopeless invalid. I had to give it all up and go and look after her. Randall died a couple of years later. I had made quite a lot of money during our association and I didn't really expect him to leave me anything, but I was very touched, yes, and very proud to find that if Belle predeceased me (and she was one of those delicate creatures whom everyone always says won't live long) I was to inherit his entire fortune. I think really the poor man didn't know who to leave it to. Belle's a dear, and she was delighted about it. She's really a very sweet person. She lives up in Scotland. I haven't seen her for years – we just write at Christmas. You see, I went with my sister to a sanatorium in Switzerland just before the war. She died of consumption out there.'

She was silent for a moment or two, then said:

'I only came back to England just over a year ago.'

'You said you might be a rich woman very soon . . . How soon?'

'I heard from the nurse attendant who looks after Belle Goedler that Belle is sinking rapidly. It may be – only a few weeks.'

She added sadly:

'The money won't mean much to me now. I've got quite enough for my rather simple needs. Once I should have enjoyed playing the markets again – but now . . . Oh, well, one grows old. Still, you do see, Inspector, don't you, that if Patrick and Julia wanted to kill me for a financial reason they'd be crazy not to wait for another few weeks.'

'Yes, Miss Blacklock, but what happens if you should predecease Mrs Goedler? Who does the money go to then?'

'D'you know, I've never really thought. Pip and Emma, I suppose . . .'

Craddock stared and Miss Blacklock smiled.

'Does that sound rather crazy? I believe, if I predecease Belle, the money would go to the legal offspring – or whatever the term is – of Randall's only sister, Sonia. Randall had quarrelled with his sister. She married a man whom he considered a crook and worse.'

'And was he a crook?'

'Oh, definitely, I should say. But I believe a very attractive person to women. He was a Greek or a Roumanian or something – what was his name now – Stamfordis, Dmitri Stamfordis.'

'Randall Goedler cut his sister out of his will when she married this man?'

'Oh, Sonia was a very wealthy woman in her own right. Randall had already settled packets of money on her, as far as possible in a way so that her husband couldn't touch it. But I believe that when the lawyers urged him to put in someone in case I predeceased Belle, he reluctantly put down Sonia's offspring, simply because he couldn't think of anyone else and he wasn't the sort of man to leave money to charities.'

'And there were children of the marriage?'

'Well, there are Pip and Emma.' She laughed. 'I know it sounds ridiculous. All I know is that Sonia wrote once to Belle after her marriage, telling her to tell Randall that she was extremely happy and that she had just had twins and was calling them Pip and Emma. As far as I know she never wrote again. But Belle, of course, may be able to tell you more.'

Miss Blacklock had been amused by her own recital. The Inspector did not look amused.

'It comes to this,' he said. 'If you had been killed the other night, there are presumably at least two people in the world who would have come into a very large fortune. You are wrong, Miss Blacklock, when you say that there is no one who has a motive for desiring your death. There are two people, at least, who are vitally interested. How old would this brother and sister be?'

Miss Blacklock frowned.

'Let me see . . . 1922 . . . no – it's difficult to remember . . . I suppose about twenty-five or twenty-six.' Her face had sobered. 'But you surely don't think –?'

'I think somebody shot at you with the intent to kill you. I think it possible that that same person or persons might try again. I would like you, if you will, to be very *very* careful, Miss Blacklock. One murder has been arranged and did not come off. I think it possible that another murder may be arranged very soon.'

Phillipa Haymes straightened her back and pushed back a tendril of hair from her damp forehead. She was cleaning a flower border.

'Yes, Inspector?'

She looked at him inquiringly. In return he gave her a rather closer scrutiny than he had done before. Yes, a good-looking girl, a very English type with her pale ash-blonde hair and her rather long face. An obstinate chin and mouth. Something of repression – of tautness about her. The eyes were blue, very steady in their glance, and told you nothing at all. The sort of girl, he thought, who would keep a secret well.

'I'm sorry always to bother you when you're at work, Mrs Haymes,' he said, 'but I didn't want to wait until you came back for lunch. Besides, I thought it might be easier to talk to you here, away from Little Paddocks.'

'Yes, Inspector?'

No emotion and little interest in her voice. But was there a note of wariness – or did he imagine it?

'A certain statement has been made to me this morning. This statement concerns you.'

Phillipa raised her eyebrows very slightly.

'You told me, Mrs Haymes, that this man, Rudi Scherz, was quite unknown to you?'

'Yes.'

'That when you saw him there, dead, it was the first time you had set eyes on him. Is that so?'

'Certainly. I had never seen him before.'

'You did not, for instance, have a conversation with him in the summer-house of Little Paddocks?'

'In the *summer*house?'

He was almost sure he caught a note of fear in her voice.

'Yes, Mrs Haymes.'

'*Who* says so?'

'I am told that you had a conversation with this man, Rudi Scherz, and that he asked you where he could hide and you replied that you would show him, and that a time, a quarter-past six, was definitely mentioned. It would be a quarter-past six, roughly, when Scherz would get here from the bus stop on the evening of the hold-up.'

There was a moment's silence. Then Phillipa gave a short scornful laugh. She looked amused.

'I don't know who told you that,' she said. 'At least I can guess. It's a very silly, clumsy story – spiteful, of course. For some reason Mitzi dislikes me even more than she dislikes the rest of us.'

'You deny it?'

'Of course it's not true . . . I never met or saw Rudi Scherz in my life, and I was nowhere near the house that morning. I was over here, working.'

Inspector Craddock said very gently:

'Which morning?'

There was a momentary pause. Her eyelids flickered.

'Every morning. I'm here every morning. I don't get away until one o'clock.'

She added scornfully:

'It's no good listening to what Mitzi tells you. She tells lies all the time.'

'And that's that,' said Craddock when he was walking away with Sergeant Fletcher. 'Two young women whose stories flatly contradict each other. Which one am I to believe?'

'Everyone seems to agree that this foreign girl tells whoppers,' said Fletcher. 'It's been my experience in dealing with aliens that lying comes more easy than truth-telling. Seems to be clear she's got a spite against this Mrs Haymes.'

'So, if you were me, you'd believe Mrs Haymes?'

'Unless you've got reason to think otherwise, sir.'

And Craddock hadn't, not really – only the remembrance of a pair of over-steady blue eyes and the glib enunciation of the words *that morning*. For to the best of his recollection he hadn't said whether the interview in the summerhouse had taken place in the morning or the afternoon.

Still, Miss Blacklock, or if not Miss Blacklock, certainly Miss Bunner, might have mentioned the visit of the young foreigner who had come to cadge his fare back to Switzerland. And Phillipa Haymes might have therefore assumed that the conversation was supposed to have taken place on that particular morning.

But Craddock still thought that there had been a note of fear in her voice as she asked:

'In the *summer*house?'

He decided to keep an open mind on the subject.

It was very pleasant in the Vicarage garden. One of those sudden spells of autumn warmth had descended upon England. Inspector Craddock could never remember if it was St Martin's or St Luke's Summer, but he knew that it was very pleasant – and also very enervating. He sat in a deck chair provided for him by an energetic Bunch, just on her way to a Mothers' Meeting, and, well protected with shawls and a large rug round her knees, Miss Marple sat knitting beside him. The sunshine, the peace, the steady click of Miss Marple's knitting needles, all combined to produce a soporific feeling in the Inspector. And yet, at the same time, there was a nightmarish feeling at the back of his mind. It was like a familiar dream where an undertone of menace grows and finally turns Ease into Terror . . .

He said abruptly, 'You oughtn't to be here.'

Miss Marple's needles stopped clicking for a moment. Her placid china-blue eyes regarded him thoughtfully.

She said, 'I know what you mean. You're a very conscientious boy. But it's perfectly all right. Bunch's father (he was vicar of our parish, a very fine scholar) and her mother (who is a most remarkable woman – real spiritual power) are very old friends of mine. It's the most natural thing in the world that when I'm at Medenham I should come on here to stay with Bunch for a little.'

'Oh, perhaps,' said Craddock. 'But – but don't snoop around . . . I've a feeling – I have really – that it isn't *safe*.'

Miss Marple smiled a little.

'But I'm afraid,' she said, 'that we old women always do snoop. It would be very odd and much more noticeable if I didn't. Questions about mutual friends in different parts of the world and whether they remember so and so, and do they remember who it was that Lady Somebody's daughter married? All that helps, doesn't it?'

'Helps?' said the Inspector, rather stupidly.

'Helps to find out if people are who they say they are,' said Miss Marple.

She went on:

'Because that's what's worrying you, isn't it? And that's really the particular way the world has changed since the war. Take this place, Chipping Cleghorn, for instance. It's very much like St Mary Mead where I live. Fifteen years ago one *knew* who everybody was. The Bantrys in the big house – and the Hartnells and the Price Ridleys and the Weatherbys . . . They were people whose fathers and mothers and grandfathers and grandmothers, or whose aunts and uncles, had lived there before them. If somebody new came to live there, they brought letters of introduction, or they'd been in the same regiment or served in the same ship as someone there already. If anybody new – really new – really a stranger – came, well, they stuck out – everybody wondered about them and didn't rest till they found out.'

She nodded her head gently.

'But it's not like that any more. Every village and small country place is full of people who've just come and settled there without any ties to bring them. The big houses have been sold, and the cottages have been converted and changed. And people just come – and all you know about them is what they say of themselves. They've come, you see, from all over the world. People from India and Hong Kong and China, and people who used to live in France and Italy in little cheap places and odd islands. And people who've made a little money and can afford to retire. But nobody *knows* any more who anyone is. You can have Benares brassware in your house and talk about *tiffin* and *chota Hazri* – and you can have pictures of Taormina and talk about the English church and the library – like Miss Hinchcliffe and Miss Murgatroyd. You can come from the South of France, or have spent your life in the East. People take you at your own valuation. They don't wait to call until they've had a letter from a friend saying that the So-and-So's are delightful people and she's known them all their lives.'

And that, thought Craddock, was exactly what *was* oppressing him. He didn't *know*. There were just faces and personalities and they were backed up by ration books and identity cards – nice neat identity cards with numbers on them, without photographs or fingerprints. Anybody who took the trouble could have a suitable identity card – and partly because of that, the subtler links that had held together English social rural life had fallen apart. In a town nobody expected to know his neighbour. In the country now nobody knew his neighbour either, though possibly he still thought he did . . .

Because of the oiled door, Craddock knew that there had been some-body in Letitia Blacklock's drawing-room who was not the pleasant friendly country neighbour he or she pretended to be . . .

And because of that he was afraid for Miss Marple who was frail and old and who noticed things . . .

He said: 'We can, to a certain extent, check up on these people . . .' But he knew that that wasn't so easy. India and China and Hong Kong and the South of France . . . It wasn't as easy as it would have been fifteen years ago. There were people, as he knew only too well, who were going about the country with borrowed identities – borrowed from people who had met sudden death by 'incidents' in the cities. There were organizations who bought up identities, who faked identity and ration cards – there were a hundred small rackets springing into being. You *could* check up – but it would take time – and time was what he hadn't got, because Randall Goedler's widow was very near death.

It was then that, worried and tired, lulled by the sunshine, he told Miss Marple about Randall Goedler and about Pip and Emma.

'Just a couple of names,' he said. 'Nicknames at that! They mayn't exist. They may be respectable citizens living in Europe somewhere. On the other hand one, or both, of them may be here in Chipping Cleghorn.'

Twenty-five years old approximately – Who filled that description? He said, thinking aloud:

'That nephew and niece of hers – or cousins or whatever they are . . . I wonder when she saw them last –'

Miss Marple said gently: 'I'll find out for you, shall I?'

'Now, please, Miss Marple, don't –'

'It will be quite simple, Inspector, you really need not worry. And it won't be noticeable if I do it, because, you see, it won't be official. If there is anything wrong you don't want to put them on their guard.'

Pip and Emma, thought Craddock, Pip and Emma? He was getting obsessed by Pip and Emma. That attractive dare-devil young man, the good-looking girl with the cool stare . . .

He said: 'I may find out more about them in the next forty-eight hours. I'm going up to Scotland. Mrs Goedler, if she's able to talk, may know a good deal more about them.'

'I think that's a very wise move.' Miss Marple hesitated. 'I hope,' she murmured, 'that you have warned Miss Blacklock to be careful?'

'I've warned her, yes. And I shall leave a man here to keep an unobtrusive eye on things.'

He avoided Miss Marple's eye which said plainly enough that a policeman keeping an eye on things would be little good if the danger was in the family circle . . .

'And remember,' said Craddock, looking squarely at her, 'I've warned *you*.'

'I assure you, Inspector,' said Miss Marple, 'that I can take care of myself.'

CHAPTER 11

MISS MARPLE COMES TO TEA

If Letitia Blacklock seemed slightly absentminded when Mrs Harmon came to tea and brought a guest who was staying with her, Miss Marple, the guest in question, was hardly likely to notice the fact since it was the first time she had met her.

The old lady was very charming in her gentle gossipy fashion. She revealed herself almost at once to be one of those old ladies who have a constant preoccupation with burglars.

'They can get in anywhere, my dear,' she assured her hostess, 'absolutely *anywhere* nowadays. So many new American methods. I myself pin my faith to a very old-fashioned device. *A cabin hook and eye.* They can pick locks and draw back bolts but a brass hook and eye defeats them. Have you ever tried that?'

'I'm afraid we're not very good at bolts and bars,' said Miss Blacklock cheerfully. 'There's really nothing much to burgle.'

'A chain on the front door,' Miss Marple advised. 'Then the maid need only open it a crack and see who is there and they can't force their way in.'

'I expect Mitzi, our Mittel European, would love that.'

'The hold-up you had must have been very, very frightening,' said Miss Marple. 'Bunch has been telling me all about it.'

'I was scared stiff,' said Bunch.

'It was an alarming experience,' admitted Miss Blacklock.

'It really seems like Providence that the man tripped himself up and shot himself. These burglars are so *violent* nowadays. How did he get in?'

'Well, I'm afraid we don't lock our doors much.'

'Oh, Letty,' exclaimed Miss Bunner. 'I forgot to tell you the Inspector was most peculiar this morning. He insisted on opening the second door – you know – the one that's never been opened – the one over there. He hunted for the key and everything and said the door had been oiled. But I can't see why because –'

Too late she got Miss Blacklock's signal to be quiet, and paused open-mouthed.

'Oh, Lotty, I'm so – sorry – I mean, oh, I *do* beg your pardon, Letty – oh, dear, how stupid I am.'

'It doesn't matter,' said Miss Blacklock, but she was annoyed. 'Only I don't think Inspector Craddock wants that talked about. I didn't know you had been there when he was experimenting, Dora. You do understand, don't you, Mrs Harmon?'

'Oh, yes,' said Bunch. 'We won't breathe a word, will we, Aunt Jane. But I wonder *why* he –'

She relapsed into thought. Miss Bunner fidgeted and looked miserable, bursting out at last: 'I always say the wrong thing – Oh, dear, I'm nothing but a trial to you, Letty.'

Miss Blacklock said quickly, 'You're my great comfort, Dora. And anyway in a small place like Chipping Cleghorn there aren't really any secrets.'

'Now that is very true,' said Miss Marple. 'I'm afraid, you know, that things do get round in the most extraordinary way. Servants, of course, and yet it can't only be that, because one has so few servants nowadays. Still, there are the daily women and perhaps they are worse, because they go to everybody in turn and pass the news round.'

'Oh!' said Bunch Harmon suddenly. 'I've got it! Of course, if that door could open too, someone might have gone out of here in the dark and done the hold-up – only of course they didn't – because it was the man from the Royal Spa Hotel. Or wasn't it? . . . No, I don't see after all . . .' She frowned.

'Did it all happen in this room then?' asked Miss Marple, adding apologetically: 'I'm afraid you must think me sadly *curious*, Miss Blacklock – but it really is so very exciting – just like something one reads about in the paper – I'm just longing to hear all about it and to picture it all, if you know what I mean –'

Immediately Miss Marple received a confused and voluble account from Bunch and Miss Bunner – with occasional emendations and corrections from Miss Blacklock.

In the middle of it Patrick came in and good-naturedly entered into the spirit of the recital – going so far as to enact himself the part of Rudi Scherz.

'And Aunt Letty was there – in the corner by the archway . . . Go and stand there, Aunt Letty.'

Miss Blacklock obeyed, and then Miss Marple was shown the actual bullet holes.

'What a marvellous – what a providential escape,' she gasped.

'I was just going to offer my guests cigarettes –' Miss Blacklock indicated the big silver box on the table.

'People are so careless when they smoke,' said Miss Bunner disapprovingly. 'Nobody really respects good furniture as they used to do. Look at the horrid burn somebody made on this beautiful table by putting a cigarette down on it. *Disgraceful.*'

Miss Blacklock sighed.

'Sometimes, I'm afraid, one thinks too much of one's possessions.'

'But it's such a lovely table, Letty.'

Miss Bunner loved her friend's possessions with as much fervour as though they had been her own. Bunch Harmon had always thought it was a very endearing trait in her. She showed no sign of envy.

'It is a lovely table,' said Miss Marple politely. 'And what a very pretty china lamp on it.'

Again it was Miss Bunner who accepted the compliment as though she and not Miss Blacklock was the owner of the lamp.

'Isn't it delightful? Dresden. There is a pair of them. The other's in the spare room, I think.'

'You know where everything in this house is, Dora – or you think you do,' said Miss Blacklock, good-humouredly. 'You care far more about my things than I do.'

Miss Bunner flushed.

'I *do* like nice things,' she said. Her voice was half defiant – half wistful.

'I must confess,' said Miss Marple, 'that my own few possessions are very dear to me, too – so many *memories*, you know. It's the same with photographs. People nowadays have so few photographs about. Now I like to keep all the pictures of my nephews and nieces as babies – and then as children – and so on.'

'You've got a horrible one of me, aged three,' said Bunch. 'Holding a fox terrier and squinting.'

'I expect your aunt has many photographs of you,' said Miss Marple, turning to Patrick.

'Oh, we're only distant cousins,' said Patrick.

'I believe Elinor did send me one of you as a baby, Pat,' said Miss Blacklock. 'But I'm afraid I didn't keep it. I'd really forgotten how many children she'd had or what their names were until she wrote me about you two being over here.'

'Another sign of the times,' said Miss Marple. 'Nowadays one so often doesn't know one's younger relations *at all*. In the old days, with all the big family reunions, that would have been impossible.'

'I last saw Pat and Julia's mother at a wedding thirty years ago,' said Miss Blacklock. 'She was a very pretty girl.'

'That's why she has such handsome children,' said Patrick with a grin.

'You've got a marvellous old album,' said Julia. 'Do you remember, Aunt Letty, we looked through it the other day. The hats!'

'And how smart we thought ourselves,' said Miss Blacklock with a sigh.

'Never mind, Aunt Letty,' said Patrick, 'Julia will come across a snapshot of herself in about thirty years' time – and won't she think she looks a guy!'

★   ★   ★

'Did you do that on purpose?' said Bunch, as she and Miss Marple were walking home. 'Talk about photographs, I mean?'

'Well, my dear, it *is* interesting to know that Miss Blacklock didn't know either of her two young relatives by sight . . . Yes – I think Inspector Craddock will be interested to hear that.'

CHAPTER 12
MORNING ACTIVITIES IN CHIPPING CLEGHORN

Edmund Swettenham sat down rather precariously on a garden roller.

'Good morning, Phillipa,' he said.

'Hallo.'

'Are you very busy?'

'Moderately.'

'What are you doing?'

'Can't you see?'

'No. I'm not a gardener. You seem to be playing with earth in some fashion.'

'I'm pricking out winter lettuce.'

'Pricking out? What a curious term! Like pinking. Do you know what pinking is? I only learnt the other day. I always thought it was a term for professional duelling.'

'Do you want anything particular?' asked Phillipa coldly.

'Yes. I want to see you.'

Phillipa gave him a quick glance.

'I wish you wouldn't come here like this. Mrs Lucas won't like it.'

'Doesn't she allow you to have followers?'

'Don't be absurd.'

'Followers. That's another nice word. It describes my attitude perfectly. Respectful – at a distance – but firmly pursuing.'

'Please go away, Edmund. You've no business to come here.'

'You're wrong,' said Edmund triumphantly. 'I *have* business here. Mrs Lucas rang up my mamma this morning and said she had a good many vegetable marrows.'

'Masses of them.'

'And would we like to exchange a pot of honey for a vegetable marrow or so.'

'That's not a fair exchange at all! Vegetable marrows are quite unsaleable at the moment – everybody has such a lot.'

'Naturally. That's why Mrs Lucas rang up. Last time, if I remember rightly, the exchange suggested was some skim milk – *skim* milk, mark you – in exchange for some lettuces. It was then very early in the season for lettuces. They were about a shilling each.'

Phillipa did not speak.

Edmund tugged at his pocket and extracted a pot of honey.

'So here,' he said, 'is my alibi. Used in a loose and quite indefensible meaning of the term. If Mrs Lucas pops her bust round the door of the potting shed, I'm here in quest of vegetable marrows. There is absolutely no question of dalliance.'

'I see.'

'Do you ever read Tennyson?' inquired Edmund conversationally.

'Not very often.'

'You should. Tennyson is shortly to make a comeback in a big way. When you turn on your wireless in the evening it will be the *Idylls of the King* you will hear and not interminable Trollope. I always thought the Trollope pose was the most unbearable affectation. Perhaps a little of Trollope, but not to drown in him. But speaking of Tennyson, have you read *Maud*?'

'Once, long ago.'

'It's got some points about it.' He quoted softly:

'"Faultily faultless, icily regular, splendidly null." That's you, Phillipa.'

'Hardly a compliment!'

'No, it wasn't meant to be. I gather Maud got under the poor fellow's skin just like you've got under mine.'

'Don't be absurd, Edmund.'

'Oh, hell, Phillipa, why are you like you are? What goes on behind your splendidly regular features? What do you think? What do you *feel*? Are you happy, or miserable, or frightened, or what? There must be *something*.'

Phillipa said quietly:

'What I feel is my own business.'

'It's mine, too. I want to make you talk. I want to know what goes on in that quiet head of yours. I've a *right* to know. I have really. I didn't want to fall in love with you. I wanted to sit quietly and write my book. Such a nice book, all about how miserable the world is. It's frightfully easy to be clever about how miserable everybody is. And it's all a habit, really. Yes, I've suddenly become convinced of that. After reading a life of Burne Jones.'

Phillipa had stopped pricking out. She was staring at him with a puzzled frown.

'What has Burne Jones got to do with it?'

'Everything. When you've read all about the Pre-Raphaelites you realize just what fashion is. They were all terrifically hearty and slangy and jolly, and laughed and joked, and everything was fine and wonderful. That was fashion, too. They weren't any happier or heartier than we are. And we're not any more miserable than they were. It's all fashion, I tell you. After the last war, we went in for sex. Now it's all frustration. None of it matters. Why are we talking about all this? I started out to talk about *us*. Only I got cold feet and shied off. Because you won't help me.'

'What do you want me to do?'

'*Talk!* Tell me things. Is it your husband? Do you adore him and he's dead and so you've shut up like a clam? Is that it? All right, you adored him, and he's dead. Well, other girls' husbands are dead – lots of them – and some of the girls loved their husbands. They tell you so in bars, and cry a bit when they're drunk enough, and then want to go to bed with you so that they'll feel better. It's one way of getting over it, I suppose. You've got to get over it, Phillipa. You're young – and you're extremely lovely – and I love you like hell. Talk about your damned husband, tell me about him.'

'There's nothing to tell. We met and got married.'

'You must have been very young.'

'Too young.'

'Then you weren't happy with him? Go *on*, Phillipa.'

'There's nothing to go on about. We were married. We were as happy as most people are, I suppose. Harry was born. Ronald went overseas. He – he was killed in Italy.'

'And now there's Harry?'

'And now there's Harry.'

'I like Harry. He's a really nice kid. He likes me. We get on. What about it, Phillipa? Shall we get married? You can go on gardening and I can go on writing my book and in the holidays we'll leave off working and enjoy ourselves. We can manage, with tact, not to have to live with Mother. She can fork out a bit to support her devoted son. I sponge, I write tripey books, I have defective eyesight and I talk too much. That's the worst. Will you try it?'

Phillipa looked at him. She saw a tall rather solemn young man with an anxious face and large spectacles. His sandy head was rumpled and he was regarding her with a reassuring friendliness.

'No,' said Phillipa.

'Definitely – no?'

'Definitely no.'

'Why?'

'You don't know anything about me.'

'Is that all?'

'No, you don't know anything about anything.'

Edmund considered.

'Perhaps not,' he admitted. 'But who does? Phillipa, my adored one –'
He broke off.

A shrill and prolonged yapping was rapidly approaching.

'Pekes in the high hall garden, (said Edmund)
When twilight was falling (only it's eleven a.m.)
Phil, Phil, Phil, Phil,
They were crying and calling

'Your name doesn't lend itself to the rhythm, does it? Sounds like an Ode to a Fountain Pen. Have you got another name?'

'Joan. *Please* go away. That's Mrs Lucas.'

'*Joan, Joan, Joan, Joan.* Better, but still not good. *When greasy Joan the pot doth keel* – that's not a nice picture of married life, either.'

'Mrs Lucas is –'

'Oh, *hell!*' said Edmund. 'Get me a blasted vegetable marrow.'

Sergeant Fletcher had the house at Little Paddocks to himself.

It was Mitzi's day off. She always went by the eleven o'clock bus into Medenham Wells. By arrangement with Miss Blacklock, Sergeant Fletcher had the run of the house. She and Dora Bunner had gone down to the village.

Fletcher worked fast. Someone in the house had oiled and prepared that door, and whoever had done it, had done it in order to be able to leave the drawing-room unnoticed as soon as the lights went out. That ruled out Mitzi who wouldn't have needed to use the door.

Who was left? The neighbours, Fletcher thought, might also be ruled out. He didn't see how they could have found an opportunity to oil and prepare the door. That left Patrick and Julia Simmons, Phillipa Haymes, and possibly Dora Bunner. The young Simmonses were in Milchester. Phillipa Haymes was at work. Sergeant Fletcher was free to search out any secrets he could. But the house was disappointingly innocent. Fletcher, who was an expert on electricity, could find nothing suggestive in the wiring or appurtenances of the electric fixtures to show how the lights had been fused. Making a rapid survey of the household bedrooms he found an irritating normality. In Phillipa Haymes' room were photographs of a small boy with serious eyes, an earlier photo of the same child, a pile of schoolboy letters, a theatre programme or two. In Julia's room there was a drawer full of snapshots of the South of France. Bathing photos, a villa set amidst mimosa. Patrick's held some souvenirs of Naval days. Dora Bunner's held few personal possessions and they seemed innocent enough.

And yet, thought Fletcher, someone in the house must have oiled that door.

His thoughts broke off at a sound below stairs. He went quickly to the top of the staircase and looked down.

Mrs Swettenham was crossing the hall. She had a basket on her arm. She looked into the drawing-room, crossed the hall and went into the dining-room. She came out again without the basket.

Some faint sound that Fletcher made, a board that creaked unexpectedly under his feet, made her turn her head. She called up:

'Is that you, Miss Blacklock?'

'No, Mrs Swettenham, it's me,' said Fletcher.

Mrs Swettenham gave a faint scream.

'Oh! how you startled me. I thought it might be another burglar.'

Fletcher came down the stairs.

'This house doesn't seem very well protected against burglars,' he said. 'Can anybody always walk in and out just as they like?'

'I just brought up some of my quinces,' explained Mrs Swettenham. 'Miss Blacklock wants to make quince jelly and she hasn't got a quince tree here. I left them in the dining-room.'

Then she smiled.

'Oh, I see, you mean how did I get in? Well, I just came in through the side door. We all walk in and out of each other's houses, Sergeant. Nobody dreams of locking a door until it's dark. I mean it would be so awkward, wouldn't it, if you brought things and couldn't get in to leave them? It's not like the old days when you rang a bell and a servant always came to answer it.' Mrs Swettenham sighed. 'In India, I remember,' she said mournfully, 'we had eighteen servants – eighteen. Not counting the ayah. Just as a matter of course. And at home, when I was a girl, we always had three – though Mother always felt it was terribly poverty-stricken not to be able to afford a kitchen-maid. I must say that I find life very odd nowadays, Sergeant, though I know one mustn't complain. So much worse for the miners always getting psitticosis (or is that parrot disease?) and having to come out of the mines and try to be gardeners though they don't know weeds from spinach.'

She added, as she tripped towards the door, 'I mustn't keep you. I expect you're very busy. Nothing else is going to happen, is it?'

'Why should it, Mrs Swettenham?'

'I just wondered, seeing you here. I thought it might be a *gang*. You'll tell Miss Blacklock about the quinces, won't you?'

Mrs Swettenham departed. Fletcher felt like a man who has received an unexpected jolt. He had been assuming – erroneously, he now perceived – that it must have been someone in the house who had done the oiling of the door. He saw now that he was wrong. An outsider had only to wait until Mitzi had departed by bus and Letitia Blacklock and Dora Bunner were both out of the house. Such an opportunity must have been simplicity itself. That meant that he couldn't rule out anybody who had been in the drawing-room that night.

'Murgatroyd!'

'Yes, Hinch?'

'I've been doing a bit of thinking.'

'Have you, Hinch?'

'Yes, the great brain has been working. You know, Murgatroyd, the whole set-up the other evening was decidedly fishy.'

'Fishy?'

'Yes. Tuck your hair up, Murgatroyd, and take this trowel. Pretend it's a revolver.'

'Oh,' said Miss Murgatroyd, nervously.

'All right. It won't bite you. Now come along to the kitchen door. You're going to be the burglar. You stand *here*. Now you're going into the kitchen to hold up a lot of nit-wits. Take the torch. Switch it on.'

'But it's broad daylight!'

'Use your imagination, Murgatroyd. Switch it on.'

Miss Murgatroyd did so, rather clumsily, shifting the trowel under one arm while she did so.

'Now then,' said Miss Hinchcliffe, 'off you go. Remember the time you played Hermia in *A Midsummer Night's Dream* at the Women's Institute?

Act. Give it all you've got. "Stick 'em up!" Those are your lines – and don't ruin them by saying "Please."'

Obediently Miss Murgatroyd raised her torch, flourished the trowel and advanced on the kitchen door.

Transferring the torch to her right hand she swiftly turned the handle and stepped forward, resuming the torch in her left hand.

'Stick 'em up!' she fluted, adding vexedly: 'Dear me, this is very difficult, Hinch.'

'Why?'

'The door. It's a swing door, it keeps coming back and I've got both hands full.'

'Exactly,' boomed Miss Hinchcliffe. 'And the drawing-room door at Little Paddocks always swings to. It isn't a swing door like this, but it won't stay open. That's why Letty Blacklock bought that absolutely delectable heavy glass doorstop from Elliot's in the High Street. I don't mind saying I've never forgiven her for getting in ahead of me there. I was beating the old brute down most successfully. He'd come down from eight guineas to six pound ten, and then Blacklock comes along and buys the damned thing. I'd never seen as attractive a doorstop, you don't often get those glass bubbles in that big size.'

'Perhaps the burglar put the doorstop against the door to keep it open,' suggested Miss Murgatroyd.

'Use your common sense, Murgatroyd. What does he do? Throw the door open, say "Excuse me a moment," stoop and put the stop into position and then resume business by saying "Hands up"? Try holding the door with your shoulder.'

'It's still very awkward,' complained Miss Murgatroyd.

'Exactly,' said Miss Hinchcliffe. 'A revolver, a torch and a door to hold open – a bit too much, isn't it? So what's the answer?'

Miss Murgatroyd did not attempt to supply an answer. She looked inquiringly and admiringly at her masterful friend and waited to be enlightened.

'We know he'd got a revolver, because he fired it,' said Miss Hinchcliffe. 'And we know he had a torch because we all saw it – that is unless we're all victims of mass hypnotism like explanations of the Indian Rope Trick (what a bore that old Easterbrook is with his Indian stories) so the question is, did someone hold that door open for him?'

'But who could have done that?'

'Well, *you* could have for one, Murgatroyd. As far as I remember, you were standing directly behind it when the lights went out.' Miss Hinchcliffe laughed heartily. 'Highly suspicious character, aren't you, Murgatroyd? But who'd think it to look at you? Here, give me that trowel – thank heavens it isn't really a revolver. You'd have shot yourself by now!'

'It's a most extraordinary thing,' muttered Colonel Easterbrook. 'Most extraordinary. Laura.'

'Yes, darling?'

'Come into my dressing-room a moment.'

'What is it, darling?'

Mrs Easterbrook appeared through the open door.

'Remember my showing you that revolver of mine?'

'Oh, yes, Archie, a nasty horrid black thing.'

'Yes. Hun souvenir. Was in this drawer, wasn't it?'

'Yes, it was.'

'Well, it's not there now.'

'Archie, how *extraordinary*!'

'You haven't moved it or anything?'

'Oh, no, I'd never dare to touch the horrid thing.'

'Think old mother whatsername did?'

'Oh, I shouldn't think so for a minute. Mrs Butt would never do a thing like that. Shall I ask her?'

'No – no, better not. Don't want to start a lot of talk. Tell me, do you remember when it was I showed it to you?'

'Oh, about a week ago. You were grumbling about your collars and the laundry and you opened this drawer wide and there it was at the back and I asked you what it was.'

'Yes, that's right. About a week ago. You don't remember the date?'

Mrs Easterbrook considered, eyelids down over her eyes, a shrewd brain working.

'Of course,' she said. 'It was Saturday. The day we were to have gone in to the pictures, but we didn't.'

'H'm – sure it wasn't before that? Wednesday? Thursday or even the week before that again?'

'No, dear,' said Mrs Easterbrook. 'I remember *quite* distinctly. It was Saturday the 30th. It just seems a long time because of all the trouble there's been. And I can tell you *how* I remember. It's because it was the day after the hold-up at Miss Blacklock's. Because when I saw your revolver it reminded me of the shooting the night before.'

'Ah,' said Colonel Easterbrook, 'then that's a great load off my mind.'

'Oh, Archie, why?'

'Just because if that revolver had disappeared before the shooting – well, it might possibly have been my revolver that was pinched by that Swiss fellow.'

'But how would he have known you had one?'

'These gangs have a most extraordinary communication service. They get to know everything about a place and who lives there.'

'What a lot you do know, Archie.'

'Ha. Yes. Seen a thing or two in my time. Still as you definitely remember seeing my revolver *after* the hold-up – well, that settles it. The revolver that Swiss fellow used can't have been mine, can it?'

'Of course it can't.'

'A great relief. I should have had to go to the police about it. And they ask a lot of awkward questions. Bound to. As a matter of fact I never took out a licence for it. Somehow, after a war, one forgets these peacetime regulations. I looked on it as a war souvenir, not as a firearm.'

'Yes, I see. Of course.'

'But all the same – where on earth can the damned thing be?'

'Perhaps Mrs Butt took it. She's always seemed quite honest, but perhaps she felt nervous after the hold-up and thought she'd like to – to have a revolver in the house. Of course, she'll never admit doing that. I shan't even ask her. She might get offended. And what should we do then? This is such a big house – I simply couldn't –'

'Quite so,' said Colonel Easterbrook. 'Better not say anything.'

···················· **CHAPTER 13** ····················

MORNING ACTIVITIES IN CHIPPING CLEGHORN (CONTINUED)

Miss Marple came out of the Vicarage gate and walked down the little lane that led into the main street.

She walked fairly briskly with the aid of the Rev. Julian Harmon's stout ashplant stick.

She passed the Red Cow and the butcher's and stopped for a brief moment to look into the window of Mr Elliot's antique shop. This was cunningly situated next door to the Bluebird Tearooms and Café so that rich motorists, after stopping for a nice cup of tea and somewhat euphemistically named 'Home Made Cakes' of a bright saffron colour, could be tempted by Mr Elliot's judiciously planned shop window.

In this antique bow frame, Mr Elliot catered for all tastes. Two pieces of Waterford glass reposed on an impeccable wine cooler. A walnut bureau, made up of various bits and pieces, proclaimed itself a Genuine Bargain and on a table, in the window itself, were a nice assortment of cheap doorknockers and quaint pixies, a few chipped bits of Dresden, a couple of sad-looking bead necklaces, a mug with 'A Present from Tunbridge Wells' on it, and some tit-bits of Victorian silver.

Miss Marple gave the window her rapt attention, and Mr Elliot, an elderly obese spider, peeped out of his web to appraise the possibilities of this new fly.

But just as he decided that the charms of the Present from Tunbridge Wells were about to be too much for the lady who was staying at the Vicarage (for of course Mr Elliot, like everybody else, knew exactly who she was), Miss Marple saw out of the corner of her eye Miss Dora Bunner entering the Bluebird Café, and immediately decided that what she needed to counteract the cold wind was a nice cup of morning coffee.

Four or five ladies were already engaged in sweetening their morning shopping by a pause for refreshment. Miss Marple, blinking a little in the gloom of the interior of the Bluebird, and hovering artistically, was greeted by the voice of Dora Bunner at her elbow.

'Oh, good morning, Miss Marple. Do sit down here. I'm all alone.'

'Thank you.'

Miss Marple subsided gratefully on to the rather angular little blue-painted armchair which the Bluebird affected.

'Such a sharp wind,' she complained. 'And I can't walk very fast because of my rheumatic leg.'

'Oh, I know. I had sciatica one year – and really most of the time I was in *agony*.'

The two ladies talked rheumatism, sciatica and neuritis for some moments with avidity. A sulky-looking girl in a pink overall with a flight of bluebirds down the front of it took their order for coffee and cakes with a yawn and an air of weary patience.

'The cakes,' Miss Bunner said in a conspiratorial whisper, 'are really *quite* good here.'

'I was so interested in that very pretty girl I met as we were coming away from Miss Blacklock's the other day,' said Miss Marple. 'I think she said she does gardening. Or is she on the land? Hynes – was that her name?'

'Oh, yes, Phillipa Haymes. Our "Lodger", as we call her.' Miss Bunner laughed at her own humour. 'Such a nice quiet girl. A *lady*, if you know what I mean.'

'I wonder now. I knew a Colonel Haymes – in the Indian cavalry. Her father perhaps?'

'She's *Mrs* Haymes. A widow. Her husband was killed in Sicily or Italy. Of course, it might be *his* father.'

'I wondered, perhaps, if there might be a little romance on the way?' Miss Marple suggested roguishly. 'With that tall young man?'

'With Patrick, do you mean? Oh, I don't –'

'No, I meant a young man with spectacles. I've seen him about.'

'Oh, of course, Edmund Swettenham. Sh! That's his mother, Mrs Swettenham, over in the corner. I don't know, I'm sure. You think he admires her? He's such an odd young man – says the most disturbing things sometimes. He's supposed to be *clever*, you know,' said Miss Bunner with frank disapproval.

'Cleverness isn't everything,' said Miss Marple, shaking her head. 'Ah, here is our coffee.'

The sulky girl deposited it with a clatter. Miss Marple and Miss Bunner pressed cakes on each other.

'I was so interested to hear you were at school with Miss Blacklock. Yours is indeed an old friendship.'

'Yes, indeed.' Miss Bunner sighed. 'Very few people would be as loyal to their old friends as dear Miss Blacklock is. Oh, dear, those days seem a long time ago. Such a pretty girl and enjoyed life so much. It all seemed so *sad*.'

Miss Marple, though with no idea of what had seemed so sad, sighed and shook her head.

'Life is indeed hard,' she murmured.

'*And sad affliction bravely borne*,' murmured Miss Bunner, her eyes suffusing with tears. 'I always think of that verse. True patience; true resignation. Such courage and patience *ought* to be rewarded, that is what I say. What I feel is that *nothing* is too good for dear Miss Blacklock, and whatever good things come to her, she truly *deserves* them.'

'Money,' said Miss Marple, 'can do a lot to ease one's path in life.'

She felt herself safe in this observation since she judged that it must be Miss Blacklock's prospects of future affluence to which her friend referred.

The remark, however, started Miss Bunner on another train of thought.

'Money!' she exclaimed with bitterness. 'I don't believe, you know, that until one has really experienced it, one can know what money, or rather the lack of it, *means*.'

Miss Marple nodded her white head sympathetically.

Miss Bunner went on rapidly, working herself up, and speaking with a flushed face:

'I've heard people say so often "I'd rather have flowers on the table than a meal without them." But how many meals have those people ever missed? They don't know what it is – nobody knows who hasn't been through it – to be really *hungry*. Bread, you know, and a jar of meat paste, and a scrape of margarine. Day after day, and how one longs for a good plate of meat and two vegetables. And the *shabbiness*. Darning one's clothes and hoping it won't show. And applying for jobs and always being told you're too old. And then perhaps getting a job and after all one isn't strong enough. One faints. And you're back again. It's the *rent* – always the *rent* – that's *got* to be paid – otherwise you're out in the street. And in these days it leaves so little over. One's old age pension doesn't go far – indeed it doesn't.'

'I know,' said Miss Marple gently. She looked with compassion at Miss Bunner's twitching face.

'I wrote to Letty. I just happened to see her name in the paper. It was a luncheon in aid of Milchester Hospital. There it was in black and white, Miss Letitia Blacklock. It brought the past back to me. I hadn't heard of her for years and years. She'd been secretary, you know, to that very rich man, Goedler. She was always a clever girl – the kind that gets on in the world. Not so much looks – as *character*. I thought – well, I thought – perhaps she'll remember me – and she's one of the people I *could* ask for a little help. I mean someone you've known as a girl – been at school with – well, they do *know* about you – they know you're not just a – begging letter-writer –'

Tears came into Dora Bunner's eyes.

'And then Lotty came and took me away – said she needed someone to help her. Of course, I was very surprised – *very* surprised – but then newspapers do get things wrong. How kind she was – and how *sympathetic*. And remembering all the old days so well . . . I'd do anything for her – I really would. And I try *very* hard, but I'm afraid sometimes I muddle things – my head's not what it was. I make mistakes. And I forget and say foolish things. She's very patient. What's so nice about her is that she always pretends that I *am* useful to her. That's real kindness, isn't it?'

Miss Marple said gently: 'Yes, that's real kindness.'

'I used to worry, you know, even after I came to Little Paddocks – about what would become of me if – if anything were to happen to Miss Blacklock. After all, there are so many accidents – these motors dashing about – one never knows, does one? But naturally I never *said* anything

– but she must have guessed. Suddenly, one day she told me that she'd left me a small annuity in her will – and – what I value far more – all her beautiful furniture. I was quite *overcome* . . . But she said nobody else would value it as I should – and that is quite true – I can't bear to see some lovely piece of china smashed – or wet glasses put down on a table and leaving a mark. I do really look after her things. Some people – some people especially, are so terribly careless – and sometimes worse than careless!

'I'm not really as stupid as I look,' Miss Bunner continued with simplicity. 'I can see, you know, when Letty's being imposed upon. Some people – I won't name names – but they take *advantage*. Dear Miss Blacklock is, perhaps, just a shade too *trusting*.'

Miss Marple shook her head.

'*That's* a mistake.'

'Yes, it is. You and I, Miss Marple, know the world. Dear Miss Black-lock –' She shook her head.

Miss Marple thought that as the secretary of a big financier Miss Blacklock might be presumed to know the world too. But probably what Dora Bunner meant was that Letty Blacklock had always been comfortably off, and that the comfortably off do not know the deeper abysses of human nature.

'That Patrick!' said Miss Bunner with a suddenness and an asperity that made Miss Marple jump. 'Twice, at least, to my knowledge, he's got money out of her. Pretending he's hard up. Run into debt. All that sort of thing. She's far too generous. All she said to me when I remonstrated with her was: "The boy's young, Dora. Youth is the time to have your fling."'

'Well, that's true enough,' said Miss Marple. 'Such a handsome young man, too.'

'Handsome is as handsome does,' said Dora Bunner. 'Much too fond of poking fun at people. And a lot of going on with girls, I expect. I'm just a figure of fun to him – that's all. He doesn't seem to realize that people have their feelings.'

'Young people *are* rather careless that way,' said Miss Marple.

Miss Bunner leaned forward suddenly with a mysterious air.

'You won't breathe a word, will you, my dear?' she demanded. 'But I can't help feeling that he *was* mixed up in this dreadful business. I think he knew that young man – else Julia did. I daren't hint at such a thing to dear Miss Blacklock – at least I did, and she just snapped my head off. And, of course, it's *awkward* – because he's her nephew – or at any rate

her *cousin* – and if the Swiss young man shot himself Patrick might be
held morally responsible, mightn't he? If he'd put him up to it, I mean.
I'm really terribly confused about the whole thing. Everyone making such
a fuss about that other door into the drawing-room. That's another thing
that worries me – the detective saying it had been oiled. Because you see,
I saw –'

She came to an abrupt stop.

Miss Marple paused to select a phrase.

'Most difficult for you,' she said sympathetically. 'Naturally you
wouldn't want anything to get round to the police.'

'That's just it,' Dora Bunner cried. 'I lie awake at nights and worry –
because, you see, I came upon Patrick in the shrubbery the other day. I
was looking for eggs – one hen lays out – and there he was holding a
feather and a cup – an oily cup. And he jumped most guiltily when he
saw me and he said: "I was just wondering what this was doing here."
Well, of course, he's a quick thinker. I should say he thought that up
quickly when I startled him. And how did he come to find a thing like
that in the shrubbery unless he was looking for it, knowing perfectly well
it was there? Of course, I didn't *say* anything.'

'No, no, of course not.'

'But I gave him a *look*, if you know what I mean.'

Dora Bunner stretched out her hand and bit abstractedly into a lurid
salmon-coloured cake.

'And then another day I happened to overhear him having a very curious
conversation with Julia. They seemed to be having a kind of quarrel. He
was saying: "If I thought you had anything to do with a thing like that!"
and Julia (she's always so calm, you know) said: "Well, little brother, what
would you do about it?" And then, *most* unfortunately, I trod on that board
that always squeaks, and they saw me. So I said, quite gaily: "You two
having a quarrel?" and Patrick said, "I'm warning Julia not to go in for
these black-market deals." Oh, it was all very slick, but I don't believe
they were talking about anything of the sort! And if you ask me, I believe
Patrick had tampered with that lamp in the drawing-room – to make the
lights go out, because I remember distinctly that it was the shepherdess –
not the shepherd. And the next day –'

She stopped and her face grew pink. Miss Marple turned her head
to see Miss Blacklock standing behind them – she must just have
come in.

'Coffee and gossip, Bunny?' said Miss Blacklock, with quite a shade of
reproach in her voice. 'Good morning, Miss Marple. Cold, isn't it?'

The doors flew open with a clang and Bunch Harmon came into the Bluebird with a rush.

'Hallo,' she said, 'am I too late for coffee?'

'No, dear,' said Miss Marple. 'Sit down and have a cup.'

'We must get home,' said Miss Blacklock. 'Done your shopping, Bunny?'

Her tone was indulgent once more, but her eyes still held a slight reproach.

'Yes – yes, thank you, Letty. I must just pop into the chemists in passing and get some aspirin and some cornplasters.'

As the doors of the Bluebird swung to behind them, Bunch asked:

'What were you talking about?'

Miss Marple did not reply at once. She waited whilst Bunch gave the order, then she said:

'Family solidarity is a very strong thing. Very strong. Do you remember some famous case – I really can't remember what it was. They said the husband poisoned his wife. In a glass of wine. Then, at the trial, the daughter said she'd drunk half her mother's glass – so that knocked the case against her father to pieces. They do say – but that may be just rumour – that she never spoke to her father or lived with him again. Of course, a father is one thing – and a nephew or a distant cousin is another. But still there it is – no one wants a member of their own family hanged, do they?'

'No,' said Bunch, considering. 'I shouldn't think they would.'

Miss Marple leaned back in her chair. She murmured under her breath, 'People are really very alike, everywhere.'

'Who am I like?'

'Well, really, dear, you are very much like yourself. I don't know that you remind me of anyone in particular. Except perhaps –'

'Here it comes,' said Bunch.

'I was just thinking of a parlourmaid of mine, dear.'

'A parlourmaid? I should make a terrible parlourmaid.'

'Yes, dear, so did she. She was no good at all at waiting at table. Put everything on the table crooked, mixed up the kitchen knives with the dining-room ones, and her cap (this was a long time ago, dear) her cap was *never* straight.'

Bunch adjusted her hat automatically.

'Anything else?' she demanded anxiously.

'I kept her because she was so pleasant to have about the house – and because she used to make me laugh. I liked the way she said things straight out. Came to me one day, "Of course, I don't know, ma'am," she says, "but Florrie, the way she sits down, it's just like a married woman." And sure enough poor Florrie was in trouble – the gentlemanly assistant at the hairdresser's. Fortunately it was in good time, and I was able to have a little talk with him, and they had a very nice wedding and settled down quite happily. She was a good girl, Florrie, but inclined to be taken in by a gentlemanly appearance.'

'She didn't do a murder, did she?' asked Bunch. 'The parlourmaid, I mean.'

'No, indeed,' said Miss Marple. 'She married a Baptist Minister and they had a family of five.'

'Just like me,' said Bunch. 'Though I've only got as far as Edward and Susan up to date.'

She added, after a minute or two:

'Who are you thinking about now, Aunt Jane?'

'Quite a lot of people, dear, quite a lot of people,' said Miss Marple, vaguely.

'In St Mary Mead?'

'Mostly ... I was really thinking about Nurse Ellerton – really an excellent kindly woman. Took care of an old lady, seemed really fond of her. Then the old lady died. And another came and *she* died. Morphia. It all came out. Done in the kindest way, and the shocking thing was that the woman herself really couldn't see that she'd done anything wrong. They hadn't long to live in any case, she said, and one of them had cancer and quite a lot of pain.'

'You mean – it was a mercy killing?'

'No, *no*. They signed their money away to her. She liked money, you know . . .

'And then there was that young man on the liner – Mrs Pusey at the paper shop, *her* nephew. Brought home stuff he'd stolen and got her to dispose of it. Said it was things that he'd bought abroad. She was quite taken in. And then when the police came round and started asking questions, he tried to bash her on the head, so that she shouldn't be able to give him away . . . Not a nice young man – but very good-looking. Had two girls in love with him. He spent a lot of money on one of them.'

'The nastiest one, I suppose,' said Bunch.

'Yes, dear. And there was Mrs Cray at the wool shop. Devoted to her son, spoilt him, of course. He got in with a very queer lot. Do you remember Joan Croft, Bunch?'

'N-no, I don't think so.'

'I thought you might have seen her when you were with me on a visit. Used to stalk about smoking a cigar or a pipe. We had a Bank hold-up once, and Joan Croft was in the Bank at the time. She knocked the man down and took his revolver away from him. She was congratulated on her courage by the Bench.'

Bunch listened attentively. She seemed to be learning by heart.

'And –?' she prompted.

'That girl at St Jean des Collines that summer. Such a quiet girl – not so much quiet as silent. Everybody liked her, but they never got to know her much better . . . We heard afterwards that her husband was a *forger*. It made her feel cut off from people. It made her, in the end, a little queer. Brooding does, you know.'

'Any Anglo-Indian Colonels in your reminiscences, darling?'

'Naturally, dear. There was Major Vaughan at The Larches and Colonel Wright at Simla Lodge. Nothing wrong with either of them. But I do remember Mr Hodgson, the Bank Manager, went on a cruise and married a woman young enough to be his daughter. No idea of where she came from – except what she told him of course.'

'And that wasn't true?'

'No, dear, it definitely wasn't.'

'Not bad,' said Bunch, nodding, and ticking people off on her fingers. 'We've had devoted Dora, and handsome Patrick, and Mrs Swettenham and Edmund, and Phillipa Haymes, and Colonel Easterbrook and Mrs Easterbrook – and if you ask me, I should say you're absolutely right about *her*. But there wouldn't be any reason for her murdering Letty Blacklock.'

'Miss Blacklock, of course, might know something about her that she didn't want known.'

'Oh, darling, that old Tanqueray stuff? Surely that's dead as the hills.'

'It might not be. You see, Bunch, you are not the kind that minds much about what people think of you.'

'I see what you mean,' said Bunch suddenly. 'If you'd been up against it, and then, rather like a shivering stray cat, you'd found a home and cream and a warm stroking hand and you were called Pretty Pussy and somebody thought the world of you . . . You'd do a lot to keep that . . . Well, I must say, you've presented me with a very complete gallery of people.'

'You didn't get them all right, you know,' said Miss Marple, mildly.

'Didn't I? Where did I slip up? Julia? *Julia, pretty Julia is peculiar.*'

'Three and sixpence,' said the sulky waitress, materializing out of the gloom.

'And,' she added, her bosom heaving beneath the bluebirds, 'I'd like to know, Mrs Harmon, why you call me peculiar. I had an Aunt who joined the Peculiar People, but I've always been good Church of England myself, as the late Rev. Hopkinson can tell you.'

'I'm terribly sorry,' said Bunch. 'I was just quoting a song. I didn't mean you at all. I didn't know your name was Julia.'

'Quite a coincidence,' said the sulky waitress, cheering up. 'No offence, I'm sure, but hearing my name, as I thought – well, naturally if you think someone's talking about you, it's only human nature to listen. Thank you.'

She departed with her tip.

'Aunt Jane,' said Bunch, 'don't look so upset. What is it?'

'But surely,' murmured Miss Marple. 'That couldn't be so. There's no *reason* –'

'Aunt Jane!'

Miss Marple sighed and then smiled brightly.

'It's nothing, dear,' she said.

'Did you think you knew who did the murder?' asked Bunch. 'Who was it?'

'I don't know at all,' said Miss Marple. 'I got an idea for a moment – but it's gone. I wish I did know. Time's so short. So terribly short.'

'What do you mean short?'

'That old lady up in Scotland may die any moment.'

Bunch said, staring:

'Then you really do believe in Pip and Emma. You think it was them – and that they'll try again?'

'Of course they'll try again,' said Miss Marple, almost absentmindedly. 'If they tried once, they'll try again. If you've made up your mind to murder someone, you don't stop because the first time it didn't come off. Especially if you're fairly sure you're not suspected.'

'But if it's Pip and Emma,' said Bunch, 'there are only two people it *could* be. It *must* be Patrick and Julia. They're brother and sister and they're the only ones who are the right age.'

'My dear, it isn't nearly as simple as that. There are all sorts of ramifications and combinations. There's Pip's wife if he's married, or Emma's husband. There's their mother – she's an interested party even if she doesn't inherit direct. If Lotty Blacklock hasn't seen her for thirty years, she'd probably not recognize her now. One elderly woman is very like another. You remember Mrs Wotherspoon drew her own and Mrs Bartlett's Old Age Pension although Mrs Bartlett had been dead for years. Anyway, Miss Blacklock's shortsighted. Haven't you noticed how she peers at people? And then there's the father. Apparently he was a real bad lot.'

'Yes, but he's a foreigner.'

'By birth. But there's no reason to believe he speaks broken English and gesticulates with his hands. I dare say he could play the part of – of an Anglo-Indian Colonel as well as anybody else.'

'Is *that* what you think?'

'No, I don't. I don't indeed, dear. I just think that there's a great deal of money at stake, a great deal of money. And I'm afraid I know only too well the really terrible things that people will do to lay their hands on a lot of money.'

'I suppose they will,' said Bunch. 'It doesn't really do them any good, does it? Not in the end?'

'No – but they don't usually know that.'

'I can understand it.' Bunch smiled suddenly, her sweet rather crooked smile. 'One feels it would be different for oneself . . . Even I feel that.' She considered: 'You pretend to yourself that you'd do a lot of good with all that money. Schemes . . . Homes for Unwanted Children . . . Tired Mothers . . . A lovely rest abroad somewhere for elderly women who have worked too hard . . .'

Her face grew sombre. Her eyes were suddenly dark and tragic.

'I know what you're thinking,' she said to Miss Marple. 'You're thinking that I'd be the worst kind. Because I'd kid myself. If you just wanted the money for selfish reasons you'd at any rate *see* what you were like. But once you began to pretend about doing good with it, you'd be able to persuade yourself, perhaps, that it wouldn't very much matter killing someone . . .'

Then her eyes cleared.

'But I shouldn't,' she said. 'I shouldn't really kill anyone. Not even if they were old, or ill, or doing a lot of harm in the world. Not even if they were blackmailers or – or absolute *beasts*.' She fished a fly carefully out of the dregs of the coffee and arranged it on the table to dry. 'Because people like living, don't they? So do flies. Even if you're old and in pain and can just crawl out in the sun. Julian says those people like living even more than young strong people do. It's harder, he says, for them to die, the struggle's greater. I like living myself – not just being happy and enjoying myself and having a good time. I mean *living* – waking up and feeling, all over me, that I'm *there* – ticking over.'

She blew on the fly gently; it waved its legs, and flew rather drunkenly away.

'Cheer up, darling Aunt Jane,' said Bunch. '*I'*d never kill anybody.'

CHAPTER 14

EXCURSION INTO THE PAST

After a night in the train, Inspector Craddock alighted at a small station in the Highlands.

It struck him for a moment as strange that the wealthy Mrs Goedler – an invalid – with a choice of a London house in a fashionable square, an estate in Hampshire, and a villa in the South of France, should have selected this remote Scottish home as her residence. Surely she was cut off here from many friends and distractions. It must be a lonely life – or was she too ill to notice or care about her surroundings?

A car was waiting to meet him. A big old-fashioned Daimler with an elderly chauffeur driving it. It was a sunny morning and the Inspector enjoyed the twenty-mile drive, though he marvelled anew at this preference for isolation. A tentative remark to the chauffeur brought partial enlightenment.

'It's her own home as a girl. Ay, she's the last of the family. And she and Mr Goedler were always happier here than anywhere, though it wasn't often he could get away from London. But when he did they enjoyed themselves like a couple of bairns.'

When the grey walls of the old keep came in sight, Craddock felt that time was slipping backwards. An elderly butler received him, and after a wash and a shave he was shown into a room with a huge fire burning in the grate, and breakfast was served to him.

After breakfast, a tall, middle-aged woman in nurse's dress, with a pleasant and competent manner, came in and introduced herself as Sister McClelland.

'I have my patient all ready for you, Mr Craddock. She is, indeed, looking forward to seeing you.'

'I'll do my best not to excite her,' Craddock promised.

'I had better warn you of what will happen. You will find Mrs Goedler apparently quite normal. She will talk and enjoy talking and then – quite suddenly – her powers will fail. Come away at once, then, and send for me. She is, you see, kept almost entirely under the influence of morphia.'

She drowses most of the time. In preparation for your visit, I have given her a strong stimulant. As soon as the effect of the stimulant wears off, she will relapse into semi-consciousness.'

'I quite understand, Miss McClelland. Would it be in order for you to tell me exactly what the state of Mrs Goedler's health is?'

'Well, Mr Craddock, she is a dying woman. Her life cannot be prolonged for more than a few weeks. To say that she should have been dead years ago would strike you as odd, yet it is the truth. What has kept Mrs Goedler alive is her intense enjoyment and love of being alive. That sounds, perhaps, an odd thing to say of someone who has lived the life of an invalid for many years and has not left her home here for fifteen years, but it is true. Mrs Goedler has never been a strong woman – but she has retained to an astonishing degree the will to live.' She added with a smile, 'She is a very charming woman, too, as you will find.'

Craddock was shown into a large bedroom where a fire was burning and where an old lady lay in a large canopied bed. Though she was only about seven or eight years older than Letitia Blacklock, her fragility made her seem older than her years.

Her white hair was carefully arranged, a froth of pale blue wool enveloped her neck and shoulders. There were lines of pain on the face, but lines of sweetness, too. And there was, strangely enough, what Craddock could only describe as a roguish twinkle in her faded blue eyes.

'Well, this is interesting,' she said. 'It's not often I receive a visit from the police. I hear Letitia Blacklock wasn't much hurt by this attempt on her? How is my dear Blackie?'

'She's very well, Mrs Goedler. She sent you her love.'

'It's a long time since I've seen her . . . For many years now, it's been just a card at Christmas. I asked her to come up here when she came back to England after Charlotte's death, but she said it would be painful after so long and perhaps she was right . . . Blackie always had a lot of sense. I had an old school friend to see me about a year ago, and, lor!' – she smiled – 'we bored each other to death. After we'd finished all the "Do you remembers?" there wasn't anything to say. *Most* embarrassing.'

Craddock was content to let her talk before pressing his questions. He wanted, as it were, to get back into the past, to get the feel of the Goedler-Blacklock ménage.

'I suppose,' said Belle shrewdly, 'that you want to ask about the money? Randall left it all to go to Blackie after my death. Really, of course, Randall never dreamed that I'd outlive him. He was a big strong man, never a day's illness, and I was always a mass of aches and pains and complaints and doctors coming and pulling long faces over me.'

'I don't think complaints would be the right word, Mrs Goedler.'

The old lady chuckled.

'I didn't mean it in the complaining sense. I've never been *too* sorry for myself. But it was always taken for granted that I, being the weakly one, would go first. It didn't work out that way. No – it didn't work out that way . . .'

'Why, exactly, did your husband leave his money the way he did?'

'You mean, why did he leave it to Blackie? Not for the reason you've probably been thinking.' The roguish twinkle was very apparent. 'What minds you policemen have! Randall was never in the least in love with her and she wasn't with him. Letitia, you know, has really got a man's mind. She hasn't any feminine feelings or weaknesses. I don't believe she was ever in love with any man. She was never particularly pretty and she didn't care for clothes. She used a little make-up in deference to prevailing custom, but not to make herself look prettier.' There was pity in the old voice as she went on: 'She never knew any of the fun of being a woman.'

Craddock looked at the frail little figure in the big bed with interest. Belle Goedler, he realized, *had* enjoyed – still enjoyed – being a woman. She twinkled at him.

'I've always thought,' she said, 'it must be terribly dull to be a man.'

Then she said thoughtfully:

'I think Randall looked on Blackie very much as a kind of younger brother. He relied on her judgment which was always excellent. She kept him out of trouble more than once, you know.'

'She told me that she came to his rescue once with money?'

'That, yes, but I meant more than that. One can speak the truth after all these years. Randall couldn't really distinguish between what was crooked and what wasn't. His conscience wasn't sensitive. The poor dear really didn't know what was just smart – and what was dishonest. Blackie kept him straight. That's one thing about Letitia Blacklock, she's absolutely dead straight. She would never do anything that was dishonest. She's a very fine character, you know. I've always admired her. They had a terrible girlhood, those girls. The father was an old country doctor – terrifically pig-headed and narrow-minded – the complete family tyrant. Letitia broke away, came to London, and trained herself as a chartered accountant. The other sister was an invalid, there was a deformity of kinds and she never saw people or went out. That's why when the old man died, Letitia gave up everything to go home and look after her sister. Randall was wild with her – but it made no difference. If Letitia thought a thing was her duty she'd do it. And you couldn't move her.'

'How long was that before your husband died?'

'A couple of years, I think. Randall made his will before she left the firm, and he didn't alter it. He said to me: "We've no one of our own." (Our little boy died, you know, when he was two years old.) "After you and I are gone, Blackie had better have the money. She'll play the markets and make 'em sit up."

'You see,' Belle went on, 'Randall enjoyed the whole money-making game so much – it wasn't just the money – it was the adventure, the risks, the excitement of it all. And Blackie liked it too. She had the same adventurous spirit and the same judgment. Poor darling, she'd never had any of the usual fun – being in love, and leading men on and teasing them – and having a home and children and all the real fun of life.'

Craddock thought it was odd, the real pity and indulgent contempt felt by this woman, a woman whose life had been hampered by illness, whose only child had died, whose husband had died, leaving her to a lonely widowhood, and who had been a hopeless invalid for years.

She nodded her head at him.

'I know what you're thinking. But I've *had* all the things that make life worth while – they may have been taken from me – but I have had them. I was pretty and gay as a girl, I married the man I loved, and he never stopped loving me . . . My child died, but I had him for two precious years . . . I've had a lot of physical pain – but if you have pain, you know how to enjoy the exquisite pleasure of the times when pain stops. And everyone's been kind to me, always . . . I'm a lucky woman, really.'

Craddock seized upon an opening in her former remarks.

'You said just now, Mrs Goedler, that your husband left his fortune to Miss Blacklock because he had no one else to leave it to. But that's not strictly true, is it? He had a sister.'

'Oh, Sonia. But they quarrelled years ago and made a clean break of it.'

'He disapproved of her marriage?'

'Yes, she married a man called – now what was his name –?'

'Stamfordis.'

'That's it. Dmitri Stamfordis. Randall always said he was a crook. The two men didn't like each other from the first. But Sonia was wildly in love with him and quite determined to marry him. And I really never saw why she shouldn't. Men have such odd ideas about these things. Sonia wasn't a mere girl – she was twenty-five, and she knew exactly what she was doing. He was a crook, I dare say – I mean really a crook. I believe he had a criminal record – and Randall always suspected the name he was passing under here wasn't his own. Sonia knew all that. The point was, which of course Randall couldn't appreciate, that Dmitri was really a wildly attractive person to women. And he was just as much in love with Sonia as she was with him. Randall insisted that he was just marrying her for her money – but that wasn't true. Sonia was very handsome, you know. And she had plenty of spirit. If the marriage had turned out badly, if Dmitri had been unkind to her or unfaithful to her, she would just have cut her losses and walked out on him. She was a rich woman and could do as she chose with her life.'

'The quarrel was never made up?'

'No. Randall and Sonia never had got on very well. She resented his trying to prevent the marriage. She said, "Very well. You're quite impossible! This is the last you hear of me!"'

'But it was not the last you heard of her?'

Belle smiled.

'No, I got a letter from her about eighteen months afterwards. She wrote from Budapest, I remember, but she didn't give an address. She told me to tell Randall that she was extremely happy and that she'd just had twins.'

'And she told you their names?'

Again Belle smiled. 'She said they were born just after midday – and she intended to call them Pip and Emma. That may have been just a joke, of course.'

'Didn't you hear from her again?'

'No. She said she and her husband and the babies were going to America on a short stay. I never heard any more . . .'

'You don't happen, I suppose, to have kept that letter?'

'No, I'm afraid not . . . I read it to Randall and he just grunted: "She'll regret marrying that fellow one of these days." That's all he ever said about it. We really forgot about her. She went right out of our lives . . .'

'Nevertheless Mr Goedler left his estate to her children in the event of Miss Blacklock predeceasing you?'

'Oh, that was my doing. I said to him, when he told me about the will: "And suppose Blackie dies before I do?" He was quite surprised. I said, "Oh, I know Blackie is as strong as a horse and I'm a delicate creature – but there's such a thing as accidents, you know, and there's such a thing as creaking gates . . ." And he said, "There's no one – absolutely no one."

I said, "There's Sonia." And he said at once, "And let that fellow get hold of my money? No – indeed!" I said, "Well, her children then. Pip and Emma, and there may be lots more by now" – and so he grumbled, but he did put it in.'

'And from that day to this,' Craddock said slowly, 'you've heard nothing of your sister-in-law or her children?'

'Nothing – they may be dead – they may be – anywhere.'

They may be in Chipping Cleghorn, thought Craddock.

As though she read his thoughts, a look of alarm came into Belle Goedler's eyes. She said, 'Don't let them hurt Blackie. Blackie's *good* – really good – you mustn't let harm come to –'

Her voice trailed off suddenly. Craddock saw the sudden grey shadows round her mouth and eyes.

'You're tired,' he said. 'I'll go.'

She nodded.

'Send Mac to me,' she whispered. 'Yes, tired . . .' She made a feeble motion of her hand. 'Look after Blackie . . . Nothing must happen to Blackie . . . look after her . . .'

'I'll do my very best, Mrs Goedler.' He rose and went to the door.

Her voice, a thin thread of sound, followed him . . .

'Not long now – until I'm dead – dangerous for her – Take care . . .'

Sister McClelland passed him as he went out. He said, uneasily:

'I hope I haven't done her harm.'

'Oh, I don't think so, Mr Craddock. I told you she would tire quite suddenly.'

Later, he asked the nurse:

'The only thing I hadn't time to ask Mrs Goedler was whether she had any old photographs? If so, I wonder –'

She interrupted him.

'I'm afraid there's nothing of that kind. All her personal papers and things were stored with their furniture from the London house at the beginning of the war. Mrs Goedler was desperately ill at the time. Then the storage despository was blitzed. Mrs Goedler was very upset at losing so many personal souvenirs and family papers. I'm afraid there's nothing of that kind.'

So that was that, Craddock thought.

Yet he felt his journey had not been in vain. Pip and Emma, those twin wraiths, were not quite wraiths.

Craddock thought, 'Here's a brother and sister brought up somewhere in Europe. Sonia Goedler was a rich woman at the time of her marriage, but money in Europe hasn't remained money. Queer things have happened to money during these war years. And so there are two young people, the son and daughter of a man who had a criminal record. Suppose they came to England, more or less penniless. What would they do? Find out about any rich relatives. Their uncle, a man of vast fortune, is dead. Possibly the first thing they'd do would be to look up their uncle's will. See if by any chance money had been left to them or to their mother. So they go to Somerset House and learn the contents of his will, and then, perhaps, they learn of the existence of Miss Letitia Blacklock. Then they make inquiries about Randall Goedler's widow. She's an invalid, living up in Scotland, and they find out she hasn't long to live. *If this Letitia Blacklock dies before her*, they will come into a vast fortune. What then?'

Craddock thought, 'They wouldn't go to Scotland. They'd find out where Letitia Blacklock is living now. And they'd go there – but not as themselves . . . They'd go together – or separately? Emma . . . I wonder? . . . Pip and Emma . . . I'll eat my hat if Pip, or Emma, or both of them, aren't in Chipping Cleghorn now . . .'

CHAPTER 15

DELICIOUS DEATH

In the kitchen at Little Paddocks, Miss Blacklock was giving instructions to Mitzi.

'Sardine sandwiches as well as the tomato ones. And some of those little scones you make so nicely. And I'd like you to make that special cake of yours.'

'Is it a party then, that you want all these things?'

'It's Miss Bunner's birthday, and some people will be coming to tea.'

'At her age one does not have birthdays. It is better to forget.'

'Well, she doesn't want to forget. Several people are bringing her presents – and it will be nice to make a little party of it.'

'That is what you say last time – and see what happened!'

Miss Blacklock controlled her temper.

'Well, it won't happen this time.'

'How do you know what may happen in this house? All day long I shiver and at night I lock my door and I look in the wardrobe to see no one is hidden there.'

'That ought to keep you nice and safe,' said Miss Blacklock, coldly.

'The cake that you want me to make, it is the –?' Mitzi uttered a sound that to Miss Blacklock's English ear sounded like Schwitzebzr or alternatively like cats spitting at each other.

'That's the one. The rich one.'

'Yes. It is rich. For it I have *nothing*! Impossible to make such a cake. I need for it chocolate and much butter, and sugar and raisins.'

'You can use this tin of butter that was sent us from America. And some of the raisins we were keeping for Christmas, and here is a slab of chocolate and a pound of sugar.'

Mitzi's face suddenly burst into radiant smiles.

'So, I make him for you good – good,' she cried, in an ecstasy. 'It will be rich, rich, of a melting richness! And on top I will put the icing – chocolate icing – I make him so nice – and write on it *Good Wishes*. These English people with their cakes that tastes of sand, never *never*, will they have tasted such a cake. Delicious, they will say – delicious –'

Her face clouded again.

'Mr Patrick. He called it Delicious Death. My cake! I will not have my cake called that!'

'It was a compliment really,' said Miss Blacklock. 'He meant it was worth dying to eat such a cake.'

Mitzi looked at her doubtfully.

'Well, I do not like that word – *death*. They are not dying because they eat my cake, no, they feel much, much better . . .'

'I'm sure we all shall.'

Miss Blacklock turned away and left the kitchen with a sigh of relief at the successful ending of the interview. With Mitzi one never knew.

She ran into Dora Bunner outside.

'Oh, Letty, shall I run in and tell Mitzi just how to cut the sandwiches?'

'No,' said Miss Blacklock, steering her friend firmly into the hall. 'She's in a good mood now and I don't want her disturbed.'

'But I could just show her –'

'Please don't show her *anything*, Dora. These central Europeans don't *like* being shown. They hate it.'

Dora looked at her doubtfully. Then she suddenly broke into smiles.

'Edmund Swettenham just rang up. He wished me many happy returns of the day and said he was bringing me a pot of honey as a present this afternoon. Isn't it kind? I can't imagine how he knew it was my birthday.'

'Everybody seems to know. You must have been talking about it, Dora.'

'Well, I did just happen to mention that today I should be fifty-nine.'

'You're sixty-four,' said Miss Blacklock with a twinkle.

'And Miss Hinchcliffe said, "You don't look it. What age do you think *I* am?" Which was rather awkward because Miss Hinchcliffe always looks so peculiar that she might be any age. She said she was bringing me some eggs, by the way. I said our hens hadn't been laying very well, lately.'

'We're not doing so badly out of your birthday,' said Miss Blacklock. 'Honey, eggs – a magnificent box of chocolates from Julia –'

'I don't know where she gets such things.'

'Better not ask. Her methods are probably strictly illegal.'

'And your lovely brooch.' Miss Bunner looked down proudly at her bosom on which was pinned a small diamond leaf.

'Do you like it? I'm glad. I never cared for jewellery.'

'I love it.'

'Good. Let's go and feed the ducks.'

'Ha,' cried Patrick dramatically, as the party took their places round the dining-room table. 'What do I see before me? *Delicious Death.*'

'Hush,' said Miss Blacklock. 'Don't let Mitzi hear you. She objects to your name for her cake very much.'

'Nevertheless, Delicious Death it is! Is it Bunny's birthday cake?'

'Yes, it is,' said Miss Bunner. 'I really am having the most wonderful birthday.'

Her cheeks were flushed with excitement and had been ever since Colonel Easterbrook had handed her a small box of sweets and declaimed with a bow, 'Sweets to the Sweet!'

Julia had turned her head away hurriedly, and had been frowned at by Miss Blacklock.

Full justice was done to the good things on the tea table and they rose from their seats after a round of crackers.

'I feel slightly sick,' said Julia. 'It's that cake. I remember I felt just the same last time.'

'It's worth it,' said Patrick.

'These foreigners certainly understand confectionery,' said Miss Hinchcliffe. 'What they can't make is a plain boiled pudding.'

Everybody was respectfully silent, though it seemed to be hovering on Patrick's lips to ask if anyone really *wanted* a plain boiled pudding.

'Got a new gardener?' asked Miss Hinchcliffe of Miss Blacklock as they returned to the drawing-room.

'No, why?'

'Saw a man snooping round the henhouse. Quite a decent-looking Army type.'

'Oh, *that*,' said Julia. 'That's our detective.'

Mrs Easterbrook dropped her handbag.

'Detective?' she exclaimed. 'But – but – why?'

'I don't know,' said Julia. 'He prowls about and keeps an eye on the house. He's protecting Aunt Letty, I suppose.'

'Absolute nonsense,' said Miss Blacklock. 'I can protect myself, thank you.'

'But surely it's all over now,' cried Mrs Easterbrook. 'Though I meant to ask you, why did they adjourn the inquest?'

'Police aren't satisfied,' said her husband. 'That's what that means.'

'But aren't satisfied of what?'

Colonel Easterbrook shook his head with the air of a man who could say a good deal more if he chose. Edmund Swettenham, who disliked the Colonel, said, 'The truth of it is, we're all under suspicion.'

'But suspicion of *what?*' repeated Mrs Easterbrook.

'Never mind, kitten,' said her husband.

'Loitering with intent,' said Edmund. 'The intent being to commit murder upon the first opportunity.'

'Oh, don't, please don't, Mr Swettenham.' Dora Bunner began to cry. 'I'm sure nobody here could possibly want to kill dear, dear Letty.'

There was a moment of horrible embarrassment. Edmund turned scarlet, murmured, 'Just a joke.' Phillipa suggested in a high clear voice that they might listen to the six o'clock news and the suggestion was received with enthusiastic assent.

Patrick murmured to Julia: 'We need Mrs Harmon here. She'd be sure to say in that high clear voice of hers, "But I suppose somebody *is* still waiting for a good chance to murder you, Miss Blacklock?"'

'I'm glad she and that old Miss Marple couldn't come,' said Julia. 'That old woman is the prying kind. And a mind like a sink, I should think. Real Victorian type.'

Listening to the news led easily into a pleasant discussion on the horrors of atomic warfare. Colonel Easterbrook said that the real menace to civilization was undoubtedly Russia, and Edmund said that he had several charming Russian friends – which announcement was coldly received.

The party broke up with renewed thanks to the hostess.

'Enjoy yourself, Bunny?' asked Miss Blacklock, as the last guest was sped.

'Oh, I did. But I've got a terrible headache. It's the excitement, I think.'

'It's the cake,' said Patrick. 'I feel a bit liverish myself. And you've been nibbling chocolates all the morning.'

'I'll go and lie down, I think,' said Miss Bunner. 'I'll take a couple of aspirins and try and have a nice sleep.'

'That would be a very good plan,' said Miss Blacklock.

Miss Bunner departed upstairs.

'Shall I shut up the ducks for you, Aunt Letty?'

Miss Blacklock looked at Patrick severely.

'If you'll be sure to latch that door properly.'

'I will. I swear I will.'

'Have a glass of sherry, Aunt Letty,' said Julia. 'As my old nurse used to say, "It will settle your stomach." A revolting phrase, but curiously apposite at this moment.'

'Well, I dare say it might be a good thing. The truth is one isn't used to rich things. Oh, Bunny, how you made me jump. What is it?'

'I can't find my aspirin,' said Miss Bunner disconsolately.

'Well, take some of mine, dear, they're by my bed.'

'There's a bottle on my dressing-table,' said Phillipa.

'Thank you – thank you very much. If I can't find mine – but I know I've got it *somewhere*. A new bottle. Now where could I have put it?'

'There's heaps in the bathroom,' said Julia impatiently. 'This house is chock full of aspirin.'

'It vexes me to be so careless and mislay things,' replied Miss Bunner, retreating up the stairs again.

'Poor old Bunny,' said Julia, holding up her glass. 'Do you think we ought to have given her some sherry?'

'Better not, I think,' said Miss Blacklock. 'She's had a lot of excitement today, and it isn't really good for her. I'm afraid she'll be the worse for it tomorrow. Still, I really do think she has enjoyed herself!'

'She's loved it,' said Phillipa.

'Let's give Mitzi a glass of sherry,' suggested Julia. 'Hi, Pat,' she called as she heard him entering the side door. 'Fetch Mitzi.'

So Mitzi was brought in and Julia poured her out a glass of sherry.

'Here's to the best cook in the world,' said Patrick.

Mitzi was gratified – but felt nevertheless that a protest was due.

'That is not so. I am not really a cook. In my country I do intellectual work.'

'Then you're wasted,' said Patrick. 'What's intellectual work compared to a *chef d'oeuvre* like Delicious Death?'

'Oo – I say to you I do not like –'

'Never mind what you like, my girl,' said Patrick. 'That's my name for it and here's to it. Let's all drink to Delicious Death and to hell with the after-effects.'

'Phillipa, my dear, I want to talk to you.'

'Yes, Miss Blacklock?'

Phillipa Haymes looked up in slight surprise.

'You're not worrying about anything, are you?'

'Worrying?'

'I've noticed that you've looked worried lately. There isn't anything wrong, is there?'

'Oh no, Miss Blacklock. Why should there be?'

'Well – I wondered. I thought, perhaps, that you and Patrick –?'

'Patrick?' Phillipa looked really surprised.

'It's not so, then. Please forgive me if I've been impertinent. But you've been thrown together a lot – and although Patrick is my cousin, I don't think he's the type to make a satisfactory husband. Not for some time to come, at all events.'

Phillipa's face had frozen into a hard immobility.

'I shan't marry again,' she said.

'Oh, yes, you will some day, my child. You're young. But we needn't discuss that. There's no other trouble. You're not worried about – money, for instance?'

'No, I'm quite all right.'

'I know you get anxious sometimes about your boy's education. That's why I want to tell you something. I drove into Milchester this afternoon to see Mr Beddingfeld, my lawyer. Things haven't been very settled lately and I thought I would like to make a new will – in view of certain eventualities. Apart from Bunny's legacy, everything goes to you, Phillipa.'

'What?' Phillipa spun round. Her eyes stared. She looked dismayed, almost frightened.

'But I don't want it – really I don't . . . Oh, I'd rather not . . . And anyway, why? Why to *me*?'

'Perhaps,' said Miss Blacklock in a peculiar voice, 'because there's no one else.'

'But there's Patrick and Julia.'

'Yes, there's Patrick and Julia.' The odd note in Miss Blacklock's voice was still there.

'They are your relations.'

'Very distant ones. They have no claim on me.'

'But I – I haven't either – I don't know what you think . . . Oh, I don't want it.'

Her gaze held more hostility than gratitude. There was something almost like fear in her manner.

'I know what I'm doing, Phillipa. I've become fond of you – and there's the boy . . . You won't get very much if I should die now – but in a few weeks' time it might be different.'

Her eyes met Phillipa's steadily.

'But you're not going to die!' Phillipa protested.

'Not if I can avoid it by taking due precautions.'

'Precautions?'

'Yes. Think it over . . . And don't worry any more.'

She left the room abruptly. Phillipa heard her speaking to Julia in the hall.

Julia entered the drawing-room a few moments later.

There was a slightly steely glitter in her eyes.

'Played your cards rather well, haven't you, Phillipa? I see you're one of those quiet ones . . . a dark horse.'

'So you heard –?'

'Yes, I heard. I rather think I was meant to hear.'

'What do you mean?'

'Our Letty's no fool . . . Well, anyway, you're all right, Phillipa. Sitting pretty, aren't you?'

'Oh, Julia – I didn't mean – I never meant –'

'Didn't you? Of course you did. You're fairly up against things, aren't you? Hard up for money. But just remember this – if anyone bumps off Aunt Letty now, *you'll* be suspect No. 1.'

'But I shan't be. It would be idiotic if I killed her now when – if I waited –'

'So you *do* know about old Mrs Whatsername dying up in Scotland? I wondered . . . Phillipa, I'm beginning to believe you're a very dark horse indeed.'

'I don't want to do you and Patrick out of anything.'

'Don't you, my dear? I'm sorry – but I don't believe you.'

CHAPTER 16
INSPECTOR CRADDOCK RETURNS

Inspector Craddock had had a bad night on his night journey home. His dreams had been less dreams than nightmares. Again and again he was racing through the grey corridors of an old-world castle in a desperate attempt to get somewhere, or to prevent something, in time. Finally he dreamt that he awoke. An enormous relief surged over him. Then the door of his compartment slid slowly open, and Letitia Blacklock looked in at him with blood running down her face, and said reproachfully: 'Why didn't you save me? You could have if you'd tried.'

This time he really awoke.

Altogether, the Inspector was thankful finally to reach Milchester. He went straight away to make his report to Rydesdale who listened carefully.

'It doesn't take us much further,' he said. 'But it confirms what Miss Blacklock told you. Pip and Emma – h'm, I wonder.'

'Patrick and Julia Simmons are the right age, sir. If we could establish that Miss Blacklock hadn't seen them since they were children –'

With a very faint chuckle, Rydesdale said: 'Our ally, Miss Marple, has established that for us. Actually Miss Blacklock had never seen either of them at all until two months ago.'

'Then, surely, sir –'

'It's not so easy as all that, Craddock. We've been checking up. On what we've got, Patrick and Julia seem definitely to be out of it. His Naval record is genuine – quite a good record bar a tendency to "insubordination". We've checked with Cannes, and an indignant Mrs Simmons says of course her son and daughter are at Chipping Cleghorn with her cousin Letitia Blacklock. So that's that!'

'And Mrs Simmons *is* Mrs Simmons?'

'She's been Mrs Simmons for a very long time, that's all I can say,' said Rydesdale dryly.

'That seems clear enough. Only – those two fitted. Right age. Not known to Miss Blacklock, personally. If we wanted Pip and Emma – well, there they were.'

The Chief Constable nodded thoughtfully, then he pushed across a paper to Craddock.

'Here's a little something we've dug up on Mrs Easterbrook.'

The Inspector read with lifted eyebrows.

'Very interesting,' he remarked. 'Hoodwinked that old ass pretty well, hasn't she? It doesn't tie in with this business though, as far as I can see.'

'Apparently not.'

'And here's an item that concerns Mrs Haymes.'

Again Craddock's eyebrows rose.

'I think I'll have another talk with the lady,' he said.

'You think this information might be relevant?'

'I think it might be. It would be a long shot, of course . . .'

The two men were silent for a moment or two.

'How has Fletcher got on, sir?'

'Fletcher has been exceedingly active. He's made a routine search of the house by agreement with Miss Blacklock – but he didn't find anything significant. Then he's been checking up on who could have had the opportunity of oiling that door. Checking who was up at the house on the days that that foreign girl was out. A little more complicated than we thought, because it appears she goes for a walk most afternoons. Usually down to the village where she has a cup of coffee at the Bluebird. So that when Miss Blacklock and Miss Bunner are out – which is most afternoons – they go blackberrying – the coast is clear.'

'And the doors are always left unlocked?'

'They used to be. I don't suppose they are now.'

'What are Fletcher's results? Who's known to have been in the house when it was left empty?'

'Practically the whole lot of them.'

Rydesdale consulted a page in front of him.

'Miss Murgatroyd was there with a hen to sit on some eggs. (Sounds complicated but that's what she says.) Very flustered about it all and contradicts herself, but Fletcher thinks that's temperamental and not a sign of guilt.'

'Might be,' Craddock admitted. 'She flaps.'

'Then Mrs Swettenham came up to fetch some horse meat that Miss Blacklock had left for her on the kitchen table because Miss Blacklock had been in to Milchester in the car that day and always gets Mrs Swettenham's horse meat for her. That make sense to you?'

Craddock considered.

'Why didn't Miss Blacklock leave the horse meat when she passed Mrs Swettenham's house on her way back from Milchester?'

'I don't know, but she didn't. Mrs Swettenham says she (Miss B.) always leaves it on the kitchen table, and she (Mrs S.) likes to fetch it when Mitzi isn't there because Mitzi is sometimes so rude.'

'Hangs together quite well. And the next?'

'Miss Hinchcliffe. Says she wasn't there at all lately. But she was. Because Mitzi saw her coming out of the side door one day and so did a Mrs Butt (she's one of the locals). Miss H. then admitted she might have been there but had forgotten. Can't remember what she went for. Says she probably just dropped in.'

'That's rather odd.'

'So was her manner, apparently. Then there's Mrs Easterbrook. She was exercising the dear dogs out that way and she just popped in to see if Miss Blacklock would lend her a knitting pattern but Miss Blacklock wasn't in. She says she waited a little.'

'Just so. Might be snooping round. Or might be oiling a door. And the Colonel?'

'Went there one day with a book on India that Miss Blacklock had expressed a desire to read.'

'Had she?'

'Her account is that she tried to get out of having to read it, but it was no use.'

'And that's fair enough,' sighed Craddock. 'If anyone is really determined to lend you a book, you never can get out of it!'

'We don't know if Edmund Swettenham was up there. He's extremely vague. Said he did drop in occasionally on errands for his mother, but thinks not lately.'

'In fact, it's all inconclusive.'

'Yes.'

Rydesdale said, with a slight grin:

'Miss Marple has also been active. Fletcher reports that she had morning coffee at the Bluebird. She's been to sherry at Boulders, and to tea at Little Paddocks. She's admired Mrs Swettenham's garden – and dropped in to see Colonel Easterbrook's Indian curios.'

'She may be able to tell us if Colonel Easterbrook's a pukka Colonel or not.'

'She'd know, I agree – he seems all right. We'd have to check with the Far Eastern Authorities to get certain identification.'

'And in the meantime' – Craddock broke off – 'do you think Miss Blacklock would consent to go away?'

'Go away from Chipping Cleghorn?'

'Yes. Take the faithful Bunner with her, perhaps, and leave for an unknown destination. Why shouldn't she go up to Scotland and stay with Belle Goedler? It's a pretty unget-at-able place.'

'Stop there and wait for her to die? I don't think she'd do that. I don't think any nice-natured woman would like that suggestion.'

'If it's a matter of saving her life –'

'Come now, Craddock, it isn't quite so easy to bump someone off as you seem to think.'

'Isn't it, sir?'

'Well – in one way – it's easy enough I agree. Plenty of methods. Weed-killer. A bash on the head when she's out shutting up the poultry, a pot shot from behind a hedge. All quite simple. But to bump someone off and not be suspected of bumping them off – that's not quite so easy. And they must realize by now that they're all under observation. The original carefully planned scheme failed. Our unknown murderer has got to think up something else.'

'I know that, sir. But there's the time element to consider. Mrs Goedler's a dying woman – she might pop off any minute. That means that our murderer can't afford to wait.'

'True.'

'And another thing, sir. He – or she – must know that we're checking up on everybody.'

'And that takes time,' said Rydesdale with a sigh. 'It means checking with the East, with India. Yes, it's a long tedious business.'

'So that's another reason for – hurry. I'm sure, sir, that the danger is very real. It's a very large sum that's at stake. If Belle Goedler dies –'

He broke off as a constable entered.

'Constable Legg on the line from Chipping Cleghorn, sir.'

'Put him through here.'

Inspector Craddock, watching the Chief Constable, saw his features harden and stiffen.

'Very good,' barked Rydesdale. 'Detective-Inspector Craddock will be coming out immediately.'

He put the receiver down.

'Is it –?' Craddock broke off.

Rydesdale shook his head.

'No,' he said. 'It's Dora Bunner. She wanted some aspirin. Apparently she took some from a bottle beside Letitia Blacklock's bed. There were only a few tablets left in the bottle. She took two and left one. The doctor's got that one and is sending it to be analysed. He says it's definitely *not* aspirin.'

'She's dead?'

'Yes, found dead in her bed this morning. Died in her sleep, doctor says. He doesn't think it was natural though her health was in a bad state. Narcotic poisoning, that's his guess. Autopsy's fixed for tonight.'

'Aspirin tablets by Letitia Blacklock's bed. The clever clever devil. Patrick told me Miss Blacklock threw away a half bottle of sherry – opened a new one. I don't suppose she'd have thought of doing that with an open bottle of aspirin. Who had been in the house this time – within the last day or two? The tablets can't have been there long.'

Rydesdale looked at him.

'All our lot were there yesterday,' he said. 'Birthday party for Miss Bunner. Any of them could have nipped upstairs and done a neat little substitution. Or of course anyone living in the house could have done it any time.'

CHAPTER 17

THE ALBUM

Standing by the Vicarage gate, well wrapped up, Miss Marple took the note from Bunch's hand.

'Tell Miss Blacklock,' said Bunch, 'that Julian is terribly sorry he can't come up himself. He's got a parishioner dying out at Locke Hamlet. He'll come up after lunch if Miss Blacklock would like to see him. The note's about the arrangements for the funeral. He suggests Wednesday if the inquest's on Tuesday. Poor old Bunny. It's so typical of her, somehow, to get hold of poisoned aspirin meant for someone else. Goodbye, darling. I hope the walk won't be too much for you. But I've simply got to get that child to hospital at once.'

Miss Marple said the walk wouldn't be too much for her, and Bunch rushed off.

Whilst waiting for Miss Blacklock, Miss Marple looked round the drawing-room, and wondered just exactly what Dora Bunner had meant that morning in the Bluebird by saying that she believed Patrick had 'tampered with the lamp' to 'make the lights go out'. What lamp? And how had he 'tampered' with it?

She must, Miss Marple decided, have meant the small lamp that stood on the table by the archway. She had said something about a shepherdess or a shepherd – and this was actually a delicate piece of Dresden china, a shepherd in a blue coat and pink breeches holding what had originally been a candlestick and had now been adapted to electricity. The shade was of plain vellum and a little too big so that it almost masked the figure. What else was it that Dora Bunner had said? 'I remember distinctly that it was the shepherdess. And the next day –' Certainly it was a shepherd now.

Miss Marple remembered that when she and Bunch had come to tea, Dora Bunner had said something about the lamp being one of a *pair*. Of course – a shepherd and a shepherdess. And it had been the shepherdess on the day of the hold-up – and the next morning it had been the *other* lamp – the lamp that was here now, the shepherd. The lamps had been changed over during the night. And Dora Bunner had had reason to believe (or had believed without reason) that it was Patrick who had changed them.

Why? Because, if the original lamp were examined, it would show just how Patrick had managed to 'make the lights go out'. How had he managed? Miss Marple looked earnestly at the lamp in front of her. The flex ran along the table over the edge and was plugged into the wall. There was a small pear-shaped switch half-way along the flex. None of it suggested anything to Miss Marple because she knew very little about electricity.

Where was the shepherdess lamp? she wondered. In the 'spare room' or thrown away, or – where was it Dora Bunner had come upon Patrick Simmons with a feather and an oily cup? In the shrubbery? Miss Marple made up her mind to put all these points to Inspector Craddock.

At the very beginning Miss Blacklock had leaped to the conclusion that her nephew Patrick had been behind the insertion of that advertisement. That kind of instinctive belief was often justified, or so Miss Marple believed. Because, if you knew people fairly well, you knew the kind of things they thought of . . .

Patrick Simmons . . .

A handsome young man. An engaging young man. A young man whom women liked, both young women and old women. The kind of man, perhaps, that Randall Goedler's sister had married. Could Patrick Simmons be 'Pip'? But he'd been in the Navy during the war. The police could soon check up on that.

Only – sometimes – the most amazing impersonations *did* happen.

You could get away with a great deal if you had enough audacity . . .

The door opened and Miss Blacklock came in. She looked, Miss Marple thought, many years older. All the life and energy had gone out of her.

'I'm very sorry, disturbing you like this,' said Miss Marple. 'But the

Vicar had a dying parishioner and Bunch had to rush a sick child to hospital. The Vicar wrote you a note.'

She held it out and Miss Blacklock took it and opened it.

'Do sit down, Miss Marple,' she said. 'It's very kind of you to have brought this.'

She read the note through.

'The Vicar's a very understanding man,' she said quietly. 'He doesn't offer one fatuous consolation . . . Tell him that these arrangements will do very well. Her – her favourite hymn was *Lead Kindly Light*.'

Her voice broke suddenly.

Miss Marple said gently:

'I am only a stranger, but I am so very very sorry.'

And suddenly, uncontrollably, Letitia Blacklock wept. It was a piteous overmastering grief, with a kind of hopelessness about it. Miss Marple sat quite still.

Miss Blacklock sat up at last. Her face was swollen and blotched with tears.

'I'm sorry,' she said. 'It – it just came over me. What I've lost. She – she was the only link with the past, you see. The only one who – who *remembered*. Now that she's gone I'm quite alone.'

'I know what you mean,' said Miss Marple. 'One *is* alone when the last one who *remembers* is gone. I have nephews and nieces and kind friends – but there's no one who knew me as a young girl – no one who belongs to the old days. I've been alone for quite a long time now.'

Both women sat silent for some moments.

'You understand very well,' said Letitia Blacklock. She rose and went over to her desk. 'I must write a few words to the Vicar.' She held the pen rather awkwardly and wrote slowly.

'Arthritic,' she explained. 'Sometimes I can hardly write at all.'

She sealed up the envelope and addressed it.

'If you wouldn't mind taking it, it would be very kind.'

Hearing a man's voice in the hall she said quickly:

'That's Inspector Craddock.'

She went to the mirror over the fireplace and applied a small powder puff to her face.

Craddock came in with a grim, angry face.

He looked at Miss Marple with disapprobation.

'Oh,' he said. 'So *you're* here.'

Miss Blacklock turned from the mantelpiece.

'Miss Marple kindly came up with a note from the Vicar.'

Miss Marple said in a flurried manner:

'I am going at once – at once. Please don't let me hamper you in *any* way.'

'Were you at the tea party here yesterday afternoon?'

Miss Marple said, nervously:

'No – no, I wasn't. Bunch drove me over to call on some friends.'

'Then there's nothing you can tell me.' Craddock held the door open in a pointed manner, and Miss Marple scuttled out in a somewhat abashed fashion.

'Nosey Parkers, these old women,' said Craddock.

'I think you're being unfair to her,' said Miss Blacklock. 'She really did come with a note from the Vicar.'

'I bet she did.'

'I don't think it was idle curiosity.'

'Well, perhaps you're right, Miss Blacklock, but my own diagnosis would be a severe attack of Nosey Parkeritis . . .'

'She's a very harmless old creature,' said Miss Blacklock.

'Dangerous as a rattlesnake if you only knew,' the Inspector thought grimly. But he had no intention of taking anyone into his confidence unnecessarily. Now that he knew definitely there was a killer at large, he felt that the less said the better. He didn't want the next person bumped off to be Jane Marple.

Somewhere – a killer . . . Where?

'I won't waste time offering sympathy, Miss Blacklock,' he said. 'As a matter of fact I feel pretty bad about Miss Bunner's death. We ought to have been able to prevent it.'

'I don't see what you could have done.'

'No – well, it wouldn't have been easy. But now we've got to work fast. Who's doing this, Miss Blacklock? Who's had two shots at killing you, and will probably, if we don't work fast enough, soon have another?'

Letitia Blacklock shivered. 'I don't know, Inspector – I don't know *at all!*'

'I've checked up with Mrs Goedler. She's given me all the help she can. It wasn't very much. There are just a few people who would definitely profit by your death. First Pip and Emma. Patrick and Julia Simmons are the right age, but their background seems clear enough. Anyway, we can't concentrate on these two alone. Tell me, Miss Blacklock, would you recognize Sonia Goedler if you saw her?'

'Recognize Sonia? Why, of course –' She stopped suddenly. 'No,' she said slowly, 'I don't know that I would. It's a long time. Thirty years . . . She'd be an elderly woman now.'

'What was she like when you remember her?'

'Sonia?' Miss Blacklock considered for some moments. 'She was rather small, dark . . .'

'Any special peculiarities? Mannerisms?'

'No – no, I don't think so. She was gay – very gay.'

'She mayn't be so gay now,' said the Inspector. 'Have you got a photograph of her?'

'Of Sonia? Let me see – not a proper photograph. I've got some old snapshots – in an album somewhere – at least I think there's one of her.'

'Ah. Can I have a look at it?'

'Yes, of course. Now where did I put that album?'

'Tell me, Miss Blacklock, do you consider it remotely possible that Mrs Swettenham might be Sonia Goedler?'

'*Mrs Swettenham?*' Miss Blacklock looked at him in lively atonishment. 'But her husband was in the Government Service – in India first, I think, and then in Hong Kong.'

'What you mean is, that that's the story she's told you. You don't, as we say in the Courts, know it of your own knowledge, do you?'

'No,' said Miss Blacklock slowly. 'When you put it like that, I don't . . . But Mrs Swettenham? Oh, it's absurd!'

'Did Sonia Goedler ever do any acting? Amateur theatricals?'

'Oh, yes. She was good.'

'There you are! Another thing, Mrs Swettenham wears a wig. At least,' the Inspector corrected himself, 'Mrs Harmon says she does.'

'Yes – yes, I suppose it might be a wig. All those little grey curls. But I still think it's absurd. She's really very nice and exceedingly funny sometimes.'

'Then there's Miss Hinchcliffe and Miss Murgatroyd. Could either of them be Sonia Goedler?'

'Miss Hinchcliffe is too tall. She's as tall as a man.'

'Miss Murgatroyd then?'

'Oh, but – oh no, I'm sure Miss Murgatroyd couldn't be Sonia.'

'You don't see very well, do you, Miss Blacklock?'

'I'm shortsighted; is that what you mean?'

'Yes. What I'd like to see is a snapshot of this Sonia Goedler, even if it's a long time ago and not a good likeness. We're trained, you know, to pick out resemblances, in a way no amateur can ever do.'

'I'll try and find it for you.'

'Now?'

'What, at once?'

'I'd prefer it.'

'Very well. Now, let me see. I saw that album when we were tidying a lot of books out of the cupboard. Julia was helping me. She laughed, I remember, at the clothes we used to wear in those days . . . The books we put in the shelf in the drawing-room. Where did we put the albums and the big bound volumes of the Art Journal? What a wretched memory I have! Perhaps Julia will remember. She's at home today.'

'I'll find her.'

The Inspector departed on his quest. He did not find Julia in any of the downstairs rooms. Mitzi, asked where Miss Simmons was, said crossly that it was not her affair.

'Me! I stay in my kitchen and concern myself with the lunch. And nothing do I eat that I have not cooked myself. Nothing, do you hear?'

The Inspector called up the stairs 'Miss Simmons,' and getting no response, went up.

He met Julia face to face just as he turned the corner of the landing. She had just emerged from a door that showed behind it a small twisty staircase.

'I was up in the attic,' she explained. 'What is it?'

Inspector Craddock explained.

'Those old photograph albums? Yes, I remember them quite well. We put them in the big cupboard in the study, I think. I'll find them for you.'

She led the way downstairs and pushed open the study door. Near the window there was a large cupboard. Julia pulled it open and disclosed a heterogenous mass of objects.

'Junk,' said Julia. 'All junk. But elderly people simply will *not* throw things away.'

The Inspector knelt down and took a couple of old-fashioned albums from the bottom shelf.

'Are these they?'

'Yes.'

Miss Blacklock came in and joined them.

'Oh, so *that's* where we put them. I couldn't remember.'

Craddock had the books on the table and was turning the pages.

Women in large cartwheel hats, women with dresses tapering down to their feet so that they could hardly walk. The photos had captions neatly printed underneath them, but the ink was old and faded.

'It would be in this one,' said Miss Blacklock. 'On about the second or third page. The other book is after Sonia had married and gone away.' She turned a page. 'It ought to be here.' She stopped.

There were several empty spaces on the page. Craddock bent down and deciphered the faded writing. 'Sonia . . . Self . . . R.G.' A little further along, 'Sonia and Belle on beach'. And again on the opposite page, 'Picnic at Skeyne'. He turned over another page, 'Charlotte, Self, Sonia, R.G.'

Craddock stood up. His lips were grim.

'*Somebody has removed these photographs* – not long ago, I should say.'

'There weren't any blank spaces when we looked at them the other day. Were there, Julia?'

'I didn't look very closely – only at some of the dresses. But no . . . you're right, Aunt Letty, there *weren't* any blank spaces.'

Craddock looked grimmer still.

'Somebody,' he said, 'has removed every photo of Sonia Goedler from this album.'

CHAPTER 18
THE LETTERS

'Sorry to worry you again, Mrs Haymes.'

'It doesn't matter,' said Phillipa coldly.

'Shall we go into this room here?'

'The study? Yes, if you like, Inspector. It's very cold. There's no fire.'

'It doesn't matter. It's not for long. And we're not so likely to be overheard here.'

'Does that matter?'

'Not to me, Mrs Haymes. It might to you.'

'What do you mean?'

'I think you told me, Mrs Haymes, that your husband was killed fighting in Italy?'

'Well?'

'Wouldn't it have been simpler to have told me the truth – that he was a deserter from his regiment.'

He saw her face grow white, and her hands close and unclose themselves.

She said bitterly:

'Do you have to rake up *everything?*'

Craddock said dryly:

'We expect people to tell us the truth about themselves.'

She was silent. Then she said:

'Well?'

'What do you mean by "Well?", Mrs Haymes?'

'I mean, what are you going to do about it? Tell everybody? Is that necessary – or fair – or kind?'

'Does nobody know?'

'Nobody here. Harry' – her voice changed – 'my son, he doesn't know. I don't want him to know. I don't want him to know – ever.'

'Then let me tell you that you're taking a very big risk, Mrs Haymes. When the boy is old enough to understand, tell him the truth. If he finds out by himself some day – it won't be good for him. If you go on stuffing him up with tales of his father dying like a hero –'

'I don't do that. I'm not completely dishonest. I just don't talk about it. His father was – killed in the war. After all, that's what it amounts to – for us.'

'But your husband is still alive?'

'Perhaps. How should I know?'

'When did you see him last, Mrs Haymes?'

Phillipa said quickly:

'I haven't seen him for years.'

'Are you quite sure that's true? You didn't, for instance, see him about a fortnight ago?'

'What are you suggesting?'

'It never seemed to me very likely that you met Rudi Scherz in the summerhouse here. But Mitzi's story was very emphatic. I suggest, Mrs Haymes, that the man you came back from work to meet that morning was your husband.'

'I didn't meet anybody in the summerhouse.'

'He was hard up for money, perhaps, and you supplied him with some?'

'I've not seen him, I tell you. I didn't meet anybody in the summerhouse.'

'Deserters are often rather desperate men. They often take part in robberies, you know. Hold-ups. Things of that kind. *And they have foreign revolvers very often that they've brought back from abroad.*'

'I don't know where my husband is. I haven't seen him for years.'

'Is that your last word, Mrs Haymes?'

'I've nothing else to say.'

Craddock came away from his interview with Phillipa Haymes feeling angry and baffled.

'Obstinate as a mule,' he said to himself angrily.

He was fairly sure that Phillipa was lying, but he hadn't succeeded in breaking down her obstinate denials.

He wished he knew a little more about ex-Captain Haymes. His information was meagre. An unsatisfactory Army record, but nothing to suggest that Haymes was likely to turn criminal.

And anyway Haymes didn't fit in with the oiled door.

Someone in the house had done that, or someone with easy access to it.

He stood looking up the staircase, and suddenly he wondered what Julia had been doing up in the attic. An attic, he thought, was an unlikely place for the fastidious Julia to visit.

What had she been doing up there?

He ran lightly up to the first floor. There was no one about. He opened the door out of which Julia had come and went up the narrow stairs to the attic.

There were trunks there, old suitcases, various broken articles of furniture, a chair with a leg off, a broken china lamp, part of an old dinner service.

He turned to the trunks and opened the lid of one.

Clothes. Old-fashioned, quite good-quality women's clothes. Clothes belonging, he supposed, to Miss Blacklock, or to her sister who had died.

He opened another trunk.

Curtains.

He passed to a small attaché-case. It had papers in it and letters. Very old letters, yellowed with time.

He looked at the outside of the case which had the initials C.L.B. on it. He deduced correctly that it had belonged to Letitia's sister Charlotte. He unfolded one of the letters. It began

Dearest Charlotte,
    Yesterday Belle felt well enough to go for a picnic. R.G.
also took a day off. The Asvogel flotation has gone splendidly,

R.G. is terribly pleased about it. The Preference shares are at a premium.

He skipped the rest and looked at the signature:
Your loving sister, Letitia.
He picked up another.

Darling Charlotte,
I wish you would sometimes make up your mind to see people. You do exaggerate, you know. It isn't nearly as bad as you think. And people really don't mind things like that. It's not the disfigurement you think it is.

He nodded his head. He remembered Belle Goedler saying that Charlotte Blacklock had a disfigurement or deformity of some kind. Letitia had, in the end, resigned her job, to go and look after her sister. These letters all breathed the anxious spirit of her affection and love for an invalid. She had written her sister, apparently, long accounts of everyday happenings, of any little detail that she thought might interest the sick girl. And Charlotte had kept these letters. Occasionally odd snapshots had been enclosed.

Excitement suddenly flooded Craddock's mind. Here, it might be, he would find a clue. In these letters there would be written down things that Letitia Blacklock herself had long forgotten. Here was a faithful picture of the past and somewhere amongst it, there might be a clue that would help him to identify the unknown. Photographs, too. There might, just possibly, be a photograph of Sonia Goedler here that the person who had taken the other photos out of the album did not know about.

Inspector Craddock packed the letters up again, carefully, closed the case, and started down the stairs.

Letitia Blacklock, standing on the landing below, looked at him in amazement.

'Was that you up in the attic? I heard footsteps. I couldn't imagine who –'

'Miss Blacklock, I have found some letters here, written by you to your sister Charlotte many years ago. Will you allow me to take them away and read them?'

She flushed angrily.

'Must you do a thing like that? Why? What good can they be to you?'

'They might give me a picture of Sonia Goedler, of her character – there may be some allusion – some incident – that will help.'

'They are private letters, Inspector.'

'I know.'

'I suppose you will take them anyway . . . You have the power to do so, I suppose, or you can easily get it. Take them – take them! But you'll find very little about Sonia. She married and went away only a year or two after I began to work for Randall Goedler.'

Craddock said obstinately:

'There may be *something*.' He added, 'We've got to try everything. I assure you the danger is very real.'

She said, biting her lips:

'I know. Bunny is dead – from taking an aspirin tablet that was meant for me. It may be Patrick, or Julia, or Phillipa, or Mitzi next – somebody young with their life in front of them. Somebody who drinks a glass of wine that is poured out for me, or eats a chocolate that is sent to me. Oh! take the letters – take them away. And afterwards burn them. They don't mean anything to anyone but me and Charlotte. It's all over – gone – past. Nobody remembers now . . .'

Her hand went up to the choker of false pearls she was wearing. Craddock thought how incongruous it looked with her tweed coat and skirt.

She said again:

'Take the letters.'

It was the following afternoon that the Inspector called at the Vicarage.

It was a dark gusty day.

Miss Marple had her chair pulled close to the fire and was knitting. Bunch was on hands and knees, crawling about the floor, cutting out material to a pattern.

She sat back and pushed a mop of hair out of her eyes, looking up expectantly at Craddock.

'I don't know if it's a breach of confidence,' said the Inspector, addressing himself to Miss Marple, 'but I'd like you to look at this letter.'

He explained the circumstances of his discovery in the attic.

'It's rather a touching collection of letters,' he said. 'Miss Blacklock poured out everything in the hopes of sustaining her sister's interest in life and keeping her health good. There's a very clear picture of an old father in the background – old Dr Blacklock. A real old pig-headed bully, absolutely set in his ways, and convinced that everything he thought and said was right. Probably killed thousands of patients through obstinacy. He wouldn't stand for any new ideas or methods.'

'I don't really know that I blame him there,' said Miss Marple. 'I always feel that the young doctors are only too anxious to experiment. After they've whipped out all our teeth, and administered quantities of very peculiar glands, and removed bits of our insides, they then confess that nothing can be done for us. I really prefer the old-fashioned remedy of big black bottles of medicine. After all, one can always pour those down the sink.'

She took the letter that Craddock handed her.

He said: 'I want you to read it because I think that that generation is more easily understood by you than by me. I don't know really quite how these people's minds worked.'

Miss Marple unfolded the fragile paper.

Dearest Charlotte,

I've not written for two days because we've been having the most terrible domestic complications. Randall's sister Sonia (you remember her? She came to take you out in the car that day? How I wish you would go out more). Sonia has declared her intention of marrying one Dmitri Stamfordis. I have only seen him once. Very attractive – not to be trusted, I should say. R.G. raves against him and says he is a crook and a swindler. Belle, bless her, just smiles and lies on her sofa. Sonia, who though she looks so impassive has really a terrific temper, is simply wild with R.G. I really thought yesterday she was going to murder him!

I've done my best. I've talked to Sonia and I've talked to R.G. and I've got them both into a more reasonable frame of mind and then they come together and it all starts over again! You've no idea how tiring it is. R.G. has been making enquiries – and it does really seem as though this Stamfordis man was thoroughly undesirable.

In the meantime business is being neglected. I carry on at the office and in a way it's rather fun because R.G. gives me a free hand. He said to me yesterday: 'Thank Heaven, there's one sane person in the world. You're never likely to fall in love with a crook, Blackie, are you?' I said I didn't think I was likely to fall in love with anybody. R.G. said: 'Let's start a few new hares in the City.' He's really rather a mischievous devil sometimes and he sails terribly near the wind. 'You're quite determined to keep me on the straight and narrow path, aren't you, Blackie?' he said the other day. And I shall too! I can't understand how people can't see when a thing's dishonest – but R.G. really and truly doesn't. He only knows what is actually against the law.

Belle only laughs at all this. She thinks the fuss about Sonia is all nonsense. 'Sonia has her own money,' she said. 'Why shouldn't she marry this man if she wants to?' I said it might turn out to be a terrible mistake and Belle said, 'It's never a mistake to marry a man you want to marry – even if you regret it.' And then she said, 'I suppose Sonia doesn't want to break with Randall because of money. Sonia's very fond of money.'

No more now. How is father? I won't say Give him my love. But you can if you think it's better to do so. Have you seen more people? You really must not be morbid, *darling.*

Sonia asks to be remembered to you. She has just come in and is closing and unclosing her hands like an angry cat sharpening its claws. I think she and R.G. have had another row. Of course Sonia can be very irritating. She stares you down with that cool stare of hers.

Lots of love, darling, and buck up. This iodine treatment may make a lot of difference. I've been enquiring about it and it really does seem to have good results.

Your loving sister,
Letitia.

Miss Marple folded the letter and handed it back. She looked abstracted.

'Well, what do you think about her?' Craddock urged. 'What picture do you get of her?'

'Of Sonia? It's difficult, you know, to see anyone through another person's mind . . . Determined to get her own way – that, definitely, I think. And wanting the best of two worlds . . .'

'*Closing and unclosing her hands like an angry cat,*' murmured Craddock. 'You know, that reminds me of someone . . .'

He frowned.

'Making enquiries . . .' murmured Miss Marple.

'If we could get hold of the result of those inquiries,' said Craddock.

'Does that letter remind you of anything in St Mary Mead?' asked Bunch, rather indistinctly since her mouth was full of pins.

'I really can't say it does, dear . . . Dr Blacklock is, perhaps, a little like Mr Curtiss the Wesleyan Minister. He wouldn't let his child wear a plate on her teeth. Said it was the Lord's Will if her teeth stuck out. "After all," I said to him, "you do trim your beard and cut your hair. It might be the Lord's Will that your hair should grow out." He said that was quite different. So like a man. But that doesn't help us with our present problem.'

'We've never traced that revolver, you know. It wasn't Rudi Scherz. If I knew who had had a revolver in Chipping Cleghorn –'

'Colonel Easterbrook has one,' said Bunch. 'He keeps it in his collar drawer.'

'How do you know, Mrs Harmon?'

'Mrs Butt told me. She's my daily. Or rather, my twice weekly. Being a military gentleman, she said, he'd naturally have a revolver and very handy it would be if burglars were to come along.'

'When did she tell you this?'

'Ages ago. About six months ago, I should think.'

'Colonel Easterbrook?' murmured Craddock.

'It's like those pointer things at fairs, isn't it?' said Bunch, still speaking through a mouthful of pins. 'Go round and round and stop at something different every time.'

'You're telling me,' said Craddock and groaned.

'Colonel Easterbrook was up at Little Paddocks to leave a book there one day. He could have oiled that door then. He was quite straightforward about being there though. Not like Miss Hinchcliffe.'

Miss Marple coughed gently. 'You must make allowances for the times we live in, Inspector,' she said.

Craddock looked at her, uncomprehendingly.

'After all,' said Miss Marple. 'you *are* the Police, aren't you? People can't say everything they'd like to say to the Police, can they?'

'I don't see why not,' said Craddock. 'Unless they've got some criminal matter to conceal.'

'She means butter,' said Bunch, crawling actively round a table leg to anchor a floating bit of paper. 'Butter and corn for hens, and sometimes cream – and sometimes, even, a side of bacon.'

'Show him that note from Miss Blacklock,' said Miss Marple. 'It's some time ago now, but it reads like a first-class mystery story.'

'What have I done with it? Is this the one you mean, Aunt Jane?'

Miss Marple took it and looked at it.

'Yes,' she said with satisfaction. 'That's the one.'

She handed it to the Inspector.

'I have made inquiries – Thursday is the day,' Miss Blacklock had written. *'Any time after three. If there is any for me leave it in the usual place.'*

Bunch spat out her pins and laughed. Miss Marple was watching the Inspector's face.

The Vicar's wife took upon herself to explain.

'Thursday is the day one of the farms round here makes butter. They let anybody they like have a bit. It's usually Miss Hinchcliffe who collects it. She's very much in with all the farmers – because of her pigs, I think. But it's all a bit hush hush, you know, a kind of local scheme of barter. One person gets butter, and sends along cucumbers, or something like that – and a little something when a pig's killed. And now and then an animal has an accident and has to be destroyed. Oh, you know the sort of thing. Only one can't, very well, say it right out to the Police. Because I suppose quite a lot of this barter is illegal – only nobody really knows because it's all so complicated. But I expect Hinch had slipped into Little Paddocks with a pound of butter or something and had put it in the *usual place*. That's a flour bin under the dresser, by the way. It doesn't have flour in it.'

Craddock sighed.

'I'm glad I came here to you ladies,' he said.

'There used to be clothing coupons, too,' said Bunch. 'Not usually bought – that wasn't considered honest. No money passes. But people like Mrs Butt or Mrs Finch or Mrs Huggins like a nice woollen dress or a winter coat that hasn't seen too much wear and they pay for it with coupons instead of money.'

'You'd better not tell me any more,' said Craddock. 'It's all against the law.'

'Then there oughtn't to be such silly laws,' said Bunch, filling her mouth up with pins again. *'I* don't do it, of course, because Julian doesn't like me to, so I don't. But I know what's going on, of course.'

A kind of despair was coming over the Inspector.

'It all sounds so pleasant and ordinary,' he said. 'Funny and petty and simple. And yet one woman and a man have been killed, and another woman may be killed before I can get anything definite to go on. I've left off worrying about Pip and Emma for the moment. I'm concentrating on Sonia. I wish I knew what she looked like. There was a snapshot or two in with these letters, but none of the snaps could have been of her.'

'How do you know it couldn't have been her? Do you know what she looked like?'

'She was small and dark, Miss Blacklock said.'

'Really,' said Miss Marple, 'that's *very* interesting.'

'There was one snap that reminded me vaguely of someone. A tall fair girl with her hair all done up on top of her head. I don't know who she could have been. Anyway, it can't have been Sonia. Do you think Mrs Swettenham could have been dark when she was a girl?'

'Not very dark,' said Bunch. 'She's got blue eyes.'

'I hoped there might be a photo of Dmitri Stamfordis – but I suppose that was too much to hope for . . . Well' – he took up the letter – 'I'm sorry this doesn't suggest anything to you, Miss Marple.'

'Oh! but it does,' said Miss Marple. 'It suggests a good deal. Just read it through again, Inspector – especially where it says that Randall Goedler was making inquiries about Dmitri Stamfordis.'

Craddock stared at her.

The telephone rang.

Bunch got up from the floor and went out into the hall where, in accordance with the best Victorian traditions, the telephone had originally been placed and where it still was.

She re-entered the room to say to Craddock:

'It's for you.'

Slightly surprised, the Inspector went out to the instrument – carefully shutting the door of the living-room behind him.

'Craddock? Rydesdale here.'

'Yes, sir.'

'I've been looking through your report. In the interview you had with Phillipa Haymes I see she states positively that she hasn't seen her husband since his desertion from the Army?'

'That's right, sir – she was most emphatic. But in my opinion she wasn't speaking the truth.'

'I agree with you. Do you remember a case about ten days ago – man run over by a lorry – taken to Milchester General with concussion and a fractured pelvis?'

'The fellow who snatched a child practically from under the wheels of a lorry, and got run down himself?'

'That's the one. No papers of any kind on him and nobody came forward to identify him. Looked as though he might be on the run. He died last night without regaining consciousness. But he's been identified – deserter from the Army – Ronald Haymes, ex-Captain in the South Loamshires.'

'Phillipa Haymes' husband?'

'Yes. He'd got an old Chipping Cleghorn bus ticket on him, by the way – and quite a reasonable amount of money.'

'So he did get money from his wife? I always thought he was the man Mitzi overheard talking to her in the summerhouse. She denied it flatly, of course. But surely, sir, that lorry accident was before –'

Rydesdale took the words out of his mouth.

'Yes, he was taken to Milchester General on the 28th. The hold-up at Little Paddocks was on the 29th. That lets him out of any possible connection with it. But his wife, of course, knew nothing about the accident. She may have been thinking all along that he *was* concerned in it. She'd hold her tongue – naturally – after all he *was* her husband.'

'It was a fairly gallant bit of work, wasn't it, sir?' said Craddock slowly.

'Rescuing that child from the lorry? Yes. Plucky. Don't suppose it was cowardice that made Haymes desert. Well, all that's past history. For a man who'd blotted his copybook, it was a good death.'

'I'm glad for her sake,' said the Inspector. 'And for that boy of theirs.'

'Yes, he needn't be too ashamed of his father. And the young woman will be able to marry again now.'

Craddock said slowly:

'I was thinking of that, sir . . . It opens up – possibilities.'

'You'd better break the news to her as you're on the spot.'

'I will, sir. I'll push along there now. Or perhaps I'd better wait until she's back at Little Paddocks. It may be rather a shock – and there's someone else I rather want to have a word with first.'

CHAPTER 19

RECONSTRUCTION OF THE CRIME

'I'll put a lamp by you before I go,' said Bunch. 'It's so dark in here. There's going to be a storm, I think.'

She lifted the small reading lamp to the other side of the table where it would throw light on Miss Marple's knitting as she sat in a wide highbacked chair.

As the flex pulled across the table, Tiglath Pileser the cat leapt upon it and bit and clawed it violently.

'No, Tiglath Pileser, you mustn't . . . He really is awful. Look, he's nearly bitten it through – it's all frayed. Don't you understand, you idiotic puss, that you may get a nasty electric shock if you do that?'

'Thank you, dear,' said Miss Marple, and put out a hand to turn on the lamp.

'It doesn't turn on there. You have to press that silly little switch half-way along the flex. Wait a minute. I'll take these flowers out of the way.'

She lifted a bowl of Christmas roses across the table. Tiglath Pileser, his tail switching, put out a mischievous paw and clawed Bunch's arm. She spilled some of the water out of the vase. It fell on the frayed area of flex and on Tiglath Pileser himself, who leapt to the floor with an indignant hiss.

Miss Marple pressed the small pear-shaped switch. Where the water had soaked the frayed flex there was a flash and a crackle.

'Oh, dear,' said Bunch. 'It's fused. Now I suppose all the lights in here are off.' She tried them. 'Yes, they are. So stupid being all on the same thingummibob. And it's made a burn on the table, too. Naughty Tiglath Pileser – it's all his fault. Aunt Jane – what's the matter? Did it startle you?'

'It's nothing, dear. Just something I saw quite suddenly which I ought to have seen before . . .'

'I'll go and fix the fuse and get the lamp from Julian's study.'

'No, dear, don't bother. You'll miss your bus. I don't want any more light. I just want to sit quietly and – think about something. Hurry dear, or you won't catch your bus.'

When Bunch had gone, Miss Marple sat quite still for about two minutes. The air of the room was heavy and menacing with the gathering storm outside.

Miss Marple drew a sheet of paper towards her.

She wrote first: *Lamp?* and underlined it heavily.

After a moment or two, she wrote another word.

Her pencil travelled down the paper, making brief cryptic notes . . .

In the rather dark living-room of Boulders with its low ceiling and latticed window panes, Miss Hinchcliffe and Miss Murgatroyd were having an argument.

'The trouble with you, Murgatroyd,' said Miss Hinchcliffe, 'is that you won't *try*.'

'But I tell you, Hinch, I can't remember a thing.'

'Now look here, Amy Murgatroyd, we're going to do some constructive thinking. So far we haven't shone on the detective angle. I was quite wrong over that door business. You didn't hold the door open for the murderer after all. You're cleared, Murgatroyd!'

Miss Murgatroyd gave a rather watery smile.

'It's just our luck to have the only silent cleaning woman in Chipping Cleghorn,' continued Miss Hinchcliffe. 'Usually I'm thankful for it, but this time it means we've got off to a bad start. Everybody else in the place knows about that second door in the drawing-room being used – and we only heard about it yesterday –'

'I still don't quite understand how –'

'It's perfectly simple. Our original premises were quite right. You can't hold open a door, wave a torch and shoot with a revolver all at the same time. We kept in the revolver and the torch and cut out the door. Well, we were wrong. It was the revolver we ought to have cut out.'

'But he *did* have a revolver,' said Miss Murgatroyd. 'I saw it. It was there on the floor beside him.'

'When he was dead, yes. It's all quite clear. *He* didn't fire that revolver –'

'Then who did?'

'That's what we're going to find out. But whoever did it, the same person put a couple of poisoned aspirin tablets by Letty Blacklock's bed – and thereby bumped off poor Dora Bunner. And that couldn't have been Rudi Scherz, because he's as dead as a doornail. It was someone who was in the room that night of the hold-up and probably someone who was at the birthday party, too. And the only person *that* lets out is Mrs Harmon.'

'You think someone put those aspirins there the day of the birthday party?'

'Why not?'

'But how could they?'

'Well, we all went to the loo, didn't we?' said Miss Hinchcliffe coarsely. 'And I washed my hands in the bathroom because of that sticky cake. And little Sweetie Easterbrook powdered her grubby little face in Blacklock's bedroom, didn't she?'

'Hinch! Do you think *she* –?'

'I don't know yet. Rather obvious, if she did. I don't think if you were going to plant some tablets, that you'd want to be seen in the bedroom at all. Oh, yes, there were plenty of opportunities.'

'The men didn't go upstairs.'

'There are back stairs. After all, if a man leaves the room, you don't follow him to see if he really is going where you think he is going. It wouldn't be delicate! Anyway, don't *argue*, Murgatroyd. I want to get back to the original attempt on Letty Blacklock. Now, to begin with, get the facts firmly into your head, because it's all going to depend upon you.'

Miss Murgatroyd looked alarmed.

'Oh, dear, Hinch, you know what a muddle I get into!'

'It's not a question of your brains, or the grey fluff that passes for brains with you. It's a question of *eyes*. It's a question of what you *saw*.'

'But I didn't see *anything*.'

'The trouble with you is, Murgatroyd, as I said just now, that you won't *try*. Now pay attention. This is what happened. Whoever it is that's got it in for Letty Blacklock was there in that room that evening. He (I say *he* because it's easier, but there's no reason why it should be a man more than a woman except, of course, that men are dirty dogs), well, he has previously oiled that second door that leads out of the drawing-room and which is supposed to be nailed up or something. Don't ask me *when* he did it, because that confuses things. Actually, by choosing my time, I could walk into any house in Chipping Cleghorn and do anything I liked there for half an hour or so with no one being the wiser. It's just a question of working out where the daily women are and when the occupiers are out and exactly where they've gone and how long they'll be. Just good staff work. Now, to continue. He's oiled that second door. It will open without a sound. Here's the set-up: Lights go out, door A (the regular door) opens with a flourish. Business with torch and hold-up lines. In the meantime, while we're all goggling, X (that's the best term to use) slips quietly out by door B into the dark hall, comes up behind that Swiss idiot, takes a couple of shots at Letty Blacklock and then shoots the Swiss. Drops the revolver, where lazy thinkers like you will assume it's evidence that the Swiss did the shooting, and nips back into the room again by the time that someone gets a lighter going. Got it?'

'Yes – ye-es, but who was it?'

'Well, if *you* don't know, Murgatroyd, nobody does!'

'*Me?*' Miss Murgatroyd fairly twittered in alarm. 'But I don't know anything *at all*. I don't *really*, Hinch!'

'Use that fluff of yours you call a brain. To begin with, where was everybody when the lights went out?'

'I don't know.'

'Yes, you do. You're maddening, Murgatroyd. You know where *you* were, don't you? You were behind the door.'

'Yes – yes, I was. It knocked against my corn when it flew open.'

'Why don't you go to a proper chiropodist instead of messing about yourself with your feet?. You'll give yourself blood poisoning one of these days. Come on, now – *you're* behind the door. *I'm* standing against the mantelpiece with my tongue hanging out for a drink. Letty Blacklock is by the table near the archway, getting the cigarettes. Patrick Simmons has gone through the archway into the small room where Letty Blacklock has had the drinks put. Agreed?'

'Yes, yes, I remember all that.'

'Good, now somebody else followed Patrick into that room or was just starting to follow him. One of the men. The annoying thing is that I can't remember whether it was Easterbrook or Edmund Swettenham. Do you remember?'

'No, I don't.'

'You wouldn't! And there was someone else who went through to the small room: Phillipa Haymes. I remember that distinctly because I remember noticing what a nice flat back she has, and I thought to myself "that girl would look well on a horse." I was watching her and thinking just that. She went over to the mantelpiece in the other room. I don't know what it was she wanted there, because at that moment the lights went out.

'So that's the position. In the drawing-room are Patrick Simmons, Phillipa Haymes, and *either* Colonel Easterbrook or Edmund Swettenham – we don't know which. Now, Murgatroyd, pay attention. The most probable thing is that it was *one of those three* who did it. If anyone wanted to get out of that far door, they'd naturally take care to put themselves in a convenient place when the lights went out. So, as I say, in all probability, it's one of those three. And in that case, Murgatroyd, there's not a thing you can do about it!'

Miss Murgatroyd brightened perceptibly.

'On the other hand,' continued Miss Hinchcliffe, 'there's the possibility that it *wasn't* one of those three. And that's where you come in, Murgatroyd.'

'But how should *I* know anything about it?'

'As I said before if you don't nobody does.'

'But I don't! I really *don't*! I couldn't see anything *at all*!'

'Oh, yes, you could. You're the only person who *could* see. You were standing behind the door. You couldn't look *at* the torch – because the door was between you and it. You were facing the other way, the same way as the torch was pointing. The rest of us were just dazzled. But *you* weren't dazzled.'

'No – no, perhaps not, but I didn't *see* anything, the torch went round and round –'

'Showing you *what*? It rested on *faces*, didn't it? And on tables? And on chairs?'

'Yes – yes, it did . . . Miss Bunner, her mouth wide open and her eyes popping out of her head, staring and blinking.'

'That's the stuff!' Miss Hinchcliffe gave a sigh of relief. 'The difficulty there is in making you use that grey fluff of yours! Now then, keep it up.'

'But I didn't see any more, I didn't, really.'

'You mean you saw an empty room? Nobody standing about? Nobody sitting down?'

'No, of course not *that*. Miss Bunner with her mouth open and Mrs Harmon was sitting on the arm of a chair. She had her eyes tight shut and her knuckles all doubled up to her face – like a child.'

'Good, that's Mrs Harmon and Miss Bunner. Don't you see yet what I'm getting at? The difficulty is that I don't want to put ideas into your head. But when we've eliminated who you *did* see – we can get on to the important point which is, was there anyone you *didn't* see. Got it? Besides the tables and the chairs and the chrysanthemums and the rest of it, there were certain people: Julia Simmons, Mrs Swettenham, Mrs Easterbrook – *either* Colonel Easterbrook or Edmund Swettenham – Dora Bunner and Bunch Harmon. All right, you saw Bunch Harmon and Dora Bunner. Cross them off. Now *think*, Murgatroyd, *think*, was there one of those people who definitely *wasn't* there?'

Miss Murgatroyd jumped slightly as a branch knocked against the open window. She shut her eyes. She murmured to herself . . .

'The flowers . . . on the table . . . the big armchair . . . the torch didn't come round as far as you, Hinch – Mrs Harmon, yes . . .'

The telephone rang sharply. Miss Hinchcliffe went to it.

'Hallo, yes? The station?'

The obedient Miss Murgatroyd, her eyes closed, was reliving the night of the 29th. The torch, sweeping slowly round . . . a group of people . . . the windows . . . the sofa . . . Dora Bunner . . . the wall . . . the table with lamp . . . the archway . . . the sudden spat of the revolver . . .

'. . . but that's *extraordinary*!' said Miss Murgatroyd.

'What?' Miss Hinchcliffe was barking angrily into the telephone. 'Been there since this morning? What time? Damn and blast you, and you only ring me up *now*? I'll set the S.P.C.A. after you. An oversight? Is *that* all you've got to say?'

She banged down the receiver.

'It's that dog,' she said. 'The red setter. Been at the station since this

morning – since this morning at eight o'clock. Without a drop of water!
And the idiots only ring me up now. I'm going to get her right away.'

She plunged out of the room, Miss Murgatroyd squeaking shrilly in
her wake.

'But listen, Hinch, a most extraordinary thing . . . I don't understand
it . . .'

Miss Hinchcliffe had dashed out of the door and across to the shed
which served as a garage.

'We'll go on with it when I come back,' she called. 'I can't wait
for you to come with me. You've got your bedroom slippers on as
usual.'

She pressed the starter of the car and backed out of the garage with a
jerk. Miss Murgatroyd skipped nimbly sideways.

'But listen, Hinch, I *must* tell you –'

'When I come back . . .'

The car jerked and shot forwards. Miss Murgatroyd's voice came faintly
after it on a high excited note.

'But, Hinch, *she wasn't there* . . .'

Overhead the clouds had been gathering thick and blue. As Miss
Murgatroyd stood looking after the retreating car, the first big drops
began to fall.

In an agitated fashion, Miss Murgatroyd plunged across to a line of
string on which she had, some hours previously, hung out a couple of
jumpers and a pair of woollen combinations to dry.

She was murmuring under her breath:

'Really *most* extraordinary . . . Oh, dear, I shall never get these down
in time – and they were nearly dry . . .'

She struggled with a recalcitrant clothes peg, then turned her head as
she heard someone approaching.

Then she smiled a pleased welcome.

'Hallo – do go inside, you'll get wet.'

'Let me help you.'

'Oh, if you don't mind . . . so annoying if they all get soaked again. I
really ought to let down the line, but I think I can just reach.'

'Here's your scarf. Shall I put it round your neck?'

'Oh, thank you . . . Yes, perhaps . . . If I could just reach this peg . . .'

The woollen scarf was slipped round her neck and then, suddenly,
pulled tight . . .

Miss Murgatroyd's mouth opened, but no sound came except a small choking gurgle.

And the scarf was pulled tighter still . . .

On her way back from the station, Miss Hinchcliffe stopped the car to pick up Miss Marple who was hurrying along the street.

'Hallo,' she shouted. 'You'll get very wet. Come and have tea with us. I saw Bunch waiting for the bus. You'll be all alone at the Vicarage. Come and join us. Murgatroyd and I are doing a bit of reconstruction of the crime. I rather think we're just getting somewhere. Mind the dog. She's rather nervous.'

'What a beauty!'

'Yes, lovely bitch, isn't she! Those fools kept her at the station since this morning without letting me know. I told them off, the lazy b – s. Oh, excuse my language. I was brought up by grooms at home in Ireland.'

The little car turned with a jerk into the small backyard of Boulders.

A crowd of eager ducks and fowls encircled the two ladies as they descended.

'Curse Murgatroyd,' said Miss Hinchcliffe, 'she hasn't given 'em their corn.'

'Is it difficult to get corn?' Miss Marple inquired.

Miss Hincliffe winked.

'I'm in with most of the farmers,' she said.

Shooing away the hens, she escorted Miss Marple towards the cottage.

'Hope you're not too wet?'

'No, this is a very good mackintosh.'

'I'll light the fire if Murgatroyd hasn't lit it. Hiyah, Murgatroyd? Where is the woman? Murgatroyd! Where's that dog? *She's* disappeared now.'

A slow dismal howl came from outside.

'Curse the silly bitch.' Miss Hinchcliffe tramped to the door and called:

'Hyoup, Cutie – Cutie. Damn' silly name but that's what they called her apparently. We must find her another name. Hiyah, Cutie.'

The red setter was sniffing at something lying below the taut string where a row of garments swirled in the wind.

'Murgatroyd's not even had the sense to bring the washing in. Where *is* she?'

Again the red setter nosed at what seemed to be a pile of clothes, and raised her nose high in the air and howled again.

'What's the *matter* with the dog?'

Miss Hinchcliffe strode across the grass.

And quickly, apprehensively, Miss Marple ran after her. They stood there, side by side, the rain beating down on them, and the older woman's arm went round the younger one's shoulders.

She felt the muscles go stiff and taut as Miss Hinchcliffe stood looking down on the thing lying there, with the blue congested face and the protruding tongue.

'I'll kill whoever did this,' said Miss Hinchcliffe in a low quiet voice, 'if I once get my hands on her . . .'

Miss Marple said questioningly:

'*Her?*'

Miss Hinchcliffe turned a ravaged face towards her.

'Yes. I know who it is – near enough . . . That is, it's one of three possibles.'

She stood for another moment, looking down at her dead friend, and then turned towards the house. Her voice was dry and hard.

'We must ring up the police,' she said. 'And while we're waiting for them, I'll tell you. My fault, in a way, that Murgatroyd's lying out there. I made a game of it . . . Murder isn't a game . . .'

'No,' said Miss Marple. 'Murder isn't a game.'

'You know something about it, don't you?' said Miss Hinchcliffe as she lifted the receiver and dialled.

She made a brief report and hung up.

'They'll be here in a few minutes . . . Yes, I heard that you'd been mixed up in this sort of business before . . . I think it was Edmund Swettenham told me so . . . Do you want to hear what we were doing, Murgatroyd and I?'

Succinctly she described the conversation held before her departure for the station.

'She called after me, you know, just as I was leaving . . . That's how I know it's a woman and not a man . . . If I'd waited – if only I'd *listened*! God dammit, the dog could have stopped where she was for another quarter of an hour.'

'Don't blame yourself, my dear. That does no good. One can't foresee.'

'No, one can't . . . Something tapped against the window, I remember. Perhaps *she* was outside there, then – yes, of course, she must have been . . . coming to the house . . . and there were Murgatroyd and I shouting at each other. Top of our voices . . . She heard . . . She heard it all . . .'

'You haven't told me yet what your friend said.'

'Just one sentence! "*She wasn't there.*"'

She paused. 'You see? There were three women we hadn't eliminated. Mrs Swettenham, Mrs Easterbrook, Julia Simmons. And one of those three – *wasn't there* . . . She wasn't there in the drawing-room because she had slipped out through the other door and was out in the hall.'

'Yes,' said Miss Marple, 'I see.'

'It's *one* of those three women. I don't know which. But I'll find out!'

'Excuse me,' said Miss Marple. 'But did she – did Miss Murgatroyd, I mean, say it exactly as you said it?'

'How d'you mean – as I said it?'

'Oh, dear, how can I explain? You said it like this. *She-wasn't-there.* An equal emphasis on every word. You see, there are three ways you could say it. You could say, "*She* wasn't there." Very personal. Or again, "She *wasn't* there." Confirming, some suspicion already held. Or else you could say (and this is nearer to the way you said it just now), "She wasn't *there* . . ." quite blankly – with the emphasis, if there was emphasis – on the "*there*".'

'I don't know.' Miss Hinchcliffe shook her head. 'I can't remember . . . How the hell can I remember? I think, yes, surely she'd say '*She* wasn't there." That would be the natural way, I should think. But I simply don't know. Does it make any difference?'

'Yes,' said Miss Marple, thoughtfully. 'I think so. It's a very *slight* indication, of course, but I think it *is* an indication. Yes, I should think it makes a lot of difference . . .'

CHAPTER 20

MISS MARPLE IS MISSING

The postman, rather to his disgust, had lately been given orders to make an afternoon delivery of letters in Chipping Cleghorn as well as a morning one.

On this particular afternoon he left three letters at Little Paddocks at exactly ten minutes to five.

One was addressed to Phillipa Haymes in a schoolboy's hand; the other two were for Miss Blacklock. She opened them as she and Phillipa sat down at the tea table. The torrential rain had enabled Phillipa to leave Dayas Hall early today, since once she had shut up the greenhouses there was nothing more to do.

Miss Blacklock tore open her first letter which was a bill for repairing a kitchen boiler. She snorted angrily.

'Dymond's prices are *preposterous* – quite preposterous. Still, I suppose all the other people are just as bad.'

She opened the second letter which was in a handwriting quite unknown to her.

Dear Cousin Letty (it said),

I hope it will be all right for me to come to you on Tuesday? I wrote to Patrick two days ago but he hasn't answered. So I presume it's all right. Mother is coming to England next month and hopes to see you then.

My train arrives at Chipping Cleghorn at 6.15 if that's convenient?

Yours affectionately,

Julia Simmons.

Miss Blacklock read the letter once with astonishment pure and simple, and then again with a certain grimness. She looked up at Phillipa who was smiling over her son's letter.

'Are Julia and Patrick back, do you know?'

Phillipa looked up.

'Yes, they came in just after I did. They went upstairs to change. They were wet.'

'Perhaps you'd not mind going and calling them.'

'Of course I will.'

'Wait a moment – I'd like you to read this.'

She handed Phillipa the letter she had received.

Phillipa read it and frowned. 'I don't understand . . .'

'Nor do I, quite . . . I think it's about time I did. Call Patrick and Julia, Phillipa.'

Phillipa called from the bottom of the stairs:

'Patrick! Julia! Miss Blacklock wants you.'

Patrick came running down the stairs and entered the room.

'Don't go, Phillipa,' said Miss Blacklock.

'Hallo, Aunt Letty,' said Patrick cheerfully. 'Want me?'

'Yes, I do. Perhaps you'll give me an explanation of *this*?'

Patrick's face showed an almost comical dismay as he read.

'I meant to telegraph her! What an ass I am!'

'This letter, I presume, is from your sister Julia?'

'Yes – yes, it is.'

Miss Blacklock said grimly:

'*Then who, may I ask, is the young woman whom you brought here as Julia Simmons*, and whom I was given to understand was your sister and my cousin?'

'Well – you see – Aunt Letty – the fact of the matter is – I can explain it all – I know I oughtn't to have done it – but it really seemed more of a lark than anything else. If you'll just let me explain –'

'I am waiting for you to explain. *Who is this young woman?*'

'Well, I met her at a cocktail party soon after I got demobbed. We got talking and I said I was coming here and then – well, we thought it might be rather a good wheeze if I brought her along . . . You see, Julia, the real Julia, was mad to go on the stage and Mother had seven fits at the idea – however, Julia got a chance to join a jolly good repertory company up in Perth or somewhere and she thought she'd give it a try – but she thought she'd keep Mum calm by letting Mum think that she was here with me studying to be a dispenser like a good little girl.'

'I still want to know who this other young woman *is*.'

Patrick turned with relief as Julia, cool and aloof, came into the room.

'The balloon's gone up,' he said.

Julia raised her eyebrows. Then, still cool, she came forward and sat down.

'O.K.,' she said. 'That's that. I suppose you're very angry?' She studied Miss Blacklock's face with almost dispassionate interest. 'I should be if I were you.'

'*Who are you?*'

Julia sighed.

'I think the moment's come when I make a clean breast of things. Here we go. I'm one half of the Pip and Emma combination. To be exact, my christened name is Emma Jocelyn Stamfordis – only Father soon dropped the Stamfordis. I think he called himself De Courcy next.

'My father and mother, let me tell you, split up about three years after Pip and I were born. Each of them went their own way. And they split us up. I was Father's part of the loot. He was a bad parent on the whole, though quite a charming one. I had various desert spells of being educated in convents – when Father hadn't any money, or was preparing to engage in some particularly nefarious deal. He used to pay the first term with every sign of affluence and then depart and leave me on the nuns' hands for a year or two. In the intervals, he and I had some very good times together, moving in cosmopolitan society. However, the war separated us completely. I've no idea of what's happened to him. I had a few adventures myself. I was with the French Resistance for a time. Quite exciting. To cut a long story short, I landed up in London and began to think about my future. I knew that Mother's brother with whom she'd had a frightful row had died a very rich man. I looked up his will to see if there was anything for me. There wasn't – not directly, that is to say. I made a few inquiries about his widow – it seemed she was quite ga-ga and kept under drugs and was dying by inches. Frankly, it looked as though *you* were my best bet. You were going to come into a hell of a lot of money and from all I could find out, you didn't seem to have anyone much to spend it on. I'll be quite frank. It occurred to me that if I could get to know you in a friendly kind of way, and if you took a fancy to me – well, after all, conditions have changed a bit, haven't they, since Uncle Randall died? I mean any money we ever had has been swept away in the cataclysm of Europe. I thought you might pity a poor orphan girl, all alone in the world, and make her, perhaps, a small allowance.'

'Oh, you did, did you?' said Miss Blacklock grimly.

'Yes. Of course, I hadn't seen you then . . . I visualized a kind of sob stuff approach . . . Then, by a marvellous stroke of luck, I met Patrick here – and he turned out to be your nephew or your cousin, or something. Well, that struck me as a marvellous chance. I went bull-headed for Patrick and he fell for me in a most gratifying way. The real Julia was all wet about this acting stuff and I soon persuaded her it was her duty to Art to go and fix herself up in some uncomfortable lodgings in Perth and train to be the new Sarah Bernhardt.

'You mustn't blame Patrick too much. He felt awfully sorry for me, all alone in the world – and he soon thought it would be a really marvellous idea for me to come here as his sister and do my stuff.'

'And he also approved of your continuing to tell a tissue of lies to the police?'

'Have a heart, Letty. Don't you see that when that ridiculous hold-up business happened – or rather after it happened – I began to feel I was in a bit of a spot. Let's face it, I've got a perfectly good motive for putting you out of the way. You've only got my word for it now that I wasn't the one who tried to do it. You can't expect me deliberately to go and incriminate myself. Even Patrick got nasty ideas about me from time to time, and if even *he* could think things like that, what on earth would the police think? That Detective-Inspector struck me as a man of singularly sceptical mind. No, I figured out the only thing for me to do was to sit tight as Julia and just fade away when term came to an end.

'How was I to know that fool Julia, the real Julia, would go and have a row with the producer, and fling the whole thing up in a fit of temperament? She writes to Patrick and asks if she can come here, and instead of wiring her "Keep away" he goes and forgets to do anything at all!' She cast an angry glance at Patrick. 'Of all the utter *idiots*!'

She sighed.

'You don't know the straits I've been put to in Milchester! Of course, I haven't been to the hospital at all. But I had to go *somewhere*. Hours and hours I've spent in the pictures seeing the most frightful films over and over again.'

'*Pip and Emma*,' murmured Miss Blacklock. 'I never believed, somehow, in spite of what the Inspector said, that they were *real –*'

She looked searchingly at Julia.

'You're Emma,' she said. 'Where's Pip?'

Julia's eyes, limpid and innocent, met hers.

'I don't know,' she said. 'I haven't the least idea.'

'I think you're lying, Julia. When did you see him last?'

Was there a momentary hesitation before Julia spoke?

She said clearly and deliberately:

'I haven't seen him since we were both three years old – when my mother took him away. I haven't seen either him or my mother. I don't know where they are.'

'And that's all you have to say?'

Julia sighed.

'I could say I was sorry. But it wouldn't really be true; because actually I'd do the same thing again – though not if I'd known about this murder business, of course.'

'Julia,' said Miss Blacklock, 'I call you that because I'm used to it. You were with the French Resistance, you say?'

'Yes. For eighteen months.'

'Then I suppose you learned to shoot?'

Again those cool blue eyes met hers.

'I can shoot all right. I'm a first-class shot. I didn't shoot at you, Letitia Blacklock, though you've only got my word for that. But I can tell you this, that if *I* had shot at you, I wouldn't have been likely to miss.'

★   ★   ★

The sound of a car driving up to the door broke through the tenseness of the moment.

'Who can that be?' asked Miss Blacklock.

Mitzi put a tousled head in. She was showing the whites of her eyes.

'It is the police come again,' she said. 'This, it is persecution! Why will they not leave us alone? I will not bear it. I will write to the Prime Minister. I will write to your King.'

Craddock's hand put her firmly and not too kindly aside. He came in with such a grim set to his lips that they all looked at him apprehensively. This was a new Inspector Craddock.

He said sternly:

'Miss Murgatroyd has been murdered. She was strangled – not more than an hour ago.' His eye singled out Julia. 'You – Miss Simmons – where have you been all day?'

Julia said warily:

'In Milchester. I've just got in.'

'And you?' The eye went on to Patrick.

'Yes.'

'Did you both come back here together?'

'Yes – yes, we did,' said Patrick.

'No,' said Julia. 'It's no good, Patrick. That's the kind of lie that will be found out at once. The bus people know us well. I came back on the earlier bus, Inspector – the one that gets here at four o'clock.'

'And what did you do then?'

'I went for a walk.'

'In the direction of Boulders?'

'No. I went across the fields.'

He stared at her. Julia, her face pale, her lips tense, stared back.

Before anyone could speak, the telephone rang.

Miss Blacklock, with an inquiring glance at Craddock, picked up the receiver.

'Yes. Who? Oh, Bunch. What? No. No, she hasn't. I've no idea . . . Yes, he's here now.'

She lowered the instrument and said:

'Mrs Harmon would like to speak to you, Inspector. Miss Marple has not come back to the Vicarage and Mrs Harmon is worried about her.'

Craddock took two strides forward and gripped the telephone.

'Craddock speaking.'

'I'm worried, Inspector.' Bunch's voice came through with a childish tremor in it. 'Aunt Jane's out somewhere – and I don't know where. And they say that Miss Murgatroyd's been killed. Is it true?'

'Yes, it's true, Mrs Harmon. Miss Marple was there with Miss Hinchcliffe when they found the body.'

'Oh, so *that's* where she is.' Bunch sounded relieved.

'No – no, I'm afraid she isn't. Not now. She left there about – let me see – half an hour ago. She hasn't got home?'

'No – she hasn't. It's only ten minutes' walk. Where can she be?'

'Perhaps she's called in on one of your neighbours?'

'I've rung them up – *all of them*. She's not there. I'm frightened, Inspector.'

'So am *I*,' thought Craddock.

He said quickly:

'I'll come round to you – at once.'

'Oh, *do* – there's a piece of paper. She was writing on it before she went out. I don't know if it means anything . . . It just seems gibberish to me.'

Craddock replaced the receiver.

Miss Blacklock said anxiously:

'Has something happened to Miss Marple? Oh, I hope not.'

'I hope not, too.' His mouth was grim.

'She's so old – and frail.'

'I know.'

Miss Blacklock, standing with her hand pulling at the choker of pearls round her neck, said in a hoarse voice:

'It's getting worse and worse. Whoever's doing these things must be mad, Inspector – quite mad . . .'

'I wonder.'

The choker of pearls round Miss Blacklock's neck broke under the clutch of her nervous fingers. The smooth white globules rolled all over the room.

Letitia cried out in an anguished tone.

'My pearls – my *pearls* –' The agony in her voice was so acute that they all looked at her in astonishment. She turned, her hand to her throat, and rushed sobbing out of the room.

Phillipa began picking up the pearls.

'I've never seen her so upset over anything,' she said. 'Of course – she always wears them. Do you think, perhaps, that someone special gave them to her? Randall Goedler, perhaps?'

'It's possible,' said the Inspector slowly.

'They're not – they couldn't be – *real* by any chance?' Phillipa asked from where, on her knees, she was still collecting the white shining globules.

Taking one in his hand, Craddock was just about to reply contemptuously, 'Real? Of course not!' when he suddenly stifled the words.

After all, *could* the pearls be real?

They were so large, so even, so white that their falseness seemed palpable, but Craddock remembered suddenly a police case where a string of real pearls had been bought for a few shillings in a pawnbroker's shop.

Letitia Blacklock had assured him that there was no jewellery of value in the house. If these pearls were, by any chance, genuine, they must be worth a fabulous sum. And if Randall Goedler had given them to her – then they might be worth any sum you cared to name.

They looked false – they *must* be false, but – if they were real?

Why not? She might herself be unaware of their value. Or she might choose to protect her treasure by treating it as though it were a cheap ornament worth a couple of guineas at most. What would they be worth if real? A fabulous sum . . . Worth doing murder for – *if anybody knew about them*.

With a start, the Inspector wrenched himself away from his speculations. Miss Marple was missing. He must go to the Vicarage.

He found Bunch and her husband waiting for him, their faces anxious and drawn.

'She hasn't come back,' said Bunch.

'Did she say she was coming back here when she left Boulders?' asked Julian.

'She didn't actually say so,' said Craddock slowly, throwing his mind back to the last time he had seen Jane Marple.

He remembered the grimness of her lips and the severe frosty light in those usually gentle blue eyes.

Grimness, an inexorable determination . . . to do what? To go where?

'She was talking to Sergeant Fletcher when I last saw her,' he said. 'Just by the gate. And then she went through it and out. I took it she was going straight home to the Vicarage. I would have sent her in the car – but there was so much to attend to, and she slipped away very quietly. Fletcher may know something! Where's Fletcher?'

But Sergeant Fletcher, it seemed, as Craddock learned when he rang up Boulders, was neither to be found there nor had he left any message where

316 • AGATHA CHRISTIE

he had gone. There was some idea that he had returned to Milchester for some reason.

The Inspector rang up headquarters in Milchester, but no news of Fletcher was to be found there.

Then Craddock turned to Bunch as he remembered what she had told him over the telephone.

'Where's that paper? You said she'd been writing something on a bit of paper.'

Bunch brought it to him. He spread it out on the table and looked down on it. Bunch leant over his shoulder and spelled it out as he read. The writing was shaky and not easy to read:

Lamp.

Then came the word '*Violets.*'

Then after a space:

Where is bottle of aspirin?

The next item in this curious list was more difficult to make out. '*Delicious death,*' Bunch read. 'That's Mitzi's cake.'

'*Making enquiries,*' read Craddock.

'Inquiries? What about, I wonder? What's this? *Severe affliction bravely borne* . . . What on earth –!'

'*Iodine,*' read the Inspector. '*Pearls.* Ah, pearls.'

'And then *Lotty* – no, Letty. Her *e*'s look like *o*'s. And then *Berne.* And what's this? *Old Age Pension* . . .'

They looked at each other in bewilderment.

Craddock recapitulated swiftly:

'Lamp. Violets. Where is bottle of aspirin? Delicious Death. Making enquiries. Severe affliction bravely borne. Iodine. Pearls. Letty. Berne. Old Age Pension.'

Bunch asked: 'Does it mean anything? Anything at all? I can't see any connection.'

Craddock said slowly: 'I've just a glimmer – but I don't see. It's odd that she should have put down that about pearls.'

'What about pearls? What does it mean?'

'Does Miss Blacklock always wear that three-tier choker of pearls?'

'Yes, she does. We laugh about it sometimes. They're so dreadfully false-looking, aren't they? But I suppose she thinks it's fashionable.'

'There might be another reason,' said Craddock slowly.

'You don't mean that they're *real.* Oh! they *couldn't* be!'

'How often have you had an opportunity of seeing real pearls of that size, Mrs Harmon?'

'But they're so glassy.'

Craddock shrugged his shoulders.

'Anyway, they don't matter now. It's Miss Marple that matters. We've got to find her.'

They'd got to find her before it was too late – but perhaps it was already too late? Those pencilled words showed that she was on the track . . . But that was dangerous – horribly dangerous. And where the hell was Fletcher?

Craddock strode out of the Vicarage to where he'd left his car. Search – that was all he could do – search.

A voice spoke to him out of the dripping laurels.

'Sir!' said Sergeant Fletcher urgently. '*Sir* . . .'

CHAPTER 21

THREE WOMEN

Dinner was over at Little Paddocks. It had been a silent and uncomfortable meal.

Patrick, uneasily aware of having fallen from grace, only made spasmodic attempts at conversation – and such as he did make were not well received. Phillipa Haymes was sunk in abstraction. Miss Blacklock herself had abandoned the effort to behave with her normal cheerfulness. She had changed for dinner and had come down wearing her necklace of cameos but for the first time fear showed from her darkly circled eyes, and betrayed itself by her twitching hands.

Julia, alone, had maintained her air of cynical detachment throughout the evening.

'I'm sorry, Letty,' she said, 'that I can't pack my bag and go. But I presume the police wouldn't allow it. I don't suppose I'll darken your roof – or whatever the expression is – for long. I should imagine that Inspector Craddock will be round with a warrant and the handcuffs any moment. In fact I can't imagine why something of the kind hasn't happened already.'

'He's looking for the old lady – for Miss Marple,' said Miss Blacklock.

'Do you think she's been murdered, too?' Patrick asked with scientific curiosity. 'But why? What could she know?'

'I don't know,' said Miss Blacklock dully. 'Perhaps Miss Murgatroyd told her something.'

'If she's been murdered too,' said Patrick, 'there seems to be logically only one person who could have done it.'

'Who?'

'Hinchcliffe, of course,' said Patrick triumphantly. 'That's where she was last seen alive – at Boulders. My solution would be that she never left Boulders.'

'My head aches,' said Miss Blacklock in a dull voice. She pressed her fingers to her forehead. 'Why should Hinch murder Miss Marple? It doesn't make sense.'

'It would if Hinch had really murdered Murgatroyd,' said Patrick triumphantly.

Phillipa came out of her apathy to say:

'Hinch wouldn't murder Murgatroyd.'

'She might have if Murgatroyd had blundered on something to show that she – Hinch – was the criminal.'

'Anyway, Hinch was at the station when Murgatroyd was killed.'

'She could have murdered Murgatroyd before she left.'

Startling them all, Letitia Blacklock suddenly screamed out:

'Murder, murder, *murder* –! Can't you talk of *anything* else? I'm frightened, don't you understand? I'm frightened. I wasn't before. I thought I could take care of myself . . . But what can you do against a murderer who's waiting – and watching – and biding his time! Oh, God!'

She dropped her head forward on her hands. A moment later she looked up and apologized stiffly.

'I'm sorry. I – I lost control.'

'That's all right, Aunt Letty,' said Patrick affectionately. 'I'll look after you.'

'You?' was all Letitia Blacklock said, but the disillusionment behind the word was almost an accusation.

That had been shortly before dinner, and Mitzi had then created a diversion by coming and declaring that she was not going to cook the dinner.

'I do not do anything more in this house. I go to my room. I lock myself in. I stay there until it is daylight. I am afraid – people are being killed – that Miss Murgatroyd with her stupid English face – who would want to kill *her*? Only a maniac! Then it is a maniac that is about! And a maniac does not care *who* he kills. But me, I do not want to be killed. There are shadows in the kitchen – and I hear noises – I think there is someone out in the yard and then I think I see a shadow by the larder door and then it is footsteps I hear. So I go now to my room and I lock the door and perhaps even I put the chest of drawers against it. And in the morning I tell that cruel hard policeman that I go away from here. And if he will not let me I say: "I scream and I scream and I scream until you have to let me go!"'

Everybody, with a vivid recollection of what Mitzi could do in the screaming line, shuddered at the threat.

'So I go to my room,' said Mitzi, repeating the statement once more to make her intentions quite clear. With a symbolic action she cast off the cretonne apron she had been wearing. 'Goodnight, Miss Blacklock. Perhaps in the morning, you may not be alive. So in case that is so, I say goodbye.'

She departed abruptly and the door, with its usual gentle little whine, closed softly after her.

Julia got up.

'I'll see to dinner,' she said in a matter-of-fact way. 'Rather a good arrangement – less embarrassing for you all than having me sit down at table with you. Patrick (since he's constituted himself your protector, Aunt Letty) had better taste every dish first. I don't want to be accused of poisoning you on top of everything else.'

So Julia had cooked and served a really excellent meal.

Phillipa had come out to the kitchen with an offer of assistance but Julia had said firmly that she didn't want any help.

'Julia, there's something I want to say –'

'This is no time for girlish confidences,' said Julia firmly. 'Go on back in the dining-room, Phillipa.'

Now dinner was over and they were in the drawing-room with coffee on the small table by the fire – and nobody seemed to have anything to say. They were waiting – that was all.

At 8.30 Inspector Craddock rang up.

'I shall be with you in about a quarter of an hour's time,' he announced. 'I'm bringing Colonel and Mrs Easterbrook and Mrs Swettenham and her son with me.'

'But really, Inspector . . . I can't cope with people tonight –'

Miss Blacklock's voice sounded as though she were at the end of her tether.

'I know how you feel, Miss Blacklock. I'm sorry. But this is urgent.'

'Have you – found Miss Marple?'

'No,' said the Inspector, and rang off.

Julia took the coffee tray out to the kitchen where, to her surprise, she found Mitzi contemplating the piled-up dishes and plates by the sink.

Mitzi burst into a torrent of words.

'See what you do in my so nice kitchen! That frying pan – only, *only* for omelettes do I use it! And you, what have you used it for?'

'Frying onions.'

'Ruined – *ruined*. It will have now to be *washed* and never – *never* – do I wash my omelette pan. I rub it carefully over with a greasy newspaper, that is all. And this saucepan here that you have used – that one, I use him only for milk –'

'Well, I don't know what pans you use for what,' said Julia crossly. 'You choose to go to bed and why on earth you've chosen to get up again, I can't imagine. Go away again and leave me to wash up in peace.'

'No, I will not let you use my kitchen.'

'Oh, Mitzi, you *are* impossible!'

Julia stalked angrily out of the kitchen and at that moment the door-bell rang.

'I do not go to the door,' Mitzi called from the kitchen. Julia muttered an impolite Continental expression under her breath and stalked to the front door.

It was Miss Hinchcliffe.

''Evening,' she said in her gruff voice. 'Sorry to barge in. Inspector's rung up, I expect?'

'He didn't tell us you were coming,' said Julia, leading the way to the drawing-room.

'He said I needn't come unless I liked,' said Miss Hinchcliffe. 'But I do like.'

Nobody offered Miss Hinchcliffe sympathy or mentioned Miss Murgatroyd's death. The ravaged face of the tall vigorous woman told its own tale, and would have made any expression of sympathy an impertinence.

'Turn all the lights on,' said Miss Blacklock. 'And put more coal on the fire. I'm cold – horribly cold. Come and sit here by the fire, Miss Hinchcliffe. The Inspector said he would be here in a quarter of an hour. It must be nearly that now.'

'Mitzi's come down again,' said Julia.

'Has she? Sometimes I think that girl's mad – quite mad. But then perhaps we're all mad.'

'I've no patience with this saying that all people who commit crimes are mad,' barked Miss Hinchcliffe. 'Horribly and intelligently sane – that's what I think a criminal is!'

The sound of a car was heard outside and presently Craddock came in with Colonel and Mrs Easterbrook and Edmund and Mrs Swettenham.

They were all curiously subdued.

Colonel Easterbrook said in a voice that was like an echo of his usual tones:

'Ha! A good fire.'

Mrs Easterbrook wouldn't take off her fur coat and sat down close to her husband. Her face, usually pretty and rather vapid, was like a little pinched weasel face. Edmund was in one of his furious moods and scowled at everybody. Mrs Swettenham made what was evidently a great effort, and which resulted in a kind of parody of herself.

'It's awful – isn't it?' she said conversationally. 'Everything, I mean. And really the less one says, the better. Because one doesn't know *who* next – like the Plague. Dear Miss Blacklock, don't you think you ought to have a little brandy? Just half a wineglass even? I always think there's nothing like brandy – such a wonderful stimulant. I – it seems so terrible of us – forcing our way in here like this, but Inspector Craddock *made* us come. And it seems too terrible – she hasn't been found, you know. That poor old thing from the Vicarage, I mean. Bunch Harmon is nearly frantic. Nobody knows *where* she went instead of going home. She didn't come to us. I've not even seen her today. And I should know if she *had* come to the house because I was in the drawing-room – at the back, you know, and Edmund was in his study writing – and that's at the front – so if she'd come either way we *should* have seen. And oh, I do hope and pray that nothing has happened to that dear sweet old thing – all her faculties still and *everything*.'

'Mother,' said Edmund in a voice of acute suffering, 'can't you shut up?'

'I'm sure, dear, I don't want to say a *word*,' said Mrs Swettenham, and sat down on the sofa by Julia.

Inspector Craddock stood near the door. Facing him, almost in a row, were the three women. Julia and Mrs Swettenham on the sofa. Mrs Easterbrook on the arm of her husband's chair. He had not brought about this arrangement, but it suited him very well.

Miss Blacklock and Miss Hinchcliffe were crouching over the fire. Edmund stood near them. Phillipa was far back in the shadows.

Craddock began without preamble.

'You all know that Miss Murgatroyd's been killed,' he began. 'We've reason to believe that the person who killed her was a woman. And for certain other reasons we can narrow it down still more. I'm about to ask certain ladies here to account for what they were doing between the hours of four and four-twenty this afternoon. I have already had an account of her movements from – from the young lady who has been calling herself Miss Simmons. I will ask her to repeat that statement. At the same time, Miss Simmons, I must caution you that you need not answer if you think your answers may incriminate you, and anything you say will be taken down by Constable Edwards and may be used as evidence in court.'

'You have to say that, don't you?' said Julia. She was rather pale, but composed. 'I repeat that between four and four-thirty I was walking along the field leading down to the brook by Compton Farm. I came back to the road by that field with three poplars in it. I didn't meet anyone as far as I can remember. I did not go near Boulders.'

'Mrs Swettenham?'

Edmund said, 'Are you cautioning all of us?'

The Inspector turned to him.

'No. At the moment only Miss Simmons. I have no reason to believe that any other statement made will be incriminating, but anyone, of course, is entitled to have a solicitor present and to refuse to answer questions unless he *is* present.'

'Oh, but that would be very silly and a complete waste of time,' cried Mrs Swettenham. 'I'm sure I can tell you at once exactly what I was doing. That's what you want, isn't it? Shall I begin now?'

'Yes, please, Mrs Swettenham.'

'Now, let me see.' Mrs Swettenham closed her eyes, opened them again. 'Of course I had nothing *at all* to do with killing Miss Murgatroyd. I'm sure *everybody* here knows *that*. But I'm a woman of the world, I know quite well that the police have to ask all the most unnecessary questions and write the answers down very carefully, because it's all for what they call "the record". That's it, isn't it?' Mrs Swettenham flashed the question at the diligent Constable Edwards, and added graciously, 'I'm not going too fast for you, I hope?'

Constable Edwards, a good shorthand writer, but with little social *savoir faire*, turned red to the ears and replied:

'It's quite all right, madam. Well, perhaps a *little* slower would be better.'

Mrs Swettenham resumed her discourse with emphatic pauses where she considered a comma or a full stop might be appropriate.

'Well, of course it's difficult to say – exactly – because I've not got, really, a very good sense of time. And ever since the war quite half our clocks haven't gone at all, and the ones that do go are often either fast or

slow or stop because we haven't wound them up.' Mrs Swettenham paused
to let this picture of confused time sink in and then went on earnestly,
'What I *think* I was doing at four o'clock was turning the heel of my sock
(and for some extraordinary reason I was going round the wrong way –
in purl, you know, not plain) but if I *wasn't* doing that, I must have been
outside snipping off the dead chrysanthemums – no, that was earlier –
before the rain.'

'The rain,' said the Inspector, 'started at 4.10 exactly.'

'Did it now? That helps a lot. Of course, I was upstairs putting a wash
basin in the passage where the rain always comes through. And it was
coming through so fast that I guessed at once that the gutter was stopped
up again. So I came down and got my mackintosh and rubber boots. I
called Edmund, but he didn't answer, so I thought perhaps he'd got to
a very important place in his novel and I wouldn't disturb him, and I've
done it quite often myself before. With the broom handle, you know, tied
on to that long thing you push up windows with.'

'You mean,' said Craddock, noting bewilderment on his subordinate's
face, 'that you were cleaning out the gutter?'

'Yes, it was all choked up with leaves. It took a long time and I got
rather wet, but I got it clear at last. And then I went in and got changed
and washed – so *smelly*, dead leaves – and then I went into the kitchen
and put the kettle on. It was 6.15 by the kitchen clock.'

Constable Edwards blinked.

'Which means,' finished Mrs Swettenham triumphantly, 'that it was
exactly twenty minutes to five.'

'Or near enough,' she added.

'Did anybody see what you were doing whilst you were out cleaning
the gutter?'

'No, indeed,' said Mrs Swettenham. 'I'd soon have roped them in to
help if they had! It's a most difficult thing to do single-handed.'

'So, by your own statement, you were outside, in a mackintosh and
boots, at the time when the rain was coming down, and according to you,
you were employed during that time in cleaning out a gutter but you have
no one who can substantiate that statement?'

'You can look at the gutter,' said Mrs Swettenham. 'It's beautifully
clear.'

'Did you hear your mother call to you, Mr Swettenham?'

'No,' said Edmund. 'I was fast asleep.'

'Edmund,' said his mother reproachfully, 'I thought you were *writing*.'

Inspector Craddock turned to Mrs Easterbrook.

'Now, Mrs Easterbrook?'

'I was sitting with Archie in his study,' said Mrs Easterbrook, fixing wide innocent eyes on him. 'We were listening to the wireless together, weren't we, Archie?'

There was a pause. Colonel Easterbrook was very red in the face. He took his wife's hand in his.

'You don't understand these things, kitten,' he said. 'I – well, I must say, Inspector, you've rather sprung this business on us. My wife, you know, has been terribly upset by all this. She's nervous and highly strung and doesn't appreciate the importance of – of taking due consideration before she makes a statement.'

'Archie,' cried Mrs Easterbrook reproachfully, 'are you going to say you weren't with me?'

'Well, I wasn't, was I, my dear? I mean one's got to stick to the facts. Very important in this sort of inquiry. I was talking to Lampson, the farmer at Croft End, about some chicken netting. That was about a quarter to four. I didn't get home until after the rain had stopped. Just before tea. A quarter to five. Laura was toasting the scones.'

'And had *you* been out also, Mrs Easterbrook?'

The pretty face looked more like a weasel's than ever. Her eyes had a trapped look.

'No – no, I just sat listening to the wireless. I didn't go out. Not then. I'd been out earlier. About – about half-past three. Just for a little walk. Not far.'

She looked as though she expected more questions, but Craddock said quietly:

'That's all, Mrs Easterbrook.'

He went on: 'These statements will be typed out. You can read them and sign them if they are substantially correct.'

Mrs Easterbrook looked at him with sudden venom.

'Why don't you ask the others where they were? That Haymes woman? And Edmund Swettenham? How do you know he *was* asleep indoors? Nobody saw him.'

Inspector Craddock said quietly:

'Miss Murgatroyd, before she died, made a certain statement. On the night of the hold-up here, *someone* was absent from this room. Someone who was supposed to have been in the room all the time. Miss Murgatroyd told her friend the names of the people she *did* see. By a process of elimination, she made the discovery that there was someone she did *not* see.'

'Nobody could see anything,' said Julia.

'Murgatroyd could,' said Miss Hinchcliffe, speaking suddenly in her deep voice. 'She was over there behind the door, where Inspector Craddock is now. She was the only person who could see anything of what was happening.'

'*Aha! That is what you think, is it!*' demanded Mitzi.

She made one of her dramatic entrances, flinging open the door and almost knocking Craddock sideways. She was in a frenzy of excitement.

'Ah, you do not ask Mitzi to come in here with the others, do you, you stiff policemen? I am only Mitzi! Mitzi in the kitchen! Let her stay in the kitchen where she belongs! But I tell you that Mitzi, as well as anyone else, and perhaps better, yes, better, can see things. Yes, I see things. I see something the night of the burglary. I see something and I do not quite believe it, and I hold my tongue till now. I think to myself I will not tell what it is I have seen, not yet. I will wait.'

'And when everything had calmed down, you meant to ask for a little money from a certain person, eh?' said Craddock.

Mitzi turned on him like an angry cat.

'And why not? Why look down your nose? Why should I not be paid for it if I have been so generous as to keep silence? Especially if some day there will be money – much *much* money. Oh! I have heard things – I know what goes on. I know this Pippemmer – this secret society of which *she'* – she flung a dramatic finger towards Julia – 'is an agent. Yes, I would have waited and asked for money – but now I am afraid. I would rather be *safe*. For soon, perhaps, someone will kill *me*. So I will tell what I know.'

'All right then,' said the Inspector sceptically. 'What *do* you know?'

'I tell you.' Mitzi spoke solemnly. 'On that night I am *not* in the pantry cleaning silver as I say – I am already in the dining-room when I hear the gun go off. I look through the keyhole. The hall it is black, but the gun go off again and the torch it falls – and it swings round as it falls – and I see *her*. I see *her* there close to him with the gun in her hand. I see Miss Blacklock.'

'Me?' Miss Blacklock sat up in astonishment. 'You must be mad!'

'But that's impossible,' cried Edmund. 'Mitzi couldn't have seen Miss Blacklock.'

Craddock cut in and his voice had the corrosive quality of a deadly acid.

'*Couldn't she, Mr Swettenham? And why not?* Because it *wasn't* Miss Blacklock who was standing there with the gun? It was *you*, wasn't it?'

'I – of course not – what the *hell*!'

'*You* took Colonel Easterbrook's revolver. *You* fixed up the business with Rudi Scherz – as a good joke. You had followed Patrick Simmons into the far room and when the lights went out, you slipped out through the carefully oiled door. You shot at Miss Blacklock and then you killed Rudi Scherz. A few seconds later you were back in the drawing-room clicking your lighter.'

For a moment Edmund seemed at a loss for words, then he spluttered out:

'The whole idea is *monstrous*. Why *me*? What earthly motive had *I* got?'

'If Miss Blacklock dies before Mrs Goedler, two people inherit, remember. The two we know of as Pip and Emma. Julia Simmons has turned out to be Emma –'

'And you think I'm Pip?' Edmund laughed. 'Fantastic – absolutely *fantastic*! I'm about the right age – nothing else. And I can prove to you, you damned fool, that I *am* Edmund Swettenham. Birth certificate, schools, university – everything.'

'He isn't Pip.' The voice came from the shadows in the corner. Phillipa Haymes came forward, her face pale. '*I'm Pip*, Inspector.'

'*You*, Mrs Haymes?'

'Yes. Everybody seems to have assumed that Pip was a boy – Julia knew, of course, that her twin was another girl – I don't know why she didn't say so this afternoon –'

'Family solidarity,' said Julia. 'I suddenly realized who you were. I'd had no idea till that moment.'

'I'd had the same idea as Julia did,' said Phillipa, her voice trembling a little. 'After I – lost my husband and the war was over, I wondered what I was going to do. My mother died many years ago. I found out about my Goedler relations. Mrs Goedler was dying and at her death the money would go to a Miss Blacklock. I found out where Miss Blacklock lived and I – I came here. I took a job with Mrs Lucas. I hoped that, since this Miss Blacklock was an elderly woman without relatives, she might, perhaps, be willing to help. Not me, because I could work, but help with Harry's education. After all, it *was* Goedler money and she'd no one particular of her own to spend it on.

'And then,' Phillipa spoke faster, it was as though, now her long reserve had broken down, she couldn't get the words out fast enough, 'that hold-up happened and I began to be frightened. Because it seemed to me that the only possible person with a motive for killing Miss Blacklock was *me*. I hadn't the least idea who Julia was – we aren't identical twins and we're not much alike to look at. No, it seemed as though I was the only one bound to be suspected.'

She stopped and pushed her fair hair back from her face, and Craddock suddenly realized that the faded snapshot in the box of letters must have been a photograph of Phillipa's mother. The likeness was undeniable. He knew too why that mention of closing and unclosing hands had seemed familiar – Phillipa was doing it now.

'Miss Blacklock has been good to me. Very *very* good to me – I didn't try to kill her. I never thought of killing her. But all the same, I'm Pip.' She added, 'You see, you needn't suspect Edmund any more.'

'Needn't I?' said Craddock. Again there was that acid biting tone in his voice. 'Edmund Swettenham's a young man who's fond of money. A young man, perhaps, who would like to marry a rich wife. But she wouldn't be a rich wife *unless Miss Blacklock died before Mrs Goedler*. And since it seemed almost certain that Mrs Goedler would die before Miss Blacklock, well – he had to do something about it – *didn't you, Mr Swettenham?*'

'It's a damned lie!' Edmund shouted.

And then, suddenly, a sound rose on the air. It came from the kitchen – a long unearthly shriek of terror.

'That isn't Mitzi!' cried Julia.

'No,' said Inspector Craddock, 'it's someone who's murdered three people . . .'

CHAPTER 22

THE TRUTH

When the Inspector turned on Edmund Swettenham, Mitzi had crept quietly out of the room and back to the kitchen. She was running water into the sink when Miss Blacklock entered.

Mitzi gave her a shamefaced sideways look.

'What a liar you are, Mitzi,' said Miss Blacklock pleasantly. 'Here – that isn't the way to wash up. The silver first, and fill the sink right up. You can't wash up in about two inches of water.'

Mitzi turned the taps on obediently.

'You are not angry at what I say, Miss Blacklock?' she asked.

'If I were to be angry at all the lies you tell, I should never be out of a temper,' said Miss Blacklock.

'I will go and say to the Inspector that I make it all up, shall I?' asked Mitzi.

'He knows that already,' said Miss Blacklock, pleasantly.

Mitzi turned off the taps and as she did so two hands came up behind her head and with one swift movement forced it down into the water-filled sink.

'Only *I* know that you're telling the truth for once,' said Miss Blacklock viciously.

Mitzi thrashed and struggled but Miss Blacklock was strong and her hands held the girl's head firmly under water.

Then, from somewhere quite close behind her, Dora Bunner's voice rose piteously on the air:

'*Oh Lotty – Lotty – don't do it . . . Lotty.*'

Miss Blacklock screamed. Her hands flew up in the air, and Mitzi, released, came up choking and spluttering.

Miss Blacklock screamed again and again. For there was no one there in the kitchen with her . . .

'*Dora, Dora, forgive me. I had to . . . I had to –*'

She rushed distractedly towards the scullery door – and the bulk of Sergeant Fletcher barred her way, just as Miss Marple stepped, flushed and triumphant, out of the broom cupboard.

'I could always mimic people's voices,' said Miss Marple.

'You'll have to come with me, Madam,' said Sergeant Fletcher. 'I was a witness of your attempt to drown this girl. And there will be other charges. I must warn you, Letitia Blacklock –'

'Charlotte Blacklock,' corrected Miss Marple. 'That's who she is, you know. Under that choker of pearls she always wears you'll find the scar of the operation.'

'Operation?'

'Operation for goitre.'

Miss Blacklock, quite calm now, looked at Miss Marple.

'So you know all about it?' she said.

'Yes, I've known for some time.'

Charlotte Blacklock sat down by the table and began to cry.

'You shouldn't have done that,' she said. 'Not made Dora's voice come. I loved Dora. I really loved Dora.'

Inspector Craddock and the others had crowded in the doorway.

Constable Edwards, who added a knowledge of first aid and artificial respiration to his other accomplishments, was busy with Mitzi. As soon as Mitzi could speak she was lyrical with self-praise.

'I do that good, do I not? I am clever! And I am brave! Oh, I am brave! Very very nearly was *I* murdered, too. But I was so brave I risk *everything.*'

With a rush Miss Hinchcliffe thrust aside the others and leapt upon the weeping figure of Charlotte Blacklock by the table.

It took all Sergeant Fletcher's strength to hold her off.

'Now then –' he said. 'Now then – no, no, Miss Hinchcliffe –'

Between clenched teeth Miss Hinchcliffe was muttering:

'Let me get at her. Just let me get at her. It was she who killed Amy Murgatroyd.'

Charlotte Blacklock looked up and sniffed.

'I didn't want to kill her. I didn't want to kill anybody – I had to – but it's Dora I mind about – after Dora was dead, I was all alone – ever since she died – I've been alone – oh, Dora – Dora –'

And once again she dropped her head on her hands and wept.

CHAPTER 23

EVENING AT THE VICARAGE

Miss Marple sat in the tall armchair. Bunch was on the floor in front of the fire with her arms round her knees.

The Reverend Julian Harmon was leaning forward and was for once looking more like a schoolboy than a man foreshadowing his own maturity. And Inspector Craddock was smoking his pipe and drinking a whisky and soda and was clearly very much off duty. An outer circle was composed of Julia, Patrick, Edmund and Phillipa.

'I think it's your story, Miss Marple,' said Craddock.

'Oh no, my dear boy. I only just helped a little, here and there. *You* were in charge of the whole thing, and conducted it all, and you know so much that I don't.'

'Well, tell it together,' said Bunch impatiently. 'Bit each. Only let Aunt Jane start because I like the muddly way her mind works. When did you first think that the whole thing was a put-up job by Blacklock?'

'Well, my dear Bunch, it's hard to say. Of course, right at the very beginning, it did seem as though the ideal person – or rather the *obvious* person, I should say – to have arranged the hold-up *was* Miss Blacklock herself. She was the only person who was known to have been in contact with Rudi Scherz, and how much easier to arrange something like that

when it's your own house. The central heating, for instance. No fires –
because that would have meant light in the room. But the only person
who could have arranged *not* to have a fire was the mistress of the house
herself.

'Not that I thought of all that at the time – it just seemed to me that it was
a pity it *couldn't* be as simple as that! Oh, no, I was taken in like everyone
else, I thought that someone really did want to kill Letitia Blacklock.'

'I think I'd like to get clear first on what really happened,' said Bunch.
'Did this Swiss boy recognize her?'

'Yes. He'd worked in –'

She hesitated and looked at Craddock.

'In Dr Adolf Koch's clinic in Berne,' said Craddock. 'Koch was a
world-famous specialist on operations for goitre. Charlotte Blacklock
went there to have her goitre removed and Rudi Scherz was one of the
orderlies. When he came to England he recognized in the hotel a lady
who had been a patient and on the spur of the moment he spoke to her.
I dare say he mightn't have done that if he'd paused to think, because he
left the place under a cloud, but that was some time after Charlotte had
been there, so she wouldn't know anything about it.'

'So he never said anything to her about Montreux and his father being
a hotel proprietor?'

'Oh, no, she made that up to account for his having spoken to her.'

'It must have been a great shock to her,' said Miss Marple, thoughtfully.
'She felt reasonably safe – and then – the almost impossible mischance
of somebody turning up who had known her – not as one of the two
Miss Blacklocks – she was prepared for *that* – but definitely as *Charlotte*
Blacklock, a patient who'd been operated on for goitre.

'But you wanted to go through it all from the beginning. Well, the
beginning, I think – if Inspector Craddock agrees with me – was when
Charlotte Blacklock, a pretty, light-hearted affectionate girl, developed
that enlargement of the thyroid gland that's called a goitre. It ruined her
life, because she was a very sensitive girl. A girl, too, who had always set a
lot of stress on her personal appearance. And girls just at that age in their
teens are particularly sensitive about themselves. If she'd had a mother, or
a reasonable father, I don't think she would have got into the morbid state
she undoubtedly did get into. She had no one, you see, to take her out of
herself, and force her to see people and lead a normal life and not think
too much about her infirmity. And, of course, in a different household,
she might have been sent for an operation many years earlier.

'But Dr Blacklock, I think, was an old-fashioned, narrow-minded, tyrannical and obstinate man. He didn't believe in these operations. Charlotte must take it from him that nothing could be done – apart from dosage with iodine and other drugs. Charlotte *did* take it from him, and I think her sister also placed more faith in Dr Blacklock's powers as a physician than he deserved.

'Charlotte was devoted to her father in a rather weak and soppy way. She thought, definitely, that her father knew best. But she shut herself up more and more as the goitre became larger and more unsightly, and refused to see people. She was actually a kindly affectionate creature.'

'That's an odd description of a murderess,' said Edmund.

'I don't know that it is,' said Miss Marple. 'Weak and kindly people are often very treacherous. And if they've got a grudge against life it saps the little moral strength that they may possess.

'Letitia Blacklock, of course, had quite a different personality. Inspector Craddock told me that Belle Goedler described her as really *good* – and I think Letitia *was* good. She was a woman of great integrity who found – as she put it herself – a great difficulty in understanding how people couldn't see what was dishonest. Letitia Blacklock, however tempted, would never have contemplated any kind of fraud for a moment.

'Letitia was devoted to her sister. She wrote her long accounts of everything that happened in an effort to keep her sister in touch with life. She was worried by the morbid state Charlotte was getting into.

'Finally Dr Blacklock died. Letitia, without hesitation, threw up her position with Randall Goedler and devoted herself to Charlotte. She took her to Switzerland, to consult authorities there on the possibility of operating. It had been left very late – but as we know the operation was successful. The deformity was gone – and the scar this operation had left was easily hidden by a choker of pearls or beads.

'The war had broken out. A return to England was difficult and the two sisters stayed in Switzerland doing various Red Cross and other work. That's right, isn't it, Inspector?'

'Yes, Miss Marple.'

'They got occasional news from England – amongst other things, I expect, they heard that Belle Goedler could not live long. I'm sure it would be only human nature for them both to have planned and talked together of the days ahead when a big fortune would be theirs to spend. One has got to realize, I think, that this prospect meant much more to *Charlotte* than it did to Letitia. For the first time in her life, Charlotte could go about feeling herself a normal woman, a woman at whom no one looked with either repulsion or pity. She was free at last to enjoy life

– and she had a whole lifetime, as it were, to crowd into her remaining years. To travel, to have a house and beautiful grounds – to have clothes and jewels, and go to plays and concerts, to gratify every whim – it was all a kind of fairy tale come true to Charlotte.

'And then Letitia, the strong healthy Letitia, got flu which turned to pneumonia and died within the space of a week! Not only had Charlotte lost her sister, but the whole dream existence she had planned for herself was cancelled. I think, you know, that she may have felt almost resentful towards Letitia. Why need Letitia have died, just then, when they had just had a letter saying Belle Goedler could not last long? Just one more month, perhaps, and the money would have been Letitia's – and hers when Letitia died . . .

'Now this is where I think the difference between the two came in. Charlotte didn't really feel that what she suddenly thought of doing was wrong – not really wrong. The money was meant to come to Letitia – it *would* have come to Letitia in the course of a few months – and she regarded herself and Letitia as one.

'Perhaps the idea didn't occur to her until the doctor or someone asked her her sister's Christian name – and then she realized how to nearly everyone they had appeared as the two Miss Blacklocks – elderly, well-bred Englishwomen, dressed much the same, with a strong family resemblance – (and, as I pointed out to Bunch, one elderly woman is *so* like another). Why shouldn't it be Charlotte who had died and *Letitia* who was alive?

'It was an impulse, perhaps, more than a plan. Letitia was buried under Charlotte's name. "Charlotte" was dead, "Letitia" came to England. All the natural initiative and energy, dormant for so many years, were now in the ascendant. As Charlotte she had played second fiddle. She now assumed the airs of command, the feeling of command that had been Letitia's. They were not really so unlike in mentality – though there was, I think, a big difference *morally*.

'Charlotte had, of course, to take one or two obvious precautions. She bought a house in a part of England quite unknown to her. The only people she had to avoid were a few people in her own native town in Cumberland (where in any case she'd lived as a recluse) and, of course, Belle Goedler who had known Letitia so well that any impersonation would have been out of the question. Handwriting difficulties were got over by the arthritic condition of her hands. It was really very easy because so few people had ever really known Charlotte.'

'But supposing she'd met people who'd known Letitia?' asked Bunch. 'There must have been plenty of those.'

'They wouldn't matter in the same way. Someone might say: "I came across Letitia Blacklock the other day. She's changed so much I really wouldn't have known her." But there still wouldn't be any suspicion in their minds that she wasn't Letitia. People *do* change in the course of ten years. *Her* failure to recognize *them* could always be put down to her short-sightedness; and you must remember that she knew every detail of Letitia's life in London – the people she met – the places she went. She'd got Letitia's letters to refer to, and she could quickly have disarmed any suspicion by mention of some incident, or an inquiry after a mutual friend. No, it was recognition as *Charlotte* that was the only thing she had to fear.

'She settled down at Little Paddocks, got to know her neighbours and, when she got a letter asking dear Letitia to be kind, she accepted with pleasure the visit of two young cousins she had never seen. Their acceptance of her as Aunt Letty increased her security.

'The whole thing was going splendidly. And then – she made her big mistake. It was a mistake that arose solely from her kindness of heart and her naturally affectionate nature. She got a letter from an old school friend who had fallen on evil days, and she hurried to the rescue. Perhaps it may have been partly because she was, in spite of everything, lonely. Her secret kept her in a way apart from people. And she had been genuinely fond of Dora Bunner and remembered her as a symbol of her own gay carefree days at school. Anyway, on an impulse, she answered Dora's letter in person. And very surprised Dora must have been! She'd written to *Letitia* and the sister who turned up in answer to her letter was *Charlotte*. There was never any question of pretending to be Letitia to Dora. Dora was one of the few old friends who had been admitted to see Charlotte in her lonely and unhappy days.

'And because she knew that Dora would look at the matter in exactly the same way as she did herself, she told Dora what she had done. Dora approved wholeheartedly. In her confused muddle-headed mind it seemed only right that dear Lotty should not be done out of her inheritance by Letty's untimely death. Lotty *deserved* a reward for all the patient suffering she had borne so bravely. It would have been most unfair if all that money should have gone to somebody nobody had ever heard of.

'She quite understood that nothing must be allowed to get out. It was like an extra pound of butter. You couldn't talk about it but there was nothing wrong about having it. So Dora came to Little Paddocks – and very soon Charlotte began to understand that she had made a terrible mistake. It was not merely the fact that Dora Bunner, with her muddles and her mistakes and her bungling, was quite maddening to live with. Charlotte could have put up with that – because she really cared for Dora, and anyway knew from the doctor that Dora hadn't got a very long time to live. But Dora very soon became a real danger. Though Charlotte and Letitia had called each other by their full names, Dora was the kind of person who always used abbreviations. To her the sisters had always been Letty and Lotty. And though she schooled her tongue resolutely to call her friend Letty – the old name often slipped out. Memories of the past, too, were rather apt to come to her tongue – and Charlotte had constantly to be on the watch to check these forgetful allusions. It began to get on her nerves.

'Still, nobody was likely to pay attention to Dora's inconsistencies. The real blow to Charlotte's security came, as I say, when she was recognized and spoken to by Rudi Scherz at the Royal Spa Hotel.

'I think that the money Rudi Scherz used to replace his earlier defalcations at the hotel may have come from Charlotte Blacklock. Inspector Craddock doesn't believe – and I don't either – that Rudi Scherz applied to her for money with any idea of blackmail in his head.'

'He hadn't the faintest idea he knew anything to blackmail her about,' said Inspector Craddock. 'He knew that he was quite a personable young man – and he was aware by experience that personable young men sometimes can get money out of elderly ladies if they tell a hard-luck story convincingly enough.

'But she may have seen it differently. She may have thought that it was a form of insidious blackmail, that perhaps he suspected something – and that later, if there was publicity in the papers as there might be after Belle Goedler's death, he would realize that in her he had found a gold mine.

'And she was committed to the fraud now. She'd established herself as Letitia Blacklock. With the Bank. With Mrs Goedler. The only snag was this rather dubious Swiss hotel clerk, an unreliable character, and possibly a blackmailer. If only he were out of the way – she'd be safe.

'Perhaps she made it all up as a kind of fantasy first. She'd been starved of emotion and drama in her life. She pleased herself by working out the details. How would she go about getting rid of him?

'She made her plan. And at last she decided to act on it. She told her story of a sham hold-up at a party to Rudi Scherz, explained that she wanted a stranger to act the part of the "gangster", and offered him a generous sum for his co-operation.

'And the fact that he agreed without any suspicion is what makes me quite certain that Scherz had no idea that he had any kind of hold over her. To him she was just a rather foolish old woman, very ready to part with money.

'She gave him the advertisement to insert, arranged for him to pay a visit to Little Paddocks to study the geography of the house, and showed him the spot where she would meet him and let him into the house on the night in question. Dora Bunner, of course, knew nothing about all this.

'The day came –' He paused.

Miss Marple took up the tale in her gentle voice.

'She must have spent a very miserable day. You see, it still wasn't too late to draw back . . . Dora Bunner told us that Letty was frightened that day and she must have been frightened. Frightened of what she was going to do, frightened of the plan going wrong – but not frightened enough to draw back.

'It had been fun, perhaps, getting the revolver out of Colonel Easterbrook's collar drawer. Taking along eggs, or jam – slipping upstairs in the empty house. It had been fun getting the second door in the drawing-room oiled, so that it would open and shut noiselessly. Fun suggesting the moving of the table outside the door so that Phillipa's flower arrangements would show to better advantage. It may have all seemed like a game. But what was going to happen next definitely wasn't a game any longer. Oh, yes, she was frightened . . . Dora Bunner was right about that.'

'All the same, she went through with it,' said Craddock. 'And it all went according to plan. She went out just after six to "shut up the ducks", and she let Scherz in then and gave him the mask and cloak and gloves and the torch. Then, at 6.30, when the clock begins to chime, she's ready by that table near the archway with her hand on the cigarette-box. It's all so natural. Patrick, acting as host, has gone for the drinks. She, the hostess, is fetching the cigarettes. She'd judged, quite correctly, that when the clock begins to chime, everyone will look at the clock. They did. Only one person, the devoted Dora, kept her eyes fixed on her friend. And she told us, in her very first statement, exactly what Miss Blacklock did. She said that Miss Blacklock had picked up the vase of violets.

'She'd previously frayed the cord of the lamp so that the wires were nearly bare. The whole thing only took a second. The cigarette-box, the vase and the little switch were all close together. She picked up the violets, spilt the water on the frayed place and switched on the lamp. Water's a good conductor of electricity. The wires fused.'

'Just like the other afternoon at the Vicarage,' said Bunch. 'That's what startled you so, wasn't it, Aunt Jane?'

'Yes, my dear. I've been puzzling about those lights. I'd realized that there were two lamps, a pair, and that one had been changed for the other – probably during the night.'

'That's right,' said Craddock. 'When Fletcher examined that lamp the next morning it was, like all the others, perfectly in order, no frayed flex or fused wires.'

'I'd understood what Dora Bunner meant by saying it had been the *shepherdess* the night before,' said Miss Marple, 'but I fell into the error of thinking, as she thought, that *Patrick* had been responsible. The interesting thing about Dora Bunner was that she was quite unreliable in repeating things she had heard – she always used her imagination to exaggerate or distort them, and she was usually wrong in what she *thought* – but she was quite accurate about the things she *saw*. She saw Letitia pick up the violets –'

'And she saw what she described as a flash and a crackle,' put in Craddock.

'And, of course, when dear Bunch spilt the water from the Christmas roses on to the lamp wire – I realized at once that only Miss Blacklock herself could have fused the lights because only she was near that table.'

'I could kick myself,' said Craddock. 'Dora Bunner even prattled about a burn on the table where someone had "put their cigarette down" – but nobody had even lit a cigarette . . . And the violets were dead because there was no water in the vase – a slip on Letitia's part – she ought to have filled it up again. But I suppose she thought nobody would notice and as a matter of fact Miss Bunner was quite ready to believe that she herself had put no water in the vase to begin with.'

He went on:

'She was highly suggestible, of course. And Miss Blacklock took advantage of that more than once. Bunny's suspicions of Patrick were, I think, induced by her.'

'Why pick on me?' demanded Patrick in an aggrieved tone.

'It was not, I think, a serious suggestion – but it would keep Bunny distracted from any suspicion that Miss Blacklock might be stage managing the business. Well, we know what happened next. As soon as the lights went and everyone was exclaiming, she slipped out through the previously oiled door and up behind Rudi Scherz who was flashing his torch round the room and playing his part with gusto. I don't suppose he realized for a moment she was there behind him with her gardening gloves pulled on and the revolver in her hand. She waits till the torch reaches the spot she must aim for – the wall near which she is supposed to be standing.

Then she fires rapidly twice and as he swings round startled, she holds the revolver close to his body and fires again. She lets the revolver fall by his body, throws her gloves carelessly on the hall table, then back through the other door and across to where she had been standing when the lights went out. She nicked her ear – I don't quite know how –'

'Nail scissors, I expect,' said Miss Marple. 'Just a snip on the lobe of the ear lets out a lot of blood. That was very good psychology, of course. The actual blood running down over her white blouse made it seem certain that she *had* been shot at, and that it had been a near miss.'

'It ought to have gone off quite all right,' said Craddock. 'Dora Bunner's insistence that Scherz had definitely aimed at Miss Blacklock had its uses. Without meaning it, Dora Bunner conveyed the impression that she'd actually seen her friend wounded. It might have been brought in Suicide or Accidental Death. And the case would have been closed. That it was kept open is due to Miss Marple here.'

'Oh, no, no.' Miss Marple shook her head energetically. 'Any little efforts on my part were quite incidental. It was you who weren't satisfied, Mr Craddock. It was *you* who wouldn't let the case be closed.'

'I wasn't happy about it,' said Craddock. 'I knew it was all wrong somewhere. But I didn't see *where* it was wrong, till you showed me. And after that Miss Blacklock had a real piece of bad luck. I discovered that that second door had been tampered with. Until that moment, whatever we agreed *might* have happened – we'd nothing to go upon but a pretty theory. But that oiled door was *evidence*. And I hit upon it by pure chance – by catching hold of a handle by mistake.'

'I think you were *led* to it, Inspector,' said Miss Marple. 'But then I'm old-fashioned.'

'So the hunt was up again,' said Craddock. 'But this time with a difference. We were looking now for someone with a motive to kill Letitia Blacklock.'

'And there *was* someone with a motive, and Miss Blacklock knew it,' said Miss Marple. 'I think she recognized Phillipa almost at once. Because Sonia Goedler seems to have been one of the very few people who had been admitted to Charlotte's privacy. And when one is old (you wouldn't know this yet, Mr Craddock) one has a much better memory for a face you've seen when you were young than you have for anyone you've only met a year or two ago. Phillipa must have been just about the same age as her mother was when Charlotte remembered her, and she was very like her mother. The odd thing is that I think Charlotte was very pleased to recognize Phillipa. She became very fond of Phillipa and

I think, unconsciously, it helped to stifle any qualms of conscience she may have had. She told herself that when she inherited the money, she was going to look after Phillipa. She would treat her as a daughter. Phillipa and Harry should live with her. She felt quite happy and beneficent about it. But once the Inspector began asking questions and finding out about "Pip and Emma" Charlotte became very uneasy. She didn't want to make a scapegoat of Phillipa. Her whole idea had been to make the business look like a hold-up by a young criminal and his accidental death. But now, with the discovery of the oiled door, the whole viewpoint was changed. And, except for Phillipa, there wasn't (as far as *she* knew, for she had absolutely no idea of Julia's identity) anyone with the least possible motive for wishing to kill her. She did her best to shield Phillipa's identity. She was quick-witted enough to tell you when you asked her, that Sonia was small and dark and she took the old snapshots out of the album so that you shouldn't notice any resemblance at the same time as she removed snapshots of Letitia herself.'

'And to think I suspected Mrs Swettenham of being Sonia Goedler,' said Craddock disgustedly.

'My poor mamma,' murmured Edmund. 'A woman of blameless life – or so I have always believed.'

'But of course,' Miss Marple went on, 'it was Dora Bunner who was the real danger. Every day Dora got more forgetful and more talkative. I remember the way Miss Blacklock looked at her the day we went to tea there. Do you know why? Dora had just called her Lotty again. It seemed to us a mere harmless slip of the tongue. But it frightened Charlotte. And so it went on. Poor Dora could not stop herself talking. That day we had coffee together in the Bluebird, I had the oddest impression that Dora was talking about *two* people, not one – and so, of course, she was. At one moment she spoke of her friend as not pretty but having so much character – but almost at the same moment she described her as a pretty light-hearted girl. She'd talk of Letty as so clever and so successful – and then say what a sad life she'd had, and then there was that quotation about stern affliction bravely borne – which really didn't seem to fit Letitia's life at all. Charlotte must, I think, have overheard a good deal that morning she came into the café. She certainly must have heard Dora mention about the lamp having been changed – about its being the shepherd and not the shepherdess. And she realized then what a very real danger to her security poor devoted Dora Bunner was.

'I'm afraid that that conversation with me in the café really sealed Dora's fate – if you'll excuse such a melodramatic expression. But I think it would have come to the same in the end . . . Because life couldn't be safe for Charlotte while Dora Bunner was alive. She loved Dora – she didn't want to kill Dora – but she couldn't see any other way. And, I expect (like Nurse Ellerton that I was telling you about, Bunch) she persuaded herself that it was almost a *kindness*. Poor Bunny – not long to live anyway and perhaps a painful end. The queer thing is that she did her best to make Bunny's last day a happy day. The birthday party – and the special cake . . .'

'Delicious Death,' said Phillipa with a shudder.

'Yes – yes, it was rather like that . . . she tried to give her friend a delicious death . . . The party, and all the things she liked to eat, and trying to stop people saying things to upset her. And then the tablets, whatever they were, in the aspirin bottle by her own bed so that Bunny, when she couldn't find the new bottle of aspirin she'd just bought, would go there to get some. And it would look, as it did look, that the tablets had been meant for *Letitia* . . .

'And so Bunny died in her sleep, quite happily, and Charlotte felt safe again. But she missed Dora Bunner – she missed her affection and her loyalty, she missed being able to talk to her about the old days . . . She cried bitterly the day I came up with that note from Julian – and her grief was quite genuine. She'd killed her own dear friend . . .'

'That's horrible,' said Bunch. 'Horrible.'

'But it's very human,' said Julian Harmon. 'One forgets how human murderers are.'

'I know,' said Miss Marple. 'Human. And often very much to be pitied. But very dangerous, too. Especially a weak kindly murderer like Charlotte Blacklock. Because, once a weak person gets *really* frightened, they get quite savage with terror and they've no self-control at all.'

'Murgatroyd?' said Julian.

'Yes, poor Miss Murgatroyd. Charlotte must have come up to the cottage and heard them rehearsing the murder. The window was open and she listened. It had never occurred to her until that moment that there was anyone else who could be a danger to her. Miss Hinchcliffe was urging her friend to remember what she'd seen and until that moment Charlotte hadn't realized that anyone could have seen anything at all. She'd assumed that everybody would automatically be looking at Rudi Scherz. She must have held her breath outside the window and listened. Was it going to be all right? And then, just as Miss Hinchcliffe rushed off to the station Miss Murgatroyd got to a point which showed that she had stumbled on the truth. She called after Miss Hinchcliffe: "She wasn't *there* . . ."'

'I asked Miss Hinchcliffe, you know, if that was the way she said it . . . Because if she'd said "*She* wasn't there" it wouldn't have meant the same thing.'

'Now that's too subtle a point for me,' said Craddock.

Miss Marple turned her eager pink and white face to him.

'Just think what's going on in Miss Murgatroyd's mind . . . One does see things, you know, and not know one sees them. In a railway accident once, I remember noticing a large blister of paint at the side of the carriage. I could have *drawn* it for you afterwards. And once, when there was a flying bomb in London – splinters of glass everywhere – and the shock – but what I remember best is a woman standing in front of me who had a big hole half-way up the leg of her stockings and the stockings didn't match. So when Miss Murgatroyd stopped thinking and just tried to remember what she *saw*, she remembered a good deal.'

'She started, I think, near the mantelpiece, where the torch must have hit first – then it went along the two windows and there were people in between the windows and her. Mrs Harmon with her knuckles screwed into her eyes for instance. She went on in her mind following the torch past Miss Bunner with her mouth open and her eyes staring – past a blank wall and a table with a lamp and a cigarette-box. And then came the shots – and quite suddenly she remembered a most incredible thing. She'd seen the wall where, later, there were the two bullet holes, the wall where Letitia Blacklock had been standing when she was shot, and at the moment when the revolver went off and Letty was shot, *Letty hadn't been there* . . .

'You see what I mean now? She'd been thinking of the three women Miss Hinchcliffe had told her to think about. If one of them hadn't been there, it would have been the *personality* she'd have fastened upon. She'd have said – in effect – "*That's* the one! *She* wasn't there;" But it was a *place* that was in her mind – a place where someone should have been – but the place wasn't filled – there wasn't anybody there. The place was there – but the person wasn't. And she couldn't take it in all at once. "How extraordinary, Hinch," she said. "She wasn't *there*" . . . So that could only mean Letitia Blacklock . . .'

'But you knew before that, didn't you?' said Bunch. 'When the lamp fused. When you wrote down those things on the paper.'

'Yes, my dear. It all came together then, you see – all the various isolated bits – and made a coherent pattern.'

Bunch quoted softly:

'*Lamp?* Yes. *Violets?* Yes. *Bottle of Aspirin.* You meant that Bunny had been going to buy a new bottle that day, and so she ought not to have needed to take Letitia's?'

'Not unless her own bottle had been taken or hidden. It had to appear as though Letitia Blacklock was the one meant to be killed.'

'Yes, I see. And then "Delicious Death". The cake – but more than the cake. The whole party set-up. A happy day for Bunny before she died. Treating her rather like a dog you were going to destroy. That's what I find the most horrible thing of all – the sort of – of spurious kindness.'

'She *was* quite a kindly woman. What she said at the last in the kitchen was quite true. "I didn't want to kill anybody." What she wanted was a great deal of money that didn't belong to her! And before that desire – (and it had become a kind of obsession – the money was to pay her back for all the suffering life had inflicted on her) – everything else went to the wall. People with a grudge against the world are always dangerous. They seem to think life owes them something. I've known many an invalid who has suffered far worse and been cut off from life much more than Charlotte Blacklock – and they've managed to lead happy contented lives. It's what in *yourself* that makes you happy or unhappy. But, oh dear, I'm afraid I'm straying away from what we were talking about. Where were we?'

'Going over your list,' said Bunch. 'What did you mean by "Making enquiries?" Inquiries about what?'

Miss Marple shook her head playfully at Inspector Craddock.

'You ought to have seen that, Inspector Craddock. You showed me that letter from Letitia Blacklock to her sister. It had the word "enquiries" in it twice – each time spelt with an *e*. But in the note I asked Bunch to show you, Miss Blacklock had written "*inquiries*" with an *i*. People don't often alter their spelling as they get older. It seemed to me very significant.'

'Yes,' Craddock agreed. 'I ought to have spotted that.'

Bunch was continuing. '*Severe afflictions bravely borne.* That's what Bunny said to you in the café and of course Letitia hadn't had any affliction. *Iodine.* That put you on the track of goitre?'

'Yes, dear. Switzerland, you know, and Miss Blacklock giving the impression that her sister had died of consumption. But I remembered then that the greatest authorities on goitre and the most skilful surgeons operating on it are Swiss. And it linked up with those really preposterous pearls that Letitia Blacklock always wore. Not really her *style* – but just right for concealing the scar.'

'I understand now her agitation the night the string broke,' said Craddock. 'It seemed at the time quite disproportionate.'

'And after that, it *was* Lotty you wrote, not Letty as we thought,' said Bunch.

'Yes, I remembered that the sister's name was Charlotte, and that Dora

Bunner had called Miss Blacklock Lotty once or twice – and that each time she did so, she had been very upset afterwards.'

'And what about Berne and Old Age Pensions?'

'Rudi Scherz had been an orderly in a hospital in Berne.'

'And Old Age Pension.'

'Oh, my dear Bunch, I mentioned that to you in the Bluebird though I didn't really see the application then. How Mrs Wotherspoon drew Mrs Bartlett's Old Age Pension as well as her own – though Mrs Bartlett had been dead for years – simply because one old woman is so like another old woman – yes, it all made a pattern and I felt so worked up I went out to cool my head a little and think what could be done about proving all this. Then Miss Hinchcliffe picked me up and we found Miss Murgatroyd . . .'

Miss Marple's voice dropped. It was no longer excited and pleased. It was quiet and remorseless.

'I knew then something had *got* to be done. Quickly! But there still wasn't any *proof*. I thought out a possible plan and I talked to Sergeant Fletcher.'

'And I have had Fletcher on the carpet for it!' said Craddock. 'He'd no business to go agreeing to your plans without reporting first to me.'

'He didn't like it, but I talked him into it,' said Miss Marple. 'We went up to Little Paddocks and I got hold of Mitzi.'

Julia drew a deep breath and said, 'I can't imagine how you ever got her to do it.'

'I worked on her, my dear,' said Miss Marple. 'She thinks far too much about herself anyway, and it will be good for her to have done something for others. I flattered her up, of course, and said I was sure if she'd been in her own country she'd have been in the Resistance movement, and she said, "Yes, indeed." And I said I could see she had got just the temperament for that sort of work. She was brave, didn't mind taking risks, and could act a part. I told her stories of deeds done by girls in the Resistance movements, some of them true, and some of them, I'm afraid, invented. She got tremendously worked up!'

'Marvellous,' said Patrick.

'And then I got her to agree to do her part. I rehearsed her till she was word perfect. Then I told her to go upstairs to her room and not come down until Inspector Craddock came. The worst of these excitable people is that they're apt to go off half-cocked and start the whole thing before the time.'

'She did it very well,' said Julia.

'I don't quite see the point,' said Bunch. 'Of course, I wasn't there –' she added apologetically.

'The point was a little complicated – and rather touch and go. The idea was that Mitzi whilst admitting, as though casually, that blackmail *had* been in her mind, was now so worked up and terrified that she was willing to come out with the truth. She'd seen, through the keyhole of the dining-room, Miss Blacklock in the hall with a revolver behind Rudi Scherz. She'd seen, that is, *what had actually taken place.* Now the only danger was that Charlotte Blacklock might have realized that, as the key was in the keyhole, Mitzi couldn't possibly have seen anything at all. But I banked on the fact that you don't think of things like that when you've just had a bad shock. All she could take in was that Mitzi had seen her.'

Craddock took over the story.

'But – and this was essential – I pretended to receive this with scepticism, and I made an immediate attack as though unmasking my batteries at last, upon someone who had not been previously suspected. I accused Edmund –'

'And very nicely *I* played *my* part,' said Edmund. 'Hot denial. All according to plan. What wasn't according to plan, Phillipa, my love, was you throwing in your little chirp and coming out into the open as "Pip". Neither the Inspector nor I had any idea you were Pip. *I* was going to be Pip! It threw us off our stride for the moment, but the Inspector made a masterly comeback and made some perfectly filthy insinuations about my wanting a rich wife which will probably stick in your subconscious and make irreparable trouble between us one day.'

'I don't see why that was necessary?'

'Don't you? It meant that, *from Charlotte Blacklock's point of view*, the only person who suspected or knew the truth, was *Mitzi*. The suspicions of the police were elsewhere. They had treated Mitzi for the moment as a liar. But if Mitzi were to persist, they might listen to her and take her seriously. So Mitzi had got to be silenced.'

'Mitzi went straight out of the room and back to the kitchen – just like I had told her,' said Miss Marple. 'Miss Blacklock came out after her almost immediately. Mitzi was apparently alone in the kitchen. Sergeant Fletcher was behind the scullery door. And I was in the broom cupboard in the kitchen. Luckily I'm very thin.'

Bunch looked at Miss Marple.

'What did you expect to happen, Aunt Jane?'

'One of two things. Either Charlotte would offer Mitzi money to hold her tongue – and Sergeant Fletcher would be a witness to that offer, or else – or else I thought she'd try to kill Mitzi.'

'But she couldn't hope to get away with *that*? She'd have been suspected at once.'

'Oh, my dear, she was past reasoning. She was just a snapping terrified cornered rat. Think what had happened that day. The scene between Miss Hinchcliffe and Miss Murgatroyd. Miss Hinchcliffe driving off to the station. As soon as she comes back Miss Murgatroyd will explain that Letitia Blacklock wasn't in the room that night. There's just a few minutes in which to make sure Miss Murgatroyd can't tell anything. No time to make a plan or set a stage. Just crude murder. She greets the poor woman and strangles her. Then a quick rush home, to change, to be sitting by the fire when the others come in, as though she'd never been out.

'And then came the revelation of Julia's identity. She breaks her pearls and is terrified they may notice her scar. Later, the Inspector telephones that he's bringing everyone there. No time to think, to rest. Up to her neck in murder now, no mercy killing – or undesirable young man to be put out of the way. Crude plain murder. Is she safe? Yes, so far. And then comes Mitzi – yet *another* danger. Kill Mitzi, stop her tongue! She's beside herself with fear. Not human any longer. Just a dangerous animal.'

'But why were you in the broom cupboard, Aunt Jane?' asked Bunch. 'Couldn't you have left it to Sergeant Fletcher?'

'It was safer with two of us, my dear. And besides, I knew I could mimic Dora Bunner's voice. If anything could break Charlotte Blacklock down – that would.'

'And it did . . . !'

'Yes . . . She went to pieces.'

There was a long silence as memory laid hold of them and then, speaking with determined lightness, to ease the strain, Julia said:

'It's made a wonderful difference to Mitzi. She told me yesterday that she was taking a post near Southampton. And she said (Julia produced a very good imitation of Mitzi's accent):

'"I go there and if they say to me you have to register with the police – you are an alien, I say to them, 'Yes, I will register! The police, they know me very well. I assist the police! Without me the police never would they have made the arrest of a very dangerous criminal. I risked my life because I am brave – brave like a lion – I do not care about risks.' 'Mitzi,' they say to me, 'you are a *heroine*, you are superb.' 'Ach, it is nothing, I say.'"'

Julia stopped.

'And a great deal more,' she added.

'I think,' said Edmund thoughtfully, 'that soon Mitzi will have assisted the police in not one but hundreds of cases!'

'She's softened towards me,' said Phillipa. 'She actually presented me with the recipe for Delicious Death as a kind of wedding present. She added that I was on no account to divulge the secret to Julia, because Julia had ruined her omelette pan.'

'Mrs Lucas,' said Edmund, 'is all over Phillipa now that since Belle Goedler's death Phillipa and Julia have inherited the Goedler millions. She sent us some silver asparagus tongs as a wedding present. I shall have enormous pleasure in *not* asking her to the wedding!'

'And so they lived happily ever after,' said Patrick. 'Edmund and Phillipa – and Julia and Patrick?' he added tentatively.

'Not with me, you won't live happily ever after,' said Julia. 'The remarks that Inspector Craddock improvised to address to Edmund apply far more aptly to you. You *are* the sort of soft young man who would like a rich wife. Nothing doing!'

'There's gratitude for you,' said Patrick. 'After all I did for that girl.'

'Nearly landed me in prison on a murder charge – that's what your forgetfulness nearly did for me,' said Julia. 'I shall never forget that evening when your sister's letter came. I really thought I was for it. I couldn't see any way out.'

'As it is,' she added musingly, 'I think I shall go on the stage.'

'What? You, too?' groaned Patrick.

'Yes. I might go to Perth. See if I can get your Julia's place in the Rep there. Then, when I've learnt my job, I shall go into theatre management – and put on Edmund's plays, perhaps.'

'I thought you wrote novels,' said Julian Harmon.

'Well, so did I,' said Edmund. 'I began writing a novel. Rather good it was. Pages about an unshaven man getting out of bed and what he smelt like, and the grey streets, and a horrible old woman with dropsy and a vicious young tart who dribbled down her chin – and they all talked interminably about the state of the world and wondered what they were alive for. And suddenly I began to wonder too . . . And then a rather comic idea occurred to me . . . and I jotted it down – and then I worked up rather a good little scene . . . All very obvious stuff. But somehow, I got interested . . . And before I knew what I was doing I'd finished a roaring farce in three acts.'

'What's it called?' asked Patrick. '*What the Butler Saw*?'

'Well, it easily might be . . . As a matter of I've called it *Elephants*

Do Forget. What's more, it's been accepted and it's going to be produced!'

'Elephants Do Forget,' murmured Bunch. 'I thought they didn't?'

The Rev. Julian Harmon gave a guilty start.

'My goodness. I've been so interested. My *sermon*!'

'Detective stories again,' said Bunch. 'Real-life ones this time.'

'You might preach on Thou Shall Do No Murder,' suggested Patrick.

'No,' said Julian Harmon quietly. 'I shan't take that as my text.'

'No,' said Bunch. 'You're quite right, Julian. I know a much nicer text, a happy text.' She quoted in a fresh voice, 'For lo the Spring is here and the Voice of the Turtle is heard in the Land – I haven't got it quite right – but you know the one I mean. Though why a *turtle* I can't think. I shouldn't think turtles have got nice voices at all.'

'The word turtle,' explained the Rev. Julian Harmon, 'is not very happily translated. It doesn't mean a reptile but the turtle dove. The Hebrew word in the original is –'

Bunch interrupted him by giving him a hug and saying:

'I know one thing – *You* think that the Ahasuerus of the Bible is Artaxerxes the Second, but between you and me it was Artaxerxes the Third.'

As always, Julian Harmon wondered why his wife should think that story so particularly funny.

'Tiglath Pileser wants to go and help you,' said Bunch. 'He ought to be a very proud cat. *He* showed us how the lights fused.'

EPILOGUE

'We ought to order some papers,' said Edmund to Phillipa upon the day of their return to Chipping Cleghorn after the honeymoon. 'Let's go along to Totman's.'

Mr Totman, a heavy-breathing, slow-moving man, received them with affability.

'Glad to see you back, sir. *And* madam.'

'We want to order some papers.'

'Certainly, sir. And your mother is keeping well, I hope? Quite settled down at Bournemouth?'

'She loves it,' said Edmund, who had not the faintest idea whether this was so or not, but like most sons, preferred to believe that all was well with those loved, but frequently irritating beings, parents.

'Yes, sir. Very agreeable place. Went there for my holiday last year. Mrs Totman enjoyed it very much.'

'I'm glad. About papers, we'd like –'

'And I hear you have a play on in London, sir. Very amusing, so they tell me.'

'Yes, it's doing very well.'

'Called *Elephants Do Forget*, so I hear. You'll excuse me, sir, asking you, but I always thought that they *didn't* – forget, I mean.'

'Yes – yes, exactly – I've begun to think it was a mistake calling it that. So many people have said just what you say.'

'A kind of natural-history fact, I've always understood.'

'Yes – yes. Like earwigs making good mothers.'

'Do they indeed, sir? Now, that's a fact I *didn't* know.'

'About the papers –'

'*The Times*, sir, I think it was?' Mr Totman paused with pencil uplifted.

'The *Daily Worker*,' said Edmund firmly. 'And the *Daily Telegraph*,' said Phillipa. 'And the *New Statesman*,' said Edmund. 'The *Radio Times*,' said Phillipa. 'The *Spectator*,' said Edmund. 'The *Gardener's Chronicle*,' said Phillipa.

They both paused to take breath.

'Thank you, sir,' said Mr Totman. '*And* the *Gazette*, I suppose?'

'No,' said Edmund.

'No,' said Phillipa.

'Excuse me, you *do* want the *Gazette*?'

'No.'

'No.'

'You mean' – Mr Totman liked to get things perfectly clear – 'You *don't* want the *Gazette*!'

'No, we don't.'

'Certainly not.'

'You don't want the *North Benham News and the Chipping Cleghorn Gazette* –'

'No.'

'You don't want me to send it along to you every week?'

'*No*.' Edmund added: 'Is that quite clear now?'

'Oh, yes, sir – yes.'

Edmund and Phillipa went out, and Mr Totman padded into his back parlour.

'Got a pencil, Mother?' he said. 'My pen's run out.'

'Here you are,' said Mrs Totman, seizing the order book. 'I'll do it. What do they want?'

'*Daily Worker, Daily Telegraph, Radio Times, New Statesman, Spectator* – let me see – *Gardener's Chronicle.*'

'*Gardener's Chronicle*,' repeated Mrs Totman, writing busily. 'And the *Gazette.*'

'They don't want the *Gazette.*'

'What?'

'They don't want the *Gazette.* They said so.'

'Nonsense,' said Mrs Totman. 'You don't hear properly. Of course they want the *Gazette*! Everybody has the *Gazette.* How else would they know what's going on round here?'

SLOTH

•

SPARKLING CYANIDE

Six people were thinking of Rosemary Barton
who had died nearly a year ago . . .

BOOK I

ROSEMARY

'What can I do to drive away remembrances from mine eyes?'

CHAPTER I

IRIS MARLE

Iris Marle was thinking about her sister, Rosemary.

For nearly a year she had deliberately tried to put the thought of Rosemary away from her. She hadn't wanted to remember.

It was too painful – too horrible!

The blue cyanosed face, the convulsed clutching fingers . . .

The contrast between that and the gay lovely Rosemary of the day before . . . Well, perhaps not exactly *gay*. She had had 'flu – she had been depressed, run down . . . All that had been brought out at the inquest. Iris herself had laid stress on it. It accounted, didn't it, for Rosemary's suicide?

Once the inquest was over, Iris had deliberately tried to put the whole thing out of her mind. Of what good was remembrance? Forget it all! Forget the whole horrible business.

But now, she realized, she had got to remember. She had got to think back into the past . . . To remember carefully every slight unimportant seeming incident . . .

That extraordinary interview with George last night necessitated remembrance.

It had been so unexpected, so frightening. Wait – *had* it been so unexpected? Hadn't there been indications beforehand? George's growing absorption, his absentmindedness, his unaccountable actions – his – well, *queerness* was the only word for it! All leading up to that moment last night when he had called her into the study and taken the letters from the drawer of the desk.

So now there was no help for it. She had got to think about Rosemary – to *remember*.

Rosemary – her sister . . .

With a shock Iris realized suddenly that it was the first time in her life she had ever thought about Rosemary. Thought about her, that is, objectively, as a *person*.

She had always accepted Rosemary without thinking about her. You didn't think about your mother or your father or your sister or your aunt. They just existed, unquestioned, in those relationships.

You didn't think about them as *people*. You didn't ask yourself, even, what they were *like*.

What had Rosemary been like?

That might be very important now. A lot might depend upon it. Iris cast her mind back into the past. Herself and Rosemary as children . . .

Rosemary had been the elder by six years.

Glimpses of the past came back – brief flashes – short scenes. Herself as a small child eating bread and milk, and Rosemary, important in pig tails, 'doing lessons' at a table.

The seaside one summer – Iris envying Rosemary who was a 'big girl' and could swim!

Rosemary going to boarding school – coming home for the holidays. Then she herself at school, and Rosemary being 'finished' in Paris. Schoolgirl Rosemary; clumsy, all arms and legs. 'Finished' Rosemary coming back from Paris with a strange new frightening elegance, soft voiced, graceful, with a swaying undulating figure, with red gold chestnut hair and big black fringed dark blue eyes. A disturbing beautiful creature – grown up – in a different world!

From then on they had seen very little of each other, the six-year gap had been at its widest.

Iris had been still at school, Rosemary in the full swing of a 'season.' Even when Iris came home, the gap remained. Rosemary's life was one of late mornings in bed, fork luncheons with other débutantes, dances most evenings of the week. Iris had been in the schoolroom with Mademoiselle, had gone for walks in the Park, had had supper at nine o'clock and gone to bed at ten. The intercourse between the sisters had been limited to such brief interchanges as:

'Hullo, Iris, telephone for a taxi for me, there's a lamb, I'm going to be devastatingly late,' or

'I don't like that new frock, Rosemary. It doesn't suit you. It's all bunch and fuss.'

Then had come Rosemary's engagement to George Barton. Excitement, shopping, streams of parcels, bridesmaids' dresses.

The wedding. Walking up the aisles behind Rosemary, hearing whispers:

'What a *beautiful* bride she makes . . .'

Why had Rosemary married George? Even at the time Iris had been vaguely surprised. There had been so many exciting young men, ringing Rosemary up, taking her out. Why choose George Barton, fifteen years older than herself, kindly, pleasant, but definitely dull?

George was well off, but it wasn't money. Rosemary had her own money, a great deal of it.

Uncle Paul's money . . .

Iris searched her mind carefully, seeking to differentiate between what she knew now and what she had known then: Uncle Paul, for instance?

He wasn't really an uncle, she had always known that. Without ever having been definitely told them she knew certain facts. Paul Bennett had been in love with their mother. She had preferred another and a poorer man. Paul Bennett had taken his defeat in a romantic spirit. He had remained the family friend, adopted an attitude of romantic platonic devotion. He had become Uncle Paul, had stood godfather to the first-born child, Rosemary. When he died, it was found that he had left his entire fortune to his little god-daughter, then a child of thirteen.

Rosemary, besides her beauty, had been an heiress. And she had married nice dull George Barton.

Why? Iris had wondered then. She wondered now. Iris didn't believe that Rosemary had ever been in love with him. But she had seemed very happy with him and she had been fond of him – yes, definitely fond of him. Iris had good opportunities for knowing, for a year after the marriage, their mother, lovely delicate Viola Marle, had died, and Iris, a girl of seventeen, had gone to live with Rosemary Barton and her husband.

A girl of seventeen. Iris pondered over the picture of herself. What had she been like? What had she felt, thought, seen?

She came to the conclusion that that young Iris Marle had been slow of development – unthinking, acquiescing in things as they were. Had she resented, for instance, her mother's earlier absorption in Rosemary? On the whole she thought not. She had accepted, unhesitatingly, the fact that Rosemary was the important one. Rosemary was 'out' – naturally her mother was occupied as far as her health permitted with her elder daughter. That had been natural enough. Her own turn would come some day. Viola Marle had always been a somewhat remote mother, preoccupied mainly with her own health, relegating her children to nurses, governesses, schools, but invariably charming to them in those brief moments when she came across them. Hector Marle had died when Iris was five years old. The knowledge that he drank more than was good for him had permeated so subtly that she had not the least idea how it had actually come to her.

Seventeen-year-old Iris Marle had accepted life as it came, had duly mourned for her mother, had worn black clothes, had gone to live with her sister and her sister's husband at their house in Elvaston Square.

Sometimes it had been rather dull in that house. Iris wasn't to come out, officially, until the following year. In the meantime she took French and German lessons three times a week, and also attended domestic science classes. There were times when she had nothing much to do and nobody to talk to. George was kind, invariably affectionate and brotherly. His attitude had never varied. He was the same now.

And Rosemary? Iris had seen very little of Rosemary. Rosemary had been out a good deal. Dressmakers, cocktail parties, bridge . . .

What did she really *know* about Rosemary when she came to think of it? Of her tastes, of her hopes, of her fears? Frightening, really, how little you might know of a person after living in the same house with them! There had been little or no intimacy between the sisters.

But she'd got to think now. She'd got to remember. It might be important.

Certainly Rosemary had *seemed* happy enough . . .

Until that day – a week before it happened.

She, Iris, would never forget that day. It stood out crystal clear – each detail, each word. The shining mahogany table, the pushed back chair, the hurried characteristic writing . . .

Iris closed her eyes and let the scene come back . . .

Her own entry into Rosemary's sitting-room, her sudden stop.

It had startled her so; what she saw! Rosemary, sitting at the writing table, her head laid down on her outstretched arms. Rosemary weeping with a deep abandoned sobbing. She'd never seen Rosemary cry before – and this bitter, violent weeping frightened her.

True, Rosemary had had a bad go of 'flu. She'd only been up a day or two. And everyone knew that 'flu *did* leave you depressed. Still –

Iris had cried out, her voice childish, startled:

'Oh, Rosemary, what is it?'

Rosemary sat up, swept the hair back from her disfigured face. She struggled to regain command of herself. She said quickly:

'It's nothing – nothing – don't stare at me like that!'

She got up and passing her sister, she ran out of the room.

Puzzled, upset, Iris went farther into the room. Her eyes, drawn wonderingly to the writing table, caught sight of her own name in her sister's handwriting. Had Rosemary been writing to her then?

She drew nearer, looked down on the sheet of blue notepaper with the big characteristic sprawling writing, even more sprawling than usual owing to the haste and agitation behind the hand that held the pen.

Darling Iris,

There isn't any point in my making a will because my money goes to you anyway, but I'd like certain of my things to be given to certain people.

To George, the jewellery he's given me, and the little enamel casket we bought together when we were engaged.

To Gloria King, my platinum cigarette case.

To Maisie, my Chinese Pottery horse that she's always admired –

It stopped there, with a frantic scrawl of the pen as Rosemary had dashed it down and given way to uncontrollable weeping.

Iris stood as though turned to stone.

What did it mean? Rosemary wasn't going to *die*, was she? She'd been very ill with influenza, but she was all right now. And anyway people didn't die of 'flu – at least sometimes they did, but Rosemary hadn't. She was quite well now, only weak and run down.

Iris's eyes went over the words again and this time a phrase stood out with startling effect:

'. . . *my money goes to you anyway* . . .'

It was the first intimation she had had of the terms of Paul Bennett's will. She had known since she was a child that Rosemary had inherited Uncle Paul's money, that Rosemary was rich whilst she herself was comparatively poor. But until this moment she had never questioned what would happen to that money on Rosemary's death.

If she had been asked, she would have replied that she supposed it would go to George as Rosemary's husband, but would have added that it seemed absurd to think of Rosemary dying before George!

But here it was, set down in black and white, in Rosemary's own hand. At Rosemary's death the money came to her, Iris. But surely that wasn't legal? A husband or wife got any money, not a *sister*. Unless, of course, Paul Bennett had left it that way in his will. Yes, that must be it. Uncle Paul had said the money was to go to her if Rosemary died. That did make it rather less unfair –

Unfair? She was startled as the word leapt to her thoughts. Had she been thinking that it was unfair for Rosemary to get *all* Uncle Paul's money? She supposed that, deep down, she must have been feeling just that. It *was* unfair. They were sisters, she and Rosemary. They were both her mother's children. Why should Uncle Paul give it all to Rosemary?

Rosemary always had everything!

Parties and frocks and young men in love with her and an adoring husband.

The only unpleasant thing that ever happened to Rosemary was having an attack of 'flu! And even *that* hadn't lasted longer than a week!

Iris hesitated, standing by the desk. That sheet of paper – would Rosemary want it left about for the servants to see?

After a minute's hesitation she picked it up, folded it in two and slipped it into one of the drawers of the desk.

It was found there after the fatal birthday party, and provided an additional proof, if proof was necessary, that Rosemary had been in a depressed and unhappy state of mind after her illness, and had possibly been thinking of suicide even then.

Depression after influenza. That was the motive brought forward at the inquest, the motive that Iris's evidence helped to establish. An inadequate motive, perhaps, but the only one available, and consequently accepted. It had been a bad type of influenza that year.

Neither Iris nor George Barton could have suggested any other motive – *then*.

Now, thinking back over the incident in the attic, Iris wondered that she could have been so blind.

The whole thing must have been going on under her eyes! And she had seen nothing, noticed nothing!

Her mind took a quick leap over the tragedy of the birthday party. No need to think of *that*! That was over – done with. Put away the horror of that and the inquest and George's twitching face and bloodshot eyes. Go straight on to the incident of the trunk in the attic.

That had been about six months after Rosemary's death.

Iris had continued to live at the house in Elvaston Square. After the funeral the Marle family solicitor, a courtly old gentleman with a shining bald head and unexpectedly shrewd eyes, had had an interview with Iris. He had explained with admirable clarity that under the will of Paul Bennett, Rosemary had inherited his estate in trust to pass at her death to any children she might have. If Rosemary died childless, the estate was to go to Iris absolutely. It was, the solicitor explained, a very large fortune which would belong to her absolutely upon attaining the age of twenty-one or on her marriage.

In the meantime, the first thing to settle was her place of residence. Mr George Barton had shown himself anxious for her to continue living with him and had suggested that her father's sister, Mrs Drake, who was in impoverished circumstances owing to the financial claims of a son (the black sheep of the Marle family), should make her home with them and chaperon Iris in society. Did Iris approve of this plan?

Iris had been quite willing, thankful not to have to make new plans. Aunt Lucilla she remembered as an amiable friendly sheep with little will of her own.

So the matter had been settled. George Barton had been touchingly pleased to have his wife's sister still with him and treated her affectionately as a younger sister. Mrs Drake, if not a stimulating companion, was completely subservient to Iris's wishes. The household settled down amicably.

It was nearly six months later that Iris made her discovery in the attic.

The attics of the Elvaston Square house were used as storage rooms for odds and ends of furniture, and a number of trunks and suitcases.

Iris had gone up there one day after an unsuccessful hunt for an old red pullover for which she had an affection. George had begged her not to wear mourning for Rosemary, Rosemary had always been opposed to the idea, he said. This, Iris knew, was true, so she acquiesced and continued to wear ordinary clothes, somewhat to the disapproval of Lucilla Drake, who was old-fashioned and liked what she called 'the decencies' to be observed. Mrs Drake herself was still inclined to wear crêpe for a husband deceased some twenty-odd years ago.

Various unwanted clothes, Iris knew, had been packed away in a trunk upstairs. She started hunting through it for her pullover, coming across, as she did so, various forgotten belongings, a grey coat and skirt, a pile of stockings, her skiing kit and one or two old bathing dresses.

It was then that she came across an old dressing-gown that had belonged to Rosemary and which had somehow or other escaped being given away with the rest of Rosemary's things. It was a mannish affair of spotted silk with big pockets.

Iris shook it out, noting that it was in perfectly good condition. Then she folded it carefully and returned it to the trunk. As she did so, her hand felt something crackle in one of the pockets. She thrust in her hand and drew out a crumpled-up piece of paper. It was in Rosemary's handwriting and she smoothed it out and read it.

> *Leopard darling, you can't mean it . . . You can't – you can't . . .*
> *We love each other! We belong together! You must know that just as*
> *I know it! We can't just say goodbye and go on coolly with our own*
> *lives. You know that's impossible, darling – quite impossible. You and*
> *I belong together – for ever and ever. I'm not a conventional woman*
> *– I don't mind about what people say. Love matters more to me than*
> *anything else. We'll go away together – and be happy – I'll make you*
> *happy. You said to me once that life without me was dust and ashes*
> *to you – do you remember, Leopard darling? And now you write*
> *calmly that all this had better end – that it's only fair to me. Fair*
> *to me? But I can't live without you! I'm sorry about George – he's*
> *always been sweet to me – but he'll understand. He'll want to give me*
> *my freedom. It isn't right to live together if you don't love each other*
> *any more. God meant us for each other, darling – I know He did.*
> *We're going to be wonderfully happy – but we must be brave. I shall*
> *tell George myself – I want to be quite straight about the whole thing –*
> *but not until after my birthday.*
>
> *I know I'm doing what's right, Leopard darling – and I can't live*
> *without you – can't, can't – CAN'T. How stupid it is of me to write*
> *all this. Two lines would have done. Just 'I love you. I'm never going*
> *to let you go.' Oh darling –*

The letter broke off.

Iris stood motionless, staring down at it.

How little one knew of one's own sister!

So Rosemary had had a lover – had written him passionate love letters – had planned to go away with him?

What had happened? Rosemary had never sent the letter after all. What letter had she sent? What had been finally decided between Rosemary and this unknown man?

('Leopard!' What extraordinary fancies people had when they were in love. So silly. *Leopard* indeed!)

Who was this man? Did he love Rosemary as much as she loved him? Surely he must have done. Rosemary was so unbelievably lovely. And yet, according to Rosemary's letter, he had suggested 'ending it all'. That suggested – what? Caution? He had evidently said that the break was for Rosemary's sake. That it was only fair to her. Yes, but didn't men say that sort of thing to save their faces? Didn't it really mean that the man, whoever he was, was tired of it all? Perhaps it had been to him a mere passing distraction. Perhaps he had never really cared. Somehow Iris got the impression that the unknown man had been very determined to break with Rosemary finally . . .

But Rosemary had thought differently. Rosemary wasn't going to count the cost. Rosemary had been determined, too . . .

Iris shivered.

And she, Iris, hadn't known a thing about it! Hadn't even guessed! Had taken it for granted that Rosemary was happy and contented and that she and George were quite satisfied with one another. Blind! She must have been blind not to know a thing like that about her own sister.

But who was the man?

She cast her mind back, thinking, remembering. There had been so many men about, admiring Rosemary, taking her out, ringing her up. There had been no one special. But there must have been – the rest of the bunch were mere camouflage for the one, the only one, that mattered. Iris frowned perplexedly, sorting her remembrances carefully.

Two names stood out. It must, yes, positively it must, be one or the other. Stephen Farraday? It must be Stephen Farraday. What could Rosemary have seen in him? A stiff pompous young man – and not so very young either. Of course people did say he was brilliant. A rising politician, an under-secretaryship prophesied in the near future, and all the weight of the influential Kidderminster connection behind him. A possible future Prime Minister! Was that what had given him glamour in Rosemary's eyes? Surely she couldn't care so desperately for the man himself – such a cold self-contained creature? But they said that his own wife was passionately in love with him, that she had gone against all the wishes of her powerful family in marrying him – a mere nobody with political ambitions! If one woman felt like that about him, another woman might also. Yes, it *must* be Stephen Farraday.

Because, if it wasn't Stephen Farraday, it must be Anthony Browne.

And Iris didn't want it to be Anthony Browne.

True, he'd been very much Rosemary's slave, constantly at her beck and call, his dark good-looking face expressing a kind of humorous desperation. But surely that devotion had been too open, too freely declared to go really deep?

Odd the way he had disappeared after Rosemary's death. They had none of them seen him since.

Still not so odd really – he was a man who travelled a lot. He had talked about the Argentine and Canada and Uganda and the U.S.A. She had an idea that he was actually an American or a Canadian, though he had hardly any accent. No, it wasn't really strange that they shouldn't have seen anything of him since.

It was Rosemary who had been his friend. There was no reason why he should go on coming to see the rest of them. He had been Rosemary's friend. But not Rosemary's lover! She didn't want him to have been Rosemary's lover! That would hurt – that would hurt terribly . . .

She looked down at the letter in her hand. She crumpled it up. She'd throw it away, burn it . . .

It was sheer instinct that stopped her.

Some day it might be important to produce that letter . . .

She smoothed it out, took it down with her and locked it away in her jewel case.

It might be important, some day, to show why Rosemary took her own life.

'And the next thing, please?'

The ridiculous phrase came unbidden into Iris's mind and twisted her lips into a wry smile. The glib shopkeeper's question seemed to represent so exactly her own carefully directed mental processes.

Was not that exactly what she was trying to do in her survey of the past? She had dealt with the surprising discovery in the attic. And now – on to 'the next thing, please!' What was the next thing?

Surely the increasingly odd behaviour of George. That dated back for a long time. Little things that had puzzled her became clear now in the light of the surprising interview last night. Disconnected remarks and actions took their proper place in the course of events.

And there was the reappearance of Anthony Browne. Yes, perhaps that ought to come next in sequence, since it had followed the finding of the letter by just one week.

Iris couldn't recall her sensations exactly . . .

Rosemary had died in November. In the following May, Iris, under the wing of Lucilla Drake, had started her social young girl's life. She had gone to luncheons and teas and dances without, however, enjoying them very much. She had felt listless and unsatisfied. It was at a somewhat dull dance towards the end of June that she heard a voice say behind her:

'It *is* Iris Marle, isn't it?'

She had turned, flushing, to look into Anthony's – Tony's – dark quizzical face.

He said:

'I don't expect you to remember me, but –'

She interrupted.

'Oh, but I do remember you. Of course I do!'

'Splendid. I was afraid you'd have forgotten me. It's such a long time since I saw you.'

'I know. Not since Rosemary's birthday par –'

She stopped. The words had come gaily, unthinkingly, to her lips. Now the colour rushed away from her cheeks, leaving them white and drained of blood. Her lips quivered. Her eyes were suddenly wide and dismayed.

Anthony Browne said quickly:

'I'm terribly sorry. I'm a brute to have reminded you.'

Iris swallowed. She said:

'It's all right.'

(Not since the night of Rosemary's birthday party. Not since the night of Rosemary's suicide. She wouldn't think of it. She would *not* think of it!)

Anthony Browne said again:

'I'm terribly sorry. Please forgive me. Shall we dance?'

She nodded. Although already engaged for the dance that was just beginning, she had floated on to the floor in his arms. She saw her partner, a blushing immature young man whose collar seemed too big for him, peering about for her. The sort of partner, she thought scornfully, that debs have to put up with. Not like this man – Rosemary's friend.

A sharp pang went through her. *Rosemary's friend.* That letter. Had it been written to this man she was dancing with now? Something in the easy feline grace with which he danced lent substance to the nickname 'Leopard'. Had he and Rosemary –

She said sharply:

'Where have you been all this time?'

He held her a little way from him, looking down into her face. He was unsmiling now, his voice held coldness.

'I've been travelling – on business.'

'I see.' She went on uncontrollably, 'Why have you come back?'

He smiled then. He said lightly:

'Perhaps – to see you, Iris Marle.'

And suddenly gathering her up a little closer, he executed a long daring glide through the dancers, a miracle of timing and steering. Iris wondered why, with a sensation that was almost wholly pleasure, she should feel afraid.

Since then Anthony had definitely become part of her life. She saw him at least once a week.

She met him in the Park, at various dances, found him put next to her at dinner.

The only place he never came to was the house in Elvaston Square. It was some time before she noticed this, so adroitly did he manage to evade or refuse invitations there. When she did realize it she began to wonder why. Was it because he and Rosemary –

Then, to her astonishment, George, easy-going, non-interfering George, spoke to her about him.

'Who's this fellow, Anthony Browne, you're going about with? What do you know about him?'

She stared at him.

'Know about him? Why, he was a friend of Rosemary's!'

George's face twitched. He blinked. He said in a dull heavy voice:

'Yes, of course, so he was.'

Iris cried remorsefully:

'I'm sorry. I shouldn't have reminded you.'

George Barton shook his head. He said gently:

'No, no, I don't want her forgotten. Never that. After all,' he spoke awkwardly, his eyes averted, 'that's what her name means. Rosemary – remembrance.' He looked full at her. 'I don't want you to forget your sister, Iris.'

She caught her breath.

'I never shall.'

George went on:

'But about this young fellow, Anthony Browne. Rosemary may have liked him, but I don't believe she knew much about him. You know, you've got to be careful, Iris. You're a very rich young woman.'

A kind of burning anger swept over her.

'Tony – Anthony – has plenty of money himself. Why, he stays at Claridge's when he's in London.'

George Barton smiled a little. He murmured:

'Eminently respectable – as well as costly. All the same, my dear, nobody seems to know much about this fellow.'

'He's an American.'

'Perhaps. If so, it's odd he isn't sponsored more by his own Embassy. He doesn't come much to this house, does he?'

'No. And I can see why, if you're so horrid about him!'

George shook his head.

'Seem to have put my foot in it. Oh well. Only wanted to give you a timely warning. I'll have a word with Lucilla.'

'Lucilla!' said Iris scornfully.

George said anxiously:

'Is everything all right? I mean, does Lucilla see to it that you get the sort of time you ought to have? Parties – all that sort of thing?'

'Yes, indeed, she works like a beaver . . .'

'Because, if not, you've only got to say, you know, child. We could get hold of someone else. Someone younger and more up to date. I want you to enjoy yourself.'

'I do, George. Oh, George, I do.'

He said rather heavily:

'Then that's all right. I'm not much hand at these shows myself – never was. But see to it you get everything you want. There's no need to stint expense.'

That was George all over – kind, awkward, blundering.

True to his promise, or threat, he 'had a word' with Mrs Drake on the subject of Anthony Browne, but as Fate would have it the moment was unpropitious for gaining Lucilla's full attention.

She had just had a cable from that ne'er-do-well son who was the apple of her eye and who knew, only too well, how to wring the maternal heartstrings to his own financial advantage.

'Can you send me two hundred pounds. Desperate. Life or death. Victor.'

'Victor is so honourable. He knows how straitened my circumstances are and he'd never apply to me except in the last resource. He never has. I'm always so afraid he'll shoot himself.'

'Not he,' said George Barton unfeelingly.

'You don't know him. I'm his mother and naturally I know what my own son is like. I should never forgive myself if I didn't do what he asked. I could manage by selling out those shares.'

George sighed.

'Look here, Lucilla. I'll get full information by cable from one of my correspondents out there. We'll find out just exactly what sort of a jam Victor's in. But my advice to you is to let him stew in his own juice. He'll never make good until you do.'

'You're so hard, George. The poor boy has always been unlucky –'

George repressed his opinions on that point. Never any good arguing with women.

He merely said:

'I'll get Ruth on to it at once. We should hear by tomorrow.'

Lucilla was partially appeased. The two hundred was eventually cut down to fifty, but that amount Lucilla firmly insisted on sending.

George, Iris knew, provided the amount himself though pretending to Lucilla that he was selling her shares. Iris admired George very much for his generosity and said so. His answer was simple.

'Way I look at it – always some black sheep in the family. Always someone who's got to be kept. Someone or other will have to fork out for Victor until he dies.'

'But it needn't be you. He's not *your* family.'

'Rosemary's family's *mine.*'

'You're a darling, George. But couldn't *I* do it? You're always telling me I'm rolling.'

He grinned at her.

'Can't do anything of that kind until you're twenty-one, young woman. And if you're wise you won't do it then. But I'll give you one tip. When a fellow wires that he'll end everything unless he gets a couple of hundred by return, you'll usually find that twenty pounds will be ample . . . I daresay a tenner would do! You can't stop a mother coughing up, but you can reduce the amount – remember that. Of course Victor Drake would never do away with himself, not he! These people who threaten suicide never do it.'

Never? Iris thought of Rosemary. Then she pushed the thought away. George wasn't thinking of Rosemary. He was thinking of an unscrupulous, plausible young man in Rio de Janeiro.

The net gain from Iris's point of view was that Lucilla's maternal preoccupations kept her from paying full attention to Iris's friendship with Anthony Browne.

So – on to the 'next thing, Madam.' The change in George! Iris couldn't put it off any longer. When had that begun? What was the cause of it?

Even now, thinking back, Iris could not put her finger definitely on the moment when it began. Ever since Rosemary's death George had been abstracted, had had fits of inattention and brooding. He had seemed older, heavier. That was all natural enough. But when exactly had his abstraction become something more than natural?

It was, she thought, after their clash over Anthony Browne, that she had first noticed him staring at her in a bemused, perplexed manner. Then he formed a new habit of coming home early from business and shutting himself up in his study. He didn't seem to be doing anything there. She had gone in once and found him sitting at his desk staring straight ahead of him. He looked at her when she came in with dull lack-lustre eyes. He behaved like a man who has had a shock, but to her question as to what was the matter, he replied briefly, 'Nothing.'

As the days went on, he went about with the careworn look of a man who has some definite worry upon his mind.

Nobody had paid very much attention. Iris certainly hadn't. Worries were always conveniently 'Business'.

Then, at odd intervals, and with no seeming reason, he began to ask questions. It was then that she began to put his manner down as definitely 'queer'.

'Look here, Iris, did Rosemary ever talk to you much?'

Iris stared at him.

'Why, of course, George. At least – well, about what?'

'Oh, herself – her friends – how things were going with her. Whether she was happy or unhappy. That sort of thing.'

She thought she saw what was in his mind. He must have got wind of Rosemary's unhappy love affair.

She said slowly:

'She never said much. I mean – she was always busy – doing things.'

'And you were only a kid, of course. Yes, I know. All the same, I thought she might have said something.'

He looked at her inquiringly – rather like a hopeful dog.

She didn't want George to be hurt. And anyway Rosemary never *had* said anything. She shook her head.

George sighed. He said heavily:

'Oh, well, it doesn't matter.'

Another day he asked her suddenly who Rosemary's best women friends had been.

Iris reflected.

'Gloria King. Mrs Atwell – Maisie Atwell. Jean Raymond.'

'How intimate was she with them?'

'Well, I don't know exactly.'

'I mean, do you think she might have confided in any of them?'

'I don't really know . . . I don't think it's awfully likely . . . What sort of confidence do you mean?'

Immediately she wished she hadn't asked that last question, but George's response to it surprised her.

'Did Rosemary ever say she was afraid of anybody?'

'Afraid?' Iris stared.

'What I'm trying to get at is, did Rosemary have any enemies?'

'Amongst other women?'

'No, no, not that kind of thing. Real enemies. There wasn't anyone – that you knew of – who – who might have had it in for her?'

Iris's frank stare seemed to upset him. He reddened, muttered:

'Sounds silly, I know. Melodramatic, but I just wondered.'

It was a day or two after that that he started asking about the Farradays.

How much had Rosemary seen of the Farradays?

Iris was doubtful.

'I really don't know, George.'

'Did she ever talk about them?'

'No, I don't think so.'

'Were they intimate at all?'

'Rosemary was very interested in politics.'

'Yes. After she met the Farradays in Switzerland. Never cared a button about politics before that.'

'No. I think Stephen Farraday interested her in them. He used to lend her pamphlets and things.'

George said:

'What did Sandra Farraday think about it?'

'About what?'

'About her husband lending Rosemary pamphlets.'

Iris said uncomfortably:

'I don't know.'

George said, 'She's a very reserved woman. Looks cold as ice. But they say she's crazy about Farraday. Sort of woman who might resent his having a friendship with another woman.'

'Perhaps.'

'How did Rosemary and Farraday's wife get on?'

Iris said slowly:

'I don't think they did. Rosemary laughed at Sandra. Said she was one of those stuffed political women like a rocking horse. (She is rather like a horse, you know.) Rosemary used to say that "if you pricked her sawdust would ooze out."'

George grunted.

Then he said:

'Still seeing a good deal of Anthony Browne?'

'A fair amount.' Iris's voice was cold, but George did not repeat his warnings. Instead he seemed interested.

'Knocked about a good deal, hasn't he? Must have had an interesting life. Does he ever talk to you about it?'

'Not much. He's travelled a lot, of course.'

'Business, I suppose.'

'I suppose so.'

'What is his business?'

'I don't know.'

'Something to do with armament firms, isn't it?'

'He's never said.'

'Well, needn't mention I asked. I just wondered. He was about a lot last Autumn with Dewsbury, who's chairman of the United Arms Ltd . . . Rosemary saw rather a lot of Anthony Browne, didn't she?'

'Yes – yes, she did.'

'But she hadn't known him very long – he was more or less of a casual acquaintance? Used to take her dancing, didn't he?'

'Yes.'

'I was rather surprised, you know, that she wanted him at her birthday party. Didn't realize she knew him so well.'

Iris said quietly:

'He dances very well . . .'

'Yes – yes, of course . . .'

Without wishing to, Iris unwillingly let a picture of that evening flit across her mind.

The round table at the Luxembourg, the shaded lights, the flowers. The dance band with its insistent rhythm. The seven people round the table, herself, Anthony Browne, Rosemary, Stephen Farraday, Ruth Lessing, George, and on George's right, Stephen Farraday's wife, Lady Alexandra Farraday with her pale straight hair and those slightly arched nostrils and her clear arrogant voice. Such a gay party it had been, or hadn't it?

And in the middle of it, Rosemary – *No, no, better not think about that.* Better only to remember herself sitting next to Tony – that was the first time she had really met him. Before that he had been only a name, a shadow in the hall, a back accompanying Rosemary down the steps in front of the house to a waiting taxi.

Tony –

She came back with a start. George was repeating a question.

'Funny he cleared off so soon after. Where did he go, do you know?'

She said vaguely, 'Oh, Ceylon, I think, or India.'

'Never mentioned it that night.'

Iris said sharply:

'Why should he? And have we got to talk about – that night?'

His face crimsoned over.

'No, no, of course not. Sorry, old thing. By the way, ask Browne to dinner one night. I'd like to meet him again.'

Iris was delighted. George was coming round. The invitation was duly given and accepted, but at the last minute Anthony had to go North on business and couldn't come.

One day at the end of July, George startled both Lucilla and Iris by announcing that he had bought a house in the country.

'Bought a *house*?' Iris was incredulous. 'But I thought we were going to rent that house at Goring for two months?'

'Nicer to have a place of one's own – eh? Can go down for weekends all through the year.'

'Where is it? On the river?'

'Not exactly. In fact, not at all. Sussex. Marlingham. Little Priors, it's called. Twelve acres – small Georgian house.'

'Do you mean you've bought it without us even seeing it?'

'Rather a chance. Just came into the market. Snapped it up.'

Mrs Drake said:

'I suppose it will need a lot of doing up and redecorating.'

George said in an off-hand way:

'Oh, that's all right. Ruth has seen to all that.'

They received the mention of Ruth Lessing, George's capable secretary, in respectful silence. Ruth was an institution – practically one of the family. Good looking in a severe black-and-white kind of way, she was the essence of efficiency combined with tact . . .

During Rosemary's lifetime, it had been usual for Rosemary to say, 'Let's get Ruth to see to it. She's marvellous. Oh, leave it to Ruth.'

Every difficulty could always be smoothed out by Miss Lessing's capable fingers. Smiling, pleasant, aloof, she surmounted all obstacles. She ran George's office and, it was suspected, ran George as well. He was devoted to her and leaned upon her judgement in every way. She seemed to have no needs, no desires of her own.

Nevertheless on this occasion Lucilla Drake was annoyed.

'My dear George, capable as Ruth is, well, I mean – the women of a family do like to arrange the colour scheme of their own drawing-room! Iris should have been consulted. I say nothing about myself. *I* do not count. But it is annoying for Iris.'

George looked conscience-stricken.

'I wanted it to be a surprise!'

Lucilla had to smile.

'What a boy you are, George.'

Iris said:

'I don't mind about colour schemes. I'm sure Ruth will have made it perfect. She's so clever. What shall we do down there? There's a tennis court, I suppose.'

'Yes, and golf links six miles away, and it's only about fourteen miles to the sea. What's more we shall have neighbours. Always wise to go to a part of the world where you know somebody, I think.'

'What neighbours?' asked Iris sharply.

George did not meet her eyes.

'The Farradays,' he said. 'They live about a mile and a half away just across the park.'

Iris stared at him. In a minute she leapt to the conviction that the whole of this elaborate business, the purchasing and equipping of a country house, had been undertaken with one object only – to bring George into close relationship with Stephen and Sandra Farraday. Near neighbours in the country, with adjoining estates, the two families were bound to be on intimate terms. Either that or a deliberate coolness!

But why? Why this persistent harping on the Farradays? Why this costly method of achieving an incomprehensible aim?

Did George suspect that Rosemary and Stephen Farraday had been something more than friends? Was this a strange manifestation of post-mortem jealousy? Surely that was a thought too far-fetched for words!

But what *did* George want from the Farradays? What was the point of all the odd questions he was continually shooting at her, Iris? Wasn't there something very queer about George lately?

The odd fuddled look he had in the evenings! Lucilla attributed it to a glass or so too much of port. Lucilla would!

No, there was something queer about George lately. He seemed to be labouring under a mixture of excitement interlarded with great spaces of complete apathy when he sunk in a coma.

Most of that August they spent in the country at Little Priors. Horrible house! Iris shivered. She hated it. A gracious well-built house, harmoniously furnished and decorated (Ruth Lessing was never at fault!). And curiously, frighteningly *vacant*. They didn't live there. They *occupied* it. As soldiers, in a war, occupied some look-out post.

What made it horrible was the overlay of ordinary normal summer living. People down for weekends, tennis parties, informal dinners with the Farradays. Sandra Farraday had been charming to them – the perfect manner to neighbours who were already friends. She introduced them to the county, advised George and Iris about horses, was prettily deferential to Lucilla as an older woman.

And behind the mask of her pale smiling face no one could know what she was thinking. A woman like a sphinx.

Of Stephen they had seen less. He was very busy, often absent on political business. To Iris it seemed certain that he deliberately avoided meeting the Little Priors party more than he could help.

So August had passed and September, and it was decided that in October they should go back to the London house.

Iris had drawn a deep breath of relief. Perhaps, once they were back George would return to his normal self.

And then, last night, she had been roused by a low tapping on her door. She switched on the light and glanced at the time. Only one o'clock. She had gone to bed at half-past ten and it had seemed to her it was much later.

She threw on a dressing-gown and went to the door. Somehow that seemed more natural than just to shout 'Come in.'

George was standing outside. He had not been to bed and was still in his evening clothes. His breath was coming unevenly and his face was a curious blue colour.

He said:

'Come down to the study, Iris. I've got to talk to you. I've got to talk to someone.'

Wondering, still dazed with sleep, she obeyed.

Inside the study, he shut the door and motioned her to sit opposite him at the desk. He pushed the cigarette box across to her, at the same time taking one and lighting it, after one or two attempts, with a shaking hand.

She said, 'Is anything the matter, George?'

She was really alarmed now. He looked ghastly.

George spoke between small gasps, like a man who has been running.

'I can't go on by myself. I can't keep it any longer. You've got to tell me what you think – whether it's true – whether it's *possible* –'

'But what is it you're talking about, George?'

'You must have noticed something, seen something. There must have been something she *said*. There must have been a *reason* –'

She stared at him.

He passed his hand over his forehead.

'You don't understand what I'm talking about. I can see that. Don't look so scared, little girl. You've got to help me. You've got to remember every damned thing you can. Now, now, I know I sound a bit incoherent, but you'll understand in a minute – when I've shown you the letters.'

He unlocked one of the drawers at the side of the desk and took out two single sheets of paper.

They were of a pale innocuous blue, with words printed on them in small prim letters.

'Read that,' said George.

Iris stared down at the paper. What it said was quite clear and devoid of circumlocution:

'*YOU THINK YOUR WIFE COMMITTED SUICIDE. SHE DIDN'T. SHE WAS KILLED.*'

The second ran:

'*YOUR WIFE ROSEMARY DIDN'T KILL HERSELF. SHE WAS MURDERED.*'

As Iris stayed staring at the words, George went on:

'They came about three months ago. At first I thought it was a joke – a cruel rotten sort of joke. Then I began to think. Why *should* Rosemary have killed herself?'

Iris said in a mechanical voice:

'Depression after influenza.'

'Yes, but really when you come to think of it, that's rather piffle, isn't it? I mean lots of people have influenza and feel a bit depressed afterwards – what?'

Iris said with an effort:

'She might – have been unhappy?'

'Yes, I suppose she might.' George considered the point quite calmly. 'But all the same I don't see Rosemary putting an end to herself because she was unhappy. She might threaten to, but I don't think she would really do it when it came to the point.'

'But she *must* have done, George! What other explanation could there be? Why, they even found the stuff in her handbag.'

'I know. It all hangs together. But ever since these came,' he tapped the anonymous letters with his finger-nail, 'I've been turning things over in my mind. And the more I've thought about it the more I feel sure there's something in it. That's why I've asked you all those questions – about Rosemary ever making any enemies. About anything she'd ever said that sounded as though she were afraid of someone. Whoever killed her must have had a *reason* –'

'But, George, you're crazy –'

'Sometimes I think I am. Other times I know that I'm on the right track. But I've got to *know*. I've got to find out. You've got to help me, Iris. You've got to *think*. You've got to remember. That's it – *remember*. Go back over that night again and again. Because you do see, don't you, that if she was killed, it *must have been someone who was at the table that night?* You do see that, don't you?'

Yes, she had seen that. There was no pushing aside the remembrance of that scene any longer. She must remember it all. The music, the roll of drums, the lowered lights, the cabaret and the lights going up again and Rosemary sprawled forward on the table, her face blue and convulsed.

Iris shivered. She was frightened now – horribly frightened . . .

She must think – go back – remember.

Rosemary, that's for remembrance.

There was to be no oblivion.

CHAPTER 2

RUTH LESSING

Ruth Lessing, during a momentary lull in her busy day, was remembering her employer's wife, Rosemary Barton.

She had disliked Rosemary Barton a good deal. She had never known quite how much until that November morning when she had first talked with Victor Drake.

That interview with Victor had been the beginning of it all, had set the whole train in motion. Before then, the things she had felt and thought had been so far below the stream of her consciousness that she hadn't really known about them.

She was devoted to George Barton. She always had been. When she had first come to him, a cool, competent young woman of twenty-three, she had seen that he needed taking charge of. She had taken charge of him. She had saved him time, money and worry. She had chosen his friends for him, and directed him to suitable hobbies. She had restrained him from ill-advised business adventures, and encouraged him to take judicious risks on occasions. Never once in their long association had George suspected her of being anything other than subservient, attentive and entirely directed by himself. He took a distinct pleasure in her appearance, the neat shining dark head, the smart tailor-mades and crisp shirts, the small pearls in her well-shaped ears, the pale discreetly powdered face and the faint restrained rose shade of her lipstick.

Ruth, he felt, was absolutely right.

He liked her detached impersonal manner, her complete absence of sentiment or familiarity. In consequence he talked to her a good deal about his private affairs and she listened sympathetically and always put in a useful word of advice.

She had nothing to do, however, with his marriage. She did not like it. However, she accepted it and was invaluable in helping with the wedding arrangements, relieving Mrs Marle of a great deal of work.

For a time after the marriage, Ruth was on slightly less confidential terms with her employer. She confined herself strictly to the office affairs. George left a good deal in her hands.

Nevertheless such was her efficiency that Rosemary soon found that George's Miss Lessing was an invaluable aid in all sorts of ways. Miss Lessing was always pleasant, smiling and polite.

George, Rosemary and Iris all called her Ruth and she often came to Elvaston Square to lunch. She was now twenty-nine and looked exactly the same as she had looked at twenty-three.

Without an intimate word ever passing between them, she was always perfectly aware of George's slightest emotional reactions. She knew when the first elation of his married life passed into an ecstatic content, she was aware when that content gave way to something else that was not so easy to define. A certain inattention to detail shown by him at this time was corrected by her own forethought.

However distrait George might be, Ruth Lessing never seemed to be aware of it. He was grateful to her for that.

It was on a November morning that he spoke to her of Victor Drake.

'I want you to do a rather unpleasant job for me, Ruth?'

She looked at him inquiringly. No need to say that certainly she would do it. That was understood.

'Every family's got a black sheep,' said George.

She nodded comprehendingly.

'This is a cousin of my wife's – a thorough bad hat, I'm afraid. He's half ruined his mother – a fatuous sentimental soul who has sold out most of what few shares she has on his behalf. He started by forging a cheque at Oxford – they got that hushed up and since then he's been shipped about the world – never making good anywhere.'

Ruth listened without much interest. She was familiar with the type. They grew oranges, started chicken farms, went as jackaroos to Australian stations, got jobs with meat-freezing concerns in New Zealand. They never made good, never stayed anywhere long, and invariably got through any money that had been invested on their behalf. They had never interested her much. She preferred success.

'He's turned up now in London and I find he's been worrying my wife. She hadn't set eyes on him since she was a schoolgirl, but he's a plausible sort of scoundrel and he's been writing to her for money, and I'm not going to stand for that. I've made an appointment with him for twelve o'clock this morning at his hotel. I want you to deal with it for me. The fact is I don't want to get into contact with the fellow. I've never met him and I never want to and I don't want Rosemary to meet him. I think the whole thing can be kept absolutely businesslike if it's fixed up through a third party.'

'Yes, that is always a good plan. What is the arrangement to be?'

'A hundred pounds cash and a ticket to Buenos Aires. The money to be given to him actually on board the boat.'

Ruth smiled.

'Quite so. You want to be sure he actually sails!'

'I see you understand.'

'It's not an uncommon case,' she said indifferently.

'No, plenty of that type about.' He hesitated. 'Are you sure you don't mind doing this?'

'Of course not.' She was a little amused. 'I can assure you I am quite capable of dealing with the matter.'

'You're capable of anything.'

'What about booking his passage? What's his name, by the way?'

'Victor Drake. The ticket's here. I rang up the steamship company yesterday. It's the *San Cristobal*, sails from Tilbury tomorrow.'

Ruth took the ticket, glanced over it to make sure of its correctness and put it into her handbag.

'That's settled. I'll see to it. Twelve o'clock. What address?'

'The Rupert, off Russell Square.'

She made a note of it.

'Ruth, my dear, I don't know what I should do without you –' He put a hand on her shoulder affectionately; it was the first time he had ever done such a thing. 'You're my right hand, my other self.'

She flushed, pleased.

'I've never been able to say much – I've taken all you do for granted –

but it's not really like that. You don't know how much I rely on you for everything –' he repeated: '*everything*. You're the kindest, dearest, most helpful girl in the world!'

Ruth said, laughing to hide her pleasure and embarrassment, 'You'll spoil me saying such nice things.'

'Oh, but I mean them. You're part of the firm, Ruth. Life without you would be unthinkable.'

She went out feeling a warm glow at his words. It was still with her when she arrived at the Rupert Hotel on her errand.

Ruth felt no embarrassment at what lay before her. She was quite confident of her powers to deal with any situation. Hard-luck stories and people never appealed to her. She was prepared to take Victor Drake as all in the day's work.

He was very much as she had pictured him, though perhaps definitely more attractive. She made no mistake in her estimate of his character. There was not much good in Victor Drake. As cold-hearted and calculating a personality as could exist, well masked behind an agreeable devilry. What she had not allowed for was his power of reading other people's souls, and the practised ease with which he could play on the emotions. Perhaps, too, she had underestimated her own resistance to his charm. For he had charm.

He greeted her with an air of delighted surprise.

'George's emissary? But how wonderful. What a surprise!'

In dry even tones, she set out George's terms. Victor agreed to them in the most amiable manner.

'A hundred pounds? Not bad at all. Poor old George. I'd have taken sixty – but don't tell him so! Conditions: – "Do not worry lovely Cousin Rosemary – do not contaminate innocent Cousin Iris – do not embarrass worthy Cousin George." All agreed to! Who is coming to see me off on the *San Cristobal*? You are, my dear Miss Lessing? Delightful.' He wrinkled up his nose, his dark eyes twinkled sympathetically. He had a lean brown face and there was a suggestion about him of a toreador – romantic conception! He was attractive to women and knew it!

'You've been with Barton some time, haven't you, Miss Lessing?'

'Six years.'

'And he wouldn't know what to do without you. Oh yes, I know all about it. And I know all about you, Miss Lessing.'

'How do you know?' asked Ruth sharply.

Victor grinned. 'Rosemary told me.'

'Rosemary? But –'

'That's all right. I don't propose to worry Rosemary any further. She's already been very nice to me – quite sympathetic. I got a hundred out of her, as a matter of fact.'

'You –'

Ruth stopped and Victor laughed. His laugh was infectious. She found herself laughing too.

'That's too bad of you, Mr Drake.'

'I'm a very accomplished sponger. Highly finished technique. The mater, for instance, will always come across if I send a wire hinting at imminent suicide.'

'You ought to be ashamed of yourself.'

'I disapprove of myself very deeply. I'm a bad lot, Miss Lessing. I'd like *you* to know just how bad.'

'Why?' She was curious.

'I don't know. You're different. I couldn't play up the usual technique to you. Those clear eyes of yours – you wouldn't fall for it. No, "More sinned against than sinning, poor fellow," wouldn't cut any ice with you. You've no pity in you.'

Her face hardened.

'I despise pity.'

'In spite of your name? Ruth *is* your name, isn't it? Piquant that. Ruth the ruthless.'

She said, 'I've no sympathy with weakness!'

'Who said I was weak? No, no, you're wrong there, my dear. Wicked, perhaps. But there's one thing to be said for me.'

Her lip curled a little. The inevitable excuse.

'Yes?'

'I enjoy myself. Yes,' he nodded, 'I enjoy myself immensely. I've seen a good deal of life, Ruth. I've done almost everything. I've been an actor and a storekeeper and a waiter and an odd job man, and a luggage porter, and a property man in a circus! I've sailed before the mast in a tramp steamer. I've been in the running for President in a South American Republic. I've been in prison! There are only two things I've never done, an honest day's work, or paid my own way.'

He looked at her, laughing. She ought, she felt, to have been revolted. But the strength of Victor Drake was the strength of the devil. He could make evil seem amusing. He was looking at her now with that uncanny penetration.

'You needn't look so smug, Ruth! You haven't as many morals as you think you have! Success is your fetish. You're the kind of girl who ends up by marrying the boss. That's what you ought to have done with George. George oughtn't to have married that little ass Rosemary. He ought to have married *you*. He'd have done a damned sight better for himself if he had.'

'I think you're rather insulting.'

'Rosemary's a damned fool, always has been. Lovely as paradise and dumb as a rabbit. She's the kind men fall for but never stick to. Now you – you're different. My God, if a man fell in love with you – he'd never tire.'

He had reached the vulnerable spot. She said with sudden raw sincerity:

'If! But he wouldn't fall in love with me!'

'You mean George didn't? Don't fool yourself, Ruth. If anything happened to Rosemary, George would marry you like a shot.'

(Yes, that was it. That was the beginning of it all.)

Victor said, watching her:

'But you know that as well as I do.'

(George's hand on hers, his voice affectionate, warm – Yes, surely it was true . . . He turned to her, depended on her . . .)

Victor said gently: 'You ought to have more confidence in yourself, my dear girl. You could twist George round your little finger. Rosemary's only a silly little fool.'

'It's true,' Ruth thought. 'If it weren't for Rosemary, I could make George ask me to marry him. I'd be good to him. I'd look after him well.'

She felt a sudden blind anger, an uprushing of passionate resentment. Victor Drake was watching her with a good deal of amusement. He liked putting ideas into people's heads. Or, as in this case, showing them the ideas that were already there . . .

Yes, that was how it started – that chance meeting with the man who was going to the other side of the globe on the following day. The Ruth who came back to the office was not quite the same Ruth who had left it, though no one could have noticed anything different in her manner or appearance.

Shortly after she had returned to the office Rosemary Barton rang up on the telephone.

'Mr Barton has just gone out to lunch. Can I do anything?'

'Oh, Ruth, would you? That tiresome Colonel Race has sent a telegram to say he won't be back in time for my party. Ask George who he'd like to ask instead. We really ought to have another man. There are four women – Iris is coming as a treat and Sandra Farraday and – who on earth's the other? I can't remember.'

'I'm the fourth, I think. You very kindly asked me.'

'Oh, of course. I'd forgotten all about you!'

Rosemary's laugh came light and tinkling. She could not see the sudden flush, the hard line of Ruth Lessing's jaw.

Asked to Rosemary's party as a favour – a concession to George! 'Oh, yes, we'll have your Ruth Lessing. After all she'll be pleased to be asked, and she is awfully useful. She looks quite presentable too.'

In that moment Ruth Lessing knew that she hated Rosemary Barton.

Hated her for being rich and beautiful and careless and brainless. No routine hard work in an office for Rosemary – everything handed to her on a golden platter. Love affairs, a doting husband – no need to work or plan –

Hateful, condescending, stuck-up, frivolous beauty . . .

'I wish you were dead,' said Ruth Lessing in a low voice to the silent telephone.

Her own words startled her. They were so unlike her. She had never been passionate, never vehement, never been anything but cool and controlled and efficient.

She said to herself: 'What's happening to me?'

She had hated Rosemary Barton that afternoon. She still hated Rosemary Barton on this day a year later.

Some day, perhaps, she would be able to forget Rosemary Barton. But not yet.

She deliberately sent her mind back to those November days.

Sitting looking at the telephone – feeling hatred surge up in her heart . . .

Giving Rosemary's message to George in her pleasant controlled voice. Suggesting that she herself should not come so as to leave the number even. George had quickly over-ridden *that*!

Coming in to report next morning on the sailing of the *San Cristobal*. George's relief and gratitude.

'So he's sailed on her all right?'

'Yes. I handed him the money just before the gangway was taken up.' She hesitated and said, 'He waved his hand as the boat backed away from the quay and called out "Love and kisses to George and tell him I'll drink his health tonight."'

'Impudence!' said George. He asked curiously, 'What did you think of him, Ruth?'

Her voice was deliberately colourless as she replied:

'Oh – much as I expected. A weak type.'

And George saw nothing, noticed nothing! She felt like crying out: 'Why did you send me to see him? Didn't you know what he might do to me? Don't you realize that I'm a different person since yesterday? Can't you see that I'm *dangerous*? That there's no knowing what I may do?'

Instead she said in her businesslike voice, 'About that San Paulo letter –'

She was the competent efficient secretary . . .

Five more days.

Rosemary's birthday.

A quiet day at the office – a visit to the hairdresser – the putting on of a new black frock, a touch of make-up skilfully applied. A face looking at her in the glass that was not quite her own face. A pale, determined, bitter face.

It was true what Victor Drake had said. There was no pity in her.

Later, when she was staring across the table at Rosemary Barton's blue convulsed face, she still felt no pity.

Now, eleven months later, thinking of Rosemary Barton, she felt suddenly afraid . . .

CHAPTER 3

ANTHONY BROWNE

Anthony Browne was frowning into the middle distance as he thought about Rosemary Barton.

A damned fool he had been ever to get mixed up with her. Though a man might be excused for that! Certainly she was easy upon the eyes. That evening at the Dorchester he'd been able to look at nothing else. As beautiful as a houri – and probably just about as intelligent!

Still he'd fallen for her rather badly. Used up a lot of energy trying to find someone who would introduce him. Quite unforgivable really when he ought to have been attending strictly to business. After all, he wasn't idling his days away at Claridge's for pleasure.

But Rosemary Barton was lovely enough in all conscience to excuse any momentary lapse from duty. All very well to kick himself now and wonder why he'd been such a fool. Fortunately there was nothing to regret. Almost as soon as he spoke to her the charm had faded a little. Things resumed their normal proportions. This wasn't love – nor yet infatuation. A good time was to be had by all, no more, no less.

Well, he'd enjoyed it. And Rosemary had enjoyed it too. She danced like an angel and wherever he took her men turned round to stare at her. It gave a fellow a pleasant feeling. So long as you didn't expect her to talk. He thanked his stars he wasn't married to her. Once you got used to all that perfection of face and form where would you be? She couldn't even listen intelligently. The sort of girl who would expect you to tell her every morning at the breakfast table that you loved her passionately!

Oh, all very well to think those things now.

He'd fallen for her all right, hadn't he?

Danced attendance on her. Rung her up, taken her out, danced with her, kissed her in the taxi. Been in a fair way to making rather a fool of himself over her until that startling, that incredible day.

He could remember just how she had looked, the piece of chestnut hair that had fallen loose over one ear, the lowered lashes and the gleam of her dark blue eyes through them. The pout of the soft red lips.

'Anthony Browne. It's a nice name!'

He said lightly:

'Eminently well established and respectable. There was a chamberlain to Henry the Eighth called Anthony Browne.'

'An ancestor, I suppose?'

'I wouldn't swear to that.'

'You'd better not!'

He raised his eyebrows.

'I'm the Colonial branch.'

'Not the Italian one?'

'Oh,' he laughed. 'My olive complexion? I had a Spanish mother.'

'That explains it.'

'Explains what?'

'A great deal, Mr Anthony Browne.'

'You're very fond of my name.'

'I said so. It's a nice name.'

And then quickly like a bolt from the blue: 'Nicer than Tony Morelli.'

For a moment he could hardly believe his ears! It was incredible! Impossible!

He caught her by the arm. In the harshness of his grip she winced away.

'Oh, you're hurting me!'

'Where did you get hold of that name?'

His voice was harsh, menacing.

She laughed, delighted with the effect she had produced. The incredible little fool!

'Who told you?'

'Someone who recognized you.'

'Who was it? This is serious, Rosemary. I've got to know.'

She shot a sideways glance at him.

'A disreputable cousin of mine, Victor Drake.'

'I've never met anyone of that name.'

'I imagine he wasn't using that name at the time you knew him. Saving the family feelings.'

Anthony said slowly. 'I see. It was – in prison?'

'Yes. I was reading Victor the riot act – telling him he was a disgrace to us all. He didn't care, of course. Then he grinned and said, "You aren't always so particular yourself, sweetheart. I saw you the other night dancing with an ex-gaol-bird – one of your best boy friends, in fact. Calls himself Anthony Browne, I hear, but in stir he was Tony Morelli."'

Anthony said in a light voice:

'I must renew my acquaintance with this friend of my youth. We old prison ties must stick together.'

Rosemary shook her head. 'Too late. He's been shipped off to South America. He sailed yesterday.'

'I see.' Anthony drew a deep breath. 'So you're the only person who knows my guilty secret?'

She nodded. 'I won't tell on you.'

'You'd better not.' His voice grew stern. 'Look here, Rosemary, this is dangerous. You don't want your lovely face carved up, do you? There are people who don't stick at a little thing like ruining a girl's beauty. And there's such a thing as being bumped off. It doesn't only happen in books and films. It happens in real life, too.'

'Are you threatening me, Tony?'

'Warning you.'

Would she take the warning? Did she realize that he was in deadly earnest? Silly little fool. No sense in that lovely empty head. You couldn't rely on her to keep her mouth shut. All the same he'd have to try and ram his meaning home.

'Forget you've ever heard the name of Tony Morelli, do you understand?'

'But I don't mind a bit, Tony. I'm quite broad-minded. It's quite a thrill for me to meet a criminal. You needn't feel ashamed of it.'

The absurd little idiot. He looked at her coldly. He wondered in that moment how he could ever have fancied he cared. He'd never been able to suffer fools gladly – not even fools with pretty faces.

'Forget about Tony Morelli,' he said grimly. 'I mean it. Never mention that name again.'

He'd have to get out. That was the only thing to do. There was no relying on this girl's silence. She'd talk whenever she felt inclined.

She was smiling at him – an enchanting smile, but it left him unmoved. 'Don't be so fierce. Take me to the Jarrows' dance next week.'

'I shan't be here. I'm going away.'

'Not before my birthday party. You can't let me down. I'm counting on you. Now don't say no. I've been miserably ill with that horrid 'flu and I'm still feeling terribly weak. I mustn't be crossed. You've got to come.'

He might have stood firm. He might have chucked it all – gone right away.

Instead, through an open door, he saw Iris coming down the stairs. Iris, very straight and slim, with her pale face and black hair and grey eyes. Iris with much less than Rosemary's beauty and with all the character that Rosemary would never have.

In that moment he hated himself for having fallen a victim, in however small a degree, to Rosemary's facile charm. He felt as Romeo felt remembering Rosaline when he had first seen Juliet.

Anthony Browne changed his mind.

In the flash of a second he committed himself to a totally different course of action.

CHAPTER 4

STEPHEN FARRADAY

Stephen Farraday was thinking of Rosemary – thinking of her with that incredulous amazement that her image always aroused in him. Usually he banished all thoughts of her from his mind as promptly as they arose – but there were times when, persistent in death as she had been in life, she refused to be thus arbitrarily dismissed.

His first reaction was always the same, a quick irresponsible shudder as he remembered the scene in the restaurant. At least he need not think again of *that*. His thoughts turned further back, to Rosemary alive, Rosemary smiling, breathing, gazing into his eyes . . .

What a fool – what an incredible fool he had been!

And amazement held him, sheer bewildered amazement. How had it all come about? He simply could not understand it. It was as though his life were divided into two parts, one, the larger part, a sane well-balanced orderly progression, the other a brief uncharacteristic madness. The two parts simply did not fit.

For with all his ability and his clever, shrewd intellect, Stephen had not the inner perception to see that actually they fitted only too well.

Sometimes he looked back over his life, appraising it coldly and without undue emotion, but with a certain priggish self-congratulation. From a very early age he had been determined to succeed in life, and in spite of difficulties and certain initial disadvantages he *had* succeeded.

He had always had a certain simplicity of belief and outlook. He believed in the Will. What a man willed, that he could do!

Little Stephen Farraday had steadfastly cultivated his Will. He could look for little help in life save that which he got by his own efforts. A small pale boy of seven, with a good forehead and a determined chin, he meant to rise – and rise high. His parents, he already knew, would be of no use to him. His mother had married beneath her station in life – and regretted it. His father, a small builder, shrewd, cunning and cheese-paring, was despised by his wife and also by his son . . . For his mother, vague, aimless, and given to extraordinary variations of mood, Stephen felt only a puzzled incomprehension until the day he found her slumped down on the corner of a table with an empty eau-de-Cologne bottle fallen from her hand. He had never thought of drink as an explanation of his mother's moods. She never drank spirits or beer, and he had never realized that her passion for eau-de-Cologne had had any other origin than her vague explanation of headaches.

He realized in that moment that he had little affection for his parents. He suspected shrewdly that they had not much for him. He was small for his age, quiet, with a tendency to stammer. Namby-pamby his father called him. A well-behaved child, little trouble in the house. His father would have preferred a more rumbustious type. 'Always getting into mischief *I* was, at his age.' Sometimes, looking at Stephen, he felt uneasily his own social inferiority to his wife. Stephen took after her folk.

Quietly, with growing determination, Stephen mapped out his own life. He was going to succeed. As a first test of will, he determined to master his stammer. He practised speaking slowly, with a slight hesitation between every word. And in time his efforts were crowned with success. He no longer stammered. In school he applied himself to his lessons. He intended to have education. Education got you somewhere. Soon his teachers became interested, encouraged him. He won a scholarship. His parents were approached by the educational authorities – the boy had promise. Mr Farraday, doing well out of a row of jerry-built houses, was persuaded to invest money in his son's education.

At twenty-two Stephen came down from Oxford with a good degree, a reputation as a good and witty speaker, and a knack of writing articles. He had also made some useful friends. Politics were what attracted him. He had learnt to overcome his natural shyness and to cultivate an admirable social manner – modest, friendly, and with that touch of brilliance that led people to say, 'That young man will go far.' Though by predilection a Liberal, Stephen realized that for the moment, at least, the Liberal Party was dead. He joined the ranks of the Labour Party. His name soon became known as that of a 'coming' young man. But the Labour Party did not satisfy Stephen. He found it less open to new ideas, more hidebound by tradition than its great and powerful rival. The Conservatives, on the other hand, were on the look-out for promising young talent.

They approved of Stephen Farraday – he was just the type they wanted. He contested a fairly solid Labour constituency and won it by a very narrow majority. It was with a feeling of triumph that Stephen took his seat in the House of Commons. His career had begun and this was the right career he had chosen. Into this he could put all his ability, all his ambition. He felt in him the ability to govern, and to govern well. He had a talent for handling people, for knowing when to flatter and when to oppose. One day, he swore it, he would be in the Cabinet.

Nevertheless, once the excitement of actually being in the House had subsided, he experienced swift disillusionment. The hardly fought election had put him in the limelight, now he was down in the rut, a mere insignificant unit of the rank and file, subservient to the party whips, and kept in his place. It was not easy here to rise out of obscurity. Youth here was looked upon with suspicion. One needed something above ability. One needed influence.

There were certain interests. Certain families. You had to be sponsored.

He considered marriage. Up to now he had thought very little about the subject. He had a dim picture in the back of his mind of some handsome creature who would stand hand in hand with him sharing his life and his ambitions; who would give him children and to whom he could unburden his thoughts and perplexities. Some woman who felt as he did and who would be eager for his success and proud of him when he achieved it.

Then one day he went to one of the big receptions at Kidderminster House.

The Kidderminster connection was the most powerful in England. They were, and always had been, a great political family. Lord Kidderminster, with his little Imperial, his tall, distinguished figure, was known by sight everywhere. Lady Kidderminster's large rocking-horse face was familiar on public platforms and on committees all over England. They had five daughters, three of them beautiful, and one son still at Eton.

The Kidderminsters made a point of encouraging likely young members of the Party. Hence Farraday's invitation.

He did not know many people there and he was standing alone near a window about twenty minutes after his arrival. The crowd by the tea table was thinning out and passing into the other rooms when Stephen noticed a tall girl in black standing alone by the table looking for a moment slightly at a loss.

Stephen Farraday had a very good eye for faces. He had picked up that very morning in the Tube a 'Home Gossip' discarded by a woman traveller and glanced over it with slight amusement. There had been a rather smudgy reproduction of Lady Alexandra Hayle, third daughter of the Earl of Kidderminster, and below a gossipy little extract about her – '. . . always been of a shy and retiring disposition – devoted to animals – Lady Alexandra has taken a course in Domestic Science as Lady Kidderminster believes in her daughters being thoroughly grounded in all domestic subjects.'

That was Lady Alexandra Hayle standing there, and with the unerring perception of a shy person, Stephen knew that she, too, was shy. The plainest of the five daughters, Alexandra had always suffered under a sense of inferiority. Given the same education and upbringing as her sisters, she had never quite attained their *savoir faire*, which annoyed her mother considerably. Sandra must make an effort – it was absurd to appear so awkward, so *gauche*.

Stephen did not know that, but he knew that the girl was ill at ease and unhappy. And suddenly a rush of conviction came to him. This was his chance! '*Take it, you fool, take it! It's now or never!*'

He crossed the room to the long buffet. Standing beside the girl he picked up a sandwich. Then, turning, and speaking nervously and with an effort (no acting, that – he *was* nervous!) he said:

'I say, do you mind if I speak to you? I don't know many people here and I can see you don't either. Don't snub me. As a matter of fact I'm awfully s-s-shy' (his stammer of years ago came back at a most opportune moment) 'and – and I think you're s-s-shy too, aren't you?'

The girl flushed – her mouth opened. But as he had guessed, she could not say it. Too difficult to find words to say 'I'm the daughter of the house.' Instead she admitted quietly:

'As a matter of fact, I – I am shy. I always have been.'

Stephen went on quickly:

'It's a horrible feeling. I don't know whether one ever gets over it. Sometimes I feel absolutely tongue-tied.'

'So do I.'

He went on – talking rather quickly, stammering a little – his manner was boyish, appealing. It was a manner that had been natural to him a few years ago and which was now consciously retained and cultivated. It was young, naïve, disarming.

He led the conversation soon to the subject of plays, mentioned one that was running which had attracted a good deal of interest. Sandra had seen it. They discussed it. It had dealt with some point of the social services and they were soon deep in a discussion of these measures.

Stephen did not overdo things. He saw Lady Kidderminster entering the room, her eyes in search of her daughter. It was no part of his plan to be introduced now. He murmured a goodbye.

'I have enjoyed talking to you. I was simply hating the whole show till I found you. Thank you.'

He left Kidderminster House with a feeling of exhilaration. He had taken his chance. Now to consolidate what he had started.

For several days after that he haunted the neighbourhood of Kidderminster House. Once Sandra came out with one of her sisters. Once she left the house alone, but with a hurried step. He shook his head. That would not do, she was obviously en route to some particular appointment. Then, about a week after the party, his patience was rewarded. She came out one morning with a small black Scottie dog and she turned with a leisurely step in the direction of the Park.

Five minutes later, a young man walking rapidly in the opposite direction pulled up short and stopped in front of Sandra. He exclaimed blithely:

'I say, what luck! I wondered if I'd ever see you again.'

His tone was so delighted that she blushed just a little.

He stooped to the dog.

'What a jolly little fellow. What's his name?'

'MacTavish.'

'Oh, very Scotch.'

They talked dog for some moments. Then Stephen said, with a trace of embarrassment:

'I never told you my name the other day. It's Farraday. Stephen Farraday. I'm an obscure M.P.'

He looked inquiringly and saw the colour come up in her cheeks again as she said: 'I'm Alexandra Hayle.'

He responded to that very well. He might have been back in the O.U.D.S. Surprise, recognition, dismay, embarrassment!

'Oh, you're – you're Lady Alexandra Hayle – you – my goodness! *What* a stupid fool you must have thought me the other day!'

Her answering move was inevitable. She was bound both by her breeding and her natural kindliness to do all she could to put him at his ease, to reassure him.

'I ought to have told you at the time.'

'I ought to have known. What an oaf you must think me!'

'How should you have known? What does it matter anyway? Please, Mr Farraday, don't look so upset. Let's walk to the Serpentine. Look, MacTavish is simply pulling.'

After that, he met her several times in the Park. He told her his ambitions. Together they discussed political topics. He found her intelligent, well-informed and sympathetic. She had good brains and a singularly unbiased mind. They were friends now.

The next advance came when he was asked to dinner at Kidderminster House and to go on to a dance. A man had fallen through at the last moment. When Lady Kidderminster was racking her brains Sandra said quietly:

'What about Stephen Farraday?'

'Stephen Farraday?'

'Yes, he was at your party the other day and I've met him once or twice since.'

Lord Kidderminster was consulted and was all in favour of encouraging the young hopefuls of the political world.

'Brilliant young fellow – quite brilliant. Never heard of his people, but he'll make a name for himself one of these days.'

Stephen came and acquitted himself well.

'A useful young man to know,' said Lady Kidderminster with unconscious arrogance.

Two months later Stephen put his fortunes to the test. They were by the Serpentine and MacTavish sat with his head on Sandra's foot.

'Sandra, you know – you must know that I love you. I want you to marry me. I wouldn't ask you if I didn't believe that I shall make a name for myself one day. I do believe it. You shan't be ashamed of your choice. I swear it.'

She said, 'I'm not ashamed.'

'Then you do care?'

'Didn't you know?'

'I hoped – but I couldn't be sure. Do you know that I've loved you since that very first moment when I saw you across the room and took my courage in both hands and came to speak to you. I was never more terrified in my life.'

She said, 'I think I loved you then, too . . .'

It was not all plain sailing. Sandra's quiet announcement that she was going to marry Stephen Farraday sent her family into immediate protests. Who was he? What did they know about him?

To Lord Kidderminster Stephen was quite frank about his family and origin. He spared a fleeting thought that it was just as well for his prospects that his parents were now both dead.

To his wife, Lord Kidderminster said, 'H'm, it might be worse.'

He knew his daughter fairly well, knew that her quiet manner hid inflexible purpose. If she meant to have the fellow she would have him. She'd never give in!

'The fellow's got a career ahead of him. With a bit of backing he'll go far. Heaven knows we could do with some young blood. He seems a decent chap, too.'

Lady Kidderminster assented grudgingly. It was not at all her idea of a good match for her daughter. Still, Sandra was certainly the most difficult of the family. Susan had been a beauty and Esther had brains. Diana, clever child, had married the young Duke of Harwich – the *parti* of the season. Sandra had certainly less charm – there was her shyness – and if this young man had a future as everyone seemed to think . . .

She capitulated, murmuring:

'But, of course, one will have to use *influence* . . .'

So Alexandra Catherine Hayle took Stephen Leonard Farraday for better and for worse, in white satin and Brussels lace, with six bridesmaids and two minute pages and all the accessories of a fashionable wedding. They went to Italy for the honeymoon and came back to a small charming house in Westminster, and a short time afterwards Sandra's godmother died and left her a very delightful small Queen Anne Manor house in the country. Everything went well for the young married pair. Stephen plunged into Parliamentary life with renewed ardour, Sandra aided and abetted him in every way, identifying herself heart and soul with his ambitions. Sometimes, Stephen would think with an almost incredulous realization of how Fortune had favoured him! His alliance with the powerful Kidderminster faction assured him of rapid rise in his career. His own ability and brilliance would consolidate the position that opportunity made for him. He believed honestly in his own powers and was prepared to work unsparingly for the good of his country.

Often, looking across the table at his wife, he felt gladly what a perfect helpmate she was – just what he had always imagined. He liked the lovely clean lines of her head and neck, the direct hazel eyes under their level brows, the rather high white forehead and the faint arrogance of her aquiline nose. She looked, he thought, rather like a racehorse – so well groomed, so instinct with breeding, so proud. He found her an ideal companion, their minds raced alike to the same quick conclusions. Yes, he thought, Stephen Farraday, that little disconsolate boy, had done very well for himself. His life was shaping exactly as he had meant it to be. He was only a year or two over thirty and already success lay in the hollow of his hand.

And in that mood of triumphant satisfaction, he went with his wife for a fortnight to St Moritz, and looking across the hotel lounge saw Rosemary Barton.

What happened to him at that moment he never understood. By a kind of poetic revenge the words he had spoken to another woman came true. Across a room he fell in love. Deeply, overwhelmingly, crazily in love. It was the kind of desperate, headlong, adolescent calf love that he should have experienced years ago and got over.

He had always assumed that he was not a passionate type of man. One or two ephemeral affairs, a mild flirtation – that, so far as he knew, was all that 'love' meant to him. Sensual pleasures simply did not appeal to him. He told himself that he was too fastidious for that sort of thing.

If he had been asked if he loved his wife, he would have replied 'Certainly' – yet he knew, well enough, that he would not have dreamed of marrying her if she had been, say, the daughter of a penniless country gentleman. He liked her, admired her and felt a deep affection for her and also a very real gratitude for what her position had brought him.

That he could fall in love with the abandon and misery of a callow boy was a revelation. He could think of nothing but Rosemary. Her lovely laughing face, the rich chestnut of her hair, her swaying voluptuous figure. He couldn't eat – he couldn't sleep. They went ski-ing together. He danced with her. And as he held her to him he knew that he wanted her more than anything on earth. So this, this misery, this aching longing agony – this was love!

Even in his preoccupation he blessed Fate for having given him a naturally imperturbable manner. No one must guess, no one must know, what he was feeling – except Rosemary herself.

The Bartons left a week earlier than the Farradays. Stephen said to Sandra that St Moritz was not very amusing. Should they cut their time short and go back to London? She agreed very amiably. Two weeks after their return, he became Rosemary's lover.

A strange ecstatic hectic period – feverish, unreal. It lasted – how long? Six months at most. Six months during which Stephen went about his work as usual, visited his constituency, asked questions in the House, spoke at various meetings, discussed politics with Sandra and thought of one thing only – Rosemary.

Their secret meetings in the little flat, her beauty, the passionate endearments he showered on her, her clinging passionate embraces. A dream. A sensual infatuated dream.

And after the dream – the awakening.

It seemed to happen quite suddenly.

Like coming out of a tunnel into the daylight.

One day he was a bemused lover, the next day he was Stephen Farraday again thinking that perhaps he ought not to see Rosemary quite so often. Dash it all, they had been taking some terrific risks. If Sandra was ever to suspect – He stole a look at her down the breakfast table. Thank goodness, she didn't suspect. She hadn't an idea. Yet some of his excuses for absence lately had been pretty thin. Some women would have begun to smell a rat. Thank goodness Sandra wasn't a suspicious woman.

He took a deep breath. Really he and Rosemary had been very reckless! It was a wonder her husband hadn't got wise to things. One of those foolish unsuspecting chaps – years older than she was.

What a lovely creature she was . . .

He thought suddenly of golf links. Fresh air blowing over sand dunes, tramping round with clubs – swinging a driver – a nice clean shot off the tee – a little chip with a mashie. Men. Men in plus fours smoking pipes. And no women allowed on the links!

He said suddenly to Sandra:

'Couldn't we go down to Fairhaven?'

She looked up, surprised.

'Do you want to? Can you get away?'

'Might take the inside of a week. I'd like to get some golf. I feel stale.'

'We could go tomorrow if you like. It will mean putting off the Astleys, and I must cancel that meeting on Tuesday. But what about the Lovats?'

'Oh, let's cancel that too. We can think of some excuse. I want to get away.'

It had been peaceful at Fairhaven with Sandra and the dogs on the terrace and in the old walled garden, and with golf at Sandley Heath, and pottering down to the farm in the evening with MacTavish at his heels.

He had felt rather like someone who is recovering from an illness.

He had frowned when he saw Rosemary's writing. He'd told her not to write. It was too dangerous. Not that Sandra ever asked him who his letters were from, but all the same it was unwise. Servants weren't always to be trusted.

He ripped open the envelope with some annoyance, having taken the letter into his study. Pages. Simply pages.

As he read, the old enchantment swept over him again. She adored him, she loved him more than ever, she couldn't endure not seeing him for five whole days. Was he feeling the same? Did the Leopard miss his Ethiopian?

He half-smiled, half-sighed. That ridiculous joke – born when he had bought her a man's spotted dressing-gown that she had admired. The Leopard changing his spots, and he had said, 'But you mustn't change your skin, darling.' And after that she had called him Leopard and he had called her his Black Beauty.

Damned silly, really. Yes, damned silly. Rather sweet of her to have written such pages and pages. But still she shouldn't have done it. Dash it all, they'd got to be *careful*! Sandra wasn't the sort of woman who would stand for anything of that kind. If she once got an inkling – Writing letters was dangerous. He'd told Rosemary so. Why couldn't she wait until he got back to town? Dash it all, he'd see her in another two or three days.

There was another letter on the breakfast table the following morning. This time Stephen swore inwardly. He thought Sandra's eyes rested on it for a couple of seconds. But she didn't say anything. Thank goodness she wasn't the sort of woman who asked questions about a man's correspondence.

After breakfast he took the car over to the market town eight miles away. Wouldn't do to put through a call from the village. He got Rosemary on the phone.

'Hullo – that you, Rosemary? Don't write any more letters.'

'Stephen, darling, how lovely to hear your voice!'

'Be careful, can anyone overhear you?'

'Of course not. Oh, angel, I have missed you. Have you missed me?'

'Yes, of course. But don't write. It's much too risky.'

'Did you like my letter? Did it make you feel I was with you? Darling, I want to be with you every minute. Do you feel that too?'

'Yes – but not on the phone, old thing.'

'You're so ridiculously cautious. What does it matter?'

'I'm thinking of you, too, Rosemary. I couldn't bear any trouble to come to you through me.'

'I don't care what happens to me. You know that.'

'Well, I care, sweetheart.'

'When are you coming back?'

'Tuesday.'

'And we'll meet at the flat, Wednesday.'

'Yes – er, yes.'

'Darling, I can hardly bear to wait. Can't you make some excuse and come up today? Oh, Stephen, you *could*! Politics or something stupid like that?'

'I'm afraid it's out of the question.'

'I don't believe you miss me half as much as I miss you.'

'Nonsense, of course I do.'

When he rang off he felt tired. Why should women insist on being so damned reckless? Rosemary and he must be more careful in future. They'd have to meet less often.

Things after that became difficult. He was busy – very busy. It was quite impossible to give as much time to Rosemary – and the trying thing was she didn't seem able to understand. He explained but she just wouldn't listen.

'Oh, your stupid old politics – as though *they* were important!'

'But they *are* –'

She didn't realize. She didn't care. She took no interest in his work, in his ambitions, in his career. All she wanted was to hear him reiterate again and again that he loved her. 'Just as much as ever? Tell me again that you *really* love me?'

Surely, he thought, she might take that for granted by this time! She was a lovely creature, lovely – but the trouble was that you couldn't *talk* to her.

The trouble was they'd been seeing too much of each other. You couldn't keep up an affair at fever heat. They must meet less often – slacken off a bit.

But that made her resentful – very resentful. She was always reproaching him now.

'You don't love me as you used to do.'

And then he'd have to reassure her, to swear that of course he did. And she *would* constantly resurrect everything he had ever said to her.

'Do you remember when you said it would be lovely if we died together? Fell asleep for ever in each other's arms? Do you remember when you said we'd take a caravan and go off into the desert? Just the stars and the camels – and how we'd forget everything in the world?'

What damned silly things one said when one was in love! They hadn't seemed fatuous at the time, but to have them hashed up in cold blood! Why couldn't women let things decently alone? A man didn't want to be continually reminded what an ass he'd made of himself.

She came out with sudden unreasonable demands. Couldn't he go abroad to the South of France and she'd meet him there? Or go to Sicily or Corsica – one of those places where you never saw anyone you knew? Stephen said grimly that there was no such place in the world. At the most unlikely spots you always met some dear old school friend that you'd never seen for years.

And then she said something that frightened him.

'Well, but it wouldn't really matter, would it?'

He was alert, watchful, suddenly cold within.

'What do you mean?'

She was smiling up at him, that same enchanting smile that had once made his heart turn over and his bones ache with longing. Now it made him merely impatient.

'Leopard, darling, I've thought sometimes that we're stupid to go on trying to carry on this hole-and-corner business. It's not worthy, somehow. Let's go away together. Let's stop pretending. George will divorce me and your wife will divorce you and then we can get married.'

Just like that! Disaster! Ruin! And she couldn't see it!

'I wouldn't let you do such a thing.'

'But, darling, I don't care. I'm not really very conventional.'

'But I am. But I am,' thought Stephen.

'I do feel that love is the most important thing in the world. It doesn't matter what people think of us.'

'It would matter to me, my dear. An open scandal of that kind would be the end of my career.'

'But would that really matter? There are hundreds of other things that you could do.'

'Don't be silly.'

'Why have you got to do anything anyway? I've got lots of money, you know. Of my own, I mean, not George's. We could wander about all over the world, going to the most enchanting out-of-the-way places – places, perhaps, where nobody else has ever been. Or to some island in the Pacific – think of it, the hot sun and the blue sea and the coral reefs.'

He did think of it. A South Sea Island! Of all the idiotic ideas. What sort of a man did she think he was – a beachcomber?

He looked at her with eyes from which the last traces of scales had fallen. A lovely creature with the brains of a hen! He'd been mad – utterly and completely mad. But he was sane again now. And he'd got to get out of this fix. Unless he was careful she'd ruin his whole life.

He said all the things that hundreds of men had said before him. They must end it all – so he wrote. It was only fair to her. He couldn't risk bringing unhappiness on her. She didn't understand – and so on and so on.

It was all over – he must make her understand that.

But that was just what she refused to understand. It wasn't to be as easy as that. She adored him, she loved him more than ever, she couldn't live without him! The only honest thing was for her to tell her husband, and for Stephen to tell his wife the truth! He remembered how cold he had felt as he sat holding her letter. The little fool! The silly clinging fool! She'd go and blab the whole thing to George Barton and then George would divorce her and cite him as co-respondent. And Sandra would perforce divorce him too. He hadn't any doubt of that. She had spoken once of a friend, had said with faint surprise, 'But of course when she found out he was having an affair with another woman, what else could she do but divorce him?' That was what Sandra would feel. She was proud. She would never share a man.

And then he would be done, finished – the influential Kidderminster backing would be withdrawn. It would be the kind of scandal that he would not be able to live down, even though public opinion was broader-minded than it used to be. But not in a flagrant case like this! Goodbye to his dreams, his ambitions. Everything wrecked, broken – all because of a crazy infatuation for a silly woman. Calf love, that was all it had been. Calf love contracted at the wrong time of life.

He'd lose everything he'd staked. Failure! Ignominy!

He'd lose Sandra . . .

And suddenly, with a shock of surprise he realized that it was that that he would mind most. *He'd lose Sandra.* Sandra with her square white forehead and her clear hazel eyes. Sandra, his dear friend and companion, his arrogant, proud, loyal Sandra. No, he couldn't lose Sandra – he couldn't . . . Anything but that.

The perspiration broke out on his forehead.

Somehow he *must* get out of this mess.

Somehow he must make Rosemary listen to reason . . . But would she? Rosemary and reason didn't go together. Supposing he were to tell her that, after all, he loved his wife? No. She simply wouldn't believe it. She was such a stupid woman. Empty-headed, clinging, possessive. And she loved him still – that was the mischief of it.

A kind of blind rage rose up in him. How on earth was he to keep her quiet? To shut her mouth? Nothing short of a dose of poison would do that, he thought bitterly.

A wasp was buzzing close at hand. He stared abstractedly. It had got inside a cut-glass jampot and was trying to get out.

Like me, he thought, entrapped by sweetness and now – he can't get out, poor devil.

But he, Stephen Farraday, was going to get out somehow. Time, he must play for time.

Rosemary was down with 'flu at the moment. He'd sent conventional inquiries – a big sheaf of flowers. It gave him a respite. Next week Sandra and he were dining with the Bartons – a birthday party for Rosemary. Rosemary had said, 'I shan't do anything until after my birthday – it would be too cruel to George. He's making such a fuss about it. He's such a dear. After it's all over we'll come to an understanding.'

Supposing he were to tell her brutally that it was all over, that he no longer cared? He shivered. No, he dare not do that. She might go to George in hysterics. She might even come to Sandra. He could hear her tearful, bewildered voice.

'He says he doesn't care any more, but I *know* it's not true. He's trying to be loyal – to play the game with *you* – but I know you'll agree with me that when people love each other honesty is the *only* way. That's why I'm asking you to give him his freedom.'

That was just the sort of nauseating stuff she would pour out. And Sandra, her face proud and disdainful, would say, 'He can have his freedom!'

She wouldn't believe – how could she believe? If Rosemary were to bring out those letters – the letters he'd been asinine enough to write to her. Heaven knew what he had said in them. Enough and more than enough to convince Sandra – letters such as he had never written to *her* –

He must think of something – some way of keeping Rosemary quiet. 'It's a pity,' he thought grimly, 'that we don't live in the days of the Borgias . . .'

A glass of poisoned champagne was about the only thing that would keep Rosemary quiet.

Yes, he had actually thought that.

Cyanide of potassium in her champagne glass, cyanide of potassium in her evening bag. Depression after influenza.

And across the table, Sandra's eyes meeting his.

Nearly a year ago – and he couldn't forget.

CHAPTER 5

ALEXANDRA FARRADAY

Sandra Farraday had not forgotten Rosemary Barton.

She was thinking of her at this very minute – thinking of her slumped forward across the table in the restaurant that night.

She remembered her own sharp indrawn breath and how then, looking up, she had found Stephen watching her . . .

Had he read the truth in her eyes? Had he seen the hate, the mingling of horror and triumph?

Nearly a year ago now – and as fresh in her mind as if it had been yesterday! *Rosemary, that's for remembrance.* How horribly true that was. It was no good a person being dead if they lived on in your mind. That was what Rosemary had done. In Sandra's mind – and in Stephen's, too? She didn't know, but she thought it probable.

The Luxembourg – that hateful place with its excellent food, its deft swift service, its luxurious *décor* and setting. An impossible place to avoid, people were always asking you there.

She would have liked to forget – but everything conspired to make her remember. Even Fairhaven was no longer exempt now that George Barton had come to live at Little Priors.

It was really rather extraordinary of him. George Barton was altogether an odd man. Not at all the kind of neighbour she liked to have. His presence at Little Priors spoiled for her the charm and peace of Fairhaven. Always, up to this summer, it had been a place of healing and rest, a place where she and Stephen had been happy – that is, if they ever had been happy?

Her lips pressed thinly together. Yes, a thousand times, yes! They could have been happy but for Rosemary. It was Rosemary who had shattered the delicate edifice of mutual trust and tenderness that she and Stephen were beginning to build. Something, some instinct, had bade her hide from Stephen her own passion, her single-hearted devotion. She had loved him from the moment he came across the room to her that day at Kidderminster House, pretending to be shy, pretending not to know who she was.

For he *had* known. She could not say when she had first accepted that fact. Some time after their marriage, one day when he was expounding some neat piece of political manipulation necessary to the passing of some Bill.

The thought had flashed across her mind then: 'This reminds me of something. What?' Later she realized that it was, in essence, the same tactics he had used that day at Kidderminster House. She accepted the knowledge without surprise, as though it were something of which she had long been aware, but which had only just risen to the surface of her mind.

From the day of their marriage she had realized that he did not love her in the same way as she loved him. But she thought it possible that he was actually incapable of such a love. That power of loving was her own unhappy heritage. To care with a desperation, an intensity that was, she knew, unusual among women! She would have died for him willingly; she was ready to lie for him, scheme for him, suffer for him! Instead she accepted with pride and reserve the place he wanted her to fill. He wanted her co-operation, her sympathy, her active and intellectual help. He wanted of her, not her heart, but her brains, and those material advantages which birth had given her.

One thing she would never do, embarrass him by the expression of a devotion to which he could make no adequate return. And she did believe honestly that he liked her, that he took pleasure in her company. She foresaw a future in which her burden would be immeasurably lightened – a future of tenderness and friendship.

In his way, she thought, he loved her.

And then Rosemary came.

She wondered sometimes, with a wry painful twist of the lips, how it was that he could imagine that she did not know. She had known from the first minute – up there at St Moritz – when she had first seen the way he looked at the woman.

She had known the very day the woman became his mistress.

She knew the scent the creature used . . .

She could read in Stephen's polite face, with eyes abstracted, just what his memories were, what he was thinking about – that woman – the woman he had just left!

It was difficult, she thought dispassionately, to assess the suffering she had been through. Enduring, day after day, the tortures of the damned, with nothing to carry her through but her belief in courage – her own natural pride. She would not show, she would never show, what she was feeling. She lost weight, grew thinner and paler, the bones of her head and shoulders showing more distinctly with the flesh stretched tightly over them. She forced herself to eat, but could not force herself to sleep. She lay long nights, with dry eyes, staring into darkness. She despised the taking of drugs as weakness. She would hang on. To show herself hurt, to plead, to protest – all these things were abhorrent to her.

She had one crumb of comfort, a meagre one – Stephen did not wish to leave her. Granted that that was for the sake of his career, not out of fondness for her, still the fact remained. He did not want to leave her.

Some day, perhaps, the infatuation would pass . . .

What could he, after all, see in the girl? She was attractive, beautiful – but so were other women. What did he find in Rosemary Barton that infatuated him?

She was brainless – silly – and not – she clung to this point especially – not even particularly amusing. If she had had wit, charm and provocation of manner – those were the things that held men. Sandra clung to the belief that the thing would end – that Stephen would tire of it.

She was convinced that the main interest in his life was his work. He was marked out for great things and he knew it. He had a fine statesmanlike brain and he delighted in using it. It was his appointed task in life. Surely once the infatuation began to wane he would realize that fact?

Never for one minute did Sandra consider leaving him. The idea never even came to her. She was his, body and soul, to take or discard. He was her life, her existence. Love burned in her with a medieval force.

There was a moment when she had hope. They went down to Fairhaven. Stephen seemed more his normal self. She felt suddenly a renewal of the old sympathy between them. Hope rose in her heart. He wanted her still, he enjoyed her company, he relied on her judgement. For the moment, he had escaped from the clutches of that woman.

He looked happier, more like his own self.

Nothing was irretrievably ruined. He was getting over it. If only he could make up his mind to break with her . . .

Then they went back to London and Stephen relapsed. He looked haggard, worried, ill. He began to be unable to fix his mind on his work.

She thought she knew the cause. Rosemary wanted him to go away with her . . . He was making up his mind to take the step – to break with everything he cared about most. Folly! Madness! He was the type of man with whom his work would always come first – a very English type. He must know that himself, deep down – Yes, but Rosemary was very lovely – and very stupid. Stephen would not be the first man who had thrown away his career for a woman and been sorry afterwards!

Sandra caught a few words – a phrase one day at a cocktail party.

'. . . Telling George – got to make up our minds.'

It was soon after that that Rosemary went down with 'flu.

A little hope rose in Sandra's heart. Suppose she were to get pneumonia – people did after 'flu – a young friend of hers had died that way only last winter. If Rosemary were to die –

She did not try to repress the thought – she was not horrified at herself. She was medieval enough to hate with a steady and untroubled mind.

She hated Rosemary Barton. If thoughts could kill, she would have killed her.

But thoughts do not kill –

Thoughts are not enough . . .

How beautiful Rosemary had looked that night at the Luxembourg with her pale fox furs slipping off her shoulders in the ladies' cloak-room. Thinner, paler since her illness – an air of delicacy made her beauty more ethereal. She had stood in front of the glass touching up her face . . .

Sandra, behind her, looked at their joint reflection in the mirror. Her own face like something sculptured, cold, lifeless. No feeling there, you would have said – a cold hard woman.

And then Rosemary said: 'Oh, Sandra, am I taking all the glass? I've finished now. This horrid 'flu has pulled me down a lot. I look a sight. And I feel quite weak still and headachy.'

Sandra had asked with quiet polite concern:

'Have you got a headache tonight?'

'Just a bit of one. You haven't got an aspirin, have you?'

'I've got a Cachet Faivre.'

She had opened her handbag, taken out the cachet. Rosemary had accepted it. 'I'll take it in my bag in case.'

That competent dark-haired girl, Barton's secretary, had watched the little transaction. She came in turn to the mirror, and just put on a slight dusting of powder. A nice-looking girl, almost handsome. Sandra had the impression that she didn't like Rosemary.

Then they had gone out of the cloak-room, Sandra first, then Rosemary, then Miss Lessing – oh, and of course, the girl Iris, Rosemary's sister, she had been there. Very excited, with big grey eyes, and a schoolgirlish white dress.

They had gone out and joined the men in the hall.

And the head waiter had come bustling forward and showed them to their table. They had passed in under the great domed arch and there had been nothing, absolutely nothing, to warn one of them that she would never come out through that door again alive . . .

CHAPTER 6

GEORGE BARTON

Rosemary . . .

George Barton lowered his glass and stared rather owlishly into the fire.

He had drunk just enough to feel maudlin with self-pity.

What a lovely girl she had been. He'd always been crazy about her. She knew it, but he'd always supposed she'd only laugh at him.

Even when he first asked her to marry him, he hadn't done it with any conviction.

Mowed and mumbled. Acted like a blithering fool.

'You know, old girl, any time – you've only got to say. I know it's no good. You wouldn't look at me. I've always been the most awful fool. Got a bit of a corporation, too. But you do know what I feel, don't you, eh? I mean – I'm always there. Know I haven't got an earthly chance, but thought I'd just mention it.'

And Rosemary had laughed and kissed the top of his head.

'You're sweet, George, and I'll remember the kind offer, but I'm not marrying anyone just at present.'

And he had said seriously: 'Quite right. Take plenty of time to look around. You can take your pick.'

He'd never had any hope – not any real hope.

That's why he had been so incredulous, so dazed when Rosemary had said she was going to marry him.

She wasn't in love with him, of course. He knew that quite well. In fact, she admitted as much.

'You do understand, don't you? I want to feel settled down and happy and safe. I shall with you. I'm so sick of being in love. It always goes wrong somehow and ends in a mess. I like you, George. You're nice and funny and sweet and you think I'm wonderful. That's what I want.'

He had answered rather incoherently:

'Steady does it. We'll be as happy as kings.'

Well, that hadn't been far wrong. They had been happy. He'd always felt humble in his own mind. He'd always told himself that there were bound to be snags. Rosemary wasn't going to be satisfied with a dull kind of chap like himself. There would be *incidents*! He'd schooled himself to accept – incidents! He would hold firm to the belief that they wouldn't be lasting! Rosemary would always come back to him. Once let him accept that view and all would be well.

For she was fond of him. Her affection for him was constant and unvarying. It existed quite apart from her flirtations and her love affairs.

He had schooled himself to accept those. He had told himself that they were inevitable with someone of Rosemary's susceptible temperament and unusual beauty. What he had not bargained for were his own reactions.

Flirtations with this young man and that were nothing, but when he first got an inkling of a serious affair –

He'd known quick enough, sensed the difference in her. The rising excitement, the added beauty, the whole glowing radiance. And then what his instinct told him was confirmed by ugly concrete facts.

There was that day when he'd come into her sitting-room and she had instinctively covered with her hand the page of the letter she was writing. He'd known then. She was writing to her lover.

Presently, when she went out of the room, he went across to the blotter. She had taken the letter with her, but the blotting sheet was nearly fresh. He'd taken it across the room and held it up to the glass – seen the words in Rosemary's dashing script, 'My own beloved darling . . .'

His blood had sung in his ears. He understood in that moment just what Othello had felt. Wise resolutions? Pah! Only the natural man counted. He'd like to choke the life out of her! He'd like to murder the fellow in cold blood. Who was it? That fellow Browne? Or that stick Stephen Farraday? They'd both of them been making sheep's eyes at her.

He caught sight of his face in the glass. His eyes were suffused with blood. He looked as though he were going to have a fit.

As he remembered that moment, George Barton let his glass fall from his hand. Once again he felt the choking sensation, the beating blood in his ears. Even now –

With an effort he pushed remembrance away. Mustn't go over that again. It was past – done with. He wouldn't ever suffer like that again.

Rosemary was dead. Dead and at peace. And he was at peace too. No more suffering . . .

Funny to think that that was what her death had meant to him. Peace . . .

He'd never told even Ruth that. Good girl, Ruth. A good headpiece on her. Really, he didn't know what he would do without her. The way she helped. The way she sympathized. And never a hint of sex. Not man mad like Rosemary . . .

Rosemary . . . Rosemary sitting at the round table in the restaurant. A little thin in the face after 'flu – a little pulled down – but lovely, so lovely. And only an hour later –

No, he wouldn't think of that. Not just now. His plan. He would think of The Plan.

He'd speak to Race first. He'd show Race the letters. What would Race make of these letters? Iris had been dumbfounded. She evidently hadn't had the slightest idea.

Well, he was in charge of the situation now. He'd got it all taped.

The Plan. All worked out. The date. The place.

Nov. 2nd. *All Souls' Day.* That was a good touch. The Luxembourg, of course. He'd try to get the same table.

And the same guests. Anthony Browne, Stephen Farraday, Sandra Farraday. Then, of course, Ruth and Iris and himself. And as the odd, the seventh guest he'd get Race. Race who was originally to have been at the dinner.

And there would be one empty place.

It would be splendid!

Dramatic!

A repetition of the crime.

Well, not quite a repetition . . .

His mind went back . . .

Rosemary's birthday . . .

Rosemary, sprawled forward on that table – dead . . .

BOOK II

ALL SOULS' DAY

'There's Rosemary, that's for remembrance.'

Lucilla Drake was twittering. That was the term always used in the family and it was really a very apt description of the sounds that issued from Lucilla's kindly lips.

She was concerned on this particular morning with many things – so many that she found it hard to pin her attention down to one at a time. There was the imminence of the move back to town and the household problems involved in that move. Servants, housekeeping, winter storage, a thousand minor details – all these contended with a concern over Iris's looks.

'Really, dear, I feel quite anxious about you – you look so white and washed out – as though you hadn't slept – did you sleep? If not, there's that nice sleeping preparation of Dr Wylie's or was it Dr Gaskell's? – which reminds me – I shall have to go and speak to the grocer *myself* – either the maids have been ordering things in on their own, or else it's deliberate swindling on his part. Packets and packets of soap flakes – and I never allow more than three a week. But perhaps a tonic would be better? Eaton's syrup, they used to give when I was a girl. And spinach, of course. I'll tell cook to have spinach for lunch today.'

Iris was too languid and too used to Mrs Drake's discursive style to inquire why the mention of Dr Gaskell should have reminded her aunt of the local grocer, though had she done so, she would have received the immediate response: 'Because the grocer's name is Cranford, my dear.' Aunt Lucilla's reasoning was always crystal clear to herself.

Iris merely said with what energy she could command, 'I'm perfectly well, Aunt Lucilla.'

'Black under the eyes,' said Mrs Drake. 'You've been doing too much.'

'I've done nothing at all – for weeks.'

'So you think, dear. But too much tennis is overtiring for young girls. And I think the air down here is inclined to be enervating. This place is in a hollow. If George had consulted *me* instead of that girl.'

'Girl?'

'That Miss Lessing he thinks so much of. All very well in the office, I daresay – but a great mistake to take her out of her place. Encourage her to think herself one of the family. Not that she needs any encouragement, I should say.'

'Oh, well, Aunt Lucilla, Ruth *is* practically one of the family.'

Mrs Drake sniffed. 'She means to be – that's quite clear. Poor George – really an infant in arms where women are concerned. But it won't do, Iris. George must be protected from himself and if I were you I should make it very clear that nice as Miss Lessing is, any idea of marriage is out of the question.'

Iris was startled for a moment out of her apathy.

'I never thought of George marrying Ruth.'

'You don't see what goes on under your nose, child. Of course you haven't had my experience of life.' Iris smiled in spite of herself. Aunt Lucilla was really very funny sometimes. 'That young woman is out for matrimony.'

'Would it matter?' asked Iris.

'Matter? Of course it would matter.'

'Wouldn't it really be rather nice?' Her aunt stared at her. 'Nice for George, I mean. I think you're right about her, you know. I think she is fond of him. And she'd be an awfully good wife to him and look after him.'

Mrs Drake snorted and an almost indignant expression appeared on her rather sheep-like amiable face.

'George is very well looked after at present. What more can he want, I should like to know? Excellent meals and his mending seen to. Very pleasant for him to have an attractive young girl like you about the house and when you marry some day I should hope I was still capable of seeing to his comfort and looking after his health. Just as well or better than a young woman out of an office could do – what does she know about housekeeping? Figures and ledgers and shorthand and typing – what good is that in a man's home?'

Iris smiled and shook her head, but she did not argue the point. She was thinking of the smooth dark satin of Ruth's head, of the clear complexion and the figure so well set off by the severe tailor-made clothes that Ruth affected. Poor Aunt Lucilla, all her mind on comfort and housekeeping, with romance so very far behind her that she had probably forgotten what it meant – if indeed, thought Iris, remembering her uncle by marriage, it had ever meant much.

Lucilla Drake had been Hector Marle's half-sister, the child of an earlier marriage. She had played the little mother to a very much younger brother when his own mother died. Housekeeping for her father, she had stiffened into a pronounced spinsterhood. She was close on forty when she met the Rev Caleb Drake, he himself a man of over fifty. Her married life had been short, a mere two years, then she had been left a widow with an infant son. Motherhood, coming late and unexpectedly, had been the supreme experience of Lucilla Drake's life. Her son had turned out an anxiety, a source of grief and a constant financial drain – but never a disappointment. Mrs Drake refused to recognize anything in her son Victor except an amiable weakness of character. Victor was too trusting – too easily led astray by bad companions because of his own belief in them. Victor was unlucky. Victor was deceived. Victor was swindled. He was the cat's-paw of wicked men who exploited his innocence. The pleasant, rather silly sheep's face hardened into obstinacy when criticism of Victor was to the fore. She knew her own son. He was a dear boy, full of high spirits, and his so-called friends took advantage of him. She knew, none better, how Victor hated having to ask her for money. But when the poor boy was really in such a terrible situation, what else could he do? It wasn't as though he had anyone but her to go to.

All the same, as she admitted, George's invitation to come and live in the house and look after Iris, had come as a god-send, at a moment when she really had been in desperate straits of genteel poverty. She had been very happy and comfortable this last year and it was not in human nature to look kindly on the possibility of being superseded by an upstart young woman, all modern efficiency and capability, who in any case, so she persuaded herself, would only be marrying George for his money. Of course that was what she was after! A good home and a rich indulgent husband. You couldn't tell Aunt Lucilla, at her age, that any young woman really *liked* working for her living! Girls were the same as they always had been – if they could get a man to keep them in comfort, they much preferred it. This Ruth Lessing was clever, worming her way into a position of confidence, advising George about house furnishing, making herself indispensable – but, thank goodness, there was *one* person at least who saw what she was up to!

Lucilla Drake nodded her head several times, causing her soft double chins to quiver, raised her eyebrows with an air of superb human sapience, and abandoned the subject for one equally interesting and possibly even more pressing.

'It's the blankets I can't make up my mind about, dear. You see, I can't get it clearly laid down whether we shan't be coming down again until next spring or whether George means to run down for weekends. He won't say.'

'I suppose he doesn't really know.' Iris tried to give her attention to a point that seemed completely unimportant. 'If it was nice weather it might be fun to come down occasionally. Though I don't think I want to particularly. Still the house will be here if we do want to come.'

'Yes, dear, but one wants to *know*. Because, you see, if we aren't coming down until next year, then the blankets ought to be put away with moth balls. But if we *are* coming down, that wouldn't be necessary, because the blankets would be *used* – and the smell of moth balls is so unpleasant.'

'Well, don't use them.'

'Yes, but it's been such a hot summer there are a lot of moths about. Everyone says it's a bad year for moths. And for wasps, of course. Hawkins told me yesterday he's taken thirty wasps' nests this summer – thirty – just fancy –'

Iris thought of Hawkins – stalking out at dusk – cyanide in hand – *Cyanide – Rosemary* – Why did everything lead back to that –?

The thin trickle of sound that was Aunt Lucilla's voice was going on – it had reached by now a different point –

'– and whether one ought to send the silver to the bank or not? Lady Alexandra was saying so many burglaries – though of course we do have good shutters – I don't like the way she does her hair myself – it makes her face look so hard – but I should think she was a hard woman. And nervy, too. Everyone is nervy nowadays. When I was a girl people didn't know what nerves were. Which reminds me that I didn't like the look of George lately – I wonder if he could be going to have 'flu? I've wondered once or twice whether he was feverish. But perhaps it is some business worry. He looks to me, you know, as though he has got something on his mind.'

Iris shivered, and Lucilla Drake exclaimed triumphantly: 'There, I said you had a chill.'

CHAPTER 2

'How I wish they had never come here.'

Sandra Farraday uttered the words with such unusual bitterness that her husband turned to look at her in surprise. It was as though his own thoughts had been put into words – the thoughts that he had been trying so hard to conceal. So Sandra, too, felt as he did? She, too, had felt that

Fairhaven was spoiled, its peace impaired, by these new neighbours a mile away across the Park. He said, voicing his surprise impulsively:

'I didn't know you felt like that about them, too.'

Immediately, or so it seemed to him, she withdrew into herself.

'Neighbours are so important in the country. One has either to be rude or friendly; one can't, as in London, just keep people as amiable acquaintances.'

'No,' said Stephen, 'one can't do that.'

'And now we're committed to this extraordinary party.'

They were both silent, running over in their minds the scene at lunch. George Barton had been friendly, even exuberant in manner, with a kind of undercurrent of excitement of which they had both been conscious. George Barton was really very odd these days. Stephen had never noticed him much in the time preceding Rosemary's death. George had just been there in the background, the kindly dull husband of a young and beautiful wife. Stephen had never even felt a pang of disquiet over the betrayal of George. George had been the kind of husband who was born to be betrayed. So much older – so devoid of the attractions necessary to hold an attractive and capricious woman. Had George himself been deceived? Stephen did not think so. George, he thought, knew Rosemary very well. He loved her, and he was the kind of man who was humble about his own powers of holding a wife's interest.

All the same, George must have suffered . . .

Stephen began to wonder just what George had felt when Rosemary died.

He and Sandra had seen little of him in the months following the tragedy. It was not until he had suddenly appeared as a near neighbour at Little Priors that he had reentered their lives and at once, so Stephen thought, he had seemed different.

More alive, more positive. And – yes, decidedly *odd*.

He had been odd today. That suddenly blurted out invitation. A party for Iris's eighteenth birthday. He did so hope Stephen and Sandra would both come. Stephen and Sandra had been so kind to them down here.

Sandra had said quickly; of course, it would be delightful. Naturally Stephen would be rather tied when they got back to London and she herself had a great many tiresome engagements, but she did hope they would be able to manage it.

'Then let's settle a day now, shall we?'

George's face – florid, smiling, insistent.

'I thought perhaps one day the week after next – Wednesday or

Thursday? Thursday is November 2nd. Would that be all right? But we'll arrange any day that suits you both.'

It had been the kind of invitation that pinned you down – there was a certain lack of social *savoir-faire*. Stephen noticed that Iris Marle had gone red and looked embarrassed. Sandra had been perfect. She had smilingly surrendered to the inevitable and said that Thursday, November 2nd, would suit them very well.

Suddenly voicing his thoughts, Stephen said sharply, 'We needn't go.'

Sandra turned her face slightly towards him. It wore a thoughtful considering air.

'You think not?'

'It's easy to make some excuse.'

'He'll only insist on us coming some other time – or change the day. He – he seems very set on our coming.'

'I can't think why. It's Iris's party – and I can't believe she is so particularly anxious for our company.'

'No – no –' Sandra sounded thoughtful.

Then she said:

'You know where this party is to be?'

'No.'

'The Luxembourg.'

The shock nearly deprived him of speech. He felt the colour ebbing out of his cheeks. He pulled himself together and met her eyes. Was it his fancy or was there meaning in the level gaze?

'But it's preposterous,' he exclaimed, blustering a little in his attempt to conceal his own personal emotion. 'The Luxembourg where – to revive all that. The man must be mad.'

'I thought of that,' said Sandra.

'But then we shall certainly refuse to go. The – the whole thing was terribly unpleasant. You remember all the publicity – the pictures in the papers.'

'I remember the unpleasantness,' said Sandra.

'Doesn't he realize how disagreeable it would be for us?'

'He has a reason, you know, Stephen. A reason that he gave me.'

'What was it?'

He felt thankful that she was looking away from him when she spoke.

'He took me aside after lunch. He said he wanted to explain. He told me that the girl – Iris – had never recovered properly from the shock of her sister's death.'

She paused and Stephen said unwillingly:

'Well, I daresay that may be true enough – she looks far from well. I thought at lunch how ill she was looking.'

'Yes, I noticed it too – although she has seemed in good health and spirits on the whole lately. But I am telling you what George Barton said. He told me that Iris has consistently avoided the Luxembourg ever since as far as she was able.'

'I don't wonder.'

'But according to him that is all wrong. It seems he consulted a nerve specialist on the subject – one of these modern men – and his advice is that after a shock of any kind, the trouble must be faced, not avoided. The principle, I gather, is like that of sending up an airman again immediately after a crash.'

'Does the specialist suggest another suicide?'

Sandra replied quietly, 'He suggests that the associations of the restaurant must be overcome. It is, after all, just a restaurant. He proposed an ordinary pleasant party with, as far as possible, the same people present.'

'Delightful for the people!'

'Do you mind so much, Stephen?'

A swift pang of alarm shot through him. He said quickly: 'Of course I don't mind. I just thought it rather a gruesome idea. Personally *I* shouldn't mind in the least . . . I was really thinking of *you*. If you don't mind –'

She interrupted him.

'I do mind. Very much. But the way George Barton put it made it very difficult to refuse. After all, I have frequently been to the Luxembourg since – so have you. One is constantly being asked there.'

'But not under these circumstances.'

'No.'

Stephen said:

'As you say, it is difficult to refuse – and if we put it off the invitation will be renewed. But there's no reason, Sandra, why *you* should have to endure it. I'll go and you can cry off at the last minute – a headache, chill – something of that kind.'

He saw her chin go up.

'That would be cowardly. No, Stephen, if you go, I go. After all,' she laid her hand on his arm, 'however little our marriage means, it should at least mean sharing our difficulties.'

But he was staring at her – rendered dumb by one poignant phrase which had escaped her so easily, as though it voiced a long familiar and not very important fact.

Recovering himself he said, 'Why do you say that? *However little our marriage means?*'

She looked at him steadily, her eyes wide and honest.

'Isn't it true?'

'No, a thousand times no. Our marriage means everything to me.'

She smiled.

'I suppose it does – in a way. We're a good team, Stephen. We pull together with a satisfactory result.'

'I didn't mean that.' He found his breath was coming unevenly. He took her hand in both of his, holding it very closely – 'Sandra, don't you know that you mean all the world to me?'

And suddenly she did know it. It was incredible – unforeseen, but it was so.

She was in his arms and he was holding her close, kissing her, stammering out incoherent words.

'Sandra – Sandra – darling. I love you . . . I've been so afraid – so afraid I'd lose you.'

She heard herself saying:

'Because of Rosemary?'

'Yes.' He let go of her, stepped back, his face was ludicrous in its dismay.

'You knew – about Rosemary?'

'Of course – all the time.'

'And you understand?'

She shook her head.

'No, I don't understand. I don't think I ever should. You loved her?'

'Not really. It was you I loved.'

A surge of bitterness swept over her. She quoted: 'From the first moment you saw me across the room? Don't repeat that lie – for it was a lie!'

He was not taken aback by that sudden attack. He seemed to consider her words thoughtfully.

'Yes, it was a lie – and yet in a queer way it wasn't. I'm beginning to believe that it was true. Oh, try and *understand*, Sandra. You know the people who always have a noble and good reason to mask their meaner actions? The people who "have to be honest" when they want to be unkind, who "thought it their duty to repeat so and so," who are such hypocrites to themselves that they go through to their life's end convinced that every mean and beastly action was done in a spirit of unselfishness! Try and realize that the opposite of those people can exist too. People who are so cynical, so distrustful of themselves and of life that they only believe in their bad motives. You were the woman I needed. That, at least, is true. And I do honestly believe, now, looking back on it, that if it hadn't been true, I should never have gone through with it.'

She said bitterly:

'You were not in love with me.'

'No. I'd never been in love. I was a starved, sexless creature who prided himself – yes, I did – on the fastidious coldness of his nature! And then I did fall in love "across a room" – a silly violent puppy love. A thing like a midsummer thunderstorm, brief, unreal, quickly over.' He added bitterly: 'Indeed a "tale told by an idiot, full of sound and fury, signifying nothing."'

He paused, and then went on:

'It was here, at Fairhaven, that I woke up and realized the truth.'

'The truth?'

'The only thing in life that mattered to me was you – and keeping your love.'

'If I had only known . . .'

'What did you think?'

'I thought you were planning to go away with her.'

'With Rosemary?' He gave a short laugh. 'That would indeed have been penal servitude for life!'

'Didn't she want you to go away with her?'

'Yes, she did.'

'What happened?'

Stephen drew a deep breath. They were back again. Facing once more that intangible menace. He said:

'The Luxembourg happened.'

They were both silent, seeing, they both knew, the same thing. The blue cyanosed face of a once lovely woman.

Staring at a dead woman, and then – looking up to meet each other's eyes . . .

Stephen said:

'Forget it, Sandra, for God's sake, let us forget it!'

'It's no use forgetting. We're not going to be allowed to forget.'

There was a pause. Then Sandra said:

'What are we going to do?'

'What you said just now. Face things – together. Go to this horrible party whatever the reason for it may be.'

'You don't believe what George Barton said about Iris?'

'No. Do you?'

'It could be true. But even if it is, it's not the real reason.'

'What do you think the real reason is?'

'I don't know, Stephen. But I'm afraid.'

'Of George Barton?'

'Yes, I think he – knows.'

Stephen said sharply:

'Knows what?'

She turned her head slowly until her eyes met his.

She said in a whisper:

'We mustn't be afraid. We must have courage – all the courage in the world. You're going to be a great man, Stephen – a man the world needs – and nothing shall interfere with that. I'm your wife and I love you.'

'What do you think this party is, Sandra?'

'I think it's a trap.'

He said slowly, 'And we walk into it?'

'We can't afford to show we know it's a trap.'

'No, that's true.'

Suddenly Sandra threw back her head and laughed. She said: 'Do your worst, Rosemary. You won't win.'

He gripped her shoulder.

'Be quiet, Sandra. Rosemary's dead.'

'Is she? Sometimes – she feels very much alive . . .'

<hr>

CHAPTER 3

Halfway across the Park Iris said:

'Do you mind if I don't come back with you, George? I feel like a walk. I thought I'd go up over Friar's Hill and come down through the wood. I've had an awful headache all day.'

'My poor child. Do go. I won't come with you – I'm expecting a fellow along some time this afternoon and I'm not quite sure when he'll turn up.'

'Right. Goodbye till tea-time.'

She turned abruptly and made off at right angles to where a belt of larches showed on the hillside.

When she came out on the brow of the hill she drew a deep breath. It was one of those close humid days common in October. A dank moisture coated the leaves of the trees and the grey cloud hung low overhead promising yet more rain shortly. There was not really much more air up here on the hill than there had been in the valley, but Iris felt nevertheless as though she could breathe more freely.

She sat down on the trunk of a fallen tree and stared down into the valley to where Little Priors nestled demurely in its wooded hollow. Farther to the left, Fairhaven Manor showed a glimpse of rose red on brick.

Iris stared out sombrely over the landscape, her chin cupped in her hand.

The slight rustle behind her was hardly louder than the drip of the leaves, but she turned her head sharply as the branches parted and Anthony Browne came through them.

She cried half angrily: 'Tony! Why do you always have to arrive like – like a demon in a pantomime?'

Anthony dropped to the ground beside her. He took out his cigarette case, offered her one and when she shook her head took one himself and lighted it. Then inhaling the first puff he replied:

'It's because I'm what the papers call a Mystery Man. I *like* appearing from nowhere.'

'How did you know where I was?'

'An excellent pair of bird glasses. I heard you were lunching with the Farradays and spied on you from the hillside when you left.'

'Why don't you come to the house like an ordinary person?'

'I'm not an ordinary person,' said Anthony in a shocked tone. 'I'm very extraordinary.'

'I think you are.'

He looked at her quickly. Then he said:

'Is anything the matter?'

'No, of course not. At least –'

She paused. Anthony said interrogatively:

'At least?'

She drew a deep breath.

'I'm tired of being down here. I hate it. I want to go back to London.'

'You're going soon, aren't you?'

'Next week.'

'So this was a farewell party at the Farradays'?'

'It wasn't a party. Just them and one old cousin.'

'Do you like the Farradays, Iris?'

'I don't know. I don't think I do very much – although I shouldn't say that because they've really been very nice to us.'

'Do you think they like you?'

'No, I don't. I think they hate us.'

'Interesting.'

'Is it?'

'Oh, not the hatred – if true. I meant the use of the word "us". My question referred to you personally.'

'Oh, I see . . . I think they like *me* quite well in a negative sort of way. I think it's us as a family living next door that they mind about. We weren't particular friends of theirs – they were Rosemary's friends.'

'Yes,' said Anthony, 'as you say they were Rosemary's friends – not that I should imagine Sandra Farraday and Rosemary were ever bosom friends, eh?'

'No,' said Iris. She looked faintly apprehensive but Anthony smoked peacefully. Presently he said:

'Do you know what strikes me most about the Farradays?'

'What?'

'Just that – that they are the Farradays. I always think of them like that – not as Stephen and Sandra, two individuals linked by the State and the Established Church – but as a definite dual entity – the Farradays. That is rarer than you would think. They are two people with a common aim, a common way of life, identical hopes and fears and beliefs. And the odd part of it is that they are actually very dissimilar in character. Stephen Farraday, I should say, is a man of very wide intellectual scope, extremely sensitive to outside opinion, horribly diffident about himself and somewhat lacking in moral courage. Sandra, on the other hand, has a narrow medieval mind, is capable of fanatical devotion, and is courageous to the point of recklessness.'

'He always seems to me,' said Iris, 'rather pompous and stupid.'

'He's not at all stupid. He's just one of the usual unhappy successes.'

'Unhappy?'

'Most successes are unhappy. That's why they are successes – they have to reassure themselves about themselves by achieving something that the world will notice.'

'What extraordinary ideas you have, Anthony.'

'You'll find they're quite true if you only examine them. The happy people are failures because they are on such good terms with themselves that they don't give a damn. Like me. They are also usually agreeable to get on with – again like me.'

'You have a very good opinion of yourself.'

'I am just drawing attention to my good points in case you mayn't have noticed them.'

Iris laughed. Her spirits had risen. The dull depression and fear had lifted from her mind. She glanced down at her watch.

'Come home and have tea, and give a few more people the benefit of your unusually agreeable society.'

Anthony shook his head.

'Not today. I must be getting back.'

Iris turned sharply on him.

'Why will you never come to the house? There must be a reason.'

Anthony shrugged his shoulders.

'Put it that I'm rather peculiar in my ideas of accepting hospitality. Your brother-in-law doesn't like me – he's made that quite clear.'

'Oh, don't bother about George. If Aunt Lucilla and I ask you – she's an old dear – you'd like her.'

'I'm sure I should – but my objection holds.'

'You used to come in Rosemary's time.'

'That,' said Anthony, 'was rather different.'

A faint cold hand touched Iris's heart. She said, 'What made you come down here today? Had you business in this part of the world?'

'Very important business – with you. I came here to ask you a question, Iris.'

The cold hand vanished. Instead there came a faint flutter, that throb of excitement that women have known from time immemorial. And with it Iris's face adopted that same look of blank inquiry that her great-grandmother might have worn prior to saying a few minutes later, 'Oh, Mr X, this is so sudden!'

'Yes?' She turned that impossibly innocent face towards Anthony.

He was looking at her, his eyes were grave, almost stern.

'Answer me truthfully, Iris. This is my question. Do you trust me?'

It took her aback. It was not what she had expected. He saw that.

'You didn't think that that was what I was going to say? But it is a very important question, Iris. The most important question in the world to me. I ask it again. Do you trust me?'

She hesitated, a bare second, then she answered, her eyes falling: 'Yes.'

'Then I'll go on and ask you something else. Will you come up to London and marry me without telling anybody about it?'

She stared.

'But I couldn't! I simply couldn't.'

'You couldn't marry me?'

'Not in that way.'

'And yet you love me. You do love me, don't you?'

She heard herself saying:

'Yes, I love you, Anthony.'

'But you won't come and marry me at the Church of Saint Elfrida, Bloomsbury, in the parish of which I have resided for some weeks and where I can consequently get married by licence at any time?'

'How can I do a thing like that? George would be terribly hurt and Aunt Lucilla would never forgive me. And anyway I'm not of age. I'm only eighteen.'

'You'd have to lie about your age. I don't know what penalties I should incur for marrying a minor without her guardian's consent. Who is your guardian, by the way?'

'George. He's my trustee as well.'

'As I was saying, whatever penalties I incurred, they couldn't unmarry us and that is really all I care about.'

Iris shook her head. 'I couldn't do it. I couldn't be so unkind. And in any case, *why*? What's the point of it?'

Anthony said: 'That's why I asked you first if you could trust me. You'd have to take my reasons on trust. Let's say that it is the simplest way. But never mind.'

Iris said timidly:

'If George only got to know you a little better. Come back now with me. It will be only he and Aunt Lucilla.'

'Are you sure? I thought –' he paused. 'As I struck up the hill I saw a man going up your drive – and the funny thing is that I believe I recognized him as a man I' – he hesitated – 'had met.'

'Of course – I forgot – George said he was expecting someone.'

'The man I thought I saw was a man called Race – Colonel Race.'

'Very likely,' Iris agreed. 'George does know a Colonel Race. He was coming to dinner on that night when Rosemary –'

She stopped, her voice quivering. Anthony gripped her hand.

'Don't go on remembering it, darling. It was beastly, I know.'

She shook her head.

'I can't help it. Anthony –'

'Yes?'

'Did it ever occur to you – did you ever think –' she found a difficulty in putting her meaning into words.

'Did it ever strike you that – that Rosemary might not have committed suicide? That she might have been – *killed*?'

'Good God, Iris, what put that idea into your head?'

She did not reply – merely persisted: 'That idea never occured to you?'

'Certainly not. Of course Rosemary committed suicide.'

Iris said nothing.

'Who's been suggesting these things to you?'

For a moment she was tempted to tell him George's incredible story, but she refrained. She said slowly:

'It was just an idea.'

'Forget it, darling idiot.' He pulled her to her feet and kissed her cheek lightly. 'Darling morbid idiot. Forget Rosemary. Only think of me.'

CHAPTER 4

Puffing at his pipe, Colonel Race looked speculatively at George Barton.

He had known George Barton ever since the latter's boyhood. Barton's uncle had been a country neighbour of the Races. There was a difference of over twenty years between the two men. Race was over sixty, a tall, erect, military figure, with sunburnt face, closely cropped iron-grey hair, and shrewd dark eyes.

There had never been any particular intimacy between the two men – but Barton remained to Race 'young George' – one of the many vague figures associated with earlier days.

He was thinking at this moment that he had really no idea what 'young George' was like. On the brief occasions when they had met in later years, they had found little in common. Race was an out-of-door man, essentially of the Empire-builder type – most of his life had been spent abroad. George was emphatically the city gentleman. Their interests were dissimilar and when they met it was to exchange rather lukewarm reminiscences of 'the old days', after which an embarrassed silence was apt to occur. Colonel Race was not good at small talk and might indeed have posed as the model of a strong silent man so beloved by an earlier generation of novelists.

Silent at this moment, he was wondering just why 'young George' had been so insistent on this meeting. Thinking, too, that there was some subtle change in the man since he had last seen him a year ago. George Barton had always struck him as the essence of stodginess – cautious, practical, unimaginative.

There was, he thought, something very wrong with the fellow. Jumpy as a cat. He'd already re-lit his cigar three times – and that wasn't like Barton at all.

He took his pipe out of his mouth.

'Well, young George, what's the trouble?'

'You're right, Race, it is trouble. I want your advice badly – and your help.'

The colonel nodded and waited.

'Nearly a year ago you were coming to dine with us in London – at the Luxembourg. You had to go abroad at the last minute.'

Again Race nodded.

'South Africa.'

'At that dinner party my wife died.'

Race stirred uncomfortably in his chair.

'I know. Read about it. Didn't mention it now or offer you sympathy because I didn't want to stir up things again. But I'm sorry, old man, you know that.'

'Oh, yes, yes. That's not the point. My wife was supposed to have committed suicide.'

Race fastened on the key word. His eyebrows rose.

'*Supposed?*'

'Read these.'

He thrust the two letters into the other's hand. Race's eyebrows rose still higher.

'Anonymous letters?'

'Yes. And I believe them.'

Race shook his head slowly.

'That's a dangerous thing to do. You'd be surprised how many lying spiteful letters get written after any event that's been given any sort of publicity in the Press.'

'I know that. But these weren't written at the time – they weren't written until six months afterwards.'

Race nodded.

'That's a point. Who do you think wrote them?'

'I don't know. I don't care. The point is that I believe what they say is true. My wife was murdered.'

Race laid down his pipe. He sat up a little straighter in his chair.

'Now just why do you think that? Had you any suspicion at the time. Had the police?'

'I was dazed when it happened – completely bowled over. I just accepted the verdict at the inquest. My wife had had 'flu, was run down. No suspicion of anything but suicide arose. The stuff was in her handbag, you see.'

'What was the stuff?'

'Cyanide.'

'I remember. She took it in champagne.'

'Yes. It seemed, at the time, all quite straightforward.'

'Had she ever threatened to commit suicide?'

'No, never. Rosemary,' said George Barton, 'loved life.'

Race nodded. He had only met George's wife once. He had thought her a singularly lovely nit-wit – but certainly not a melancholic type.

'What about the medical evidence as to state of mind, etcetera?'

'Rosemary's own doctor – an elderly man who has attended the Marle family since they were young children – was away on a sea voyage. His partner, a young man, attended Rosemary when she had 'flu. All he said, I remember, was that the type of 'flu about was inclined to leave serious depression.'

George paused and went on.

'It wasn't until after I got these letters that I talked with Rosemary's own doctor. I said nothing of the letters, of course – just discussed what had happened. He told me then that he was very surprised at what had happened. He would never have believed it, he said. Rosemary was not at all a suicidal type. It showed, he said, how even a patient one knew well might act in a thoroughly uncharacteristic manner.'

Again George paused and then went on:

'It was after talking to him that I realized how absolutely unconvincing to *me* Rosemary's suicide was. After all, I knew her very well. She was a person who was capable of violent fits of unhappiness. She could get very worked up over things, and she would on occasions take very rash and unconsidered action, but I have never known her in the frame of mind that "wanted to get out of it all."'

Race murmured in a slightly embarrassed manner:

'Could she have had a motive for suicide apart from mere depression? Was she, I mean, definitely unhappy about anything?'

'I – no – she was perhaps rather nervy.'

Avoiding looking at his friend, Race said:

'Was she at all a melodramatic person? I only saw her once, you know. But there is a type that – well – might get a kick out of attempted suicide – usually if they've quarrelled with someone. The rather childish motive of – "I'll make them sorry!"'

'Rosemary and I hadn't quarrelled.'

'No. And I must say that the fact of cyanide having been used rather rules that possibility out. It's not the kind of thing you can monkey about with safely – and everybody knows it.'

'That's another point. If by any chance Rosemary *had* contemplated doing away with herself, surely she'd never do it that way? Painful and – and ugly. An overdose of some sleeping stuff would be far more likely.'

'I agree. Was there any evidence as to her purchasing or getting hold of the cyanide?'

'No. But she had been staying with friends in the country and they had taken a wasps' nest one day. It was suggested that she might have taken a handful of potassium cyanide crystals then.'

'Yes – it's not a difficult thing to get hold of. Most gardeners keep a stock of it.'

He paused and then said:

'Let me summarize the position. There was no positive evidence as to a disposition to suicide, or to any preparation for it. The whole thing was negative. But there can also have been no positive evidence pointing to murder, or the police would have got hold of it. They're quite wide awake, you know.'

'The mere idea of murder would have seemed fantastic.'

'But it didn't seem fantastic to you six months later?'

George said slowly:

'I think I must have been unsatisfied all along. I think I must have been subconsciously preparing myself so that when I saw the thing written down in black and white I accepted it without doubt.'

'Yes.' Race nodded. 'Well, then, let's have it. Who do you suspect?'

George leaned forward – his face twitching.

'That's what is so terrible. *If* Rosemary was killed, one of those people round the table, one of our friends, must have done it. No one else came near the table.'

'Waiters? Who poured out the wine?'

'Charles, the head waiter at the Luxembourg. You know Charles?'

Race assented. Everybody knew Charles. It seemed quite impossible to imagine that Charles could have deliberately poisoned a client.

'And the waiter who looked after us was Giuseppe. We know Giuseppe well. I've known him for years. He always looks after me there. He's a delightful cheery little fellow.'

'So we come to the dinner party. Who was there?'

'Stephen Farraday, the M.P. His wife, Lady Alexandra Farraday. My secretary, Ruth Lessing. A fellow called Anthony Browne. Rosemary's sister, Iris, and myself. Seven in all. We should have been eight if you had come. When you dropped out we couldn't think of anybody suitable to ask at the last minute.'

'I see. Well, Barton, who do you think did it?'

George cried out: 'I don't know – I tell you I don't know. If I had any idea –'

'All right – all right. I just thought you might have a definite suspicion. Well, it oughtn't to be difficult. How did you sit – starting with yourself?'

'I had Sandra Farraday on my right, of course. Next to her, Anthony Browne. Then Rosemary. Then Stephen Farraday, then Iris, then Ruth Lessing who sat on my left.'

'I see. And your wife had drunk champagne earlier in the evening?'

'Yes. The glasses had been filled up several times. It – it happened while the cabaret show was on. There was a lot of noise – it was one of those negro shows and we were all watching it. She slumped forward on the table just before the lights went up. She may have cried out – or gasped – but nobody heard anything. The doctor said that death must have been practically instantaneous. Thank God for that.'

'Yes, indeed. Well, Barton – on the face of it, it seems fairly obvious.'

'You mean?'

'Stephen Farraday of course. He was on her right hand. Her champagne glass would be close to his left hand. Easiest thing in the world to put the stuff in as soon as the lights were lowered and general attention went to the raised stage. I can't see that anybody else had anything like as good an opportunity. I know those Luxembourg tables. There's plenty of room round them – I doubt very much if anybody could have leaned across the table, for instance, without being noticed even if the lights were down. The same thing applies to the fellow on Rosemary's left. He would have had to lean across her to put anything in her glass. There *is* one other possibility, but we'll take the obvious person first. Any reason why Stephen Farraday, M.P., should want to do away with your wife?'

George said in a stifled voice:

'They – they had been rather close friends. If – if Rosemary had turned him down, for instance, he might have wanted revenge.'

'Sounds highly melodramatic. That is the only motive you can suggest?'

'Yes,' said George. His face was very red. Race gave him the most fleeting of glances. Then he went on:

'We'll examine possibility No. 2. One of the women.'

'Why the women?'

'My dear George, has it escaped your notice that in a party of seven, four women and three men, there will probably be one or two periods during the evening when three couples are dancing and one woman is sitting alone at the table? You did all dance?'

'Oh, yes.'

'Good. Now before the cabaret, can you remember who was sitting alone at any moment?'

George thought a minute.

'I think – yes, Iris was odd man out last, and Ruth the time before.'

'You don't remember when your wife drank champagne last?'

'Let me see, she had been dancing with Browne. I remember her coming back and saying that had been pretty strenuous – he's rather a fancy dancer. She drank up the wine in her glass then. A few minutes later they played a waltz and she – she danced with me. She knew a waltz is the only dance I'm really any good at. Farraday danced with Ruth and Lady Alexandra with Browne. Iris sat out. Immediately after that, they had the cabaret.'

'Then let's consider your wife's sister. Did she come into any money on your wife's death?'

George began to splutter.

'My dear Race – don't be absurd. Iris was a mere child, a schoolgirl.'

'I've known two schoolgirls who committed murder.'

'But Iris! She was devoted to Rosemary.'

'Never mind, Barton. She had opportunity. I want to know if she had motive. Your wife, I believe, was a rich woman. Where did her money go – to you?'

'No, it went to Iris – a trust fund.'

He explained the position, to which Race listened attentively.

'Rather a curious position. The rich sister and the poor sister. Some girls might have resented that.'

'I'm sure Iris never did.'

'Maybe not – but she had a motive all right. We'll try that tack now. Who else had a motive?'

'Nobody – nobody at all. Rosemary hadn't an enemy in the world, I'm sure. I've been looking into all that – asking questions – trying to find out. I've even taken this house near the Farradays' so as to –'

He stopped. Race took up his pipe and began to scratch at its interior.

'Hadn't you better tell me everything, young George?'

'What do you mean?'

'You're keeping something back – it sticks out a mile. You can sit there defending your wife's reputation – or you can try and find out if she was murdered or not – but if the latter matters most to you, you'll have to come clean.'

There was a silence.

'All right then,' said George in a stifled voice. 'You win.'

'You'd reason to believe your wife had a lover, is that it?'

'Yes.'

'Stephen Farraday?'

'I don't know! I swear to you I don't know! It might have been him or it might have been the other fellow, Browne. I couldn't make up my mind. It was hell.'

'Tell me what you know about this Anthony Browne? Funny, I seem to have heard the name.'

'I don't know anything about him. Nobody does. He's a good-looking, amusing sort of chap – but nobody knows the first thing about him. He's supposed to be an American but he's got no accent to speak of.'

'Oh, well, perhaps the Embassy will know something about him. You've no idea – which?'

'No – no, I haven't. I'll tell you, Race. She was writing a letter – I – I examined the blotting-paper afterwards. It – it was a love letter all right – but there was no name.'

Race turned his eyes away carefully.

'Well, that gives us a bit more to go on. Lady Alexandra, for instance – she comes into it, if her husband was having an affair with your wife. She's the kind of woman, you know, who feels things rather intensely. The quiet, deep type. It's a type that will do murder at a pinch. We're getting on. There's Mystery Browne and Farraday and his wife, and young Iris Marle. What about this other woman, Ruth Lessing?'

'Ruth couldn't have had anything to do with it. She at least had no earthly motive.'

'Your secretary, you say? What sort of a girl is she?'

'The dearest girl in the world.' George spoke with enthusiasm. 'She's practically one of the family. She's my right hand – I don't know anyone I think more highly of, or have more absolute faith in.'

'You're fond of her,' said Race, watching him thoughtfully.

'I'm devoted to her. That girl, Race, is an absolute trump. I depend upon her in every way. She's the truest, dearest creature in the world.'

Race murmured something that sounded liked 'Umhum' and left the subject. There was nothing in his manner to indicate to George that he had mentally chalked down a very definite motive to the unknown Ruth Lessing. He could imagine that this 'dearest girl in the world' might have a very decided reason for wanting the removal of Mrs George Barton to another world. It might be a mercenary motive – she might have envisaged herself as the second Mrs Barton. It might be that she was genuinely in love with her employer. But the motive for Rosemary's death was there.

Instead he said gently: 'I suppose it's occurred to you, George, that you had a pretty good motive yourself.'

'I?' George looked flabbergasted.

'Well, remember Othello and Desdemona.'

'I see what you mean. But – but it wasn't like that between me and Rosemary. I adored her, of course, but I always knew that there would be things that – that I'd have to endure. Not that she wasn't fond of me – she was. She was very fond of me and sweet to me always. But of course I'm a dull stick, no getting away from it. Not romantic, you know. Anyway, I'd made up my mind when I married her that it wasn't going to be all beer and skittles. She as good as warned me. It hurt, of course, when it happened – but to suggest that I'd have touched a hair of her head –'

He stopped, and then went on in a different tone:

'Anyway, if I'd done it, why on earth should I go raking it all up? I mean, after a verdict of suicide, and everything all settled and over. It would be madness.'

'Absolutely. That's why I don't seriously suspect you, my dear fellow. If you were a successful murderer and got a couple of letters like these, you'd put them quietly in the fire and say nothing at all about it. And that brings me to what I think is the one really interesting feature of the whole thing. Who wrote those letters?'

'Eh?' George looked rather startled. 'I haven't the least idea.'

'The point doesn't seem to have interested you. It interests me. It's the first question I asked you. We can assume, I take it, that they weren't written by the murderer. Why should he queer his own pitch when, as you say, everything had settled down and suicide was universally accepted? Then who wrote them? Who is it who is interested in stirring the whole thing up again?'

'Servants?' hazarded George vaguely.

'Possibly. If so, what servants, and what do they know? Did Rosemary have a confidential maid?'

George shook his head.

'No. At the time we had a cook – Mrs Pound – we've still got her, and a couple of maids. I think they've both left. They weren't with us very long.'

'Well, Barton, if you want my advice, which I gather you do, I should think the matter over very carefully. On one side there's the fact that Rosemary is dead. You can't bring her back to life whatever you do. If the evidence for suicide isn't particularly good, neither is the evidence for murder. Let us say, for the sake of argument, that Rosemary *was* murdered. Do you really wish to rake up the whole thing? It may mean a lot of unpleasant publicity, a lot of washing of dirty linen in public, your wife's love affairs becoming public property –'

George Barton winced. He said violently:

'Do you really advise me to let some swine get away with it? That stick Farraday, with his pompous speeches, and his precious career – and all the time, perhaps, a cowardly murderer.'

'I only want you to be clear what it involves.'

'I want to get at the truth.'

'Very well. In that case, I should go to the police with these letters. They'll probably be able to find out fairly easily who wrote them and if the writer knows anything. Only remember that once you've started them on the trail, you won't be able to call them off.'

'I'm not going to the police. That's why I wanted to see you. I'm going to set a trap for the murderer.'

'What on earth do you mean?'

'Listen, Race. I'm going to have a party at the Luxembourg. I want you to come. The same people, the Farradays, Anthony Browne, Ruth, Iris, myself. I've got it all worked out.'

'What are you going to do?'

George gave a faint laugh.

'That's my secret. It would spoil it if I told anyone beforehand – even you. I want you to come with an unbiased mind and – see what happens.'

Race leant forward. His voice was suddenly sharp.

'I don't like it, George. These melodramatic ideas out of books don't work. Go to the police – there's no better body of men. They know how to deal with these problems. They're professionals. Amateur shows in crime aren't advisable.'

'That's why I want you there. You're not an amateur.'

'My dear fellow. Because I once did work for M.I.5? And anyway you propose to keep me in the dark.'

'That's necessary.'

Race shook his head.

'I'm sorry. I refuse. I don't like your plan and I won't be a party to it. Give it up, George, there's a good fellow.'

'I'm not going to give it up. I've got it all worked out.'

'Don't be so damned obstinate. I know a bit more about these shows than you do. I don't like the idea. It won't work. It may even be dangerous. Have you thought of that?'

'It will be dangerous for somebody all right.'

Race sighed.

'You don't know what you're doing. Oh, well, don't say I haven't warned you. For the last time I beg you to give up this crack-brained idea of yours.'

George Barton only shook his head.

CHAPTER 5

The morning of November 2nd dawned wet and gloomy. It was so dark in the dining-room of the house in Elvaston Square that they had to have the lights on for breakfast.

Iris, contrary to her habit, had come down instead of having her coffee and toast sent up to her and sat there white and ghostlike pushing uneaten food about her plate. George rustled his *Times* with a nervy hand and at the other end of the table Lucilla Drake wept copiously into a handkerchief.

'I know the dear boy will do something dreadful. He's so sensitive – and he wouldn't say it was a matter of life and death if it wasn't.'

Rustling his paper, George said sharply:

'Please don't worry, Lucilla. I've said I'll see to it.'

'I know, dear George, you are always so kind. But I do feel any delay might be fatal. All these inquiries you speak of making – they will all take *time*.'

'No, no, we'll hurry them through.'

'He says: "without fail by the 3rd" and tomorrow *is* the 3rd. I should never forgive myself if anything happened to the darling boy.'

'It won't.' George took a long drink of coffee.

'And there is still that Conversion Loan of mine –'

'Look here, Lucilla, you leave it all to me.'

'Don't worry, Aunt Lucilla,' put in Iris. 'George will be able to arrange it all. After all, this has happened before.'

'Not for a long time' ('Three months,' said George), 'not since the poor boy was deceived by those dreadful swindling friends of his on that horrid ranch.'

George wiped his moustache on his napkin, got up, patted Mrs Drake kindly on the back as he made his way out of the room.

'Now do cheer up, my dear. I'll get Ruth to cable right away.'

As he went out in the hall, Iris followed him.

'George, don't you think we ought to put off the party tonight? Aunt Lucilla is so upset. Hadn't we better stay at home with her?'

'Certainly not!' George's pink face went purple. 'Why should that damned swindling young crook upset our whole lives? It's blackmail – sheer blackmail, that's what it is. If I had my way, he shouldn't get a penny.'

'Aunt Lucilla would never agree to that.'

'Lucilla's a fool – always has been. These women who have children when they're over forty never seem to learn any sense. Spoil the brats from the cradle by giving them every damned thing they want. If young Victor had once been told to get out of this mess by himself it might have been the making of him. Now don't argue, Iris. I'll get something fixed up before tonight so that Lucilla can go to bed happy. If necessary we'll take her along with us.'

'Oh, no, she hates restaurants – and gets so sleepy, poor darling. And she dislikes the heat and the smoky air gives her asthma.'

'I know. I wasn't serious. Go and cheer her up, Iris. Tell her everything will be all right.'

He turned away and out of the front door. Iris turned slowly back towards the dining-room. The telephone rang and she went to answer it.

'Hallo – who?' Her face changed, its white hopelessness dissolved into pleasure. 'Anthony!'

'Anthony himself. I rang you up yesterday but couldn't get you. Have you been putting in a spot of work with George?'

'What do you mean?'

'Well, George was so pressing over his invitation to your party tonight. Quite unlike his usual style of "hands off my lovely ward"! Absolutely insistent that I should come. I thought perhaps it was the result of some tactful work on your part.'

'No – no – it's nothing to do with me.'

'A change of heart all on his own?'

'Not exactly. It's –'

'Hallo – have you gone away?'

'No, I'm here.'

'You were saying something. What's the matter, darling? I can hear you sighing through the telephone. Is anything the matter?'

'No – nothing. I shall be all right tomorrow. Everything will be all right tomorrow.'

'What touching faith. Don't they say "tomorrow never comes"?'

'Don't.'

'Iris – something *is* the matter?'

'No, nothing. I can't tell you. I promised, you see.'

'Tell me, my sweet.'

'No – I can't really. Anthony, will you tell *me* something?'

'If I can.'

'Were you – ever in love with Rosemary?'

A momentary pause and then a laugh.

'So that's it. Yes, Iris, I was a bit in love with Rosemary. She was very lovely, you know. And then one day I was talking to her and I saw you coming down the staircase – and in a minute it was all over, blown away. There was nobody but you in the world. That's the cold sober truth. Don't brood over a thing like that. Even Romeo, you know, had his Rosaline before he was bowled over for good and all by Juliet.'

'Thank you, Anthony. I'm glad.'

'See you tonight. It's your birthday, isn't it?'

'Actually not for a week – it's my birthday party though.'

'You don't sound very enthusiastic about it.'

'I'm not.'

'I suppose George knows what he's doing, but it seems to me a crazy idea to have it at the same place where –'

'Oh, I've been to the Luxembourg several times since – since Rosemary – I mean, one can't avoid it.'

'No, and it's just as well. I've got a birthday present for you, Iris. I hope you'll like it. *Au revoir.*'

He rang off.

Iris went back to Lucilla Drake, to argue, persuade and reassure.

George, on his arrival at his office, sent at once for Ruth Lessing.

His worried frown relaxed a little as she entered, calm and smiling, in her neat black coat and skirt.

'Good morning.'

'Good morning, Ruth. Trouble again. Look at this.'

She took the cable he held out.

'Victor Drake again!'

'Yes, curse him.'

She was silent a minute, holding the cable. A lean, brown face wrinkling up round the nose when he laughed. A mocking voice saying, 'the sort of girl who ought to marry the Boss . . .' How vividly it all came back.

She thought:

'It might have been yesterday . . .'

George's voice recalled her.

'Wasn't it about a year ago that we shipped him out there?'

She reflected.

'I think so, yes. Actually I believe it was October 27th.'

'What an amazing girl you are. What a memory!'

She thought to herself that she had a better reason for remembering than he knew. It was fresh from Victor Drake's influence that she had listened to Rosemary's careless voice over the phone and decided that she hated her employer's wife.

'I suppose we're lucky,' said George, 'that he's lasted as long as he has out there. Even if it did cost us fifty pounds three months ago.'

'Three hundred pounds now seems a lot.'

'Oh, yes. He won't get as much as that. We'll have to make the usual investigations.'

'I'd better communicate with Mr Ogilvie.'

Alexander Ogilvie was their agent in Buenos Aires – a sober, hard-headed Scotsman.

'Yes. Cable at once. His mother is in a state, as usual. Practically hysterical. Makes it very difficult with the party tonight.'

'Would you like me to stay with her?'

'No.' He negatived the idea emphatically. 'No, indeed. You're the one person who's got to be there. I need you, Ruth.' He took her hand. 'You're too unselfish.'

'I'm not unselfish at all.'

She smiled and suggested:

'Would it be worth trying telephonic communication with Mr Ogilvie? We might get the whole thing cleared up by tonight.'

'A good idea. Well worth the expense.'

'I'll get busy at once.'

Very gently she disengaged her hand from his and went out.

George dealt with various matters awaiting his attention.

At half-past twelve he went out and took a taxi to the Luxembourg.

Charles, the notorious and popular head waiter, came towards him, bending his stately head and smiling in welcome.

'Good morning, Mr Barton.'

'Good morning, Charles. Everything all right for tonight?'

'I think you will be satisfied, sir.'

'The same table?'

'The middle one in the alcove, that is right, is it not?'

'Yes – and you understand about the extra place?'

'It is all arranged.'

'And you've got the – the rosemary?'

'Yes, Mr Barton. I'm afraid it won't be very decorative. You wouldn't like some red berries incorporated – or say a few chrysanthemums?'

'No, no, only the rosemary.'

'Very good, sir. You would like to see the menu. Giuseppe.'

With a flick of the thumb Charles produced a smiling little middle-aged Italian.

'The menu for Mr Barton.'

It was produced.

Oysters, Clear Soup, Sole Luxembourg, Grouse, Poires Hélène, Chicken Livers in Bacon.

George cast an indifferent eye over it.

'Yes, yes, quite all right.'

He handed it back. Charles accompanied him to the door.

Sinking his voice a little, he murmured:

'May I just mention how appreciative we are, Mr Barton, that you are – er – coming back to us?'

A smile, rather a ghastly smile, showed on George's face. He said:

'We've got to forget the past – can't dwell on the past. All that is over and done with.'

'Very true, Mr Barton. You know how shocked and grieved we were at the time. I'm sure I hope that Mademoiselle will have a very happy birthday party and that everything will be as you like it.'

Gracefully bowing, Charles withdrew and darted like an angry dragon-fly on some very inferior grade of waiter who was doing the wrong thing at a table near the window.

George went out with a wry smile on his lips. He was not an imaginative enough man to feel a pang of sympathy for the Luxembourg. It was not, after all, the fault of the Luxembourg that Rosemary had decided to commit suicide there or that someone had decided to murder her there. It had been decidedly hard on the Luxembourg. But like most people with an idea, George thought only of that idea.

He lunched at his club and went afterwards to a directors' meeting.

On his way back to the office, he put through a phone call to a Maida Vale number from a public call box. He came out with a sigh of relief. Everything was set according to schedule.

He went back to the office.

Ruth came to him at once.

'About Victor Drake.'

'Yes?'

'I'm afraid it's rather a bad business. A possibility of criminal prosecution. He's been helping himself to the firm's money over a considerable period.'

'Did Ogilvie say so?'

'Yes. I got through to him this morning and he got a call through to us this afternoon ten minutes ago. He says Victor was quite brazen about the whole thing.'

'He would be!'

'But he insists that they won't prosecute if the money is refunded. Mr Ogilvie saw the senior partner and that seems to be correct. The actual sum in question is one hundred and sixty-five pounds.'

'So that Master Victor was hoping to pocket a clear hundred and thirty-five on the transaction?'

'I'm afraid so.'

'Well, we've scotched that, at any rate,' said George with grim satisfaction. 'I told Mr Ogilvie to go ahead and settle the business. Was that right?'

'Personally I should be delighted to see that young crook go to prison – but one has to think of his mother. A fool – but a dear soul. So Master Victor scores as usual.'

'How good you are,' said Ruth.

'Me?'

'I think you're the best man in the world.'

He was touched. He felt pleased and embarrassed at the same time. On an impulse he picked up her hand and kissed it.

'Dearest Ruth. My dearest and best of friends. What would I have done without you?'

They stood very close together.

She thought: 'I could have been happy with him. I could have made him happy. If only –'

He thought: 'Shall I take Race's advice? Shall I give it all up? Wouldn't that really be the best thing?'

Indecision hovered over him and passed. He said:

'9.30 at the Luxembourg.'

CHAPTER 6

They had all come.

George breathed a sigh of relief. Up to the last moment he had feared some last minute defection – but they were all here. Stephen Farraday, tall and stiff, a little pompous in manner. Sandra Farraday in a severe black velvet gown wearing emeralds around her neck. The woman had breeding, not a doubt of it. Her manner was completely natural, possibly a little more gracious than usual. Ruth also in black with no ornament save one jewelled clip. Her raven black hair smooth and lying close to her head, her neck and arms very white – whiter than those of the other women. Ruth was a working girl, she had no long leisured ease in which to acquire sun tan. His eyes met hers and, as though she saw the anxiety in his, she smiled reassurance. His heart lifted. Loyal Ruth. Beside him Iris was unusually silent. She alone showed consciousness of this being an unusual party. She was pale but in some way it suited her, gave her a grave steadfast beauty. She wore a straight simple frock of leaf-green. Anthony Browne came last, and to George's mind, he came with the quick stealthy step of a wild creature – a panther, perhaps, or a leopard. The fellow wasn't really quite civilized.

They were all there – all safe in George's trap. Now, the play could begin . . .

Cocktails were drained. They got up and passed through the open arch into the restaurant proper.

Dancing couples, soft negro music, deft hurrying waiters.

Charles came forward and smilingly piloted them to their table. It was at the far end of the room, a shallow arched alcove which held three tables – a big one in the middle and two small ones for two people either side of it. A middle-aged sallow foreigner and a blonde lovely were at one, a slip of a boy and a girl at the other. The middle table was reserved for the Barton party.

George genially assigned them to their places.

'Sandra, will you sit here, on my right. Browne next to her. Iris, my dear, it's your party. I must have you here next to me, and you beyond her, Farraday. Then you, Ruth –'

He paused – between Ruth and Anthony was a vacant chair – the table had been laid for seven.

'My friend Race may be a bit late. He said we weren't to wait for him. He'll be along some time. I'd like you all to know him – he's a splendid fellow, knocked about all over the world and can tell you some good yarns.'

Iris was conscious of a feeling of anger as she seated herself. George had done it on purpose – separated her from Anthony. Ruth ought to have been sitting where she was, next to her host. So George still disliked and mistrusted Anthony.

She stole a glance across the table. Anthony was frowning. He did not look across at her. Once he directed a sharp sideways glance at the empty chair beside him. He said:

'Glad you've got another man, Barton. There's just a chance I may have to go off early. Quite unavoidable. But I ran into a man here I know.'

George said smilingly:

'Running business into pleasure hours? You're too young for that, Browne. Not that I've ever known exactly what your business is?'

By chance there was a lull in the conversation. Anthony's reply came deliberately and coolly.

'Organized crime, Barton, that's what I always say when I'm asked. Robberies arranged. Larcenies a feature. Families waited upon at their private addresses.'

Sandra Farraday laughed as she said:

'You're something to do with armaments, aren't you, Mr Browne? An armament king is always the villain of the piece nowadays.'

Iris saw Anthony's eyes momentarily widen in a stare of quick surprise. He said lightly:

'You mustn't give me away, Lady Alexandra, it's all very hush-hush. The spies of a foreign power are everywhere. Careless talk.'

He shook his head with mock solemnity.

The waiter took away the oyster plates. Stephen asked Iris if she would like to dance.

Soon they were all dancing. The atmosphere lightened.

Presently Iris's turn came to dance with Anthony.

She said: 'Mean of George not to let us sit together.'

'Kind of him. This way I can look at you all the time across the table.'

'You won't really have to go early?'

'I might.'

Presently he said:

'Did you know that Colonel Race was coming?'

'No, I hadn't the least idea.'

'Rather odd, that.'

'Do you know him? Oh, yes, you said so, the other day.'

She added:

'What sort of a man is he?'

'Nobody quite knows.'

They went back to the table. The evening wore on. Slowly the tension, which had relaxed, seemed to close again. There was an atmosphere of taut nerves about the table. Only the host seemed genial and unconcerned.

Iris saw him glance at his watch.

Suddenly there was a roll of drums – the lights went down. A stage rose in the room. Chairs were pushed a little back, turned sideways. Three men and three girls took the floor, dancing. They were followed by a man who could make noises. Trains, steam rollers, aeroplanes, sewing machines, cows coughing. He was a success. Lenny and Flo followed in an exhibition dance which was more of a trapeze act than a dance. More applause. Then another ensemble by the Luxembourg Six. The lights went up.

Everyone blinked.

At the same time a wave of sudden freedom from restraint seemed to pass over the party at the table. It was as though they had been subconsciously expecting something that had failed to happen. For on an earlier occasion the going up of the lights had coincided with the discovery of a dead body lying across the table. It was as though now the past was definitely past – vanished into oblivion. The shadow of a bygone tragedy had lifted.

Sandra turned to Anthony in an animated way. Stephen made an observation to Iris and Ruth leaned forward to join in. Only George sat in his chair staring – staring, his eyes fixed on the empty chair opposite him. The place in front of it was laid. There was champagne in the glass. At any moment, someone might come, might sit down there –

A nudge from Iris recalled him:

'Wake up, George. Come and dance. You haven't danced with me yet.'

He roused himself. Smiling at her he lifted his glass.

'We'll drink a toast first – to the young lady whose birthday we're celebrating. Iris Marle, may her shadow never grow less!'

They drank it laughing, then they all got up to dance, George and Iris, Stephen and Ruth, Anthony and Sandra.

It was a gay jazz melody.

They all came back together, laughing and talking. They sat down.

Then suddenly George leaned forward.

'I've something I want to ask you all. A year ago, more or less, we were here before on an evening that ended tragically. I don't want to recall past sadness, but it's just that I don't want to feel that Rosemary is completely forgotten. I'll ask you to drink to her memory – for Remembrance sake.'

He raised his glass. Everyone else obediently raised theirs. Their faces were polite masks.

George said:

'*To Rosemary for remembrance.*'

The glasses were raised to their lips. They drank.

There was a pause – then George swayed forward and slumped down in his chair, his hands rising frenziedly to his neck, his face turning purple as he fought for breath.

It took him a minute and a half to die.

BOOK III

IRIS

'For I thought that the dead had peace
But it is not so . . .'

CHAPTER I

Colonel Race turned into the doorway of New Scotland Yard. He filled in the form that was brought forward and a very few minutes later he was shaking hands with Chief Inspector Kemp in the latter's room.

The two men were well acquainted. Kemp was slightly reminiscent of that grand old veteran, Battle, in type. Indeed, since he had worked under Battle for many years, he had perhaps unconsciously copied a good many of the older man's mannerisms. He bore about him the same suggestion of being carved all in one piece – but whereas Battle had suggested some wood such as teak or oak, Chief Inspector Kemp suggested a somewhat more showy wood – mahogany, say, or good old-fashioned rosewood.

'It was good of you to ring us, colonel,' said Kemp. 'We shall want all the help we can get on this case.'

'It seems to have got us into exalted hands,' said Race.

Kemp did not make modest disclaimers. He accepted quite simply the indubitable fact that only cases of extreme delicacy, wide publicity or supreme importance came his way. He said seriously:

'It's the Kidderminster connection. You can imagine that means careful going.'

Race nodded. He had met Lady Alexandra Farraday several times. One of those quiet women of unassailable position whom it seems fantastic to associate with sensational publicity. He had heard her speak on public platforms – without eloquence, but clearly and competently, with a good grasp of her subject, and with an excellent delivery.

The kind of woman whose public life was in all the papers, and whose private life was practically non-existent except as a bland domestic background.

Nevertheless, he thought, such women *have* a private life. They know despair, and love, and the agonies of jealousy. They can lose control and risk life itself on a passionate gamble.

He said curiously:

'Suppose she "done it", Kemp?'

'Lady Alexandra? Do you think she did, sir?'

'I've no idea. But suppose she did. Or her husband – who comes under the Kidderminster mantle.'

The steady sea-green eyes of Chief Inspector Kemp looked in an untroubled way into Race's dark ones.

'If either of them did murder, we'll do our level best to hang him or her. *You* know that. There's no fear and no favour for murderers in this country. But we'll have to be absolutely sure of our evidence – the public prosecutor will insist on that.'

Race nodded.

Then he said, 'Let's have the doings.'

'George Barton died of cyanide poisoning – same thing as his wife a year ago. You said you were actually in the restaurant?'

'Yes. Barton had asked me to join his party. I refused. I didn't like what he was doing. I protested against it and urged him, if he had doubts about his wife's death, to go to the proper people – to you.'

Kemp nodded.

'That's what he ought to have done.'

'Instead he persisted in an idea of his own – setting a trap for the murderer. He wouldn't tell me what that trap was. I was uneasy about the whole business – so much so that I went to the Luxembourg last night so as to keep an eye on things. My table, necessarily, was some distance away – I didn't want to be spotted too obviously. Unfortunately I can tell you nothing. I saw nothing in the least suspicious. The waiters and his own party were the only people who approached the table.'

'Yes,' said Kemp, 'it narrows it down, doesn't it? It was one of them, or it was the waiter, Giuseppe Bolsano. I've got him on the mat again this morning – thought you might like to see him – but I can't believe he had anything to do with it. Been at the Luxembourg for twelve years – good reputation, married, three children, good record behind him. Gets on well with all the clients.'

'Which leaves us with the guests.'

'Yes. The same party as was present when Mrs Barton – died.'

'What about that business, Kemp?'

'I've been going into it since it seems pretty obvious that the two hang together. Adams handled it. It wasn't what we call a clear case of suicide, but suicide was the most probable solution and in the absence of any direct evidence suggesting murder, one had to let it go as suicide. Couldn't do anything else. We've a good many cases like that in our records, as you know. Suicide with a query mark. The public doesn't know about the query mark – but we keep it in mind. Sometimes we go on quite a bit hunting about quietly.

'Sometimes something crops up – sometimes it doesn't. In this case it didn't.'

'Until now.'

'Until now. Somebody tipped Mr Barton off to the fact that his wife had been murdered. He got busy on his own – he as good as announced that he was on the right track – whether he was or not I don't know – but the murderer must have thought so – so the murderer gets rattled and bumps off Mr Barton. That seems the way of it as far as I can see – I hope you agree?'

'Oh, yes – that part of it seems straightforward enough. God knows what the "trap" was – I noticed that there was an empty chair at the table. Perhaps it was waiting for some unexpected witness. Anyhow it accomplished rather more than it was meant to do. It alarmed the guilty person so much that he or she didn't wait for the trap to be sprung.'

'Well,' said Kemp, 'we've got five suspects. And we've got the first case to go on – Mrs Barton.'

'You're definitely of the opinion now that it was *not* suicide?'

'This murder seems to prove that it wasn't. Though I don't think you can blame us at the time for accepting the suicide theory as the most probable. There was some evidence for it.'

'Depression after influenza?'

Kemp's wooden face showed a ripple of a smile.

'That was for the coroner's court. Agreed with the medical evidence and saved everybody's feelings. That's done every day. And there was a half-finished letter to the sister directing how her personal belongings were to be given away – showed she'd had the idea of doing away with herself in her mind. She was depressed all right, I don't doubt, poor lady – but nine times out of ten, with women, it's a love affair. With men it's mostly money worries.'

'So you knew Mrs Barton had a love affair.'

'Yes, we soon found that out. It had been discreet – but it didn't take much finding.'

'Stephen Farraday?'

'Yes. They used to meet in a little flat out Earls Court way. It had been going on for over six months. Say they'd had a quarrel – or possibly he was getting tired of her – well, she wouldn't be the first woman to take her life in a fit of desperation.'

'By potassium cyanide in a public restaurant?'

'Yes – if she wanted to be dramatic about it – with him looking on and all. Some people have a feeling for the spectacular. From what I could find out she hadn't much feeling for the conventions – all the precautions were on his side.'

'Any evidence as to whether his wife knew what was going on?'

'As far as we could learn she knew nothing about it.'

'She may have, for all that, Kemp. Not the kind of woman to wear her heart on her sleeve.'

'Oh, quite so. Count them both in as possibles. She for jealousy. He for his career. Divorce would have dished that. Not that divorce means as much as it used to, but in his case it would have meant the antagonism of the Kidderminster clan.'

'What about the secretary girl?'

'She's a possible. Might have been sweet on George Barton. They were pretty thick at the office and there's an idea there that she was keen on him. Actually yesterday afternoon one of the telephone girls was giving an imitation of Barton holding Ruth Lessing's hand and saying he couldn't do without her, and Miss Lessing came out and caught them and sacked the girl there and then – gave her a month's money and told her to go. Looks as though she was sensitive about it all. Then the sister came into a peck of money – one's got to remember that. Looked a nice kid, but you can never tell. And there was Mrs Barton's other boy friend.'

'I'm rather anxious to hear what you know about him?'

Kemp said slowly:

'Remarkably little – but what there is isn't too good. His passport's in order. He's an American citizen about whom we can't find anything, detrimental or otherwise. He came over here, stayed at Claridge's and managed to strike up an acquaintance with Lord Dewsbury.'

'Confidence man?'

'Might be. Dewsbury seems to have fallen for him – asked him to stay. Rather a critical time just then.'

'Armaments,' said Race. 'There was that trouble about the new tank trials in Dewsbury's works.'

'Yes. This fellow Browne represented himself as interested in armaments. It was soon after he'd been up there that they discovered that sabotage business – just in the nick of time. Browne met a good many cronies of Dewsbury – he seemed to have cultivated all the ones who were connected with the armament firms. As a result he's been shown a lot of stuff that in my opinion he ought never to have seen – and in one or two cases there's been serious trouble in the works not long after he's been in the neighbourhood.'

'An interesting person, Mr Anthony Browne?'

'Yes. He's got a lot of charm, apparently, and plays it for all he's worth.'

'And where did Mrs Barton come in? George Barton hasn't anything to do with the armament world?'

'No. But they seem to have been fairly intimate. He may have let out something to her. *You* know, colonel, none better, what a pretty woman can get out of a man.'

Race nodded, taking the chief inspector's words, as meant, to refer to the Counter-Espionage Department which he had once controlled and not – as some ignorant person might have thought – to some personal indiscretions of his own.

He said after a minute or two:

'Have you had a go at those letters that George Barton received?'

'Yes. Found them in his desk at his house last night. Miss Marle found them for me.'

'You know I'm interested in those letters, Kemp. What's the expert opinion on them?'

'Cheap paper, ordinary ink – fingerprints show George Barton and Iris Marle handled them – and a horde of unidentified dabs on the envelope, postal employees, etc. They were printed and the experts say by someone of good education in normal health.'

'Good education. Not a servant?'

'Presumably not.'

'That makes it more interesting still.'

'It means that somebody else had suspicions, at least.'

'Someone who didn't go to the police. Someone who was prepared to arouse George's suspicions but who didn't follow the business up. There's something odd there, Kemp. He couldn't have written them himself, could he?'

'He could have. But why?'

'As a preliminary to suicide – a suicide which he intended to look like murder.'

'With Stephen Farraday booked for the hangman's rope? It's an idea – but he'd have made quite sure that everything pointed to Farraday as the murderer. As it is we've nothing against Farraday at all.'

'What about cyanide? Was there any container found?'

'Yes. A small white paper packet under the table. Traces of cyanide crystals inside. No fingerprints on it. In a detective story, of course, it would be some special kind of paper or folded in some special way. I'd like to give these detective story writers a course of routine work. They'd soon learn how most things are untraceable and nobody ever notices anything anywhere!'

Race smiled.

'Almost too sweeping a statement. Did anybody notice anything last night?'

'Actually that's what I'm starting on today. I took a brief statement from everyone last night and I went back to Elvaston Square with Miss Marle and had a look through Barton's desk and papers. I shall get fuller statements from them all today – also statements from the people sitting at the other two tables in the alcove –' He rustled through some papers – 'Yes, here they are. Gerald Tollington, Grenadier Guards, and the Hon. Patricia Brice-Woodworth. Young engaged couple. I'll bet they didn't see anything but each other. And Mr Pedro Morales – nasty bit of goods from Mexico – even the whites of his eyes are yellow – and Miss Christine Shannon – a gold-digging blonde lovely – I'll bet she didn't see anything – dumber than you'd believe possible except where money is concerned. It's a hundred to one chance that any of them saw anything, but I took their names and addresses on the off chance. We'll start off with the waiter chap, Giuseppe. He's here now. I'll have him sent in.'

CHAPTER 2

Giuseppe Bolsano was a middle-aged man, slight with a rather monkey-like intelligent face. He was nervous, but not unduly so. His English was fluent since he had, he explained, been in the country since he was sixteen and had married an English wife.

Kemp treated him sympathetically.

'Now then, Giuseppe, let's hear whether anything more has occurred to you about this.'

'It is for me very unpleasant. It is I who serve that table. I who pour out the wine. People will say that I am off my head, that I put poison into the wine glasses. It is not so, but that is what people will say. Already, Mr Goldstein says it is better that I take a week away from work – so that people do not ask me questions there and point me out. He is a fair man, and just, and he knows it is not my fault, and that I have been there for many years, so he does not dismiss me as some restaurant owners would do. M. Charles, too, he has been kind, but all the same it is a great misfortune for me – and it makes me afraid. Have I an enemy, I ask myself?'

'Well,' said Kemp at his most wooden, 'have you?'

The sad monkey-face twitched into laughter. Giuseppe stretched out his arms.

'I? I have not an enemy in the world. Many good friends but no enemies.'

Kemp grunted.

'Now about last night. Tell me about the champagne.'

'It was Clicquot, 1928 – very good and expensive wine. Mr Barton was like that – he liked good food and drink – the best.'

'Had he ordered the wine beforehand?'

'Yes. He had arranged everything with Charles.'

'What about the vacant place at the table?'

'That, too, he had arranged for. He told Charles and he told me. A young lady would occupy it later in the evening.'

'A young lady?' Race and Kemp looked at each other. 'Do you know who the young lady was?'

Giuseppe shook his head.

'No, I know nothing about that. She was to come later, that is all I heard.'

'Go on about the wine. How many bottles?'

'Two bottles and a third to be ready if needed. The first bottle was finished quite quickly. The second I open not long before the cabaret. I fill up the glasses and put the bottle in the ice bucket.'

'When did you last notice Mr Barton drinking from his glass?'

'Let me see, when the cabaret was over, they drink the young lady's health. It is her birthday so I understand. Then they go and dance. It is after that, when they come back, that Mr Barton drinks and in a minute, like *that*! he is dead.'

'Had you filled up the glasses during the time they were dancing?'

'No, monsieur. They were full when they drank to mademoiselle and they did not drink much, only a few mouthfuls. There was plenty left in the glasses.'

'Did anyone – *anyone* at all – come near the table whilst they were dancing?'

'No one at all, sir. I am sure of that.'

'Did they all go to dance at the same time?'

'Yes.'

'And came back at the same time?'

Giuseppe screwed up his eyes in an effort of memory.

'Mr Barton he came back first – with the young lady. He was stouter than the rest – he did not dance quite so long, you comprehend. Then came the fair gentleman, Mr Farraday, and the young lady in black. Lady Alexandra Farraday and the dark gentleman came last.'

'You know Mr Farraday and Lady Alexandra?'

'Yes, sir. I have seen them in the Luxembourg often. They are very distinguished.'

'Now, Giuseppe, would you have seen if one of those people had put something in Mr Barton's glass?'

'That I cannot say, sir. I have my service, the other two tables in the alcove, and two more in the main restaurant. There are dishes to serve. I do not watch at Mr Barton's table. After the cabaret everyone nearly gets up and dances, so at that time I am standing still – and that is why I can be sure that no one approached the table then. But as soon as people sit down, I am at once very busy.'

Kemp nodded.

'But I think,' Giuseppe continued, 'that it would be very difficult to do without being observed. It seems to me that only Mr Barton himself could do it. But you do not think so, no?'

He looked inquiringly at the police officer.

'So that's your idea, is it?'

'Naturally I know nothing – but I wonder. Just a year ago that beautiful lady, Mrs Barton, she kills herself. Could it not be that Mr Barton he grieves so much that he too decides to kill himself the same way? It would be poetic. Of course it is not good for the restaurant – but a gentleman who is going to kill himself would not think of that.'

He looked eagerly from one to the other of the two men.

Kemp shook his head.

'I doubt if it's as easy as that,' he said.

He asked a few more questions, then Giuseppe was dismissed.

As the door closed behind Giuseppe, Race said:

'I wonder if that's what we are meant to think?'

'Grieving husband kills himself on anniversary of wife's death? Not that it was the anniversary – but near enough.'

'It was All Souls' Day,' said Race.

'True. Yes, it's possible that *was* the idea – but if so, whoever it was can't have known about those letters being kept and that Mr Barton had consulted you and shown them to Iris Marle.'

He glanced at his watch.

'I'm due at Kidderminster House at 12.30. We've time before that to go and see those people at the other two tables – some of them at any rate. Come with me, won't you, colonel?'

CHAPTER 3

Mr Morales was staying at the Ritz. He was hardly a pretty sight at this hour in the morning, still unshaven, the whites of his eyes bloodshot and with every sign of a severe hangover.

Mr Morales was an American subject and spoke a variant of the American language. Though professing himself willing to remember anything he could, his recollections of the previous evening were of the vaguest description.

'Went with Chrissie – that baby is sure hard-boiled! She said it was a good joint. Honey pie, I said, we'll go just where you say. It was a classy joint, that I'll admit – and do they know how to charge you! Set me back the best part of thirty dollars. But the band was punk – they just couldn't seem to swing it.'

Diverted from his recollections of his own evening, Mr Morales was pressed to remember the table in the middle of the alcove. Here he was not very helpful.

'Sure there was a table and some people at it. I don't remember what they looked like, though. Didn't take much account of them till the guy there croaked. Thought at first he couldn't hold his liquor. Say now, I remember one of the dames. Dark hair and she had what it takes, I should say.'

'You mean the girl in the green velvet dress?'

'No, not that one. She was skinny. This baby was in black with some good curves.'

It was Ruth Lessing who had taken Mr Morales' roving eye.

He wrinkled up his nose appreciatively.

'I watched her dancing – and say, could that baby dance! I gave her the high sign once or twice, but she had a frozen eye – just looked through me in your British way.'

Nothing more of value could be extracted from Mr Morales and he admitted frankly that his alcoholic condition was already well advanced by the time the cabaret was on.

Kemp thanked him and prepared to take his leave.

'I'm sailing for New York tomorrow,' said Morales. 'You wouldn't,' he asked wistfully, 'care for me to stay on?'

'Thank you, but I don't think your evidence will be needed at the inquest.'

'You see I'm enjoying it right here – and if it was police business the firm couldn't kick. When the police tell you to stay put, you've got to stay put. Maybe I *could* remember something if I thought hard enough?'

But Kemp declined to rise to this wistful bait, and he and Race drove to Brook Street where they were greeted by a choleric gentleman, the father of the Hon. Patricia Brice-Woodworth.

General Lord Woodworth received them with a good deal of outspoken comment.

What on earth was the idea of suggesting that his daughter – *his* daughter! – was mixed up in this sort of thing? If a girl couldn't go out with her fiancé to dine in a restaurant without being subjected to annoyance by detectives and Scotland Yard, what was England coming to? She didn't even know these people what was their name – Hubbard – Barton? Some City fellow or other! Showed you couldn't be too careful where you went – Luxembourg was always supposed to be all right – but apparently this was the second time a thing of this sort had happened there. Gerald must be a fool to have taken Pat there – these young men thought they knew everything. But in any case he wasn't going to have his daughter badgered and bullied and cross-questioned – not without a solicitor's say so. He'd ring up old Anderson in Lincoln's Inn and ask him –

Here the general paused abruptly and staring at Race said, 'Seen you somewhere. Now where –?'

Race's answer was immediate and came with a smile.

'Badderpore. 1923.'

'By Jove,' said the general. 'If it isn't Johnny Race! What are you doing mixed up in this show?'

Race smiled.

'I was with Chief Inspector Kemp when the question of interviewing your daughter came up. I suggested it would be much pleasanter for her if Inspector Kemp came round here than if she had to come down to Scotland Yard, and I thought I'd come along too.'

'Oh – er – well, very decent, of you, Race.'

'We naturally wanted to upset the young lady as little as possible,' put in Chief Inspector Kemp.

But at this moment the door opened and Miss Patricia Brice-Woodworth

walked in and took charge of the situation with the coolness and detachment of the very young.

'Hallo,' she said. 'You're from Scotland Yard, aren't you? About last
night? I've been longing for you to come. Is father being tiresome? Now
don't, daddy – you know what the doctor said about your blood pressure.
Why you want to get into such states about everything, I can't think. I'll
just take the inspectors or superintendents or whatever they are into my
room and I'll send Walters to you with a whisky and soda.'

The general had a choleric desire to express himself in several blistering
ways at once, but only succeeded in saying, 'Old friend of mine, Major
Race,' at which introduction, Patricia lost interest in Race and bent a
beatific smile on Chief Inspector Kemp.

With cool generalship, she shepherded them out of the room and into
her own sitting-room, firmly shutting her father in his study.

'Poor daddy,' she observed. 'He *will* fuss. But he's quite easy to
manage really.'

The conversation then proceeded on most amicable lines but with very
little result.

'It's maddening really,' said Patricia. 'Probably the only chance in my
life that I shall ever have of being right on the spot when a murder was
done – it is a murder, isn't it? The papers were very cautious and vague,
but I said to Gerry on the telephone that it must be murder. Think of it,
a murder done right close by me and I wasn't even looking!'

The regret in her voice was unmistakable.

It was evident enough that, as the chief inspector had gloomily prognos-
ticated, the two young people who had got engaged only a week previously
had had eyes only for each other.

With the best will in the world, a few personalities were all that Patricia
Brice-Woodworth could muster.

'Sandra Farraday was looking very smart, but then she always does.
That was a Schiaparelli model she had on.'

'You know her?' Race asked.

Patricia shook her head.

'Only by sight. He looks rather a bore, I always think. So pompous, like
most politicians.'

'Did you know any of the others by sight?'

She shook her head.

'No, I'd never seen any of them before – at least I don't think so. In
fact, I don't suppose I would have noticed Sandra Farraday if it hadn't
been for the Schiaparelli.'

'And you'll find,' said Chief Inspector Kemp grimly as they left the house, 'that Master Tollington will be exactly the same – only there won't even have been a Skipper – skipper what – sounds like a sardine – to attract his attention.'

'I don't suppose,' agreed Race, 'that the cut of Stephen Farraday's dress suit will have caused him any heart pangs.'

'Oh, well,' said the inspector. 'Let's try Christine Shannon. Then we'll have finished with the outside chances.'

Miss Shannon was, as Chief Inspector Kemp had stated, a blonde lovely. The bleached hair, carefully arranged, swept back from a soft vacant baby-like countenance. Miss Shannon might be as Inspector Kemp had affirmed, dumb – but she was eminently easy to look at, and a certain shrewdness in the large baby-blue eyes indicated that her dumbness only extended in intellectual directions and that where horse sense and a knowledge of finance were indicated, Christine Shannon was right on the spot.

She received the two men with the utmost sweetness, pressing drinks upon them and when these were refused, urging cigarettes. Her flat was small and cheaply modernistic.

'I'd just love to be able to help you, chief inspector. Do ask me any questions you like.'

Kemp led off with a few conventional questions about the bearing and demeanour of the party at the centre table.

At once Christine showed herself to be an unusually keen and shrewd observer.

'The party wasn't going well – you could see that. Stiff as stiff could be. I felt quite sorry for the old boy – the one who was giving it. Going all out he was to try and make things go – and just as nervous as a cat on wires – but all he could do didn't seem to cut any ice. The tall woman he'd got on his right was as stiff as though she'd swallowed the poker and the kid on his left was just mad, you could see, because she wasn't sitting next to the nice-looking dark boy opposite. As for the tall fair fellow next to her he looked as though his tummy was out of order, ate his food as though he thought it would choke him. The woman next to him was doing her best, she pegged away at him, but she looked rather as though she had the jumps herself.'

'You seem to have been able to notice a great deal, Miss Shannon,' said Colonel Race.

'I'll let you into a secret. I wasn't being so much amused myself. I'd been out with that boy friend of mine three nights running, and was I getting tired of him! He was all out for seeing London – especially what he called the classy spots – and I will say for him he wasn't mean. Champagne every time. We went to the Compradour and the Mille Fleurs and finally the Luxembourg, and I'll say he enjoyed himself. In a way it was kind of pathetic. But his conversation wasn't what you'd call interesting. Just long histories of business deals he'd put through in Mexico and most of those I heard three times – and going on to all the dames he'd known and how mad they were about him. A girl gets kind of tired listening after a while and you'll admit that Pedro is nothing much to look at – so I just concentrated on the eats and let my eyes roam round.'

'Well, that's excellent from our point of view, Miss Shannon,' said the chief inspector. 'And I can only hope that you will have seen something that may help us solve our problem.'

Christine shook her blonde head.

'I've no idea who bumped the old boy off – no idea at all. He just took a drink of champagne, went purple in the face and sort of collapsed.'

'Do you remember when he had last drunk from his glass before that?'

The girl reflected.

'Why – yes – it was just after the cabaret. The lights went up and he picked up his glass and said something and the others did it too. Seemed to me it was a toast of some kind.'

The chief inspector nodded.

'And then?'

'Then the music began and they all got up and went off to dance, pushing their chairs back and laughing. Seemed to get warmed up for the first time. Wonderful what champagne will do for the stickiest parties.'

'They all went together – leaving the table empty?'

'Yes.'

'And no one touched Mr Barton's glass.'

'No one at all.' Her reply came promptly. 'I'm perfectly certain of that.'

'And no one – no one at all came near the table while they were away.'

'No one – except the waiter, of course.'

'A waiter? Which waiter?'

'One of the half-fledged ones with an apron, round about sixteen. Not the real waiter. He was an obliging little fellow rather like a monkey – Italian I guess he was.'

Chief Inspector Kemp acknowledged this description of Giuseppe Bolsano with a nod of the head.

'And what did he do, this young waiter? He filled up the glasses?'

Christine shook her head.

'Oh, no. He didn't touch anything on the table. He just picked up an evening bag that one of the girls had dropped when they all got up.'

'Whose bag was it?'

Christine took a minute or two to think. Then she said:

'That's right. It was the kid's bag – a green and gold thing. The other two women had black bags.'

'What did the waiter do with the bag?'

Christine looked surprised.

'He just put it back on the table, that's all.'

'You're quite sure he didn't touch any of the glasses?'

'Oh, no. He just dropped the bag down very quick and ran off because one of the real waiters was hissing at him to go somewhere or get something and everything was going to be his fault!'

'And that's the only time anyone went near the table?'

'That's right.'

'But of course someone might have gone to the table without your noticing?'

But Christine shook her head very determinedly.

'No, I'm quite sure they didn't. You see Pedro had been called to the telephone and hadn't got back yet, so I had nothing to do but look around and feel bored. I'm pretty good at noticing things and from where I was sitting there wasn't much else to see but the empty table next to us.'

Race asked:

'Who came back first to the table?'

'The girl in green and the old boy. They sat down and then the fair man and the girl in black came back and after them the haughty piece of goods and the good-looking dark boy. Some dancer, he was. When they were all back and the waiter was warming up a dish like mad on the spirit lamp, the old boy leaned forward and made a kind of speech and then they all picked up their glasses again. And then it happened.' Christine paused and added brightly, 'Awful, wasn't it? Of course I thought it was a stroke. My aunt had a stroke and she went down just like that. Pedro came back just then and I said, "Look, Pedro, that man's had a stroke." And all Pedro would say was, "Just passing out – just passing out – that's all" which was about what *he* was doing. I had to keep my eye on him. They don't like you passing out at a place like the Luxembourg. That's why I don't like Dagoes. When they've drunk too much they're not a bit refined any more – a girl never knows what unpleasantness she may be let in for.' She brooded for a moment and then glancing at a showy looking bracelet on her right wrist, she added, 'Still, I must say they're generous enough.'

Gently distracting her from the trials and compensations of a girl's existence Kemp took her through her story once more.

'That's our last chance of outside help gone,' he said to Race when they had left Miss Shannon's flat. 'And it would have been a good chance if it had come off. That girl's the right kind of witness. Sees things and remembers them accurately. If there had been anything to see, she'd have seen it. So the answer is that there wasn't anything to see. It's incredible. It's a conjuring trick! George Barton drinks champagne and goes and dances. He comes back, drinks from the same glass that no one has touched and Hey Presto it's full of cyanide. It's crazy – I tell you – it couldn't have happened except that it did.'

He stopped a minute.

'That waiter. The little boy. Giuseppe never mentioned him. I might look into that. After all, he's the one person who was near the table whilst they were all away dancing. There *might* be something in it.'

Race shook his head.

'If he'd put anything in Barton's glass, that girl would have seen him. She's a born observer of detail. Nothing to think about inside her head and so she uses her eyes. No, Kemp, there must be some quite simple explanation if only we could get it.'

'Yes, there's one. He dropped it in himself.'

'I'm beginning to believe that that *is* what happened – that it's the only thing that can have happened. But if so, Kemp, I'm convinced he didn't know it was cyanide.'

'You mean someone gave it to him? Told him it was for indigestion or blood pressure – something like that?'

'It could be.'

'Then who was the someone? Not either of the Farradays.'

'That would certainly seem unlikely.'

'And I'd say Mr Anthony Browne is equally unlikely. That leaves us two people – an affectionate sister-in-law –'

'And a devoted secretary.'

Kemp looked at him.

'Yes – she could have planted something of the kind on him – I'm due now to go to Kidderminster House – What about you? Going round to see Miss Marle?'

'I think I'll go and see the other one – at the office. Condolences of an old friend. I might take her out to lunch.'

'So that *is* what you think.'

'I don't think anything yet. I'm casting about for spoor.'

'You ought to see Iris Marle, all the same.'

'I'm going to see her – but I'd rather go to the house first when she isn't there. Do you know why, Kemp?'

'I'm sure I couldn't say.'

'Because there's someone there who twitters – twitters like a little bird . . . A little bird told me – was a saying of my youth. It's very true, Kemp – these twitterers can tell one a lot if one just lets them – twitter!'

CHAPTER 4

The two men parted. Race halted a taxi and was driven to George Barton's office in the city. Chief Inspector Kemp, mindful of his expense account, took a bus to within a stone's throw of Kidderminster House.

The inspector's face was rather grim as he mounted the steps and pushed the bell. He was, he knew, on difficult ground. The Kidderminster faction had immense political influence and its ramifications spread out like a network throughout the country. Chief Inspector Kemp had full belief in the impartiality of British justice. If Stephen or Alexandra Farraday had been concerned in the death of Rosemary Barton or in that of George Barton no 'pull' or 'influence' would enable them to escape the consequences. But if they were guiltless, or the evidence against them was too vague to ensure conviction, then the responsible officer must be careful how he trod or he would be liable to get a rap over the knuckles from his superiors. In these circumstances it can be understood that the chief inspector did not much relish what lay before him. It seemed to him highly probable that the Kidderminsters would, as he phrased it to himself, 'cut up rough'.

Kemp soon found, however, that he had been somewhat naïve in his assumption. Lord Kidderminster was far too experienced a diplomat to resort to crudities.

On stating his business, Chief Inspector Kemp was taken at once by a pontifical butler to a dim book-lined room at the back of the house where he found Lord Kidderminster and his daughter and son-in-law awaiting him.

Coming forward, Lord Kidderminster shook hands and said courteously:

'You are exactly on time, chief inspector. May I say that I much appreciate your courtesy in coming here instead of demanding that my daughter and her husband should come to Scotland Yard which, of course, they would have been quite prepared to do if necessary – that goes without saying – but they appreciate your kindness.'

Sandra said in a quiet voice:

'Yes, indeed, inspector.'

She was wearing a dress of some soft dark red material, and sitting as she was with the light from the long narrow window behind her, she reminded Kemp of a stained glass figure he had once seen in a cathedral abroad. The long oval of her face and the slight angularity of her shoulders helped the illusion. Saint Somebody or other, they had told him – but Lady Alexandra Farraday was no saint – not by a long way. And yet some of these old saints had been funny people from his point of view, not kindly ordinary decent Christian folk, but intolerant, fanatical, cruel to themselves and others.

Stephen Farraday stood close by his wife. His face expressed no emotion whatever. He looked correct and formal, an appointed legislator of the people. The natural man was well buried. But the natural man was there, as the chief inspector knew.

Lord Kidderminster was speaking, directing with a good deal of ability the trend of the interview.

'I won't disguise from you, chief inspector, that this is a very painful and disagreeable business for us all. This is the second time that my daughter and son-in-law have been connected with a violent death in a public place – the same restaurant and two members of the same family. Publicity of such a kind is always harmful to a man in the public eye. Publicity, of course, cannot be avoided. We all realize that, and both my daughter and Mr Farraday are anxious to give you all the help they can in the hope that the matter may be cleared up speedily and public interest in it die down.'

'Thank you, Lord Kidderminster. I much appreciate the attitude you have taken up. It certainly makes things easier for us.'

Sandra Farraday said:

'Please ask us any questions you like, chief inspector.'

'Thank you, Lady Alexandra.'

'Just one point, chief inspector,' said Lord Kidderminster. 'You have, of course, your own sources of information and I gather from my friend the Commissioner that this man Barton's death is regarded as murder rather than suicide, though on the face of it, to the outside public, suicide would seem a more likely explanation. *You* thought it was suicide, didn't you, Sandra, my dear?'

The Gothic figure bowed its head slightly. Sandra said in a thoughtful voice:

'It seemed to me so obvious last night. We were there in the same restaurant and actually at the same table where poor Rosemary Barton poisoned herself last year. We have seen something of Mr Barton during the summer in the country and he has really been very odd – quite unlike himself – and we all thought that his wife's death was preying on his mind. He was very fond of her, you know, and I don't think he ever got over her death. So that the idea of suicide seemed, if not natural, at least possible – whereas I can't imagine why *anyone* should want to murder George Barton.'

Stephen Farraday said quickly:

'No more can I. Barton was an excellent fellow. I'm sure he hadn't got an enemy in the world.'

Chief Inspector Kemp looked at the three inquiring faces turned towards him and reflected a moment before speaking. 'Better let 'em have it,' he thought to himself.

'What you say is quite correct, I am sure, Lady Alexandra. But you see there are a few things that you probably don't know yet.'

Lord Kidderminster interposed quickly:

'We mustn't force the chief inspector's hand. It is entirely in his discretion what facts he makes public.'

'Thanks, m'lord, but there's no reason I shouldn't explain things a little more clearly. I'll boil it down to this. George Barton, before his death, expressed to two people his belief that his wife had not, as was believed, committed suicide, but had instead been poisoned by some third party. He also thought that he was on the track of that third party, and the dinner and celebration last night, ostensibly in honour of Miss Marle's birthday, was really some part of a plan he had made for finding out the identity of his wife's murderer.'

There was a moment's silence – and in that silence Chief Inspector Kemp, who was a sensitive man in spite of his wooden appearance, felt the presence of something that he classified as dismay. It was not apparent on any face, but he could have sworn that it was there.

Lord Kidderminster was the first to recover himself. He said:

'But surely – that belief in itself might point to the fact that poor Barton was not quite – er – himself? Brooding over his wife's death might have slightly unhinged him mentally.'

'Quite so, Lord Kidderminster, but it at least shows that his frame of mind was definitely not suicidal.'

'Yes – yes, I take your point.'

And again there was silence. Then Stephen Farraday said sharply:

'But how did Barton get such an idea into his head? After all, Mrs Barton *did* commit suicide.'

Chief Inspector Kemp transferred a placid gaze to him.

'Mr Barton didn't think so.'

Lord Kidderminster interposed.

'But the police were satisfied? There was no suggestion of anything but suicide at the time?'

Chief Inspector Kemp said quietly:

'The facts were compatible with suicide. There was no evidence that her death was due to any other agency.'

He knew that a man of Lord Kidderminster's calibre would seize on the exact meaning of that.

Becoming slightly more official, Kemp said, 'I would like to ask you some questions now, if I may, Lady Alexandra?'

'Certainly.' She turned her head slightly towards him.

'You had no suspicions at the time of Mr Barton's death that it might be murder, not suicide?'

'Certainly not. I was quite sure it was suicide.' She added, 'I still am.'

Kemp let that pass. He said:

'Have you received any anonymous letters in the past year, Lady Alexandra?'

The calm of her manner seemed broken by pure astonishment.

'Anonymous letters? Oh, no.'

'You're quite sure? Such letters are very unpleasant things and people usually prefer to ignore them, but they may be particularly important in this case, and that is why I want to stress that if you did receive any such letters it is most essential that I should know about them.'

'I see. But I can only assure you, chief inspector, that I have received nothing of the kind.'

'Very well. Now you say Mr Barton's manner has been odd this summer. In what way?'

She considered a minute.

'Well, he was jumpy, nervous. It seemed difficult for him to focus his attention on what was said to him.' She turned her head towards her husband. 'Was that how it struck you, Stephen?'

'Yes, I should say that was a very fair description. The man looked physically ill, too. He had lost weight.'

'Did you notice any difference in his attitude towards you and your husband? Any less cordiality, for instance?'

'No. On the contrary. He had bought a house, you know, quite close to us, and he seemed very grateful for what we were able to do for him – in the way of local introductions, I mean, and all that. Of course we were only too pleased to do everything we could in that line, both for him and for Iris Marle who is a charming girl.'

'Was the late Mrs Barton a great friend of yours, Lady Alexandra?'

'No, we were not very intimate.' She gave a light laugh. 'She was really mostly Stephen's friend. She became interested in politics and he helped to – well, educate her politically – which I'm sure he enjoyed. She was a very charming and attractive woman, you know.'

'And you're a very clever one,' thought Chief Inspector Kemp to himself appreciatively. 'I wonder how much you know about those two – a good deal, I shouldn't wonder.'

He went on:

'Mr Barton never expressed to *you* the view that his wife did not commit suicide?'

'No, indeed. That was why I was so startled just now.'

'And Miss Marle? She never talked about her sister's death, either?'

'No.'

'Any idea what made George Barton buy a house in the country? Did you or your husband suggest the idea to him?'

'No. It was quite a surprise.'

'And his manner to you was always friendly?'

'Very friendly indeed.'

'And what do you know about Mr Anthony Browne, Lady Alexandra?'

'I really know nothing at all. I have met him occasionally and that is all.'

'What about you, Mr Farraday?'

'I think I know probably less about Browne than my wife does. She at any rate has danced with him. He seems a likeable chap – American, I believe.'

'Would you say from observation at the time that he was on special terms of intimacy with Mrs Barton?'

'I have absolutely no knowledge on that point, chief inspector.'

'I am simply asking you for your impression, Mr Farraday.'

Stephen frowned.

'They were friendly – that is all I can say.'

'And you, Lady Alexandra?'

'Simply my impression, chief inspector?'

'Simply your impression.'

'Then, for what it is worth, I did form the impression that they knew each other well and were on intimate terms. Simply, you understand, from the way they looked at each other – I have no concrete evidence.'

'Ladies have often very good judgement on these matters,' said Kemp. That somewhat fatuous smile with which he delivered this remark would have amused Colonel Race if he had been present. 'Now, what about Miss Lessing, Lady Alexandra?'

'Miss Lessing, I understand, was Mr Barton's secretary. I met her for the first time on the evening that Mrs Barton died. After that I met her once when she was staying down in the country, and last night.'

'If I may ask you another informal question, did you form the impression that she was in love with George Barton?'

'I really haven't the least idea.'

'Then we'll come to the events of last night.'

He questioned both Stephen and his wife minutely on the course of the tragic evening. He had not hoped for much from this, and all he got was confirmation of what he had already been told. All accounts agreed on the important points – Barton had proposed a toast to Iris, had drunk it and immediately afterwards had got up to dance. They had all left the table together and George and Iris had been the first to return to it. Neither of them had any explanation to offer as to the empty chair except that George Barton had distinctly said that he was expecting a friend of his, a Colonel Race, to occupy it later in the evening – a statement which, as the inspector knew, could not possibly be the truth. Sandra Farraday said, and her husband agreed, that when the lights went up after the cabaret, George had stared at the empty chair in a peculiar manner and had for some moments seemed so absent-minded as not to hear what was said to him – then he had rallied himself and proposed Iris's health.

The only item that the chief inspector could count as an addition to his knowledge, was Sandra's account of her conversation with George at Fairhaven – and his plea that she and her husband would collaborate with him over this party for Iris's sake.

It was a reasonably plausible pretext, the chief inspector thought, though not the true one. Closing his notebook in which he had jotted down one or two hieroglyphics, he rose to his feet.

'I'm very grateful to you, my lord, and to Mr Farraday and Lady Alexandra for your help and collaboration.'

'Will my daughter's presence be required at the inquest?'

'The proceedings will be purely formal on this occasion. Evidence of identification and the medical evidence will be taken and the inquest will then be adjourned for a week. By then,' said the chief inspector, his tone changing slightly, 'we shall, I hope, be further on.'

He turned to Stephen Farraday:

'By the way, Mr Farraday, there are one or two small points where I think you could help me. No need to trouble Lady Alexandra. If you will give me a ring at the Yard, we can settle a time that will suit you. You are, I know, a busy man.'

It was pleasantly said, with an air of casualness, but on three pairs of ears the words fell with deliberate meaning.

With an air of friendly co-operation Stephen managed to say:

'Certainly, chief inspector.' Then he looked at his watch and murmured: 'I must go along to the House.'

When Stephen had hurried off, and the chief inspector had likewise departed, Lord Kidderminster turned to his daughter and asked a question with no beating about the bush.

'Had Stephen been having an affair with that woman?'

There was a split second of a pause before his daughter answered.

'Of course not. I should have known it if he had. And anyway, Stephen's not that kind.'

'Now, look here, my dear, no good laying your ears back and digging your hoofs in. These things are bound to come out. We want to know where we are in this business.'

'Rosemary Barton was a friend of that man, Anthony Browne. They went about everywhere together.'

'Well,' said Lord Kidderminster slowly. 'You should know.'

He did not believe his daughter. His face, as he went slowly out of the room, was grey and perplexed. He went upstairs to his wife's sitting-room. He had vetoed her presence in the library, knowing too well that her arrogant methods were apt to arouse antagonism and at this juncture he felt it vital that relations with the official police should be harmonious.

'Well?' said Lady Kidderminster. 'How did it go off?'

'Quite well on the face of it,' said Lord Kidderminster slowly. 'Kemp is a courteous fellow – very pleasant in his manner – he handled the whole thing with tact – just a little too much tact for my fancy.'

'It's serious, then?'

'Yes, it's serious. We should never have let Sandra marry that fellow, Vicky.'

'That's what I said.'

'Yes – yes . . .' He acknowledged her claim. 'You were right – and I was wrong. But, mind you, she would have had him anyway. You can't turn Sandra when her mind is fixed on a thing. Her meeting Farraday was a disaster – a man of whose antecedents and ancestors we know nothing. When a crisis comes how does one know how a man like that will react?'

'I see,' said Lady Kidderminster. 'You think we've taken a murderer into the family?'

'I don't know. I don't want to condemn the fellow off-hand – but it's what the police think – and they're pretty shrewd. He had an affair with this Barton woman – that's plain enough. Either she committed suicide on his account, or else he – Well, whatever happened, Barton got wise to it and was heading for an exposé and scandal. I suppose Stephen simply couldn't take it – and –'

'Poisoned him?'

'Yes.'

Lady Kidderminster shook her head.

'I don't agree with you.'

'I hope you're right. But somebody poisoned him.'

'If you ask me,' said Lady Kidderminster, 'Stephen simply wouldn't have the nerve to do a thing like that.'

'He's in deadly earnest about his career – he's got great gifts, you know, and the makings of a true statesman. You can't say what anyone will do when they're forced into a corner.'

His wife still shook her head.

'I still say he hasn't got the nerve. You want someone who's a gambler and capable of being reckless. I'm afraid, William, I'm horribly afraid.'

He stared at her. 'Are you suggesting that Sandra – *Sandra* –?'

'I hate even to suggest such a thing – but it's no use being cowardly and refusing to face possibilities. She's besotted about that man – she always has been – and there's a queer streak in Sandra. I've never really understood her – but I've always been afraid for her. She'd risk anything – *anything* – for Stephen. Without counting the cost. And if she's been mad enough and wicked enough to do this thing, she's got to be protected.'

'Protected? What do you mean – protected?'

'By you. We've got to do something about our own daughter, haven't we? Mercifully you can pull any amount of strings.'

Lord Kidderminster was staring at her. Though he had thought he knew his wife's character well, he was nevertheless appalled at the force and courage of her realism – at her refusal to blink at unpalatable facts – and also at her unscrupulousness.

'If my daughter's a murderess, do you suggest that I should use my official position to rescue her from the consequences of her act?'

'Of course,' said Lady Kidderminster.

'My dear Vicky! You don't understand! One can't do things like that. It would be a breach of – of honour.'

'Rubbish!' said Lady Kidderminster.

They looked at each other – so far divided that neither could see the other's point of view. So might Agamemnon and Clytemnestra have stared at each other with the word Iphigenia on their lips.

'You could bring government pressure to bear on the police so that the whole thing is dropped and a verdict of suicide brought in. It has been done before – don't pretend.'

'That has been when it was a matter of public policy – in the interests of the State. This is a personal and private matter. I doubt very much whether I could do such a thing.'

'You can if you have sufficient determination.'

Lord Kidderminster flushed angrily.

'If I could, I wouldn't! It would be abusing my public position.'

'If Sandra were arrested and tried, wouldn't you employ the best counsel and do everything possible to get her off however guilty she was?'

'Of course, of course. That's entirely different. You women never grasp these things.'

Lady Kidderminster was silent, unperturbed by the thrust. Sandra was the least dear to her of her children – nevertheless she was at this moment a mother, and a mother only – willing to defend her young by any means, honourable or dishonourable. She would fight with tooth and claw for Sandra.

'In any case,' said Lord Kidderminster, 'Sandra will not be charged unless there is an absolutely convincing case against her. And I, for one, refuse to believe that a daughter of mine is a murderess. I'm astonished at you, Vicky, for entertaining such an idea for a moment.'

His wife said nothing, and Lord Kidderminster went uneasily out of the room. To think that Vicky – *Vicky* – whom he had known intimately for so many years – should prove to have such unsuspected and really very disturbing depths in her!

CHAPTER 5

Race found Ruth Lessing busy with papers at a large desk. She was dressed in a black coat and skirt and a white blouse and he was impressed by her quiet unhurried efficiency. He noticed the dark circles under her eyes and the unhappy set line of her mouth, but her grief, if it was grief, was as well controlled as all her other emotions.

Race explained his visit and she responded at once.

'It is very good of you to come. Of course I know who you are. Mr Barton was expecting you to join us last night, was he not? I remember his saying so.'

'Did he mention that before the evening itself?'

She thought for a moment.

'No. It was when we were actually taking our seats round the table. I remember that I was a little surprised –' She paused and flushed slightly. 'Not, of course, at his inviting you. You are an old friend, I know. And you were to have been at the other party a year ago. All I meant was that I was surprised, if you were coming, that Mr Barton hadn't invited another woman to balance the numbers – but of course if you were going to be late and might perhaps not come at all –' She broke off. 'How stupid I am. Why go over all these petty things that don't matter? I *am* stupid this morning.'

'But you have come to work as usual?'

'Of course.' She looked surprised – almost shocked. 'It is my job. There is so much to clear up and arrange.'

'George always told me how much he relied upon you,' said Race gently.

She turned away. He saw her swallow quickly and blink her eyes. Her absence of any display of emotion almost convinced him of her entire innocence. Almost, but not quite. He had met women who were good actresses before now, women whose reddened eyelids and the black circles underneath whose eyes had been due to art and not to natural causes.

Reserving judgement, he said to himself:

'At any rate she's a cool customer.'

Ruth turned back to the desk and in answer to his last remark she said quietly:

'I was with him for many years – it will be eight years next April – and I knew his ways, and I think he – trusted me.'

'I'm sure of that.'

He went on: 'It is nearly lunch-time. I hoped you would come out and lunch quietly with me somewhere? There is a good deal I would like to say to you.'

'Thank you. I should like to very much.'

He took her to a small restaurant that he knew of, where the tables were set far apart and where a quiet conversation was possible.

He ordered, and when the waiter had gone, looked across the table at his companion.

She was a good-looking girl, he decided, with her sleek dark head and her firm mouth and chin.

He talked a little on desultory topics until the food was brought, and she followed his lead, showing herself intelligent and sensible.

Presently, after a pause, she said:

'You want to talk to me about last night? Please don't hesitate to do so. The whole thing is so incredible that I would like to talk about it. Except that it happened and I saw it happen, I would not have believed it.'

'You've seen Chief Inspector Kemp, of course?'

'Yes, last night. He seems intelligent and experienced.' She paused. 'Was it really *murder*, Colonel Race?'

'Did Kemp tell you so?'

'He didn't volunteer any information, but his questions made it plain enough what he had in mind.'

'*Your* opinion as to whether or not it was suicide should be as good as anyone's, Miss Lessing. You knew Barton well and you were with him most of yesterday, I imagine. How did he seem? Much as usual? Or was he disturbed – upset – excited?'

She hesitated.

'It's difficult. He was upset and disturbed – but then there was a reason for that.'

She explained the situation that had arisen in regard to Victor Drake and gave a brief sketch of that young man's career.

'H'm,' said Race. 'The inevitable black sheep. And Barton was upset about him?'

Ruth said slowly:

'It's difficult to explain. I knew Mr Barton so well, you see. He was annoyed and bothered about the business – and I gather Mrs Drake had been very tearful and upset, as she always was on these occasions – so of course he wanted to straighten it all out. But I had the impression –'

'Yes, Miss Lessing? I'm sure your impressions will be accurate.'

'Well, then, I fancied that his annoyance was not quite the usual annoyance, if I may put it like that. Because we had had this same business before, in one form or another. Last year Victor Drake was in this country and in trouble, and we had to ship him off to South America, and only last June he cabled home for money. So you see I was familiar with Mr Barton's reactions. And it seemed to me this time that his annoyance was principally at the cable having arrived just at this moment when he was entirely preoccupied with the arrangements for the party he was giving. He seemed so taken up by the preparations for it that he grudged any other preoccupation arising.'

'Did it strike you that there was anything odd about this party of his, Miss Lessing?'

'Yes, it did. Mr Barton was really most peculiar about it. He was excited – like a child might have been.'

'Did it occur to you that there might have been a special purpose for such a party?'

'You mean that it was a replica of the party a year ago when Mrs Barton committed suicide?'

'Yes.'

'Frankly, I thought it a most extraordinary idea.'

'But George didn't volunteer any explanation – or confide in you in any way?'

She shook her head.

'Tell me, Miss Lessing, has there ever been any doubt in your mind as to Mrs Barton's having committed suicide?'

She looked astonished. 'Oh, no.'

'George Barton didn't tell you that he believed his wife had been murdered?'

She stared at him.

'George believed *that*?'

'I see that is news to you. Yes, Miss Lessing. George had received anonymous letters stating that his wife had not committed suicide but had been killed.'

'So that is why he became so odd this summer? I couldn't think what was the matter with him.'

'You knew nothing about these anonymous letters?'

'Nothing. Were there many of them?'

'He showed me two.'

'And I knew nothing about them!'

There was a note of bitter hurt in her voice.

He watched her for a moment or two, then he said:

'Well, Miss Lessing, what do you say? Is it possible, in your opinion, for George to have committed suicide?'

She shook her head.

'No – oh, no.'

'But you said he was excited – upset?'

'Yes, but he had been like that for some time. I see why now. And I see why he was so excited about last night's party. He must have had some special idea in his head – he must have hoped that by reproducing the conditions, he would gain some additional knowledge – poor George, he must have been so muddled about it all.'

'And what about Rosemary Barton, Miss Lessing? Do you still think her death was suicide?'

She frowned.

'I've never dreamt of it being anything else. It seemed so natural.'

'Depression after influenza?'

'Well, rather more than that, perhaps. She was definitely very unhappy. One could see that.'

'And guess the cause?'

'Well – yes. At least I did. Of course I may have been wrong. But women like Mrs Barton are very transparent – they don't trouble to hide their feelings. Mercifully I don't think Mr Barton knew anything . . . Oh, yes, she was very unhappy. And I know she had a bad headache that night besides being run down with 'flu.'

'How did you know she had a headache?'

'I heard her telling Lady Alexandra so – in the cloakroom when we were taking off our wraps. She was wishing she had a Cachet Faivre and luckily Lady Alexandra had one with her and gave it to her.'

Colonel Race's hand stopped with a glass in mid air.

'And she took it?'

'Yes.'

He put his glass down untasted and looked across the table. The girl looked placid and unaware of any significance in what she had said. But it *was* significant. It meant that Sandra who, from her position at table, would have had the most difficulty in putting anything unseen in Rosemary's glass, had had another opportunity of administering the poison. She could have given it to Rosemary in a cachet. Ordinarily a cachet would take only a few minutes to dissolve, but possibly this had been a special kind of cachet, it might have had a lining of gelatine or some other substance. Or Rosemary might possibly not have swallowed it then but later.

He said abruptly:

'Did you see her take it?'

'I beg your pardon?'

He saw by her puzzled face that her mind had gone on elsewhere.

'Did you see Rosemary Barton swallow that cachet?'

Ruth looked a little startled.

'I – well, no, I didn't actually see her. She just thanked Lady Alexandra.'

So Rosemary might have slipped the cachet in her bag and then, during the cabaret, with a headache increasing, she might have dropped it into her champagne glass and let it dissolve. Assumption – pure assumption – but a possibility.

Ruth said:

'Why do you ask me that?'

Her eyes were suddenly alert, full of questions. He watched, so it seemed to him, her intelligence working.

Then she said:

'Oh, I see. I see why George took that house down there near the Farradays. And I see why he didn't tell me about those letters. It seemed to me so extraordinary that he hadn't. But of course if he believed them, it meant that one of us, one of those five people round the table must have killed her. It might – it might even have been *me!*'

Race said in a very gentle voice:

'Had you any reason for killing Rosemary Barton?'

He thought at first that she hadn't heard the question. She sat so very still with her eyes cast down.

But suddenly with a sigh, she raised them and looked straight at him.

'It is not the sort of thing one cares to talk about,' she said. 'But I think you had better know. I was in love with George Barton. I was in love with him before he even met Rosemary. I don't think he ever knew – certainly he didn't care. He was fond of me – very fond of me – but I suppose never in that way. And yet I used to think that I would have made him a good wife – that I could have made him happy. He loved Rosemary, but he wasn't happy with her.'

Race said gently:

'And you disliked Rosemary?'

'Yes, I did. Oh! She was very lovely and very attractive and could be very charming in her way. She never bothered to be charming to me! I disliked her a good deal. I was shocked when she died – and at the way she died, but I wasn't really sorry. I'm afraid I was rather glad.'

She paused.

'Please, shall we talk about something else?'

Race responded quickly:

'I'd like you to tell me exactly, in detail, everything you can remember about yesterday – from the morning onwards – especially anything George did or said.'

Ruth replied promptly, going over the events of the morning – George's annoyance over Victor's importunity, her own telephone calls to South America and the arrangements made and George's pleasure when the matter was settled. She then described her arrival at the Luxembourg and George's flurried excited bearing as host. She carried her narrative up to the final moment of the tragedy. Her account tallied in every respect with those he had already heard.

With a worried frown, Ruth voiced his own perplexity.

'It wasn't suicide – I'm sure it wasn't suicide – but how can it have been murder? I mean, how can it have been done? The answer is, it couldn't, not by one of us! Then was it someone who slipped the poison into George's glass while we were away dancing? But if so, who could it have been? It doesn't seem to make sense.'

'The evidence is that *no one* went near the table while you were dancing.'

'Then it really doesn't make sense! Cyanide doesn't get into a glass by itself!'

'Have you absolutely no idea – no suspicion, even, who might have put the cyanide in the glass? Think back over last night. Is there nothing, no small incident, that awakens your suspicions in any degree, however small?'

He saw her face change, saw for a moment uncertainty come into her eyes. There was a tiny, almost infinitesimal pause before she answered 'Nothing.'

But there *had* been something. He was sure of that. Something she had seen or heard or noticed that, for some reason or other, she had decided not to tell.

He did not press her. He knew that with a girl of Ruth's type that would be no good. If, for some reason, she had made up her mind to keep silence, she would not, he felt sure, change her mind.

But there had been *something*. That knowledge cheered him and gave him fresh assurance. It was the first sign of a crevice in the blank wall that confronted him.

He took leave of Ruth after lunch and drove to Elvaston Square thinking of the woman he had just left.

Was it possible that Ruth Lessing was guilty? On the whole, he was prepossessed in her favour. She had seemed entirely frank and straightforward.

Was she capable of murder? Most people were, if you came to it. Capable not of murder in general, but of one particular individual murder. That was what made it so difficult to weed anyone out. There was a certain quality of ruthlessness about that young woman. And she had a motive – or rather a choice of motives. By removing Rosemary she had a very good chance of becoming Mrs George Barton. Whether it was a question of marrying a rich man, or of marrying the man she had loved, the removal of Rosemary was the first essential.

Race was inclined to think that marrying a rich man was not enough. Ruth Lessing was too cool-headed and cautious to risk her neck for mere comfortable living as a rich man's wife. Love? Perhaps. For all her cool and detached manner, he suspected her of being one of those women who can be kindled to unlikely passion by one particular man. Given love of George and hate of Rosemary, she might have coolly planned and executed Rosemary's death. The fact that it had gone off without a hitch, and that suicide had been universally accepted without demur, proved her inherent capability.

And then George had received anonymous letters (From whom? Why? That was the teasing vexing problem that never ceased to nag at him) and had grown suspicious. He had planned a trap. And Ruth had silenced him.

No, that wasn't right. That didn't ring true. That spelt panic – and Ruth Lessing was not the kind of woman who panicked. She had better brains than George and could have avoided any trap that he was likely to set with the greatest of ease.

It looked as though Ruth didn't add up after all.

CHAPTER 6

Lucilla Drake was delighted to see Colonel Race.

The blinds were all down and Lucilla came into the room draped in black and with a handkerchief to her eyes and explained, as she advanced a tremulous hand to meet his, how of course she couldn't have seen anyone – anyone at all – except such an old friend of dear, *dear* George's – and it was so dreadful to have no man in the house! Really without a man in the house one didn't know how to tackle *anything*. Just herself, a poor lonely widow, and Iris, just a helpless young girl, and George had always looked after everything. So kind of dear Colonel Race and really she was so grateful – no idea what they ought to do. Of course Miss Lessing would attend to all business matters – and the funeral to arrange for – but how about the inquest? and so dreadful having the police – actually in the house – plain clothes, of course, and really very considerate. But she was so bewildered and the whole thing was such an absolute tragedy and didn't Colonel Race think it must be all due to *suggestion* – that was what the psychoanalyst said, wasn't it, that everything is *suggestion*? And poor George at that horrid place, the Luxembourg, and practically the same party and remembering how poor Rosemary had died there – and it must have come over him quite suddenly, only if he'd listened to what she, Lucilla, had said, and taken that excellent tonic of dear Dr Gaskell's – run down, all the summer – yes, thoroughly run down.

Whereupon Lucilla herself ran down temporarily, and Race had a chance to speak.

He said how deeply he sympathized and how Mrs Drake must count upon him in every way.

Whereupon Lucilla started off again and said it was indeed kind of him, and it was the shock that had been so terrible – here today, and gone tomorrow, as it said in the Bible, cometh up like grass and cut down in the evening – only that wasn't quite right, but Colonel Race would know what she meant, and it was so nice to feel there was someone on whom they could rely. Miss Lessing meant well, of course, and was very efficient, but rather an unsympathetic manner and sometimes took things upon herself a little too much, and in her, Lucilla's, opinion, George had always relied upon her *far too much*, and at one time she had been really afraid that he might do something foolish which would have been a great pity and probably she would have bullied him unmercifully once they were married. Of course she, Lucilla, had seen what was in the wind. Dear Iris was so unworldly, and it was nice, didn't Colonel Race think, for young girls to be unspoilt and simple? Iris had really always been very young for her age and very quiet – one didn't know half the time what she was thinking about. Rosemary being so pretty and so gay had been out a great deal, and Iris had mooned about the house which wasn't really right for a young girl – they should go to classes – cooking and perhaps dressmaking. It occupied their minds and one never knew when it might come in useful. It had really been a mercy that she, Lucilla, had been free to come and live here after poor Rosemary's death – that horrid 'flu, quite an unusual kind of 'flu, Dr Gaskell had said. Such a clever man and such a nice, breezy manner.

She had wanted Iris to see him this summer. The girl had looked so white and pulled down. 'But really, Colonel Race, I think it was the situation of the house. *Low*, you know, and *damp*, with quite a *miasma* in the evenings.' Poor George had gone off and bought it all by himself without asking anyone's advice – such a pity. He had said he wanted it to be a surprise, but really it would have been better if he had taken some older woman's advice. Men knew nothing about houses. George might have realized that she, Lucilla, would have been willing to take any *amount* of trouble. For, after all, what was her life now? Her dear husband dead many years ago, and Victor, her dear boy, far away in the Argentine – she meant Brazil, or was it the Argentine? Such an affectionate, handsome boy.

Colonel Race said he had heard she had a son abroad.

For the next quarter of an hour, he was regaled with a full account of Victor's multitudinous activities. Such a spirited boy, willing to turn his hand to anything – here followed a list of Victor's varied occupations. Never unkind, or bearing malice to anyone. 'He's always been unlucky, Colonel Race. He was misjudged by his house-master and I consider the authorities at Oxford behaved quite disgracefully. People don't seem to understand that a clever boy with a taste for drawing would think it an excellent joke to imitate someone's handwriting. He did it for the fun of the thing, not for money.' But he'd always been a good son to his mother, and he never failed to let her know when he was in trouble which showed, didn't it, that he trusted her? Only it did seem curious, didn't it, that the jobs people found for him so often seemed to take him out of England. She couldn't help feeling that if only he could be given a nice job, in the Bank of England say, he would settle down much better. He might perhaps live a little out of London and have a little car.

It was quite twenty minutes before Colonel Race, having heard all Victor's perfections and misfortunes, was able to switch Lucilla from the subject of sons to that of servants.

Yes, it was very true what he said, the old-fashioned type of servant didn't exist any longer. Really the trouble people had nowadays! Not that she ought to complain, for really they had been very lucky. Mrs Pound, though she had the misfortune to be slightly deaf, was an excellent woman. Her pastry sometimes a little heavy and a tendency to over-pepper the soup, but really on the whole most reliable – and economical too. She had been there ever since George married and she had made no fuss about going to the country this year, though there had been trouble with the others over that and the parlourmaid had left – but that really was all for the best – an impertinent girl who answered back – besides breaking six of the best wineglasses, not one by one at odd times which might happen to *anybody*, but all at once which really meant gross carelessness, didn't Colonel Race think so?

'Very careless indeed.'

'That is what I told her. And I said to her that I should be obliged to say so in her reference – for I really feel one has a *duty*, Colonel Race. I mean, one should not mislead. Faults should be mentioned as well as good qualities. But the girl was – really – well, quite *insolent* and said that at any rate she hoped that in her next place she wouldn't be in the kind of house where people got bumped off – a dreadful common expression, acquired at the cinema, I believe, and ludicrously inappropriate since poor dear Rosemary took her own life – though not at the time responsible for her actions as the coroner very rightly pointed out – and that dreadful expression refers, I believe, to gangsters executing each other with tommy-guns. I am so thankful that we have nothing of that kind in England. And so, as I say, I put in her reference that Betty Archdale thoroughly understood her duties as parlourmaid and was sober and honest, but that she was inclined to have too many breakages and was not always respectful in her manner. And personally, if *I* had been Mrs Rees-Talbot, I should have read between the lines and not engaged her. But people nowadays just jump at anything they can get, and will sometimes take a girl who has only stayed her month in three places running.'

Whilst Mrs Drake paused to take breath, Colonel Race asked quickly whether that was Mrs Richard Rees-Talbot? If so, he had known her, he said, in India.

'I really couldn't say. Cadogan Square was the address.'

'Then it *is* my friends.'

Lucilla said that the world was such a small place, wasn't it? And that there were no friends like old friends. Friendship was a wonderful thing. She had always thought it had been so romantic about Viola and Paul. Dear Viola, she had been a lovely girl, and so many men in love with her, but, oh dear, Colonel Race wouldn't even know who she was talking about. One did so tend to re-live the past.

Colonel Race begged her to go on and in return for this politeness received the life history of Hector Marle, of his upbringing by his sister, of his peculiarities and his weaknesses and finally, when Colonel Race had almost forgotten her, of his marriage to the beautiful Viola. 'She was an orphan, you know, and a ward in Chancery.' He heard how Paul Bennett, conquering his disappointment at Viola's refusal, had transformed himself from lover to family friend, and of his fondness for his godchild, Rosemary, and of his death and the terms of his will. 'Which I have always felt *most* romantic – such an enormous fortune! Not of course that money is everything – no, indeed. One has only to think of poor Rosemary's tragic death. And even dear Iris I am not quite happy about!'

Race gave her an inquiring look.

'I find the responsibility most worrying. The fact that she is a great heiress is of course well known. I keep a very sharp eye on the undesirable type of young man, but what can one do, Colonel Race? One can't look after girls nowadays as one used to do. Iris has friends I know next to nothing about. "Ask them to the house, dear," is what I always say – but I gather that some of these young men simply will *not* be brought. Poor George was worried, too. About a young man called Browne. I myself have never seen him, but it seems that he and Iris have been seeing a good deal of each other. And one does feel that she could do better. George didn't like him – I'm quite sure of that. And I always think, Colonel Race, that men are so much better judges of other men. I remember thinking Colonel Pusey, one of our churchwardens, such a charming man, but my husband always preserved a very distant attitude towards him and enjoined on me to do the same – and sure enough one Sunday when he was handing round the offertory plate, he fell right down – completely intoxicated, it seems. And of course afterwards – one always hears these things *afterwards*, so much better if one heard them *before* – we found out that dozens of empty brandy bottles were taken out of the house every week! It was very sad really, because he was truly religious, though inclined to be Evangelical in his views. He and my husband had a terrific battle over the details of the service on All Saints' Day. Oh, dear, All Saints' Day. To think that yesterday was All Souls' Day.'

A faint sound made Race look over Lucilla's head at the open doorway. He had seen Iris before – at Little Priors. Nevertheless he felt that he was seeing her now for the first time. He was struck by the extraordinary tension behind her stillness and her wide eyes met his with something in their expression that he felt he ought to recognize, yet failed to do so.

In her turn, Lucilla Drake turned her head.

'Iris, dear, I didn't hear you come in. You know Colonel Race? He is being so very kind.'

Iris came and shook hands with him gravely, the black dress she wore made her look thinner and paler than he remembered her.

'I came to see if I could be of any help to you,' said Race.

'Thank you. That was kind of you.'

She had had a bad shock, that was evident, and was still suffering from the effects of it. But had she been so fond of George that his death could affect her so powerfully?

She turned her eyes to her aunt and Race realized that they were watchful eyes. She said:

'What were you talking about – just now, as I came in?'

Lucilla became pink and flustered. Race guessed that she was anxious to avoid any mention of the young man, Anthony Browne. She exclaimed:

'Now let me see – oh, yes, All Saints' Day – and yesterday being All Souls'. All Souls' – that seems to me such an *odd* thing – one of those coincidences one never believes in in real life.'

'Do you mean,' said Iris, 'that Rosemary came back yesterday to fetch George?'

Lucilla gave a little scream.

'Iris, dear, don't. What a terrible thought – so un-Christian.'

'Why un-Christian? It's the Day of the Dead. In Paris people used to go and put flowers on the graves.'

'Oh, I know, dear, but then they are Catholics, aren't they?'

A faint smile twisted Iris's lips. Then she said directly:

'I thought, perhaps, you were talking of Anthony – Anthony Browne.'

'Well,' Lucilla's twitter became very high and birdlike, 'as a matter of fact we did just *mention* him. I happened to say, you know, that we know *nothing about* him –'

Iris interrupted, her voice hard:

'Why should you know anything about him?'

'No, dear, of course not. At least, I mean, well, it would be rather nice, wouldn't it, if we did?'

'You'll have every chance of doing so in future,' said Iris, 'because I'm going to marry him.'

'Oh, Iris!' It was halfway between a wail and a bleat. 'You mustn't do anything rash – I mean nothing can be settled at present.'

'It *is* settled, Aunt Lucilla.'

'No, dear, one can't talk about things like marriage when the funeral hasn't even taken place yet. It wouldn't be decent. And this dreadful inquest and everything. And really, Iris, I don't think dear George would have approved. He didn't like this Mr Browne.'

'No,' said Iris, 'George wouldn't have liked it and he didn't like Anthony, but that doesn't make any difference. It's my life, not George's – and anyway George is dead . . .'

Mrs Drake gave another wail.

'Iris, Iris. What has come over you? Really that was a most unfeeling thing to say.'

'I'm sorry, Aunt Lucilla.' The girl spoke wearily. 'I know it must have sounded like that but I didn't mean it that way. I only meant that George is at peace somewhere and hasn't got to worry about me and my future any more. I must decide things for myself.'

'Nonsense, dear, nothing can be decided at a time like this – it would be most unfitting. The question simply doesn't arise.'

Iris gave a sudden short laugh.

'But it has arisen. Anthony asked me to marry him before we left Little Priors. He wanted me to come up to London and marry him the next day without telling anyone. I wish now that I had.'

'Surely that was a very curious request,' said Colonel Race gently.

She turned defiant eyes to him.

'No, it wasn't. It would have saved a lot of fuss. Why couldn't I trust him? He asked me to trust him and I didn't. Anyway, I'll marry him now as soon as he likes.'

Lucilla burst out in a stream of incoherent protest. Her plump cheeks quivered and her eyes filled.

Colonel Race took rapid charge of the situation.

'Miss Marle, might I have a word with you before I go? On a strictly business matter?'

Rather startled, the girl murmured 'Yes,' and found herself moving to the door. As she passed through, Race took a couple of strides back to Mrs Drake.

'Don't upset yourself, Mrs Drake. Least said, you know, soonest mended. We'll see what we can do.'

Leaving her slightly comforted he followed Iris who led him across the hall and into a small room giving out on the back of the house where a melancholy plane-tree was shedding its last leaves.

Race spoke in a business-like tone.

'All I had to say, Miss Marle, was that Chief Inspector Kemp is a personal friend of mine, and that I am sure you will find him most helpful and kindly. His duty is an unpleasant one, but I'm sure he will do it with the utmost consideration possible.'

She looked at him for a moment or two without speaking, then she said abruptly:

'Why didn't you come and join us last night as George expected you to do?'

He shook his head.

'George didn't expect me.'

'But he said he did.'

'He may have said so, but it wasn't true. George knew perfectly well that I wasn't coming.'

She said: 'But that empty chair . . . Who was it for?'

'Not for me.'

Her eyes half-closed and her face went very white.

She whispered:

'It was for Rosemary . . . I see . . . It was for Rosemary . . .'

He thought she was going to fall. He came quickly to her and steadied her, then forced her to sit down.

'Take it easy . . .'

She said in a low breathless voice:

'I'm all right . . . But I don't know what to do . . . I don't know what to do.'

'Can I help you?'

She raised her eyes to his face. They were wistful and sombre.

Then she said: 'I must get things clear. I must get them' – she made a groping gesture with her hands – 'in sequence. First of all, George believed Rosemary didn't kill herself – but was killed. He believed that because of those letters. Colonel Race, who wrote those letters?'

'I don't know. Nobody knows. Have you yourself any idea?'

'I simply can't imagine. Anyway, George believed what they said, and he arranged this party last night, and he had an empty chair and it was All Souls' Day . . . that's the Day of the Dead – and it was a day when Rosemary's spirit could have come back and – and told him the truth.'

'You mustn't be too imaginative.'

'But I've felt her myself – felt her quite near sometimes – I'm her sister – and I think she's trying to tell me something.'

'Take it easy, Iris.'

'I *must* talk about it. George drank Rosemary's health and he – died. Perhaps – she came and took him.'

'The spirits of the dead don't put potassium cyanide in a champagne glass, my dear.'

The words seemed to restore her balance. She said in a more normal tone:

'But it's so incredible. George was killed – yes, *killed*. That's what the police think and it must be true. Because there isn't any other alternative. But it doesn't make sense.'

'Don't you think it does? If Rosemary was killed, and George was beginning to suspect by whom –'

She interrupted him.

'Yes, but Rosemary *wasn't* killed. That's why it doesn't make sense. George believed those stupid letters partly because depression after influenza isn't a very convincing reason for killing yourself. But Rosemary *had* a reason. Look, I'll show you.'

She ran out of the room and returned a few moments later with a folded letter in her hand. She thrust it on him.

'Read it. See for yourself.'

He unfolded the slightly crumpled sheet.

'Leopard darling . . .'

He read it twice before handing it back.

The girl said eagerly:

'You see? She was unhappy – broken-hearted. She didn't want to go on living.'

'Do you know to whom that letter was written?'

Iris nodded.

'Stephen Farraday. It wasn't Anthony. She was in love with Stephen and he was cruel to her. So she took the stuff with her to the restaurant and drank it there where he could see her die. Perhaps she hoped he'd be sorry then.'

Race nodded thoughtfully, but said nothing. After a moment or two he said:

'When did you find this?'

'About six months ago. It was in the pocket of an old dressing-gown.'

'You didn't show it to George?'

Iris cried passionately:

'How could I? How could I? Rosemary was my sister. How could I give her away to George? He was so sure that she loved him. How could I show him this after she was dead? He'd got it all wrong, but I couldn't tell *him* so. But what I want to know is, what am I to do *now*? I've shown it to you because you were George's friend. Has Inspector Kemp got to see it?'

'Yes. Kemp must have it. It's evidence, you see.'

'But then they'll – they might read it out in court?'

'Not necessarily. That doesn't follow. It's George's death that is being investigated. Nothing will be made public that is not strictly relevant. You had better let me take this now.'

'Very well.'

She went with him to the front door. As he opened it she said abruptly:

'It does show, doesn't it, that Rosemary's death *was* suicide?'

Race said:

'It certainly shows that she had a motive for taking her own life.'

She gave a deep sigh. He went down the steps. Glancing back once, he saw her standing framed in the open doorway, watching him walk away across the square.

CHAPTER 7

Mary Rees-Talbot greeted Colonel Race with a positive shriek of unbelief.

'My dear, I haven't seen you since you disappeared so mysteriously from Allahabad that time. And why are you here now? It isn't to see me, I'm quite sure. You never pay social calls. Come on now, own up, you needn't be diplomatic about it.'

'Diplomatic methods would be a waste of time with you, Mary. I always have appreciated your X-ray mind.'

'Cut the cackle and come to the horses, my pet.'

Race smiled.

'Is the maid who let me in Betty Archdale?' he inquired.

'So that's it! Now don't tell me that the girl, a pure Cockney if ever there was one, is a well-known European spy because I simply don't believe it.'

'No, no, nothing of the kind.'

'And don't tell me she's one of our counter-espionage either, because I don't believe that.'

'Quite right. The girl is simply a parlourmaid.'

'And since when have you been interested in simple parlourmaids – not that Betty is simple – an artful dodger is more like it.'

'I think,' said Colonel Race, 'that she might be able to tell me something.'

'If you asked her nicely? I shouldn't be surprised if you're right.

She has the close-to-the-door-when-there's-anything-interesting-going-on technique very highly developed. What does M. do?'

'M. very kindly offers me a drink and rings for Betty and orders it.'

'And when Betty brings it?'

'By then M. has very kindly gone away.'

'To do some listening outside the door herself?'

'If she likes.'

'And after that I shall be bursting with Inside Information about the latest European crisis?'

'I'm afraid not. There is no political situation involved in this.'

'What a disappointment! All right. I'll play!'

Mrs Rees-Talbot, who was a lively near-brunette of forty-nine, rang the bell and directed her good-looking parlourmaid to bring Colonel Race a whisky and soda.

When Betty Archdale returned, with a salver and the drink upon it, Mrs Rees-Talbot was standing by the far door into her own sitting-room.

'Colonel Race has some questions to ask you,' she said and went out.

Betty turned her impudent eyes on the tall grey-haired soldier with some alarm in their depths. He took the glass from the tray and smiled.

'Seen the papers today?' he asked.

'Yes, sir.' Betty eyed him warily.

'Did you see that Mr George Barton died last night at the Luxembourg Restaurant?'

'Oh, yes, sir.' Betty's eyes sparkled with the pleasure of public disaster. 'Wasn't it dreadful?'

'You were in service there, weren't you?'

'Yes, sir. I left last winter, soon after Mrs Barton died.'

'She died at the Luxembourg, too.'

Betty nodded. 'Sort of funny, that, isn't it, sir?'

Race did not think it funny, but he knew what the words were intended to convey. He said gravely:

'I see you've got brains. You can put two and two together.'

Betty clasped her hands and cast discretion to the winds.

'Was he done in, too? The papers didn't say exactly.'

'Why do you say "too"? Mrs Barton's death was brought in by the coroner's jury as suicide.'

She gave him a quick look out of the corner of her eye. Ever so old, she thought, but he's nice looking. That quiet kind. A real gentleman. Sort of gentleman who'd have given you a gold sovereign when he was young. Funny, I don't even know what a sovereign looks like! What's he after, exactly?

She said demurely: 'Yes, sir.'

'But perhaps you never thought it *was* suicide?'

'Well, no, sir. I didn't – not really.'

'That's very interesting – very interesting indeed. Why didn't you think so?'

She hesitated, her fingers began pleating her apron.

So nicely he said that, so gravely. Made you feel important and as though you wanted to help him. And anyway she *had* been smart over Rosemary Barton's death. Never been taken in, she hadn't!

'She was done in, sir, wasn't she?'

'It seems possible that it may be so. But how did you come to think so?'

'Well,' Betty hesitated. 'It was something I heard one day.'

'Yes?'

His tone was quietly encouraging.

'The door wasn't shut or anything. I mean I'd never go and listen at a door. I don't like that sort of thing,' said Betty virtuously. 'But I was going through the hall to the dining-room and carrying the silver on a tray and they were speaking quite loud. Saying something she was – Mrs Barton I mean – about Anthony Browne not being his name. And then he got really nasty, Mr Browne did. I wouldn't have thought he had it in him – so nice-looking and so pleasant spoken as he was as a rule. Said something about carving up her face – ooh! and then he said if she didn't do what he told her he'd bump her off. Just like that! I didn't hear any more because Miss Iris was coming down the stairs, and of course I didn't think very much of it at the time, but after there was all the fuss about her committing suicide at that party and I heard he'd been there at the time – well, it gave me shivers all down my back – it did indeed!'

'But you didn't say anything?'

The girl shook her head.

'I didn't want to get mixed up with the police – and anyway I didn't know anything – not really. And perhaps if I had said anything I'd have been bumped off too. Or taken for a ride as they call it.'

'I see.' Race paused a moment and then said in his gentlest voice: 'So you just wrote an anonymous letter to Mr George Barton?'

She stared at him. He detected no uneasy guilt – nothing but pure astonishment.

'Me? Write to Mr Barton? Never.'

'Now don't be afraid to tell about it. It was really a very good idea. It warned him without your having to give yourself away. It was very clever of you.'

'But I didn't, sir. I never thought of such a thing. You mean write to Mr Barton and say that his wife had been done in? Why, the idea never came into my head!'

She was so earnest in her denial that, in spite of himself, Race was shaken. But it all fitted in so well – it could all be explained so naturally if only the girl had written the letters. But she persisted in her denials, not vehemently or uneasily, but soberly and without undue protestation. He found himself reluctantly believing her.

He shifted his ground.

'Whom did you tell about this?'

She shook her head.

'I didn't tell anyone. I'll tell you honest, sir, I was scared. I thought I'd better keep my mouth shut. I tried to forget it. I only brought it up once – that was when I gave Mrs Drake my notice – fussing terribly she'd been, more than a girl could stand, and now wanting me to go and bury myself in the dead of the country and not even a bus route! And then she turned nasty about my reference, saying I broke things, and I said sarcastic-like that at any rate I'd find a place where people didn't get bumped off – and I felt scared when I'd said it, but she didn't pay any real attention. Perhaps I ought to have spoken out at the time, but I couldn't really tell. I mean the whole thing might have been a joke. People do say all sorts of things, and Mr Browne was ever so nice really, and quite a one for joking, so I couldn't tell, sir, could I?'

Race agreed that she couldn't. Then he said:

'Mrs Barton spoke of Browne not being his real name. Did she mention what his real name was?'

'Yes, she did. Because he said, "Forget about Tony" – now what was it? Tony something . . . Reminded me of the cherry jam cook had been making.'

'Tony Cheriton? Cherable.'

She shook her head.

'More of a fancy name than that. Began with an M. And sounded foreign.'

'Don't worry. It will come back to you, perhaps. If so, let me know. Here is my card with my address. If you remember the name write to me at that address.'

He handed her the card and a treasury note.

'I will, sir, thank you, sir.'

A gentleman, she thought, as she ran downstairs. A pound note, not ten shillings. It must have been nice when there were gold sovereigns . . .

Mary Rees-Talbot came back into the room.

'Well, successful?'

'Yes, but there's still one snag to surmount. Can your ingenuity help me? Can you think of a name that would remind you of cherry jam?'

'What an extraordinary proposition.'

'Think Mary. I'm not a domestic man. Concentrate on jam making, cherry jam in particular.'

'One doesn't often make cherry jam.'

'Why not?'

'Well, it's inclined to go sugary – unless you use cooking cherries, Morello cherries.'

Race gave an exclamation.

'That's it – I bet that's it. Goodbye, Mary, I'm endlessly grateful. Do you mind if I ring that bell so that the girl comes and shows me out?'

Mrs Rees-Talbot called after him as he hurried out of the room:

'Of all the ungrateful wretches! Aren't you going to tell me what it's all about?'

He called back:

'I'll come and tell you the whole story later.'

'Sez you,' murmured Mrs Rees-Talbot.

Downstairs, Betty waited with Race's hat and stick.

He thanked her and passed out. On the doorstep he paused.

'By the way,' he said, 'was the name Morelli?'

Betty's face lighted up.

'Quite right, sir. That was it. Tony Morelli that's the name he told her to forget. And he said he'd been in prison, too.'

Race walked down the steps smiling.

From the nearest call-box he put through a call to Kemp.

Their interchange was brief but satisfactory. Kemp said:

'I'll send off a cable at once. We ought to hear by return. I must say it will be a great relief if you're right.'

'I think I'm right. The sequence is pretty clear.'

CHAPTER 8

Chief Inspector Kemp was not in a very good humour.

For the last half-hour he had been interviewing a frightened white rabbit of sixteen who, by virtue of his uncle Charles's great position, was aspiring to be a waiter of the class required by the Luxembourg. In the meantime, he was one of six harried underlings who ran about with aprons round their waists to distinguish them from the superior article, and whose duty it was to bear the blame for everything, fetch and carry, provide rolls and pats of butter and be occasionally and unceasingly hissed at in French, Italian and occasionally English. Charles, as befitted a great man, so far from showing favour to a blood relation, hissed, cursed and swore at him even more than he did at the others. Nevertheless Pierre aspired in his heart to be no less than the head waiter of a *chic* restaurant himself one day in the far future.

At the moment, however, his career had received a check, and he gathered that he was suspected of no less than murder.

Kemp turned the lad inside out and disgustedly convinced himself that the boy had done no less and no more than what he had said – namely, picked up a lady's bag from the floor and replaced it by her plate.

'It is as I am hurrying with sauce to M. Robert and already he is impatient, and the young lady sweeps her bag off the table as she goes to dance, so I pick it up and put it on the table, and then I hurry on, for already M. Robert he is making the signs frantically to me. That is all, monsieur.'

And that *was* all. Kemp disgustedly let him go, feeling strongly tempted to add, 'But don't let me catch you doing that sort of thing again.'

Sergeant Pollock made a distraction by announcing that they had telephoned up to say that a young lady was asking for him or rather for the officer in charge of the Luxembourg case.

'Who is she?'

'Her name is Miss Chloe West.'

'Let's have her up,' said Kemp resignedly. 'I can give her ten minutes. Mr Farraday's due after that. Oh, well, won't do any harm to keep *him* waiting a few minutes. Makes them jittery, that does.'

When Miss Chloe West walked into the room, Kemp was at once assailed by the impression that he recognized her. But a minute later he abandoned that impression. No, he had never seen this girl before, he was sure of that. Nevertheless the vague haunting sense of familiarity remained to plague him.

Miss West was about twenty-five, tall, brown-haired and very pretty.
Her voice was rather conscious of its diction and she seemed decidedly
nervous.

'Well, Miss West, what can I do for you?'

Kemp spoke briskly.

'I read in the paper about the Luxembourg – the man who died
there.'

'Mr George Barton? Yes? Did you know him?'

'Well, no, not exactly. I mean I didn't really *know* him.'

Kemp looked at her carefully and discarded his first deduction.
Chloe West was looking extremely refined and virtuous – severely so.
He said pleasantly:

'Can I have your exact name and address first, please, so that we know
where we are?'

'Chloe Elizabeth West. 15 Merryvale Court, Maida Vale. I'm an
actress.'

Kemp looked at her again out of the corner of his eye, and decided that
that was what she really was. Repertory, he fancied – in spite of her looks
she was the earnest kind.

'Yes, Miss West?'

'When I read about Mr Barton's death and that the – the police were
inquiring into it, I thought perhaps I ought to come and tell you something.
I spoke to my friend about it and she seemed to think so. I don't suppose
it's really anything to do with it, but –' Miss West paused.

'We'll be the judge of that,' said Kemp pleasantly. 'Just tell me about
it.'

'I'm not acting just at the moment,' explained Miss West.

Inspector Kemp nearly said 'Resting' to show that he knew the proper
terms, but restrained himself.

'But my name is down at the agencies and my picture in *Spotlight* . . .
That, I understand, is where Mr Barton saw it. He got into touch with
me and explained what he wanted me to do.'

'Yes?'

'He told me he was having a dinner party at the Luxembourg and that
he wanted to spring a surprise on his guests. He showed me a photograph
and told me that he wanted me to make up as the original. I was very much
the same colouring, he said.'

Illumination flashed across Kemp's mind. The photograph of Rosemary
he had seen on the desk in George's room in Elvaston Square. That was
who the girl reminded him of. She *was* like Rosemary Barton – not

perhaps startlingly so – but the general type and cast of features was the same.

'He also brought me a dress to wear – I've brought it with me. A greyish green silk. I was to do my hair like the photograph (it was a coloured one) and accentuate the resemblance with make-up. Then I was to come to the Luxembourg and go into the restaurant during the first cabaret show and sit down at Mr Barton's table where there would be a vacant place. He took me to lunch there and showed me where the table would be.'

'And why didn't you keep the appointment, Miss West?'

'Because about eight o'clock that night – someone – Mr Barton – rang up and said the whole thing had been put off. He said he'd let me know next day when it was coming off. Then, the next morning, I saw his death in the papers.'

'And very sensibly you came along to us,' said Kemp pleasantly. 'Well, thank you very much, Miss West. You've cleared up one mystery – the mystery of the vacant place. By the way, you said just now – "someone" – and then, "Mr Barton". Why is that?'

'Because at first I didn't think it *was* Mr Barton. His voice sounded different.'

'It was a man's voice?'

'Oh, yes, I think so – at least – it was rather husky as though he had a cold.'

'And that's all he said?'

'That's all.'

Kemp questioned her a little longer, but got no further.

When she had gone, he said to the sergeant:

'So that was George Barton's famous "plan". I see now why they all said he stared at the empty chair after the cabaret and looked queer and absent-minded. His precious plan had gone wrong.'

'You don't think it was he who put her off?'

'Not on your life. And I'm not so sure it was a man's voice, either. Huskiness is a good disguise through the telephone. Oh, well, we're getting on. Send in Mr Farraday if he's here.'

CHAPTER 9

Outwardly cool and unperturbed, Stephen Farraday had turned into Great Scotland Yard full of inner shrinking. An intolerable weight burdened his spirits. It had seemed that morning as though things were going so well. Why had Inspector Kemp asked for his presence here with such significance? What did he know or suspect? It *could* be only vague suspicion. The thing to do was to keep one's head and admit nothing.

He felt strangely bereft and lonely without Sandra. It was as though when the two faced a peril together it lost half its terrors. Together they had strength, courage, power. Alone, he was nothing, less than nothing. And Sandra, did she feel the same? Was she sitting now in Kidderminster House, silent, reserved, proud and inwardly feeling horribly vulnerable?

Inspector Kemp received him pleasantly but gravely. There was a uniformed man sitting at a table with a pencil and a pad of paper. Having asked Stephen to sit down, Kemp spoke in a strongly formal manner.

'I propose, Mr Farraday, to take a statement from you. That statement will be written down and you will be asked to read it over and sign it before you leave. At the same time it is my duty to tell you that you are at liberty to refuse to make such a statement and that you are entitled to have your solicitor present if you so desire.'

Stephen was taken aback but did not show it. He forced a wintry smile. 'That sounds very formidable, chief inspector.'

'We like everything to be clearly understood, Mr Farraday.'

'Anything I say may be used against me, is that it?'

'We don't use the word against. Anything you say will be liable to be used in evidence.'

Stephen said quietly:

'I understand, but I cannot imagine, inspector, why you should need any further statement from me? You heard all I had to say this morning.'

'That was a rather informal session – useful as a preliminary starting-off point. And also, Mr Farraday, there are certain facts which I imagined you would prefer to discuss with me here. Anything irrelevant to the case we try to be as discreet about as is compatible with the attainment of justice. I daresay you understand what I am driving at.'

'I'm afraid I don't.'

Chief Inspector Kemp sighed.

'Just this. You were on very intimate terms with the late Mrs Rosemary Barton –'

Stephen interrupted him.

'Who says so?'

Kemp leaned forward and took a typewritten document from his desk.

'This is a copy of a letter found amongst the late Mrs Barton's belongings. The original is filed here and was handed to us by Miss Iris Marle, who recognizes the writing as that of her sister.'

Stephen read:

'Leopard darling –'

A wave of sickness passed over him. Rosemary's voice . . . speaking – pleading . . . Would the past never die – never consent to be buried?

He pulled himself together and looked at Kemp.

'You may be correct in thinking Mrs Barton wrote this letter – but there is nothing to indicate that it was written to me.'

'Do you deny that you paid the rent of 21 Malland Mansions, Earls Court?'

So they knew! He wondered if they had known all the time.

He shrugged his shoulders.

'You seem very well informed. May I ask why my private affairs should be dragged into the limelight?'

'They will not unless they prove to be relevant to the death of George Barton.'

'I see. You are suggesting that I first made love to his wife, and then murdered him.'

'Come, Mr Farraday, I'll be frank with you. You and Mrs Barton were very close friends – you parted by your wish, not the lady's. She was proposing, as this letter shows, to make trouble. Very conveniently, she died.'

'She committed suicide. I daresay I may have been partly to blame. I may reproach myself, but it is no concern of the law's.'

'It may have been suicide – it may not. George Barton thought not. He started to investigate – and he died. The sequence is rather suggestive.'

'I do not see why you should – well, pitch on me.'

'You admit that Mrs Barton's death came at a very convenient moment for you? A scandal, Mr Farraday, would have been highly prejudicial to your career.'

'There would have been no scandal. Mrs Barton would have seen reason.'

'I wonder! Did your wife know about this affair, Mr Farraday?'

'Certainly not.'

'You are quite sure of that statement?'

'Yes, I am. My wife has no idea that there was anything but friendship between myself and Mrs Barton. I hope she will never learn otherwise.'

'Is your wife a jealous woman, Mr Farraday?'

'Not at all. She has never displayed the least jealousy where I am concerned. She is far too sensible.'

The inspector did not comment on that. Instead he said:

'Have you at any time in the past year had cyanide in your possession, Mr Farraday?'

'No.'

'But you keep a supply of cyanide at your country property?'

'The gardener may. I know nothing about it.'

'You have never purchased any yourself at a chemist's or for photography?'

'I know nothing of photography, and I repeat that I have never purchased cyanide.'

Kemp pressed him a little further before he finally let him go.

To his subordinate he said thoughtfully, 'He was very quick denying that his wife knew about his affair with the Barton woman. Why was that, I wonder?'

'Daresay he's in a funk in case she should get to hear of it, sir.'

'That may be, but I should have thought he'd got the brains to see that if his wife was in ignorance, and would cut up rough, that gives him an additional motive for wanting to silence Rosemary Barton. To save his skin his line ought to have been that his wife more or less knew about the affair but was content to ignore it.'

'I daresay he hadn't thought of that, sir.'

Kemp shook his head. Stephen Farraday was not a fool. He had a clear and astute brain. And he had been passionately keen to impress on the inspector that Sandra knew nothing.

'Well,' said Kemp, 'Colonel Race seems pleased with the line he's dug up and if he's right, the Farradays are out – both of them. I shall be glad if they are. I like this chap. And personally I don't think he's a murderer.'

Opening the door of their sitting-room, Stephen said, 'Sandra?'

She came to him out of the darkness, suddenly holding him, her hands on his shoulders.

'Stephen?'

'Why are you all in the dark?'

'I couldn't bear the light. Tell me.'

He said:

'They know.'

'About Rosemary?'

'Yes.'

'And what do they think?'

'They see, of course, that I had a motive. . . . Oh, my darling, see what I've dragged you into. It's all my fault. If only I'd cut loose after Rosemary's death – gone away – left you free – so that at any rate *you* shouldn't be mixed up in all this horrible business.'

'No, not that . . . Never leave me . . . never leave me.'

She clung to him – she was crying, the tears coursing down her cheeks. He felt her shudder.

'You're my life, Stephen, all my life – never leave me . . .'

'Do you care so much, Sandra? I never knew . . .'

'I didn't want you to know. But now –'

'Yes, now . . . We're in this together, Sandra . . . we'll face it together . . . whatever comes, together!'

Strength came to them as they stood there, clasped together in the darkness.

Sandra said with determination:

'This shall *not* wreck our lives! It shall not. It shall not!'

CHAPTER 10

Anthony Browne looked at the card the little page was holding out to him.

He frowned, then shrugged his shoulders. He said to the boy:

'All right, show him up.'

When Colonel Race came in, Anthony was standing by the window with the bright sun striking obliquely over his shoulder.

He saw a tall soldierly man with a lined bronze face and iron-grey hair – a man whom he had seen before, but not for some years, and a man whom he knew a great deal about.

Race saw a dark graceful figure and the outline of a well-shaped head. A pleasant indolent voice said:

'Colonel Race? You were a friend of George Barton's, I know. He talked about you on that last evening. Have a cigarette.'

'Thank you, I will.'

Anthony said as he held a match:

'You were the unexpected guest that night who did not turn up – just as well for you.'

'You are wrong there. That empty place was not for me.'

Anthony's eyebrows went up.

'Really? Barton said –'

Race cut in.

'George Barton may have said so. His plans were quite different. That chair, Mr Browne, was intended to be occupied when the lights went down by an actress called Chloe West.'

Anthony stared.

'Chloe West? Never heard of her. Who is she?'

'A young actress not very well known but who possesses a certain superficial resemblance to Rosemary Barton.'

Anthony whistled.

'I begin to see.'

'She had been given a photograph of Rosemary so that she could copy the style of hairdressing and she also had the dress which Rosemary wore the night she died.'

'So that was George's plan? Up go the lights – Hey Presto, gasps of supernatural dread! *Rosemary has come back.* The guilty party gasps out: "It's true – it's true – I dunnit."' He paused and added: 'Rotten – even for an ass like poor old George.'

'I'm not sure I understand you.'

Anthony grinned.

'Oh, come now, sir – a hardened criminal isn't going to behave like a hysterical schoolgirl. If somebody poisoned Rosemary Barton in cold blood, and was preparing to administer the same fatal dose of cyanide to George Barton, that person had a certain amount of nerve. It would take more than an actress dressed up as Rosemary to make him or her spill the beans.'

'Macbeth, remember, a decidedly hardened criminal, went to pieces when he saw the ghost of Banquo at the feast.'

'Ah, but what Macbeth saw really *was* a ghost! It wasn't a ham actor wearing Banquo's duds! I'm prepared to admit that a real ghost might bring its own atmosphere from another world. In fact I am willing to admit that I believe in ghosts – have believed in them for the last six months – one ghost in particular.'

'Really – and whose ghost is that?'

'Rosemary Barton's. You can laugh if you like. I've not seen her – but I've felt her presence. For some reason or other Rosemary, poor soul, can't stay dead.'

'I could suggest a reason.'

'Because she was murdered?'

'To put it in another idiom, because she was bumped off. *How about that, Mr Tony Morelli?*'

There was a silence. Anthony sat down, chucked his cigarette into the grate and lighted another one.

Then he said:

'How did you find out?'

'You admit that you are Tony Morelli?'

'I shouldn't dream of wasting time by denying it. You've obviously cabled to America and got all the dope.'

'And you admit that when Rosemary Barton discovered your identity you threatened to bump her off unless she held her tongue.'

'I did everything I could think of to scare her into holding her tongue,' agreed Tony pleasantly.

A strange feeling stole over Colonel Race. This interview was not going as it should. He stared at the figure in front of him lounging back in its chair – and an odd sense of familiarity came to him.

'Shall I recapitulate what I know about you, Morelli?'

'It might be amusing.'

'You were convicted in the States of attempted sabotage in the Ericsen aeroplane works and were sentenced to a term of imprisonment. After serving your sentence, you came out and the authorities lost sight of you. You were next heard of in London staying at Claridge's and calling yourself Anthony Browne. There you scraped acquaintance with Lord Dewsbury and through him you met certain other prominent armaments manufacturers. You stayed in Lord Dewsbury's house and by means of your position as his guest you were shown things which you ought never to have seen! It is curious coincidence, Morelli, that a trail of unaccountable accidents and some very near escapes from disaster on a large scale followed very closely after your visits to various important works and factories.'

'Coincidences,' said Anthony, 'are certainly extraordinary things.'

'Finally, after another lapse of time, you reappeared in London and renewed your acquaintance with Iris Marle, making excuses not to visit her home, so that her family should not realize how intimate you were becoming. Finally you tried to induce her to marry you secretly.'

'You know,' said Anthony, 'it's really extraordinary the way you have found out all these things – I don't mean the armaments business – I mean my threats to Rosemary, and the tender nothings I whispered to Iris. Surely those don't come within the province of M.I.5?'

Race looked sharply at him.

'You've got a good deal to explain, Morelli.'

'Not at all. Granted your facts are all correct, what of them? I've served my prison sentence. I've made some interesting friends. I've fallen in love with a very charming girl and am naturally impatient to marry her.'

'So impatient that you would prefer the wedding to take place before her family have the chance of finding out anything about your antecedents. Iris Marle is a very rich young woman.'

Anthony nodded his head agreeably.

'I know. When there's money, families are inclined to be abominably nosy. And Iris, you see, doesn't know anything about my murky past. Frankly, I'd rather she didn't.'

'I'm afraid she is going to know all about it.'

'A pity,' said Anthony.

'Possibly you don't realize –'

Anthony cut in with a laugh.

'Oh! I can dot the i's and cross the t's. Rosemary Barton knew my criminal past, so I killed her. George Barton was growing suspicious of me, so I killed him! Now I'm after Iris's money! It's all very agreeable and it hangs together nicely, but you haven't got a mite of proof.'

Race looked at him attentively for some minutes. Then he got up.

'Everything I have said is true,' he said. *'And it's all wrong.'*

Anthony watched him narrowly.

'What's wrong?'

'You're wrong.' Race walked slowly up and down the room. 'It hung together all right until I saw you – but now I've seen you, *it won't do. You're not a crook.* And if you're not a crook, you're one of *our* kind. I'm right, aren't I?'

Anthony looked at him in silence while a smile slowly broadened on his face. Then he hummed softly under his breath.

'*"For the Colonel's lady and Judy O'Grady are sisters under the skin."* Yes, funny how one knows one's own kind. That's why I've tried to avoid meeting you. I was afraid you'd spot me for what I am. It was important then that nobody should know – important up to yesterday.

Now, thank goodness, the balloon's gone up! We've swept our gang of international saboteurs into the net. I've been working on this assignment for three years. Frequenting certain meetings, agitating among workmen, getting myself the right reputation. Finally it was fixed that I pulled an important job and got sentenced. The business had to be genuine if I was to establish my *bona fides*.

'When I came out, things began to move. Little by little I got further into the centre of things – a great international net run from Central Europe. It was as *their* agent I came to London and went to Claridge's. I had orders to get on friendly terms with Lord Dewsbury – that was my lay, the social butterfly! I got to know Rosemary Barton in my character of attractive young man about town. Suddenly, to my horror, I found that she knew I had been in prison in America as Tony Morelli. I was terrified for *her*! The people I was working with would have had her killed without a moment's hesitation if they had thought she knew that. I did my best to scare her into keeping her mouth shut, but I wasn't very hopeful. Rosemary was born to be indiscreet. I thought the best thing I could do was to sheer off – and then I saw Iris coming down a staircase, and I swore that after my job was done I would come back and marry her.

'When the active part of my work was over, I turned up again and got into touch with Iris, but I kept aloof from the house and her people for I knew they'd want to make inquiries about me and I had to keep under cover for a bit longer. But I got worried about her. She looked ill and afraid – and George Barton seemed to be behaving in a very odd fashion. I urged her to come away and marry me. Well, she refused. Perhaps she was right. And then I was roped in for this party. It was as we sat down to dinner that George mentioned *you* were to be there. I said rather quickly that I'd met a man I knew and might have to leave early. Actually I *had* seen a fellow I knew in America – Monkey Coleman – though he didn't remember me – but I really wanted to avoid meeting you. I was still on my job.

'You know what happened next – George died. I had nothing to do with his death or with Rosemary's. I don't know now who did kill them.'

'Not even an idea?'

'It must have been either the waiter or one of the five people round the table. I don't think it was the waiter. It wasn't me and it wasn't Iris. It could have been Sandra Farraday or it could have been Stephen Farraday, or it could have been both of them together. But the best bet, in my opinion, is Ruth Lessing.'

'Have you anything to support that belief?'

'No. She seems to me the most likely person – but I don't see in the least how she did it! In both tragedies she was so placed at the table that it would be practically impossible for her to tamper with the champagne glass – and the more I think over what happened the other night, the more it seems to me impossible that George could have been poisoned at all – and yet he was!' Anthony paused. 'And there's another thing that gets me – have you found out who wrote those anonymous letters that started him on the track?'

Race shook his head.

'No. I thought I had – but I was wrong.'

'Because the interesting thing is that it means that there is *someone, somewhere,* who knows that Rosemary was murdered, so that, unless you're careful – that person will be murdered next!'

CHAPTER 11

From information received over the telephone Anthony knew that Lucilla Drake was going out at five o'clock to drink a cup of tea with a dear old friend. Allowing for possible contingencies (returning for a purse, determination after all to take an umbrella just in case, and last-minute chats on the doorstep) Anthony timed his own arrival at Elvaston Square at precisely twenty-five minutes past five. It was Iris he wanted to see, not her aunt. And by all accounts once shown into Lucilla's presence, he would have had very little chance of uninterrupted conversation with his lady.

He was told by the parlourmaid (a girl lacking the impudent polish of Betty Archdale) that Miss Iris had just come in and was in the study.

Anthony said with a smile, 'Don't bother. I'll find my way,' and went past her and along to the study door.

Iris spun round at his entrance with a nervous start.

'Oh, it's you.'

He came over to her swiftly.

'What's the matter, darling?'

'Nothing.' She paused, then said quickly, 'Nothing. Only I was nearly run over. Oh, my own fault, I expect I was thinking so hard and mooning across the road without looking, and the car came tearing round a corner and just missed me.'

He gave her a gentle little shake.

'You mustn't do that sort of thing, Iris. I'm worried about you – oh! not about your miraculous escape from under the wheels of a car, but about the reason that lets you moon about in the midst of traffic. What is it, darling? There's something special, isn't there?'

She nodded. Her eyes, raised mournfully to his, were large and dark with fear. He recognized their message even before she said very low and quick:

'*I'm afraid.*'

Anthony recovered his calm smiling poise. He sat down beside Iris on a wide settee.

'Come on,' he said, 'let's have it.'

'I don't think I want to tell you, Anthony.'

'Now then, funny, don't be like the heroines of third-rate thrillers who start in the very first chapter by having something they can't possibly tell for no real reason except to gum up the hero and make the book spin itself out for another fifty thousand words.'

She gave a faint pale smile.

'I want to tell you, Anthony, but I don't know what you'd think – I don't know if you'd believe –'

Anthony raised a hand and began to check off the fingers.

'One, an illegitimate baby. Two, a blackmailing lover. Three –'

She interrupted him indignantly:

'Of course not. Nothing of *that* kind.'

'You relieve my mind,' said Anthony. 'Come on, little idiot.'

Iris's face clouded over again.

'It's nothing to laugh at. It's – it's about the other night.'

'Yes?' His voice sharpened.

Iris said:

'You were at the inquest this morning – you heard –'

She paused.

'Very little,' said Anthony. 'The police surgeon being technical about cyanides generally and the effect of potassium cyanide on George, and the police evidence as given by that first inspector, not Kemp, the one with the smart moustache who arrived first at the Luxembourg and took charge. Identification of the body by George's chief clerk. The inquest was then adjourned for a week by a properly docile coroner.'

'It's the inspector I mean,' said Iris. 'He described finding a small paper packet under the table containing traces of potassium cyanide.'

Anthony looked interested.

'Yes. Obviously whoever slipped that stuff into George's glass just dropped the paper that had contained it under the table. Simplest thing to do. Couldn't risk having it found on him – or her.'

To his surprise Iris began to tremble violently.

'Oh, no, Anthony. Oh, no, it wasn't like that.'

'What do you mean, darling? What do you know about it?'

Iris said, '*I* dropped that packet under the table.'

He turned astonished eyes upon her.

'Listen, Anthony. You remember how George drank off that champagne and then it happened?'

He nodded.

'It was awful – like a bad dream. Coming just when everything had seemed to be all right. I mean that, after the cabaret, when the lights went up – I felt so relieved. Because it was *then*, you know, that we found Rosemary dead – and somehow, I don't know why, I felt I'd see it all happen again . . . I felt she was there, dead, at the table . . .'

'Darling . . .'

'Oh, I know. It was just nerves. But anyway, there we were, and there was nothing awful and suddenly it seemed the whole thing was really done with at last and one could – I don't know how to explain it – *begin again*. And so I danced with George and really felt I was enjoying myself at last, and we came back to the table. And then George suddenly talked about Rosemary and asked us to drink to her memory and then *he* died and all the nightmare had come back.

'I just felt paralysed I think. I stood there, shaking. You came round to look at him, and I moved back a little, and the waiters came and someone asked for a doctor. And all the time I was standing there frozen. Then suddenly a big lump came in my throat and tears began to run down my cheeks and I jerked open my bag to get my handkerchief. I just fumbled in it, not seeing properly, and got out my handkerchief, but there was something caught up inside the handkerchief – a folded stiff bit of white paper, like the kind you get powders in from the chemist. Only, you see, Anthony, *it hadn't been in my bag when I started from home.* I hadn't had anything like that! I'd put the things in myself when the bag was quite empty – a powder compact, a lip-stick, my handkerchief, my evening comb in its case and a shilling and a couple of sixpences. *Somebody had put that packet in my bag* – they must have done. And I remembered how they'd found a packet like that in Rosemary's bag after she died and how it had had cyanide in it. I was frightened, Anthony, I was horribly frightened. My fingers went limp and the packet fluttered down from my handkerchief under the table. I let it go. And I didn't say anything. I was too frightened. Somebody meant it to look as though *I* had killed George, and I *didn't*.'

Anthony gave vent to a long and prolonged whistle.

'And nobody saw you?' he said.

Iris hesitated.

'I'm not sure,' she said slowly. 'I believe Ruth noticed. But she was looking so dazed that I don't know whether she really *noticed* – or if she was just staring at me blankly.'

Anthony gave another whistle.

'This,' he remarked, 'is a pretty kettle of fish.'

Iris said:

'It's got worse and worse. I've been so afraid they'd find out.'

'Why weren't your fingerprints on it, I wonder? The first thing they'd do would be to fingerprint it.'

'I suppose it was because I was holding it through the handkerchief.'

Anthony nodded.

'Yes, you had luck there.'

'But who could have put it in my bag? I had my bag with me all the evening.'

'That's not so impossible as you think. When you went to dance after the cabaret, you left your bag on the table. Somebody may have tampered with it then. And there are the women. Could you get up and give me an imitation of just how a woman behaves in the ladies' cloakroom? It's the sort of thing I wouldn't know. Do you congregate and chat or do you drift off to different mirrors?'

Iris considered.

'We all went to the same table – a great long glass-topped one. And we put our bags down and looked at our faces, you know.'

'Actually I don't. Go on.'

'Ruth powdered her nose and Sandra patted her hair and pushed a hairpin in and I took off my fox cape and gave it to the woman and then I saw I'd got some dirt on my hand – a smear of mud and I went over to the washbasins.'

'Leaving your bag on the glass table?'

'Yes. And I washed my hands. Ruth was still fixing her face I think and Sandra went and gave up her cloak and then she went back to the glass and Ruth came and washed her hands and I went back to the table and just fixed my hair a little.'

'So either of those two could have put something in your bag without your seeing?'

'Yes, but I can't believe either Ruth or Sandra would do such a thing.'

'You think too highly of people. Sandra is the kind of Gothic creature who would have burned her enemies at the stake in the Middle Ages – and Ruth would make the most devastatingly practical poisoner that ever stepped this earth.'

'If it was Ruth why didn't she say she saw me drop it?'

'You have me there. If Ruth deliberately planted cyanide on you, she'd take jolly good care you didn't get rid of it. So it looks as though it wasn't Ruth. In fact the waiter is far and away the best bet. The waiter, the waiter! If only we had a strange waiter, a peculiar waiter, a waiter hired for that evening only. But instead we have Giuseppe and Pierre and they just don't fit . . .'

Iris sighed.

'I'm glad I've told you. No one will ever know now, will they? Only you and I?'

Anthony looked at her with a rather embarrassed expression.

'It's not going to be just like that, Iris. In fact you're coming with me now in a taxi to old man Kemp. We can't keep this under our hats.'

'Oh, no, Anthony. They'll think I killed George.'

'They'll certainly think so if they find out later that you sat tight and said nothing about all this! Your explanation will then sound extremely thin. If you volunteer it now there's a likelihood of its being believed.'

'Please, Anthony.'

'Look here, Iris, you're in a tight place. But apart from anything else, there's such a thing as *truth*. You can't play safe and take care of your own skin when it's a question of justice.'

'Oh, Anthony, must you be so grand?'

'That,' said Anthony, 'was a very shrewd blow! But all the same we're going to Kemp! Now!'

Unwillingly she came with him out into the hall. Her coat was lying tossed on a chair and he took it and held it out for her to put on.

There was both mutiny and fear in her eyes, but Anthony showed no sign of relenting. He said:

'We'll pick up a taxi at the end of the Square.'

As they went towards the hall door the bell was pressed and they heard it ringing in the basement below.

Iris gave an exclamation.

'I forgot. It's Ruth. She was coming here when she left the office to settle about the funeral arrangements. It's to be the day after tomorrow.

I thought we could settle things better while Aunt Lucilla was out. She does confuse things so.'

Anthony stepped forward and opened the door, forestalling the parlour-maid who came running up the stairs from below.

'It's all right, Evans,' said Iris, and the girl went down again.

Ruth was looking tired and rather dishevelled. She was carrying a large-sized attaché case.

'I'm sorry I'm late, but the tube was so terribly crowded tonight and then I had to wait for three buses and not a taxi in sight.'

It was, thought Anthony, unlike the efficient Ruth to apologize. Another sign that George's death had succeeded in shattering that almost inhuman efficiency.

Iris said:

'I can't come with you now, Anthony. Ruth and I must settle things.'

Anthony said firmly:

'I'm afraid this is more important . . . I'm awfully sorry, Miss Lessing, to drag Iris off like this, but it really *is* important.'

Ruth said quickly:

'That's quite all right, Mr Browne. I can arrange everything with Mrs Drake when she comes in.' She smiled faintly. 'I can really manage her quite well, you know.'

'I'm sure you could manage anyone, Miss Lessing,' said Anthony admiringly.

'Perhaps, Iris, if you can tell me any special points?'

'There aren't any. I suggested our arranging this together simply because Aunt Lucilla changes her mind about everything every two minutes, and I thought it would be rather hard on you. You've had so much to do. But I really don't care what sort of funeral it is! Aunt Lucilla *likes* funerals, but I hate them. You've got to bury people, but I hate making a fuss about it. It can't matter to the people themselves. They've got away from it all. The dead don't come back.'

Ruth did not answer, and Iris repeated with a strange defiant insistence: 'The dead don't come back!'

'Come on,' said Anthony, and pulled her out through the open door.

A cruising taxi was coming slowly along the Square. Anthony hailed it and helped Iris in.

'Tell me, beautiful,' he said, after he had directed the driver to go to Scotland Yard. 'Who exactly did you feel was there in the hall when you found it so necessary to affirm that the dead are dead? Was it George or Rosemary?'

'Nobody! Nobody at all! I just hate funerals, I tell you.'

Anthony sighed.

'Definitely,' he said. 'I must be psychic!'

CHAPTER 12

Three men sat at a small round marble-topped table.

Colonel Race and Chief Inspector Kemp were drinking cups of dark brown tea, rich in tannin. Anthony was drinking an English café's idea of a nice cup of coffee. It was not Anthony's idea, but he endured it for the sake of being admitted on equal terms to the other two men's conference. Chief Inspector Kemp, having painstakingly verified Anthony's credentials, had consented to recognize him as a colleague.

'If you ask me,' said the chief inspector, dropping several lumps of sugar into his black brew and stirring it, 'this case will never be brought to trial. We'll never get the evidence.'

'You think not?' asked Race.

Kemp shook his head and took an approving sip of his tea.

'The only hope was to get evidence concerning the actual purchasing or handling of cyanide by one of those five. I've drawn a blank everywhere. It'll be one of those cases where you *know* who did it, and can't ever prove it.'

'So you know who did it?' Anthony regarded him with interest.

'Well, I'm pretty certain in my own mind. Lady Alexandra Farraday.'

'So that's your bet,' said Race. 'Reasons?'

'You shall have 'em. I'd say she's the type that's madly jealous. And autocratic, too. Like that queen in history – Eleanor of Something, that followed the clue to Fair Rosamund's Bower and offered her the choice of a dagger or a cup of poison.'

'Only in this case,' said Anthony, 'she didn't offer Fair Rosemary any choice.'

Chief Inspector Kemp went on:

'Someone tips Mr Barton off. He becomes suspicious – and I should say his suspicions were pretty definite. He wouldn't have gone so far as actually buying a house in the country unless he wanted to keep an eye on the Farradays. He must have made it pretty plain to her – harping on this party and urging them to come to it. She's not the kind to Wait and See. Autocratic again, she finished him off! That, you say so far, is all theory and based on character. But I'll say that the *only* person who could have had any chance whatever of dropping something into Mr Barton's glass just before he drank would be the lady on his right.'

'And nobody saw her do it?' said Anthony.

'Quite. They might have – but they didn't. Say, if you like, she was pretty adroit.'

'A positive conjurer.'

Race coughed. He took out his pipe and began stuffing the bowl.

'Just one minor point. Granted Lady Alexandra is autocratic, jealous and passionately devoted to her husband, granted that she'd not stick at murder, do you think she is the type to slip incriminating evidence into a girl's handbag? A perfectly innocent girl, mind, who has never harmed her in any way? Is that in the Kidderminster tradition?'

Inspector Kemp squirmed uneasily in his seat and peered into his teacup.

'Women don't play cricket,' he said. 'If that's what you mean.'

'Actually, a lot of them do,' said Race, smiling. 'But I'm glad to see you look uncomfortable.'

Kemp escaped from his dilemma by turning to Anthony with an air of gracious patronage.

'By the way, Mr Browne (I'll still call you that, if you don't mind), I want to say that I'm very much obliged to you for the prompt way you brought Miss Marle along this evening to tell that story of hers.'

'I had to do it promptly,' said Anthony. 'If I'd waited I should probably not have brought her along at all.'

'She didn't want to come, of course,' said Colonel Race.

'She's got the wind up badly, poor kid,' said Anthony. 'Quite natural, I think.'

'Very natural,' said the inspector and poured himself out another cup of tea. Anthony took a gingerly sip of coffee.

'Well,' said Kemp. 'I think we relieved her mind – she went off home quite happily.'

'After the funeral,' said Anthony, 'I hope she'll get away to the country for a bit. Twenty-four hours' peace and quiet away from Auntie Lucilla's non-stop tongue will do her good, I think.'

'Aunt Lucilla's tongue has its uses,' said Race.

'You're welcome to it,' said Kemp. 'Lucky I didn't think it necessary to have a shorthand report made when I took her statement. If I had, the poor fellow would have been in hospital with writer's cramp.'

'Well,' said Anthony. 'I daresay you're right, chief inspector, in saying that the case will never come to trial – but that's a very unsatisfactory finish – and there's one thing we still don't know – who wrote those letters to George Barton telling him his wife was murdered? We haven't the least idea who that person is.'

Race said: 'Your suspicions still the same, Browne?'

'Ruth Lessing? Yes, I stick to her as my candidate. You told me that she admitted to you she was in love with George. Rosemary by all accounts was pretty poisonous to her. Say she saw suddenly a good chance of getting rid of Rosemary, and was fairly convinced that with Rosemary out of the way, she could marry George out of hand.'

'I grant you all that,' said Race. 'I'll admit that Ruth Lessing has the calm practical efficiency that can contemplate and carry out murder, and that she perhaps lacks that quality of pity which is essentially a product of imagination. Yes, I give you the first murder. But I simply can't see her committing the second one. I simply cannot see her panicking and poisoning the man she loved and wanted to marry! Another point that rules her out – why did she hold her tongue when she saw Iris throw the cyanide packet under the table?'

'Perhaps she didn't see her do it,' suggested Anthony, rather doubtfully.

'I'm fairly sure she did,' said Race. 'When I was questioning her, I had the impression that she was keeping something back. And Iris Marle herself thought Ruth Lessing saw her.'

'Come now, colonel,' said Kemp. 'Let's have your "spot". You've got one, I suppose?'

Race nodded.

'Out with it. Fair's fair. You've listened to ours – *and* raised objections.'

Race's eyes went thoughtfully from Kemp's face to Anthony and rested there.

Anthony's eyebrows rose.

Don't say you still think I am the villain of the piece?'

Slowly Race shook his head.

'I can imagine no possible reason why you should kill George Barton. I think I know who did kill him – and Rosemary Barton too.'

'Who is it?'

Race said musingly:

'Curious how we have all selected women as suspects. I suspect a woman, too.' He paused and said quietly: 'I think the guilty person is Iris Marle.'

With a crash Anthony pushed his chair back. For a moment his face went dark crimson – then with an effort, he regained command of himself. His voice, when he spoke, had a slight tremor but was deliberately as light and mocking as ever.

'By all means let us discuss the possibility,' he said. 'Why Iris Marle? And if so, why should she, of her own accord, tell me about dropping the cyanide paper under the table?'

'Because,' said Race, 'she knew that Ruth Lessing had seen her do it.'

Anthony considered the reply, his head on one side. Finally he nodded.

'Passed,' he said. 'Go on. Why did you suspect her in the first place?'

'Motive,' said Race. 'An enormous fortune had been left to Rosemary in which Iris was not to participate. For all we know she may have struggled for years with a sense of unfairness. She was aware that if Rosemary died childless, all that money came to her. And Rosemary was depressed, unhappy, run down after 'flu, just the mood when a verdict of suicide would be accepted without question.'

'That's right, make the girl out a monster!' said Anthony.

'Not a monster,' said Race. 'There is another reason why I suspected her – a far-fetched one, it may seem to you – Victor Drake.'

'Victor Drake?' Anthony stared.

'Bad blood. You see, I didn't listen to Lucilla Drake for nothing. I know all about the Marle family. Victor Drake – not so much weak as positively evil. His mother, feeble in intellect and incapable of concentration. Hector Marle, weak, vicious and a drunkard. Rosemary, emotionally unstable. A family history of weakness, vice and instability. Predisposing causes.'

Anthony lit a cigarette. His hands trembled.

'Don't you believe that there may be a sound blossom on a weak or even a bad stock?'

'Of course there may. But I am not sure that Iris Marle *is* a sound blossom.'

'And my word doesn't count,' said Anthony slowly, 'because I'm in love with her. George showed her those letters, and she got in a funk and killed him? That's how it goes on, is it?'

'Yes. Panic *would* obtain in her case.'

'And how did she get the stuff into George's champagne glass?'

'That, I confess, I do not know.'

'I'm thankful there's something you don't know.' Anthony tilted his chair back and then forward. His eyes were angry and dangerous. 'You've got a nerve saying all this to me.'

Race replied quietly:

'I know. But I consider it had to be said.'

Kemp watched them both with interest, but he did not speak. He stirred his tea round and round absent-mindedly.

'Very well.' Anthony sat upright. 'Things have changed. It's no longer a question of sitting round a table, drinking disgusting fluids, and airing academic theories. This case has *got* to be solved. We've *got* to resolve all the difficulties and get at the truth. That's got to be my job – and I'll do it somehow. I've got to hammer at the things we don't know – because when we do know them, the whole thing will be clear.

'I'll re-state the problem. Who knew that Rosemary had been murdered? Who wrote to George telling him so? Why did they write to him?

'And now the murders themselves. Wash out the first one. It's too long ago, and we don't know exactly what happened. But the second murder took place in front of my eyes. I *saw* it happen. Therefore I ought to know *how* it happened. The ideal time to put the cyanide in George's glass was during the cabaret – but it couldn't have been put in then because he drank from his glass immediately afterwards. I *saw* him drink. After he drank, nobody put anything in his glass. Nobody touched his glass, nevertheless next time he drank, it was full of cyanide. He *couldn't* have been poisoned – but he was! There was cyanide in his glass – *but nobody could have put it there!* Are we getting on?'

'No,' said Chief Inspector Kemp.

'Yes,' said Anthony. 'The thing has now entered into the realm of a conjuring trick. Or a spirit manifestation. I will now outline my psychic theory. Whilst we were dancing, the ghost of Rosemary hovers near George's glass and drops in some cleverly materialized cyanide – any spirit can make cyanide out of ectoplasm. George comes back and drinks her health and – oh, *Lord!*'

The other two stared curiously at him. His hands were holding his head. He rocked to and fro in apparent mental agony. He said:

'That's it . . . that's it . . . the bag . . . the waiter . . .'

'The waiter?' Kemp was alert.

Anthony shook his head.

'No, no. I don't mean what you mean. I did think once that what we needed was a waiter who was not a waiter but a conjurer – a waiter who had been engaged the day before. Instead we had a waiter who had always been a waiter – and a little waiter who was of the royal line of waiters – a cherubic waiter – a waiter above suspicion. And he's still above suspicion – but he played his part! Oh, Lord, yes, he played a star part.'

He stared at them.

'Don't you see it? *A* waiter could have poisoned the champagne but *the* waiter didn't. Nobody touched George's glass but George was poisoned. *A*, indefinite article. *The*, definite article. George's glass! George! Two separate things. And the money – lots and lots of money! And who knows – perhaps love as well? Don't look at me as though I'm mad. Come on, I'll show you.'

Thrusting his chair back he sprang to his feet and caught Kemp by the arm.

'Come with me.'

Kemp cast a regretful glance at his half-full cup.

'Got to pay,' he muttered.

'No, no, we'll be back in a moment. Come on. I must show you outside. Come on, Race.'

Pushing the table aside, he swept them away with him to the vestibule.

'You see that telephone box there?'

'Yes?'

Anthony felt in his pockets.

'Damn, I haven't got twopence. Never mind. On second thoughts I'd rather not do it that way. Come back.'

They went back into the café, Kemp first, Race following with Anthony's hand on his arm.

Kemp had a frown on his face as he sat down and picked up his pipe. He blew down it carefully and began to operate on it with a hairpin which he brought out of his waistcoat pocket.

Race was frowning at Anthony with a puzzled face. He leaned back and picked up his cup, draining the remaining fluid in it.

'Damn,' he said violently. 'It's got sugar in it!'

He looked across the table to meet Anthony's slowly widening smile.

'Hallo,' said Kemp, as he took a sip from his cup. 'What the hell's this?'

'Coffee,' said Anthony. 'And I don't think you'll like it. I didn't.'

CHAPTER 13

Anthony had the pleasure of seeing instant comprehension flash into the eyes of both his companions.

His satisfaction was short-lived, for another thought struck him with the force of a physical blow.

He ejaculated out loud:

'My God – that *car*!'

He sprang up.

'Fool that I was – idiot! She told me that a car had nearly run her down – and I hardly listened. Come on, quick!'

Kemp said:

'She said she was going straight home when she left the Yard.'

'Yes. Why didn't I go with her?'

'Who's at the house?' asked Race.

'Ruth Lessing was there, waiting for Mrs Drake. It's possible that they're both discussing the funeral still!'

'Discussing everything else as well if I know Mrs Drake,' said Race. He added abruptly, 'Has Iris Marle any other relations?'

'Not that I know of.'

'I think I see the direction in which your thoughts, ideas, are leading you. But – is it physically possible?'

'I think so. Consider for yourself how much has been taken for granted *on one person's word.*'

Kemp was paying the check. The three men hurried out as Kemp said:

'You think the danger is acute? To Miss Marle?'

'Yes, I do.'

Anthony swore under his breath and hailed a taxi. The three men got in and the driver was told to go to Elvaston Square as quickly as possible.

Kemp said slowly:

'I've only got the general idea as yet. It washes the Farradays right out.'

'Yes.'

'Thank goodness for that. But surely there wouldn't be another attempt – so soon?'

'The sooner the better,' said Race. 'Before there's any chance of our minds running on the right track. Third time lucky – that will be the idea.' He added: 'Iris Marle told me, in front of Mrs Drake, that she would marry you as soon as you wanted her to.'

They spoke in spasmodic jerks, for the taxi-driver was taking their directions literally and was hurtling round corners and cutting through traffic with immense enthusiasm.

Turning with a final spurt into Elvaston Square, he drew up with a terrific jerk in front of the house.

Elvaston Square had never looked more peaceful.

Anthony, with an effort regained his usual cool manner, murmured:

'Quite like the movies. Makes one feel rather a fool, somehow.'

But he was on the top step ringing the bell while Race paid off the taxi and Kemp followed up the steps.

The parlourmaid opened the door.

Anthony said sharply:

'Has Miss Iris got back?'

Evans looked a little surprised.

'Oh, yes, sir. She came in half an hour ago.'

Anthony breathed a sigh of relief. Everything in the house was so calm and normal that he felt ashamed of his recent melodramatic fears.

'Where is she?'

'I expect she's in the drawing-room with Mrs Drake.'

Anthony nodded and took the stairs in easy strides, Race and Kemp close behind him.

In the drawing-room, placid under its shaded electric lights, Lucilla Drake was hunting through the pigeon holes of the desk with the hopeful absorption of a terrier and murmuring audibly:

'Dear, dear, now where *did* I put Mrs Marsham's letter? Now, let me see . . .'

'Where's Iris?' demanded Anthony abruptly.

Lucilla turned and stared.

'Iris? She – I beg your pardon!' She drew herself up. 'May I ask who you *are*?'

Race came forward from behind him and Lucilla's face cleared. She did not yet see Chief Inspector Kemp who was the third to enter the room.

'Oh, dear, Colonel Race! How kind of you to come! But I do wish you could have been here a little earlier – I *should* have liked to consult you about the funeral arrangements – a man's advice, so valuable – and really I was feeling so upset, as I said to Miss Lessing, that really I couldn't even *think* – and I must say that Miss Lessing was really very sympathetic for once and offered to do everything she could to take the burden off my shoulders – only, as she put it very reasonably, naturally *I* should be the person most likely to know what were George's favourite hymns – not that I actually *did*, because I'm afraid George didn't very often go to church – but naturally, as a clergyman's wife – I mean widow – I do know what is *suitable* –'

Race took advantage of a momentary pause to slip in his question: 'Where is Miss Marle?'

'Iris? She came in some time ago. She said she had a headache and was

going straight up to her room. Young girls, you know, do not seem to me
to have very much stamina nowadays – they don't eat enough spinach –
and she seems positively to dislike talking about the funeral arrangements,
but after all, *someone* has to do these things – and one does want to feel
that everything has been done for the best, and proper respect shown to
the dead – not that I have ever thought motor hearses really *reverent* – if
you know what I mean – not like horses with their long black tails – but,
of course, I said at once that it was quite all right, and Ruth – I called
her Ruth and not Miss Lessing – and I were managing splendidly, and
she could leave everything to us.'

Kemp asked:

'Miss Lessing has gone?'

'Yes, we settled everything, and Miss Lessing left about ten minutes
ago. She took the announcements for the papers with her. No flowers,
under the circumstances – and Canon Westbury to take the service –'

As the flow went on, Anthony edged gently out of the door. He had
left the room before Lucilla, suddenly interrupting her narrative, paused
to say: 'Who *was* that young man who came with you? I didn't realize at
first that *you* had brought him. I thought possibly he might have been one
of those dreadful reporters. We have had such *trouble* with them.'

Anthony was running lightly up the stairs. Hearing footsteps behind
him, he turned his head, and grinned at Chief Inspector Kemp.

'You deserted too? Poor old Race!'

Kemp muttered.

'He does these things so nicely. I'm not popular in that quarter.'

They were on the second floor and just preparing to start up the third
when Anthony heard a light footstep descending. He pulled Kemp inside
an adjacent bathroom door.

The footsteps went on down the stairs.

Anthony emerged and ran up the next flight of stairs. Iris's room,
he knew, was the small one at the back. He rapped lightly on the
door.

'Hi – Iris.' There was no reply – and he knocked and called again. Then
he tried the handle but found the door locked.

With real urgency now he beat upon it.

'Iris – Iris –'

After a second or two, he stopped and glanced down. He was standing
on one of those woolly old-fashioned rugs made to fit outside doors
to obviate draughts. This one was close up against the door. Anthony
kicked it away. The space under the door at the bottom was quite wide

– sometime, he deduced, it had been cut to clear a fitted carpet instead of stained boards.

He stooped to the keyhole but could see nothing, but suddenly he raised his head and sniffed. Then he lay down flat and pressed his nose against the crack under the door.

Springing up, he shouted: 'Kemp!'

There was no sign of the chief inspector. Anthony shouted again.

It was Colonel Race, however, who came running up the stairs. Anthony gave him no chance to speak. He said:

'Gas – pouring out! We'll have to break the door down.'

Race had a powerful physique. He and Anthony made short shrift of the obstacle. With a splintering, cracking noise, the lock gave.

They fell back for a moment, then Race said:

'She's there by the fireplace. I'll dash in and break the window. You get her.'

Iris Marle was lying by the gas fire – her mouth and nose lying on the wide open gas jet.

A minute or two later, choking and spluttering, Anthony and Race laid the unconscious girl on the landing floor in the draught of the passage window.

Race said:

'I'll work on her. You get a doctor quickly.'

Anthony swung down the stairs. Race called after him:

'Don't worry. I think she'll be all right. We got here in time.'

In the hall Anthony dialled and spoke into the mouthpiece, hampered by a background of exclamations from Lucilla Drake.

He turned at last from the telephone to say with a sigh of relief:

'Caught him. He lives just across the Square. He'll be here in a couple of minutes.'

'– but I must know what has *happened*! Is Iris ill?'

It was a final wail from Lucilla.

Anthony said:

'She was in her room. Door locked. Her head in the gas fire and the gas full on.'

'Iris?' Mrs Drake gave a piercing shriek. 'Iris has committed *suicide*? I can't believe it. I *don't* believe it!'

A faint ghost of Anthony's grin returned to him.

'You don't need to believe it,' he said. 'It isn't true.'

CHAPTER 14

'And now, please, Tony, will you tell me all about it?'

Iris was lying on a sofa, and the valiant November sunshine was making a brave show outside the windows of Little Priors.

Anthony looked across at Colonel Race who was sitting on the window-sill, and grinned engagingly:

'I don't mind admitting, Iris, that I've been waiting for this moment. If I don't explain to someone soon how clever I've been, I shall burst. There will be no modesty in this recital. It will be shameless blowing of my own trumpet with suitable pauses to enable you to say "Anthony, how clever of you" or "Tony, how wonderful" or some phrase of a like nature. Ahem! The performance will now begin. Here we go.

'The thing as a whole *looked* simple enough. What I mean is, that it looked like a clear case of cause and effect. Rosemary's death, accepted at the time as suicide, was not suicide. George became suspicious, started investigating, was presumably getting near the truth, and before he could unmask the murderer was, in his turn, murdered. The sequence, if I may put it that way, seems perfectly clear.

'But almost at once we came across some apparent contradictions. Such as: A. George could not be poisoned. B. George *was* poisoned. And: A. Nobody touched George's glass. B. George's glass was tampered with.

'Actually I was overlooking a very significant fact – the varied use of the possessive case. George's ear is George's ear indisputably because it is attached to his head and cannot be removed without a surgical operation! But by George's watch, I only mean the watch that George is wearing – the question might arise whether it is his or maybe one lent him by someone else. And when I come to George's glass, or George's teacup, I begin to realize that I mean something very vague indeed. All I actually mean is the glass or cup out of which George has lately been drinking – and which has nothing to distinguish it from several other cups and glasses of the same pattern.

'To illustrate this, I tried an experiment. Race was drinking tea without sugar, Kemp was drinking tea with sugar, and I was drinking coffee. In appearance the three fluids were of much the same colour. We were sitting round a small marble-topped table among several other round marble-topped tables. On the pretext of an urgent brainwave I urged the other two out of their seats and out into the vestibule, pushing the chairs aside as we went, and also managing to move Kemp's pipe which

508 · AGATHA CHRISTIE

was lying by his plate to a similar position by my plate but without letting him see me do it. As soon as we were outside I made an excuse and we returned, Kemp slightly ahead. He pulled the chair to the table and sat down opposite the plate that was marked by the pipe he had left behind him. Race sat on his right as before and I on his left – *but mark what had happened* – a new A. and B. contradiction! A. Kemp's cup has sugared tea in it. B. Kemp's cup has coffee in it. Two conflicting statements that *cannot* both be true – But they *are* both true. The misleading term is *Kemp's* cup. Kemp's cup when he *left* the table and Kemp's cup when he *returned* to the table are *not the same.*

'And that, Iris, *is what happened at the Luxembourg that night.* After the cabaret, when you all went to dance, you dropped your bag. A waiter picked it up – not *the* waiter, the waiter attending on that table who knew just where you had been sitting – but *a* waiter, an anxious hurried little waiter with everybody bullying him, running along with a sauce, and who quickly stooped, picked up the bag and placed it by a plate – actually by the plate one place to the left of where you had been sitting. You and George came back first and you went without a thought straight to the place marked by your bag – just as Kemp did to the place marked by his pipe. George sat down in what he thought to be his place, on your right. And when he proposed his toast in memory of Rosemary, he drank from what he thought was *his* glass but was in reality *your glass* – the glass that can quite easily have been poisoned without needing a conjuring trick to explain it, because the only person who did *not* drink after the cabaret, was necessarily the *person whose health was being drunk*!

'Now go over the whole business again and the set-up is entirely different! *You* are the intended victim, not George! So it looks, doesn't it, as though George is being *used.* What, if things had not gone wrong, would have been the story as the world would see it? A repetition of the party a year ago – and a repetition of – suicide! Clearly, people would say, a suicidal streak in that family! Bit of paper which has contained cyanide found in your bag. Clear case! Poor girl has been brooding over her sister's death. Very sad – but these rich girls are sometimes very neurotic!'

Iris interrupted him. She cried out:

'But why should anyone want to kill me? Why? *Why?*'

'All that lovely money, angel. Money, money, money! Rosemary's money went to you on her death. Now suppose you were to die – unmarried. What would happen to that money? The answer was it would go to your next of kin – to your aunt, Lucilla Drake. Now from all accounts of the dear lady, I could hardly see Lucilla Drake as First

Murderess. But is there anyone else who would benefit? Yes, indeed. Victor Drake. If Lucilla has money, it will be exactly the same as Victor having it – Victor will see to that! He has always been able to do what he likes with his mother. And there is nothing difficult about seeing Victor as First Murderer. All along, from the very start of the case, there have been references to Victor, mentions of Victor. He has been in the offing, a shadowy, unsubstantial, evil figure.'

'But Victor's in the Argentine! He's been in South America for over a year.'

'Has he? We're coming now to what has been said to be the fundamental plot of every story. "Girl meets Boy!" When Victor met Ruth Lessing, this particular story started. He got hold of her. I think she must have fallen for him pretty badly. Those quiet, level-headed, law-abiding women are the kind that often fall for a real bad lot.

'Think a minute and you'll realize that all the evidence for Victor's being in South America depends on Ruth's word. None of it was verified because it was never a main issue! *Ruth* said that she had seen Victor off on the S.S. *Cristobal* before Rosemary's death! It was *Ruth* who suggested putting a call through to Buenos Aires on the day of George's death – and later sacked the telephone girl who might have inadvertently let out that she did no such thing.

'Of course it's been easy to check up now! Victor Drake arrived in Buenos Aires by a boat leaving England the day *after* Rosemary's death a year ago. Ogilvie, in Buenos Aires, had no telephone conversation with Ruth on the subject of Victor Drake on the day of George's death. *And Victor Drake left Buenos Aires for New York some weeks ago.* Easy enough for him to arrange for a cable to be sent off in his name on a certain day – one of those well-known cables asking for money that seemed proof positive that he was many thousands of miles away. Instead of which –'

'Yes, Anthony?'

'Instead of which,' said Anthony, leading up to his climax with intense pleasure, 'he was sitting at the next table to ours at the Luxembourg with a not so dumb blonde!'

'Not that awful looking man?'

'A yellow blotchy complexion and bloodshot eyes are easy things to assume, and they make a lot of difference to a man. Actually, of our party, *I* was the only person (apart from Ruth Lessing) who had ever seen Victor Drake – and I had never known him under *that name*! In any case I was sitting with my back to him. I did think I recognized, in the cocktail lounge outside, as we came in, a man I had known in my prison days – Monkey Coleman. But as I was now leading a highly respectable life I was not too anxious that he should recognize me. I never for one moment suspected that Monkey Coleman had had anything to do with the crime – much less that he and Victor Drake were one and the same.'

'But I don't see now how he did it?'

Colonel Race took up the tale.

'In the easiest way in the world. During the cabaret he went out to telephone, passing our table. Drake had been an actor and he had been something more important – a *waiter*. To assume the make-up and play the part of Pedro Morales was child's play to an actor, but to move deftly round a table, with the step and gait of a waiter, filling up the champagne glasses, needed the definite knowledge and technique of a man who had actually *been* a waiter. A clumsy action or movement would have drawn your attention to him, but as a *bona fide* waiter none of you noticed or saw him. You were looking at the Cabaret, not noticing that portion of the restaurant's furnishings – the waiter!'

Iris said in a hesitating voice:

'And Ruth?'

Anthony said:

'It was Ruth, of course, who put the cyanide paper in your bag – probably in the cloak-room at the beginning of the evening. The same technique she had adopted a year ago – with Rosemary.'

'I always thought it odd,' said Iris, 'that George hadn't told Ruth about those letters. He consulted her about everything.'

Anthony gave a short laugh.

'Of course he told her – first thing. She knew he would. That's why she wrote them. Then she arranged all his "plan" for him – having first got him well worked up. And so she had the stage set – all nicely arranged for suicide No. 2 – and if George chose to believe that you had killed Rosemary and were committing suicide out of remorse or panic – well, that wouldn't make any difference to Ruth!'

'And to think I liked her – liked her very much! And actually wanted her to marry George.'

'She'd probably have made him a very good wife, if she hadn't come across Victor,' said Anthony. 'Moral: every murderess was a nice girl once.'

Iris shivered. 'All that for money!'

'You innocent, money is what these things are done for! Victor certainly did it for money. Ruth partly for money, partly for Victor, and partly, I think, because she hated Rosemary. Yes, she'd travelled a long way by the time she deliberately tried to run you down in a car, and still further when she left Lucilla in the drawing-room, banged the front door and then ran up to your bedroom. What did she seem like? Excited at all?'

Iris considered.

'I don't think so. She just tapped on the door, came in and said everything was fixed up and she hoped I was feeling all right. I said yes, I was just a bit tired. And then she picked up my big rubber-covered torch and said what a nice torch that was and after that I don't seem to remember anything.'

'No, dear,' said Anthony. 'Because she hit you a nice little crack, not too hard, on the back of the neck with your nice torch. Then she arranged you artistically by the gas fire, shut the windows tight, turned on the gas, went out, locking the door and passing the key underneath it, pushed the woolly mat close up against the crack so as to shut out any draught and tripped gently down the stairs. Kemp and I just got into the bathroom in time. I raced on up to you and Kemp followed Miss Ruth Lessing unbeknownst to where she had left that car parked – you know, I felt at the time there was something fishy and uncharacteristic about the way Ruth tried to force it on our minds that she had come by bus and tube!'

Iris gave a shudder.

'It's horrible – to think anyone was as determined to kill me as all that. Did she hate me too by then?'

'Oh, I shouldn't think so. But Miss Ruth Lessing is a very efficient young woman. She'd already been an accessory in two murders and she didn't fancy having risked her neck for nothing. I've no doubt Lucilla Drake bleated out your decision to marry me at a moment's notice, and in that case there was no time to lose. Once married, I should be your next of kin and not Lucilla.'

'Poor Lucilla. I'm so terribly sorry for her.'

'I think we all are. She's a harmless, kindly soul.'

'Is he really arrested?'

Anthony looked at Race, who nodded and said:

'This morning, when he landed in New York.'

'Was he going to marry Ruth – afterwards?'

'That was Ruth's idea. I think she would have brought it off too.'

'Anthony – I don't think I like my money very much.'

'All right, sweet – we'll do something noble with it if you like. I've got enough money to live on – and to keep a wife in reasonable comfort. We'll give it all away if you like – endow homes for children, or provide free tobacco for old men, or – how about a campaign for serving better coffee all over England?'

'I shall keep a little,' said Iris. 'So that if I ever wanted to, I could be grand and walk out and leave you.'

'I don't think, Iris, that is the right spirit in which to enter upon married life. And, by the way, you didn't once say "Tony, how wonderful" or "Anthony, how clever of you"!'

Colonel Race smiled and got up.

'Going over to the Farradays for tea,' he exclaimed. There was a faint twinkle in his eye as he said to Anthony: 'Don't suppose you're coming?'

Anthony shook his head and Race went out of the room. He paused in the doorway to say, over his shoulder:

'Good show.'

'That,' said Anthony as the door closed behind him, 'denotes supreme British approval.'

Iris asked in a calm voice:

'He thought I'd done it, didn't he?'

'You mustn't hold that against him,' said Anthony. 'You see, he's known so many beautiful spies, all stealing secret formulas and wheedling secrets out of major-generals, that it's soured his nature and warped his judgement. He thinks it's just got to be the beautiful girl in the case!'

'Why did you know I hadn't, Tony?'

'Just love, I suppose,' said Anthony lightly.

Then his face changed, grew suddenly serious. He touched a little vase by Iris's side in which was a single sprig of grey-green with a mauve-flower.

'What's that doing in flower at this time of year?'

'It does sometimes – just an odd sprig – if it's a mild autumn.'

Anthony took it out of the glass and held it for a moment against his cheek. He half-closed his eyes and saw rich chestnut hair, laughing blue eyes and a red passionate mouth . . .

He said in a quiet conversational tone:

'She's not around now any longer, is she?'

'Who do you mean?'

'You know who I mean. Rosemary . . . I think she knew, Iris, that you were in danger.'

He touched the sprig of fragrant green with his lips and threw it lightly out of the window.

'Good-bye, Rosemary, thank you . . .'

Iris said softly:
'*That's for remembrance . . .*'
And more softly still:
'*Pray love remember . . .*'

LUST
•
EVIL UNDER THE SUN

To John
In memory of our last season in Syria

When Captain Roger Angmering built himself a house in the year 1782 on the island off Leathercombe Bay, it was thought the height of eccentricity on his part. A man of good family such as he was should have had a decorous mansion set in wide meadows with, perhaps, a running stream and good pasture.

But Captain Roger Angmering had only one great love, the sea. So he built his house – a sturdy house too, as it needed to be, on the little windswept gull-haunted promontory – cut off from land at each high tide.

He did not marry, the sea was his first and last spouse, and at his death the house and island went to a distant cousin. That cousin and his descendants thought little of the bequest. Their own acres dwindled, and their heirs grew steadily poorer.

In 1922 when the great cult of the Seaside for Holidays was finally established and the coast of Devon and Cornwall was no longer thought too hot in the summer, Arthur Angmering found his vast inconvenient late Georgian house unsaleable, but he got a good price for the odd bit of property acquired by the seafaring Captain Roger.

The sturdy house was added to and embellished. A concrete causeway was laid down from the mainland to the island. 'Walks' and 'Nooks' were cut and devised all round the island. There were two tennis courts, sun-terraces leading down to a little bay embellished with rafts and diving boards. The Jolly Roger Hotel, Smugglers' Island, Leathercombe Bay, came triumphantly into being. And from June till September (with a short season at Easter) the Jolly Roger Hotel was usually packed to the attics. It was enlarged and improved in 1934 by the addition of a cocktail bar, a bigger dining-room and some extra bathrooms. The prices went up.

People said:

'Ever been to Leathercombe Bay? Awfully jolly hotel there, on a sort of island. Very comfortable and no trippers or charabancs. Good cooking and all that. You ought to go.'

And people did go.

★   ★   ★

There was one very important person (in his own estimation at least) staying at the Jolly Roger. Hercule Poirot, resplendent in a white duck suit, with a panama hat tilted over his eyes, his moustaches magnificently befurled, lay back in an improved type of deck-chair and surveyed the bathing beach. A series of terraces led down to it from the hotel. On the beach itself were floats, lilos, rubber and canvas boats, balls and rubber toys. There was a long springboard and three rafts at varying distances from the shore.

Of the bathers, some were in the sea, some were lying stretched out in the sun, and some were anointing themselves carefully with oil.

On the terrace immediately above, the non-bathers sat and commented on the weather, the scene in front of them, the news in the morning papers and any other subject that appealed to them.

On Poirot's left a ceaseless flow of conversation poured in a gentle monotone from the lips of Mrs Gardener while at the same time her needles clacked as she knitted vigorously. Beyond her, her husband, Odell C. Gardener, lay in a hammock chair, his hat tilted forward over his nose, and occasionally uttered a brief statement when called upon to do so.

On Poirot's right, Miss Brewster, a tough athletic woman with grizzled hair and a pleasant weather-beaten face, made gruff comments. The result sounded rather like a sheepdog whose short stentorian barks interrupted the ceaseless yapping of a Pomeranian.

Mrs Gardener was saying:

'And so I said to Mr Gardener, why, I said, sight-seeing is all very well, and I do like to do a place thoroughly. But, after all, I said, we've done England pretty well and all I want now is to get to some quiet spot by the seaside and just relax. That's what I said, wasn't it, Odell? Just *relax*. I feel I must relax, I said. That's so, isn't it, Odell?'

Mr Gardener, from behind his hat, murmured:

'Yes, darling.'

Mrs Gardener pursued the theme.

'And so, when I mentioned it to Mr Kelso, at Cook's – He's arranged all our itinerary for us and been *most* helpful in every way. I don't really know what we'd have done without him! – well, as I say, when I mentioned it to him, Mr Kelso said that we couldn't do better than come here. A most picturesque spot, he said, quite out of the world, and at the same time very comfortable and most exclusive in every way. And, of course, Mr Gardener, he chipped in there and said what about the sanitary arrangements? Because, if you'll believe me, M. Poirot, a sister of Mr Gardener's went to stay at a guesthouse once, very exclusive they said it was, and in the heart of the moors, but would you believe me, *nothing but an earth closet*! So naturally that made Mr Gardener suspicious of these out-of-the-world places, didn't it, Odell?'

'Why, yes, darling,' said Gardener.

'But Mr Kelso reassured us at once. The sanitation, he said, was absolutely the latest word, and the cooking was excellent. And I'm sure that's so. And what I like about it is, it's *intime*, if you know what I mean. Being a small place we all talk to each other and everybody knows everybody. If there is a fault about the British it is that they're inclined to be a bit stand-offish until they've known you a couple of years. After that nobody could be nicer. Mr Kelso said that interesting people came here, and I see he was right. There's you, M. Poirot and Miss Darnley. Oh! I was just tickled to death when I found out who you were, wasn't I, Odell?'

'You were, darling.'

'Ha!' said Miss Brewster, breaking in explosively. 'What a thrill, eh, M. Poirot?'

Hercule Poirot raised his hands in deprecation. But it was no more than a polite gesture. Mrs Gardener flowed smoothly on.

'You see, M. Poirot, I'd heard a lot about you from Cornelia Robson who was. Mr Gardener and I were at Badenhof in May. And of course Cornelia told us all about that business in Egypt when Linnet Ridgeway was killed. She said you were wonderful and I've always been simply crazy to meet you, haven't I, Odell?'

'Yes, darling.'

'And then Miss Darnley, too. I get a lot of my things at Rose Mond's and of course she *is* Rose Mond, isn't she? I think her clothes are ever so clever. Such a marvellous line. That dress I had on last night was one of hers. She's just a lovely woman in every way, I think.'

From beyond Miss Brewster, Major Barry, who had been sitting with protuberant eyes glued to the bathers, grunted out:

'Distinguished lookin' gal!'

Mrs Gardener clacked her needles.

'I've just got to confess one thing, M. Poirot. It gave me a kind of a *turn* meeting you here – not that I wasn't just thrilled to meet you, because I was. Mr Gardener knows that. But it just came to me that you might be here – well, *professionally*. You know what I mean? Well, I'm just terribly sensitive, as Mr Gardener will tell you, and I just couldn't bear it if I was to be mixed up in crime of any kind. You see –'

Mr Gardener cleared his throat. He said:

'You see, M. Poirot, Mrs Gardener is very sensitive.'

The hands of Hercule Poirot shot into the air.

'But let me assure you, Madame, that I am here simply in the same way that you are here yourselves – to enjoy myself – to spend the holiday. I do not think of crime even.'

Miss Brewster said again, giving her short gruff bark:

'No bodies on Smugglers' Island.'

Hercule Poirot said:

'Ah! but that, it is not strictly true.' He pointed downward. 'Regard them there, lying out in rows. What are they? They are not men and women. There is nothing personal about them. They are just – bodies!'

Major Barry said appreciatively:

'Good-looking fillies, some of 'em. Bit on the thin side, perhaps.'

Poirot cried:

'Yes, but what appeal is there? What mystery? I, I am old, of the old school. When I was young, one saw barely the ankle. The glimpse of a foamy petticoat, how alluring! The gentle swelling of the calf – a knee – a beribboned garter –'

'Naughty, naughty!' said Major Barry hoarsely.

'Much more sensible – the things we wear nowadays,' said Miss Brewster.

'Why, yes, M. Poirot,' said Mrs Gardener. 'I do think, you know, that our girls and boys nowadays lead a much more natural healthy life. They just romp about together and they – well, they –' Mrs Gardener blushed slightly for she had a nice mind – 'they think nothing *of* it, if you know what I mean?'

'I do know,' said Hercule Poirot. 'It is deplorable!'

'Deplorable?' squeaked Mrs Gardener.

'To remove all the romance – all the mystery! Today everything is *standardized*!' He waved a hand towards the recumbent figures. 'That reminds me very much of the Morgue in Paris.'

'M. Poirot!' Mrs Gardener was scandalized.

'Bodies – arranged on slabs – like butcher's meat!'

'But M. Poirot, isn't that too far-fetched for words?'

Hercule Poirot admitted:

'It may be, yes.'

'All the same,' Mrs Gardener knitted with energy, 'I'm inclined to agree with you on one point. These girls that lie out like that in the sun will grow hair on their legs and arms. I've said so to Irene – that's my daughter, M. Poirot. Irene, I said to her, if you lie out like that in the sun, you'll have hair all over you, hair on your arms and hair on your legs and hair on your bosom, and what will you look like then? I said to her. Didn't I, Odell?'

'Yes, darling,' said Mr Gardener.

Everyone was silent, perhaps making a mental picture of Irene when the worst had happened.

Mrs Gardener rolled up her knitting and said:

'I wonder now –'

Mr Gardener said:

'Yes, darling?'

He struggled out of the hammock chair and took Mrs Gardener's knitting and her book. He asked:

'What about joining us for a drink, Miss Brewster?'

'Not just now, thanks.'

The Gardeners went up to the hotel.

Miss Brewster said:

'American husbands are wonderful!'

Mrs Gardener's place was taken by the Reverend Stephen Lane.

Mr Lane was a tall vigorous clergyman of fifty odd. His face was tanned and his dark grey flannel trousers were holidayfied and disreputable.

He said with enthusiasm:

'Marvellous country! I've been from Leathercombe Bay to Harford and back over the cliffs.'

'Warm work walking today,' said Major Barry who never walked.

'Good exercise,' said Miss Brewster. 'I haven't been for my row yet. Nothing like rowing for your stomach muscles.'

The eyes of Hercule Poirot dropped somewhat ruefully to a certain protuberance in his middle.

Miss Brewster, noting the glance, said kindly:

'You'd soon get that off, M. Poirot, if you took a rowing-boat out every day.'

'*Merci*, Mademoiselle. I detest boats!'

'You mean small boats?'

'Boats of all sizes!' He closed his eyes and shuddered. 'The movement of the sea, it is not pleasant.'

'Bless the man, the sea is as calm as a mill pond today.'

Poirot replied with conviction:

'There is no such thing as a really calm sea. Always, always, there is motion.'

'If you ask me,' said Major Barry, 'seasickness is nine-tenths nerves.'

'There,' said the clergyman, smiling a little, 'speaks the good sailor – eh, Major?'

'Only been ill once – and that was crossing the Channel! Don't think about it, that's my motto.'

'Seasickness is really a very odd thing,' mused Miss Brewster. 'Why should some people be subject to it and not others? It seems so unfair. And nothing to do with one's ordinary health. Quite sickly people are good sailors. Someone told me once it was something to do with one's spine. Then there's the way some people can't stand heights. I'm not very good myself, but Mrs Redfern is far worse. The other day, on the cliff path to Harford, she turned quite giddy and simply clung to me. She told me she once got stuck halfway down that outside staircase on Milan Cathedral. She'd gone up without thinking but coming down did for her.'

'She'd better not go down the ladder to Pixy Cove, then,' observed Lane.

Miss Brewster made a face.

'I funk that myself. It's all right for the young. The Cowan boys and the young Mastermans, they run up and down and enjoy it.'

Lane said.

'Here comes Mrs Redfern now, coming up from her bathe.'

Miss Brewster remarked:

'M. Poirot ought to approve of her. She's no sun-bather.'

Young Mrs Redfern had taken off her rubber cap and was shaking out her hair. She was an ash blonde and her skin was of that dead fairness that goes with that colouring. Her legs and arms were very white.

With a hoarse chuckle, Major Barry said:

'Looks a bit uncooked among the others, doesn't she?'

Wrapping herself in a long bath-robe Christine Redfern came up the beach and mounted the steps towards them.

She had a fair serious face, pretty in a negative way and small dainty hands and feet.

She smiled at them and dropped down beside them, tucking her bath-wrap round her.

Miss Brewster said:

'You have earned M. Poirot's good opinion. He doesn't like the sun-tanning crowd. Says they're like joints of butcher's meat, or words to that effect.'

Christine Redfern smiled ruefully. She said:

'I wish I *could* sun-bathe! But I don't go brown. I only blister and get the most frightful freckles all over my arms.'

'Better than getting hair all over them like Mrs Gardener's Irene,' said Miss Brewster. In answer to Christine's inquiring glance she went on: 'Mrs Gardener's been in grand form this morning. Absolutely non-stop. "Isn't that so, Odell?" "Yes, darling."' She paused and then said: 'I wish, though, M. Poirot, that you'd played up to her a bit. Why didn't you? Why didn't you tell her that you were down here investigating a particularly gruesome murder, and that the murderer, a homicidal maniac, was certainly to be found among the guests of the hotel?'

Hercule Poirot sighed. He said:

'I very much fear she would have believed me.'

Major Barry gave a wheezy chuckle. He said:

'She certainly would.'

Emily Brewster said:

'No, I don't believe even Mrs Gardener would have believed in a crime staged here. This isn't the sort of place you'd get a body!'

Hercule Poirot stirred a little in his chair. He protested. He said:

'But why not, Mademoiselle? Why should there not be what you call a "body" here on Smugglers' Island?'

Emily Brewster said:

'I don't know. I suppose some places *are* more unlikely than others. This isn't the kind of spot –' She broke off, finding it difficult to explain her meaning.

'It is romantic, yes,' agreed Hercule Poirot. 'It is peaceful. The sun shines. The sea is blue. But you forget, Miss Brewster, there is evil everywhere under the sun.'

The clergyman stirred in his chair. He leaned forward. His intensely blue eyes lighted up.

Miss Brewster shrugged her shoulders.

'Oh! of course I realize that, but all the same –'

'But all the same this still seems to you an unlikely setting for crime? You forget one thing, Mademoiselle.'

'Human nature, I suppose?'

'That, yes. That, always. But that was not what I was going to say. I was going to point out to you that here everyone is on holiday.'

Emily Brewster turned a puzzled face to him.

'I don't understand.'

Hercule Poirot beamed kindly at her. He made dabs in the air with an emphatic forefinger.

'Let us say, you have an enemy. If you seek him out in his flat, in his office, in the street – *eh bien*, you must have a *reason* – you must account for yourself. But here at the seaside it is necessary for no one to account for himself. You are at Leathercombe Bay, why? *Parbleu!* it is August – one goes to the seaside in August – one is on one's holiday. It is quite natural, you see, for you to be here and for Mr Lane to be here and for Major Barry to be here and for Mrs Redfern and her husband to be here. Because it is the custom in England to go to the seaside in August.'

'Well,' admitted Miss Brewster, 'that's certainly a very ingenious idea. But what about the Gardeners? They're American.'

Poirot smiled.

'Even Mrs Gardener, as she told us, feels the need to *relax*. Also, since she is "doing" England, she must certainly spend a fortnight at the seaside – as a good tourist, if nothing else. She enjoys watching people.'

Mrs Redfern murmured:

'You like watching the people too, I think?'

'Madame, I will confess it. I do.'

She said thoughtfully: 'You see – a good deal.'

There was a pause. Stephen Lane cleared his throat and said with a trace of self-consciousness.

'I was interested, M. Poirot, in something you said just now. You said that there was evil done everywhere under the sun. It was almost a quotation from Ecclesiastes.' He paused and then quoted himself: '*Yea, also the heart of the sons of men is full of evil, and madness is in their heart while they live.*' His face lit up with an almost fanatical light. 'I was glad to hear you say that. Nowadays, no one believes in evil. It is considered, at most, a mere negation of good. Evil, people say, is done by those who know no better – who are undeveloped – who are to be pitied rather than blamed. But M. Poirot, evil is *real*! It is a *fact*! I believe in Evil like I believe in Good. It exists! It is powerful! It walks the earth!'

He stopped. His breath was coming fast. He wiped his forehead with his handkerchief and looked suddenly apologetic.

'I'm sorry. I got carried away.'

Poirot said calmly:

'I understand your meaning. Up to a point I agree with you. Evil does walk the earth and can be recognized as such.'

Major Barry cleared his throat.

'Talking of that sort of thing, some of these fakir fellers in India –'

Major Barry had been long enough at the Jolly Roger for everyone to be on their guard against his fatal tendency to embark on long Indian stories. Both Miss Brewster and Mrs Redfern burst into speech.

'That's your husband swimming in now, isn't it, Mrs Redfern? How magnificent his crawl stroke is. He's an awfully good swimmer.'

At the same moment Mrs Redfern said:

'Oh look! What a lovely little boat that is out there with the red sails. It's Mr Blatt's, isn't it?'

The sailing boat with the red sails was just crossing the end of the bay.

Major Barry grunted:

'Fanciful idea, red sails,' but the menace of the story about the fakir was avoided.

Hercule Poirot looked with appreciation at the young man who had just swum to shore. Patrick Redfern was a good specimen of humanity. Lean, bronzed with broad shoulders and narrow thighs, there was about him a kind of infectious enjoyment and gaiety – a native simplicity that endeared him to all women and most men.

He stood there shaking the water from him and raising a hand in gay salutation to his wife.

She waved back calling out:

'Come up here, Pat.'

'I'm coming.'

He went a little way along the beach to retrieve the towel he had left there.

It was then that a woman came down past them from the hotel to the beach.

Her arrival had all the importance of a stage entrance.

Moreover, she walked as though she knew it. There was no self-consciousness apparent. It would seem that she was too used to the invariable effect her presence produced.

She was tall and slender. She wore a simple backless white bathing dress and every inch of her exposed body was tanned a beautiful even shade of bronze. She was as perfect as a statue. Her hair was a rich flaming auburn curling richly and intimately into her neck. Her face had that slight hardness which is seen when thirty years have come and gone, but the whole effect of her was one of youth – of superb and triumphant vitality. There was a Chinese immobility about her face, and an upward slant of the dark blue eyes. On her head she wore a fantastic Chinese hat of jade green cardboard.

There was that about her which made every other woman on the beach seem faded and insignificant. And with equal inevitability, the eye of every male present was drawn and riveted on her.

The eyes of Hercule Poirot opened, his moustache quivered appreciatively, Major Barry sat up and his protuberant eyes bulged even farther with excitement; on Poirot's left the Reverend Stephen Lane drew in his breath with a little hiss and his figure stiffened.

Major Barry said in a hoarse whisper:

'Arlena Stuart (that's who she was before she married Marshall) – I saw her in *Come and Go* before she left the stage. Something worth looking at, eh?'

Christine Redfern said slowly and her voice was cold: 'She's handsome – yes. I think – she looks rather a beast!'

Emily Brewster said abruptly:

'You talked about evil just now, M. Poirot. Now to my mind that woman's a personification of evil! She's a bad lot through and through. I happen to know a good deal about her.'

Major Barry said reminiscently:

'I remember a gal out in Simla. *She* had red hair too. Wife of a subaltern. Did she set the place by the ears? I'll say she did! Men went mad about her! All the women, of course, would have liked to gouge her eyes out! She upset the apple cart in more homes than one.'

He chuckled reminiscently.

'Husband was a nice quiet fellow. Worshipped the ground she walked on. Never saw a thing – or made out he didn't.'

Stephen Lane said in a low voice full of intense feeling:

'Such women are a menace – a menace to –'

He stopped.

Arlena Stuart had come to the water's edge. Two young men, little more than boys, had sprung up and come eagerly towards her. She stood smiling at them.

Her eyes slid past them to where Patrick Redfern was coming along the beach.

It was, Hercule Poirot thought, like watching the needle of a compass. Patrick Redfern was deflected, his feet changed their direction. The needle, do what it will, must obey the law of magnetism and turn to the north. Patrick Redfern's feet brought him to Arlena Stuart.

She stood smiling at him. Then she moved slowly along the beach by the side of the waves. Patrick Redfern went with her. She stretched herself out by a rock. Redfern dropped to the shingle beside her.

Abruptly, Christine Redfern got up and went into the hotel.

$\star$ $\star$ $\star$

There was an uncomfortable little silence after she had left.

Then Emily Brewster said:

'It's rather too bad. She's a nice little thing. They've only been married a year or two.'

'Gal I was speaking of,' said Major Barry, 'the one in Simla. She upset a couple of really happy marriages. Seemed a pity, what?'

'There's a type of woman,' said Miss Brewster, 'who *likes* smashing up homes.' She added after a minute or two, 'Patrick Redfern's a fool!'

Hercule Poirot said nothing. He was gazing down the beach, but he was not looking at Patrick Redfern and Arlena Stuart.

Miss Brewster said:

'Well, I'd better go and get hold of my boat.'

She left them.

Major Barry turned his boiled gooseberry eyes with mild curiosity on Poirot.

'Well, Poirot,' he said. 'What are you thinking about? You've not opened your mouth. What do you think of the siren? Pretty hot?'

Poirot said:

'*C'est possible.*'

'Now then, you old dog. I know you Frenchmen!'

Poirot said coldly:

'I am *not* a Frenchman!'

'Well, don't tell me you haven't got an eye for a pretty girl! What do you think of her, eh?'

Hercule Poirot said:

'She is not young.'

'What does that matter? A woman's as old as she looks! *Her* looks are all right.'

Hercule Poirot nodded. He said:

'Yes, she is beautiful. But it is not beauty that counts in the end. It is not beauty that makes every head (except one) turn on the beach to look at her.'

'It's IT, my boy,' said the Major. 'That's what it is – IT.'

Then he said with sudden curiosity.

'What are you looking at so steadily?'

Hercule Poirot replied: 'I am looking at the exception. At the one man who did not look up when she passed.'

Major Barry followed his gaze to where it rested on a man of about forty, fair-haired and sun-tanned. He had a quiet pleasant face and was sitting on the beach smoking a pipe and reading *The Times*.

'Oh, *that!*' said Major Barry. 'That's the husband, my boy. That's Marshall.'

Hercule Poirot said:

'Yes, I know.'

Major Barry chuckled. He himself was a bachelor. He was accustomed to think of The Husband in three lights only – as 'the Obstacle', 'the Inconvenience' or 'the Safeguard'.

He said:

'Seems a nice fellow. Quiet. Wonder if my *Times* has come?'

He got up and went up towards the hotel.

Poirot's glance shifted slowly to the face of Stephen Lane.

Stephen Lane was watching Arlena Marshall and Patrick Redfern. He turned suddenly to Poirot. There was a stern fanatical light in his eyes.

He said:

'That woman is evil through and through. Do you doubt it?'

Poirot said slowly:

'It is difficult to be sure.'

Stephen Lane said:

'But, man alive, don't you feel it in the air? All round you? The presence of Evil.'

Slowly, Hercule Poirot nodded his head.

CHAPTER 2

When Rosamund Darnley came and sat down by him, Hercule Poirot made no attempt to disguise his pleasure.

As he has since admitted, he admired Rosamund Darnley as much as any woman he had ever met. He liked her distinction, the graceful lines of her figure, the alert proud carriage of her head. He liked the neat sleek waves of her dark hair and the ironic quality of her smile.

She was wearing a dress of some navy blue material with touches of white. It looked very simple owing to the expensive severity of its line. Rosamund Darnley as Rose Mond Ltd was one of London's best-known dressmakers.

She said:

'I don't think I like this place. I'm wondering why I came here!'

'You have been here before, have you not?'

'Yes, two years ago, at Easter. There weren't so many people then.'

Hercule Poirot looked at her. He said gently:

'Something has occurred to worry you. That is right, is it not?'

She nodded. Her foot swung to and fro. She stared down at it. She said:

'I've met a ghost. That's what it is.'

'A ghost, Mademoiselle?'

'Yes.'

'The ghost of what? Or of whom?'

'Oh, the ghost of myself.'

Poirot asked gently:

'Was it a painful ghost?'

'Unexpectedly painful. It took me back, you know . . .'

She paused, musing. Then she said:

'Imagine my childhood. No, you can't! You're not English!'

Poirot asked:

'Was it a very English childhood?'

'Oh, incredibly so! The country – a big shabby house – horses, dogs – walks in the rain – wood fires – apples in the orchard – lack of money – old tweeds – evening dresses that went on from year to year – a neglected garden – with Michaelmas daisies coming out like great banners in the autumn . . .'

Poirot asked gently:

'And you want to go back?'

Rosamund Darnley shook her head. She said:

'One can't go back, can one? That – never. But I'd like to have gone on – a different way.'

Poirot said:

'I wonder.'

Rosamund Darnley laughed.

'So do I, really!'

Poirot said:

'When I was young (and that, Mademoiselle, is indeed a long time ago) there was a game entitled, "*If not yourself, who would you be?*" One wrote the answer in young ladies' albums. They had gold edges and were bound in blue leather. The answer? Mademoiselle, is not really very easy to find.'

Rosamund said:

'No – I suppose not. It would be a big risk. One wouldn't like to take on being Mussolini or Princess Elizabeth. As for one's friends, one knows too much about them. I remember once meeting a charming husband and wife. They were so courteous and delightful to one another and seemed on such good terms after years of marriage that I envied the woman. I'd have changed places with her willingly. Somebody told me afterwards that in private they'd never spoken to each other for eleven years!'

She laughed.

'That shows, doesn't it, that you never know?'

After a moment or two Poirot said:

'Many people, Mademoiselle, must envy you.'

Rosamund Darnley said coolly:

'Oh, yes. Naturally.'

She thought about it, her lips curved upward in their ironic smile.

'Yes, I'm really the perfect type of the successful woman! I enjoy the artistic satisfaction of the successful creative artist (I really do like designing clothes) and the financial satisfaction of the successful business woman. I'm very well off, I've a good figure, a passable face, and a not too malicious tongue.'

She paused. Her smile widened.

'Of course – I haven't got a husband! I've failed there, haven't I, M. Poirot?'

Poirot said gallantly:

'Mademoiselle, if you are not married, it is because none of my sex have been sufficiently eloquent. It is from choice, not necessity, that you remain single.'

Rosamund Darnley said:

'And yet, like all men, I'm sure you believe in your heart that no woman is content unless she is married and has children.'

Poirot shrugged his shoulders.

'To marry and have children, that is the common lot of women. Only one woman in a hundred – more, in a thousand, can make for herself a name and a position as you have done.'

Rosamund grinned at him.

'And yet, all the same, I'm nothing but a wretched old maid! That's what I feel today, at any rate. I'd be happier with twopence a year and a big silent brute of a husband and a brood of brats running after me. That's true, isn't it?'

Poirot shrugged his shoulders.

'Since you say so, then, yes, Mademoiselle.'

Rosamund laughed, her equilibrium suddenly restored. She took out a cigarette and lit it.

She said:

'You certainly know how to deal with women, M. Poirot. I now feel like taking the opposite point of view and arguing with you in favour of careers for women. Of course I'm damned well off as I am – and I know it!'

'Then everything in the garden – or shall we say at the seaside? is lovely, Mademoiselle.'

'Quite right.'

Poirot, in his turn, extracted his cigarette case and lit one of those tiny cigarettes which it was his affection to smoke.

Regarding the ascending haze with a quizzical eye, he murmured:

'So Mr – no, Captain Marshall is an old friend of yours, Mademoiselle?'

Rosamund sat up. She said:

'Now how do you know that? Oh, I suppose Ken told you.'

Poirot shook his head.

'Nobody has told me anything. After all, Mademoiselle, I am a detective. It was the obvious conclusion to draw.'

Rosamund Darnley said: 'I don't see it.'

'But consider!' The little man's hands were eloquent. 'You have been here a week. You are lively, gay, without a care. Today, suddenly, you speak of ghosts, of old times. What has happened? For several days there have been no new arrivals until last night when Captain Marshall and his wife and daughter arrive. Today the change! It is obvious!'

Rosamund Darnley said:

'Well, it's true enough. Kenneth Marshall and I were more or less children together. The Marshalls lived next door to us. Ken was always nice to me – although condescending, of course, since he was four years older. I've not seen anything of him for a long time. It must be – fifteen years at least.'

Poirot said thoughtfully:

'A long time.'

Rosamund nodded.

There was a pause and then Hercule Poirot said:

'He is sympathetic, yes?'

Rosamund said warmly:

'Ken's a dear. One of the best. Frightfully quiet and reserved. I'd say his only fault is a *penchant* for making unfortunate marriages.'

Poirot said in a tone of great understanding: 'Ah –'

Rosamund Darnley went on.

'Kenneth's a fool – an utter fool where women are concerned! Do you remember the Martingdale case?'

Poirot frowned.

'Martingdale? Martingdale? Arsenic, was it not?'

'Yes. Seventeen or eighteen years ago. The woman was tried for the murder of her husband.'

'And he was proved to have been an arsenic eater and she was acquitted?'

'That's right. Well, after her acquittal, Ken married her. That's the sort of damn silly thing he does.'

Hercule Poirot murmured:

'But if she was innocent?'

Rosamund Darnley said impatiently:

'Oh, I dare say she *was* innocent. Nobody really knows! But there are plenty of women to marry in the world without going out of your way to marry one who's stood her trial for murder.'

Poirot said nothing. Perhaps he knew that if he kept silence Rosamund Darnley would go on. She did so.

'He was very young, of course, only just twenty-one. He was crazy about her. She died when Linda was born – a year after their marriage. I believe Ken was terribly cut up by her death. Afterwards he racketed around a lot – trying to forget, I suppose.'

She paused.

'And then came this business of Arlena Stuart. She was in Revue at the time. There was the Codrington divorce case. Lady Codrington divorced Codrington, citing Arlena Stuart. They say Lord Codrington was absolutely infatuated with her. It was understood they were to be married as soon as the decree was made absolute. Actually, when it came to it, he didn't marry her. Turned her down flat. I believe she actually sued him for breach of promise. Anyway, the thing made a big stir at the time. The next thing that happens is that Ken goes and marries her. The fool – the complete fool!'

Hercule Poirot murmured:

'A man might be excused such a folly – she is beautiful, Mademoiselle.'

'Yes, there's no doubt of that. There was another scandal about three years ago. Old Sir Roger Erskine left her every penny of his money. I should have thought that would have opened Ken's eyes if anything would.'

'And did it not?'

Rosamund Darnley shrugged her shoulders.

'I tell you I've seen nothing of him for years. People say, though, that he took it with absolute equanimity. Why, I should like to know? Has he got an absolutely blind belief in her?'

'There might be other reasons.'

'Yes. Pride! Keeping a stiff upper lip! I don't know what he really feels about her. Nobody does.'

'And she? What does she feel about him?'

Rosamund stared at him.

She said:

'She? She's the world's first gold-digger. And a man-eater as well! If anything personable in trousers comes within a hundred yards of her, it's fresh sport for Arlena! She's that kind.'

Poirot nodded his head slowly in complete agreement.

'Yes,' he said. 'That is true what you say . . . Her eyes look for one thing only – men.'

Rosamund said:

'She's got her eye on Patrick Redfern now. He's a good-looking man – and rather the simple kind – you know, fond of his wife, and not a philanderer. That's the kind that's meat and drink to Arlena. I like little Mrs Redfern – she's nice-looking in her fair washed-out way – but I don't think she'll stand a dog's chance against that man-eating tiger, Arlena.'

Poirot said:

'No, it is as you say.'

He looked distressed.

Rosamund said:

'Christine Redfern was a school teacher, I believe. She's the kind that thinks that mind has a pull over matter. She's got a rude shock coming to her.'

Poirot shook his head vexedly.

Rosamund got up. She said:

'It's a shame, you know.' She added vaguely: 'Somebody ought to do something about it.'

Linda Marshall was examining her face dispassionately in her bedroom mirror. She disliked her face very much. At this minute it seemed to her to be mostly bones and freckles. She noted with distaste her heavy bush of soft brown hair (mouse, she called it in her own mind), her greenish-grey eyes, her high cheek-bones and the long aggressive line of the chin. Her mouth and teeth weren't perhaps quite so bad – but what were teeth after all? And was that a spot coming on the side of her nose?

She decided with relief that it wasn't a spot. She thought to herself:
'It's awful to be sixteen – simply *awful*.'

One didn't, somehow, know where one was. Linda was as awkward as a
young colt and as prickly as a hedgehog. She was conscious the whole time
of her ungainliness and of the fact that she was neither one thing nor the
other. It hadn't been so bad at school. But now she had left school. Nobody
seemed to know quite what she was going to do next. Her father talked
vaguely of sending her to Paris next winter. Linda didn't want to go to
Paris – but then she didn't want to be at home either. She'd never realized
properly, somehow, until now, how very much she disliked Arlena.

Linda's young face grew tense, her green eyes hardened.

Arlena . . .

She thought to herself:

'She's a beast – a *beast* . . .'

Stepmothers! It was rotten to have a stepmother, everybody said so.
And it was true! Not that Arlena was unkind to her. Most of the time
she hardly noticed the girl. But when she did, there was a contemptuous
amusement in her glance, in her words. The finished grace and poise
of Arlena's movements emphasized Linda's own adolescent clumsiness.
With Arlena about, one felt, shamingly, just how immature and crude
one was.

But it wasn't that only. No, it wasn't only that.

Linda groped haltingly in the recesses of her mind. She wasn't very
good at sorting out her emotions and labelling them. It was something
that Arlena *did* to people – to the house –

'She's bad,' thought Linda with decision. 'She's quite, quite bad.'

But you couldn't even leave it at that. You couldn't just elevate
your nose with a sniff of moral superiority and dismiss her from your
mind.

It was something she did to people. Father, now, Father was quite
different . . .

She puzzled over it. Father coming down to take her out from school.
Father taking her once for a cruise. And Father at home – with Arlena
there. All – all sort of bottled up and not – and not *there*.

Linda thought:

'And it'll go on like this. Day after day – month after month. I can't
bear it.'

Life stretched before her – endless – in a series of days darkened and
poisoned by Arlena's presence. She was childish enough still to have little
sense of proportion. A year, to Linda, seemed like an eternity.

A big dark burning wave of hatred against Arlena surged up in her mind. She thought:

'I'd like to kill her. Oh! I wish she'd die . . .'

She looked out above the mirror on to the sea below.

This place was really rather fun. Or it could be fun. All those beaches and coves and queer little paths. Lots to explore. And places where one could go off by oneself and muck about. There were caves, too, so the Cowan boys had told her.

Linda thought:

'If only Arlena would go away, I could enjoy myself.'

Her mind went back to the evening of their arrival. It had been exciting coming from the mainland. The tide had been up over the causeway. They had come in a boat. The hotel had looked exciting, unusual. And then on the terrace a tall dark woman had jumped up and said:

'Why, Kenneth!'

And her father, looking frightfully surprised, had exclaimed:

'Rosamund!'

Linda considered Rosamund Darnley severely and critically in the manner of youth.

She decided that she approved of Rosamund. Rosamund, she thought, was sensible. And her hair grew nicely – as though it fitted her – most people's hair didn't fit them. And her clothes were nice. And she had a kind of funny amused face – as though it were amused at herself, not at you. Rosamund had been nice to her, Linda. She hadn't been gushing or *said* things. (Under the term of 'saying things' Linda grouped a mass of miscellaneous dislikes.) And Rosamund hadn't looked as though she thought Linda a fool. In fact she'd treated Linda as though she was a real human being. Linda so seldom felt like a real human being that she was deeply grateful when anyone appeared to consider her one.

Father, too, had seemed pleased to see Miss Darnley.

Funny – he'd looked quite different, all of a sudden. He'd looked – he'd looked – Linda puzzled it out – why, *young*, that was it! He'd laughed – a queer boyish laugh. Now Linda came to think of it, she'd very seldom heard him laugh.

She felt puzzled. It was as though she'd got a glimpse of quite a different person. She thought:

'I wonder what Father was like when he was my age . . .'

But that was too difficult. She gave it up.

An idea flashed across her mind.

What fun it would have been if they'd come here and found Miss Darnley here – just she and Father.

A vista opened out just for a minute. Father, boyish and laughing, Miss Darnley, herself – and all the fun one could have on the island – bathing – caves –

The blackness shut down again.

Arlena. One couldn't enjoy oneself with Arlena about. Why not? Well, she, Linda, couldn't anyway. You couldn't be happy when there was a person there you – hated. Yes, hated. She hated Arlena.

Very slowly again that black burning wave of hatred rose up again.

Linda's face went very white. Her lips parted a little. The pupils of her eyes contracted. And her fingers stiffened and clenched themselves . . .

Kenneth Marshall tapped on his wife's door. When her voice answered, he opened the door and went in.

Arlena was just putting the finishing touches to her toilet. She was dressed in glittering green and looked a little like a mermaid. She was standing in front of the glass applying mascara to her eyelashes. She said:

'Oh, it's you, Ken.'

'Yes. I wondered if you were ready.'

'Just a minute.'

Kenneth Marshall strolled to the window. He looked out on the sea. His face, as usual, displayed no emotion of any kind. It was pleasant and ordinary.

Turning round, he said:

'Arlena?'

'Yes?'

'You've met Redfern before, I gather?'

Arlena said easily:

'Oh yes, darling. At a cocktail party somewhere. I thought he was rather a pet.'

'So I gather. Did you know that he and his wife were coming down here?'

Arlena opened her eyes very wide.

'Oh no, darling. It was the *greatest* surprise!'

Kenneth Marshall said quietly:

'I thought, perhaps, that that was what put the idea of this place into your head. You were very keen we should come here.'

Arlena put down the mascara. She turned towards him. She smiled – a soft seductive smile. She said:

'Somebody told me about this place. I think it was the Rylands. They said it was simply too marvellous – so unspoilt! Don't you like it?'

Kenneth Marshall said:

'I'm not sure.'

'Oh, darling, but you adore bathing and lazing about. I'm sure you'll simply adore it here.'

'I can see that you mean to enjoy yourself.'

Her eyes widened a little. She looked at him uncertainly.

Kenneth Marshall said:

'I suppose the truth of it is that you told young Redfern that you were coming here?'

Arlena said:

'Kenneth darling, you're not going to be horrid, are you?'

Kenneth Marshall said:

'Look here, Arlena. I know what you're like. They're rather a nice young couple. That boy's fond of his wife, really. Must you upset the whole blinking show?'

Arlena said:

'It's so unfair blaming *me*. *I* haven't done anything – anything at all. I can't help it if –'

He prompted her.

'If what?'

Her eyelids fluttered.

'Well, of course. I know people do go crazy about me. But it's not my doing. They just get like that.'

'So you do admit that young Redfern is crazy about you?'

Arlena murmured:

'It's really rather stupid of him.'

She moved a step towards her husband.

'But you know, don't you, Ken, that I don't really care for anyone but you?'

She looked up at him through her darkened lashes.

It was a marvellous look – a look that few men could have resisted.

Kenneth Marshall looked down at her gravely. His face was composed. His voice quiet. He said:

'I think I know you pretty well, Arlena . . .'

★　　★　　★

When you came out of the hotel on the south side the terraces and the bathing beach were immediately below you. There was also a path that led off round the cliff on the south-west side of the island. A little way along it, a few steps led down to a series of recesses cut into the cliff and labelled on the hotel map of the island as Sunny Ledge. Here cut out of the cliff were niches with seats in them.

To one of these, immediately after dinner, came Patrick Redfern and his wife. It was a lovely clear night with a bright moon.

The Redferns sat down. For a while they were silent.

At last Patrick Redfern said:

'It's a glorious evening, isn't it, Christine?'

'Yes.'

Something in her voice may have made him uneasy. He sat without looking at her.

Christine Redfern asked in her quiet voice:

'Did you know that woman was going to be here?'

He turned sharply. He said:

'I don't know what you mean.'

'I think you do.'

'Look here, Christine. I don't know what has come over you –'

She interrupted. Her voice held feeling now. It trembled.

'Over *me*? It's what has come over *you*!'

'Nothing's come over me.'

'Oh! Patrick! it *has*! You insisted so on coming here. You were quite vehement. I wanted to go to Tintagel again where – where we had our honeymoon. You were bent on coming here.'

'Well, why not? It's a fascinating spot.'

'Perhaps. But you wanted to come here because *she* was going to be here.'

'She? Who is she?'

'Mrs Marshall. You – you're infatuated with her.'

'For God's sake, Christine, don't make a fool of yourself. It's not like you to be jealous.'

His bluster was a little uncertain. He exaggerated it.

She said:

'We've been so happy.'

'Happy? Of course we've been happy! We *are* happy. But we shan't go on being happy if I can't even speak to another woman without you kicking up a row.'

'It's not like that.'

'Yes, it is. In marriage one has got to have – well – friendships with other people. This suspicious attitude is all wrong. I – I can't speak to a pretty woman without your jumping to the conclusion that I'm in love with her –'

He stopped. He shrugged his shoulders.

Christine Redfern said:

'You *are* in love with her . . .'

'Oh, don't be a fool, Christine! I've – I've barely spoken to her.'

'That's not true.'

'Don't for goodness' sake get into the habit of being jealous of every pretty woman we come across.'

Christine Redfern said:

'She's not just any pretty woman! She's – she's *different*! She's a bad lot! Yes, she is. She'll do you harm, Patrick, please, *give it up*. Let's go away from here.'

Patrick Redfern stuck out his chin mutinously. He looked, somehow, very young as he said defiantly:

'Don't be ridiculous, Christine. And – and don't let's quarrel about it.'

'I don't want to quarrel.'

'Then behave like a reasonable human being. Come on, let's go back to the hotel.'

He got up. There was a pause, then Christine Redfern got up too. She said:

'Very well . . .'

In the recess adjoining, on the seat there, Hercule Poirot sat and shook his head sorrowfully.

Some people might have scrupulously removed themselves from earshot of a private conversation. But not Hercule Poirot. He had no scruples of that kind.

'Besides,' as he explained to his friend Hastings at a later date, 'it was a question of murder.'

Hastings said, staring:

'But the murder hadn't happened, then.'

Hercule Poirot sighed. He said:

'But already, *mon cher*, it was very clearly indicated.'

'Then why didn't you stop it?'

And Hercule Poirot, with a sigh, said as he had said once before in Egypt, that if a person is determined to commit murder it is not easy to prevent them. He does not blame himself for what happened. It was, according to him, inevitable.

CHAPTER 3

Rosamund Darnley and Kenneth Marshall sat on the short springy turf of the cliff overlooking Gull Cove. This was on the east side of the island. People came here in the morning sometimes to bathe when they wanted to be peaceful.

Rosamund said:

'It's nice to get away from people.'

Marshall murmured inaudibly:

'M – m, yes.'

He rolled over, sniffing at the short turf.

'Smells good. Remember the downs at Shipley?'

'Rather.'

'Pretty good, those days.'

'Yes.'

'You've not changed much, Rosamund.'

'Yes, I have. I've changed enormously.'

'You've been very successful and you're rich and all that, but you're the same old Rosamund.'

Rosamund murmured:

'I wish I were.'

'What's that?'

'Nothing. It's a pity, isn't it, Kenneth, that we can't keep the nice natures and high ideals that we had when we were young?'

'I don't know that your nature was ever particularly nice, my child. You used to get into the most frightful rages. You half-choked me once when you flew at me in a temper.'

Rosamund laughed. She said:

'Do you remember the day that we took Toby down to get water rats?'

They spent some minutes in recalling old adventures.

Then there came a pause.

Rosamund's fingers played with the clasp of her bag. She said at last:

'Kenneth?'

'Um.' His reply was indistinct. He was still lying on his face on the turf.

'If I say something to you that is probably outrageously impertinent will you never speak to me again?'

He rolled over and sat up.

'I don't think,' he said seriously, 'that I would ever regard anything you said as impertinent. You see, you *belong*.'

She nodded in acceptance of all that last phrase meant. She concealed only the pleasure it gave her.

'Kenneth, why don't you get a divorce from your wife?'

His face altered. It hardened – the happy expression died out of it. He took a pipe from his pocket and began filling it.

Rosamund said:

'I'm sorry if I've offended you.'

He said quietly:

'You haven't offended me.'

'Well then, why don't you?'

'You don't understand, my dear girl.'

'Are you – so frightfully fond of her?'

'It's not just a question of that. You see, I married her.'

'I know. But she's – pretty notorious.'

He considered that for a moment, ramming in the tobacco carefully.

'Is she? I suppose she is.'

'You *could* divorce her, Ken.'

'My dear girl, you've got no business to say a thing like that. Just because men lose their heads about her a bit isn't to say that she loses hers.'

Rosamund bit off a rejoinder. Then she said:

'You could fix it so that she divorced you – if you prefer it that way.'

'I dare say I could.'

'You ought to, Ken. Really, I mean it. There's the child.'

'Linda?'

'Yes, Linda.'

'What's Linda to do with it?'

'Arlena's not good for Linda. She isn't really. Linda, I think, *feels* things a good deal.'

Kenneth Marshall applied a match to his pipe. Between puffs he said:

'Yes – there's something in that. I suppose Arlena and Linda aren't very good for each other. Not the right thing for a girl perhaps. It's a bit worrying.'

Rosamund said:

'I like Linda – very much. There's something – fine about her.'

Kenneth said:

'She's like her mother. She takes things hard like Ruth did.'

Rosamund said:

'Then don't you think – really – that you ought to get rid of Arlena?'

'Fix up a divorce?'

'Yes. People are doing that all the time.'

Kenneth Marshall said with sudden vehemence:

'Yes, and that's just what I hate.'

'Hate?' She was startled.

'Yes. Sort of attitude to life there is nowadays. If you take on a thing and don't like it, then you get yourself out of it as quick as possible! Dash it all, there's got to be such a thing as good faith. If you marry a woman and engage yourself to look after her, well it's up to you to do it. It's your show. You've taken it on. I'm sick of quick marriage and easy divorce. Arlena's my wife, that's all there is to it.'

Rosamund leaned forward. She said in a low voice:

'So it's like that with you? "Till death do us part"?'

Kenneth Marshall nodded his head.

He said:

'That's just it.'

Rosamund said:

'I see.'

Mr Horace Blatt, returning to Leathercombe Bay down a narrow twisting lane, nearly ran down Mrs Redfern at a corner.

As she flattened herself into the hedge, Mr Blatt brought his Sunbeam to a halt by applying the brakes vigorously.

'Hullo-ullo-ullo,' said Mr Blatt cheerfully.

He was a large man with a red face and a fringe of reddish hair round a shining bald spot.

It was Mr Blatt's apparent ambition to be the life and soul of any place he happened to be in. The Jolly Roger Hotel, in his opinion, given somewhat loudly, needed brightening up. He was puzzled at the way people seemed to melt and disappear when he himself arrived on the scene.

'Nearly made you into strawberry jam, didn't I?' said Mr Blatt gaily.

Christine Redfern said:

'Yes, you did.'

'Jump in,' said Mr Blatt.

'Oh, thanks – I think I'll walk.'

'Nonsense,' said Mr Blatt. 'What's a car for?'

Yielding to necessity Christine Redfern got in.

Mr Blatt restarted the engine which had stopped owing to the suddenness with which he had previously pulled up.

Mr Blatt inquired:

'And what are you doing walking about all alone? That's all wrong, a nice-looking girl like you.'

Christine said hurriedly:

'Oh! I like being alone.'

Mr Blatt gave her a terrific dig with his elbow, nearly sending the car into the hedge at the same time.

'Girls always say that,' he said. 'They don't mean it. You know, that place, the Jolly Roger, wants a bit of livening up. Nothing jolly about it. No *life* in it. Of course there's a good amount of duds staying there. A lot of kids, to begin with and a lot of old fogeys too. There's that old Anglo-Indian bore and that athletic parson and those yapping Americans and that foreigner with the moustache – makes me laugh that moustache of his! I should say he's a hairdresser, something of that sort.'

Christine shook her head.

'Oh no, he's a detective.'

Mr Blatt nearly let the car go into the hedge again.

'A detective? D'you mean he's in *disguise*?'

Christine smiled faintly.

She said:

'Oh no, he really *is* like that. He's Hercule Poirot. You must have heard of him.'

Mr Blatt said:

'Didn't catch his name properly. Oh yes, I've *heard* of him. But I thought he was dead. Dash it, he *ought* to be dead. What's he after down here?'

'He's not after anything – he's just on a holiday.'

'Well, I suppose that might be so,' Mr Blatt seemed doubtful about it. 'Looks a bit of a bounder, doesn't he?'

'Well,' said Christine and hesitated. 'Perhaps a little peculiar.'

'What I say is,' said Mr Blatt, 'what's wrong with Scotland Yard? Buy British every time for me.'

He reached the bottom of the hill and with a triumphant fanfare of the horn ran the car into the Jolly Roger's garage which was situated, for tidal reasons, on the mainland opposite the hotel.

Linda Marshall was in the small shop which catered for the wants of visitors to Leathercombe Bay. One side of it was devoted to shelves on which were books which could be borrowed for the sum of twopence.

The newest of them was ten years old, some were twenty years old and others older still.

Linda took first one and then another doubtfully from the shelf and glanced into it. She decided that she couldn't possibly read *The Four Feathers* or *Vice Versa*. She took out a small squat volume in brown calf.

The time passed . . .

With a start Linda shoved the book back in the shelf as Christine Redfern's voice said:

'What are you reading, Linda?'

Linda said hurriedly:

'Nothing. I'm looking for a book.'

She pulled out *The Marriage of William Ashe* at random and advanced to the counter fumbling for twopence.

Christine said:

'Mr Blatt just drove me home – after nearly running over me first. I really felt I couldn't walk all across the causeway with him, so I said I had to buy some things.'

Linda said:

'He's awful, isn't he? Always saying how rich he is and making the most terrible jokes.'

Christine said:

'Poor man. One really feels rather sorry for him.'

Linda didn't agree. She didn't see anything to be sorry for in Mr Blatt. She was young and ruthless.

She walked with Christine Redfern out of the shop and down towards the causeway.

She was busy with her own thoughts. She liked Christine Redfern. She and Rosamund Darnley were the only bearable people on the island in Linda's opinion. Neither of them talked much to her for one thing. Now, as they walked, Christine didn't say anything. That, Linda thought, was sensible. If you hadn't anything worth saying why go chattering all the time?

She lost herself in her own perplexities.

She said suddenly:

'Mrs Redfern, have you ever felt that everything's so awful – so terrible – that you'll – oh, *burst* . . . ?'

The words were almost comic, but Linda's face, drawn and anxious, was not. Christine Redfern, looking at her at first vaguely, with scarcely comprehending eyes, certainly saw nothing to laugh at . . .

She caught her breath sharply.

She said:

'Yes – yes – I have felt – just that . . .'

Mr Blatt said:

'So you're the famous sleuth, eh?'

They were in the cocktail bar, a favourite haunt of Mr Blatt's.

Hercule Poirot acknowledged the remark with his usual lack of modesty.

Mr Blatt went on.

'And what are you doing down here – on a job?'

'No, no. I repose myself. I take the holiday.'

Mr Blatt winked.

'You'd say that anyway, wouldn't you?'

Poirot replied:

'Not necessarily.'

Horace Blatt said:

'Oh! Come now. As a matter of fact you'd be safe enough with *me*. I don't repeat all I hear! Learnt to keep my mouth shut years ago. Shouldn't have got on the way I have if I hadn't known how to do that. But you know what most people are – yap, yap, yap about everything they hear! Now you can't afford that in your trade! That's why you've got to keep it up that you're here holiday-making and nothing else.'

Poirot asked:

'And why should you suppose the contrary?'

Mr Blatt closed one eye.

He said:

'I'm a man of the world. I know the cut of a fellow's jib. A man like you would be at Deauville or Le Touquet or down at Juan les Pins. That's your – what's the phrase? – spiritual home.'

Poirot sighed. He looked out of the window. Rain was falling and mist encircled the island. He said:

'It is possible that you are right! There, at least, in wet weather there are the distractions.'

'Good old Casino!' said Mr Blatt. 'You know, I've had to work pretty hard most of my life. No time for holidays or kickshaws. I meant to make good and I have made good. Now I can do what I please. My money's as good as any man's. I've seen a bit of life in the last few years, I can tell you.'

Poirot murmured:

'Ah, yes?'

'Don't know why I came to this place,' Mr Blatt continued.

Poirot observed:

'I, too, wondered?'

'Eh, what's that?'

Poirot waved an eloquent hand.

'I, too, am not without observation. I should have expected *you* most certainly to choose Deauville or Biarritz.'

'Instead of which, we're both here, eh?'

Mr Blatt gave a hoarse chuckle.

'Don't really know why I came here,' he mused. 'I think, you know, it sounded *romantic*. Jolly Roger Hotel, Smugglers' Island. That kind of address tickles you up, you know. Makes you think of when you were a boy. Pirates, smuggling, all that.'

He laughed, rather self-consciously.

'I used to sail quite a bit as a boy. Not this part of the world. Off the East coast. Funny how a taste for that sort of thing never quite leaves you. I could have a tip-top yacht if I liked, but somehow I don't really fancy it. I like mucking about in that little yawl of mine. Redfern's keen on sailing, too. He's been out with me once or twice. Can't get hold of him now – always hanging round that red-haired wife of Marshall's.'

He paused, then lowering his voice, he went on:

'Mostly a dried up lot of sticks in this hotel! Mrs Marshall's about the only lively spot! I should think Marshall's got his hands full looking after her. All sorts of stories about her in her stage days – *and* after! Men go crazy about her. You'll see, there'll be a spot of trouble one of these days.'

Poirot asked: 'What kind of trouble?'

Horace Blatt replied:

'That depends. I'd say, looking at Marshall, that he's a man with a funny kind of temper. As a matter of fact, I know he is. Heard something about him. I've met that quiet sort. Never know where you are with that kind. Redfern had better look out –'

He broke off, as the subject of his words came into the bar. He went on speaking loudly and self-consciously.

'And, as I say, sailing round this coast is good fun. Hullo, Redfern, have one with me? What'll you have? Dry Martini? Right. What about you, M. Poirot?'

Poirot shook his head.

Patrick Redfern sat down and said:

'Sailing? It's the best fun in the world. Wish I could do more of it. Used to spend most of my time as a boy in a sailing dinghy round this coast.'

Poirot said:

'Then you know this part of the world well?'

'Rather! I knew this place before there was a hotel on it. There were just a few fishermen's cottages at Leathercombe Bay and a tumbledown old house, all shut up, on the island.'

'There was a house here?'

'Oh, yes, but it hadn't been lived in for years. Was practically falling down. There used to be all sorts of stories of secret passages from the house to Pixy's Cave. We were always looking for that secret passage, I remember.'

Horace Blatt spilt his drink. He cursed, mopped himself and asked:

'What is this Pixy's Cave?'

Patrick said:

'Oh, don't you know it? It's on Pixy Cove. You can't find the entrance to it easily. It's among a lot of piled up boulders at one end. Just a long thin crack. You can just squeeze through it. Inside it widens out into quite a big cave. You can imagine what fun it was to a boy! An old fisherman showed it to me. Nowadays, even the fishermen don't know about it. I asked one the other day why the place was called Pixy Cove and he couldn't tell me.'

Hercule Poirot said:

'But I still do not understand. What is this pixy?'

Patrick Redfern said:

'Oh! that's typically Devonshire. There's the pixy's cave at Sheepstor on the Moor. You're supposed to leave a pin, you know, as a present for the pixy. A pixy is a kind of moor spirit.'

Hercule Poirot said:

'Ah! but it is interesting, that.'

Patrick Redfern went on.

'There's a lot of pixy lore on Dartmoor still. There are tors that are said to be pixy ridden, and I expect that farmers coming home after a thick night still complain of being pixy led.'

Horace Blatt said:

'You mean when they've had a couple?'

Patrick Redfern said with a smile:

'That's certainly the commonsense explanation!'

Blatt looked at his watch. He said:

'I'm going in to dinner. On the whole, Redfern, pirates are my favourites, not pixies.'

Patrick Redfern said with a laugh as the other went out:

'Faith, I'd like to see the old boy pixy led himself!'

Poirot observed meditatively:

'For a hard-bitten business man, M. Blatt seems to have a very romantic imagination.'

Patrick Redfern said:

'That's because he's only half educated. Or so my wife says. Look at what he reads! Nothing but thrillers or Wild West stories.'

Poirot said:

'You mean that he has still the mentality of a boy?'

'Well, don't you think so, sir?'

'Me, I have not seen very much of him.'

'I haven't either. I've been out sailing with him once or twice – but he doesn't really like having anyone with him. He prefers to be on his own.'

Hercule Poirot said:

'That is indeed curious. It is singularly unlike his practice on land.'

Redfern laughed. He said:

'I know. We all have a bit of trouble keeping out of his way. He'd like to turn this place into a cross between Margate and Le Touquet.'

Poirot said nothing for a minute or two. He was studying the laughing face of his companion very attentively. He said suddenly and unexpectedly:

'I think, M. Redfern, that you enjoy living.'

Patrick stared at him, surprised.

'Indeed I do. Why not?'

'Why not indeed,' agreed Poirot. 'I make you my felicitation on the fact.'

Smiling a little, Patrick Redfern said:

'Thank you, sir.'

'That is why, as an older man, a very much older man, I venture to offer you a piece of advice.'

'Yes, sir?'

'A very wise friend of mine in the Police Force said to me years ago: "Hercule, my friend, if you would know tranquillity, avoid women."'

Patrick Redfern said:

'I'm afraid it's a bit late for that, sir. I'm married, you know.'

'I do know. Your wife is a very charming, a very accomplished woman. She is, I think, very fond of you.'

Patrick Redfern said sharply:

'I'm very fond of her.'

'Ah,' said Hercule Poirot, 'I am delighted to hear it.'

Patrick's brow was suddenly like thunder.

'Look here, M. Poirot, what are you getting at?'

'*Les Femmes.*' Poirot leaned back and closed his eyes. 'I know something of them. They are capable of complicating life unbearably. And the English, they conduct their affairs indescribably. If it was necessary for you to come here, M. Redfern, why, in the name of heaven, did you bring your wife?'

Patrick Redfern said angrily:

'I don't know what you mean.'

Hercule Poirot said calmly:

'You know perfectly. I am not so foolish as to argue with an infatuated man. I utter only the word of caution.'

'You've been listening to these damned scandal-mongers. Mrs Gardener, the Brewster woman – nothing to do but to clack their tongues all day. Just because a woman's good-looking – they're down on her like a sack of coals.'

Hercule Poirot got up. He murmured:

'Are you really as young as all that?'

Shaking his head, he left the bar. Patrick Redfern stared angrily after him.

Hercule Poirot paused in the hall on his way from the dining-room. The doors were open – a breath of soft night air came in.

The rain had stopped and the mist had dispersed. It was a fine night again.

Hercule Poirot found Mrs Redfern in her favourite seat on the cliff ledge. He stopped by her and said:

'This seat is damp. You should not sit here. You will catch the chill.'

'No, I shan't. And what does it matter anyway.'

'Tscha, tscha, you are not a child! You are an educated woman. You must look at things sensibly.'

She said coldly:

'I can assure you I never take cold.'

Poirot said:

'It has been a wet day. The wind blew, the rain came down, and the mist was everywhere so that one could not see through it. *Eh bien*, what is it like now? The mists have rolled away, the sky is clear and up above the stars shine. That is like life, Madame.'

Christine said in a low fierce voice:

'Do you know what I am most sick of in this place?'

'What, Madame?'

'Pity.'

She brought the word out like the flick of a whip.

She went on:

'Do you think I don't know? That I can't see? All the time people are saying: "Poor Mrs Redfern – that poor little woman." And anyway I'm not little, I'm tall. They say little because they are sorry for me. And I can't bear it!'

Cautiously, Hercule Poirot spread his handkerchief on the seat and sat down. He said thoughtfully:

'There is something in that.'

'That woman –' said Christine and stopped.

Poirot said gravely:

'Will you allow me to tell you something, Madame? Something that is as true as the stars above us? The Arlena Stuarts – or Arlena Marshalls – of this world – do not count.'

Christine Redfern said:

'Nonsense.'

'I assure you, it is true. Their Empire is of the moment and for the moment. To count – really and truly to count – a woman must have goodness or brains.'

Christine said scornfully:

'Do you think men care for goodness or brains?'

Poirot said gravely:

'Fundamentally, yes.'

Christine laughed shortly.

'I don't agree with you.'

Poirot said:

'Your husband loves you, Madame. I know it.'

'You can't know it.'

'Yes, yes. I know it. I have seen him looking at you.'

Suddenly she broke down. She wept stormily and bitterly against Poirot's accommodating shoulder.

She said:

'I can't bear it . . . I can't bear it . . .'

Poirot patted her arm. He said soothingly:

'Patience – only patience.'

She sat up and pressed her handkerchief to her eyes. She said in a stifled voice:

'It's all right. I'm better now. Leave me. I'd – I'd rather be alone.'

He obeyed and left her sitting there while he himself followed the winding path down to the hotel.

He was nearly there when he heard the murmur of voices.

He turned a little aside from the path. There was a gap in the bushes.

He saw Arlena Marshall and Patrick Redfern beside her. He heard the man's voice, with the throb in it of emotion.

'I'm crazy about you – crazy – you've driven me mad . . . You do care a little – you do care?'

He saw Arlena Marshall's face – it was, he thought, like a sleek happy cat – it was animal, not human. She said softly:

'Of course, Patrick darling, I adore you. You know that . . .'

For once Hercule Poirot cut his eavesdropping short. He went back to the path and on down to the hotel.

A figure joined him suddenly. It was Captain Marshall.

Marshall said:

'Remarkable night, what? After that foul day.' He looked up at the sky. 'Looks as though we should have fine weather tomorrow.'

<hr />

CHAPTER 4

The morning of the 25th of August dawned bright and cloudless. It was a morning to tempt even an inveterate sluggard to rise early.

Several people rose early that morning at the Jolly Roger.

It was eight o'clock when Linda, sitting at her dressing-table, turned a little thick calf bound volume face downwards, sprawling it open and looked at her own face in the mirror.

Her lips were set tight together and the pupils of her eyes contracted.

She said below her breath:

'I'll do it . . .'

She slipped out of her pyjamas and into her bathing-dress. Over it she flung on a bath-robe and laced espadrilles on her feet.

She went out of her room and along the passage. At the end of it a door on to the balcony led to an outside staircase leading directly down to the rocks below the hotel. There was a small iron ladder clamped on to the rocks leading down into the water which was used by many of the hotel guests for a before-breakfast dip as taking up less time than going down to the main bathing beach.

As Linda started down from the balcony she met her father coming up. He said:

'You're up early. Going to have a dip?'

Linda nodded.

They passed each other.

Instead of going on down the rocks, however, Linda skirted round the hotel to the left until she came to the path down to the causeway connecting the hotel with the mainland. The tide was high and the causeway under water, but the boat that took hotel guests across was tied to a little jetty. The man in charge of it was absent at the moment. Linda got in, untied it and rowed herself across.

She tied up the boat on the other side, walked up the slope, past the hotel garage and along until she reached the general shop.

The woman had just taken down the shutters and was engaged in sweeping out the floor. She looked amazed at the sight of Linda.

'Well, Miss, you *are* up early.'

Linda put her hand in the pocket of her bath-wrap and brought out some money. She proceeded to make her purchases.

Christine Redfern was standing in Linda's room when the girl returned.

'Oh, there you are,' Christine exclaimed. 'I thought you couldn't be really up yet.'

Linda said:

'No, I've been bathing.'

Noticing the parcel in her hand, Christine said with surprise:

'The post has come early today.'

Linda flushed. With her habitual nervous clumsiness the parcel slipped from her hand. The flimsy string broke and some of the contents rolled over the floor.

Christine exclaimed:

'What have you been buying *candles* for?'

But to Linda's relief she did not wait for an answer, but went on, as she helped to pick the things up from the floor.

'I came in to ask whether you would like to come with me to Gull Cove this morning. I want to sketch there.'

Linda accepted with alacrity.

In the last few days she had accompanied Christine Redfern more than once on sketching expeditions. Christine was a most indifferent artist, but it is possible that she found the excuse of painting a help to her pride since her husband now spent most of his time with Arlena Marshall.

Linda Marshall had been increasingly morose and bad tempered. She liked being with Christine who, intent on her work, spoke very little. It was, Linda felt, nearly as good as being by oneself, and in a curious way she craved for company of some kind. There was a subtle kind of sympathy between her and the elder woman, probably based on the fact of their mutual dislike of the same person.

Christine said:

'I'm playing tennis at twelve, so we'd better start fairly early. Half-past ten?'

'Right. I'll be ready. Meet you in the hall.'

Rosamund Darnley, strolling out of the dining-room after a very late breakfast, was cannoned into by Linda as the latter came tearing down the stairs.

'Oh! sorry, Miss Darnley.'

Rosamund said: 'Lovely morning, isn't it? One can hardly believe it after yesterday.'

'I know. I'm going with Mrs Redfern to Gull Cove. I said I'd meet her at half-past ten. I thought I was late.'

'No, it's only twenty-five past.'

'Oh! good.'

She was panting a little and Rosamund looked at her curiously.

'You're not feverish, are you, Linda?'

The girl's eyes were very bright and she had a vivid patch of colour in each cheek.

'Oh! *no*. I'm never feverish.'

Rosamund smiled and said:

'It's such a lovely day I got up for breakfast. Usually I have it in bed. But today I came down and faced eggs and bacon like a man.'

'I know – it's heavenly after yesterday. Gull Cove is nice in the morning. I shall put a lot of oil on and get really brown.'

Rosamund said:

'Yes, Gull Cove is nice in the morning. And it's more peaceful than the beach here.'

Linda said, rather shyly:

'Come too.'

Rosamund shook her head.

554 • AGATHA CHRISTIE

She said:

'Not this morning. I've other fish to fry.'

Christine Redfern came down the stairs.

She was wearing beach pyjamas of a loose floppy pattern with long sleeves and wide legs. They were made of some green material with a yellow design. Rosamund's tongue itched to tell her that yellow and green were the most unbecoming colours possible for her fair, slightly anaemic complexion. It always annoyed Rosamund when people had no clothes sense.

She thought: 'If I dressed that girl, *I'd* soon make her husband sit up and take notice. However much of a fool Arlena is, she does know how to dress. This wretched girl looks just like a wilting lettuce.'

Aloud she said:

'Have a nice time. I'm going to Sunny Ledge with a book.'

Hercule Poirot breakfasted in his room as usual off coffee and rolls.

The beauty of the morning, however, tempted him to leave the hotel earlier than usual. It was ten o'clock, at least half an hour before his usual appearance, when he descended to the bathing beach. The beach itself was empty save for one person.

That person was Arlena Marshall.

Clad in her white bathing-dress, the green Chinese hat on her head, she was trying to launch a white wooden float. Poirot came gallantly to the rescue, completely immersing a pair of white suède shoes in doing so.

She thanked him with one of those sideways glances of hers.

Just as she was pushing off, she called him.

'M. Poirot?'

Poirot leaped to the water's edge.

'Madame.'

Arlena Marshall said:

'Do something for me, will you?'

'Anything.'

She smiled at him. She murmured:

'Don't tell any one where I am.' She made her glance appealing. 'Every one *will* follow me about so. I just want for once to be *alone*.'

She paddled off vigorously.

Poirot walked up the beach. He murmured to himself:

'*Ah ça, jamais!* That, *par exemple*, I do not believe.'

He doubted if Arlena Stuart, to give her her stage name, had ever wanted to be alone in her life.

Hercule Poirot, that man of the world, knew better. Arlena Marshall was doubtless keeping a rendezvous, and Poirot had a very good idea with whom.

Or thought he had, but there he found himself proved wrong.

For just as she floated round the point of the bay and disappeared out of sight, Patrick Redfern closely followed by Kenneth Marshall, came striding down the beach from the hotel.

Marshall nodded to Poirot, ''Morning, Poirot. Seen my wife anywhere about?'

Poirot's answer was diplomatic.

'Has Madame then risen so early?'

Marshall said:

'She's not in her room.' He looked up at the sky. 'Lovely day. I shall have a bathe right away. Got a lot of typing to do this morning.'

Patrick Redfern, less openly, was looking up and down the beach. He sat down near Poirot and prepared to wait for the arrival of his lady.

Poirot said:

'And Madame Redfern? Has she too risen early?'

Patrick Redfern said:

'Christine? Oh, she's going off sketching. She's rather keen on art just now.'

He spoke impatiently, his mind clearly elsewhere. As time passed he displayed his impatience for Arlena's arrival only too crudely. At every footstep he turned an eager head to see who it was coming down from the hotel.

Disappointment followed disappointment.

First Mr and Mrs Gardener complete with knitting and book and then Miss Brewster arrived.

Mrs Gardener, industrious as ever, settled herself in her chair, and began to knit vigorously and talk at the same time.

'Well, M. Poirot. The beach seems very deserted this morning. Where *is* everybody?'

Poirot replied that the Mastermans and the Cowans, two families with young people in them, had gone off on an all-day sailing excursion.

'Why that certainly does make all the difference, not having them about laughing and calling out. And only one person bathing, Captain Marshall.'

Marshall had just finished his swim. He came up the beach swinging his towel.

'Pretty good in the sea this morning,' he said. 'Unfortunately I've got a lot of work to do. Must go and get on with it.'

'Why, if that isn't too bad, Captain Marshall. On a beautiful day like this, too. My, wasn't yesterday too terrible? I said to Mr Gardener that if the weather was going to continue like that we'd just have to leave. It's the melancholy, you know, with the mist right up around the island. Gives you a kind of ghostly feeling, but then I've always been very susceptible to atmosphere ever since I was a child. Sometimes, you know, I'd feel I just had to scream and scream. And that, of course, was very trying to my parents. But my mother was a lovely woman and she said to my father, "Sinclair, if the child feels like that, we must let her do it. Screaming is her way of expressing herself." And of course, my father agreed. He was devoted to my mother and just did everything she said. They were a perfectly lovely couple, as I'm sure Mr Gardener will agree. They were a very remarkable couple, weren't they, Odell?'

'Yes, darling,' said Mr Gardener.

'And where's your girl this morning, Captain Marshall?'

'Linda? I don't know. I expect she's mooning round the island somewhere.'

'You know, Captain Marshall, that girl looks kind of peaky to me. She needs feeding up and very very sympathetic treatment.'

Kenneth Marshall said curtly:

'Linda's all right.'

He went up to the hotel.

Patrick Redfern did not go into the water. He sat about, frankly looking up towards the hotel. He was beginning to look a shade sulky.

Miss Brewster was brisk and cheerful when she arrived.

The conversation was much as it had been on a previous morning. Gentle yapping from Mrs Gardener and short staccato barks from Miss Brewster.

She remarked at last: 'Beach seems a bit empty. Everyone off on excursions?'

Mrs Gardener said:

'I was saying to Mr Gardener only this morning that we simply must make an excursion to Dartmoor. It's quite near and the associations are all so romantic. And I'd like to see that convict prison – Princetown, isn't it? I think we'd better fix up right away and go there tomorrow, Odell.'

Mr Gardener said:

'Yes, darling.'

Hercule Poirot said to Miss Brewster:

'You are going to bathe, Mademoiselle?'

'Oh I've had my morning dip before breakfast. Somebody nearly brained me with a bottle, too. Chucked it out of one of the hotel windows.'

'Now that's a very dangerous thing to do,' said Mrs Gardener. 'I had a very dear friend who got concussion by a toothpaste tin falling on him in the street – thrown out of a thirty-fifth storey window it was. A most dangerous thing to do. He got very substantial damages.' She began to hunt among her skeins of wool. 'Why, Odell, I don't believe I've got that second shade of purple wool. It's in the second drawer of the bureau in our bedroom or it might be the third.'

'Yes, darling.'

Mr Gardener rose obediently and departed on his search.

Mrs Gardener went on:

'Sometimes, you know, I do think that maybe we're going a little too far nowadays. What with all our great discoveries and all the electrical waves there must be in the atmosphere, I do think it leads to a great deal of mental unrest, and I just feel that maybe the time has come for a new message to humanity. I don't know, M. Poirot, if you've ever interested yourself in the prophecies from the Pyramids.'

'I have not,' said Poirot.

'Well, I do assure you that they're very, very interesting. What with Moscow being exactly a thousand miles due north of – now what was it? – would it be Nineveh? – but anyway you take a circle and it just shows the most surprising things – and one can just see that there must have been special guidance, and that those ancient Egyptians couldn't have thought of what they did all by themselves. And when you've gone into the theory of the numbers and their repetition, why it's all just so clear that I can't see how anyone can doubt the truth of it for a moment.'

Mrs Gardener paused triumphantly but neither Poirot nor Miss Emily Brewster felt moved to argue the point.

Poirot studied his white suède shoes ruefully.

Emily Brewster said:

'You been paddling with your shoes on, M. Poirot?'

Poirot murmured:

'Alas! I was precipitate.'

Emily Brewster lowered her voice. She said:

'Where's our vamp this morning? She's late.'

Mrs Gardener, raising her eyes from her knitting to study Patrick Redfern, murmured:

'He looks just like a thundercloud. Oh dear, I do feel the whole thing is such a pity. I wonder what Captain Marshall thinks about it all. He's such a nice quiet man – very British and unassuming. You just never know what he's thinking about things.'

Patrick Redfern rose and began to pace up and down the beach.

Mrs Gardener murmured:

'Just like a tiger.'

Three pairs of eyes watched his pacing. Their scrutiny seemed to make Patrick Redfern uncomfortable. He looked more than sulky now. He looked in a flaming temper.

In the stillness a faint chime from the mainland came to their ears.

Emily Brewster murmured:

'Wind's from the east again. That's a good sign when you can hear the church clock strike.'

Nobody said any more until Mr Gardener returned with a skein of brilliant magenta wool.

'Why, Odell, what a long time you have been?'

'Sorry darling, but you see it wasn't in your bureau at all. I found it on your wardrobe shelf.'

'Why, isn't that too extraordinary? I could have declared I put it in that bureau drawer. I do think it's fortunate that I've never had to give evidence in a court case. I'd just worry myself to death in case I wasn't remembering a thing just right.'

Mr Gardener said:

'Mrs Gardener is very conscientious.'

It was some five minutes later that Patrick Redfern said:

'Going for your row this morning, Miss Brewster? Mind if I come with you?'

Miss Brewster said heartily:

'Delighted.'

'Let's row right round the island,' proposed Redfern.

Miss Brewster consulted her watch.

'Shall we have time? Oh yes, it's not half-past eleven yet. Come on, then, let's start.'

They went down the beach together.

Patrick Redfern took first turn at the oars. He rowed with a powerful stroke. The boat leapt forward.

Emily Brewster said approvingly:

'Good. We'll see if you can keep that up.'

He laughed into her eyes. His spirits had improved.

'I shall probably have a fine crop of blisters by the time we get back.' He threw up his head, tossing back his black hair. 'God, it's a marvellous day! If you do get a real summer's day in England there's nothing to beat it.'

Emily Brewster said gruffly:

'Can't beat England anyway in my opinion. Only place in the world to live in.'

'I'm with you.'

They rounded the point of the bay to the west and rowed under the cliffs. Patrick Redfern looked up.

'Any one on Sunny Ledge this morning? Yes, there's a sunshade. Who is it, I wonder?'

Emily Brewster said:

'It's Miss Darnley, I think. She's got one of those Japanese affairs.'

They rowed up the coast. On their left was the open sea.

Emily Brewster said:

'We ought to have gone the other way round. This way we've got the current against us.'

'There's very little current. I've swum out here and not noticed it. Anyway we couldn't go the other way, the causeway wouldn't be covered.'

'Depends on the tide, of course. But they always say that bathing from Pixy Cove is dangerous if you swim out too far.'

Patrick was rowing vigorously still. At the same time he was scanning the cliffs attentively.

Emily Brewster thought suddenly:

'He's looking for the Marshall woman. That's why he wanted to come with me. She hasn't shown up this morning and he's wondering what she's up to. Probably she's done it on purpose. Just a move in the game – to make him keener.'

They rounded the jutting point of rock to the south of the little bay named Pixy's Cove. It was quite a small cove, with rocks dotted fantastically about the beach. It faced nearly north-west and the cliff overhung it a good deal. It was a favourite place for picnic teas. In the morning, when the sun was off, it was not popular and there was seldom anyone there.

On this occasion, however, there was a figure on the beach.

Patrick Redfern's stroke checked and recovered.

He said in a would-be casual tone:

'Hullo, who's that?'

Miss Brewster said dryly:

'It looks like Mrs Marshall.'

Patrick Redfern said, as though struck by the idea.

'So it does.'

He altered his course, rowing inshore.

Emily Brewster protested.

'We don't want to land here, do we?'

Patrick Redfern said quickly:

'Oh, plenty of time.'

His eyes looked into hers – something in them, a naïve pleading look rather like that of an importunate dog, silenced Emily Brewster. She thought to herself:

'Poor boy, he's got it badly. Oh well, it can't be helped. He'll get over it in time.'

The boat was fast approaching the beach.

Arlena Marshall was lying face downwards on the shingle, her arms outstretched. The white float was drawn up nearby.

Something was puzzling Emily Brewster. It was as though she was looking at something she knew quite well but which was in one respect quite wrong.

It was a minute or two before it came to her.

Arlena Marshall's attitude was the attitude of a sun-bather. So had she lain many a time on the beach by the hotel, her bronzed body outstretched and the green cardboard hat protecting her head and neck.

But there was no sun on Pixy's Beach and there would be none for some hours yet. The overhanging cliff protected the beach from the sun in the morning. A vague feeling of apprehension came over Emily Brewster.

The boat grounded on the shingle. Patrick Redfern called:

'Hullo, Arlena.'

And then Emily Brewster's foreboding took definite shape. For the recumbent figure did not move or answer.

Emily saw Patrick Redfern's face change. He jumped out of the boat and she followed him. They dragged the boat ashore then set off up the beach to where that white figure lay so still and unresponsive near the bottom of the cliff.

Patrick Redfern got there first but Emily Brewster was close behind him.

She saw, as one sees in a dream, the bronzed limbs, the white backless bathing-dress – the red curl of hair escaping under the jade-green hat – saw something else too – the curious unnatural angle of the outspread arms. Felt, in that minute, that this body had not *lain* down but had been thrown . . .

She heard Patrick's voice – a mere frightened whisper. He knelt down beside that still form – touched the hand – the arm . . .

He said in a low shuddering whisper:

'*My God, she's dead . . .*'

And then, as he lifted the hat a little, peered at the neck:

'*Oh, God, she's been strangled . . . murdered.*'

It was one of those moments when time stands still.

With an odd feeling of unreality Emily Brewster heard herself saying:

'We mustn't touch anything . . . Not until the police come.'

Redfern's answer came mechanically.

'No – no – of course not.' And then in a deep agonized whisper. 'Who? *Who?* Who could have done that to Arlena. She can't have – have been murdered. It can't be true!'

Emily Brewster shook her head, not knowing quite what to answer.

She heard him draw in his breath – heard the low controlled rage in his voice as he said:

'My God, if I get my hands on the foul fiend who did this.'

Emily Brewster shivered. Her imagination pictured a lurking murderer behind one of the boulders. Then she heard her voice saying:

'Whoever did it wouldn't be hanging about. We must get the police. Perhaps –' she hesitated – 'one of us ought to stay with – with the body.'

Patrick Redfern said:

'I'll stay.'

Emily Brewster drew a little sigh of relief. She was not the kind of woman who would ever admit to feeling fear, but she was secretly thankful not to have to remain on that beach alone with the faint possibility of a homicidal maniac lingering close at hand.

She said:

'Good. I'll be as quick as I can. I'll go in the boat. Can't face that ladder. There's a constable at Leathercombe Bay.'

Patrick Redfern murmured mechanically:

'Yes – yes, whatever you think best.'

As she rowed vigorously away from the shore, Emily Brewster saw Patrick drop down beside the dead woman and bury his head in his hands. There was something so forlorn about his attitude that she felt an unwilling sympathy. He looked like a dog watching by its dead master. Nevertheless her robust common sense was saying to her:

'Best thing that could have happened for him and his wife – and for Marshall and the child – but I don't suppose *he* can see it that way, poor devil.'

Emily Brewster was a woman who could always rise to an emergency.

CHAPTER 5

Inspector Colgate stood back by the cliff waiting for the police-surgeon to finish with Arlena's body. Patrick Redfern and Emily Brewster stood a little to one side.

Dr Neasden rose from his knees with a quick deft movement.

He said:

'Strangled – and by a pretty powerful pair of hands. She doesn't seem to have put up much of a struggle. Taken by surprise. H'm – well – nasty business.'

Emily Brewster had taken one look and then quickly averted her eyes from the dead woman's face. That horrible purple convulsed countenance.

Inspector Colgate asked:

'What about time of death?'

Neasden said irritably:

'Can't say definitely without knowing more about her. Lots of factors to take into account. Let's see, it's quarter to one now. What time was it when you found her?'

Patrick Redfern, to whom the question was addressed, said vaguely:

'Some time before twelve. I don't know exactly.'

Emily Brewster said:

'It was exactly a quarter to twelve when we found she was dead.'

'Ah, and you came here in the boat. What time was it when you caught sight of her lying here?'

Emily Brewster considered.

'I should say we rounded the point about five or six minutes earlier.' She turned to Redfern. 'Do you agree?'

He said vaguely:

'Yes – yes – about that, I should think.'

Neasden asked the Inspector in a low voice:

'This the husband? Oh! I see, my mistake. Thought it might be. He seems rather done in over it.'

He raised his voice officially.

'Let's put it at twenty minutes to twelve. She cannot have been killed very long before that. Say between then and eleven – quarter to eleven at the earliest outside limit.'

The Inspector shut his notebook with a snap.

'Thanks,' he said. 'That ought to help us considerably. Puts it within very narrow limits – less than an hour all told.'

He turned to Miss Brewster.

'Now then, I think it's all clear so far. You're Miss Emily Brewster and this is Mr Patrick Redfern, both staying at the Jolly Roger Hotel. You identify this lady as a fellow guest of yours at the hotel – the wife of a Captain Marshall?'

Emily Brewster nodded.

'Then, I think,' said Inspector Colgate, 'that we'll adjourn to the hotel.'

He beckoned to a constable.

'Hawkes, you stay here and don't allow anyone on to this cove. I'll be sending Phillips along later.'

'Upon my soul!' said Colonel Weston. 'This is a surprise finding you here!'

Hercule Poirot replied to the Chief Constable's greeting in a suitable manner. He murmured:

'Ah, yes, many years have passed since that affair at St Loo.'

'I haven't forgotten it, though,' said Weston. 'Biggest surprise of my life. The thing I've never got over, though, is the way you got round me about that funeral business. Absolutely unorthodox, the whole thing. Fantastic!'

'*Tout de même, mon Colonel*,' said Poirot. 'It produced the goods, did it not?'

'Er – well, possibly. I dare say we should have got there by more orthodox methods.'

'It is possible,' agreed Poirot diplomatically.

'And here you are in the thick of another murder,' said the Chief Constable. 'Any ideas about this one?'

Poirot said slowly:

'Nothing definite – but it is interesting.'

'Going to give us a hand?'

'You would permit it, yes?'

'My dear fellow, delighted to have you. Don't know enough yet to decide whether it's a case for Scotland Yard or not. Off-hand it looks as though our murderer must be pretty well within a limited radius. On the other hand, all these people are strangers down here. To find out about them and their motives you've got to go to London.'

Poirot said:

'Yes, that is true.'

'First of all,' said Weston, 'we've got to find out who last saw the dead woman alive. Chambermaid took her her breakfast at nine. Girl in the bureau downstairs saw her pass through the lounge and go out about ten.'

'My friend,' said Poirot, 'I suspect that I am the man you want.'

'You saw her this morning? What time?'

'At five minutes past ten. I assisted her to launch her float from the bathing beach.'

'And she went off on it?'

'Yes.'

'Alone?'

'Yes.'

'Did you see which direction she took?'

'She paddled round that point there to the right.'

'In the direction of Pixy's Cove, that is?'

'Yes.'

'And the time then was –?'

'I should say she actually left the beach at a quarter past ten.'

Weston considered.

'That fits in well enough. How long should you say that it would take her to paddle round to the Cove?'

'Ah me, I am not an expert. I do not go in boats or expose myself on floats. Perhaps half an hour?'

'That's about what I think,' said the Colonel. 'She wouldn't be hurrying, I presume. Well, if she arrived there at a quarter to eleven, that fits in well enough.'

'At what time does your doctor suggest she died?'

'Oh, Neasden doesn't commit himself. He's a cautious chap. A quarter to eleven is his earliest outside limit.'

Poirot nodded. He said:

'There is one other point that I must mention. As she left, Mrs Marshall asked me not to say I had seen her.'

Weston stared.

He said:

'H'm, that's rather suggestive, isn't it?'

Poirot murmured.

'Yes. I thought so myself.'

Weston tugged at his moustache. He said:

'Look here, Poirot. You're a man of the world. What sort of a woman was Mrs Marshall?'

A faint smile came to Poirot's lips.

He asked:

'Have you not already heard?'

The Chief Constable said dryly:

'I know what the women say of her. They would. How much truth is there in it? *Was* she having an affair with this fellow Redfern?'

'I should say undoubtedly *yes*.'

'He followed her down here, eh?'

'There is reason to suppose so.'

'And the husband? Did he know about it? What did he feel?'

Poirot said slowly:

'It is not easy to know what Captain Marshall feels or thinks. He is a man who does not display his emotions.'

Weston said sharply:

'But he might have 'em, all the same.'

Poirot nodded. He said:

'Oh yes, he might have them.'

The Chief Constable was being as tactful as it was in his nature to be with Mrs Castle.

Mrs Castle was the owner and proprietress of the Jolly Roger Hotel. She was a woman of forty odd with a large bust, rather violent henna red hair, and an almost offensively refined manner of speech.

She was saying:

'That such a thing should happen in my hotel! Ay am sure it has always been the quayettest place imaginable! The people who come here are such naice people. No *rowdiness* – if you know what ay mean. Not like the big hotels in St Loo.'

'Quite so, Mrs Castle,' said Colonel Weston. 'But accidents happen in the best regulated – er households.'

'Ay'm sure Inspector Colgate will bear me out,' said Mrs Castle, sending an appealing glance towards the Inspector who was sitting looking very official. 'As to the laycensing laws, ay am *most* particular. There has never been *any* irregularity!'

'Quite, quite,' said Weston. 'We're not blaming you in any way, Mrs Castle.'

'But it does so reflect upon an establishment,' said Mrs Castle, her large bust heaving. 'When ay think of the noisy gaping crowds. Of course no one but hotel guests are allowed upon the island – but all the same they will no doubt come and *point* from the shore.'

She shuddered.

Inspector Colgate saw his chance to turn the conversation to good account.

He said:

'In regard to that point you've just raised. Access to the island. How do you keep people off?'

'Ay am *most* particular about it.'

'Yes, but what measures do you take? *What* keeps 'em off? Holiday crowds in summer time swarm everywhere like flies.'

Mrs Castle shrugged slightly again.

She said:

'That is the fault of the charabancs. Ay have seen eighteen at one time parked by the quay at Leathercombe Bay. Eighteen!'

'Just so. How do you stop them coming here?'

'There are notices. And then, of course, at high tide, we are cut off.'

'Yes, but at low tide?'

Mrs Castle explained. At the island end of the causeway there was a gate. This said 'Jolly Roger Hotel. Private. No entry except to Hotel.' The rocks rose sheer out of the sea on either side there and could not be climbed.

'Anyone could take a boat, though, I suppose, and row round and land on one of the coves? You couldn't stop them doing that. There's a right of access to the foreshore. You can't stop people being on the beach between low and high watermark.'

But this, it seemed, very seldom happened. Boats could be obtained at Leathercombe Bay harbour, but from there it was a long row to the island, and there was also a strong current just outside Leathercombe Bay harbour.

There were notices, too, on both Gull Cove and Pixy Cove by the ladder. She added that George or William were always on the look out at the bathing beach proper which was the nearest to the mainland.

'Who are George and William?'

'George attends to the bathing beach. He sees to the costumes and the floats. William is the gardener. He keeps the paths and marks the tennis courts and all that.'

Colonel Weston said impatiently:

'Well, that seems clear enough. That's not to say that nobody could have come from outside, but anyone who did so took a risk – the risk of being noticed. We'll have a word with George and William presently.'

Mrs Castle said:

'Ay do not care for trippers – a very noisy crowd, and they frequently leave orange peel and cigarette boxes on the causeway and down by the rocks, but all the same ay never thought one of them would turn out to be a murderer. Oh dear! it really is too terrible for words. A lady like Mrs Marshall murdered and what's so horrible, actually – er – strangled . . .'

Mrs Castle could hardly bring herself to say the word. She brought it out with the utmost reluctance.

Inspector Colgate said soothingly:

'Yes, it's a nasty business.'

'And the newspapers. *My* hotel in the newspapers!'

Colgate said, with a faint grin:

'Oh well, it's advertisement, in a way.'

Mrs Castle drew herself up. Her bust heaved and whalebone creaked. She said icily:

'That is not the kind of advertisement ay care about, Mr Colgate.'

Colonel Weston broke in. He said:

'Now then, Mrs Castle, you've got a list of the guests staying here, as I asked you?'

'Yes, sir.'

Colonel Weston pored over the hotel register. He looked over to Poirot who made the fourth member of the group assembled in the manageress's office.

'This is where you'll probably be able to help us presently.'

He read down the names.

'What about servants?'

Mrs Castle produced a second list.

'There are four chambermaids, the head waiter and three under him and Henry in the bar. William does the boots and shoes. Then there's the cook and two under her.'

'What about the waiters?'

'Well, sir, Albert, the Mater Dotel, came to me from the Vincent at

Plymouth. He was there for some years. The three under him have been here for three years – one of them four. They are very naise lads and most respectable. Henry has been here since the hotel opened. He is quite an institution.'

Weston nodded. He said to Colgate:

'Seems all right. You'll check up on them, of course. Thank you, Mrs Castle.'

'That will be all you require?'

'For the moment, yes.'

Mrs Castle creaked out of the room.

Weston said:

'First thing to do is to talk with Captain Marshall.'

Kenneth Marshall sat quietly answering the questions put to him. Apart from a slight hardening of his features he was quite calm. Seen here, with the sunlight falling on him from the window, you realized that he was a handsome man. Those straight features, the steady blue eyes, the firm mouth. His voice was low and pleasant.

Colonel Weston was saying:

'I quite understand, Captain Marshall, what a terrible shock this must be to you. But you realize that I am anxious to get the fullest information as soon as possible.'

Marshall nodded.

He said:

'I quite understand. Carry on.'

'Mrs Marshall was your second wife?'

'Yes.'

'And you have been married how long?'

'Just over four years.'

'And her name before she was married?'

'Helen Stuart. Her acting name was Arlena Stuart.'

'She was an actress?'

'She appeared in Revue and musical shows.'

'Did she give up the stage on her marriage?'

'No. She continued to appear. She actually retired only about a year and a half ago.'

'Was there any special reason for her retirement?'

Kenneth Marshall appeared to consider.

'No,' he said. 'She simply said that she was tired of it all.'

'It was not – er – in obedience to your special wish?'

Marshall raised his eyebrows.

'Oh, no.'

'You were quite content for her to continue acting after your marriage?'

Marshall smiled very faintly.

'I should have preferred her to give it up – that, yes. But I made no fuss about it.'

'It caused no point of dissension between you?'

'Certainly not. My wife was free to please herself.'

'And – the marriage was a happy one?'

Kenneth Marshall said coldly:

'Certainly.'

Colonel Weston paused a minute. Then he said:

'Captain Marshall, have you any idea who could possibly have killed your wife?'

The answer came without the least hesitation.

'None whatever.'

'Had she any enemies?'

'Possibly.'

'Ah?'

The other went on quickly. He said:

'Don't misunderstand me, sir. My wife was an actress. She was also a very good-looking woman. In both capacities she aroused a certain amount of jealousy and envy. There were fusses over parts – there was rivalry from other women – there was a good deal, shall we say, of general envy, hatred, malice, and all uncharitableness! But that is not to say that there was anyone who was capable of deliberately murdering her.'

Hercule Poirot spoke for the first time. He said:

'What you really mean, Monsieur, is that her enemies were mostly or entirely, *women*?'

Kenneth Marshall looked across at him.

'Yes,' he said. 'That is so.'

The Chief Constable said:

'You know of no man who had a grudge against her?'

'No.'

'Was she previously acquainted with anyone in this hotel?'

'I believe she had met Mr Redfern before – at some cocktail party. Nobody else to my knowledge.'

Weston paused. He seemed to deliberate as to whether to pursue the subject. Then he decided against that course. He said:

'We now come to this morning. When was the last time you saw your wife?'

Marshall paused a minute, then he said:

'I looked in on my way down to breakfast –'

'Excuse me, you occupied separate rooms?'

'Yes.'

'And what time was that?'

'It must have been about nine o'clock.'

'What was she doing?'

'She was opening her letters.'

'Did she say anything?'

'Nothing of any particular interest. Just good morning – and that it was a nice day – that sort of thing.'

'What was her manner? Unusual at all?'

'No, perfectly normal.'

'She did not seem excited, or depressed, or upset in any way?'

'I certainly didn't notice it.'

Hercule Poirot said:

'Did she mention at all what were the contents of her letters?'

Again a faint smile appeared on Marshall's lips. He said:

'As far as I can remember, she said they were all bills.'

'Your wife breakfasted in bed?'

'Yes.'

'Did she always do that?'

'Invariably.'

Hercule Poirot said:

'What time did she usually come downstairs?'

'Oh! between ten and eleven – usually nearer eleven.'

Poirot went on:

'If she was to descend at ten o'clock exactly, that would be rather surprising?'

'Yes. She wasn't often down as early as that.'

'But she was this morning. Why do you think that was, Captain Marshall?'

Marshall said unemotionally:

'Haven't the least idea. Might have been the weather – extra fine day and all that.'

'You missed her?'

Kenneth Marshall shifted a little in his chair. He said:

'Looked in on her again after breakfast. Room was empty. I was a bit surprised.'

'And then you came down on the beach and asked me if I had seen her?'

'Er – yes.' He added with a faint emphasis in his voice. 'And you said you hadn't . . .'

The innocent eyes of Hercule Poirot did not falter. Gently he caressed his large and flamboyant moustache.

Weston asked:

'Had you any special reason for wanting to find your wife this morning?'

Marshall shifted his glance amiably to the Chief Constable.

He said:

'No, just wondered where she was, that's all.'

Weston paused. He moved his chair slightly. His voice fell into a different key. He said:

'Just now, Captain Marshall, you mentioned that your wife had a previous acquaintance with Mr Patrick Redfern. How well did your wife know Mr Redfern?'

Kenneth Marshall said:

'Mind if I smoke?' He felt through his pockets. 'Dash! I've mislaid my pipe somewhere.'

Poirot offered him a cigarette which he accepted. Lighting it, he said:

'You were asking about Redfern. My wife told me she had come across him at some cocktail party or other.'

'He was, then, just a casual acquaintance?'

'I believe so.'

'Since then –' the Chief Constable paused. 'I understand that that acquaintanceship has ripened into something rather closer.'

Marshall said sharply:

'You understand that, do you? Who told you so?'

'It is the common gossip of the hotel.'

For a moment Marshall's eyes went to Hercule Poirot. They dwelt on him with a kind of cold anger. He said:

'Hotel gossip is usually a tissue of lies!'

'Possibly. But I gather that Mr Redfern and your wife gave some grounds for the gossip.'

'What grounds?'

'They were constantly in each other's company.'

'Is that all?'

'You do not deny that that was so?'

'May have been. I really didn't notice.'

'You did not – excuse me, Captain Marshall – object to your wife's friendship with Mr Redfern?'

'I wasn't in the habit of criticizing my wife's conduct.'

'You did not protest or object in any way?'

'Certainly not.'

'Not even though it was becoming a subject of scandal and an estrangement was growing up between Mr Redfern and his wife?'

Kenneth Marshall said coldly:

'I mind my own business and I expect other people to mind theirs. I don't listen to gossip and tittle tattle.'

'You won't deny that Mr Redfern admired your wife?'

'He probably did. Most men did. She was a very beautiful woman.'

'But you yourself were persuaded that there was nothing serious in the affair?'

'I never thought about it, I tell you.'

'And suppose we have a witness who can testify that they were on terms of the greatest intimacy?'

Again those blue eyes went to Hercule Poirot. Again an expression of dislike showed on that usually impassive face.

Marshall said:

'If you want to listen to these tales, listen to 'em. My wife's dead and can't defend herself.'

'You mean that you, personally, don't believe them?'

For the first time a faint dew of sweat was observable on Marshall's brow. He said:

'I don't propose to believe anything of the kind.'

He went on:

'Aren't you getting a good way from the essentials of this business? What I believe or don't believe is surely not relevant to the plain fact of murder?'

Hercule Poirot answered before either of the others could speak. He said:

'You do not comprehend, Captain Marshall. There is no such thing as a plain fact of murder. Murder springs, nine times out of ten, out of the character and circumstances of the murdered person. *Because* the victim was the kind of person he or she was, *therefore* was he or she murdered! Until we can understand fully and completely *exactly what kind of a person*

Arlena Marshall was, we shall not be able to see clearly exactly *the kind of person who murdered her*. From that springs the necessity of our questions.'

Marshall turned to the Chief Constable. He said:

'That your view, too?'

Weston boggled a little. He said:

'Well, up to a point – that is to say –'

Marshall gave a short laugh. He said:

'Thought you wouldn't agree. This character stuff is M. Poirot's speciality, I believe.'

Poirot said, smiling:

'You can at least congratulate yourself on having done nothing to assist me!'

'What do you mean?'

'What have you told us about your wife? Exactly nothing at all. You have told us only what everyone could see for themselves. That she was beautiful and admired. Nothing more.'

Kenneth Marshall shrugged his shoulders. He said simply:

'You're crazy.'

He looked towards the Chief Constable and said with emphasis:

'Anything else, sir, that *you'd* like me to tell you?'

'Yes, Captain Marshall, your own movements this morning, please.'

Kenneth Marshall nodded. He had clearly expected this.

He said:

'I breakfasted downstairs about nine o'clock as usual and read the paper. As I told you I went up to my wife's room afterwards and found she had gone out. I came down to the beach, saw M. Poirot and asked if he had seen her. Then I had a quick bathe and went up to the hotel again. It was then, let me see, about twenty to eleven – yes, just about that. I saw the clock in the lounge. It was just after twenty minutes to. I went up to my room, but the chambermaid hadn't quite finished it. I asked her to finish as quickly as she could. I had some letters to type which I wanted to get off by the post. I went downstairs again and had a word or two with Henry in the bar. I went up again to my room at ten minutes to eleven. There I typed my letters. I typed until ten minutes to twelve. I then changed into tennis kit as I had a date to play tennis at twelve. We'd booked the court the day before.'

'Who was we?'

'Mrs Redfern, Miss Darnley, Mr Gardener and myself. I came down at twelve o'clock and went up to the court. Miss Darnley was there and Mr Gardener. Mrs Redfern arrived a few minutes later. We played tennis for an hour. Just as we came into the hotel afterwards I – I – got the news.'

'Thank you, Captain Marshall. Just as a matter of form, is there anyone who can corroborate the fact that you were typing in your room between – er – ten minutes to eleven and ten minutes to twelve?'

Kenneth Marshall said with a faint smile:

'Have you got some idea that I killed my own wife? Let me see now. The chambermaid was about doing the rooms. She must have heard the typewriter going. And then there are the letters themselves. With all this upset I haven't posted them. I should imagine they are as good evidence as anything.'

He took three letters from his pocket. They were addressed, but not stamped. He said:

'Their contents, by the way, are strictly confidential. But when it's a case of murder, one is forced to trust in the discretion of the police. They contain lists of figures and various financial statements. I think you will find that if you put one of your men on to type them out, he won't do it in much under an hour.'

He paused.

'Satisfied, I hope?'

Weston said smoothly:

'It is no question of suspicion. Everyone on the island will be asked to account for his or her movements between a quarter to eleven and twenty minutes to twelve this morning.'

Kenneth Marshall said:

'Quite.'

Weston said:

'One more thing, Captain Marshall. Do you know anything about the way your wife was likely to have disposed of any property she had?'

'You mean a will? I don't think she ever made a will.'

'But you are not sure?'

'Her solicitors are Barkett, Markett & Applegood, Bedford Square. They saw to all her contracts, etc. But I'm fairly certain she never made a will. She said once that doing a thing like that would give her the shivers.'

'In that case, if she has died intestate, you, as her husband, succeed to her property.'

'Yes, I suppose I do.'

'Had she any near relatives?'

'I don't think so. If she had, she never mentioned them. I know that her father and mother died when she was a child and she had no brothers or sisters.'

'In any case, I suppose, she had nothing very much to leave?'

Kenneth Marshall said coldly:

'On the contrary. Only two years ago, Sir Robert Erskine, who was an old friend of hers, died and left her most of his fortune. It amounted, I think, to about fifty thousand pounds.'

Inspector Colgate looked up. An alertness came into his glance. Up to now he had been silent. Now he asked:

'Then actually, Captain Marshall, your wife was a rich woman?'

Kenneth Marshall shrugged his shoulders.

'I suppose she was really.'

'And you still say she did not make a will?'

'You can ask the solicitors. But I'm pretty certain she didn't. As I tell you, she thought it unlucky.'

There was a pause then Marshall added:

'Is there anything further?'

Weston shook his head.

'Don't think so – eh Colgate? No. Once more, Captain Marshall, let me offer you all my sympathy in your loss.'

Marshall blinked. He said jerkily:

'Oh – thanks.'

He went out.

The three men looked at each other.

Weston said:

'Cool customer. Not giving anything away, is he? What do you make of him, Colgate?'

The Inspector shook his head.

'It's difficult to tell. He's not the kind that shows anything. That sort makes a bad impression in the witness-box, and yet it's a bit unfair on them really. Sometimes they're as cut up as anything and yet can't show it. That kind of manner made the jury bring in a verdict of Guilty against Wallace. It wasn't the evidence. They just couldn't believe that a man could lose his wife and talk and act so coolly about it.'

Weston turned to Poirot.

'What do you think, Poirot?'

Hercule Poirot raised his hands.

He said:

'What can one say? He is the closed box – the fastened oyster. He has chosen his rôle. He has heard nothing, he has seen nothing, he knows nothing!'

'We've got a choice of motives,' said Colgate. 'There's jealousy and there's the money motive. Of course, in a way, a husband's the obvious suspect. One naturally thinks of him first. If he knew his missus was carrying on with the other chap –'

Poirot interrupted.

He said:

'I think he knew that.'

'Why do you say so?'

'Listen, my friend. Last night I had been talking with Mrs Redfern on Sunny Ledge. I came down from there to the hotel and on my way I saw those two together – Mrs Marshall and Patrick Redfern. And a moment or two after I met Captain Marshall. His face was very stiff. It says nothing – but nothing at all! It is almost *too* blank, if you understand me. Oh! he knew all right.'

Colgate grunted doubtfully.

He said:

'Oh well, if you think so –'

'I am sure of it! But even then, what does that tell us? What did Kenneth Marshall *feel* about his wife?'

Colonel Weston said:

'Takes her death coolly enough.'

Poirot shook his head in a dissatisfied manner.

Inspector Colgate said:

'Sometimes these quiet ones are the most violent underneath, so to speak. It's all bottled up. He may have been madly fond of her – and madly jealous. But he's not the kind to show it.'

Poirot said slowly:

'That is possible – yes. He is a very interesting character this Captain Marshall. I interest myself in him greatly. And in his *alibi*.'

'Alibi by typewriter,' said Weston with a short bark of a laugh. 'What have you got to say about that, Colgate?'

Inspector Colgate screwed up his eyes. He said:

'Well, you know, sir, I rather fancy that alibi. It's not too good, if you know what I mean. It's – well, it's *natural*. And if we find the chambermaid was about, and did hear the typewriter going, well then, it seems to me that it's all right and that we'll have to look elsewhere.'

'H'm,' said Colonel Weston. 'Where are you going to look?'

★   ★   ★

For a minute or two the three men pondered the question.

Inspector Colgate spoke first. He said:

'It boils down to this – was it an outsider, or a guest at the hotel? I'm not eliminating the servants entirely, mind, but I don't expect for a minute that we'll find any of them had a hand in it. No, it's a hotel guest, or it's someone from right outside. We've got to look at it this way. First of all – motive. There's gain. The only person to gain by her death was the lady's husband, it seems. What other motives are there? First and foremost – jealousy. It seems to me – just looking at it – that if ever you've got a *crime passionnel* – (he bowed to Poirot) this is one.'

Poirot murmured as he looked up at the ceiling:

'There are so many passions.'

Inspector Colgate went on:

'Her husband wouldn't allow that she had any enemies – real enemies, that is, but I don't believe for a minute that that's so! I should say that a lady like her would – well, would make some pretty bad enemies – eh, sir, what do you say?'

Poirot responded. He said:

'*Mais oui*, that is so. Arlena Marshall would make enemies. But in my opinion, the enemy theory is not tenable, for you see, Inspector, Arlena Marshall's enemies would, I think, as I said just now, always be *women*.'

Colonel Weston grunted and said:

'Something in that. It's the women who've got their knife into her here all right.'

Poirot went on.

'It seems to be hardly possible that this crime was committed by a woman. What does the medical evidence say?'

Weston grunted again. He said:

'Neasden's pretty confident that she was strangled by a man. Big hands – powerful grip. It's just possible, of course, that an unusually athletic woman might have done it – but it's damned unlikely.'

Poirot nodded.

'Exactly. Arsenic in a cup of tea – a box of poisoned chocolates – a knife – even a pistol – but strangulation – no! It is a man we have to look for.

'And immediately,' he went on, 'it becomes more difficult. There are two people here in this hotel who have a motive for wishing Arlena Marshall out of the way – but both of them are women.'

Colonel Weston asked:

'Redfern's wife is one of them, I suppose?'

'Yes. Mrs Redfern might have made up her mind to kill Arlena Stuart.

She had, let us say, ample cause. I think, too, that it would be possible for Mrs Redfern to commit a murder. But not this kind of murder. For all her unhappiness and jealousy, she is not, I should say, a woman of strong passions. In love, she would be devoted and loyal – not passionate. As I said just now – arsenic in the teacup, possibly – strangulation, no. I am sure, also, that she is physically incapable of committing this crime, her hands and feet are small, below the average.'

Weston nodded. He said:

'This isn't a woman's crime. No, a man did this.'

Inspector Colgate coughed.

'Let me put forward a solution, sir. Say that prior to meeting this Mr Redfern the lady had had another affair with someone – call him X. She turns X down for Mr Redfern. X is mad with rage and jealousy. He follows her down here, stays somewhere in the neighbourhood, comes over to the island, does her in. It's a possibility!'

Weston said:

'It's *possible*, all right. And if it's true, it ought to be easy to prove. Did he come on foot or in a boat? The latter seems more likely. If so, he must have hired a boat somewhere. You'd better make inquiries.'

He looked across at Poirot.

'What do you think of Colgate's suggestion?'

Poirot said slowly:

'It leaves, somehow, too much to chance. And besides – somewhere the picture is not true. I cannot, you see, imagine this man . . . the man who is mad with rage and jealousy.'

Colgate said:

'People *did* go potty about her, though, sir. Look at Redfern.'

'Yes, yes . . . But all the same –'

Colgate looked at him questioningly.

Poirot shook his head.

He said, frowning:

'Somewhere, there is something that we have missed . . .'

CHAPTER 6

Colonel Weston was poring over the hotel register.

He read aloud:

'*Major and Mrs Cowan,*
Miss Pamela Cowan,
Master Robert Cowan,
Master Evan Cowan,
  Rydal's Mount, Leatherhead.
Mr and Mrs Masterman,
Mr Edward Masterman,
Miss Jennifer Masterman,
Mr Roy Masterman,
Master Frederick Masterman,
  5 Marlborough Avenue, London, N.W.
Mr and Mrs Gardener,
  New York.
Mr and Mrs Redfern,
  Crossgates, Seldon, Princes Risborough.
Major Barry,
  18 Cardon St., St James, London, S.W.1.
Mr Horace Blatt,
  5 Pickersgill Street, London, E.C.2.
M. Hercule Poirot,
  Whitehaven Mansions, London, W.1.
Miss Rosamund Darnley,
  8 Cardigan Court, W.1.
Miss Emily Brewster,
  Southgates, Sunbury-on-Thames.
Rev. Stephen Lane,
  London.
Captain and Mrs Marshall,
Miss Linda Marshall,
  73 Upcott Mansions, London, S.W.7.'

He stopped.

Inspector Colgate said:

'I think, sir, that we can wash out the first two entries. Mrs Castle tells me that the Mastermans and the Cowans come here regularly every summer with their children. This morning they went off on an all-day excursion sailing, taking lunch with them. They left just after nine o'clock. A man called Andrew Baston took them. We can check up from him, but I think we can put them right out of it.'

Weston nodded.

'I agree. Let's eliminate everyone we can. Can you give us a pointer on any of the rest of them, Poirot?'

Poirot said:

'Superficially, that is easy. The Gardeners are a middle-aged married couple, pleasant, travelled. All the talking is done by the lady. The husband is acquiescent. He plays tennis and golf and has a form of dry humour that is attractive when one gets him to oneself.'

'Sounds quite O.K.'

'Next – the Redferns. Mr Redfern is young, attractive to women, a magnificent swimmer, a good tennis player and accomplished dancer. His wife I have already spoken of to you. She is quiet, pretty in a washed-out way. She is, I think, devoted to her husband. She has something that Arlena Marshall did not have.'

'What is that?'

'Brains.'

Inspector Colgate sighed. He said:

'Brains don't count for much when it comes to an infatuation, sir.'

'Perhaps not. And yet I do truly believe that in spite of his infatuation for Mrs Marshall, Patrick Redfern really cares for his wife.'

'That may be, sir. It wouldn't be the first time that's happened.'

Poirot murmured:

'That is the pity of it! It is always the thing women find hardest to believe.'

He went on:

'Major Barry. Retired Indian Army. An admirer of women. A teller of long and boring stories.'

Inspector Colgate sighed.

'You needn't go on. I've met a few, sir.'

'Mr Horace Blatt. He is, apparently, a rich man. He talks a good deal – about Mr Blatt. He wants to be everybody's friend. It is sad. For nobody likes him very much. And there is something else. Mr Blatt last night asked me a good many questions. Mr Blatt was uneasy. Yes, there is something not quite right about Mr Blatt.'

He paused and went on with a change of voice:

'Next comes Miss Rosamund Darnley. Her business name is Rose Mond Ltd. She is a celebrated dressmaker. What can I say of her? She has brains and charm and chic. She is very pleasing to look at.' He paused and added. 'And she is a very old friend of Captain Marshall's.'

Weston sat up in his chair.

'Oh, she is, is she?'

'Yes. They had not met for some years.'

Weston asked:

'Did she know he was going to be down here?'

'She says not.'

Poirot paused and then went on.

'Who comes next? Miss Brewster. I find her just a little alarming.' He shook his head. 'She has a voice like a man's. She is gruff and what you call hearty. She rows boats and has a handicap of four at golf.' He paused. 'I think, though, that she has a good heart.'

Weston said:

'That leaves only the Reverend Stephen Lane. Who's the Reverend Stephen Lane?'

'I can only tell you one thing. He is a man who is in a condition of great nervous tension. Also he is, I think, a fanatic.'

Inspector Colgate said:

'Oh, that kind of person.'

Weston said:

'And that's the lot!' He looked at Poirot. 'You seem very lost in thought, my friend?'

Poirot said:

'Yes. Because, you see, when Mrs Marshall went off this morning and asked me not to tell anyone I had seen her. I jumped at once in my own mind to a certain conclusion. I thought that her friendship with Patrick Redfern had made trouble between her and her husband. I thought that she was going to meet Patrick Redfern somewhere, and that she did not want her husband to know where she was.'

He paused.

'But that, you see, was where I was wrong. Because, although her husband appeared almost immediately on the beach and asked if I had seen her, Patrick Redfern arrived also – and was most patently and obviously looking for her! And therefore, my friends, I am asking myself, *who was it that Arlena Marshall went off to meet?*'

Inspector Colgate said:

'That fits in with *my* idea. A man from London or somewhere.'

Hercule Poirot shook his head. He said:

'But, my friend, according to your theory, Arlena Marshall had broken with this mythical man. Why, then, should she take such trouble and pains to meet him?'

Inspector Colgate shook his head. He said:

'Who do *you* think it was?'

'That is just what I cannot imagine. We have just read through the list of hotel guests. They are all middle-aged – dull. Which of them would Arlena Marshall prefer to Patrick Redfern? No, that is impossible. And yet, all the same, she *did* go to meet someone – and that someone was not Patrick Redfern.'

Weston murmured:

'You don't think she just went off by herself?'

Poirot shook his head.

'*Mon cher*,' he said. 'It is very evident that you never met the dead woman. Somebody once wrote a learned treatise on the difference that solitary confinement would mean to Beau Brummel or to a man like Newton. Arlena Marshall, my dear friend, would practically not exist in solitude. She only lived in the light of a man's admiration. No, Arlena Marshall went to meet *someone* this morning. *Who was it?*'

Colonel Weston sighed, shook his head and said:

'Well, we can go into theories later. Got to get through these interviews now. Got to get it down in black and white where everyone was. I suppose we'd better see the Marshall girl now. She might be able to tell us something useful.'

Linda Marshall came into the room clumsily, knocking against the doorpost. She was breathing quickly and the pupils of her eyes were dilated. She looked like a startled young colt. Colonel Weston felt a kindly impulse towards her.

He thought:

'Poor kid – she's nothing but a kid after all. This must have been a pretty bad shock to her.'

He drew up a chair and said in a reassuring voice:

'Sorry to put you through this, Miss – Linda, isn't it?'

'Yes, Linda.'

Her voice had that indrawn breathy quality that is often characteristic of schoolgirls. Her hands rested helplessly on the table in front of him – pathetic hands, big and red, with large bones and long wrists. Weston thought:

'A kid oughtn't to be mixed up in this sort of thing.'

He said reassuringly.

'There's nothing very alarming about all this. We just want you to tell us anything you know that might be useful, that's all.'

Linda said:

'You mean – about Arlena?'

'Yes. Did you see her this morning at all?'

The girl shook her head.

'No. Arlena always gets down rather late. She has breakfast in bed.'

Hercule Poirot said:

'And you, Mademoiselle?'

'Oh, I get up. Breakfast in bed's so *stuffy*.'

Weston said:

'Will you tell us what you did this morning?'

'Well, I had a bathe first and then breakfast, and then I went with Mrs Redfern to Gull Cove.'

Weston said:

'What time did you and Mrs Redfern start?'

'She said she'd be waiting for me in the hall at half-past ten. I was afraid I was going to be late, but it was all right. We started off at about three minutes to the half-hour.'

Poirot said:

'And what did you do at Gull Cove?'

'Oh, I oiled myself and sunbathed and Mrs Redfern sketched. Then, later, I went into the sea and Christine went back to the hotel to get changed for tennis.'

Weston said, keeping his voice quite casual:

'Do you remember what time that was?'

'When Mrs Redfern went back to the hotel? Quarter to twelve.'

'Sure of that time – quarter to twelve?'

Linda, opening her eyes wide, said:

'Oh *yes*. I looked at my watch.'

'The watch you have on now?'

Linda glanced down at her wrist.

'Yes.'

Weston said:

'Mind if I see?'

She held out her wrist. He compared the watch with his own and with the hotel clock on the wall.

He said, smiling:

'Correct to a second. And after that you had a bathe?'

'Yes.'

'And you got back to the hotel – when?'

'Just about one o'clock. And – and then – I heard – about Arlena . . .'

Her voice changed.

Colonel Weston said:

'Did you – er – get on with your stepmother all right?'

She looked at him for a minute without replying. Then she said:

'Oh yes.'

Poirot asked:

'Did you like her, Mademoiselle?'

Linda said again:

'Oh yes.' She added: 'Arlena was quite kind to me.'

Weston said with rather uneasy facetiousness:

'Not the cruel stepmother, eh?'

Linda shook her head without smiling.

Weston said:

'That's good. That's good. Sometimes, you know, there's a bit of difficulty in families – jealousy – all that. Girl and her father great pals and then she resents it a bit when he's all wrapped up in the new wife. You didn't feel like that, eh?'

Linda stared at him. She said with obvious sincerity:

'Oh no.'

Weston said:

'I suppose your father was – er – very wrapped up in her?'

Linda said simply:

'I don't know.'

Weston went on:

'All sorts of difficulties, as I say, arise in families. Quarrels – rows – that sort of thing. If husband and wife get ratty with each other, that's a bit awkward for a daughter too. Anything of that sort?'

Linda said clearly:

'Do you mean, did Father and Arlena quarrel?'

'Well – yes.'

Weston thought to himself:

'Rotten business – questioning a child about her father. Why is one a policeman? Damn it all, it's got to be done, though.'

Linda said positively:

'Oh no.' She added: 'Father doesn't quarrel with people. He's not like that at all.'

Weston said:

'Now, Miss Linda, I want you to think very carefully. Have you any idea at all who might have killed your stepmother? Is there anything you've ever heard or anything you know that could help us on that point?'

Linda was silent a minute. She seemed to be giving the question a serious unhurried consideration. She said at last:

'No, I don't know who could have wanted to kill Arlena.' She added: 'Except, of course, Mrs Redfern.'

Weston said:

'You think Mrs Redfern wanted to kill her? Why?'

Linda said:

'Because her husband was in love with Arlena. But I don't think she would really want to *kill* her. I mean she'd just feel that she wished she was dead – and that isn't the same thing at all, is it?'

Poirot said gently:

'No, it is not at all the same.'

Linda nodded. A queer sort of spasm passed across her face. She said:

'And anyway, Mrs Redfern could never do a thing like that – kill anybody. She isn't – she isn't *violent*, if you know what I mean.'

Weston and Poirot nodded. The latter said:

'I know exactly what you mean, my child, and I agree with you. Mrs Redfern is not of those who, as your saying goes, "sees red". She would not be' – he leaned back half closing his eyes, picking his words with care – 'shaken by a storm of feeling – seeing life narrowing in front of her – seeing a hated face – a hated white neck – feeling her hands clench – longing to feel them press into flesh –'

He stopped.

Linda moved jerkily back from the table. She said in a trembling voice:

'Can I go now? Is that all?'

Colonel Weston said:

'Yes, yes, that's all. Thank you, Miss Linda.'

He got up to open the door for her. Then came back to the table and lit a cigarette.

'Phew,' he said. 'Not a nice job, ours. I can tell you I felt a bit of a cad questioning that child about the relations between her father and her stepmother. More or less inviting a daughter to put a rope round her father's neck. All the same, it had to be done. Murder is murder. And she's the person most likely to know the truth of things. I'm rather thankful, though, that she'd nothing to tell us in that line.'

Poirot said:

'Yes, I thought you were.'

Weston said with an embarrassed cough:

'By the way, Poirot, you went a bit far, I thought at the end. All that hands sinking into flesh business! Not quite the sort of idea to put into a kid's head.'

Hercule Poirot looked at him with thoughtful eyes. He said:

'So you thought I put ideas into her head?'

'Well, didn't you? Come now.'

Poirot shook his head.

Weston sheered away from the point. He said:

'On the whole we got very little useful stuff out of her. Except a more or less complete *alibi* for the Redfern woman. If they were together from half-past ten to a quarter to twelve that lets Christine Redfern out of it. Exit the jealous wife suspect.'

Poirot said:

'There are better reasons than that for leaving Mrs Redfern out of it. It would, I am convinced, be physically impossible and mentally impossible for her to strangle anyone. She is cold rather than warm blooded, capable of deep devotion and unswerving constancy, but not of hot blooded passion or rage. Moreover, her hands are far too small and delicate.'

Colgate said:

'I agree with M. Poirot. She's out of it. Dr Neasden says it was a full-sized pair of hands that throttled that dame.'

Weston said:

'Well, I suppose we'd better see the Redferns next. I expect he's recovered a bit from the shock now.'

Patrick Redfern had recovered full composure by now. He looked pale and haggard and suddenly very young, but his manner was quite composed.

'You are Mr Patrick Redfern of Crossgates, Seldon, Princes Risborough?'

'Yes.'

'How long had you known Mrs Marshall?'

Patrick Redfern hesitated, then said:

'Three months.'

Weston went on:

'Captain Marshall has told us that you and she met casually at a cocktail party. Is that right?'

'Yes, that's how it came about.'

Weston said:

'Captain Marshall has implied that until you both met down here you did not know each other well. Is that the truth, Mr Redfern?'

Again Patrick Redfern hesitated a minute. Then he said:

'Well – not exactly. As a matter of fact I saw a fair amount of her one way and another.'

'Without Captain Marshall's knowledge?'

Redfern flushed slightly. He said:

'I don't know whether he knew about it or not.'

Hercule Poirot spoke. He murmured:

'And was it also without your wife's knowledge, Mr Redfern?'

'I believe I mentioned to my wife that I had met the famous Arlena Stuart.'

Poirot persisted.

'But she did not know how often you were seeing her?'

'Well, perhaps not.'

Weston said:

'Did you and Mrs Marshall arrange to meet down here?'

Redfern was silent a minute or two. Then he shrugged his shoulders.

'Oh well,' he said, 'I suppose it's bound to come out now. It's no good my fencing with you. I was crazy about the woman – mad – infatuated – anything you like. She wanted me to come down here. I demurred a bit and then I agreed. I – I – well, I would have agreed to do any mortal thing she liked. She had that kind of effect on people.'

Hercule Poirot murmured:

'You paint a very clear picture of her. She was the eternal Circe. Just that!'

Patrick Redfern said bitterly:

'She turned men into swine all right!' He went on: 'I'm being frank with you, gentlemen. I'm not going to hide anything. What's the use? As I say, I was infatuated with her. Whether she cared for me or not, I don't know. She pretended to, but I think she was one of those women who lose interest in a man once they've got him body and soul. She knew she'd got me all right. This morning, when I found her there on the beach, dead, it was as though' – he paused – 'as though something had hit me straight between the eyes. I was dazed – knocked out!'

Poirot leaned forward. 'And now?'

Patrick Redfern met his eyes squarely.

He said:

'I've told you the truth. What I want to ask is this – *how much of it has got to be made public*? It's not as though it could have any bearing on her death. And if it all comes out, it's going to be pretty rough on my wife.

'Oh, I know,' he went on quickly. 'You think I haven't thought much about her up to now? Perhaps that's true. But, though I may sound the worst kind of hypocrite, the real truth is that I care for my wife – care for her very deeply. The other' – he twitched his shoulders – 'it was a madness – the kind of idiotic fool thing men do – but Christine is different. She's *real*. Badly as I've treated her, I've known all along, deep down, that she was the person who really counted.' He paused – sighed – and said rather pathetically: 'I wish I could make you believe that.'

Hercule Poirot leant forward. He said:

'But I do believe it. Yes, yes, I do believe it!'

Patrick Redfern looked at him gratefully. He said:

'Thank you.'

Colonel Weston cleared his throat. He said:

'You may take it, Mr Redfern, that we shall not go into irrelevancies. If your infatuation for Mrs Marshall played no part in the murder then there will be no point in dragging it into the case. But what you don't seem to realize is that that – er – intimacy – may have a very direct bearing on the murder. It might establish, you understand, a *motive* for the crime.'

Patrick Redfern said:

'Motive?'

Weston said:

'Yes, Mr Redfern, *motive*! Captain Marshall, perhaps, was unaware of the affair. Suppose that he suddenly found out?'

Redfern said:

'Oh God! You mean he got wise and – and killed her?'

The Chief Constable said rather dryly:

'That solution had not occurred to you?'

Redfern shook his head. He said:

'No – funny. I never thought of it. You see, Marshall's such a quiet chap. I – oh, it doesn't seem likely.'

Weston asked:

'What was Mrs Marshall's attitude to her husband in all this? Was she – well, uneasy – in case it should come to his ears? Or was she indifferent?'

Redfern said slowly:

'She was – a bit nervous. She didn't want him to suspect anything.'

'Did she seem afraid of him?'

'Afraid. No, I wouldn't say that.'

Poirot murmured:

'Excuse me, M. Redfern, there was not, at any time, the question of a divorce?'

Patrick Redfern shook his head decisively.

'Oh no, there was no question of anything like that. There was Christine, you see. And Arlena, I am sure, never thought of such a thing. She was perfectly satisfied married to Marshall. He's – well, rather a big bug in his way –' He smiled suddenly. 'County – all that sort of thing, and quite well off. She never thought of me as a possible *husband*. No, I was just one of a succession of poor mutts – just something to pass the time with. I knew that all along, and yet, queerly enough, it didn't alter my feeling towards her . . .'

His voice trailed off. He sat there thinking.

Weston recalled him to the needs of the moment.

'Now, Mr Redfern, had you any particular appointment with Mrs Marshall this morning?'

Patrick Redfern looked slightly puzzled.

He said:

'Not a particular appointment, no. We usually met every morning on the beach. We used to paddle about on floats.'

'Were you surprised not to find Mrs Marshall there this morning?'

'Yes, I was. Very surprised. I couldn't understand it at all.'

'What did you think?'

'Well, I didn't know what to think. I mean, all the time I thought she would be coming.'

'If she were keeping an appointment elsewhere you had no idea with whom that appointment might be?'

Patrick Redfern merely stared and shook his head.

'When you had a *rendezvous* with Mrs Marshall, where did you meet?'

'Well, sometimes I'd meet her in the afternoon down at Gull Cove. You see the sun is off Gull Cove in the afternoon and so there aren't usually many people there. We met there once or twice.'

'Never on the other cove? Pixy Cove?'

'No. You see Pixy Cove faces west and people go round there in boats or on floats in the afternoon. We never tried to meet in the morning. It would have been too noticeable. In the afternoon people go and have a sleep or mouch around and nobody knows much where any one else is.'

Weston nodded:

Patrick Redfern went on:

'After dinner, of course, on the fine nights, we used to go off for a stroll together to different parts of the island.'

Hercule Poirot murmured:

'Ah, yes!' and Patrick Redfern shot him an inquiring glance.

Weston said:

'Then you can give us no help whatsoever as to the cause that took Mrs Marshall to Pixy Cove this morning?'

Redfern shook his head. He said, and his voice sounded honestly bewildered:

'I haven't the faintest idea! It wasn't like Arlena.'

Weston said:

'Had she any friends down here staying in the neighbourhood?'

'Not that I know of. Oh, I'm sure she hadn't.'

'Now, Mr Redfern, I want you to think very carefully. You knew Mrs Marshall in London. You must be acquainted with various members of her circle. Is there anyone you know of who could have had a grudge against her? Someone, for instance, whom you may have supplanted in her fancy?'

Patrick Redfern thought for some minutes. Then he shook his head.

'Honestly,' he said. 'I can't think of anyone.'

Colonel Weston drummed with his fingers on the table.

He said at last:

'Well, that's that. We seem to be left with three possibilities. That of an unknown killer – some monomaniac – who happened to be in the neighbourhood – and that's a pretty tall order –'

Redfern said, interrupting:

'And yet surely, it's by far the most likely explanation.'

Weston shook his head. He said:

'This isn't one of the "lonely copse" murders. This cove place was pretty inaccessible. Either the man would have to come up from the causeway past the hotel, over the top of the island and down by that ladder contraption, or else he came there by boat. Either way is unlikely for a casual killing.'

Patrick Redfern said:

'You said there were three possibilities.'

'Um – yes,' said the Chief Constable. 'That's to say, there were two people on this island who had a motive for killing her. Her husband, for one, and your wife for another.'

Redfern stared at him. He looked dumbfounded. He said:

'My wife? Christine? D'you mean that *Christine* had anything to do with this?'

He got up and stood there stammering slightly in his incoherent haste to get the words out.

'You're mad – quite mad – Christine? Why, it's *impossible*. It's laughable!'

Weston said:

'All the same, Mr Redfern, jealousy is a very powerful motive. Women who are jealous lose control of themselves completely.'

Redfern said earnestly:

'Not Christine. She's – oh she's not like that. She was unhappy, yes. But she's not the kind of person to – Oh, there's no violence in her.'

Hercule Poirot nodded thoughtfully. Violence. The same word that Linda Marshall had used. As before, he agreed with the sentiment.

'Besides,' went on Redfern confidently. 'It would be absurd. Arlena was twice as strong physically as Christine. I doubt if Christine could strangle a kitten – certainly not a strong wiry creature like Arlena. And then Christine could never have got down that ladder to the beach. She has no head for that sort of thing. And – oh, the whole thing is fantastic!'

Colonel Weston scratched his ear tentatively.

'Well,' he said. 'Put like that it doesn't seem likely. I grant you that. But motive's the first thing we've got to look for.' He added: 'Motive and opportunity.'

When Redfern had left the room, the Chief Constable observed with a slight smile:

'Didn't think it necessary to tell the fellow his wife had got an alibi. Wanted to hear what he'd have to say to the idea. Shook him up a bit, didn't it?'

Hercule Poirot murmured:

'The arguments he advanced were quite as strong as any alibi.'

'Yes. Oh! she didn't do it! She couldn't have done it – physically impossible as you said. Marshall *could* have done it – but apparently he didn't.'

Inspector Colgate coughed. He said:

'Excuse me, sir, I've been thinking about that alibi. It's possible, you know, if he'd thought this thing out, that those letters were got ready *beforehand*.'

Weston said:

'That's a good idea. We must look into –'

He broke off as Christine Redfern entered the room.

She was, as always, calm and a little precise in manner. She was wearing a white tennis frock and a pale blue pullover. It accentuated her fair, rather anaemic prettiness. Yet, Hercule Poirot thought to himself, it was neither a silly face nor a weak one. It had plenty of resolution, courage and good sense. He nodded appreciatively.

Colonel Weston thought:

'Nice little woman. Bit wishy-washy, perhaps. A lot too good for that philandering young ass of a husband of hers. Oh well, the boy's young. Women usually make a fool of you once!'

He said:

'Sit down, Mrs Redfern. We've got to go through a certain amount of routine, you see. Asking everybody for an account of their movements this morning. Just for our records.'

Christine Redfern nodded.

She said in her quiet precise voice:

'Oh yes, I quite understand. Where do you want me to begin?'

Hercule Poirot said:

'As early as possible, Madame. What did you do when you first got up this morning?'

Christine said:

'Let me see. On my way down to breakfast I went into Linda Marshall's room and fixed up with her to go to Gull Cove this morning. We agreed to meet in the lounge at half-past ten.'

Poirot asked:

'You did not bathe before breakfast, Madame?'

'No. I very seldom do.' She smiled. 'I like the sea well warmed before I get into it. I'm rather a chilly person.'

'But your husband bathes then?'

'Oh, yes. Nearly always.'

'And Mrs Marshall, she also?'

A change came over Christine's voice. It became cold and almost acrid.

She said:

'Oh no, Mrs Marshall was the sort of person who never made an appearance before the middle of the morning.'

With an air of confusion, Hercule Poirot said:

'Pardon, Madame, I interrupted you. You were saying that you went to Miss Linda Marshall's room. What time was that?'

'Let me see – half-past eight – no, a little later.'

'And was Miss Marshall up then?'

'Oh yes, she had been out.'

'Out?'

'Yes, she said she'd been bathing.'

There was a faint – a very faint note of embarrassment in Christine's voice. It puzzled Hercule Poirot.

Weston said:

'And then?'

'Then I went down to breakfast.'

'And after breakfast?'

'I went upstairs, collected my sketching box and sketching book and we started out.'

'You and Miss Linda Marshall?'

'Yes.'

'What time was that?'

'I think it was just on half-past ten.'

'And what did you do?'

'We went to Gull Cove. You know, the cove on the east side of the island. We settled ourselves there. I did a sketch and Linda sunbathed.'

'What time did you leave the cove?'

'At a quarter to twelve. I was playing tennis at twelve and had to change.'

'You had your watch with you?'

'No, as a matter of fact I hadn't. I asked Linda the time.'

'I see. And then?'

'I packed up my sketching things and went back to the hotel.'

Poirot said:

'And Mademoiselle Linda?'

'Linda?' Oh, Linda went into the sea.'

Poirot said:

'Were you far from the sea where you were sitting?'

'Well, we were well above high-water mark. Just under the cliff – so that I could be a little in the shade and Linda in the sun.'

Poirot said:

'Did Linda Marshall actually enter the sea before you left the beach?'

Christine frowned a little in the effort to remember. She said:

'Let me see. She ran down the beach – I fastened my box – Yes, I heard her splashing in the waves as I was on the path up the cliff.'

'You are sure of that, Madame? That she really entered the sea?'

'Oh yes.'

She stared at him in surprise.

Colonel Weston also stared at him.

Then he said:

'Go on, Mrs Redfern.'

'I went back to the hotel, changed, and went to the tennis courts where I met the others.'

'Who were?'

'Captain Marshall, Mr Gardener and Miss Darnley. We played two sets. We were just going in again when the news came about – about Mrs Marshall.'

Hercule Poirot leant forward. He said:

'And what did you think, Madame, when you heard that news?'

'What did I think?'

Her face showed a faint distaste for the question.

'Yes.'

Christine Redfern said slowly:

'It was – a horrible thing to happen.'

'Ah, yes, your fastidiousness was revolted. I understand that. But what did it mean to *you* – personally?'

She gave him a quick look – a look of appeal. He responded to it. He said in a matter-of-fact voice.

'I am appealing to you, Madame, as a woman of intelligence with plenty of good sense and judgment. You had doubtless during your stay here formed an opinion of Mrs Marshall, of the kind of woman she was?'

Christine said cautiously:

'I suppose one always does that more or less when one is staying in hotels.'

'Certainly, it is the natural thing to do. So I ask you, Madame, were you really very surprised at the manner of her death?'

Christine said slowly:

'I think I see what you mean. No, I was not, perhaps, surprised. Shocked, yes. But she was the kind of woman –'

Poirot finished the sentence for her.

'She was the kind of woman to whom such a thing might happen . . . Yes, Madame, that is the truest and most significant thing that has been said in this room this morning. Laying all – er (he stressed it carefully) *personal* feeling aside, what did you really think of the late Mrs Marshall?'

Christine Redfern said calmly:

'Is it really worth while going into all that now?'

'I think it might be, yes.'

'Well, what shall I say?' Her fair skin was suddenly suffused with colour. The careful poise of her manner was relaxed. For a short space the natural raw woman looked out. 'She's the kind of woman that to my mind is absolutely worthless! She did nothing to justify her existence. She had no mind – no brains. She thought of nothing but men and clothes and admiration. Useless, a parasite! She was attractive to men, I suppose – Oh, of course, she was. And she lived for that kind of life. And so, I suppose, I wasn't really surprised at her coming to a sticky end. She was the sort of woman who would be mixed up with everything sordid – blackmail – jealousy – violence – every kind of crude emotion. She – she appealed to the worst in people.'

She stopped, panting a little. Her rather short top lip lifted itself in a kind of fastidious disgust. It occurred to Colonel Weston that you could not have found a more complete contrast to Arlena Stuart than Christine Redfern. It also occurred to him that if you were married to Christine Redfern, the atmosphere might be so rarefied that the Arlena Stuarts of this world would hold a particular attraction for you.

And then, immediately following on these thoughts, a single word out of the words she had spoken fastened on his attention with particular intensity.

He leaned forward and said:

'Mrs Redfern, why, in speaking of her, did you mention the word *blackmail*?'

CHAPTER 7

Christine stared at him, not seeming at once to take in what he meant. She answered almost mechanically.

'I suppose – because she *was* being blackmailed. She was the sort of person who would be.'

Colonel Weston said earnestly:

'But – do you know she was being blackmailed?'

A faint colour rose in the girl's cheeks. She said rather awkwardly:

'As a matter of fact I do happen to know it. I – I overheard something.'

'Will you explain, Mrs Redfern?'

Flushing still more, Christine Redfern said:

'I – I didn't mean to overhear. It was an accident. It was two – no, three nights ago. We were playing bridge.' She turned towards Poirot. 'You remember? My husband and I, M. Poirot and Miss Darnley. I was dummy. It was very stuffy in the card room, and I slipped out of the window for a breath of fresh air. I went down towards the beach and I suddenly heard voices. One – it was Arlena Marshall's – I knew it at once – said: "It's no good pressing me. I can't get any more money now. My husband will suspect something." And then a man's voice said: "I'm not taking any excuses. You've got to cough up." And then Arlena Marshall said: "You blackmailing brute!" And the man said: "Brute or not, you'll pay up, my lady."'

Christine paused.

'I'd turned back and a minute after Arlena Marshall rushed past me. She looked – well, frightfully upset.'

Weston said:

'And the man? Do you know who he was?'

Christine Redfern shook her head.

She said:

'He was keeping his voice low. I barely heard what he said.'

'It didn't suggest the voice to you of anyone you knew?'

She thought again, but once more shook her head. She said:

'No, I don't know. It was gruff and low. It – oh, it might have been anybody's.'

Colonel Weston said:

'Thank you, Mrs Redfern.'

When the door had closed behind Christine Redfern Inspector Colgate said:

'Now we are getting somewhere!'

Weston said:

'You think so, eh?'

'Well, it's suggestive, sir, you can't get away from it. Somebody in this hotel was blackmailing the lady.'

Poirot murmured:

'But it is not the wicked blackmailer who lies dead. It is the victim.'

'That's a bit of a setback, I agree,' said the Inspector. 'Blackmailers aren't in the habit of bumping off their victims. But what it does give us is this, it suggests a reason for Mrs Marshall's curious behaviour this morning. She'd got a *rendezvous* with this fellow who was blackmailing her, and she didn't want either her husband or Redfern to know about it.'

'It certainly explains that point,' agreed Poirot.

Inspector Colgate went on:

'And think of the place chosen. The very spot for the purpose. The lady goes off in her float. That's natural enough. It's what she does every day. She goes round to Pixy Cove where no one ever goes in the morning and which will be a nice quiet place for an interview.'

Poirot said:

'But yes, I too was struck by that point. It is as you say, an ideal spot for a *rendezvous*. It is deserted, it is only accessible from the land side by descending a vertical steel ladder which is not everybody's money, *bien entendu*. Moreover most of the beach is invisible from above because of the overhanging cliff. And it has another advantage. Mr Redfern told me of that one day. There is a cave on it, the entrance to which is not easy to find but where anyone could wait unseen.'

Weston said:

'Of course, the Pixy's Cave – remember hearing about it.'

Inspector Colgate said:

'Haven't heard it spoken of for years, though. We'd better have a look inside it. Never know, we might find a pointer of some kind.'

Weston said:

'Yes, you're right, Colgate, we've got the solution to part one of the puzzle. *Why did Mrs Marshall go to Pixy's Cove?* We want the other half of that solution, though. *Who did she go there to meet?* Presumably someone staying in this hotel. None of them fitted as a lover – but a blackmailer's a different proposition.'

He drew the register towards him.

'Excluding the waiters, boots, etc., whom I don't think likely, we've got the following. The American – Gardener, Major Barry, Mr Horace Blatt, and the Reverend Stephen Lane.'

Inspector Colgate said:

'We can narrow it down a bit, sir. We might almost rule out the American, I think. He was on the beach all the morning. That's so, isn't it, M. Poirot?'

Poirot replied:

'He was absent for a short time when he fetched a skein of wool for his wife.'

Colgate said:

'Oh well, we needn't count that.'

Weston said:

'And what about the other three?'

'Major Barry went out at ten o'clock this morning. He returned at one-thirty. Mr Lane was earlier still. He breakfasted at eight. Said he was going for a tramp. Mr Blatt went off for a sail at nine-thirty same as he does most days. Neither of them are back yet.'

'A sail, eh?' Colonel Weston's voice was thoughtful.

Inspector Colgate's voice was responsive. He said:

'Might fit in rather well, sir.'

Weston said:

'Well, we'll have a word with this Major bloke – and let me see, who else is there? Rosamund Darnley. And there's the Brewster woman who found the body with Redfern. What's she like, Colgate?'

'Oh, a sensible party, sir. No nonsense about her.'

'She didn't express any opinions on the death?'

The Inspector shook his head.

'I don't think she'll have anything more to tell us, sir, but we'll have to make sure. Then there are the Americans.'

Colonel Weston nodded. He said: 'Let's have 'em all in and get it over as soon as possible. Never know, might learn something. About the blackmailing stunt if about nothing else.'

Mr and Mrs Gardener came into the presence of authority together.

Mrs Gardener explained immediately.

'I hope you'll understand how it is, Colonel Weston (that is the name, I think?).' Reassured on this point she went on: 'But this has been a very bad shock to me and Mr Gardener is always very, very careful of my health –'

Mr Gardener here interpolated:

'Mrs Gardener,' he said, 'is very sensitive.'

'– and he said to me, "Why, Carrie," he said, "naturally I'm coming right along with you." It's not that we haven't the highest admiration for British police methods because we have. I've been told that British police procedure is most refined and delicate, and I've never doubted it, and certainly when I once had a bracelet missing at the Savoy Hotel nothing could have been more lovely and sympathetic than the young man who came to see me about it, and, of course, I hadn't really lost the bracelet at all, but just mislaid it; that's the worst of rushing about so much, it makes you kind of forgetful where you put things –' Mrs Gardener paused, inhaled gently and started off again. 'And what I say is, and I know Mr Gardener agrees with me, that we're only too anxious to do anything to help the British police in every way. So go right ahead and ask me anything at all you want to know –'

Colonel Weston opened his mouth to comply with this invitation, but had momentarily to postpone speech while Mrs Gardener went on.

'That's what I said, Odell, isn't it? And that's so, isn't it?'

'Yes, darling,' said Mr Gardener.

Colonel Weston spoke hastily.

'I understand, Mrs Gardener, that you and your husband were on the beach all the morning?'

For once Mr Gardener was able to get in first.

'That's so,' he said.

'Why, certainly we were,' said Mrs Gardener. 'And a lovely peaceful morning it was, just like any other morning if you get me, perhaps even more so, and not the slightest idea in our minds of what was happening round the corner on that lonely beach.'

'Did you see Mrs Marshall at all today?'

'We did not. And I said to Odell, why wherever can Mrs Marshall have got to this morning? I said. And first her husband coming looking for her and then that good-looking young man, Mr Redfern, and so impatient he was, just sitting there on the beach scowling at everyone and everything. And I said to myself why, when he has that nice pretty little wife of his own, must he go running after that dreadful woman? Because that's just what I felt she was. I always felt that about her, didn't I, Odell?'

'Yes, darling.'

'However that nice Captain Marshall came to marry such a woman I just cannot imagine and with that nice young daughter growing up, and it's so important for girls to have the right influence. Mrs Marshall was not at all the right person – no breeding at all – and I should say a very animal nature. Now if Captain Marshall had had any sense he'd have married Miss Darnley, who's a very very charming woman and a very distinguished one. I must say I admire the way she's gone straight ahead and built up a first-class business as she has. It takes brains to do a thing like that – and you've only got to look at Rosamund Darnley to see she's just frantic with brains. She could plan and carry out any mortal thing she liked. I just admire that woman more than I can say. And I said to Mr Gardener the other day that any one could see she was very much in love with Captain Marshall – crazy about him was what I said, didn't I, Odell?'

'Yes, darling.'

'It seems they knew each other as children, and why now, who knows, it may all come right after all with that woman out of the way. I'm not a

narrow-minded woman, Colonel Weston, and it isn't that I disapprove of
the stage as such – why, quite a lot of my best friends are actresses – but
I've said to Mr Gardener all along that there was something evil about
that woman. And you see, I've been proved right.'

She paused triumphantly.

The lips of Hercule Poirot quivered in a little smile. His eyes met for
a minute the shrewd grey eyes of Mr Gardener.

Colonel Weston said rather desperately:

'Well, thank you, Mrs Gardener. I suppose there's nothing that either
of you has noticed since you've been here that might have a bearing upon
the case?'

'Why no, I don't think so.' Mr Gardener spoke with a slow drawl. 'Mrs
Marshall was around with young Redfern most of the time – but everybody
can tell you that.'

'What about her husband? Did he mind, do you think?'

Mr Gardener said cautiously:

'Captain Marshall is a very reserved man.'

Mrs Gardener confirmed this by saying:

'Why, yes, he is a real Britisher!'

On the slightly apoplectic countenance of Major Barry various emotions
seemed contending for mastery. He was endeavouring to look properly
horrified but could not subdue a kind of shamefaced gusto.

He was saying in his hoarse, slightly wheezy voice:

'Glad to help you any way I can. 'Course I don't know anythin' about
it – nothin' at all. Not acquainted with the parties. But I've knocked about
a bit in my time. Lived a lot in the East, you know. And I can tell you that
after being in an Indian hill station what you don't know about human
nature isn't worth knowin'.'

He paused, took a breath and was off again.

'Matter of fact this business reminds me of a case in Simla. Fellow called
Robinson, or was it Falconer? Anyway he was in the East Wilts, or was it
the North Surreys? Can't remember now, and anyway it doesn't matter.
Quiet chap, you know, great reader – mild as milk you'd have said. Went
for his wife one evening in their bungalow. Got her by the throat. She'd
been carryin' on with some feller or other and he'd got wise to it. By Jove,
he nearly did for her! It was touch and go. Surprised us all! Didn't think
he had it in him.'

Hercule Poirot murmured:

'And you see there an analogy to the death of Mrs Marshall?'

'Well, what I mean to say – strangled, you know. Same idea. Feller suddenly sees red!'

Poirot said:

'You think that Captain Marshall felt like that?'

'Oh, look here, I never said that.' Major Barry's face went even redder. 'Never said anything about Marshall. Thoroughly nice chap. Wouldn't say a word against him for the world.'

Poirot murmured:

'Ah, *pardon*, but you *did* refer to the natural reactions of a husband.'

Major Barry said:

'Well, I mean to say, I should think she'd been pretty hot stuff. Eh? Got young Redfern on a string all right. And there were probably others before him. But the funny thing is, you know, that husbands are a dense lot. Amazin'. I've been surprised by it again and again. They see a feller sweet on their wife but they don't see that *she's* sweet on *him*! Remember a case like that in Poona. Very pretty woman, Jove, she led her husband a dance –'

Colonel Weston stirred a little restively. He said:

'Yes, yes, Major Barry. For the moment we've just got to establish the facts. You don't know of anything personally – that you've seen or noticed that might help us in this case?'

'Well, really, Weston, I can't say I do. Saw her and young Redfern one afternoon on Gull Cove' – here he winked knowingly and gave a deep hoarse chuckle – 'very pretty it was, too. But it's not evidence of that kind you're wanting. Ha, ha!'

'You did not see Mrs Marshall at all this morning?'

'Didn't see anybody this morning. Went over to St Loo. Just my luck. Sort of place here where nothin' happens for months and when it does you miss it!'

The Major's voice held a ghoulish regret.

Colonel Weston prompted him.

'You went to St Loo, you say?'

'Yes, wanted to do some telephonin'. No telephone here and that post-office place at Leathercombe Bay isn't very private.'

'Were your telephone calls of a very private nature?'

The Major winked again cheerfully.

'Well, they were and they weren't. Wanted to get through to a pal of mine and get him to put somethin' on a horse. Couldn't get through to him, worse luck.'

'Where did you telephone from?'

'Call box in the G.P.O. at St Loo. Then on the way back I got lost – these confounded lanes – twistin' and turnin' all over the place. Must have wasted an hour over that at least. Damned confusing part of the world. I only got back half an hour ago.'

Colonel Weston said:

'Speak to anyone or meet anyone in St Loo?'

Major Barry said with a chuckle:

'Wantin' me to prove an alibi? Can't think of anythin' useful. Saw about fifty thousand people in St Loo – but that's not to say they'll remember seein' me.'

The Chief Constable said:

'We have to ask these things, you know.'

'Right you are. Call on me at any time. Glad to help you. Very fetchin' woman, the deceased. Like to help you catch the feller who did it. The Lonely Beach Murder – bet you that's what the papers will call it. Reminds me of the time –'

It was Inspector Colgate who firmly nipped this latest reminiscence in the bud and manoeuvred the garrulous Major out of the door.

Coming back he said:

'Difficult to check up on anything in St Loo. It's the middle of the holiday season.'

The Chief Constable said:

'Yes, we can't take him off the list. Not that I seriously believe he's implicated. Dozens of old bores like him going about. Remember one or two of them in my army days. Still – he's a possibility. I leave all that to you, Colgate. Check what time he took the car out – petrol – all that. It's humanly possible that he parked the car somewhere in a lonely spot, walked back here and went to the cove. But it doesn't seem feasible to me. He'd have run too much risk of being seen.'

Colgate nodded.

He said:

'Of course there are a good many charabancs here today. Fine day. They start arriving round about half-past eleven. High tide was at seven. Low tide would be about one o'clock. People would be spread out over the sands and the causeway.'

Weston said:

'Yes. But he'd have to come up from the causeway past the hotel.'

'Not right past it. He could branch off on the path that leads up over the top of the island.'

Weston said doubtfully:

'I'm not saying that he mightn't have done it without being seen. Practically all the hotel guests were on the bathing beach except for Mrs Redfern and the Marshall girl who were down in Gull Cove, and the beginning of that path would only be overlooked by a few rooms of the hotel and there are plenty of chances against anyone looking out of those windows just at that moment. For the matter of that, I dare say it's possible for a man to walk up to the hotel, through the lounge and out again without anyone happening to see him. But what I say is, he couldn't *count* on no one seeing him.'

Colgate said:

'He could have gone round to the cove by boat.'

Weston nodded. He said:

'That's much sounder. If he'd had a boat handy in one of the coves nearby, he could have left the car, rowed or sailed to Pixy Cove, done the murder, rowed back, picked up the car and arrived back with this tale about having been to St Loo and lost his way – a story that he'd know would be pretty hard to disprove.'

'You're right, sir.'

The Chief Constable said:

'Well, I leave it to you, Colgate. Comb the neighbourhood thoroughly. You know what to do. We'd better see Miss Brewster now.'

Emily Brewster was not able to add anything of material value to what they already knew.

Weston said after she had repeated her story:

'And there's nothing you know of that could help us in any way?'

Emily Brewster said shortly:

'Afraid not. It's a distressing business. However, I expect you'll soon get to the bottom of it.'

Weston said:

'I hope so, I'm sure.'

Emily Brewster said dryly:

'Ought not to be difficult.'

'Now what do you mean by that, Miss Brewster?'

'Sorry. Wasn't attempting to teach you your business. All I meant was that with a woman of that kind it ought to be easy enough.'

Hercule Poirot murmured:

'That is your opinion?'

Emily Brewster snapped out:

'Of course. *De mortuis nil nisi bonum* and all that, but you can't get away from *facts*. That woman was a bad lot through and through. You've only got to hunt round a bit in her unsavoury past.'

Hercule Poirot said gently:

'You did not like her?'

'I know a bit too much about her.' In answer to the inquiring looks she went on: 'My first cousin married one of the Erskines. You've probably heard that that woman induced old Sir Robert when he was in his dotage to leave most of his fortune to her away from his own family.'

Colonel Weston said:

'And the family – er – resented that?'

'Naturally. His association with her was a scandal anyway, and on top of that, to leave her a sum like fifty thousand pounds shows just the kind of woman she was. I dare say I sound hard, but in my opinion the Arlena Stuarts of this world deserve very little sympathy. I know of something else too – a young fellow who lost his head about her completely – he'd always been a bit wild, naturally his association with her pushed him over the edge. He did something rather fishy with some shares – solely to get money to spend on her – and only just managed to escape prosecution. That woman contaminated everyone she met. Look at the way she was ruining young Redfern. No, I'm afraid I can't have any regret for her death – though of course it would have been better if she'd drowned herself, or fallen over a cliff. Strangling is rather unpleasant.'

'And you think the murderer was someone out of her past?'

'Yes, I do.'

'Someone who came from the mainland with no one seeing him?'

'Why should any one see him? We were all on the beach. I gather the Marshall child and Christine Redfern were down on Gull Cove out of the way. Captain Marshall was in his room in the hotel. Then who on earth was there to see him except possibly Miss Darnley.'

'Where was Miss Darnley?'

'Sitting up on the cutting at the top of the cliff. Sunny Ledge it's called. We saw her there, Mr Redfern and I, when we were rowing round the island.'

Colonel Weston said:

'You may be right, Miss Brewster.'

Emily Brewster said positively:

'I'm sure I'm right. When a woman's neither more nor less than a nasty mess, then she herself will provide the best possible clue. Don't you agree with me, M. Poirot?'

Hercule Poirot looked up. His eyes met her confident grey ones. He said:

'Oh, yes – I agree with that which you have just this minute said. Arlena Marshall herself is the best, the only clue, to her own death.'

Miss Brewster said sharply:

'Well, then!'

She stood there, an erect sturdy figure, her cool self-confident glance going from one man to the other.

Colonel Weston said:

'You may be sure, Miss Brewster, that any clue there may be in Mrs Marshall's past life will not be overlooked.'

Emily Brewster went out.

Inspector Colgate shifted his position at the table. He said in a thoughtful voice:

'She's a determined one, she is. And she'd got her knife into the dead lady, proper, she had.'

He stopped a minute and said reflectively:

'It's a pity in a way that she's got a cast-iron alibi for the whole morning. Did you notice her hands, sir? As big as a man's. And she's a hefty woman – as strong and stronger than many a man, I'd say . . .'

He paused again. His glance at Poirot was almost pleading.

'And you say she never left the beach this morning, M. Poirot?'

Slowly Poirot shook his head. He said:

'My dear Inspector, she came down to the beach before Mrs Marshall could have reached Pixy Cove and she was within my sight until she set off with Mr Redfern in the boat.'

Inspector Colgate said gloomily:

'Then that washes her out.'

He seemed upset about it.

As always, Hercule Poirot felt a keen sense of pleasure at the sight of Rosamund Darnley.

Even to a bare police inquiry into the ugly facts of murder she brought a distinction of her own.

She sat down opposite Colonel Weston and turned a grave and intelligent face to him.

She said:

'You want my name and address? Rosamund Anne Darnley. I carry on a dressmaking business under the name of Rose Mond Ltd at 622 Brook Street.'

'Thank you, Miss Darnley. Now can you tell us anything that may help us?'

'I don't really think I can.'

'Your own movements –'

'I had breakfast about nine-thirty. Then I went up to my room and collected some books and my sunshade and went out to Sunny Ledge. That must have been about twenty-five past ten. I came back to the hotel about ten minutes to twelve, went up and got my tennis racquet and went out to the tennis courts, where I played tennis until lunch-time.'

'You were in the cliff recess, called by the hotel Sunny Ledge, from about half-past ten until ten minutes to twelve?'

'Yes.'

'Did you see Mrs Marshall at all this morning?'

'No.'

'Did you see her from the cliff as she paddled her float round to Pixy Cove?'

'No, she must have gone by before I got there.'

'Did you notice anyone on a float or in a boat at all this morning?'

'No, I don't think I did. You see, I was reading. Of course I looked up from my book from time to time, but as it happened the sea was quite bare each time I did so.'

'You didn't even notice Mr Redfern and Miss Brewster when they went round?'

'No.'

'You were, I think, acquainted with Mr Marshall?'

'Captain Marshall is an old family friend. His family and mine lived next door to each other. I had not seen him, however, for a good many years – it must be something like twelve years.'

'And Mrs Marshall?'

'I'd never exchanged half a dozen words with her until I met her here.'

'Were Captain and Mrs Marshall, as far as you knew, on good terms with each other?'

'On perfectly good terms, I should say.'

'Was Captain Marshall very devoted to his wife?'

Rosamund said:

'He may have been. I can't really tell you anything about that. Captain

Marshall is rather old-fashioned – he hasn't got the modern habit of shouting matrimonial woes upon the housetop.'

'Did you like Mrs Marshall, Miss Darnley?'

'No.'

The monosyllable came quietly and evenly. It sounded what it was – a simple statement of fact.

'Why was that?'

A half smile came to Rosamund's lips. She said:

'Surely you've discovered that Arlena Marshall was not popular with her own sex? She was bored to death with women and showed it. Nevertheless I should like to have had the dressing of her. She had a great gift for clothes. Her clothes were always just right and she wore them well. I should like to have had her as a client.'

'She spent a good deal on clothes?'

'She must have done. But then she had money of her own and of course Captain Marshall is quite well off.'

'Did you ever hear or did it ever occur to you that Mrs Marshall was being blackmailed, Miss Darnley?'

A look of intense astonishment came over Rosamund Darnley's expressive face.

She said:

'Blackmailed? Arlena?'

'The idea seems to surprise you.'

'Well, yes, it does rather. It seems so incongruous.'

'But surely it is possible?'

'Everything's possible, isn't it? The world soon teaches one that. But I wondered what any one could blackmail Arlena about?'

'There are certain things, I suppose, that Mrs Marshall might be anxious should not come to her husband's ears?'

'We-ll, yes.'

She explained the doubt in her voice by saying with a half smile:

'I sound sceptical, but then, you see, Arlena was rather notorious in her conduct. She never made much of a pose of respectability.'

'You think, then, that her husband was aware of her – intimacies with other people?'

There was a pause. Rosamund was frowning. She spoke at last in a slow, reluctant voice. She said:

'You know, I don't really know what to think. I've always assumed that Kenneth Marshall accepted his wife, quite frankly, for what she was. That he had no illusions about her. But it may not be so.'

'He may have believed in her absolutely?'

Rosamund said with semi-exasperation:

'Men are such fools. And Kenneth Marshall is unworldly under his sophisticated manner. He *may* have believed in her blindly. He may have thought she was just – admired.'

'And you know of no one – that is, you have heard of no one who was likely to have had a grudge against Mrs Marshall?'

Rosamund Darnley smiled. She said:

'Only resentful wives. And I presume, since she was strangled, that it was a man who killed her.'

'Yes.'

Rosamund said thoughtfully:

'No, I can't think of any one. But then I probably shouldn't know. You'll have to ask someone in her own intimate set.'

'Thank you, Miss Darnley.'

Rosamund turned a little in her chair. She said:

'Hasn't M. Poirot any questions to ask?'

Her faintly ironic smile flashed out at him.

Hercule Poirot smiled and shook his head.

He said:

'I can think of nothing.'

Rosamund Darnley got up and went out.

CHAPTER 8

They were standing in the bedroom that had been Arlena Marshall's.

Two big bay windows gave on to a balcony that overlooked the bathing beach and the sea beyond. Sunshine poured into the room, flashing over the bewildering array of bottles and jars on Arlena's dressing-table.

Here there was every kind of cosmetic and unguent known to beauty parlours. Amongst this panoply of woman's affairs three men moved purposefully. Inspector Colgate went about shutting and opening drawers.

Presently he gave a grunt. He had come upon a packet of folded letters. He and Weston ran through them together.

Hercule Poirot had moved to the wardrobe. He opened the door of the hanging cupboard and looked at the multiplicity of gowns and sports suits that hung there. He opened the other side. Foamy lingerie lay in piles. On a wide shelf were hats. Two more beach cardboard hats in lacquer red and pale yellow – a Big Hawaiian straw hat – another of drooping dark-blue linen and three or four little absurdities for which, no doubt, several guineas had been paid apiece – a kind of beret in dark blue – a tuft, no more, of black velvet – a pale grey turban.

Hercule Poirot stood scanning them – a faintly indulgent smile came to his lips. He murmured:

'*Les femmes!*'

Colonel Weston was refolding the letters.

'Three from young Redfern,' he said. 'Damned young ass. He'll learn not to write letters to women in a few more years. Women always keep letters and then swear they've burnt them. There's one other letter here. Same line of country.'

He held it out and Poirot took it.

Darling Arlena, – God, I feel blue. To be going out to China – and perhaps not seeing you again for years and years. I didn't know any man could go on feeling crazy about a woman like I feel about you. Thanks for the cheque. They won't prosecute now. It was a near shave, though, and all because I wanted to make big money for you. Can you forgive me? I wanted to set diamonds in your ears – your lovely ears – and clasp great milk-white pearls round your throat, only they say pearls are no good nowadays. A fabulous emerald, then? Yes, that's the thing. A great emerald, cool and green and full of hidden fire. Don't forget me – but you won't, I know. You're mine – always.

Goodbye – goodbye – goodbye.

J.N.

Inspector Colgate said:

'Might be worth while to find out if J.N. really did go to China. Otherwise – well, he might be the person we're looking for. Crazy about the woman, idealizing her, suddenly finding out he'd been played for a sucker. It sounds to me as though this is the boy Miss Brewster mentioned. Yes, I think this might be useful.'

Hercule Poirot nodded. He said: 'Yes, that letter is important. I find it very important.'

He turned round and stared at the room – at the bottles on the dressing-table – at the open wardrobe and at a big Pierrot doll that lolled insolently on the bed.

They went into Kenneth Marshall's room.

It was next door to his wife's but with no communicating door and no balcony. It faced the same way and had two windows, but it was much smaller. Between the two windows a gilt mirror hung on the wall. In the corner beyond the right-hand window was the dressing-table. On it were two ivory brushes, a clothes brush and a bottle of hair lotion. In the corner by the left-hand window was a writing-table. An open typewriter stood on it and papers were ranged in a stack beside it.

Colgate went through them rapidly.

He said:

'All seems straightforward enough. Ah, here's the letter he mentioned this morning. Dated the 24th – that's yesterday. And here's the envelope postmarked Leathercombe Bay this morning. Seems all square. Now we'll have an idea if he could have prepared that answer of his beforehand.'

He sat down.

Colonel Weston said:

'We'll leave you to it, for a moment. We'll just glance through the rest of the rooms. Everyone's been kept out of this corridor until now, and they're getting a bit restive about it.'

They went next into Linda Marshall's room. It faced east, looking out over the rocks down to the sea below.

Weston gave a glance round. He murmured:

'Don't suppose there's anything to see here. But it's possible Marshall might have put something in his daughter's room that he didn't want us to find. Not likely, though. It isn't as though there had been a weapon or anything to get rid of.'

He went out again.

Hercule Poirot stayed behind. He found something that interested him in the grate. Something had been burnt there recently. He knelt down, working patiently. He laid out his finds on a sheet of paper. A large irregular blob of candle grease – some fragments of green paper or cardboard, possibly a pull-off calendar for with it was an unburnt fragment bearing a large figure 5 and a scrap of printing . . . *noble deeds* . . . There was also an ordinary pin and some burnt animal matter which might have been hair.

Poirot arranged them neatly in a row and stared at them.

He murmured:

'*Do noble deeds, not dream them all day long. C'est possible.* But what is one to make of this collection? *C'est fantastique!*'

And then he picked up the pin and his eyes grew sharp and green.

He murmured:

'*Pour l'amour de Dieu!* Is it possible?'

Hercule Poirot got up from where he had been kneeling by the grate.

Slowly he looked round the room and this time there was an entirely new expression on his face. It was grave and almost stern.

To the left of the mantelpiece there were some shelves with a row of books. Hercule Poirot looked thoughtfully along the titles.

A Bible, a battered copy of Shakespeare's plays, *The Marriage of William Ashe*, by Mrs Humphry Ward. *The Young Stepmother*, by Charlotte Yonge. *The Shropshire Lad*. Eliot's *Murder in the Cathedral*. Bernard Shaw's *St Joan*. *Gone With the Wind*, by Margaret Mitchell. *The Burning Court*, by Dickson Carr.

Poirot took out two books. *The Young Stepmother* and *William Ashe*, and glanced inside at the blurred stamp affixed to the title page. As he was about to replace them, his eye caught sight of a book that had been shoved behind the other books. It was a small dumpy volume bound in brown calf.

He took it out and opened it. Very slowly he nodded his head.

He murmured:

'*So I was right* . . . Yes, I was right. But for the other – is that possible too? No, it is not possible, unless . . .'

He stayed there, motionless, stroking his moustaches whilst his mind ranged busily over the problem.

He said again, softly:

'*Unless* –'

Colonel Weston looked in at the door.

'Hullo, Poirot, still there?'

'I arrive. I arrive,' cried Poirot.

He hurried out into the corridor.

The room next to Linda's was that of the Redferns.

Poirot looked into it, noting automatically the trace of two different individualities – a neatness and tidiness which he associated with Christine, and a picturesque disorder which was characteristic of Patrick. Apart from these sidelights on personality the room did not interest him.

Next to it again was Rosamund Darnley's room, and here he lingered for a moment in the sheer pleasure of the owner's personality.

He noted the few books that lay on the table next to the bed, the expensive simplicity of the toilet set on the dressing-table. And there came gently to his nostrils the elusive expensive perfume that Rosamund Darnley used.

Next to Rosamund Darnley's room at the northern end of the corridor was an open window leading to a balcony from which an outside stair led down to the rocks below.

Weston said:

'That's the way people go down to bathe before breakfast – that is, if they bathe off the rocks as most of them do.'

Interest came into Hercule Poirot's eyes. He stepped outside and looked down.

Below, a path led to steps cut zigzag leading down the rocks to the sea. There was also a path that led round the hotel to the left. He said:

'One could go down these stairs, go to the left round the hotel and join the main path up from the causeway.'

Weston nodded. He amplified Poirot's statement.

'One could go right across the island without going through the hotel at all.' He added: 'But one might still be seen from a window.'

'What window?'

'Two of the public bathrooms look out that way – north – and the staff bathroom, and the cloakrooms on the ground floor. Also the billiard room.'

Poirot nodded. He said:

'And all the former have frosted glass windows, and one does not play billiards on a fine morning.'

'Exactly.'

Weston paused and said:

'If he did it, that's the way he went.'

'You mean Captain Marshall?'

'Yes. Blackmail, or no blackmail. I still feel it points to him. And his manner – well, his manner is unfortunate.'

Hercule Poirot said dryly:

'Perhaps – but a manner does not make a murderer!'

Weston said:

'Then you think he's out of it?'

Poirot shook his head. He said:

'No, I would not say that.'

Weston said:

'We'll see what Colgate can make out of the typewriting alibi. In the meantime I've got the chambermaid of this floor waiting to be interviewed. A good deal may depend on her evidence.'

The chambermaid was a woman of thirty, brisk, efficient and intelligent. Her answers came readily.

Captain Marshall had come up to his room not long after ten-thirty. She was then finishing the room. He had asked her to be as quick as possible. She had not seen him come back but she had heard the sound of the typewriter a little later. She put it at about five minutes to eleven. She was then in Mr and Mrs Redfern's room. After she had done that she moved on to Miss Darnley's room at the end of the corridor. She could not hear the typewriter from there. She went to Miss Darnley's room, as near as she could say, at just after eleven o'clock. She remembered hearing Leathercombe Church strike the hour as she went in. At a quarter-past eleven she had gone downstairs for her eleven o'clock cup of tea and 'snack'. Afterwards she had gone to do the rooms in the other wing of the hotel. In answer to the Chief Constable's question she explained that she had done the rooms in this corridor in the following order:

Miss Linda Marshall's, the two public bathrooms, Mrs Marshall's room and private bath, Captain Marshall's room. Mr and Mrs Redfern's room and private bath, Miss Darnley's room and private bath. Captain Marshall's and Miss Marshall's rooms had no adjoining bathrooms.

During the time she was in Miss Darnley's room and bathroom she had not heard any one pass the door or go out by the staircase to the rocks, but it was quite likely she wouldn't have heard if any one went quietly.

Weston then directed his questions to the subject of Mrs Marshall.

No, Mrs Marshall wasn't one for rising early as a rule. She, Gladys Narracott, had been surprised to find the door open and Mrs Marshall gone down at just after ten. Something quite unusual, that was.

'Did Mrs Marshall always have her breakfast in bed?'

'Oh yes, sir, always. Not very much of it either. Just tea and orange juice and one piece of toast. Slimming like so many ladies.'

No, she hadn't noticed anything unusual in Mrs Marshall's manner that morning. She'd seemed quite as usual.

Hercule Poirot murmured:

'What did you think of Mrs Marshall, Mademoiselle?'

Gladys Narracott stared at him. She said:

'Well, that's hardly for me to say, is it, sir?'

'But yes, it is for you to say. We are anxious – very anxious – to hear your impression.'

Gladys gave a slightly uneasy glance towards the Chief Constable, who endeavoured to make his face sympathetic and approving, though actually he felt slightly embarrassed by his foreign colleague's methods of approach. He said:

'Er – yes, certainly. Go ahead.'

For the first time Gladys Narracott's brisk efficiency deserted her. Her fingers fumbled with her print dress. She said:

'Well, Mrs Marshall – she wasn't exactly a lady, as you might say. What I mean is she was more like an actress.'

Colonel Weston said:

'She was an actress.'

'Yes, sir, that's what I'm saying. She just went on exactly as she felt like it. She didn't – well, she didn't trouble to be polite if she wasn't feeling polite. And she'd be all smiles one minute and then, if she couldn't find something or the bell wasn't answered at once or her laundry wasn't back, well, be downright rude and nasty about it. None of us you might say *liked* her. But her clothes were beautiful, and, of course, she was a very handsome lady, so it was only natural she should be admired.'

Colonel Weston said:

'I am sorry to have to ask you what I am going to ask you, but it is a very vital matter. Can you tell me how things were between her and her husband?'

Gladys Narracott hesitated a minute.

She said:

'You don't – it wasn't – you don't think as *he* did it?'

Hercule Poirot said quickly:

'Do you?'

'Oh! I wouldn't like to think so. He's such a nice gentleman, Captain Marshall. He couldn't do a thing like that – I'm sure he couldn't.'

'But you are *not* very sure – I hear it in your voice.'

Gladys Narracott said reluctantly:

'You do read such things in the papers! When there's jealousy. If there's been goings on – and, of course, everyone's been talking about it – about her and Mr Redfern, I mean. And Mrs Redfern such a nice quiet lady! It does seem a shame! And Mr Redfern's a nice gentleman too, but it seems men can't help themselves when it's a lady like Mrs Marshall – one who's used to having her own way. Wives have to put up with a lot, I'm sure.' She sighed and paused. 'But if Captain Marshall found out about it –'

Colonel Weston said sharply:

'Well?'

Gladys Narracott said slowly:

'I did think sometimes that Mrs Marshall was frightened of her husband knowing.'

'What makes you say that?'

'It wasn't anything definite, sir. It was only I felt – that sometimes she was – afraid of him. He was a very quiet gentleman but he wasn't – he wasn't *easy*.'

Weston said:

'But you've nothing definite to go on? Nothing either of them ever said to each other.'

Slowly Gladys Narracott shook her head.

Weston sighed. He went on.

'Now, as to letters received by Mrs Marshall this morning. Can you tell us anything about those?'

'There were about six or seven, sir. I couldn't say exactly.'

'Did you take them up to her?'

'Yes, sir. I got them from the office as usual and put them on her breakfast tray.'

'Do you remember anything about the look of them?'

The girl shook her head.

'They were just ordinary-looking letters. Some of them were bills and circulars, I think, because they were torn up on the tray.'

'What happened to them?'

'They went into the dustbin, sir. One of the police gentlemen is going through that now.'

Weston nodded.

'And the contents of the waste-paper baskets, where are they?'

'They'll be in the dustbin too.'

Weston said: 'H'm – well, I think that is all at present.' He looked inquiringly at Poirot.

Poirot leaned forward.

'When you did Miss Linda Marshall's room this morning, did you do the fireplace?'

'There wasn't anything to do, sir. There had been no fire lit.'

'And there was nothing in the fireplace itself?'

'No sir, it was perfectly all right.'

'What time did you do her room?'

'About a quarter-past nine, sir, when she'd gone down to breakfast.'

'Did she come up to her room after breakfast, do you know?'

'Yes, sir. She came up about a quarter to ten.'

'Did she stay in her room?'

'I think so, sir. She came out, hurrying rather, just before half-past ten.'

'You didn't go into her room again?'

'No, sir. I had finished with it.'

Poirot nodded. He said:

'There is another thing I want to know. What people bathed before breakfast this morning?'

'I couldn't say about the other wing and the floor above. Only about this one.'

'That is all I want to know.'

'Well, sir, Captain Marshall and Mr Redfern were the only ones this morning, I think. They always go down for an early dip.'

'Did you see them?'

'No, sir, but their wet bathing things were hanging over the balcony rail as usual.'

'Miss Linda Marshall did not bathe this morning?'

'No, sir. All her bathing dresses were quite dry.'

'Ah,' said Poirot. 'That is what I wanted to know.'

Gladys Narracott volunteered:

'She does most mornings, sir.'

'And the other three, Miss Darnley, Mrs Redfern and Mrs Marshall?'

'Mrs Marshall never, sir. Miss Darnley has once or twice, I think. Mrs Redfern doesn't often bathe before breakfast – only when it's very hot, but she didn't this morning.'

Again Poirot nodded. Then he asked:

'I wonder if you have noticed whether a bottle is missing from any of the rooms you look after in this wing?'

'A bottle, sir? What kind of a bottle?'

'Unfortunately I do not know. But have you noticed – or would you be likely to notice – if one had gone?'

Gladys said frankly:

'I shouldn't from Mrs Marshall's room, sir, and that's a fact. She has ever so many.'

'And the other rooms?'

'Well, I'm not sure about Miss Darnley. She has a good many creams and lotions. But from the other rooms, yes, I would, sir. I mean if I were to look special. If I were noticing, so to speak.'

'But you haven't actually noticed?'

'No, because I wasn't looking special, as I say.'

'Perhaps you would go and look now, then.'

'Certainly, sir.'

She left the room, her print dress rustling. Weston looked at Poirot. He said: 'What's all this?'

Poirot murmured:

'My orderly mind, that is vexed by trifles! Miss Brewster, this morning, was bathing off the rocks before breakfast, and she says that a bottle was thrown from above and nearly hit her. *Eh bien*, I want to know who threw that bottle and why?'

'My dear man, any one may have chucked a bottle away.'

'Not at all. To begin with, it could only have been thrown from a window on the east side of the hotel – that is, one of the windows of the rooms we have just examined. Now I ask you, if you have an empty bottle on your dressing-table or in your bathroom what do you do with it? I will tell you, you drop it into the waste-paper basket. You do not take the trouble to go out on your balcony and hurl it into the sea! For one thing you might hit someone, for another it would be too much trouble. No, you would only do that *if you did not want any one to see that particular bottle.*'

Weston stared at him.

Weston said:

'I know that Chief Inspector Japp, whom I met over a case not long ago, always says you have a damned tortuous mind. You're not going to tell me now that Arlena Marshall wasn't strangled at all, but poisoned out of some mysterious bottle with a mysterious drug?'

'No, no, I do not think there was poison in that bottle.'

'Then what was there?'

'I do not know at all. That's why I am interested.'

Gladys Narracott came back. She was a little breathless. She said:

'I'm sorry, sir, but I can't find anything missing. I'm sure there's nothing gone from Captain Marshall's room, or Miss Linda Marshall's room, or Mr and Mrs Redfern's room, and I'm pretty sure there's nothing gone from Miss Darnley's either. But I couldn't say about Mrs Marshall's. As I say, she's got such a lot.'

Poirot shrugged his shoulders.

He said:

'No matter. We will leave it.'

Gladys Narracott said:

'Is there anything more, sir?'

She looked from one to the other of them.

Weston said:

'Don't think so. Thank you.'

Poirot said:

'I thank you, no. You are sure, are you not, that there is nothing – nothing at all, that you have forgotten to tell us?'

'About Mrs Marshall, sir?'

'About anything at all. Anything unusual, out of the way, unexplained, slightly peculiar, rather curious – *enfin*, something that has made you say to yourself or to one of your colleagues: "That's funny!"?'

Gladys said doubtfully:

'Well, not the sort of thing that you would mean, sir.'

Hercule Poirot said:

'Never mind what I mean. You do not know what I mean. It is true, then, that you have said to yourself or to a colleague today, "that is funny!"?'

He brought out the three words with ironic detachment.

Gladys said:

'It was nothing really. Just a bath being run. And I did pass the remark to Elsie, downstairs, that it was funny somebody having a bath round about twelve o'clock.'

'Whose bath, who had a bath?'

'That I couldn't say, sir. We heard it going down the waste from this wing, that's all, and that's when I said what I did to Elsie.'

'You're sure it was a bath? Not one of the hand-basins?'

'Oh! quite sure, sir. You can't mistake bath-water running away.'

Poirot displaying no further desire to keep her, Gladys Narracott was permitted to depart.

Weston said:

'You don't think this bath question is important, do you, Poirot? I mean, there's no point to it. No bloodstains or anything like that to wash off. That's the –' He hesitated.

Poirot cut in:

'That, you would say, is the advantage of strangulation! No bloodstains, no weapon – nothing to get rid of or conceal! Nothing is needed but physical strength – *and the soul of a killer!*'

His voice was so fierce, so charged with feeling, that Weston recoiled a little.

Hercule Poirot smiled at him apologetically.

'No one,' he said, 'the bath is probably of no importance. Anyone may have had a bath. Mrs Redfern before she went to play tennis, Captain Marshall, Miss Darnley. As I say, anyone. There is nothing in that.'

A police constable knocked at the door, and put in his head.

'It's Miss Darnley, sir. She says she'd like to see you again for a minute. There's something she forgot to tell you, she says.'

Weston said:

'We're coming down – now.'

The first person they saw was Colgate. His face was gloomy.

'Just a minute, sir.'

Weston and Poirot followed him into Mrs Castle's office.

Colgate said:

'I've been checking-up with Heald on this type-writing business. Not a doubt of it, it couldn't be done under an hour. Longer, if you had to stop and think here and there. That seems to me pretty well to settle it. And look at this letter.'

He held it out.

'*My dear Marshall – Sorry to worry you on your holiday but an entirely unforseen situation has arisen over the Burley and Tender contracts . . .*'

'Etcetera, etcetera,' said Colgate. 'Dated the 24th – that's yesterday. Envelope postmarked yesterday evening E.C.1. and Leathercombe Bay this morning. Same typewriter used on envelope and in letter. And by the contents it was clearly impossible for Marshall to prepare his answer beforehand. The figures arise out of the ones in the letter – the whole thing is quite intricate.'

'H'm,' said Weston gloomily. 'That seems to let Marshall out. We'll have to look elsewhere.' He added: 'I've got to see Miss Darnley again. She's waiting now.'

Rosamund came in crisply. Her smile held an apologetic *nuance*.

She said:

'I'm frightfully sorry. Probably it isn't worth bothering about. But one does forget things so.'

'Yes, Miss Darnley?'

The Chief Constable indicated a chair.

She shook her shapely black head.

'Oh, it isn't worth sitting down. It's simply this. I told you that I spent the morning lying out on Sunny Ledge. That isn't quite accurate. I forgot that once during the morning I went back to the hotel and out again.'

'What time was that, Miss Darnley?'

'It must have been about a quarter-past eleven.'

'You went back to the hotel, you said?'

'Yes, I'd forgotten my glare glasses. At first I thought I wouldn't bother and then my eyes got tired and I decided to go in and get them.'

'You went straight to your room and out again?'

'Yes. At least, as a matter of fact, I just looked in on Ken – Captain Marshall. I heard his machine going and I thought it was so stupid of him to stay indoors typing on such a lovely day. I thought I'd tell him to come out.'

'And what did Captain Marshall say?'

Rosamund smiled rather shamefacedly.

'Well, when I opened the door he was typing so vigorously, and frowning and looking so concentrated, that I just went away quietly. I don't think he even saw me come in.'

'And that was – at what time, Miss Darnley?'

'Just about twenty-past eleven. I noticed the clock in the hall as I went out again.'

'And that puts the lid on it finally,' said Inspector Colgate. 'The chambermaid heard him typing up till five minutes to eleven. Miss Darnley saw him at twenty minutes past, and the woman was dead at a quarter to twelve. He says he spent that hour typing in his room, and it seems quite clear that he *was* typing in his room. That washes Captain Marshall right out.'

He stopped, then looking at Poirot with some curiosity, he asked:

'M. Poirot's looking very serious over something.'

Poirot said thoughtfully:

'I was wondering why Miss Darnley suddenly volunteered this extra evidence.'

Inspector Colgate cocked his head alertly.

'Think there's something fishy about it? That it isn't just a question of "forgetting"?'

He considered for a minute or two, then he said slowly:

'Look here, sir, let's look at it this way. Supposing Miss Darnley wasn't on Sunny Ledge this morning as she says. That story's a lie. Now suppose that *after* telling us her story, she finds that somebody saw her somewhere else or alternatively that someone went to the Ledge and didn't find her there. Then she thinks up this story quick and comes and tells it to us to account for her absence. You'll notice that she was careful to say Captain Marshall didn't *see* her when she looked into his room.'

Poirot murmured:

'Yes, I noticed that.'

Weston said incredulously:

'Are you suggesting that Miss Darnley's mixed up in this? Nonsense, seems absurd to me. Why should she be?'

Inspector Colgate coughed.

He said:

'You'll remember what the American lady, Mrs Gardener, said. She sort of hinted that Miss Darnley was sweet on Captain Marshall. There'd be a motive there, sir.'

Weston said impatiently:

'Arlena Marshall wasn't killed by a woman. It's a man we've got to look for. We've got to stick to the men in the case.'

Inspector Colgate sighed. He said:

'Yes, that's true, sir. We always come back to that, don't we?'

Weston went on:

'Better put a constable on to timing one or two things. From the hotel across the island to the top of the ladder. Let him do it running and walking. Same thing with the ladder itself. And somebody had better check the time it takes to go on a float from the bathing beach to the cove.'

Inspector Colgate nodded.

'I'll attend to all that, sir,' he said confidently.

The Chief Constable said:

'Think I'll go along to the cove now. See if Phillips has found anything. Then there's that Pixy's Cave we've been hearing about. Ought to see if there are any traces of a man waiting in there. Eh, Poirot? What do you think?'

'By all means. It is a possibility.'

Weston said:

'If somebody from outside had nipped over to the island that would be a good hiding-place – if he knew about it. I suppose the locals know?'

Colgate said:

'Don't believe the younger generation would. You see, ever since this hotel was started the coves have been private property. Fishermen don't go there, or picnic parties. And the hotel people aren't local. Mrs Castle's a Londoner.'

Weston said:

'We might take Redfern with us. He told us about it. What about you, M. Poirot?'

Hercule Poirot hesitated. He said, his foreign intonation very pronounced:

'Me, I am like Miss Brewster and Mrs Redfern, I do not like to descend perpendicular ladders.'

Weston said: 'You can go round by boat.'

Again Hercule Poirot sighed.

'My stomach, it is not happy on the sea.'

'Nonsense, man, it's a beautiful day. Calm as a mill pond. You can't let us down, you know.'

Hercule Poirot hardly looked like responding to this British adjuration. But at that moment, Mrs Castle poked her ladylike face and elaborate coiffure round the door.

'Ay'm sure ay hope ay am not intruding,' she said. 'But Mr Lane, the clergyman, you know, has just returned. Ay thought you might like to know.'

'Ah yes, thanks, Mrs Castle. We'll see him right away.'

Mrs Castle came a little farther into the room. She said:

'Ay don't know if it is worth mentioning, but ay *have* heard that the smallest incident should not be ignored –'

'Yes, yes?' said Weston impatiently.

'It is only that there was a lady and gentleman here about one o'clock. Came over from the mainland. For luncheon. They were informed that there had been an accident and that under the circumstances no luncheons could be served.'

'Any idea who they were?'

'Ay couldn't say at all. Naturally no name was given. They expressed disappointment and a certain amount of curiosity as to the nature of the accident. Ay couldn't tell them anything, of course. Ay should say, myself, they were summer visitors of the better class.'

Weston said brusquely:

'Ah well, thank you for telling us. Probably not important but quite right – er – to remember everything.'

'Naturally,' said Mrs Castle, 'ay wish to do my Duty!'

'Quite, quite. Ask Mr Lane to come here.'

Stephen Lane strode into the room with his usual vigour.

Weston said:

'I'm the Chief Constable of the County, Mr Lane. I suppose you've been told what has occurred here?'

'Yes – oh yes – I heard as soon as I got here. Terrible . . . Terrible . . .' His thin frame quivered. He said in a low voice: 'All along – ever since I arrived here – I have been conscious – very conscious – of the forces of evil close at hand.'

His eyes, burning eager eyes, went to Hercule Poirot.

He said:

'You remember, M. Poirot? Our conversation some days ago? About the reality of evil?'

Weston was studying the tall, gaunt figure in some perplexity. He found it difficult to make this man out. Lane's eyes came back to him. The clergyman said with a slight smile:

'I dare say that seems fantastic to you, sir. We have left off believing in evil in these days. We have abolished Hell fire! We no longer believe in the Devil! But Satan and Satan's emissaries were never more powerful than they are today!'

Weston said:

'Er – er – yes, perhaps. That, Mr Lane, is your province. Mine is more prosaic – to clear up a case of murder.'

Stephen Lane said:

'An awful word. Murder! One of the earliest sins known on earth – the ruthless shedding of an innocent brother's blood . . .' He paused, his eyes half closed. Then, in a more ordinary voice he said:

'In what way can I help you?'

'First of all, Mr Lane, will you tell me your own movements today?'

'Willingly. I started off early on one of my usual tramps. I am fond of walking. I have roamed over a good deal of the countryside round here. Today I went to St Petrock-in-the-Combe. That is about seven miles from here – a very pleasant walk along winding lanes, up and down the Devon hills and valleys. I took some lunch with me and ate it in a spinney. I visited the church – it has some fragments – only fragments alas, of early glass – also a very interesting painted screen.'

'Thank you, Mr Lane. Did you meet anyone on your walk?'

'Not to speak to. A cart passed me once and a couple of boys on bicycles and some cows. However,' he smiled, 'if you want proof of my statement, I wrote my name in the book at the church. You will find it there.'

'You did not see anyone at the church itself – the Vicar, or the verger?'

Stephen Lane shook his head. He said:

'No, there was no one about and I was the only visitor. St Petrock is a very remote spot. The village itself lies on the far side of it about half a mile farther on.'

Colonel Weston said pleasantly:

'You mustn't think we're – er – doubting what you say. Just a matter of checking-up on everybody. Just routine, you know, routine. Have to stick to routine in cases of this kind.'

Stephen Lane said gently:

'Oh yes, I quite understand.'

Weston went on:

'Now the next point. Is there anything you know that would assist us at all? Anything about the dead woman? Anything that could give us a pointer as to who murdered her? Anything you heard or saw?'

Stephen Lane said:

'I heard nothing. All I can tell you is this: that I knew instinctively as soon as I saw her that Arlena Marshall was a focus of evil. She *was* Evil! Evil personified! Woman can be man's help and inspiration in life – she can also be man's downfall. She can drag a man down to the level of the beast. The dead woman was just such a woman. She appealed to everything base in a man's nature. She was a woman such as Jezebel and Aholibah. Now – she has been struck down in the middle of her wickedness!'

Hercule Poirot stirred. He said:

'Not struck down – *strangled!* Strangled, Mr Lane, by a pair of human hands.'

The clergyman's own hands trembled. The fingers writhed and twitched. He said, and his voice came low and choked:

'That's horrible – horrible – Must you put it like that?'

Hercule Poirot said:

'It is the simple truth. Have you any idea, Mr Lane, whose hands those were?'

The other shook his head. He said: 'I know nothing – nothing . . .'

Weston got up. He said, after a glance at Colgate to which the latter replied by an almost imperceptible nod, 'Well, we must get on to the Cove.'

Lane said:

'Is that where – it happened?'

Weston nodded.

Lane said:

'Can – can I come with you?'

About to return a curt negative, Weston was forestalled by Poirot.

'But certainly,' said Poirot. 'Accompany me there in a boat, Mr Lane. We start immediately.'

CHAPTER 9

For the second time that morning Patrick Redfern was rowing a boat into Pixy Cove. The other occupants of the boat were Hercule Poirot, very pale with a hand to his stomach, and Stephen Lane. Colonel Weston had taken the land route. Having been delayed on the way he arrived on the beach at the same time as the boat grounded. A police constable and a plainclothes sergeant were on the beach already. Weston was questioning the latter as the three from the boat walked up and joined him.

Sergeant Phillips said:

'I think I've been over every inch of the beach, sir.'

'Good, what did you find?'

'It's all together here, sir, if you'd like to come and see.'

A small collection of objects was laid out neatly on a rock. There was a pair of scissors, an empty Gold Flake packet, five patent bottle tops, a number of used matches, three pieces of string, one or two fragments of newspaper, a fragment of a smashed pipe, four buttons, the drumstick bone of a chicken and an empty bottle of sun-bathing oil.

Weston looked down appraisingly on the objects.

'H'm,' he said. 'Rather moderate for a beach nowadays! Most people seem to confuse a beach with a public rubbish dump! Empty bottle's been here some time by the way the label's blurred – so have most of the other things, I should say. The scissors are new, though. Bright and shining. *They* weren't out in yesterday's rain! Where were they?'

'Close by the bottom of the ladder, sir. Also this bit of pipe.'

'H'm, probably dropped by someone going up or down. Nothing to say who they belong to?'

'No, sir. Quite an ordinary pair of nail scissors. Pipe's a good quality brier – expensive.'

Poirot murmured thoughtfully:

'Captain Marshall told us, I think, that he had mislaid his pipe.'

Weston said:

'Marshall's out of the picture. Anyway, he's not the only person who smokes a pipe.'

Hercule Poirot was watching Stephen Lane as the latter's hand went to his pocket and away again. He said pleasantly:

'You also smoke a pipe, do you not, Mr Lane?'

The clergyman started. He looked at Poirot.

He said:

'Yes. Oh yes. My pipe is an old friend and companion.' Putting his hand into his pocket again he drew out a pipe, filled it with tobacco and lighted it.

Hercule Poirot moved away to where Redfern was standing, his eyes blank.

He said in a low voice:

'I'm glad – they've taken *her* away . . .'

Stephen Lane asked:

'Where was she found?'

The Sergeant said cheerfully:

'Just about where you're standing, sir.'

Lane moved swiftly aside. He stared at the spot he had just vacated.

The Sergeant went on:

'Place where the float was drawn up agrees with putting the time she arrived here at 10.45. That's going by the tide. It's turned now.'

'Photography all done?' asked Weston.

'Yes, sir.'

Weston turned to Redfern.

'Now then, man, where's the entrance to this cave of yours?'

Patrick Redfern was still staring down at the beach where Lane had been standing. It was as though he was seeing that sprawling body that was no longer there.

Weston's words recalled him to himself.

He said: 'It's over here.'

He led the way to where a great mass of tumbled-down rocks were massed picturesquely against the cliff side. He went straight to where two big rocks, side by side, showed a straight narrow cleft between them. He said:

'The entrance is here.'

Weston said:

'Here? Doesn't look as though a man could squeeze through.'

'It's deceptive, you'll find, sir. It can just be done.'

Weston inserted himself gingerly into the cleft. It was not as narrow as it looked. Inside, the space widened and proved to be a fairly roomy recess with room to stand upright and to move about.

Hercule Poirot and Stephen Lane joined the Chief Constable. The other stayed outside. Light filtered in through the opening, but Weston had also got a powerful torch which he played freely over the interior.

He observed:

'Handy place. You'd never suspect it from the outside.'

He played the torch carefully over the floor.

Hercule Poirot was delicately sniffing the air.

Noticing this, Weston said:

'Air quite fresh, not fishy or seaweedy, but of course this place is well above high water mark.'

But to Poirot's sensitive nose, the air was more than fresh. It was delicately scented. He knew two people who used that elusive perfume . . .

Weston's torch came to rest. He said:

'Don't see anything out of the way in here.'

Poirot's eyes rose to a ledge a little way above his head. He murmured:

'One might perhaps see that there is nothing up there?'

Weston said: 'If there's anything up there it would have to be deliberately put there. Still, we'd better have a look.'

Poirot said to Lane:

'You are, I think, the tallest of us, Monsieur. Could we venture to ask you to make sure there is nothing resting on that ledge?'

Lane stretched up, but he could not quite reach to the back of the shelf. Then, seeing a crevice in the rock, he inserted a toe in it and pulled himself up by one hand.

He said:

'Hullo, there's a box up here.'

In a minute or two they were out in the sunshine examining the clergyman's find.

Weston said:

'Careful, don't handle it more than you can help. May be fingerprints.'

It was a dark-green tin box and bore the word Sandwiches on it.

Sergeant Phillips said:

'Left from some picnic or other, I suppose.'

He opened the lid with his handkerchief.

Inside were small tin containers marked salt, pepper, mustard and two larger square tins evidently for sandwiches. Sergeant Phillips lifted the lid of the salt container. It was full to the brim. He raised the next one, commenting:

'H'm, got salt in the pepper one too.'

The mustard compartment also contained salt.

His face suddenly alert, the police sergeant opened one of the bigger square tins. That, too, contained the same white crystalline powder.

Very gingerly, Sergeant Phillips dipped a finger in and applied it to his tongue.

His face changed. He said – and his voice was excited:

'This isn't *salt*, sir. Not by a long way! Bitter taste! Seems to me it's some kind of *drug*.'

'The third angle,' said Colonel Weston with a groan.

They were back at the hotel again.

The Chief Constable went on:

'If by any chance there's a dope gang mixed up in this, it opens up several possibilities. First of all, the dead woman may have been in with the gang herself. Think that's likely?'

Hercule Poirot said cautiously:

'It is possible.'

'She may have been a drug addict?'

Poirot shook his head.

He said:

'I should doubt that. She had steady nerves, radiant health, there were no marks of hypodermic injections (not that that proves anything. Some people sniff the stuff). No, I do not think she took drugs.'

'In that case,' said Weston, 'she may have run into the business accidentally, and she was deliberately silenced by the people running the show. We'll know presently just what the stuff is. I've sent it to Neasden. If we're on to some dope ring, they're not the people to stick at trifles –'

He broke off as the door opened and Mr Horace Blatt came briskly into the room.

Mr Blatt was looking hot. He was wiping the perspiration from his forehead. His big hearty voice billowed out and filled the small room.

'Just this minute got back and heard the news! You the Chief Constable? They told me you were in here. My name's Blatt – Horace Blatt. Any way I can help you? Don't suppose so. I've been out in my boat since early this morning. Missed the whole blinking show. The one day that something *does* happen in this out-of-the-way spot, I'm not there. Just like life, that, isn't it? Hullo, Poirot, didn't see you at first. So you're in on this? Oh well, I suppose you would be. Sherlock Holmes *v.* the local police, is that it? Ha, ha! Lestrade – all that stuff. I'll enjoy seeing you do a bit of fancy sleuthing.'

Mr Blatt came to anchor in a chair, pulled out a cigarette case and offered it to Colonel Weston, who shook his head.

He said, with a slight smile:

'I'm an inveterate pipe smoker.'

'Same here. I smoke cigarettes as well – but nothing beats a pipe.'

Colonel Weston said with suddenly geniality:

'Then light up, man.'

Blatt shook his head.

'Not got my pipe on me at the moment. But put me wise about all this. All I've heard so far is that Mrs Marshall was found murdered on one of the beaches here.'

'On Pixy Cove,' said Colonel Weston, watching him.

But Mr Blatt merely asked excitedly:

'And she was strangled?'

'Yes, Mr Blatt.'

'Nasty – very nasty. Mind you, she asked for it! Hot stuff – *trés moustarde* – eh, M. Poirot? Any idea who did it, or mustn't I ask that?'

With a faint smile Colonel Weston said:

'Well, you know, it's we who are supposed to ask the questions.'

Mr Blatt waved his cigarette.

'Sorry – sorry – my mistake. Go ahead.'

'You went out sailing this morning. At what time?'

'Left here at a quarter to ten.'

'Was any one with you?'

'Not a soul. All on my little lonesome.'

'And where did you go?'

'Along the coast in the direction of Plymouth. Took lunch with me. Not much wind so I didn't actually get very far.'

After another question or two, Weston asked:

'Now about the Marshalls? Do you know anything that might help us?'

'Well, I've given you my opinion. *Crime passionnel!* All I can tell you is, it wasn't *me*! The fair Arlena had no use for me. Nothing doing in that quarter. She had her own blue-eyed boy! And if you ask me, Marshall was getting wise to it.'

'Have you any evidence for that?'

'Saw him give young Redfern a dirty look once or twice. Dark horse, Marshall. Looks very meek and mild and as though he were half asleep all the time – but that's not his reputation in the City. I've heard a thing or two about him. Nearly had up for assault once. Mind you, the fellow in question had put up a pretty dirty deal. Marshall had trusted him and the fellow had let him down cold. Particularly dirty business, I believe. Marshall went for him and half killed him. Fellow didn't prosecute – too afraid of what might come out. I give you that for what it's worth.'

'So you think it possible,' said Poirot, 'that Captain Marshall strangled his wife?'

'Not at all. Never said anything of the sort. Just letting you know that he's the sort of fellow who could go berserk on occasions.'

Poirot said:

'Mr Blatt, there is reason to believe that Mrs Marshall went this morning to Pixy Cove to meet someone. Have you any idea who that someone might be?'

Mr Blatt winked.

'It's not a guess. It's a certainty. Redfern!'

'It was not Mr Redfern.'

Mr Blatt seemed taken aback. He said hesitatingly:

'Then I don't know . . . No, I can't imagine . . .'

He went on, regaining a little of his aplomb:

'As I said before, it wasn't *me*! No such luck! Let me see, couldn't have been Gardener – his wife keeps far too sharp an eye on him! That old ass Barry? Rot! And it would hardly be the parson. Although, mind you, I've seen his Reverence watching her a good bit. All holy disapproval, but perhaps an eye for the contours all the same! Eh? Lot of hypocrites, most parsons. Did you read that case last month? Parson and the churchwarden's daughter! Bit of an eye-opener.'

Mr Blatt chuckled.

Colonel Weston said coldly:

'There is nothing you can think of that might help us?'

The other shook his head.

'No. Can't think of a thing.' He added: 'This will make a bit of a stir, I imagine. The Press will be on to it like hot cakes. There won't be quite so much of this high-toned exclusiveness about the Jolly Roger in future. Jolly Roger indeed. Precious little jollity about it.'

Hercule Poirot murmured:

'You have not enjoyed your stay here?'

Mr Blatt's red face got slightly redder. He said:

'Well, no, I haven't. The sailing's all right and the scenery and the service and the food – but there's no *matiness* in the place, you know what I mean! What I say is, my money's as good as another man's. We're all here to enjoy ourselves. Then why not get together and *do* it? All these cliques

and people sitting by themselves and giving you frosty good-mornings –
and good-evenings – and yes, very pleasant weather. No joy de viver. Lot
of stuck-up dummies!'

Mr Blatt paused – by now very red indeed.

He wiped his forehead once more and said apologetically:

'Don't pay any attention to me. I get all worked up.'

Hercule Poirot murmured:

'And what do we think of Mr Blatt?'

Colonel Weston grinned and said:

'What do *you* think of him? You've seen more of him than I have.'

Poirot said softly:

'There are many of your English idioms that describe him. The rough
diamond! The self-made man! The social climber! He is, as you choose
to look at it, pathetic, ludicrous, blatant! It is a matter of opinion. But I
think, too, that he is something else.'

'And what is that?'

Hercule Poirot, his eyes raised to the ceiling, murmured:

'I think that he is – *nervous*!'

Inspector Colgate said:

'I've got those times worked out. From the hotel to the ladder down to
Pixy Cove three minutes. That's walking till you are out of sight of the
hotel and then running like hell.'

Weston raised his eyebrows. He said:

'That's quicker than I thought.'

'Down ladder to beach one minute and three-quarters. Up same two
minutes. That's P.C. Flint. He's a bit of an athlete. Walking and taking
the ladder in the normal way, the whole business takes close on a quarter
of an hour.'

Weston nodded. He said:

'There's another thing we must go into, the pipe question.'

Colgate said:

'Blatt smokes a pipe, so does Marshall, so does the parson. Redfern
smokes cigarettes, the American prefers a cigar. Major Barry doesn't
smoke at all. There's one pipe in Marshall's room, two in Blatt's, and
one in the parson's. Chambermaid says Marshall has two pipes. The other
chambermaid isn't a very bright girl. Doesn't know how many pipes the

other two have. Says vaguely she's noticed two or three about in their rooms.'

Weston nodded.

'Anything else?'

'I've checked up on the staff. They all seem quite O.K. Henry, in the bar, checks Marshall's statement about seeing him at ten to eleven. William, the beach attendant, was down repairing the ladder on the rocks by the hotel most of the morning. He seems all right. George marked the tennis court and then bedded out some plants round by the dining-room. Neither of them would have seen anyone who came across the causeway to the island.'

'When was the causeway uncovered?'

'Round about 9.30, sir.'

Weston pulled at his moustache.

'It's possible somebody did come that way. We've got a new angle, Colgate.'

He told of the discovery of the sandwich box in the cave.

There was a tap on the door.

'Come in,' said Weston.

It was Captain Marshall.

He said:

'Can you tell me what arrangements I can make about the funeral?'

'I think we shall manage the inquest for the day after tomorrow, Captain Marshall.'

'Thank you.'

Inspector Colgate said:

'Excuse me, sir, allow me to return you these.'

He handed over the three letters.

Kenneth Marshall smiled rather sardonically.

He said:

'Has the police department been testing the speed of my typing? I hope my character is cleared.'

Colonel Weston said pleasantly:

'Yes, Captain Marshall, I think we can give you a clean bill of health. Those sheets take fully an hour to type. Moreover you were heard typing them by the chambermaid up till five minutes to eleven and you were seen by another witness at twenty minutes past.'

Captain Marshall murmured:

'Really? That all seems very satisfactory!'

'Yes. Miss Darnley came to your room at twenty minutes past eleven. You were so busy typing that you did not observe her entry.'

Kenneth Marshall's face took on an impassive expression. He said:

'Does Miss Darnley say that?' He paused. 'As a matter of fact she is wrong. I *did* see her, though she may not be aware of the fact. I saw her in the mirror.'

Poirot murmured:

'But you did not interrupt your typing?'

Marshall said shortly:

'No. I wanted to get finished.'

He paused a minute, then, in an abrupt voice, he said:

'Nothing more I can do for you?'

'No, thank you, Captain Marshall.'

Kenneth Marshall nodded and went out.

Weston said with a sigh:

'There goes our most hopeful suspect – cleared! Hullo, here's Neasden.'

The doctor came in with a trace of excitement in his manner. He said:

'That's a nice little death lot you sent me along.'

'What is it?'

'What is it? Diamorphine Hydrochloride. Stuff that's usually called Heroin.'

Inspector Colgate whistled. He said:

'Now we're getting places, all right! Depend upon it, this dope stunt is at the bottom of the whole business.'

<hr>

CHAPTER 10

The little crowd of people flocked out of the Red Bull. The brief inquest was over – adjourned for a fortnight.

Rosamund Darnley joined Captain Marshall. She said in a low voice:

'That wasn't so bad, was it, Ken?'

He did not answer at once. Perhaps he was conscious of the staring eyes of the villagers, the fingers that nearly pointed to him and only just did not quite do so!

'*That's 'im, my dear.*' '*See, that's 'er 'usband.*' '*That be the 'usband.*' '*Look, there 'e goes . . .*'

The murmurs were not loud enough to reach his ears, but he was none the less sensitive to them. This was the modern-day pillory. The Press he had already encountered – self-confident, persuasive young men, adept at battering down his wall of silence of 'Nothing to say' that he had endeavoured to erect. Even the curt monosyllables that he had uttered, thinking that they at least could not lead to misapprehension, had reappeared in his morning's papers in a totally different guise. 'Asked whether he agreed that the mystery of his wife's death could only be explained on the assumption that a homicidal murderer had found his way on to the island, Captain Marshall declared that –' and so on and so forth.

Cameras had clicked ceaselessly. Now, at this minute, the well-known sound caught his ear. He half turned – a smiling young man was nodding cheerfully, his purpose accomplished.

Rosamund murmured:

'*Captain Marshall and a friend leaving the Red Bull after the inquest.*'

Marshall winced.

Rosamund said:

'It's no use, Ken! You've got to face it! I don't mean just the fact of Arlena's death – I mean all the attendant beastliness. The staring eyes and gossiping tongues, the fatuous interviews in the papers – and the best way to meet it is to find it funny! Come out with all the old inane cliches and curl a sardonic lip at them.'

He said:

'Is that your way?'

'Yes.' She paused. 'It isn't yours, I know. Protective colouring is your line. Remain rigidly non-active and fade into the background! But you can't do that here – you've no background to fade into. You stand out clear for all to see – like a striped tiger against a white backcloth. *The husband of the murdered woman!*'

'For God's sake, Rosamund –'

She said gently:

'My dear, I'm trying to be good for you!'

They walked for a few steps in silence. Then Marshall said in a different voice:

'I know you are. I'm not really ungrateful, Rosamund.'

They had progressed beyond the limits of the village. Eyes followed them but there was no one very near. Rosamund Darnley's voice dropped as she repeated a variant of her first remark.

'It didn't really go so badly, did it?'

He was silent for a moment, then he said:

'I don't know.'

'What do the police think?'

'They're non-committal.'

After a minute Rosamund said:

'That little man – Poirot – is he really taking an active interest!'

Kenneth Marshall said:

'Seemed to be sitting in the Chief Constable's pocket all right the other day.'

'I know – but is he *doing* anything?'

'How the hell should I know, Rosamund?'

She said thoughtfully:

'He's pretty old. Probably more or less ga ga.'

'Perhaps.'

They came to the causeway. Opposite them, serene in the sun, lay the island.

Rosamund said suddenly:

'Sometimes – things seem unreal. I can't believe, this minute, that it ever happened . . .'

Marshall said slowly:

'I think I know what you mean. Nature is so regardless! One ant the less – that's all it is in Nature!'

Rosamund said:

'Yes – and that's the proper way to look at it really.'

He gave her one very quick glance. Then he said in a low voice:

'Don't worry, my dear. It's all right. *It's all right.*'

Linda came down to the causeway to meet them. She moved with the spasmodic jerkiness of a nervous colt. Her young face was marred by deep black shadows under her eyes. Her lips were dry and rough.

She said breathlessly:

'What happened – what – what did they say?'

Her father said abruptly:

'Inquest adjourned for a fortnight.'

'That means they – they haven't decided?'

'Yes. More evidence is needed.'

'But – but what do they think?'

Marshall smiled a little in spite of himself.

'Oh, my dear child – who knows? And whom do you mean by they?

The coroner, the jury, the police, the newspaper reporters, the fishing folk of Leathercombe Bay?'

Linda said slowly:

'I suppose I mean – the police.'

Marshall said dryly:

'Whatever the police think, they're not giving it away at present.'

His lips closed tightly after the sentence. He went into the hotel.

As Rosamund Darnley was about to follow suit, Linda said:

'Rosamund!'

Rosamund turned. The mute appeal in the girl's unhappy face touched her. She linked her arm through Linda's and together they walked away from the hotel, taking the path that led to the extreme end of the island.

Rosamund said gently:

'Try not to mind so much, Linda. I know it's all very terrible and a shock and all that, but it's no use brooding over these things. And it can be only the – horror of it, that is worrying you. You weren't in the least *fond* of Arlena, you know.'

She felt the tremor that ran through the girl's body as Linda answered:

'No, I wasn't fond of her . . .'

Rosamund went on:

'Sorrow for a person is different – one can't put *that* behind one. But one *can* get over shock and horror by just not letting your mind *dwell* on it all the time.'

Linda said sharply:

'You don't understand.'

'I think I do, my dear.'

Linda shook her head.

'No, you don't. You don't understand in the least – and Christine doesn't understand either! Both of you have been nice to me, but you can't understand what I'm feeling. You just think it's morbid – that I'm dwelling on it all when I needn't.'

She paused.

'But it isn't that at all. If you knew what I know –'

Rosamund stopped dead. Her body did not tremble – on the contrary it stiffened. She stood for a minute or two, then she disengaged her arm from Linda's.

She said:

'What is it that you know, Linda?'

The girl gazed at her. Then she shook her head.

She muttered:

'Nothing.'

Rosamund caught her by the arm. The grip hurt and Linda winced slightly.

Rosamund said:

'Be careful, Linda. Be damned careful.'

Linda had gone dead white.

She said:

'I *am* very careful – all the time.'

Rosamund said urgently:

'Listen, Linda, what I said a minute or two ago applies just the same – only a hundred times more so. *Put the whole business out of your mind.* Never think about it. Forget – forget . . . You can if you try! Arlena is dead and nothing can bring her back to life . . . Forget everything and live in the future. And above all, *hold your tongue.*'

Linda shrank a little. She said:

'You – you seem to know all about it?'

Rosamund said energetically:

'I don't know *anything*! In my opinion a wandering maniac got on to the island and killed Arlena. That's much the most probable solution. I'm fairly sure that the police will have to accept that in the end. That's what *must* have happened! That's what *did* happen!'

Linda said:

'If Father –'

Rosamund interrupted her.

'Don't talk about it.'

Linda said:

'I've got to say one thing. My mother –'

'Well, what about her?'

'She – she was tried for murder, wasn't she?'

'Yes.'

Linda said slowly:

'And then Father married her. That looks, doesn't it, as though Father didn't really think murder was very wrong – not always, that is.'

Rosamund said sharply:

'Don't say things like that – even to me! The police haven't got anything against your father. He's got an alibi – an alibi that they can't break. He's perfectly safe.'

Linda whispered:

'Did they think at first that Father –?'

Rosamund cried:

'I don't know what they thought! But they know now *that he couldn't have done it.* Do you understand? *He couldn't have done it.*'

She spoke with authority, her eyes commanded Linda's acquiescence. The girl uttered a long fluttering sigh.

Rosamund said:

'You'll be able to leave here soon. You'll forget everything – everything!'

Linda said with sudden unexpected violence.

'*I shall never forget.*'

She turned abruptly and ran back to the hotel. Rosamund stared after her.

'There is something I want to know, Madame?'

Christine Redfern glanced up at Poirot in a slightly abstracted manner. She said:

'Yes?'

Hercule Poirot took very little notice of her abstraction. He had noted the way her eyes followed her husband's figure where he was pacing up and down on the terrace outside the bar, but for the moment he had no interest in purely conjugal problems. He wanted information.

He said:

'Yes, Madame. It was a phrase – a chance phrase of yours the other day which roused my attention.'

Christine, her eyes still on Patrick, said:

'Yes? What did I say?'

'It was in answer to a question from the Chief Constable. You described how you went into Miss Linda Marshall's room on the morning of the crime and how you found her absent from it and how she returned there, and it was then that the Chief Constable asked you where she had been.'

Christine said rather impatiently:

'And I said she had been bathing? Is that it?'

'Ah, but you did not say quite that. You did not say "she had been bathing". Your words were, "she said she had been bathing".'

Christine said:

'It's the same thing, surely.'

'No, it is not the same! The form of your answer suggests a certain attitude of mind on your part. Linda Marshall came into the room – she was wearing a bathing-wrap and yet – for some reason – you did not at once assume she had been bathing. That is shown by your words, "she *said* she had been bathing". What was there about her appearance – was it her manner, or something that she was wearing or something she said – that led you to feel surprised when she said she had been bathing?'

Christine's attention left Patrick and focused itself entirely on Poirot. She was interested. She said:

'That's clever of you. It's quite true, now I remember . . . I *was*, just faintly, surprised when Linda said she had been bathing.'

'But why, Madame, why?'

'Yes, why? That's just what I'm trying to remember. Oh yes, I think it was the parcel in her hand.'

'She had a parcel?'

'Yes.'

'You do not know what was in it?'

'Oh yes, I do. The string broke. It was loosely done up in the way they do in the village. It was *candles* – they were scattered on the floor. I helped her to pick them up.'

'Ah,' said Poirot. 'Candles.'

Christine stared at him. She said:

'You seem excited, M. Poirot.'

Poirot asked:

'Did Linda say why she had bought candles?'

Christine reflected.

'No, I don't think she did. I suppose it was to read by at night – perhaps the electric light wasn't good.'

'On the contrary, Madame, there was a bedside electric lamp in perfect order.'

Christine said:

'Then I don't know what she wanted them for.'

Poirot said:

'What was her manner – when the string broke and the candles fell out of the parcel?'

Christine said slowly:

'She was – upset – embarrassed.'

Poirot nodded his head. Then he asked:

'Did you notice a calendar in her room?'

'A calendar? What kind of a calendar?'

Poirot said:

'Possibly a green calendar – with tear-off leaves.'

Christine screwed up her eyes in an effort of memory.

'A green calendar – rather a bright green. Yes, I have seen a calendar like that – but I can't remember where. It may have been in Linda's room, but I can't be sure.'

'But you have definitely seen such a thing.'

'Yes.'

Again Poirot nodded.

Christine said rather sharply:

'What are you hinting at, M. Poirot? What is the meaning of all this?'

For answer Poirot produced a small volume bound in faded brown calf. He said:

'Have you ever seen this before?'

'Why – I think – I'm not sure – yes, Linda was looking into it in the village lending library the other day. But she shut it up and thrust it back quickly when I came up to her. It made me wonder what it was.'

Silently Poirot displayed the title.

A History of Witchcraft, Sorcery and of the Compounding of Untraceable Poisons.

Christine said:

'I don't understand. What does all this mean?'

Poirot said gravely.

'It may mean, Madame, a good deal.'

She looked at him inquiringly, but he did not go on. Instead he asked:

'One more question, Madame, did you take a bath that morning before you went out to play tennis?'

Christine stared again.

'A bath? No. I would have had no time and, anyway, I didn't want a bath – not before tennis. I might have had one after.'

'Did you use your bathroom at all when you came in?'

'I sponged my face and hands, that's all.'

'You did not turn on the bath at all?'

'No, I'm sure I didn't.'

Poirot nodded. He said:

'It is of no importance.'

Hercule Poirot stood by the table where Mrs Gardener was wrestling with a jig-saw. She looked up and jumped.

'Why, M. Poirot, how very quietly you came up beside me! I never heard you. Have you just come back from the inquest? You know, the very thought of that inquest makes me so nervous, I don't know what to do. That's why I'm doing this puzzle. I just felt I couldn't sit outside on the beach as usual. As Mr Gardener knows, when my nerves are all upset, there's nothing like one of these puzzles for calming me. There now, where *does* this white piece fit in? It must be part of the fur rug, but I don't seem to see . . .'

Gently Poirot's hand took the piece from her. He said:

'It fits, Madame, *here*. It is part of the cat.'

'It can't be. It's a black cat.'

'A black cat, yes, but you see the tip of the black cat's tail happens to be white.'

'Why, so it does! How clever of you! But I do think the people who make puzzles are kind of mean. They just go out of their way to deceive you.'

She fitted in another piece and then resumed.

'You know, M. Poirot, I've been watching you this last day or two. I just wanted to watch you detecting if you know what I mean – not that it doesn't sound rather heartless put like that, as though it were all a game – and a poor creature killed. Oh dear, every time *I* think of it I get the shivers! I told Mr Gardener this morning I'd just *got* to get away from here, and now the inquest's over he thinks we'll be able to leave tomorrow, and that's a blessing, I'm sure. But about detecting, I would so like to know your methods – you know, I'd feel privileged if you'd just *explain* it to me.'

Hercule Poirot said:

'It is a little like your puzzle, Madame. One assembles the pieces. It is like a mosaic – many colours and patterns – and every strange-shaped little piece must be fitted into its own place.'

'Now isn't that interesting? Why, I'm sure you explain it just too beautifully.'

Poirot went on:

'And sometimes it is like that piece of your puzzle just now. One arranges very methodically the pieces of the puzzle – one sorts the colours – and then perhaps a piece of one colour that should fit in with – say, the fur rug, fits in instead in a black cat's tail.'

'Why, if that doesn't sound too fascinating! And are there a great many pieces, M. Poirot?'

'Yes, Madame. Almost everyone here in this hotel has given me a piece for my puzzle. You amongst them.'

'Me?' Mrs Gardener's tone was shrill.

'Yes, a remark of yours, Madame, was exceedingly helpful. I might say it was illuminating.'

'Well, if that isn't too lovely! Can't you tell me some more, M. Poirot?'

'Ah! Madame, I reserve the explanations for the last chapter.'

Mrs Gardener murmured:

'If that isn't just too bad!'

Hercule Poirot tapped gently on the door of Captain Marshall's room. Inside there was the sound of a typewriter.

A curt 'Come in' came from the room and Poirot entered.

Captain Marshall's back was turned to him. He was sitting typing at the table between the windows. He did not turn his head but his eyes met Poirot's in the mirror that hung on the wall directly in front of him. He said irritably:

'Well, M. Poirot, what is it?'

Poirot said quickly:

'A thousand apologies for intruding. You are busy?'

Marshall said shortly: 'I am rather.'

Poirot said:

'It is one little question that I would like to ask you.'

Marshall said:

'My God, I'm sick of answering questions. I've answered the police questions. I don't feel called upon to answer yours.'

Poirot said:

'Mine is a very simple one. Only this. On the morning of your wife's death, did you have a bath after you finished typing and before you went out to play tennis?'

'A bath? No, of course I didn't! I'd had a bathe only an hour earlier!'

Hercule Poirot said:

'Thank you. That is all.'

'But look here. Oh –' the other paused irresolutely.

Poirot withdrew, gently closing the door.

Kenneth Marshall said:

'The fellow's crazy!'

Just outside the bar Poirot encountered Mr Gardener. He was carrying two cocktails and was clearly on his way to where Mrs Gardener was ensconced with her jig-saw.

He smiled at Poirot in genial fashion.

'Care to join us, M. Poirot?'

Poirot shook his head. He said:

'What did you think of the inquest, Mr Gardener?'

Mr Gardener lowered his voice. He said:

'Seemed kind of indeterminate to me. Your police, I gather, have got something up their sleeves.'

'It is possible,' said Hercule Poirot.

Mr Gardener lowered his voice still further.

'I shall be glad to get Mrs Gardener away. She's a very, very sensitive woman, and this affair has got on her nerves. She's very highly strung.'

Hercule Poirot said:

'Will you permit me, Mr Gardener, to ask you one question?'

'Why, certainly, M. Poirot. Delighted to assist in any way I can.'

Hercule Poirot said:

'You are a man of the world – a man, I think, of considerable acumen. What, frankly, was your opinion of the late Mrs Marshall?'

Mr Gardener's eyebrows rose in surprise. He glanced cautiously round and lowered his voice.

'Well, M. Poirot, I've heard a few things that have been kind of going around, if you get me, especially among the women.' Poirot nodded. 'But if you ask me I'll tell you my candid opinion and that is that that woman was pretty much of a darned fool!'

Hercule Poirot said thoughtfully:

'Now that is very interesting.'

Rosamund Darnley said: 'So it's my turn, is it?'

'Pardon?'

She laughed.

'The other day the Chief Constable held his inquisition. You sat by. Today, I think, you are conducting your own unofficial inquiry. I've been watching you. First Mrs Redfern, then I caught a glimpse of you through the lounge window where Mrs Gardener is doing her hateful jig-saw puzzle. Now it's my turn.'

Hercule Poirot sat down beside her. They were on Sunny Ledge. Below them the sea showed a deep-glowing green. Farther out it was a pale dazzling blue.

Poirot said:

'You are very intelligent, Mademoiselle. I have thought so ever since I arrived here. It would be a pleasure to discuss this business with you.'

Rosamund Darnley said softly:

'You want to know what I think about the whole thing?'

'It would be most interesting.'

Rosamund said:

'I think it's really very simple. The clue is in the woman's past.'

'The past? Not the present?'

'Oh! not necessarily the very remote past. I look at it like this. Arlena Marshall was attractive, fatally attractive, to men. It's possible, I think, that she also tired of them rather quickly. Amongst her – followers, shall we say – was one who resented that. Oh, don't misunderstand me, it won't be someone who sticks out a mile. Probably some tepid little man, vain and sensitive – the kind of man who broods. I think he followed her down here, waited his opportunity and killed her.'

'You mean that he was an outsider, that he came from the mainland?'

'Yes. He probably hid in that cave until he got his chance.'

Poirot shook his head. He said:

'Would she go there to meet such a man as you describe? No, she would laugh and not go.'

Rosamund said:

'She mayn't have known she was going to meet him. He may have sent her a message in some other person's name.'

Poirot murmured:

'That is possible.'

Then he said:

'But you forget one thing, Mademoiselle. A man bent on murder could not risk coming in broad daylight across the causeway and past the hotel. Someone might have seen him.'

'They might have – but I don't think that it's certain. I think it's quite possible that he could have come without anyone noticing him at all.'

'It would be *possible*, yes, that I grant you. But the point is that he could not *count* on that possibility.'

Rosamund said:

'Aren't you forgetting something? The weather.'

'The weather?'

'Yes. The day of the murder was a glorious day, but the day before, remember, there was rain and thick mist. Anyone could come on to the island then without being seen. He had only to go down to the beach and spend the night in the cave. That mist, M. Poirot, is important.'

Poirot looked at her thoughtfully for a minute or two. He said:

'You know, there is a good deal in what you have just said.'

Rosamund flushed. She said:

'That's my theory, for what it is worth. Now tell me yours.'

'Ah,' said Hercule Poirot. He stared down at the sea.

'*Eh bien*, Mademoiselle. I am a very simple person. I always incline to the belief that the most likely person committed the crime. At the very beginning it seemed to me that one person was very clearly indicated.'

Rosamund's voice hardened a little. She said:

'Go on.'

Hercule Poirot went on.

'But you see, there is what you call a snag in the way! It seems that it was *impossible* for that person to have committed the crime.'

He heard the quick expulsion of her breath. She said rather breathlessly:

'Well?'

Hercule Poirot shrugged his shoulders.

'Well, what do we do about it? That is my problem.' He paused and then went on. 'May I ask you a question?'

'Certainly.'

She faced him, alert and vigilant. But the question that came was an unexpected one.

'When you came in to change for tennis that morning, did you have a bath?'

Rosamund stared at him.

'A bath? What do you mean?'

'That is what I mean. A bath! The receptacle of porcelain, one turns the taps and fills it, one gets in, one gets out and ghoosh – ghoosh – ghoosh, the water goes down the waste-pipe!'

'M. Poirot, are you quite mad?'

'No, I am extremely sane.'

'Well, anyway, I *didn't* take a bath.'

'Ha!' said Poirot. 'So nobody took a bath. That is extremely interesting.'

'But why should anyone take a bath?'

Hercule Poirot said: 'Why, indeed?'

Rosamund said with some exasperation:

'I suppose this is the Sherlock Holmes touch!'

Hercule Poirot smiled.

Then he sniffed the air delicately.

'Will you permit me to be impertinent, Mademoiselle?'

'I'm sure you couldn't be impertinent, M. Poirot.'

'That is very kind of you. Then may I venture to say that the scent you use is delicious – it has a *nuance* – a delicate elusive charm.' He waved his hands, and then added in a practical voice, 'Gabrielle, No 8, I think?'

'How clever you are. Yes, I always use it.'

'So did the late Mrs Marshall. It is chic, eh? And very expensive?'

Rosamund shrugged her shoulders with a faint smile.

Poirot said:

'You sat here where we are now, Mademoiselle, on the morning of the crime. You were seen here, or at least your sunshade was seen by Miss Brewster and Mr Redfern as they passed on the sea. During the morning, Mademoiselle, are you sure you did not happen to go down to Pixy Cove and enter the cave there – the famous Pixy's Cave?'

Rosamund turned her head and stared at him.

She said in a quiet level voice:

'Are you asking me if I killed Arlena Marshall?'

'No, I am asking you if you went into the Pixy's Cave?'

'I don't even know where it is. Why should I go into it? For what reason?'

'On the day of the crime, Mademoiselle, somebody had been in that cave who used Gabrielle No 8.'

Rosamund said sharply:

'You've just said yourself, M. Poirot, that Arlena Marshall used Gabrielle No 8. She was on the beach there that day. Presumably she went into the cave.'

'Why should she go into the cave? It is dark there and narrow and very uncomfortable.'

Rosamund said impatiently:

'Don't ask me for reasons. Since she was actually at the cove she was by far the most likely person. I've told you already I never left this place the whole morning.'

'Except for the time when you went into the hotel to Captain Marshall's room.' Poirot reminded her.

'Yes, of course. I'd forgotten that.'

Poirot said:

'And you were wrong, Mademoiselle, when you thought that Captain Marshall did not see you.'

Rosamund said incredulously:

'Kenneth did see me? Did – did he say so?'

Poirot nodded.

'He saw you, Mademoiselle, in the mirror that hangs over the table.'

Rosamund caught her breath. She said:

'Oh! I see.'

Poirot was no longer looking out to sea. He was looking at Rosamund Darnley's hands as they lay folded in her lap. They were well-shaped hands, beautifully moulded with very long fingers.

Rosamund, shooting a quick look at him, followed the direction of his eyes. She said sharply:

'What are you looking at my hands for? Do you think – do you think –?'

Poirot said:

'Do I think – what, Mademoiselle?'

Rosamund Darnley said:

'Nothing.'

It was perhaps an hour later that Hercule Poirot came to the top of the path leading to Gull Cove. There was someone sitting on the beach. A slight figure in a red shirt and dark blue shorts.

Poirot descended the path, stepping carefully in his tight smart shoes.

Linda Marshall turned her head sharply. He thought that she shrank a little.

Her eyes, as he came and lowered himself gingerly to the shingle beside her, rested on him with the suspicion and alertness of a trapped animal. He realized, with a pang, how young and vulnerable she was.

She said:

'What is it? What do you want?'

Hercule Poirot did not answer for a minute or two. Then he said:

'The other day you told the Chief Constable that you were fond of your stepmother and that she was kind to you.'

'Well?'

'That was not true, was it, Mademoiselle?'

'Yes, it was.'

Poirot said:

'She may not have been actively unkind – that I will grant. But you were not fond of her – Oh no – I think you disliked her very much. That was very plain to see.'

Linda said:

'Perhaps I didn't like her very much. But one can't say that when a person is dead. It wouldn't be decent.'

Poirot sighed. He said:

'They taught you that at your school?'

'More or less, I suppose.'

Hercule Poirot said:

'When a person has been murdered, it is more important to be truthful than to be decent.'

Linda said:

'I suppose you *would* say a thing like that.'

'I would say it and I do say it. It is my business, you see, to find out who killed Arlena Marshall.'

Linda muttered:

'I want to forget it all. It's so horrible.'

Poirot said gently:

'*But you can't forget, can you?*'

Linda said:

'I suppose some beastly madman killed her.'

Hercule Poirot murmured:

'No, I do not think it was quite like that.'

Linda caught her breath. She said:

'You sound – as though you *know*?'

Poirot said:

'Perhaps I do know.' He paused and went on: 'Will you trust me, my child, to do the best I can for you in your bitter trouble?'

Linda sprang up. She said:

'I haven't any trouble. There is nothing you can do for me. I don't know what you are talking about.'

Poirot said, watching her:

'I am talking about *candles* . . .'

He saw the terror leap into her eyes. She cried:

'I won't listen to you. I won't listen.'

She ran across the beach, swift as a young gazelle and went flying up the zigzag path.

Poirot shook his head. He looked grave and troubled.

CHAPTER 11

Inspector Colgate was reporting to the Chief Constable.

'I've got on to one thing, sir, and something pretty sensational. It's about Mrs Marshall's money. I've been into it with her lawyers. I'd say it's a bit of a shock to them. I've got proof of the blackmail story. You remember she was left fifty thousand pounds by old Erskine? Well, all that's left of that is about fifteen thousand.'

The Chief Constable whistled.

'Whew, what's become of the rest?'

'That's the interesting point, sir. She's sold out stuff from time to time, and each time she's handled it in cash or negotiable securities – that's to say she's handed out money to someone that she didn't want traced. Blackmail all right.'

The Chief Constable nodded.

'Certainly looks like it. And the blackmailer is here in this hotel. That means it must be one of those three men. Got anything fresh on any of them?'

'Can't say I've got anything definite, sir. Major Barry's a retired Army man, as he says. Lives in a small flat, has a pension and a small income from stocks. *But* he's paid in pretty considerable sums into his account in the last year.'

'That sounds promising. What's his explanation?'

'Says they're betting gains. It's perfectly true that he goes to all the large race meetings. Places his bets on the course too, doesn't run an account.'

The Chief Constable nodded.

'Hard to disprove that,' he said. 'But it's suggestive.'

Colgate went on.

'Next, the Reverend Stephen Lane. He's *bona fide* all right – had a living at St Helen's, Whiteridge, Surrey – resigned his living just over a year ago owing to ill-health. His ill-health amounted to his going into a nursing home for mental patients. He was there for over a year.'

'Interesting,' said Weston.

'Yes, sir. I tried to get as much as I could out of the doctor in charge but you know what these medicos are – it's difficult to pin them down to anything you can get hold of. But as far as I can make out, his reverence's trouble was an obsession about the devil – especially the devil in the guise of a woman – scarlet woman – whore of Babylon.'

'H'm,' said Weston. 'There have been precedents for murder there.'

'Yes, sir. It seems to me that Stephen Lane is at least a possibility. The late Mrs Marshall was a pretty good example of what a clergyman would call a Scarlet Woman – hair and goings on and all. Seems to me it's not impossible he may have felt it his appointed task to dispose of her. That is if he is really batty.'

'Nothing to fit in with the blackmail theory?'

'No, sir, I think we can wash him out as far as that's concerned. Has some private means of his own, but not very much, and no sudden increase lately.'

'What about his story of his movements on the day of the crime?'

'Can't get any confirmation of them. Nobody remembers meeting a parson in the lanes. As to the book at the church, the last entry was three days before and nobody had looked at it for about a fortnight. He could have quite easily gone over the day before, say, or even a couple of days before, and dated his entry the 25th.'

Weston nodded. He said:

'And the third man?'

'Horace Blatt? It's my opinion, sir, that there's definitely something fishy there. Pays income-tax on a sum far exceeding what he makes out of his hardware business. And mind you, he's a slippery customer. He could probably cook up a reasonable statement – he gambles a bit on the Stock Exchange, and he's in with one or two shady deals. Oh, yes, there may be plausible explanations, but there's no getting away from it that he's been making pretty big sums from unexplained sources for some years now.'

'In fact,' said Weston, 'the idea is that Mr Horace Blatt is a successful blackmailer by profession?'

'Either that, sir, or it's dope. I saw Chief Inspector Ridgeway who's in charge of the dope business, and he was no end keen. Seems there's been a good bit of heroin coming in lately. They're on to the small distributors, and they know more or less who's running it the other end, but it's the way it's coming into the country that's baffled them so far.'

Weston said:

'If the Marshall woman's death is the result of her getting mixed up, innocently or otherwise, with the dope-running stunt, then we'd better hand the whole thing over to Scotland Yard. It's their pigeon. Eh? What do you say?'

Inspector Colgate said rather regretfully:

'I'm afraid you're right, sir. If it's dope, then it's a case for the Yard.'

Weston said after a moment or two's thought:

'It really seems the most likely explanation.'

Colgate nodded gloomily.

'Yes, it does. Marshall's right out of it – though I did get some information that might have been useful if his alibi hadn't been so good. Seems his firm is very near the rocks. Not his fault or his partner's, just the general result of the crisis last year and the general state of trade and finance. And as far as he knew, he'd come into fifty thousand pounds if his wife died. And fifty thousand would have been a very useful sum.'

He sighed.

'Seems a pity when a man's got two perfectly good motives for murder, that he can be proved to have had nothing to do with it!'

Weston smiled.

'Cheer up, Colgate. There's still a chance we may distinguish ourselves. There's the blackmail angle still and there's the batty parson, but, personally, I think the dope solution is far the most likely.' He added: 'And if it was one of the dope gang who put her out we'll have been instrumental in helping Scotland Yard to solve the dope problem. In fact, take it all round, one way or another, we've done pretty well.'

An unwilling smile showed on Colgate's face.

He said:

'Well, that's the lot, sir. By the way, I checked up on the writer of that letter we found in her room. The one signed J.N. Nothing doing. He's in China safe enough. Same chap as Miss Brewster was telling us about. Bit of a young scallywag. I've checked up on the rest of Mrs Marshall's friends. No leads there. Everything there is to get, we've got, sir.'

Weston said:

'So now it's up to us.' He paused and then added: 'Seen anything of our Belgian colleague? Does he know all you've told me?'

Colgate said with a grin:

'He's a queer little cuss, isn't he? D'you know what he asked me day before yesterday? He wanted particulars of any cases of strangulation in the last three years.'

Colonel Weston sat up.

'He did, did he? Now I wonder –' he paused a minute. 'When did you say the Reverend Stephen Lane went into that mental home?'

'A year ago last Easter, sir.'

Colonel Weston was thinking deeply. He said:

'There was a case – body of a young woman found somewhere near Bagshot. Going to meet her husband somewhere and never turned up. And there was what the papers called the Lonely Copse Mystery. Both in Surrey if I remember rightly.'

His eyes met those of his Inspector. Colgate said:

'Surrey? My word, sir, it fits, doesn't it? I wonder . . .'

★   ★   ★

Hercule Poirot sat on the turf on the summit of the island.

A little to his left was the beginning of the steel ladder that led down to Pixy Cove. There were several rough boulders near the head of the ladder, he noted, forming easy concealment for anyone who proposed to descend to the beach below. Of the beach itself little could be seen from the top owing to the overhang of the cliff.

Hercule Poirot nodded his head gravely.

The pieces of his jig-saw were fitting into position.

Mentally he went over those pieces, considering each as a detached item.

A morning on the bathing beach some few days before Arlena Marshall's death.

One, two, three, four, five separate remarks uttered on that morning.

The evening of a bridge game. He, Patrick Redfern and Rosamund Darnley had been at the table. Christine had wandered out while dummy and had overheard a certain conversation. Who else had been in the lounge at that time? Who had been absent?

The evening before the crime. The conversation he had had with Christine on the cliff and the scene he had witnessed on his way back to the hotel.

Gabrielle No 8.

A pair of scissors.

A broken pipe stem.

A bottle thrown from a window.

A green calendar.

A packet of candles.

A mirror and a typewriter.

A skein of magenta wool.

A girl's wristwatch.

Bathwater rushing down the waste-pipe.

Each of these unrelated facts must fit into its appointed place. There must be no loose ends.

And then, with each concrete fact fitted into position, on to the next stop: his own belief in the presence of evil on the island.

Evil . . .

He looked down at a typewritten paper in his hands.

Nellie Parsons – found strangled in a lonely copse near Chobham. No clue to her murderer ever discovered.

Nellie Parsons?

Alice Corrigan.

He read very carefully the details of Alice Corrigan's death.

To Hercule Poirot, sitting on the ledge overlooking the sea, came Inspector Colgate.

Poirot liked Inspector Colgate. He liked his rugged face, his shrewd eyes, and his slow unhurried manner.

Inspector Colgate sat down. He said, glancing down at the typewritten sheets in Poirot's hand:

'Done anything with those cases, sir?'

'I have studied them – yes.'

Colgate got up, he walked along and peered into the next niche. He came back, saying:

'One can't be too careful. Don't want to be overheard.'

Poirot said:

'You are wise.'

Colgate said:

'I don't mind telling you, M. Poirot, that I've been interested in those cases myself – though perhaps I shouldn't have thought about them if you hadn't asked for them.' He paused: 'I've been interested in one case in particular.'

'Alice Corrigan?'

'Alice Corrigan.' He paused. 'I've been on to the Surrey police about that case – wanted to get all the ins and outs of it.'

'Tell me, my friend. I am interested – very interested.'

'I thought you might be. Alice Corrigan was found strangled in Caesar's Grove on Blackridge Heath – not ten miles from Marley Copse where Nellie Parsons was found – and both those places are within twelve miles of Whiteridge where Mr Lane was vicar.'

Poirot said:

'Tell me more about the death of Alice Corrigan.'

Colgate said:

'The Surrey police didn't at first connect her death with that of Nellie Parsons. That's because they'd pitched on the husband as the guilty party. Don't quite know why except that he was a bit of what the Press calls a "mystery man" – not much known about him – who he was or where he came from. She'd married him against her people's wishes, she'd a bit of money of her own – and she'd insured her life in his favour – all that was enough to raise suspicion, as I think you'll agree, sir?'

Poirot nodded.

'But when it came down to brass tacks the husband was washed right out of the picture. The body was discovered by one of these women hikers – hefty young women in shorts. She was an absolutely competent and reliable witness – games mistress at a school in Lancashire. She noted the time when she found the body – it was exactly four-fifteen – and gave it as her opinion that the woman had been dead quite a short time – not more than ten minutes. That fitted in well enough with the police surgeon's view when he examined the body at 5.45. She left everything as it was and tramped across country to Bagshot police station where she reported the death. Now from three o'clock to four-ten, Edward Corrigan was in the train coming down from London where he'd gone up for the day on business. Four other people were in the carriage with him. From the station he took the local bus, two of his fellow passengers travelling by it also. He got off at the Pine Ridge Café where he'd arranged to meet his wife for tea. Time then was four twenty-five. He ordered tea for them both, but said not to bring it till she came. Then he walked about outside waiting for her. When, by five o'clock she hadn't turned up, he was getting alarmed – thought she might have sprained her ankle. The arrangement was that she was to walk across the moors from the village where they were staying to the Pine Ridge Café and go home by bus. Caesar's Grove is not far from the café, and it's thought that as she was ahead of time she sat down there to admire the view for a bit before going on, and that some tramp or madman came upon her there and caught her unawares. Once the husband was proved to be out of it, naturally they connected up her death with that of Nellie Parsons – that rather flighty servant girl who was found strangled in Marley Copse. They decided that the same man was responsible for both crimes, but they never caught him – and what's more they never came near to catching him! Drew a blank everywhere.'

He paused and then he said slowly:

'And now – here's a third woman strangled – and a certain gentleman we won't name right on the spot.'

He stopped.

His small shrewd eyes came round to Poirot. He waited hopefully.

Poirot's lips moved. Inspector Colgate leaned forward.

Poirot was murmuring:

'– so difficult to know which pieces are part of the fur rug and which are the cat's tail.'

'I *beg* pardon, sir?' said Inspector Colgate, startled.

Poirot said quickly:

'I apologize. I was following a train of thought of my own.'

'What's this about a fur rug and a cat?'

'Nothing – nothing at all.' He paused. 'Tell me, Inspector Colgate, if you suspected someone of telling lies – many, many lies but you had no proof, what would you do?'

Inspector Colgate considered.

'It's difficult, that is. But it's my opinion that if anyone tells enough lies, they're bound to trip up in the end.'

Poirot nodded.

'Yes, that is very true. You see, it is only in my mind that certain statements are lies. I *think* that they are lies, but I cannot *know* that they are lies. But one might perhaps make a test – a test of one little not very noticeable lie. And if that were proved to be a lie – why then, one would know that all the rest were lies, too!'

Inspector Colgate looked at him curiously.

'Your mind works a funny way, doesn't it, sir? But I dare say it comes out all right in the end. If you'll excuse me asking, what put you on to asking about strangulation cases in general?'

Poirot said slowly:

'You have a word in your language – *slick*. This crime seemed to me a very slick crime! It made me wonder if, perhaps, it was not a first attempt.'

Inspector Colgate said:

'I see.'

Poirot went on:

'I said to myself, let us examine past crimes of a similar kind and if there is a crime that closely resembles this one – *eh bien*, we shall have there a very valuable clue.'

'You mean using the same method of death, sir?'

'No, no, I mean more than that. The death of Nellie Parsons for instance tells me nothing. But the death of Alice Corrigan – tell me, Inspector Colgate, do you not notice one striking form of similarity in this crime?'

Inspector Colgate turned the problem over in his mind. He said at last:

'No, sir, I can't say that I do really. Unless it's that in each case the husband has got a cast-iron alibi.'

Poirot said softly:

'Ah, so you *have* noticed that?'

★   ★   ★

'Ha, Poirot. Glad to see you. Come in. Just the man I want.'

Hercule Poirot responded to the invitation.

The Chief Constable pushed over a box of cigarettes, took one himself and lighted it. Between puffs he said:

'I've decided, more or less, on a course of action. But I'd like your opinion on it before I act decisively.'

Hercule Poirot said:

'Tell me, my friend.'

Weston said:

'I've decided to call in Scotland Yard and hand the case over to them. In my opinion, although there have been grounds for suspicion against one or two people, the whole case hinges on dope smuggling. It seems clear to me that that place, Pixy's Cave, was a definite rendezvous for the stuff.'

Poirot nodded.

'I agree.'

'Good man. And I'm pretty certain who our dope smuggler is. Horace Blatt.'

Again Poirot assented. He said:

'That, too, is indicated.'

'I see our minds have both worked the same way. Blatt used to go sailing in that boat of his. Sometimes he'd invite people to go with him, but most of the time he went out alone. He had some rather conspicuous red sails on that boat, but we've found that he had some white sails as well stowed away. I think he sailed out on a good day to an appointed spot, and was met by another boat – sailing boat or motor yacht – something of the kind and the stuff was handed over. Then Blatt would run ashore into Pixy Cove at a suitable time of day –'

Hercule Poirot smiled:

'Yes, yes, at half-past one. The hour of the British lunch when everyone is quite sure to be in the dining-room. The island is private. It is not a place where outsiders come for picnics. People take their tea sometimes from the hotel to Pixy Cove in the afternoon when the sun is on it, or if they want a picnic they would go somewhere far afield, many miles away.'

The Chief Constable nodded.

'Quite,' he said. 'Therefore, Blatt ran ashore there and stowed the stuff on that ledge in the cave. Somebody else was to pick it up there in due course.'

Poirot murmured:

'There was a couple, you remember, who came to the island for lunch on the day of the murder? That would be a way of getting the stuff. Some summer visitors from a hotel on the Moor or at St Loo come over to Smugglers' Island. They announce that they will have lunch. They walk round the island first. How easy to descend to the beach, pick up the sandwich box, place it, no doubt, in Madame's bathing-bag which she carries – and return for lunch to the hotel – a little late, perhaps, say at ten minutes to two, having enjoyed their walk whilst everyone else was in the dining-room.'

Weston said:

'Yes, it all sounds practicable enough. Now these dope organizations are pretty ruthless. If any one blundered in and got wise to things they wouldn't make any bones about silencing that person. It seems to me that that is the right explanation of Arlena Marshall's death. It's possible that on that morning Blatt was actually at the cove stowing the stuff away. His accomplices were to come for it that very day. Arlena arrives on her float and sees him going into the cave with the box. She asks him about it and he kills her then and there and sheers off in his boat as quick as possible.'

Poirot said:

'You think definitely that Blatt is the murderer?'

'It seems the most probable solution. Of course it's possible that Arlena might have got on to the truth earlier, said something to Blatt about it, and some other member of the gang fixed a fake appointment with her and did her in. As I say, I think the best course is to hand the case over to Scotland Yard. They've a far better chance than we have of proving Blatt's connection with the gang.'

Hercule Poirot nodded thoughtfully.

Weston said:

'You think that's the wise thing to do – eh?'

Poirot was thoughtful. He said at last: 'It may be.'

'Dash it all, Poirot, have you got something up your sleeve, or haven't you?'

Poirot said gravely:

'If I have, I am not sure that I can prove it.'

Weston said:

'Of course, I know that you and Colgate have other ideas. Seems a bit fantastic to me, but I'm bound to admit there may be something in it. But even if you're right, I still think it's a case for the Yard. We'll give them the facts and they can work in with the Surrey police. What I feel is that it isn't really a case for us. It's not sufficiently localized.'

He paused.

'What do you think, Poirot? What do you feel ought to be done about it?'

Poirot seemed lost in thought. At last he said:

'I know what I should like to do.'

'Yes, man.'

Poirot murmured:

'I should like to go for a picnic.'

Colonel Weston stared at him.

CHAPTER 12

'A picnic, M. Poirot?'

Emily Brewster stared at him as though he were out of his senses.

Poirot said engagingly:

'It sounds to you, does it not, very outrageous? But indeed it seems to me a most admirable idea. We need something of the every day, the usual, to restore life to the normal. I am most anxious to see something of Dartmoor, the weather is good. It will – how shall I say, it will cheer everybody up! So aid me in this matter. Persuade everyone.'

The idea met with unexpected success. Everyone was at first dubious and then grudgingly admitted it might not be such a bad idea after all.

It was not suggested that Captain Marshall should be asked. He had himself announced that he had to go to Plymouth that day. Mr Blatt was of the party, enthusiastically so. He was determined to be the life and soul of it. Besides him there was Emily Brewster, the Redferns, Stephen Lane, the Gardeners, who were persuaded to delay their departure by one day, Rosamund Darnley and Linda.

Poirot had been eloquent to Rosamund and had dwelt on the advantage it would be to Linda to have something to take her out of herself. To this Rosamund agreed. She said:

'You're quite right. The shock has been very bad for a child of that age. It has made her terribly jumpy.'

'That is only natural, Mademoiselle. But at any age one soon forgets. Persuade her to come. You can, I know.'

Major Barry had refused firmly. He said he didn't like picnics. 'Lots of baskets to carry,' he said. 'And darned uncomfortable. Eating my food at a table's good enough for me.'

The party assembled at ten o'clock. Three cars had been ordered. Mr Blatt was loud and cheerful, imitating a tourist guide.

'This way, ladies and gentlemen – this way for Dartmoor. Heather and bilberries, Devonshire cream and convicts. Bring your wives, gentlemen, or bring the other thing! Everyone welcome! Scenery guaranteed. Walk up. Walk up.'

At the last minute Rosamund Darnley came down looking concerned. She said:

'Linda's not coming. She says she's got a frightful headache.'

Poirot cried:

'But it will do her good to come. Persuade her, Mademoiselle.'

Rosamund said firmly:

'It's no good. She's absolutely determined. I've given her some aspirin and she's gone to bed.'

She hesitated and said:

'I think, perhaps, I won't go, either.'

'Can't allow that, dear lady, can't allow that,' cried Mr Blatt, seizing her facetiously by the arm. '*La haute Mode* must grace the occasion. No refusals! I've taken you into custody, ha, ha. Sentenced to Dartmoor.'

He led her firmly to the first car. Rosamund threw a black look at Hercule Poirot.

'I'll stay with Linda,' said Christine Redfern. 'I don't mind a bit.'

Patrick said: 'Oh, come on, Christine.'

And Poirot said:

'No, no, you must come, Madame. With a headache one is better alone. Come, let us start.'

The three cars drove off. They went first to the real Pixy's Cave on Sheepstor, and had a good deal of fun looking for the entrance and at last finding it, aided by a picture postcard.

It was precarious going on the big boulders and Hercule Poirot did not attempt it. He watched indulgently while Christine Redfern sprang lightly from stone to stone and observed that her husband was never far from her. Rosamund Darnley and Emily Brewster had joined in the search though the latter slipped once and gave a slight twist to her ankle. Stephen Lane was indefatigable, his long lean figure turning and twisting among the boulders. Mr Blatt contented himself with going a little way and shouting encouragement, also taking photographs of the searchers.

The Gardeners and Poirot remained staidly sitting by the wayside whilst Mrs Gardener's voice upraised itself in a pleasant even-toned monologue, punctuated now and then by the obedient 'Yes, darlings' of her spouse.

'– and what I always have felt, M. Poirot, and Mr Gardener agrees with me, is that snapshots can be very annoying. Unless, that is to say, they are taken among friends. That Mr Blatt has just no sensitiveness of any kind. He just comes right up to everyone and talks away and takes pictures of you and, as I said to Mr Gardener, that really is very ill-bred. That's what I said, Odell, wasn't it?'

'Yes, darling.'

'That group he took of us all sitting on the beach. Well, that's all very well, but he should have asked first. As it was, Miss Brewster was just getting up from the beach, and it certainly makes her look a very peculiar shape.'

'I'll say it does,' said Mr Gardener with a grin.

'And there's Mr Blatt giving round copies to everybody without so much as asking first. He gave one to you, M. Poirot, I noticed.'

Poirot nodded. He said:

'I value that group very much.'

Mrs Gardener went on:

'And look at his behaviour today – so loud and noisy and common. Why, it just makes me shudder. You ought to have arranged to leave that man at home, M. Poirot.'

Hercule Poirot murmured:

'Alas, Madame, that would have been difficult.'

'I should say it would. That man just pushes his way in anywhere. He's just not sensitive at all.'

At this moment the discovery of the Pixy's Cave was hailed from below with loud cries.

The party now drove on, under Hercule Poirot's directions, to a spot where a short walk from the car down a hillside of heather led to a delightful spot by a small river.

A narrow plank bridge crossed the river and Poirot and her husband induced Mrs Gardener to cross it to where a delightful heathery spot free from prickly furze looked an ideal spot for a picnic lunch.

Talking volubly about her sensations when crossing on a plank bridge Mrs Gardener sank down. Suddenly there was a slight outcry.

The others had run across the bridge lightly enough, but Emily Brewster was standing in the middle of the plank, her eyes shut, swaying to and fro.

Poirot and Patrick Redfern rushed to the rescue.

Emily Brewster was gruff and ashamed.

'Thanks, thanks. Sorry. Never was good at crossing running water. Get giddy. Stupid, very.'

Lunch was spread out and the picnic began.

All the people concerned were secretly surprised to find how much they enjoyed this interlude. It was, perhaps, because it afforded an escape from an atmosphere of suspicion and dread. Here, with the trickling of the water, the soft peaty smell in the air and the warm colouring of bracken and heather, a world of murder and police inquiries and suspicion seemed blotted out as though it had never existed. Even Mr Blatt forgot to be the life and soul of the party. After lunch he went to sleep a little distance away and subdued snores testified to his blissful unconsciousness.

It was quite a grateful party of people who packed up the picnic baskets and congratulated Hercule Poirot on his good idea.

The sun was sinking as they returned along the narrow winding lanes. From the top of the hill above Leathercombe Bay they had a brief glimpse of the island with the white hotel on it.

It looked peaceful and innocent in the setting sun.

Mrs Gardener, not loquacious for once, sighed and said:

'I really do thank you, M. Poirot. I feel so calm. It's just wonderful.'

Major Barry came out to greet them on arrival.

'Hullo,' he said. 'Had a good day?'

Mrs Gardener said:

'Indeed we did. The moors were just too lovely for anything. So English and old world. And the air delicious and invigorating. You ought to be ashamed of yourself for being so lazy as to stay behind.'

The Major chuckled.

'I'm too old for that kind of thing – sitting on a patch of bog and eating sandwiches.'

A chambermaid had come out of the hotel. She was a little out of breath. She hesitated for a moment then came swiftly up to Christine Redfern.

Hercule Poirot recognized her as Gladys Narracott. Her voice came quick and uneven.

'Excuse me, Madam, but I'm worried about the young lady. About Miss Marshall. I took her up some tea just now and I couldn't get her to wake, and she looks so – so queer somehow.'

Christine looked round helplessly. Poirot was at her side in a moment. His hand under her elbow he said quietly:

'We will go up and see.'

They hurried up the stairs and along the passage to Linda's room.

One glance at her was enough to tell them both that something was very wrong. She was an odd colour and her breathing was hardly perceptible.

Poirot's hand went to her pulse. At the same time he noticed an envelope stuck up against the lamp on the bedside table. It was addressed to himself.

Captain Marshall came quickly into the room. He said:

'What's this about Linda? What's the matter with her?'

A small frightened sob came from Christine Redfern.

Hercule Poirot turned from the bed. He said to Marshall:

'Get a doctor – as quick as you possibly can. But I'm afraid – very much afraid – it may be too late.'

He took the letter with his name on it and ripped open the envelope. Inside were a few lines of writing in Linda's prim schoolgirl hand.

I think this is the best way out. Ask Father to try and forgive me. I killed Arlena. I thought I should be glad – but I'm not. I am very sorry for everything.

They were assembled in the lounge – Marshall, the Redferns, Rosamund Darnley and Hercule Poirot.

They sat there silent – waiting . . .

The door opened and Dr Neasden came in. He said curtly:

'I've done all I can. She may pull through – but I'm bound to tell you that there's not much hope.'

He paused. Marshall, his face stiff, his eyes a cold frosty blue, asked:

'How did she get hold of the stuff?'

Neasden opened the door again and beckoned.

The chambermaid came into the room. She had been crying.

Neasden said:

'Just tell us again what you saw.'

Sniffing, the girl said:

'I never thought – I never thought for a minute there was anything wrong – though the young lady did seem rather strange about it.' A slight gesture of impatience from the doctor started her off again. 'She was in the other lady's room. Mrs Redfern's. Your room, Madam. Over at the washstand, and she took up a little bottle. She did give a bit of a jump when I came in, and I thought it was queer her taking things from your room, but then, of course, it might be something she'd lent you. She just said: "Oh, this is what I'm looking for –" and went out.'

Christine said almost in a whisper.

'My sleeping tablets.'

The doctor said brusquely:

'How did she know about them?'

Christine said:

'I gave her one. The night after it happened. She told me she couldn't sleep. She – I remember her saying – "Will one be enough?" – and I said, Oh yes, they were very strong – that I'd been cautioned never to take more than two at most.' Neasden nodded: 'She made pretty sure,' he said. 'Took six of them.'

Christine sobbed again.

'Oh dear, I feel it's my fault. I should have kept them locked up.'

The doctor shrugged his shoulders.

'It might have been wiser, Mrs Redfern.'

Christine said despairingly:

'She's dying – and it's my fault . . .'

Kenneth Marshall stirred in his chair. He said:

'No, you can't blame yourself. Linda knew what she was doing. She took them deliberately. Perhaps – perhaps it was best.'

He looked down at the crumpled note in his hand – the note that Poirot had silently handed to him.

Rosamund Darnley cried out.

'I don't believe it. I don't believe Linda killed her. Surely it's impossible – on the evidence!'

Christine said eagerly:

'Yes, she *can't* have done it! She must have got overwrought and imagined it all.'

The door opened and Colonel Weston came in. He said:

'What's all this I hear?'

Dr Neasden took the note from Marshall's hand and handed it to the Chief Constable. The latter read it. He exclaimed incredulously:

'What? But this is nonsense – absolute nonsense! It's impossible.' He repeated with assurance. 'Impossible! Isn't it, Poirot?'

Hercule Poirot moved for the first time. He said in a slow sad voice:

'No, I'm afraid it is not impossible.'

Christine Redfern said:

'But I was with her, M. Poirot. I was with her up to a quarter to twelve. I told the police so.'

Poirot said:

'Your evidence gave her an alibi – yes. But what was your evidence based on? It was based on *Linda Marshall's own wristwatch.* You do not know *of your own knowledge* that it was a quarter to twelve when you left her – you only know that she told you so. You said yourself the time seemed to have gone very fast.'

She stared at him, stricken.

He said:

'Now, think, Madame, when you left the beach, did you walk back to the hotel fast or slow?'

'I – well, fairly slowly, I think.'

'Do you remember much about that walk back?'

'Not very much, I'm afraid. I – I was thinking.'

Poirot said:

'I am sorry to ask you this, but will you tell just what you were thinking about during that walk?'

Christine flushed.

'I suppose – if it is necessary . . . I was considering the question of – of leaving here. Just going away without telling my husband. I – I was very unhappy just then, you see.'

Patrick Redfern cried:

'Oh, Christine! I know . . . I know . . .'

Poirot's precise voice cut in.

'Exactly. You were concerned over taking a step of some importance. You were, I should say, deaf and blind to your surroundings. You probably walked very slowly and occasionally stopped for some minutes whilst you puzzled things out.'

Christine nodded.

'How clever you are. It was just like that. I woke up from a kind of dream just outside the hotel and hurried in thinking I should be very late, but when I saw the clock in the lounge I realized I had plenty of time.'

Hercule Poirot said again:

'Exactly.'

He turned to Marshall.

'I must now describe to you certain things I found in your daughter's room after the murder. In the grate was a large blob of melted wax, some burnt hair, fragments of cardboard and paper and an ordinary household pin. The paper and the cardboard might not be relevant, but the other three things were suggestive – particularly when I found tucked away in the bookshelf a volume from the local library here dealing with witchcraft and magic. It opened very easily at a certain page. On that page were described various methods of causing death by moulding in wax a figure supposed to represent the victim. This was then slowly roasted till it melted away – or alternatively you would pierce the wax figure to the heart with a pin. Death of the victim would ensue. I later heard from Mrs Redfern that Linda Marshall had been out early that morning and had bought a packet of candles, and had seemed embarrassed when her purchase was revealed. I had no doubt what had happened after that. Linda had made a crude figure of the candle wax – possibly adorning it with a snip of Arlena's red hair to give the magic force – had then stabbed it to the heart with a pin and finally melted the figure away by lighting strips of cardboard under it.

'It was crude, childish, superstitious, but it revealed one thing: the desire to kill.

'Was there any possibility that there had been more than a desire? Could Linda Marshall have *actually* killed her stepmother?

'At first sight it seemed as though she had a perfect alibi – but in actuality, as I have just pointed out, the time evidence was supplied *by Linda herself*. She could easily have declared the time to be a quarter of an hour later than it really was.

'It was quite possible once Mrs Redfern had left the beach for Linda to follow her up and then strike across the narrow neck of land to the ladder, hurry down it, meet her stepmother there, strangle her and return up the ladder before the boat containing Miss Brewster and Patrick Redfern came in sight. She could then return to Gull Cove, take her bathe and return to the hotel at her leisure.

'But that entailed two things. She must have definite knowledge that Arlena Marshall would be at Pixy Cove and she must be physically capable of the deed.

'Well, the first was quite possible – if Linda Marshall had written a note to Arlena herself in someone else's name. As to the second, Linda has very large strong hands. They are as large as a man's. As to the strength, she is at the age when one is prone to be mentally unbalanced. Mental derangement often is accompanied by unusual strength. There was one other small point. Linda Marshall's mother had actually been accused and tried for murder.'

Kenneth Marshall lifted his head. He said fiercely: 'She was also acquitted.'

'She was acquitted,' Poirot agreed.

Marshall said:

'And I'll tell you this, M. Poirot. Ruth – my wife – was innocent. That I know with complete and absolute certainty. In the intimacy of our life I could not have been deceived. She was an innocent victim of circumstances.'

He paused.

'And I don't believe that Linda killed Arlena. It's ridiculous – absurd!'

Poirot said:

'Do you believe that letter, then, to be a forgery?'

Marshall held out his hand for it and Weston gave it to him. Marshall studied it attentively. Then he shook his head.

'No,' he said unwillingly. 'I believe Linda did write this.'

Poirot said:

'Then if she wrote it, there are only two explanations. Either she wrote it in all good faith, knowing herself to be the murderess or – or, I say – *she wrote it deliberately to shield someone else*, someone whom she feared was suspected.'

Kenneth Marshall said:

'You mean me?'

'It is possible, is it not?'

Marshall considered for a moment or two, then he said quietly:

'No, I think that idea is absurd. Linda may have realized that I was regarded with suspicion at first. But she knew definitely by now that that was over and done with – that the police had accepted my alibi and turned their attention elsewhere.'

Poirot said:

'And supposing that it was not so much that she thought that you were suspected as that she *knew* you were guilty.'

Marshall stared at him. He gave a short laugh.

'That's absurd.'

Poirot said:

'I wonder. There are, you know, several possibilities about Mrs Marshall's death. There is the theory that she was being blackmailed, that she went that morning to meet the blackmailer and that the blackmailer killed her. There is the theory that Pixy Cove and Cave were being used for drug-running, and that she was killed because she accidentally learned something about that. There is a third possibility – that she was killed by a religious maniac. And there is a fourth possibility – you stood to gain a lot of money by your wife's death, Captain Marshall?'

'I've just told you –'

'Yes, yes – I agree that it is impossible that you could have killed your wife – *if you were acting alone.* But supposing someone helped you?'

'What the devil do you mean?'

The quiet man was roused at last. He half rose from his chair. His voice was menacing. There was a hard angry light in his eyes.

Poirot said:

'I mean that this is not a crime that was committed single-handed. Two people were in it. It is quite true that you could not have typed that letter and at the same time gone to the cove – but there would have been time for you to have jotted down that letter in shorthand – and for *someone else* to have typed it in your room while you yourself were absent on your murderous errand.'

Hercule Poirot looked towards Rosamund Darnley. He said:

'Miss Darnley states that she left Sunny Ledge at ten minutes past eleven and saw you typing in your room. But just about that time Mr Gardener went up to the hotel to fetch a skein of wool for his wife. He did not meet Miss Darnley or see her. That is rather remarkable. It looks as though either Miss Darnley never left Sunny Ledge, or else she had left it much earlier and was in your room typing industriously. Another point, you stated that when Miss Darnley looked into your room at a quarter past eleven *you saw her in the mirror.* But on the day of the murder your typewriter and papers were all on the writing-desk across the corner of the room, whereas the mirror was between the windows. So that statement was a deliberate lie. Later, you moved your typewriter to the table under the mirror so as to substantiate your story – but it was too late. I was aware that both you and Miss Darnley had lied.'

Rosamund Darnley spoke. Her voice was low and clear.

She said:

'How devilishly ingenious you are!'

Hercule Poirot said, raising his voice:

'But not so devilish and so ingenious as the man who killed Arlena Marshall! Think back for a moment. Who did I think – who did everybody think – that Arlena Marshall had gone to meet that morning? We all jumped to the same conclusion. *Patrick Redfern.* It was not to meet a blackmailer that she went. Her face alone would have told me that. Oh no, it was a lover she was going to meet – or thought she was going to meet.

'Yes, I was quite sure of that. Arlena Marshall was going to meet Patrick Redfern. But a minute later Patrick Redfern appeared on the beach and was obviously looking for her. So what then?'

Patrick Redfern said with subdued anger:

'Some devil used my name.'

Poirot said:

'You were very obviously upset and surprised by her non-appearance. Almost too obviously, perhaps. It is *my* theory, Mr Redfern, that she went to Pixy Cove to meet *you*, and that she *did* meet you, and that *you killed her there as you had planned to do.*'

Patrick Redfern stared. He said in his high good-humoured Irish voice:

'Is it daft you are? I was with you on the beach until I went round in the boat with Miss Brewster and found her dead.'

Hercule Poirot said:

'You killed her after Miss Brewster had gone off in the boat to fetch the police. Arlena Marshall was not dead when you got to the beach. She was waiting hidden in the cave until the coast could be clear.'

'But the body! Miss Brewster and I both saw the body.'

'*A* body – yes. But not a *dead* body. The *live* body of the woman who helped you, her arms and legs stained with tan, her face hidden by a green cardboard hat. Christine, your wife (or possibly not your wife – but still your partner), helping you to commit this crime as she helped you to commit that crime in the past when she "discovered" the body of Alice Corrigan at least twenty minutes before Alice Corrigan died – killed by her husband Edward Corrigan – you!'

Christine spoke. Her voice was sharp – cold. She said:

'Be careful, Patrick, don't lose your temper.'

Poirot said:

'You will be interested to hear that both you and your wife Christine were easily recognized and picked out by the Surrey police from a group of people photographed here. They identified you both at once as Edward Corrigan and Christine Deverill, the young woman who found the body.'

Patrick Redfern had risen. His handsome face was transformed, suffused with blood, blind with rage. It was the face of a killer – of a tiger. He yelled:

'You damned interfering murdering lousy little worm!'

He hurled himself forward, his fingers stretching and curling, his voice raving curses, as he fastened his fingers round Hercule Poirot's throat . . .

CHAPTER 13

Poirot said reflectively:

'It was on a morning when we were sitting out here that we talked of sun-tanned bodies lying like meat upon a slab, and it was then that I reflected how little difference there was between one body and another. If one looked closely and appraisingly – yes – but to the casual glance? One moderately well-made young woman is very like another. Two brown legs, two brown arms, a little piece of bathing suit in between – just a body lying out in the sun. When a woman walks, when she speaks, laughs, turns her head, moves a hand – then, yes then, there is personality – individuality. But in the sun ritual – no.

'It was that day that we spoke of evil – *evil under the sun* as Mr Lane put it. Mr Lane is a very sensitive person – evil affects him – he perceives its presence – but though he is a good recording instrument, he did not really know exactly where the evil was. To him, evil was focused in the person of Arlena Marshall, and practically everyone present agreed with him.

'But to my mind, though evil was present, it was not centralized in Arlena Marshall at all. It was connected with her, yes – but in a totally different way. I saw her, first, last and all the time, as an eternal and predestined *victim*. Because she was beautiful, because she had glamour, because men turned their heads to look at her, it was assumed that she was the type of woman who wrecked lives and destroyed souls. But I saw her very differently. It was not she who fatally attracted men – it was men who fatally attracted her. She was the type of woman whom men care for easily and of whom they as easily tire. And everything that I was told or found out about her strengthened my conviction on this point. The first thing that was mentioned about her was how the man in whose divorce case she had been cited refused to marry her. It was then that Captain Marshall, one of those incurably chivalrous men, stepped in and asked her to marry him. To a shy retiring man of Captain Marshall's type, a public ordeal of any kind would be the worst torture – hence his love and pity for his first wife who was publicly accused and tried for a murder she had not committed. He married her and found himself amply justified in his estimate of her character. After her death another beautiful woman, perhaps something of the same type (since Linda has red hair which she probably inherited from her mother), is held up to public ignominy. Again Marshall performs a rescue act. But this time he finds little to sustain his infatuation. Arlena is stupid, unworthy of his sympathy and protection, mindless. Nevertheless, I think he always had a fairly true vision of her. Long after he ceased to love her and was irked by her presence, he remained sorry for her. She was to him like a child who cannot get farther than a certain page in the book of life.

'I saw in Arlena Marshall with her passion for men, a predestined prey for an unscrupulous man of a certain type. In Patrick Redfern, with his good looks, his easy assurance, his undeniable charm for women, I recognized at once that type. The adventurer who makes his living, one way or another, out of women. Looking on from my place on the beach I was quite certain that Arlena was Patrick's victim, not the other way about. And I associated that focus of evil with Patrick Redfern, not with Arlena Marshall.

'Arlena had recently come into a large sum of money, left her by an elderly admirer who had not had time to grow tired of her. She was the type of woman who is invariably defrauded of money by some man or other. Miss Brewster mentioned a young man who had been "ruined" by Arlena, but a letter from him which was found in her room, though it expressed a wish (which cost nothing) to cover her with jewels, in actual *fact* acknowledged a cheque from *her* by means of which he hoped to escape prosecution. A clear case of a young waster sponging on her. I have no doubt that Patrick Redfern found it easy to induce her to hand him large sums from time to time "for investment". He probably dazzled her with stories of great opportunities – how he would make her fortune and his own. Unprotected women, living alone, are easy prey to that type of man – and he usually escapes scot free with the booty. If, however, there is a husband, or a brother, or a father about, things are apt to take an unpleasant turn for the swindler. Once Captain Marshall was to find out what had happened to his wife's fortune, Patrick Redfern might expect short shrift.

'That did not worry him, however, because he contemplated quite calmly doing away with her when he judged it necessary – encouraged by having already got away with one murder – that of a young woman whom he had married in the name of Corrigan and whom he had persuaded to insure her life for a large sum.

'In his plans he was aided and abetted by the woman who down here passed as his wife and to whom he was genuinely attached. A young woman as unlike the type of his victims as could well be imagined – cool, calm, passionless, but steadfastly loyal to him and an actress of no mean ability. From the time of her arrival here Christine Redfern played a part, the part of the "poor little wife" – frail, helpless, intellectual rather than athletic. Think of the points she made one after another. Her tendency to blister in the sun and her consequent white skin, her giddiness at heights – stories of getting stuck on Milan Cathedral, etc. An emphasis on her frailty and delicacy – nearly every one spoke of her as a "little woman". She was actually as tall as Arlena Marshall, but with very small hands and feet. She spoke of herself as a former school-teacher, and thereby emphasized an impression of book learning and lack of athletic prowess. Actually, it is quite true that she had worked in a school, but the position she held there was that of *games mistress*, and she was an extremely active young woman who could climb like a cat and run like an athlete.

'The crime itself was perfectly planned and timed. It was, as I mentioned before, a very slick crime. The timing was a work of genius.

'First of all there were certain preliminary scenes – one played on the cliff ledge when they knew me to be occupying the next recess – a conventional jealous wife dialogue between her and her husband. Later she played the same part in a scene with me. At the time I remember a vague feeling of having read all this in a book. It did not seem *real*. Because, of course, it was *not* real. Then came the day of the crime. It was a fine day – an essential. Redfern's first act was to slip out very early – by the balcony door which he unlocked from the inside (if found open it would only be thought someone had gone for an early bathe). Under his bathing-wrap he concealed a green Chinese hat, the duplicate of the one Arlena was in the habit of wearing. He slipped across the island, down the ladder and stowed it away in an appointed place behind some rocks. Part I.

'On the previous evening he had arranged a rendezvous with Arlena. They were exercising a good deal of caution about meeting as Arlena was slightly afraid of her husband. She agreed to go round to Pixy Cove early. Nobody went there in the morning. Redfern was to join her there, taking a chance to slip away unobtrusively. If she heard anyone descending the ladder or a boat came in sight she was to slip inside the Pixy's Cave, the secret of which he had told her, and wait there until the coast was clear. Part II.

'In the meantime Christine went to Linda's room at a time when she judged Linda would have gone for her early morning dip. She would then alter Linda's watch, putting it on twenty minutes. There was, of course, a risk that Linda might notice her watch was wrong, but it did not much matter if she did. Christine's real alibi was the size of her hands which made it a physical impossibility for her to have committed the crime. Nevertheless, an additional alibi would be desirable. Then in

Linda's room she noticed the book on witchcraft and magic, open at a certain page. She read it, and when Linda came in and dropped a parcel of candles she realized what was in Linda's mind. It opened up some new ideas to her. The original idea of the guilty pair had been to cast a reasonable amount of suspicion on Kenneth Marshall, hence the abstracted pipe, a fragment of which was to be planted on the Cove underneath the ladder.

'On Linda's return Christine easily arranged an outing together to Gull Cove. She then returned to her own room, took out from a locked suitcase a bottle of artificial suntan, applied it carefully and threw the empty bottle out of the window where it narrowly escaped hitting Emily Brewster who was bathing. Part II successfully accomplished.

'Christine then dressed herself in a white bathing-suit, and over it a pair of beach trousers and coat with long floppy sleeves which effectually concealed her newly-browned arms and legs.

'At 10.15 Arlena departed for her rendezvous, a minute or two later Patrick Redfern came down and registered surprise, annoyance etc. Christine's task was easy enough. Keeping her own watch concealed she asked Linda at twenty-five past eleven what time it was. Linda looked at her watch and replied that it was a quarter to twelve. She then starts down to the sea and Christine packs up her sketching things. As soon as Linda's back is turned Christine picks up the girl's watch which she has necessarily discarded before going into the sea and alters it back to the correct time. Then she hurries up the cliff path, runs across the narrow neck of land to the top of the ladder, strips off her pyjamas and shoves them and her sketching box behind a rock and swarms rapidly down the ladder in her best gymnastic fashion.

'Arlena is on the beach below wondering why Patrick is so long in coming. She sees or hears someone on the ladder, takes a cautious observation, and to her annoyance sees that inconvenient person – the wife! She hurries along the beach and into the Pixy's Cave.

'Christine takes the hat from its hiding-place, a false red curl pinned underneath the brim at the back, and disposes herself in a sprawling attitude with the hat and curl shielding her face and neck. The timing is perfect. A minute or two later the boat containing Patrick and Emily Brewster comes round the point. Remember it is *Patrick* who bends down and examines the body, *Patrick* who is stunned – shocked – broken down by the death of his lady love! His witness has been carefully chosen. Miss Brewster has not got a good head, she will not attempt to go up the ladder. She will leave the Cove by boat, Patrick naturally being the one to remain with the body – "in case the murderer may still be about". Miss Brewster rows off to fetch the police. Christine, as soon as the boat has disappeared, springs up, cuts the hat into pieces with the scissors Patrick has carefully brought, stuffs them into her bathing-suit and swarms up the ladder in double quick time, slips into her beach-pyjamas and runs back to the hotel. Just time to have a quick bath, washing off the brown suntan application, and into her tennis dress. One other thing she does. She burns the pieces of the green cardboard hat and the hair in Linda's grate, adding a leaf of a calendar so that it may be associated with the cardboard. Not a *Hat* but a *Calendar* has been burnt. As she suspected, Linda has been experimenting in magic – the blob of wax and the pin shows that.

'Then, down to the tennis court, arriving the last, but showing no signs of flurry or haste.

'And, meanwhile, Patrick has gone to the cave. Arlena has seen nothing and heard very little – a boat – voices – she has prudently remained hidden. But now it is Patrick calling.

'"All clear, darling," and she comes out, and his hands fasten round her neck – and that is the end of poor foolish beautiful Arlena Marshall . . .'

His voice died away.

For a moment there was silence, then Rosamund Darnley said with a little shiver:

'Yes, you make one see it all. But that's the story from the other side. You haven't told us how *you* came to get at the truth?'

Hercule Poirot said:

'I told you once that I had a very simple mind. Always, from the beginning, it seemed to me that *the most likely person* had killed Arlena Marshall. And the most likely person was Patrick Redfern. He was the type, *par excellence* – the type of man who exploits women like her – and the type of the killer – the kind of man who will take a woman's savings and cut her throat into the bargain. Who was Arlena going to meet that morning? By the evidence of her face, her smile, her manner, her words to me – *Patrick Redfern*. And therefore, in the very nature of things, it should be Patrick who killed her.

'But at once I came up, as I told you, against impossibility. Patrick Redfern could not have killed her since he was on the beach and in Miss Brewster's company until the actual discovery of the body. So I looked about for other solutions – and there were several. She could have been killed by her husband – with Miss Darnley's connivance. (They too had both lied as to one point which looked suspicious.) She could have been killed as a result of her having stumbled on the secret of the dope smuggling. She could have been killed, as I said, by a religious maniac, and she could have been killed by her stepdaughter. The latter seemed to me at one time to be the real solution. Linda's manner in her very first interview with the police was significant. An interview that I had with her later assured me of one point. Linda considered herself guilty.'

'You mean she imagined that she had actually killed Arlena?'

Rosamund's voice was incredulous.

Hercule Poirot nodded.

'Yes. Remember – she is really little more than a child. She read that book on witchcraft and she half believed it. She hated Arlena. She deliberately made the wax doll, cast her spell, pierced it to the heart, melted it away – *and that very day Arlena dies*. Older and wiser people than Linda have believed fervently in magic. Naturally, she believed that it was all true – that by using magic she had killed her stepmother.'

Rosamund cried:

'Oh, poor child, poor child. And I thought – I imagined – something quite different – that she knew something which would –'

Rosamund stopped. Poirot said:

'I know what it was you thought. Actually your manner frightened Linda still further. She believed that her action had really brought about Arlena's death and that you knew it. Christine Redfern worked on her too, introducing the idea of the sleeping tablets to her mind, showing her the way to a speedy and painless expiation of her crime. You see, once Captain Marshall was proved to have an alibi, it was vital for a new suspect to be found. Neither she nor her husband knew about the dope smuggling. They fixed on Linda to be the scapegoat.'

Rosamund said:

'What a devil!'

Poirot nodded.

'Yes, you are right. A cold-blooded and cruel woman. For me, I was in great difficulty. Was Linda guilty only of the childish attempt at witchcraft, or had her hate carried her still further – to the actual act? I tried to get her to confess to me. But it was no good. At that moment I was in grave uncertainty. The Chief Constable was inclined to accept the dope smuggling explanation. I couldn't let it go at that. I went over the facts again very carefully. I had, you see, a collection of jig-saw puzzle pieces, isolated happenings – plain facts. The whole must fit into a complete and harmonious pattern. There were the scissors found on the beach – a bottle thrown from a window – a bath that no one would admit to having taken – all perfectly harmless occurrences in themselves, but rendered significant by the fact that no one would admit to them. Therefore, they *must* be of significance. Nothing about them fitted in with the theories of either Captain Marshall's or Linda's, or of a dope gang's being responsible. And yet they *must* have meaning. I went back again to my first solution – that Patrick Redfern had committed the murder. Was there anything in support of that? Yes, the fact that a very large sum of money was missing from Arlena's account. Who had got that money? Patrick Redfern of course. She was the type of woman easily swindled by a handsome young man – but she was not at all the type of woman to be blackmailed. She was far too transparent, not good enough at keeping a secret. The blackmailer story had never rung true to my mind. And yet there *had* been that conversation overheard – ah, but overheard by whom? *Patrick Redfern's wife.* It was her story – unsupported by any outside evidence. Why was it invented? The answer came to me like lightning. To account for the absence of Arlena's money!

'Patrick and Christine Redfern. The two of them were in it together. Christine hadn't got the physical strength to strangle her or the mental make up. No, it was Patrick who had done it – but that was impossible! Every minute of his time was accounted for until the body was found.

'Body – the word stirred something in my mind – bodies lying on the beach – *all alike.* Patrick Redfern and Emily Brewster had got to the Cove and seen *a body* lying there. A body – suppose it was not Arlena's body but somebody else's? The face was hidden by the great Chinese hat.

'But there *was* only one dead body – Arlena's. Then, could it be – a *live* body – someone pretending to be dead? Could it be Arlena herself, inspired by Patrick to play some kind of a joke. I shook my head – no, too risky. A live body – whose? Was there any woman who would help Redfern? Of course – his wife. But she was a white-skinned delicate creature. Ah yes, but suntan can be applied out of bottles – bottles – I had one of my jig-saw pieces. Yes, and afterwards, of course, a bath – to wash that tell-tale stain off before she went out to play tennis. And the scissors? Why, to cut up that duplicate cardboard hat – an unwieldy thing that must be got out of the way, and in the haste the scissors were left behind – the one thing that the pair of murderers forgot.

'But where was Arlena all the time? That again was perfectly clear. Either Rosamund Darnley or Arlena Marshall had been in the Pixy's Cave, the scent they both used told me that. It was certainly not Rosamund Darnley. Then it was Arlena, hiding till the coast should clear.

'When Emily Brewster went off in the boat, Patrick had the beach to himself and full opportunity to commit the crime. Arlena Marshall was killed after a quarter to twelve, but the medical evidence was only concerned with the earliest possible time the crime could have been committed. That Arlena was dead at a quarter to twelve was what was told to the doctor, not what he told the police.

'Two more points had to be settled. Linda Marshall's evidence gave Christine Redfern an alibi. Yes, but that evidence depended on Linda Marshall's wristwatch. All that was needed was to prove that Christine had had two opportunities of tampering with the watch. I found those easily enough. She had been alone in Linda's room that morning – and there was an indirect proof. Linda was heard to say that she was "afraid she was going to be late", but when she got down it was only twenty-five past ten by the lounge clock. The second opportunity was easy – she could alter the watch back again as soon as Linda turned her back and went down to bathe.

'Then there was the question of the ladder. Christine had always declared she had no head for heights. Another carefully prepared lie.

'I had my mosaic now – each piece beautifully fitted into its place. But, unfortunately, I had no definite proof. It was all in my mind.

'It was then that an idea came to me. There was an assurance – a slickness about the crime. I had no doubt that in the future Patrick Redfern would repeat his crime. What about the past? It was remotely possible that this was not his first killing. The method employed, strangulation, was in harmony with his nature – a killer for pleasure as well as for profit. If he was already a murderer I was sure that he would have used the same means. I asked Inspector Colgate for a list of women victims of strangulation. The result filled me with joy. The death of Nellie Parson found strangled in a lonely copse might or might not be Patrick Redfern's work – it might merely have suggested choice of locality to him, but in Alice Corrigan's death I found exactly what I was looking for. In essence the same method. Juggling with time – a murder committed not, as is the usual way, *before* it is supposed to have happened, but *afterwards*. A body supposedly discovered at a quarter past four. A husband with an alibi up to twenty-five past four.

'What really happened? It was said that Edward Corrigan arrived at the Pine Ridge, found his wife not there, *and went out* and *walked up and down*. Actually, of course, he ran full speed to the rendezvous, Caesar's Grove (which you will remember was quite nearby), killed her and returned to the café. The girl hiker who reported the crime was a most respectable young lady, games mistress in a well-known girls' school. Apparently she had no connection with Edward Corrigan. She had to walk some way to report the death. The police surgeon only examined the body at a quarter to six. As in this case the time of death was accepted without question.

'I made one final test. I must know definitely if Mrs Redfern was a liar. I arranged our little excursion to Dartmoor. If anyone has a bad head for heights, they are never comfortable crossing a narrow bridge over running water. Miss Brewster, a genuine sufferer, showed giddiness. But Christine Redfern, unconcerned, ran across without a qualm. It was a small point, but it was a definite test. If she had told one unnecessary lie – then all the other lies were possible. In the meantime Colgate had got the photograph identified by the Surrey Police. I played my hand in the only way I thought likely to succeed. Having lulled Patrick Redfern into security, I turned on him and did my utmost to make him lose his self-control. The knowledge that he had been identified with Corrigan caused him to lose his head completely.'

Hercule Poirot stroked his throat reminiscently.

'What I did,' he said with importance, 'was exceedingly dangerous – but I do not regret it. I succeeded! I did not suffer in vain.'

There was a moment's silence. Then Mrs Gardener gave a deep sigh.

'Why, M. Poirot,' she said. 'It's just been too wonderful – hearing just exactly how you got your results. It's every bit as fascinating as a lecture on criminology – in fact it *is* a lecture on criminology. And to think my magenta wool and that sun-bathing conversation actually had something to do with it? That really makes me too excited for words, and I'm sure Mr Gardener feels the same, don't you, Odell?'

'Yes, darling,' said Mr Gardener.

Hercule Poirot said:

'Mr Gardener too was of assistance to me. I wanted the opinion of a sensible man about Mrs Marshall. I asked Mr Gardener what he thought of her.'

'Is that so,' said Mrs Gardener. 'And what did you say about her, Odell?'

Mr Gardener coughed. He said:

'Well, darling, I never did think very much of her, you know.'

'That's the kind of thing men always say to their wives,' said Mrs Gardener. 'And if you ask me, even M. Poirot here is what I should call a shade on the indulgent side about her, calling her a natural victim and all that. Of course it's true that she wasn't a cultured woman at all, and as Captain Marshall isn't here I don't mind saying that she always did seem to me kind of dumb. I said so to Mr Gardener, didn't I, Odell?'

'Yes, darling,' said Mr Gardener.

Linda Marshall sat with Hercule Poirot on Gull Cove.

She said:

'Of course I'm glad I didn't die after all. But you know, M. Poirot, it's just the same as if I'd killed her, isn't it? I meant to.'

Hercule Poirot said energetically:

'It is not at all the same thing. The wish to kill and the action of killing are two different things. If in your bedroom instead of a little wax figure you had had your stepmother bound and helpless and a dagger in your hand instead of a pin, you would not have pushed it into her heart! Something within you would have said "no". It is the same with me. I enrage myself at an imbecile. I say, "I would like to kick him." Instead, I kick the table. I say, "This table, it is the imbecile, I kick him so." And then, if I have not hurt my toe too much, I feel much better and the table it is not usually damaged. But if the imbecile himself was there I should not kick him. To make the wax figures and stick in the pins, it is silly, yes, it is childish, yes – but it does something useful too. You took the hate out of yourself and put it into that little figure. And with the pin and the fire you destroyed – not your stepmother – but the hate you bore her. Afterwards, even before you heard of her death, you felt cleansed, did you not – you felt lighter – happier?'

Linda nodded. She said:

'How did you know? That's just how I did feel.'

Poirot said:

'Then do not repeat to yourself the imbecilities. Just make up your mind not to hate your next stepmother.'

Linda said startled:

'Do you think I'm going to have another? Oh, I see, you mean Rosamund. I don't mind her.' She hesitated a minute. 'She's *sensible*.'

It was not the adjective that Poirot himself would have selected for Rosamund Darnley, but he realized that it was Linda's idea of high praise.

★   ★   ★

Kenneth Marshall said:

'Rosamund, did you get some extraordinary idea into your head that I'd killed Arlena.'

Rosamund looked rather shamefaced. She said:

'I suppose I was a damned fool.'

'Of course you were.'

'Yes, but Ken, you are such an oyster. I never knew what you really felt about Arlena. I didn't know if you accepted her as she was and were just frightfully decent about her, or whether you – well, just believed in her blindly. And I thought if it was that, and you suddenly found out that she was letting you down you might go mad with rage. I've heard stories about you. You're always very quiet but you're rather frightening sometimes.'

'So you thought I just took her by the throat and throttled the life out of her?'

'Well – yes – that's just exactly what I did think. And your alibi seemed a bit on the light side. That's when I suddenly decided to take a hand, and made up that silly story about seeing you typing in your room. And when I heard that you said you'd seen me look in – well, that made me quite sure you'd done it. That, and Linda's queerness.'

Kenneth Marshall said with a sigh:

'Don't you realize that I said I'd seen you in the mirror in order to back up *your* story. I – I thought you needed it corroborated.'

Rosamund stared at him.

'You don't mean you thought that I killed your wife?'

Kenneth Marshall shifted uneasily. He mumbled:

'Dash it all, Rosamund, don't you remember how you nearly killed that boy about that dog once? How you hung on to his throat and wouldn't let go.'

'But that was years ago.'

'Yes, I know –'

Rosamund said sharply:

'What earthly motive do you think I had to kill Arlena?'

His glance shifted. He mumbled something again.

Rosamund cried:

'Ken, you mass of conceit! You thought I killed her out of altruism on your behalf, did you? Or – did you think I killed her because I wanted you myself?'

'Not at all,' said Kenneth Marshall indignantly. 'But you know what you said that day – about Linda and everything – and – and you seemed to care what happened to me.'

Rosamund said:

'I've always cared about that.'

'I believe you have. You know, Rosamund – I can't usually talk about things – I'm not good at talking – but I'd like to get this clear. I didn't care for Arlena – only just a little at first – and living with her day after day was a pretty nerve-racking business. In fact it was absolute hell, but I *was* awfully sorry for her. She was such a damned fool – crazy about men – she just couldn't help it – and they always let her down and treated her rottenly. I simply felt I couldn't be the one to give her the final push. I'd married her and it was up to me to look after her as best I could. I think she knew that and was grateful to me really. She was – she was a pathetic sort of creature really.'

Rosamund said gently:

'It's all right, Ken. I understand now.'

Without looking at her Kenneth Marshall carefully filled a pipe. He mumbled:

'You're – pretty good at understanding, Rosamund.'

A faint smile curved Rosamund's ironic mouth. She said:

'Are you going to ask me to marry you now, Ken, or are you determined to wait six months?'

Kenneth Marshall's pipe dropped from his lips and crashed on the rocks below.

He said:

'Damn, that's the second pipe I've lost down here. And I haven't got another with me. How the devil did you know I'd fixed six months as the proper time?'

'I suppose because it *is* the proper time. But I'd rather have something definite now, please. Because in the intervening months you may come across some other persecuted female and rush to the rescue in chivalrous fashion again.'

He laughed.

'You're going to be the persecuted female this time, Rosamund. You're going to give up that damned dress-making business of yours and we're going to live in the country.'

'Don't you know that I make a very handsome income out of my business? Don't you realize that it's *my* business – that I created it and worked it up, and that I'm proud of it! And you've got the damned nerve to come along and say, "Give it all up, dear."'

'I've got the damned nerve to say it, yes.'

'And you think I care enough for you to do it?'

'If you don't,' said Kenneth Marshall, 'you'd be no good to me.'

Rosamund said softly:

'Oh, my dear, I've wanted to live in the country with you all my life. Now – it's going to come true . . .'

GLUTTONY

•

AT BERTRAM'S HOTEL

For Harry Smith
because I appreciate the scientific way
he reads my books

In the heart of the West End, there are many quiet pockets, unknown to almost all but taxi drivers who traverse them with expert knowledge, and arrive triumphantly thereby at Park Lane, Berkeley Square or South Audley Street.

If you turn off on an unpretentious street from the Park, and turn left and right once or twice, you will find yourself in a quiet street with Bertram's Hotel on the right hand side. Bertram's Hotel has been there a long time. During the war, houses were demolished on the right of it, and a little farther down on the left of it, but Bertram's itself remained unscathed. Naturally it could not escape being, as house agents would say, scratched, bruised and marked, but by the expenditure of only a reasonable amount of money it was restored to its original condition. By 1955 it looked precisely as it had looked in 1939 – dignified, unostentatious, and quietly expensive.

Such was Bertram's, patronized over a long stretch of years by the higher *échelons* of the clergy, dowager ladies of the aristocracy up from the country, girls on their way home for the holidays from expensive finishing schools. ('So few places where a girl can stay alone in London but of course it is *quite* all right at Bertram's. We have stayed there for *years*.')

There had, of course, been many other hotels on the model of Bertram's. Some still existed, but nearly all had felt the wind of change. They had had necessarily to modernize themselves, to cater for a different clientele. Bertram's, too, had had to change, but it had been done so cleverly that it was not at all apparent at the first casual glance.

Outside the steps that led up to the big swing doors stood what at first sight appeared to be no less than a Field-Marshal. Gold braid and medal ribbons adorned a broad and manly chest. His deportment was perfect. He received you with tender concern as you emerged with rheumatic difficulty from a taxi or a car, guided you carefully up the steps and piloted you through the silently swinging doorway.

Inside, if this was the first time you had visited Bertram's, you felt, almost with alarm, that you had re-entered a vanished world. Time had gone back. You were in Edwardian England once more.

There was, of course, central heating, but it was not apparent. As there had always been, in the big central lounge, there were two magnificent coal fires; beside them big brass coal scuttles shone in the way they used to shine when Edwardian housemaids polished them, and they were filled with exactly the right sized lumps of coal. There was a general appearance of rich red velvet and plushy cosiness. The arm-chairs were not of this time and age. They were well above the level of the floor, so that rheumatic old ladies had not to struggle in an undignified manner in order to get to their feet. The seats of the chairs did not, as in so many modern high-priced arm-chairs, stop half-way between the thigh and the knee, thereby inflicting agony on those suffering from arthritis and sciatica; and they were not all of a pattern. There were straight backs and reclining backs, different widths to accommodate the slender and the obese. People of almost any dimension could find a comfortable chair at Bertram's.

Since it was now the tea hour, the lounge hall was full. Not that the lounge hall was the only place where you could have tea. There was a drawing-room (chintz), a smoking-room (by some hidden influence reserved for gentlemen only), where the vast chairs were of fine leather, two writing-rooms, where you could take a special friend and have a cosy little gossip in a quiet corner – and even write a letter as well if you wanted to. Besides these amenities of the Edwardian age, there were other retreats, not in any way publicized, but known to those who wanted them. There was a double bar, with two bar attendants, an American barman to make the Americans feel at home and to provide them with bourbon, rye, and every kind of cocktail, and an English one to deal with sherries and Pimm's No. 1, and to talk knowledgeably about the runners at Ascot and Newbury to the middle-aged men who stayed at Bertram's for the more serious race meetings. There was also, tucked down a passage, in a secretive way, a television-room for those who asked for it.

But the big entrance lounge was the favourite place for the afternoon tea drinking. The elderly ladies enjoyed seeing who came in and out, recognizing old friends, and commenting unfavourably on how these had aged. There were also American visitors fascinated by seeing the titled English really getting down to their traditional afternoon tea. For afternoon tea was quite a feature of Bertram's.

It was nothing less than splendid. Presiding over the ritual was Henry, a large and magnificent figure, a ripe fifty, avuncular, sympathetic, and with the courtly manners of that long vanished species: the perfect butler. Slim youths performed the actual work under Henry's austere direction. There were large crested silver trays, and Georgian silver teapots. The china, if not actually Rockingham and Davenport, looked like it. The Blind Earl services were particular favourites. The tea was the best Indian, Ceylon, Darjeeling, Lapsang, etc. As for eatables, you could ask for anything you liked – and get it!

On this particular day, November the 17th, Lady Selina Hazy, sixty-five, up from Leicestershire, was eating delicious well-buttered muffins with all an elderly lady's relish.

Her absorption with muffins, however, was not so great that she failed to look up sharply every time the inner pair of swing doors opened to admit a newcomer.

So it was that she smiled and nodded to welcome Colonel Luscombe – erect, soldierly, race glasses hanging round his neck. Like the old autocrat that she was, she beckoned imperiously and, in a minute or two, Luscombe came over to her.

'Hallo, Selina, what brings you up to Town?'

'Dentist,' said Lady Selina, rather indistinctly, owing to muffin. 'And I thought as I *was* up, I might as well go and see that man in Harley Street about my arthritis. You know who I mean.'

Although Harley Street contained several hundreds of fashionable practitioners for all and every ailment, Luscombe did know whom she meant.

'Do you any good?' he asked.

'I rather think he did,' said Lady Selina grudgingly. 'Extraordinary fellow. Took me by the neck when I wasn't expecting it, and wrung it like a chicken.' She moved her neck gingerly.

'Hurt you?'

'It must have done, twisting it like that, but really I hadn't time to know.' She continued to move her neck gingerly. 'Feels all right. Can look over my right shoulder for the first time in years.'

She put this to a practical test and exclaimed, 'Why I do believe that's old Jane Marple. Thought she was dead years ago. Looks a hundred.'

Colonel Luscombe threw a glance in the direction of Jane Marple thus resurrected, but without much interest: Bertram's always had a sprinkling of what he called fluffy old pussies.

Lady Selina was continuing.

'Only place in London you can still get muffins. Real muffins. Do you know when I went to America last year they had something *called* muffins on the breakfast menu. Not real muffins at all. Kind of teacake with raisins in them. I mean, why call them muffins?'

She pushed in the last buttery morsel and looked round vaguely. Henry materialized immediately. Not quickly or hurriedly. It seemed that, just suddenly, he was there.

'Anything further I can get you, my lady? Cake of any kind?'

'Cake?' Lady Selina thought about it, was doubtful.

'We are serving very good seed cake, my lady. I can recommend it.'

'Seed cake? I haven't eaten seed cake for *years*. It is *real* seed cake?'

'Oh, yes, my lady. The cook has had the recipe for years. You'll enjoy it, I'm sure.'

Henry gave a glance at one of his retinue, and the lad departed in search of seed cake.

'I suppose you've been at Newbury, Derek?'

'Yes. Darned cold, I didn't wait for the last two races. Disastrous day. That filly of Harry's was no good at all.'

'Didn't think she would be. What about Swanhilda?'

'Finished fourth.' Luscombe rose. 'Got to see about my room.'

He walked across the lounge to the reception desk. As he went he noted the tables and their occupants. Astonishing number of people having tea here. Quite like old days. Tea as a meal had rather gone out of fashion since the war. But evidently not at Bertram's. Who *were* all these people? Two Canons and the Dean of Chislehampton. Yes, and another pair of gaitered legs over in the corner, a Bishop, no less! Mere Vicars were scarce. 'Have to be at least a Canon to afford Bertram's,' he thought. The rank and file of the clergy certainly couldn't, poor devils. As far as that went, he wondered how on earth people like old Selina Hazy could. She'd only got twopence or so a year to bless herself with. And there was old Lady Berry, and Mrs Posselthwaite from Somerset, and Sybil Kerr – all poor as church mice.

Still thinking about this he arrived at the desk and was pleasantly greeted by Miss Gorringe the receptionist. Miss Gorringe was an old friend. She knew every one of the clientele and, like Royalty, never forgot a face. She looked frumpy but respectable. Frizzled yellowish hair (old-fashioned tongs, it suggested), black silk dress, a high bosom on which reposed a large gold locket and a cameo brooch.

'Number fourteen,' said Miss Gorringe. 'I think you had fourteen last time, Colonel Luscombe, and liked it. It's quiet.'

'How you always manage to remember these things, I can't imagine, Miss Gorringe.'

'We like to make our old friends comfortable.'

'Takes me back a long way, coming in here. Nothing seems to have changed.'

He broke off as Mr Humfries came out from an inner sanctum to greet him.

Mr Humfries was often taken by the uninitiated to be Mr Bertram in person. Who the actual Mr Bertram was, or indeed, if there ever *had* been a Mr Bertram was now lost in the mists of antiquity. Bertram's had existed since about 1840, but nobody had taken any interest in tracing its past history. It was just there, solid, in fact. When addressed as Mr Bertram, Mr Humfries never corrected the impression. If they wanted him to be Mr Bertram he would be Mr Bertram. Colonel Luscombe knew his name, though he didn't know if Humfries was the manager or the owner. He rather fancied the latter.

Mr Humfries was a man of about fifty. He had very good manners, and the presence of a Junior Minister. He could, at any moment, be all things to all people. He could talk racing shop, cricket, foreign politics, tell anecdotes of Royalty, give Motor Show information, knew the most interesting plays on at present – advise on places Americans ought really to see in England however short their stay. He had knowledgeable information about where it would suit persons of all incomes and tastes to dine. With all this, he did not make himself too cheap. He was not on tap all the time. Miss Gorringe had all the same facts at her fingertips and could retail them efficiently. At brief intervals Mr Humfries, like the sun, made his appearance above the horizon and flattered someone by his personal attention.

This time it was Colonel Luscombe who was so honoured. They exchanged a few racing platitudes, but Colonel Luscombe was absorbed by his problem. And here was the man who could give him the answer.

'Tell me, Humfries, how do all these old dears manage to come and stay here?'

'Oh you've been wondering about that?' Mr Humfries seemed amused. 'Well, the answer's simple. They couldn't afford it. Unless –'

He paused.

'Unless you make special prices for them? Is that it?'

'More or less. They don't know, usually, that they *are* special prices, or if they do realize it, they think it's because they're old customers.'

'And it isn't just that?'

'Well, Colonel Luscombe, I *am* running a hotel. I couldn't afford actually to lose money.'

'But how can that pay you?'

'It's a question of atmosphere . . . Strangers coming to this country (Americans, in particular, because they are the ones who have the money) have their own rather queer ideas of what England is like. I'm not talking, you understand, of the rich business tycoons who are always crossing the Atlantic. They usually go to the Savoy or the Dorchester. They want modern décor, American food, all the things that will make them feel at home. But there are a lot of people who come abroad at rare intervals and who expect this country to be – well, I won't go back as far as Dickens, but they've read *Cranford* and Henry James, and they don't want to find this country just the same as their own! So they go back home afterwards and say: "There's a wonderful place in London; Bertram's Hotel, it's called. It's just like stepping back a hundred years. It just *is* old England! And the people who stay there! People you'd never come across anywhere else. Wonderful old Duchesses. They serve all the old English dishes, there's a marvellous old-fashioned beef-steak pudding! You've never tasted anything like it; and great sirloins of beef and saddles of mutton, and an old-fashioned English tea and a wonderful English breakfast. And of course all the usual things as well. And it's wonderfully comfortable. *And* warm. Great log fires."'

Mr Humfries ceased his impersonation and permitted himself something nearly approaching a grin.

'I see,' said Luscombe thoughtfully. 'These people; decayed aristocrats, impoverished members of the old County families, they are all so much *mise en scène*?'

Mr Humfries nodded agreement.

'I really wonder no one else has thought of it. Of course I found Bertram's ready made, so to speak. All it needed was some rather expensive restoration. All the people who come here think it's something that they've discovered for themselves, that no one else knows about.'

'I suppose,' said Luscombe, 'that the restoration *was* quite expensive?'

'Oh yes. The place has got to *look* Edwardian, but it's got to have the modern comforts that we take for granted in these days. Our old dears – if you will forgive me referring to them as that – have got to feel that nothing has changed since the turn of the century, and our travelling clients have got to feel they can have period surroundings, and still have what they are used to having at home, and can't really live without!'

'Bit difficult sometimes?' suggested Luscombe.

'Not really. Take central heating for instance. Americans require – need, I should say – at least ten degrees Fahrenheit higher than English people do. We actually have two quite different sets of bedrooms. The English we put in one lot, the Americans in the other. The rooms all look alike, but they are full of actual differences – electric razors, and showers as well as tubs in some of the bathrooms, and if you want an American breakfast, it's there – cereals and iced orange juice and all – or if you prefer you can have the English breakfast.'

'Eggs and bacon?'

'As you say – but a good deal more than that if you want it. Kippers, kidneys and bacon, cold grouse, York ham. Oxford marmalade.'

'I must remember all that tomorrow morning. Don't get that sort of thing any more at home.'

Humfries smiled.

'Most gentlemen only ask for eggs and bacon. They've – well, they've got out of the way of thinking about the things there used to be.'

'Yes, yes . . . I remember when I was a child . . . Sideboards groaning with hot dishes. Yes, it was a luxurious way of life.'

'We endeavour to give people anything they ask for.'

'Including seed cake and muffins – yes, I see. To each according to his need – I see . . . Quite Marxian.'

'I beg your pardon?'

'Just a thought, Humfries. Extremes meet.'

Colonel Luscombe turned away, taking the key Miss Gorringe offered him. A page-boy sprang to attention and conducted him to the lift. He saw in passing that Lady Selina Hazy was now sitting with her friend Jane Something or other.

CHAPTER 2

'And I suppose you're still living at that dear St Mary Mead?' Lady Selina was asking. 'Such a sweet unspoilt village. I often think about it. Just the same as ever, I suppose?'

'Well, not quite.' Miss Marple reflected on certain aspects of her place of residence. The new Building Estate. The additions to the Village Hall, the altered appearance of the High Street with its up-to-date shop fronts – She sighed. 'One has to accept change, I suppose.'

'Progress,' said Lady Selina vaguely. 'Though it often seems to me that it isn't progress. All these smart plumbing fixtures they have nowadays. Every shade of colour and superb what they call "finish" – but do any of them really *pull*? Or *push*, when they're that kind. Every time you go to a friend's house, you find some kind of a notice in the loo – "Press sharply and release," "Pull to the *left*," "Release *quickly*." But in the old days, one just pulled up a handle *any* kind of way, and cataracts of water came *at once* – There's the dear Bishop of Medmenham,' Lady Selina broke off to say, as a handsome, elderly cleric passed by. 'Practically quite blind, I believe. But such a splendid *militant* priest.'

A little clerical talk was indulged in, interspersed by Lady Selina's recognition of various friends and acquaintances, many of whom were not the people she thought they were. She and Miss Marple talked a little of 'old days', though Miss Marple's upbringing, of course, had been quite different from Lady Selina's, and their reminiscences were mainly confined to the few years when Lady Selina, a recent widow of severely straitened means, had taken a small house in the village of St Mary Mead during the time her second son had been stationed at an airfield nearby.

'Do you always stay here when you come up, Jane? Odd I haven't seen you here before.'

'Oh no, indeed. I couldn't afford to, and anyway, I hardly ever leave home these days. No, it was a very kind niece of mine who thought it would be a treat for me to have a short visit to London. Joan is a very kind girl – at least perhaps hardly a girl.' Miss Marple reflected with a qualm that Joan must now be close on fifty. 'She is a painter, you know. Quite a well-known painter. Joan West. She had an exhibition not long ago.'

Lady Selina had little interest in painters, or indeed in anything artistic. She regarded writers, artists and musicians as a species of clever performing animal; she was prepared to feel indulgent towards them, but to wonder privately why they wanted to do what they did.

'This modern stuff, I suppose,' she said, her eyes wandering. 'There's Cicely Longhurst – dyed her hair again, I see.'

'I'm afraid dear Joan *is* rather modern.'

Here Miss Marple was quite wrong. Joan West had been modern about twenty years ago, but was now regarded by the young *arriviste* artists as completely old-fashioned.

Casting a brief glance at Cicely Longhurst's hair, Miss Marple relapsed into a pleasant remembrance of how kind Joan had been. Joan had actually said to her husband, 'I wish we could do something for poor old Aunt Jane. She never gets away from home. Do you think she'd like to go to Bournemouth for a week or two?'

'Good idea,' said Raymond West. His last book was doing very well indeed, and he felt in a generous mood.

'She enjoyed her trip to the West Indies, I think, though it was a pity she had to get mixed up in a murder case. Quite the wrong thing at her age.'

'That sort of thing seems to happen to her.'

Raymond was very fond of his old aunt and was constantly devising treats for her, and sending her books that he thought might interest her. He was surprised when she often politely declined the treats, and though she always said the books were 'so interesting' he sometimes suspected that she had not read them. But then, of course, her eyes were failing.

In this last he was wrong. Miss Marple had remarkable eyesight for her age, and was at this moment taking in everything that was going on round her with keen interest and pleasure.

To Joan's proffer of a week or two at one of Bournemouth's best hotels, she had hesitated, murmured, 'It's very, very kind of you, my dear, but I really don't think –'

'But it's *good* for you, Aunt Jane. Good to get away from home sometimes. It gives you new ideas, and new things to think about.'

'Oh yes, you are quite right there, and I *would* like a little visit somewhere for a change. Not, perhaps, Bournemouth.'

Joan was slightly surprised. She had thought Bournemouth would have been Aunt Jane's Mecca.

'Eastbourne? Or Torquay?'

'What I would really like –' Miss Marple hesitated.

'Yes?'

'I dare say you will think it rather silly of me.'

'No, I'm sure I shan't.' (Where *did* the old dear want to go?)

'I would really like to go to Bertram's Hotel – in London.'

'Bertram's Hotel?' The name was vaguely familiar.

Words came from Miss Marple in a rush.

'I stayed there once – when I was fourteen. With my uncle and aunt, Uncle Thomas, that was, he was Canon of Ely. And I've never forgotten it. If I could stay there – a week would be quite enough – two weeks might be too expensive.'

'Oh, that's all right. Of course you shall go. I ought to have thought that you might want to go to London – the shops and everything. We'll fix it up – if Bertram's Hotel still exists. So many hotels have vanished, sometimes bombed in the war and sometimes just given up.'

'No, I happen to know Bertram's Hotel is still going. I had a letter from there – from my American friend Amy McAllister of Boston. She and her husband were staying there.'

'Good, then I'll go ahead and fix it up.' She added gently, 'I'm afraid you may find it's changed a good deal from the days when you knew it. So don't be disappointed.'

But Bertram's Hotel had not changed. It was just as it had always been. Quite miraculously so, in Miss Marple's opinion. In fact, she wondered . . .

It really seemed too good to be true. She knew quite well, with her usual clear-eyed common sense, that what she wanted was simply to refurbish her memories of the past in their old original colours. Much of her life had, perforce, to be spent recalling past pleasures. If you could find someone to remember them with, that was indeed happiness. Nowadays that was not easy to do; she had outlived most of her contemporaries. But she still sat and remembered. In a queer way, it made her come to life again – Jane Marple, that pink and white eager young girl . . . Such a silly girl in many ways . . . now who was that very unsuitable young man whose name – oh dear, she couldn't even remember it now! How wise her mother had been to nip that friendship so firmly in the bud. She had come across him years later – and really he was quite dreadful! At the time she had cried herself to sleep for at least a week!

Nowadays, of course – she considered nowadays . . . These poor young things. Some of them had mothers, but never mothers who seemed to be any good – mothers who were quite incapable of protecting their daughters from silly affairs, illegitimate babies, and early and unfortunate marriages. It was all very sad.

Her friend's voice interrupted these meditations.

'Well, I never. It is – yes, it is – Bess Sedgwick over there! Of all the unlikely places –'

Miss Marple had been listening with only half an ear to Lady Selina's comments on her surroundings. She and Miss Marple moved in entirely different circles, so that Miss Marple had been unable to exchange scandalous tit-bits about the various friends or acquaintances that Lady Selina recognized or thought she recognized.

But Bess Sedgwick was different. Bess Sedgwick was a name that almost everyone in England knew. For over thirty years now, Bess Sedgwick had been reported by the Press as doing this or that outrageous or extraordinary thing. For a good part of the war she had been a member of the French Resistance, and was said to have six notches on her gun representing dead Germans. She had flown solo across the Atlantic years ago, had ridden on horseback across Europe and fetched up at Lake Van. She had driven racing cars, had once saved two children from a burning house, had several marriages to her credit and discredit and was said to be the second best-dressed woman in Europe. It was also said that she had successfully smuggled herself aboard a nuclear submarine on its test voyage.

It was therefore with the most intense interest that Miss Marple sat up and indulged in a frankly avid stare.

Whatever she had expected of Bertram's Hotel, it was not to find Bess Sedgwick there. An expensive night club, or a lorry drivers' pull up – either of those would be quite in keeping with Bess Sedgwick's wide range of interests. But this highly respectable and old world hostelry seemed strangely alien.

Still there she was – no doubt of it. Hardly a month passed without Bess Sedgwick's face appearing in the fashion magazines or the popular press. Here she was in the flesh, smoking a cigarette in a quick impatient manner and looking in a surprised way at the large tea tray in front of her as though she had never seen one before. She had ordered – Miss Marple screwed up her eyes and peered – it was rather far away – yes, *doughnuts*. Very interesting.

As she watched, Bess Sedgwick stubbed out her cigarette in her saucer, lifted a doughnut and took an immense bite. Rich red real strawberry jam gushed out over her chin. Bess threw back her head and laughed, one of the loudest and gayest sounds to have been heard in the lounge of Bertram's Hotel for some time.

Henry was immediately beside her, a small delicate napkin proffered. She took it, scrubbed her chin with the vigour of a schoolboy, exclaiming: 'That's what I call a *real* doughnut. Gorgeous.'

She dropped the napkin on the tray and stood up. As usual every eye was on her. She was used to that. Perhaps she liked it, perhaps she no longer noticed it. She was worth looking at – a striking woman rather than a beautiful one. The palest of platinum hair fell sleek and smooth to her shoulders. The bones of her head and face were exquisite. Her nose was faintly aquiline, her eyes deep set and a real grey in colour. She had the wide mouth of a natural comedian. Her dress was of such simplicity that it puzzled most men. It looked like the coarsest kind of sacking, had no ornamentation of any kind, and no apparent fastening or seams. But women knew better. Even the provincial old dears in Bertram's knew, quite certainly, that it had cost the earth!

Striding across the lounge towards the lift, she passed quite close to Lady Selina and Miss Marple, and she nodded to the former.

'Hello, Lady Selina. Haven't seen you since Crufts. How are the Borzois?'

'What on earth are you doing here, Bess?'

'Just staying here. I've just driven up from Land's End. Four hours and three quarters. Not bad.'

'You'll kill yourself one of these days. Or someone else.'

'Oh I hope not.'

'But why are you staying *here*?'

Bess Sedgwick threw a swift glance round. She seemed to see the point and acknowledged it with an ironic smile.

'Someone told me I ought to try it. I think they're right. I've just had the most marvellous doughnut.'

'My dear, they have *real* muffins too.'

'Muffins,' said Lady Sedgwick thoughtfully. 'Yes . . .' She seemed to concede the point. 'Muffins!'

She nodded and went on towards the lift.

'Extraordinary girl,' said Lady Selina. To her, like to Miss Marple, every woman under sixty was a girl. 'Known her ever since she was a child. Nobody could do anything with her. Ran away with an Irish groom when she was sixteen. They managed to get her back in time – or perhaps not in time. Anyway they bought him off and got her safely married to old Coniston – thirty years older than she was, awful old rip, quite dotty about her. *That* didn't last long. She went off with Johnnie Sedgwick. That *might* have stuck if he hadn't broken his neck steeplechasing. After that she married Ridgway Becker, the American yacht owner. He divorced her three years ago and I hear she's taken up with some Racing Motor Driver – a Pole or something. I don't know whether she's actually married or not. After the American divorce she went back to calling herself Sedgwick. She goes about with *the* most extraordinary people. They *say* she takes drugs . . . I don't know, I'm sure.'

'One wonders if she is happy,' said Miss Marple.

Lady Selina, who had clearly never wondered anything of the kind, looked rather startled.

'She's got packets of money, I suppose,' she said doubtfully. 'Alimony and all that. Of course that isn't everything . . .'

'No, indeed.'

'And she's usually got a man – or several men – in tow.'

'Yes?'

'Of course when some women get to that age, that's all they want . . . But somehow –'

She paused.

'No,' said Miss Marple. '*I* don't think so either.'

There were people who would have smiled in gentle derision at this pronouncement on the part of an old-fashioned old lady who could hardly be expected to be an authority on nymphomania, and indeed it was not a word that Miss Marple would have used – her own phrase would have been 'always too fond of men'. But Lady Selina accepted her opinion as a confirmation of her own.

'There have been a lot of men in her life,' she pointed out.

'Oh yes, but I should say, wouldn't you, that men were an adventure to her, not a need?'

And would any woman, Miss Marple wondered, come to Bertram's Hotel for an assignation with a man? Bertram's was very definitely not that sort of place. But possibly that could be, to someone of Bess Sedgwick's disposition, the very reason for choosing it.

She sighed, looked up at the handsome grandfather clock decorously ticking in the corner, and rose with the careful effort of the rheumatic to her feet. She walked slowly towards the lift. Lady Selina cast a glance around her and pounced upon an elderly gentleman of military appearance who was reading the *Spectator*.

'How nice to see you again. Er – it is General Arlington, isn't it?'

But with great courtesy the old gentleman declined being General Arlington. Lady Selina apologized, but was not unduly discomposed. She combined short sight with optimism and since the thing she enjoyed most was meeting old friends and acquaintances, she was always making this kind of mistake. Many other people did the same, since the lights were pleasantly dim and heavily shaded. But nobody ever took offence – usually indeed it seemed to give them pleasure.

Miss Marple smiled to herself as she waited for the lift to come down. So like Selina! Always convinced that she knew everybody. She herself could not compete. Her solitary achievement in that line had been the handsome and well-gaitered Bishop of Westchester whom she had addressed affectionately as 'dear Robbie' and who had responded with equal affection and with memories of himself as a child in a Hampshire vicarage calling out lustily 'Be a crocodile now, Aunty Janie. Be a crocodile and eat me.'

The lift came down, the uniformed middle-aged man threw open the door. Rather to Miss Marple's surprise the alighting passenger was Bess Sedgwick whom she had seen go up only a minute or two before.

And then, one foot poised, Bess Sedgwick stopped dead, with a suddenness that surprised Miss Marple and made her own forward step falter. Bess Sedgwick was staring over Miss Marple's shoulder with such concentration that the old lady turned her own head.

The commissionaire had just pushed open the two swing doors of the entrance and was holding them to let two women pass through into the lounge. One of them was a fussy looking middle-aged lady wearing a rather unfortunate flowered violet hat, the other was a tall, simply but smartly dressed, girl of perhaps seventeen or eighteen with long straight flaxen hair.

Bess Sedgwick pulled herself together, wheeled round abruptly and re-entered the lift. As Miss Marple followed her in, she turned to her and apologized.

'I'm so sorry. I nearly ran into you.' She had a warm friendly voice. 'I just remembered I'd forgotten something – which sounds nonsense but isn't really.'

'Second floor?' said the operator. Miss Marple smiled and nodded in acknowledgment of the apology, got out and walked slowly along to her room, pleasurably turning over sundry little unimportant problems in her mind as was so often her custom.

For instance what Lady Sedgwick had said wasn't true. She had only just gone up to her room, and it must have been then that she 'remembered she had forgotten something' (if there had been any truth in that statement at all) and had come down to find it. Or had she perhaps come down to meet someone or look for someone? But if so, what she had seen as the lift door opened had startled and upset her, and she had immediately swung into the lift again and gone up so as *not* to meet whoever it was she had seen.

It must have been the two newcomers. The middle-aged woman and the girl. Mother and daughter? No, Miss Marple thought, *not* mother and daughter.

Even at Bertram's, thought Miss Marple, happily, interesting things could happen . . .

CHAPTER 3

'Er – is Colonel Luscombe –?'

The woman in the violet hat was at the desk. Miss Gorringe smiled in a welcoming manner and a page, who had been standing at the ready, was immediately dispatched but had no need to fulfil his errand, as Colonel

Luscombe himself entered the lounge at that moment and came quickly across to the desk.

'How do you do, Mrs Carpenter.' He shook hands politely, then turned to the girl. 'My dear Elvira.' He took both hands affectionately in his. 'Well, well, this *is* nice. Splendid – splendid. Come and let's sit down.' He led them to chairs, established them. 'Well, well,' he repeated, 'this is nice.'

The effort he made was somewhat palpable as was his lack of ease. He could hardly go on saying how nice this was. The two ladies were not very helpful. Elvira smiled very sweetly. Mrs Carpenter gave a meaningless little laugh, and smoothed her gloves.

'A good journey, eh?'

'Yes, thank you,' said Elvira.

'No fog. Nothing like that?'

'Oh no.'

'Our flight was five minutes ahead of time,' said Mrs Carpenter.

'Yes, yes. Good, very good.' He took a pull upon himself. 'I hope this place will be all right for you?'

'Oh, I'm sure it's *very* nice,' said Mrs Carpenter warmly, glancing round her. 'Very comfortable.'

'Rather old-fashioned, I'm afraid,' said the Colonel apologetically. 'Rather a lot of old fogies. No – er – dancing, anything like that.'

'No, I suppose not,' agreed Elvira.

She glanced round in an expressionless manner. It certainly seemed impossible to connect Bertram's with dancing.

'Lot of old fogies here, I'm afraid,' said Colonel Luscombe, repeating himself. 'Ought, perhaps, to have taken you somewhere more modern. Not very well up in these things, you see.'

'This is very nice,' said Elvira politely.

'It's only for a couple of nights,' went on Colonel Luscombe. 'I thought we'd go to a show this evening. A musical –' he said the word rather doubtfully, as though not sure he was using the right term. '*Let Down Your Hair Girls*. I hope that will be all right?'

'How delightful,' exclaimed Mrs Carpenter. 'That will be a treat, won't it, Elvira?'

'Lovely,' said Elvira, tonelessly.

'And then supper afterwards? At the Savoy?'

Fresh exclamations from Mrs Carpenter. Colonel Luscombe, stealing a glance at Elvira, cheered up a little. He thought that Elvira was pleased, though quite determined to express nothing more than polite approval in front of Mrs Carpenter. 'And I don't blame her,' he said to himself.

He said to Mrs Carpenter:

'Perhaps you'd like to see your rooms – see they're all right and all that –'

'Oh, I'm sure they will be.'

'Well, if there's anything you don't like about them, we'll make them change it. They know me here very well.'

Miss Gorringe, in charge at the desk, was pleasantly welcoming. Nos 28 and 29 on the second floor with an adjoining bathroom.

'I'll go up and get things unpacked,' said Mrs Carpenter. 'Perhaps, Elvira, you and Colonel Luscombe would like to have a little gossip.'

Tact, thought Colonel Luscombe. A bit obvious, perhaps, but anyway it would get rid of her for a bit. Though what he was going to gossip about to Elvira, he really didn't know. A very nice-mannered girl, but he wasn't used to girls. His wife had died in childbirth and the baby, a boy, had been brought up by his wife's family whilst an elder sister had come to keep house for him. His son had married and gone to live in Kenya, and his grandchildren were eleven, five and two and a half and had been entertained on their last visit by football and space science talk, electric trains, and a ride on his foot. Easy! But young girls!

He asked Elvira if she would like a drink. He was about to propose a bitter lemon, ginger ale, or orangeade, but Elvira forestalled him.

'Thank you. I should like a gin and vermouth.'

Colonel Luscombe looked at her rather doubtfully. He supposed girls of – what was she? sixteen? seventeen? – did drink gin and vermouth. But he reassured himself that Elvira knew, so to speak, correct Greenwich social time. He ordered a gin and vermouth and a dry sherry.

He cleared his throat and asked:

'How was Italy?'

'Very nice, thank you.'

'And that place you were at, the Contessa what's-her-name? Not too grim?'

'She is rather strict. But I didn't let that worry me.'

He looked at her, not quite sure whether the reply was not slightly ambiguous.

He said, stammering a little, but with a more natural manner than he had been able to manage before:

'I'm afraid we don't know each other as well as we ought to, seeing I'm your guardian as well as your godfather. Difficult for me, you know

– difficult for a man who's an old buffer like me – to know what a girl wants – at least – I mean to know what a girl ought to have. Schools and then after school – what they used to call finishing in my day. But now, I suppose it's all more serious. Careers eh? Jobs? All that? We'll have to have a talk about all that sometime. Anything in particular you want to do?'

'I suppose I shall take a secretarial course,' said Elvira without enthusiasm.

'Oh. You want to be a secretary?'

'Not particularly –'

'Oh – well, then –'

'It's just what you start with,' Elvira explained.

Colonel Luscombe had an odd feeling of being relegated to his place.

'These cousins of mine, the Melfords. You think you'll like living with them? If not –'

'Oh I think so. I like Nancy quite well. And Cousin Mildred is rather a dear.'

'That's all right then?'

'Quite, for the present.'

Luscombe did not know what to say to that. Whilst he was considering what next to say, Elvira spoke. Her words were simple and direct.

'Have I any money?'

Again he took his time before answering, studying her thoughtfully. Then he said:

'Yes. You've got quite a lot of money. That is to say, you will have when you are twenty-one.'

'Who has got it now?'

He smiled. 'It's held in trust for you; a certain amount is deducted each year from the income to pay for your maintenance and education.'

'And you are the trustee?'

'One of them. There are three.'

'What happens if I die?'

'Come, come, Elvira, you're not going to die. What nonsense!'

'I hope not – but one never knows, does one? An airliner crashed only last week and everyone was killed.'

'Well, it's not going to happen to you,' said Luscombe firmly.

'You can't really know that,' said Elvira. 'I was just wondering who would get my money if I died?'

'I haven't the least idea,' said the Colonel irritably. 'Why do you ask?'

'It might be interesting,' said Elvira thoughtfully. 'I wondered if it would be worth anyone's while to kill me.'

'Really, Elvira! This is a most unprofitable conversation. I can't understand why your mind dwells on such things.'

'Oh. Just ideas. One wants to know what the facts really are.'

'You're not thinking of the *Mafia* – or something like that?'

'Oh no. That would be silly. Who would get my money if I was married?'

'Your husband, I suppose. But really –'

'Are you sure of that?'

'No, I'm not in the least sure. It depends on the wording of the Trust. But you're not married, so why worry?'

Elvira did not reply. She seemed lost in thought. Finally she came out of her trance and asked:

'Do you ever see my mother?'

'Sometimes. Not very often.'

'Where is she now?'

'Oh – abroad.'

'Where abroad?'

'France – Portugal. I don't really know.'

'Does she ever want to see me?'

Her limpid gaze met his. He didn't know what to reply. Was this a moment for truth? Or for vagueness? Or for a good thumping lie? What could you say to a girl who asked a question of such simplicity, when the answer was of great complexity? He said unhappily:

'I don't know.'

Her eyes searched him gravely. Luscombe felt thoroughly ill at ease. He was making a mess of this. The girl must wonder – clearly was wondering. Any girl would.

He said, 'You mustn't think – I mean it's difficult to explain. Your mother is, well, rather different from –' Elvira was nodding energetically.

'I know. I'm always reading about her in the papers. She's something rather special, isn't she? In fact, she's rather a wonderful person.'

'Yes,' agreed the Colonel. 'That's exactly right. She's a wonderful person.' He paused and then went on. 'But a wonderful person is very often –' He stopped and started again – 'it's not always a happy thing to have a wonderful person for a mother. You can take that from me because it's the truth.'

'You don't like speaking the truth very much, do you? But I think what you've just said *is* the truth.'

They both sat staring towards the big brass-bound swing doors that led to the world outside.

Suddenly the doors were pushed open with violence – a violence quite unusual in Bertram's Hotel – and a young man strode in and went straight across to the desk. He wore a black leather jacket. His vitality was such that Bertram's Hotel took on the atmosphere of a museum by way of contrast. The people were the dust-encrusted relics of a past age. He bent towards Miss Gorringe and asked:

'Is Lady Sedgwick staying here?'

Miss Gorringe on this occasion had no welcoming smile. Her eyes were flinty. She said:

'Yes.' Then, with definite unwillingness, she stretched out her hand towards the telephone. 'Do you want to –?'

'No,' said the young man. 'I just wanted to leave a note for her.'

He produced it from a pocket of his leather coat and slid it across the mahogany counter.

'I only wanted to be sure this was the right hotel.'

There might have been some slight incredulity in his voice as he looked round him, then turned back towards the entrance. His eyes passed indifferently over the people sitting round him. They passed over Luscombe and Elvira in the same way, and Luscombe felt a sudden unsuspected anger. 'Dammit all,' he thought to himself, 'Elvira's a pretty girl. When I was a young chap I'd have noticed a pretty girl, especially among all these fossils.' But the young man seemed to have no interested eyes to spare for pretty girls. He turned back to the desk and asked, raising his voice slightly as though to call Miss Gorringe's attention:

'What's the telephone number here? 1129 isn't it?'

'No,' said Miss Gorringe, '3925.'

'Regent?'

'No. Mayfair.'

He nodded. Then swiftly he strode across to the door and passed out, swinging the doors to behind him with something of the same explosive quality he had shown on entering.

Everybody seemed to draw a deep breath; to find difficulty in resuming their interrupted conversations.

'Well,' said Colonel Luscombe, rather inadequately, as if at a loss for words. 'Well, really! These young fellows nowadays . . .'

Elvira was smiling.

'You recognized him, didn't you?' she said. 'You know who he is?' She spoke in a slightly awed voice. She proceeded to enlighten him. 'Ladislaus Malinowski.'

'Oh, that chap.' The name was indeed faintly familiar to Colonel Luscombe. 'Racing driver.'

'Yes. He was world champion two years running. He had a bad crash a year ago. Broke lots of things. But I believe he's driving again now.' She raised her head to listen. 'That's a racing car he's driving now.'

The roar of the engine had penetrated through to Bertram's Hotel from the street outside. Colonel Luscombe perceived that Ladislaus Malinowski was one of Elvira's heroes. 'Well,' he thought to himself, 'better that than one of those pop singers or crooners or long-haired Beatles or whatever they call themselves.' Luscombe was old-fashioned in his views of young men.

The swing doors opened again. Both Elvira and Colonel Luscombe looked at them expectantly but Bertram's Hotel had reverted to normal. It was merely a white-haired elderly cleric who came in. He stood for a moment looking round him with a slightly puzzled air as of one who fails to understand where he was or how he had come there. Such an experience was no novelty to Canon Pennyfather. It came to him in trains when he did not remember where he had come from, where he was going, or why! It came to him when he was walking along the street, it came to him when he found himself sitting on a committee. It had come to him before now when he was in his cathedral stall, and did not know whether he had already preached his sermon or was about to do so.

'I believe I know that old boy,' said Luscombe, peering at him. 'Who is he now? Stays here fairly often, I believe. Abercrombie? Archdeacon Abercrombie – no, it's not Abercrombie, though he's rather like Abercrombie.'

Elvira glanced round at Canon Pennyfather without interest. Compared with a racing driver he had no appeal at all. She was not interested in ecclesiastics of any kind although, since being in Italy, she admitted to a mild admiration for Cardinals whom she considered as at any rate properly picturesque.

Canon Pennyfather's face cleared and he nodded his head appreciatively. He had recognized where he was. In Bertram's Hotel, of course; where he was going to spend the night on his way to – now where was he on his way to? Chadminster? No, no, he had just *come* from Chadminster. He was going to – of course – to the Congress at Lucerne. He stepped forward, beaming, to the reception desk and was greeted warmly by Miss Gorringe.

'So glad to see you, Canon Pennyfather. How well you are looking.'

'Thank you – thank you – I had a severe cold last week but I've got over it now. You have a room for me. I *did* write?'

Miss Gorringe reassured him.

'Oh yes, Canon Pennyfather, we got your letter. We've reserved No. 19 for you, the room you had last time.'

'Thank you – thank you. For – let me see – I shall want it for four days. Actually I am going to Lucerne and I shall be away for one night, but please keep the room. I shall leave most of my things here and only take a small bag to Switzerland. There won't be any difficulty over that?'

Again Miss Gorringe reassured him.

'Everything's going to be quite all right. You explained very clearly in your letter.'

Other people might not have used the word 'clearly'. 'Fully' would have been better, since he had certainly written at length.

All anxieties set at rest, Canon Pennyfather breathed a sigh of relief and was conveyed, together with his baggage, to Room 19.

In Room 28 Mrs Carpenter had removed her crown of violets from her head and was carefully adjusting her nightdress on the pillow of her bed. She looked up as Elvira entered.

'Ah, there you are, my dear. Would you like me to help you with your unpacking?'

'No, thank you,' said Elvira politely. 'I shan't unpack very much, you know.'

'Which of the bedrooms would you like to have? The bathroom is between them. I told them to put your luggage in the far one. I thought this room might be a little noisy.'

'That was very kind of you,' said Elvira in her expressionless voice.

'You're sure you wouldn't like me to help you?'

'No, thanks, really I wouldn't. I think I might perhaps have a bath.'

'Yes, I think that's a very good idea. Would you like to have the first bath? I'd rather finish putting my things away.'

Elvira nodded. She went into the adjoining bathroom, shut the door behind her and pushed the bolts across. She went into her own room, opened her suitcase and flung a few things on the bed. Then she undressed, put on a dressing-gown, went into the bathroom and turned the taps on. She went back into her own room and sat down on the bed by the telephone. She listened a moment or two in case of interruption, then lifted the receiver.

'This is Room 29. Can you give me Regent 1129 please?'

CHAPTER 4

Within the confines of Scotland Yard a conference was in progress. It was by way of being an informal conference. Six or seven men were sitting easily around a table and each of those six men was a man of some importance in his own line. The subject that occupied the attention of these guardians of the law was a subject that had grown terrifically in importance during the last two or three years. It concerned a branch of crime whose success had been overwhelmingly disquieting. Robbery on a big scale was increasing. Bank hold-ups, snatches of pay-rolls, thefts of consignments of jewels sent through the mail, train robberies. Hardly a month passed but some daring and stupendous coup was attempted and brought off successfully.

Sir Ronald Graves, Assistant Commissioner of Scotland Yard, was presiding at the head of the table. According to his usual custom he did more listening than talking. No formal reports were being presented on this occasion. All that belonged to the ordinary routine of CID work. This was a high level consultation, a general pooling of ideas between men looking at affairs from slightly different points of view. Sir Ronald Graves' eyes went slowly round his little group, then he nodded his head to a man at the end of the table.

'Well, Father,' he said, 'let's hear a few homely wisecracks from you.'

The man addressed as 'Father' was Chief-Inspector Fred Davy. His retirement lay not long ahead and he appeared to be even more elderly than he was. Hence his nickname of 'Father'. He had a comfortable spreading presence, and such a benign and kindly manner that many criminals had been disagreeably surprised to find him a less genial and gullible man than he had seemed to be.

'Yes, Father, let's hear your views,' said another Chief-Inspector.

'It's big,' said Chief-Inspector Davy with a deep sigh. 'Yes, it's big. Maybe it's growing.'

'When you say big, do you mean numerically?'

'Yes, I do.'

Another man, Comstock, with a sharp, foxy face and alert eyes, broke in to say:

'Would you say that was an advantage to them?'

'Yes and no,' said Father. 'It *could* be a disaster. But so far, devil take it, they've got it all well under control.'

Superintendent Andrews, a fair, slight, dreamy-looking man said, thoughtfully:

'I've always thought there's a lot more to size than people realize. Take a little one-man business. If that's well run and if it's the right size, it's a sure and certain winner. Branch out, make it bigger, increase personnel, and perhaps you'll get it suddenly to the *wrong* size and down the hill it goes. The same way with a great big chain of stores. An empire in industry. If that's *big* enough it will succeed. If it's *not* big enough it just won't manage it. Everything has got its right size. When it is its right size and well run it's the tops.'

'How big do you think this show is?' Sir Ronald barked.

'Bigger than we thought at first,' said Comstock.

A tough looking man, Inspector McNeill, said:

'It's growing, I'd say. Father's right. Growing all the time.'

'That may be a good thing,' said Davy. 'It may grow a bit *too* fast, and then it'll get out of hand.'

'The question is, Sir Ronald,' said McNeill, 'who we pull in and when?'

'There's a round dozen or so we could pull in,' said Comstock. 'The Harris lot are mixed up in it, we know that. There's a nice little pocket down Luton way. There's a garage at Epsom, there's a pub near Maidenhead, and there's a farm on the Great North Road.'

'Any of them worth pulling in?'

'I don't think so. Small fry all of them. Links. Just links here and there in the chain. A spot where cars are converted, and turned over quickly; a respectable pub where messages get passed; a second-hand clothes shop where appearance can be altered, a theatrical costumier in the East End, also very useful. They're paid, these people. Quite well paid but they don't really *know* anything!'

The dreamy Superintendent Andrews said again:

'We're up against some good brains. We haven't got near them yet. We know some of their affiliations and that's all. As I say, the Harris crowd are in it and Marks is in on the financial end. The foreign contacts are in touch with Weber but he's only an agent. We've nothing actually *on* any of these people. We know that they all have ways of maintaining contact with each other, and with the different branches of the concern, but we don't know exactly how they do it. We watch them and follow them, and they know we're watching them. *Somewhere* there's a great central exchange. What we want to get at is the planners.'

Comstock said:

'It's like a giant network. I agree that there must be an operational headquarters somewhere. A place where each operation is planned and detailed and dovetailed completely. Somewhere, someone plots it all, and produces a working blueprint of Operation Mailbag or Operation Payroll. Those are the people we're out to get.'

'Possibly they are not even in this country,' said Father quietly.

'No, I dare say that's true. Perhaps they're in an igloo somewhere, or in a tent in Morocco or in a chalet in Switzerland.'

'I don't believe in these master-minds,' said McNeill, shaking his head; 'they sound all right in a story. There's got to *be* a head, of course, but I don't believe in a Master Criminal. I'd say there was a very clever little Board of Directors behind this. Centrally planned, with a Chairman. They've got on to something good, and they're improving their technique all the time. All the same –'

'Yes?' said Sir Ronald encouragingly.

'Even in a right tight little team, there are probably expendables. What I call the Russian Sledge principle. From time to time, if they think we might be getting hot on the scent, they throw off one of them, the one they think they can best afford.'

'Would they dare to do that? Wouldn't it be rather risky?'

'I'd say it could be done in such a way that whoever it was wouldn't even know he *had* been pushed off the sledge. He'd just think he'd fallen off. He'd keep quiet because he'd think it was worth his while to keep quiet. So it would be, of course. They've got plenty of money to play with, and they can afford to be generous. Family looked after, if he's got one, whilst he's in prison. Possibly an escape engineered.'

'There's been too much of that,' said Comstock.

'I think, you know,' said Sir Ronald, 'that it's not much good going over and over our speculations again. We always say much the same thing.'

McNeill laughed.

'What is it you really wanted us for, sir?'

'Well –' Sir Ronald thought a moment, 'we're all agreed on the main things,' he said slowly. 'We're agreed on our main policy, on what we're trying to do. I think it *might* be profitable to have a look around for some of the small things, the things that don't matter much, that are just a bit out of the usual run. It's hard to explain what I mean, but like that business some years ago in the Culver case. An ink stain. Do you remember? An ink stain round a mouse-hole. Now why on earth should a man empty a bottle of ink into a mouse-hole? It didn't seem important. It was hard to get at the answer. But when we did hit on the answer, it led somewhere. That's – roughly – the sort of thing I was thinking about. Odd things. Don't mind saying if you come across something that strikes you as a bit out of the usual. Petty if you like, but irritating, because it doesn't quite fit in. I see Father's nodding his head.'

'Couldn't agree with you more,' said Chief-Inspector Davy. 'Come on, boys, try to come up with something. Even if it's only a man wearing a funny hat.'

There was no immediate response. Everyone looked a little uncertain and doubtful.

'Come on,' said Father. 'I'll stick my neck out first. It's just a funny story, really, but you might as well have it for what it's worth. The London and Metropolitan Bank hold-up. Carmolly Street Branch. Remember it? A whole list of car numbers and car colours and makes. We appealed to people to come forward and they responded – how they responded! About a hundred and fifty pieces of misleading information! Got it sorted out in the end to about seven cars that had been seen in the neighbourhood, any one of which *might* have been concerned in the robbery.'

'Yes,' said Sir Ronald, 'go on.'

'There were one or two we couldn't get tags on. Looked as though the numbers might have been changed. Nothing out of the way in that. It's often done. Most of them got tracked down in the end. I'll just bring up one instance. Morris Oxford, black saloon, number CMG 265, reported by a probation officer. He said it was being driven by Mr Justice Ludgrove.'

He looked round. They were listening to him, but without any manifest interest.

'I know,' he said, 'wrong as usual. Mr Justice Ludgrove is a rather noticeable old boy, ugly as sin for one thing. Well, it wasn't Mr Justice Ludgrove because at that exact time he was actually in Court. He *has* got a Morris Oxford, but its number isn't CMG 256.' He looked round. 'All right. All right. So there's no point in it, you'll say. But do you know what the number *was*? CMG 265. Near enough, eh? Just the sort of mistake one does make when you're trying to remember a car number.'

'I'm sorry,' said Sir Ronald, 'I don't quite see –'

'No,' said Chief-Inspector Davy, 'there's nothing *to* see really, is there? Only – it was very like the actual car number, wasn't it? 265 – 256 CMG. Really rather a coincidence that there should be a Morris Oxford car of the right colour with the number just one digit wrong, and with a man in it closely resembling the owner of the car.'

'Do you mean –?'

'Just one little digit difference. Today's "deliberate mistake". It almost seems like that.'

'Sorry, Davy. I still don't get it.'

'Oh, I don't suppose there's anything *to* get. There's a Morris Oxford car, CMG 265, proceeding along the street two and a half minutes after the bank snatch. In it, the probation officer recognizes Mr Justice Ludgrove.'

'Are you suggesting it really *was* Mr Justice Ludgrove? Come now, Davy.'

'No, I'm not suggesting that it was Mr Justice Ludgrove and that he was mixed up in a bank robbery. He was staying at Bertram's Hotel in Pond Street, and he was at the Law Courts at that exact time. All proved up to the hilt. I'm saying the car number and make and the identification by a probation officer who knows old Ludgrove quite well by sight is the kind of coincidence that *ought* to mean something. Apparently it doesn't. Too bad.'

Comstock stirred uneasily.

'There was another case like that in connection with the jewellery business at Brighton. Some old Admiral or other. I've forgotten his name now. Some woman identified him most positively as having been on the scene.'

'And he wasn't?'

'No, he'd been in London that night. Went up for some Naval dinner or other, I think.'

'Staying at his club?'

'No, he was staying at a hotel – I believe it was that one you mentioned just now, Father, Bertram's, isn't it? Quiet place. A lot of old service geezers go there, I believe.'

'Bertram's Hotel,' said Chief-Inspector Davy, thoughtfully.

CHAPTER 5

Miss Marple awoke early because she always woke early. She was appreciative of her bed. Most comfortable.

She pattered across to the window and pulled the curtains, admitting a little pallid London daylight. As yet, however, she did not try to dispense with the electric light. A very nice bedroom they had given her, again quite in the tradition of Bertram's. A rose-flowered wallpaper, a large well-polished mahogany chest of drawers – a dressing-table to correspond. Two upright chairs, one easy chair of a reasonable height from the ground. A connecting door led to a bathroom which was modern but which had a tiled wallpaper of roses and so avoided any suggestion of over-frigid hygiene.

Miss Marple got back into bed, plumped her pillows up, glanced at her clock, half-past seven, picked up the small devotional book that always accompanied her, and read as usual the page and a half allotted to the day. Then she picked up her knitting and began to knit, slowly at first, since her fingers were stiff and rheumatic when she first awoke, but very soon her pace grew faster, and her fingers lost their painful stiffness.

'Another day,' said Miss Marple to herself, greeting the fact with her usual gentle pleasure. Another day – and who knew what it might bring forth?

She relaxed, and abandoning her knitting, let thoughts pass in an idle stream through her head . . . Selina Hazy . . . what a pretty cottage she had had in St Mary Mead – and now someone had put on that ugly green roof . . . Muffins . . . very wasteful in butter . . . but very good . . . And fancy serving old-fashioned seed cake! She had never expected, not for a moment, that things would be as much like they used to be . . . because, after all, Time didn't stand still . . . And to have made it stand still in this way must really have cost a lot of money . . . Not a bit of plastic in the place! . . . It must pay them, she supposed. The out-of-date returns in due course as the picturesque . . . Look how people wanted old-fashioned roses now, and scorned hybrid teas! . . . None of this place seemed real at all . . . Well, why should it? . . . It was fifty – no, nearer sixty years since she had stayed here. And it didn't seem real to her because she was now acclimatized in this present year of Our Lord – Really, the whole thing opened up a very interesting set of problems . . . The atmosphere and the *people* . . . Miss Marple's fingers pushed her knitting farther away from her.

'Pockets,' she said aloud . . . 'Pockets, I suppose . . . And quite difficult to find . . .'

Would that account for that curious feeling of uneasiness she had had last night? That feeling that something was wrong . . .

All those elderly people – really very much like those she remembered when she had stayed here fifty years ago. They had been natural then – but they weren't very natural now. Elderly people nowadays weren't like elderly people then – they had that worried harried look of domestic anxieties with which they are too tired to cope, or they rushed around to committees and tried to appear bustling and competent, or they dyed their hair gentian blue, or wore wigs, and their hands were not the hands she remembered, tapering, delicate hands – they were harsh from washing up and detergents . . .

And so – well, so these people didn't look real. But the point was that they *were* real. Selina Hazy was real. And that rather handsome old military man in the corner was real – she had met him once, although she did not recall his name – and the Bishop (dear Robbie!) was dead.

Miss Marple glanced at her little clock. It was eight-thirty. Time for her breakfast.

She examined the instructions given by the hotel – splendid big print so that it wasn't necessary to put one's spectacles on.

Meals could be ordered through the telephone by asking for Room Service, or you could press the bell labelled Chambermaid.

Miss Marple did the latter. Talking to Room Service always flustered her.

The result was excellent. In no time at all there was a tap on the door and a highly satisfactory chambermaid appeared. A real chambermaid looking unreal, wearing a striped lavender print dress and actually a *cap*, a freshly laundered cap. A smiling, rosy, positively *countrified* face. (Where did they *find* these people?)

Miss Marple ordered her breakfast. Tea, poached eggs, fresh rolls. So adept was the chambermaid that she did not even mention cereals or orange juice.

Five minutes later breakfast came. A comfortable tray with a big pot-bellied teapot, creamy-looking milk, a silver hot water jug. Two beautifully poached eggs on toast, poached the proper way, not little round hard bullets shaped in tin cups, a good-sized round of butter stamped with a thistle. Marmalade, honey and strawberry jam. Delicious-looking rolls, not the hard kind with papery interiors – they *smelt* of fresh bread (the most delicious smell in the world!). There was also an apple, a pear and a banana.

Miss Marple inserted a knife gingerly but with confidence. She was not disappointed. Rich deep yellow yolk oozed out, thick and creamy. *Proper* eggs!

Everything's piping hot. A *real* breakfast. She could have cooked it herself but she hadn't had to! It was brought to her as if – no, not as though she were a queen – as though she were a middle-aged lady staying in a good but not unduly expensive hotel. In fact – back to

1909. Miss Marple expressed appreciation to the chambermaid who replied smiling,

'Oh, yes, Madam, the Chef is very particular about his breakfasts.'

Miss Marple studied her appraisingly. Bertram's Hotel could certainly produce marvels. A *real* housemaid. She pinched her left arm surreptitiously.

'Have you been here long?' she asked.

'Just over three years, Madam.'

'And before that?'

'I was in a hotel at Eastbourne. Very modern and up-to-date – but I prefer an old-fashioned place like this.'

Miss Marple took a sip of tea. She found herself humming in a vague way – words fitting themselves to a long-forgotten song.

'Oh where have you been all my life . . .'

The chambermaid was looking slightly startled.

'I was just remembering an old song,' twittered Miss Marple apologetically. 'Very popular at one time.'

Again she sang softly. 'Oh where have you been all my life . . .'

'Perhaps you know it?' she asked.

'Well –' The chambermaid looked rather apologetic.

'Too long ago for you,' said Miss Marple. 'Ah well, one gets to remembering things – in a place like this.'

'Yes, Madam, a lot of the ladies who stay here feel like that, I think.'

'It's partly why they come, I expect,' said Miss Marple.

The chambermaid went out. She was obviously used to old ladies who twittered and reminisced.

Miss Marple finished her breakfast, and got up in a pleasant leisurely fashion. She had a plan ready made for a delightful morning of shopping. Not too much – to over-tire herself. Oxford Street today, perhaps. And tomorrow Knightsbridge. She planned ahead happily.

It was about ten o'clock when she emerged from her room fully equipped: hat, gloves, umbrella – just in case, though it looked fine – handbag – her smartest shopping bag –

The door next but one on the corridor opened sharply and someone looked out. It was Bess Sedgwick. She withdrew back into the room and closed the door sharply.

Miss Marple wondered as she went down the stairs. She preferred the stairs to the lift first thing in the morning. It limbered her up. Her steps grew slower and slower . . . she stopped.

As Colonel Luscombe strode along the passage from his room, a door at the top of the stairs opened sharply and Lady Sedgwick spoke to him.

'There you are at last! I've been on the look-out for you – waiting to pounce. Where can we go and talk? That is to say without falling over some old pussy every second.'

'Well, really, Bess, I'm not quite sure – I think on the mezzanine floor there's a sort of writing-room.'

'You'd better come in here. Quick now, before the chambermaid gets peculiar ideas about us.'

Rather unwillingly, Colonel Luscombe stepped across the threshold and had the door shut firmly behind him.

'I'd no idea you would be staying here, Bess, I hadn't the faintest idea of it.'

'I don't suppose you had.'

'I mean – I would never have brought Elvira here. I *have* got Elvira here, you know?'

'Yes, I saw her with you last night.'

'But I really didn't know that you were here. It seemed such an unlikely place for you.'

'I don't see why,' said Bess Sedgwick, coldly. 'It's far and away the most comfortable hotel in London. Why shouldn't I stay here?'

'You must understand that I hadn't any idea of . . . I mean –'

She looked at him and laughed. She was dressed ready to go out in a well cut dark suit and a shirt of bright emerald green. She looked gay and very much alive. Beside her, Colonel Luscombe looked rather old and faded.

'Darling Derek, don't look so worried. I'm not accusing you of trying to stage a mother and daughter sentimental meeting. It's just one of those things that happen; where people meet each other in unsuspected places. But you *must* get Elvira out of here, Derek. You must get her out of it at once – today.'

'Oh, she's going. I mean, I only brought her here just for a couple of nights. Do a show – that sort of thing. She's going down to the Melfords' tomorrow.'

'Poor girl, that'll be boring for her.'

Luscombe looked at her with concern. 'Do you think she will be very bored?'

Bess took pity on him.

'Probably not after duress in Italy. She might even think it wildly thrilling.'

Luscombe took his courage in both hands.

'Look here, Bess, I was startled to find you here, but don't you think it – well, you know, it might be *meant* in a way. I mean that it might be an opportunity – I don't think you really know how – well, how the girl might feel.'

'What are you trying to say, Derek?'

'Well, you *are* her mother, you know.'

'Of course I'm her mother. She's my daughter. And what good has that fact ever been to either of us, or ever will be?'

'You can't be sure. I think – I think she feels it.'

'What gives you that idea?' said Bess Sedgwick sharply.

'Something she said yesterday. She asked where you were, what you were doing.'

Bess Sedgwick walked across the room to the window. She stood there a moment tapping on the pane.

'You're so nice, Derek,' she said. 'You have such nice ideas. But they don't work, my poor angel. That's what you've got to say to yourself. They don't work and they might be dangerous.'

'Oh come now, Bess. Dangerous?'

'Yes, yes, yes. Dangerous. *I'm* dangerous. I've always been dangerous.'

'When I think of some of the things you've done,' said Colonel Luscombe.

'That's my own business,' said Bess Sedgwick. 'Running into danger has become a kind of habit with me. No, I wouldn't say habit. More an addiction. Like a drug. Like that nice little dollop of heroin addicts have to have every so often to make life seem bright coloured and worth living. Well, that's all right. That's my funeral – or not – as the case may be. I've never taken drugs – never needed them – Danger has been my drug. But people who live as I do can be a source of harm to others. Now don't be an obstinate old fool, Derek. You keep that girl well away from me. I can do her no good. Only harm. If possible, don't even let her know I was staying in the same hotel. Ring up the Melfords and take her down there *today*. Make some excuse about a sudden emergency –'

Colonel Luscombe hesitated, pulling his moustaches.

'I think you're making a mistake, Bess.' He sighed. 'She asked where you were. I told her you were abroad.'

'Well, I shall be in another twelve hours, so that all fits very nicely.'

She came up to him, kissed him on the point of his chin, turned him smartly around as though they were about to play Blind Man's Buff, opened the door, gave him a gentle little propelling shove out of it. As the door shut behind him, Colonel Luscombe noticed an old lady turning the corner from the stairs. She was muttering to herself as she looked into her handbag. 'Dear, dear me. I suppose I must have left it in my room. Oh dear.'

She passed Colonel Luscombe without paying much attention to him apparently, but as he went on down the stairs Miss Marple paused by her room door and directed a piercing glance after him. Then she looked towards Bess Sedgwick's door. 'So that's who she was waiting for,' said Miss Marple to herself. 'I wonder why.'

Canon Pennyfather, fortified by breakfast, wandered across the lounge, remembered to leave his key at the desk, pushed his way through the swinging doors, and was neatly inserted into a taxi by the Irish commissionaire who existed for this purpose.

'Where to, sir?'

'Oh dear,' said Canon Pennyfather in sudden dismay. 'Now let me see – where *was* I going?'

The traffic in Pond Street was held up for some minutes whilst Canon Pennyfather and the commissionaire debated this knotty point.

Finally Canon Pennyfather had a brainwave and the taxi was directed to go to the British Museum.

The commissionaire was left on the pavement with a broad grin on his face, and since no other exits seemed to be taking place, he strolled a little way along the façade of the hotel whistling an old tune in a muted manner.

One of the windows on the ground floor of Bertram's was flung up – but the commissionaire did not even turn his head until a voice spoke unexpectedly through the open window.

'So this is where you've landed up, Micky. What on earth brought you to this place?'

He swung round, startled – and stared.

Lady Sedgwick thrust her head through the open window.

'Don't you know me?' she demanded.

A sudden gleam of recognition came across the man's face.

'Why, if it isn't little Bessie now! Fancy that! After all these years. Little Bessie.'

'Nobody but you ever called me Bessie. It's a revolting name. What have you been doing all these years?'

'This and that,' said Micky with some reserve. 'I've not been in the news like you have. I've read of your doings in the paper time and again.'

Bess Sedgwick laughed. 'Anyway, I've worn better than you have,' she said. 'You drink too much. You always did.'

'You've worn well because you've always been in the money.'

'Money wouldn't have done you any good. You'd have drunk even more and gone to the dogs completely. Oh yes, you would! What brought you *here*? That's what I want to know. How did you ever get taken on at this place?'

'I wanted a job. I had these −' his hand flicked over the row of medals.

'Yes, I see.' She was thoughtful. 'All genuine too, aren't they?'

'Sure they're genuine. Why shouldn't they be?'

'Oh I believe you. You always had courage. You've always been a good fighter. Yes, the army suited you. I'm sure of that.'

'The army's all right in time of war, but it's no good in peace time.'

'So you took to this stuff. I hadn't the least idea −' she stopped.

'You hadn't the least idea what, Bessie?'

'Nothing. It's queer seeing you again after all these years.'

'*I* haven't forgotten,' said the man. 'I've never forgotten you, little Bessie. Ah! A lovely girl you were! A lovely slip of a girl.'

'A damn' fool of a girl, that's what I was,' said Lady Sedgwick.

'That's true now. You hadn't much sense. If you had, you wouldn't have taken up with me. What hands you had for a horse. Do you remember that mare − what was her name now? − Molly O'Flynn. Ah, she was a wicked devil, that one was.'

'You were the only one that could ride her,' said Lady Sedgwick.

'She'd have had me off if she could! When she found she couldn't, she gave in. Ah, she was a beauty, now. But talking of sitting a horse, there wasn't one lady in those parts better than you. A lovely seat you had, lovely hands. Never any fear in you, not for a minute! And it's been the same ever since, so I judge. Aeroplanes, racing cars.'

Bess Sedgwick laughed.

'I must get on with my letters.'

She drew back from the window.

Micky leaned over the railing. 'I've not forgotten Ballygowlan,' he said with meaning. 'Sometimes I've thought of writing to you −'

Bess Sedgwick's voice came out harshly.

'And what do you mean by that, Mick Gorman?'

'I was just saying as I haven't forgotten – anything. I was just – reminding you like.'

Bess Sedgwick's voice still held its harsh note.

'If you mean what I think you mean, I'll give you a piece of advice. Any trouble from you, and I'd shoot you as easily as I'd shoot a rat. I've shot men before –'

'In foreign parts, maybe –'

'Foreign parts or here – it's all the same to me.'

'Ah, good Lord, now, and I believe you would do just that!' His voice held admiration. 'In Ballygowlan –'

'In Ballygowlan,' she cut in, 'they paid you to keep your mouth shut and paid you well. You took the money. You'll get no more from me so don't think it.'

'It would be a nice romantic story for the Sunday papers . . .'

'You heard what I said.'

'Ah,' he laughed, 'I'm not serious, I was just joking. I'd never do anything to hurt my little Bessie. I'll keep my mouth shut.'

'Mind you do,' said Lady Sedgwick.

She shut down the window. Staring down at the desk in front of her she looked at her unfinished letter on the blotting paper. She picked it up, looked at it, crumpled it into a ball and slung it into the waste-paper basket. Then abruptly she got up from her seat and walked out of the room. She did not even cast a glance around her before she went.

The smaller writing-rooms at Bertram's often had an appearance of being empty even when they were not. Two well-appointed desks stood in the windows, there was a table on the right that held a few magazines, on the left were two very high-backed arm-chairs turned towards the fire. These were favourite spots in the afternoon for elderly military or naval gentlemen to ensconce themselves and fall happily asleep until tea-time. Anyone coming in to write a letter did not usually even notice them. The chairs were not so much in demand during the morning.

As it happened, however, they were on this particular morning both occupied. An old lady was in one and a young girl in the other. The young girl rose to her feet. She stood a moment looking uncertainly towards the door through which Lady Sedgwick had passed out, then she moved slowly towards it. Elvira Blake's face was deadly pale.

It was another five minutes before the old lady moved. Then Miss Marple decided that the little rest which she always took after dressing and coming downstairs had lasted quite long enough. It was time to go out and enjoy the pleasures of London. She might walk as far as Piccadilly, and take a No. 9 bus to High Street, Kensington, or she might walk along to Bond Street and take a 25 bus to Marshall & Snelgrove's, or she might take a 25 the other way which as far as she remembered would land her up at the Army & Navy Stores. Passing through the swing doors she was still savouring these delights in her mind. The Irish commissionaire, back on duty, made up her mind for her.

'You'll be wanting a taxi, Ma'am,' he said with firmness.

'I don't think I do,' said Miss Marple. 'I think there's a 25 bus I could take quite near here – or a 2 from Park Lane.'

'You'll not be wanting a bus,' said the commissionaire firmly. 'It's very dangerous springing on a bus when you're getting on in life. The way they start and stop and go on again. Jerk you off your feet, they do. No heart at all, these fellows, nowadays. I'll whistle you along a taxi and you'll go to wherever you want to like a queen.'

Miss Marple considered and fell.

'Very well then,' she said, 'perhaps I *had* better have a taxi.'

The commissionaire had no need even to whistle. He merely clicked his thumb and a taxi appeared like magic. Miss Marple was helped into it with every possible care and decided on the spur of the moment to go to Robinson & Cleaver's and look at their splendid offer of real linen sheets. She sat happily in her taxi feeling indeed as the commissionaire had promised her, just like a queen. Her mind was filled with pleasurable anticipation of linen sheets, linen pillow cases and proper glass- and kitchen-cloths without pictures of bananas, figs or performing dogs and other pictorial distractions to annoy you when you were washing up.

Lady Sedgwick came up to the Reception desk.

'Mr Humfries in his office?'

'Yes, Lady Sedgwick.' Miss Gorringe looked startled.

Lady Sedgwick passed behind the desk, tapped on the door and went in without waiting for any response.

Mr Humfries looked up startled.

'What –'

'Who engaged the man Michael Gorman?'

Mr Humfries spluttered a little.

'Parfitt left – he had a car accident a month ago. We had to replace him quickly. This man seemed all right. References OK – ex-Army –

quite good record – not very bright perhaps – but that's all the better sometimes – you don't know anything against him, do you?'

'Enough not to want him here.'

'If you insist,' Humfries said slowly, 'we'll give him his notice –'

'No,' said Lady Sedgwick slowly. 'No – it's too late for that – Never mind.'

CHAPTER 6

'Elvira.'

'Hallo, Bridget.'

The Hon. Elvira Blake pushed her way through the front door of 180 Onslow Square, which her friend Bridget had rushed down to open for her, having been watching through the window.

'Let's go upstairs,' said Elvira.

'Yes, we'd better. Otherwise we'll get entangled by Mummy.'

The two girls rushed up the stairs, thereby circumventing Bridget's mother, who came out on to the landing from her own bedroom just too late.

'You really are lucky not to have a mother,' said Bridget, rather breathlessly as she took her friend into her bedroom and shut the door firmly. 'I mean, Mummy's quite a pet and all that, but the *questions* she asks! Morning, noon and night. Where are you going, and who have you met? And are they cousins of somebody else of the same name in Yorkshire? I mean, the *futility* of it all.'

'I suppose they have nothing else to think about,' said Elvira vaguely. 'Look here, Bridget, there's something terribly important I've got to do, and you've got to help me.'

'Well, I will if I can. What is it – a man?'

'No, it isn't, as a matter of fact.' Bridget looked disappointed. 'I've got to get away to Ireland for twenty-four hours or perhaps longer, and you've got to cover up for me.'

'To Ireland? Why?'

'I can't tell you all about it now. There's no time. I've got to meet my guardian, Colonel Luscombe, at Prunier's for lunch at half-past one.'

'What have you done with the Carpenter?'

'Gave her the slip in Debenhams.'

Bridget giggled.

'And after lunch they're taking me down to the Melfords. I'm going to live with them until I'm twenty-one.'

'How ghastly!'

'I expect I shall manage. Cousin Mildred is fearfully easy to deceive. It's arranged I'm to come up for classes and things. There's a place called World of Today. They take you to lectures and to Museums and to Picture Galleries and the House of Lords, and all that. The whole point is that nobody will know whether you're where you ought to be or not! We'll manage lots of things.'

'I expect we will.' Bridget giggled. 'We managed in Italy, didn't we? Old Macaroni thought she was so strict. Little did she know what we got up to when we tried.'

Both girls laughed in the pleasant consciousness of successful wickedness.

'Still, it did need a lot of planning,' said Elvira.

'And some splendid lying,' said Bridget. 'Have you heard from Guido?'

'Oh yes, he wrote me a long letter signed Ginevra as though he was a girl friend. But I do wish you'd stop talking so much, Bridget. We've got a lot to do and only about an hour and a half to do it in. Now first of all just *listen*. I'm coming up tomorrow for an appointment with the dentist. That's easy, I can put it off by telephone – or you can from here. Then, about midday, you can ring up the Melfords pretending to be your mother and explain that the dentist wants to see me again the next day and so I'm staying over with you here.'

'That ought to go down all right. They'll say how very kind and gush. But supposing you're *not* back the next day?'

'Then you'll have to do some more ringing up.'

Bridget looked doubtful.

'We'll have lots of time to think up something before then,' said Elvira impatiently. 'What's worrying me now is *money*. You haven't got any, I suppose?' Elvira spoke without much hope.

'Only about two pounds.'

'That's no good. I've got to buy my air ticket. I've looked up the flights. It only takes about two hours. A lot depends upon how long it takes me when I get there.'

'Can't you tell me what you're going to do?'

'No, I can't. But it's terribly, terribly important.'

Elvira's voice was so different that Bridget looked at her in some surprise.

'Is anything really the matter, Elvira?'

'Yes, it is.'

'Is it something nobody's got to know about?'

'Yes, that's the sort of thing. It's frightfully, frightfully secret. I've got to find out if something is really true or not. It's a bore about the money. What's maddening is that I'm really quite rich. My guardian told me so. But all they give me is a measly dress allowance. And that seems to go as soon as I get it.'

'Wouldn't your guardian – Colonel Thingummybob – lend you some money?'

'That wouldn't do at all. He'd ask a lot of questions and want to know what I wanted it for.'

'Oh, dear, I suppose he would. I can't think why everybody wants to ask so many questions. Do you know that if somebody rings me up, Mummy has to ask *who it is*? When it really is *no* business of hers!'

Elvira agreed, but her mind was on another tack.

'Have you ever pawned anything, Bridget?'

'Never. I don't think I'd know how to.'

'It's quite easy, I believe,' said Elvira. 'You go to the sort of jeweller who has three balls over the door, isn't that right?'

'I don't think I've got anything that would be any good taking to a pawnbroker,' said Bridget.

'Hasn't your mother got some jewellery somewhere?'

'I don't think we'd better ask her to help.'

'No, perhaps not – But we could pinch something perhaps.'

'Oh, I don't think we could do that,' said Bridget, shocked.

'No? Well, perhaps you're right. But I bet she wouldn't notice. We could get it back before she missed it. *I* know. We'll go to Mr Bollard.'

'Who's Mr Bollard?'

'Oh, he's a sort of family jeweller. I take my watch there always to have it mended. He's known me ever since I was six. Come on, Bridget, we'll go there right away. We'll just have time.'

'We'd better go out the back way,' said Bridget, 'and then Mummy won't ask us where we're going.'

Outside the old-established business of Bollard and Whitley in Bond Street the two girls made their final arrangements.

'Are you sure you understand, Bridget?'

'I think so,' said Bridget in a far from happy voice.

'First,' said Elvira, 'we synchronize our watches.'

Bridget brightened up a little. This familiar literary phrase had a heartening effect. They solemnly synchronized their watches, Bridget adjusting hers by one minute.

'Zero hour will be twenty-five past exactly,' said Elvira.

'That will give me plenty of time. Perhaps even more than I need, but it's better that way about.'

'But supposing –' began Bridget.

'Supposing what?' asked Elvira.

'Well, I mean, supposing I *really* got run over?'

'Of course you won't get run over,' said Elvira. 'You know how nippy you are on your feet, and all London traffic is used to pulling up suddenly. It'll be all right.'

Bridget looked far from convinced.

'You won't let me down, Bridget, will you?'

'All right,' said Bridget, 'I won't let you down.'

'Good,' said Elvira.

Bridget crossed to the other side of Bond Street and Elvira pushed open the doors of Messrs Bollard and Whitley, old-established jewellers and watchmakers. Inside there was a beautiful and hushed atmosphere. A frock-coated nobleman came forward and asked Elvira what he could do for her.

'Could I see Mr Bollard?'

'Mr Bollard. What name shall I say?'

'Miss Elvira Blake.'

The nobleman disappeared and Elvira drifted to a counter where, below plate glass, brooches, rings and bracelets showed off their jewelled proportions against suitable shades of velvet. In a very few moments Mr Bollard made his appearance. He was the senior partner of the firm, an elderly man of sixty odd. He greeted Elvira with warm friendliness.

'Ah, Miss Blake, so you are in London. It's a great pleasure to see you. Now what can I do for you?'

Elvira produced a dainty little evening wrist-watch.

'This watch doesn't go properly,' said Elvira. 'Could you do something to it?'

'Oh yes, of course. There's no difficulty about *that*.' Mr Bollard took it from her. 'What address shall I send it to?'

Elvira gave the address.

'And there's another thing,' she said. 'My guardian – Colonel Luscombe you know –'

'Yes, yes, of course.'

'He asked me what I'd like for a Christmas present,' said Elvira. 'He suggested I should come in here and look at some different things. He said would I like him to come with me, and I said I'd rather come along first – because I always think it's rather embarrassing, don't you? I mean, prices and all that.'

'Well, that's certainly one aspect,' said Mr Bollard, beaming in an avuncular manner. 'Now what had you in mind, Miss Blake? A brooch, bracelet – a ring?'

'I think really brooches are more useful,' said Elvira. 'But I wonder – could I look at a *lot* of things?' She looked up at him appealingly. He smiled sympathetically.

'Of course, of course. No pleasure at all if one has to make up one's mind too quickly, is it?'

The next five minutes were spent very agreeably. Nothing was too much trouble for Mr Bollard. He fetched things from one case and another, brooches and bracelets piled up on the piece of velvet spread in front of Elvira. Occasionally she turned aside to look at herself in a mirror, trying the effect of a brooch or a pendant. Finally, rather uncertainly, a pretty little bangle, a small diamond wrist-watch and two brooches were laid aside.

'We'll make a note of these,' said Mr Bollard, 'and then when Colonel Luscombe is in London next, perhaps he'll come in and see what he decides himself he'd like to give you.'

'I think that way will be very nice,' said Elvira. 'Then he'll feel more that he's chosen my present himself, won't he?' Her limpid blue gaze was raised to the jeweller's face. That same blue gaze had registered a moment earlier that the time was now exactly twenty-five minutes past the hour.

Outside there was the squealing of brakes and a girl's loud scream. Inevitably the eyes of everyone in the shop turned towards the windows of the shop giving on Bond Street. The movement of Elvira's hand on the counter in front of her and then to the pocket of her neat tailor-made coat and skirt was so rapid and unobtrusive as to be almost unnoticeable, even if anybody had been looking.

'Tcha, tcha,' said Mr Bollard, turning back from where he had been peering out into the street. 'Very nearly an accident. Silly girl! Rushing across the road like that.'

Elvira was already moving towards the door. She looked at her wrist-watch and uttered an exclamation.

'Oh dear, I've been far too long in here. I shall miss my train back to the country. Thank you *so* much, Mr Bollard, and you won't forget which the four things are, will you?'

In another minute, she was out of the door. Turning rapidly to the left and then to the left again, she stopped in the arcade of a shoe shop until Bridget, rather breathless, rejoined her.

'Oh,' said Bridget, 'I was terrified. I thought I was going to be killed. And I've torn a hole in my stocking, too.'

'Never mind,' said Elvira and walked her friend rapidly along the street and round yet another corner to the right. 'Come on.'

'Is it – was it – all right?'

Elvira's hand slipped into her pocket and out again showing the diamond and sapphire bracelet in her palm.

'Oh, Elvira, how you dared!'

'Now, Bridget, you've got to get along to that pawnshop we marked down. Go in and see how much you can get for this. Ask for a hundred.'

'Do you think – supposing they say – I mean – I mean, it might be on a list of stolen things –'

'Don't be silly. How could it be on a list so soon? They haven't even noticed it's gone yet.'

'But Elvira, when they *do* notice it's gone, they'll think – perhaps they'll know – that you must have taken it.'

'They *might* think so – if they discover it soon.'

'Well, then they'll go to the police and –'

She stopped as Elvira shook her head slowly, her pale yellow hair swinging to and fro and a faint enigmatic smile curving up the corners of her mouth.

'They won't go to the police, Bridget. Certainly not if they think *I* took it.'

'Why – you mean –?'

'As I told you, I'm going to have a lot of money when I'm twenty-one. I shall be able to buy lots of jewels from them. *They* won't make a scandal. Go on and get the money quick. Then go to Aer Lingus and book the ticket – I must take a taxi to Prunier's. I'm already ten minutes late. I'll be with you tomorrow morning by half-past ten.'

'Oh, Elvira, I wish you wouldn't take such frightful risks,' moaned Bridget.

But Elvira had hailed a taxi.

Miss Marple had a very enjoyable time at Robinson & Cleaver's. Besides purchasing expensive but delicious sheets – she loved linen sheets with their texture and their coolness – she also indulged in a purchase of good quality red-bordered glass-cloths. Really the difficulty in getting proper glass-cloths nowadays! Instead, you were offered things that might as well have been ornamental table-cloths, decorated with radishes or lobsters or the *Tour Eiffel* or Trafalgar Square, or else littered with lemons and oranges. Having given her address in St Mary Mead, Miss Marple found a convenient bus which took her to the Army & Navy Stores.

The Army & Navy Stores had been a haunt of Miss Marple's aunt in days long gone. It was not, of course, quite the same nowadays. Miss Marple cast her thoughts back to Aunt Helen seeking out her own special man in the grocery department, settling herself comfortably in a chair, wearing a bonnet and what she always called her 'black poplin' mantle. Then there would ensue a long hour with nobody in a hurry and Aunt Helen thinking of every conceivable grocery that could be purchased and stored up for future use. Christmas was provided for, and there was even a far-off look towards Easter. The young Jane had fidgeted somewhat, and had been told to go and look at the glass department by way of amusement.

Having finished her purchases, Aunt Helen would then proceed to lengthy inquiries about her chosen shop-assistant's mother, wife, second boy and crippled sister-in-law. Having had a thoroughly pleasant morning, Aunt Helen would say in the playful manner of those times, 'And how would a little girl feel about some luncheon?' Whereupon they went up in the lift to the fourth floor and had luncheon which always finished with a strawberry ice. After that, they bought half a pound of coffee chocolate creams and went to a matinée in a four wheeler.

Of course, the Army & Navy Stores had had a good many face lifts since those days. In fact, it was now quite unrecognizable from the old times. It was gayer and much brighter. Miss Marple, though throwing a kindly and indulgent smile at the past, did not object to the amenities of the present. There was still a restaurant, and there she repaired to order her lunch.

As she was looking carefully down the menu and deciding what to have, she looked across the room and her eyebrows went up a little. How extraordinary coincidence was! Here was a woman she had never seen till the day before, though she had seen plenty of newspaper photographs of her – at race meetings, in Bermuda, or standing by her own plane or car. Yesterday, for the first time, she had seen her in the flesh. And now, as was so often the case, there was the coincidence of running into her again in a most unlikely place. For somehow she did not connect lunch at the Army & Navy Stores with Bess Sedgwick. She would not have been surprised to see Bess Sedgwick emerging from a den in Soho, or stepping out of Covent Garden Opera House in evening dress with a diamond tiara on her head. But somehow, not in the Army & Navy Stores which in Miss Marple's mind was, and always would be, connected with the armed forces, their wives, daughters, aunts and grandmothers. Still, there Bess Sedgwick was, looking as usual very smart, in her dark suit and her emerald shirt, lunching at a table with a man. A young man with a lean hawklike face, wearing a black leather jacket. They were leaning forward talking earnestly together, forking in mouthfuls of food as though they were quite unaware what they were eating.

An assignation, perhaps? Yes, probably an assignation. The man must be fifteen or twenty years younger than she was – but Bess Sedgwick was a magnetically attractive woman.

Miss Marple looked at the young man consideringly and decided that he was what she called a 'handsome fellow'. She also decided that she didn't like him very much. 'Just like Harry Russell,' said Miss Marple to herself, dredging up a prototype as usual from the past. 'Never up to any good. Never did any woman who had anything to do with him any good either.

'She wouldn't take advice from me,' thought Miss Marple, 'but I could give her some.' However, other people's love affairs were no concern of hers, and Bess Sedgwick, by all accounts, could take care of herself very well when it came to love affairs.

Miss Marple sighed, ate her lunch, and meditated a visit to the stationery department.

Curiosity, or what she preferred herself to call 'taking an interest' in other people's affairs, was undoubtedly one of Miss Marple's characteristics.

Deliberately leaving her gloves on the table, she rose and crossed the floor to the cash desk, taking a route that passed close to Lady Sedgwick's table. Having paid her bill she 'discovered' the absence of her gloves and returned to get them – unfortunately dropping her handbag on the return route. It came open and spilled various oddments. A waitress rushed to assist her in picking them up, and Miss Marple was forced to show a great shakiness and dropped coppers and keys a second time.

She did not get very much by these subterfuges but they were not entirely in vain – and it was interesting that neither of the two objects of her curiosity spared as much as a glance for the dithery old lady who kept dropping things.

As Miss Marple waited for the lift down she memorized such scraps as she had heard.

'*What about the weather forecast?*'

'*OK. No fog.*'

'*All set for Lucerne?*'

'*Yes. Plane leaves 9.40.*'

That was all she had got the first time. On the way back it had lasted a little longer.

Bess Sedgwick had been speaking angrily.

'*What possessed you to come to Bertram's yesterday – you shouldn't have come near the place.*'

'*It's all right. I asked if you were staying there and everyone knows we're close friends –*'

'*That's not the point. Bertram's is all right for me – Not for you. You stick out like a sore thumb. Everyone stares at you.*'

'*Let them!*'

'*You really are an idiot. Why – why? What reasons did you have? You had a reason – I know you . . .*'

'*Calm down, Bess.*'

'*You're such a liar!*'

That was all she had been able to hear. She found it interesting.

CHAPTER 7

On the evening of 19th November Canon Pennyfather had finished an early dinner at the Athenaeum, he had nodded to one or two friends, had had a pleasant acrimonious discussion on some crucial points of the dating of the Dead Sea Scrolls and now, glancing at his watch, saw that it was time to leave to catch his plane to Lucerne. As he passed through the hall he was greeted by one more friend: Dr Whittaker of the SOAS, who said cheerfully:

'How are you, Pennyfather? Haven't seen you for a long time. How did you get on at the Congress? Any points of interest come up?'

'I am sure there will be.'

'Just come back from it, haven't you?'

'No, no, I am on my way there. I'm catching a plane this evening.'

'Oh I see.' Whittaker looked slightly puzzled. 'Somehow or other I thought the Congress was today.'

'No, no. Tomorrow, the 19th.'

Canon Pennyfather passed out through the door while his friend, looking after him, was just saying:

'But my dear chap, *today* is the 19th, isn't it?'

Canon Pennyfather, however, had gone beyond earshot. He picked up a taxi in Pall Mall, and was driven to the air terminal in Kensington. There was quite a fair crowd this evening. Presenting himself at the desk it at last came to his turn. He managed to produce ticket and passport and other necessities for the journey. The girl behind the desk, about to stamp these credentials, paused abruptly.

'I beg your pardon, sir, this seems to be the wrong ticket.'

'The wrong ticket? No, no, that is quite right. Flight one hundred and – well, I can't really read without my glasses – one hundred and something to Lucerne.'

'It's the date, sir. This is dated Wednesday the 18th.'

'No, no, surely. At least – I mean – today is Wednesday the 18th.'

'I'm sorry, sir. Today is the 19th.'

'The 19th!' The Canon was dismayed. He fished out a small diary, turning the pages eagerly. In the end he had to be convinced. Today *was* the 19th. The plane he had meant to catch had gone yesterday.

'Then that means – that means – dear me, it means the Congress at Lucerne has taken place *today*.'

He stared in deep dismay across the counter; but there were many others travelling; the Canon and his perplexities were elbowed aside. He stood sadly, holding the useless ticket in his hand. His mind ranged over various possibilities. Perhaps his ticket could be changed? But that would be no use – no indeed – what time was it now? Going on for 9 o'clock? The conference had actually taken place; starting at 10 o'clock this morning. Of course, that was what Whittaker had meant at the Athenaeum. He thought Canon Pennyfather had already *been* to the Congress.

'Oh dear, oh dear,' said Canon Pennyfather, to himself. 'What a muddle I have made of it all!' He wandered sadly and silently into the Cromwell Road, not at its best a very cheerful place.

He walked slowly along the street carrying his bag and revolving perplexities in his mind. When at last he had worked out to his satisfaction the various reasons for which he had made a mistake in the day, he shook his head sadly.

'Now, I suppose,' he said to himself, 'I suppose – let me see, it's after nine o'clock, yes, I suppose I had better have something to eat.'

It was curious, he thought, that he did not feel hungry.

Wandering disconsolately along the Cromwell Road he finally settled upon a small restaurant which served Indian curries. It seemed to him that though he was not quite as hungry as he ought to be, he had better keep his spirits up by having a meal, and after that he must find a hotel and – but no, there was no need to do *that*. He had a hotel! Of course. He was staying at Bertram's; and had reserved his room for four days. What a piece of luck! What a splendid piece of luck! So his room was there, waiting for him. He had only to ask for his key at the desk and – here another reminiscence assailed him. Something heavy in his pocket?

He dipped his hand in and brought out one of those large and solid keys with which hotels try and discourage their vaguer guests from taking them away in their pockets. It had not prevented the Canon from doing so!

'No. 19,' said the Canon, in happy recognition. 'That's right. It's very fortunate that I haven't got to go and find a room in a hotel. They say they're very crowded just now. Yes, Edmunds was saying so at the Athenaeum this evening. He had a terrible job finding a room.'

Somewhat pleased with himself and the care he had taken over his travelling arrangements by booking a hotel beforehand, the Canon abandoned his curry, remembered to pay for it, and strode out once more into the Cromwell Road.

It seemed a little tame to go home just like this when he ought to have been dining in Lucerne and talking about all sorts of interesting and fascinating problems. His eye was caught by a cinema.

Walls of Jericho.

It seemed an eminently suitable title. It would be interesting to see if biblical accuracy had been preserved.

He bought himself a seat and stumbled into the darkness. He enjoyed the film, though it seemed to him to have no relationship to the biblical story whatsoever. Even Joshua seemed to have been left out. The walls of Jericho seemed to be a symbolical way of referring to a certain lady's marriage vows. When they had tumbled down several times, the beautiful star met the dour and uncouth hero whom she had secretly loved all along and between them they proposed to build up the walls in a way that would stand the test of time better. It was not a film destined particularly to appeal to an elderly clergyman; but Canon Pennyfather enjoyed it very much. It was not the sort of film he often saw and he felt it was enlarging his knowledge of life. The film ended, the lights went up, the National Anthem was played and Canon Pennyfather stumbled out into the lights of London, slightly consoled for the sad events of earlier in the evening.

It was a fine night and he walked home to Bertram's Hotel after first getting into a bus which took him in the opposite direction. It was midnight when he got in and Bertram's Hotel at midnight usually preserved a decorous appearance of everyone having gone to bed. The lift was on a higher floor so the Canon walked up the stairs. He came to his room, inserted the key in the lock, threw the door open and entered!

Good gracious, was he seeing things? But who – how – he saw the upraised arm too late . . .

Stars exploded in a kind of Guy Fawkes' display within his head . . .

CHAPTER 8

The Irish Mail rushed through the night. Or, more correctly, through the darkness of the early morning hours.

At intervals the diesel engine gave its weird banshee warning cry. It was travelling at well over eighty miles an hour. It was on time.

Then, with some suddenness, the pace slackened as the brakes came on. The wheels screamed as they gripped the metals. Slower . . . slower . . . The guard put his head out of the window noting the red signal ahead as the train came to a final halt. Some of the passengers woke up. Most did not.

One elderly lady, alarmed by the suddenness of the deceleration, opened the door and looked out along the corridor. A little way along one of the doors to the line was open. An elderly cleric with a thatch of thick white hair was climbing up from the permanent way. She presumed he had previously climbed down to the line to investigate. The morning air was distinctly chilly. Someone at the end of the corridor said: 'Only a signal.' The elderly lady withdrew into her compartment and tried to go to sleep again.

Farther up the line, a man waving a lantern was running towards the train from a signal box. The fireman climbed down from the engine. The guard who had descended from the train came along to join him. The man with the lantern arrived, rather short of breath and spoke in a series of gasps.

'Bad crash ahead . . . Goods train derailed . . .'

The engine driver looked out of his cab, then climbed down also to join the others.

At the rear of the train, six men who had just climbed up the embankment boarded the train through a door left open for them in the last coach. Six passengers from different coaches met them. With well rehearsed speed, they proceeded to take charge of the postal van, isolating it from the rest of the train. Two men in Balaclava helmets at front and rear of the compartment stood on guard, coshes in hand.

A man in railway uniform went forward along the corridor of the stationary train, uttering explanations to such as demanded them.

'Block on the line ahead. Ten minutes' delay, maybe, not much more . . .' It sounded friendly and reassuring.

By the engine, the driver and the fireman lay neatly gagged and trussed up. The man with the lantern called out:

'Everything OK here.'

The guard lay by the embankment, similarly gagged and tied.

The expert cracksmen in the postal van had done their work. Two more neatly trussed bodies lay on the floor. The special mailbags sailed out to where other men on the embankment awaited them.

In their compartments, passengers grumbled to each other that the railways were not what they used to be.

Then, as they settled themselves to sleep again, there came through the darkness the roar of an exhaust.

'Goodness,' murmured a woman. 'Is that a jet plane?'

'Racing car, I should say.'

The roar died away . . .

On the Bedhampton Motorway, nine miles away, a steady stream of night lorries was grinding its way north. A big white racing car flashed past them.

Ten minutes later, it turned off the motorway.

The garage on the corner of the B road bore the sign CLOSED. But the big doors swung open and the white car was driven straight in, the doors closing again behind it. Three men worked at lightning speed. A fresh set of number-plates were attached. The driver changed his coat and cap. He had worn white sheepskin before. Now he wore black leather. He drove out again. Three minutes after his departure, an old Morris Oxford, driven by a clergyman, chugged out on to the road and proceeded to take a route through various turning and twisting country lanes.

A station wagon, driven along a country road, slowed up as it came upon an old Morris Oxford stationary by the hedge, with an elderly man standing over it.

The driver of the station wagon put out a head.

'Having trouble? Can I help?'

'Very good of you. It's my lights.'

The two drivers approached each other – listened. 'All clear.'

Various expensive American-style cases were transferred from the Morris Oxford to the station wagon.

A mile or two farther on, the station wagon turned off on what looked like a rough track but which presently turned out to be the back way to a large and opulent mansion. In what had been a stableyard, a big white Mercedes car was standing. The driver of the station wagon opened its boot with a key, transferred the cases to the boot, and drove away again in the station wagon.

In a nearby farmyard a cock crowed noisily.

CHAPTER 9

Elvira Blake looked up at the sky, noted that it was a fine morning and went into a telephone box. She dialled Bridget's number in Onslow Square. Satisfied by the response, she said:

'Hallo? Bridget?'

'Oh Elvira, is that you?' Bridget's voice sounded agitated.

'Yes. Has everything been all right?'

'Oh no. It's been *awful*. Your cousin, Mrs Melford, rang up Mummy yesterday afternoon.'

'What, about me?'

'Yes. I thought I'd done it so well when I rang her up at lunch-time. But it seems she got worried about your teeth. Thought there might be something really wrong with them. Abscesses or something. So she rang up the dentist herself and found, of course, that you'd never been there at all. So then she rang up Mummy and unfortunately Mummy was right there by the telephone. So I couldn't get there first. And naturally Mummy said *she* didn't know anything about it, and that you certainly weren't staying *here*. I didn't know *what* to do.'

'What *did* you do?'

'Pretended I knew nothing about it. I did say that I thought you'd said something about going to see some friends at Wimbledon.'

'Why Wimbledon?'

'It was the first place came into my head.'

Elvira sighed. 'Oh well, I suppose I'll have to cook up something. An old governess, perhaps, who lives at Wimbledon. All this fussing does make things so *complicated*. I hope Cousin Mildred doesn't make a real fool of herself and ring up the police or something like that.'

'Are you going down there now?'

'Not till this evening. I've got a lot to do first.'

'You got to Ireland. Was it – all right?'

'I found out what I wanted to know.'

'You sound – sort of grim.'

'I'm feeling grim.'

'Can't I help you, Elvira? Do anything?'

'Nobody can help me really . . . It's a thing I have to do myself. I hoped something wasn't true, but it *is* true. I don't know quite what to do about it.'

'Are you in danger, Elvira?'

'Don't be melodramatic, Bridget. I'll have to be careful, that's all. I'll have to be very careful.'

'Then you *are* in danger.'

Elvira said after a moment's pause, 'I expect I'm just imagining things, that's all.'

'Elvira, what are you going to do about that bracelet?'

'Oh, that's all right. I've arranged to get some money from someone, so I can go and – what's the word – redeem it. Then just take it back to Bollards.'

'D'you think they'll be all right about it? – No, Mummy, it's just the laundry. They say we never sent that sheet. Yes, Mummy, yes, I'll tell the manageress. All right then.'

At the other end of the line Elvira grinned and put down the receiver. She opened her purse, sorted through her money, counted out the coins she needed and arranged them in front of her and proceeded to put through a call. When she got the number she wanted she put in the necessary coins, pressed Button A and spoke in a small rather breathless voice.

'Hallo, Cousin Mildred. Yes, it's me . . . I'm terribly sorry . . . Yes, I know . . . well I was going to . . . yes it was dear old Maddy, you know our old Mademoiselle . . . yes I wrote a postcard, then I forgot to post it. It's still in my pocket now . . . well, you see she was ill and there was no one to look after her and so I just stopped to see she was all right. Yes,

I *was* going to Bridget's but this changed things . . . I don't understand about the message you got. Someone must have jumbled it up . . . Yes, I'll explain it all to you when I get back . . . yes, this afternoon. No, I shall just wait and see the nurse who's coming to look after old Maddy – well, not really a nurse. You know one of those – er – practical aid nurses or something like that. No, she would hate to go to hospital . . . But I *am* sorry, Cousin Mildred, I really am very, very sorry.' She put down the receiver and sighed in an exasperated manner. 'If only,' she murmured to herself, 'one didn't have to tell so many lies to everybody.'

She came out of the telephone box, noting as she did so the big newspaper placards – BIG TRAIN ROBBERY, IRISH MAIL ATTACKED BY BANDITS.

Mr Bollard was serving a customer when the shop door opened. He looked up to see the Honourable Elvira Blake entering.

'No,' she said to an assistant who came forward to her. 'I'd rather wait until Mr Bollard is free.'

Presently Mr Bollard's customer's business was concluded and Elvira moved into the vacant place.

'Good morning, Mr Bollard,' she said.

'I'm afraid your watch isn't done quite as soon as this, Miss Elvira,' said Mr Bollard.

'Oh, it's not the watch,' said Elvira. 'I've come to apologize. A dreadful thing happened.' She opened her bag and took out a small box. From it she extracted the sapphire and diamond bracelet. 'You will remember when I came in with my watch to be repaired that I was looking at things for a Christmas present and there was an accident outside in the street. Somebody was run over I think, or nearly run over. I suppose I must have had the bracelet in my hand and put it into the pocket of my suit without thinking, although I only found it this morning. So I rushed along *at once* to bring it back. I'm so terribly sorry, Mr Bollard, I don't know how I came to do such an idiotic thing.'

'Why, that's quite all right, Miss Elvira,' said Mr Bollard, slowly.

'I suppose you thought someone had stolen it,' said Elvira.

Her limpid blue eyes met him.

'We *had* discovered its loss,' said Mr Bollard. 'Thank you very much, Miss Elvira, for bringing it back so promptly.'

'I felt simply awful about it when I found it,' said Elvira. 'Well, thank you very much, Mr Bollard, for being so nice about it.'

'A lot of strange mistakes do occur,' said Mr Bollard. He smiled at her in an avuncular manner. 'We won't think of it any more. But don't do it again, though.' He laughed with the air of one making a genial little joke.

'Oh no,' said Elvira, 'I shall be terribly careful in future.'

She smiled at him, turned and left the shop.

'Now I wonder,' said Mr Bollard to himself, 'I really do wonder . . .'

One of his partners, who had been standing near, moved nearer to him.

'So she *did* take it?' he said.

'Yes. She took it all right,' said Mr Bollard.

'But she brought it back,' his partner pointed out.

'She brought it back,' agreed Mr Bollard. 'I didn't actually expect that.'

'You mean you didn't expect her to bring it back?'

'No, not if it was she who'd taken it.'

'Do you think her story is true?' his partner inquired curiously. 'I mean, that she slipped it into her pocket by accident?'

'I suppose it's possible,' said Bollard, thoughtfully.

'Or it *could* be kleptomania, I suppose.'

'Or it could be kleptomania,' agreed Bollard. 'It's more likely that she took it on purpose . . . But if so, why did she bring it back so soon? It's curious –'

'Just as well we didn't notify the police. I admit *I* wanted to.'

'I know, I know. You haven't got as much experience as I have. In this case, it was definitely better not.' He added softly to himself, 'The thing's interesting, though. Quite interesting. I wonder how old she is? Seventeen or eighteen I suppose. She might have got herself in a jam of some kind.'

'I thought you said she was rolling in money.'

'You may be an heiress and rolling in money,' said Bollard, 'but at seventeen you can't always get your hands on it. The funny thing is, you know, they keep heiresses much shorter of cash than they keep the more impecunious. It's not always a good idea. Well, I don't suppose we shall ever know the truth of it.'

He put the bracelet back in its place in the display case and shut down the lid.

CHAPTER 10

The offices of Egerton, Forbes & Wilborough were in Bloomsbury, in one of those imposing and dignified squares which have as yet not felt the wind of change. Their brass plate was suitably worn down to illegibility. The firm had been going for over a hundred years and a good proportion of the landed gentry of England were their clients. There was no Forbes in the firm any more and no Wilboroughs. Instead there were Atkinsons, father and son, and a Welsh Lloyd and a Scottish McAllister. There was, however, still an Egerton, descendant of the original Egerton. This particular Egerton was a man of fifty-two and he was adviser to several families which had in their day been advised by his grandfather, his uncle, and his father.

At this moment he was sitting behind a large mahogany desk in his handsome room on the first floor, speaking kindly but firmly to a dejected looking client. Richard Egerton was a handsome man, tall, dark with a touch of grey at the temples and very shrewd grey eyes. His advice was always good advice, but he seldom minced his words.

'Quite frankly you haven't got a leg to stand upon, Freddie,' he was saying. 'Not with those letters you've written.'

'You don't think –' Freddie murmured dejectedly.

'No, I don't,' said Egerton. 'The only hope is to settle out of court. It might even be held that you've rendered yourself liable to criminal prosecution.'

'Oh, look here, Richard, that's carrying things a bit far.'

There was a small discreet buzz on Egerton's desk. He picked up the telephone receiver with a frown.

'I thought I said I wasn't to be disturbed.'

There was a murmur at the other end. Egerton said, 'Oh. Yes – Yes, I see. Ask her to wait, will you.'

He replaced the receiver and turned once more to his unhappy looking client.

'Look here, Freddie,' he said, 'I know the law and you don't. You're in a nasty jam. I'll do my best to get you out of it, but it's going to cost you a bit. I doubt if they'd settle for less than twelve thousand.'

'Twelve thousand!' The unfortunate Freddie was aghast. 'Oh, I say! I haven't got it, Richard.'

'Well, you'll have to raise it then. There are always ways and means. If she'll settle for twelve thousand, you'll be lucky, and if you fight the case it'll cost you a lot more.'

'You lawyers!' said Freddie. 'Sharks, all of you!'

He rose to his feet. 'Well,' he said, 'do your bloody best for me, Richard old boy.'

He took his departure, shaking his head sadly. Richard Egerton put Freddie and his affairs out of his mind, and thought about his next client. He said softly to himself, 'The Honourable Elvira Blake. I wonder what she's like . . .' He lifted his receiver. 'Lord Frederick's gone. Send up Miss Blake, will you.'

As he waited he made little calculations on his desk pad. How many years since –? She must be fifteen – seventeen – perhaps even more than that. Time went so fast. 'Coniston's daughter,' he thought, 'and Bess's daughter. I wonder which of them she takes after?'

The door opened, the clerk announced Miss Elvira Blake and the girl walked into the room. Egerton rose from his chair and came towards her. In appearance, he thought, she did not resemble either of her parents. Tall, slim, very fair, Bess's colouring but none of Bess's vitality, with an old-fashioned air about her; though that was difficult to be sure of, since the fashion in dress happened at the moment to be ruffles and baby bodices.

'Well, well,' he said, as he shook hands with her. 'This is a surprise. Last time I saw you, you were eleven years old. Come and sit here.' He pulled forward a chair and she sat down.

'I suppose,' said Elvira, a little uncertainly, 'that I ought to have written first. Written and made an appointment. Something like that, but I really made up my mind very suddenly and it seemed an opportunity, since I was in London.'

'And what are you doing in London?'

'Having my teeth seen to.'

'Beastly things, teeth,' said Egerton. 'Give us trouble from the cradle to the grave. But I am grateful for the teeth, if it gives me an opportunity of seeing you. Let me see now; you've been in Italy, haven't you, finishing your education there at one of these places all girls go to nowadays?'

'Yes,' said Elvira, 'the Contessa Martinelli. But I've left there now for good. I'm living with the Melfords in Kent until I make up my mind if there's anything I'd like to do.'

'Well, I hope you'll find something satisfactory. You're not thinking of a university or anything like that?'

'No,' said Elvira, 'I don't think I'd be clever enough for that.' She paused before saying, 'I suppose *you'd* have to agree to anything if I did want to do it?'

Egerton's keen eyes focused sharply.

'I am one of your guardians, and a trustee under your father's will, yes,' he said. 'Therefore, you have a perfect right to approach me at any time.'

Elvira said, 'Thank you,' politely. Egerton asked:

'Is there anything worrying you?'

'No. Not really. But you see, I don't *know* anything. Nobody's ever told me things. One doesn't always like to ask.'

He looked at her attentively.

'You mean things about yourself?'

'Yes,' said Elvira. 'It's kind of you to understand. Uncle Derek –' she hesitated.

'Derek Luscombe, you mean?'

'Yes. I've always called him uncle.'

'I see.'

'He's very kind,' said Elvira, 'but he's not the sort of person who ever tells you anything. He just arranges things, and looks a little worried in case they mightn't be what I'd like. Of course he listens to a lot of people – women, I mean – who tell him things. Like Contessa Martinelli. He arranges for me to go to schools or to finishing places.'

'And they haven't been where you wanted to go?'

'No, I didn't mean that. They've been quite all right. I mean they've been more or less where everyone else goes.'

'I see.'

'But I don't know anything about *myself*, I mean what money I've got, and how much, and what I could do with it if I wanted.'

'In fact,' said Egerton, with his attractive smile, 'you want to talk business. Is that it? Well, I think you're quite right. Let's see. How old are you? Sixteen – seventeen?'

'I'm nearly twenty.'

'Oh dear. I'd no idea.'

'You see,' explained Elvira, 'I feel all the time that I'm being shielded and sheltered. It's nice in a way, but it can get very irritating.'

'It's an attitude that's gone out of date,' agreed Egerton, 'but I can quite see that it would appeal to Derek Luscombe.'

'He's a dear,' said Elvira, 'but very difficult, somehow, to talk to seriously.'

'Yes, I can see that that might be so. Well, how much *do* you know about yourself, Elvira? About your family circumstances?'

'I know that my father died when I was five and that my mother had run away from him with someone when I was about two, I don't remember her at all. I barely remember my father. He was very old and had his leg up on a chair. He used to swear. I was rather scared of him. After he died I lived first with an aunt or a cousin or something of my father's, until *she* died, and then I lived with Uncle Derek and his sister. But then she died and I went to Italy. Uncle Derek has arranged for me, now, to live with the Melfords who are his cousins and very kind and nice and have two daughters about my age.'

'You're happy there?'

'I don't know yet. I've barely got there. They're all very dull. I really wanted to know how much money I've got.'

'So it's financial information you really want?'

'Yes,' said Elvira. 'I've got *some* money. Is it a lot?'

Egerton was serious now.

'Yes,' he said. 'You've got a lot of money. Your father was a very rich man. You were his only child. When he died, the title and the estate went to a cousin. He didn't like the cousin, so he left all his personal property, which was considerable, to his daughter – to you, Elvira. You're a very rich woman, or will be, when you are twenty-one.'

'You mean I am not rich *now*?'

'Yes,' said Egerton, 'you're rich now, but the money is not yours to dispose of until you are twenty-one or marry. Until that time it is in the hands of your Trustees. Luscombe, myself and another.' He smiled at her. 'We haven't embezzled it or anything like that. It's still there. In fact, we've increased your capital considerably by investments.'

'How much will I have?'

'At the age of twenty-one or upon your marriage, you will come into a sum which at a rough estimate would amount to six or seven hundred thousand pounds.'

'That *is* a lot,' said Elvira, impressed.

'Yes, it is a lot. Probably it is because it is such a lot that nobody has ever talked to you about it much.'

He watched her as she reflected upon this. Quite an interesting girl, he thought. Looked an unbelievably milk-and-water Miss, but she was more than that. A good deal more. He said, with a faintly ironic smile:

'Does that satisfy you?'

She gave him a sudden smile.

'It ought to, oughtn't it?'

'Rather better than winning the pools,' he suggested.

She nodded, but her mind was elsewhere. Then she came out abruptly with a question.

'Who gets it if I die?'

'As things stand now, it would go to your next of kin.'

'I mean – I couldn't make a will now, could I? Not until I was twenty-one. That's what someone told me.'

'They were quite right.'

'That's really rather annoying. If I was married and died I suppose my husband would get the money?'

'Yes.'

'And if I wasn't married my mother would be my next of kin and get it. I really seem to have very few relations – I don't even know my mother. What is she like?'

'She's a very remarkable woman,' said Egerton shortly. 'Everybody would agree to that.'

'Didn't she ever *want* to see me?'

'She may have done . . . I think it's very possible that she did. But having made in – certain ways – rather a mess of her own life, she may have thought that it was better for you that you should be brought up quite apart from her.'

'Do you actually *know* that she thinks that?'

'No. I don't really know anything about it.'

Elvira got up.

'Thank you,' she said. 'It's very kind of you to tell me all this.'

'I think perhaps you ought to have been told more about things before,' said Egerton.

'It's humiliating *not* to know things,' said Elvira. 'Uncle Derek, of course, thinks I'm just a *child*.'

'Well, he's not a very young man himself. He and I, you know, are well advanced in years. You must make allowances for us when we look at things from the point of view of our advanced age.'

Elvira stood looking at him for a moment or two.

'But *you* don't think I'm really a child, do you?' she said shrewdly, and added, 'I expect you know rather more about girls than Uncle Derek does. He just lived with his sister.' Then she stretched out her hand and said, very prettily, 'Thank you so much. I hope I haven't interrupted some important work you had to do,' and went out.

Egerton stood looking at the door that had closed behind her. He pursed up his lips, whistled a moment, shook his head and sat down again, picked up a pen and tapped thoughtfully on his desk. He drew some papers towards him, then thrust them back and picked up his telephone.

'Miss Cordell, get me Colonel Luscombe, will you? Try his club first. And then the Shropshire address.'

He put back the receiver. Again he drew his papers towards him and started reading them but his mind was not on what he was doing. Presently his buzzer went.

'Colonel Luscombe is on the wire now, Mr Egerton.'

'Right. Put him through. Hallo, Derek. Richard Egerton here. How are you? I've just been having a visit from someone you know. A visit from your ward.'

'From Elvira?' Derek Luscombe sounded very surprised.

'Yes.'

'But why – what on earth – what did she come to you for? Not in any trouble?'

'No, I wouldn't say so. On the contrary, she seemed rather – well, pleased with herself. She wanted to know all about her financial position.'

'You didn't tell her, I hope?' said Colonel Luscombe, in alarm.

'Why not? What's the point of secrecy?'

'Well, I can't help feeling it's a little unwise for a girl to know that she is going to come into such a large amount of money.'

'Somebody else will tell her that, if we don't. She's got to be prepared, you know. Money is a responsibility.'

'Yes, but she's so much of a child still.'

'Are you sure of that?'

'What do you mean? Of course she's a child.'

'I wouldn't describe her as such. Who's the boy friend?'

'I beg your pardon.'

'I said who's the boy friend? There *is* a boy friend in the offing, isn't there?'

'No, indeed. Nothing of the sort. What on earth makes you think that?'

'Nothing that she actually said. But I've got some experience, you know. I think you'll find there *is* a boy friend.'

'Well, I can assure you you're quite wrong. I mean, she's been most carefully brought up, she's been at very strict schools, she's been in a very select finishing establishment in Italy. I should know if there was anything of that kind going on. I dare say she's met one or two pleasant young fellows and all that, but I'm sure there's been nothing of the kind you suggest.'

'Well, my diagnosis is a boy friend – and probably an undesirable one.'

'But why, Richard, why? What do *you* know about young girls?'

'Quite a lot,' said Egerton dryly. 'I've had three clients in the last year, two of whom were made wards of court and the third one managed to bully her parents into agreeing to an almost certainly disastrous marriage. Girls don't get looked after the way they used to be. Conditions are such that it's very difficult to look after them at all –'

'But I assure you Elvira has been most carefully looked after.'

'The ingenuity of the young female of the species is beyond anything you could conjecture! You keep an eye on her, Derek. Make a few inquiries as to what she's been up to.'

'Nonsense. She's just a sweet simple girl.'

'What you don't know about sweet simple girls would fill an album! Her mother ran away and caused a scandal – remember? – when she was younger than Elvira is today. As for old Coniston, he was one of the worst rips in England.'

'You upset me, Richard. You upset me very much.'

'You might as well be warned. What I didn't quite like was one of her other questions. Why is she so anxious to know who'd inherit her money if she dies?'

'It's queer your saying that, because she asked me that same question.'

'Did she now? Why should her mind run on early death? She asked me about her mother, by the way.'

Colonel Luscombe's voice sounded worried as he said: 'I wish Bess would get in touch with the girl.'

'Have you been talking to her on the subject – to Bess, I mean?'

'Well, yes . . . Yes I did. I ran across her by chance. We were staying in the same hotel, as a matter of fact. I urged Bess to make some arrangements to see the girl.'

'What did she say?' asked Egerton curiously.

'Refused point blank. She more or less said that she wasn't a safe person for the girl to know.'

'Looked at from one point of view I don't suppose she is,' said Egerton. 'She's mixed up with that racing fellow, isn't she?'

'I've heard rumours.'

'Yes, I've heard them too. I don't know if there's much in it really. There might be, I suppose. That could be why she feels as she does. Bess's friends are strong meat from time to time! But what a woman she is, eh Derek? What a woman.'

'Always been her own worst enemy,' said Derek Luscombe, gruffly.

'A really nice conventional remark,' said Egerton. 'Well, sorry I bothered you, Derek, but keep a look out for undesirables in the background. Don't say you haven't been warned.'

He replaced the receiver and drew the pages on his desk towards him once more. This time he was able to put his whole attention on what he was doing.

CHAPTER 11

Mrs McCrae, Canon Pennyfather's housekeeper, had ordered a Dover sole for the evening of his return. The advantages attached to a good Dover sole were manifold. It need not be introduced to the grill or frying pan until the Canon was safely in the house. It could be kept until the next day if necessary. Canon Pennyfather was fond of Dover sole; and, if a telephone call or telegram arrived saying that the Canon would after all be elsewhere on this particular evening, Mrs McCrae was fond of a good Dover sole herself. All therefore was in good trim for the Canon's return. The Dover sole would be followed by pancakes. The sole sat on the kitchen table, the batter for the pancakes was ready in a bowl. All was in readiness. The brass shone, the silver sparkled, not a minuscule of dust showed anywhere. There was only one thing lacking. The Canon himself.

The Canon was scheduled to return on the train arriving at 6.30 from London.

At 7 o'clock he had not returned. No doubt the train was late. At 7.30 he still had not returned. Mrs McCrae gave a sigh of vexation. She suspected that this was going to be another of these things. Eight o'clock came and no Canon. Mrs McCrae gave a long, exasperated sigh. Soon, no doubt, she would get a telephone call, though it was quite within the bounds of possibility that there would not be even a telephone call. He might have written to her. No doubt he had written, but he had probably omitted to post the letter.

'Dear, dear!' said Mrs McCrae.

At 9 o'clock she made herself three pancakes with the pancake batter. The sole she put carefully away in the Frigidaire. 'I wonder where the good man's got to now,' she said to herself. She knew by experience that he might be anywhere. The odds were that he would discover his mistake in time to telegraph her or telephone her before she retired to bed. 'I shall sit up until 11 o'clock but no longer,' said Mrs McCrae. Ten-thirty was her bed-time, an extension to eleven she considered her duty, but if at eleven there was nothing, no word from the Canon, then Mrs McCrae would duly lock up the house and betake herself to bed.

It cannot be said that she was worried. This sort of thing had happened before. There was nothing to be done but wait for news of some kind. The possibilities were numerous. Canon Pennyfather might have got on the wrong train and failed to discover his mistake until he was at Land's End or John o' Groats, or he might still be in London having made some mistake in the date, and was therefore convinced he was not returning until tomorrow. He might have met a friend or friends at this foreign conference he was going to and been induced to stay out there perhaps over the weekend. He would have meant to let her know but had entirely forgotten to do so. So, as has been already said, she was not worried. The day after tomorrow his old friend, Archdeacon Simmons, was coming to stay. That was the sort of thing the Canon *did* remember, so no doubt he himself or a telegram from him would arrive tomorrow and at latest he would be home on the day after, or there would be a letter.

The morning of the day after, however, arrived without a word from him. For the first time Mrs McCrae began to be uneasy. Between 9 a.m. and 1 p.m. she eyed the telephone in a doubtful manner. Mrs McCrae had her own fixed views about the telephone. She used it and recognized its convenience but she was not fond of the telephone. Some of her household shopping was done by telephone, though she much preferred to do it in person owing to a fixed belief that if you did not see what you were being given, a shopkeeper was sure to try and cheat you. Still, telephones were useful for domestic matters. She occasionally, though rarely, telephoned her friends or relations in the near neighbourhood. To make a call of any distance, or a London call, upset her severely. It was a shameful waste of money. Nevertheless, she began to meditate facing that problem.

Finally, when yet another day dawned without any news of him, she decided to act. She knew where the Canon was staying in London. Bertram's Hotel. A nice old-fashioned place. It might be as well, perhaps, if she rang up and made certain inquiries. They would probably know where the Canon was. It was not an ordinary hotel. She would ask to be put through to Miss Gorringe. Miss Gorringe was always efficient and thoughtful. The Canon might, of course, return by the twelve-thirty. If so he would be here any minute now.

But the minutes passed and there was no Canon. Mrs McCrae took a deep breath, nerved herself and asked for a call to London. She waited, biting her lips and holding the receiver clamped firmly to her ear.

'Bertram's Hotel, at your service,' said a voice.

'I would like, if you please, to speak to Miss Gorringe,' said Mrs McCrae.

'Just a moment. What name shall I say?'

'It's Canon Pennyfather's housekeeper. Mrs McCrae.'

'Just a moment please.'

Presently the calm and efficient voice of Miss Gorringe came through.

'Miss Gorringe here. Did you say Canon Pennyfather's housekeeper?'

'That's right. Mrs McCrae.'

'Oh yes. Of course. What can I do for you, Mrs McCrae?'

'Is Canon Pennyfather staying at the hotel still?'

'I'm glad you've rung up,' said Miss Gorringe. 'We have been rather worried as to what exactly to do.'

'Do you mean something's happened to Canon Pennyfather? Has he had an accident?'

'No, no, nothing of that kind. But we expected him back from Lucerne on Friday or Saturday.'

'Eh – that'd be right.'

'But he didn't arrive. Well, of course that wasn't really surprising. He had booked his room on – booked it, that is, until yesterday. He didn't come back yesterday or send any word and his things are still here. The major part of his baggage. We hadn't been quite sure what to do about it. Of course,' Miss Gorringe went on hastily, 'we know the Canon is, well – somewhat forgetful sometimes.'

'You may well say that!'

'It makes it a little difficult for us. We are so fully booked up. His room is actually booked for another guest.' She added: 'You have no idea where he is?'

With bitterness Mrs McCrae said:

'The man might be anywhere!' She pulled herself together. 'Well, thank you, Miss Gorringe.'

'Anything I can do –' Miss Gorringe suggested helpfully.

'I dare say I'll hear soon enough,' said Mrs McCrae. She thanked Miss Gorringe again and rang off.

She sat by the telephone, looking upset. She did not fear for the Canon's personal safety. If he had had an accident she would by now have been notified. She felt sure of that. On the whole the Canon was not what one could call accident prone. He was what Mrs McCrae called to herself 'one of the scatty ones', and the scatty ones seemed always to be looked after by a special providence. Whilst taking no care or thought, they could still survive even a Panda crossing. No, she did not visualize Canon Pennyfather as lying groaning in a hospital. He was *somewhere*, no doubt innocently and happily prattling with some friend or other. Maybe he was abroad still. The difficulty was that Archdeacon Simmons was arriving this evening and Archdeacon Simmons would expect to find a host to receive him. She couldn't put Archdeacon Simmons off because she didn't know where he was. It was all very difficult, but it had, like most difficulties, its bright spot. Its bright spot was Archdeacon Simmons. Archdeacon Simmons would know what to do. She would place the matter in his hands.

Archdeacon Simmons was a complete contrast to her employer. He knew where he was going, and what he was doing, and was always cheerfully sure of knowing the right thing to be done and doing it. A confident cleric. Archdeacon Simmons, when he arrived, to be met by Mrs McCrae's explanations, apologies and perturbation, was a tower of strength. He, too, was not alarmed.

'Now don't you worry, Mrs McCrae,' he said in his genial fashion, as he sat down to the meal she had prepared for his arrival. 'We'll hunt the absent-minded fellow down. Ever heard that story about Chesterton? G. K. Chesterton, you know, the writer. Wired to his wife when he'd gone on a lecture tour "Am at Crewe Station. Where ought I to be?"'

He laughed. Mrs McCrae smiled dutifully. She did not think it was very funny because it was so exactly the sort of thing that Canon Pennyfather might have done.

'Ah,' said Archdeacon Simmons, with appreciation, 'one of your excellent veal cutlets! You're a marvellous cook, Mrs McCrae. I hope my old friend appreciates you.'

Veal cutlets having been succeeded by some small castle puddings with a blackberry sauce which Mrs McCrae had remembered was one of the Archdeacon's favourite sweets, the good man applied himself in earnest to the tracking down of his missing friend. He addressed himself to the telephone with vigour and a complete disregard for expense, which made Mrs McCrae purse her lips anxiously, although not really disapproving, because definitely her master had got to be tracked down.

Having first dutifully tried the Canon's sister who took little notice of her brother's goings and comings and as usual had not the faintest idea where he was or might be, the Archdeacon spread his net farther afield. He addressed himself once more to Bertram's Hotel and got details as precisely as possible. The Canon had definitely left there on the early evening of the 19th. He had with him a small BEA handbag, but his other luggage had remained behind in his room, which he had duly retained. He had mentioned that he was going to a conference of some kind at Lucerne. He had not gone direct to the airport from the hotel. The commissionaire, who knew him well by sight, had put him into a taxi and had directed it as told by the Canon, to the Athenaeum Club. That was the last time that anyone at Bertram's Hotel had seen Canon Pennyfather. Oh yes, a small detail – he had omitted to leave his key behind but had taken it with him. It was not the first time that that had happened.

Archdeacon Simmons paused for a few minutes' consideration before the next call. He could ring up the air station in London. That would no doubt take some time. There might be a short cut. He rang up Dr Weissgarten, a learned Hebrew scholar who was almost certain to have been at the conference.

Dr Weissgarten was at his home. As soon as he heard who was speaking to him he launched out into a torrent of verbiage consisting mostly of disparaging criticism of two papers that had been read at the conference in Lucerne.

'Most unsound, that fellow Hogarov,' he said, 'most unsound. How he gets away with it I don't know! Fellow isn't a scholar at all. Do you know what he actually said?'

The Archdeacon sighed and had to be firm with him. Otherwise there was a good chance that the rest of the evening would be spent in listening to criticism of fellow scholars at the Lucerne Conference. With some reluctance Dr Weissgarten was pinned down to more personal matters.

'Pennyfather?' he said. 'Pennyfather? He ought to have been there. Can't think why he wasn't there. Said he was going. Told me so only a week before when I saw him in the Athenaeum.'

'You mean he wasn't at the conference at all?'

'That's what I've just said. He *ought* to have been there.'

'Do you know *why* he wasn't there? Did he send an excuse?'

'How should I know? He certainly talked about being there. Yes, now I remember. He was expected. Several people remarked on his absence. Thought he might have had a chill or something. Very treacherous weather.' He was about to revert to his criticisms of his fellow scholars but Archdeacon Simmons rang off.

He had got a fact but it was a fact that for the first time awoke in him an uneasy feeling. Canon Pennyfather had not been at the Lucerne Conference. He had meant to go to that conference. It seemed very extraordinary to the Archdeacon that he had not been there. He might, of course, have taken the wrong plane, though on the whole BEA were pretty careful of you and shepherded you away from such possibilities. Could Canon Pennyfather have forgotten the actual day that he was going to the conference? It was always possible, he supposed. But if so where had he gone instead?

He addressed himself now to the air terminal. It involved a great deal of patient waiting and being transferred from department to department. In the end he got a definite fact. Canon Pennyfather had booked as a passenger on the 21.40 plane to Lucerne on the 18th but he had not been on the plane.

'We're getting on,' said Archdeacon Simmons to Mrs McCrae, who was hovering in the background. 'Now, let me see. Who shall I try next?'

'All this telephoning will cost a fearful lot of money,' said Mrs McCrae.

'I'm afraid so. I'm afraid so,' said Archdeacon Simmons. 'But we've got to get on his track, you know. He's not a very young man.'

'Oh, sir, you don't think there's anything could really have happened to him?'

'Well, I hope not . . . I don't think so, because I think you'd have heard if so. He – er – always had his name and address on him, didn't he?'

'Oh yes, sir, he had cards on him. He'd have letters too, and all sorts of things in his wallet.'

'Well, I don't think he's in a hospital then,' said the Archdeacon. 'Let me see. When he left the hotel he took a taxi to the Athenaeum. I'll ring them up next.'

Here he got some definite information. Canon Pennyfather, who was well known there, had dined there at seven-thirty on the evening of the 19th. It was then that the Archdeacon was struck by something he had overlooked until then. The aeroplane ticket had been for the 18th but the Canon had left Bertram's Hotel by taxi to the Athenaeum, having mentioned he was going to the Lucerne Conference, on the 19th. Light began to break. 'Silly old ass,' thought Archdeacon Simmons to himself, but careful not to say it aloud in front of Mrs McCrae. 'Got his dates wrong. The conference was on the 19th. I'm sure of it. He must have thought that he was leaving on the 18th. He was one day wrong.'

He went over the next bit carefully. The Canon would have gone to the Athenaeum, he would have dined, he would have gone on to Kensington Air Station. There, no doubt, it would have been pointed out to him that his ticket was for the day before and he would then have realized that the conference he was going to attend was now over.

'That's what happened,' said Archdeacon Simmons, 'depend upon it.' He explained it to Mrs McCrae, who agreed that it was likely enough. 'Then what would he do?'

'Go back to his hotel,' said Mrs McCrae.

'He wouldn't have come straight down here – gone straight to the station, I mean.'

'Not if his luggage was at the hotel. At any rate, he would have called there for his luggage.'

'True enough,' said Simmons. 'All right. We'll think of it like this. He left the airport with his little bag and he went back to the hotel, or started for the hotel at all events. He might have had dinner perhaps – no, he'd dined at the Athenaeum. All right, he went back to the hotel. *But* he never arrived there.' He paused a moment or two and then said doubtfully, 'Or did he? Nobody seems to have seen him there. So what happened to him on the way?'

'He could have met someone,' said Mrs McCrae, doubtfully.

'Yes. Of course that's perfectly possible. Some old friend he hadn't seen for a long time . . . He could have gone off with a friend to the friend's hotel or the friend's house, but he wouldn't have stayed there three days, would he? He couldn't have forgotten for three whole days that his luggage was at the hotel. He'd have rung up about it, he'd have called for it, or in a supreme fit of absent-mindedness he might have come straight home. Three days' silence. That's what's so inexplicable.'

'If he had an accident –'

'Yes, Mrs McCrae, of course that's possible. We can try the hospitals. You say he had plenty of papers on him to identify him? Hm – I think there's only one thing for it.'

Mrs McCrae looked at him apprehensively.

'I think, you know,' said the Archdeacon gently, 'that we've got to go to the police.'

CHAPTER 12

Miss Marple had found no difficulty in enjoying her stay in London. She did a lot of the things that she had not had the time to do in her hitherto brief visits to the capital. It has to be regretfully noted that she did not avail herself of the wide cultural activities that would have been possible to her. She visited no picture galleries and no museums. The idea of patronizing a dress show of any kind would not even have occurred to her. What she did visit were the glass and china departments of the large stores, and the household linen departments, and she also availed herself of some marked down lines in furnishing fabrics. Having spent what she considered a reasonable sum upon these household investments, she indulged in various excursions of her own. She went to places and shops she remembered from her young days, sometimes merely with the curiosity of seeing whether they were still there. It was not a pursuit that she had ever had time for before, and she enjoyed it very much. After a nice little nap after lunch, she would go out, and, avoiding the attentions of the commissionaire if possible, because he was so firmly imbued with the idea that a lady of her age and frailty should always go in a taxi, she walked towards a bus stop, or tube station. She had bought a small guide to buses and their routes – and an Underground Transport Map; and she would plan her excursion carefully. One afternoon she could be seen walking happily and nostalgically round Evelyn Gardens or Onslow Square murmuring softly, 'Yes, that was Mrs Van Dylan's house. Of course it looks *quite* different now. They seem to have remodelled it. Dear me, I see it's got four bells. Four flats, I suppose. Such a nice old-fashioned square this always was.'

Rather shamefacedly she paid a visit to Madame Tussaud's, a well-remembered delight of her childhood. In Westbourne Grove she looked in vain for Bradley's. Aunt Helen had always gone to Bradley's about her sealskin jacket.

Window shopping in the general sense did not interest Miss Marple, but she had a splendid time rounding up knitting patterns, new varieties of knitting wool, and such-like delights. She made a special expedition to Richmond to see the house that had been occupied by Great-Uncle Thomas, the retired admiral. The handsome terrace was still there but here again each house seemed to be turned into flats. Much more painful was the house in Lowndes Square where a distant cousin, Lady Merridew, had lived in some style. Here a vast skyscraper building of modernistic design appeared to have arisen. Miss Marple shook her head sadly and said firmly to herself, 'There must *be* progress I suppose. If Cousin Ethel knew, she'd turn in her grave, I'm sure.'

It was on one particularly mild and pleasant afternoon that Miss Marple embarked on a bus that took her over Battersea Bridge. She was going to combine the double pleasure of taking a sentimental look at Princes Terrace Mansions where an old governess of hers had once lived, and visiting Battersea Park. The first part of her quest was abortive. Miss

Ledbury's former home had vanished without trace and had been replaced by a great deal of gleaming concrete. Miss Marple turned into Battersea Park. She had always been a good walker but had to admit that nowadays her walking powers were not what they were. Half a mile was quite enough to tire her. She could manage, she thought, to cross the Park and go out over Chelsea Bridge and find herself once more on a convenient bus route, but her steps grew gradually slower and slower, and she was pleased to come upon a tea enclosure situated on the edge of the lake.

Teas were still being served there in spite of the autumn chill. There were not many people today, a certain amount of mothers and prams, and a few pairs of young lovers. Miss Marple collected a tray with tea and two sponge cakes. She carried her tray carefully to a table and sat down. The tea was just what she needed. Hot, strong and very reviving. Revived, she looked round her, and, her eyes stopping suddenly at a particular table, she sat up very straight in her chair. Really, a very strange coincidence, very strange indeed! First the Army & Navy Stores and now here. Very unusual places those particular two people chose! But no! She was wrong. Miss Marple took a second and stronger pair of glasses from her bag. Yes, she had been mistaken. There was a certain similarity, of course. That long straight blonde hair; but this was not Bess Sedgwick. It was someone years younger. Of course! It was the daughter! The young girl who had come into Bertram's with Lady Selina Hazy's friend, Colonel Luscombe. But the man was the same man who had been lunching with Lady Sedgwick in the Army & Navy Stores. No doubt about it, the same handsome, hawklike look, the same leanness, the same predatory toughness and – yes, the same strong, virile attraction.

'Bad!' said Miss Marple. 'Bad all through! Cruel! Unscrupulous. I don't *like* seeing this. First the mother, now the daughter. What does it mean?'

It meant no good. Miss Marple was sure of that. Miss Marple seldom gave anyone the benefit of the doubt; she invariably thought the worst, and nine times out of ten, so she insisted, she was right in so doing. Both these meetings, she was sure, were more or less secret meetings. She observed now the way these two bent forward over the table until their heads nearly touched; and the earnestness with which they talked. The girl's face – Miss Marple took off her spectacles, rubbed the lenses carefully, then put them on again. Yes, this girl was in love. Desperately in love, as only the young can be in love. But what were her guardians about to let her run about London and have these clandestine assignments in Battersea Park? A nicely brought up, well-behaved girl like that. *Too* nicely brought up, no doubt! Her people probably believed her to be in some quite other spot. She had to tell lies.

On the way out Miss Marple passed the table where they were sitting, slowing down as much as she could without its being too obvious. Unfortunately, their voices were so low that she could not hear what they said. The man was speaking, the girl was listening, half pleased, half afraid. 'Planning to run away together, perhaps?' thought Miss Marple. 'She's still under age.'

Miss Marple passed through the small gate in the fence that led to the side-walk of the park. There were cars parked along there and presently she stopped beside one particular car. Miss Marple was not particularly knowledgeable over cars but such cars as this one did not come her way very often, so she had noted and remembered it. She had acquired a little information about cars of this style from an enthusiastic great-nephew. It was a racing car. Some foreign make – she couldn't remember the name now. Not only that, she had seen this car, or one exactly like it, seen it only yesterday in a side street close to Bertram's Hotel. She had noticed it not only because of its size and its powerful and unusual appearance but because the number had awakened some vague memory, some trace of association in her memory. FAN 2266. It had made her think of her cousin Fanny Godfrey. Poor Fanny who stuttered, who had said 'I have got t-t-t-wo s-s-s-potz . . .'

She walked along and looked at the number of this car. Yes, she was quite right. FAN 2266. It was the same car. Miss Marple, her footsteps growing more painful every moment, arrived deep in thought at the other side of Chelsea Bridge and by then was so exhausted that she hailed the first taxi she saw with decision. She was worried by the feeling that there was something she ought to do about things. But what things and what to do about them? It was all so indefinite. She fixed her eyes absently on some newsboards.

'Sensational developments in train robbery,' they ran. 'Engine driver's story,' said another one. Really! Miss Marple thought to herself, every day there seemed to be a bank hold-up or a train robbery or a wage pay snatch.

Crime seemed to have got above itself.

CHAPTER 13

Vaguely reminiscent of a large bumble bee, Chief-Inspector Fred Davy wandered around the confines of the Criminal Investigation Department, humming to himself. It was a well-known idiosyncrasy of his, and caused no particular notice except to give rise to the remark that 'Father was on the prowl again.'

His prowling led him at last to the room where Inspector Campbell was sitting behind a desk with a bored expression. Inspector Campbell was an ambitious young man and he found much of his occupation tedious in the extreme. Nevertheless, he coped with the duties appointed to him and achieved a very fair measure of success in so doing. The powers that be approved of him, thought he should do well and doled out from time to time a few words of encouraging commendation.

'Good morning, sir,' said Inspector Campbell, respectfully, when Father entered his domain. Naturally he called Chief-Inspector Davy 'Father' behind his back as everyone else did; but he was not yet of sufficient seniority to do such a thing to his face.

'Anything I can do for you, sir?' he inquired.

'La, la, boom, boom,' hummed the Chief-Inspector, slightly off key. 'Why must they call me Mary when my name's Miss Gibbs?' After this rather unexpected resurrection of a by-gone musical comedy, he drew up a chair and sat down.

'Busy?' he asked.

'Moderately so.'

'Got some disappearance case or other on, haven't you, to do with some hotel or other. What's the name of it now? Bertram's. Is that it?'

'Yes, that's right, sir. Bertram's Hotel.'

'Contravening the licensing hours? Call girls?'

'Oh no, sir,' said Inspector Campbell, slightly shocked at hearing Bertram's Hotel being referred to in such a connection. 'Very nice, quiet, old-fashioned place.'

'Is it now?' said Father. 'Yes, is it now? Well, that's interesting, really.'

Inspector Campbell wondered why it was interesting. He did not like to ask, as tempers in the upper hierarchy were notoriously short since the mail train robbery, which had been a spectacular success for the criminals. He looked at Father's large, heavy, bovine face and wondered, as he had once or twice wondered before, how Chief-Inspector Davy had reached his present rank and why he was so highly thought of in the department.

'All right in his day, I suppose,' thought Inspector Campbell, 'but there are plenty of go-ahead chaps about who could do with some promotion, once the dead wood is cleared away.' But the dead wood had begun another song, partly hummed, with an occasional word or two here and there.

'*Tell me, gentle stranger, are there any more at home like you?*' intoned Father and then in a sudden falsetto, '*A few, kind sir, and nicer girls you never knew*. No, let's see, I've got the sexes mixed up. *Floradora*. That was a good show, too.'

'I believe I've heard of it, sir,' said Inspector Campbell.

'Your mother sang you to sleep in the cradle with it, I expect,' said Chief-Inspector Davy. 'Now then, what's been going on at Bertram's Hotel? Who has disappeared and how and why?'

'A Canon Pennyfather, sir. Elderly clergyman.'

'Dull case, eh?'

Inspector Campbell smiled.

'Yes, sir, it *is* rather dull in a way.'

'What did he look like?'

'Canon Pennyfather?'

'Yes – you've got a description, I suppose?'

'Of course.' Campbell shuffled papers and read: 'Height 5 ft 8. Large thatch of white hair – stoops . . .'

'And he disappeared from Bertram's Hotel – when?'

'About a week ago – November 19th.'

'And they've just reported it. Took their time about it, didn't they?'

'Well, I think there was a general idea that he'd turn up.'

'Any idea what's behind it?' asked Father. 'Has a decent God-fearing man suddenly gone off with one of the church-wardens' wives? Or does he do a bit of secret drinking, or has he embezzled church funds? Or is he the sort of absent-minded old chap who goes in for this sort of thing?'

'Well, from all I can hear, sir, I should say the latter. He's done it before.'

'What – disappeared from a respectable West End hotel?'

'No, not exactly that, but he's not always returned home when he was expected. Occasionally he's turned up to stay with friends on a day when they haven't asked him, or not turned up on the date when they *had* asked him. That sort of thing.'

'Yes,' said Father. 'Yes. Well that sounds very nice and natural and according to plan, doesn't it? When exactly did you say he disappeared?'

'Thursday. November 19th. He was supposed to be attending a congress at –' He bent down and studied some papers on his desk. '– oh yes, Lucerne. Society of Biblical Historical Studies. That's the English translation of it. I think it's actually a German society.'

'And it was held at Lucerne? The old boy – I suppose he *is* an old boy?'

'Sixty-three, sir, I understand.'

'The old boy didn't turn up, is that it?'

Inspector Campbell drew his papers towards him and gave Father the ascertainable facts in so far as they had been ascertained.

'Doesn't sound as if he'd gone off with a choirboy,' observed Chief-Inspector Davy.

'I expect he'll turn up all right,' said Campbell, 'but we're looking into it, of course. Are you – er – particularly interested in the case, sir?' He could hardly restrain his curiosity on this point.

'No,' said Davy thoughtfully. 'No, I'm not interested in the *case*. I don't see anything to be interested about in it.'

There was a pause, a pause which clearly contained the words, 'Well, then?' with a question mark after it from Inspector Campbell, which he was too well trained to utter in audible tones.

'What I'm *really* interested in,' said Father, 'is the date. And Bertram's Hotel, of course.'

'It's always been very well conducted, sir. No trouble there.'

'That's very nice, I'm sure,' said Father. He added thoughtfully, 'I'd rather like to have a look at the place.'

'Of course, sir,' said Inspector Campbell. 'Any time you like. I was thinking of going round there myself.'

'I might as well come along with you,' said Father. 'Not to butt in, nothing like that. But I'd just rather like to have a look at the place, and this disappearing Archdeacon of yours, or whatever he is, makes rather a good excuse. No need to call me "sir" when we're there – you throw your weight about. I'll just be your stooge.'

Inspector Campbell became interested.

'Do you think there's something that might tie in there, sir, something that might tie in with something else?'

'There's no reason to believe so, so far,' said Father. 'But you know how it is. One gets – I don't know what to call them – whims, do you think? Bertram's Hotel, somehow, sounds almost too good to be true.'

He resumed his impersonation of a bumble bee with a rendering of 'Let's All Go Down the Strand'.

The two detective officers went off together, Campbell looking smart in a lounge suit (he had an excellent figure), and Chief-Inspector Davy carrying with him a tweedy air of being up from the country. They fitted in quite well. Only the astute eye of Miss Gorringe, as she raised it from her ledgers, singled out and appreciated them for what they were. Since she had reported the disappearance of Canon Pennyfather herself and had already had a word with a lesser personage in the police force, she had been expecting something of this kind.

A faint murmur to the earnest-looking girl assistant whom she kept handy in the background, enabled the latter to come forward and deal with any ordinary inquiries or services while Miss Gorringe gently shifted herself a little farther along the counter and looked up at the two men. Inspector Campbell laid down his card on the desk in front of her and she nodded. Looking past him to the large tweed-coated figure behind him, she noted that he had turned slightly sideways, and was observing the lounge and its occupants with an apparently naïve pleasure at beholding such a well bred, upper-class world in action.

'Would you like to come into the office?' said Miss Gorringe. 'We can talk better there perhaps.'

'Yes, I think that would be best.'

'Nice place you've got here,' said the large, fat, bovine-looking man, turning his head back towards her. 'Comfortable,' he added, looking approvingly at the large fire. 'Good old-fashioned comfort.'

Miss Gorringe smiled with an air of pleasure.

'Yes, indeed. We pride ourselves on making our visitors comfortable,' she said. She turned to her assistant. 'Will you carry on, Alice? There is the ledger. Lady Jocelyn will be arriving quite soon. She is sure to want to change her room as soon as she sees it but you must explain to her we are really full up. If necessary, you can show her number 340 on the third floor and offer her that instead. It's not a very pleasant room and I'm sure she will be content with her present one as soon as she sees that.'

'Yes, Miss Gorringe. I'll do just that, Miss Gorringe.'

'And remind Colonel Mortimer that his field glasses are here. He asked me to keep them for him this morning. Don't let him go off without them.'

'No, Miss Gorringe.'

These duties accomplished, Miss Gorringe looked at the two men, came out from behind the desk and walked along to a plain mahogany door with no legend on it. Miss Gorringe opened it and they went into a small, rather sad-looking office. All three sat down.

'The missing man is Canon Pennyfather, I understand,' said Inspector

Campbell. He looked at his notes. 'I've got Sergeant Wadell's report. Perhaps you'll tell me in your own words just what occurred.'

'I don't think that Canon Pennyfather has really disappeared in the sense in which one would usually use that word,' said Miss Gorringe. 'I think, you know, that he's just met someone somewhere, some old friend or something like that, and has perhaps gone off with him to some scholarly meeting or reunion or something of that kind, on the Continent – he is so very vague.'

'You've known him for a long time?'

'Oh yes, he's been coming here to stay for – let me see – oh five or six years at least, I should think.'

'You've been here some time yourself, ma'am,' said Chief-Inspector Davy, suddenly putting in a word.

'I have been here, let me think, fourteen years,' said Miss Gorringe.

'It's a nice place,' repeated Davy again. 'And Canon Pennyfather usually stayed here when he was in London? Is that right?'

'Yes. He always came to us. He wrote well beforehand to retain his room. He was much less vague on paper than he was in real life. He asked for a room from the 17th to the 21st. During that time he expected to be away for one or two nights, and he explained that he wished to keep his room on while he was away. He quite often did that.'

'When did you begin to get worried about him?' asked Campbell.

'Well, I didn't really. Of course it was awkward. You see, his room was let on from the 23rd and when I realized – I didn't at first – that he hadn't come back from Lugano –'

'I've got Lucerne here in my notes,' said Campbell.

'Yes, yes, I think it *was* Lucerne. Some Archaeological Congress or other. Anyway, when I realized he hadn't come back here and that his baggage was still here waiting in his room, it made things rather awkward. You see, we are very booked up at this time of year and I had someone else coming into his room. The Honourable Mrs Saunders, who lives at Lyme Regis. She always has that room. And then his housekeeper rang up. She was worried.'

'The housekeeper's name is Mrs McCrae, so I understand from Archdeacon Simmons. Do you know her?'

'Not personally, no, but I have spoken to her on the telephone once or twice. She is, I think, a very reliable woman and has been with Canon Pennyfather for some years. She was worried naturally. I believe she and Archdeacon Simmons got in touch with near friends and relations but they knew nothing of Canon Pennyfather's movements. And since he was expecting the Archdeacon to stay with him it certainly seemed very odd – in fact it still does – that the Canon should not have returned home.'

'Is this Canon usually as absent-minded as that?' asked Father.

Miss Gorringe ignored him. This large man, presumably the accompanying sergeant, seemed to her to be pushing himself forward a little too much.

'And now I understand,' continued Miss Gorringe, in an annoyed voice, 'and now I understand from Archdeacon Simmons that the Canon never even went to this conference in Lucerne.'

'Did he send any message to say he wouldn't go?'

'I don't think so – not from here. No telegram or anything like that. I really know nothing about Lucerne – I am really only concerned with *our* side of the matter. It has got into the evening papers, I see – the fact that he is missing, I mean. They haven't mentioned he was staying *here*. I hope they won't. We don't want the Press here, our visitors wouldn't like that at all. If you can keep them off us, Inspector Campbell, we should be very grateful. I mean it's not as if he had disappeared from *here*.'

'His luggage is still here?'

'Yes. In the baggage-room. If he didn't go to Lucerne, have you considered the possibility of his being run over? Something like that?'

'Nothing like that has happened to him.'

'It really does seem very, very curious,' said Miss Gorringe, a faint flicker of interest appearing in her manner, to replace the annoyance. 'I mean, it does make one wonder where he *could* have gone and why?'

Father looked at her comprehendingly.

'Of course,' he said. 'You've only been thinking of it from the hotel angle. Very natural.'

'I understand,' said Inspector Campbell, referring once more to his notes, 'that Canon Pennyfather left here about six-thirty on the evening of Thursday the 19th. He had with him a small overnight bag and he left here in a taxi, directing the commissionaire to tell the driver to drive to the Athenaeum Club.'

Miss Gorringe nodded her head.

'Yes, he dined at the Athenaeum Club – Archdeacon Simmons told me that *that* was the place he was last seen.'

There was a firmness in Miss Gorringe's voice as she transferred the responsibility of seeing the Canon last from Bertram's Hotel to the Athenaeum Club.

'Well, it's nice to get the facts straight,' said Father in a gentle rumbling voice. 'We've got 'em straight now. He went off with his little blue BOAC bag or whatever he'd got with him – it *was* a blue BOAC bag, yes? He went off and he didn't come back, and that's that.'

'So you see, really I cannot help you,' said Miss Gorringe, showing a disposition to rise to her feet and get back to work.

'It doesn't *seem* as if you could help us,' said Father, 'but someone else might be able to,' he added.

'Someone else?'

'Why, yes,' said Father. 'One of the staff perhaps.'

'I don't think anyone knows *anything*; or they would certainly have reported it to me.'

'Well, perhaps they might. Perhaps they mightn't. What I mean is, they'd have told you if they'd distinctly *known* anything. But I was thinking more of something he might have *said*.'

'What sort of thing?' said Miss Gorringe, looking perplexed.

'Oh, just some chance word that might give one a clue. Something like "I'm going to see an old friend tonight that I haven't seen since we met in Arizona." Something like that. Or "I'm going to stay next week with a niece of mine for her daughter's confirmation." With absent-minded people, you know, clues like that are a great help. They show what was in the person's mind. It may be that after his dinner at the Athenaeum, he gets into a taxi and thinks "Now where am I going?" and having got – say – the confirmation in his mind – thinks he's going off there.'

'Well, I see what you mean,' said Miss Gorringe doubtfully. 'It seems a little unlikely.'

'Oh, one never knows one's luck,' said Father cheerfully. 'Then there are the various guests here. I suppose Canon Pennyfather knew some of them since he came here fairly often.'

'Oh yes,' said Miss Gorringe. 'Let me see now. I've seen him talking to – yes, Lady Selina Hazy. Then there was the Bishop of Norwich. They're old friends, I believe. They were at Oxford together. And Mrs Jameson and her daughters. They come from the same part of the world. Oh yes, quite a lot of people.'

'You see,' said Father, 'he might have talked to one of *them*. He might have just mentioned some little thing that would give us a clue. Is there anyone staying here now that the Canon knew fairly well?'

Miss Gorringe frowned in thought.

'Well, I think General Radley is here still. And there's an old lady who came up from the country – who used to stay here as a girl, so she told me. Let me see, I can't remember her name at the moment, but I can find it for you. Oh yes, Miss Marple, that's her name. I believe she knew him.'

'Well, we could make a start with those two. And there'd be a chamber-maid, I suppose.'

'Oh yes,' said Miss Gorringe. 'But she has been interviewed already by Sergeant Wadell.'

'I know. But not perhaps from this angle. What about the waiter who attended on his table. Or the head waiter?'

'There's Henry, of course,' said Miss Gorringe.

'Who's Henry?' asked Father.

Miss Gorringe looked almost shocked. It was to her impossible that anyone should not know Henry.

'Henry has been here for more years than I can say,' she said. 'You must have noticed him serving teas as you came in.'

'Kind of personality,' said Davy. 'I remember noticing him.'

'I don't know what we should do without Henry,' said Miss Gorringe with feeling. 'He really is wonderful. He sets the tone of the place, you know.'

'Perhaps he might like to serve tea to me,' said Chief-Inspector Davy. 'Muffins, I saw he'd got there. I'd like a good muffin again.'

'Certainly if you like,' said Miss Gorringe, rather coldly. 'Shall I order two teas to be served to you in the lounge?' she added, turning to Inspector Campbell.

'That would –' the inspector began, when suddenly the door opened and Mr Humfries appeared in his Olympian manner.

He looked slightly taken aback, then looked inquiringly at Miss Gorringe. Miss Gorringe explained.

'These are two gentlemen from Scotland Yard, Mr Humfries,' she said.

'Detective-Inspector Campbell,' said Campbell.

'Oh yes. Yes, of course,' said Mr Humfries. 'The matter of Canon Pennyfather, I suppose? Most extraordinary business. I hope nothing's happened to him, poor old chap.'

'So do I,' said Miss Gorringe. 'Such a dear old man.'

'One of the old school,' said Mr Humfries approvingly.

'You seem to have quite a lot of the old school here,' observed Chief-Inspector Davy.

'I suppose we do, I suppose we do,' said Mr Humfries. 'Yes, in many ways we are quite a survival.'

'We have our regulars you know,' said Miss Gorringe. She spoke proudly. 'The same people come back year after year. We have a lot of Americans. People from Boston, and Washington. Very quiet, nice people.'

'They like our English atmosphere,' said Mr Humfries, showing his very white teeth in a smile.

Father looked at him thoughtfully. Inspector Campbell said:

'You're quite sure that no message came here from the Canon? I mean it might have been taken by someone who forgot to write it down or to pass it on.'

'Telephone messages are always taken down *most* carefully,' said Miss Gorringe with ice in her voice. 'I cannot conceive it possible that a message would not have been passed on to me or to the appropriate person on duty.'

She glared at him.

Inspector Campbell looked momentarily taken aback.

'We've really answered all these questions before, you know,' said Mr Humfries, also with a touch of ice in his voice. 'We gave all the information at our disposal to your sergeant – I can't remember his name for the moment.'

Father stirred a little and said, in a kind of homely way:

'Well you see, things have begun to look rather more serious. It looks like a bit more than absent-mindedness. That's why, I think, it would be a good thing if we could have a word or two with those two people you mentioned – General Radley and Miss Marple.'

'You want me to – to arrange an interview with them?' Mr Humfries looked rather unhappy. 'General Radley's very deaf.'

'I don't think it will be necessary to make it too formal,' said Chief-Inspector Davy. 'We don't want to worry people. You can leave it quite safely to us. Just point out those two you mentioned. There is just a chance, you know, that Canon Pennyfather *might* have mentioned some plan of his, or some person he was going to meet at Lucerne or who was going with him to Lucerne. Anyway, it's worth trying.'

Mr Humfries looked somewhat relieved.

'Nothing more we can do for you?' he asked. 'I'm sure you understand that we wish to help you in every way, only you do understand how we feel about any Press publicity.'

'Quite,' said Inspector Campbell.

'And I'll just have a word with the chambermaid,' said Father.

'Certainly, if you like. I doubt very much whether she can tell you anything.'

'Probably not. But there might be some detail – some remark the Canon made about a letter or an appointment. One never knows.'

Mr Humfries glanced at his watch.

'She'll be on duty at six,' he said. 'Second floor. Perhaps, in the meantime, you'd care for tea?'

'Suits me,' said Father promptly.

They left the office together.

Miss Gorringe said, 'General Radley will be in the smoking-room. The first room down that passage on the left. He'll be in front of the fire there with *The Times*. I think,' she added discreetly, 'he might be asleep. You're sure you don't want me to –'

'No, no, I'll see to it,' said Father. 'And what about the other one – the old lady?'

'She's sitting over there, by the fireplace,' said Miss Gorringe.

'The one with white fluffy hair and the knitting?' said Father, taking a look. 'Might almost be on the stage, mightn't she? Everybody's universal great-aunt.'

'Great-aunts aren't much like that nowadays,' said Miss Gorringe, 'nor grandmothers nor great-grandmothers, if it comes to that. We had the Marchioness of Barlowe in yesterday. She's a great-grandmother. Honestly, I didn't know her when she came in. Just back from Paris. Her face a mask of pink and white and her hair platinum blonde and I suppose an entirely false figure, but it looked wonderful.'

'Ah,' said Father, 'I prefer the old-fashioned kind myself. Well, thank you, ma'am.' He turned to Campbell. 'I'll look after it, shall I, sir? I know you've got an important appointment.'

'That's right,' said Campbell, taking his cue. 'I don't suppose anything much will come of it, but it's worth trying.'

Mr Humfries disappeared into his inner sanctum, saying as he did so:

'Miss Gorringe – just a moment, please.'

Miss Gorringe followed him in and shut the door behind her.

Humfries was walking up and down. He demanded sharply:

'What do they want to see Rose for? Wadell asked all the necessary questions.'

'I suppose it's just routine,' said Miss Gorringe, doubtfully.

'You'd better have a word with her first.'

Miss Gorringe looked a little startled.

'But surely Inspector Campbell –'

'Oh, I'm not worried about Campbell. It's the other one. Do you know who he is?'

'I don't think he gave his name. Sergeant of some kind, I suppose. He looks rather a yokel.'

'Yokel, my foot,' said Mr Humfries, abandoning his elegance. 'That's

Chief-Inspector Davy, an old fox if there ever was one. They think a lot of him at the Yard. I'd like to know what *he's* doing here, nosing about and playing the genial hick. I don't like it at all.'

'You can't think –'

'I don't know what to think. But I tell you I don't like it. Did he ask to see anyone else besides Rose?'

'I think he's going to have a word with Henry.'

Mr Humfries laughed. Miss Gorringe laughed too.

'We needn't worry about Henry.'

'No, indeed.'

'And the visitors who knew Canon Pennyfather?'

Mr Humfries laughed again.

'I wish him joy of old Radley. He'll have to shout the place down and then he won't get anything worth having. He's welcome to Radley and that funny old hen, Miss Marple. All the same, I don't much like his poking his nose in . . .'

CHAPTER 14

'You know,' said Chief-Inspector Davy thoughtfully, 'I don't much like that chap Humfries.'

'Think there's something wrong with him?' asked Campbell.

'Well –' Father sounded apologetic, 'you know the sort of feeling one gets. Smarmy sort of chap. I wonder if he's the owner or only the manager.'

'I could ask him.' Campbell took a step back towards the desk.

'No, don't ask him,' said Father. 'Just find out – quietly.'

Campbell looked at him curiously.

'What's on your mind, sir?'

'Nothing in particular,' said Father. 'I just think I'd like to have a good deal more information about this place. I'd like to know who is behind it, what its financial status is. All that sort of thing.'

Campbell shook his head.

'I should have said if there was one place in London that was absolutely above suspicion –'

'I know, I know,' said Father. 'And what a useful thing it is to have that reputation!'

Campbell shook his head and left. Father went down the passage to the smoking-room. General Radley was just waking up. *The Times* had slipped from his knees and disintegrated slightly. Father picked it up and reassembled the sheets and handed it to him.

'Thank ye, sir. Very kind,' said General Radley gruffly.

'General Radley?'

'Yes.'

'You'll excuse me,' said Father, raising his voice, 'but I want to speak to you about Canon Pennyfather.'

'Eh – what's that?' The General approached a hand to his ear.

'Canon Pennyfather,' bellowed Father.

'My father? Dead years ago.'

'Canon *Penny*father.'

'Oh. What about him? Saw him the other day. He was staying here.'

'There was an address he was going to give me. Said he'd leave it with you.'

That was rather more difficult to get over but he succeeded in the end.

'Never gave me any address. Must have mixed me up with somebody else. Muddle-headed old fool. Always was. Scholarly sort of chap, you know. They're always absent-minded.'

Father persevered for a little longer but soon decided that conversation with General Radley was practically impossible and almost certainly unprofitable. He went and sat down in the lounge at a table adjacent to that of Miss Jane Marple.

'Tea, sir?'

Father looked up. He was impressed, as everyone was impressed, by Henry's personality. Though such a large and portly man he had appeared, as it were, like some vast travesty of Ariel who could materialize and vanish at will. Father ordered tea.

'Did I see you've got muffins here?' he asked.

Henry smiled benignly.

'Yes, sir. Very good indeed our muffins are, if I may say so. Everyone enjoys them. Shall I order you muffins, sir? Indian or China tea?'

'Indian,' said Father. 'Or Ceylon if you've got it.'

'Certainly we have Ceylon, sir.'

Henry made the faintest gesture with a finger and the pale young man who was his minion departed in search of Ceylon tea and muffins. Henry moved graciously elsewhere.

'You're *Someone*, you are,' thought Father. 'I wonder where they got hold of you and what they pay you. A packet, I bet, *and* you'd be worth it.' He watched Henry bending in a fatherly manner over an elderly lady. He wondered what Henry thought, if he thought anything, about Father. Father considered that he fitted into Bertram's Hotel reasonably well. He might have been a prosperous gentleman farmer or he might have been a peer of the realm with a resemblance to a bookmaker. Father knew two peers who were very like that. On the whole, he thought, he passed muster, but he also thought it possible that he had not deceived Henry. 'Yes, you're *Someone* you are,' Father thought again.

Tea came and the muffins. Father bit deeply. Butter ran down his chin. He wiped it off with a large handkerchief. He drank two cups of tea with plenty of sugar. Then he leaned forward and spoke to the lady sitting in the chair next to him.

'Excuse me,' he said, 'but aren't you Miss Jane Marple?'

Miss Marple transferred her gaze from her knitting to Chief Detective-Inspector Davy.

'Yes,' she said, 'I am Miss Marple.'

'I hope you don't mind my speaking to you. As a matter of fact I am a police officer.'

'Indeed? Nothing seriously wrong here, I hope?'

Father hastened to reassure her in his best paternal fashion.

'Now, don't you worry, Miss Marple,' he said. 'It's not the sort of thing you mean at all. No burglary or anything like that. Just a little difficulty about an absent-minded clergyman, that's all. I think he's a friend of yours. Canon Pennyfather.'

'Oh, Canon Pennyfather. He was here only the other day. Yes, I've known him slightly for many years. As you say, he *is* very absent-minded.' She added, with some interest, 'What has he done now?'

'Well, as you might say in a manner of speaking, he's lost himself.'

'Oh dear,' said Miss Marple. 'Where ought he to be?'

'Back at home in his Cathedral Close,' said Father, 'but he isn't.'

'He told *me*,' said Miss Marple, 'he was going to a conference at Lucerne. Something to do with the Dead Sea Scrolls, I believe. He's a great Hebrew and Aramaic scholar, you know.'

'Yes,' said Father. 'You're quite right. That's where he – well, that's where he was supposed to be going.'

'Do you mean he didn't turn up there?'

'No,' said Father, 'he didn't turn up.'

'Oh, well,' said Miss Marple, 'I expect he got his dates wrong.'

'Very likely, very likely.'

'I'm afraid,' said Miss Marple, 'that that's not the first time that that's happened. I went to have tea with him in Chadminster once. He was actually absent from home. His housekeeper told me then how very absent-minded he was.'

'He didn't say anything to you when he was staying here that might give us a clue, I suppose?' asked Father, speaking in an easy and confidential way. 'You know the sort of thing I mean, any old friend he'd met or any plans he'd made apart from this Lucerne Conference?'

'Oh no. He just mentioned the Lucerne Conference. I think he said it was on the 19th. Is that right?'

'That was the date of the Lucerne Conference, yes.'

'I didn't notice the date particularly. I mean –' like most old ladies, Miss Marple here became slightly involved – 'I *thought* he said the 19th and he *might* have said the 19th, but at the same time he might have *meant* the 19th and it might really have been the *20th*. I mean, he may have thought the 20th *was* the 19th or he may have thought the 19th was the 20th.'

'Well –' said Father, slightly dazed.

'I'm putting it badly,' said Miss Marple, 'but I mean people like Canon Pennyfather, if they say they're going somewhere on a Thursday, one is quite prepared to find that they didn't mean Thursday, it may be Wednesday or Friday they really mean. Usually they find out in time but sometimes they just don't. I thought at the time that something like that must have happened.'

Father looked slightly puzzled.

'You speak as though you knew already, Miss Marple, that Canon Pennyfather hadn't gone to Lucerne.'

'I knew he wasn't in Lucerne on *Thursday*,' said Miss Marple. 'He was here all day – or most of the day. That's why I thought, of course, that though he may have said Thursday to me, it was really Friday he meant. He certainly left here on Thursday evening carrying his BEA bag.'

'Quite so.'

'I took it he was going off to the airport then,' said Miss Marple. 'That's why I was so surprised to see he was back again.'

'I beg your pardon, what do you mean by "back again"?'

'Well, that he was back here again, I mean.'

'Now, let's get this quite clear,' said Father, careful to speak in an agreeable and reminiscent voice, and not as though it was really important. 'You saw the old idio – you saw the Canon, that is to say, leave as you thought for the airport with his overnight bag, fairly early in the evening. Is that right?'

'Yes. About half-past six, I would say, or quarter to seven.'

'But you say he came *back*.'

'Perhaps he missed the plane. That would account for it.'

'*When* did he come back?'

'Well, I don't really know. I didn't see him come back.'

'Oh,' said Father, taken aback. 'I thought you said you *did* see him.'

'Oh, I did see him *later*,' said Miss Marple. 'I meant I didn't see him actually come into the hotel.'

'You saw him later? When?'

Miss Marple thought.

'Let me see. It was about 3 a.m. I couldn't sleep very well. Something woke me. Some sound. There are so many queer noises in London. I looked at my little clock, it was ten minutes past three. For some reason – I'm not quite sure what – I felt uneasy. Footsteps, perhaps, outside my door. Living in the country, if one hears footsteps in the middle of the night it makes one nervous. So I just opened my door and looked out. There was Canon Pennyfather leaving his room – it's next door to mine – and going off down the stairs wearing his overcoat.'

'He came out of his room wearing his overcoat and went down the stairs at 3 a.m. in the morning?'

'Yes,' said Miss Marple and added: 'I thought it odd at the time.'

Father looked at her for some moments.

'Miss Marple,' he said, 'why haven't you told anyone this before?'

'Nobody asked me,' said Miss Marple simply.

CHAPTER 15

Father drew a deep breath.

'No,' he said. 'No, I suppose nobody would ask you. It's as simple as that.'

He relapsed into silence again.

'You think something has happened to him, don't you?' asked Miss Marple.

'It's over a week now,' said Father. 'He didn't have a stroke and fall down in the street. He's not in a hospital as a result of an accident. So where *is* he? His disappearance has been reported in the Press, but nobody's come forward with any information yet.'

'They may not have seen it. *I* didn't.'

'It looks – it really looks –' Father was following out his own line of thought – 'as though he *meant* to disappear. Leaving this place like that in the middle of the night. You're quite sure about it, aren't you?' he demanded sharply. 'You didn't dream it?'

'I am absolutely sure,' said Miss Marple with finality.

Father heaved himself to his feet.

'I'd better go and see that chambermaid,' he said.

Father found Rose Sheldon on duty and ran an approving eye over her pleasant person.

'I'm sorry to bother you,' he said. 'I know you've seen our sergeant already. But it's about that missing gentleman, Canon Pennyfather.'

'Oh yes, sir, a very nice gentleman. He often stays here.'

'Absent-minded,' said Father.

Rose Sheldon permitted a discreet smile to appear on her respectful mask of a face.

'Now let me see.' Father pretended to consult some notes. 'The last time you saw Canon Pennyfather – was –'

'On the Thursday morning, sir. Thursday the 19th. He told me that he would not be back that night and possibly not the next either. He was going, I think, to Geneva. Somewhere in Switzerland, anyway. He gave me two shirts he wanted washed and I said they would be ready for him on the morning of the following day.'

'And that's the last you saw of him, eh?'

'Yes, sir. You see, I'm not on duty in the afternoons. I come back again at 6 o'clock. By then he must have left, or at any rate he was downstairs. Not in his room. He had left two suitcases behind.'

'That's right,' said Father. The contents of the suitcases had been examined, but had given no useful lead. He went on: 'Did you call him the next morning?'

'Call him? No, sir, he was away.'

'What did you do ordinarily – take him early tea? Breakfast?'

'Early tea, sir. He breakfasted downstairs always.'

'So you didn't go into his room at all the next day?'

'Oh yes, sir.' Rose sounded shocked. 'I went into his room as usual. I took his shirts in for one thing. And of course I dusted the room. We dust all the rooms every day.'

'Had the bed been slept in?'

She stared at him. 'The bed, sir? Oh no.'

'Was it rumpled – creased in any way?'

She shook her head.

'What about the bathroom?'

'There was a damp hand towel, sir, that had been used. I presume that would be the evening before. He may have washed his hands last thing before going off.'

'And there was nothing to show that he had come back into the room – perhaps quite late – after midnight?'

She stared at him with an air of bewilderment. Father opened his mouth, then shut it again. Either she knew nothing about the Canon's return or she was a highly accomplished actress.

'What about his clothes – suits. Were they packed up in his suitcases?'

'No, sir, they were hanging up in the cupboards. He was keeping his room on, you see, sir.'

'Who did pack them up?'

'Miss Gorringe gave orders, sir. When the room was wanted for the new lady coming in.'

A straightforward coherent account. But if that old lady was correct in stating that she saw Canon Pennyfather leaving his room at 3 a.m. on Friday morning, then he must have come back to that room sometime. Nobody had seen him enter the hotel. Had he, for some reason, deliberately avoided being seen? He had left no traces in the room. He hadn't even lain down on the bed. Had Miss Marple dreamed the whole thing? At her age it was possible enough. An idea struck him.

'What about the airport bag?'

'I beg your pardon, sir?'

'A small bag, dark blue – a BEA or BOAC bag – you must have seen it?'

'Oh that – yes, sir. But of course he'd take that with him abroad.'

'But he didn't *go* abroad. He never went to Switzerland after all. So he must have left it behind. Or else he came back and left it here with his other luggage.'

'Yes – yes – I think – I'm not quite sure – I believe he did.'

Quite unsolicited, the thought raced into Father's mind: *They didn't brief you on that, did they?*

Rose Sheldon had been calm and competent up till now. But that question had rattled her. She hadn't known the right answer to it. *But she ought to have known.*

The Canon had taken his bag to the airport, had been turned away from the airport. If he had come back to Bertram's, the bag would have been with him. *But Miss Marple had made no mention of it when she had described the Canon leaving his room and going down the stairs.*

Presumably it was left in the bedroom, but it had not been put in the baggage-room with the suitcases. Why not? *Because the Canon was supposed to have gone to Switzerland?*

He thanked Rose genially and went downstairs again.

Canon Pennyfather! Something of an enigma, Canon Pennyfather. Talked a lot about going to Switzerland, muddled up things so that he didn't go to Switzerland, came back to his hotel so secretly that nobody saw him, left it again in the early hours of the morning. (To go where? To do what?)

Could absent-mindedness account for all this?

If not, then what was Canon Pennyfather up to? And more important, where was he?

From the staircase, Father cast a jaundiced eye over the occupants of the lounge, and wondered whether *anyone* was what they seemed to be. He had got to that stage! Elderly people, middle-aged people (nobody very young) nice old-fashioned people, nearly all well-to-do, all highly respectable. Service people, lawyers, clergymen; American husband and wife near the door, a French family near the fireplace. Nobody flashy, nobody out of place; most of them enjoying an old-fashioned English afternoon tea. Could there really be anything seriously wrong with a place that served old-fashioned afternoon teas?

The Frenchman made a remark to his wife that fitted in appositively enough.

'*Le Five-o'-clock,*' he was saying. '*C'est bien Anglais ça, n'est ce pas?*' He looked round him with approval.

'*Le Five-o'-clock,*' thought Davy as he passed through the swing doors to the street. 'That chap doesn't know that "*le Five-o'-clock*" is as dead as the Dodo!'

Outside, various vast American wardrobe cases and suitcases were being loaded on to a taxi. It seemed that Mr and Mrs Elmer Cabot were on their way to the Hotel Vendôme, Paris.

Beside him on the kerb, Mrs Elmer Cabot was expressing her views to her husband.

'The Pendleburys were quite right about this place, Elmer. It just *is* old England. So beautifully Edwardian. I just feel Edward the Seventh could walk right in any moment and sit down there for his afternoon tea. I mean to come back here next year – I really do.'

'If we've got a million dollars or so to spare,' said her husband dryly.

'Now, Elmer, it wasn't as bad as all *that.*'

The baggage was loaded, the tall commissionaire helped them in, murmuring 'Thank you, sir' as Mr Cabot made the expected gesture. The taxi drove off. The commissionaire transferred his attention to Father.

'Taxi, sir?'

Father looked up at him.

Over six feet. Good-looking chap. A bit run to seed. Ex-Army. Lot of medals – genuine, probably. A bit shifty? Drinks too much.

Aloud he said: 'Ex-Army man?'

'Yes, sir. Irish Guards.'

'Military Medal, I see. Where did you get that?'

'Burma.'

'What's your name?'

'Michael Gorman. Sergeant.'

'Good job here?'

'It's a peaceful spot.'

'Wouldn't you prefer the Hilton?'

'I would not. I like it here. Nice people come here, and quite a lot of racing gentlemen – for Ascot and Newbury. I've had good tips from them now and again.'

'Ah, so you're an Irishman and gambler, is that it?'

'Och! Now, what would life be without a gamble?'

'Peaceful and dull,' said Chief-Inspector Davy, 'like mine.'

'Indeed, sir?'

'Can you guess what my profession is?' asked Father.

The Irishman grinned.

'No offence to you, sir, but if I may guess I'd say you were a cop.'

'Right first time,' said Chief-Inspector Davy. 'You remember Canon Pennyfather?'

'Canon Pennyfather now, I don't seem to mind the name –'

'Elderly clergyman.'

Michael Gorman laughed.

'Ah now, clergyman are as thick as peas in a pod in there.'

'This one disappeared from here.'

'Oh, *that* one!' The commissionaire seemed slightly taken aback.

'Did you know him?'

'I wouldn't remember him if it hadn't been for people asking me questions about him. All I know is, I put him into a taxi and he went to the Athenaeum Club. That's the last I saw of him. Somebody told me he'd gone to Switzerland, but I hear he never got there. Lost himself, it seems.'

'You didn't see him later that day?'

'Later – No, indeed.'

'What time do you go off duty?'

'Eleven-thirty.'

Chief-Inspector Davy nodded, refused a taxi and moved slowly away along Pond Street. A car roared past him close to the kerb, and pulled up outside Bertram's Hotel, with a scream of brakes. Chief-Inspector Davy turned his head soberly and noted the number plate. FAN 2266. There was something reminiscent about that number, though he couldn't for the moment place it.

Slowly he retraced his steps. He had barely reached the entrance before the driver of the car, who had gone through the doors a moment or two before, came out again. He and the car matched each other. It was a racing model, white with long gleaming lines. The young man had the same eager greyhound look with a handsome face and a body with not a superfluous inch of flesh on it.

The commissionaire held the car door open, the young man jumped in, tossed a coin to the commissionaire and drove off with a burst of powerful engine.

'You know who *he* is?' said Michael Gorman to Father.

'A dangerous driver, anyway.'

'Ladislaus Malinowski. Won the Grand Prix two years ago – world champion he was. Had a bad smash last year. They say he's all right again now.'

'Don't tell me *he's* staying at Bertram's. Highly unsuitable.'

Michael Gorman grinned.

'He's not staying here, no. But a friend of his is –' He winked.

A porter in a striped apron came out with more American luxury travel equipment.

Father stood absent-mindedly watching them being ensconced in a Daimler Hire Car whilst he tried to remember what he knew about Ladislaus Malinowski. A reckless fellow – said to be tied up with some well-known woman – what was her name now? Still staring at a smart wardrobe case, he was just turning away when he changed his mind and re-entered the hotel again.

He went to the desk and asked Miss Gorringe for the hotel register. Miss Gorringe was busy with departing Americans, and pushed the book along the counter towards him. He turned the pages.

Lady Selina Hazy, Little Cottage, Merryfield, Hants.
Mr and Mrs Hennessey King, Elderberries, Essex.
Sir John Woodstock, 5 Beaumont Crescent, Cheltenham.
Lady Sedgwick, Hurstings House, Northumberland.
Mr and Mrs Elmer Cabot, Connecticut.
General Radley, 14, The Green, Chichester.
Mr and Mrs Woolmer Pickington, Marble Head, Connecticut.

La Comtesse de Beauville, Les Sapins, St Germain en Laye.
Miss Jane Marple, St Mary Mead, Much Benham.
Colonel Luscombe, Little Green, Suffolk.
Mrs Carpenter, The Hon. Elvira Blake.
Canon Pennyfather, The Close, Chadminster.
Mrs Holding, Mr Holding, Miss Audrey Holding, The Manor House,
*   Carmanton.*
Mr and Mrs Ryesville, Valley Forge, Pennsylvania.
The Duke of Barnstable, Doone Castle, N. Devon . . .

A cross-section of the kind of people who stayed at Bertram's Hotel. They formed, he thought, a kind of pattern . . .

As he shut the book, a name on an earlier page caught his eye. Sir William Ludgrove.

Mr Justice Ludgrove who had been recognized by a probation officer near the scene of a bank robbery. Mr Justice Ludgrove – Canon Pennyfather – both patrons of Bertram's Hotel . . .

'I hope you enjoyed your tea, sir?' It was Henry, standing at his elbow. He spoke courteously, and with the slight anxiety of the perfect host.

'The best tea I've had for years,' said Chief-Inspector Davy.

He remembered he hadn't paid for it. He attempted to do so; but Henry raised a deprecating hand.

'Oh no, sir. I was given to understand that your tea was on the house. Mr Humfries' orders.'

Henry moved away. Father was left uncertain whether he ought to have offered Henry a tip or not. It was galling to think that Henry knew the answer to that social problem much better than he did!

As he moved away along the street, he stopped suddenly. He took out his note-book and put down a name and an address – no time to lose. He went into a telephone box. He was going to stick out his neck. Come hell or high water, he was going all out on a hunch.

CHAPTER 16

It was the wardrobe that worried Canon Pennyfather. It worried him before he was quite awake. Then he forgot it and he fell asleep again. But when his eyes opened once more, there the wardrobe still was in the wrong place. He was lying on his left side facing the window and the wardrobe ought to have been there between him and the window on the left wall. But it wasn't. It was on the right. It worried him. It worried him so much that it made him feel tired. He was conscious of his head aching badly, and on top of that, to have the wardrobe in the wrong place. At this point once more his eyes closed.

There was rather more light in the room the next time he woke. It was not daylight yet. Only the faint light of dawn. 'Dear me,' said Canon Pennyfather to himself, suddenly solving the problem of the wardrobe. 'How stupid I am! Of course, I'm not at home.'

He moved gingerly. No, this wasn't his own bed. He was away from home. He was – where was he? Oh, of course. He'd gone to London, hadn't he? He was in Bertram's Hotel and – but no, he *wasn't* in Bertram's Hotel. In Bertram's Hotel his bed was facing the window. So that was wrong, too.

'Dear me, where can I be?' said Canon Pennyfather.

Then he remembered that he was going to Lucerne. 'Of course,' he said to himself, 'I'm in Lucerne.' He began thinking about the paper he was going to read. He didn't think about it long. Thinking about his paper seemed to make his head ache so he went to sleep again.

The next time he woke his head was a great deal clearer. Also there was a good deal more light in the room. He was not at home, he was not at Bertram's Hotel and he was fairly sure that he was not in Lucerne. This wasn't a hotel bedroom at all. He studied it fairly closely. It was an entirely strange room with very little furniture in it. A kind of cupboard (what he'd taken for the wardrobe) and a window with flowered curtains through which the light came. A chair and a table and a chest of drawers. Really, that was about all.

'Dear me,' said Canon Pennyfather, 'this is *most* odd. Where am I?'

He was thinking of getting up to investigate but when he sat up in bed his headache began again so he lay down.

'I must have been ill,' decided Canon Pennyfather. 'Yes, definitely I must have been ill.' He thought a minute or two and then said to himself, 'As a matter of fact, I think perhaps I'm still ill. Influenza, perhaps?' Influenza, people often said, came on very suddenly. Perhaps – perhaps it had come on at dinner at the Athenaeum. Yes, that was right. He remembered that he had dined at the Athenaeum.

There were sounds of moving about in the house. Perhaps they'd taken him to a nursing home. But no, he didn't think this was a nursing home. With the increased light it showed itself as a rather shabby and ill-furnished small bedroom. Sounds of movement went on. From downstairs a voice called out, 'Goodbye, ducks. Sausage and mash this evening.'

Canon Pennyfather considered this. Sausage and mash. The words had a faintly agreeable quality.

'I believe,' he said to himself, 'I'm *hungry*.'

The door opened. A middle-aged woman came in, went across to the curtains, pulled them back a little and turned towards the bed.

'Ah, you're awake now,' she said. 'And how are you feeling?'

'Really,' said Canon Pennyfather, rather feebly, 'I'm not quite sure.'

'Ah, I expect not. You've been quite bad, you know. Something hit you a nasty crack, so the doctor said. These motorists! Not even stopping after they'd knocked you down.'

'Have I had an accident?' said Canon Pennyfather. 'A motor accident?'

'That's right,' said the woman. 'Found you by the side of the road when we come home. Thought you was drunk at first.' She chuckled pleasantly at the reminiscence. 'Then my husband said he'd better take a look. It may have been an accident, he said. There wasn't no smell of drink or anything. No blood or anything neither. Anyway, there you was, out like a log. So my husband said, "We can't leave him here lying like that," and he carried you in here. See?'

'Ah,' said Canon Pennyfather, faintly, somewhat overcome by all these revelations. 'A good Samaritan.'

'And he saw you were a clergyman so my husband said, "It's all quite respectable." Then he said he'd better not call the police because being a clergyman and all that you mightn't like it. That's if you was drunk, in spite of there being no smell of drink. So then we hit upon getting Dr Stokes to come and have a look at you. We still call him Dr Stokes although he's been struck off. A very nice man he is, embittered a bit, of course, by being struck off. It was only his kind heart really, helping a lot of girls who were no better than they should be. Anyway, he's a good enough doctor and we got him to come and take a look at you. He says you've come to no real harm, says it's mild concussion. All we'd got to do was to keep you lying flat and quiet in a dark room. "Mind you," he said, "I'm not giving an opinion or anything like that. This is unofficial. I've no right to prescribe or to say anything. By rights I dare say you ought to report it to the police, but if you don't want to, why should you?" Give the poor old geezer a chance, that's what he said. Excuse me if I'm speaking disrespectful. He's a rough and ready speaker, the doctor is. Now what about a drop of soup or some hot bread and milk?'

'Either,' said Canon Pennyfather faintly, 'would be very welcome.'

He relapsed on to his pillows. An accident? So *that* was it. An accident, and he couldn't remember a thing about it! A few minutes later the good woman returned bearing a tray with a steaming bowl on it.

'You'll feel better after this,' she said. 'I'd like to have put a drop of whisky or a drop of brandy in it but the doctor said you wasn't to have nothing like that.'

'Certainly not,' said Canon Pennyfather, 'not with concussion. No. It would have been unadvisable.'

'I'll put another pillow behind your back, shall I, ducks? There, is that all right?'

Canon Pennyfather was a little startled by being addressed as 'ducks'. He told himself that it was kindly meant.

'Upsydaisy,' said the woman, 'there we are.'

'Yes, but where are we?' said Canon Pennyfather. 'I mean, where am I? Where is this place?'

'Milton St John,' said the woman. 'Didn't you know?'

'Milton St John?' said Canon Pennyfather. He shook his head. 'I never heard the name before.'

'Oh well, it's not much of a place. Only a village.'

'You have been very kind,' said Canon Pennyfather. 'May I ask your name?'

'Mrs Wheeling. Emma Wheeling.'

'You are most kind,' said Canon Pennyfather again. 'But this accident now. I simply cannot remember –'

'You put yourself outside that, luv, and you'll feel better and up to remembering things.'

'Milton St John,' said Canon Pennyfather to himself, in a tone of wonder. 'The name means nothing to me *at all*. How very extraordinary!'

CHAPTER 17

Sir Ronald Graves drew a cat upon his blotting pad. He looked at the large portly figure of Chief-Inspector Davy sitting opposite him and drew a bulldog.

'Ladislaus Malinowski?' he said. 'Could be. Got any evidence?'

'No. He'd fit the bill, would he?'

'A daredevil. No nerves. Won the World Championship. Bad crash about a year ago. Bad reputation with women. Sources of income doubtful. Spends money here and abroad freely. Always going to and fro to the Continent. Have you got some idea that he's the man behind these organized robberies and hold-ups?'

'I don't think he's the planner. But I think he's in with them.'

'Why?'

'For one thing, he runs a Mercedes-Otto car. Racing model. A car answering to that description was seen near Bedhampton on the morning of the mail robbery. Different number plates – but we're used to that. And it's the same stunt – unlike, but not too unlike. FAN 2299 instead of 2266. There aren't so many Mercedes-Otto models of that type about. Lady Sedgwick has one and young Lord Merrivale.'

'You don't think Malinowski runs the show?'

'No – I think there are better brains than his at the top. But he's in it. I've looked back over the files. Take the hold-up at the Midland and West London. Three vans happened – just happened – to block a certain street. A Mercedes-Otto that was on the scene got clear away owing to that block.'

'It was stopped later.'

'Yes. And given a clean bill of health. Especially as the people who'd reported it weren't sure of the correct number. It was reported as FAM 3366 – Malinowski's registration number is FAN 2266 – It's all the same picture.'

'And you persist in tying it up with Bertram's Hotel. They dug up some stuff about Bertram's for you –'

Father tapped his pocket.

'Got it here. Properly registered company. Balance – paid up capital – directors – etcetera, etcetera, etcetera. Doesn't mean a thing! These financial shows are all the same – just a lot of snakes swallowing each other! Companies, and holding companies – makes your brain reel!'

'Come now, Father. That's just a way they have in the City. Has to do with taxation –'

'What I want is the real dope. If you'll give me a chit, sir, I'd like to go and see some top brass.'

The AC stared at him.

'And what exactly do you mean by top brass?'

Father mentioned a name.

The AC looked upset. 'I don't know about that. I hardly think we dare approach *him*.'

'It might be very helpful.'

There was a pause. The two men looked at each other. Father looked bovine, placid, and patient. The AC gave in.

'You're a stubborn old devil, Fred,' he said. 'Have it your own way. Go and worry the top brains behind the international financiers of Europe.'

'*He'll* know,' said Chief-Inspector Davy. 'He'll *know*. And if he doesn't, he can find out by pressing one buzzer on his desk or making one telephone call.'

'I don't know that he'll be pleased.'

'Probably not,' said Father, 'but it won't take much of his time. I've got to have authority behind me, though.'

'You're really serious about this place, Bertram's, aren't you? But what have you got to go on? It's well run, has a good respectable clientele – no trouble with the licensing laws.'

'I know – I know. No drinks, no drugs, no gambling, no accommodation for criminals. All pure as the driven snow. No beatniks, no thugs, no juvenile delinquents. Just sober Victorian-Edwardian old ladies, county families, visiting travellers from Boston and the more respectable parts of the USA. All the same, a respectable Canon of the church is seen to leave it at 3 a.m. in the morning in a somewhat surreptitious manner –'

'Who saw that?'

'An old lady.'

'How did she manage to see him. Why wasn't she in bed and asleep?'

'Old ladies are like that, sir.'

'You're not talking of – what's his name – Canon Pennyfather?'

'That's right, sir. His disappearance was reported and Campbell has been looking into it.'

'Funny coincidence – his name's just come up in connection with the mail robbery at Bedhampton.'

'Indeed? In what way, sir?'

'Another old lady – or middle-aged anyway. When the train was stopped by that signal that had been tampered with, a good many people woke up and looked out into the corridor. This woman, who lives in Chadminster and knows Canon Pennyfather by sight, says she saw him entering the train by one of the doors. She thought he'd got out to see what was wrong and was getting in again. We were going to follow it up because of his disappearance being reported –'

'Let's see – the train was stopped at 5.30 a.m. Canon Pennyfather left

780 • AGATHA CHRISTIE

Bertram's Hotel not long after 3 a.m. Yes, it could be done. If he were driven there – say – in a racing car . . .'

'So we're back again to Ladislaus Malinowski!'

The AC looked at his blotting pad doodles. 'What a bulldog you are, Fred,' he said.

Half an hour later Chief-Inspector Davy was entering a quiet and rather shabby office.

The large man behind the desk rose and put forward a hand.

'Chief-Inspector Davy? Do sit down,' he said. 'Do you care for a cigar?'

Chief-Inspector Davy shook his head.

'I must apologize,' he said, in his deep countryman's voice, 'for wasting your valuable time.'

Mr Robinson smiled. He was a fat man and very well dressed. He had a yellow face, his eyes were dark and sad looking and his mouth was large and generous. He frequently smiled to display over-large teeth. 'The better to eat you with,' thought Chief-Inspector Davy irrelevantly. His English was perfect and without accent but he was not an Englishman. Father wondered, as many others had wondered before him, what nationality Mr Robinson really was.

'Well, what can I do for you?'

'I'd like to know,' said Chief-Inspector Davy, 'who owns Bertram's Hotel.'

The expression on Mr Robinson's face did not change. He showed no surprise at hearing the name nor did he show recognition. He said thoughtfully:

'You want to know who owns Bertram's Hotel. That, I think, is in Pond Street, off Piccadilly.'

'Quite right, sir.'

'I have occasionally stayed there myself. A quiet place. Well run.'

'Yes,' said Father, 'particularly well run.'

'And you want to know who owns it? Surely that is easy to ascertain?'

There was a faint irony behind his smile.

'Through the usual channels, you mean? Oh yes.' Father took a small piece of paper from his pocket and read out three or four names and addresses.

'I see,' said Mr Robinson, 'someone has taken quite a lot of trouble. Interesting. And you come to me?'

'If anyone knows, you would, sir.'

'Actually I do not know. But it is true that I have ways of obtaining information. One has –' he shrugged his very large, fat shoulders – 'one has contacts.'

'Yes, sir,' said Father with an impassive face.

Mr Robinson looked at him, then he picked up the telephone on his desk.

'Sonia? Get me Carlos.' He waited a minute or two then spoke again. 'Carlos?' He spoke rapidly half a dozen sentences in a foreign language. It was not a language that Father could even recognize.

Father could converse in good British French. He had a smattering of Italian and he could make a guess at plain travellers' German. He knew the sounds of Spanish, Russian and Arabic, though he could not understand them. This language was none of those. At a faint guess he hazarded it might be Turkish or Persian or Armenian, but even of that he was by no means sure. Mr Robinson replaced the receiver.

'I do not think,' he said genially, 'that we shall have long to wait. I am interested, you know. Very much interested. I have occasionally wondered myself –'

Father looked inquiring.

'About Bertram's Hotel,' said Mr Robinson. 'Financially, you know. One wonders how it can pay. However, it has never been any of my business. And one appreciates –' he shrugged his shoulders – 'a comfortable hostelry with an unusually talented personnel and staff . . . Yes, I have wondered.' He looked at Father. 'You know how and why?'

'Not yet,' said Father, 'but I mean to.'

'There are several possibilities,' said Mr Robinson, thoughtfully. 'It is like music, you know. Only so many notes to the octave, yet one can combine them in – what is it – several million different ways? A musician told me once that you do not get the same tune twice. Most interesting.'

There was a slight buzz on his desk and he picked up the receiver once more.

'Yes? Yes, you have been very prompt. I am pleased. I see. Oh! Amsterdam yes . . . Ah . . . Thank you . . . Yes. You will spell that? Good.'

He wrote rapidly on a pad at his elbow.

'I hope this will be useful to you,' he said, as he tore off the sheet and passed it across the table to Father, who read the name out loud. 'Wilhelm Hoffman.'

'Nationality Swiss,' said Mr Robinson. 'Though not, I would say, born in Switzerland. Has a good deal of influence in Banking circles and though keeping strictly on the right side of the law, he has been behind a great many – questionable deals. He operates solely on the Continent, not in this country.'

'Oh.'

'But he has a brother,' said Mr Robinson. 'Robert Hoffman. Living in London – a diamond merchant – most respectable business – His wife is Dutch – He also has offices in Amsterdam – Your people may know about him. As I say, he deals mainly in diamonds, but he is a very rich man, and he owns a lot of property, not usually in his own name. Yes, he is behind quite a lot of enterprises. He and his brother are the real owners of Bertram's Hotel.'

'Thank you, sir.' Chief-Inspector Davy rose to his feet. 'I needn't tell you that I'm much obliged to you. It's wonderful,' he added, allowing himself to show more enthusiasm than was normal.

'That I should know?' inquired Mr Robinson, giving one of his larger smiles. 'But this is one of my specialities. Information. I like to know. That is why you came to me, is it not?'

'Well,' said Chief-Inspector Davy, 'we do know about you. The Home Office. The Special Branch and all the rest of it.' He added almost naïvely, 'It took a bit of nerve on my part to approach you.'

Again Mr Robinson smiled.

'I find you an interesting personality, Chief-Inspector Davy,' he said. 'I wish you success in whatever you are undertaking.'

'Thank you, sir. I think I shall need it. By the way, these two brothers, would you say they were violent men?'

'Certainly not,' said Mr Robinson. 'It would be quite against their policy. The brothers Hoffman do not apply violence in business matters. They have other methods that serve them better. Year by year, I would say, they get steadily richer, or so my information from Swiss Banking circles tells me.'

'It's a useful place, Switzerland,' said Chief-Inspector Davy.

'Yes, indeed. What we should all do without it I do not know! So much rectitude. Such a fine business sense! Yes, we businessmen must all be very grateful to Switzerland. I myself,' he added, 'have also a high opinion of Amsterdam.' He looked hard at Davy, then smiled again, and the Chief-Inspector left.

When he got back to headquarters again, he found a note awaiting him.

Canon Pennyfather has turned up – safe if not sound. Apparently was knocked down by a car at Milton St John and has concussion.

CHAPTER 18

Canon Pennyfather looked at Chief-Inspector Davy and Inspector Campbell, and Chief-Inspector Davy and Inspector Campbell looked at him. Canon Pennyfather was at home again. Sitting in the big arm-chair in his library, a pillow behind his head and his feet up on a pouffe, with a rug over his knees to emphasize his invalid status.

'I'm afraid,' he was saying politely, 'that I simply cannot remember anything at all.'

'You can't remember the accident when the car hit you?'

'I'm really afraid not.'

'Then how did you know a car did hit you?' demanded Inspector Campbell acutely.

'The woman there, Mrs – Mrs – was her name Wheeling? – told me about it.'

'And how did she know?'

Canon Pennyfather looked puzzled.

'Dear me, you are quite right. She couldn't have known, could she? I suppose she thought it was what must have happened.'

'And you really cannot remember *anything*? How did you come to be in Milton St John?'

'I've no idea,' said Canon Pennyfather. 'Even the name is quite unfamiliar to me.'

Inspector Campbell's exasperation was mounting, but Chief-Inspector Davy said in his soothing, homely voice:

'Just tell us again the last thing you do remember, sir.'

Canon Pennyfather turned to him with relief. The inspector's dry scepticism had made him uncomfortable.

'I was going to Lucerne to a congress. I took a taxi to the airport – at least to Kensington Air Station.'

'Yes. And then?'

'That's all. I can't remember any more. The next thing I remember is the wardrobe.'

'What wardrobe?' demanded Inspector Campbell.

'It was in the wrong place.'

Inspector Campbell was tempted to go into this question of a wardrobe in the wrong place. Chief-Inspector Davy cut in.

'Do you remember arriving at the air station, sir?'

'I suppose so,' said Canon Pennyfather, with the air of one who has a great deal of doubt on the matter.

'And you duly flew to Lucerne.'

'Did I? I don't remember anything about it if so.'

'Do you remember arriving back at Bertram's Hotel that night?'

'No.'

'You do remember Bertram's Hotel?'

'Of course. I was staying there. Very comfortable. I kept my room on.'

'Do you remember travelling in a train?'

'A train? No, I can't recall a train.'

'There was a hold-up. The train was robbed. Surely, Canon Pennyfather, you can remember *that*.'

'I ought to, oughtn't I?' said Canon Pennyfather. 'But somehow –' he spoke apologetically – 'I don't.' He looked from one to the other of the officers with a bland gentle smile.

'Then your story is that you remember nothing after going in a taxi to the air station until you woke up in the Wheelings' cottage at Milton St John.'

'There is nothing unusual in that,' the Canon assured him. 'It happens quite often in cases of concussion.'

'What did you think had happened to you when you woke up?'

'I had such a headache I really couldn't think. Then of course I began to wonder where I was and Mrs Wheeling explained and brought me some excellent soup. She called me "love" and "dearie" and "ducks",' said the Canon with slight distaste, 'but she was very kind. Very kind indeed.'

'She ought to have reported the accident to the police. Then you would have been taken to hospital and properly looked after,' said Campbell.

'She looked after me very well,' the Canon protested, with spirit, 'and I understand that with concussion there is very little you *can* do except keep the patient quiet.'

'If you should remember anything more, Canon Pennyfather –'

The Canon interrupted him.

'Four whole days I seem to have lost out of my life,' he said. 'Very curious. Really very curious indeed. I wonder so much where I was and what I was doing. The doctor tells me it may all come back to me. On the other hand it may not. Possibly I shall never know what happened to me during those days.' His eyelids flickered. 'You'll excuse me. I think I am rather tired.'

'That's quite enough now,' said Mrs McCrae, who had been hovering by the door, ready to intervene if she thought it necessary. She advanced upon them. 'Doctor says he wasn't to be worried,' she said firmly.

The policemen rose and moved towards the door. Mrs McCrae shepherded them out into the hall rather in the manner of a conscientious sheep-dog. The Canon murmured something and Chief-Inspector Davy, who was the last to pass through the door, wheeled round at once.

'What was that?' he asked, but the Canon's eyes were now closed.

'What did you think he said?' said Campbell as they left the house after refusing Mrs McCrae's lukewarm offer of refreshment.

Father said thoughtfully:

'I thought he said "the Walls of Jericho".'

'What could he mean by that?'

'It sounds biblical,' said Father.

'Do you think we'll ever know,' asked Campbell, 'how that old boy got from the Cromwell Road to Milton St John?'

'It doesn't seem as if we shall get much help from him,' agreed Davy.

'That woman who says she saw him on the train after the hold-up. Can she possibly be right? Can he be mixed up in some way with these robberies? It seems impossible. He's such a thoroughly respectable old boy. Can't very well suspect a Canon of Chadminster Cathedral of being mixed up with a train robbery, can one?'

'No,' said Father thoughtfully, 'no. No more than one can imagine Mr Justice Ludgrove being mixed up with a bank hold-up.'

Inspector Campbell looked at his superior officer curiously.

The expedition to Chadminster concluded with a short and unprofitable interview with Dr Stokes.

Dr Stokes was aggressive, uncooperative and rude.

'I've known the Wheelings quite a while. They're by way of being neighbours of mine. They'd picked some old chap off the road. Didn't know whether he was dead drunk, or ill. Asked me in to have a look. I told them he wasn't drunk – that it was concussion –'

'And you treated him after that.'

'Not at all. I didn't treat him, or prescribe for him or attend him. I'm not a doctor – I was once, but I'm not now – I told them what they ought to do was ring up the police. Whether they did or not I don't know. Not my business. They're a bit dumb, both of them – but kindly folk.'

'You didn't think of ringing up the police yourself?'

786 · AGATHA CHRISTIE

'No, I did not. I'm not a doctor. Nothing to do with me. As a human being I told them not to pour whisky down his throat and keep him quiet and flat until the police came.'

He glared at them and, reluctantly, they had to leave it at that.

Mr Hoffman was a big solid-looking man. He gave the appearance of being carved out of wood – preferably teak.

His face was so expressionless as to give rise to surmise – could such a man be capable of thinking – of feeling emotion? It seemed impossible.

His manner was highly correct.

He rose, bowed, and held out a wedge-like hand.

'Chief-Inspector Davy? It is some years since I had the pleasure – you may not even remember –'

'Oh yes I do, Mr Hoffman. The Aaronberg Diamond Case. You were a witness for the Crown – a most excellent witness, let me say. The defence was quite unable to shake you.'

'I am not easily shaken,' said Mr Hoffman gravely.

He did not look a man who would easily be shaken.

'What can I do for you?' he went on. 'No trouble, I hope – I always want to agree well with the police. I have the greatest admiration for your superb police force.'

'Oh! There is no trouble. It is just that we wanted you to confirm a little information.'

'I shall be delighted to help you in any way I can. As I say, I have the highest opinion of your London Police Force. You have such a splendid class of men. So full of integrity, so fair, so just.'

'You'll make me embarrassed,' said Father.

'I am at your service. What is it that you want to know?'

'I was just going to ask you to give me a little dope about Bertram's Hotel.'

Mr Hoffman's face did not change. It was possible that his entire attitude became for a moment or two even more static than it had been before – that was all.

'Bertram's Hotel?' he said. His voice was inquiring, slightly puzzled. It might have been that he had never heard of Bertram's Hotel or that he could not quite remember whether he knew Bertram's Hotel or not.

'You have a connection with it, have you not, Mr Hoffman?'

Mr Hoffman moved his shoulders.

'There are so many things,' he said. 'One cannot remember them all. So much business – so much – it keeps me very busy.'

'You have your fingers in a lot of pies, I know that.'

'Yes.' Mr Hoffman smiled a wooden smile. 'I pull out many plums, that is what you think? And so you believe I have a connection with this – Bertram's Hotel?'

'I shouldn't have said a connection. As a matter of fact, you own it, don't you?' said Father genially.

This time, Mr Hoffman definitely did stiffen.

'Now who told you *that*, I wonder?' he said softly.

'Well, it's true, isn't it?' said Chief-Inspector Davy, cheerfully. 'Very nice place to own, I should say. In fact, you must be quite proud of it.'

'Oh yes,' said Hoffman. 'For the moment – I could not quite remember – you see –' he smiled deprecatingly – 'I own quite a lot of property in London. It is a good investment – property. If something comes on the market in what I think is a good position, and there is a chance of snapping it up cheap, I invest.'

'And was Bertram's Hotel going cheap?'

'As a running concern, it had gone down the hill,' said Mr Hoffman, shaking his head.

'Well, it's on its feet now,' said Father. 'I was in there just the other day. I was very much struck with the atmosphere there. Nice old-fashioned clientele, comfortable, old-fashioned premises, nothing rackety about it, a lot of luxury without looking luxurious.'

'I know very little about it personally,' explained Mr Hoffman. 'It is just one of my investments – but I believe it is doing well.'

'Yes, you seem to have a first-class fellow running it. What is his name? Humfries? Yes, Humfries.'

'An excellent man,' said Mr Hoffman. 'I leave everything to him. I look at the balance sheet once a year to see that all is well.'

'The place was thick with titles,' said Father. 'Rich travelling Americans too.' He shook his head thoughtfully. 'Wonderful combination.'

'You say you were in there the other day?' Mr Hoffman inquired. 'Not – not officially, I hope?'

'Nothing serious. Just trying to clear up a little mystery.'

'A mystery? In Bertram's Hotel?'

'So it seems. The Case of the Disappearing Clergyman, you might label it.'

'That is a joke,' Mr Hoffman said. 'That is your Sherlock Holmes language.'

'This clergyman walked out of the place one evening and was never seen again.'

'Peculiar,' said Mr Hoffman, 'but such things happen. I remember many, many years ago now, a great sensation. Colonel – now let me think of his name – Colonel Fergusson I think, one of the equerries of Queen Mary. He walked out of his club one night and he, too, was never seen again.'

'Of course,' said Father, with a sigh, 'a lot of these disappearances are voluntary.'

'You know more about that than I do, my dear Chief-Inspector,' said Mr Hoffman. He added, 'I hope they gave you every assistance at Bertram's Hotel?'

'They couldn't have been nicer,' Father assured him. 'That Miss Gorringe, she has been with you some time, I believe?'

'Possibly. I really know so very little about it. I take no *personal* interest, you understand. In fact –' he smiled disarmingly – 'I was surprised that you even knew it belonged to me.'

It was not quite a question; but once more there was a slight uneasiness in his eyes. Father noted it without seeming to.

'The ramifications that go on in the City are like a gigantic jigsaw,' he said. 'It would make my head ache if I had to deal with that side of things. I gather that a company – Mayfair Holding Trust or some name like that – is the registered owner. They're owned by another company and so on and so on. The real truth of the matter is that it belongs to *you*. Simple as that. I'm right, aren't I?'

'I and my fellow directors are what I dare say you'd call behind it, yes,' admitted Mr Hoffman rather reluctantly.

'Your fellow directors. And who might they be? Yourself and, I believe, a brother of yours?'

'My brother Wilhelm is associated with me in this venture. You must understand that Bertram's is only a part of a chain of various hotels, offices, clubs and other London properties.'

'Any other directors?'

'Lord Pomfret, Abel Isaacstein.' Hoffman's voice was suddenly edged. 'Do you really need to know all these things? Just because you are looking into the Case of the Disappearing Clergyman?'

Father shook his head and looked apologetic.

'I suppose it's really curiosity. Looking for my disappearing clergyman

was what took me to Bertram's, but then I got – well, interested if
you understand what I mean. One thing leads to another sometimes,
doesn't it?'

'I suppose that could be so, yes. And now?' He smiled. 'Your curiosity
is satisfied?'

'Nothing like coming to the horse's mouth when you want information,
is there?' said Father, genially. He rose to his feet. 'There's only one thing
I'd really like to know – and I don't suppose you'll tell me that.'

'Yes, Chief-Inspector?' Hoffman's voice was wary.

'Where do Bertram's get hold of their staff? Wonderful! That fellow
what's-his-name – Henry. The one that looks like an Archduke or an
Archbishop, I'm not sure which. Anyway, he serves you tea and muffins
– most wonderful muffins! An unforgettable experience.'

'You like muffins with much butter, yes?' Mr Hoffman's eyes rested
for a moment on the rotundity of Father's figure with disapprobation.

'I expect you can see I do,' said Father. 'Well, I mustn't be keeping
you. I expect you're pretty busy taking over take-over bids, or something
like that.'

'Ah. It amuses you to pretend to be ignorant of all these things. No, I
am not busy. I do not let business absorb me too much. My tastes are
simple. I live simply, with leisure, with growing of roses, and my family
to whom I am much devoted.'

'Sounds ideal,' said Father. 'Wish I could live like that.'

Mr Hoffman smiled and rose ponderously to shake hands with him.

'I hope you will find your disappearing clergyman very soon.'

'Oh! That's all right. I'm sorry I didn't make myself clear. He's found –
disappointing case, really. Had a car accident and got concussion – simple
as that.'

Father went to the door, then turned and asked:

'By the way, is Lady Sedgwick a director of your company?'

'Lady Sedgwick?' Hoffman took a moment or two. 'No. Why should
she be?'

'Oh well, one hears things – Just a shareholder?'

'I – yes.'

'Well, goodbye, Mr Hoffman. Thanks very much.'

Father went back to the Yard and straight to the AC.

'The two Hoffman brothers are the ones behind Bertram's Hotel –
financially.'

'What? Those scoundrels?' demanded Sir Ronald.

'Yes.'

'They've kept it very dark.'

'Yes – and Robert Hoffman didn't half like our finding it out. It was a shock to him.'

'What did he say?'

'Oh, we kept it all very formal and polite. He tried, not too obviously, to learn how I had found out about it.'

'And you didn't oblige him with that information, I suppose.'

'I certainly did not.'

'What excuse did you give for going to see him?'

'I didn't give any,' said Father.

'Didn't he think that a bit odd?'

'I expect he did. On the whole I thought that was a good way to play it, sir.'

'If the Hoffmans are behind all this, it accounts for a lot. They're never concerned in anything crooked themselves – oh no! *They* don't organize crime – they finance it though!

'Wilhelm deals with the banking side from Switzerland. He was behind those foreign currency rackets just after the war – we knew it – but we couldn't prove it. Those two brothers control a great deal of money and they use it for backing all kinds of enterprises – some legitimate – some not. But they're careful – they know every trick of the trade. Robert's diamond broking is straightforward enough – but it makes a suggestive picture – diamonds – banking interests, and property – clubs, cultural foundations, office buildings, restaurants, hotels – all apparently owned by somebody else.'

'Do you think Hoffman is the planner of these organized robberies?'

'No, I think those two deal only with finance. No, you'll have to look elsewhere for your planner. Somewhere there's a first-class brain at work.'

CHAPTER 20

The fog had come down over London suddenly that evening. Chief-Inspector Davy pulled up his coat collar and turned into Pond Street. Walking slowly, like a man who was thinking of something else, he did not look particularly purposeful but anyone who knew him well would realize that his mind was wholly alert. He was prowling as a cat prowls before the moment comes for it to pounce on its prey.

Pond Street was quiet tonight. There were few cars about. The fog had been patchy to begin with, had almost cleared, then had deepened again. The noise of the traffic from Park Lane was muted to the level of a suburban side road. Most of the buses had given up. Only from time to time individual cars went on their way with determined optimism. Chief-Inspector Davy turned up a cul-de-sac, went to the end of it and came back again. He turned again, aimlessly as it seemed, first one way, then the other, but he was not aimless. Actually his cat prowl was taking him in a circle round one particular building. Bertram's Hotel. He was appraising carefully just what lay to the east of it, to the west of it, to the north of it and to the south of it. He examined the cars that were parked by the pavement, he examined the cars that were in the cul-de-sac. He examined a mews with special care. One car in particular interested him and he stopped. He pursed his lips and said softly, 'So you're here again, you beauty.' He checked the number and nodded to himself. 'FAN 2266 tonight, are you?' He bent down and ran his fingers over the number plate delicately, then nodded approval. 'Good job they made of it,' he said under his breath.

He went on, came out at the other end of the mews, turned right and right again and came out in Pond Street once more, fifty yards from the entrance of Bertram's Hotel. Once again he paused, admiring the handsome lines of yet another racing car.

'You're a beauty, too,' said Chief-Inspector Davy. 'Your number plate's the same as the last time I saw you. I rather fancy your number plate always *is* the same. And that should mean –' he broke off – 'or should it?' he muttered. He looked up towards what could have been the sky. 'Fog's getting thicker,' he said to himself.

Outside the door to Bertram's, the Irish commissionaire was standing swinging his arms backwards and forwards with some violence to keep himself warm. Chief-Inspector Davy said good evening to him.

'Good evening, sir. Nasty night.'

'Yes. I shouldn't think anyone would want to go out tonight who hadn't got to.'

The swing doors were pushed open and a middle-aged lady came out and paused uncertainly on the step.

'Want a taxi, ma'am?'

'Oh dear. I meant to walk.'

'I wouldn't if I were you, ma'am. It's very nasty, this fog. Even in a taxi it won't be too easy.'

'Do you think you could find me a taxi?' asked the lady doubtfully.

'I'll do my best. You go inside now and keep warm, and I'll come in and tell you if I've got one.' His voice changed, modulated to a persuasive tone. 'Unless you *have* to, ma'am, I wouldn't go out tonight at all.'

'Oh dear. Perhaps you're right. But I'm expected at some friends in Chelsea. I don't know. It might be very difficult getting back here. What do you think?'

Michael Gorman took charge.

'If I were you, ma'am,' he said firmly, 'I'd go in and telephone to your friends. It's not nice for a lady like you to be out on a foggy night like this.'

'Well – really – yes, well, perhaps you're right.'

She went back in again.

'I have to look after them,' said Micky Gorman, turning in an explanatory manner to Father. 'That kind would get her bag snatched, she would. Going out this time of night in a fog and wandering about Chelsea or West Kensington or wherever she's trying to go.'

'I suppose you've had a good deal of experience of dealing with elderly ladies?' said Davy.

'Ah yes, indeed. This place is a home from home to them, bless their ageing hearts. How about you, sir? Were you wanting a taxi?'

'Don't suppose you could get me one if I did,' said Father. 'There don't seem to be many about in this. And I don't blame them.'

'Ah, no, I might lay my hand on one for you. There's a place round the corner where there's usually a taxi driver got his cab parked, having a warm up and a drop of something to keep the cold out.'

'A taxi's no good to me,' said Father with a sigh.

He jerked his thumb towards Bertram's Hotel.

'I've got to go inside. I've got a job to do.'

'Indeed now? Would it be still the missing Canon?'

'Not exactly. He's been found.'

'Found?' The man stared at him. 'Found where?'

'Wandering about with concussion after an accident.'

'Ah, that's just what one might expect of him. Crossed the road without looking, I expect.'

'That seems to be the idea,' said Father.

He nodded, and pushed through the doors into the hotel. There were not very many people in the lounge this evening. He saw Miss Marple sitting in a chair near the fire and Miss Marple saw him. She made, however, no sign of recognition. He went towards the desk. Miss Gorringe, as usual, was behind her books. She was, he thought, faintly discomposed to see him. It was a very slight reaction, but he noted the fact.

'You remember me, Miss Gorringe,' he said. 'I came here the other day.'

'Yes, of course I remember you, Chief-Inspector. Is there anything more you want to know? Do you want to see Mr Humfries?'

'No thank you. I don't think that'll be necessary. I'd just like one more look at your register if I may.'

'Of course.' She pushed it along to him.

He opened it and looked slowly down the pages. To Miss Gorringe he gave the appearance of a man looking for one particular entry. In actuality this was not the case. Father had an accomplishment which he had learnt early in life and had developed into a highly skilled art. He could remember names and addresses with a perfect and photographic memory. That memory would remain with him for twenty-four or even forty-eight hours. He shook his head as he shut the book and returned it to her.

'Canon Pennyfather hasn't been in, I suppose?' he said in a light voice.

'Canon Pennyfather?'

'You know he's turned up again?'

'No indeed. Nobody has told *me*. Where?'

'Some place in the country. Car accident it seems. Wasn't reported to us. Some good Samaritan just picked him up and looked after him.'

'Oh! I am pleased. Yes, I really am very pleased. I was worried about him.'

'So were his friends,' said Father. 'Actually I was looking to see if one of them might be staying here now. Archdeacon – Archdeacon – I can't remember his name now, but I'd know it if I saw it.'

'Tomlinson?' said Miss Gorringe helpfully. 'He is due next week. From Salisbury.'

'No, not Tomlinson. Well, it doesn't matter.' He turned away.

It was quiet in the lounge tonight.

An ascetic-looking middle-aged man was reading through a badly typed thesis, occasionally writing a comment in the margin in such small crabbed handwriting as to be almost illegible. Every time he did this, he smiled in vinegary satisfaction.

There were one or two married couples of long standing who had little need to talk to each other. Occasionally two or three people were gathered together in the name of the weather conditions, discussing anxiously how they or their families were going to get where they wanted to be.

'– I rang up and begged Susan not to come by car . . . it means the M1 and always so dangerous in fog –'

'They say it's clearer in the Midlands . . .'

Chief-Inspector Davy noted them as he passed. Without haste, and with no seeming purpose, he arrived at his objective.

Miss Marple was sitting near the fire and observing his approach.

'So you're still here, Miss Marple. I'm glad.'

'I go tomorrow,' said Miss Marple.

That fact had, somehow, been implicit in her attitude. She had sat, not relaxed, but upright, as one sits in an airport lounge, or a railway waiting-room. Her luggage, he was sure, would be packed, only toilet things and night wear to be added.

'It is the end of my fortnight's holiday,' she explained.

'You've enjoyed it, I hope?'

Miss Marple did not answer at once.

'In a way – yes . . .' She stopped.

'And in another way, no?'

'It's difficult to explain what I mean –'

'Aren't you, perhaps, a little too near the fire? Rather hot, here. Wouldn't you like to move – into that corner perhaps?'

Miss Marple looked at the corner indicated, then she looked at Chief-Inspector Davy.

'I think you are quite right,' she said.

He gave her a hand up, carried her handbag and her book for her and established her in the quiet corner he had indicated.

'All right?'

'Quite all right.'

'You know why I suggested it?'

'You thought – very kindly – that it was too hot for me by the fire. Besides,' she added, 'our conversation cannot be overheard here.'

'Have you got something you want to tell me, Miss Marple?'

'Now why should you think that?'

'You looked as though you had,' said Davy.

'I'm sorry I showed it so plainly,' said Miss Marple. 'I didn't mean to.'

'Well, what about it?'

'I don't know if I ought to do so. I would like you to believe, Inspector, that I am not really fond of interfering. I am against interference. Though often well meant, it can cause a great deal of harm.'

'It's like that, is it? I see. Yes, it's quite a problem for you.'

'Sometimes one sees people doing things that seem to one unwise – even dangerous. But has one any right to interfere? Usually not, I think.'

'Is this Canon Pennyfather you're talking about?'

'Canon Pennyfather?' Miss Marple sounded very surprised. 'Oh no. Oh dear me no, nothing whatever to do with him. It concerns – a girl.'

'A girl, indeed? And you thought I could help?'

'I don't know,' said Miss Marple. 'I simply don't know. But I'm worried, very worried.'

Father did not press her. He sat there looking large and comfortable and rather stupid. He let her take her time. She had been willing to do her best to help him, and he was quite prepared to do anything he could to help her. He was not, perhaps, particularly interested. On the other hand, one never knew.

'One reads in the papers,' said Miss Marple in a low clear voice, 'accounts of proceedings in court; of young people, children or girls "in need of care and protection". It's just a sort of legal phrase, I suppose, but it could mean something real.'

'This girl you mentioned, you feel she is in need of care and protection?'

'Yes. Yes I do.'

'Alone in the world?'

'Oh no,' said Miss Marple. 'Very much not so, if I may put it that way. She is to all outward appearances very heavily protected and very well cared for.'

'Sounds interesting,' said Father.

'She was staying in this hotel,' said Miss Marple, 'with a Mrs Carpenter, I think. I looked in the register to see the name. The girl's name is Elvira Blake.'

Father looked up with a quick air of interest.

'She was a lovely girl. Very young, very much, as I say, sheltered and protected. Her guardian was a Colonel Luscombe, a very nice man. Quite charming. Elderly of course, and I am afraid terribly innocent.'

'The guardian or the girl?'

'I meant the guardian,' said Miss Marple. 'I don't know about the girl. But I do think she is in danger. I came across her quite by chance in Battersea Park. She was sitting at a refreshment place there with a young man.'

'Oh, that's it, is it?' said Father. 'Undesirable, I suppose. Beatnik – spiv – thug –'

'A very handsome man,' said Miss Marple. 'Not so very young.

Thirty-odd, the kind of man that I should say is very attractive to women, but his face is a bad face. Cruel, hawklike, predatory.'

'He mayn't be as bad as he looks,' said Father soothingly.

'If anything he is worse than he looks,' said Miss Marple. 'I am convinced of it. He drives a large racing car.'

Father looked up quickly.

'Racing car?'

'Yes. Once or twice I've seen it standing near this hotel.'

'You don't remember the number, do you?'

'Yes, indeed I do. FAN 2266. I had a cousin who stuttered,' Miss Marple explained. 'That's how I remember it.'

Father looked puzzled.

'Do you know who he is?' demanded Miss Marple.

'As a matter of fact I do,' said Father slowly. 'Half French, half Polish. Very well-known racing driver, he was world champion three years ago. His name is Ladislaus Malinowski. You're quite right in some of your views about him. He has a bad reputation where women are concerned. That is to say, he is not a suitable friend for a young girl. But it's not easy to do anything about that sort of thing. I suppose she is meeting him on the sly, is that it?'

'Almost certainly,' said Miss Marple.

'Did you approach her guardian?'

'I don't know him,' said Miss Marple. 'I've only just been introduced to him once by a mutual friend. I don't like the idea of going to him in a tale-bearing way. I wondered if perhaps in some way *you* could do something about it.'

'I can try,' said Father. 'By the way, I thought you might like to know that your friend, Canon Pennyfather, has turned up all right.'

'Indeed!' Miss Marple looked animated. 'Where?'

'A place called Milton St John.'

'How very odd. What was he doing there? Did he know?'

'*Apparently* –' Chief-Inspector Davy stressed the word – 'he had had an accident.'

'What kind of an accident?'

'Knocked down by a car – concussed – or else, of course, he might have been conked on the head.'

'Oh! I see.' Miss Marple considered the point. 'Doesn't he know himself?'

'He *says* –' again the Chief-Inspector stressed the word – 'that he does not know anything.'

'Very remarkable.'

'Isn't it? The last thing he remembers is driving in a taxi to Kensington Air Station.'

Miss Marple shook her head perplexedly.

'I know it does happen that way in concussion,' she murmured. 'Didn't he say anything – useful?'

'He murmured something about the Walls of Jericho.'

'Joshua?' hazarded Miss Marple, 'or Archaeology – excavations? – or I remember, long ago, a play – by Mr Sutro, I think.'

'And all this week north of the Thames, Gaumont Cinemas – *The Walls of Jericho*, featuring Olga Radbourne and Bart Levinne,' said Father.

Miss Marple looked at him suspiciously.

'He could have gone to that film in the Cromwell Road. He could have come out about eleven and come back here – though if so, someone ought to have seen him – it would be well before midnight –'

'Took the wrong bus,' Miss Marple suggested. 'Something like that –'

'Say he got back here *after* midnight,' Father said – 'he could have walked up to his room without anyone seeing him – But if so, what happened then – and why did he go out again three hours later?'

Miss Marple groped for a word.

'The only idea that occurs to me is – oh!'

She jumped as a report sounded from the street outside.

'Car backfiring,' said Father soothingly.

'I'm sorry to be so jumpy – I am nervous tonight – that feeling one has –'

'That something's going to happen? I don't think you need worry.'

'I have never liked fog.'

'I wanted to tell you,' said Chief-Inspector Davy, 'that you've given me a lot of help. The things you've noticed here – just little things – they've added up.'

'So there *was* something wrong with this place?'

'There was and is everything wrong with it.'

Miss Marple sighed.

'It seemed wonderful at first – unchanged you know – like stepping back into the past – to the part of the past that one had loved and enjoyed.'

She paused.

'But of course, it wasn't really like that. I learned (what I suppose I really knew already) that one can never go back, that one should not ever try to go back – that the essence of life is going forward. Life is really a One Way Street, isn't it?'

'Something of the sort,' agreed Father.

'I remember,' said Miss Marple, diverging from her main topic in a characteristic way, 'I remember being in Paris with my mother and my grandmother, and we went to have tea at the Elysée Hotel. And my grandmother looked round, and she said suddenly, "Clara, I do believe I am the only woman here in a *bonnet*!" And she was, too! When she got home she packed up all her bonnets, and her headed mantles too – and sent them off –'

'To the Jumble Sale?' inquired Father, sympathetically.

'Oh no. Nobody would have wanted them at a jumble sale. She sent them to a theatrical Repertory Company. They appreciated them very much. But let me see –' Miss Marple recovered her direction. '– Where was I?'

'Summing up this place.'

'Yes. It seemed all right – but it wasn't. It was mixed up – real people and people who weren't real. One couldn't always tell them apart.'

'What do you mean by not real?'

'There were retired military men, but there were also what seemed to be military men but who had never been in the Army. And clergymen who weren't clergymen. And admirals and sea captains who've never been in the Navy. My friend, Selina Hazy – it amused me at first how she was always so anxious to recognize people she knew (quite natural, of course) and how often she was mistaken and they weren't the people she thought they were. But it happened too often. And so – I began to wonder. Even Rose, the chambermaid – so nice – but I began to think that perhaps *she* wasn't real, either.'

'If it interests you to know, she's an ex-actress. A good one. Gets a better salary here than she ever drew on the stage.'

'But – why?'

'Mainly, as part of the décor. Perhaps there's more than that to it.'

'I'm glad to be leaving here,' said Miss Marple. She gave a little shiver. 'Before anything happens.'

Chief-Inspector Davy looked at her curiously.

'What do you expect to happen?' he asked.

'Evil of some kind,' said Miss Marple.

'Evil is rather a big word –'

'You think it is too melodramatic? But I have some experience – seem to have been – so often – in contact with murder.'

'Murder?' Chief-Inspector Davy shook his head. 'I'm not suspecting murder. Just a nice cosy round-up of some remarkably clever criminals –'

'That's not the same thing. Murder – the wish to do murder – is something quite different. It – how shall I say? – it defies God.'

He looked at her and shook his head gently and reassuringly.

'There won't be any murders,' he said.

A sharp report, louder than the former one, came from outside. It was followed by a scream and another report.

Chief-Inspector Davy was on his feet, moving with a speed surprising in such a bulky man. In a few seconds he was through the swing doors and out in the street.

The screaming – a woman's – was piercing the mist with a note of terror. Chief-Inspector Davy raced down Pond Street in the direction of the screams. He could dimly visualize a woman's figure backed against a railing. In a dozen strides he had reached her. She wore a long pale fur coat, and her shining blonde hair hung down each side of her face. He thought for a moment that he knew who she was, then he realized that this was only a slip of a girl. Sprawled on the pavement at her feet was the body of a man in uniform. Chief-Inspector Davy recognized him. It was Michael Gorman.

As Davy came up to the girl, she clutched at him, shivering all over, stammering out broken phrases.

'Someone tried to kill me . . . Someone . . . they shot at me . . . If it hadn't been for *him* –' She pointed down at the motionless figure at her feet. 'He pushed me back and got in front of me – and then the second shot came . . . and he fell . . . He saved my life. I think he's hurt – badly hurt . . .'

Chief-Inspector Davy went down on one knee. His torch came out. The tall Irish commissionaire had fallen like a soldier. The left hand side of his tunic showed a wet patch that was growing wetter as the blood oozed out into the cloth. Davy rolled up an eyelid, touched a wrist. He rose to his feet again.

'He's had it all right,' he said.

The girl gave a sharp cry. 'Do you mean he's *dead?* Oh no, no! He can't be *dead.*'

'Who was it shot at you?'

'I don't know . . . I'd left my car just round the corner and was feeling my way along by the railings – I was going to Bertram's Hotel. And then suddenly there was a shot – and a bullet went past my cheek and then – he – the porter from Bertram's – came running down the street towards me, and shoved me behind him, and then another shot came . . . I think – I think whoever it was must have been hiding in that area there.'

Chief-Inspector Davy looked where she pointed. At this end of Bertram's Hotel there was an old-fashioned area below the level of the street, with a gate and some steps down to it. Since it gave only on some store-rooms it was not much used. But a man could have hidden there easily enough.

'You didn't see him?'

'Not properly. He rushed past me like a shadow. It was all thick fog.'

Davy nodded.

The girl began to sob hysterically.

'But who could possibly want to kill me? Why should anyone want to kill me? That's the second time. I don't understand . . . why . . .'

One arm round the girl, Chief-Inspector Davy fumbled in his pocket with the other hand.

The shrill notes of a police whistle penetrated the mist.

In the lounge of Bertram's Hotel, Miss Gorringe had looked up sharply from the desk.

One or two of the visitors had looked up also. The older and deafer did not look up.

Henry, about to lower a glass of old brandy to a table, stopped poised with it still in his hand.

Miss Marple sat forward, clutching the arms of her chair. A retired admiral said derisively:

'Accident! Cars collided in the fog, I expect.'

The swing doors from the street were pushed open. Through them came what seemed like an outsize policeman, looking a good deal larger than life.

He was supporting a girl in a pale fur coat. She seemed hardly able to walk. The policeman looked round for help with some embarrassment.

Miss Gorringe came out from behind the desk, prepared to cope. But at that moment the lift came down. A tall figure emerged, and the girl shook herself free from the policeman's support, and ran frantically across the lounge.

'Mother,' she cried. 'Oh *Mother, Mother . . .*' and threw herself, sobbing, into Bess Sedgwick's arms.

CHAPTER 21

Chief-Inspector Davy settled himself back in his chair and looked at the two women sitting opposite him. It was past midnight. Police officials had come and gone. There had been doctors, fingerprint men, an ambulance to remove the body; and now everything had narrowed to this one room dedicated for the purposes of the law by Bertram's Hotel. Chief-Inspector Davy sat one side of the table. Bess Sedgwick and Elvira sat the other side. Against the wall a policeman sat unobtrusively writing. Detective-Sergeant Wadell sat near the door.

Father looked thoughtfully at the two women facing him. Mother and daughter. There was, he noted, a strong superficial likeness between them. He could understand how for one moment in the fog he had taken Elvira Blake for Bess Sedgwick. But now, looking at them, he was more struck by the points of difference than the points of resemblance. They were not really alike save in colouring, yet the impression persisted that here he had a positive and a negative version of the same personality. Everything about Bess Sedgwick was positive. Her vitality, her energy, her magnetic attraction. He admired Lady Sedgwick. He always had admired her. He had admired her courage and had always been excited over her exploits; had said, reading his Sunday papers: 'She'll never get away with *that,*' and invariably she had got away with it! He had not thought it possible that she would reach journey's end and she had reached journey's end. He admired particularly the indestructible quality of her. She had had one air crash, several car crashes, had been thrown badly twice from her horse, but at the end of it here she was. Vibrant, alive, a personality one could not ignore for a moment. He took off his hat to her mentally. Some day, of course, she would come a cropper. You could only bear a charmed life for so long. His eyes went from mother to daughter. He wondered. He wondered very much.

In Elvira Blake, he thought, everything had been driven inward. Bess Sedgwick had got through life by imposing her will on it. Elvira, he guessed, had a different way of getting through life. She submitted, he thought. She obeyed. She smiled in compliance and behind that, he thought, she slipped away through your fingers. 'Sly,' he said to himself, appraising that fact. 'That's the only way she can manage, I expect. She can never brazen things out or impose herself. That's why, I expect, the people who've looked after her have never had the least idea of what she might be up to.'

He wondered what she had been doing slipping along the street to Bertram's Hotel on a late foggy evening. He was going to ask her presently. He thought it highly probable that the answer he would get would not be the true one. 'That's the way,' he thought, 'that the poor child defends herself.' Had she come here to meet her mother or to find her mother? It was perfectly possible, but he didn't think so. Not for a moment. Instead he thought of the big sports car tucked away round the corner – the car with the number plate FAN 2266. Ladislaus Malinowski must be somewhere in the neighbourhood since his car was there.

'Well,' said Father, addressing Elvira in his most kindly and fatherlike manner, 'well, and how are you feeling now?'

'I'm quite all right,' said Elvira.

'Good. I'd like you to answer a few questions if you feel up to it; because, you see, time is usually the essence of these things. You were shot at twice and a man was killed. We want as many clues as we can get to the person who killed him.'

'I'll tell you everything I can, but it all came so suddenly. And you can't *see* anything in a fog. I've no idea myself who it could have been – or even what he looked like. That's what was so frightening.'

'You said this was the second time somebody had tried to kill you. Does that mean there was an attempt on your life before?'

'Did I say that? I can't remember.' Her eyes moved uneasily. 'I don't think I said that.'

'Oh, but you did, you know,' said Father.

'I expect I was just being – hysterical.'

'No,' said Father, 'I don't think you were. I think you meant just what you said.'

'I might have been imagining things,' said Elvira. Her eyes shifted again.

Bess Sedgwick moved. She said quietly:

'You'd better tell him, Elvira.'

Elvira shot a quick, uneasy look at her mother.

'You needn't worry,' said Father, reassuringly. 'We know quite well in the police force that girls don't tell their mothers or their guardians everything. We don't take those things too seriously, but we've got to *know* about them, because, you see, it all helps.'

Bess Sedgwick said:

'Was it in Italy?'

'Yes,' said Elvira.

Father said: 'That's where you've been at school, isn't it, or a finishing place or whatever they call it nowadays?'

'Yes. I was at Contessa Martinelli's. There were about eighteen or twenty of us.'

'And you thought that somebody tried to kill you. How was that?'

'Well, a big box of chocolates and sweets and things came for me. There was a card with it written in Italian in a flowery hand. The sort of thing they say, you know, "To the bellissima Signorina". Something like that. And my friends and I – well – we laughed about it a bit, and wondered who'd sent it.'

'Did it come by post?'

'No. No, it couldn't have come by post. It was just there in my room. Someone must have put it there.'

'I see. Bribed one of the servants, I suppose. I am to take it that you didn't let the Contessa whoever-it-was in on this?'

A faint smile appeared on Elvira's face. 'No. No. We certainly didn't. Anyway we opened the box and they were lovely chocolates. Different kinds, you know, but there were some violet creams. That's the sort of chocolate that has a crystallized violet on top. My favourite. So of course I ate one or two of those first. And then afterwards, in the night, I felt terribly ill. I didn't think it was the chocolates, I just thought it was something perhaps that I'd eaten at dinner.'

'Anybody else ill?'

'No. Only me. Well, I was very sick and all that, but I felt all right by the end of the next day. Then a day or two later I ate another of the same chocolates, and the same thing happened. So I talked to Bridget about it. Bridget was my special friend. And we looked at the chocolates, and we found that the violet creams had got a sort of hole in the bottom that had been filled up again, so we thought that someone had put some poison in and they'd only put it in the violet creams so that I would be the one who ate them.'

'Nobody else was ill?'

'No.'

'So presumably nobody else ate the violet creams?'

'No. I don't think they could have. You see, it was my present and they knew I liked the violet ones, so they'd leave them for me.'

'The chap took a risk, whoever he was,' said Father. 'The whole place might have been poisoned.'

'It's absurd,' said Lady Sedgwick sharply. 'Utterly absurd! I never heard of anything so crude.'

Chief-Inspector Davy made a slight gesture with his hand. 'Please,' he said, then he went on to Elvira: 'Now I find that very interesting, Miss Blake. And you still didn't tell the Contessa?'

'Oh no, we didn't. She'd have made a terrible fuss.'

'What did you do with the chocolates?'

'We threw them away,' said Elvira. 'They were lovely chocolates,' she added, with a tone of slight grief.

'You didn't try and find out who sent them?'

Elvira looked embarrassed.

'Well, you see, I thought it might have been Guido.'

'Yes?' said Chief-Inspector Davy, cheerfully. 'And who is Guido?'

'Oh, Guido . . .' Elvira paused. She looked at her mother.

'Don't be stupid,' said Bess Sedgwick. 'Tell Chief-Inspector Davy about Guido, whoever he is. Every girl of your age has a Guido in her life. You met him out there, I suppose?'

'Yes. When we were taken to the opera. He spoke to me there. He was nice. Very attractive. I used to see him sometimes when we went to classes. He used to pass me notes.'

'And I suppose,' said Bess Sedgwick, 'that you told a lot of lies, and made plans with some friends and you managed to get out and meet him? Is that it?'

Elvira looked relieved by this short cut to confession. 'Sometimes Guido managed to –'

'What was Guido's other name?'

'I don't know,' said Elvira. 'He never told me.'

Chief-Inspector Davy smiled at her.

'You mean you're not going to tell? Never mind. I dare say we'll be able to find out quite all right without your help, if it should really matter. But why should you think that this young man, who was presumably fond of you, should want to kill you?'

'Oh, because he used to threaten things like that. I mean, we used to have rows now and then. He'd bring some of his friends with him, and I'd pretend to like them better than him, and then he'd get very, very wild and angry. He said I'd better be careful what I did. I couldn't give him up just like that! That if I wasn't faithful to him he'd kill me! I just thought he was being melodramatic and theatrical.' Elvira smiled suddenly and unexpectedly. 'But it was all rather fun. I didn't think it was *real* or *serious.*'

'Well,' said Chief-Inspector Davy, 'I don't think it *does* seem very likely that a young man such as you describe would really poison chocolates and send them to you.'

'Well, I don't think so really either,' said Elvira, 'but it must have been him because I can't see that there's anyone else. It worried me. And then, when I came back here, I got a note –' She stopped.

'What sort of a note?'

'It just came in an envelope and was printed. It said *"Be on your guard. Somebody wants to kill you."*'

Chief-Inspector Davy's eyebrows went up.

'Indeed? Very curious. Yes, very curious. And it worried you. You were frightened?'

'Yes. I began to – to wonder who could possibly want me out of the way. That's why I tried to find out if I was really very rich.'

'Go on.'

'And the other day in London something else happened. I was in the tube and there were a lot of people on the platform. I thought someone tried to push me on to the line.'

'My dear child!' said Bess Sedgwick. 'Don't romance.'

Again Father made that slight gesture of his hand.

'Yes,' said Elvira apologetically. 'I expect I *have* been imagining it all but – I don't know – I mean, after what happened this evening it seems, doesn't it, as though it might all be true?' She turned suddenly to Bess Sedgwick, speaking with urgency, '*Mother!* You *might* know. *Does* anyone want to kill me? *Could* there be anyone? Have I got an enemy?'

'Of course you've not got an enemy,' said Bess Sedgwick, impatiently. 'Don't be an idiot. Nobody wants to kill you. Why should they?'

'Then who shot at me tonight?'

'In that fog,' said Bess Sedgwick, 'you might have been mistaken for someone else. That's possible, don't you think?' she said, turning to Father.

'Yes, I think it might be quite possible,' said Chief-Inspector Davy.

Bess Sedgwick was looking at him very intently. He almost fancied the motion of her lips saying 'later'.

'Well,' he said cheerfully, 'we'd better get down to some more facts now. Where had you come from tonight? What were you doing walking along Pond Street on such a foggy evening?'

'I came up for an Art class at the Tate this morning. Then I went to lunch with my friend Bridget. She lives in Onslow Square. We went to a film and when we came out, there was this fog – quite thick and getting worse, and I thought perhaps I'd better not drive home.'

'You drive a car, do you?'

'Yes. I took my driving test last summer. Only, I'm not a very good driver and I hate driving in fog. So Bridget's mother said I could stay the night, so I rang up Cousin Mildred – that's where I live in Kent –'

Father nodded.

'– and I said I was going to stay up over-night. She said that was very wise.'

'And what happened next?' asked Father.

'And then the fog seemed lighter suddenly. You know how patchy fogs are. So I said I would drive down to Kent after all. I said goodbye to Bridget and started off. But then it began to come down again. I didn't like it very much. I ran into a very thick patch of it and I lost my way and I didn't know where I was. Then after a bit I realized I was at Hyde Park Corner and I thought "I really *can't* go down to Kent in this." At first, I thought I'd go back to Bridget's but then I remembered how I'd lost my way already. And then I realized that I was quite close to this nice hotel where Uncle Derek took me when I came back from Italy and I thought, "I'll go there and I'm sure they can find me a room." That was fairly easy, I found a place to leave the car and then I walked back up the street towards the hotel.'

'Did you meet anyone or did you hear anyone walking near you?'

'It's funny you saying that, because I did think I heard someone walking behind me. Of course, there must be lots of people walking about in London. Only in a fog like this, it gives you a nervous feeling. I waited and listened but I didn't hear any footsteps and I thought I'd imagined them. I was quite close to the hotel by then.'

'And then?'

'And then quite suddenly there was a shot. As I told you, it seemed to go right past my ear. The commissionaire man who stands outside the hotel came running down towards me and he pushed me behind him and then – then – the other shot came . . . He – he fell down and I screamed.' She was shaking now. Her mother spoke to her.

'Steady, girl,' said Bess in a low, firm voice. 'Steady now.' It was the voice Bess Sedgwick used for her horses and it was quite as efficacious when used on her daughter. Elvira blinked at her, drew herself up a little, and became calm again.

'Good girl,' said Bess.

'And then *you* came,' said Elvira to Father. 'You blew your whistle, you told the policeman to take me into the hotel. And as soon as I got in, I saw – I saw Mother.' She turned and looked at Bess Sedgwick.

'And that brings us more or less up to date,' said Father. He shifted his bulk a little in the chair.

'Do you know a man called Ladislaus Malinowski?' he asked. His tone was even, casual, without any direct inflection. He did not look at the girl, but he was aware, since his ears were functioning at full attention, of a quick little gasp she gave. His eyes were not on the daughter but on the mother.

'No,' said Elvira, having waited just a shade too long to say it. 'No, I don't.'

'Oh,' said Father. 'I thought you might. I thought he might have been here this evening.'

'Oh? Why should he be here?'

'Well, his car is here,' said Father. 'That's why I thought he might be.'

'I don't know him,' said Elvira.

'My mistake,' said Father. 'You do, of course?' He turned his head towards Bess Sedgwick.

'Naturally,' said Bess Sedgwick. 'Known him for many years.' She added, smiling slightly, 'He's a madman, you know. Drives like an angel or a devil – he'll break his neck one of these days. Had a bad smash eighteen months ago.'

'Yes, I remember reading about it,' said Father. 'Not racing again yet, is he?'

'No, not yet. Perhaps he never will.'

'Do you think I could go to bed now?' asked Elvira, plaintively. 'I'm – really terribly tired.'

'Of course. You must be,' said Father. 'You've told us all you can remember?'

'Oh. Yes.'

'I'll go up with you,' said Bess.

Mother and daughter went out together.

'*She* knows him all right,' said Father.

'Do you really think so?' asked Sergeant Wadell.

'I know it. She had tea with him in Battersea Park only a day or two ago.'

'How did you find that out?'

'Old lady told me – distressed. Didn't think he was a nice friend for a young girl. He isn't of course.'

'Especially if he and the mother –' Wadell broke off delicately. 'It's pretty general gossip –'

'Yes. May be true, may not. Probably *is*.'

'In that case which one is he really after?'

Father ignored that point. He said:

'I want him picked up. I want him badly. His car's here – just round the corner.'

'Do you think he might be actually staying in this hotel?'

'Don't think so. It wouldn't fit into the picture. He's not supposed to be here. *If* he came here, he came to meet the girl. She definitely came to meet him, I'd say.'

The door opened and Bess Sedgwick reappeared.

'I came back,' she said, 'because I wanted to speak to you.'

She looked from him to the other two men.

'I wonder if I could speak to you alone? I've given you all the information I have, such as it is; but I would like a word or two with you in private.'

'I don't see any reason why not,' said Chief-Inspector Davy. He motioned with his head, and the young detective-constable took his note-book and went out. Wadell went with him. 'Well?' said Chief-Inspector Davy.

Lady Sedgwick sat down again opposite him.

'That silly story about poisoned chocolates,' she said. 'It's nonsense. Absolutely ridiculous. I don't believe anything of the kind ever happened.'

'You don't, eh?'

'Do you?'

Father shook his head doubtfully. 'You think your daughter cooked it up?'

'Yes. But why?'

'Well, if you don't know why,' said Chief-Inspector Davy, 'how should I know? She's your daughter. Presumably you know her better than I do.'

'I don't know her at all,' said Bess Sedgwick bitterly. 'I've not seen her or had anything to do with her since she was two years old, when I ran away from my husband.'

'Oh yes. I know all that. I find it curious. You see, Lady Sedgwick, courts usually give the mother, even if she is a guilty party in a divorce, custody of a young child if she asks for it. Presumably then you didn't ask for it? You didn't want it.'

'I thought it – better not.'

'Why?'

'I didn't think it was – safe for her.'

'On moral grounds?'

'No. Not on moral grounds. Plenty of adultery nowadays. Children have to learn about it, have to grow up with it. No. It's just that *I* am not really a safe person to be with. The life I'd lead wouldn't be a safe life. You can't help the way you're born. I was born to live dangerously. I'm not law-abiding or conventional. I thought it would be better for Elvira, happier, to have a proper English conventional bringing-up. Shielded, looked after . . .'

'But minus a mother's love?'

'I thought if she learned to love me it might bring sorrow to her. Oh, you mayn't believe me, but that's what I felt.'

'I see. Do you still think you were right?'

'No,' said Bess. 'I don't. I think now I may have been entirely wrong.'

'*Does* your daughter know Ladislaus Malinowski?'

'I'm sure she doesn't. She said so. You heard her.'

'I heard her, yes.'

'Well, then?'

'She was afraid, you know, when she was sitting here. In our profession we get to know fear when we meet up with it. She was afraid – why? Chocolates or no chocolates, her life *has* been attempted. That tube story may be true enough –'

'It was ridiculous. Like a thriller –'

'Perhaps. But that sort of thing does happen, Lady Sedgwick. Oftener than you'd think. Can you give me any idea who might want to kill your daughter?'

'Nobody – nobody at all!'

She spoke vehemently.

Chief-Inspector Davy sighed and shook his head.

CHAPTER 22

Chief-Inspector Davy waited patiently until Mrs Melford had finished talking. It had been a singularly unprofitable interview. Cousin Mildred had been incoherent, unbelieving and generally feather-headed. Or that was Father's private view. Accounts of Elvira's sweet manners, nice nature, troubles with her teeth, odd excuses told through the telephone, had led on to serious doubts whether Elvira's friend Bridget was really a suitable friend for her. All these matters had been presented to the Chief-Inspector in a kind of general hasty pudding. Mrs Melford knew nothing, had heard nothing, had seen nothing and had apparently deduced very little.

A short telephone call to Elvira's guardian, Colonel Luscombe, had been even more unproductive, though fortunately less wordy. 'More Chinese monkeys,' he muttered to his sergeant as he put down the receiver. 'See no evil, hear no evil, speak no evil.

'The trouble is that everyone who's had anything to do with this girl has been far too nice – if you get my meaning. Too many nice people who don't know anything about evil. Not like my old lady.'

'The Bertram's Hotel one?'

'Yes, that's the one. She's had a long life of experience in noticing evil, fancying evil, suspecting evil and going forth to do battle with evil. Let's see what we can get out of girl friend Bridget.'

The difficulties in this interview were represented first, last, and most of the time by Bridget's mamma. To talk to Bridget without the assistance of her mother took all Chief-Inspector Davy's adroitness and cajolery. He was, it must be admitted, ably seconded by Bridget. After a certain amount of stereotyped questions and answers and expressions of horror on the part of Bridget's mother at hearing of Elvira's narrow escape from death, Bridget said, 'You know it's time for that committee meeting, Mum. You said it was very important.'

'Oh dear, dear,' said Bridget's mother.

'You know they'll get into a frightful mess without you, Mummy.'

'Oh they will, they certainly will. But perhaps I ought –'

'Now that's quite all right, Madam,' said Chief-Inspector Davy, putting on his kindly old father look. 'You don't want to worry. Just you get off. I've finished all the important things. You've told me really everything I wanted to know. I've just one or two routine inquiries about people in Italy which I think your daughter, Miss Bridget, might be able to help me with.'

'Well, if you think you can manage, Bridget –'

'Oh, I can manage, Mummy,' said Bridget.

Finally, with a great deal of fuss, Bridget's mother went off to her committee.

'Oh, dear,' said Bridget, sighing, as she came back after closing the front door. 'Really! I do think mothers are *difficult*.'

'So they tell me,' said Chief-Inspector Davy. 'A lot of young ladies I come across have a lot of trouble with their mothers.'

'I'd have thought you'd put it the other way round,' said Bridget.

'Oh I do, I do,' said Davy. 'But that's not how the young ladies see it. Now you can tell me a little more.'

'I couldn't really speak frankly in front of Mummy,' explained Bridget. 'But I do feel, of course, that it is really important that you should know as much as possible about all this. I do know Elvira was terribly worried about something and afraid. She wouldn't exactly admit she was in danger, but she was.'

'I thought that might have been so. Of course I didn't like to ask you too much in front of your mother.'

'Oh no,' said Bridget, 'we don't want *Mummy* to hear about it. She gets in such a frightful state about things and she'd go and *tell* everyone. I mean, if Elvira doesn't want things like this to be known . . .'

'First of all,' said Chief-Inspector Davy, 'I want to know about a box of chocolates in Italy. I gather there was some idea that a box was sent to her which might have been poisoned.'

Bridget's eyes opened wide. 'Poisoned,' she said. 'Oh no. I don't think so. At least . . .'

'There was something?'

'Oh yes. A box of chocolates came and Elvira did eat a lot of them and she was rather sick that night. Quite ill.'

'But she didn't suspect poison?'

'No. At least – oh yes, she did say that someone was trying to poison one of us and we looked at the chocolates to see, you know, if anything had been injected into them.'

'And had it?'

'No, it hadn't,' said Bridget. 'At least, not as far as we could see.'

'But perhaps your friend, Miss Elvira, might still have thought so?'

'Well, she might – but she didn't *say* any more.'

'But you think she was afraid of someone?'

'I didn't think so at the time or notice anything. It was only here, later.'

'What about this man, Guido?'

Bridget giggled.

'He had a terrific crush on Elvira,' she said.

'And you and your friend used to meet him places?'

'Well, I don't mind telling *you*,' said Bridget. 'After all you're the police. It isn't important to you, that sort of thing and I expect you understand. Countess Martinelli was frightfully strict – or thought she was. And of course we had all sorts of dodges and things. We all stood in with each other. You know.'

'And told the right lies, I suppose?'

'Well, I'm afraid so,' said Bridget. 'But what can one do when anyone is so suspicious?'

'So you did meet Guido and all that. And used he to threaten Elvira?'

'Oh, not seriously, I don't think.'

'Then perhaps there was someone else she used to meet?'

'Oh – that – well, I don't know.'

'Please tell me, Miss Bridget. It might be – vital, you know.'

'Yes. Yes I can see that. Well there was *someone*. I don't know who it was, but there was someone else – she really minded about. She was deadly serious. I mean it was a really *important* thing.'

'She used to meet him?'

'I think so. I mean she'd *say* she was meeting Guido but it wasn't Guido. It was this other man.'

'Any idea who it was?'

'No.' Bridget sounded a little uncertain.

'It wouldn't be a racing motorist called Ladislaus Malinowski?'

Bridget gaped at him.

'So you *know*?'

'Am I right?'

'Yes – I think so. She'd got a photograph of him torn out of a paper. She kept it under her stockings.'

'That might have been just a pin-up hero, mightn't it?'

'Well it *might*, of course, but I don't think it was.'

'Did she meet him here in this country, do you know?'

'I don't know. You see I don't know really what she's been doing since she came back from Italy.'

'She came up to London to the dentist,' Davy prompted her. 'Or so she said. Instead she came to you. She rang up Mrs Melford with some story about an old governess.'

A faint giggle came from Bridget.

'That wasn't true, was it?' said the Chief-Inspector, smiling. 'Where did she really go?'

Bridget hesitated and then said, 'She went to Ireland.'

'She went to Ireland, did she? Why?'

'She wouldn't tell me. She said there was something she had to find out.'

'Do you know where she went in Ireland?'

'Not exactly. She mentioned a name. Bally something. Ballygowlan, I think it was.'

'I see. You're sure she went to Ireland?'

'I saw her off at Kensington Airport. She went by Aer Lingus.'

'She came back when?'

'The following day.'

'Also by air?'

'Yes.'

'You're quite sure, are you, that she came back by air?'

'Well – I suppose she did!'

'Had she taken a return ticket?'

'No. No, she didn't. I remember.'

'She might have come back another way, mightn't she?'

'Yes, I suppose so.'

'She might have come back for instance by the Irish Mail?'

'She didn't say she had.'

'But she didn't *say* she'd come by air, did she?'

'No,' Bridget agreed. 'But why should she come back by boat and train instead of by air?'

'Well, if she had found out what she wanted to know and had had nowhere to stay, she might think it would be easier to come back by the Night Mail.'

'Why, I suppose she *might*.'

Davy smiled faintly.

'I don't suppose you young ladies,' he said, 'think of going anywhere except in terms of flying, do you, nowadays?'

'I suppose we don't really,' agreed Bridget.

'Anyway, she came back to England. Then what happened? Did she come to you or ring you up?'

'She rang up.'

'What time of day?'

'Oh, in the morning sometime. Yes, it must have been about eleven or twelve o'clock, I think.'

'And she said, what?'

'Well, she just asked if everything was all right.'

'And was it?'

'No, it wasn't, because, you see, Mrs Melford had rung up and Mummy had answered the phone and things had been very difficult and I hadn't known what to say. So Elvira said she would not come to Onslow Square, but that she'd ring up her cousin Mildred and try to fix up some story or other.'

'And that's all that you can remember?'

'That's all,' said Bridget, making certain reservations. She thought of Mr Bollard and the bracelet. That was certainly a thing she was not going to tell Chief-Inspector Davy. Father knew quite well that something was being kept from him. He could only hope that it was not something pertinent to his inquiry. He asked again:

'You think your friend was really frightened of someone or something?'

'Yes I do.'

'Did she mention it to you or did you mention it to her?'

'Oh, I asked her outright. At first she said no and then she admitted that she *was* frightened. And I know she was,' went on Bridget violently. 'She was in danger. She was quite sure of it. But I don't know why or how or anything about it.'

'Your surety on this point relates to that particular morning, does it, the morning she had come back from Ireland?'

'Yes. Yes, that's when I was so sure about it.'

'On the morning when she *might* have come back on the Irish Mail?'

'I don't think it's very likely that she did. Why don't you ask her?'

'I probably shall do in the end. But I don't want to call attention to that point. Not at the moment. It might just possibly make things more dangerous for her.'

Bridget opened round eyes.

'What do you mean?'

'You may not remember it, Miss Bridget, but that was the night, or rather the early morning, of the Irish Mail robbery.'

'Do you mean that Elvira was in *that* and never told me a thing about it?'

'I agree it's unlikely,' said Father. 'But it just occurred to me that she might have seen something or someone, or some incident might have occurred connected with the Irish Mail. She might have seen someone she knew, for instance, and that might have put her in danger.'

'Oh!' said Bridget. She thought it over. 'You mean – someone she knew was mixed up in the robbery.'

Chief-Inspector Davy got up.

'I think that's all,' he said. 'Sure there's nothing more you can tell me? Nowhere where your friend went that day? Or the day before?'

Again visions of Mr Bollard and the Bond Street shop rose before Bridget's eyes.

'No,' she said.

'I think there is something you haven't told me,' said Chief-Inspector Davy.

Bridget grasped thankfully at a straw.

'Oh, I forgot,' she said. 'Yes. I mean she did go to some lawyers. Lawyers who were trustees, to find out something.'

'Oh, she went to some lawyers who were her trustees. I don't suppose you know their name?'

'Their name was Egerton – Forbes Egerton and Something,' said Bridget. 'Lots of names. I think that's more or less right.'

'I see. And she wanted to find out something, did she?'

'She wanted to know how much money she'd got,' said Bridget.

Inspector Davy's eyebrows rose.

'Indeed!' he said. 'Interesting. Why didn't she know herself?'

'Oh, because people never told her anything about money,' said Bridget. 'They seem to think it's bad for you to know actually how much money you have.'

'And she wanted to know badly, did she?'

'Yes,' said Bridget. 'I think she thought it was important.'

'Well, thank you,' said Chief-Inspector Davy. 'You've helped me a good deal.'

CHAPTER 23

Richard Egerton looked again at the official card in front of him, then up into the Chief-Inspector's face.

'Curious business,' he said.

'Yes, sir,' said Chief-Inspector Davy, 'a very curious business.'

'Bertram's Hotel,' said Egerton, 'in the fog. Yes it was a bad fog last night. I suppose you get a lot of that sort of thing in fogs, don't you? Snatch and grab – handbags – that sort of thing?'

'It wasn't quite like that,' said Father. 'Nobody attempted to snatch anything from Miss Blake.'

'Where did the shot come from?'

'Owing to the fog we can't be sure. She wasn't sure herself. But we think – it seems the best idea – that the man may have been standing in the area.'

'He shot at her twice, you say?'

'Yes. The first shot missed. The commissionaire rushed along from where he was standing outside the hotel door and shoved her behind him just before the second shot.'

'So that he got hit instead, eh?'

'Yes.'

'Quite a brave chap.'

'Yes. He was brave,' said the Chief-Inspector. 'His military record was very good. An Irishman.'

'What's his name?'

'Gorman. Michael Gorman.'

'Michael Gorman.' Egerton frowned for a minute. 'No,' he said. 'For a moment I thought the name meant something.'

'It's a very common name, of course. Anyway, he saved the girl's life.'

'And why exactly have you come to me, Chief-Inspector?'

'I hoped for a little information. We always like full information, you know, about the victim of a murderous assault.'

'Oh, naturally, naturally. But really, I've only seen Elvira twice since she was a child.'

'You saw her when she came to call upon you about a week ago, didn't you?'

'Yes, that's quite right. What exactly do you want to know? If it's anything about her personality, who her friends were or about boy friends, or lovers' quarrels – all that sort of thing – you'd do better to go to one of the women. There's a Mrs Carpenter who brought her back from Italy, I believe, and there's Mrs Melford with whom she lives in Kent.'

'I've seen Mrs Melford.'

'Oh.'

'No good. Absolutely no good at all, sir. And I don't so much want to know about the girl personally – after all, I've seen her for myself and I've heard what she can tell me – or rather what she's willing to tell me –'

At a quick movement of Egerton's eyebrows he saw that the other had appreciated the point of the word 'willing'.

'I've been told that she was worried, upset, afraid about something, and convinced that her life was in danger. Was that your impression when she came to see you?'

'No,' said Egerton, slowly, 'no, I wouldn't go as far as that; though she did say one or two things that struck me as curious.'

'Such as?'

'Well, she wanted to know who would benefit if she were to die suddenly.'

'Ah,' said Chief-Inspector Davy, 'so she had that possibility in her mind, did she? That she might die suddenly. Interesting.'

'She'd got something in her head but I didn't know what it was. She also wanted to know how much money she had – or would have when she was twenty-one. That, perhaps, is more understandable.'

'It's a lot of money I believe.'

'It's a very large fortune, Chief-Inspector.'

'Why do you think she wanted to know?'

'About the money?'

'Yes, and about who would inherit it.'

'I don't know,' said Egerton. 'I don't know at all. She also brought up the subject of marriage –'

'Did you form the impression that there was a man in the case?'

'I've no evidence – but – yes, I did think just that. I felt sure there was a boy friend somewhere in the offing. There usually is! Luscombe – that's Colonel Luscombe, her guardian, doesn't seem to know anything about a boy friend. But then dear old Derek Luscombe wouldn't. He was quite upset when I suggested that there was such a thing in the background and probably an unsuitable one at that.'

'He is unsuitable,' said Chief-Inspector Davy.

'Oh. Then you know who he is?'

'I can have a very good guess at it. Ladislaus Malinowski.'

'The racing motorist? Really! A handsome dare-devil. Women fall for him easily. I wonder how he came across Elvira. I don't see very well where their orbits would meet except – yes, I believe he was in Rome a couple of months ago. Possibly she met him there.'

'Very possibly. Or could she have met him through her mother?'

'What, through Bess? I wouldn't say that was at all likely.'

Davy coughed.

'Lady Sedgwick and Malinowski are said to be close friends, sir.'

'Oh yes, yes, I know that's the gossip. May be true, may not. They are close friends – thrown together constantly by their way of life. Bess has had her affairs, of course; though, mind you, she's not the nymphomaniac type. People are ready enough to say that about a woman, but it's not true in Bess's case. Anyway, as far as I know, Bess and her daughter are practically not even acquainted with each other.'

'That's what Lady Sedgwick told me. And you agree?'

Egerton nodded.

'What other relatives has Miss Blake got?'

'For all intents and purposes, none. Her mother's two brothers were killed in the war – and she was old Coniston's only child. Mrs Melford, though the girl calls her "Cousin Mildred", is actually a cousin of Colonel Luscombe's. Luscombe's done his best for the girl in his conscientious old-fashioned way – but it's difficult . . . for a man.'

'Miss Blake brought up the subject of marriage, you say? There's no possibility, I suppose, that she may actually already *be* married –'

'She's well under age – she'd have to have the assent of her guardian and trustees.'

'Technically, yes. But they don't always wait for that,' said Father.

'I know. Most regrettable. One has to go through all the machinery of making them Wards of Court, and all the rest of it. And even that has its difficulties.'

'And once they're married, they're married,' said Father. 'I suppose, if she *were* married, and died suddenly, her husband would inherit?'

'This idea of marriage is most unlikely. She has been most carefully looked after and . . .' He stopped, reacting to Chief-Inspector Davy's cynical smile.

However carefully Elvira had been looked after, she seemed to have succeeded in making the acquaintance of the highly unsuitable Ladislaus Malinowski.

He said dubiously, 'Her mother bolted, it's true.'

'Her mother bolted, yes – that's what she would do – but Miss Blake's a different type. She's just as set on getting her own way, but she'd go about it differently.'

'You don't really think –'

'I don't think anything – *yet*,' said Chief-Inspector Davy.

CHAPTER 24

Ladislaus Malinowski looked from one to the other of the two police officers and flung back his head and laughed.

'It is very amusing!' he said. 'You look solemn as owls. It is ridiculous that you should ask me to come here and wish to ask me questions. You have nothing against me, nothing.'

'We think you may be able to assist us in our inquiries, Mr Malinowski.' Chief-Inspector Davy spoke with official smoothness. 'You own a car, Mercedes-Otto, registration number FAN 2266.'

'Is there any reason why I should not own such a car?'

'No reason at all, sir. There's just a little uncertainty as to the correct number. Your car was on a motor road, M7, and the registration plate on that occasion was a different one.'

'Nonsense. It must have been some other car.'

'There aren't so many of that make. We have checked up on those there are.'

'You believe everything, I suppose, that your traffic police tell you! It is laughable! Where was all this?'

'The place where the police stopped you and asked to see your licence is not very far from Bedhampton. It was on the night of the Irish Mail robbery.'

'You really do amuse me,' said Ladislaus Malinowski.

'You have a revolver?'

'Certainly, I have a revolver and an automatic pistol. I have proper licences for them.'

'Quite so. They are both still in your possession?'

'Certainly.'

'I have already warned you, Mr Malinowski.'

'The famous policeman's warning! Anything you say will be taken down and used against you at your trial.'

'That's not quite the wording,' said Father mildly. 'Used, yes. Against, no. You don't want to qualify that statement of yours?'

'No, I do not.'

'And you are sure you don't want your solicitor here?'

'I do not like solicitors.'

'Some people don't. Where are those firearms now?'

'I think you know very well where they are, Chief-Inspector. The small pistol is in the pocket of my car, the Mercedes-Otto whose registered number is, as I have said, FAN 2266. The revolver is in a drawer in my flat.'

'You're quite right about the one in the drawer in your flat,' said Father, 'but the other – the pistol – is not in your car.'

'Yes, it is. It is in the left-hand pocket.'

Father shook his head. 'It may have been once. It isn't now. Is this it, Mr Malinowski?'

He passed a small automatic pistol across the table. Ladislaus Malinowski, with an air of great surprise, picked it up.

'Ah-ha, yes. This is it. So it was *you* who took it from my car?'

'No,' said Father, 'we didn't take it from your car. It was not in your car. We found it somewhere else.'

'Where did you find it?'

'We found it,' said Father, 'in an area in Pond Street, which – as you no doubt know – is a street near Park Lane. It could have been dropped by a man walking down that street – or running perhaps.'

Ladislaus Malinowski shrugged his shoulders. 'That is nothing to do with me – I did not put it there. It was in my car a day or two ago. One does not continually look to see if a thing is still where one has put it. One assumes it will be.'

'Do you know, Mr Malinowski, that this is the pistol which was used to shoot Michael Gorman on the night of November 26th?'

'Michael Gorman? I do not know a Michael Gorman.'

'The commissionaire from Bertram's Hotel.'

'Ah yes, the one who was shot. I read about it. And you say *my* pistol shot him? Nonsense!'

'It's not nonsense. The ballistic experts have examined it. You know enough of firearms to be aware that their evidence is reliable.'

'You are trying to frame me. I know what you police do!'

'I think you know the police of this country better than that, Mr Malinowski.'

'Are you suggesting that I shot Michael Gorman?'

'So far we are only asking for a statement. No charge has been made.'

'But that is what you think – that I shot that ridiculous dressed-up military figure. Why should I? I didn't owe him money, I had no grudge against him.'

'It was a young lady who was shot at. Gorman ran to protect her and received the second bullet in his chest.'

'A young lady?'

'A young lady whom I think you know. Miss Elvira Blake.'

'Do you say someone tried to shoot Elvira with *my* pistol?'

He sounded incredulous.

'It could be that you had had a disagreement.'

'You mean that I quarrelled with Elvira and shot her? What madness! Why should I shoot the girl I am going to marry?'

'Is that part of your statement? That you are going to marry Miss Elvira Blake?'

Just for a moment or two Ladislaus hesitated. Then he said, shrugging his shoulders:

'She is still very young. It remains to be discussed.'

'Perhaps she had promised to marry you, and then – she changed her mind. There was *someone* she was afraid of. Was it you, Mr Malinowski?'

'Why should *I* want her to die? Either I am in love with her and want to marry her or if I do not want to marry her I need not marry her. It is as simple as that. So why should I kill her?'

'There aren't many people close enough to her to want to kill her.' Davy waited a moment and then said, almost casually: 'There's her mother, of course.'

'What!' Malinowski sprang up. '*Bess?* Bess kill her own daughter? You are mad! Why should Bess kill Elvira?'

'Possibly because, as next of kin, she might inherit an enormous fortune.'

'Bess? You mean Bess would kill for money? She has plenty of money from her American husband. Enough, anyway.'

'Enough is not the same as a great fortune,' said Father. 'People do do murder for a large fortune, mothers have been known to kill their children, and children have killed their mothers.'

'I tell you, you are mad!'

'You say that you may be going to marry Miss Blake. Perhaps you have already married her? If so, then *you* would be the one to inherit a vast fortune.'

'What more crazy, stupid things can you say! No, I am not married to Elvira. She is a pretty girl. I like her, and she is in love with me. Yes, I admit it. I met her in Italy. We had fun – but that is all. No more, do you understand?'

'Indeed? Just now, Mr Malinowski, you said quite definitely that she was the girl you were going to marry.'

'Oh that.'

'Yes – that. Was it true?'

'I said it because – it sounded more respectable that way. You are so – prudish in this country –'

'That seems to me an unlikely explanation.'

'You do not understand anything at all. The mother and I – we are lovers – I did not wish to say so – I suggest instead that the daughter and I – we are engaged to be married. That sounds very English and proper.'

'It sounds to me even more far-fetched. You're rather badly in need of money, aren't you, Mr Malinowski?'

'My dear Chief-Inspector, I am always in need of money. It is very sad.'

'And yet a few months ago I understand you were flinging money about in a very carefree way.'

'Ah. I had had a lucky flutter. I am a gambler. I admit it.'

'I find that quite easy to believe. Where did you have this "flutter"?'

'That I do not tell. You can hardly expect it.'

'I don't expect it.'

'Is that all you have to ask me?'

'For the moment, yes. You have identified the pistol as yours. That will be very helpful.'

'I don't understand – I can't conceive –' He broke off and stretched out his hand. 'Give it me please.'

'I'm afraid we'll have to keep it for the present, so I'll write you out a receipt for it.'

He did so and handed it to Malinowski.

The latter went out slamming the door.

'Temperamental chap,' said Father.

'You didn't press him on the matter of the false number plate and Bedhampton?'

'No. I wanted him rattled. But not too badly rattled. We'll give him one thing to worry about at a time – And he *is* worried.'

'The Old Man wanted to see you, sir, as soon as you were through.'

Chief-Inspector Davy nodded and made his way to Sir Ronald's room.

'Ah! Father. Making progress?'

'Yes. Getting along nicely – quite a lot of fish in the net. Small fry mostly. But we're closing in on the big fellows. Everything's in train –'

'Good show, Fred,' said the AC.

CHAPTER 25

Miss Marple got out of her train at Paddington and saw the burly figure of Chief-Inspector Davy standing on the platform waiting for her.

He said, 'Very good of you, Miss Marple,' put his hand under her elbow and piloted her through the barrier to where a car was waiting. The driver opened the door, Miss Marple got in, Chief-Inspector Davy followed her and the car drove off.

'Where are you taking me, Chief-Inspector Davy?'

'To Bertram's Hotel.'

'Dear me, Bertram's Hotel again. Why?'

'The official reply is: because the police think you can assist them in their inquiries.'

'That sounds familiar, but surely rather sinister? So often the prelude to an arrest, is it not?'

'I am not going to arrest you, Miss Marple.' Father smiled. 'You have an alibi.'

Miss Marple digested this in silence. Then she said, 'I see.'

They drove to Bertram's Hotel in silence. Miss Gorringe looked up from the desk as they entered, but Chief-Inspector Davy piloted Miss Marple to the lift.

'Second floor.'

The lift ascended, stopped, and Father led the way along the corridor. As he opened the door of No. 18 Miss Marple said:

'This is the same room I had when I was staying here before.'

'Yes,' said Father.

Miss Marple sat down in the arm-chair.

'A very comfortable room,' she observed, looking round with a slight sigh.

'They certainly know what comfort is here,' Father agreed.

'You look tired, Chief-Inspector,' said Miss Marple unexpectedly.

'I've had to get around a bit. As a matter of fact I've just got back from Ireland.'

'Indeed. From Ballygowlan?'

'Now how the devil did *you* know about Ballygowlan? I'm sorry – I beg your pardon.'

Miss Marple smiled forgiveness.

'I suppose Michael Gorman happened to tell you he came from there – was that it?'

'No, not exactly,' said Miss Marple.

'Then how, if you'll excuse me asking you, *did* you know?'

'Oh dear,' said Miss Marple, 'it's really very embarrassing. It was just something I – happened to overhear.'

'Oh, I see.'

'I wasn't eavesdropping. It was in a public room – at least technically a public room. Quite frankly, I enjoy listening to people talking. One does. Especially when one is old and doesn't get about very much. I mean, if people are talking near you, you listen.'

'Well, that seems to me quite natural,' said Father.

'Up to a point, yes,' said Miss Marple. 'If people do not choose to lower their voices, one must assume that they are prepared to be overheard. But of course matters may develop. The situation sometimes arises when you realize that though it *is* a public room, other people talking do not realize that there is anyone else in it. And then one has to decide what to do about it. Get up and cough, or just stay quite quiet and hope they won't realize you've been there. Either way is embarrassing.'

Chief-Inspector Davy glanced at his watch.

'Look here,' he said, 'I want to hear more about this – but I've got Canon Pennyfather arriving at any moment. I must go and collect him. You don't mind?'

Miss Marple said she didn't mind. Chief-Inspector Davy left the room.

Canon Pennyfather came through the swing doors into the hall of Bertram's Hotel. He frowned slightly, wondering what it was that seemed a little different about Bertram's today. Perhaps it had been painted or done up in some way? He shook his head. That was not it, but there was *something*. It did not occur to him that it was the difference between a six foot commissionaire with blue eyes and dark hair and a five foot seven commissionaire with sloping shoulders, freckles and a sandy thatch of hair bulging out under his commissionaire's cap. He just knew something was different. In his usual vague way he wandered up to the desk. Miss Gorringe was there and greeted him.

'Canon Pennyfather. How nice to see you. Have you come to fetch your baggage? It's all ready for you. If you'd only let us know we could have sent it to you to any address you like.'

'Thank you,' said Canon Pennyfather, 'thank you very much. You're always most kind, Miss Gorringe. But as I had to come up to London anyway today I thought I might as well call for it.'

'We were so worried about you,' said Miss Gorringe. 'Being missing, you know. Nobody able to find you. You had a car accident, I hear?'

'Yes,' said Canon Pennyfather. 'Yes. People drive much too fast nowadays. Most dangerous. Not that I can remember much about it. It affected my head. Concussion, the doctor says. Oh well, as one is getting on in life, one's memory –' He shook his head sadly. 'And how are you, Miss Gorringe?'

'Oh, I'm very well,' said Miss Gorringe.

At that moment it struck Canon Pennyfather that Miss Gorringe also was different. He peeered at her, trying to analyse where the difference lay. Her hair? That was the same as usual. Perhaps even a little frizzier. Black dress, large locket, cameo brooch. All there as usual. But there was a difference. Was she perhaps a little thinner? Or was it – yes, surely, she looked *worried*. It was not often that Canon Pennyfather noticed whether people looked worried, he was not the kind of man who noticed emotion in the faces of others, but it struck him today, perhaps because Miss Gorringe had so invariably presented exactly the same countenance to guests for so many years.

'You've not been ill, I hope?' he asked solicitously. 'You look a little thinner.'

'Well, we've had a good deal of worry, Canon Pennyfather.'

'Indeed. Indeed. I'm sorry to hear it. Not due to my disappearance, I hope?'

'Oh no,' said Miss Gorringe. 'We were worried, of course, about that, but as soon as we heard that you were all right –' She broke off and said, 'No. No – it's this – well, perhaps you haven't read about it in the papers. Gorman, our outside porter, got killed.'

'Oh yes,' said Canon Pennyfather. 'I remember now. I did see it mentioned in the paper – that you had had a murder here.'

Miss Gorringe shuddered at this blunt mention of the word murder. The shudder went all up her black dress.

'Terrible,' she said, 'terrible. Such a thing has *never* happened at Bertram's. I mean, we're not the sort of hotel where murders happen.'

'No, no, indeed,' said Canon Pennyfather quickly. 'I'm sure you're not. I mean it would never have occurred to me that anything like that could happen *here*.'

'Of course it wasn't *inside* the hotel,' said Miss Gorringe, cheering up a little as this aspect of the affair struck her. 'It was outside in the street.'

'So really nothing to do with you at all,' said the Canon, helpfully.

That apparently was not quite the right thing to say.

'But it was connected with Bertram's. We had to have the police here questioning people, since it was our commissionaire who was shot.'

'So that's a new man you have outside. D'you know, I thought somehow things looked a little strange.'

'Yes, I don't know that he's very satisfactory. I mean, not quite the style we're used to here. But of course we had to get someone quickly.'

'I remember all about it now,' said Canon Pennyfather, assembling some rather dim memories of what he had read in the paper a week ago. 'But I thought it was a *girl* who was shot.'

'You mean Lady Sedgwick's daughter? I expect you remember seeing her here with her guardian, Colonel Luscombe. Apparently she was attacked by someone in the fog. I expect they wanted to snatch her bag. Anyway they fired a shot at her and then Gorman, who of course had been a soldier and was a man with a lot of presence of mind, rushed down, got in front of her and got shot himself, poor fellow.'

'Very sad, very sad,' said the Canon, shaking his head.

'It makes everything terribly difficult,' complained Miss Gorringe. 'I mean, the police constantly in and out. I suppose that's to be expected, but we don't *like* it here, though I must say Chief-Inspector Davy and Sergeant Wadell are very respectable-looking. Plain clothes, and very good style, not the sort with boots and mackintoshes like one sees on films. Almost like one of *us*.'

'Er – yes,' said Canon Pennyfather.

'Did you have to go to hospital?' inquired Miss Gorringe.

'No,' said the Canon, 'some very nice people, really good Samaritans – a market gardener, I believe – picked me up and his wife nursed me back to health. I'm most grateful, most grateful. It is refreshing to find that there is still human kindness in the world. Don't you think so?'

Miss Gorringe said she thought it was very refreshing. 'After all one reads about the increase in crime,' she added, 'all those dreadful young men and girls holding up banks and robbing trains and ambushing people.' She looked up and said, 'There's Chief-Inspector Davy coming down the stairs now. I think he wants to speak to you.'

'I don't know why he should want to speak to me,' said Canon Pennyfather, puzzled. 'He's already been to see me, you know,' he said, 'at Chadminster. He was very disappointed, I think, that I couldn't tell him anything useful.'

'You couldn't?'

The Canon shook his head sorrowfully.

'I couldn't remember. The accident took place somewhere near a place called Bedhampton and really I don't understand *what* I can have been doing there. The Chief-Inspector kept asking me why I was there and I couldn't tell him. Very odd, isn't it? He seemed to think I'd been driving a car from somewhere near a railway station to a vicarage.'

'That sounds very possible,' said Miss Gorringe.

'It doesn't seem possible at all,' said Canon Pennyfather. 'I mean, why should I be driving about in a part of the world that I don't really know?'

Chief-Inspector Davy had come up to them.

'So here you are, Canon Pennyfather,' he said. 'Feeling quite yourself again?'

'Oh, I feel quite well now,' said the Canon, 'but rather inclined to have headaches still. And I've been told not to do too much. But I still don't seem to remember what I ought to remember and the doctor says it may never come back.'

'Oh well,' said Chief-Inspector Davy, 'we mustn't give up hope.' He led the Canon away from the desk. 'There's a little experiment I want you to try,' he said. 'You don't mind helping me, do you?'

When Chief-Inspector Davy opened the door of No. 18, Miss Marple was still sitting in the arm-chair by the window.

'A good many people in the street today,' she observed. 'More than usual.'

'Oh well – this is a way through to Berkeley Square and Shepherd Market.'

'I didn't mean only passers-by. Men doing things – road repairs, a telephone repair van – meat trolley – a couple of private cars –'

'And what – may I ask – do you deduce from that?'

'I didn't say that I deduced anything.'

Father gave her a look. Then he said:

'I want you to help me.'

'Of course. That is why I am here. What do you want me to do?'

'I want you to do exactly what you did on the night of November 19th. You were asleep – you woke up – possibly awakened by some unusual noise. You switched on the light, looked at the time, got out of bed, opened the door and looked out. Can you repeat those actions?'

'Certainly,' said Miss Marple. She got up and went across to the bed.

'Just a moment.'

Chief-Inspector Davy went and tapped on the connecting walls of the next room.

'You'll have to do that louder,' said Miss Marple. 'This place is very well built.'

The Chief-Inspector redoubled the force of his knuckles.

'I told Canon Pennyfather to count ten,' he said, looking at his watch. 'Now then, off you go.'

Miss Marple touched the electric lamp, looked at an imaginary clock, got up, walked to the door, opened it and looked out. To her right, just leaving his room, walking to the top of the stairs, was Canon Pennyfather. He arrived at the top of the stairs and started down them. Miss Marple gave a slight catch of her breath. She turned back.

'Well?' said Chief-Inspector Davy.

'The man I saw that night can't have been Canon Pennyfather,' said Miss Marple. 'Not if that's Canon Pennyfather now.'

'I thought you said –'

'I know. He looked like Canon Pennyfather. His hair and his clothes and everything. But he didn't walk the same way. I think – I think he must have been a younger man. I'm sorry, very sorry, to have misled you, but it wasn't Canon Pennyfather that I saw that night. I'm quite sure of it.'

'You really are quite sure this time, Miss Marple?'

'Yes,' said Miss Marple. 'I'm sorry,' she added again, 'to have misled you.'

'You were very nearly right. Canon Pennyfather did come back to the hotel that night. Nobody saw him come in – but that wasn't remarkable. He came in after midnight. He came up the stairs, he opened the door of his room next door and he went in. What he saw or what happened next we don't know, because he can't or won't tell us. If there was only some way we could jog his memory . . .'

'There's that German word of course,' said Miss Marple, thoughtfully.

'What German word?'

'Dear me, I've forgotten it now, but –'

There was a knock at the door.

'May I come in?' said Canon Pennyfather. He entered. 'Was it satisfactory?'

'Most satisfactory,' said Father. 'I was just telling Miss Marple – you know Miss Marple?'

'Oh yes,' said Canon Pennyfather, really slightly uncertain as to whether he did or not.

'I was just telling Miss Marple how we have traced your movements. You came back to the hotel that night after midnight. You came upstairs and you opened the door of your room and went in –' He paused.

Miss Marple gave an exclamation.

'I remember now,' she said, 'what the German word is. *Doppelgänger!*'

Canon Pennyfather uttered an exclamation. 'But of course,' he said, 'of *course*! How could I have forgotten? You're quite right, you know. After that film, *The Walls of Jericho*, I came back here and I came upstairs and I opened my room and I saw – extraordinary, I distinctly saw *myself* sitting in a chair facing me. As you say, dear lady, a *doppelgänger*. How very remarkable! And then – let me see –' He raised his eyes, trying to think.

'And then,' said Father, 'startled out of their lives to see you, when they thought you were safely in Lucerne, somebody hit you on the head.'

CHAPTER 26

Canon Pennyfather had been sent on his way in a taxi to the British Museum. Miss Marple had been ensconced in the lounge by the Chief-Inspector. Would she mind waiting for him there for about ten minutes? Miss Marple had not minded. She welcomed the opportunity to sit and look around her and think.

Bertram's Hotel. So many memories . . . The past fused itself with the present. A French phrase came back to her. *Plus ça change, plus c'est la même chose.* She reversed the wording. *Plus c'est la même chose, plus ça change.* Both true, she thought.

She felt sad – for Bertram's Hotel and for herself. She wondered what Chief-Inspector Davy wanted of her next. She sensed in him the excitement of purpose. He was a man whose plans were at last coming to fruition. It was Chief-Inspector Davy's D-Day.

The life of Bertram's went on as usual. No, Miss Marple decided, *not* as usual. There was a difference, though she could not have defined where the difference lay. An underlying uneasiness, perhaps?

'All set?' he inquired genially.

'Where are you taking me now?'

'We're going to pay a call on Lady Sedgwick.'

'Is she staying here?'

'Yes. With her daughter.'

Miss Marple rose to her feet. She cast a glance round her and murmured: 'Poor Bertram's.'

'What do you mean – poor Bertram's?'

'I think you know quite well what I mean.'

'Well – looking at it from your point of view, perhaps I do.'

'It is always sad when a work of art has to be destroyed.'

'You call this place a work of art?'

'Certainly I do. So do you.'

'I see what you mean,' admitted Father.

'It is like when you get ground elder really badly in a border. There's nothing else you can do about it – except dig the whole thing up.'

'I don't know much about gardens. But change the metaphor to dry rot and I'd agree.'

They went up in the lift and along a passage to where Lady Sedgwick and her daughter had a corner suite.

Chief-Inspector Davy knocked on the door, a voice said, 'Come in,' and he entered with Miss Marple behind him.

Bess Sedgwick was sitting in a high-backed chair near the window. She had a book on her knee which she was not reading.

'So it's you again, Chief-Inspector.' Her eyes went past him towards Miss Marple, and she looked slightly surprised.

'This is Miss Marple,' explained Chief-Inspector Davy. 'Miss Marple – Lady Sedgwick.'

'I've met you before,' said Bess Sedgwick. 'You were with Selina Hazy the other day, weren't you? Do sit down,' she added. Then she turned towards Chief-Inspector Davy again. 'Have you any news of the man who shot at Elvira?'

'Not actually what you'd call *news*.'

'I doubt if you ever will have. In a fog like that, predatory creatures come out and prowl around looking for women walking alone.'

'True up to a point,' said Father. 'How is your daughter?'

'Oh, Elvira is quite all right again.'

'You've got her here with you?'

'Yes. I rang up Colonel Luscombe – her guardian. He was delighted that I was willing to take charge.' She gave a sudden laugh. 'Dear old boy. He's always been urging a mother-and-daughter reunion act!'

'He may be right at that,' said Father.

'Oh no, he isn't. Just at the moment, yes, I think it is the best thing.' She turned her head to look out of the window and spoke in a changed voice. 'I hear you've arrested a friend of mine – Ladislaus Malinowski. On what charge?'

'Not *arrested*,' Chief-Inspector Davy corrected her. 'He's just assisting us with our inquiries.'

'I've sent my solicitor to look after him.'

'Very wise,' said Father approvingly. 'Anyone who's having a little difficulty with the police is very wise to have a solicitor. Otherwise they may so easily say the wrong thing.'

'Even if completely innocent?'

'Possibly it's even more necessary in that case,' said Father.

'You're quite a cynic, aren't you? What are you questioning him about, may I ask? Or mayn't I?'

'For one thing we'd like to know just exactly what his movements were on the night when Michael Gorman died.'

Bess Sedgwick sat up sharply in her chair.

'Have you got some ridiculous idea that *Ladislaus* fired those shots at Elvira? They didn't even know each other.'

'He could have done it. His car was just round the corner.'

'Rubbish,' said Lady Sedgwick robustly.

'How much did that shooting business the other night upset you, Lady Sedgwick?'

She looked faintly surprised.

'Naturally I was upset when my daughter had a narrow escape of her life. What do you expect?'

'I didn't mean that. I mean how much did the death of Michael Gorman upset you?'

'I was very sorry about it. He was a brave man.'

'Is that all?'

'What more would you expect me to say?'

'You knew him, didn't you?'

'Of course. He worked here.'

'You knew him a little better than that, though, didn't you?'

'What do you mean?'

'Come, Lady Sedgwick. He was your husband, wasn't he?'

She did not answer for a moment or two, though she displayed no signs of agitation or surprise.

'You know a good deal, don't you, Chief-Inspector?' She sighed and sat back in her chair. 'I hadn't seen him for – let me see – a great many years. Twenty – more than twenty. And then I looked out of the window one day, and suddenly recognized Micky.'

'And he recognized you?'

'Quite surprising that we did recognize each other,' said Bess Sedgwick. 'We were only together for about a week. Then my family caught up with us, paid Micky off, and took me home in disgrace.'

She sighed.

'I was very young when I ran away with him. I knew very little. Just a fool of a girl with a head full of romantic notions. He was a hero to me, mainly because of the way he rode a horse. He didn't know what fear was. And he was handsome and gay with an Irishman's tongue! I suppose really *I* ran away with *him*! I doubt if he'd have thought of it himself! But I was wild and headstrong and madly in love!' She shook her head. 'It didn't last long . . . The first twenty-four hours were enough to disillusion me. He drank and he was coarse and brutal. When my family turned up and took me back with them, I was thankful. I never wanted to see him or hear of him again.'

'Did your family know that you were married to him?'

'No.'

'You didn't tell them?'

'I didn't think I *was* married.'

'How did that come about?'

'We were married in Ballygowlan, but when my people turned up, Micky came to me and told me the marriage had been a fake. He and his friends had cooked it up between them, he said. By that time it seemed to me quite a natural thing for him to have done. Whether he wanted the money that was being offered him, or whether he was afraid he'd committed a breach of the law by marrying me when I wasn't of age, I don't know. Anyway, I didn't doubt for a moment that what he said was true – not then.'

'And later?'

She seemed lost in her thoughts. 'It wasn't until – oh, quite a number of years afterwards, when I knew a little more of life, and of legal matters, that it suddenly occurred to me that probably I was married to Micky Gorman after all!'

'In actual fact, then, when you married Lord Coniston, you committed bigamy.'

'And when I married Johnnie Sedgwick, and again when I married my American husband, Ridgway Becker.' She looked at Chief-Inspector Davy and laughed with what seemed like genuine amusement.

'So much bigamy,' she said. 'It really does seem very ridiculous.'

'Did you never think of getting a divorce?'

She shrugged her shoulders. 'It all seemed like a silly dream. Why rake it up? I told Johnnie, of course.' Her voice softened and mellowed as she said his name.

'And what did he say?'

'He didn't care. Neither Johnnie nor I were ever very law-abiding.'

'Bigamy carries certain penalties, Lady Sedgwick.'

She looked at him and laughed.

'Who was ever going to worry about something that had happened in Ireland years ago? The whole thing was over and done with. Micky had taken his money and gone off. Oh, don't you understand? It seemed just a silly little incident. An incident I wanted to forget. I put it aside with the things – the very many things – that don't matter in life.'

'And then,' said Father, in a tranquil voice, 'one day in November, Michael Gorman turned up again and blackmailed you?'

'Nonsense! Who said he blackmailed me?'

Slowly Father's eyes went round to the old lady sitting quietly, very upright in her chair.

'You.' Bess Sedgwick stared at Miss Marple. 'What can *you* know about it?'

Her voice was more curious than accusing.

'The arm-chairs in this hotel have very high backs,' said Miss Marple. 'Very comfortable they are. I was sitting in one in front of the fire in the writing-room. Just resting before I went out one morning. You came in to write a letter. I suppose you didn't realize there was anyone else in the room. And so – I heard your conversation with this man Gorman.'

'You listened?'

'Naturally,' said Miss Marple. 'Why not? It was a public room. When you threw up the window and called to the man outside, I had no idea that it was going to be a private conversation.'

Bess stared at her for a moment, then she nodded her head slowly.

'Fair enough,' she said. 'Yes, I see. But all the same you misunderstood what you heard. Micky didn't blackmail me. He might have thought of it – but I warned him off before he could try!' Her lips curled up again in that wide generous smile that made her face so attractive. 'I frightened him off.'

'Yes,' agreed Miss Marple. 'I think you probably did. You threatened to shoot him. You handled it – if you won't think it impertinent of me to say so – very well indeed.'

Bess Sedgwick's eyebrows rose in some amusement.

'But I wasn't the only person to hear you,' Miss Marple went on.

'Good gracious! Was the whole hotel listening?'

'The other arm-chair was also occupied.'

'By whom?'

Miss Marple closed her lips. She looked at Chief-Inspector Davy, and it was almost a pleading glance. 'If it *must* be done, *you* do it,' the glance said, 'but I can't . . .'

'Your daughter was in the other chair,' said Chief-Inspector Davy.

'Oh no!' The cry came out sharply. 'Oh *no*. Not Elvira! I see – yes, I see. She must have thought –'

'She thought seriously enough of what she had overheard to go to Ireland and search for the truth. It wasn't difficult to discover.'

Again Bess Sedgwick said softly: 'Oh no . . .' And then: 'Poor child . . . Even now, she's never asked me a thing. She's kept it all to herself. Bottled it up inside herself. If she'd only told me I could have explained it all to her – showed her how it didn't matter.'

'She mightn't have agreed with you there,' said Chief-Inspector Davy. 'It's a funny thing, you know,' he went on, in a reminiscent, almost gossipy manner, looking like an old farmer discussing his stock and his land, 'I've learnt after a great many years' trial and error – I've learned to distrust a pattern when it's simple. Simple patterns are often too good to be true. The pattern of this murder the other night was like that. Girl says someone shot at her and missed. The commissionaire came running to save her, and copped it with a second bullet. That may be all true enough. That may be the way the girl saw it. But actually behind the appearances, things might be rather different.

'You said pretty vehemently just now, Lady Sedgwick, that there could be no reason for Ladislaus Malinowski to attempt your daughter's life. Well, I'll agree with you. I don't think there was. He's the sort of young man who might have a row with a woman, pull out a knife and stick it into her. But I don't think he'd hide in an area, and wait cold-bloodedly to shoot her. But supposing he wanted to shoot *someone else*. Screams and shots – but what actually has happened is that *Michael Gorman* is dead. Suppose that was actually what was *meant* to happen. Malinowski plans it very carefully. He chooses a foggy night, hides in the area and waits until your daughter comes up the street. He knows she's coming because he has managed to arrange it that way. He fires a shot. It's not meant to hit the girl. He's careful not to let the bullet go anywhere near her, but *she* thinks it's aimed at her all right. She screams. The porter from the hotel, hearing the shot and the scream, comes rushing down the street and *then Malinowski shoots the person he's come to shoot. Michael Gorman.*'

'I don't believe a word of it! Why on earth should Ladislaus want to shoot Micky Gorman?'

'A little matter of blackmail, perhaps,' said Father.

'Do you mean that Micky was blackmailing *Ladislaus*? What about?'

'Perhaps,' said Father, 'about the things that go on at Bertram's Hotel. Michael Gorman might have found out quite a lot about that.'

'Things that go on at Bertram's Hotel? What *do* you mean?'

'It's been a good racket,' said Father. 'Well planned, beautifully executed. But nothing lasts for ever. Miss Marple here asked me the other day what was wrong with this place. Well, I'll answer that question now. Bertram's Hotel is to all intents and purposes the headquarters of one of the best and biggest crime syndicates that's been known for years.'

CHAPTER 27

There was silence for about a minute and a half. Then Miss Marple spoke.

'How *very* interesting,' she said conversationally.

Bess Sedgwick turned on her. 'You don't seem surprised, Miss Marple.'

'I'm not. Not really. There were so many curious things that didn't seem quite to fit in. It was all too good to be true – if you know what I mean. What they call in theatrical circles, a beautiful performance. But it *was* a performance – not real.

'And there were a lot of little things, people claiming a friend or an acquaintance – and turning out to be wrong.'

'These things happen,' said Chief-Inspector Davy, 'but they happened too often. Is that right, Miss Marple?'

'Yes,' agreed Miss Marple. 'People like Selina Hazy do make that kind of mistake. But there were so many other people doing it too. One couldn't help *noticing* it.'

'She notices a lot,' said Chief-Inspector Davy, speaking to Bess Sedgwick as though Miss Marple was his pet performing dog.

Bess Sedgwick turned on him sharply.

'What did you mean when you said this place was the headquarters of a Crime Syndicate? I should have said that Bertram's Hotel was the most respectable place in the world.'

'Naturally,' said Father. 'It would have to be. A lot of money, time, and thought has been spent on making it just what it is. The genuine and the phony are mixed up very cleverly. You've got a superb actor manager running the show in Henry. You've got that chap, Humfries, wonderfully plausible. He hasn't got a record in this country but he's been mixed up in some rather curious hotel dealings abroad. There are some very good character actors playing various parts here. I'll admit, if you like, that I can't help feeling a good deal of admiration for the whole set-up. It has cost this country a mint of money. It's given the CID and the provincial police forces constant headaches. Every time we seemed to be getting somewhere, and put our finger on some particular incident – it turned out to be the kind of incident that had nothing to do with anything else. But we've gone on working on it, a piece there, a piece here. A garage where stacks of number plates were kept, transferable at a moment's notice to certain cars. A firm of furniture vans, a butcher's van, a grocer's van, even one or two phony postal vans. A racing driver with a racing car covering incredible distances in incredibly few minutes, and at the other end of the scale an old clergyman jogging along in his old Morris Oxford. A cottage with a market gardener in it who lends first aid if necessary and who is in touch with a useful doctor. I needn't go into it all. The ramifications seem unending. That's one half of it. The foreign visitors who come to Bertram's are the other half. Mostly from America, or from the Dominions. Rich people above suspicion, coming here with a good lot of luxury luggage, leaving here with a good lot of luxury luggage which looks the same but isn't. Rich tourists arriving in France and not worried unduly by the Customs because the Customs don't worry tourists when they're bringing money into the country. Not the same tourists too many times. The pitcher mustn't go to the well too often. None of it's going to be easy to prove or to tie up, but it will all tie up in the end. We've made a beginning. The Cabots, for instance –'

'What about the Cabots?' asked Bess sharply.

'You remember them? Very nice Americans. Very nice indeed. They stayed here last year and they've been here again this year. They wouldn't have come a third time. Nobody ever comes here more than twice on the same racket. Yes, we arrested them when they arrived at Calais. Very well-made job, that wardrobe case they had with them. It had over three hundred thousand pounds neatly stashed. Proceeds of the Bedhampton train robbery. Of course, that's only a drop in the ocean.

'Bertram's Hotel, let me tell you, is the headquarters of the whole thing! Half the staff are in on it. Some of the guests are in on it. Some of the guests are who they say they are – some are not. The real Cabots, for instance, are in Yucatan just now. Then there was the identification racket. Take

Mr Justice Ludgrove. A familiar face, bulbous nose and a wart. Quite easy to impersonate. Canon Pennyfather. A mild country clergyman, with a great white thatch of hair and notable absent-minded behaviour. His mannerisms, his way of peering over his spectacles – all very easily imitated by a good character actor.'

'But what was the use of all that?' asked Bess.

'Are you really asking me? Isn't it obvious? Mr Justice Ludgrove is seen near the scene of a bank hold-up. Someone recognizes him, mentions it. We go into it. It's all a mistake. He was somewhere else at the time. But it wasn't for a while that we realized that these were all what is sometimes called "deliberate mistakes". Nobody's bothered about the man who had looked so like him. And doesn't look particularly like him really. He takes off his make-up and stops acting his part. The whole thing brings about confusion. At one time we had a High Court judge, an Archdeacon, an Admiral, a Major-General, all seen near the scene of a crime.

'After the Bedhampton train robbery at least four vehicles were concerned before the loot arrived in London. A racing car driven by Malinowski took part in it, a false Metal Box lorry, an old-fashioned Daimler with an admiral in it, and an old clergyman with a thatch of white hair in a Morris Oxford. The whole thing was a splendid operation, beautifully planned.

'And then one day the gang had a bit of bad luck. That muddle-headed old ecclesiastic, Canon Pennyfather, went off to catch his plane on the wrong day, they turned him away from the air station, he wandered out into Cromwell Road, went to a film, arrived back here after midnight, came up to his room, of which he had the key in his pocket, opened the door, and walked in to get the shock of his life when he saw what appeared to be *himself* sitting in a chair facing him! The last thing the gang expected was to see the real Canon Pennyfather, supposed to be safely in Lucerne, walk in! His double was just getting ready to start off to play his part at Bedhampton when in walked the real man. They didn't know what to do but there was a quick reflex action from one member of the party. Humfries, I suspect. He hit the old man on the head, and he went down unconscious. Somebody, I think, was angry over that. Very angry. However, they examined the old boy, decided he was only knocked out, and would probably come round later and they went on with their plans. The false Canon Pennyfather left his room, went out of the hotel and drove to the scene of activities where he was to play his part in the relay race. What they did with the real Canon Pennyfather I don't know. I can only guess. I presume he too was moved later that night, driven down in a car, taken to the market gardener's cottage which was at a spot not too far from where the train was to be held up and where a doctor could attend to him. Then, if reports came through about Canon Pennyfather having been seen in the neighbourhood, it would all fit in. It must have been an anxious moment for all concerned until he regained consciousness and they found that at least three days had been knocked out of his remembrance.'

'Would they have killed him otherwise?' asked Miss Marple.

'No,' said Father. 'I don't think they would have killed him. Someone wouldn't have let that happen. It had seemed very clear all along that whoever ran this show had an objection to murder.'

'It sounds fantastic,' said Bess Sedgwick. 'Utterly fantastic! And I don't believe you have any evidence whatever to link Ladislaus Malinowski with this rigmarole.'

'I've got plenty of evidence against Ladislaus Malinowski,' said Father. 'He's careless, you know. He hung around here when he shouldn't have. On the first occasion he came to establish connection with your daughter. They had a code arranged.'

'Nonsense. She told you herself that she didn't know him.'

'She may have told me that but it wasn't true. She's in love with him. She wants the fellow to marry her.'

'I don't believe it!'

'You're not in a position to know,' Chief-Inspector Davy pointed out. 'Malinowski isn't the sort of person who tells all his secrets and your daughter you don't know at all. You admitted as much. You were angry, weren't you, when you found out Malinowski had come to Bertram's Hotel.'

'Why should I be angry?'

'*Because you're the brains of the show,*' said Father. 'You and Henry. The financial side was run by the Hoffman brothers. They made all the arrangements with the Continental banks and accounts and that sort of thing, but the boss of the syndicate, the brains that run it, and plan it, are your brains, Lady Sedgwick.'

Bess looked at him and laughed. 'I never heard anything so ridiculous!' she said.

'Oh no, it's not ridiculous at all. You've got brains, courage and daring. You've tried most things; you thought you'd turn your hand to crime. Plenty of excitement in it, plenty of risk. It wasn't the money that attracted you, I'd say, it was the fun of the whole thing. But you wouldn't stand for murder, or for undue violence. There were no killings, no brutal assaults, only nice quiet scientific taps on the head if necessary. You're a very interesting woman, you know. One of the few really interesting great criminals.'

There was silence for some few minutes. Then Bess Sedgwick rose to her feet.

'I think you must be mad.' She put her hand out to the telephone.

'Going to ring up your solicitor? Quite the right thing to do before you say too much.'

With a sharp gesture she slammed the receiver back on the hook.

'On second thoughts I hate solicitors . . . All right. Have it your own way. Yes, I ran this show. You're quite correct when you say it was fun. I loved every minute of it. It was fun scooping money from banks, trains and post offices and so-called security vans! It was fun planning and deciding; glorious fun and I'm glad I had it. The pitcher goes to the well once too often? That's what you said just now, wasn't it? I suppose it's true. Well, I've had a good run for my money! But you're wrong about Ladislaus Malinowski shooting Michael Gorman! He didn't. *I did.*' She laughed a sudden high, excited laugh. 'Never mind what it was he did, what he threatened . . . I told him I'd shoot him – Miss Marple heard me – and I *did* shoot him. I did very much what you suggested Ladislaus did. I hid in that area. When Elvira passed, I fired one shot wild, and when she screamed and Micky came running down the street, I'd got him where I wanted him, and I let him have it! I've got keys to all the hotel entrances, of course. I just slipped in through the area door and up to my room. It never occurred to me you'd trace the pistol to Ladislaus – or would even suspect him. I'd pinched it from his car without his knowing. But not, I can assure you, with any idea of throwing suspicion on *him.*'

She swept round on Miss Marple. 'You're a witness to what I've said, remember. *I killed Gorman.*'

'Or perhaps you are saying so because you're in love with Malinowski,' suggested Davy.

'I'm not.' Her retort came sharply. 'I'm his good friend, that's all. Oh yes, we've been lovers in a casual kind of way, but I'm not in love with him. In all my life, I've only loved one person – John Sedgwick.' Her voice changed and softened as she pronounced the name.

'But Ladislaus is my friend. I don't want him railroaded for something he didn't do. *I killed Michael Gorman.* I've said so, and Miss Marple has heard me . . . And now, dear Chief-Inspector Davy –' her voice rose excitedly, and her laughter rang out – '*catch me if you can.*'

With a sweep of her arm, she smashed the window with the heavy telephone set, and before Father could get to his feet, she was out of the window and edging her way rapidly along the narrow parapet. With surprising quickness in spite of his bulk, Davy had moved to the other window and flung up the sash. At the same time he blew the whistle he had taken from his pocket.

Miss Marple, getting to her feet with rather more difficulty a moment or two later, joined him. Together they stared out along the façade of Bertram's Hotel.

'She'll fall. She's climbing up a drainpipe,' Miss Marple exclaimed. 'But why *up*?'

'Going to the roof. It's her only chance and she knows it. Good God, look at her. Climbs like a cat. She looks like a fly on the side of the wall. The risks she's taking!'

Miss Marple murmured, her eyes half closing, 'She'll fall. She can't do it . . .'

The woman they were watching disappeared from sight. Father drew back a little into the room.

Miss Marple asked:

'Don't you want to go and –'

Father shook his head. 'What good am I with my bulk? I've got my men posted ready for something like this. They know what to do. In a few minutes we shall know . . . I wouldn't put it past her to beat the lot of them! She's a woman in a thousand, you know.' He sighed. 'One of the wild ones. Oh, we've some of them in every generation. You can't tame them, you can't bring them into the community and make them live in law and order. They go their own way. If they're saints they go and tend lepers or something, or get themselves martyred in jungles. If they're bad lots they commit the atrocities that you don't like hearing about: and sometimes – they're just wild! They'd have been all right, I suppose, born in another age when it was everyone's hand for himself, everyone fighting to keep life in their veins. Hazards at every turn, danger all round them, and they themselves perforce dangerous to others. That world would have suited them; they'd have been at home in it. This one doesn't.'

'Did you know what she was going to do?'

'Not really. That's one of her gifts. The unexpected. She must have thought this out, you know. She knew what was coming. So she sat looking at us – keeping the ball rolling – and thinking. Thinking and planning hard. I expect – ah –' He broke off as there came the sudden roar of a car's exhaust, the screaming of wheels, and the sound of a big racing engine. He leaned out. 'She's made it, she's got to her car.'

There was more screaming as the car came round the corner on two wheels, a great roar, and the beautiful white monster came tearing up the street.

'She'll kill someone,' said Father, 'she'll kill a lot of people . . . even if she doesn't kill herself.'

'I wonder,' said Miss Marple.

'She's a good driver, of course. A damn good driver. Whoof, that was a near one!'

They heard the roar of the car racing away with the horn blaring, heard it grow fainter. Heard cries, shouts, the sound of brakes, cars hooting and pulling up and finally a great scream of tyres and a roaring exhaust and –

'She's crashed,' said Father.

He stood there very quietly waiting with the patience that was characteristic of his whole big patient form. Miss Marple stood silent beside him. Then, like a relay race, word came down along the street. A man on the pavement opposite looked up at Chief-Inspector Davy and made rapid signs with his hands.

'She's had it,' said Father heavily. 'Dead! Went about ninety miles an hour into the park railings. No other casualties bar a few slight collisions. Magnificent driving. Yes, she's dead.' He turned back into the room and said heavily, 'Well, she told her story first. You heard her.'

'Yes,' said Miss Marple. 'I heard her.' There was a pause. 'It wasn't true, of course,' said Miss Marple quietly.

Father looked at her. 'You didn't believe her, eh?'

'Did you?'

'No,' said Father. 'No, it wasn't the right story. She thought it out so that it would meet the case exactly, but it wasn't true. She didn't shoot Michael Gorman. D'you happen to know who did?'

'Of course I know,' said Miss Marple. 'The girl.'

'Ah! When did you begin to think that?'

'I always wondered,' said Miss Marple.

'So did I,' said Father. 'She was full of fear that night. And the lies she told were poor lies. But I couldn't see a motive at first.'

'That puzzled me,' said Miss Marple. 'She had found out her mother's marriage was bigamous, but would a girl do murder for that? Not nowadays! I suppose there was a money side to it?'

'Yes, it was money,' said Chief-Inspector Davy. 'Her father left her a colossal fortune. When she found out that her mother was married to Michael Gorman she realized that the marriage to Coniston hadn't been legal. She thought that meant that the money wouldn't come to her because, though she was his daughter, she wasn't legitimate. She was wrong, you know. We had a case something like that before. Depends on the terms of a will. Coniston left it quite clearly to her, naming her by name. She'd get it all right, but she didn't know that. And she wasn't going to let go of the cash.'

'Why did she need it so badly?'

Chief-Inspector Davy said grimly, 'To buy Ladislaus Malinowski. He would have married her for her money. He wouldn't have married her without it. She wasn't a fool, that girl. She knew that. But she wanted him on any terms. She was desperately in love with him.'

'I know,' said Miss Marple. She explained: 'I saw her face that day in Battersea Park . . .'

'She knew that with the money she'd get him, and without the money she'd lose him,' said Father. 'And so she planned a cold-blooded murder. She didn't hide in the area, of course. There was nobody in the area. She just stood by the railings and fired a shot and screamed, and when Michael Gorman came racing down the street from the hotel, she shot him at close quarters. Then she went on screaming. She was a cool hand. She'd no idea of incriminating young Ladislaus. She pinched his pistol because it was the only way she could get hold of one easily; and she never dreamed that he would be suspected of the crime, or that he would be anywhere in the neighbourhood that night. She thought it would be put down to some thug taking advantage of the fog. Yes, she was a cool hand. But she was afraid that night – afterwards! And her mother was afraid for her . . .'

'And now – what will you do?'

'I know she did it,' said Father, 'but I've no evidence. Maybe she'll have beginner's luck . . . Even the law seems to go on the principle now of allowing a dog to have one bite – translated into human terms. An experienced counsel could make great play with the sob stuff – so young a girl, unfortunate upbringing – and she's beautiful, you know.'

'Yes,' said Miss Marple. 'The children of Lucifer are often beautiful – And as we know, they flourish like the green bay tree.'

'But as I tell you, it probably won't even come to that – there's no evidence – take yourself – you'll be called as a witness – a witness to what her mother said – to her mother's confession of the crime.'

'I know,' said Miss Marple. 'She impressed it on me, didn't she? She chose death for herself, at the price of her daughter going free. She forced it on me as a dying request . . .'

The connecting door to the bedroom opened. Elvira Blake came through. She was wearing a straight shift dress of pale blue. Her fair hair fell down each side of her face. She looked like one of the angels in an early primitive Italian painting. She looked from one to the other of them. She said:

'I heard a car and a crash and people shouting . . . Has there been an accident?'

'I'm sorry to tell you, Miss Blake,' said Chief-Inspector Davy formally, 'that your mother is dead.'

Elvira gave a little gasp. 'Oh no,' she said. It was a faint uncertain protest.

'Before she made her escape,' said Chief-Inspector Davy, 'because it *was* an escape – she confessed to the murder of Michael Gorman.'

'You mean – she said – that it was *she* –'

'Yes,' said Father. 'That is what she *said*. Have you anything to add?'

Elvira looked for a long time at him. Very faintly she shook her head.

'No,' she said, 'I haven't anything to add.'

Then she turned and went out of the room.

'Well,' said Miss Marple. 'Are you going to let her get away with it?'

There was a pause, then Father brought down his fist with a crash on the table.

'No,' he roared – 'No, by God I'm not!'

Miss Marple nodded her head slowly and gravely.

'May God have mercy on her soul,' she said.

AVARICE

•

ENDLESS NIGHT

To Nora Prichard
from whom I first heard
the legend of Gipsy's Acre

Every Night and every Morn
Some to Misery are born.
Every Morn and every Night
Some are born to Sweet Delight,
Some are born to Sweet Delight,
Some are born to Endless Night.

William Blake
Auguries of Innocence

BOOK I

CHAPTER I

In my end is my beginning . . . That's a quotation I've often heard people say. It sounds all right – but what does it really mean?

Is there ever any particular spot where one can put one's finger and say: 'It all began that day, at such a time and such a place, with such an incident?'

Did my story begin, perhaps, when I noticed the Sale Bill hanging on the wall of the George and Dragon, announcing Sale by Auction of that valuable property 'The Towers', and giving particulars of the acreage, the miles and furlongs, and the highly idealized portrait of 'The Towers' as it might have been perhaps in its prime, anything from eighty to a hundred years ago?

I was doing nothing particular, just strolling along the main street of Kingston Bishop, a place of no importance whatever, killing time. I noticed the Sale Bill. Why? Fate up to its dirty work? Or dealing out its golden handshake of good fortune? You can look at it either way.

Or you could say, perhaps, that it all had its beginnings when I met Santonix, during the talks I had with him; I can close my eyes and see: his flushed cheeks, the over-brilliant eyes, and the movement of the strong yet delicate hand that sketched and drew plans and elevations of houses. One house in particular, a beautiful house, a house that would be wonderful to own!

My longing for a house, a fine and beautiful house, such a house as I could never hope to have, flowered into life then. It was a happy fantasy shared between us, the house that Santonix would build for me – if he lasted long enough . . .

A house that in my dreams I would live in with the girl that I loved, a house in which just like a child's silly fairy story we should live together 'happy ever afterwards'. All pure fantasy, all nonsense, but it started that tide of longing in me. Longing for something I was never likely to have.

Or if this is a love story – and it *is* a love story, I swear – then why not begin where I first caught sight of Ellie standing in the dark fir trees of Gipsy's Acre?

Gipsy's Acre. Yes, perhaps I'd better begin there, at the moment when I turned away from the Sale board with a little shiver because a black cloud had come over the sun, and asked a question carelessly enough of one of the locals, who was clipping a hedge in a desultory fashion nearby.

'What's this house, The Towers, like?'

I can still see the queer face of the old man, as he looked at me sideways and said:

'That's not what us calls it here. What sort of a name is that?' He snorted disapproval. 'It's many a year now since folks lived in it and called it The Towers.' He snorted again.

I asked him then what *he* called it, and again his eyes shifted away from me in his old wrinkled face in that queer way country folk have of not speaking to you direct, looking over your shoulder or round the corner, as it were, as though they saw something you didn't; and he said:

'It's called hereabouts Gipsy's Acre.'

'Why is it called that?' I asked.

'Some sort of a tale. I dunno rightly. One says one thing, one says another.' And then he went on, 'Anyway, it's where the accidents take place.'

'Car accidents?'

'All kinds of accidents. Car accidents mainly nowadays. It's a nasty corner there, you see.'

'Well,' I said, 'if it's a nasty curve, I can well see there might be accidents.'

'Rural Council put up a Danger sign, but it don't do no good, that don't. There are accidents just the same.'

'Why Gipsy?' I asked him.

Again his eyes slipped past me and his answer was vague.

'Some tale or other. It was gipsies' land once, they say, and they were turned off, and they put a curse on it.'

I laughed.

'Aye,' he said, 'you can laugh but there's places as *is* cursed. You smart-Alecks in town don't know about them. But there's places as is cursed all right, and there's a curse on this place. People got killed here in the quarry when they got the stone out to build. Old Geordie he fell over the edge there one night and broke his neck.'

'Drunk?' I suggested.

'He may have been. He liked his drop, he did. But there's many drunks as fall – nasty falls – but it don't do them no lasting harm. But Geordie, he got his neck broke. In there,' he pointed up behind him to the pine-covered hill, 'in Gipsy's Acre.'

Yes, I suppose that's how it began. Not that I paid much attention to it at the time. I just happened to remember it. That's all. I think – that is, when I think properly – that I built it up a bit in my mind. I don't know if it was before or later that I asked if there were still gipsies about there. He said there weren't many anywhere nowadays. The police were always moving them on, he said. I asked:

'Why doesn't anybody like gipsies?'

'They're a thieving lot,' he said, disapprovingly. Then he peered more closely at me. 'Happen you've got gipsy blood yourself?' he suggested, looking hard at me.

I said not that I knew of. It's true, I do look a bit like a gipsy. Perhaps that's what fascinated me about the name of Gipsy's Acre. I thought to myself as I was standing there, smiling back at him, amused by our conversation, that perhaps I *had* a bit of gipsy blood.

Gipsy's Acre. I went up the winding road that led out of the village and wound up through the dark trees and came at last to the top of the hill so that I could see out to sea and the ships. It was a marvellous view and I thought, just as one does think things: I wonder how it would be if Gipsy's Acre was *my* acre . . . Just like that . . . It was only a ridiculous thought. When I passed my hedge clipper again, he said:

'If you want gipsies, there's old Mrs Lee of course. The Major, he gives her a cottage to live in.'

'Who's the Major?' I asked.

He said, in a shocked voice, 'Major Phillpot, of course.' He seemed quite upset that I should ask! I gathered that Major Phillpot was God locally. Mrs Lee was some kind of dependent of his, I suppose, whom he provided for. The Phillpots seemed to have lived there all their lives and more or less to have run the place.

As I wished my old boy good day and turned away he said:

'She's got the last cottage at the end of the street. You'll see her outside, maybe. Doesn't like the inside of houses. Them as has got gipsy blood don't.'

So there I was, wandering down the road, whistling and thinking about Gipsy's Acre. I'd almost forgotten what I'd been told when I saw a tall black-haired old woman staring at me over a garden hedge. I knew at once it must be Mrs Lee. I stopped and spoke to her.

'I hear you can tell me about Gipsy's Acre up there,' I said.

She stared at me through a tangled fringe of black hair and she said:

'Don't have nought to do with it, young man. You listen to me. Forget about it. You're a good-looking lad. Nothing good comes out of Gipsy's Acre and never will.'

'I see it's up for sale,' I said.

'Aye, that's so, and more fool he who buys it.'

'Who's likely to buy it?'

'There's a builder after it. More than one. It'll go cheap. You'll see.'

'Why should it go cheap?' I asked curiously. 'It's a fine site.'

She wouldn't answer that.

'Supposing a builder buys it cheap, what will he do with it?'

She chuckled to herself. It was malicious, unpleasant laughter.

'Pull down the old ruined house and build, of course. Twenty – thirty houses, maybe – and all with a curse on them.'

I ignored the last part of the sentence. I said, speaking before I could stop myself:

'That would be a shame. A great shame.'

'Ah, you needn't worry. *They'll* get no joy of it, not those who buys and not those who lays the bricks and mortar. There'll be a foot that slips on the ladder, and there'll be the lorry that crashes with a load, and the slate that falls from the roof of a house and finds its mark. And the trees too. Crashing, maybe, in a sudden gale. Ah, you'll see! There's none that'll get any good out of Gipsy's Acre. They'd do best to leave it alone. You'll see. You'll see.' She nodded vigorously and then she repeated softly to herself, '*There's no luck for them as meddles with Gipsy's Acre.* There never has been.'

I laughed. She spoke sharply.

'Don't laugh, young man. It comes to me as may-be one of these days you'll laugh on the wrong side of your mouth. There's never been no luck there, not in the house nor yet in the land.'

'What happened in the house?' I asked. 'Why has it been empty so long? Why was it left to fall down?'

'The last people that lived there died, all of them.'

'How did they die?' I asked out of curiosity.

'Best not to speak of it again. But no one cared to come and live in it afterwards. It was left to moulder and decay. It's forgot by now and best that it should be.'

'But you could tell me the story,' I said, wheedlingly. 'You know all about it.'

'I don't gossip about Gipsy's Acre.' Then she let her voice drop to a kind of phoney beggar's whine. 'I'll tell your fortune now, my pretty lad, if you like. Cross my palm with silver and I'll tell your fortune. You're one of those that'll go far one of these days.'

'I don't believe nonsense about fortune-telling,' I said, 'and I haven't any silver. Not to spare, anyway.'

She came nearer to me and went on in a wheedling voice. 'Sixpence now. Sixpence now. I'll do it for sixpence. What's that? Nothing at all. I'll do it for sixpence because you're a handsome lad with a ready tongue and a way with you. It could be that you'll go far.'

I fished a sixpence out of my pocket, not because I believed in any of her foolish superstitions but because for some reason I liked the old fraud even if I did see through her. She grabbed the coin from me, and said:

'Give me your hand then. Both hands.'

She took my hands in her withered claw and stared down at the open palms. She was silent for a minute or two, staring. Then she dropped my hands abruptly, almost pushing them away from her. She retreated a step and spoke harshly.

'If you know what's good for you, you'll get out of Gipsy's Acre here and now and you won't come back! That's the best advice I can give you. Don't come back.'

'Why not? Why shouldn't I come back?'

'Because if you do you'll come back to sorrow and loss and danger maybe. There's trouble, black trouble waiting for you. Forget you ever saw this place. I'm warning you.'

'Well of all the –'

But she had turned away and was retreating to the cottage. She went in and slammed the door. I'm not superstitious. I believe in luck, of course, who doesn't? But not a lot of superstitious nonsense about ruined houses with curses on them. And yet I had an uneasy feeling that the sinister old creature had seen *something* in my hands. I looked down at my two palms spread out in front of me. What could anyone see in the palms of anyone's hands? Fortune-telling was arrant nonsense – just a trick to get money out of you – money out of your silly credulity. I looked up at the sky. The sun had gone in, the day seemed different now. A sort of shadow, a kind of menace. Just an approaching storm, I thought. The wind was beginning to blow, the backs of the leaves were showing on the trees. I whistled to keep my spirits up and walked along the road through the village.

I looked again at the pasted-up bill advertising the auction of The Towers. I even made a note of the date. I had never attended a property sale in my life but I thought to myself that I'd come and attend this one. It would be interesting to see who bought The Towers. That is to say interesting to see who became the owner of Gipsy's Acre. Yes, I think that's really where it all began . . . A fantastic notion occurred to me. I'd come and pretend to myself that I was the man who was going to bid for Gipsy's Acre! I'd bid against the local builders! They'd drop out, disappointed in their hopes of buying it cheap. *I'd* buy it and I'd go to Rudolf Santonix and say, 'Build me a house. I've bought the site for you.' And I'd find a girl, a wonderful girl, and we'd live in it together happy ever after.

I often had dreams of that kind. Naturally they never came to anything but they were fun. That's what I thought then. Fun! Fun, my God! If I'd only known!

CHAPTER 2

It was pure chance that had brought me to the neighbourhood of Gipsy's Acre that day. I was driving a hired car, taking some people down from London to attend a sale, a sale not of a house but its contents. It was a big house just at the outskirts of the town, a particularly ugly one. I drove an elderly couple there who were interested, from what I could overhear of their conversation, in a collection of *papier mâché*, whatever *papier mâché* was. The only time I ever heard it mentioned before was by my mother in connection with washing-up bowls. She'd said that a *papier mâché* washing-up bowl was far better than a plastic one any day! It seemed an odd thing for rich people to want to come down and buy a collection of the stuff.

However I stored the fact away in my mind and I thought I would look in a dictionary or read up somewhere what *papier mâché* really was. Something that people thought worthwhile to hire a car for, and go down to a country sale and bid for. I liked to know about things. I was twenty-two years of age at that time and I had picked up a fair amount of knowledge one way and another. I knew a good deal about cars, was a fair mechanic and a careful driver. Once I'd worked with horses in Ireland. I nearly got entangled with a dope gang but I got wise and quit in time. A job as a chauffeur to a classy car hire firm isn't bad at all. Good money to be made with tips. And not usually too strenuous. But the work itself was boring.

Once I'd gone fruit picking in summer time. That didn't pay much, but

I enjoyed myself. I'd tried a lot of things. I'd been a waiter in a third-class hotel, life guard on a summer beach, I'd sold encyclopaedias and vacuum cleaners and a few other things. I'd once done horticultural work in a botanical garden and had learnt a little about flowers.

I never stuck to anything. Why should I? I'd found nearly everything I did interesting. Some things were harder work than others but I didn't really mind that. I'm not really lazy. I suppose what I really am is restless. I want to go everywhere, see everything, do everything. I want to *find* something. Yes, that's it. I want to find something.

From the time I left school I wanted to find something, but I didn't yet know what that something was going to be. It was just something I was looking for in a vague, unsatisfied sort of way. It was *somewhere*. Sooner or later I'd know all about it. It might perhaps be a girl . . . I like girls, but no girl I'd met so far had been important . . . You liked them all right but then you went to the next one quite gladly. They were like the jobs I took. All right for a bit and then you got fed up with them and you wanted to move on to the next one. I'd gone from one thing to another ever since I'd left school.

A lot of people disapproved of my way of life. I suppose they were what you might call my well-wishers. That was because they didn't understand the first thing about me. They wanted me to go steady with a nice girl, save money, get married to her and then settle down to a nice steady job. Day after day, year after year, world without end, amen. Not for yours truly! There must be something better than that. Not just all this tame security, the good old welfare state limping along in its half-baked way! Surely, I thought, in a world where man has been able to put satellites in the sky and where men talk big about visiting the stars, there must be *something* that rouses you, that makes your heart beat, that's worthwhile searching all over the world to find! One day, I remember, I was walking down Bond Street. It was during my waiter period and I was due on duty. I'd been strolling looking at some shoes in a shop window. Very natty they were. Like they say in the advertisements in newspapers: '*What smart men are wearing today*' and there's usually a picture of the smart man in question. My word, he usually looks a twerp! Used to make me laugh, advertisements like that did.

I passed on from the shoes to the next window. It was a picture shop. Just three pictures in the window artily arranged with a drape of limp velvet in some neutral colour arranged over a corner of a gilt frame. Cissy, if you know what I mean. I'm not much of a one for Art. I dropped in to the National Gallery once out of curiosity. Fair gave me the pip, it did. Great big shiny coloured pictures of battles in rocky glens, or emaciated saints getting themselves stuck with arrows. Portraits of simpering great ladies sitting smirking in silks and velvets and lace. I decided then and there that Art wasn't for me. But the picture I was looking at now was somehow different. There were three pictures in the window. One a landscape, nice bit of country for what I call everyday. One of a woman drawn in such a funny way, so much out of proportion, that you could hardly see she *was* a woman. I suppose that's what you call *art nouveau*. I don't know what it was about. The third picture was my picture. There wasn't really much to it, if you know what I mean. It was – how can I describe it? It was kind of *simple*. A lot of space in it and a few great widening circles all round each other if you can put it that way. All in different colours, odd colours that you wouldn't expect. And here and there, there were sketchy bits of colour that didn't seem to mean anything. Only somehow they *did* mean something! I'm no good at description. All I can say is that one wanted terribly to go on looking at it.

I just stood there, feeling queer as though something very unusual had happened to me. Those fancy shoes now, I'd have liked them to wear. I mean I take quite a bit of trouble with my clothes. I like to dress well so as to make an impression, but I never seriously thought in my life of buying a pair of shoes in Bond Street. I know the kind of fancy prices they ask there. Fifteen pounds a pair those shoes might be. Hand-made or something, they call it, making it more worthwhile for some reason. Sheer waste of money that would be. A classy line in shoes, yes, but you can pay too much for class. I've got my head screwed on the right way.

But this picture, what would *that* cost? I wondered. Suppose *I* were to buy that picture? You're crazy, I said to myself. You don't go for pictures, not in a general way. That was true enough. But I wanted this picture . . . I'd like it to be *mine*. I'd like to be able to hang it and sit and look at it as long as I liked and know that *I* owned it! Me! Buying pictures. It seemed a crazy idea. I took a look at the picture again. Me wanting that picture didn't make sense, and anyway, I probably couldn't afford it. Actually I was in funds at just that moment. A lucky tip on a horse. This picture would probably cost a packet. Twenty pounds? Twenty-five? Anyway, there would be no harm in asking. They couldn't eat me, could they? I went in, feeling rather aggressive and on the defensive.

The inside of the place was all very hushed and grand. There was a sort of muted atmosphere with neutral-colour walls and a velvet settee on which you could sit and look at the pictures. A man who looked a little like the model for the perfectly dressed man in advertisements came and attended to me, speaking in a rather hushed voice to match the scenery. Funnily, he didn't look superior as they usually do in high-grade Bond Street shops. He listened to what I said and then he took the picture out of the window and displayed it for me against a wall, holding it there for me to look at as long as I wanted. It came to me then – in the way you sometimes know just exactly how things are, that the same rules didn't apply over pictures as they do about other things. Somebody might come into a place like this dressed in shabby old clothes and a frayed shirt and turn out to be a millionaire who wanted to add to his collection. Or he could come in looking cheap and flashy, rather like me perhaps, but somehow or other he'd got such a yen for a picture that he managed to get the money together by some kind of sharp practice.

'A very fine example of the artist's work,' said the man who was holding the picture.

'How much?' I said briskly.

The answer took my breath away.

'Twenty-five thousand,' he said in his gentle voice.

I'm quite good at keeping a poker face. I didn't show anything. At least I don't think I did. He added some name that sounded foreign. The artist's name, I suppose, and that it had just come on the market from a house in the country, where the people who lived there had had no idea what it was. I kept my end up and sighed.

'It's a lot of money but it's worth it, I suppose,' I said.

Twenty-five thousand pounds. What a laugh!

'Yes,' he said and sighed. 'Yes indeed.' He lowered the picture very gently and carried it back to the window. He looked at me and smiled. 'You have good taste,' he said.

I felt that in some way he and I understood each other. I thanked him and went out into Bond Street.

CHAPTER 3

I don't know much about writing things down – not, I mean, in the way a proper writer would do. The bit about that picture I saw, for instance. It doesn't really have anything to do with anything. I mean, nothing came of it, it didn't lead to anything and yet I feel somehow that it is important, that it has a place somewhere. It was one of the things that happened to me that *meant* something. Just like

Gipsy's Acre meant something to me. Like Santonix meant something to me.

I haven't really said much about him. He was an architect. Of course you'll have gathered that. Architects are another thing I'd never had much to do with, though I knew a few things about the building trade. I came across Santonix in the course of my wanderings. It was when I was working as a chauffeur, driving the rich around places. Once or twice I drove abroad, twice to Germany – I knew a bit of German – and once or twice to France – I had a smattering of French too – and once to Portugal. They were usually elderly people, who had money and bad health in about equal quantities.

When you drive people like that around, you begin to think that money isn't so hot after all. What with incipient heart attacks, lots of bottles of little pills you have to take all the time, and losing your temper over the food or the service in hotels. Most of the rich people I've known have been fairly miserable. They've got their worries, too. Taxation and investments. You hear them talking together or to friends. Worry! That's what's killing half of them. And their sex life's not so hot either. They've either got long-legged blonde sexy wives who are playing them up with boyfriends somewhere, or they're married to the complaining kind of woman, hideous as hell, who keeps telling them where they get off. No. I'd rather be myself. Michael Rogers, seeing the world, and getting off with good-looking girls when he feels like it!

Everything a bit hand-to-mouth, of course, but I put up with that. Life was good fun, and I'd been content to go on with life being fun. But I suppose I would have in any case. That attitude goes with youth. When youth begins to pass fun isn't fun any longer.

Behind it, I think, was always the other thing – wanting someone and something . . . However, to go on with what I was saying, there was one old boy I used to drive down to the Riviera. He'd got a house being built there. He went down to look how it was getting on. Santonix was the architect. I don't really know what nationality Santonix was. English I thought at first, though it was a funny sort of name I'd never heard before. But I don't think he was English. Scandinavian of some kind I guess. He was an ill man. I could see that at once. He was young and very fair and thin with an odd face, a face that was askew somehow. The two sides of it didn't match. He could be quite bad-tempered to his clients. You'd have thought as they were paying the money that they'd call the tune and do the bullying. That wasn't so. Santonix bullied *them* and he was always quite sure of himself although they weren't.

This particular old boy of mine was frothing with rage, I remember, as soon as he arrived and had seen how things were going. I used to catch snatches here and there when I was standing by ready to assist in my chauffeurly and handyman way. It was always on the cards that Mr Constantine would have a heart attack or a stroke.

'You have not done as I said,' he half screamed. 'You have spent too much money. Much too much money. It is not as we agreed. It is going to cost me more than I thought.'

'You're absolutely right,' said Santonix. 'But the money's got to be spent.'

'It shall not be spent! It shall not be spent. You have got to keep within the limits I laid down. You understand?'

'Then you won't get the kind of house you want,' said Santonix. 'I *know* what you want. The house I build you will be the house you want. I'm quite sure of that and you're quite sure of it, too. Don't give me any of your pettifogging middle-class economies. You want a house of quality and you're going to *get* it, and you'll boast about it to your friends and they'll envy you. I don't build a house for anyone, I've told you that. There's more to it than money. This house isn't going to be like other people's houses!'

'It is going to be terrible. Terrible.'

'Oh no it isn't. The trouble with you is that *you* don't know what you want. Or at least so anyone might think. But you do know what you want really, only you can't bring it out into your mind. You can't *see* it clearly. But I *know*. That's the one thing I always know. What people are after and what they want. There's a feeling in you for quality. I'm going to *give* you quality.'

He used to say things like that. And I'd stand by and listen. Somehow or other I could see for myself that this house that was being built there amongst pine trees looking over the sea, wasn't going to be the usual house. Half of it didn't look out towards the sea in a conventional way. It looked inland, up to a certain curve of mountains, up to a glimpse of sky between hills. It was odd and unusual and very exciting.

Santonix used to talk to me sometimes when I was off duty. He said:

'I only build houses for people I *want* to build for.'

'Rich people, you mean?'

'They have to be rich or they couldn't pay for the houses. But it's not the money I'm going to make out of it I care about. My clients have to be rich because I want to make the kind of houses that cost money. The house only isn't enough, you see. It has to have the setting. That's just as important. It's like a ruby or an emerald. A beautiful stone is only a beautiful stone. It doesn't lead you anywhere further. It doesn't mean anything, it has no form or significance until it has its setting. And the setting has to have a beautiful jewel to be worthy of it. I take the setting, you see, out of the landscape, where it exists only in its own right. It has no meaning until there is my house sitting proudly like a jewel within its grasp.' He looked at me and laughed. 'You don't understand?'

'I suppose not,' I said slowly, 'and yet – in a way – I think I do . . .'

'That may be.' He looked at me curiously.

We came down to the Riviera again later. By then the house was nearly finished. I won't describe it because I couldn't do it properly, but it was – well – something special – and it was *beautiful*. I could see that. It was a house you'd be proud of, proud to show to people, proud to look at yourself, proud to be in with the right person perhaps. And then suddenly one day Santonix said to me:

'I could build a house for *you*, you know. I'd know the kind of house you'd want.'

I shook my head.

'I shouldn't know myself,' I said, honestly.

'Perhaps you wouldn't. I'd know for you.' Then he added, 'It's a thousand pities you haven't got the money.'

'And never shall have,' I said.

'You can't say that,' said Santonix. 'Born poor doesn't mean you've got to stay poor. Money's queer. It goes where it's wanted.'

'I'm not sharp enough,' I said.

'You're not ambitious enough. Ambition hasn't woken up in you, but it's there, you know.'

'Oh, well,' I said, 'some day when I've woken up ambition and I've made money, then I'll come to you and say "build me a house".'

He sighed then. He said:

'I can't wait . . . No, I can't afford to wait. I've only a short time to go now. One house – two houses more. Not more than that. One doesn't *want* to die young . . . Sometimes one has to . . . It doesn't really matter, I suppose.'

'I'll have to wake up my ambition quick.'

'No,' said Santonix. 'You're healthy, you're having fun, don't change your way of life.'

I said: 'I couldn't if I tried.'

I thought that was true then. I liked my way of life and I was having fun and there was never anything wrong with my health. I've driven a lot of people who've made money, who've worked hard and who've got ulcers and coronary thrombosis and many other things as a result of working hard. I didn't want to work hard. I could do a job as well as another but that was all there was to it. And I hadn't got ambition, or I didn't think I had ambition. Santonix had had ambition, I suppose. I could see that designing houses and building them, the planning of the drawing and something else that I couldn't quite get hold of, all that had taken it out of him. He hadn't been a strong man to begin with. I had a fanciful idea sometimes that he was killing himself before his time by the work he had put out to drive his ambition. I didn't *want* to work. It was as simple as that. I distrusted work, disliked it. I thought it was a very bad thing, that the human race had unfortunately invented for itself.

I thought about Santonix quite often. He intrigued me almost more than anyone I knew. One of the oddest things in life, I think, is the things one remembers. One chooses to remember, I suppose. Something in one must choose. Santonix and his house were one of the things and the picture in Bond Street and visiting that ruined house, The Towers, and hearing the story of Gipsy's Acre, all those were the things that I'd chosen to remember! Sometimes girls that I met, and journeys to the foreign places in the course of driving clients about. The clients were all the same. Dull. They always stayed at the same kind of hotels and ate the same kind of unimaginative food.

I still had that queer feeling in me of waiting for something, waiting for something to be offered to me, or to happen to me, I don't quite know which way describes it best. I suppose really I was looking for a girl, the right sort of girl – by which I don't mean a nice, suitable girl to settle down with, which is what my mother would have meant or my Uncle Joshua or some of my friends. I didn't know at that time anything about love. All I knew about was sex. That was all anybody of my generation seemed to know about. We talked about it too much, I think, and heard too much about it and took it too seriously. We didn't know – any of my friends or myself – what it was really going to be when it happened. Love I mean. We were young and virile and we looked the girls over we met and we appreciated their curves and their legs and the kind of eye they gave you, and you thought to yourself: 'Will they or won't they? Should I be wasting my time?' And the more girls you made the more you boasted and the finer fellow you were thought to be, and the finer fellow you thought yourself.

I'd no real idea that that wasn't all there was to it. I suppose it happens to everyone sooner or later and it happens suddenly. You don't think as you imagine you're going to think: 'This might be the girl for me . . . This is the girl who is going to be mine.' At least, I didn't feel it that way. I didn't know that when it happened it would happen quite suddenly. That I would say: 'That's the girl I belong to. I'm *hers*. I belong to *her*, utterly, for always.' No. I never dreamed it would be like that. Didn't one of the old comedians say once – wasn't it one of his stock jokes? 'I've been in love once and if I felt it coming on again I tell you I'd emigrate.' It was the same with me. If I had known, if I had only known what it could all come to mean *I'd* have emigrated too! If I'd been wise, that is.

CHAPTER 4

I hadn't forgotten my plan of going to the auction.

There was three weeks to go. I'd had two more trips to the Continent, one to France and the other to Germany. It was when I was in Hamburg that things came to a crisis. For one thing I took a violent dislike to the man and his wife I was driving. They represented everything I disliked most. They were rude, inconsiderate, unpleasant to look at, and I suppose they developed in me a feeling of being unable to stand this life of sycophancy any longer. I was careful, mind you. I thought I couldn't stand them another day but I didn't tell them so. No good running yourself in bad with the firm that employs you. So I telephoned up their hotel, said I was ill and I wired London saying the same thing. I said I might be in quarantine and it would be advisable if they sent out a driver to replace me. Nobody could blame me for that. They wouldn't care enough about me to make further inquiries and they'd merely think that I was too feverish to send them any more news. Later, I'd turn up in London again, spinning them a yarn of how ill I'd been! But I didn't think I should do that. I was fed up with the driving racket.

That rebellion of mine was an important turning-point in my life. Because of that and of other things, I turned up at the auction rooms on the appointed date.

'Unless sold before by private treaty' had been pasted across the original board. But it was still there, so it hadn't been sold by private treaty. I was so excited I hardly knew what I was doing.

As I say, I had never been to a public auction of property before. I was imbued with the idea that it would be exciting but it wasn't exciting. Not in the least. It was one of the most moribund performances I have ever attended. It took place in a semi-gloomy atmosphere and there were only about six or seven people there. The auctioneer was quite different from those auctioneers that I had seen presiding at furniture sales or things of that kind; men with facetious voices and very hearty and full of jokes. This one, in a dead and alive voice, praised the property and described the acreage and a few things like that and then he went half-heartedly into the bidding. Somebody made a bid of £5,000. The auctioneer gave a tired smile rather as one who hears a joke that isn't really funny. He made a few remarks and there were a few more bids. They were mostly country types standing around. Someone who looked like a farmer, someone who I guessed to be one of the competitive builders, a couple of lawyers, I think, one a man who looked as though he was a stranger from London, well dressed and professional-looking. I don't know if he made an actual bid, he may have done. If so it was very quietly and done more by gesture. Anyway the bidding petered to an end, the auctioneer announced in a melancholy voice that the reserve price had not been reached and the thing broke up.

'That was a dull business,' I said to one of the country-looking fellows whom I was next to as I went out.

'Much the same as usual,' he said. 'Been to many of these?'

'No,' I said, 'actually it's the first.'

'Come out of curiosity, did you? I didn't notice you doing any bidding.'

'No fear,' I said. 'I just wanted to see how it would go.'

'Well, it's the way it runs very often. They just want to see who's interested, you know.'

I looked at him inquiringly.

'Only three of 'em in it, I should say,' said my friend. 'Whetherby from Helminster. He's the builder, you know. Then Dakham and Coombe, bidding on behalf of some Liverpool firm, I understand, and a dark horse from London, too, I should say a lawyer. Of course there may be more in it than that, but those seemed the main ones to me. It'll go cheap. That's what everyone says.'

'Because of the place's reputation?' I asked.

'Oh, you've heard about Gipsy's Acre, have you? That's only what the country people say. Rural Council ought to have altered that road years ago – it's a death trap.'

'But the place *has* got a bad reputation?'

'I tell you that's just superstition. Anyway, as I say, the real business'll happen now behind the scenes, you know. They'll go and make offers.

I'd say the Liverpool people might get it. I don't think Whetherby'll go high enough. He likes buying cheap. Plenty of properties coming into the market nowadays for development. After all, it's not many people who could afford to buy the place, pull that ruined house down and put up another house there, could they?'

'Doesn't seem to happen very often nowadays,' I said.

'Too difficult. What with taxation and one thing and another, and you can't get domestic help in the country. No, people would rather pay thousands for a luxury flat in a town nowadays up on the sixteenth floor of a modern building. Big unwieldy country houses are a drag on the market.'

'But you could build a modern house,' I argued. 'Labour-saving.'

'You *could*, but it's an expensive business and people aren't so fond of living lonely.'

'Some people might be,' I said.

He laughed and we parted. I walked along, frowning, puzzling to myself. My feet took me without my really noticing where I was going along the road between the trees and up, up to the curving road that led between the trees to the moorlands.

And so I came to the spot in the road where I first saw Ellie. As I said, she was standing just by a tall fir tree and she had the look, if I can explain it, of someone who hadn't been there a moment before but had just materialized, as it were, out of the tree. She was wearing a sort of dark green tweed and her hair was the soft brown colour of an autumn leaf and there was something a bit unsubstantial about her. I saw her and I stopped. She was looking at me, her lips just parted, looking slightly startled. I suppose I looked startled too. I wanted to say something and I didn't quite know what to say. Then I said:

'Sorry. I – I didn't mean to startle you. I didn't know there was anyone here.'

She said, and her voice was very soft and gentle, it might have been a little girl's voice but not quite. She said:

'It's quite all right. I mean, I didn't think anyone would be here either.' She looked round her and said, 'It – it's a lonely spot.' And she shivered just a little.

There was rather a chilly wind that afternoon. But perhaps it wasn't the wind. I don't know. I came a step or two nearer.

'It is a sort of scary place rather, isn't it?' I said. 'I mean, the house being a ruin the way it is.'

'The Towers,' she said thoughtfully. 'That was the name of it, wasn't it – only I mean, there don't seem to have been any towers.'

'I expect that was just a name,' I said. 'People call their houses names like The Towers to make them sound grander than they are.'

She laughed just a little. 'I suppose that was it,' she said. 'This – perhaps you know, I'm not sure – this is the place that they're selling today or putting up for auction?'

'Yes,' I said. 'I've come from the auction now.'

'Oh.' She sounded startled. 'Were you – are you – interested?'

'I'm not likely to buy a ruined house with a few hundred acres of woodland land,' I said. 'I'm not in that class.'

'Was it sold?' she asked.

'No, it didn't come up to reserve.'

'Oh. I see.' She sounded relieved.

'You didn't want to buy it either, did you?' I said.

'Oh no,' she said, 'of course not.' She sounded nervous about it.

I hesitated and then I blurted out the words that came to my lips.

'I'm pretending,' I said. 'I can't buy it, of course, because I haven't got any money, but I'm interested. I'd *like* to buy it. I *want* to buy it. Open your mouth and laugh at me if you like but that's the way it is.'

'But isn't it rather too decrepit, too –'

'Oh yes,' I said. 'I don't mean I want it like it is *now*. I want to pull this down, cart it all away. It's an ugly house and I think it must have been a sad house. But this *place* isn't sad or ugly. It's beautiful. Look here. Come a little this way, through the trees. Look out at the view that way where it goes to the hills and the moors. D'you see? Clear away a vista *here* – and then you come this way –'

I took her by the arm and led her to a second point of the compass. If we were behaving unconventionally she did not notice it. Anyway, it wasn't that kind of way I was holding her. I wanted to show her what I saw.

'Here,' I said, 'here you see where it sweeps down to the sea and where the rocks show out *there*. There's a town between us and that but we can't see it because of the hills bulging out farther down the slope. And then you can look a third way, to a vague foresty valley. Do you see now if you cut down trees and make big vistas and clear this space round the house, do you see what a beautiful house you could have *here*? You wouldn't site it where the old one is. You'd go about fifty – a hundred yards to the right, here. This is where you could have a house, a wonderful house. A house built by an architect who's a genius.'

'Do you know any architects who are geniuses?' She sounded doubtful.

'I know one,' I said.

Then I started telling her about Santonix. We sat down side by side on a fallen tree and I talked. Yes, I talked to that slender woodland girl whom I'd never seen before and I put all I had into what I was telling her. I told her the dream that one could build up.

'It won't happen,' I said, 'I know that. It couldn't happen. But think. Think into it just like I'm thinking into it. There we'd cut the trees and there we'd open up, and we'd plant things, rhododendrons and azaleas, and my friend Santonix would come. He'd cough a good deal because I think he's dying of consumption or something but he could do it. He could do it before he died. He could build the most wonderful house. You don't know what his houses are like. He builds them for very rich people and they have to be people who want the right thing. I don't mean the right thing in the conventional sense. Things people who want a dream come true want. Something wonderful.'

'I'd want a house like that,' said Ellie. 'You make me see it, feel it . . . Yes, this would be a lovely place to live. Everything one has dreamed of come true. One could live here and be free, not hampered, not tied round by people pushing you into doing everything you don't want, keeping you from doing anything you do want. Oh I am so sick of my life and the people who are round me and *everything*!'

That's the way it began, Ellie and I together. Me with my dreams and she with her revolt against her life. We stopped talking and looked at each other.

'What's your name?' she said.

'Mike Rogers,' I said. 'Michael Rogers,' I amended. 'What's yours?'

'Fenella.' She hesitated and then said, 'Fenella Goodman,' looking at me with a rather troubled expression.

This didn't seem to take us much further but we went on looking at each other. We both wanted to see each other again – but just for the moment we didn't know how to set about it.

CHAPTER 5

Well, that's how it began between Ellie and myself. It didn't really go along so very quickly, because we both had our secrets. Both had things we wanted to keep from the other and so we couldn't tell each other as much about ourselves as we might have done, and that kept bringing us up sharp, as it were, against a kind of barrier. We couldn't bring things into the open and say, 'When shall we meet again? Where can I find you?

Where do you live?' Because, you see, if you ask the other person that, they'd expect you to tell the same.

Fenella looked apprehensive when she gave me her name. So much so that I thought for a moment that it mightn't be her real name. I almost thought that she might have made it up! But of course I knew that that was impossible. I'd given her my real name.

We didn't know quite how to take leave of each other that day. It was awkward. It had become cold and we wanted to wander down from The Towers – but what then? Rather awkwardly, I said tentatively:

'Are you staying round here?'

She said she was staying in Market Chadwell. That was a market town not very far away. It had, I knew, a large hotel, three-starred. She'd be staying there, I guessed. She said, with something of the same awkwardness, to me:

'Do you live here?'

'No,' I said, 'I don't live here. I'm only here for the day.'

Then a rather awkward silence fell. She gave a faint shiver. A cold little wind had come up.

'We'd better walk,' I said, 'and keep ourselves warm. Are you – have you got a car or are you going by bus or train?'

She said she'd left the car in the village.

'But I'll be quite all right,' she said.

She seemed a little nervous. I thought perhaps she wanted to get rid of me but didn't quite know how to manage it. I said:

'We'll walk down, shall we, just as far as the village?'

She gave me a quick grateful look then. We walked slowly down the winding road on which so many car accidents had happened. As we came round a corner, a figure stepped suddenly from beneath the shelter of the fir tree. It appeared so suddenly that Ellie gave a start and said, 'Oh!' It was the old woman I had seen the other day in her cottage garden. Mrs Lee. She looked a great deal wilder today with a tangle of black hair blowing in the wind and a scarlet cloak round her shoulders; the commanding stance she took up made her look taller.

'And what would you be doing, my dears?' she said. 'What brings you to Gipsy's Acre?'

'Oh,' Ellie said, 'we aren't trespassing, are we?'

'That's as may be. Gipsies' land this used to be. Gipsies' land and they drove us off it. You'll do no good here, and no good will come to you prowling about Gipsy's Acre.'

There was no fight in Ellie, she wasn't that kind. She said gently and politely:

'I'm very sorry if we shouldn't have come here. I thought this place was being sold today.'

'And bad luck it will be to anyone who buys it!' said the old woman. 'You listen, my pretty, for you're pretty enough, bad luck will come to whoever buys it. There's a curse on this land, a curse put on it long ago, many years ago. You keep clear of it. Don't have nought to do with Gipsy's Acre. Death it will bring you and danger. Go away home across the sea and don't come back to Gipsy's Acre. Don't say I didn't warn you.'

'We're doing no harm.'

'Come now, Mrs Lee,' I said, 'don't frighten this young lady.'

I turned in an explanatory way to Ellie.

'Mrs Lee lives in the village. She's got a cottage there. She tells fortunes and prophesies the future. All that, don't you, Mrs Lee?' I spoke to her in a jocular way.

'I've got the gift,' she said simply, drawing her gipsy-like figure up straighter still. 'I've got the gift. It's born in me. We all have it. I'll tell your fortune, young lady. Cross my palm with silver and I'll tell your fortune for you.'

'I don't think I want my fortune told.'

'It'd be a wise thing to do. Know something about the future. Know what to avoid, know what's coming to you if you don't take care. Come now, there's plenty of money in your pocket. Plenty of money. I know things it would be wise for you to know.'

I believe the urge to have one's fortune told is almost invariable in women. I've noticed it before with girls I knew. I nearly always had to pay for them to go into the fortune-tellers' booths if I took them to a fair. Ellie opened her bag and laid two half-crowns in the old woman's hand.

'Ah, my pretty, that's right now. You hear what old Mother Lee will tell you.'

Ellie drew off her glove and laid her small delicate palm in the old woman's hand. She looked down at it, muttering to herself. 'What do I see now? What do I see?'

Suddenly she dropped Ellie's hand abruptly.

'I'd go away from here if I were you. Go – and don't come back! That's what I told you just now and it's true. I've seen it again in your palm. Forget Gipsy's Acre, forget you ever saw it. And it's not just the ruined house up there, it's the land itself that's cursed.'

'You've got a mania about that,' I said roughly. 'Anyway the young lady has nothing to do with the land here. She's only here for a walk today, she's nothing to do with the neighbourhood.'

The old woman paid no attention to me. She said dourly:

'I'm telling you, my pretty. I'm warning you. You can have a happy life – but you must avoid danger. Don't come to a place where there's danger or where there's a curse. Go away where you're loved and taken care of and looked after. You've got to keep yourself safe. Remember that. Otherwise – otherwise –' she gave a short shiver. 'I don't like to see it, I don't like to see what's in your hand.'

Suddenly with a queer brisk gesture she pushed back the two half-crowns into Ellie's palm, mumbling something we could hardly hear. It sounded like 'It's cruel. It's cruel, what's going to happen.' Turning, she stalked away at a rapid pace.

'What a – what a frightening woman,' said Ellie.

'Pay no attention to her,' I said gruffly. 'I think she's half off her head anyway. She just wants to frighten you off. They've got a sort of feeling, I think, about this particular piece of land.'

'Have there been accidents here? Have bad things happened?'

'Bound to be accidents. Look at the curve and the narrowness of the road. The Town Council ought to be shot for not doing something about it. Of course there'll be accidents here. There aren't enough signs warning you.'

'Only accidents – or other things?'

'Look here,' I said, 'people like to collect disasters. There are plenty of disasters always to collect. That's the way stories build themselves up about a place.'

'Is that one of the reasons why they say this property which is being sold will go cheap?'

'Well, it may be, I suppose. Locally, that is. But I don't suppose it'll be sold locally. I expect it'll be bought for developing. You're shivering,' I said. 'Don't shiver. Come on, we'll walk fast.' I added, 'Would you rather I left you before you got back into the town?'

'No. Of course not. Why should I?'

I made a desperate plunge.

'Look here,' I said, 'I shall be in Market Chadwell tomorrow. I – I suppose – I don't know whether you'll still be there . . . I mean, would there be any chance of – seeing you?' I shuffled my feet and turned my head away. I got rather red, I think. But if I didn't say something *now*, how was I going to go on with this?

'Oh yes,' she said, 'I shan't be going back to London until the evening.'

'Then perhaps – would you – I mean, I suppose it's rather cheek –'

'No, it isn't.'

'Well, perhaps you'd come and have tea at a café – the Blue Dog I think it's called. It's quite nice,' I said. 'It's – I mean, it's –' I couldn't get hold of the word I wanted and I used the word that I'd heard my mother use once or twice – 'it's quite ladylike,' I said anxiously.

Then Ellie laughed. I suppose it sounded rather peculiar nowadays.

'I'm sure it'll be very nice,' she said. 'Yes. I'll come. About half past four, will that be right?'

'I'll be waiting for you,' I said. 'I – I'm glad.' I didn't say what I was glad about.

We had come to the last turn of the road where the houses began.

'Goodbye, then,' I said, 'till tomorrow. And – don't think again about what that old hag said. She just likes scaring people, I think. She's not all there,' I added.

'Do you feel it's a frightening place?' Ellie asked.

'Gipsy's Acre? No, I don't,' I said. I said it perhaps a trifle too decidedly, but I didn't think it was frightening. I thought as I'd thought before, that it was a beautiful place, a beautiful setting for a beautiful house . . .

Well, that's how my first meeting with Ellie went. I was in Market Chadwell the next day waiting in the Blue Dog and she came. We had tea together and we talked. We still didn't say much about ourselves, not about our lives, I mean. We talked mostly about things we thought, and felt; and then Ellie glanced at her wrist-watch and said she must be going because her train to London left at 5.30 –

'I thought you had a car down here,' I said.

She looked slightly embarrassed then and she said no, no, that hadn't been her car yesterday. She didn't say whose it had been. That shadow of embarrassment came over us again. I raised a finger to the waitress and paid the bill, then I said straight out to Ellie:

'Am I – am I ever going to see you again?'

She didn't look at me, she looked down at the table. She said:

'I shall be in London for another fortnight.'

I said:

'Where? How?'

We made a date to meet in Regent's Park in three days' time. It was a fine day. We had some food in the open-air restaurant and we walked in Queen Mary's Gardens and we sat there in two deck-chairs and we talked. From that time on, we began to talk about ourselves. I'd had some good schooling, I told her, but otherwise I didn't amount to much. I told her about the jobs I'd had, some of them at any rate, and how I'd never stuck to things and how I'd been restless and wandered about trying this and that. Funnily enough, she was entranced to hear all this.

'So different,' she said, 'so wonderfully different.'

'Different from what?'

'From me.'

'You're a rich girl?' I said teasingly – 'A poor little rich girl.'

'Yes,' she said, 'I'm a poor little rich girl.'

She talked then in a fragmentary way about her background of riches, of stifling comfort, of boredom, of not really choosing your own friends, of never doing what you wanted. Sometimes looking at people who seemed to be enjoying themselves, when she wasn't. Her mother had died when she was a baby and her father had married again. And then, not many years after, he had died, she said. I gathered she didn't care much for her stepmother. She'd lived mostly in America but also travelling abroad a fair amount.

It seemed fantastic to me listening to her that any girl in this age and time could live this sheltered, confined existence. True, she went to parties and entertainments, but it might have been fifty years ago it seemed to me from the way she talked. There didn't seem to be any intimacy, any *fun*! Her life was as different from mine as chalk from cheese. In a way it was fascinating to hear about it but it sounded stultifying to me.

'You haven't really got any friends of your own then?' I said, incredulously. 'What about boyfriends?'

'They're chosen for me,' she said rather bitterly. 'They're deadly dull.'

'It's like being in prison,' I said.

'That's what it seems like.'

'And really no friends of your own?'

'I have now. I've got Greta.'

'Who's Greta?' I said.

'She came first as an *au pair* – no, not quite that, perhaps. But anyway I'd had a French girl who lived with us for a year, for French, and then Greta came from Germany, for German. Greta was different. Everything was different once Greta came.'

'You're very fond of her?' I asked.

'She helps me,' said Ellie. 'She's on my side. She arranges so that I can do things and go places. She'll tell lies for me. I couldn't have got away to come down to Gipsy's Acre if it hadn't been for Greta. She's keeping me company and looking after me in London while my stepmother's in Paris.

I write two or three letters and if I go off anywhere Greta posts them every three or four days so that they have a London postmark.'

'Why did you want to go down to Gipsy's Acre though?' I asked. 'What for?'

She didn't answer at once.

'Greta and I arranged it,' she said. 'She's rather wonderful,' she went on. 'She thinks of things, you know. She suggests ideas.'

'What's this Greta like?' I asked.

'Oh, Greta's beautiful,' she said. 'Tall and blonde. She can do anything.'

'I don't think I'd like her,' I said.

Ellie laughed.

'Oh yes you would. I'm sure you would. She's very clever, too.'

'I don't like clever girls,' I said. 'And I don't like tall blonde girls. I like small girls with hair like autumn leaves.'

'I believe you're jealous of Greta,' said Ellie.

'Perhaps I am. You're very fond of her, aren't you?'

'Yes, I am *very* fond of her. She's made all the difference in my life.'

'And it was she who suggested you went down there. Why, I wonder? There's not much to see or do in that part of the world. I find it rather mysterious.'

'It's our secret,' said Ellie and looked embarrassed.

'Yours and Greta's? Tell me.'

She shook her head. 'I must have *some* secrets of my own,' she said.

'Does your Greta know you're meeting me?'

'She knows I'm meeting someone. That's all. She doesn't ask questions. She knows I'm happy.'

After that there was a week when I didn't see Ellie. Her stepmother had come back from Paris, also someone whom she called Uncle Frank, and she explained almost casually that she was having a birthday, and that they were giving a big party for her in London.

'I shan't be able to get away,' she said. 'Not for the next week. But after that – after that, it'll be different.'

'Why will it be different after that?'

'I shall be able to do what I like then.'

'With Greta's help as usual?' I said.

It used to make Ellie laugh the way I talked about Greta. She'd say, 'You're so silly to be jealous of her. One day you must meet her. You'll like her.'

'I don't like bossy girls,' I said obstinately.

'Why do you think she's bossy?'

'By the way you talk about her. She's always busy arranging something.'

'She's very efficient,' said Ellie. 'She arranges things very well. That's why my stepmother relies on her so much.'

I asked what her Uncle Frank was like.

She said, 'I don't know him really so very well. He was my father's sister's husband, not a real relation. I think he's always been rather a rolling stone and got into trouble once or twice. You know the way people talk about someone and sort of hint things.'

'Not socially acceptable?' I asked. 'Bad lot?'

'Oh, nothing really bad I think, but he used to get into scrapes, I believe. Financial ones. And trustees and lawyers and people used to have to get him out of them. Pay up for things.'

'That's it,' I said. 'He's the bad hat of the family. I expect I'd get on better with him than I would with the paragon Greta.'

'He can make himself very agreeable when he likes,' said Ellie. 'He's good company.'

'But you don't really like him?' I asked sharply.

'I think I do . . . It's just that sometimes, oh I can't explain it. I just feel I don't know what he's thinking or planning.'

'One of our planners, is he?'

'I don't know what he's really like,' said Ellie again.

She didn't ever suggest that I should meet any of her family. I wondered sometimes if I ought to say something about it myself. I didn't know how she felt about the subject. I asked her straight out at last.

'Look here, Ellie,' I said, 'do you think I ought to – meet your family or would you rather I didn't?'

'I don't want you to meet them,' she said at once.

'I know I'm not much –' I said.

'I don't mean it *that* way, not a bit! I mean they'd make a *fuss*. I can't stand a fuss.'

'I sometimes feel,' I said, 'that this is rather a hole and corner business. It puts me in a rather bad light, don't you think?'

'I'm old enough to have my own friends,' said Ellie. 'I'm nearly twenty-one. When I am twenty-one I can have my own friends and nobody can stop me. But now you see – well, as I say there'd be a terrible fuss and they'd cart me off somewhere so that I couldn't meet you. There'd be – oh do, *do* let's go on as we are now.'

'Suits me if it suits you,' I said. 'I just didn't want to be, well, too underhand about everything.'

'It's not being underhand. It's just having a friend one can talk to and say things to. It's someone one can –' she smiled suddenly, 'one can make-believe with. You don't know how wonderful that is.'

Yes, there was a lot of that – make-believe! More and more our times together were to turn out that way. Sometimes it was me. More often it was Ellie who'd say, 'Let's suppose that we've bought Gipsy's Acre and that we're building a house there.'

I had told her a lot about Santonix and about the houses he'd built. I tried to describe to her the kind of houses they were and the way he thought about things. I don't think I described it very well because I'm not good at describing things. Ellie no doubt had her own picture of the house – our house. We didn't *say* 'our house' but we knew that's what we meant . . .

So for over a week I wasn't to see Ellie. I had taken out what savings I had (there weren't many), and I'd bought her a little green shamrock ring made of some Irish bog stone. I'd given it to her for a birthday present and she'd loved it and looked very happy.

'It's beautiful,' she said.

She didn't wear much jewellery and when she did I had no doubt it was real diamonds and emeralds and things like that but she liked my Irish ring.

'It will be the birthday present I like best,' she said.

Then I got a hurried note from her. She was going abroad with her family to the South of France immediately after her birthday.

'But don't worry,' she wrote, 'we shall be back again in two or three weeks' time, on our way to America this time. But anyway we'll meet again then. I've got something special I want to talk to you about.'

I felt restless and ill at ease not seeing Ellie and knowing she'd gone abroad to France. I had a bit of news about the Gipsy's Acre property too. Apparently it *had* been sold by private treaty but there wasn't much information about who'd bought it. Some firm of London solicitors apparently were named as the purchasers. I tried to get more information about it, but I couldn't. The firm in question were very cagey. Naturally I didn't approach the principals. I palled up to one of their clerks and so got a little vague information. It had been bought for a very rich client who was going to hold it as a good investment capable of appreciation when the land in that part of the country was becoming more developed.

It's very hard to find out about things when you're dealing with really exclusive firms. Everything is as much of a deadly secret as though they were M.I.5 or something! Everyone is always acting on behalf of someone else who can't be named or spoken of! Takeover bids aren't in it!

I got into a terrible state of restlessness. I stopped thinking about it all and I went and saw my mother.

I hadn't been to see her for a good long time.

CHAPTER 6

My mother lived in the same street she had lived in for the last twenty years, a street of drab houses all highly respectable and devoid of any kind of beauty or interest. The front doorstep was nicely whitened and it looked just the same as usual. It was No. 46. I pressed the front-door bell. My mother opened the door and stood there looking at me. She looked just the same as usual, too. Tall and angular, grey hair parted in the middle, mouth like a rattrap, and eyes that were eternally suspicious. She looked hard as nails. But where I was concerned there was a core of softness somewhere in her. She never showed it, not if she could help it, but I'd found out that it was there. She'd never stopped for a moment wanting me to be different but her wishes were never going to come true. There was a perpetual state of stalemate between us.

'Oh,' she said, 'so it's you.'

'Yes,' I said, 'it's me.'

She drew back a little to let me pass and I came into the house and went on past the sitting-room door and into the kitchen. She followed me and stood looking at me.

'It's been quite a long time,' she said. 'What have you been doing?'

I shrugged my shoulders.

'This and that,' I said.

'Ah,' said my mother, 'as usual, eh?'

'As usual,' I agreed.

'How many jobs have you had since I saw you last?'

I thought a minute. 'Five,' I said.

'I wish you'd grow up.'

'I'm fully adult,' I said. 'I have chosen my way of life. How have things been with you?' I added.

'Also as usual,' said my mother.

'Quite well and all that?'

'I've no time to waste being ill,' said my mother. Then she said abruptly, 'What have you come for?'

'Should I have come for anything in particular?'

'You usually do.'

'I don't see why you should disapprove so strongly of my seeing the world,' I said.

'Driving luxurious cars all over the Continent! Is that your idea of seeing the world?'

'Certainly.'

'You won't make much of a success in that. Not if you throw up the job at a day's notice and go sick, dumping your clients in some heathen town.'

'How did you know about that?'

'Your firm rang up. They wanted to know if I knew your address.'

'What did they want me for?'

'They wanted to re-employ you I suppose,' said my mother. 'I can't think why.'

'Because I'm a good driver and the clients like me. Anyway, I couldn't help it if I went sick, could I?'

'I don't know,' said my mother.

Her view clearly was that I could have helped it.

'Why didn't you report to them when you got back to England?'

'Because I had other fish to fry,' I said.

She raised her eyebrows. 'More notions in your head? More wild ideas? What jobs have you been doing since?'

'Petrol pump. Mechanic in a garage. Temporary clerk, washer-up in a sleazy night-club restaurant.'

'Going down the hill in fact,' said my mother with a kind of grim satisfaction.

'Not at all,' I said. 'It's all part of the plan. My plan!'

She sighed. 'What would you like, tea or coffee? I've got both.'

I plumped for coffee. I've grown out of the tea-drinking habit. We sat there with our cups in front of us and she took a home-made cake out of a tin and cut us each a slice.

'You're different,' she said, suddenly.

'Me, how?'

'I don't know, but you're different. What's happened?'

'Nothing's happened. What should have happened?'

'You're excited,' she said.

'I'm going to rob a bank,' I said.

She was not in the mood to be amused. She merely said:

'No, I'm not afraid of your doing that.'

'Why not? Seems a very easy way of getting rich quickly nowadays.'

'It would need too much work,' she said. 'And a lot of planning. More brainwork than you'd like to have to do. Not safe enough, either.'

'You think you know all about me,' I said.

'No, I don't. I don't really know anything about you, because you and I are as different as chalk and cheese. But I know when you're up to something. You're up to something now. What is it, Micky? Is it a girl?'

'Why should you think it's a girl?'

'I've always known it would happen some day.'

'What do you mean by "some day"? I've had lots of girls.'

'Not the way I mean. It's only been the way of a young man with nothing to do. You've kept your hand in with girls but you've never been really serious till now.'

'But you think I'm serious now?'

'Is it a girl, Micky?'

I didn't meet her eyes. I looked away and said, 'In a way.'

'What kind of a girl is she?'

'The right kind for me,' I said.

'Are you going to bring her to see me?'

'No,' I said.

'It's like that, is it?'

'No, it isn't. I don't want to hurt your feelings but –'

'You're not hurting my feelings. You don't want me to see her in case I should say to you "Don't". Is that it?'

'I wouldn't pay any attention if you did.'

'Maybe not, but it would shake you. It would shake you somewhere inside because you take notice of what I say and think. There are things I've guessed about you – and maybe I've guessed right and you know it. I'm the only person in the world who can shake your confidence in yourself. Is this girl a bad lot who's got hold of you?'

'Bad lot?' I said and laughed. 'If you only saw her! You make me laugh.'

'What do you want from me? You want something. You always do.'

'I want some money,' I said.

'You won't get it from me. What do you want it for – to spend on this girl?'

'No,' I said, 'I want to buy a first-class suit to get married in.'

'You're going to marry her?'

'If she'll have me.'

That shook her.

'If you'd only tell me something!' she said. 'You've got it badly, I can see that. It's the thing I always feared, that you'd choose the wrong girl.'

'Wrong girl! Hell!' I shouted. I was angry.

I went out of the house and I banged the door.

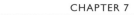

CHAPTER 7

When I got home there was a telegram waiting for me – it had been sent from Antibes.

Meet me tomorrow four-thirty usual place.

Ellie was different. I saw it at once. We met as always in Regent's Park and at first we were a bit strange and awkward with each other. I had something I was going to say to her and I was in a bit of a state as to how to put it. I suppose any man is when he comes to the point of proposing marriage.

And she was strange about something too. Perhaps she was considering the nicest and kindest way of saying No to me. But somehow I didn't think that. My whole belief in life was based on the fact that Ellie loved me. But there was a new independence about her, a new confidence in herself which I could hardly feel was simply because she was a year older. One more birthday can't make that difference to a girl. She and her family had been in the South of France and she told me a little about it. And then rather awkwardly she said:

'I – I saw that house there, the one you told me about. The one that architect friend of yours had built.'

'What – Santonix?'

'Yes. We went there to lunch one day.'

'How did you do that? Does your stepmother know the man who lives there?'

'Dmitri Constantine? Well – not exactly but she met him and – well – Greta fixed it up for us to go there as a matter of fact.'

'Greta again,' I said, allowing the usual exasperation to come into my voice.

'I told you,' she said, 'Greta is very good at arranging things.'

'Oh all right. So she arranged that you and your stepmother –'

'And Uncle Frank,' said Ellie.

'Quite a family party,' I said, 'and Greta too, I suppose.'

'Well, no, Greta didn't come because, well –' Ellie hesitated, '– Cora, my stepmother, doesn't treat Greta exactly like that.'

'She's not one of the family, she's a poor relation, is she?' I said. 'Just the *au pair* girl, in fact. Greta must resent being treated that way sometimes.'

'She's not an *au pair* girl, she's a kind of companion to me.'

'A chaperone,' I said, 'a cicerone, a duenna, a governess. There are lots of words.'

'Oh do be quiet,' said Ellie, 'I want to tell you. I know now what you mean about your friend Santonix. It's a wonderful house. It's – it's quite *different*. I can see that if he built a house for us it would be a wonderful house.'

She had used the word quite unconsciously. *Us*, she had said. She had gone to the Riviera and had made Greta arrange things so as to see the house I had described, because she wanted to visualize more clearly the house that we would, in the dream world we'd built ourselves, have built for us by Rudolf Santonix.

'I'm glad you felt like that about it,' I said.

She said: 'What have you been doing?'

'Just my dull job,' I said, 'and I've been to a race meeting and I put some money on an outsider. Thirty to one. I put every penny I had on it and it won by a length. Who says my luck isn't in?'

'I'm glad you won,' said Ellie, but she said it without excitement, because putting all you had in the world on an outsider and the outsider winning didn't mean anything to Ellie's world. Not the kind of thing it meant in mine.

'And I went to see my mother,' I added.

'You've never spoken much of your mother.'

'Why should I?' I said.

'Aren't you fond of her?'

I considered. 'I don't know,' I said. 'Sometimes I don't think I am. After all, one grows up and – outgrows parents. Mothers and fathers.'

'I think you do care about her,' said Ellie. 'You wouldn't be so uncertain when you talk about her otherwise.'

'I'm afraid of her in a way,' I said. 'She knows me too well. She knows the worst of me, I mean.'

'Somebody has to,' said Ellie.

'What do you mean?'

'There's a saying by some great writer or other that no man is a hero to his valet. Perhaps everyone ought to have a valet. It must be so hard otherwise, always living up to people's good opinion of one.'

'Well, you certainly have ideas, Ellie,' I said. I took her hand. 'Do you know all about me?' I said.

'I think so,' said Ellie. She said it quite calmly and simply.

'I never told you much.'

'You mean you never told me anything at all, you always clammed up. That's different. But I know quite well what you are *like*, you yourself.'

'I wonder if you do,' I said. I went on, 'It sounds rather silly saying I love you. It seems too late for that, doesn't it? I mean, you've known about it a long time, practically from the beginning, haven't you?'

'Yes,' said Ellie, 'and you knew, too, didn't you, about me?'

'The thing is,' I said, 'what are we going to do about it? It's not going to be easy, Ellie. You know pretty well what I am, what I've done, the sort of life I've led. I went back to see my mother and the grim, respectable little street she lives in. It's not the same world as yours, Ellie. I don't know that we can ever make them meet.'

'You could take me to see your mother.'

'Yes, I could,' I said, 'but I'd rather not. I expect that sounds very harsh to you, perhaps cruel, but you see we've got to lead a queer life together, you and I. It's not going to be the life that you've led and it's not going to be the life that I've led either. It's got to be a new life where we have a sort of meeting ground between my poverty and ignorance and your money and culture and social knowledge. My friends will think you're stuck up and your friends will think I'm socially unpresentable. So what are we going to do?'

'I'll tell you,' said Ellie, 'exactly what we're going to do. We're going to live on Gipsy's Acre in a house – a dream house – that your friend Santonix will build for us. That's what we're going to do.' She added, 'We'll get married first. That's what you mean, isn't it?'

'Yes,' I said, 'that's what I mean. If you're sure it's all right with you.'

'It's quite easy,' said Ellie, 'we can get married next week. I'm of age, you see. I can do what I like now. That makes all the difference. I think perhaps you're right about relations. I shan't tell my people and you won't tell your mother, not until it's all over and then they can throw fits and it won't matter.'

'That's wonderful,' I said, 'wonderful, Ellie. But there's one thing. I hate telling you about it. We can't live at Gipsy's Acre, Ellie. Wherever we build our house it can't be there because it's sold.'

'I know it's sold,' said Ellie. She was laughing. 'You don't understand, Mike. *I'm* the person who's bought it.'

CHAPTER 8

I sat there, on the grass by the stream among the water flowers with the little paths and the stepping stones all round us. A good many other people were sitting round about us, but we didn't notice them or even see they were there, because we were like all the others. Young couples, talking about their future. I stared at her and stared at her. I just couldn't speak.

'Mike,' she said. 'There's something, something I've got to tell you. Something about me, I mean.'

'You don't need to,' I said, 'no need to tell me anything.'

'Yes, but I must. I ought to have told you long ago but I didn't want to because – because I thought it might drive you away. But it explains in a way, about Gipsy's Acre.'

'You *bought* it?' I said. 'But how did you buy it?'

'Through lawyers,' she said, 'the usual way. It's a perfectly good investment, you know. The land will appreciate. My lawyers were quite happy about it.'

It was odd suddenly to hear Ellie, the gentle and timid Ellie, speaking with such knowledge and confidence of the business world of buying and selling.

'You bought it for us?'

'Yes. I went to a lawyer of my own, not the family one. I told him what I wanted to do, I got him to look into it, I got everything set up and in train. There were two other people after it but they were not really desperate and they wouldn't go very high. The important thing was that the whole thing had to be set up and arranged ready for me to sign as soon as I came of age. It's signed and finished.'

'But you must have made some deposit or something beforehand. Had you enough money to do that?'

'No,' said Ellie, 'no, I hadn't control of much money beforehand, but of course there are people who will advance you money. And if you go to a new firm of legal advisers, they will want you to go on employing

them for business deals once you've come into what money you're going
to have so they're willing to take the risk that you might drop down dead
before your birthday comes.'

'You sound so businesslike,' I said, 'you take my breath away!'

'Never mind business,' said Ellie, 'I've got to get back to what I'm
telling you. In a way I've told it you already, but I don't suppose really
you realize it.'

'I don't want to know,' I said. My voice rose, I was almost shouting.
'Don't tell me *anything*. I don't want to know anything about what you've
done or who you've been fond of or what has happened to you.'

'It's nothing of that kind,' she said. 'I didn't realize that that was what you
were fearing it might be. No, there's nothing of that kind. No sex secrets.
There's nobody but you. The thing is that I'm – well – I'm rich.'

'I know that,' I said, 'you've told me already.'

'Yes,' said Ellie with a faint smile, 'and you said to me, "poor little rich
girl". But in a way it's more than that. My grandfather, you see, was
enormously rich. Oil. Mostly oil. And other things. The wives he paid
alimony to are dead, there was only my father and myself left because his
two other sons were killed. One in Korea and one in a car accident. And
so it was all left in a great big huge trust and when my father died suddenly,
it all came to *me*. My father had made provision for my stepmother before,
so she didn't get anything more. It was all *mine*. I'm – actually one of the
richest women in America, Mike.'

'Good Lord,' I said. 'I didn't know . . . Yes, you're right, I didn't know
it was like *that*.'

'I didn't want you to know. I didn't want to tell you. That was why
I was afraid when I said my name – Fenella Goodman. We spell it
G-u-t-e-m-a-n, and I thought you might know the name of Guteman
so I slurred over it and made it into Goodman.'

'Yes,' I said, 'I've seen the name Guteman vaguely. But I don't think
I'd have recognized it even then. Lots of people are called names rather
like that.'

'That's why,' she said, 'I've been so hedged around all the time and
fenced in, and imprisoned. I've had detectives guarding me and young
men being vetted before they're allowed even to speak to me. Whenever
I've made a friend they've had to be quite sure it wasn't an unsuitable one.
You don't know what a terrible, terrible prisoner's life it is! But now that's
all over, and if you don't mind –'

'Of course I don't mind,' I said, 'we shall have lots of fun. In fact,' I
said, 'you couldn't be *too* rich a girl for me!'

We both laughed. She said: 'What I like about you is that you can be natural about things.'

'Besides,' I said, 'I expect you pay a lot of tax on it, don't you? That's one of the few nice things about being like me. Any money I make goes into my pocket and nobody can take it away from me.'

'We'll have our house,' said Ellie, 'our house on Gipsy's Acre.' Just for a moment she gave a sudden little shiver.

'You're not cold, darling,' I said. I looked up at the sunshine.

'No,' she said.

It was really very hot. We'd been basking. It might almost have been the South of France.

'No,' said Ellie, 'it was just that – that woman, that gipsy that day.'

'Oh, don't think of her,' I said, 'she was crazy anyway.'

'Do you think she *really* thinks there's a curse on the land?'

'I think gipsies are like that. You know – always wanting to make a song and dance about some curse or something.'

'Do you know much about gipsies?'

'Absolutely nothing,' I said truthfully. 'If you don't want Gipsy's Acre, Ellie, we'll buy a house somewhere else. On the top of a mountain in Wales, on the coast of Spain or an Italian hillside, and Santonix can build us a house there just as well.'

'No,' said Ellie, 'that's how I want it to be. It's where I first saw you walking up the road, coming round the corner very suddenly, and then you saw me and stopped and stared at me. I'll never forget that.'

'Nor will I,' I said.

'So that's where it's going to be. And your friend Santonix will build it.'

'I hope he's still alive,' I said with an uneasy pang. 'He was a sick man.'

'Oh yes,' said Ellie, 'he's alive. I went to see him.'

'You went to see him?'

'Yes. When I was in the South of France. He was in a sanitorium there.'

'Every minute, Ellie, you seem to be more and more amazing. The things you do and manage.'

'He's rather a wonderful person I think,' said Ellie, 'but rather frightening.'

'Did he frighten you?'

'Yes, he frightened me very much for some reason.'

'Did you talk to him about us?'

'Yes. Oh yes, I told him all about us and about Gipsy's Acre and about the house. He told me then that we'd have to take a chance with him. He's a very ill man. He said he thought he still had the life left in him to go and see the site, to draw the plans, to visualize it and get it all sketched out. He said he wouldn't mind really if he died before the house was finished, but I told him,' added Ellie, 'that he mustn't die before the house was finished because I wanted him to see us live in it.'

'What did he say to that?'

'He asked me if I knew what I was doing marrying you, and I said of course I did.'

'And then?'

'He said he wondered if *you* knew what you were doing.'

'I know all right,' I said.

'He said "You will always know where you're going, Miss Guteman." He said "You'll be going always where you want to go and because it's your chosen way."

'"But Mike," he said, "might take the wrong road. He hasn't grown up enough yet to know where he's going."

'I said,' said Ellie, '"He'll be quite safe with me."'

She had superb self-confidence. I was angry though at what Santonix had said. He was like my mother. She always seemed to know more about me than I knew myself.

'I know where I'm going,' I said. 'I'm going the way I want to go and we're going it together.'

'They've started pulling down the ruins of The Towers already,' said Ellie.

She began to talk practically.

'It's to be a rush-job as soon as the plans are finished. We must hurry. Santonix said so. Shall we be married next Tuesday?' said Ellie. 'It's a nice day of the week.'

'With nobody else there,' I said.

'Except Greta,' said Ellie.

'To hell with Greta,' I said, 'she's not coming to our wedding. You and I and nobody else. We can pull the necessary witnesses out of the street.'

I really think, looking back, that that was the happiest day of my life . . .

BOOK II

So that was that, and Ellie and I got married. It sounds abrupt just putting it like that, but you see it was really just the way things happened. We decided to be married and we got married.

It was part of the whole thing – not just an end to a romantic novel or a fairy story. 'And so they got married and lived happily ever afterwards.' You can't, after all, make a big drama out of living happily ever afterwards. We were married and we were both happy and it was really quite a time before anyone got on to us and began to make the usual difficulties and commotions and we'd made up our minds to those.

The whole thing was really extraordinarily simple. In her desire for freedom Ellie had covered her tracks very cleverly up to now. The useful Greta had taken all the necessary steps, and was always on guard behind her. And I had realized fairly soon on that there was nobody really whose business it was to care terribly about Ellie and what she was doing. She had a stepmother who was engrossed in her own social life and love affairs. If Ellie didn't wish to accompany her to any particular spot on the globe there was no need for Ellie to do so. She'd had all the proper governesses and ladies' maids and scholastic advantages and if she wanted to go to Europe, why not? If she chose to have her twenty-first birthday in London, again why not? Now that she had come into her vast fortune she had the whip hand of her family in so far as spending her money went. If she'd wanted a villa on the Riviera or a castle on the Costa Brava or a yacht or any of those things, she had only to mention the fact and someone among the retinues that surrounded millionaires would put everything in hand immediately.

Greta, I gather, was regarded by her family as an admirable stooge. Competent, able to make all arrangements with the utmost efficiency, subservient no doubt and charming to the stepmother, the uncle and a few odd cousins who seemed to be knocking about. Ellie had no fewer than three lawyers at her command, from what she let fall every now and then. She was surrounded by a vast financial network of bankers and lawyers and the administrators of trust funds. It was a world that I just got glimpses of every now and then, mostly from things that Ellie let fall carelessly in the course of conversation. It didn't occur to her, naturally, that I wouldn't know about all those things. She had been brought up in the midst of them and she naturally concluded that the whole world knew what they were and how they worked and all the rest of it.

In fact, getting glimpses of the special peculiarities of each other's lives were unexpectedly what we enjoyed most in our early married life. To put it quite crudely – and I did put things crudely to myself, for that was the only way to get to terms with my new life – the poor don't really know how the rich live and the rich don't know how the poor live, and to find out is really enchanting to both of them. Once I said uneasily:

'Look here, Ellie, is there going to be an awful schemozzle over all this, over our marriage, I mean?'

Ellie considered without, I noticed, very much interest.

'Oh yes,' she said, 'they'll probably be awful.' And she added, 'I hope you won't mind *too* much.'

'I won't mind – why should I? – But you, will they bully you over it?'

'I expect so,' said Ellie, 'but one needn't listen. The point is that they can't *do* anything.'

'But they'll try?'

'Oh yes,' said Ellie. 'They'll try.' Then she added thoughtfully, 'They'll probably try and buy you off.'

'Buy me off?'

'Don't look so shocked,' said Ellie, and she smiled, a rather happy little girl's smile. 'It isn't put exactly like that.' Then she added, 'They bought off Minnie Thompson's first, you know.'

'Minnie Thompson? Is that the one they always call the oil heiress?'

'Yes, that's right. She ran off and married a life guard off the beach.'

'Look here, Ellie,' I said uneasily, '*I* was a life guard at Littlehampton once.'

'Oh, were you? What fun! Permanently?'

'No, of course not. Just one summer, that's all.'

'I wish you wouldn't worry,' said Ellie.

'What happened about Minnie Thompson?'

'They had to go up to 200,000 dollars, I think,' said Ellie, 'he wouldn't take less. Minnie was man-mad and really a half-wit,' she added.

'You take my breath away, Ellie,' I said. 'I've not only acquired a wife, I've got something I can trade for solid cash at any time.'

'That's right,' said Ellie. 'Send for a high-powered lawyer and tell him you're willing to talk turkey. Then he fixes up the divorce and the amount of alimony,' said Ellie, continuing my education. 'My stepmother's been married four times,' she added, 'and she's made quite a lot out of it.' And then she said, 'Oh, Mike, don't look so *shocked.*'

The funny thing is that I was shocked. I felt a priggish distaste for the corruption of modern society in its richer phases. There had been something so little-girl-like about Ellie, so simple, almost touching in her attitude that I was astonished to find how well up she was in worldly affairs and how much she took for granted. And yet I knew that I was right about her fundamentally. I knew quite well the kind of creature that Ellie was. Her simplicity, her affection, her natural sweetness. That didn't mean she had to be ignorant of things. What she did know and took for granted was a fairly limited slice of humanity. She didn't know much about my world, the world of scrounging for jobs, of race-course gangs and dope gangs, the rough and tumble dangers of life, the sharp-Aleck flashy type that I knew so well from living amongst them all my life. She didn't know what it was to be brought up decent and respectable but always hard up for money, with a mother who worked her fingers to the bone in the name of respectability, determining that her son should do well in life. Every penny scrimped for and saved, and the bitterness when your gay carefree son threw away his chances or gambled his all on a good tip for the 3.30.

She enjoyed hearing about my life as much as I enjoyed hearing about hers. Both of us were exploring a foreign country.

Looking back I see what a wonderfully happy life it was, those early days with Ellie. At the time I took them for granted and so did she. We were married in a registry office in Plymouth. Guteman is not an uncommon name. Nobody, reporters or otherwise, knew the Guteman heiress was in England. There had been vague paragraphs in papers occasionally, describing her as in Italy or on someone's yacht. We were married in the Registrar's office with his clerk and a middle-aged typist as witnesses. He gave us a serious little harangue on the serious responsibilities of married life, and wished us happiness. Then we went out, free and married. Mr and Mrs Michael Rogers! We spent a week in a seaside hotel and then we went abroad. We had a glorious three weeks travelling about wherever the fancy took us and no expense spared.

We went to Greece and we went to Florence, and to Venice and lay on the Lido, then to the French Riviera and then to the Dolomites. Half the places I forget the names of now. We took planes or chartered a yacht or hired large and handsome cars. And while we enjoyed ourselves, Greta, I gathered from Ellie, was still on the Home Front doing her stuff.

Travelling about in her own way, sending letters and forwarding all the various post-cards and letters that Ellie had left with her.

'There'll be a day of reckoning, of course,' said Ellie. 'They'll come down on us like a cloud of vultures. But we might as well enjoy ourselves until that happens.'

'What about Greta?' I said. 'Won't they be rather angry with her when they find out?'

'Oh, of course,' said Ellie, 'but Greta won't mind. She's tough.'

'Mightn't it stop her getting another job?'

'Why should she get another job?' said Ellie. 'She'll come and live with us.'

'No!' I said.

'What do you mean, *no*, Mike?'

'We don't want anyone living with us,' I said.

'Greta wouldn't be in the way,' said Ellie, 'and she'd be very useful. Really, I don't know what I'd do without her. I mean, she manages and arranges everything.'

I frowned. 'I don't think I'd like that. Besides, we want our own house – our dream house, after all, Ellie – we want it to ourselves.'

'Yes,' said Ellie, 'I know what you mean. But all the same –' She hesitated. 'I mean, it would be very hard on Greta not to have anywhere to live. After all, she's been with me, done everything for me for four years now. And look how she's helped me to get married and all that.'

'I won't have her butting in between us all the time!'

'But she's not *like* that at all, Mike. You haven't even met her yet.'

'No. No, I know I haven't but – but it's nothing to do with, oh with liking her or not. We want to be by *ourselves*, Ellie.'

'Darling Mike,' said Ellie softly.

We left it at that for the moment.

During the course of our travels we had met Santonix. That was in Greece. He had been in a small fisherman's cottage near the sea. I was startled by how ill he looked, much worse than when I had seen him a year ago. He greeted both Ellie and myself very warmly.

'So you've done it, you two,' he said.

'Yes,' said Ellie, 'and now we're going to have our house built, aren't we?'

'I've got the drawings for you here, the plans,' he said to me. 'She's told you, hasn't she, how she came and ferreted me out and gave me her – commands,' he said, choosing the words thoughtfully.

'Oh! not commands,' said Ellie. 'I just pleaded.'

'You know we've bought the site?' I said.

'Ellie wired and told me. She sent me dozens of photographs.'

'Of course you've got to come and see it first,' said Ellie. 'You mightn't like the site.'

'I do like it.'

'You can't *really* know till you've seen it.'

'But I have seen it, child. I flew over five days ago. I met one of your hatchet-faced lawyers there – the English one.'

'Mr Crawford?'

'That's the man. In fact, operations have already started: clearing the ground, removing the ruins of the old house, foundations – drains – When you get back to England I'll be there to meet you.' He got out his plans then and we sat talking and looking at our house to be. There was even a rough water-colour sketch of it as well as the architectural elevations and plans.

'Do you like it, Mike?'

I drew a deep breath.

'Yes,' I said, 'that's it. That's absolutely *it*.'

'You used to talk about it enough, Mike. When I was in a fanciful mood I used to think that piece of land had laid a spell upon you. You were a man in love with a house that you might never own, that you might never see, that might never even be built.'

'But it's going to be built,' said Ellie. 'It's going to be built, isn't it?'

'If God or the devil wills it,' said Santonix. 'It doesn't depend on me.'

'You're not any – any better?' I asked doubtfully.

'Get it into your thick head. I shall never be *better*. That's not on the cards.'

'Nonsense,' I said. 'People are finding cures for things all the time. Doctors are gloomy brutes. They give people up for dead and then the people laugh and cock a snook at them and live for another fifty years.'

'I admire your optimism, Mike, but my malady isn't one of that kind. They take you to hospital and give you a change of blood and back you come again with a little leeway of life, a little span of time gained. And so on, getting weaker each time.'

'You are very brave,' said Ellie.

'Oh no, I'm not brave. When a thing is certain there's nothing to be brave about. All you can do is find your consolation.'

'Building houses?'

'No, not that. You've less vitality all the time, you see, and there-fore building houses becomes more difficult, not easier. The strength keeps giving out. No. But there *are* consolations. Sometimes very queer ones.'

'I don't understand you,' I said.

'No, you wouldn't, Mike. I don't know really that Ellie would. She might.' He went on, speaking not so much to us as to himself. 'Two things run together, side by side. Weakness and strength. The weakness of fading vitality and the strength of frustrated power. It doesn't matter, you see, *what* you do now! You're going to die anyway. So you can do *anything you choose*. There's nothing to deter you, there's nothing to hold you back. I could walk through the streets of Athens shooting down every man or woman whose face I didn't like. Think of that.'

'The police could arrest you just the same,' I pointed out.

'Of course they could. But what could they do? At the most take my life. Well my life's going to be taken by a greater power than the law in a very short time. What else could they do? Send me to prison for twenty – thirty years? That's rather ironical, isn't it, there aren't twenty or thirty years for me to serve. Six months – one year – eighteen months at the utmost. There's nothing anyone can do to me. So in the span that's left to me I am king. I can do what I like. Sometimes it's a very heady thought. Only – only, you see, there's not much temptation because there's nothing particularly exotic or lawless that I want to do.'

After we had left him, as we were driving back to Athens, Ellie said to me:

'He's an odd person. Sometimes you know, I feel frightened of him.'

'Frightened, of Rudolf Santonix – why?'

'Because he isn't like other people and because he has a – I don't know – a ruthlessness and an arrogance about him somewhere. And I think that he was trying to tell us, really, that knowing he's going to die soon has increased his arrogance. Supposing,' said Ellie, looking at me in an animated way, with almost a rapt and emotional expression on her face, 'supposing he built us our lovely castle, our lovely house on the cliff's edge there in the pines, supposing we were coming to live in it. There he was on the doorstep and he welcomed us in and then –'

'Well, Ellie?'

'Then supposing he came in after us, he slowly closed the doorway behind us and sacrificed us there on the threshold. Cut our throats or something.'

'You frighten me, Ellie. The things you think of!'

'The trouble with you and me, Mike, is that we don't live in the real world. We dream of fantastic things that may never happen.'

'Don't think of sacrifices in connection with Gipsy's Acre.'

'It's the name, I suppose, and the curse upon it.'

'There isn't any curse,' I shouted. 'It's all nonsense. Forget it.'

That was in Greece.

CHAPTER 10

It was, I think, the day after that. We were in Athens. Suddenly, on the steps of the Acropolis Ellie ran into people that she knew. They had come ashore from one of the Hellenic cruises. A woman of about thirty-five detached herself from the group and rushed along the steps to Ellie exclaiming:

'Why, I never did. It's really you, Ellie Guteman? Well, what are you doing here? I'd no *idea*. Are you on a cruise?'

'No,' said Ellie, 'just staying here.'

'My, but it's lovely to see you. How's Cora, is she here?'

'No, Cora is at Salzburg I believe.'

'Well, well.' The woman was looking at me and Ellie said quietly, 'Let me introduce – Mr Rogers, Mrs Bennington.'

'How d'you do. How long are you here for?'

'I'm leaving tomorrow,' said Ellie.

'Oh dear! My, I'll lose my party if I don't go, and I just don't want to miss a word of the lecture and the descriptions. They do hustle one a bit, you know. I'm just dead beat at the end of the day. Any chance of meeting you for a drink?'

'Not today,' said Ellie, 'we're going on an excursion.'

Mrs Bennington rushed off to rejoin her party. Ellie, who had been going with me up the steps of the Acropolis, turned round and moved down again.

'That rather settles things, doesn't it?' she said to me.

'What does it settle?'

Ellie did not answer for a minute or two and then she said with a sigh, 'I must write tonight.'

'Write to whom?'

'Oh, to Cora, and to Uncle Frank, I suppose, and Uncle Andrew.'

'Who's Uncle Andrew? He's a new one.'

'Andrew Lippincott. Not really an uncle. He's my principal guardian or trustee or whatever you call it. He's a lawyer – a very well-known one.'

'What are you going to say?'

'I'm going to tell them I'm married. I couldn't say suddenly to Nora Bennington "Let me introduce my husband." There would have been frightful shrieks and exclamations and "I never heard you were married. Tell me all about it, darling" etcetera, etcetera. It's only fair that my stepmother and Uncle Frank and Uncle Andrew should be the first to know.' She sighed. 'Oh well, we've had a lovely time up to now.'

'What will they say or do?' I asked.

'Make a fuss, I expect,' said Ellie, in her placid way. 'It doesn't matter if they do and they'll have sense enough to know that. We'll have to have a meeting, I expect. We could go to New York. Would you like that?' She looked at me inquiringly.

'No,' I said, 'I shouldn't like it in the least.'

'Then they'll come to London probably, or some of them will. I don't know if you'd like that any better.'

'I shouldn't like any of it. I want to be with you and see our house going up brick by brick as soon as Santonix gets there.'

'So we can,' said Ellie. 'After all, meetings with the family won't take long. Possibly just one big splendid row would do. Get it over in one. Either we fly over there or they fly over here.'

'I thought you said your stepmother was at Salzburg.'

'Oh, I just said that. It sounded odd to say I didn't know where she was. Yes,' said Ellie with a sigh, 'we'll go home and meet them all. Mike, I hope you won't mind too much.'

'Mind what – your family?'

'Yes. You won't mind if they're nasty to you.'

'I suppose it's the price I have to pay for marrying you,' I said. 'I'll bear it.'

'There's your mother,' said Ellie thoughtfully.

'For heaven's sake, Ellie, you're not going to try and arrange a meeting between your stepmother in her frills and her furbelows and my mother from her back street. What do you think they'd have to say to each other?'

'If Cora was my own mother they might have quite a lot to say to each other,' said Ellie. 'I wish you wouldn't be so obsessed with class distinctions, Mike!'

'Me!' I said incredulously. 'What's your American phrase – I come from the wrong side of the tracks, don't I?'

'You don't want to write it on a placard and put it on yourself.'

'I don't know the right clothes to wear,' I said bitterly. 'I don't know the right way to talk about things and I don't know anything really about pictures or art or music. I'm only just learning who to tip and how much to give.'

'Don't you think, Mike, that that makes it all much more exciting for you? I think so.'

'Anyway,' I said, 'you're not to drag my mother into your family party.'

'I wasn't proposing to drag anyone into anything, but I think, Mike, *I* ought to go and see your mother when we go back to England.'

'No,' I said explosively.

She looked at me rather startled.

'Why not, Mike, though? I mean, apart from anything else, I mean it's just very rude not to. Have you told her you're married?'

'Not yet.'

'Why not?'

I didn't answer.

'Wouldn't the simplest way be to tell her you're married and take me to see her when we get back to England?'

'No,' I said again. It was not so explosive this time but it was still fairly well underlined.

'You don't want me to meet her,' said Ellie, slowly.

I didn't of course. I suppose it was obvious enough but the last thing I could do was to explain. I didn't see how I could explain.

'It wouldn't be the right thing to do,' I said slowly. 'You must see that. I'm sure it would lead to trouble.'

'You think she wouldn't like me?'

'Nobody could help liking you, but it wouldn't be – oh I don't know how to put it. But she might be upset and confused. After all, well, I mean I've married out of my station. That's the old-fashioned term. She wouldn't like *that*.'

Ellie shook her head slowly.

'Does anybody really think like that nowadays?'

'Of course they do. They do in your country too.'

'Yes,' she said, 'in a way that's true but – if anyone makes good there –'

'You mean if a man makes a lot of money.'

'Well, not only money.'

'Yes,' I said, 'it's money. If a man makes a lot of money he's admired and looked up to and it doesn't matter where he was born.'

'Well, that's the same everywhere,' said Ellie.

'Please, Ellie,' I said. 'Please don't go and see my mother.'

'I still think it's unkind.'

'No it isn't. Can't you let me know what's best for my own mother? She'd be upset. I tell you she would.'

'But you must tell her you've got married.'

'All right,' I said. 'I'll do that.'

It occurred to me it would be easier to write to my mother from abroad. That evening when Ellie was writing to Uncle Andrew and Uncle Frank and her stepmother Cora van Stuyvesant, I, too, was writing my own letter. It was quite short.

'Dear Mum,' I wrote. 'I ought to have told you before but I felt a bit awkward. I got married three weeks ago. It was all rather sudden. She's a very pretty girl and very sweet. She's got a lot of money which makes things a bit awkward sometimes. We're going to build ourselves a house somewhere in the country. Just at present we're travelling around Europe. All the best, Yours, Mike.'

The results of our evening's correspondence were somewhat varied. My mother let a week elapse before she sent a letter remarkably typical of her.

"Dear Mike. I was glad to get your letter. I hope you'll be very happy. Your affectionate mother."

As Ellie had prophesied, there was far more fuss on her side. We'd stirred up a regular hornet's nest of trouble. We were beset by reporters who wanted news of our romantic marriage, there were articles in the papers about the Guteman heiress and her romantic elopement, there were letters from bankers and lawyers. And finally official meetings were arranged. We met Santonix on the site of Gipsy's Acre and we looked at the plans there and discussed things, and then having seen things under way we came to London, took a suite at Claridge's and prepared, as they say in old world books, to receive cavalry.

The first to arrive was Mr Andrew P. Lippincott. He was an elderly man, dry and precise in appearance. He was long and lean with suave and courteous manners. He was a Bostonian and from his voice I wouldn't have known he was an American. By arrangement through the telephone he called upon us in our suite at 12 o'clock. Ellie was nervous, I could tell, although she concealed it very well.

Mr Lippincott kissed Ellie and extended a hand and a pleasant smile to me.

'Well, Ellie my dear, you are looking very well. Blooming, I might say.'

'How are you, Uncle Andrew? How did you come? Did you fly?'

'No, I had a very pleasant trip across on the *Queen Mary*. And this is your husband?'

'This is Mike, yes.'

I played up, or thought I did. 'How are you, sir?' I said. Then I asked him if he'd have a drink, which he refused pleasantly. He sat down in an upright chair with gilt arms to it and looked, still smiling, from Ellie to me.

'Well,' he said, 'you young people have been giving us shocks. All very romantic, eh?'

'I'm sorry,' said Ellie, 'I really am sorry.'

'Are you?' said Mr Lippincott, rather dryly.

'I thought it was the best way,' said Ellie.

'I am not altogether of your opinion there, my dear.'

'Uncle Andrew,' Ellie said, 'you know perfectly well that if I'd done it any other way there would have been the most frightful fuss.'

'Why should there have been such a frightful fuss?'

'You know what they'd have been like,' said Ellie. 'You too,' she added accusingly. She added, 'I've had two letters from Cora. One yesterday and one this morning.'

'You must discount a certain amount of agitation, my dear. It's only natural under the circumstances, don't you think?'

'It's my business who I get married to and how and where.'

'You may think so, but you will find that the women of any family would rarely agree as to that.'

'Really, I've saved everyone a lot of trouble.'

'You may put it that way.'

'But it's true, isn't it?'

'But you practised, did you not, a good deal of deception, helped by someone who should have known better than to do what she did.'

Ellie flushed.

'You mean Greta? She only did what I asked her to. Are they all very upset with her?'

'Naturally. Neither she nor you could expect anything else, could you? She was, remember, in a position of trust.'

'I'm of age. I can do what I like.'

'I am speaking of the period of time before you were of age. The deceptions began then, did they not?'

'You mustn't blame Ellie, sir,' I said. 'To begin with I didn't know what was going on and since all her relations are in another country it wasn't easy for me to get in touch with them.'

'I quite realize,' said Mr Lippincott, 'that Greta posted certain letters and gave certain information to Mrs van Stuyvesant and to myself as she was requested to do by Ellie here, and made, if I may say so, a very competent job of it. You have met Greta Andersen, Michael? I may call you Michael, since you are Ellie's husband?'

'Of course,' I said, 'call me Mike. No, I haven't met Miss Andersen –'

'Indeed? That seems to me surprising.' He looked at me with a long thoughtful gaze. 'I should have thought that she would have been present at your marriage.'

'No, Greta wasn't there,' said Ellie. She threw me a look of reproach and I shifted uncomfortably.

Mr Lippincott's eyes were still resting on me thoughtfully. He made me uncomfortable. He seemed about to say something more then changed his mind.

'I'm afraid,' he said after a moment or two, 'that you two, Michael and Ellie, will have to put up with a certain amount of reproaches and criticism from Ellie's family.'

'I suppose they are going to descend on me in a bunch,' said Ellie.

'Very probably,' said Mr Lippincott. 'I've tried to pave the way,' he added.

'You're on our side, Uncle Andrew?' said Ellie, smiling at him.

'You must hardly ask a prudent lawyer to go as far as that. I have learnt that in life it is wise to accept what is a *fait accompli.* You two have fallen in love with each other and have got married and have, I understood you to say, Ellie, bought a piece of property in the South of England and have already started building a house on it. You propose, therefore, to live in this country?'

'We want to make our home here, yes. Do you object to our doing that?' I said with a touch of anger in my voice. 'Ellie's married to me and she's a British subject now. So why shouldn't she live in England?'

'No reason at all. In fact, there is no reason why Fenella should not live in any country she chooses, or indeed have property in more than one country. The house in Nassau belongs to you, remember, Ellie.'

'I always thought it was Cora's. She always has behaved as though it was.'

'But the actual property rights are vested in you. You also have the house in Long Island whenever you care to visit it. You are the owner of a great deal of oil-bearing property in the West.' His voice was amiable, pleasant, but I had the feeling that the words were directed at me in some curious way. Was it his idea of trying to insinuate a wedge between me and Ellie? I was not sure. It didn't seem very sensible, rubbing it in to a man that his wife owned property all over the world and was fabulously rich. If anything I should have thought that he would have played down Ellie's property rights and her money and all the rest of it. If I was a fortune hunter as he obviously thought, that would be all the more grist to my mill. But I did realize that Mr Lippincott was a subtle man. It would be hard at any time to know what he was driving at; what he had in his mind behind his even and pleasant manner. Was he trying in a way of his own to make me feel uncomfortable, to make me feel that I was going to be branded almost publicly as a fortune hunter? He said to Ellie:

'I've brought over a certain amount of legal stuff which you'll have to go through with me, Ellie. I shall want your signature to many of these things.'

'Yes, of course, Uncle Andrew. Any time.'

'As you say, any time. There's no hurry. I have other business in London and I shall be over here for about ten days.'

Ten days, I thought. That's a long time. I rather wished that Mr Lippincott wasn't going to be here for ten days. He appeared friendly enough towards me, though, as you might say, indicating that he still reserved his judgment on certain points, but I wondered at that moment whether he was really my enemy. If he was, he would not be the kind of man to show his hand.

'Well,' he went on, 'now that we've all met and come to terms, as you might say, for the future, I would like to have a short interview with this husband of yours.'

Ellie said, 'You can talk to us both.' She was up in arms. I put a hand on her arm.

'Now don't flare up, ducks, you're not a mother hen protecting a chicken.' I propelled her gently to the door in the wall that led into the bedroom. 'Uncle Andrew wants to size me up,' I said. 'He's well within his rights.'

I pushed her gently through the double doors. I shut them both and came back into the room. It was a large handsome sitting-room. I came back and took a chair and faced Mr Lippincott. 'All right,' I said. 'Shoot.'

'Thank you, Michael,' he said. 'First of all I want to assure you that I am not, as you may be thinking, your enemy in any way.'

'Well,' I said, 'I'm glad to hear that.' I didn't sound very sure about it.

'Let me speak frankly,' said Mr Lippincott, 'more frankly than I could do before that dear child to whom I am guardian and of whom I am very fond. You may not yet appreciate it fully, Michael, but Ellie is a most unusually sweet and lovable girl.'

'Don't you worry. I'm in love with her all right.'

'That is not at all the same thing,' said Mr Lippincott in his dry manner. 'I hope that as well as being in love with her you can also appreciate what a really dear and in some ways very vulnerable person she is.'

'I'll try,' I said. 'I don't think I'll have to try very hard. She's the tops, Ellie is.'

'So I will go on with what I was about to say. I shall put my cards on the table with the utmost frankness. You are not the kind of young man that I should have wished Ellie to marry. I should like her, as her family would have liked her, to marry someone of her own surroundings, of her own set —'

'A toff in other words,' I said.

'No, not only that. A similar background is, I think, to be desired as a basis for matrimony. And I am not referring to the snob attitude. After all, Herman Guteman, her grandfather, started life as a dockhand. He ended up as one of the richest men in America.'

'For all you know I might do the same,' I said. 'I may end up one of the richest men in England.'

'Everything is possible,' said Mr Lippincott. 'Do you have ambitions that way?'

'It's not just the money,' I said. 'I'd like to — I'd like to get somewhere and do things and —' I hesitated, stopped.

'You have ambitions, shall we say? Well, that is a very good thing, I am sure.'

'I'm starting at long odds,' I said, 'starting from scratch. I'm nothing and nobody and I won't pretend otherwise.'

He nodded approval.

'Very frankly and handsomely said, I appreciate it. Now, Michael, I am no relation to Ellie, but I have acted as her guardian, I am a trustee, left so by her grandfather, of her affairs, I manage her fortune and her investments. And I assume therefore a certain responsibility for them. Therefore I want to know all that I can know about the husband she has chosen.'

'Well,' I said, 'you can make inquiries about me, I suppose, and find out anything you like easily enough.'

'Quite so,' said Mr Lippincott. 'That would be one way of doing it. A wise precaution to take. But actually, Michael, I should like to know all that I can about you from your own lips. I should like to hear your own story of what your life has been up to now.'

Of course I didn't like it. I expect he knew I wouldn't. Nobody in my position would like that. It's second nature to make the best of yourself. I'd made a point of that at school and onwards, boasted about things a bit, said a few things, stretching the truth a bit. I wasn't ashamed of it. I think it's natural. I think it's the sort of thing that you've got to do if you want to get on. Make out a good case for yourself. People take you at your own valuation and I didn't want to be like that chap in Dickens. They read it out on the television, and I must say it's a good yarn on its own. Uriah something his name was, always going on about being humble and rubbing his hands, and actually planning and scheming behind that humility. I didn't want to be like that.

I was ready enough to boast a bit with the chaps I met or to put up a good case to a prospective employer. After all, you've *got* a best side and a worst side of yourself and it's no good showing the worst side and harping on it. No, I'd always done the best for myself describing my activities up to date. But I didn't fancy doing that sort of thing with Mr Lippincott. He'd rather pooh-poohed the idea of making private inquiries about me but I wasn't at all sure that he wouldn't do so all the same. So I gave him the truth unvarnished, as you might say.

Squalid beginnings, the fact that my father had been a drunk, but that I'd had a good mother, that she'd slaved a good bit to help me get educated. I made no secret of the fact that I'd been a rolling stone, that I'd moved from one job to another. He was a good listener, encouraging, if you know what I mean. Every now and then, though, I realized how shrewd he was. Just little questions that he slipped in, or comments, some comments that I might have rushed in unguardedly either to admit or to deny.

Yes, I had a sort of feeling that I'd better be wary and on my toes. And after ten minutes I was quite glad when he leaned back in his chair and the inquisition, if you could call it that, and it wasn't in the least like one, seemed to be over.

'You have an adventurous attitude to life, Mr Rogers – Michael. Not a bad thing. Tell me more about this house that you and Ellie are building.'

'Well,' I said, 'it's not far from a town called Market Chadwell.'

'Yes,' he said, 'I know just where it is. As a matter of fact I ran down to see it. Yesterday, to be exact.'

That startled me a little. It showed he was a devious kind of fellow who got round to more things than you might think he would.

'It's a beautiful site,' I said defensively, 'and the house we're building is going to be a beautiful house. The architect's a chap called Santonix. Rudolf Santonix. I don't know if you've ever heard of him but –'

'Oh yes,' said Mr Lippincott, 'he's quite a well-known name among architects.'

'He's done work in the States I believe.'

'Yes, an architect of great promise and talent. Unfortunately I believe his health is not good.'

'He thinks he's a dying man,' I said, 'but I don't believe it. I believe he'll get cured, get well again. Doctors – they'll say anything.'

'I hope your optimism is justified. You are an optimist.'

'I am about Santonix.'

'I hope all you wish will come true. I may say that I think you and Ellie have made an extremely good purchase in the piece of property that you have bought.'

I thought it was nice of the old boy to use the pronoun 'you'. It wasn't rubbing it in that Ellie had done the buying on her own.

'I have had a consultation with Mr Crawford –'

'Crawford?' I frowned slightly.

'Mr Crawford of Reece & Crawford, a firm of English solicitors. Mr Crawford was the member of the firm who put the purchase in hand. It is a good firm of solicitors and I gather that this property was acquired at a cheap figure. I may say that I wondered slightly at that. I am familiar with the present prices of land in this country and I really felt rather at a loss to account for it. I think Mr Crawford himself was surprised to get it at so low a figure. I wondered if you knew at all why this property happened to go so cheaply. Mr Crawford did not advance any opinion on that. In fact he seemed slightly embarrassed when I put the question to him.'

'Oh well,' I said, 'it's got a curse on it.'

'I beg your pardon, Michael, what did you say?'

'A curse, sir,' I explained. 'The gipsy's warning, that sort of thing. It is known locally as Gipsy's Acre.'

'Ah. A story?'

'Yes. It seems rather confused and I don't know how much people have made up and how much is true. There was a murder or something long ago. A man and his wife and another man. Some story that the husband shot the other two and then shot himself. At least that's the verdict that was brought in. But all sorts of other stories go flying about. I don't think any-one really knows what happened. It was a good long time ago. It's changed hands about four or five times since, but nobody stays there long.'

'Ah,' said Mr Lippincott appreciatively, 'yes, quite a piece of English folklore.' He looked at me curiously. 'And you and Ellie are not afraid of the curse?' He said it lightly, with a slight smile.

'Of course not,' I said. 'Neither Ellie nor I would believe in any rubbish of that kind. Actually it's a lucky thing since because of it we got it cheap.' When I said that a sudden thought struck me. It was lucky in one sense, but I thought that with all Ellie's money and her property and all the rest of it, it couldn't matter to her very much whether she bought a piece of land cheap or at the top price. Then I thought, no, I was wrong. After all, she'd had a grandfather who came up from being a dock labourer to a millionaire. Anyone of that kind would always wish to buy cheap and sell dear.

'Well, I am not superstitious,' said Mr Lippincott, 'and the view from your property is quite magnificent.' He hesitated. 'I only hope that when you come to move into your house to live there, that Ellie will not hear too many of these stories that are going about.'

'I'll keep everything from her that I can,' I said. 'I don't suppose anybody will say anything to her.'

'People in country villages are very fond of repeating stories of that kind,' said Mr Lippincott. 'And Ellie, remember, is not as tough as you are, Michael. She can be influenced easily. Only in some ways. Which brings me –' he stopped without going on to say what he had been going to. He tapped on the table with one finger. 'I'm going to speak to you now on a matter of some difficulty. You said just now that you had *not* met this Greta Andersen.'

'No, as I said, I haven't met her yet.'

'Odd. Very curious.'

'Well?' I looked at him inquiringly.

'I should have thought you'd have been almost sure to have met her,' he said slowly. 'How much do you know about her?'

'I know that she's been with Ellie some time.'

'She has been with Ellie since Ellie was seventeen. She has occupied a post of some responsibility and trust. She came first to the States in the capacity of secretary and companion. A kind of chaperone to Ellie when Mrs van Stuyvesant, her stepmother, was away from home, which I may say was a quite frequent occurrence.' He spoke particularly dryly when he said this. 'She is, I gather, a well-born girl with excellent references, half-Swedish half-German. Ellie became, quite naturally, very much attached to her.'

'So I gather,' I said.

'In some way Ellie was, I suppose, almost too much attached to her. You don't mind my saying that?'

'No. Why should I mind? As a matter of fact I've – well, I've thought so myself once or twice. Greta this and Greta that. I got – well, I know I've no business to, but I used to get fed up sometimes.'

'And yet she expressed no wish for you to meet Greta?'

'Well,' I said, 'it's rather difficult to explain. But I think, yes, I think she probably did suggest it in a mild way once or twice but, well, we were too taken up with having met each other. Besides, oh well, I suppose I didn't really want to meet Greta. I didn't want to share Ellie with anyone.'

'I see. Yes, I see. And Ellie did not suggest Greta being present at your wedding?'

'She did suggest it,' I said.

'But – but you didn't want her to come. Why?'

'I don't know. I really don't know. I just felt that this Greta, this girl or woman I'd never met, she was always horning in on everything. You know, arranging Ellie's life for her. Sending post-cards and letters and filling in for Ellie, arranging a whole itinerary and passing it on to the family. I felt that Ellie was dependent on Greta in a way, that she let Greta run her, that she wanted to do everything that Greta wanted. I – oh, I'm sorry, Mr Lippincott, I oughtn't to be saying all these things perhaps. Say I was just plain jealous. Anyway I blew up and I said I didn't want Greta at the wedding, that the wedding was ours, that it was just our business and nobody else's. And so we went along to the Registrar's office and his clerk and the typist from his office were the two witnesses. I dare say it was mean of me to refuse to have Greta there, but I wanted to have Ellie to myself.'

'I see. Yes, I see, and I think, if I may say so, that you were wise, Michael.'

'You don't like Greta either,' I said shrewdly.

'You can hardly use the word "either", Michael, if you have not even met her.'

'No, I know but, well, I mean if you hear a lot about a person you can form some sort of idea of them, some judgment of them. Oh well, call it plain jealousy. Why don't *you* like Greta?'

'This is without prejudice,' said Mr Lippincott, 'but you are Ellie's husband, Michael, and I have Ellie's happiness very much at heart. I don't think that the influence that Greta has over Ellie is a very desirable one. She takes too much upon herself.'

'Do you think she'll try and make trouble between us?' I asked.

'I think,' said Mr Lippincott, 'that I have no right to say anything of that kind.'

He sat looking cautiously at me, and blinking like a wrinkled old tortoise.

I didn't know quite what to say next. He spoke first, choosing his words with some care.

'There has been, then, no suggestion that Greta Andersen might take up her residence with you?'

'Not if I can help it,' I said.

'Ah. So that is what you feel? The idea *has* been mooted.'

'Ellie did say something of the kind. But we're newly married, Mr Lippincott. We want our house – our new home – to ourselves. Of course she'll come and stay sometimes, I suppose. That'll only be natural.'

'As you say, that would be only natural. But you realize, perhaps, that Greta is going to be in a somewhat difficult position as regards further employment. I mean, it is not a question of what *Ellie* thinks of her, but of what the people who engaged her and reposed trust in her feel.'

'You mean that you or Mrs van What's-her-name won't recommend her for another post of the same kind?'

'They are hardly likely to do so except so far as to satisfy purely legal requirements.'

'And you think that she'll want to come to England and live on Ellie.'

'I don't want to prejudice you too much against her. After all, this is mostly in my mind. I dislike some of the things she has done and the way she has done them. I think that Ellie who has a very generous heart will be upset at having, shall we say, blighted Greta's prospects in many ways. She might impulsively insist on her coming to live with you.'

'I don't think Ellie will insist,' I said slowly. I sounded a little worried all the same, and I thought Lippincott noticed it. 'But couldn't we – Ellie, I mean – couldn't Ellie pension her off?'

'We should not put it precisely like that,' said Mr Lippincott. 'There is a suggestion of age about pensioning anyone off and Greta is a young woman, and I may say a very handsome young woman. Beautiful, in fact,' he added in a deprecating, disapproving voice. 'She's very attractive to men, too.'

'Well, perhaps she'll marry,' I said. 'If she's all that, why hasn't she got married before this?'

'There have been people attracted, I believe, but she has not considered them. I think, however, that your suggestion is a very sound one. I think it might be carried out in a way that would not hurt anyone's susceptibilities.

It might seem quite a natural thing to do on Ellie's having attained her majority and having had her marriage helped on by Greta's good offices – settle a sum of money upon her in a fit of gratitude.' Mr Lippincott made the last two words sound as sour as lemon juice.

'Well, then, that's all right,' I said cheerfully.

'Again I see that you are an optimist. Let us hope that Greta will accept what is offered to her.'

'Why shouldn't she? She'd be mad if she didn't.'

'I don't know,' said Mr Lippincott. 'I should say it would be extraordinary if she did not accept, and they will remain on terms of friendship, of course.'

'You think – what *do* you think?'

'I would like to see her influence over Ellie broken,' said Mr Lippincott. He got up. 'You will, I hope, assist me and do everything you can to further that end?'

'You bet I will,' I said. 'The last thing I want is to have Greta in our pockets all the time.'

'You might change your mind when you see her,' said Mr Lippincott.

'I don't think so,' I said. 'I don't like managing females, however efficient and even handsome they are.'

'Thank you, Michael, for listening to me so patiently. I hope you will give me the pleasure of dining with me, both of you. Possibly next Tuesday evening? Cora van Stuyvesant and Frank Barton will probably be in London by that time.'

'And I've got to meet them, I suppose?'

'Oh yes, that will be quite inevitable.' He smiled at me and this time his smile seemed more genuine than it had before. 'You mustn't mind too much,' he said. 'Cora, I expect, will be very rude to you. Frank will be merely tactless. Reuben won't be over just at present.'

I didn't know who Reuben was – another relation I supposed.

I went across to the connecting doors and opened them. 'Come on, Ellie,' I said, 'the grilling is over.'

She came back in the room and looked quickly from Lippincott to myself, then she went across and kissed him.

'Dear Uncle Andrew,' she said. 'I can see you've been nice to Michael.'

'Well, my dear, if I weren't nice to your husband you wouldn't have much use for me in the future, would you? I do reserve the right to give a few words of advice now and then. You're very young you know, both of you.'

'All right,' said Ellie, 'we'll listen patiently.'

'Now, my dear, I'd like to have a word with *you* if I may.'

'My turn to be odd man out,' I said, and I too went into the bedroom.

I shut the two double doors ostentatiously but I opened the inner one again after I got inside. I hadn't been as well brought up as Ellie so I felt a bit anxious to find out how double-faced Mr Lippincott might turn out to be. But actually there was nothing I need have listened to. He gave Ellie one or two wise words of advice. He said she must realize that I might find it difficult to be a poor man married to a rich wife and then he went on to sound her about making a settlement on Greta. She agreed to it eagerly and said she'd been going to ask him that herself. He also suggested that she should make an additional settlement on Cora van Stuyvesant.

'There is no earthly need that you should do so,' he said. 'She has been very well provided for in the matter of alimony from several husbands. And she is as you know paid an income, though not a very big one, from the trust fund left by your grandfather.'

'But you think I ought to give her more still?'

'I think there is no legal or moral obligation to do so. What I think is that you will find her far less tiresome and shall I say catty if you do so. I should make it in the form of an increased income, which you could revoke at any time. If you find that she has been spreading malicious rumours about Michael or yourself or your life together, the knowledge that you can do that will keep her tongue free of those more poisonous barbs that she so well knows how to plant.'

'Cora has always hated me,' said Ellie. 'I've known that.' She added rather shyly, 'You do like Mike, don't you, Uncle Andrew?'

'I think he's an extremely attractive young man,' said Mr Lippincott. 'And I can quite see how you came to marry him.'

That, I suppose, was as good as I could expect. I wasn't really his type and I knew it. I eased the door gently to and in a minute or two Ellie came to fetch me.

We were both standing saying goodbye to Lippincott when there was a knock on the door and a page boy came in with a telegram. Ellie took it and opened it. She gave a little surprised cry of pleasure.

'It's Greta,' she said, 'she's arriving in London tonight and she'll be coming to see us tomorrow. How lovely.' She looked at us both. 'Isn't it?' she said.

She saw two sour faces and heard two polite voices saying, one: 'Yes indeed, my dear,' the other one, 'Of course.'

I had been out shopping the next morning and I arrived back at the hotel rather later than I had meant. I found Ellie sitting in the central lounge and opposite her was a tall blonde young woman. In fact Greta. Both of them were talking nineteen to the dozen.

I'm never any hand at describing people but I'll have a shot at describing Greta. To begin with one couldn't deny that she was, as Ellie had said, very beautiful and also, as Mr Lippincott had reluctantly admitted, very handsome. The two things are not exactly the same. If you say a woman is handsome it does not mean that actually you yourself admire her. Mr Lippincott, I gathered, had not admired Greta. All the same when Greta walked across the lounge into a hotel or in a restaurant, men's heads turned to look at her. She was a Nordic type of blonde with pure gold-corn-coloured hair. She wore it piled high on her head in the fashion of the time, not falling straight down on each side of her face in the Chelsea tradition. She looked what she was, Swedish or north German. In fact, pin on a pair of wings and she could have gone to a fancy dress ball as a Valkyrie. Her eyes were a bright clear blue and her contours were admirable. Let's admit it. She was something!

I came along to where they were sitting and joined them, greeting them both in what I hope was a natural, friendly manner, though I couldn't help feeling a bit awkward. I'm not always very good at acting a part. Ellie said immediately:

'At last, Mike, this is Greta.'

I said I guessed it might be, in a rather facetious, not very happy manner. I said:

'I'm very glad to meet you at last, Greta.'

Ellie said:

'As you know very well, if it hadn't been for Greta we would never have been able to get married.'

'All the same we'd have managed it somehow,' I said.

'Not if the family had come down on us like a ton of coals. They'd have broken it up somehow. Tell me, Greta, have they been very awful?' Ellie asked. 'You haven't written or said anything to me about that.'

'I know better,' said Greta, 'than to write to a happy couple when they're on their honeymoon.'

'But were they very angry with you?'

'Of course! What do you imagine? But I was prepared for that, I can assure you.'

'What have they said or done?'

'Everything they could,' said Greta cheerfully. 'Starting with the sack naturally.'

'Yes, I suppose that was inevitable. But – but what have you done? After all they can't refuse to give you references.'

'Of course they can. And after all, from their point of view I was placed in a position of trust and abused it shamefully.' She added, 'Enjoyed abusing it too.'

'But what are you going to do now?'

'Oh I've got a job ready to walk into.'

'In New York?'

'No. Here in London. Secretarial.'

'But are you all right?'

'Darling Ellie,' said Greta, 'how can I not be all right with that lovely cheque you sent me in anticipation of what was going to happen when the balloon went up?'

Her English was very good with hardly any trace of accent though she used a lot of colloquial terms which sometimes didn't run quite right.

'I've seen a bit of the world, fixed myself up in London and bought a good many things as well.'

'Mike and I have bought a lot of things too,' said Ellie, smiling at the recollection.

It was true. We'd done ourselves pretty well with our continental shopping. It was really wonderful that we had dollars to spend, no niggling Treasury restrictions. Brocades and fabrics in Italy for the house. And we'd bought pictures too, both in Italy and in Paris, paying what seemed fabulous sums for them. A whole world had opened up to me that I'd never dreamt would have come my way.

'You both look remarkably happy,' said Greta.

'You haven't seen our house yet,' said Ellie. 'It's going to be wonderful. It's going to be just like we dreamed it would be, isn't it, Mike?'

'I have seen it,' said Greta. 'The first day I got back to England I hired a car and drove down there.'

'Well?' said Ellie.

I said Well? too.

'Well,' said Greta consideringly. She shifted her head from side to side.

Ellie looked grief-stricken, horribly taken aback. But I wasn't taken in. I saw at once that Greta was having a bit of fun with us. If the thought of fun wasn't very kind, it hardly had time to take root. Greta burst out laughing, a high musical laugh that made people turn their heads and look at us.

'You should have seen your faces,' she said, 'especially yours, Ellie. I have to tease you just a little. It's a wonderful house, lovely. That man's a genius.'

'Yes,' I said, 'he's something out of the ordinary. Wait till you meet him.'

'I have met him,' said Greta. 'He was down there the day I went. Yes, he's an extraordinary person. Rather frightening, don't you think?'

'Frightening?' I said, surprised. 'In what way?'

'Oh I don't know. It's as though he looks through you and – well, sees right through to the other side. That's always disconcerting.' Then she added, 'He looks rather ill.'

'He is ill. Very ill,' I said.

'What a shame. What's the matter with him, tuberculosis, something like that?'

'No,' I said, 'I don't think it's tuberculosis. I think it's something to do with – oh with blood.'

'Oh I see. Doctors can do almost anything nowadays, can't they, unless they kill you first while they're trying to cure you. But don't let's think of that. Let's think of the house. When will it be finished?'

'Quite soon, I should think, by the look of it. I'd never imagined a house could go up so quickly,' I said.

'Oh,' said Greta carelessly, 'that's money. Double shifts and bonuses – all the rest of it. You don't really know yourself, Ellie, how wonderful it is to have all the money you have.'

But *I* did know. I had been learning, learning a great deal in the last few weeks. I'd stepped as a result of marriage into an entirely different world and it wasn't the sort of world I'd imagined it to be from the outside. So far in my life, a lucky double had been my highest knowledge of affluence. A whack of money coming in, and spending it as fast as I could on the biggest blow-out I could find. Crude, of course. The crudeness of my class. But Ellie's world was a different world. It wasn't what I should have thought it to be. Just more and more super luxury. It wasn't bigger bathrooms and larger houses and more electric light fittings and bigger meals and faster cars. It wasn't just spending for spending's sake and showing off to everyone in sight. Instead, it was curiously simple. The sort of simplicity that comes when you get beyond the point of splashing for splashing's sake. You don't want three yachts or four cars and you can't eat more than three meals a day and if you buy a really top-price picture you don't want more than perhaps one of them in a room. It's as simple as that. Whatever you have is just the best of its kind, not so much because it is the best, but because there is no reason if you like or want any particular thing, why you shouldn't have it. There is no moment when you say, 'I'm afraid I can't afford that one.' So in a strange way it makes sometimes for such a curious simplicity that I couldn't understand it. We were considering a French Impressionist picture, a Cézanne, I think it was. I had to learn that name carefully. I always mixed it up with a tzigane which I gather is a gipsy orchestra. And then as we walked along the streets of Venice, Ellie stopped to look at some pavement artists. On the whole they were doing some terrible pictures for tourists which all looked the same. Portraits with great rows of shining teeth and usually blonde hair falling down their necks.

And then she bought quite a tiny picture, just a picture of a little glimpse through to a canal. The man who had painted it appraised the look of us and she bought it for £6 by English exchange. The funny thing was that I knew quite well that Ellie had just the same longing for that £6 picture that she had for the Cézanne.

It was the same way one day in Paris. She'd said to me suddenly:

'What fun it would be – let's get a really nice crisp French loaf of bread and have that with butter and one of those cheeses wrapped up in leaves.'

So we did and Ellie I think enjoyed it more than the meal we'd had the night before which had come to about £20 English. At first I couldn't understand it, then I began to see. The awkward thing was that I could see now that being married to Ellie wasn't just fun and games. You have to do your homework, you have to learn how to go into a restaurant and the sort of things to order and the right tips, and when for some reason you gave more than usual. You have to memorize what you drink with certain foods. I had to do most of it by observation. I couldn't ask Ellie because that was one of the things she wouldn't have understood. She'd have said 'But, darling Mike, you can have anything you like. What does it matter if waiters think you ought to have one particular wine with one particular thing?' It wouldn't have mattered to her because she was born to it but it mattered to me because I couldn't do just as I liked. I wasn't simple enough. Clothes too. Ellie was more helpful there, for she could understand better. She just guided me to the right places and told me to let them have their head.

Of course I didn't look right and sound right yet. But that didn't matter much. I'd got the hang of it, enough so that I could pass muster with people like old Lippincott, and shortly, presumably, when Ellie's stepmother and uncles were around, but actually it wasn't going to matter in the future at all. When the house was finished and when we'd moved in, we were going to be far away from everybody. It could be our kingdom. I looked at Greta sitting opposite me. I wondered what she'd really thought of our house. Anyway, it was what I wanted. It satisfied me utterly. I wanted to drive down and go through a private path through the trees which led down to a small cove which would be our own beach which nobody could come to on the land side. It would be a thousand times better, I thought, plunging into the sea there. A thousand times better than a lido spread along a beach with hundreds of bodies lying there. I didn't want all the *senseless* rich things. I wanted – there were the words again, my own particular words – I want, I want . . . I could feel all the feeling surging up in me. I wanted a wonderful woman and a wonderful house like nobody else's house and I wanted my wonderful house to be full of wonderful things. Things that belonged to *me*. Everything would belong to me.

'He's thinking of our house,' said Ellie.

It seemed that she had twice suggested to me that we should go now into the dining-room. I looked at her affectionately.

Later in the day – it was that evening – when we were dressing to go out to dinner, Ellie said a little tentatively:

'Mike, you do – you do like Greta, don't you?'

'Of course I do,' I said.

'I couldn't bear it if you didn't like her.'

'But I do,' I protested. 'What makes you think I don't?'

'I'm not quite sure. I think it's the way you hardly look at her even when you're talking to her.'

'Well, I suppose that's because – well, because I feel nervous.'

'Nervous of Greta?'

'Yes, she's a bit awe-inspiring, you know.'

And I told Ellie how I thought Greta looked rather like a Valkyrie.

'Not as stout as an operatic one,' said Ellie and laughed. We both laughed. I said:

'It's all very well for you because you've known her for years. But she is just a bit – well, I mean she's very efficient and practical and sophisticated.' I struggled with a lot of words which didn't seem to be quite the right ones. I said suddenly, 'I feel – I feel at a disadvantage with her.'

'Oh Mike!' Ellie was conscience-stricken. 'I know we've got a lot of things to talk about. Old jokes and old things that happened and all that.

I suppose – yes, I suppose it might make you feel rather shy. But you'll soon get to be friends. She likes you. She likes you very much. She told me so.'

'Listen, Ellie, she'd probably tell you that anyway.'

'Oh no she wouldn't. Greta's very outspoken. You heard her. Some of the things she said today.'

It was true that Greta had not minced her words during luncheon. She had said, addressing me rather than Ellie:

'You must have thought it queer sometimes, the way I was backing Ellie up when I'd not even seen you. But I got so mad – so mad with the life that they were making her lead. All tied up in a cocoon with their money, their traditional ideas. She never had a chance to enjoy herself, go anywhere really by herself and do what she wanted. She wanted to rebel but she didn't know how. And so – yes, all right, I urged her on. I suggested she should look at properties in England. Then I said when she was twenty-one she could buy one of her own and say goodbye to all that New York lot.'

'Greta always has wonderful ideas,' said Ellie. 'She thinks of things I'd probably never have thought of myself.'

What were those words Mr Lippincott had said to me? 'She has too much influence over Ellie.' I wondered if it was true. Queerly enough I didn't really think so. I felt that there was a core somewhere in Ellie that Greta, for all that she knew her so well, had never quite appreciated. Ellie, I was sure, would always accept any ideas that matched with the ideas she wanted to have herself. Greta had preached rebellion to Ellie but Ellie herself wanted to rebel, only she was not sure how to do so. But I felt that Ellie, now that I was coming to know her better, was one of those very simple people who have unexpected reserves. I thought Ellie would be quite capable of taking a stand of her own if she wished to. The point was that she wouldn't very often wish to and I thought then how difficult everyone was to understand. Even Ellie. Even Greta. Even perhaps my own mother . . . The way she looked at me with fear in her eyes.

I wondered about Mr Lippincott. I said, as we were peeling some outsize peaches:

'Mr Lippincott seems to have taken our marriage very well really. I was surprised.'

'Mr Lippincott,' said Greta, 'is an old fox.'

'You always say so, Greta,' said Ellie, 'but I think he's rather a dear. Very strict and proper and all that.'

'Well, go on thinking so if you like,' said Greta. 'Myself, I wouldn't trust him an inch.'

'Not trust him!' said Ellie.

Greta shook her head. 'I know. He's a pillar of respectability and trustworthiness. He's everything a trustee and a lawyer should be.'

Ellie laughed and said, 'Do you mean he's embezzled my fortune? Don't be silly, Greta. There are thousands of auditors and banks and check-ups and all that sort of thing.'

'Oh, I expect he's all right really,' said Greta. 'All the same, those are the people that do embezzle. The trustworthy ones. And then everyone says afterwards, "I'd never have believed it of Mr A. or Mr B. The last man in the world." Yes, that's what they say. "The last man in the world".'

Ellie said thoughtfully that her Uncle Frank, she thought, was much more likely to go in for dishonest practices. She did not seem unduly worried or surprised by the idea.

'Oh well he looks like a crook,' said Greta. 'That handicaps him to start with. All that geniality and bonhomie. But he'll never be in a position to be a crook in a big way.'

'Is he your mother's brother?' I asked. I always got confused over Ellie's relations.

'He's my father's sister's husband,' said Ellie. 'She left him and married someone else and died about six or seven years ago. Uncle Frank has more or less stuck on with the family.'

'There are three of them,' said Greta kindly and helpfully. 'Three leeches hanging round, as you might say. Ellie's actual uncles were killed, one in Korea and one in a car accident, so what she's got is a much-damaged stepmother, an Uncle Frank, an amiable hanger-on in the family home, and her cousin Reuben whom she calls Uncle but he's only a cousin and Andrew Lippincott, and Stanford Lloyd.'

'Who is Stanford Lloyd?' I asked, bewildered.

'Oh another sort of trustee, isn't he, Ellie? At any rate he manages your investments and things like that. Which can't really be very difficult because when you've got as much money as Ellie has, it sort of makes more money all the time without anyone having to do much about it. Those are the main surrounding group,' Greta added, 'and I have no doubt that you will be meeting them fairly soon. They'll be over here to have a look at you.'

I groaned, and looked at Ellie. Ellie said very gently and sweetly:

'Never mind, Mike, they'll go away again.'

CHAPTER 12

They did come over. None of them stayed very long. Not that time, not on a first visit. They came over to have a look at me. I found them difficult to understand because of course they were all Americans. They were types with which I was not well acquainted. Some of them were pleasant enough. Uncle Frank, for instance. I agreed with Greta about him. I wouldn't have trusted him a yard. I had come across the same type in England. He was a big man with a bit of a paunch and pouches under his eyes that gave him a dissipated look which was not far from the truth, I imagine. He had an eye for women, I thought, and even more of an eye for the main chance. He borrowed money from me once or twice, quite small amounts, just, as it were, something to tide him over for a day or two. I thought it was not so much that he needed the money but he wanted to test me out, to see if I lent money easily. It was rather worrying because I wasn't sure which was the best way to take it. Would it have been better to refuse point blank and let him know I was a skinflint or was it better to assume an appearance of careless generosity, which I was very far from feeling? To hell with Uncle Frank, I thought.

Cora, Ellie's stepmother, was the one that interested me most. She was a woman of about forty, well turned out with tinted hair and a rather gushing manner. She was all sweetness to Ellie.

'You mustn't mind those letters I wrote you, Ellie,' she said. 'You must admit that it came as a terrible shock, your marrying like that. So secretly. But of course I know it was Greta who put you up to it, doing it that way.'

'You mustn't blame Greta,' said Ellie. 'I didn't mean to upset you all so much. I just thought that – well, the less fuss –'

'Well, of course, Ellie dear, you have something there. All the men of business were simply livid. Stanford Lloyd and Andrew Lippincott. I suppose they thought everyone would blame them for not looking after you better. And of course they'd no idea what Mike would be like. They didn't realize how charming he was going to be. I didn't myself.'

She smiled across at me, a very sweet smile and one of the falsest ones I'd ever seen! I thought to myself that if ever a woman hated a man, it was Cora who hated me. I thought her sweetness to Ellie was understandable enough. Andrew Lippincott had gone back to America and had, no doubt, given her a few words of caution. Ellie was selling some of her property in America, since she herself had definitely decided to live in England, but she was going to make a large allowance to Cora so that the latter could live where she chose. Nobody mentioned Cora's husband much. I gathered he'd already taken himself off to some other part of the world, and had not gone there alone. In all probability, I gathered, another divorce was pending. There wouldn't be much alimony out of this one. Cora's last marriage had been to a man a good many years younger than herself with more attractions of a physical kind than cash.

Cora wanted that allowance. She was a woman of extravagant tastes. No doubt old Andrew Lippincott had hinted clearly enough that it could be discontinued any time if Ellie chose, or if Cora so far forgot herself as to criticize Ellie's new husband too virulently.

Cousin Reuben, or Uncle Reuben, did not make the journey. He wrote instead to Ellie a pleasant, non-committal letter hoping she'd be very happy, but doubted if she would like living in England. 'If you don't, Ellie, you come right back to the States. Don't think you won't get a welcome here because you will. Certainly you will from your Uncle Reuben.'

'He sounds rather nice,' I said to Ellie.

'Yes,' said Ellie meditatively. She wasn't, it seemed, quite so sure about it.

'Are you fond of any of them, Ellie?' I asked, 'or oughtn't I to ask that?'

'Of course you can ask me anything.' But she didn't answer for a moment or two all the same. Then she said, with a sort of finality and decision, 'No, I don't think I am. It seems odd, but I suppose it's because they don't really belong to me. Only by environment, not by relationship. They none of them are my flesh and blood relations. I loved my father, what I remembered of him. I think he was rather a weak man and I think my grandfather was disappointed in him because he hadn't got much head for business. He didn't want to go into the business life. He liked going to Florida and fishing, that sort of thing. And then later he married Cora and I never cared for Cora much – or Cora for me, for that matter. My own mother, of course, I don't remember. I liked Uncle Henry and Uncle Joe. They were fun. In some ways more fun than my father was. He, I think, was in some ways a quiet and rather sad man. But the uncles enjoyed themselves. Uncle Joe was, I think, a bit wild, the kind that is wild just because they've got lots of money. Anyway, he was the one who got smashed up in the car, and the other one was killed fighting in the war. My grandfather was a sick man by that time and it was a terrible blow to him that all his three sons were dead. He didn't like Cora and he didn't care much for any of his more distant relatives. Uncle Reuben for instance. He said you could never tell what Reuben was up to. That's why he made arrangements to put his money in trust. A lot of it went to museums and hospitals. He left Cora well provided for, and his daughter's husband Uncle Frank.'

'But most of it to you?'

'Yes. And I think that worried him a little bit. He did his best to get it looked after for me.'

'By Uncle Andrew and by Mr Stanford Lloyd. A lawyer and a banker.'

'Yes. I suppose he didn't think I could look after it very well by myself. The odd thing is that he let me come into it at the age of twenty-one. He didn't keep it in trust till I was twenty-five, as lots of people do. I expect that was because I was a girl.'

'That's odd,' I said, 'it would seem to me that it ought to be the other way round?'

Ellie shook her head. 'No,' she said, 'I think my grandfather thought that young males were always wild and hit things up and that blondes with evil designs got hold of them. I think he thought it would be a good thing if they had plenty of time to sow their wild oats. That's your English saying, isn't it? But he said once to me, "If a girl is going to have any sense at all, she'll have it at twenty-one. It won't make any difference making her wait four years longer. If she's going to be a fool she'll be a fool by then just as much." He said, too,' Ellie looked at me and smiled, 'that he didn't think I *was* a fool. He said, "You mayn't know very much about life, but you've got good sense, Ellie. Especially about people. I think you always will have."'

'I don't suppose he would have liked me,' I said thoughtfully.

Ellie has a lot of honesty. She didn't try and reassure me by saying anything but what was undoubtedly the truth.

'No,' she said, 'I think he'd have been rather horrified. To begin with, that is. He'd have had to get used to you.'

'Poor Ellie,' I said suddenly.

'Why do you say that?'

'I said it to you once before, do you remember?'

'Yes. You said poor little rich girl. You were quite right too.'

'I didn't mean it the same way this time,' I said. 'I didn't mean that you were poor because you were rich. I think I meant –' I hesitated. 'You've too many people,' I said, '*at* you. All round you. Too many people who want things from you but who don't really care about you. That's true, isn't it?'

'I think Uncle Andrew really cares about me,' said Ellie, a little doubt-fully. 'He's always been nice to me, sympathetic. The others – no, you're quite right. They only want *things*.'

'They come and cadge off you, don't they? Borrow money off you, want favours. Want you to get them out of jams, that sort of thing. They're *at* you, *at* you, *at* you!'

'I suppose it's quite natural,' said Ellie calmly, 'but I've done with them all now. I'm coming to live here in England. I shan't see much of them.'

She was wrong there, of course, but she hadn't grasped that fact yet. Stanford Lloyd came over later by himself. He brought a great many documents and papers and things for Ellie to sign and wanted her agreement on investments. He talked to her about investments and shares and property that she owned, and the disposal of trust funds. It was all Double Dutch to me. I couldn't have helped her or advised her. I couldn't have stopped Stanford Lloyd from cheating her, either. I hoped he wasn't, but how could anyone ignorant like myself be sure?

There was something about Stanford Lloyd that was almost too good to be true. He was a banker, and he looked like a banker. He was rather a handsome man though not young. He was very polite to me and thought dirt of me though he tried not to show it.

'Well,' I said when he had finally taken his departure, 'that's the last of the bunch.'

'You didn't think much of any of them, did you?'

'I think your stepmother, Cora, is a double-faced bitch if I ever knew one. Sorry, Ellie, perhaps I oughtn't to say that.'

'Why not, if that's what you think? I expect you're not far wrong.'

'You must have been lonely, Ellie,' I said.

'Yes, I was lonely. I knew girls of my own age. I went to a fashionable school but I was never really *free*. If I made friends with people, somehow or other they'd get me separated, push another girl at me instead. You know? Everything was governed by the social register. If I'd cared enough about anybody to make a fuss – but I never got far enough. There was never anybody I *really* cared for. Not until Greta came, and then everything was different. For the first time someone was really fond of *me*. It was wonderful.' Her face softened.

'I wish,' I said, as I turned away towards the window.

'What do you wish?'

'Oh I don't know . . . I wish perhaps that you weren't – weren't quite so dependent on Greta. It's a bad thing to be as dependent as that on anyone.'

'You don't like her, Mike,' said Ellie.

'I do,' I protested hurriedly. 'Indeed I do. But you must realize, Ellie, that she is – well, she's quite a stranger to me. I suppose, let's face it, I'm a bit jealous of her. Jealous because she and you – well, I didn't understand before – how linked together you were.'

'Don't be jealous. She's the only person who was good to me, who cared about me – till I met you.'

'But you have met me,' I said, 'and you've married me.' Then I said again what I'd said before. 'And we're going to live happily ever afterwards.'

CHAPTER 13

I'm trying as best I can, though that isn't saying much, to paint a picture of the people who came into our lives, that is to say: who came into *my* life because, of course, they were in Ellie's life already. Our mistake was that we thought they'd go out of Ellie's life. But they didn't. They'd no intention of doing so. However, we didn't know that then.

The English side of our life was the next thing that happened. Our house was finished, we had a telegram from Santonix. He'd asked us to keep away for about a week, then the telegram came. It said: 'Come tomorrow.'

We drove down there, and we arrived at sunset. Santonix heard the car and came out to meet us, standing in front of the house. When I saw our house, finished, something inside me leaped up, leaped up as though to burst out of my skin! It was *my house* – and I'd got it at last! I held Ellie's arm very tight.

'Like it?' said Santonix.

'It's the tops,' I said. A silly thing to say but he knew what I meant.

'Yes,' he said, 'it's the best thing I've done . . . It's cost you a mint of money and it's worth every penny of it. I've exceeded my estimates all round. Come on, Mike,' he said, 'pick her up and carry her over the threshold. That's the thing to do when you enter into possession with your bride!'

I flushed and then I picked up Ellie – she was quite a light weight – and carried her as Santonix had suggested, over the threshold. As I did so, I stumbled just a little and I saw Santonix frown.

'There you are,' said Santonix, 'be good to her, Mike. Take care of her.

Don't let harm come to her. She can't take care of herself. She thinks she can.'

'Why should any harm happen to me?' said Ellie.

'Because it's a bad world and there are bad people in it,' said Santonix, 'and there are some bad people around you, my girl. I know. I've seen one or two of them. Seen them down here. They come nosing around, sniffing around like the rats they are. Excuse my French but somebody's got to say it.'

'They won't bother us,' said Ellie, 'they've all gone back to the States.'

'Maybe,' said Santonix, 'but it's only a few hours by plane, you know.'

He put his hands on her shoulders. They were very thin now, very white-looking. He looked terribly ill.

'I'd look after you myself, child, if I could,' he said, 'but I can't. It won't be long now. You'll have to fend for yourself.'

'Cut out the gipsy's warning, Santonix,' I said, 'and take us round the house. Every inch of it.'

We went round the house. Some of the rooms were still empty but most of the things we'd bought, pictures and the furniture and the curtains, were there.

'We haven't got a name for it,' said Ellie suddenly. 'We can't call it The Towers, that was a ridiculous name. What was the other name for it that you told me once?' she said to me. 'Gipsy's Acre, wasn't it?'

'We won't call it that,' I said sharply. 'I don't like that name.'

'It'll always be called that hereabouts,' said Santonix.

'They're a lot of silly superstitious people,' I said.

And then we sat down on the terrace looking at the setting sun and the view, and we thought of names for the house. It was a kind of game. We started quite seriously and then we began to think of every silly name we possibly could. 'Journey's End', 'Heart's Delight' and names like boarding-houses. 'Seaview', 'Fairhome', 'The Pines'. Then suddenly it grew dark and cold, and we went indoors. We didn't draw the curtains, just closed the windows. We'd brought down provisions with us. On the following day an expensively acquired domestic staff was coming.

'They'll probably hate it and say it's lonely and they'll all go away,' said Ellie.

'And then you'll give them double the money to stay on,' said Santonix.

'*You* think,' said Ellie, 'that everyone can be bought!' But she only said it laughingly.

We had brought *pâté en croûte* with us and French bread and large red prawns. We sat round the table laughing and eating and talking. Even Santonix looked strong and animated, and there was a kind of wild excitement in his eyes.

And then it happened suddenly. A stone crashed in through the window and dropped on the table. Smashed a wineglass too, and a sliver of glass slit Ellie's cheek. For a moment we sat paralysed, then I sprang up, rushed to the window, unbolted it and went out on the terrace. There was no one to be seen. I came back into the room again.

I picked up a paper napkin and bent over Ellie, wiping away a trickle of blood I saw coursing down her cheek.

'It's hurt you . . . There, dear, it's nothing much. It's just a wee cut from a sliver of glass.'

My eyes met those of Santonix.

'Why did anyone do it?' said Ellie. She looked bewildered.

'Boys,' I said, 'you know, young hooligans. They knew, perhaps, we were settling in. I dare say you were lucky that they only threw a stone. They might have had an air gun or something like that.'

'But *why* should they do it to us? *Why?*'

'I don't know,' I said. 'Just beastliness.'

Ellie got up suddenly. She said:

'I'm frightened. I'm afraid.'

'We'll find out tomorrow,' I said. 'We don't know enough about the people round here.'

'Is it because we're rich and they're poor?' said Ellie. She asked it not of me but of Santonix as though he would know the answer to the question better than I did.

'No,' said Santonix slowly, 'I don't think it's that . . .'

Ellie said:

'It's because they hate us . . . Hate Mike and hate me. *Why?* Because we're happy?'

Again Santonix shook his head.

'No,' Ellie said, as though she were agreeing with him, 'no, it's something else. Something we don't know about. Gipsy's Acre. Anyone who lives here is going to be hated. Going to be persecuted. Perhaps they will succeed in the end in driving us away . . .'

I poured out a glass of wine and gave it to her.

'Don't, Ellie,' I begged her. 'Don't say such things. Drink this. It's a nasty thing to happen, but it was only silliness, crude horseplay.'

'I wonder,' said Ellie, 'I wonder . . .' She looked hard at me. 'Somebody is trying to drive us away, Mike. To drive us away from the house we've built, the house we love.'

'We won't let them drive us away,' I said. I added, 'I'll take care of you. Nothing shall hurt you.'

She looked again at Santonix.

'You should know,' she said, 'you've been here while the house was building. Didn't anyone ever say anything to you? Come and throw stones – interfere with the building of the house?'

'One can imagine things,' said Santonix.

'There *were* accidents, then?'

'There are always a few accidents in the building of a house. Nothing serious or tragic. A man falls off a ladder, someone drops a load on his foot, someone gets a splinter in his thumb and it goes septic.'

'Nothing more than that? Nothing that might have been *meant*?'

'No,' said Santonix, '*no*. I swear to you, no!'

Ellie turned to me.

'You remember that gipsy woman, Mike. How queer she was that day, how she warned me not to come here.'

'She's just a bit crazy, a bit off her head.'

'We've built on Gipsy's Acre,' said Ellie. 'We've done what she told us not to do.' Then she stamped her foot. 'I won't let them drive me away. I won't let *anyone* drive me away!'

'Nobody shall drive us away,' I said. 'We're going to be happy here.'

We said it like a challenge to fate.

CHAPTER 14

That's how our life began at Gipsy's Acre. We didn't find another name for the house. That first evening fixed Gipsy's Acre in our heads.

'We'll call it Gipsy's Acre,' said Ellie, 'just to show! A kind of challenge, don't you think? It's *our* Acre, and to hell with the gipsy's warning.'

She was her old gay self again the next day and soon we were busy getting ourselves settled in, and getting also to know the neighbourhood and the neighbours. Ellie and I walked down to the cottage where the gipsy woman lived. I felt it would be a good thing if we found her digging in her garden. The only time Ellie had seen her before was when she told our fortunes. If Ellie saw she was just an ordinary old woman – digging up potatoes – but we didn't see her. The cottage was shut up. I asked if she were dead but the neighbour I asked shook her head.

'She must have gone away,' she said. 'She goes away from time to time, you know. She's a gipsy really. That's why she can't stay in houses. She wanders away and comes back again.' She tapped her forehead. 'Not quite right up here.'

Presently she said, trying to mask curiosity, 'You've come from the new house up there, haven't you, the one on the top of the hill, that's just been built?'

'That's right,' I said, 'we moved in last night.'

'Wonderful-looking place it is,' she said. 'We've all been up to look at it while it was building. Makes a difference, doesn't it, seeing a house like that where all those gloomy trees used to be?' She said to Ellie rather shyly, 'You're an American lady, aren't you, so we heard?'

'Yes,' said Ellie, 'I'm American – or I was, but now I'm married to an Englishman so I'm an Englishwoman.'

'And you've come here to settle down and live, haven't you?'

We said we had.

'Well, I hope you'll like it, I'm sure.' She sounded doubtful.

'Why shouldn't we?'

'Oh well, it's lonely up there, you know. People don't always like living in a lonely place among a lot of trees.'

'Gipsy's Acre,' said Ellie.

'Ah, you know the local name, do you? But the house that was there before was called The Towers. I don't know why. It hadn't any towers, at least not in my time.'

'I think The Towers is a silly name,' said Ellie. 'I think we'll go on calling it Gipsy's Acre.'

'We'll have to tell the post office if so,' I said, 'or we shan't get any letters.'

'No, I suppose we shan't.'

'Though when I come to think of it,' I said, 'would that matter, Ellie? Wouldn't it be much nicer if we *didn't* get any letters?'

'It might cause a lot of complications,' said Ellie. 'We shouldn't even get our bills.'

'That would be a splendid idea,' I said.

'No, it wouldn't,' said Ellie. 'Bailiffs would come in and camp there. Anyway,' she said, 'I wouldn't like not to get any letters. I'd want to hear from Greta.'

'Never mind Greta,' I said. 'Let's go on exploring.'

So we explored Kingston Bishop. It was a nice village, nice people in the shops. There was nothing sinister about the place. Our domestic help didn't take to it much, but we soon arranged that hired cars should take them into the nearest seaside town or into Market Chadwell on their days out. They were not enthusiastic about the location of the house, but it was not superstition that worried them. I pointed out to Ellie nobody could say the house was haunted because it had been just built.

'No,' Ellie agreed, 'it's not the house. There's nothing wrong with the house. It's outside. It's that road where it curves round through the trees and that bit of rather gloomy wood where that woman stood and made me jump so that day.'

'Well, next year,' I said, 'we might cut down those trees and plant a lot of rhododendrons or something like that.'

We went on making plans.

Greta came and stayed with us for a weekend. She was enthusiastic about the house, and congratulated us on all our furnishings and pictures and colour schemes. She was very tactful. After the weekend she said she wouldn't disturb the honeymooners any longer, and anyway she'd got to get back to her job.

Ellie enjoyed showing her the house. I could see how fond Ellie was of her. I tried to behave very sensibly and pleasantly but I was glad when Greta went back to London, because her staying there had been a strain on me.

When we'd been there a couple of weeks we were accepted locally and made the acquaintance of God. He came one afternoon to call upon us. Ellie and I were arguing about where we'd have a flower border when our correct, to me slightly phoney-looking, manservant came out from the house to announce that Major Phillpot was in the drawing-room. It was then that I said in a whisper to Ellie: 'God!' Ellie asked me what I meant.

'Well, the locals treat him like that,' I said.

So we went in and there was Major Phillpot. He was just a pleasant, nondescript man of close on sixty. He was wearing country clothes, rather shabby, he had grey hair going a little thin on top and a short bristly moustache. He apologized for his wife not being able to come and call on us. She was something of an invalid, he said. He sat down and chatted with us. Nothing he said was remarkable or particularly interesting. He had the knack of making people feel at their ease. He touched quite lightly on a variety of subjects. He didn't ask any direct questions, but he soon got it into his head where our particular interests lay. He talked to me about racing and to Ellie about making a garden and what things did well in this particular soil. He had been to the States once or twice. He found out that though Ellie didn't care much for race meetings, she was fond of riding. He told her that if she was going to keep horses she could go up a particular track through the pine woods and she would come out on a good stretch of moor where she could have a gallop. Then we came to the subject of our house and the stories about Gipsy's Acre.

'I see you know the local name,' he said, 'and all the local superstitions, too, I expect.'

'Gipsies' warnings in profusion,' I said. 'Far too many of them. Mostly old Mrs Lee.'

'Oh dear,' said Phillpot. 'Poor old Esther: she's been a nuisance, has she?'

'Is she a bit dotty?' I asked.

'Not so much as she likes to make out. I feel more or less responsible for her. I settled her in that cottage,' he said, 'not that she's grateful for it. I'm fond of the old thing though she can be a nuisance sometimes.'

'Fortune-telling?'

'No, not particularly. Why, has she told your fortune?'

'I don't know if you can call it a fortune,' said Ellie. 'It was more a warning to us against coming here.'

'That seems rather odd to me.' Major Phillpot's rather bristly eyebrows rose. 'She's usually got a honeyed tongue in fortunes. Handsome stranger, marriage bells, six children and a heap of good fortune and money in your hand, pretty lady.' He imitated rather unexpectedly the gipsy whine of her voice. 'The gipsies used to camp here a lot when I was a boy,' he said. 'I suppose I got fond of them then, though they were a thieving lot, of course. But I've always been attracted to them. As long as you don't expect them to be law-abiding, they're all right. Many a tin mug of gipsy stew I've had as a schoolboy. We felt the family owed Mrs Lee something, she saved the life of a brother of mine when he was a child. Fished him out of a pond when he'd gone through the ice.'

I made a clumsy gesture and knocked a glass ashtray off a table. It smashed into fragments.

I picked up the pieces and Major Phillpot helped me.

'I expect Mrs Lee's quite harmless really,' said Ellie. 'I was very foolish to have been so scared.'

'Scared, were you?' His eyebrows rose again. 'It was as bad as that, was it?'

'I don't wonder she was afraid,' I said quickly. 'It was almost more like a threat than a warning.'

'A threat!' He sounded incredulous.

'Well, it sounded that way to me. And then the first night we moved in here something else happened.'

I told him about the stone crashing through the window.

'I'm afraid there are a good many young hooligans about nowadays,' he said, 'though we haven't got many of them round here – not nearly as bad as some places. Still, it happens, I'm sorry to say.' He looked at Ellie. 'I'm very sorry you were frightened. It was a beastly thing to happen, your first night moving in.'

'Oh, I've got over it now,' said Ellie. 'It wasn't only that, it was – it was something else that happened not long afterwards.'

I told him about that too. We had come down one morning and we had found a dead bird skewered through with a knife and a small piece of paper with it which said in an illiterate scrawl, 'Get out of here if you know what's good for you.'

Phillpot looked really angry then. He said, 'You should have reported that to the police.'

'We didn't want to,' I said. 'After all, that would only have put whoever it is even more against us.'

'Well, that kind of thing has got to be stopped,' said Phillpot. Suddenly he became the magistrate. 'Otherwise, you know, people will go on with the thing. Think it's funny, I suppose. Only – only this sounds a bit more than fun. Nasty – malicious – It's not,' he said, rather as though he was talking to himself, 'it's not as though anyone round here could have a grudge against you, a grudge against either of you personally, I mean.'

'No,' I said, 'it couldn't be that because we're both strangers here.'

'I'll look into it,' Phillpot said.

He got up to go, looking round him as he did.

'You know,' he said, 'I like this house of yours. I didn't think I should. I'm a bit of an old square, you know, what used to be called old fogey. I like old houses and old buildings. I don't like all these matchbox factories that are going up all over the country. Big boxes. Like beehives. I like buildings with some ornament on them, some grace. But I like this house. It's plain and very modern, I suppose, but it's got shape and light. And when you look out from it you see things – well, in a different way from the way you've seen them before. It's interesting. Very interesting. Who designed it? An English architect or a foreigner?'

I told him about Santonix.

'Mm,' he said, 'I think I read about him somewhere. Would it have been in *House and Garden*?'

I said he was fairly well known.

'I'd like to meet him sometime, though I don't suppose I'd know what to say to him. I'm not artistic.'

Then he asked us to settle a day to come and have lunch with him and his wife.

'You can see how you like my house,' he said.

'It's an old house, I suppose?' I said.

'Built 1720. Nice period. The original house was Elizabethan. That was burnt down about 1700 and a new one built on the same spot.'

'You've always lived here then?' I said. I didn't mean him personally, of course, but he understood.

'Yes. We've been here since Elizabethan times. Sometimes prosperous, sometimes down and out, selling land when things have gone badly, buying it back when things went well. I'll be glad to show it to you both,' he said, and looking at Ellie he said with a smile, 'Americans like old houses, I know. *You're* the one who probably won't think much of it,' he said to me.

'I won't pretend I know much about old things,' I said.

He stumped off then. In his car there was a spaniel waiting for him. It was a battered old car with the paint rubbed off, but I was getting my values by now. I knew that in this part of the world he was still God all right, and he'd set the seal of his approval on us. I could see that. He liked Ellie. I was inclined to think that he'd liked me, too, although I'd noticed the appraising glances which he shot over me from time to time, as though he was making a quick snap judgment on something he hadn't come across before.

Ellie was putting splinters of glass carefully in the waste-paper basket when I came back into the drawing-room.

'I'm sorry it's broken,' she said regretfully. 'I liked it.'

'We can get another like it,' I said. 'It's modern.'

'I know! What startled you, Mike?'

I considered for a moment.

'Something Phillpot said. It reminded me of something that happened when I was a kid. A pal of mine at school and I played truant and went out skating on a local pond. Ice wouldn't bear us, silly little asses that we were. He went through and was drowned before anyone could get him out.'

'How horrible.'

'Yes. I'd forgotten all about it until Phillpot mentioned about his own brother.'

'I like him, Mike, don't you?'

'Yes, very much. I wonder what his wife is like.'

We went to lunch with the Phillpots early the following week. It was a white Georgian house, rather beautiful in its lines, though not particularly exciting. Inside it was shabby but comfortable. There were pictures of what I took to be ancestors on the walls of the long dining-room. Most of them were pretty bad, I thought, though they might have looked better if they had been cleaned. There was one of a fair-haired girl in pink satin that I rather took to. Major Phillpot smiled and said:

'You've picked one of our best. It's a Gainsborough, and a good one, though the subject of it caused a bit of trouble in her time. Strongly suspected of having poisoned her husband. May have been prejudice, because she was a foreigner. Gervase Phillpot picked her up abroad somewhere.'

A few other neighbours had been invited to meet us. Dr Shaw, an elderly man with a kindly but tired manner. He had to rush away before we had finished our meal. There was the Vicar who was young and earnest, and a middle-aged woman with a bullying voice who bred corgis. And there was a tall handsome dark girl called Claudia Hardcastle who seemed to live for horses, though hampered by having an allergy which gave her violent hay fever.

She and Ellie got on together rather well. Ellie adored riding and she too was troubled by an allergy.

'In the States it's mostly ragwort gives it to me,' she said – 'but horses too, sometimes. It doesn't trouble me much nowadays because they have such wonderful things that doctors can give you for different kinds of allergies. I'll give you some of my capsules. They're bright orange. And if you remember to take one before you start out you don't as much as sneeze once.'

Claudia Hardcastle said that would be wonderful.

'Camels do it to me worse than horses,' she said. 'I was in Egypt last year – and the tears just streamed down my face all the way round the Pyramids.'

Ellie said some people got it with cats.

'And pillows.' They went on talking about allergies.

I sat next to Mrs Phillpot who was tall and willowy and talked exclusively about her health in the intervals of eating a hearty meal. She gave me a full account of all her various ailments and of how puzzled many eminent members of the medical profession had been by her case. Occasionally she made a social diversion and asked me what I *did*. I parried that one, and she made half-hearted efforts to find out whom I *knew*. I could have answered truthfully 'Nobody,' but I thought it would be well to refrain – especially as she wasn't a real snob and didn't really want to know. Mrs Corgi, whose proper name I hadn't caught, was much more thorough in her queries but I diverted her to the general iniquity and ignorance of vets! It was all quite pleasant and peaceful, if rather dull.

Later, as we were making a rather desultory tour of the garden, Claudia Hardcastle joined me.

She said, rather abruptly, 'I've heard about you – from my brother.'

I looked surprised. I couldn't imagine it to be possible that I knew a brother of Claudia Hardcastle's.

'Are you sure?' I said.

She seemed amused.

'As a matter of fact, he built your house.'

'Do you mean *Santonix* is your brother?'

'Half-brother. I don't know him very well. We rarely meet.'

'He's wonderful,' I said.

'Some people think so, I know.'

'Don't you?'

'I'm never sure. There are two sides to him. At one time he was going right down the hill . . . People wouldn't have anything to do with him. And then – he seemed to change. He began to succeed in his profession in the most extraordinary way. It was as though he was –' she paused for a word – 'dedicated.'

'I think he is – just that.'

Then I asked her if she had seen our house.

'No – not since it was finished.'

I told her she must come and see it.

'I shan't like it, I warn you. I don't like modern houses. Queen Anne is my favourite period.'

She said she was going to put Ellie up for the golf club. And they were going to ride together. Ellie was going to buy a horse, perhaps more than one. She and Ellie seemed to have made friends.

When Phillpot was showing me his stables he said a word or two about Claudia.

'Good rider to hounds,' he said. 'Pity she's mucked up her life.'

'Has she?'

'Married a rich man, years older than herself. An American. Name of

Lloyd. It didn't take. Came apart almost at once. She went back to her own name. Don't think she'll ever marry again. She's anti man. Pity.'

When we were driving home, Ellie said: 'Dull – but nice. Nice people. We're going to be very happy here, aren't we, Mike?'

I said: 'Yes, we are.' And took my hand from the steering wheel and laid it over hers.

When we got back, I dropped Ellie at the house, and put away the car in the garage.

As I walked back to the house, I heard a faint twanging of Ellie's guitar. She had a rather beautiful old Spanish guitar that must have been worth a lot of money. She used to sing to it in a soft low crooning voice. Very pleasant to hear. I didn't know what most of the songs were. American spirituals partly, I think, and some old Irish and Scottish ballads – sweet and rather sad. They weren't pop music or anything of that kind. Perhaps they were folk songs.

I went round by the terrace and paused by the window before going in.

Ellie was singing one of my favourites. I don't know what it was called. She was crooning the words softly to herself, bending her head down over the guitar and gently plucking the strings. It had a sweet-sad haunting little tune.

> *Man was made for Joy and Woe*
> *And when this we rightly know*
> *Thro' the World we safely go . . .*
>
> *Every Night and every Morn*
> *Some to Misery are born.*
> *Every Morn and every Night*
> *Some are born to Sweet Delight,*
> *Some are born to Sweet Delight,*
> *Some are born to Endless Night . . .*

She looked up and saw me.

'Why are you looking at me like that, Mike?'

'Like what?'

'You're looking at me as though you loved me . . .'

'Of course I love you. How else should I be looking at you?'

'But what were you thinking just then?'

I answered slowly and truthfully: 'I was thinking of you as I saw you first – standing by a dark fir tree.' Yes, I'd been remembering that first moment of seeing Ellie, the surprise of it and the excitement . . .

Ellie smiled at me and sang softly:

'*Every Morn and every Night*
Some are born to Sweet Delight,
Some are born to Sweet Delight,
Some are born to Endless Night.'

One doesn't recognize in one's life the really important moments – not until it's too late.

That day when we'd been to lunch with the Phillpots and came back so happily to our home was such a moment. But I didn't know then – not until afterwards.

I said: 'Sing the song about the Fly.' And she changed to a gay little dance tune and sang:

'*Little Fly,*
Thy Summer's play
My thoughtless hand
Has brushed away.

Am not I
A fly like thee?
Or art not thou
A man like me?

For I dance
And drink, and sing
Till some blind hand
Shall brush my wing.

If thought is life
And strength and breath
And the want
Of thought is death;

Then am I
A happy fly
If I live
Or if I die.'

Oh, Ellie – Ellie . . .

CHAPTER 15

It's astonishing in this world how things don't turn out at all the way you expect them to!

We'd moved into our house and were living there and we'd got away from everyone just the way I'd meant and planned. Only of course we *hadn't* got away from everyone. Things crowded back upon us across the ocean and in other ways.

First of all there was Ellie's blasted stepmother. She sent letters and cables and asked Ellie to go and see estate agents. She'd been so fascinated, she said, by our house that she really must have a house of her own in England. She said she'd love to spend a couple of months every year in England. And hard on her last cable she arrived and had to be taken round the neighbourhood with lots of orders to view. In the end she more or less settled on a house. A house about fifteen miles away from us. We didn't want her there, we hated the idea – but we couldn't tell her so. Or rather, what I really mean is even if we *had* told her so, it wouldn't have stopped her taking it if she'd wanted to. We couldn't order her *not* to come there. It was the last thing Ellie wanted. I knew that. However, while she was still awaiting a surveyor's report, some cables arrived.

Uncle Frank, it seemed, had got himself into a jam of some kind. Something crooked and fraudulent, I gathered, which would mean a big sum of money to get him out. More cables passed to and fro between Mr Lippincott and Ellie. And then there turned out to be some trouble between Stanford Lloyd and Lippincott. There was a row about some of Ellie's investments. I had felt, in my ignorance and credulity, that people who were in America were a long way away. I'd never realized that Ellie's relations and business connections thought nothing of taking a plane over to England for twenty-four hours and then flying back again. First Stanford Lloyd flew over and back again. Then Andrew Lippincott flew over.

Ellie had to go up to London and meet them. I hadn't got the hang of these financial things. I think everybody was being fairly careful in what they said. But it was something to do with the settling up of the trusts on Ellie, and a kind of sinister suggestion that either Mr Lippincott had delayed the matter or it was Stanford Lloyd who was holding up the accounting.

In the lull between these worries Ellie and I discovered our Folly. We hadn't really explored all our property yet (only the part just round the house). We used to follow up tracks through the woods and see where they led. One day we followed a sort of path that had been so overgrown that you couldn't really see where it was at first. But we tracked it out and in the end it came out at what Ellie said was a Folly. A sort of little white ridiculous temple-looking place. It was in fairly good condition so we cleared it up and had it painted and we put a table, and a few chairs in it, and a divan and a corner cupboard in which we put china and glasses, and some bottles. It was fun really. Ellie said we'd have the path cleared and made easier to climb and I said no, it would be more fun if no one knew where it was except us. Ellie thought that was a romantic idea.

'We certainly won't let Cora know,' I said and Ellie agreed.

It was when we were coming down from there, not the first time but later, after Cora had gone away and we were hoping to be peaceful again, that Ellie, who was skipping along ahead of me, suddenly tripped over the root of a tree and fell and sprained her ankle.

Dr Shaw came and said she'd taken a nasty sprain but that she'd be able to get about again all right in perhaps a week. Ellie sent for Greta then. I couldn't object. There was no one really to look after her properly, no woman I mean. The servants we had were pretty useless and anyway Ellie wanted Greta. So Greta came.

She came and she was a great blessing of course to Ellie. And to me as far as that went. She arranged things and kept the household working properly. Our servants gave notice about now. They said it was too lonely – but really I think Cora had upset them. Greta put in advertisements and got another couple almost at once. She looked after Ellie's ankle, amused her, fetched things for her that she knew she liked, the kind of books and fruit and things like that – things I knew nothing about. And they seemed frightfully happy together. Ellie was certainly delighted to see Greta. And somehow or other Greta just didn't go away again . . . She stopped on. Ellie said to me:

'You don't mind, do you, if Greta stays on for a bit?'

I said, 'Oh no. No, of course not.'

'It's such a comfort having her,' said Ellie. 'You see, there are so many sort of *female* things we can do together. One's awfully lonely without another woman about.'

Every day I noticed Greta was taking a bit more upon herself, giving orders, queening it over things. I pretended I liked having Greta there, but one day when Ellie was lying with her foot up inside the drawing-room and Greta and I were out on the terrace, we suddenly got into a row together. I can't remember the exact words that started it. Something that Greta said, it annoyed me and I answered sharply back. And then we went on, hammer and tongs. Our voices rose. She let me have it, saying all the vicious, unkind things she could think of, and I pretty well gave her as good as I was getting. Told her she was a bossy, interfering female, that she'd far too much influence over Ellie, that I wasn't going to stand having Ellie bossed about the whole time. We shouted at each other and then suddenly Ellie came hobbling out on the terrace looking from one to the other of us, and I said:

'Darling, I'm sorry. I'm terribly sorry.'

I went back into the house and settled Ellie on the sofa again. She said:

'I didn't realize. I didn't realize a bit that you – that you really hated having Greta here.'

I soothed her and calmed her and said she mustn't take any notice, that I just lost my temper, that I was rather quarrelsome sometimes. I said all that was the matter was that I thought Greta was just a bit bossy. Perhaps that was natural enough because she'd been used to being so. And in the end I said I really liked Greta very much, it was just that I'd lost my temper because I'd been upset and worried. So it ended that I practically begged Greta to stay on.

It was quite a scene we'd had. I think quite a good many other people in the house had heard it as well. Our new manservant and his wife certainly did. When I get angry I do shout. I dare say I really overdid it a bit. I'm like that.

Greta seemed to make a point of worrying a great deal about Ellie's health, saying she oughtn't to do this, or that.

'She isn't really very strong, you know,' she said to me.

'There's nothing wrong with Ellie,' I said, 'she's always perfectly well.'

'No, she isn't, Mike. She's delicate.'

When Dr Shaw next came to have a look at Ellie's ankle and to tell her, by the way, that it was quite all right again, just bind it up if she was going to walk over rough ground, I said to him, I suppose in rather the foolish way that men do:

'She isn't delicate or anything, is she, Dr Shaw?'

'Who says she's delicate?' Dr Shaw was the kind of practitioner that is fairly rare nowadays and was, indeed, known locally as 'Leave-it-to-Nature Shaw'.

'Nothing wrong with her as far as I can see,' he said. 'Anyone can sprain an ankle.'

'I didn't mean her ankle. I wondered if she had a weak heart or anything like that.'

He looked at me through the top of his spectacles. 'Don't start imagining things, young man. What put it into your head? You're not the type that worries usually about women's ailments.'

'It was only what Miss Andersen said.'

'Ah. Miss Andersen. What does she know about it? Not medically qualified, is she?'

'Oh no,' I said.

'Your wife's a woman of great wealth,' he said, 'according to local gossip anyway. Of course some people just imagine all Americans are rich.'

'She is wealthy,' I said.

'Well, you must remember this. Rich women get the worst of it in many ways. Some doctor or other is always giving them powders and pills, stimulants or pep pills, or tranquillizers, things that on the whole they'd be better without. Now the village women are much healthier because nobody worries about their health in the same way.'

'She does take some capsules or something,' I said.

'I'll give her a check-up if you like. Might as well find out what muck she's been given. I can tell you, before now I've said to people "chuck the whole lot in the wastepaper basket".'

He spoke to Greta before he left. He said:

'Mr Rogers asked me to give Mrs Rogers a general check-up. I can't find anything much wrong with her. I think more exercise in the open air might do her good. What does she take in the way of medicines?'

'She has some tablets that she takes when she's tired, and some that she takes for sleeping if she wants them.'

She and Dr Shaw went and had a look at Ellie's prescriptions. Ellie was smiling a little.

'I don't take all these things, Dr Shaw,' she said. 'Only the allergy capsules.'

Shaw took a look at the capsules, read the prescription and said there was no harm in that, and passed on to a prescription for sleeping pills.

'Any trouble with sleeping?'

'Not living in the country. I don't think I've taken a single sleeping pill since I've been here.'

'Well, that's a good thing.' He patted her on the shoulder. 'There's nothing wrong with you, my dear. Inclined to worry a bit sometimes, I should say. That's all. These capsules are mild enough. Lots of people take them nowadays and they don't do them any harm. Go on with them but leave the sleeping pills alone.'

'I don't know why I worried,' I said to Ellie apologetically. 'I suppose it was Greta.'

'Oh,' said Ellie and laughed, 'Greta fusses about me. She never takes any remedies herself.' She said, 'We'll have a turn-out, Mike, and throw most of these things away.'

Ellie was getting on very friendly terms with most of our neighbours now. Claudia Hardcastle came over quite often and she and Ellie went riding together occasionally. I didn't ride, I'd dealt with cars and mechanical things all my life. I didn't know the first thing about a horse in spite of mucking out stables in Ireland for a week or two once, but I thought to myself that some time or other when we were in London I'd go to a posh riding stable and learn how to ride properly. I didn't want to start down here. People would laugh at me very likely. I thought riding was perhaps good for Ellie. She seemed to enjoy it.

Greta encouraged her to ride, although Greta herself also knew nothing about horses.

Ellie and Claudia went together to a sale and on Claudia's advice Ellie bought herself a horse, a chestnut called Conquer. I urged Ellie to be careful when she went out riding by herself but she laughed at me.

'I've ridden since I was three years old,' she said.

So she usually went for a ride about two or three times a week. Greta used to drive the car and go into Market Chadwell to do the shopping.

One day Greta said at lunchtime: 'You and your gipsies! There was a terrible-looking old woman this morning. She stood in the middle of the road. I might have run over her. Just stood smack in front of the car. I had to pull up. Coming up the hill too.'

'Why, what did she want?'

Ellie was listening to us both but she didn't say anything. I thought, though, that she looked rather worried.

'Damn' cheek, she threatened me,' said Greta.

'Threatened you?' I said sharply.

'Well, she told me to get out of here. She said: "This is gipsy land here. Go back. Go back the lot of you. Go back to where you came from if you wish to be safe." And she lifted up her fist and shook it at me. She said: "If I curse you," she said, "there'll be no good luck for you ever again. Buying our land and raising houses on our land. We don't want houses where tent dwellers should be."'

Greta said a lot more. Ellie said to me afterwards, frowning a little:

'It all sounded most improbable, didn't you think so, Mike?'

'I think Greta was exaggerating a bit,' I said.

'It didn't sound right somehow,' said Ellie. 'I wonder if Greta was making some of it up.'

I considered. 'Why would she want to make things up?' Then I asked sharply, '*You* haven't seen our Esther lately, have you? Not when you are out riding?'

'The gipsy woman? No.'

'You don't sound quite sure, Ellie,' I said.

'I think I've caught glimpses of her,' said Ellie. 'You know, standing among the trees peering out but never near enough for me to be sure.'

But Ellie came back from a ride one day, white and shaking. The old woman had come out from in between the trees. Ellie had reined up and stopped to speak to her. She said the old woman was shaking her fist and muttering under her breath. Ellie said, 'This time I was angry, I said to her:

"What do you want here? This land doesn't belong to you. It's our land and our house."'

The old woman had said then:

'It'll never be your land and it'll never belong to you. I warned you once and I've warned you twice. I shan't warn you again. It won't be long now – I can tell you that. It's Death I see. There behind your left shoulder. It's Death standing by you and it's Death will have you. That horse you're riding has got one white foot. Don't you know that it's bad luck to ride a horse with one white foot? It's Death I see and the grand house you've built falling in ruins!'

'This has got to be stopped,' I said angrily.

Ellie didn't laugh it off this time. Both she and Greta looked upset. I went straight down to the village. I went first to Mrs Lee's cottage. I hesitated for a moment but there was no light there and I went on to the police station. I knew the Sergeant in Charge, Sergeant Keene, a square, sensible man. He listened to me, then he said:

'I'm sorry you've had this trouble. She's a very old woman and she may be getting tiresome. We've never had much real trouble with her up to now. I'll speak to her and tell her to lay off.'

'If you would,' I said.

He hesitated a minute and then said:

'I don't like to suggest things – but as far as you know, Mr Rogers, is there anyone around here who might – perhaps for some trivial cause – have it in for you or your wife?'

'I should think it most unlikely. Why?'

'Old Mrs Lee has been flush of money lately – I don't know where it's coming from –'

'What are you suggesting?'

'It could be someone is paying her – someone who wants you out of here. There was an incident – a good many years ago. She took money from someone in the village – to frighten a neighbour away. Doing this same sort of stuff – threats – warnings – evil eye business – Village people are superstitious. You'd be surprised at the number of villages in England that have got their private witch, so to speak. She got a warning then and so far as I know she's never tried it on since – but it could be like that. She's fond of money – they'll do a lot for money –'

But I couldn't accept that idea. I pointed out to Keene that we were complete strangers here. 'We've not had time to make enemies,' I said.

I walked back to the house worried and perplexed. As I turned the corner of the terrace, I heard the faint sound of Ellie's guitar, and a tall figure, who had been standing by the window looking in, wheeled round and came towards me. For a moment I thought it was a gipsy, then I relaxed as I recognized Santonix.

'Oh,' I said with a slight gasp, 'it's you. Where have you sprung from? We've not heard from you for ages.'

He didn't answer me directly. He just caught my arm and drew me away from the window.

'So she's here!' he said. 'I'm not surprised. I thought she'd come sooner or later. Why did you let her? She's dangerous. You ought to know that.'

'You mean Ellie?'

'No, no, not Ellie. The other one! What's her name? Greta?'

I stared at him.

'Do you know what Greta's like or don't you? She's *come*, hasn't she? Taken possession! You won't get rid of her now. She's come to *stay*.'

'Ellie sprained her ankle,' I said. 'Greta came to look after her. She's – I suppose she's going soon.'

'You don't know anything of the kind. She always meant to come. I knew that. I took her measure when she came down while the house was building.'

'Ellie seems to want her,' I muttered.

'Oh yes, she's been with Ellie some time, hasn't she? She knows how to manage Ellie.'

That was what Lippincott had said. I'd seen for myself lately how true it was.

'Do you want her here, Mike?'

'I can't throw her out of the house,' I said irritably. 'She's Ellie's old friend. Her best friend. What the hell can I do about it?'

'No,' said Santonix, 'I suppose you can't do anything, can you?'

He looked at me. It was a very strange glance. Santonix was a strange man. You never knew what his words really meant.

'Do you know where you're going, Mike?' he said. 'Have you any idea? Sometimes I don't think you know anything at all.'

'Of course I know,' I said. 'I'm doing what I want to. I'm going where I wanted.'

'Are you? I wonder. I wonder if you really know what you want yourself. I'm afraid for you with Greta. She's stronger than you are, you know.'

'I don't see how you make that out. It isn't a question of strength.'

'Isn't it? I think it is. She's the strong kind, the kind that always gets her way. You didn't mean to have her here. That's what you said. But here she is, and I've been watching them. She and Ellie sitting together, at home together, chattering and settled in. What are *you*, Mike? The outsider? Or aren't you an outsider?'

'You're crazy, the things you say. What do you mean – I'm an outsider? I'm Ellie's husband, aren't I?'

'*Are* you Ellie's husband or is Ellie *your* wife?'

'You're daft,' I said. 'What's the difference?'

He sighed. Suddenly, his shoulders sagged as though vigour went out of him.

'I can't reach you,' said Santonix. 'I can't make you hear me. I can't make you understand. Sometimes I think you do understand, sometimes I think you don't know anything at all about yourself or anyone else.'

'Look here,' I said, 'I'll take so much from you, Santonix. You're a wonderful architect – but –'

His face changed in the queer way it had.

'Yes,' he said, 'I'm a good architect. This house is the best thing I have done. I'm as near as possible satisfied with it. You wanted a house like this. And Ellie wanted a house like this, too, to live in with you. She's got it and you've got it. Send that other woman away, Mike, before it's too late.'

'How can I upset Ellie?'

'That woman's got you where she wants you,' said Santonix.

'Look here,' I said, 'I don't like Greta. She gets on my nerves. The other day I even had a frightful row with her. But none of it's as simple as you think.'

'No, it won't be simple with her.'

'Whoever called this place Gipsy's Acre and said it had a curse on it may have had something,' I said angrily. 'We've got gipsies who jump out from behind trees and shake fists at us and warn us that if we don't get out of here, some awful fate will happen to us. *This place that ought to be good and beautiful.*'

They were queer words to say, those last ones. I said them as though it was somebody else saying them.

'Yes, it should be like that,' said Santonix. 'It should be. But it can't be, can it, if there is something evil possessing it?'

'You don't believe, surely, in –'

'There are many queer things I believe . . . I know something about evil. Don't you realize, haven't you often felt, that *I* am partly evil myself? Always have been. That's why I know when it's near me, although I don't always know exactly where it is . . . *I want the house I built purged of evil.* You understand that?' His tone was menacing. 'You understand that? It matters to me.'

Then his whole manner changed.

'Come on,' he said, 'don't let's talk a lot of nonsense. Let's come in and see Ellie.'

So we went in through the window and Ellie greeted Santonix with enormous pleasure.

Santonix showed all his normal manner that evening. There were no more histrionics, he was his own self, charming, light-hearted. He talked mostly to Greta, giving her as it were the special benefit of his charm. And he had a lot of charm. Anyone would have sworn that he was impressed by her, that he liked her, that he was anxious to please her. It made me feel that Santonix was really a dangerous man, there was a great deal more to him than I had ever glimpsed.

Greta always responded to admiration. She showed herself at her best. She could on occasion dim her beauty or else reveal it and tonight she looked as beautiful as I'd ever seen her. Smiling at Santonix, listening to him as though spellbound. I wondered what lay behind his manner. You never knew with Santonix. Ellie said she hoped he was staying for several days but he shook his head. He had to leave on the following day, he said.

'Are you building something now, are you busy?'

He said no, he'd just come out of hospital.

'They've patched me up once more,' he said, 'but it's probably for the last time.'

'Patched you up? What do they do to you?'

'Drain the bad blood out of my body and put some good, fresh red blood in,' he said.

'Oh.' Ellie gave a little shudder.

'Don't worry,' said Santonix, 'it will never happen to you.'

'But why has it got to happen to you?' said Ellie. 'It's cruel.'

'Not cruel, no,' said Santonix. 'I heard what you were singing just now.

'Man was made for Joy and Woe
And when this we rightly know
Thro' the World we safely go.

'I go safely because I know why I'm here. And for you, Ellie:

'Every Morn and every Night
Some are born to Sweet Delight.

'That's *you.*'

'I wish I could feel safe,' said Ellie.

'Don't you feel safe?'

'I don't like to be threatened,' said Ellie. 'I don't like anyone to put a curse on me.'

'You're talking about your gipsy?'

'Yes.'

'Forget it,' said Santonix. 'Forget it for tonight. Let's be happy. Ellie – your health – Long life to you – and a quick and merciful end to me – and good luck to Mike here –' He stopped, his glass raised towards Greta.

'Yes?' said Greta. 'And to me?'

'And to you, what's coming to you! Success, perhaps?' he added, half quizzically with an ironic question in his tone.

He went away next morning early.

'What a strange man he is,' Ellie said. 'I've never understood him.'

'I never understand half of what he says,' I answered.

'He knows things,' said Ellie thoughtfully.

'You mean he knows the future?'

'No,' said Ellie, 'I didn't mean that. He knows people. I said it to you once before. He knows people better than they know themselves. Sometimes he hates them because of that, and sometimes he's sorry for them. He's not sorry for me, though,' she added meditatively.

'Why should he be?' I demanded.

'Oh, because –' said Ellie.

CHAPTER 16

It was the next day in the afternoon that as I was walking rather rapidly in the darkest part of the wood where the shade of the pine trees was more menacing than anywhere else, I saw the figure of a tall woman standing in the drive. I took a quick impulsive step off the path. I'd taken it for granted that she was our gipsy but I stopped in sudden recoil when I saw who it actually was. It was my mother. She stood there tall and grim and grey-haired.

'Good Lord,' I said, 'you startled me, Mum. What are you doing here? Come to see us? We've asked you often enough, haven't we?'

We hadn't actually. I'd extended one rather lukewarm invitation, that was all. I'd put it, too, in a way which made it pretty sure that my mother wouldn't accept. I didn't want her here. I'd never wanted her here.

'You're right,' she said. 'I've come to see you at last. To see all's well with you. So this is the grand house you've built, and it is a grand house,' she said, looking over my shoulder.

I thought I detected in her voice the disapproving acidity that I'd expected to find.

'Too grand for the likes of me, eh?' I said.

'I didn't say that, lad.'

'But you thought it.'

'It wasn't what you were born to, and no good comes from getting out of your station in life.'

'Nobody'd ever get anywhere if they listened to you.'

'Aye, I know that's what you say and think, but I don't know what good ambition's ever done to anybody. It's the kind of thing that turns to dead-sea fruit in your mouth.'

'Ah, for God's sake don't croak,' I said. 'Come on. Come along up to see our grand house for yourself and turn up your nose at it. And come and see my grand wife, too, and turn up your nose at her if you dare.'

'Your wife? I've seen her already.'

'What do you mean, you've seen her already?' I demanded.

'So she didn't tell you, eh?'

'What?' I demanded.

'That she came to see me.'

'She came to see you?' I asked, dumbfounded.

'Yes. There she was one day standing outside the door, ringing the bell and looking a little scared. She's a pretty lass and a sweet one for all the fine clothes she had on. She said, "You're Mike's mother, aren't you?" and I said, "Yes, and who are you?" and she said, "I'm his wife." She said, "I had to come to see you. It didn't seem right that I shouldn't know Mike's mother . . ." And I said, "I bet *he* didn't want you to" and she hesitated, and I said: "You don't need to mind telling me that. I know my boy and I know what he'd want or not want." She said, "You think – perhaps he's ashamed of you because he and you are poor and I'm rich, but it isn't like that at all. That isn't like him at all. It isn't, really it isn't." I said again, "You don't need to tell me, lass. I know what faults my boy has. That's not one of his faults. He's not ashamed of his mother and he's not ashamed of his beginnings.

'"He's not ashamed of me," I said to her. "He's *afraid* of me if anything. I know too much about him, you see." And that seemed to amuse her. She said, "I expect mothers always feel like that – that they know all about their sons. And I expect sons always feel embarrassed just because of that!"

'I said in a way that might be true. When you're young, you're always putting on an act to the world. I mind myself, when I was a child in my auntie's house. On the wall over my bed there was a great big eye in a gilt frame. It said "Thou God seest me." Gave me the creeps it did all up my spine before I went to sleep.'

'Ellie should have told me she'd been to see you,' I said. 'I don't see why she should keep it such a secret. She should have told me.'

I was angry. I was very angry. I'd had no idea that Ellie would keep secrets like that from me.

'She was a little scared of what she'd done, maybe, but she'd no call to be frightened of you, my boy.'

'Come on,' I said, 'come on and see our house.'

I don't know whether she liked our house or not. I think not. She looked round the rooms and raised her eyebrows and then she went into the terrace room. Ellie and Greta were sitting there. They'd just come in from outside and Greta had a scarlet wool cloak half over her shoulders. My mother looked at them both. She just stood there for a moment as though rooted to the spot. Ellie jumped up and came forward and across the room.

'Oh, it's Mrs Rogers,' she said, then turning to Greta, she said, 'It's Mike's mother come to see our house and us. Isn't that nice? This is my friend Greta Andersen.'

And she held out both her hands and took Mum's and Mum looked hard at her and then looked over her shoulder at Greta very hard.

'I see,' she said to herself, 'I see.'

'What do you see?' asked Ellie.

'I wondered,' said Mum. 'I wondered what it would all be like here.' She looked round her. 'Yes, it's a fine house. Fine curtains and fine chairs and fine pictures.'

'You must have some tea,' said Ellie.

'You look as if you've finished tea.'

'Tea's a thing that need never be finished,' said Ellie, then she said to Greta, 'I won't ring the bell. Greta, will you go out to the kitchen and make a fresh pot of tea?'

'Of course, darling,' said Greta and went out of the room looking over her shoulder once in a sharp, almost scared way at my mother.

My mother sat down.

'Where's your luggage?' said Ellie. 'Have you come to stay? I hope you have.'

'No, lass, I won't stay. I'm going back by train in half an hour's time. I just wanted to look in on you.' Then she added rather quickly, probably because she wished to get it out before Greta came back, 'Now don't worry yourself, love, I told him how you came to see me and paid me a visit.'

'I'm sorry, Mike, that I didn't tell you,' said Ellie firmly, 'only I thought perhaps I'd better not.'

'She came out of the kindness of her heart, she did,' said my mother. 'She's a good girl you've married, Mike, and a pretty one. Yes, a very pretty one.' Then she added half audibly, 'I am sorry.'

'Sorry,' said Ellie, faintly puzzled.

'Sorry for thinking the things I did,' said my mother and added with a slight air of strain, 'Well, as you say, mothers are like that. Always inclined to be suspicious of daughters-in-law. But when I saw you, I knew he'd been lucky. It seemed too good to be true to me, that it did.'

'What impertinence,' I said, but I smiled at her as I said it. 'I always had excellent taste.'

'You've always had expensive taste, that's what you mean,' said my mother and looked at the brocade curtains.

'I'm not really the worse for being an expensive taste,' said Ellie, smiling at her.

'You make him save a bit of money from time to time,' said Mum, 'it'll be good for his character.'

'I refuse to have my character improved,' I said. 'The advantage of taking a wife is that the wife thinks everything you do is perfect. Isn't that so, Ellie?'

Ellie was looking happy again now. She laughed and said:

'You're above yourself, Mike! The conceit of you.'

Greta came back then with the teapot. We'd been a little ill at ease and we were just getting over it. Somehow when Greta came back the strain came out again. My mother resisted all endeavours on Ellie's part to make her stay over and Ellie didn't insist after a short while. She and I walked down together with my mother along the winding drive through the trees and to the gateway.

'What do you call it?' my mother asked abruptly.

Ellie said, 'Gipsy's Acre.'

'Ah,' said my mother, 'yes you've got gipsies around here, haven't you?'

'How did you know that?' I asked.

'I saw one as I came up. She looked at me queer, she did.'

'She's all right really,' I said, 'a little half-baked, that's all.'

'Why do you say she's half-baked? She'd a funny look to her when she looked at me. She's got a grievance against you of some kind?'

'I don't think it's real,' said Ellie. 'I think she's imagined it all. That we've done her out of her land or something like that.'

'I expect she wants money,' said my mother. 'Gipsies are like that. Make a big song and dance sometimes of how they've been done down one way or another. But they soon stop when they get some money in their itching palms.'

'You don't like gipsies,' said Ellie.

'They're a thieving lot. They don't work steady and they don't keep their hands off what doesn't belong to them.'

'Oh well,' Ellie said, 'we – we – don't worry any more now.'

My mother said goodbye and then added, 'Who's the young lady that lives with you?'

Ellie explained how Greta had been with her for three years before she married and how but for Greta she would have had a miserable life.

'Greta's done everything to help us. She's a wonderful person,' said Ellie. 'I wouldn't know how – how to get on without her.'

'She's living with you or on a visit?'

'Oh well,' said Ellie. She avoided the question. 'She – she's living with us at present because I sprained my ankle and had to have someone to look after me. But I'm all right again now.'

'Married people do best alone together when they're starting,' my mother said.

We stood by the gate watching my mother march away.

'She's got a very strong personality,' said Ellie thoughtfully.

I was angry with Ellie, really very angry because she'd gone and found out my mother and visited her without telling me. But when she turned and stood looking at me with one eyebrow raised a little and the funny half-timid, half-satisfied little-girl smile on her face, I couldn't help relenting.

'What a deceitful little thing you are,' I said.

'Well,' said Ellie, 'I've had to be sometimes, you see.'

'That's like a Shakespeare play I once saw. They did it at a school I was at.' I quoted self-consciously, '"She has deceiv'd her father and may thee."'

'What did you play – Othello?'

'No,' I said, 'I played the girl's father. That's why I remember that speech, I suppose. It's practically the only thing I had to say.'

'"She has deceiv'd her father and may thee,"' said Ellie thoughtfully. 'I didn't even deceive my father as far as I know. Perhaps I would have later.'

'I don't suppose he would have taken very kindly to your marrying me,' I said, 'any more than your stepmother did.'

'No,' said Ellie, 'I don't suppose he would. He was pretty conventional I think.' Then she gave that funny little-girl smile again. 'So I suppose I'd have had to be like Desdemona and deceived my father and run away with you.'

'Why did you want to see my mother so much, Ellie?' I asked curiously.

'It's not so much I wanted to see her,' said Ellie, 'but I felt terribly bad not doing anything about it. You haven't mentioned your mother very often but I did gather that she's always done everything she could for you. Come to the rescue about things and worked very hard to get you extra schooling and things like that. And I thought it seemed so mean and purse-proud of me not to go near her.'

'Well, it wouldn't have been your fault,' I said, 'it would have been mine.'

'Yes,' said Ellie. 'I can understand that perhaps you didn't want me to go and see her.'

'You think I've got an inferiority complex about my mother? That's not true at all, Ellie, I assure you it isn't. It wasn't that.'

'No,' said Ellie thoughtfully, 'I know that now. It was because you didn't want her to do a lot of mother stuff.'

'Mother stuff?' I queried.

'Well,' said Ellie, 'I can see that she's the kind of person who would know quite well what other people ought to do. I mean, she'd want you to go in for certain kinds of jobs.'

'Quite right,' I said. 'Steady jobs. Settling down.'

'It wouldn't have mattered very much now,' said Ellie. 'I dare say it was very good advice. But it wouldn't have been the right advice ever for *you*, Mike. You're not a settler down. You don't want to be steady. You want to go and see things and do things – be on top of the world.'

'I want to stay here in this house with you,' I said.

'For a while, perhaps . . . And I think – I think you'll always want to come back here. And so shall I. I think we shall come here every year and I think we shall be happier here than anywhere else. But you'll want to go places too. You'll want to travel and see things and buy things. Perhaps think up new plans for doing the garden here. Perhaps we'll go and look at Italian gardens, Japanese gardens, landscape gardens of all kinds.'

'You make life seem very exciting, Ellie,' I said. 'I'm sorry I was cross.'

'Oh, I don't mind your being cross,' said Ellie. 'I'm not afraid of you.' Then she added, with a frown: 'Your mother didn't like Greta.'

'A lot of people don't like Greta,' I said.

'Including you.'

'Now look here, Ellie, you're always saying that. It's not true. I was just a bit jealous of her at first, that was all. We get on very well now.' And I added, 'I think perhaps she makes people get rather on the defensive.'

'Mr Lippincott doesn't like her either, does he? He thinks she's got too much influence over me,' said Ellie.

'Has she?'

'I wonder why you should ask that. Yes, I think perhaps she has. It's only natural, she's rather a dominant personality and I had to have someone I could trust in and rely on. Someone who'd stand up for me.'

'And see you got your own way?' I asked her, laughing.

We went into the house arm in arm. For some reason it seemed dark that afternoon. I suppose because the sun had just left the terrace and left a feeling of darkness behind it. Ellie said:

'What's the matter, Mike?'

'I don't know,' I said. 'Just suddenly I felt as though someone were walking over my grave.'

'A goose is walking over your grave. That's the real saying, isn't it?' said Ellie.

Greta wasn't about anywhere. The servants said she'd gone out for a walk.

Now that my mother knew all about my marriage and had seen Ellie, I did what I had really wanted to do for some time. I sent her a large cheque. I told her to move into a better house and to buy herself any additional furniture she wanted. Things like that. I had doubts of course as to whether she would accept it or not. It wasn't money that I'd worked for and I couldn't honestly pretend it was. As I expected, she sent the cheque back torn in two with a scrawled note. 'I'll have naught to do with any of this,' she wrote. 'You'll never be different. I know that now, heaven help you.' I flung it down in front of Ellie.

'You see what my mother's like,' I said. 'I married a rich girl, and I'm living on my rich wife's money and the old battleaxe disapproves of it!'

'Don't worry,' said Ellie. 'Lots of people think that way. She'll get over it. She loves you very much, Mike,' she added.

'Then why does she want to alter me all the time? Make me into *her* pattern. I'm myself. I'm not anybody else's pattern. I'm not mother's little boy to be moulded the way she likes. I'm *myself*. I'm an adult. I'm *me*!'

'You're you,' said Ellie, 'and I love you.'

And then, perhaps to distract me, she said something rather disquieting.

'What do you think,' she said, 'of this new manservant of ours?'

I hadn't thought about him. What was there to think? If anything I preferred him to our last one who had not troubled to conceal his low opinion of my social status.

'He's all right,' I said. 'Why?'

'I just wondered whether he might be a security man.'

'A security man? What do you mean?'

'A detective. I thought Uncle Andrew might have arranged it.'

'Why should he?'

'Well – possible kidnapping, I suppose. In the States, you know, we usually had guards – especially in the country.'

Another of the disadvantages of having money that I hadn't known about!

'What a beastly idea!'

'Oh, I don't know . . . I suppose I'm used to it. What does it matter? One doesn't really notice.'

'Is the wife in it, too?'

'She'd have to be, I think, though she cooks very well. I should think that Uncle Andrew, or perhaps Stanford Lloyd, whichever one of them thought of it, must have paid our last ones to leave, and had these two all lined up ready to take their place. It would have been quite easy.'

'Without telling you?' I was still incredulous.

'They'd never dream of telling me. I might have kicked up a fuss. Anyway, I may be quite wrong about them.' She went on dreamily. 'It's only that one gets a kind of feeling when one's been used to people of that kind always being around.'

'Poor little rich girl,' I said savagely.

Ellie did not mind at all.

'I suppose that does describe it rather well,' she said.

'The things I'm learning about you all the time, Ellie,' I said.

CHAPTER 17

What a mysterious thing sleep is. You go to bed worrying about gipsies and secret enemies, and detectives planted in your house and the possibilities of kidnapping and a hundred other things; and sleep whisks you away from it all. You travel very far and you don't know where you've been, but when you wake up, it's to a totally new world. No worries, no apprehensions. Instead, when I woke up on the 17th September I was in a mood of boisterous excitement.

'A wonderful day,' I said to myself with conviction. 'This is going to be a wonderful day.' I meant it. I was like those people in advertisements that offer to go anywhere and do anything. I went over plans in my head. I had arranged to meet Major Phillpot at a sale at a country house about fifteen miles away. They had some very nice stuff there and I'd already marked down two or three items in the catalogue. I was quite excited about the whole thing.

Phillpot was very knowledgeable about period furniture and silver and things of that kind, not because he was artistic – he was entirely a sporting man – but simply because he knew. His whole family was knowledgeable.

I looked over the catalogue at breakfast. Ellie had come down in a riding habit. She rode most mornings now – sometimes alone, sometimes with Claudia. She had the American habit of drinking coffee and a glass of orange juice and nothing much else for breakfast. My tastes, now that I hadn't got to restrain them in any way, were very much those of a Victorian squire! I liked lots of hot dishes on the sideboard. I ate kidneys this morning and sausages and bacon as well. Delicious.

'What are you doing, Greta?' I asked.

Greta said she was meeting Claudia Hardcastle at the station at Market Chadwell and they were going up to London to a white sale. I asked what a white sale was.

'Does there really have to be white in it?' I asked.

Greta looked scornful and said that a white sale meant a sale of household linen and blankets and towels and sheets, etc. There were some very good bargains at a special shop in Bond Street of which she had been sent a catalogue.

I said to Ellie, 'Well, if Greta is going to London for the day, why don't you drive in and meet us at the George in Bartington. The food there's very good, so old Phillpot said. He suggested you might come. One o'clock. You go through Market Chadwell and then you take a turning about three miles after that. It's sign-posted, I think.'

'All right,' said Ellie, 'I'll be there.'

I mounted her and she went off riding through the trees. Ellie loved riding. She usually rode up one of the winding tracks and came out on the Downs and had a gallop before returning home. I left the smaller car for Ellie as it was easier to park and took the big Chrysler myself. I got to Bartington Manor just before the sale began. Phillpot was there already and had kept a place for me.

'Some quite nice stuff here,' he said. 'One or two good pictures. A Romney and a Reynolds. I don't know if you're interested?'

I shook my head. My taste at the moment was entirely for modern artists.

'Several dealers here,' Phillpot went on, 'a couple down from London. See that thin man over there with the pinched lips? That's Cressington. Pretty well known. Not brought your wife?'

'No,' I said, 'she's not awfully keen on sales. Anyway, I didn't particularly want her to come this morning.'

'Oh? Why not?'

'There's going to be a surprise for Ellie,' I said. 'Did you notice Lot 42?'

He took a glance at the catalogue and then looked across the room.

'Hm. That *papier mâché* desk? Yes. Rather a beautiful little piece. One of the best examples of *papier mâché* I've seen. Desk rather rare too. Plenty of hand desks to stand on tables. But this is an early example. Never seen one quite like it before.'

The little piece was inlaid with a design of Windsor Castle and the sides of it had bouquets of roses and thistles and shamrock.

'Beautiful condition,' said Phillpot. He looked at me curiously. 'I shouldn't have thought it was your taste but –'

'Oh, it isn't,' I said. 'It's a little too flowery and ladylike for me. But Ellie loves the stuff. It's her birthday next week and I want it as a present for her. A surprise. That's why I didn't want her to know I was bidding for it today. But I know there's nothing I could give her that she'd like more. She'll be really surprised.'

We went in and took seats and the sale began. Actually, the piece I wanted was run up pretty high. Both the London dealers seemed keen on it although one of them was so practised and reserved about it that you could hardly notice the almost infinitesimal motion of his catalogue which the auctioneer was observing closely. I bought a carved Chippendale chair as well which I thought would look well in our hall and some enormous brocade curtains in good condition.

'Well, you seem to have enjoyed yourself all right,' said Phillpot, rising to his feet when the auctioneer completed the morning's sale. 'Want to come back this afternoon?'

I shook my head.

'No, there's nothing in the second half of the sale that I want. Mostly bedroom furniture and carpets and things like that.'

'No, I didn't think you'd be interested. Well –' he looked at his watch, 'we'd better be getting along. Is Ellie meeting us at the George?'

'Yes, she'll be there.'

'And – er – Miss Andersen?'

'Oh, Greta's gone to London,' I said. 'She's gone to what they call a white sale. With Miss Hardcastle, I believe.'

'Oh yes, Claudia said something about it the other day. Price of sheets and things are fantastic nowadays. Do you know what a linen pillow case costs? Thirty-five shillings. Used to buy 'em for six bob.'

'You're very knowledgeable on household purchases,' I said.

'Well, I hear my wife complaining about them.' Phillpot smiled. 'You're looking in the pink of condition, Mike. Happy as a sandboy.'

'That's because I've got the *papier mâché* desk,' I said, 'or at any rate that's partly it. I just woke up feeling happy this morning. You know those days when everything in the world seems right.'

'Mm,' said Phillpot, 'be careful. That's what's known as being fey.'

'Fey?' I said. 'That's something Scottish, isn't it?'

'It comes before disaster, my boy,' said Phillpot. 'Better curb your exuberance.'

'Oh, I don't believe those silly superstitions,' I said.

'Nor in gipsies' prophecies, eh?'

'We haven't seen our gipsy lately,' I said. 'Well, not for a week at least.'

'Perhaps she's away from the place,' said Phillpot.

He asked me if I'd give him a lift in my car and I said I would.

'No use taking the two of them. You can drop me here on your way back, can't you? What about Ellie, will she be bringing her car over?'

'Yes, she's bringing the little one.'

'Hope the George will put on a good meal,' said Major Phillpot. 'I'm hungry.'

'Did you buy anything?' I asked. 'I was too excited to notice.'

'Yes, you've got to keep your wits about you when you're bidding. Have to notice what the dealers are doing. No. I made a bid or two but everything went far above my price.'

I gathered that although Phillpot owned enormous quantities of land round about, his actual income did not amount to much. He was what you might describe as a poor man though a large landowner. Only by selling a good portion of his land would he have had money to spend and he didn't want to sell his land. He loved it.

We got to the George and found a good many cars standing there already. Possibly some of the people from the auction. I didn't see Ellie's though. We went inside and I looked around for her but she hadn't turned up yet. However, it was only just past one.

We went and had a drink at the bar while we were waiting for Ellie to arrive. The place was pretty crowded. I looked into the dining-room but they were still holding our table. There were a good many local faces that I knew and sitting at a table by the window was a man whose face seemed familiar to me. I was sure I knew him but I couldn't remember when and where we'd met. I didn't think he was a local, because his clothes didn't fit in with these parts. Of course I've knocked up against a great many people in my time and it is unlikely that I can remember them all easily. He hadn't been at the sale as far as I could remember, though, oddly enough, there had been one face that I thought I'd recognized but couldn't place. Faces are tricky unless you can connect up when and where you'd seen them.

The presiding goddess of the George, rustling in her usual black silk of affected Edwardian style which she always wore, came to me and said:

'Will you be coming to your table soon, Mr Rogers? There's one or two waiting.'

'My wife will be here in a minute or two,' I said.

I went back to rejoin Phillpot. I thought perhaps that Ellie might have had a puncture.

'We'd better go in,' I said, 'they seem to be getting rather upset about it. They've got quite a crowd today. I'm afraid,' I added, 'that Ellie isn't the most punctual of people.'

'Ah,' said Phillpot in his old-fashioned style, 'the ladies make a point of keeping us waiting, don't they? All right, Mike, if that's all right by you. We'll go in and start lunch.'

We went into the dining-room, chose steak and kidney pie off the menu and started.

'It's too bad of Ellie,' I said, 'to stand us up like this.' I added that it was possibly because Greta was in London. 'Ellie's very used, you know,' I said, 'to Greta helping her to keep appointments, reminding her of them, and getting her off in time and all that.'

'Is she very dependent on Miss Andersen?'

'In that way, yes,' I said.

We went on eating and passed from the steak and kidney pie to apple tart with a self-conscious piece of phoney pastry on top of it.

'I wonder if she's forgotten all about it,' I said suddenly.

'Perhaps you'd better ring up.'

'Yes, I think I'd better.'

I went out to the phone and rang. Mrs Carson, the cook, answered.

'Oh, it's you, Mr Rogers, Mrs Rogers hasn't come home yet.'

'What do you mean, hasn't come home? Home from where?'

'She hasn't come back from her ride yet.'

'But that was after breakfast. She can't have been riding the whole morning.'

'She didn't say anything different. I was expecting her back.'

'Why didn't you ring up sooner and let me know about it?' I asked.

'Well, I wouldn't know where to get at you, you see. I didn't know where you'd gone.'

I told her I was at the George at Bartington and gave her the number. She was to ring up the moment Ellie came in or she had news of her. Then I went back to join Phillpot. He saw from my face at once that something was wrong.

'Ellie hasn't come home,' I said. 'She went off riding this morning. She usually does most mornings but it only lasts half an hour to an hour.'

'Now don't worry before you need to, boy,' he said kindly. 'Your place is in a very lonely part, you know. Maybe her horse went lame and she might be walking it home. All that moorland and downs above the woods. There's nobody much in that part to send a message by.'

'If she decided to change her plans and ride over and see anyone, anything like that,' I said, 'she'd have rung here. She'd have left a message for us.'

'Well, don't get het up yet,' Phillpot said. 'I think we'd better go now, right away, and see what we can find out.'

As we went out to the car park, another car drove away. In it was the man I had noticed in the dining-room and suddenly it came to me who it was. Stanford Lloyd or someone just like him. I wondered what he could be doing down here. Could he be coming to see us? If so, it was odd he hadn't let us know. In the car with him was a woman who had looked like Claudia Hardcastle, but surely she was in London with Greta, shopping. It all floored me rather . . .

As we drove away Phillpot looked at me once or twice. I caught his eye once and said rather bitterly:

'All right. You said I was fey this morning.'

'Well, don't think of that yet. She may have had a fall and sprained an ankle or something like that. She's a good horsewoman, though,' he said. 'I've seen her. I can't feel an accident is really likely.'

I said, 'Accidents can happen at any time.'

We drove fast and came at last to the road over the downs above our property, looking about us as we went. Now and again we stopped to ask people. We stopped a man who was digging peat and there we got the first news.

'Seen a riderless horse I have,' he said. 'Two hours ago maybe or longer. I would-a caught it but it galloped off when I got near it. Didn't see anyone though.'

'Best drive home,' suggested Phillpot, 'there may be news of her there.'

We drove home but there was no news. We got hold of the groom and sent him off to ride the moorland in search of Ellie. Phillpot telephoned his own house and sent a man from there too. He and I went up a path together and through the wood, the one that Ellie often took, and came out on the downs there.

At first there was nothing to be seen. Then we walked along the edge of the wood near where some of the other paths came out and so – we found her. We saw what looked like a huddled heap of clothes. The horse had come back and was now standing cropping near that huddled heap. I began to run. Phillpot followed me faster than I'd have thought a man of his age could have kept up.

She was there – lying in a crumpled-up heap, her little white face turned up to the sky. I said:

'I can't – I can't –' and turned my face away.

Phillpot went and knelt down by her. He got up almost at once.

'We'll get hold of a doctor,' he said. 'Shaw. He's the nearest. But – I don't think it's any use, Mike.'

'You mean – she's dead?'

'Yes,' he said, 'it's no good pretending anything else.'

'Oh God!' I said and turned away. 'I can't believe it. Not Ellie.'

'Here, have this,' said Phillpot.

He took a flask out of his pocket, unscrewed it and handed it to me. I took a good deep pull at it.

'Thanks,' I said.

The groom came along then and Phillpot sent him off to fetch Dr Shaw.

CHAPTER 18

Shaw came up in a battered old Land-Rover. I suppose it was the car he used for going to visit isolated farms in bad weather. He barely looked at either of us. He went straight and bent over Ellie. Then he came over to us.

'She's been dead at least three or four hours,' he said. 'How did it happen?'

I told him how she'd gone off riding as usual after breakfast that morning.

'Has she had any accidents up to this time when she's been out riding?'

'No,' I said, 'she was a good rider.'

'Yes, I know she's a good rider. I've seen her once or twice. She's ridden since she was a child, I understand. I wondered if she might have had an accident lately and that that might have affected her nerve a bit. If the horse had shied –'

'Why should the horse shy? It's a quiet brute –'

'There's nothing vicious about this particular horse,' said Major Phillpot. 'He's well behaved, not nervy. Has she broken any bones?'

'I haven't made a complete examination yet but she doesn't seem physically injured in any way. There may be some internal injury. Might be shock, I suppose.'

'But you can't die of shock,' I said.

'People have died of shock before now. If she'd had a weak heart –'

'They said in America that she had a weak heart – some kind of weakness at least.'

'Hm. I couldn't find much trace of it when I examined her. Still, we didn't have a cardiograph. Anyway no point in going into that now. We shall know later. After the inquest.'

He looked at me consideringly, then he patted me on the shoulder.

'You go home and go to bed,' he said. 'You're the one who's suffering from shock.'

In the queer way people materialize out of nowhere in the country, we had three or four people standing near us, by this time. One a hiker who had come along from the main road seeing our little group, one a rosy-faced woman who I think was going to a farm over a short cut and an old roadman. They were making exclamations and remarks.

'Poor young lady.'

'So young too. Thrown from her horse, was she?'

'Ah well, you never know with horses.'

'It's Mrs Rogers, isn't it, the American lady from The Towers?'

It was not until everyone else had exclaimed in their astonished fashion, that the aged roadman spoke. He gave us information. Shaking his head he said:

'I must-a seen it happen. I must-a seen it happen.'

The doctor turned sharply on him.

'What did you see happen?'

'I saw a horse bolting across country.'

'Did you see the lady fall?'

'No. No, I didn't. She were riding along the top of the woods when I saw her and after that I'd got me back turned and I was cutting the stones for the road. And then I heard hoofs and I looked up and there was the horse a-galloping. I didn't think there'd been an accident. I thought the lady perhaps had got off and let go of the horse in some way. It wasn't coming towards me, it was going in the other direction.'

'You didn't see the lady lying on the ground?'

'No, I don't see very well far. I saw the horse because it showed against the sky line.'

'Was she riding alone? Was there anyone with her, or near her?'

'Nobody near her. No. She was all alone. She rode not very far from me, past me, going along that way. She was bearing towards the woods, I think. No, I didn't see anyone at all except her and the horse.'

'Might have been the gipsy who frightened her,' said the rosy-faced woman.

I swung round.

'What gipsy? When?'

'Oh, must have been – well, it must have been three or four hours ago when I went down the road this morning. About quarter to ten maybe, I saw that gipsy woman. The one as lives in the cottages in the village. Least I think it was she. I wasn't near enough to be sure. But she's the only one as goes about hereabouts in a red cloak. She was walking up a path through the trees. Somebody told me as she'd said nasty things to the poor American young lady. Threatened her. Told her something bad would happen if she didn't get out of this place. Very threatening, I hear she was.'

'The gipsy,' I said. Then, bitterly, to myself, though out loud, 'Gipsy's Acre. I wish I'd never seen the place.'

BOOK III

It's extraordinary how difficult it is for me to remember what happened after that. I mean, the sequence of it all. Up to then, you see, it's all clear in my mind. I was a little doubtful where to begin, that was all. But from then on it was as though a knife fell, cutting my life into two halves. What I went on to from the moment of Ellie's death seems to me now like something for which I was not prepared. A confusion of thrusting people and elements and happenings where I wasn't myself in control of anything any more. Things happened not to me, but all around me. That's what it seemed like.

Everybody was very kind to me. That seems the thing I remember best. I stumbled about and looked dazed and didn't know what to do. Greta, I remember, came into her element. She had that amazing power that women have to take charge of a situation and deal with it. Deal, I mean, with all the small unimportant details that someone has to see to. I would have been incapable of seeing to them.

I think the first thing I remembered clearly after they'd taken Ellie away and I'd got back to my house – our house – *the* house – was when Dr Shaw came along and talked to me. I don't know how long after that was. He was quiet, kind, reasonable. Just explaining things clearly and gently.

Arrangements. I remember his using the word arrangements. What a hateful word it is and all the things it stands for. The things in life that have grand words – Love – sex – life – death – hate – those aren't the things that govern existence at all. It's lots of other pettifogging, degrading things. Things you have to endure, things you never think about until they happen to you. Undertakers, arrangements for funerals, inquests. And servants coming into rooms and pulling the blinds down. Why should blinds be pulled down because Ellie was dead? Of all the stupid things!

That was why, I remember, I felt quite grateful to Dr Shaw. He dealt with such things so kindly and sensibly, explaining gently why certain things like an inquest had to be. Talking rather slowly, I remember, so that he could be quite sure I was taking them in.

I didn't know what an inquest would be like. I'd never been to one. It seemed to me curiously unreal, amateurish. The Coroner was a small fussy little man with pincenez. I had to give evidence of identification, to describe the last time I had seen Ellie at the breakfast table and her departure for her usual morning ride and the arrangement we had made to meet later for lunch. She had seemed, I said, exactly the same as usual, in perfectly good health.

Dr Shaw's evidence was quiet, inconclusive. No serious injuries, a wrenched collar bone and bruises such as would result from a fall from the horse – not of a very serious nature, and inflicted at the time of death. She did not appear to have moved again after she had fallen. Death, he thought, had been practically instantaneous. There was no specific organic injury to have caused death, and he could give no other explanation of it than that she had died from heart failure caused by shock. As far as I could make out from the medical language used Ellie had died simply as a result of absence of breath – of asphyxia of some kind. Her organs were healthy, her stomach contents normal.

Greta, who also gave evidence, stressed rather more forcibly than she had done to Dr Shaw before, that Ellie had suffered from some form of heart malady three or four years ago. She had never heard anything definite mentioned but Ellie's relations had occasionally said that her heart was weak and that she must take care not to over-do things. She had never heard anything more definite than that.

Then we came to the people who had seen or been in the vicinity at the time the accident happened. The old man who had been cutting peat was the first of them. He had seen the lady pass him, she'd been about fifty yards or so away. He knew who she was though he'd never spoken to her. She was the lady from the new house.

'You knew her by sight?'

'No, not exactly by sight but I knew the horse, sir. It's got a white fetlock. Used to belong to Mr Carey over at Shettlegroom. I've never heard it anything but quiet and well behaved, suitable for a lady to ride.'

'Was the horse giving any trouble when you saw it? Playing up in any way?'

'No, it was quiet enough. It was a nice morning.'

There hadn't been many people about, he said. He hadn't noticed many.

That particular track across the moor wasn't much used except as a short cut occasionally to one of the farms. Another track crossed it about a mile farther away. He'd seen one or two passers-by that morning but not to notice. One man on a bicycle, another man walking. They were too far away for him to see who they were and he hadn't noticed much anyway. Earlier, he said, before he'd seen the lady riding, he'd seen old Mrs Lee, or so he thought. She was coming up the track towards him and then she turned off and went into the woods. She often walked across the moors and in and out of the woods.

The Coroner asked why Mrs Lee was not in court. He understood that she'd been summoned to attend. He was told, however, that Mrs Lee had left the village some days ago – nobody knew exactly when. She had not left any address behind. It was not her habit to do so, she often went away and came back without notifying anyone. So there was nothing unusual about this. In fact one or two people said they thought she'd already left the village *before* the day the accident happened. The Coroner asked the old man again.

'You think, however, that it *was* Mrs Lee you saw?'

'Couldn't say, I'm sure. Wouldn't like to be certain. It was a tall woman and striding along, and had on a scarlet cloak, like Mrs Lee wears sometimes. But I didn't look particular. I was busy with what I was doing. Could have been she, it could have been someone else. Who's to say?'

As for the rest he repeated very much what he had said to us. He'd seen the lady riding nearby, he'd often seen her riding before. He hadn't paid any particular attention. Only later did he see the horse galloping alone. It looked as though something had frightened it, he said. 'At least, it could be that way.' He couldn't tell what time that was. Might have been eleven, might have been earlier. He saw the horse much later, farther away. It seemed to be returning towards the woods.

Then the Coroner recalled me and asked me a few more questions about Mrs Lee, Mrs Esther Lee of Vine Cottage.

'You and your wife knew Mrs Lee by sight?'

'Yes,' I said, 'quite well.'

'Did you talk with her?'

'Yes, several times. Or rather,' I added, 'she talked to us.'

'Did she at any time threaten you or your wife?'

I paused a moment or two.

'In a sense she did,' I said slowly, 'but I never thought –'

'You never thought what?'

'I never thought she really meant it,' I said.

'Did she sound as though she had any particular grudge against your wife?'

'My wife said so once. She said she thought she had some special grudge against her but she couldn't see why.'

'Had you or your wife at any time ordered her off your land, threatened her, treated her roughly in any way?'

'Any aggression came from her side,' I said.

'Did you ever have the impression that she was mentally unbalanced?'

I considered. 'Yes,' I said, 'I did. I thought she had come to believe that the land on which we had built our house belonged to her, or belonged to her tribe or whatever they call themselves. She had a kind of obsession about it.' I added slowly, 'I think she was getting worse, more and more obsessed by the idea.'

'I see. She never offered your wife physical violence at any time?'

'No,' I said, slowly, 'I don't think it would be fair to say that. It was all – well all a sort of gipsy's warning stuff. "You'll have bad luck if you stay here. There'll be a curse on you unless you go away."'

'Did she mention the word death?'

'Yes, I think so. We didn't take her seriously. At least,' I corrected myself, 'I didn't.'

'Do you think your wife did?'

'I'm afraid she did sometimes. The old woman, you know, could be rather alarming. I don't think she was really responsible for what she was saying or doing.'

The proceedings ended with the Coroner adjourning the inquest for a fortnight. Everything pointed to death being due to accidental causes but there was not sufficient evidence to show what had caused the accident to occur. He would adjourn the proceedings until he had heard the evidence of Mrs Esther Lee.

CHAPTER 20

The day after the inquest I went to see Major Phillpot and I told him point-blank that I wanted his opinion. Someone whom the old peat-cutting man had taken to be Mrs Esther Lee had been seen going up towards the woods that morning.

'You know the old woman,' I said. 'Do you actually think that she would have been capable of causing an accident by deliberate malice?'

'I can't really believe so, Mike,' he said. 'To do a thing like that you need a very strong motive. Revenge for some personal injury caused to you. Something like that. And what had Ellie ever done to her? Nothing.'

'It seems crazy, I know. Why was she constantly appearing in that queer way, threatening Ellie, telling her to go away? She seemed to have a grudge against her, but how could she have had a grudge? She'd never met Ellie or seen her before. What was Ellie to her but a perfectly strange American? There's no past history, no link between them.'

'I know, I know,' said Phillpot. 'I can't help feeling, Mike, that there's something here that we don't understand. I don't know how much your wife was over in England previous to her marriage. Did she ever live in this part of the world for any length of time?'

'No, I'm sure of that. It's all so difficult. *I* don't really know anything about Ellie. I mean, who she knew, where she went. We just – met.' I checked myself and looked at him. I said, 'You don't know how we came to meet, do you? No,' I went on, 'you wouldn't guess in a hundred years how we met.' And suddenly, in spite of myself, I began to laugh. Then I pulled myself together. I could feel that I was very near hysteria.

I could see his kind patient face just waiting till I was myself again. He was a helpful man. There was no doubt about that.

'We met here,' I said. 'Here at Gipsy's Acre. I had been reading the notice board of the sale of The Towers and I walked up the road, up the hill because I was curious about this place. And that's how I first saw her. She was standing there under a tree. I startled her – or perhaps it was she who startled me. Anyway, that's how it all began. That's how we came to live here in this damned, cursed, unlucky place.'

'Have you felt that all along? That it would be unlucky?'

'No. Yes. No, I don't know really. I've never admitted it. I've never wanted to admit it. But I think *she* knew. I think she's been frightened all along.' Then I said slowly, 'I think somebody deliberately wanted to frighten her.'

He said rather sharply, 'What do you mean by that? Who wanted to frighten her?'

'Presumably the gipsy woman. But somehow I'm not quite sure about it . . . She used to lie in wait for Ellie, you know, tell her this place would bring her bad luck. Tell her she ought to go away from it.'

'Tcha!' He spoke angrily. 'I wish I'd been told more about that. I'd have spoken to old Esther. Told her she couldn't do things like that.'

'Why did she?' I asked. 'What made her?'

'Like so many people,' said Phillpot, 'she likes to make herself important. She likes either to give people warnings or else tell their fortunes and
prophesy happy lives for them. She likes to pretend she knows the future.'

'Supposing,' I said slowly, 'somebody gave her money. I've been told
she's fond of money.'

'Yes, she was very fond of money. If someone paid her – that's what
you're suggesting – what put that idea into your head?'

'Sergeant Keene,' I said. 'I should never have thought of it myself.'

'I see.' He shook his head doubtfully.

'I can't believe,' he said, 'that she would deliberately try to frighten your
wife to the extent of causing an accident.'

'She mayn't have counted on a fatal accident. She might have done
something to frighten the horse,' I said. 'Let off a squib or flapped a sheet
of white paper or something. Sometimes, you know, I did feel that she had
some entirely personal grudge against Ellie, a grudge for some reason that
I don't know about.'

'That sounds very far-fetched.'

'This place never belonged to her?' I asked. 'The land, I mean.'

'No. Gipsies may have been warned off this property, probably more
than once. Gipsies are always getting turned off places, but I doubt if they
keep up a life-long resentment about it.'

'No,' I said, 'that would be far-fetched. But I do wonder if for some
reason that we don't know about – she was paid –'

'A reason we don't know about – what reason?'

I reflected a moment or two.

'Everything I say will just sound fantastic. Let's say that, as Keene
suggested, someone paid her to do the things she did. What did that
someone want? Say they wanted to make us both go away from here.
They concentrated on Ellie, not on me, because I wouldn't be scared in
the way Ellie would be. They frightened her to get her – and through her
both of us – to leave here. If so, there must be some reason for wanting
the land to come on the market again. Somebody, shall we say, for some
reason wants our land.' I stopped.

'It's a logical suggestion,' Phillpot said, 'but I know of no reason why
anyone should.'

'Some important mineral deposit,' I suggested, 'that nobody knows
about.'

'Hm, I doubt it.'

'Something like buried treasure. Oh, I know it sounds absurd. Or – well,
say the proceeds of some big bank robbery.'

Phillpot was still shaking his head but rather less vehemently now.

'The only other proposition,' I said, 'is to go one step farther back as you did just now. Behind Mrs Lee to the person who paid Mrs Lee. That might be some unknown enemy of Ellie's.'

'But you can't think of anyone it would be likely to be?'

'No. She didn't know anyone down here. That I'm sure of. She had no links with this place.' I got up. 'Thank you for listening to me,' I said.

'I wish I could have been more helpful.'

I went out of the door, fingering the thing that I was carrying in my pocket. Then, taking a sudden decision, I turned on my heels and went back into the room.

'There's something I'd like to show you,' I said. 'Actually, I was going to take it down to show Sergeant Keene and see what he could make of it.'

I dived into my pocket and brought out a stone round which was wrapped a crumpled bit of paper with printed writing on it.

'This was thrown through our breakfast window this morning,' I said. 'I heard the crash of the glass as I came down the stairs. A stone was thrown through the window once before when we first came here. I don't know if this is the same person or not.'

I took off the wrapping paper and held it out for him. It was a dirty, coarse bit of paper. There was some printing on it in rather faint ink. Phillpot put on his spectacles and bent over the piece of paper. The message on it was quite short. All it said was, '*It was a woman who killed your wife.*'

Phillpot's eyebrows went up.

'Extraordinary,' he said. 'Was the first message you got printed?'

'I can't remember now. It was just a warning to go away from here. I can't even remember the exact wording of it now. Anyway, it seems pretty certain that that was hooligans. This doesn't seem quite the same.'

'Do you think it was thrown in by someone who knew something?'

'Probably just a bit of silly cruel malice in the anonymous letter class. You get it, you know, a good deal in villages.'

He handed it back to me.

'But I think your instinct was right,' he said, 'to take it to Sergeant Keene. He'll know more about these anonymous things than I should.'

I found Sergeant Keene at the police station and he was definitely interested.

'There's queer things going on here,' he said.

'What do you think it means?' I asked.

'Hard to say. Might be just malice leading up to accusing some particular person.'

'It might be just accusing Mrs Lee, I suppose?'

'No, I don't think it would have been put that way. It might be – I'd like to think it was – it might be that someone saw or heard something. Heard a noise or a cry or the horse bolted right past someone, and they saw or met a woman soon afterwards. But it sounds as though it was a different woman from the gipsy, because everyone thinks the gipsy's mixed up in this anyway. So this sounds as though another, an entirely different woman was meant.'

'What about the gipsy?' I said. 'Have you had news of her, found her?'

He shook his head slowly.

'We know some of the places she used to go when she left here. East Anglia, that way. She'd friends there among the gipsy clan. She's not been there, they say, but they'd say that anyway. They clam up, you know. She's fairly well known by sight in those parts but nobody's seen her. All the same, I don't think she's as far away as East Anglia.'

There was something peculiar about the way he said the words.

'I don't quite understand,' I said.

'Look at it this way, she's scared. She's got good reason to be. She's been threatening your wife, frightening her, and now, say, she caused an accident and your wife died. The police'll be after her. She knows that, so she'll go to earth, as you might say. She'll put as big a distance between herself and us as she possibly can. But she won't want to show herself. She'd be afraid of public transport.'

'But you'll find her? She's a woman of striking appearance.'

'Ah yes, we shall find her eventually. These things take a little time. That is, if it *was* that way.'

'But you think it was some other way.'

'Well, you know what I've wondered all along. Whether somebody was paying her to say the things she did?'

'Then she might be even more anxious to get away,' I pointed out.

'But somebody else would be anxious too. You've got to think of that, Mr Rogers.'

'You mean,' I said slowly, 'the person who paid her.'

'Yes.'

'Supposing it was a – a woman who paid her.'

'And supposing somebody else has some idea of that. And so they start sending anonymous messages. The woman would be scared too.

She needn't have *meant* this to happen, you know. However much she got that gipsy woman to frighten your wife away from this place she wouldn't have meant it to result in Mrs Rogers' death.'

'No,' I said. 'Death wasn't meant. It was just to frighten us. To frighten my wife and to frighten me into leaving here.'

'And now who's going to be frightened? The woman who caused the accident. And that's Mrs Esther Lee. And so she's going to come clean, isn't she? Say it wasn't really her doing. She'll admit even that she was paid money to do it. And she'll mention a name. She'll say who paid her. And somebody wouldn't like that would they, Mr Rogers?'

'You mean this unknown woman that we've more or less postulated without even knowing there's any such person?'

'Man or woman, say someone paid her. Well, that someone would want her silenced pretty quickly, wouldn't they?'

'You're thinking she might be dead?'

'It's a possibility, isn't it?' said Keene. Then he made what seemed quite an abrupt change of subject. 'You know that kind of Folly place, Mr Rogers, that you've got up at the top of your woods?'

'Yes,' I said, 'what of it? My wife and I had it repaired and fixed up a bit. We used to go up there occasionally but not very often. Not lately certainly. Why?'

'Well, we've been hunting about, you know. We looked into this Folly. It wasn't locked.'

'No,' I said, 'we never bothered to lock it. There was nothing of value in there, just a few odd bits of furniture.'

'We thought it possible old Mrs Lee had been using it but we found no traces of her. We did find this, though. I was going to show it to you anyway.' He opened a drawer and took out a small delicate gold-chased lighter. It was a woman's lighter and it had an initial on it in diamonds. The letter C. 'It wouldn't be your wife's, would it?'

'Not with the initial C. No, it's not Ellie's,' I said. 'She hadn't any-thing of that kind. And it's not Miss Andersen's either. Her name is Greta.'

'It was up there where somebody had dropped it. It's a classy bit of goods – cost money.'

'C,' I said, repeating the initial thoughtfully. 'I can't think of anyone who's been with us whose initial is C except Cora,' I said. 'That's my wife's stepmother. Mrs van Stuyvesant, but I really can't see her scrambling up to the Folly along that overgrown path. And anyway she hasn't been staying with us for quite a long time. About a month. I don't think I've ever seen her using this lighter. Perhaps I wouldn't notice anyway,' I said. 'Miss Andersen might know.'

'Well, take it up with you and show it to her.'

'I will. But if so, if it's Cora's, it seems odd that we've never seen it when we've been in the Folly lately. There's not much stuff there. You'd notice something like this lying on the floor – it was on the floor?'

'Yes, quite near the divan. Of course anybody might use that Folly. It's a handy place, you know, for a couple of lovers to meet any time. The locals I'm talking about. But they wouldn't be likely to have an expensive thing of this kind.'

'There's Claudia Hardcastle,' I said, 'but I doubt if she'd have anything as fancy as this. And what would she be doing in the Folly?'

'She was quite a friend of your wife's, wasn't she?'

'Yes,' I said, 'I think she was Ellie's best friend down here. And she'd know we wouldn't mind her using the Folly any time.'

'Ah,' said Sergeant Keene.

I looked at him rather hard. 'You don't think Claudia Hardcastle was a – an enemy of Ellie's do you? That would be absurd.'

'Doesn't seem any reason why she should be, I agree, but you never know with ladies.'

'I suppose –' I began and then stopped because what I was going to say would seem perhaps rather odd.

'Yes, Mr Rogers?'

'I believe that Claudia Hardcastle was originally married to an American – an American named Lloyd. Actually – the name of my wife's principal trustee in America is Stanford Lloyd. But there must be hundreds of Lloyds and anyway it would only be a coincidence if it was the same person. And what would it have to do with all this?'

'It doesn't seem likely. But then –' he stopped.

'The funny thing is that I thought I saw Stanford Lloyd down here on the day of the – the accident – Having lunch in the George at Bartington –'

'He didn't come to see you?'

I shook my head.

'He was with someone who looked rather like Miss Hardcastle. But probably it was just a mistake on my part. You know, I suppose, that it was her brother who built our house?'

'Does she take an interest in the house?'

'No,' I said, 'I don't think she likes her brother's type of architecture.' Then I got up. 'Well, I won't take any more of your time. Try and find the gipsy.'

'We shan't stop looking, I can tell you that. Coroner wants her too.'

I said goodbye and went out of the police station. In the queer way that so often happens when you suddenly meet someone you've been talking about, Claudia Hardcastle came out of the post office just as I was passing it. We both stopped. She said with that slight embarrassment that you have when you meet someone that's been recently bereaved:

'I'm so terribly sorry, Mike, about Ellie. I won't say any more. It's beastly when people say things to you. But I have just – just to say that.'

'I know,' I said. 'You were very nice to Ellie. You made her feel at home here. I've been grateful.'

'There was one thing I wanted to ask you and I thought perhaps I'd better do it now before you go to America. I hear you're going quite soon.'

'As soon as I can. I've got a lot to see to there.'

'It was only – if you *were* putting your house on the market I thought it might be a thing you'd set in motion before you went away . . . And if so – if so, I'd rather like to have the first refusal of it.'

I stared at her. This really did surprise me. It was the last thing I'd expected.

'You mean you'd like to buy it? I thought you didn't even care for that type of architecture?'

'My brother Rudolf said to me that it was the best thing he'd done. I dare say he knows. I expect you'll want a very large price for it but I could pay it. Yes, I'd like to have it.'

I couldn't help thinking it was odd. She'd never shown the faintest appreciation of our house when she'd come to it. I wondered as I'd wondered once or twice before what her links with her half-brother really were. Had she really a great devotion to him? Sometimes I'd almost thought that she disliked him, perhaps hated him. She spoke of him certainly in a very odd way. But whatever her actual emotions were, he *meant* something to her. Meant something important. I shook my head slowly.

'I can see that you might think I'd want to sell the place and leave here because of Ellie's death,' I said. 'But actually that's not so at all. We lived here and were happy and this is the place I shall remember her best. *I shan't sell Gipsy's Acre* – not for any consideration! You can be quite sure of that.'

Our eyes met. It was like a kind of tussle between us. Then hers dropped.

I took my courage in both hands and spoke.

'It's no business of mine, but you were married once. Was the name of your husband Stanford Lloyd?'

She looked at me for a moment without speaking. Then she said abruptly:

'Yes,' and turned away.

CHAPTER 21

Confusion – That's all I can remember when I look back. Newspapermen asking questions – wanting interviews – masses of letters and telegrams – Greta coping with them –

The first really startling thing was that Ellie's family were not as we supposed in America. It was quite a shock to find that most of them were actually in England. It was understandable, perhaps, that Cora van Stuyvesant should be. She was a very restless woman, always dashing across to Europe, to Italy, to Paris, to London and back again to America, to Palm Beach, out West to the ranch; here, there and everywhere. On the actual day of Ellie's death she had been not more than fifty miles away, still pursuing her whim of having a house in England. She had rushed over to stay in London for two or three days and gone to fresh house agents for fresh orders to view and had been touring round the country seeing half a dozen on that particular day.

Stanford Lloyd, it turned out, had flown over in the same plane ostensibly for a business meeting in London. These people learnt of Ellie's death, not from the cables which we had dispatched to the United States but from the public Press.

An ugly wrangle developed about where Ellie should be buried. I had assumed it was only natural that she'd be buried here where she had died. Here where she and I had lived.

But Ellie's family objected violently to this. They wanted the body brought to America to be buried with her forebears. Where her grandfather and her father, her mother and others had been laid to rest. I suppose it was natural, really, when one comes to think of it.

Andrew Lippincott came down to talk to me about it. He put the matter in a reasonable way.

'She never left any directions as to where she wished to be buried,' he pointed out to me.

'Why should she?' I demanded hotly. 'How old was she – twenty-one?

You don't think at twenty-one you're going to die. You don't start thinking then the way you want to be buried. If we'd ever thought about it we'd assume we'd be buried together somewhere even if we didn't die at the same time. But who thinks of death in the middle of life?'

'A very just observation,' said Mr Lippincott. Then he said, 'I'm afraid you'll also have to come to America, you know. There's a great deal of business interests you'll have to look into.'

'What sort of business? What have I got to do with business?'

'You could have a great deal to do with it,' he said. 'Don't you realize that you're the principal beneficiary under the will?'

'You mean because I'm Ellie's next of kin or something?'

'No. Under her will.'

'I didn't know she ever made a will.'

'Oh yes,' said Mr Lippincott. 'Ellie was quite a businesslike young woman. She'd had to be, you know. She'd lived in the middle of that kind of thing. She made a will on coming of age and almost immediately after she was married. It was lodged with her lawyer in London with a request that one copy should be sent to me.' He hesitated and then said, 'If you do come to the States, which I advise, I also think that you should place your affairs in the hands of some reputable lawyer there.'

'Why?'

'Because in the case of a vast fortune, large quantities of real estate, stocks, controlling interests in varying industries, you will need technical advice.'

'I'm not qualified to deal with things like that,' I said. 'Really I'm not.'

'I quite understand,' said Mr Lippincott.

'Couldn't I place the whole thing in your hands?'

'You could do so.'

'Well then, why don't I?'

'All the same, I think you should be separately represented. I am already acting for some members of the family and a conflict of interests might arise. If you will leave it in my hands, I will see that your interests are safeguarded by your being represented by a thoroughly able attorney.'

'Thank you,' I said, 'you're very kind.'

'If I may be slightly indiscreet –' he looked a little uncomfortable – it pleased me rather thinking of Lippincott being indiscreet.

'Yes?' I said.

'I should advise you to be very careful of anything you sign. Any business documents. Before you sign anything, read it thoroughly and carefully.'

'Would the kind of document you're talking about mean anything to me if I do read it?'

'If it is not all clear to you, you will then hand it over to your legal adviser.'

'Are you warning me against somebody or someone?' I said, with a suddenly aroused interest.

'That is not at all a proper question for me to answer,' said Mr Lippincott. 'I will go this far. Where large sums of money are concerned it is advisable to trust *nobody*.'

So he *was* warning me against someone, but he wasn't going to give me any names. I could see that. Was it against Cora? Or had he had suspicions – perhaps suspicions of some long standing – of Stanford Lloyd, that florid banker so full of bonhomie, so rich and carefree, who had recently been over here 'on business'? Might it be Uncle Frank who might approach me with some plausible documents? I had a sudden vision of myself, a poor innocent boob, swimming in a lake surrounded by evilly disposed crocodiles, all smiling false smiles of amity.

'The world,' said Mr Lippincott, 'is a very evil place.'

It was perhaps a stupid thing to say, but quite suddenly I asked him a question.

'Does Ellie's death benefit anyone?' I asked.

He looked at me sharply.

'That's a very curious question. Why do you ask that?'

'I don't know,' I said, 'it just came into my head.'

'It benefits you,' he said.

'Of course,' I said. 'I take that for granted. I really meant – does it benefit anyone else?'

Mr Lippincott was silent for quite a long time.

'If you mean,' he said, 'does Fenella's will benefit certain other people in the way of legacies, that is so in a minor degree. Some old servants, an old governess, one or two charities but nothing of any particular moment. There's a legacy to Miss Andersen but not a large one for she has already, as you probably know, settled a very considerable sum on Miss Andersen.'

I nodded. Ellie had told me she was doing that.

'You were her husband. She had no other near relations. But I take it that your question did not mean specifically that.'

'I don't know quite what I meant by it,' I said. 'But somehow or other, you've succeeded, Mr Lippincott, in making me feel suspicious. Suspicious of I don't know who, or why. Only – well, suspicious. I don't understand finance,' I added.

'No, that is quite apparent. Let me say only that I have no exact knowledge, no exact suspicions of any kind. At someone's death there is usually an accounting of their affairs. This may take place quickly or it may be delayed for a period of many years.'

'What you really mean,' I said, 'is that some of the others quite likely might put a few fast ones over and ball up things generally. Get me perhaps to sign releases – whatever you call the things.'

'If Fenella's affairs were not, shall we say, in the healthy state they ought to be, then – yes, possibly her premature death might be, shall we say, fortunate for someone, we will name no names, someone perhaps who could cover his traces more easily if he had a fairly simple person, if I may say so, like yourself to deal with. I will go that far but I do not wish to speak further on the matter. It would not be equitable to do so.'

There was a simple funeral service held in the little church. If I could have stayed away I would have done so. I hated all those people who were staring at me lining up outside the church. Curious eyes. Greta pulled me through things. I don't think I'd realized until now what a strong, reliable character she was. She made the arrangements, ordered flowers, arranged everything. I understood better now how Ellie had come to depend upon Greta as she had done. There aren't many Gretas in the world.

The people in the church were mostly our neighbours – some, even, that we had hardly known. But I noticed one face that I had seen before, but which I could not at the moment place. When I got back to the house, Carson told me there was a gentleman in the drawing-room waiting to see me.

'I can't see anyone today. Send him away. You shouldn't have let him in!'

'Excuse me, sir. He said he was a relation.'

'A relation?'

Suddenly I remembered the man I'd seen in the church.

Carson was handing me a card.

It meant nothing to me for a moment. Mr William R. Pardoe. I turned it over and shook my head. Then I handed it to Greta.

'Do you know by any chance who this is?' I said. 'His face seemed familiar but I couldn't place it. Perhaps it's one of Ellie's friends.'

Greta took it from me and looked at it. Then she said:

'Of course.'

'Who is it?'

'Uncle Reuben. You remember. Ellie's cousin. She's spoken of him to you, surely?'

I remembered then why the face had seemed familiar to me. Ellie had had several photographs in her sitting-room of her various relations carelessly placed about the room. That was why the face had been so familiar. I had seen it so far only in a photograph.

'I'll come,' I said.

I went out of the room and into the drawing-room. Mr Pardoe rose to his feet, and said:

'Michael Rogers? You may not know my name but your wife was my cousin. She called me Uncle Reuben always, but we haven't met, I know. This is the first time I've been over since your marriage.'

'Of course I know who you are,' I said.

I don't know quite how to describe Reuben Pardoe. He was a big burly man with a large face, wide and rather absent-looking as though he were thinking of something else. Yet after you had talked to him for a few moments you got the feeling that he was more on the ball than you would have thought.

'I don't need to tell you how shocked and grieved I was to hear of Ellie's death,' he said.

'Let's skip that,' I said. 'I'm not up to talking about it.'

'No, no, I can understand that.'

He had a certain sympathetic personality and yet there was something about him that made me vaguely uneasy. I said, as Greta entered:

'You know Miss Andersen?'

'Of course,' he said, 'how are you, Greta?'

'Not too bad,' said Greta. 'How long have you been over?'

'Just a week or two. Touring around.'

Then it came to me. On an impulse I went in. 'I saw you the other day.'

'Really? Where?'

'At an auction sale at a place called Bartington Manor.'

'I remember now,' he said, 'yes, yes I think I remember your face. You were with a man about sixty with a brown moustache.'

'Yes,' I said. 'A Major Phillpot.'

'You seemed in good spirits,' he said, 'both of you.'

'Never better,' I said, and repeated with the strange wonder that I always felt, 'Never better.'

'Of course – at that time you didn't know what had happened. That was the date of the accident, wasn't it?'

'Yes, we were expecting Ellie to join us for lunch.'

'Tragic,' said Uncle Reuben. 'Really tragic . . .'

'I had no idea,' I said, 'that you were in England. I don't think Ellie had any idea either?' I paused, waiting for what he would tell me.

'No,' he said, 'I hadn't written. In fact, I didn't know how much time I should have over here, but actually I'd concluded my business earlier than I thought and I was wondering if after the sale I'd have the time to drive over and see you.'

'You came over from the States on business?' I asked.

'Well, partly yes and partly no. Cora wanted some advice from me on one or two matters. One concerning this house she's thinking of buying.'

It was then that he told me where Cora had been staying in England. Again I said:

'We didn't know that.'

'She was actually staying not far from here that day,' he said.

'Near here? Was she in a hotel?'

'No, she was staying with a friend.'

'I didn't know she had any friends in this part of the world.'

'A woman called – now what was her name? – Hard – something. Hardcastle.'

'Claudia Hardcastle?' I was surprised.

'Yes. She was quite a friend of Cora's. Cora knew her well when she was in the States. Didn't you know?'

'I know very little,' I said. 'Very little about the family.'

I looked at Greta.

'Did *you* know that Cora knew Claudia Hardcastle?'

'I don't think I ever heard her speak of her,' said Greta. 'So that's why Claudia didn't turn up that day.'

'Of course,' I said, 'she was going with you to shop in London. You were to meet at Market Chadwell station –'

'Yes – and she wasn't there. She rang up the house just after I'd left. Said some American visitor had turned up unexpectedly and she couldn't leave home.'

'I wonder,' I said, 'if the American visitor could have been Cora.'

'Obviously,' said Reuben Pardoe. He shook his head. 'It all seems so confused,' he said. He went on, 'I understand the inquest was adjourned.'

'Yes,' I said.

He drained his cup and got up.

'I won't stay to worry you any more,' he said. 'If there's anything I can do, I'm staying at the Majestic Hotel in Market Chadwell.'

I said I was afraid there wasn't anything he could do and thanked him. When he had gone away, Greta said:

'What does he want, I wonder? Why did he come over?' And then sharply: 'I wish they'd all go back where they belong.'

'I wonder if it was really Stanford Lloyd I saw at the George – I only got a glimpse.'

'You said he was with someone who looked like Claudia so it probably was him. Perhaps he called to see *her* and Reuben came to see Cora – what a mix-up!'

'I don't like it – all of them milling round that day.'

Greta said things often happened that way – as usual she was quite cheerful and reasonable about it.

<hr />

CHAPTER 22

There was nothing more for me to do at Gipsy's Acre. I left Greta in charge of the house while I sailed to New York to wind up things there and to take part in what I felt with some dread were going to be the most ghastly gold-plated obsequies for Ellie.

'You're going into the jungle,' Greta warned me. 'Look after yourself. Don't let them skin you alive.'

She was right about that. It *was* the jungle. I felt it when I got there. I didn't know about jungles – not that kind of jungle. I was out of my depth and I knew it. I wasn't the hunter, I was the hunted. There were people all round me in the undergrowth, gunning for me. Sometimes, I expect, I imagined things. Sometimes my suspicions were justified. I remember going to the lawyer supplied for me by Mr Lippincott (a most urbane man who treated me rather as a general practitioner might have done in the medical profession). I had been advised to get rid of certain mining properties to which the title deeds were not too clear.

He asked me who had told me so and I said it was Stanford Lloyd.

'Well, we must look into it,' he said. 'A man like Mr Lloyd ought to know.'

He said to me afterwards:

'There's nothing wrong with your title deeds, and there is certainly no point in your selling the land in a hurry, as he seems to have advised you. Hang on to it.'

I had the feeling then that I'd been right, everybody *was* gunning for me. They all knew I was a simpleton when it came to finance.

The funeral was splendid and, I thought, quite horrible. Gold-plated, as I had surmised. At the cemetery, masses of flowers, the cemetery itself like a public park and all the trimmings of wealthy mourning expressed in monumental marble. Ellie would have hated it, I was sure of that. But I suppose her family had a certain right to her.

Four days after my arrival in New York I had news from Kingston Bishop.

The body of old Mrs Lee had been found in the disused quarry on the far side of the hill. She had been dead some days. There had been accidents there before, and it had been said that the place ought to be fenced in – but nothing had been done. A verdict of Accidental Death had been brought in and a further recommendation to the Council to fence the place off. In Mrs Lee's cottage a sum of three hundred pounds had been found hidden under the floorboards, all in one-pound notes.

Major Phillpot had added in a postscript, 'I'm sure you will be sorry to hear that Claudia Hardcastle was thrown from her horse and killed out hunting yesterday.'

Claudia – killed? I couldn't believe it! It gave me a very nasty jolt. Two people – within a fortnight, killed in a riding accident. It seemed like an almost impossible coincidence.

I don't want to dwell on that time I spent in New York. I was a stranger in an alien atmosphere. I felt all the time that I had to be wary of what I said and what I did. The Ellie that I had known, the Ellie that had belonged peculiarly to me was not there. I saw her now only as an American girl, heiress to a great fortune, surrounded by friends and connections and distant relatives, one of a family that had lived there for five generations. She had come from there as a comet might have come, visiting my territory.

Now she had gone back to be buried with her own folk, to where her own home was. I was glad to have it that way. I shouldn't have been easy feeling her there in the prim little cemetery at the foot of the pine woods just outside the village. No, I shouldn't have been easy.

'Go back where you belong, Ellie,' I said to myself.

Now and again that haunting little tune of the song she used to sing to her guitar came into my mind. I remembered her fingers twanging the strings.

Every Morn and every Night
Some are born to Sweet Delight

and I thought 'That was true of you. You were born to Sweet Delight. You had Sweet Delight there at Gipsy's Acre. Only it didn't last very long. Now it's over. You've come back to where perhaps there wasn't much delight, where you weren't happy. But you're *at home* here anyway. You're among your own folk.'

I wondered suddenly where *I* should be when the time came for me to die. Gipsy's Acre? It could be. My mother would come and see me laid in my grave – if she wasn't dead already. But I couldn't think of my mother being dead. I could think more easily of death for myself. Yes, she'd come and see me buried. Perhaps the sternness of her face would relax. I took my thoughts away from her. I didn't want to think of her. I didn't want to go near her or see her.

That last isn't quite true. It wasn't a question of seeing *her*. It was always with my mother a question of *her* seeing *me*, of her eyes looking through me, of an anxiety that swept out like a miasma embracing me. I thought: 'Mothers are the devil! Why have they got to brood over their children? Why do they feel they know all about their children? They don't. They *don't*! She ought to be proud of me, happy for me, happy for the wonderful life that I've achieved. She ought –' Then I wrenched thoughts away from her again.

How long was I over in the States? I can't even remember. It seemed an age of walking warily, of being watched by people with false smiles and enmity in their eyes. I said to myself every day, 'I've got to get *through* this. I've got to get *through* this – and then.' Those were the two words I used. Used in my own mind, I mean. Used them every day several times. *And then* – They were the two words of the future. I used them in the same way that I had once used those other two words. *I want* . . .

Everyone went out of their way to be nice to me because I was rich! Under the terms of Ellie's will I was an extremely rich man. I felt very odd. I had investments I didn't understand, shares, stocks, property. And I didn't know in the least what to do with them all.

The day before I went back to England I had a long conversation with Mr Lippincott. I always thought of him like that in my mind – as Mr Lippincott. He'd never become Uncle Andrew to me. I told him that I thought of withdrawing the charge of my investments from Stanford Lloyd.

'Indeed!' His grizzled eyebrows rose. He looked at me with his shrewd eyes and his poker face and I wondered what exactly his 'indeed' meant.

'Do you think it's all right to do that?' I asked anxiously.

'You have reasons, I presume?'

'No,' I said, 'I haven't got reasons. A feeling, that's all. I suppose I can say anything to you?'

'The communication will be privileged, naturally.'

'All right,' I said, 'I just feel that he's a crook!'

'Ah.' Mr Lippincott looked interested. 'Yes, I should say your instinct was possibly sound.'

So I knew then that I was right. Stanford Lloyd had been playing hanky-panky with Ellie's bonds and investments and all the rest of it. I signed a power of attorney and gave it to Andrew Lippincott.

'You're willing,' I said, 'to accept it?'

'As far as financial matters are concerned,' said Mr Lippincott, 'you can trust me absolutely. I will do my best for you in that respect. I don't think you will have any reason to complain of my stewardship.'

I wondered exactly what he meant by that. He meant something. I think he meant that he didn't like me, had never liked me, but financially he would do his best for me because I had been Ellie's husband. I signed all necessary papers. He asked me how I was going back to England. Flying? I said no, I wasn't flying, I was going by sea. 'I've got to have a little time to myself,' I said. 'I think a sea voyage will do me good.'

'And you are going to take up your residence – where?'

'Gipsy's Acre,' I said.

'Ah. You propose to live there.'

'Yes,' I said.

'I thought perhaps you might have put it on the market for sale.'

'No,' I said, and the no came out rather stronger than I meant. I wasn't going to part with Gipsy's Acre. Gipsy's Acre had been part of my dream, the dream that I'd cherished since I'd been a callow boy.

'Is anybody looking after it while you have been away in the States?'

I said that I'd left Greta Andersen in charge.

'Ah,' said Mr Lippincott, 'yes. Greta.'

He meant something in the way he said 'Greta' but I didn't take him up on it. If he disliked her, he disliked her. He always had. It left an awkward pause, then I changed my mind. I felt that I'd got to say *something*.

'She was very good to Ellie,' I said. 'She nursed her when she was ill, she came and lived with us and looked after Ellie. I – I can't be grateful enough to her. I'd like you to understand that. You don't know what she's been like. You don't know how she helped and did everything after Ellie was killed. I don't know what I'd have done without her.'

'Quite so, quite so,' said Mr Lippincott. He sounded drier than you could possibly imagine.

'So you see I owe her a lot.'

'A very competent girl,' said Mr Lippincott.

I got up and said goodbye and I thanked him.

'You have nothing for which to thank me,' said Mr Lippincott, dry as ever.

He added, 'I wrote you a short letter. I have sent it by air mail to Gipsy's Acre. If you are going by sea you will probably find it waiting there on arrival.' Then he said, 'Have a good voyage.'

I asked him, rather hesitantly, if he'd known Stanford Lloyd's wife – a girl called Claudia Hardcastle.

'Ah, you mean his first wife. No I never met her. The marriage I believe broke up quite soon. After the divorce, he remarried. That too ended in divorce.'

So that was that.

When I got back to my hotel I found a cable. It asked me to come to a hospital in California. It said a friend of mine, Rudolf Santonix, had asked for me, he had not long to live and he wished to see me before he died.

I changed my passage to a later boat and flew to San Francisco. He wasn't dead yet, but he was sinking very fast. They doubted, they said, if he would recover consciousness before he died, but he had asked for me very urgently. I sat there in that hospital room watching him, watching what looked like a shell of the man I knew. He'd always looked ill, he'd always had a kind of queer transparency about him, a delicacy, a frailness. He lay now looking a deadly, waxen figure. I sat there thinking: 'I wish he'd speak to me. I wish he'd say something. Just *something* before he dies.'

I felt so alone, so horribly alone. I'd escaped from enemies now, I'd got to a friend. My only friend, really. He was the only person who knew anything about me, except Mum, but I didn't want to think of Mum.

Once or twice I spoke to a nurse, asked her if there wasn't anything they could do, but she shook her head and said non-committally:

'He might recover consciousness or might not.'

I sat there. And then at last he stirred and sighed. The nurse raised him up very gently. He looked at me but I didn't know whether he recognized me or not. He was just looking at me as though he looked past me and beyond me. Then suddenly a difference came into his eyes. I thought, 'He *does* know me, he *does* see me.' He said something very faintly and I bent over the bed so as to catch it. But they didn't seem words that had any meaning. Then his body had a sudden spasm and twitch, and he threw his head back and shouted out:

'You damned fool . . . Why didn't you go the other way?'

Then he just collapsed and died.

I don't know what he meant – or even if he knew himself what he was saying.

So that was the last I saw of Santonix. I wonder if he'd have heard me if I had said anything to him? I'd like to have told him once more that the house he'd built me was the best thing I had in the world. The thing that mattered most to me. Funny that a house could mean that. I suppose it was a sort of symbolism about it. Something you want. Something you want so much that you don't quite know what it is. But he'd known what it was and he'd given it to me. And I'd got it. And I was going home to it.

Going home. That's all I could think about when I got on the boat. That and a deadly tiredness at first . . . And then a rising tide of happiness oozing up as it were from the depths . . . I was going home. I was going home . . .

Home is the sailor, home from the sea
And the hunter home from the hill . . .

CHAPTER 23

Yes, that was what I was doing. It was all over now. The last of the fight, the last of the struggle. The last phase of the journey.

It seemed so long ago to the time of my restless youth. The days of '*I want, I want.*' But it wasn't long. Less than a year . . .

I went over it all – lying there in my bunk, and thinking.

Meeting Ellie – our times in Regent's Park – our marriage in the Registrar's Office. The house – Santonix building it – the house completed. Mine, all mine. I was me – me – me as I wanted to be. As I'd always wanted to be. I'd got everything I'd wanted and I was going home to it.

Before I left New York I'd written one letter and sent it off by air mail to get there ahead of me. I'd written to Phillpot. Somehow I felt that Phillpot would understand, though others mightn't.

It was easier to write than to tell him. Anyway, he'd got to know. Everyone had got to know. Some people probably wouldn't understand, but I thought he would. He'd seen for himself how close Ellie and Greta had been, how Ellie had depended on Greta. I thought he'd realize how I'd come to depend upon her also, how it would be impossible for me to live alone in the house where I'd lived with Ellie unless there was someone there to help me. I don't know if I put it very well. I did my best.

'I'd like you,' I wrote, 'to be the first to know. You've been so kind to us, and I think you'll be the only person to understand. I can't face living alone at Gipsy's Acre. I've been thinking all the time I've been in America and I've decided that as soon as I get home I'm going to ask Greta to marry me. She's the only person I can really talk to about Ellie, you see. She'll understand. Perhaps she won't marry me, but I think she will . . . It will make everything as though there were the three of us together still.'

I wrote the letter three times before I could get it to express just what I wanted to say. Phillpot ought to get it two days before my return.

I came up on deck as we were approaching England. I looked out as the land came nearer. I thought, 'I wish Santonix was with me.' I did wish it. I wished he could know how everything was all coming true. Everything I'd planned – everything I'd thought – everything I'd wanted.

I'd shaken off America, I'd shaken off the crooks and the sycophants and all the whole lot of them whom I hated and whom I was pretty sure hated me and looked down on me for being so low class! I was back in triumph. I was coming back to the pine trees and the curling dangerous road that made its way up through Gipsy's Acre to the house on the hilltop. *My* house! I was coming back to the two things I wanted. My house – the house that I'd dreamed of, that I'd planned, that I'd wanted above everything. That and a wonderful woman . . . I'd known always that I'd meet one day a wonderful woman. I had met her. I'd seen her and she'd seen me. We'd come together. A wonderful woman. I'd known the moment I saw her that I belonged to her, belonged to her absolutely and for always. I was hers. And now – at last – I was going to her.

Nobody saw me arrive at Kingston Bishop. It was almost dark and I came by train and I walked from the station, taking a roundabout side road. I didn't want to meet any of the people in the village. Not that night . . .

The sun had set when I came up the road to Gipsy's Acre. I'd told Greta the time I'd arrive. She was up there in the house waiting for me. At last! We'd done with subterfuges now and all the pretences – the pretence of disliking her – I thought now, laughing to myself, of the part I'd played, a part I'd played carefully right from the beginning. Disliking Greta, not wanting her to come and stay with Ellie. Yes, I'd been very careful. Everyone must have been taken in by the pretence. I remembered the quarrel we'd faked up so that Ellie should overhear it.

Greta had known me for what I was the first moment we met. We'd never had any silly illusions about each other. She had the same kind of mind, the same kind of desires as I had. We wanted the World, nothing less! We wanted to be on top of the World. We wanted to fulfil every ambition. We wanted to have everything, deny ourselves nothing. I remembered how I'd poured out my heart to her when I first met her in Hamburg, telling her my frenzied desire for things. I hadn't got to conceal my inordinate greed for life from Greta, she had the same greed herself. She said:

'For all you want out of life you've got to have money.'

'Yes,' I said, 'and I don't see how I'm going to get it.'

'No,' said Greta, 'you won't get it by hard work. You're not the kind.'

'Work!' I said. 'I'd have to work for years! I don't want to wait. I don't want to be middle-aged.' I said, 'You know the story about that chap Schliemann how he worked, toiled, and made a fortune so that he could have his life's dream come true and go to Troy and dig it up and find the graves of Troy. He got his dream but he had to wait till he was forty. But I don't want to wait till I'm a middle-aged man. Old. One foot in the grave. I want it now when I'm young and strong. You do too, don't you?'

'Yes. And I know the way you can do it. It's easy. I wonder you haven't thought of it already. You can get girls easily enough, can't you? I can see that. I can feel it.'

'Do you think I care about girls – or ever have really? There's only one girl I want,' I said. 'You. And you know that. I belong to you. I knew it the moment I saw you. I knew always that I'd meet someone like you. And I have. I belong to you.'

'Yes,' said Greta, 'I think you do.'

'We both want the same things out of life,' I said.

'I tell you it's easy,' said Greta. 'Easy. All you've got to do is to marry a rich girl, one of the richest girls in the world. I can put you in the way of doing that.'

'Don't be fantastic,' I said.

'It's not fantastic, it'll be easy.'

'No,' I said, 'that's no good to me. I don't want to be the husband of a rich wife. She'll buy me things and we'll do things and she'll keep me in a golden cage, but that's not what I want. I don't want to be a tied-up slave.'

'You needn't be. It's the sort of thing that needn't last for long. Just long enough. Wives do die, you know.'

I stared at her.

'Now you're shocked,' she said.

'No,' I said, 'I'm not shocked.'

'I thought you wouldn't be. I thought perhaps already?' She looked at me inquiringly, but I wasn't going to answer that. I still had some self-preservation left. There are some secrets one doesn't want anyone to know. Not that they were much in the way of secrets, but I didn't like to think of them. I didn't like to think of the first one. Silly though. Puerile. Nothing that mattered. I had had a boy's passion for a classy wrist-watch that a boy . . . a friend of mine at school – had been given. I wanted it. I wanted it badly. It had cost a lot of money. A rich godfather had given it to him. Yes, I wanted that, but I didn't think I'd ever have a chance of getting it. Then there was the day we went skating together. The ice wasn't strong enough to bear. Not that we thought of it beforehand. It just happened. The ice cracked. I skated across to him. He was hanging on. He had gone through a hole and he was hanging on to the ice which was cutting his hands. I went across to pull him out, of course, but just as I got there I saw the glint of the wrist-watch. I thought 'Supposing he goes under and drowns.' I thought how easy it would be . . .

It seemed almost unconsciously, I think, that I unfastened the strap, grabbed the watch and pushed his head under instead of trying to pull him out . . . Just held his head under. He couldn't struggle much, he was under the ice. People saw and came towards us. They thought I was trying to pull him out! They got him out in due course, with some difficulty. They tried artificial respiration on him but it was too late. I hid my treasure away in a special place where I kept things now and then. Things I didn't want Mum to see because she'd ask me where I got them. She came across that watch one day when she was fooling about with my socks. Asked me if that wasn't Pete's watch? I said of course it wasn't – it was one I'd swopped with a boy at school.

I was always nervous with Mum – I always felt she knew too much about me. I was nervous with her when she found the watch. She suspected, I think. She couldn't *know*, of course. Nobody *knew*. But she used to look at me. In a funny way. Everybody thought I'd tried to rescue Pete. I don't think she ever thought so. I think she knew. She didn't want to know, but her trouble was that she knew too much about me. I felt a bit guilty sometimes, but it wore off, fairly soon.

And then later on, when I was in camp. It was during our military training time. Chap called Ed and I had been to a sort of gambling place. I'd had no luck at all, lost everything I had, but Ed had won a packet. He changed his chips and he and I were coming home and he was stuffed up with notes. His pockets were bulging with them. Then a couple of toughs came round the corner and went for us. They were pretty handy with the flick knives they'd got. I got cut in the arm but Ed got a proper sort of stab. He went down under it. Then there was a noise of people coming. The toughs hooked it. I could see that if I was quick . . . I *was* quick! My reflexes are pretty good – I wrapped a handkerchief round my hand and I pulled out the knife from Ed's wound and I stuck the knife in again a couple of times in better places. He gave a gasp and passed out. I was scared, of course, scared for a second or two and then I knew it was going to be all right. So I felt – well – naturally I felt proud of myself for thinking and acting quick! I thought 'Poor old Ed, he always was a fool.' It took me no time at all to transfer those notes to my own pocket! Nothing like having quick reflexes, seizing your opportunity. The trouble is the opportunities don't come very often. Some people, I suppose, get scared when they know they've killed someone. But I wasn't scared. Not this time.

Mind you, it's not a thing you want to do too often. Not unless it might be really worth your while. I don't know how Greta sensed that about me. But she'd known. I don't mean that she'd known that I'd actually killed a couple of people. But I think she knew the idea of killing wouldn't shock or upset me. I said:

'What's all this fantastic story, Greta?'

She said, 'I am in a position to help you. I can bring you in touch with one of the richest girls in America. I more or less look after her. I live with her. I have a lot of influence over her.'

'Do you think she'd look at someone like me?' I said. I didn't believe it for a moment. Why should a rich girl who could have her pick of any attractive, sexy man she liked go for me?

'You've got a lot of sex appeal,' said Greta. 'Girls go for you, don't they?'

I grinned and said I didn't do too badly.

'She's never had that kind of thing. She's been looked after too well. The only young men she's been allowed to meet are conventional kids, bankers' sons, tycoons' sons. She's groomed to make a good marriage in the moneyed class. They're terrified of her meeting handsome foreigners who might be after her money. But naturally she's keener on people like that. They'd be new to her, something she's never seen before. You've got to make a big play for her. You've got to fall in love with her at first sight and sweep her off her feet! It'll be easy enough. She's never had anyone to make a real sexy approach to her. You could do it.'

'I could try,' I said doubtfully.

'We could set it up,' said Greta.

'Her family would step in and stop it.'

'No they wouldn't,' said Greta, 'they wouldn't know anything about it. Not until it was too late. Not until you'd got married secretly.'

'So that's your idea.'

So we talked about it. We planned. Not in detail, mind you. Greta went back to America, but she kept in touch with me. I went on with various jobs. I'd told her about Gipsy's Acre and that I wanted it, and she said that was just fine for setting up a romantic story. We laid our plans so that my meeting with Ellie would take place there. Greta would work Ellie up about having a house in England and getting away from the family as soon as she came of age.

Oh yes, we set it up. Greta was a great planner. I don't think I could have planned it, but I knew I could play my part all right. I'd always enjoyed playing a part. And so that's how it happened. That's how I met Ellie.

It was fun, all of it. Mad fun because of course there was always a risk, there was always a danger that it wouldn't come off. The thing that made me really nervous were the times that I had to meet Greta. I had to be sure, you see, that I never gave myself away, by looking at Greta. I tried *not* to look at her. We agreed it was best that I should take a dislike to her, pretend jealousy of her. I carried that out all right. I remember the day she came down to stay. We staged a quarrel, a quarrel that Ellie could hear. I don't know whether we overdid it a bit. I don't think so. Sometimes I was nervous that Ellie might guess or something, but I don't think she did. I don't know. I don't know really. I never did know about Ellie.

It was very easy to make love to Ellie. She was very sweet. Yes, she was really sweet. Just sometimes I was afraid of her because she did things sometimes without telling me. And she knew things that I never dreamt she knew. But she loved me. Yes, she loved me. Sometimes – I think I loved her too . . .

I don't mean it was ever like Greta. Greta was the woman I belonged to. She was sex personified. I was made for her and I had to hold myself in. Ellie was something different. I enjoyed living with her, you know. Yes, that sounds very queer now I think back to it. I enjoyed living with her very much.

I'm putting this down now because this is what I was thinking that evening when I arrived back from America. When I arrived back on top of the world, having got all I'd longed for in spite of the risks, in spite of the dangers, in spite of having done a pretty good murder, though I say it myself!

Yes, it was tricky, I thought once or twice, but nobody could tell, not the way we'd done it. Now the risks were over, the dangers were over and here I was coming up to Gipsy's Acre. Coming as I'd come up to it that day after I'd first seen the poster on the walls, and gone up to look at the ruins of the old house. Coming up and rounding the bend –

And then – *it was then I saw her*. I mean it was then I saw Ellie. Just as I came round the corner of the road in the dangerous place where the accidents happened. *She was there* in the same place just where she'd been before, standing in the shadow of the fir tree. Just as she'd stood, when she'd started a little as she saw me and I'd started, seeing her. There we'd looked at each other first and I'd come up and spoken to her, played the part of the young man who's fallen suddenly in love. Played it jolly well too! Oh, I tell you I'm a fine actor!

But I hadn't expected to see her now . . . I mean, I *couldn't* see her now, could I? But I *was* seeing her . . . She was looking – looking straight at me. Only – there was something that frightened me – something that frightened me very much. It was, you see, just as though she *didn't* see me – I mean I knew she couldn't really be there. I knew she was dead – *but I saw her*. She was dead and her body was buried in the cemetery in the U.S.A. But all the same she was standing under the fir tree and she was looking at me. No, *not* at me. She was looking as though she expected to see me and there was love in her face. The same love that I had seen one day, one day when she'd been plucking the strings of her guitar. That day when she'd said to me, 'What were you thinking of?' And I said, 'Why do you ask me?' and she said, 'You were looking at me as though you loved me.' I'd said something silly like 'Of course I love you.'

I stopped dead. I stopped dead there in the road. I was shaking. I said out loud:

'Ellie.'

She didn't move, she just stayed there, *looking* . . . Looking straight through me. That's what frightened me because I knew if I thought for a minute I'd know why she didn't see me, and I didn't want to know. No, I didn't want to know that. I was quite sure that I didn't want to know that. Looking straight at the place where I was – *not seeing me*. I ran then. I ran like a coward, up the rest of the road to where the lights were shining in my house, until I pulled myself out of the silly panic that I was in. This was my triumph. I'd got home. I was the hunter home from the hills, back to my house, back to the things that I'd wanted more than anything in the world, to the wonderful woman whom I belonged to body and soul.

And now we'd get married and we'd live in the House. We'd get all we'd played for! We'd won – Won hands down!

The door wasn't latched. I went in, stamping my feet, and through the open door of the library. And there was Greta standing by the window waiting for me. She was glorious. She was the most glorious and the most lovely thing I'd ever seen. She was like a Brünnhilde, a super Valkyrie with shining golden hair. She smelt and looked and tasted of sex. We'd denied ourselves so long except for occasional brief meetings up in the Folly.

I came straight into her arms, a sailor home from the sea to where he belonged. Yes, it was one of the most wonderful moments of my life.

Presently we came down to earth. I sat down and she shoved a small pile of letters towards me. I picked out almost automatically one with an American stamp. It was the air mail letter from Lippincott. I wondered what he'd put in it, why he'd had to write me a letter.

'Well,' said Greta with a deep satisfied sigh, 'we've made it.'

'V-Day all right,' I said.

We both laughed, laughed wildly. There was champagne on the table. I opened it and we drank to each other.

'This place is wonderful,' I said, looking round. 'It's more beautiful than I remember it. Santonix – But I haven't told you. Santonix is dead.'

'Oh dear,' said Greta, 'what a pity. So he really *was* ill?'

'Of course he was ill. I never wanted to think so. I went and saw him when he was dying.'

Greta gave a little shiver.

'I shouldn't like to do that. Did he say anything?'

'Not really. He said I was a damned fool – I ought to have gone the other way.'

'What did he mean – what way?'

'I don't know what he meant,' I said. 'I suppose he was delirious. Didn't know what he was talking about.'

'Well, this house is a fine monument to his memory,' said Greta. 'I think we'll stick to it, don't you?'

I stared at her. 'Of course. Do you think I'm going to live anywhere else?'

'We can't live here all the time,' said Greta. 'Not all the year round. Buried in a hole like this village?'

'But it's where I want to live – it's where I always meant to live.'

'Yes, of course. But after all, Mike, we've got all the money in the world. We can go anywhere! We can go all over the Continent – we'll go on safari in Africa. We'll have adventures. We'll go and look for things – exciting pictures. We'll go to the Angkor Vat. Don't you want to have an adventurous life?'

'Well, I suppose so . . . But we'll always come back here, won't we?'

I had a queer feeling, a queer feeling that something had gone wrong somewhere. That's all I'd ever thought of. My House and Greta. I hadn't wanted anything else. But she did. I saw that. She was just beginning. Beginning to want things. Beginning to know she could have them. I had a sudden cruel foreboding. I began to shiver.

'What's the matter with you, Mike – you're shivering. Have you caught a cold or something?'

'It's not that,' I said.

'What's happened, Mike?'

'I saw Ellie,' I said.

'What do you mean, you saw Ellie?'

'As I was walking up the road I turned the corner and there she was, standing under a fir tree, looking at – I mean looking towards me.'

Greta stared.

'Don't be ridiculous. You – you imagined things.'

'Perhaps one does imagine things. This is Gipsy's Acre after all. Ellie was there all right, looking – looking quite happy. Just like herself as though she'd – she'd always been there and was always going to be there.'

'Mike!' Greta took hold of my shoulder. She shook me. 'Mike, don't say things like that. Had you been drinking before you got here?'

'No, I waited till I got here to you. I knew you'd have champagne waiting for us.'

'Well, let's forget Ellie and drink to ourselves.'

'It *was* Ellie,' I said obstinately.

'Of course it wasn't Ellie! It was just a trick of the light – something like that.'

'It was Ellie, and she was standing there. She was looking – looking for me and at me. But she couldn't see me. Greta, *she couldn't see me.*' My voice rose. 'And I know why. I know *why* she couldn't see me.'

'What do you mean?'

It was then that I whispered for the first time under my breath:

'Because that wasn't me. I wasn't there. There was nothing for her to see but Endless Night.' Then I shouted out in a panic-stricken voice, 'Some are born to Sweet Delight, and some are born to Endless Night. *Me*, Greta, *me*.

'Do you remember, Greta,' I said, 'how she sat on that sofa? She used to play that song on her guitar, singing it in her gentle voice. You must remember.

'"*Every night and every morn*,"' I sang it under my breath, '"*Some to misery are born. Every morn and every night some are born to sweet delight.*" That's Ellie, Greta. She was born to sweet delight. "*Some are born to sweet delight, some are born to endless night.*" That's what Mum knew about me. She knew I was born to endless night. I hadn't got there yet. But she knew. And Santonix knew. He knew I was heading that way. But it mightn't have happened. There was just a moment, just one moment, the time Ellie sang that song. I could have been quite happy, couldn't I, really, married to Ellie? I could have gone on being married to Ellie.'

'No, you couldn't,' said Greta. 'I never thought you were the type of person who lost your nerve, Mike.' She shook me roughly by the shoulder again. 'Wake up.'

I stared at her.

'I'm sorry, Greta. What have I been saying?'

'I suppose they got you down over there in the States. But you did all right, didn't you? I mean, all the investments are all right?'

'Everything's fixed,' I said. 'Everything's fixed for our future. Our glorious, glorious future.'

'You speak very queerly. I'd like to know what Lippincott says in his letter.'

I pulled his letter towards me and opened it. There was nothing inside except a cutting from a paper. Not a new cutting, it was old and rather rubbed. I stared down at it. It was a picture of a street. I recognized the street, with rather a grand building in the background. It was a street in Hamburg with some people coming towards the photographer. Two people in the forefront walking arm in arm. They were Greta and myself. *So Lippincott had known.* He'd known all along that I already knew Greta. Somebody must have sent him this cutting some time, probably with no nefarious intention. Just amused perhaps to recognize Miss Greta Andersen walking along the streets of Hamburg. He had known I knew Greta and I remembered how particularly he had asked me whether I had met or not met Greta Andersen. I had denied it, of course, but he'd known I was lying. It must have begun his suspicion of me.

I was suddenly afraid of Lippincott. He couldn't suspect, of course, that I'd killed Ellie. He suspected something, though. Perhaps he suspected even that.

'Look,' I said to Greta, 'he knew we knew each other. He's known it all along. I've always hated that old fox and he's always hated you,' I said. 'When he knows that we're going to marry, he'll suspect.' But then I knew that Lippincott had certainly suspected Greta and I were going to marry, he suspected that we knew each other, he suspected perhaps that we were lovers.

'Mike, will you stop being a panic-stricken rabbit? Yes, that's what I said. A panic-stricken rabbit. I admired you. I've always admired you. But now you're falling to pieces. You're afraid of everyone.'

'Don't say that to me.'

'Well, it's true.'

'*Endless night.*'

I couldn't think of anything else to say. I was still wondering just what it meant. Endless night. It meant blackness. It meant that I wasn't there to be seen. I could see the dead but the dead couldn't see me although I was living. They couldn't see me because I wasn't really there. The man who loved Ellie wasn't really there. He'd entered of his own accord into endless night. I bent my head lower towards the ground.

'*Endless night,*' I said again.

'Stop saying that,' Greta screamed. 'Stand up! Be a man, Mike. Don't give in to this absurd superstitious fancy.'

'How can I help it?' I said. 'I've sold my soul to Gipsy's Acre, haven't I? Gipsy's Acre's never been safe. It's never been safe for anyone. It wasn't safe for Ellie and it isn't safe for me. Perhaps it isn't safe for you.'

'What do you mean?'

I got up. I went towards her. I loved her. Yes, I loved her still with a last tense sexual desire. But love, hate, desire – aren't they all the same? Three in one and one in three. I could never have hated Ellie, but I hated Greta. I enjoyed hating her. I hated her with all my heart and with a leaping joyous wish – I couldn't wait for the safe ways, I didn't want to wait for them, I came nearer to her.

'You filthy bitch!' I said. 'You hateful, glorious, golden-haired bitch. You're not safe, Greta. You're not safe from *me*. Do you understand? I've learnt to enjoy – to enjoy killing people. I was excited the day that I knew Ellie had gone out with that horse to her death. I enjoyed myself all the morning because of killing, but I've never got near enough to killing until now. This is different. I want more than just knowing that someone's going to die because of a capsule they swallowed at breakfast time. I want more than pushing an old woman over a quarry. I want *to use my hands.*'

Greta was afraid now. She, whom I'd belonged to ever since I met her that day in Hamburg, met her and gone on to pretend illness, to throw up my job, to stay there with her. Yes, I'd belonged to her then, body and soul. I didn't belong to her now. I was myself. I was coming into another kind of kingdom to the one I'd dreamed of.

She was afraid. I loved seeing her afraid and I fastened my hands round her neck. Yes, even now when I am sitting here writing down all about myself (which, mind you, is a very happy thing to do) – to write all about yourself and what you've been through and what you felt and thought and how you deceived everyone – yes, it's wonderful to do, yes I was wonderfully happy when I killed Greta . . .

CHAPTER 24

There isn't really very much to say after that. I mean, things came to a climax there. One forgets, I suppose, that there can't be anything better to follow – that you've had it all. I just sat there for a long time. I don't know when *They* came. I don't know whether They all came at once . . . They couldn't have been there all along because they wouldn't have let me kill Greta. I noticed that God was there first. I don't mean God, I'm confused, I mean Major Phillpot. I'd liked him always, he'd been nice to me. He was rather like God in some ways, I think. I mean if God had been a human being and not something supernatural – up in the sky somewhere. He was a very fair man, very fair and kind. He looked after things and people. Tried to do his best for people.

I don't know how much he'd known about me. I remembered the curious way he looked at me that morning in the sale room when he said that I was 'fey'. I wonder why he thought I happened to be fey that day.

Then when we were there with that little crumpled heap on the ground that was Ellie in her riding habit . . . I wonder if he knew then or had some idea that I'd had something to do with it.

After Greta's death, as I say I just sat there in my chair, staring down at my champagne glass. It was empty. Everything was very empty, very empty indeed. There was just one light that we'd switched on, Greta and I, but it was in the corner. It didn't give much light and the sun – I think the sun must have set a long time ago. I just sat there and wondered what was going to happen next with a sort of dull wonder.

Then, I suppose, the people began coming. Perhaps a lot of people came at once. They came very quietly, if so, or else I wasn't hearing or noticing anybody.

Perhaps if Santonix had been there he would have told me what to do. Santonix was dead. He'd gone a different way to my way, so he wouldn't be any help. Nobody really would be any help.

After a bit I noticed Dr Shaw. He was so quiet I hardly knew he was there at first. He was sitting quite near me, just waiting for something. After a while I thought he was waiting for me to speak. I said to him:

'I've come home.'

There were one or two other people moving somewhere behind him. They seemed to be waiting, to be waiting for something that he was going to do.

'Greta's dead,' I said. 'I killed her. I expect you'd better take the body away, hadn't you?'

Somebody somewhere let off a flash bulb. It must have been a police photographer photographing the body. Dr Shaw turned his head and said sharply:

'Not yet.'

He turned his head round back to me again. I leaned towards him and said:

'I saw Ellie tonight.'

'Did you? Where?'

'Outside standing under a fir tree. It was the place I first saw her, you know.' I paused a moment and then said, 'She didn't see me . . . She couldn't see me because I wasn't there.' And after a while I said, 'That upset me. It upset me very much.'

Dr Shaw said, 'It was in the capsule, wasn't it? Cyanide in the capsule? That's what you gave Ellie that morning?'

'It was for her hay fever,' I said, 'she always took a capsule as a preventative against her allergy when she went riding. Greta and I fixed up one or two of the capsules with wasp stuff from the garden shed and joined them together again. We did it up in the Folly. Smart, wasn't it?' And I laughed. It was an odd sort of laugh, I heard it myself. It was more like a queer little giggle. I said, 'You'd examined all the things she took, hadn't you, when you came to see her ankle? Sleeping pills, the allergy capsules, and they were all quite all right, weren't they? No harm in any of them.'

'No harm,' said Dr Shaw. 'They were quite innocent.'

'That was rather clever really, wasn't it?' I said.

'You've been quite clever, yes, but not clever enough.'

'All the same I don't see how you found out.'

'We found out when there was a second death, the death you didn't mean to happen.'

'Claudia Hardcastle?'

'Yes. She died the same way as Ellie. She fell from her horse in the hunting field. Claudia was a healthy girl too, but she just fell from her horse and died. The time wasn't so long there, you see. They picked her up almost at once and there was still the smell of cyanide to go by. If she'd lain in the open air like Ellie for a couple of hours, there'd have been nothing – nothing to smell, nothing to find. I don't see how Claudia got the capsule, though. Unless you'd left one behind in the Folly. Claudia used to go to the Folly sometimes. Her fingerprints were there and she dropped a lighter there.'

'We must have been careless. Filling them was rather tricky.'

Then I said:

'You suspected I had something to do with Ellie's death, didn't you? All of you?' I looked round at the shadowy figures. 'Perhaps all of you.'

'Very often one knows. But I wasn't sure whether we'd be able to do anything about it.'

'You ought to caution me,' I said reprovingly.

'I'm not a police officer,' said Dr Shaw.

'What are you then?'

'I'm a doctor.'

'I don't need a doctor,' I said.

'That remains to be seen.'

I looked at Phillpot then, and I said:

'What are *you* doing? Come here to judge me, to preside at my trial?'

'I'm only a Justice of the Peace,' he said. 'I'm here as a friend.'

'A friend of mine?' That startled me.

'A friend of Ellie's,' he said.

I didn't understand. None of it made sense to me but I couldn't help feeling rather important. All of them there! Police and doctor, Shaw and Phillpot who was a busy man in his way. The whole thing was very complicated. I began to lose count of things. I was very tired, you see. I used to get tired suddenly and go to sleep . . .

And all the coming and going. People came to see me, all sorts of people. Lawyers, a solicitor, I think, and another kind of lawyer with him and doctors. Several doctors. They bothered me and I didn't want to answer them.

One of them kept asking me if there was anything I wanted. I said there was. I said there was only one thing I wanted. I said I wanted a ballpen and a lot of paper. I wanted, you see, to write all about it, how it all came to happen. I wanted to tell them what I'd felt, what I'd thought. The more I thought about myself, the more interesting I thought it would be to everybody. Because I *was* interesting. I was a really interesting person and I'd done interesting things.

The doctors – one doctor, anyway – seemed to think it was a good idea. I said:

'You always let people make a statement, so why can't I write my statement out? Some day, perhaps, everybody can read it.'

They let me do it. I couldn't write very long on end. I used to get tired. Somebody used a phrase like 'diminished responsibility' and somebody else disagreed. All sorts of things you hear. Sometimes they don't think you're even listening. Then I had to appear in court and I wanted them to fetch me my best suit because I had to make a good figure there. It seemed they had had detectives watching me. For some time. Those new servants. I think they'd been engaged or put on my trail by Lippincott. They found out too many things about me and Greta. Funny, after she was dead I never thought of Greta much . . . After I'd killed her she didn't seem to matter any more.

I tried to bring back the splendid triumphant feeling that I'd had when I strangled her. But even that was gone away . . .

They brought my mother to see me quite suddenly one day. There she was looking at me from the doorway. She didn't look as anxious as she used to look. I think all she looked now was sad. She hadn't much to say and nor had I. All she said was:

'I tried, Mike. I tried very hard to keep you safe. I failed. I was always afraid that I should fail.'

I said, 'All right, Mum, it wasn't your fault. I chose to go the way I wanted.'

And I thought suddenly, 'That's what Santonix said. He was afraid for me, too. He hadn't been able to do anything either. Nobody could have done anything – except perhaps I myself . . . I don't know. I'm not sure. But every now and then I remember – I remember that day when Ellie said to me, "What are you thinking of when you look at me like that?" and I said, "Like what?" She said, "As though you loved me." I suppose in a way I did love her. I could have loved her. She was so sweet, Ellie. Sweet delight . . .'

I suppose the trouble with me was that I wanted things too much, always. Wanted them, too, the easy way, the greedy way.

That first time, that first day I came to Gipsy's Acre and met Ellie. As we were going down the road again we met Esther. It put it into my head that day, the warning she gave Ellie, put it in my head to pay her. I knew she was the kind who would do anything for money. I'd pay her. She'd start warning Ellie and frightening her, making her feel that she was in danger. I thought it might make it seem more possible then that Ellie had died from shock. That first day, I know now, I'm sure of it, Esther was really frightened. She was really frightened for Ellie. She warned her, warned her to go away, have nothing to do with Gipsy's Acre. She was warning her, of course, to have nothing to do with *me*. I didn't understand that. Ellie didn't understand either.

Was it *me* Ellie was afraid of? I think it must have been though she didn't know it herself. She knew there was something threatening her, she knew there was danger. Santonix knew the evil in me, too, just like my mother. Perhaps all three of them knew. Ellie knew but she didn't mind, she never minded. It's odd, very odd. I know now. We were very happy together. Yes, very happy. I wish I'd known then that we were happy . . . I had my chance. Perhaps everyone has a chance. I – turned my back on it.

It seems odd, doesn't it, that Greta doesn't matter at all?

And even my beautiful house doesn't matter.

Only Ellie . . . And Ellie can never find me again – Endless Night . . . That's the end of my story –

In my end is the beginning – that's what people are always saying. But what does it *mean*?

And just where does my story begin? I must try and think . . .

WRATH

•

FIVE LITTLE PIGS

To Stephen Glanville

CARLA LEMARCHANT

Hercule Poirot looked with interest and appreciation at the young woman who was being ushered into the room.

There had been nothing distinctive in the letter she had written. It had been a mere request for an appointment, with no hint of what lay behind that request. It had been brief and business-like. Only the firmness of the handwriting had indicated that Carla Lemarchant was a young woman.

And now here she was in the flesh – a tall, slender young woman in the early twenties. The kind of young woman that one definitely looked at twice. Her clothes were good, an expensive well-cut coat and skirt and luxurious furs. Her head was well poised on her shoulders, she had a square brow, a sensitively cut nose and a determined chin. She looked very much alive. It was her aliveness, more than her beauty, which struck the predominant note.

Before her entrance, Hercule Poirot had been feeling old – now he felt rejuvenated – alive – keen!

As he came forward to greet her, he was aware of her dark grey eyes studying him attentively. She was very earnest in that scrutiny.

She sat down and accepted the cigarette that he offered her. After it was lit she sat for a minute or two smoking, still looking at him with that earnest, thoughtful gaze.

Poirot said gently:

'Yes, it has to be decided, does it not?'

She started. 'I beg your pardon?'

Her voice was attractive, with a faint, agreeable huskiness in it.

'You are making up your mind, are you not, whether I am a mere mountebank, or the man you need?'

She smiled. She said:

'Well, yes – something of that kind. You see, M. Poirot, you – you don't look exactly the way I pictured you.'

'And I am old, am I not? Older than you imagined?'

'Yes, that too.' She hesitated. 'I'm being frank, you see. I want – I've got to have – the best.'

'Rest assured,' said Hercule Poirot. 'I *am* the best!'

Carla said: 'You're not modest . . . All the same, I'm inclined to take you at your word.'

Poirot said placidly:

'One does not, you know, employ merely the muscles. I do not need to bend and measure the footprints and pick up the cigarette ends and examine the bent blades of grass. It is enough for me to sit back in my chair and *think*. It is this' – he tapped his egg-shaped head – '*this* that functions!'

'I know,' said Carla Lemarchant. 'That's why I've come to you. I want you, you see, to do something fantastic!'

'That,' said Hercule Poirot, 'promises well!'

He looked at her in encouragement.

Carla Lemarchant drew a deep breath.

'My name,' she said, 'isn't Carla. It's Caroline. The same as my mother's. I was called after her.' She paused. 'And though I've always gone by the name of Lemarchant – my real name is Crale.'

Hercule Poirot's forehead creased a moment perplexedly. He murmured: 'Crale – I seem to remember . . .'

She said:

'My father was a painter – rather a well-known painter. Some people say he was a great painter. *I* think he was.'

Hercule Poirot said: 'Amyas Crale?'

'Yes.' She paused, then she went on: 'And my mother, Caroline Crale, was tried for murdering him!'

'Aha,' said Hercule Poirot. 'I remember now – but only vaguely. I was abroad at the time. It was a long time ago.'

'Sixteen years,' said the girl.

Her face was very white now and her eyes two burning lights.

She said:

'Do you understand? *She was tried and convicted* . . . She wasn't hanged because they felt that there were extenuating circumstances – so the sentence was commuted to penal servitude for life. But she died only a year after the trial. You see? It's all over – done – finished with . . .'

Poirot said quietly: 'And so?'

The girl called Carla Lemarchant pressed her hands together. She spoke slowly and haltingly but with an odd, pointed emphasis.

She said:

'You've got to understand – exactly – where I come in. I was five years old at the time it – happened. Too young to know anything about it. I remember my mother and my father, of course, and I remember leaving home suddenly – being taken to the country. I remember the pigs and a nice fat farmer's wife – and everybody being very kind – and I remember, quite clearly, the funny way they used to look at me – everybody – a sort of furtive look. I knew, of course, children do, that there was something wrong – but I didn't know what.

'And then I went on a ship – it was exciting – it went on for days, and then I was in Canada and Uncle Simon met me, and I lived in Montreal with him and with Aunt Louise, and when I asked about Mummy and Daddy they said they'd be coming soon. And then – and then I think I forgot – only I sort of knew that they were dead without remembering any one actually telling me so. Because by that time, you see, I didn't think about them any more. I was very happy, you know. Uncle Simon and Aunt Louise were sweet to me, and I went to school and had a lot of friends, and I'd quite forgotten that I'd ever had another name, not Lemarchant. Aunt Louise, you see, told me that that was my name in Canada and that seemed quite sensible to me at the time – it was just my Canadian name – but as I say I forgot in the end that I'd ever had any other.'

She flung up her defiant chin. She said:

'Look at me. You'd say – wouldn't you? if you met me: "There goes a girl who's got nothing to worry about!" I'm well off, I've got splendid health, I'm sufficiently good to look at, I can enjoy life. At twenty, there wasn't a girl anywhere I'd have changed places with.

'But already, you know, I'd begun to ask questions. About my own mother and father. Who they were and what they did? I'd have been bound to find out in the end –

'As it was, they told me the truth. When I was twenty-one. They had to then, because for one thing I came into my own money. And then, you see, there was the letter. The letter my mother left for me when she died.'

Her expression changed, dimmed. Her eyes were no longer two burning points, they were dark dim pools. She said:

'That's when I learnt the truth. That my mother had been convicted of murder. It was – rather horrible.'

She paused.

'There's something else I must tell you. I was engaged to be married. They said we must wait – that we couldn't be married until I was twenty-one. When I knew, I understood why.'

Poirot stirred and spoke for the first time. He said:

'And what was your fiancé's reaction?'

'John? John didn't care. He said it made no difference – not to him. He and I were John and Carla – and the past didn't matter.'

She leaned forward.

'We're still engaged. But all the same, you know, it *does* matter. It matters to me. And it matters to John too . . . It isn't the past that matters to us – it's the future.' She clenched her hands. 'We want children, you see. We both want children. And we don't want to watch our children growing up and be afraid.'

Poirot said:

'Do you not realize that amongst every one's ancestors there has been violence and evil?'

'You don't understand. That's so, of course. But then, one doesn't usually know about it. We do. It's very near to us. And sometimes – I've seen John just look at me. Such a quick glance – just a flash. Supposing we were married and we'd quarrelled – and I saw him look at me and – and *wonder*?'

Hercule Poirot said: 'How was your father killed?'

Carla's voice came clear and firm.

'He was poisoned.'

Hercule Poirot said: 'I see.'

There was a silence.

Then the girl said in a calm, matter-of-fact voice:

'Thank goodness you're sensible. You see that it does matter – and what it involves. You don't try and patch it up and trot out consoling phrases.'

'I understand very well,' said Poirot. 'What I do not understand is what you want of *me*?'

Carla Lemarchant said simply:

'I want to marry John! And I mean to marry John! And I want to have at least two girls and two boys. And you're going to make that possible!'

'You mean – you want me to talk to your fiancé? Ah no, it is idiocy what I say there! It is something quite different that you are suggesting. Tell me what is in your mind.'

'Listen, M. Poirot. Get this – and get it clearly. I'm hiring you to investigate a case of murder.'

'Do you mean –?'

'Yes, I do mean. A case of murder is a case of murder whether it happened yesterday or sixteen years ago.'

'But my dear young lady –'

'Wait, M. Poirot. You haven't got it all yet. There's a very important point.'

'Yes?'

'My mother was innocent,' said Carla Lemarchant.

Hercule Poirot rubbed his nose. He murmured:

'Well, naturally – I comprehend that –'

'It isn't sentiment. There's her letter. She left it for me before she died. It was to be given to me when I was twenty-one. She left it for that one reason – that I should be quite sure. That's all that was in it. That she hadn't done it – that she was innocent – that I could be sure of that always.'

Hercule Poirot looked thoughtfully at the young vital face staring so earnestly at him. He said slowly:

'*Tout de même –*'

Carla smiled.

'No, mother wasn't like that! You're thinking that it might be a lie – a sentimental lie?' She leaned forward earnestly. 'Listen, M. Poirot, there are some things that children know quite well. I can remember my mother – a patchy remembrance, of course, but I remember quite well the *sort* of person she was. She didn't tell lies – kind lies. If a thing was going to hurt she always told you so. Dentists, or thorns in your finger – all that sort of thing. Truth was a – a natural impulse to her. I wasn't, I don't think, especially fond of her – but I trusted her. I *still* trust her! If she says she didn't kill my father then she didn't kill him! She wasn't the sort of person who would solemnly write down a lie when she knew she was dying.'

Slowly, almost reluctantly, Hercule Poirot bowed his head.

Carla went on.

'That's why it's all right for *me* marrying John. *I* know it's all right. *But he doesn't.* He feels that naturally I would think my mother was innocent. It's got to be cleared up, M. Poirot. And *you're* going to do it!'

Hercule Poirot said slowly:

'Granted that what you say is true, mademoiselle, sixteen years have gone by!'

Carla Lemarchant said: 'Oh! of course it's going to be *difficult*! Nobody but *you* could do it!'

Hercule Poirot's eyes twinkled slightly. He said:

'You give me the best butter – *hein?*'

Carla said:

'I've heard about you. The things you've done. The *way* you have done them. It's psychology that interests you, isn't it? Well, that doesn't change with time. The tangible things are gone – the cigarette-end and the footprints and the bent blades of grass. You can't look for those any more. But you can go over all the facts of the case, and perhaps talk to the people who were there at the time – they're all alive still – and then – and then, as you said just now, you can lie back in your chair and *think. And you'll know what really happened . . .'*

Hercule Poirot rose to his feet. One hand caressed his moustache. He said:

'Mademoiselle, I am honoured! I will justify your faith in me. I will investigate your case of murder. I will search back into the events of sixteen years ago and I will find out the truth.'

Carla got up. Her eyes were shining. But she only said:

'Good.'

Hercule Poirot shook an eloquent forefinger.

'One little moment. I have said I will find out the truth. I do not, you understand, have the bias. I do not accept your assurance of your mother's innocence. If she was guilty – *eh bien*, what then?'

Carla's proud head went back. She said:

'I'm her daughter. I want the *truth*!'

Hercule Poirot said:

'*En avant*, then. Though it is not that, that I should say. On the contrary. *En arrière . . .'*

BOOK I

COUNSEL FOR THE DEFENCE

'Do I remember the Crale case?' asked Sir Montague Depleach. 'Certainly I do. Remember it very well. Most attractive woman. But unbalanced, of course. No self-control.'

He glanced sideways at Poirot.

'What makes you ask me about it?'

'I am interested.'

'Not really tactful of you, my dear man,' said Depleach, showing his teeth in his sudden famous 'wolf's smile', which had been reputed to have such a terrifying effect upon witnesses. 'Not one of my successes, you know. I didn't get her off.'

'I know that.'

Sir Montague shrugged his shoulders. He said:

'Of course I hadn't quite as much experience then as I have now. All the same I think I did all that could humanly be done. One can't do much without *co-operation*. We *did* get it commuted to penal servitude. Provocation, you know. Lots of respectable wives and mothers got up a petition. There was a lot of sympathy for her.'

He leaned back stretching out his long legs. His face took on a judicial, appraising look.

'If she'd shot him, you know, or even knifed him – I'd have gone all out for manslaughter. But poison – no, you can't play tricks with that. It's tricky – very tricky.'

'What was the defence?' asked Hercule Poirot.

He knew because he had already read the newspaper files, but he saw no harm in playing the complete ignorant to Sir Montague.

'Oh, suicide. Only thing you *could* go for. But it didn't go down well. Crale simply wasn't that kind of man! You never met him, I suppose? No? Well, he was a great blustering, vivid sort of chap. Great womanizer, beer drinker – all the rest of it. Went in for the lusts of the flesh and enjoyed them. You can't persuade a jury that a man like that is going to sit down and quietly do away with himself. It just doesn't fit. No, I was afraid I was up against a losing proposition from the first. And she wouldn't play up! I knew we'd lost as soon as she went into the box. No fight in her at all. But there it is – if you *don't* put your client into the box, the jury draw their own conclusions.'

Poirot said:

'Is that what you meant when you said just now that one cannot do much without co-operation?'

'Absolutely, my dear fellow. We're not magicians, you know. Half the battle is the impression the accused makes on the jury. I've known juries time and again bring in verdicts dead against the judge's summing up. "'E did it, all right" – that's the point of view. Or "*He* never did a thing like that – don't tell me!" Caroline Crale didn't even *try* to put up a fight.'

'Why was that?'

Sir Montague shrugged his shoulders.

'Don't ask me. Of course, she was fond of the fellow. Broke her all up when she came to and realized what she'd done. Don't believe she ever rallied from the shock.'

'So in your opinion she was guilty?'

Depleach looked rather startled. He said:

'Er – well, I thought we were taking that for granted.'

'Did she ever admit to you that she was guilty?'

Depleach looked shocked.

'Of course not – of course not. We have our code, you know. Innocence is always – er – assumed. If you're so interested it's a pity you can't get hold of old Mayhew. Mayhews were the solicitors who briefed me. Old Mayhew could have told you more than I can. But there – he's joined the great majority. There's young George Mayhew, of course, but he was only a boy at the time. It's a long time ago, you know.'

'Yes, I know. It is fortunate for me that you remember so much. You have a remarkable memory.'

Depleach looked pleased. He murmured:

'Oh well, one remembers the main headings, you know. Especially when it's a capital charge. And, of course, the Crale case got a lot of publicity from the press. Lot of sex interest and all that. The girl in the case was pretty striking. Hard-boiled piece of goods, I thought.'

'You will forgive me if I seem too insistent,' said Poirot, 'but I repeat once more, you had no doubt of Caroline Crale's guilt?'

Depleach shrugged his shoulders. He said:

'Frankly – as man to man – I don't think there's much doubt about it. Oh yes, she did it all right.'

'What was the evidence against her?'

'Very damning indeed. First of all there was motive. She and Crale had led a kind of cat and dog life for years – interminable rows. He was always getting mixed up with some woman or other. Couldn't help it. He was that kind of man. She stood it pretty well on the whole. Made allowances for him on the score of temperament – and the man really was a first-class painter, you know. His stuff's gone up enormously in price – enormously. Don't care for that style of painting myself – ugly forceful stuff, but it's *good* – no doubt of that.

'Well, as I say, there had been trouble about women from time to time. Mrs Crale wasn't the meek kind who suffers in silence. There were rows all right. But he always came back to her in the end. These affairs of his blew over. But this final affair was rather different. It was a girl, you see – and quite a young girl. She was only twenty.

'Elsa Greer, that was her name. She was the only daughter of some Yorkshire manufacturer. She'd got money and determination, and she knew what she wanted. What she wanted was Amyas Crale. She got him to paint her – he didn't paint regular Society portraits, "Mrs Blinkety Blank in satin and pearls", but he painted figures. I don't know that most women would have cared to be painted by him – he didn't spare them! But he painted the Greer girl, and he ended by falling for her good and proper. He was getting on for forty, you know, and he'd been married a good many years. He was just ripe for making a fool of himself over some chit of a girl. Elsa Greer was the girl. He was crazy about her, and his idea was to get a divorce from his wife and marry Elsa.

'Caroline Crale wasn't standing for that. She threatened him. She was overheard by two people to say that if he didn't give the girl up she'd kill him. And she meant it all right! The day before it happened, they'd been having tea with a neighbour. He was by way of dabbling in herbs and home-brewed medicines. Amongst his patent brews was one of coniine – spotted hemlock. There was some talk about it and its deadly properties.

'The next day he noticed that half the contents of the bottle had gone. Got the wind up about it. They found an almost empty bottle of it in Mrs Crale's room, hidden away at the bottom of a drawer.'

Hercule Poirot moved uncomfortably. He said:

'Somebody else might have put it there.'

'Oh! She admitted to the police she'd taken it. Very unwise, of course, but she didn't have a solicitor to advise her at that stage. When they asked her about it, she admitted quite frankly that she had taken it.'

'For what reason?'

'She made out that she'd taken it with the idea of doing herself in. She couldn't explain how the bottle came to be empty – nor how it was that there were only her fingerprints on it. That part of it was pretty damaging. She contended, you see, that Amyas Crale had committed suicide. But if he'd taken the coniine from the bottle she'd hidden in her room, *his* fingerprints would have been on the bottle as well as hers.'

'It was given him in beer, was it not?'

'Yes. She got out the bottle from the refrigerator and took it down herself to where he was painting in the garden. She poured it out and gave it to him and watched him drink it. Every one went up to lunch and left him – he often didn't come in to meals. Afterwards she and the governess found him there dead. Her story was that the beer *she* gave him was all right. Our theory was that he suddenly felt so worried and remorseful that he slipped the poison in himself. All poppycock – he wasn't that kind of man! And the fingerprint evidence was the most damning of all.'

'They found her fingerprints on the bottle?'

'No, they didn't – they found only *his* – and they were phoney ones. She was alone with the body, you see, while the governess went to call up a doctor. And what she must have done was to wipe the bottle and glass and then press his fingers on them. She wanted to pretend, you see, that she'd never even handled the stuff. Well, that didn't work. Old Rudolph, who was prosecuting, had a lot of fun with that – proved quite definitely by demonstration in court that a man *couldn't* hold a bottle with his fingers in that position! Of course *we* did our best to prove that he *could* – that his hands would take up a contorted attitude when he was dying – but frankly our stuff wasn't very convincing.'

Hercule Poirot said:

'The coniine in the bottle must have been put there before she took it down to the garden.'

'There was no coniine in the bottle at all. Only in the glass.'

He paused – his large handsome face suddenly altered – he turned his head sharply. 'Hallo,' he said. 'Now then, Poirot, *what are you driving at?*'

Poirot said:

'*If* Caroline Crale was innocent, how did that coniine get into the beer? The defence said at the time that Amyas Crale himself put it there. But you say to me that that was in the highest degree unlikely – and for my part I agree with you. He was not that kind of man. Then, if Caroline Crale did not do it, *someone else did.*'

Depleach said with almost a splutter:

'Oh, damn it all, man, you can't flog a dead horse. It's all over and done with years ago. Of course she did it. You'd know that well enough if you'd seen her at the time. It was written all over her! I even fancy that the verdict was a relief to her. She wasn't frightened. No nerves at all. Just wanted to get through the trial and have it over. A very brave woman, really . . .'

'And yet,' said Hercule Poirot, 'when she died she left a letter to be given to her daughter in which she swore solemnly that she was innocent.'

'I dare say she did,' said Sir Montague Depleach. 'You or I would have done the same in her place.'

'Her daughter says she was not that kind of woman.'

'The daughter says – pah! What does *she* know about it? My dear Poirot, the daughter was a mere infant at the time of the trial. What was she – four – five? They changed her name and sent her out of England somewhere to some relatives. What can *she* know or remember?'

'Children know people very well sometimes.'

'Maybe they do. But that doesn't follow in this case. Naturally the girl wants to believe her mother didn't do it. Let her believe it. It doesn't do any harm.'

'But unfortunately she demands proof.'

'Proof that Caroline Crale didn't kill her husband?'

'Yes.'

'Well,' said Depleach. 'She won't get it.'

'You think not?'

The famous K.C. looked thoughtfully at his companion.

'I've always thought you were an honest man, Poirot. What are you doing? Trying to make money by playing on a girl's natural affections?'

'You do not know the girl. She is an unusual girl. A girl of great force of character.'

'Yes, I should imagine the daughter of Amyas and Caroline Crale might be that. What does she want?'

'She wants the truth.'

'Hm – I'm afraid she'll find the truth unpalatable. Honestly, Poirot, I don't think there's any doubt about it. She killed him.'

'You will forgive me, my friend, but I must satisfy myself on that point.'

'Well, I don't know what more you can do. You can read up the newspaper accounts of the trial. Humphrey Rudolph appeared for the Crown. He's dead – let me see, who was his junior? Young Fogg, I think.

Yes, Fogg. You can have a chat with him. And then there are the people who were there at the time. Don't suppose they'll enjoy your butting in and raking the whole thing up, but I dare say you'll get what you want out of them. You're a plausible devil.'

'Ah yes, the people concerned. That is very important. You remember, perhaps, who they were?'

Depleach considered.

'Let me see – it's a long time ago. There were only five people who were really in it, so to speak – I'm not counting the servants – a couple of faithful old things, scared-looking creatures – they didn't know anything about anything. No one could suspect them.'

'There are five people, you say. Tell me about them.'

'Well, there was Philip Blake. He was Crale's greatest friend – had known him all his life. He was staying in the house at the time. *He's* alive. I see him now and again on the links. Lives at St George's Hill. Stockbroker. Plays the markets and gets away with it. Successful man, running to fat a bit.'

'Yes. And who next?'

'Then there was Blake's elder brother. Country squire – stay at home sort of chap.'

A jingle ran through Poirot's head. He repressed it. He must *not* always be thinking of nursery rhymes. It seemed an obsession with him lately. And yet the jingle persisted.

'*This little pig went to market, this little pig stayed at home . . .*'

He murmured:

'He stayed at home – yes?'

'He's the fellow I was telling you about – messed about with drugs – and herbs – bit of a chemist. His hobby. What was his name now? Literary sort of name – I've got it. Meredith. Meredith Blake. Don't know whether he's alive or not.'

'And who next?'

'Next? Well, there's the cause of all the trouble. The girl in the case. Elsa Greer.'

'*This little pig ate roast beef,*' murmured Poirot.

Depleach stared at him.

'They've fed her meat all right,' he said. 'She's been a go-getter. She's had three husbands since then. In and out of the divorce court as easy as you please. And every time she makes a change, it's for the better. Lady Dittisham – that's who she is now. Open any *Tatler* and you're sure to find her.'

'And the other two?'

'There was the governess woman. I don't remember her name. Nice capable woman. Thompson – Jones – something like that. And there was the child. Caroline Crale's half-sister. She must have been about fifteen. She's made rather a name for herself. Digs up things and goes trekking to the back of beyond. Warren – that's her name. Angela Warren. Rather an alarming young woman nowadays. I met her the other day.'

'She is not, then, the little pig who cried Wee Wee Wee . . . ?'

Sir Montague Depleach looked at him rather oddly. He said drily:

'She's had something to cry Wee-Wee about in her life! She's disfigured, you know. Got a bad scar down one side of her face. She – Oh well, you'll hear all about it, I dare say.'

Poirot stood up. He said:

'I thank you. You have been very kind. If Mrs Crale did *not* kill her husband –'

Depleach interrupted him:

'But she did, old boy, she did. Take my word for it.'

Poirot continued without taking any notice of the interruption.

'Then it seems logical to suppose that one of these five people must have done so.'

'One of them *could* have done it, I suppose,' said Depleach, doubtfully. 'But I don't see why any of them *should*. No reason at all! In fact, I'm quite sure none of them *did* do it. Do get this bee out of your bonnet, old boy!'

But Hercule Poirot only smiled and shook his head.

CHAPTER 2

COUNSEL FOR THE PROSECUTION

'Guilty as Hell,' said Mr Fogg succinctly.

Hercule Poirot looked meditatively at the thin clear-cut face of the barrister.

Quentin Fogg, K.C. was a very different type from Montague Depleach. Depleach had force, magnetism, an over-bearing and slightly bullying personality. He got his effects by a rapid and dramatic change of manner. Handsome, urbane, charming one minute – then an almost magical transformation, lips back, snarling smile – out for your blood.

Quentin Fogg was thin, pale, singularly lacking in what is called personality. His questions were quiet and unemotional – but steadily persistent. If Depleach was like a rapier, Fogg was like an auger. He bored steadily. He had never reached spectacular fame, but he was known as a first-class man on law. He usually won his cases.

Hercule Poirot eyed him meditatively.

'So that,' he said, 'was how it struck you?'

Fogg nodded. He said:

'You should have seen her in the box. Old Humpie Rudolph (he was leading, you know) simply made mincement of her. Mincemeat!'

He paused and then said unexpectedly:

'On the whole, you know, it was rather too much of a good thing.'

'I am not sure,' said Hercule Poirot, 'that I quite understand you?'

Fogg drew his delicately marked brows together. His sensitive hand stroked his bare upper lip. He said:

'How shall I put it? It's a very English point of view. "Shooting the sitting bird" describes it best. Is that intelligible to you?'

'It is, as you say, a very English point of view, but I think I understand you. In the Central Criminal Court, as on the playing fields of Eton, and in the hunting country, the Englishman likes the victim to have a sporting chance.'

'That's it, exactly. Well, in this case, the accused *didn't* have a chance. Humpie Rudolph did as he liked with her. It started with her examination by Depleach. She stood up there, you know – as docile as a little girl at a party, answering Depleach's questions with the answers she'd learnt off by heart. Quite docile, word perfect – and absolutely unconvincing! She'd been told what to say and she said it. It wasn't Depleach's fault. That old mountebank played his part perfectly – but in any scene that needs two actors, one alone can't carry it. She didn't play up to him. It made the worst possible effect on the jury. And then old Humpie got up. I expect you've seen him? He's a great loss. Hitching his gown up, swaying back on his feet – and then – straight off the mark!

'As I tell you, he made mincemeat of her! Led up to this and that – and she fell into the pitfall every time. He got her to admit the absurdities of her own statements, he got her to contradict herself, she floundered in deeper and deeper. And then he wound up with his usual stuff. Very compelling – very convinced: "I suggest to you, Mrs Crale, that this story of yours about stealing coniine in order to commit suicide is a tissue of falsehood. I suggest that you took it in order to administer it to your husband who was about to leave you for another woman, and that you *did* deliberately administer it to him." And she looked at him – such a pretty creature –

graceful, delicate – and she said: "Oh, no – no, I didn't." It was the flattest thing you ever heard – the most unconvincing. I saw old Depleach squirm in his seat. He knew it was all up then.'

Fogg paused a minute – then he went on:

'And yet – I don't know. In some ways it was the cleverest thing she could have done! It appealed to chivalry – to that queer chivalry closely allied to blood sports which makes most foreigners think us such almighty humbugs! The jury felt – the whole court felt – that she hadn't got a chance. She couldn't even fight for herself. She certainly couldn't put up any kind of a show against a great big clever brute like old Humpie. That weak, unconvincing: "*Oh no – no, I didn't,*" it was pathetic – simply pathetic. She was done for!

'Yes, in a way, it was the best thing she could have done. The jury were only out just over half an hour. They brought her in: Guilty with a recommendation to mercy.

'Actually, you know, she made a good contrast to the other woman in the case. The girl. The jury were unsympathetic to *her* from the start. She never turned a hair. Very good looking, hard-boiled, modern. To the women in the court she stood for a type – type of the home-breaker. Homes weren't safe when girls like that were wandering abroad. Girls damn full of sex and contemptuous of the rights of wives and mothers. She didn't spare herself, I will say. She was honest. Admirably honest. She'd fallen in love with Amyas Crale and he with her, and she'd no scruples at all about taking him away from his wife and child.

'I admired her in a way. She had guts. Depleach put in some nasty stuff in cross-examination and she stood up well to it. But the court was unsympathetic. And the judge didn't like her. Old Avis, it was. Been a bit of a rip himself when young – but he's very hot on morality when he's presiding in his robes. His summing up against Caroline Crale was mildness itself. He couldn't deny the facts but he threw out pretty strong hints as to provocation and all that.'

Hercule Poirot asked:

'He did not support the suicide theory of the defence?'

Fogg shook his head.

'*That* never really had a leg to stand upon. Mind you, I don't say Depleach didn't do his best with it. He was magnificent. He painted a most moving picture of a great-hearted, pleasure-loving, temperamental man, suddenly overtaken by a passion for a lovely young girl, conscience stricken, yet unable to resist. Then his recoil, his disgust with himself, his remorse for the way he was treating his wife and child and his sudden decision to end it all! The honourable way out. I can tell you, it was a most moving performance; Depleach's voice brought tears to your eyes. You saw the poor wretch torn by his passions and his essential decency. The effect was terrific. Only – when it was all over – and the spell was broken, you couldn't quite square that mythical figure with Amyas Crale. Everybody knew too much about Crale. He wasn't at all that kind of man. And Depleach hadn't been able to get hold of any evidence to show that he was. I should say Crale came as near as possible to being a man without even a rudimentary conscience. He was a ruthless, selfish, good-tempered happy egoist. Any ethics he had would have applied to painting. He wouldn't, I'm convinced, have painted a sloppy, bad picture – no matter what the inducement. But for the rest, he was a full-blooded man and he loved life – he had a zest for it. Suicide? Not he!'

'Not, perhaps, a very good defence to have chosen?'

Fogg shrugged his thin shoulders. He said:

'What else was there? Couldn't sit back and plead that there was no case for the jury – that the prosecution had got to prove their case against the accused. There was a great deal too much proof. She'd handled the poison – admitted pinching it, in fact. There was means, motive, opportunity – everything.'

'One might have attempted to show that these things were artificially arranged?'

Fog said bluntly:

'She admitted most of them. And, in any case, it's too far-fetched. You're implying, I presume, that somebody else murdered him and fixed it up to look as though she had done it.'

'You think that quite untenable?'

Fogg said slowly:

'I'm afraid I do. You're suggesting the mysterious X. Where do we look for him?'

Poirot said:

'Obviously in a close circle. There were five people, were there not, who *could* have been concerned?'

'Five? Let me see. There was the old duffer who messed about with his herb brewing. A dangerous hobby – but an amiable creature. Vague sort of person. Don't see him as X. There was the girl – she might have polished off Caroline, but certainly not Amyas. Then there was the stockbroker – Crale's best friend. That's popular in detective stories, but I don't believe in it in real life. There's no one else – oh yes, the kid sister, but one doesn't seriously consider her. That's four.'

Hercule Poirot said:

'You forget the governess.'

'Yes, that's true. Wretched people, governesses, one never does remember them. I do recall her dimly though. Middle-aged, plain, competent. I suppose a psychologist would say that she had a guilty passion for Crale and therefore killed him. The repressed spinster! It's no good – I just don't believe it. As far as my dim remembrance goes she wasn't the neurotic type.'

'It is a long time ago.'

'Fifteen or sixteen years, I suppose. Yes, quite that. You can't expect my memories of the case to be very acute.'

Hercule Poirot said:

'But on the contrary, you remember it amazingly well. That astounds me. You can see it, can you not? When you talk the picture is there before your eyes.'

Fogg said slowly:

'Yes, you're right – I do see it – quite plainly.'

Poirot said:

'It would interest me, my friend, very much, if you would tell me *why?*'

'Why?' Fogg considered the question. His thin intellectual face was alert – interested. 'Yes, now *why?*'

Poirot asked:

'*What* do you see so plainly? The witnesses? The counsel? The judge? The accused standing in the dock?'

Fogg said quietly:

'That's the reason, of course! You've put your finger on it. I shall always see *her* . . . Funny thing, romance. She had the quality of it. I don't know if she was really beautiful . . . She wasn't very young – tired looking – circles under her eyes. But it all centred round her. The interest – the drama. And yet, half the time, *she wasn't there*. She'd gone away somewhere, quite far away – just left her body there, quiescent, attentive, with the little polite smile on her lips. She was all half tones, you know, lights and shades. And yet, with it all, she was more alive than the other – that girl with the perfect body, and the beautiful face, and the crude young strength. I admired Elsa Greer because she had guts, because she could fight, because she stood up to her tormentors and never quailed! But I admired Caroline Crale because she didn't fight, because she retreated into her world of half lights and shadows. She was never defeated because she never gave battle.'

He paused:

'I'm only sure of one thing. She loved the man she killed. Loved him so much that half of her died with him . . .'

Mr Fogg, K.C., paused and polished his glasses.

'Dear me,' he said. 'I seem to be saying some very strange things! I was quite a young man at the time, you know. Just an ambitious youngster. These things make an impression. But all the same I'm sure that Caroline Crale was a very remarkable woman. I shall never forget her. No – I shall never forget her . . .'

CHAPTER 3

THE YOUNG SOLICITOR

George Mayhew was cautious and non-committal.

He remembered the case, of course, but not at all clearly. His father had been in charge – he himself had been only nineteen at the time.

Yes, the case had made a great stir. Because of Crale being such a well-known man. His pictures were very fine – very fine indeed. Two of them were in the Tate. Not that that meant anything.

M. Poirot would excuse him, but he didn't see quite what M. Poirot's interest was in the matter. Oh, the *daughter*! Really? Indeed? Canada? He had always heard it was New Zealand.

George Mayhew became less rigid. He unbent.

A shocking thing in a girl's life. He had the deepest sympathy for her. Really it would have been better if she had never learned the truth. Still, it was no use saying that *now*.

She wanted to know? Yes, but what *was* there to know? There were the reports of the trial, of course. He himself didn't really know anything.

No, he was afraid there wasn't much doubt as to Mrs Crale's being guilty. There was a certain amount of excuse for her. These artists – difficult people to live with. With Crale, he understood, it had always been some woman or other.

And she herself had probably been the possessive type of woman. Unable to accept facts. Nowadays she'd simply have divorced him and got over it. He added cautiously:

'Let me see – er – Lady Dittisham, I believe, was the girl in the case.'

Poirot said that he believed that that was so.

'The newspapers bring it up from time to time,' said Mayhew. 'She's been in the divorce court a good deal. She's a very rich woman, as I expect you know. She was married to that explorer fellow before Dittisham. She's always more or less in the public eye. The kind of woman who likes notoriety, I should imagine.'

'Or possibly a hero worshipper,' suggested Poirot.

The idea was upsetting to George Mayhew. He accepted it dubiously.

'Well, possibly – yes, I suppose that might be so.'

He seemed to be turning the idea over in his mind.

Poirot said:

'Had your firm acted for Mrs Crale for a long period of years?'

George Mayhew shook his head.

'On the contrary. Jonathan and Jonathan were the Crale solicitors. Under the circumstances, however, Mr Jonathan felt that he could not very well act for Mrs Crale, and he arranged with us – with my father – to take over her case. You would do well, I think, M. Poirot, to arrange a meeting with old Mr Jonathan. He has retired from active work – he is over seventy – but he knew the Crale family intimately, and he could tell you far more than I can. Indeed, I myself can tell you nothing at all. I was a boy at the time. I don't think I was even in court.'

Poirot rose and George Mayhew, rising too, added:

'You might like to have a word with Edmunds, our managing clerk. He was with the firm then and took a great interest in the case.'

Edmunds was a man of slow speech. His eyes gleamed with legal caution. He took his time in sizing up Poirot before he let himself be betrayed into speech. He said:

'Ay, I mind the Crale case.'

He added severely: 'It was a disgraceful business.'

His shrewd eyes rested appraisingly on Hercule Poirot.

He said:

'It's a long time since to be raking things up again.'

'A court verdict is not always an ending.'

Edmunds's square head nodded slowly.

'I'd not say that you weren't in the right of it there.'

Hercule Poirot went on: 'Mrs Crale left a daughter.'

'Ay, I mind there was a child. Sent abroad to relatives, was she not?'

Poirot went on:

'That daughter believes firmly in her mother's innocence.'

The huge bushy eyebrows of Mr Edmunds rose.

'That's the way of it, is it?'

Poirot asked:

'Is there anything you can tell me to support that belief?'

Edmunds reflected. Then, slowly, he shook his head.

'I could not conscientiously say there was. I admired Mrs Crale. Whatever else she was, she was a lady! Not like the other. A hussy – no more, no less. Bold as brass! Jumped-up trash – that's what *she* was – and showed it! Mrs Crale was quality.'

'But none the less a murderess?'

Edmunds frowned. He said, with more spontaneity than he had yet shown:

'That's what I used to ask myself, day after day. Sitting there in the dock so calm and gentle. "I'll not believe it," I used to say to myself. But, if you take my meaning, Mr Poirot, there wasn't anything else to believe. That hemlock didn't get into Mr Crale's beer by accident. It was put there. And if Mrs Crale didn't put it there, who did?'

'That is the question,' said Poirot. 'Who did?'

Again those shrewd old eyes searched his face.

'So that's your idea?' said Mr Edmunds.

'What do you think yourself?'

There was a pause before the officer answered. Then he said:

'There was nothing that pointed that way – nothing at all.'

Poirot said:

'You were in court during the hearing of the case?'

'Every day.'

'You heard the witnesses give evidence?'

'I did.'

'Did anything strike you about them – any abnormality, any insincerity?'

Edmunds said bluntly:

'Was one of them lying, do you mean? Had one of them a reason to wish Mr Crale dead? If you'll excuse me, Mr Poirot, that's a very *melodramatic* idea.'

'At least consider it,' Poirot urged.

He watched the shrewd face, the screwed-up, thoughtful eyes. Slowly, regretfully, Edmunds shook his head.

'That Miss Greer,' he said, 'she was bitter enough, *and* vindictive! I'd say she overstepped the mark in a good deal she said, but it was Mr Crale alive she wanted. He was no use to her dead. She wanted Mrs Crale hanged all right – but that was because death had snatched her man away from her. Like a baulked tigress she was! But, as I say, it was Mr Crale alive she'd wanted. Mr Philip Blake, *he* was against Mrs Crale too. Prejudiced. Got his knife into her whenever he could. But I'd say he was honest according to his lights. He'd been Mr Crale's great friend. His brother, Mr Meredith Blake – a bad witness he was – vague, hesitating – never seemed sure of his answers. I've seen many witnesses like that. Look as though they're lying when all the time they're telling the truth. Didn't want to say anything more than he could help, Mr Meredith Blake didn't. Counsel got all the more out of him on that account. One of these quiet gentlemen who get easily flustered. The governess now, she stood up well to them. Didn't waste words and answered pat and to the point. You couldn't have told, listening to her, which side she was on. Got all her wits about her, she had. The brisk kind.' He paused. 'Knew a lot more than she ever let on about the whole thing, I shouldn't wonder.'

'I, too, should not wonder,' said Hercule Poirot.

He looked sharply at the wrinkled, shrewd face of Mr Alfred Edmunds. It was quite bland and impassive. But Hercule Poirot wondered if he had been vouchsafed a hint.

CHAPTER 4

THE OLD SOLICITOR

Mr Caleb Jonathan lived in Essex. After a courteous exchange of letters, Poirot received an invitation, almost royal in its character, to dine and sleep. The old gentleman was decidedly a character. After the insipidity of young George Mayhew, Mr Jonathan was like a glass of his own vintage port.

He had his own methods of approach to a subject, and it was not until well on towards midnight, when sipping a glass of fragrant old brandy, that Mr Jonathan really unbent. In oriental fashion he had appreciated Hercule Poirot's courteous refusal to rush him in any way. Now, in his own good time, he was willing to elaborate the theme of the Crale family.

'Our firm, of course, has known many generations of the Crales. I knew Amyas Crale and his father, Richard Crale, and I can remember Enoch Crale – the grandfather. Country squires, all of them, thought more of horses than human beings. They rode straight, liked women, and had no truck with ideas. They distrusted ideas. But Richard Crale's wife was cram full of ideas – more ideas than sense. She was poetical and musical – she played the harp, you know. She enjoyed poor health and looked very picturesque on her sofa. She was an admirer of Kingsley. That's why she called her son Amyas. His father scoffed at the name – but he gave in.

'Amyas Crale profited by his mixed inheritance. He got his artistic trend from his weakly mother, and his driving power and ruthless egoism from his father. All the Crales were egoists. They never by any chance saw any point of view but their own.'

Tapping with a delicate finger on the arm of his chair, the old man shot a shrewd glance at Poirot.

'Correct me if I am wrong, M. Poirot, but I think you are interested in – character, shall we say?'

Poirot replied:

'That, to me, is the principal interest of all my cases.'

'I can conceive of it. To get under the skin, as it were, of your criminal. How interesting. How absorbing. Our firm, of course, have never had a criminal practice. We should not have been competent to act for Mrs Crale, even if taste had allowed. Mayhews, however, were a very adequate firm. They briefed Depleach – they didn't perhaps show much imagination there – still, he was very expensive and, of course, exceedingly dramatic! What they hadn't the wits to see was that Caroline would never play up in the way he wanted her to. She wasn't a dramatic woman.'

'What was she?' asked Poirot. 'It is that that I am chiefly anxious to know.'

'Yes, yes – of course. How did she come to do what she did? That is the really vital question. I knew her, you know, before she married. Caroline Spalding, she was. A turbulent unhappy creature. Very alive. Her mother was left a widow early in life and Caroline was devoted to her mother. Then the mother married again – there was another child. Yes – yes, very sad, very painful. These young, ardent, adolescent jealousies.'

'She was jealous?'

'Passionately so. There was a regrettable incident. Poor child, she blamed herself bitterly afterwards. But you know, M. Poirot, these things happen. There is an inability to put on the brakes. It comes – it comes with maturity.'

Poirot said:

'What happened?'

'She struck the child – the baby – flung a paperweight at her. The child lost the sight of one eye and was permanently disfigured.'

Mr Jonathan sighed. He said:

'You can imagine the effect a simple question on that point had at the trial.'

He shook his head:

'It gave the impression that Caroline Crale was a woman of ungovernable temper. That was not true. No, that was not true.'

He paused and then resumed:

'Caroline Spalding came often to stay at Alderbury. She rode well, and was keen. Richard Crale was fond of her. She waited on Mrs Crale and was deft and gentle – Mrs Crale also liked her. The girl was not happy at home. She was happy at Alderbury. Diana Crale, Amyas's sister, and she were by way of being friends. Philip and Meredith Blake, boys from the adjoining estate, were frequently at Alderbury. Philip was always a nasty, money-grubbing little brute. I must confess I have always had a distaste for him. But I am told that he tells a very good story and that he has the reputation of being a staunch friend. Meredith was what my contemporaries used to call Namby Pamby. Liked botany and butterflies and observing birds and beasts. Nature study they call it nowadays. Ah, dear – all the young people were a disappointment to their parents. None of them ran true to type – huntin', shootin', fishin'. Meredith preferred watching birds and animals to shooting or hunting them, Philip definitely preferred town to country and went into the business of money-making. Diana married a fellow who wasn't a gentleman – one of the temporary officers in the war. And Amyas, strong, handsome, virile Amyas, blossomed into being a painter, of all things in the world. It's my opinion that Richard Crale died of the shock.

'And in due course Amyas married Caroline Spalding. They'd always fought and sparred, but it was a love match all right. They were both crazy about each other. And they continued to care. But Amyas was like all the Crales, a ruthless egoist. He loved Caroline but he never once considered her in any way. He did as he pleased. It's my opinion that he was as fond of her as he could be of anybody – but she came a long way behind his art. That came first. And I should say at no time did his art give place to a woman. He had affairs with women – they stimulated him – but he left them high and dry when he'd finished with them. He wasn't a sentimental man, nor a romantic one. And he wasn't entirely a sensualist either. The only woman he cared a button for was his own wife. And because she knew that she put up with a lot. He was a very fine painter, you know. She realized that, and respected it. He chased off in his amorous pursuits and came back again – usually with a picture to show for it.

'It might have gone on like that if it hadn't come to Elsa Greer. Elsa Greer –'

Mr Jonathan shook his head.

Poirot said: 'What of Elsa Greer?'

Mr Jonathan said unexpectedly:

'Poor child. Poor child.'

Poirot said: 'So you feel like that about her?'

Jonathan said:

'Maybe it is because I am an old man, but I find, M. Poirot, that there is something about the defencelessness of youth that moves me to tears. Youth is so vulnerable. It is so ruthless – so sure. So generous and so demanding.'

Getting up, he crossed to the bookcase. Taking out a volume he opened it, turned the pages, and then read out:

> *'"If that thy bent of love be honourable,*
> *The purpose marriage, send me word tomorrow*
> *By one that I'll procure to come to thee,*
> *Where and what time thou wilt perform the rite,*
> *And all my fortunes at thy foot I'll lay,*
> *And follow thee my lord throughout the world."*

'There speaks love allied to youth, in Juliet's words. No reticence, no holding back, no so-called maiden modesty. It is the courage, the insistence, the ruthless force of youth. Shakespeare knew youth. Juliet singles out Romeo. Desdemona claims Othello. They have no doubts, the young, no fear, no pride.'

Poirot said thoughtfully:

'So to you Elsa Greer spoke in the words of Juliet?'

'Yes. She was a spoiled child of fortune – young, lovely, rich. She found her mate and claimed him – no young Romeo, a married, middle-aged painter. Elsa Greer had no code to restrain her, she had the code of modernity. *"Take what you want – we shall only live once!"*'

He sighed, leaned back, and again tapped gently on the arm of his chair.

'A predatory Juliet. Young, ruthless, but horribly vulnerable! Staking everything on the one audacious throw. And seemingly she won . . . and then – at the last moment – death steps in – and the living, ardent, joyous Elsa died also. There was left only a vindictive, cold, hard woman, hating with all her soul the woman whose hand had done this thing.'

His voice changed:

'Dear, dear. Pray forgive this little lapse into melodrama. A crude young woman – with a crude outlook on life. Not, I think, an interesting character. *Rose white youth, passionate, pale,* etc. Take that away and what remains? Only a somewhat mediocre young woman seeking for another life-sized hero to put on an empty pedestal.'

Poirot said:

'If Amyas Crale had not been a famous painter –'

Mr Jonathan agreed quickly. He said:

'Quite – quite. You have taken the point admirably. The Elsas of this world are hero-worshippers. A man must have *done* something, must be somebody ... Caroline Crale, now, could have recognized quality in a bank clerk or an insurance agent! Caroline loved Amyas Crale the man, not Amyas Crale the painter. Caroline Crale was not crude – Elsa Greer was.'

He added:

'But she was young and beautiful and to my mind infinitely pathetic.'

Hercule Poirot went to bed thoughtful. He was fascinated by the problem of personality.

To Edmunds, the clerk, Elsa Greer was a hussy, no more, no less.

To old Mr Jonathan she was the eternal Juliet.

And Caroline Crale?

Each person had seen her differently. Montague Depleach had despised her as a defeatist – a quitter. To young Fogg she had represented Romance. Edmunds saw her simply as a 'lady'. Mr Jonathan had called her a stormy, turbulent creature.

How would he, Hercule Poirot, have seen her?

On the answer to that question depended, he felt, the success of his quest.

So far, not one of the people he had seen had doubted that whatever else she was, Caroline Crale was also a murderess.

CHAPTER 5

THE POLICE SUPERINTENDENT

Ex-Superintendent Hale pulled thoughtfully at his pipe.

He said:

'This is a funny fancy of yours, M. Poirot.'

'It is, perhaps, a little unusual,' Poirot agreed cautiously.

'You see,' said Hale, 'it's all such a long time ago.'

Hercule Poirot foresaw that he was going to get a little tired of that particular phrase. He said mildly:

'That adds to the difficulty, of course.'

'Raking up the past,' mused the other. 'If there were an *object* in it, now . . .'

'There is an object.'

'What is it?'

'One can enjoy the pursuit of truth for its own sake. I do. And you must not forget the young lady.'

Hale nodded.

'Yes, I see *her* side of it. But – you'll excuse me, M. Poirot – you're an ingenious man. You could cook her up a tale.'

Poirot replied:

'You do not know the young lady.'

'Oh, come now – a man of your experience!'

Poirot drew himself up.

'I may be, *mon cher*, an artistic and competent liar – you seem to think so. But it is not my idea of ethical conduct. I have my standards.'

'Sorry, M. Poirot. I didn't mean to hurt your feelings. But it would be all in a good cause, so to speak.'

'Oh I wonder, would it really?'

Hale said slowly:

'It's tough luck on a happy innocent girl who's just going to get married to find that her mother was a murderess. If I were you I'd go to her and say that, after all, suicide was what it was. Say the case was mishandled by Depleach. Say that there's no doubt in *your* mind that Crale poisoned himself!'

'But there is every doubt in my mind! I do not believe for one minute that Crale poisoned himself. Do you consider it even reasonably possible yourself?'

Slowly Hale shook his head.

'You see? No, it is the truth I must have – not a plausible – or not very plausible – lie.'

Hale turned and looked at Poirot. His square rather red face grew a little redder and even appeared to get a little squarer. He said:

'You talk about the *truth*. I'd like to make it plain to you that we think we *got* the truth in the Crale case.'

Poirot said quickly:

'That pronouncement from you means a great deal. I know you for what you are, an honest and capable man. Now tell me this, was there no doubt at any time in your mind as to the guilt of Mrs Crale?'

The Superintendent's answer came promptly.

'No doubt at all, M. Poirot. The circumstances pointed to her straight away, and every single fact that we uncovered supported that view.'

'You can give me an outline of the evidence against her?'

'I can. When I received your letter I looked up the case.' He picked up a small notebook. 'I've jotted down all the salient facts here.'

'Thank you, my friend. I am all eagerness to hear.'

Hale cleared his throat. A slight official intonation made itself heard in his voice.

He said:

'At two forty-five on the afternoon of September 18th, Inspector Conway was rung up by Dr Andrew Faussett. Dr Faussett stated that Mr Amyas Crale of Alderbury had died suddenly and that in consequence of the circumstances of that death and also of a statement made to him by a Mr Blake, a guest staying in the house, he considered that it was a case for the police.

'Inspector Conway, in company with a sergeant and the police surgeon, came over to Alderbury straight away. Dr Faussett was there and took him to where the body of Mr Crale had not been disturbed.

'Mr Crale had been painting in a small enclosed garden, known as the Battery garden, from the fact that it overlooked the sea, and had some miniature cannon placed in embattlements. It was situated at about four minutes' walk from the house. Mr Crale had not come up to the house for lunch as he wanted to get certain effects of light on the stone – and the sun would have been wrong for this later. He had, therefore, remained alone in the Battery garden, painting. This was stated not to be an unusual occurrence. Mr Crale took very little notice of meal times. Sometimes a sandwich would be sent down to him, but more often he preferred to remain undisturbed. The last people to see him alive were Miss Elsa Greer (staying in the house) and Mr Meredith Blake (a near neighbour). These two went up together to the house and went with the rest of the household in to lunch. After lunch, coffee was served on the terrace. Mrs Crale finished drinking her coffee and then observed that she would "go down and see how Amyas was getting on." Miss Cecilia Williams, governess, got up and accompanied her. She was looking for a pullover belonging to her pupil, Miss Angela Warren, sister of Mrs Crale, which the latter had mislaid and she thought it possible it might have been left down on the beach.

'These two started off together. The path led downwards, through some woods, until it emerged at the door leading into the Battery garden. You could either go into the Battery garden or you could continue on the same path, which led down to the seashore.

'Miss Williams continued on down and Mrs Crale went into the Battery garden. Almost at once, however, Mrs Crale screamed and Miss Williams hurried back. Mr Crale was reclining on a seat and he was dead.

'At Mrs Crale's urgent request Miss Williams left the Battery garden and hurried up to the house to telephone for a doctor. On her way, however, she met Mr Meredith Blake and entrusted her errand to him, herself returning to Mrs Crale whom she felt might be in need of someone. Dr Faussett arrived on the scene a quarter of an hour later. He saw at once that Mr Crale had been dead for some time – he placed the probable time of death at between one and two o'clock. There was nothing to show what had caused death. There was no sign of any wound and Mr Crale's attitude was a perfectly natural one. Nevertheless Dr Faussett, who was well acquainted with Mr Crale's state of health, and who knew positively that there was no disease or weakness of any kind, was inclined to take a grave view of the situation. It was at this point that Mr Philip Blake made a certain statement to Dr Faussett.'

Superintendent Hale paused, drew a deep breath and passed, as it were, to Chapter Two.

'Subsequently Mr Blake repeated this statement to Inspector Conway. It was to this effect. He had that morning received a telephone message from his brother, Mr Meredith Blake (who lived at Handcross Manor, a mile and a half away). Mr Meredith Blake was an amateur chemist – or perhaps herbalist would describe it best. On entering his laboratory that morning, Mr Meredith Blake had been startled to note that a bottle containing a preparation of hemlock, which had been quite full the day before, was now nearly empty. Worried and alarmed by this fact he had rung up his brother to ask his advice as to what he should do about it. Mr Philip Blake had urged his brother to come over to Alderbury at once and they would talk the matter over. He himself walked part way to meet his brother and they had come up to the house together. They had come to no decision as to what course to adopt and had left the matter in order to consult again after lunch.

'As a result of further inquiries, Inspector Conway ascertained the following facts: On the preceding afternoon five people had walked over from Alderbury to tea at Handcross Manor. There were Mr and Mrs Crale, Miss Angela Warren, Miss Elsa Greer and Mr Philip Blake. During the time spent there, Mr Meredith Blake had given quite a dissertation on his hobby and had taken the party into his little laboratory and "shown them round". In the course of this tour, he had mentioned certain specific drugs – one of which was coniine, the active principle of the spotted hemlock. He had explained its properties, had lamented the fact that it had now disappeared from the Pharmacopœia and boasted that he had known small doses of it to be very efficacious in whooping cough and asthma. Later he had mentioned its lethal properties and had actually read to his guests some passage from a Greek author describing its effects.'

Superintendent Hale paused, refilled his pipe and passed on to Chapter Three.

'Colonel Frere, the Chief Constable, put the case into my hands. The result of the autopsy put the matter beyond any doubt. Coniine, I understand, leaves no definite post-mortem appearances, but the doctors knew what to look for, and an ample amount of the drug was recovered. The doctor was of the opinion that it had been administered two or three hours before death. In front of Mr Crale, on the table, there had been an empty glass and an empty beer bottle. The dregs of both were analysed. There was no coniine in the bottle, but there was in the glass. I made inquiries and learned that although a case of beer and glasses were kept in a small summerhouse in the Battery garden in case Mr Crale should feel thirsty when painting, on this particular morning Mrs Crale had brought down from the house a bottle of freshly iced beer. Mr Crale was busy painting when she arrived and Miss Greer was posing for him, sitting on one of the battlements.

'Mrs Crale opened the beer, poured it out and put the glass into her husband's hand as he was standing before the easel. He tossed it off in one draught – a habit of his, I learned. Then he made a grimace, set down the glass on the table, and said: "Everything tastes foul to me today!" Miss Greer upon that laughed and said, "Liver!" Mr Crale said: "Well, at any rate it was *cold*."'

Hale paused. Poirot said:

'At what time did this take place?'

'At about a quarter-past eleven. Mr Crale continued to paint. According to Miss Greer, he later complained of stiffness in the limbs and grumbled that he must have got a touch of rheumatism. But he was the type of man who hates to admit to illness of any kind, and he undoubtedly tried not to admit that he was feeling ill. His irritable demand that he should be left alone and the others go up to lunch was quite characteristic of the man, I should say.'

Poirot nodded.

Hale continued.

'So Crale was left alone in the Battery garden. No doubt he dropped down on the seat and relaxed as soon as he was alone. Muscular paralysis would then set in. No help was at hand, and death supervened.'

Again Poirot nodded.

Hale said:

'Well, I proceeded according to routine. There wasn't much difficulty in getting down to the facts. On the preceding day there had been a set-to between Mrs Crale and Miss Greer. The latter had pretty insolently described some change in the arrangement of the furniture "when I am living here." Mrs Crale took her up, and said, "What do you mean? When *you* are living here." Miss Greer replied: "Don't pretend you don't know what I mean, Caroline. You're just like an ostrich that buries its head in the sand. You know perfectly well that Amyas and I care for each other and are going to be married." Mrs Crale said: "I know nothing of the kind." Miss Greer then said: "Well, you know it now." Whereupon, it seems, Mrs Crale turned to her husband who had just come into the room and said: "Is it true, Amyas, that you are going to marry Elsa?"'

Poirot said with interest:

'And what did Mr Crale say to that?'

'Apparently he turned on Miss Greer and shouted at her: "What the devil do you mean by blurting that out? Haven't you got the sense to hold your tongue?"'

'Miss Greer said: "I think Caroline ought to recognize the truth."'

'Mrs Crale said to her husband: "Is it true, Amyas?"'

'He wouldn't look at her, it seems, turned his face away and mumbled something.

'She said: "Speak out. I've got to know." Whereupon he said:

'"Oh, it's true enough – but I don't want to discuss it now."

'Then he flounced out of the room again and Miss Greer said:

'"You see!" and went on – with something about its being no good for Mrs Crale to adopt a dog-in-the-manger attitude about it. They must all behave like rational people. She herself hoped that Caroline and Amyas would always remain good friends.'

'And what did Mrs Crale say to that?' asked Poirot curiously.

'According to the witnesses she laughed. She said: "Over my dead body, Elsa." She went to the door and Miss Greer called after her: "What do you mean?" Mrs Crale looked back and said: "I'll kill Amyas before I give him up to *you*."'

Hale paused.

'Pretty damning – eh?'

'Yes.' Poirot seemed thoughtful. 'Who overheard this scene?'

'Miss Williams was in the room and Philip Blake. Very awkward for them.'

'Their accounts of the scene agree?'

'Near enough – you never got two witnesses to remember a thing exactly alike. *You* know that just as well as I do, M. Poirot.'

Poirot nodded. He said thoughtfully:

'Yes, it will be interesting to see –' He stopped with the sentence unfinished.

Hale went on: 'I instituted a search of the house. In Mrs Crale's bedroom I found in a bottom drawer, tucked away underneath some winter stockings, a small bottle labelled jasmine scent. It was empty. I fingerprinted it. The only prints on it were those of Mrs Crale. On analysis it was found to contain faint traces of oil of jasmine, and a strong solution of coniine hydrobromide.

'I cautioned Mrs Crale and showed her the bottle. She replied readily. She had, she said, been in a very unhappy state of mind. After listening to Mr Meredith Blake's description of the drug she had slipped back to the laboratory, had emptied out a bottle of jasmine scent which was in her bag and had filled the bottle up with coniine solution. I asked her why she had done this and she said: "I don't want to speak of certain things more than I can help, but I had received a bad shock. My husband was proposing to leave me for another woman. If that was so, I didn't want to live. That is why I took it."'

Hale paused.

Poirot said: 'After all – it is likely enough.'

'Perhaps, M. Poirot. But it doesn't square with what she was overheard to say. And then there was a further scene on the following morning. Mr Philip Blake overheard a portion of it. Miss Greer overheard a different portion of it. It took place in the library between Mr and Mrs Crale. Mr Blake was in the hall and caught a fragment or two. Miss Greer was sitting outside near the open library window and heard a good deal more.'

'And what did they hear?'

'Mr Blake heard Mrs Crale say: "You and your women. I'd like to kill you. Some day I will kill you."'

'No mention of suicide?'

'Exactly. None at all. No words like "If you do this thing, I'll kill *myself*." Miss Greer's evidence was much the same. According to her, Mr Crale said: "Do try and be reasonable about this, Caroline. I'm fond of you and will always wish you well – you and the child. But I'm going to marry Elsa. We've always agreed to leave each other free." Mrs Crale answered to that: "Very well, don't say I haven't warned you." He said: "What do you mean?" And she said: "I mean that I love you and I'm not going to lose you. I'd rather kill you than let you go to that girl."'

Poirot made a slight gesture.

'It occurs to me,' he murmured, 'that Miss Greer was singularly unwise to raise this issue? Mrs Crale could easily have refused her husband a divorce.'

'We had some evidence bearing on that point,' said Hale. 'Mrs Crale, it seems, confided partly in Mr Meredith Blake. He was an old and trusted friend. He was very distressed and managed to get a word with Mr Crale about it. This, I may say, was on the preceding afternoon. Mr Blake remonstrated delicately with his friend, said how distressed he would be if the marriage between Mr and Mrs Crale was to break up so disastrously. He also stressed the point that Miss Greer was a very young girl and that it was a very serious thing to drag a young girl through the divorce court. To this Mr Crale replied, with a chuckle (callous sort of brute he must have been): "That isn't Elsa's idea at all. *She* isn't going to appear. We shall fix it up in the usual way."'

Poirot said: 'Therefore even more imprudent of Miss Greer to have broken out the way she did.'

Superintendent Hale said:

'Oh, you know what women are! Have to get at each other's throats. It must have been a difficult situation anyhow. I can't understand Mr Crale allowing it to happen. According to Mr Meredith Blake he wanted to finish his picture. Does that make sense to you?'

'Yes, my friend, I think it does.'

'It doesn't to me. The man was asking for trouble!'

'He was probaby seriously annoyed with his young woman for breaking out the way she did.'

'Oh, he was. Meredith Blake said so. If he had to finish the picture I don't see why he couldn't have taken some photographs and worked from them. I know a chap – does watercolours of places – *he* does that.'

Poirot shook his head.

'No – I can understand Crale the artist. You must realize, my friend, that at that moment, probably, his picture was all that mattered to Crale. However much he wanted to marry the girl, the picture came first. That's why he hoped to get through her visit without its coming to an open issue. The girl, of course, didn't see it that way. With women, love always comes first.'

'Don't I know it?' said Superintendent Hale with feeling.

'Men,' continued Poirot, 'and especially artists – are different.'

'Art!' said the Superintendent with scorn. 'All this talk about *Art*! I never *have* understood it and I never shall! You should have seen that picture Crale was painting. All lopsided. He'd made the girl look as though she'd got toothache, and the battlements were all cock-eyed. Unpleasant looking, the whole thing. I couldn't get it out of my mind for a long time afterwards. I even dreamt about it. And what's more it affected my eyesight – I began to see battlements and walls and things all out of drawing. Yes, and women too!'

Poirot smiled. He said:

'Although you do not know it, you are paying a tribute to the greatness of Amyas Crale's art.'

'Nonsense. Why can't a painter paint something nice and cheerful to look at? Why go out of your way to look for ugliness?'

'Some of us, *mon cher*, see beauty in curious places.'

'The girl was a good looker, all right,' said Hale. 'Lots of make-up and next to no clothes on. It isn't decent the way these girls go about. And that was sixteen years ago, mind you. Nowadays one wouldn't think anything of it. But then – well, it shocked me. Trousers and one of those canvas shirts, open at the neck – and not another thing, I should say!'

'You seem to remember these points very well,' murmured Poirot slyly.

Superintendent Hale blushed. 'I'm just passing on the impression I got,' he said austerely.

'Quite – quite,' said Poirot soothingly. He went on:

'So it would seem that the principal witnesses against Mrs Crale were Philip Blake and Elsa Greer?'

'Yes. Vehement, they were, both of them. But the governess was called by the prosecution too, and what she said carried more weight than the other two. She was on Mrs Crale's side entirely, you see. Up in arms for her. But she was an honest woman and gave her evidence truthfully without trying to minimize it in any way.'

'And Meredith Blake?'

'He was very distressed by the whole thing, poor gentleman. As well he might be! Blamed himself for his drug brewing – and the coroner blamed him for it too. Coniine and AE Salts comes under Schedule I of the Poisons Acts. He came in for some pretty sharp censure. He was a friend of both parties, and it hit him very hard – besides being the kind of county gentleman who shrinks from notoriety and being in the public eye.'

'Did not Mrs Crale's young sister give evidence?'

'No. It wasn't necessary. She wasn't there when Mrs Crale threatened her husband, and there was nothing she could tell us that we couldn't get from someone else equally well. She saw Mrs Crale go to the refrigerator and get the iced beer out and, of course, the Defence could have subpœnaed her to say that Mrs Crale took it straight down without tampering with it in any way. But that point wasn't relevant because we never claimed that the coniine was in the beer bottle.'

'How did she manage to put it in the glass with those two looking on?'

'Well, first of all, they weren't looking on. That is to say, Mr Crale was painting – looking at his canvas and at the sitter. And Miss Greer was posed, sitting with her back almost to where Mrs Crale was standing, and her eyes looking over Mr Crale's shoulder.'

Poirot nodded.

'As I say neither of the two was looking at Mrs Crale. She had the stuff in one of those pipette things – one used to fill fountain pens with them. We found it crushed to splinters on the path up to the house.'

Poirot murmured:

'You have an answer to everything.'

'Well, come now, M. Poirot! Without prejudice. *She* threatens to kill him. *She* takes the stuff from the laboratory. The empty bottle is found in *her* room and *nobody has handled it but her*. She deliberately takes down iced beer to him – a funny thing, anyway, when you realize that they weren't on speaking terms –'

'A very curious thing. I had already remarked on it.'

'Yes. Bit of a give away. *Why* was she so amiable all of a sudden? He complains of the taste of the stuff – and coniine *has* a nasty taste. She arranges to find the body and she sends the other woman off to telephone. Why? So that she can wipe that bottle and glass and then press *his* fingers on it. After that she can pipe up and say that it was remorse and that he committed suicide. A likely story.'

'It was certainly not very well imagined.'

'No. If you ask me she didn't take the trouble to *think*. She was so eaten up with hate and jealousy. All she thought of was doing him in. And then, when it's over, when she sees him there dead – well, *then*, I should say, she suddenly comes to herself and realizes that what she's done is murder – and that you get hanged for murder. And desperately she goes bald-headed for the only thing she can think of – which is suicide.'

Poirot said:

'It is very sound what you say there – yes. Her mind might work that way.'

'In a way it was a premeditated crime and in a way it wasn't,' said Hale. 'I don't believe she really thought it out, you know. Just went on with it blindly.'

Poirot murmured:

'I wonder . . .'

Hale looked at him curiously. He said:

'Have I convinced you, M. Poirot, that it was a straightforward case?'

'Almost. Not quite. There are one or two peculiar points . . . !'

'Can you suggest an alternative solution – that will hold water?'

Poirot said:

'What were the movements of the other people on that morning?'

'We went into them, I can assure you. We checked up on everybody. Nobody had what you could call an alibi – you can't have with poisoning. Why, there's nothing to prevent a would-be murderer from handing his victim some poison in a capsule the day before, telling him it's a specific cure for indigestion and he must take it before lunch – and then going away to the other end of England.'

'But you don't think that happened in this case?'

'Mr Crale didn't suffer from indigestion. And in any case I can't see that kind of thing happening. It's true that Mr Meredith Blake was given to recommending quack nostrums of his own concocting, but I don't see Mr Crale trying any of them. And if he did he'd probably talk and joke about it. Besides, why *should* Mr Meredith Blake want to kill Mr Crale? Everything goes to show that he was on very good terms with him. They all were. Mr Philip Blake was his best friend. Miss Greer was in love with him. Miss Williams disapproved of him, I imagine, very strongly – but moral disapprobation doesn't lead to poisoning. Little Miss Warren scrapped with him a lot, she was at a tiresome age – just off to school, I believe, but he was quite fond of her and she of him. She was treated, you know, with particular tenderness and consideration in that house. You may have heard why. She was badly injured when she was a child – injured by Mrs Crale in a kind of maniacal fit of rage. That rather shows, doesn't it, that she was a pretty uncontrolled sort of person? To go for a child – and maim her for life!'

'It might show,' said Poirot thoughtfully, 'that Angela Warren had good reason to bear a grudge against Caroline Crale.'

'Perhaps – but not against Amyas Crale. And anyway Mrs Crale was devoted to her young sister – gave her a home when her parents died, and, as I say, treated her with special affection – spoiled her badly, so they say. The girl was obviously fond of Mrs Crale. She was kept away from the trial and sheltered from it all as far as possible – Mrs Crale was very insistent about that, I believe. But the girl was terribly upset and longed to be taken to see her sister in prison. Caroline Crale wouldn't agree. She said that sort of thing might injure a girl's mentality for life. She arranged for her to go to school abroad.'

He added:

'Miss Warren's turned out a very distinguished woman. Traveller to weird places. Lectures at the Royal Geographical – all that sort of thing.'

'And no one remembers the trial?'

'Well, it's a different name for one thing. They hadn't even the same maiden name. They had the same mother but different fathers. Mrs Crale's name was Spalding.'

'This Miss Williams, was she the child's governess, or Angela Warren's?'

'Angela's. There was a nurse for the child – but she used to do a few little lessons with Miss Williams every day, I believe.'

'Where was the child at the time?'

'She'd gone with the nurse to pay a visit to her grandmother. A Lady Tressillian. A widow lady who'd lost her own two little girls and who was devoted to this kid.'

Poirot nodded. 'I see.'

Hale continued:

'As to the movements of the other people on the day of the murder, I can give them to you.

'Miss Greer sat on the terrace near the library window after breakfast. There, as I say, she overheard the quarrel between Crale and his wife. After that she accompanied Crale down to the Battery and sat for him until lunch time with a couple of breaks to ease her muscles.

'Philip Blake was in the house after breakfast, and overheard part of the quarrel. After Crale and Miss Greer went off, he read the paper until his brother telephoned him. Thereupon he went down to the shore to meet his brother. They walked together up the path again past the Battery garden. Miss Greer had just gone up to the house to fetch a pullover as she felt chilly and Mrs Crale was with her husband discussing arrangements for Angela's departure to school.'

'Ah, an amicable interview.'

'Well, no, not amicable. Crale was fairly shouting at her, I understand. Annoyed at being bothered with domestic details. I suppose she wanted to get things straightened up if there *was* going to be a break.'

Poirot nodded.

Hale went on:

'The two brothers exchanged a few words with Amyas Crale. Then Miss Greer reappeared and took up her position, and Crale picked up his brush again, obviously wanting to get rid of them. They took the hint and went up to the house. It was when they were at the Battery, by the way, that Amyas Crale complained all the beer down there was hot and his wife promised to send him down some iced beer.'

'Aha!'

'Exactly – Aha! Sweet as sugar she was about it. They went up to the house and sat on the terrace outside. Mrs Crale and Angela Warren brought them out beer there.

'Later, Angela Warren went down to bathe and Philip Blake went with her.

'Meredith Blake went down to a clearing with a seat just above the Battery garden. He could just see Miss Greer as she posed on the battlements and could hear her voice and Crale's as they talked. He sat there and thought over the coniine business. He was still very worried about it and didn't know quite what to do. Elsa Greer saw him and waved her hand to him. When the bell went for lunch he came down to the Battery and Elsa Greer and he went back to the house together. He noticed then that Crale was looking, as he put it, very queer, but he didn't really think anything of it at the time. Crale was the kind of man who is never ill – and so one didn't imagine he would be. On the other hand, he *did* have moods of fury and despondency according as to whether his painting was not going as he liked it. On those occasions one left him alone and said as little as possible to him. That's what these two did on this occasion.

'As to the others, the servants were busy with housework and cooking lunch. Miss Williams was in the schoolroom part of the morning correcting some exercise books. Afterwards she took some household mending to the terrace. Angela Warren spent most of the morning wandering about the garden, climbing trees and eating things – you know what a girl of fifteen is! Plums, sour apples, hard pears, etc. After she came back to the house and, as I say, went down with Philip Blake to the beach and had a bathe before lunch.'

Superintendent Hale paused:

'Now then,' he said belligerently, 'do you find anything phoney about that?'

Poirot said: 'Nothing at all.'

'Well, then!'

The two words expressed volumes.

'But all the same,' said Hercule Poirot. 'I am going to satisfy myself. I –'

'What are you going to do?'

'I am going to visit these five people – and from each one I am going to get his or her own story.'

Superintendent Hale sighed with a deep melancholy.

He said:

'Man, you're nuts! None of their stories are going to agree! Don't you grasp that elementary fact? No two people remember a thing in the same order anyway. And after all this time! Why, you'll hear five accounts of five separate murders!'

'That,' said Poirot, 'is what I am counting upon. It will be very instructive.'

CHAPTER 6

THIS LITTLE PIG WENT TO MARKET . . .

Philip Blake was recognizably like the description given of him by Montague Depleach. A prosperous, shrewd, jovial-looking man – slightly running to fat.

Hercule Poirot had timed his appointment for half-past six on a Saturday afternoon. Philip Blake had just finished his eighteen holes, and he had been on his game – winning a fiver from his opponent. He was in the mood to be friendly and expansive.

Hercule Poirot explained himself and his errand. On this occasion at least he showed no undue passion for unsullied truth. It was a question, Blake gathered, of a series of books dealing with famous crimes.

Philip Blake frowned. He said:

'Good Lord, why make up these things?'

Hercule Poirot shrugged his shoulders. He was at his most foreign today. He was out to be despised but patronized.

He murmured:

'It is the public. They eat it up – yes, eat it up.'

'Ghouls,' said Philip Blake.

But he said it good-humouredly – not with the fastidiousness and the distaste that a more sensitive man might have displayed.

Hercule Poirot said with a shrug of the shoulders:

'It is human nature. You and I, Mr Blake, who know the world, have no illusions about our fellow human beings. Not bad people, most of them, but certainly not to be idealized.'

Blake said heartily:

'I've parted with my illusions long ago.'

'Instead, you tell a very good story, so I have been told.'

'Ah!' Blake's eyes twinkled. 'Heard this one?'

Poirot's laugh came at the right place. It was not an edifying story, but it was funny.

Philip Blake lay back in his chair, his muscles relaxed, his eyes creased with good humour.

Hercule Poirot thought suddenly that he looked rather like a contented pig.

A pig. *This little pig went to market . . .*

What was he like, this man, this Philip Blake? A man, it would seem, without cares. Prosperous, contented. No remorseful thoughts, no uneasy twinges of conscience from the past, no haunting memories here. No, a well-fed pig who had gone to market – and fetched the full market price . . .

But once, perhaps, there had been more to Philip Blake. He must have been, when young, a handsome man. Eyes always a shade too small, a fraction too near together, perhaps – but otherwise a well made, well set up young man. How old was he now? At a guess between fifty and sixty. Nearing forty, then, at the time of Crale's death. Less stultified, then, less sunk in the gratifications of the minute. Asking more of life, perhaps, and receiving less . . .

Poirot murmured as a mere catch-phrase:

'You comprehend my position.'

'No, really, you know, I'm hanged if I do.' The stockbroker sat upright again, his glance was once more shrewd. 'Why *you*? You're not a writer?'

'Not precisely – no. Actually I am a detective.'

The modesty of this remark had probably not been equalled before in Poirot's conversation.

'Of course you are. We all know that. The famous Hercule Poirot!'

But his tone held a subtly mocking note. Intrinsically, Philip Blake was too much of an Englishman to take the pretensions of a foreigner seriously.

To his cronies he would have said:

'Quaint little mountebank. Oh well, I expect his stuff goes down with the women all right.'

And although that derisive patronizing attitude was exactly the one which Hercule Poirot had aimed at inducing, nevertheless he found himself annoyed by it.

This man, this successful man of affairs, was unimpressed by Hercule Poirot! It was a scandal.

'I am gratified,' said Poirot untruly, 'that I am so well known to you. My success, let me tell you, has been founded on the psychology – the eternal *why*? of human behaviour. That, M. Blake, is what interests the world in crime today. It used to be romance. Famous crimes were retold from one angle only – the love-story connected with them. Nowadays it is very different. People read with interest that Dr Crippen murdered his wife because she was a big bouncing woman and he was little and insignificant and therefore she made him feel inferior. They read of some famous woman criminal that she killed because she'd been snubbed by her father when she was three years old. It is, as I say, the *why* of crime that interests nowadays.'

Philip Blake said, with a slight yawn:

'The why of most crimes is obvious enough, I should say. Usually money.'

Poirot cried:

'Ah, but my dear sir, the why must never be obvious. That is the whole point!'

'And that's where *you* come in?'

'And that, as you say, is where I come in! It is proposed to rewrite the stories of certain bygone crimes – from the psychological angle. Psychology in crime, it is my speciality. I have accepted the commission.'

Philip Blake grinned.

'Pretty lucrative, I suppose?'

'I hope so – I certainly hope so.'

'Congratulations. Now, perhaps, you'll tell me where *I* come in?'

'Most certainly. The Crale case, Monsieur.'

Philip Blake did not look startled. But he looked thoughtful. He said:

'Yes, of course, the Crale case . . .'

Hercule Poirot said anxiously:

'It is not displeasing to you, Mr Blake?'

'Oh, as to that.' Philip Blake shrugged his shoulders. 'It's no use resenting a thing that you've no power to stop. The trial of Caroline Crale is public property. Any one can go ahead and write it up. It's no use *my* objecting. In a way – I don't mind telling you – I do dislike it a good deal. Amyas Crale was one of my best friends. I'm sorry the whole unsavoury business has to be raked up again. But these things happen.'

'You are a philosopher, Mr Blake.'

'No, no. I just know enough not to start kicking against the pricks. I dare say you'll do it less offensively than many others.'

'I hope, at least, to write with delicacy and good taste,' said Poirot.

Philip Blake gave a loud guffaw but without any real amusement. 'Makes me chuckle to hear you say that.'

'I assure you, Mr Blake, I am really interested. It is not just a matter of money with me. I genuinely want to recreate the past, to feel and see the events that took place, to see behind the obvious and to visualize the thoughts and feelings of the actors in the drama.'

Philip Blake said:

'I don't know that there was much subtlety about it. It was a pretty obvious business. Crude female jealousy, that was all there was to it.'

'It would interest me enormously, Mr Blake, if I could have your own reactions to the affair.'

Philip Blake said with sudden heat, his face deepening in colour:

'Reactions! Reactions! Don't speak so pedantically. I didn't just stand there and react! You don't seem to understand that my friend – *my friend*, I tell you, had been killed – poisoned! And that if I'd acted quicker I could have saved him.'

'How do you make that out, Mr Blake?'

'Like this. I take it that you've already read up the facts of the case?' Poirot nodded. 'Very well. Now on that morning my brother Meredith called me up. He was in a pretty good stew. One of his Hell brews was missing – and it was a fairly deadly Hell brew. What did I do? I told him to come along and we'd talk it over. Decide what was best to be done. "Decide what was best." It beats me now how I could have been such a hesitating fool! I ought to have realized that there was no time to lose. I ought to have gone to Amyas straight away and warned him. I ought to have said: "Caroline's pinched one of

Meredith's patent poisons, and you and Elsa had better look out for yourselves."'

Blake got up. He strode up and down in his excitement.

'Good God, man. Do you suppose I haven't gone over it in my mind again and again? I *knew*. I had the chance to save him – and I dallied about – waiting for Meredith! Why hadn't I the sense to realize that Caroline wasn't going to have any qualms or hesitancies. She'd taken that stuff to use – and, by God, she'd used it at the very first opportunity. She wouldn't wait till Meredith discovered his loss. I knew – of course I knew – that Amyas was in deadly danger – and I did nothing!'

'I think you reproach yourself unduly, Monsieur. You had not much time –'

The other interrupted him:

'Time? I had plenty of time. Any amount of courses open to me. I could have gone to Amyas, as I say – but there was the chance, of course, that he wouldn't believe me. Amyas wasn't the sort of man who'd believe easily in his own danger. He'd have scoffed at the notion. And he never thoroughly understood the sort of devil Caroline was. But I could have gone to her. I could have said: "I know what you're up to. I know what you're planning to do. But if Amyas or Elsa die of coniine poisoning, you'll be hanged by your neck!" That would have stopped her. Or I might have rung up the police. Oh! there were things that could have been done – and instead, I let myself be influenced by Meredith's slow, cautious methods. "We must be sure – talk it over – make quite certain who could have taken it . . ." Damned old fool – never made a quick decision in his life! A good thing for him he was the eldest son and has an estate to live on. If he'd ever tried to *make* money he'd have lost every penny he had.'

Poirot asked:

'You had no doubt yourself who had taken the poison?'

'Of course not. I knew at once it must be Caroline. You see, I knew Caroline very well.'

Poirot said:

'That is very interesting. I want to know, Mr Blake, what kind of a woman Caroline Crale was?'

Philip Blake said sharply:

'She wasn't the injured innocent people thought she was at the time of the trial!'

'What was she, then?'

Blake sat down again. He said seriously:

'Would you really like to know?'

'I would like to know very much indeed.'

'Caroline was a rotter. She was a rotter through and through. Mind you, she had charm. She had that kind of sweetness of manner that deceives people utterly. She had a frail, helpless look about her that appealed to people's chivalry. Sometimes, when I've read a bit of history, I think Mary Queen of Scots must have been a bit like her. Always sweet and unfortunate and magnetic – and actually a cold calculating woman, a scheming woman who planned the murder of Darnley and got away with it. Caroline was like that – a cold, calculating planner. And she had a wicked temper.

'I don't know whether they've told you – it isn't a vital point of the trial, but it shows her up – what she did to her baby sister? She was jealous, you know. Her mother had married again, and all the notice and affection went to little Angela. Caroline couldn't stand that. She tried to kill the baby with a crowbar – smash its head in. Luckily the blow wasn't fatal. But it was a pretty ghastly thing to do.'

'Yes, indeed.'

'Well, that was the real Caroline. She had to be first. That was the thing she simply could not stand – not being first. And there was a cold, egotistical devil in her that was capable of being stirred to murderous lengths.

'She appeared impulsive, you know, but she was really calculating. When she stayed at Alderbury as a girl, she gave us all the once over and made her plans. She'd no money of her own. I was never in the running – a younger son with his way to make. (Funny, that, I could probably buy up Meredith and Crale, if he'd lived, nowadays!) She considered Meredith for a bit, but she finally fixed on Amyas. Amyas would have Alderbury, and though he wouldn't have much money with it, she realized that his talent as a painter was something quite out of the way. She gambled on his being not only a genius but a financial success as well.

'And she won. Recognition came to Amyas early. He wasn't a fashionable painter exactly – but his genius was recognized and his pictures were bought. Have you seen any of his paintings? There's one here. Come and look at it.'

He led the way into the dining-room and pointed to the left-hand wall.

'There you are. That's Amyas.'

Poirot looked in silence. It came to him with fresh amazement that a man could so imbue a conventional subject with his own particular magic. A vase of roses on a polished mahogany table. That hoary old set-piece. How then did Amyas Crale contrive to make his roses flame and burn with a riotous almost obscene life. The polished wood of the table trembled and took on sentient life. How explain the excitement the picture roused? For it was exciting. The proportions of the table would have distressed Superintendent Hale, he would have complained that no known roses were precisely of that shape or colour. And afterwards he would have gone about wondering vaguely why the roses he saw were unsatisfactory, and round mahogany tables would have annoyed him for no known reason.

Poirot gave a little sigh.

He murmured:

'Yes – it is all there.'

Blake led the way back. He mumbled:

'Never have understood anything about art myself. Don't know why I like looking at that thing so much, but I do. It's – oh, damn it all, it's *good*.'

Poirot nodded emphatically.

Blake offered his guest a cigarette and lit one himself. He said:

'And that's the man – the man who painted those roses – the man who painted the "Woman with a Cocktail Shaker" – the man who painted that amazing painful "Nativity", *that's* the man who was cut short in his prime, deprived of his vivid forceful life all because of a vindictive mean-natured woman!'

He paused:

'You'll say that I'm bitter – that I'm unduly prejudiced against Caroline. She *had* charm – I've felt it. But I knew – I always knew – the real woman behind. And that woman, M. Poirot, was evil. She was cruel and malignant and a grabber!'

'And yet it has been told me that Mrs Crale put up with many hard things in her married life?'

'Yes, and didn't she let everybody know about it! Always the martyr! Poor old Amyas. His married life was one long hell – or rather it would have been if it hadn't been for his exceptional quality. His art, you see – he always had that. It was an escape. When he was painting he didn't care, he shook off Caroline and her nagging and all the ceaseless rows and quarrels. They were endless, you know. Not a week passed without a thundering row over one thing or another. *She* enjoyed it. Having rows stimulated her, I believe. It was an outlet. She could say all the hard bitter stinging things she wanted to say. She'd positively purr after one of those set-tos – go off looking as sleek and well-fed as a cat. But it took it out of *him. He* wanted peace – rest – a quiet life. Of course a man like that ought never to marry – he isn't out for domesticity. A man like Crale should have affairs but no binding ties. They're bound to chafe him.'

'He confided in you?'

'Well – he knew that I was a pretty devoted pal. He let me see things. He didn't complain. He wasn't that kind of man. Sometimes he'd say, "Damn all women." Or he'd say, "Never get married, old boy. Wait for hell till after this life."'

'You knew about his attachment to Miss Greer?'

'Oh yes – at least I saw it coming on. He told me he'd met a marvellous girl. She was different, he said, from anything or any one he'd ever met before. Not that I paid much attention to that. Amyas was always meeting one woman or other who was "different". Usually a month later he'd stare at you if you mentioned them, and wonder who you were talking about! But this Elsa Greer really was different. I realized that when I came down to Alderbury to stay. She'd got him, you know, hooked him good and proper. The poor mutt fairly ate out of her hand.'

'You did not like Elsa Greer either?'

'No, I didn't like her. She was definitely a predatory creature. She, too, wanted to own Crale body and soul. But I think, all the same, that she'd have been better for him than Caroline. She might conceivably have let him alone once she was sure of him. Or she might have got tired of him and moved on to someone else. The best thing for Amyas would have been to be quite free of female entanglements.'

'But that, it would seem, was not to his taste?'

Philip Blake said with a sigh:

'The damned fool was always getting himself involved with some woman or other. And yet, in a way, women really meant very little to him. The only two women who really made any impression on him at all in his life were Caroline and Elsa.'

Poirot said:

'Was he fond of the child?'

'Angela? Oh! we all liked Angela. She was such a sport. She was always game for anything. What a life she led that wretched governess of hers. Yes, Amyas liked Angela all right – but sometimes she went too far and then he used to get really mad with her – and then Caroline would step in – Caro was always on Angela's side and that would finish Amyas altogether. He hated it when Caro sided with Angela against him. There was a bit of jealousy all round, you know. Amyas was jealous of the way Caro always put Angela first and would do anything for her. And Angela was jealous of

Amyas and rebelled against his overbearing ways. It was his decision that she should go to school that autumn, and she was furious about it. Not, I think, because she didn't like the idea of school, she really rather wanted to go, I believe – but it was Amyas's high-handed way of settling it all offhand that infuriated her. She played all sorts of tricks on him in revenge. Once she put ten slugs in his bed. On the whole, I think Amyas was right. It was time she got some discipline. Miss Williams was very efficient, but even she confessed that Angela was getting too much for her.'

He paused. Poirot said:

'When I asked if Amyas was fond of the child – I referred to his own child, his daughter?'

'Oh, you mean little Carla? Yes, she was a great pet. He enjoyed playing with her when he was in the mood. But his affection for her wouldn't have deterred him from marrying Elsa, if that's what you mean. He hadn't *that* kind of feeling for her.'

'Was Caroline Crale very devoted to the child?'

A kind of spasm contorted Philip's face. He said:

'I can't say that she wasn't a good mother. No, I can't say that. It's the one thing –'

'Yes, Mr Blake?'

Philip said slowly and painfully:

'It's the one thing I really – regret – in this affair. The thought of that child. Such a tragic background to her young life. They sent her abroad to Amyas's cousin and her husband. I hope – I sincerely hope – they managed to keep the truth from her.'

Poirot shook his head. He said:

'The truth, Mr Blake, has a habit of making itself known. Even after many years.'

The stockbroker murmured: 'I wonder.'

Poirot went on:

'In the interests of truth, Mr Blake, I am going to ask you to do something.'

'What is it?'

'I am going to beg that you will write me out an exact account of what happened on those days at Alderbury. That is to say, I am going to ask you to write me out a full account of the murder and its attendant circumstances.'

'But, my dear fellow, after all this time? I should be hopelessly inaccurate.'

'Not necessarily.'

'Surely.'

'No, for one thing, with the passage of time, the mind retains a hold on essentials and rejects superficial matters.'

'Ho! You mean a mere broad outline?'

'Not at all. I mean a detailed conscientious account of each event as it occurred, and every conversation you can remember.'

'And supposing I remember them wrong?'

'You can give the wording at least to the best of your reflection. There may be gaps, but that cannot be helped.'

Blake looked at him curiously.

'But what's the idea? The police files will give you the whole thing far more accurately.'

'No, Mr Blake. We are speaking now from the psychological point of view. I do not want bare *facts*. *I want your own selections of facts*. Time and your memory are responsible for that selection. There may have been things done, words spoken, that I should seek for in vain in the police files. Things and words that you never mentioned because, maybe, you judged them irrelevant, or because you preferred not to repeat them.'

Blake said sharply:

'Is this account of mine for publication?'

'Certainly not. It is for my eye only. To assist me to draw my own deductions.'

'And you won't quote from it without my consent?'

'Certainly not.'

'Hm,' said Philip Blake. 'I'm a very busy man, M. Poirot.'

'I appreciate that there will be time and trouble involved. I should be happy to agree to a – reasonable fee.'

There was a moment's pause. Then Philip Blake said suddenly:

'No, if I do it – I'll do it for nothing.'

'And you will do it?'

Philip said warningly:

'Remember, I can't vouch for the accuracy of my memory.'

'That is perfectly understood.'

'Then I think,' said Philip Blake, 'that I should *like* to do it. I feel I owe it – in a way – to Amyas Crale.'

CHAPTER 7

THIS LITTLE PIG STAYED AT HOME

Hercule Poirot was not a man to neglect details.

His advance towards Meredith Blake was carefully thought out. Meredith Blake was, he already felt sure, a very different proposition from Philip Blake. Rush tactics would not succeed here. The assault must be leisurely.

Hercule Poirot knew that there was only one way to penetrate the stronghold. He must approach Meredith Blake with the proper credentials. Those credentials must be social, not professional. Fortunately, in the course of his career, Hercule Poirot had made friends in many counties. Devonshire was no exception. He sat down to review what resources he had in Devonshire. As a result he discovered two people who were acquaintances or friends of Mr Meredith Blake. He descended upon him therefore armed with two letters, one from Lady Mary Lytton-Gore, a gentle widow lady of restricted means, the most retiring of creatures; and the other from a retired Admiral, whose family had been settled in the county for four generations.

Meredith Blake received Poirot in a state of some perplexity.

As he had often felt lately, things were not what they used to be. Dash it all, private detectives used to be private detectives – fellows you got to guard wedding presents at country receptions, fellows you went to – rather shame-facedly – when there was some dirty business afoot and you'd got to get the hang of it.

But here was Lady Mary Lytton-Gore writing: 'Hercule Poirot is a very old and valued friend of mine. Please do all you can to help him, won't you?' And Mary Lytton-Gore wasn't – no, decidedly she wasn't – the sort of woman you associate with private detectives and all that they stand for. And Admiral Cronshaw wrote: 'Very good chap – absolutely sound. Grateful if you will do what you can for him. Most entertaining fellow, can tell you lots of good stories.'

And now here was the man himself. Really a most impossible person – the wrong clothes – button boots! – an incredible moustache! Not his – Meredith Blake's – kind of fellow at all. Didn't look as though he'd ever hunted or shot – or even played a decent game. A foreigner.

Slightly amused, Hercule Poirot read accurately these thoughts passing through the other's head.

He had felt his own interest rising considerably as the train brought him into the West Country. He would see now, with his own eyes, the actual place where these long past events happened.

It was here, at Handcross Manor, that two young brothers had lived and gone over to Alderbury and joked and played tennis and fraternized with a young Amyas Crale and a girl called Caroline. It was from here that Meredith had started out to Alderbury on that fatal morning. That had been sixteen years ago. Hercule Poirot looked with interest at the man who was confronting him with somewhat uneasy politeness.

Very much what he had expected. Meredith Blake resembled superficially every other English country gentleman of straitened means and outdoor tastes.

A shabby old coat of Harris tweed, a weather-beaten, pleasant, middle-aged face with somewhat faded blue eyes, a weak mouth, half hidden by a rather straggly moustache. Poirot found Meredith Blake a great contrast to his brother. He had a hesitating manner, his mental processes were obviously leisurely. It was as though his tempo had slowed down with the years just as his brother's had been accelerated.

As Poirot had already guessed, he was a man whom you could not hurry. The leisurely life of the English countryside was in his bones.

He looked, the detective thought, a good deal older than his brother, though, from what Mr Jonathan had said, it would seem that only a couple of years separated them.

Hercule Poirot prided himself on knowing how to handle an 'old school tie'. It was no moment for trying to seem English. No, one must be a foreigner – frankly a foreigner – and be magnanimously forgiven for the fact. 'Of course, these foreigners don't quite know the ropes. *Will* shake hands at breakfast. Still, a decent fellow really . . .'

Poirot set about creating this impression of himself. The two men talked, cautiously, of Lady Mary Lytton-Gore and of Admiral Cronshaw. Other names were mentioned. Fortunately Poirot knew someone's cousin and had met somebody else's sister-in-law. He could see a kind of warmth dawning in the Squire's eye. The fellow seemed to know the right people.

Gracefully, insidiously, Poirot slid into the purpose of his visit. He was quick to counteract the inevitable recoil. This book was, alas! going to be written. Miss Crale – Miss Lemarchant, as she was now called – was anxious for him to exercise a judicious editorship. The facts, unfortunately, were public property. But much could be done in their presentation to avoid wounding susceptibilities. Poirot murmured that before now he had been able to use discreet influence to avoid certain purple passages in a book of memoirs.

Meredith Blake flushed angrily. His hand shook a little as he filled a pipe. He said, a slight stammer in his voice:

'It's – it's g-ghoulish the way they dig these things up. S-sixteen years ago. Why can't they let it be?'

Poirot shrugged his shoulders. He said:

'I agree with you. But what will you? There is a demand for such things. And any one is at liberty to reconstruct a proved crime and to comment on it.'

'Seems disgraceful to me.'

Poirot murmured:

'Alas – we do not live in a delicate age . . . You would be surprised, Mr Blake, if you knew the unpleasant publications I had succeeded in – shall we say – softening. I am anxious to do all I can to save Miss Crale's feeling in the matter.'

Meredith Blake murmured: 'Little Carla! That child! A grown-up woman. One can hardly believe it.'

'I know. Time flies swiftly, does it not?'

Meredith Blake sighed. He said: 'Too quickly.'

Poirot said:

'As you will have seen in the letter I handed you from Miss Crale, she is very anxious to know everything possible about the sad events of the past.'

Meredith Blake said with a touch of irritation:

'Why? Why rake up everything again? How much better to let it all be forgotten.'

'You say that, Mr Blake, because you know all the past too well. Miss Crale, remember, knows nothing. That is to say she knows only the story as she has learnt it from the official accounts.'

Meredith Blake winced. He said:

'Yes, I forgot. Poor child. What a detestable position for her. The shock of learning the truth. And then – those soulless, callous reports of the trial.'

'The truth,' said Hercule Poirot, 'can never be done justice to in a mere legal recital. It is the things that are left out that are the things that matter. The emotions, the feelings – the characters of the actors in the drama. The extenuating circumstances –'

He paused and the other man spoke eagerly like an actor who had received his cue.

'Extenuating circumstances! That's just it. If ever there were extenuating circumstances, there were in this case. Amyas Crale was an old friend –

his family and mine had been friends for generations, but one has to admit that his conduct was, frankly, outrageous. He was an artist, of course, and presumably that explains it. But there it is – he allowed a most extraordinary set of affairs to arise. The position was one that no ordinary decent man could have contemplated for a moment.'

Hercule Poirot said:

'I am interested that you should say that. It had puzzled me, that situation. Not so does a well-bred man, a man of the world, go about his affairs.'

Blake's thin, hesitating face had lit up with animation. He said:

'Yes, but the whole point is that Amyas never was an ordinary man! He was a painter, you see, and with him painting came first – really sometimes in the most extraordinary way! I don't understand these so-called artistic people myself – never have. I understood Crale a little because, of course, I'd known him all my life. His people were the same sort as my people. And in many ways Crale ran true to type – it was only where art came in that he didn't conform to the usual standards. He wasn't, you see, an amateur in any way. He was first-class – really first-class. Some people say he's a genius. They may be right. But as a result, he was always what I should describe as unbalanced. When he was painting a picture – nothing else mattered, nothing could be allowed to get in the way. He was like a man in a dream. Completely obsessed by what he was doing. Not till the canvas was finished did he come out of this absorption and start to pick up the threads of ordinary life again.'

He looked questioningly at Poirot and the latter nodded.

'You understand, I see. Well, that explains, I think, why this particular situation arose. He was in love with this girl. He wanted to marry her. He was prepared to leave his wife and child for her. But he'd started painting her down here, and he wanted to finish that picture. Nothing else mattered to him. He didn't *see* anything else. And the fact that the situation was a perfectly impossible one for the two women concerned, doesn't seem to have occurred to him.'

'Did either of them understand his point of view?'

'Oh yes – in a way. Elsa did, I suppose. She was terrifically enthusiastic about his painting. But it was a difficult position for her – naturally. And as for Caroline –'

He stopped. Poirot said:

'For Caroline – yes, indeed.'

Meredith Blake said, speaking with a little difficulty:

'Caroline – I had always – well, I had always been very fond of Caroline.

There was a time when – when I hoped to marry her. But that was soon nipped in the bud. Still, I remained, if I may say so, devoted to – to her service.'

Poirot nodded thoughtfully. That slightly old-fashioned phrase expressed, he felt, the man before him very typically. Meredith Blake was the kind of man who would devote himself readily to a romantic and honourable devotion. He would serve his lady faithfully and without hope of reward. Yes, it was all very much in character.

He said, carefully weighing the words:

'You must have resented this – attitude – on *her* behalf?'

'I did. Oh, I did. I – I actually remonstrated with Crale on the subject.'

'When was this?'

'Actually the day before – before it all happened. They came over to tea here, you know. I got Crale aside and I – I put it to him. I even said, I remember, that it wasn't fair on either of them.'

'Ah, you said that?'

'Yes. I didn't think – you see, that he *realized*.'

'Possibly not.'

'I said to him that it was putting Caroline in a perfectly unendurable position. If he meant to marry this girl, he ought not to have her staying in the house and – well – more or less flaunt her in Caroline's face. It was, I said, an unendurable insult.'

Poirot asked curiously: 'What did he answer?'

Meredith Blake replied with distaste:

'He said: "Caroline must lump it."'

Hercule Poirot's eyebrows rose.

'Not,' he said, 'a very sympathetic reply.'

'I thought it abominable. I lost my temper. I said that no doubt, not caring for his wife, he didn't mind how much he made her suffer, but what, I said, about the girl? Hadn't he realized it was a pretty rotten position for *her*? His reply to that was that Elsa must lump it too!

'Then he went on: "You don't seem to understand, Meredith, that this thing I'm painting is the best thing I've done. It's *good*, I tell you. And a couple of jealous quarrelling women aren't going to upset it – no, by hell, they're not."

'It was hopeless talking to him. I said he seemed to have taken leave of all ordinary decency. Painting, I said, wasn't everything. He interrupted there. He said: "Ah, but it is to *me*."

'I was still very angry. I said it was perfectly disgraceful the way he had always treated Caroline. She had had a miserable life with him. He said he knew that and he was sorry about it. Sorry! He said: "I know, Merry, you don't believe that – but it's the truth. I've given Caroline the hell of a life and she's been a saint about it. But she did know, I think, what she might be letting herself in for. I told her candidly the sort of damnable egoistic, loose-living kind of chap I was."

'I put it to him then very strongly that he ought not to break up his married life. There was the child to be considered and everything. I said that I could understand that a girl like Elsa could bowl a man over, but that even for her sake he ought to break off the whole thing. She was very young. She was going into this bald-headed, but she might regret it bitterly afterwards. I said couldn't he pull himself together, make a clean break and go back to his wife?'

'And what did he say?'

Blake said: 'He just looked – embarrassed. He patted me on the shoulder and said: "You're a good chap, Merry. But you're too sentimental. You wait till the picture's finished and you'll admit that I was right."

'I said: "Damn your picture." And he grinned and said all the neurotic women in England couldn't do that. Then I said that it would have been more decent to have kept the whole thing from Caroline until after the picture was finished. He said that that wasn't *his* fault. It was Elsa who had insisted on spilling the beans. I said, Why? And he said that she had had some idea that it wasn't straight otherwise. She wanted everything to be clear and above board. Well, of course, in a way, one could understand that and respect the girl for it. However badly she was behaving, she did at least want to be honest.'

'A lot of additional pain and grief is caused by honesty,' remarked Hercule Poirot.

Meredith Blake looked at him doubtfully. He did not quite like the sentiment. He sighed:

'It was a – a most unhappy time for us all.'

'The only person who does not seem to have been affected by it was Amyas Crale,' said Poirot.

'And why? Because he was a rank egoist. I remember him now. Grinning at me as he went off saying: "Don't worry, Merry. Everything's going to pan out all right!"'

'The incurable optimist,' murmured Poirot.

Meredith Blake said:

'He was the kind of man who didn't take women seriously. *I* could have told him that Caroline was desperate.'

1048 • AGATHA CHRISTIE

'Did she tell you so?'

'Not in so many words. But I shall always see her face as it was that afternoon. White and strained with a kind of desperate gaiety. She talked and laughed a lot. But her eyes – there was a kind of anguished grief in them that was the most moving thing I have ever known. Such a gentle creature, too.'

Hercule Poirot looked at him for a minute or two without speaking. Clearly the man in front of him felt no incongruity in speaking thus of a woman who on the day after had deliberately killed her husband.

Meredith Blake went on. He had by now quite overcome his first suspicious hostility. Hercule Poirot had the gift of listening. To men such as Meredith Blake, the reliving of the past has a definite attraction. He spoke now almost more to himself than to his guest.

'I ought to have suspected something, I suppose. It was Caroline who turned the conversation to – to my little hobby. It was, I must confess, an enthusiasm of mine. The old English herbalists, you know, are a very interesting study. There are so many plants that were formerly used in medicine and which have now disappeared from the official Pharmacopœia. And it's astonishing, really, how a simple decoction of something or other will really work wonders. No need for doctors half the time. The French understand these things – some of their *tisanes* are first rate.' He was well away now on his hobby.

'Dandelion tea, for instance; marvellous stuff. And a decoction of hips – I saw the other day somewhere that that's coming into fashion with the medical profession again. Oh yes, I must confess, I got a lot of pleasure out of my brews. Gathering the plants at the right time, drying them – macerating them – all the rest of it. I've even dropped to superstition sometimes and gathered my roots at the full of the moon or whatever it was the ancients advised. On that day I gave my guests, I remember, a special disquisition on the spotted hemlock. It flowers biennially. You gather the fruits when they're ripening, just before they turn yellow. Coniine, you know, is a drug that's dropped out – I don't believe there's any official preparation of it in the last Pharmacopœia – but I've proved the usefulness of it in whooping cough – and in asthma too, for that matter –'

'You talked of all this in your laboratory?'

'Yes, I showed them round – explained the various drugs to them – valerian and the way it attracts cats – one sniff at that was enough for them! Then they asked about deadly nightshade and I told them about belladonna and atropine. They were very much interested.'

'They? What is comprised in that word?'

Meredith Blake looked faintly surprised as though he had forgotten that his listener had no first-hand knowledge of the scene.

'Oh, the whole party. Let me see, Philip was there and Amyas, and Caroline, of course. Angela. And Elsa Greer.'

'That was all?'

'Yes – I think so. Yes, I am sure of it,' Blake looked at him curiously. 'Who else should there be?'

'I thought perhaps the governess –'

'Oh, I see. No, she wasn't there that afternoon. I believe I've forgotten her name now. Nice woman. Took her duties very seriously. Angela worried her a good deal I think.'

'Why was that?'

'Well, she was a nice kid, but she was inclined to run wild. Always up to something or other. Put a slug or something down Amyas's back one day when he was hard at work painting. He went up in smoke. Cursed her up and down dale. It was after that that he insisted on this school idea.'

'Sending her to school?'

'Yes. I don't mean he wasn't fond of her, but he found her a bit of a nuisance sometimes. And I think – I've always thought –'

'Yes?'

'That he was a bit jealous. Caroline, you see, was a slave to Angela. In a way, perhaps, Angela came first with her – and Amyas didn't like that. There was a reason for it of course. I won't go into that, but –'

Poirot interrupted.

'The reason being that Caroline Crale reproached herself for an action that had disfigured the girl?'

Blake exclaimed: 'Oh, you know that? I wasn't going to mention it. All over and done with. But yes, that was the cause of her attitude I think. She always seemed to feel that there was nothing too much she could do – to make up, as it were.'

Poirot nodded thoughtfully. He asked:

'And Angela? Did she bear a grudge against her half sister?'

'Oh no, don't run away with that idea. Angela was devoted to Caroline. She never gave that old business a thought, I'm sure. It was just Caroline who couldn't forgive herself.'

'Did Angela take kindly to the idea of boarding school?'

'No, she didn't. She was furious with Amyas. Caroline took her side, but Amyas had absolutely made his mind up about it. In spite of a hot temper, Amyas was an easy man in most respects, but when he really got his back up, everyone had to give in. Both Caroline and Angela knuckled under.'

'She was to go to school – when?'

'The autumn term – they were getting her kit together, I remember. I suppose, if it hadn't been for the tragedy, she would have gone off a few days later. There was some talk of her packing on the morning of that day.'

Poirot said: 'And the governess?'

'What do you mean – the governess?'

'How did she like the idea? It deprived her of a job, did it not?'

'Yes – well, I suppose it did in a way. Little Carla used to do a few lessons, but of course she was only – what? Six or thereabouts. She had a nurse. They wouldn't have kept Miss Williams on for her. Yes, that's the name – Williams. Funny how things come back to you when you talk them over.'

'Yes, indeed. You are back now, are you not, in the past? You relive the scenes – the words that people said, their gestures – the expressions on their faces?'

Meredith Blake said slowly:

'In a way – yes . . . But there are gaps, you know . . . Great chunks missed out. I remember, for instance, the shock it was to me when I first learned that Amyas was going to leave Caroline – but I can't remember whether it was he who told me or Elsa. I do remember arguing with Elsa on the subject – trying to show her, I mean, that it was a pretty rotten thing to do. And she only laughed at me in that cool way of hers and said I was old fashioned. Well, I dare say I *am* old fashioned, but I still think I was right. Amyas had a wife and child – he ought to have stuck to them.'

'But Miss Greer thought that point of view out of date?'

'Yes. Mind you, sixteen years ago, divorce wasn't looked on quite so much as a matter of course as it is now. But Elsa was the kind of girl who went in for being modern. Her point of view was that when two people weren't happy together it was better to make a break. She said that Amyas and Caroline never stopped having rows and that it was far better for the child that she shouldn't be brought up in an atmosphere of disharmony.'

'And her argument did not impress you?'

Meredith Blake said slowly:

'I felt, all the time, that she didn't really know what she was talking about. She was rattling these things off – things she'd read in books or heard from her friends – it was like a parrot. She was – it's a queer thing to say – pathetic somehow. So young and so self-confident.' He paused.

'There is something about youth, M. Poirot, that is – that can be – terribly moving.'

Hercule Poirot said, looking at him with some interest: 'I know what you mean . . .'

Blake went on, speaking more to himself than to Poirot.

'That's partly, I think, why I tackled Crale. He was nearly twenty years older than the girl. It didn't seem fair.'

Poirot murmured:

'Alas – how seldom one makes any effect. When a person has determined on a certain course – it is not easy to turn them from it.'

Meredith Blake said:

'That is true enough.' His tone was a shade bitter. 'I certainly did no good by my interference. But then, I am not a very convincing person. I never have been.'

Poirot threw him a quick glance. He read into that slight acerbity of tone the dissatisfaction of a sensitive man with his own lack of personality. And he acknowledged to himself the truth of what Blake had just said. Meredith Blake was not the man to persuade any one into or out of any course. His well-meaning attempts would always be set aside – indulgently usually, without anger, but definitely set aside. They would not carry weight. He was essentially an ineffective man.

Poirot said, with an appearance of changing a painful subject: 'You still have your laboratory of medicines and cordials, yes?'

'No.'

The word came sharply – with an almost anguished rapidity Meredith Blake said, his face flushing:

'I abandoned the whole thing – dismantled it. I couldn't go on with it – how could I? – after what had happened. The whole thing, you see, might have been said to be *my* fault.'

'No, no, Mr Blake, you are too sensitive.'

'But don't you see? If I hadn't collected those damned drugs? If I hadn't laid stress on them – boasted about them – forced them on those people's notice that afternoon? But I never thought – I never dreamed – how could I –'

'How indeed.'

'But I went bumbling on about them. Pleased with my little bit of knowledge. Blind, conceited fool. I pointed out that damned coniine. I even, fool that I was, took them back into the library and read them out that passage from the Phaedo describing Socrates' death. A beautiful piece of writing – I've always admired it. But it's haunted me ever since.'

Poirot said:

'Did they find any fingerprints on the coniine bottle?'

'Hers.'

'Caroline Crale's?'

'Yes.'

'Not yours?'

'No. I didn't handle the bottle, you see. Only pointed to it.'

'But at the same time, surely, you had handled it?'

'Oh, of course, but I gave the bottles a periodic dusting from time to time – I never allowed the servants in there, of course – and I had done that about four or five days previously.'

'You kept the room locked up?'

'Invariably.'

'When did Caroline Crale take the coniine from the bottle?'

Meredith Blake replied reluctantly:

'She was the last to leave the room. I called her, I remember, and she came hurrying out. Her cheeks were just a little pink – and her eyes wide and excited. Oh, God, I can see her now.'

Poirot said: 'Did you have any conversation with her at all that afternoon? I mean by that, did you discuss the situation as between her and her husband at all?'

Blake said slowly in a low voice:

'Not directly. She was looking as I've told you – very upset. I said to her at a moment when we were more or less by ourselves: "Is anything the matter, my dear?" she said: "Everything's the matter . . ." I wish you could have heard the desperation in her voice. Those words were the absolute literal truth. There's no getting away from it – Amyas Crale was Caroline's whole world. She said, "Everything's gone – finished. I'm finished, Meredith." And then she laughed and turned to the others and was suddenly wildly and very unnaturally gay.'

Hercule Poirot nodded his head slowly. He looked very like a china mandarin. He said:

'Yes – I see – it was like that . . .'

Meredith Blake pounded suddenly with his fist. His voice rose. It was almost a shout.

'And I'll tell you this, M. Poirot – when Caroline Crale said at the trial that she took the stuff for herself, I'll swear she was speaking the truth! There was no thought in her mind of murder at that time. I swear there wasn't. That came later.'

Hercule Poirot asked:

'Are you sure that it *did* come later?'

Blake stared. He said:

'I beg your pardon? I don't quite understand –'

Poirot said:

'I ask you whether you are sure that the thought of murder ever did come? Are you perfectly convinced in your own mind that Caroline Crale did deliberately commit murder?'

Meredith Blake's breath came unevenly. He said: 'But if not – if not – are you suggesting an – well, accident of some kind?'

'Not necessarily.'

'That's a very extraordinary thing to say.'

'Is it? You have called Caroline Crale a gentle creature. Do gentle creatures commit murder?'

'She was a gentle creature – but all the same – well, there were very violent quarrels, you know.'

'Not such a gentle creature, then?'

'But she *was* – Oh, how difficult these things are to explain.'

'I am trying to understand.'

'Caroline had a quick tongue – a vehement way of speaking. She might say "I hate you. I wish you were dead." But it wouldn't mean – it wouldn't entail – *action*.'

'So in your opinion, it was highly uncharacteristic of Mrs Crale to commit murder?'

'You have the most extraordinary ways of putting things, M. Poirot. I can only say that – yes – it does seem to me uncharacteristic of her. I can only explain it by realizing that the provocation was extreme. She adored her husband. Under those circumstances a woman might – well – kill.'

Poirot nodded. 'Yes, I agree . . .'

'I was dumbfounded at first. I didn't feel it *could* be true. And it wasn't true – if you know what I mean – it wasn't the real Caroline who did that.'

'But you are quite sure that – in the legal sense – Caroline Crale did do it?'

Again Meredith Blake stared at him.

'My dear man – if she didn't –'

'Well, if she didn't?'

'I can't imagine any alternative solution. Accident? Surely impossible.'

'Quite impossible, I should say.'

'And I can't believe in the suicide theory. It had to be brought forward, but it was quite unconvincing to any one who knew Crale.'

'Quite.'

'So what remains?' asked Meredith Blake.

Poirot said coolly: 'There remains the possibility of Amyas Crale having been killed by somebody else.'

'But that's absurd!'

'You think so?'

'I'm sure of it. Who would have wanted to kill him? Who *could* have killed him?'

'You are more likely to know than I am.'

'But you don't seriously believe –'

'Perhaps not. It interests me to examine the possibility. Give it your serious consideration. Tell me what you think.'

Meredith stared at him for a minute or two. Then he lowered his eyes. After a minute or two he shook his head. He said:

'I can't imagine *any* possible alternative. I should like to do so. If there were any reason for suspecting anybody else I would readily believe Caroline innocent. I don't want to think she did it. I couldn't believe it at first. But who else is there? Who else was there. Philip? Crale's best friend. Elsa? Ridiculous. Myself? Do I look like a murderer? A respectable governess? A couple of old faithful servants? Perhaps you'd suggest that the child Angela did it? No, M. Poirot, there's *no* alternative. *Nobody* could have killed Amyas Crale but his wife. But he drove her to it. And so, in a way, it was suicide after all, I suppose.'

'Meaning that he died by the result of his own actions, though not by his own hand?'

'Yes, it's a fanciful point of view, perhaps. But – well – cause and effect, you know.'

Hercule Poirot said:

'Have you ever reflected, Mr Blake, that the reason for murder is nearly always to be found by a study of the person murdered?'

'I hadn't exactly – yes, I suppose I see what you mean.'

Poirot said:

'Until you know exactly *what sort of a person the victim was*, you cannot begin to see the circumstances of a crime clearly.'

He added:

'That is what I am seeking for – and what you and your brother have helped to give me – a reconstruction of the man Amyas Crale.'

Meredith Blake passed the main point of the remark over. His attention had been attracted by a single word. He said quickly:

'Philip?'

'Yes.'

'You have talked with him also?'

'Certainly.'

Meredith Blake said sharply:

'You should have come to me first.'

Smiling a little, Poirot made a courteous gesture.

'According to the laws of primogeniture, that is so,' he said. 'I am aware that you are the elder. But you comprehend that as your brother lives near London, it was easier to visit him first.'

Meredith Blake was still frowning. He pulled uneasily at his lip. He repeated:

'You should have come to me first.'

This time, Poirot did not answer. He waited. And presently Meredith Blake went on:

'Philip,' he said, 'is prejudiced.'

'Yes?'

'As a matter of fact he's a mass of prejudices – always has been.' He shot a quick uneasy glance at Poirot. 'He'll have tried to put you against Caroline.'

'Does that matter, so long – after?'

Meredith Blake gave a sharp sigh.

'I know. I forget that it's so long ago – that it's all over. Caroline is beyond being harmed. But all the same I shouldn't like you to get a false impression.'

'And you think your brother might give me a false impression?'

'Frankly, I do. You see, there was always a certain – how shall I put it? – antagonism between him and Caroline.'

'Why?'

The question seemed to irritate Blake. He said:

'Why? How should I know *why*? These things are so. Philip always crabbed her whenever he could. He was annoyed, I think, when Amyas married her. He never went near them for over a year. And yet Amyas was almost his best friend. That was the reason really, I suppose. He didn't feel that any woman was good enough. And he probably felt that Caroline's influence would spoil their friendship.'

'And did it?'

'No, of course it didn't. Amyas was always just as fond of Philip – right up to the end. Used to twit him with being a money grabber and with growing a corporation and being a Philistine generally. Philip didn't care.

He just used to grin and say it was a good thing Amyas had one respectable friend.'

'How did your brother react to the Elsa Greer affair?'

'Do you know, I find it rather difficult to say. His attitude wasn't really easy to define. He was annoyed, I think, with Amyas for making a fool of himself over the girl. He said more than once that it wouldn't work and that Amyas would live to regret it. At the same time I have a feeling – yes, very definitely I have a feeling that he was just faintly pleased at seeing Caroline let down.'

Poirot's eyebrows rose. He said:

'He really felt like that?'

'Oh, don't misunderstand me. I wouldn't go further than to say that I believe that feeling was at the back of his mind. I don't know that he ever quite realized himself that that is what he felt. Philip and I have nothing much in common, but there is a link, you know, between people of the same blood. One brother often knows what the other brother is thinking.'

'And after the tragedy?'

Meredith Blake shook his head. A spasm of pain crossed his face. He said:

'Poor Phil. He was terribly cut up. Just broken up by it. He'd always been devoted to Amyas, you see. There was an element of hero worship about it, I think. Amyas Crale and I are the same age. Philip was two years younger. And he looked up to Amyas always. Yes – it was a great blow to him. He was – he was terribly bitter against Caroline.'

'He, at least, had no doubts, then?'

Meredith Blake said:

'None of us had any doubts . . .'

There was a silence. Then Blake said with the irritable plaintiveness of a weak man:

'It was all over – forgotten – and now *you* come – raking it all up . . .'

'Not I. Caroline Crale.'

Meredith stared at him: '*Caroline?* What do you mean?'

Poirot said, watching him:

'Caroline Crale the second.'

Meredith's face relaxed.

'Ah yes, the child. Little Carla. I – I misunderstood you for a moment.'

'You thought I meant the original Caroline Crale? You thought that it was she who would not – how shall I say it – rest easy in her grave?'

Meredith Blake shivered.

'Don't, man.'

'You know that she wrote to her daughter – the last words she ever wrote – that she was innocent?'

Meredith stared at him. He said – and his voice sounded utterly incredulous:

'Caroline wrote *that*?'

'Yes.'

Poirot paused and said:

'It surprises you?'

'It would surprise you if you'd seen her in court. Poor, hunted, defenceless creature. Not even struggling.'

'A defeatist?'

'No, no. She wasn't that. It was, I think, the knowledge that she'd killed the man she loved – or I thought it was that.'

'You are not so sure now?'

'To write a thing like that – solemnly – when she was dying.'

Poirot suggested:

'A pious lie, perhaps.'

'Perhaps.' But Meredith was dubious. 'That's not – that's not like Caroline . . .'

Hercule Poirot nodded. Carla Lemarchant had said that. Carla had only a child's obstinate memory. But Meredith Blake had known Caroline well. It was the first confirmation Poirot had got that Carla's belief was to be depended upon.

Meredith Blake looked up at him. He said slowly:

'If – *if* Caroline was innocent – why, the whole thing's madness! I don't see – any other possible solution . . .'

He turned sharply on Poirot.

'And you? What do you think?'

There was a silence.

'As yet,' said Poirot at last, 'I think nothing. I collect only the impressions. What Caroline Crale was like. What Amyas Crale was like. What the other people who were there at the time were like. What happened exactly on those two days. *That* is what I need. To go over the facts laboriously one by one. Your brother is going to help me there. He is sending me an account of the events as he remembers them.'

Meredith Blake said sharply:

'You won't get much from that. Philip's a busy man. Things slip his memory once they're past and done with. Probably he'll remember things all wrong.'

'There will be gaps, of course. I realize that.'

'I tell you what –' Meredith paused abruptly, then went on, reddening a little as he spoke. 'If you like, I – I could do the same. I mean, it would be a kind of check, wouldn't it?'

Hercule Poirot said warmly:

'It would be most valuable. An idea of the first excellence!'

'Right. I will. I've got some old diaries somewhere. Mind you,' he laughed awkwardly. 'I'm not much of a hand at literary language. Even my spelling's not too good. You – you won't expect too much?'

'Ah, it is not the style I demand. Just a plain recital of everything you can remember. What every one said, how they looked – just what happened. Never mind if it doesn't seem relevant. It all helps with the atmosphere, so to speak.'

'Yes, I can see that. It must be difficult visualizing people and places you have never seen.'

Poirot nodded.

'There is another thing I wanted to ask you. Alderbury is the adjoining property to this, is it not? Would it be possible to go there – to see with my own eyes where the tragedy occurred?'

Meredith Blake said slowly:

'I can take you over there right away. But, of course, it is a good deal changed.'

'It has not been built over?'

'No, thank goodness – not quite so bad as that. But it's a kind of hostel now – it was bought by some society. Hordes of young people come down to it in the summer, and of course all the rooms have been cut up and partitioned into cubicles, and the grounds have been altered a good deal.'

'You must reconstruct it for me by your explanations.'

'I'll do my best. I wish you could have seen it in the old days. It was one of the loveliest properties I know.'

He led the way out through the window and began walking down a slope of lawn.

'Who was responsible for selling it?'

'The executors on behalf of the child. Everything Crale had came to her. He hadn't made a will, so I imagine that it would be divided automatically between his wife and the child. Caroline's will left what she had to the child also.'

'Nothing to her half-sister?'

'Angela had a certain amount of money of her own left her by her father.'

Poirot nodded. 'I see.'

Then he uttered an exclamation:

'But where is it that you take me? This is the seashore ahead of us!'

'Ah, I must explain our geography to you. You'll see for yourself in a minute. There's a creek, you see, Camel Creek, they call it, runs inland – looks almost like a river mouth, but it isn't – it's just sea. To get to Alderbury by land you have to go right inland and round the creek, but the shortest way from one house to the other is to row across this narrow bit of the creek. Alderbury is just opposite – there, you can see the house through the trees.'

They had come out on a little beach. Opposite them was a wooded headland and a white house could just be distinguished high up amongst the trees.

Two boats were drawn up on the beach. Meredith Blake, with Poirot's somewhat awkward assistance, dragged one of them down to the water and presently they were rowing across to the other side.

'We always went this way in the old days,' Meredith explained. 'Unless, of course, there was a storm or it was raining, and then we'd take the car. But it's nearly three miles if you go round that way.'

He ran the boat neatly alongside a stone quay on the other side. He cast a disparaging eye on a collection of wooden huts and some concrete terraces.

'All new, this. Used to be a boathouse – tumbledown old place – and nothing else. And one walked along the shore and bathed off those rocks over there.'

He assisted his guest to alight, made fast the boat, and led the way up a steep path.

'Don't suppose we'll meet any one,' he said over his shoulder. 'Nobody here in April – except for Easter. Doesn't matter if we do. I'm on good terms with my neighbours. Sun's glorious today. Might be summer. It was a wonderful day then. More like July than September. Brilliant sun – but a chilly little wind.'

The path came out of the trees and skirted an outcrop of rock. Meredith pointed up with his hand.

'That's what they called the Battery. We're more or less underneath it now – skirting round it.'

They plunged into trees again and then the path took another sharp turn and they emerged by a door set in a high wall. The path itself continued to zigzag upwards, but Meredith opened the door and the two men passed through it.

For a moment Poirot was dazzled coming in from the shade outside. The Battery was an artificially cleared plateau with battlements set with cannon. It gave one the impression of overhanging the sea. There were trees above it and behind it, but on the sea side there was nothing but the dazzling blue water below.

'Attractive spot,' said Meredith. He nodded contemptuously towards a kind of pavilion set back against the back wall. 'That wasn't there, of course – only an old tumbledown shed where Amyas kept his painting muck and some bottled beer and a few deck chairs. It wasn't concreted then, either. There used to be a bench and a table – painted iron ones. That was all. Still – it hasn't changed much.'

His voice held an unsteady note.

Poirot said: 'And it was here that it happened?'

Meredith nodded.

'The bench was there – up against the shed. He was sprawled on that. He used to sprawl there sometimes when he was painting – just fling himself down and stare and stare – and then suddenly up he'd jump and start laying the paint on the canvas like mad.'

He paused.

'That's why, you know, he looked – almost natural. As though he might be asleep – just have dropped off. But his eyes were open – and he'd – just stiffened up. Stuff sort of paralyses you, you know. There isn't any pain . . . I've – I've always been glad of that . . .'

Poirot asked a thing that he already knew.

'Who found him?'

'She did. Caroline. After lunch. I and Elsa, I suppose, were the last ones to see him alive. It must have been coming on then. He – looked queer. I'd rather not talk about it. I'll write it to you. Easier that way.'

He turned abruptly and went out of the Battery. Poirot followed him without speaking.

The two men went on up the zigzag path. At a higher level than the Battery there was another small plateau. It was over-shadowed with trees and there was a bench there and a table.

Meredith said:

'They haven't changed this much. But the bench used not to be Ye Olde Rustic. It was just a painted iron business. A bit hard for sitting, but a lovely view.'

Poirot agreed. Through a framework of trees one looked down over the Battery to the creek mouth.

'I sat up here part of the morning,' Meredith explained. 'Trees weren't quite so overgrown then. One could see the battlements of the Battery quite plainly. That's where Elsa was posing, you know. Sitting on one with her head twisted round.'

He gave a slight twitch of his shoulders.

'Trees grow faster than one thinks,' he muttered. 'Oh well, suppose I'm getting old. Come on up to the house.'

They continued to follow the path till it emerged near the house. It had been a fine old house, Georgian in style. It had been added to and on a green lawn near it were set some fifty little wooden bathing hutches.

'Young men sleep there, girls in the house,' Meredith explained. 'I don't suppose there's anything you want to see here. All the rooms have been cut about. Used to be a little conservatory tacked on here. These people have built a loggia. Oh well – I suppose they enjoy their holidays. Can't keep everything as it used to be – more's the pity.'

He turned away abruptly.

'We'll go down another way. It – it all comes back to me, you know. Ghosts. Ghosts everywhere.'

They returned to the quay by a somewhat longer and more rambling route. Neither of them spoke. Poirot respected his companion's mood.

When they reached Handcross Manor once more, Meredith Blake said abruptly:

'I bought that picture, you know. The one that Amyas was painting. I just couldn't stand the idea of its being sold for – well – publicity value – a lot of dirty-minded brutes gaping at it. It was a fine piece of work. Amyas said it was the best thing he'd ever done. I shouldn't be surprised if he was right. It was practically finished. He only wanted to work on it another day or so. Would – would you care to see it?'

Hercule Poirot said quickly: 'Yes, indeed.'

Blake led the way across the hall and took a key from his pocket. He unlocked a door and they went into a fair-sized, dusty smelling room. It was closely shuttered. Blake went across to the windows and opened the wooden shutters. Then, with a little difficulty, he flung up a window and a breath of fragrant spring air came wafting into the room.

Meredith said: 'That's better.'

He stood by the window inhaling the air and Poirot joined him. There was no need to ask what the room had been. The shelves were empty but there were marks upon them where bottles had stood. Against one wall was some derelict chemical apparatus and a sink. The room was thick in dust.

Meredith Blake was looking out of the window. He said:

'How easily it all comes back. Standing here, smelling the jasmine – and talking – talking – like the damned fool I was – about my precious potions and distillations!'

Absently, Poirot stretched a hand through the window. He pulled off a spray of jasmine leaves just breaking from their woody stem.

Meredith Blake moved resolutely across the floor. On the wall was a picture covered with a dust sheet. He jerked the dust sheet away.

Poirot caught his breath. He had seen so far, four pictures of Amyas Crale's: two at the Tate, one at a London dealer's, one, the still life of roses. But now he was looking at what the artist himself had called his best picture, and Poirot realized at once what a superb artist the man had been.

The painting had an old superficial smoothness. At first sight it might have been a poster, so seemingly crude were its contrasts. A girl, a girl in a canary-yellow shirt and dark-blue slacks, sitting on a grey wall in full sunlight against a background of violent blue sea. Just the kind of subject for a poster.

But the first appearance was deceptive; there was a subtle distortion – an amazing brilliance and clarity in the light. And the girl –

Yes, here was life. All there was, all there could be of life, of youth, of sheer blazing vitality. The face was alive and the eyes . . .

So much life! Such passionate youth! That, then, was what Amyas Crale had seen in Elsa Greer, which had made him blind and deaf to the gentle creature, his wife. Elsa *was* life. Elsa was youth.

A superb, slim, straight creature, arrogant, her head turned, her eyes insolent with triumph. Looking at you, watching you – waiting . . .

Hercule Poirot spread out his hands. He said:

'It is a great – yes, it is great –'

Meredith Blake said, a catch in his voice:

'She was so young –'

Poirot nodded. He thought to himself.

'What do most people mean when they say that? *So young*. Something innocent, something appealing, something helpless. But youth is not that! Youth is crude, youth is strong, youth is powerful – yes, and cruel! And one thing more – youth is vulnerable.'

He followed his host to the door. His interest was quickened now in Elsa Greer whom he was to visit next. What would the years have done to that passionate, triumphant crude child?

He looked back at the picture.

Those eyes. Watching him . . . watching him . . . Telling him something . . .

Supposing he couldn't understand what they were telling him? Would the real woman be able to tell him? Or were those eyes saying something that the real woman did not know?

Such arrogance, such triumphant anticipation.

And then Death had stepped in and taken the prey out of those eager, clutching young hands . . .

And the light had gone out of those passionately anticipating eyes. What were the eyes of Elsa Greer like now?

He went out of the room with one last look.

He thought: 'She was too much alive.'

He felt – a little – frightened . . .

CHAPTER 8

THIS LITTLE PIG HAD ROAST BEEF

The house in Brook Street had Darwin tulips in the window boxes. Inside the hall a great vase of white lilac sent eddies of perfume towards the open front door.

A middle-aged butler relieved Poirot of his hat and stick. A footman appeared to take them and the butler murmured deferentially:

'Will you come this way, sir?'

Poirot followed him along the hall and down three steps. A door was opened, the butler pronounced his name with every syllable correct.

Then the door closed behind him and a tall thin man got up from a chair by the fire and came towards him.

Lord Dittisham was a man just under forty. He was not only a Peer of the Realm, he was a poet. Two of his fantastical poetic dramas had been staged at vast expense and had had a *succès d'estime*. His forehead was rather prominent, his chin was eager, and his eyes and his mouth unexpectedly beautiful.

He said:

'Sit down, M. Poirot.'

Poirot sat down and accepted a cigarette from his host. Lord Dittisham shut the box, struck a match and held it for Poirot to light his cigarette, then he himself sat down and looked thoughtfully at his visitor.

Then he said:

'It is my wife you have come to see, I know.'

Poirot answered:

'Lady Dittisham was so kind as to give me an appointment.'

'Yes.'

There was a pause. Poirot hazarded:

'You do not, I hope, object, Lord Dittisham?'

The thin dreamy face was transformed by a sudden quick smile.

'The objections of husbands, M. Poirot, are never taken seriously in these days.'

'Then you do object?'

'No. I cannot say that. But I am, I must confess it, a little fearful of the effect upon my wife. Let me be quite frank. A great many years ago, when my wife was only a young girl, she passed through a terrible ordeal. She has, I hope, recovered from the shock. I have come to believe that she has forgotten it. Now you appear and necessarily your questions will reawaken these old memories.'

'It is regrettable,' said Hercule Poirot politely.

'I do not know quite what the result will be.'

'I can only assure you, Lord Dittisham, that I shall be as discreet as possible, and do all I can not to distress Lady Dittisham. She is, no doubt, of a delicate and nervous temperament.'

Then, suddenly and surprisingly, the other laughed. He said:

'Elsa? Elsa's as strong as a horse!'

'Then –' Poirot paused diplomatically. The situation intrigued him.

Lord Dittisham said:

'My wife is equal to any amount of shocks. I wonder if you know her reason for seeing you?'

Poirot replied placidly: 'Curiosity?'

A kind of respect showed in the other man's eyes.

'Ah, you realize that?'

Poirot said:

'It is inevitable. Women will *always* see a private detective! Men will tell him to go to the devil.'

'Some women might tell him to go to the devil too.'

'After they have seen him – not before.'

'Perhaps.' Lord Dittisham paused. 'What is the idea behind this book?'

Hercule Poirot shrugged his shoulders.

'One resurrects the old tunes, the old stage turns, the old costumes. One resurrects, too, the old murders.'

'Faugh!' said Lord Dittisham.

'Faugh! If you like. But you will not alter human nature by saying

Faugh. Murder is a drama. The desire for drama is very strong in the human race.'

Lord Dittisham murmured:

'I know – I know . . .'

'So you see,' said Poirot, 'the book will be written. It is my part to make sure that there shall be no gross mis-statements, no tampering with the known facts.'

'The facts are public property I should have thought.'

'Yes. But not the interpretation of them.'

Dittisham said sharply:

'Just what do you mean by that, M. Poirot?'

'My dear Lord Dittisham, there are many ways of regarding, for instance, a historical fact. Take an example: many books have been written on your Mary Queen of Scots, representing her as a martyr, as an unprincipled and wanton woman, as a rather simple-minded saint, as a murderess and an intriguer, or again as a victim of circumstance and fate! One can take one's choice.'

'And in this case? Crale was killed by his wife – that is, of course, undisputed. At the trial my wife came in for some, in my opinion, undeserved calumny. She had to be smuggled out of court afterwards. Public opinion was very hostile to her.'

'The English,' said Poirot, 'are a very moral people.'

Lord Dittisham said: 'Confound them, they are!'

He added – looking at Poirot: 'And you?'

'Me,' said Poirot. 'I lead a very moral life. That is not quite the same thing as having moral ideas.'

Lord Dittisham said:

'I've wondered sometimes what this Mrs Crale was really like. All this injured wife business – I've a feeling there was something *behind* that.'

'Your wife might know,' agreed Poirot.

'My wife,' said Lord Dittisham, 'has never mentioned the case once.'

Poirot looked at him with quickened interest. He said:

'Ah, I begin to see –'

The other said sharply:

'What do you see?'

Poirot replied with a bow:

'The creative imagination of the poet . . .'

Lord Dittisham rose and rang the bell. He said brusquely:

'My wife will be waiting for you.'

The door opened.

'You rang, my lord?'

'Take M. Poirot up to her ladyship.'

Up two flights of stairs, feet sinking into soft pile carpets. Subdued flood lighting. Money, money everywhere. Of taste, not so much. There had been a sombre austerity in Lord Dittisham's room. But here, in the house, there was only a solid lavishness. The best. Not necessarily the showiest, or the most startling. Merely 'expense no object', allied to a lack of imagination.

Poirot said to himself: 'Roast beef? Yes, roast beef!'

It was not a large room into which he was shown. The big drawing-room was on the first floor. This was the personal sitting-room of the mistress of the house and the mistress of the house was standing against the mantelpiece as Poirot was announced and shown in.

A phrase leapt into his startled mind and refused to be driven out.

She died young . . .

That was his thought as he looked at Elsa Dittisham who had been Elsa Greer.

He would never have recognized her from the picture Meredith Blake had shown him. That had been, above all, a picture of youth, a picture of vitality. Here there was no youth – there might never have been youth. And yet he realized, as he had not realized from Crale's picture, that Elsa was beautiful. Yes, it was a very beautiful woman who came forward to meet him. And certainly not old. After all, what was she? Not more than thirty-six now if she had been twenty at the time of the tragedy. Her black hair was perfectly arranged round her shapely head, her features were almost classic, her make-up was exquisite.

He felt a strange pang. It was, perhaps, the fault of old Mr Jonathan, speaking of Juliet . . . No Juliet here – unless perhaps one could imagine Juliet a survivor – living on, deprived of Romeo . . . Was it not an essential part of Juliet's make-up that she should die young?

Elsa Greer had been left alive . . .

She was greeting him in a level rather monotonous voice.

'I am so interested, M. Poirot. Sit down and tell me what you want me to do?'

He thought:

'But she isn't interested. Nothing interests her.'

Big grey eyes – like dead lakes.

Poirot became, as was his way, a little obviously foreign.

He exclaimed:

'I am confused, madame, veritably I am confused.'

'Oh no, why?'

'Because I realize that this – this reconstruction of a past drama must be excessively painful to you!'

She looked amused. Yes, it was amusement. Quite genuine amusement. She said:

'I suppose my husband put that idea into your head? He saw you when you arrived. Of course he doesn't understand in the least. He never has. I'm not at all the sensitive sort of person he imagines I am.'

The amusement was still in her voice. She said:

'My father, you know, was a mill hand. He worked his way up and made a fortune. You don't do that if you're thin-skinned. I'm the same.'

Poirot thought to himself: Yes, that is true. A thin-skinned person would not have come to stay in Caroline Crale's house.

Lady Dittisham said:

'What is it you want me to do?'

'You are sure, madame, that to go over the past would not be painful to you?'

She considered a minute, and it struck Poirot suddenly that Lady Dittisham was a very frank woman. She might lie from necessity but never from choice.

Elsa Dittisham said slowly:

'No, not *painful*. In a way, I wish it were.'

'Why?'

She said impatiently:

'It's so stupid never to feel anything . . .'

And Hercule Poirot thought:

'Yes, Elsa Greer is dead . . .'

Aloud he said:

'At all events, Lady Dittisham, it makes my task very much easier.'

She said cheerfully:

'What do you want to know?'

'Have you a good memory, madame?'

'Reasonably good, I think.'

'And you are sure it will not pain you to go over those days in detail?'

'It won't pain me at all. Things can only pain you when they are happening.'

'It is so with some people, I know.'

Lady Dittisham said:

'That's what Edward – my husband – can't understand. He thinks the trial and all that was a terrible ordeal for me.'

'Was it not?'

Elsa Dittisham said:

'No, I enjoyed it.' There was a reflective satisfied quality in her voice. She went on: 'God, how that old brute Depleach went for me. He's a devil, if you like. I enjoyed fighting him. He didn't get me down.'

She looked at Poirot with a smile.

'I hope I'm not upsetting your illusions. A girl of twenty, I ought to have been prostrated, I suppose – agonized with shame or something. I wasn't. I didn't care what they said to me. I only wanted one thing.'

'What?'

'To get her hanged, of course,' said Elsa Dittisham.

He noticed her hands – beautiful hands but with long curving nails. Predatory hands.

She said:

'You're thinking me vindictive? So I am vindictive – to any one who has injured me. That woman was to my mind the lowest kind of woman there is. She knew that Amyas cared for me – that he was going to leave her and she killed him so that *I* shouldn't have him.'

She looked across at Poirot.

'Don't you think that's pretty mean?'

'You do not understand or sympathize with jealousy?'

'No, I don't think I do. If you've lost, you've lost. If you can't keep your husband, let him go with a good grace. It's possessiveness I don't understand.'

'You might have understood it if you had ever married him.'

'I don't think so. We weren't –' She smiled suddenly at Poirot. Her smile was, he felt, a little frightening. It was so far removed from any real feeling. 'I'd like you to get this right,' she said. 'Don't think that Amyas Crale seduced an innocent young girl. It wasn't like that at all! Of the two of us, *I* was responsible. I met him at a party and I fell for him – I knew I'd got to have him –'

A travesty – a grotesque travesty but –

And all my fortunes at thy foot I'll lay
And follow thee, my lord, throughout the world . . .

'Although he was married?'

'Trespassers will be prosecuted? It takes more than a printed notice to keep you from reality. If he was unhappy with his wife and could be happy with me, then why not? We've only one life to live.'

'But it has been said he was happy with his wife.'

Elsa shook her head.

'No. They quarrelled like cat and dog. She nagged at him. She was – oh, she was a horrible woman!'

She got up and lit a cigarette. She said with a little smile:

'Probably I'm unfair to her. But I really *do* think she was rather hateful.'

Poirot said slowly: 'It was a great tragedy.'

'Yes, it was a great tragedy.' She turned on him suddenly, into the dead monotonous weariness of her face something came quiveringly alive.

'It killed *me*, do you understand? It killed me. Ever since there's been nothing – nothing at all.' Her voice dropped. 'Emptiness!' She waved her hands impatiently. 'Like a stuffed fish in a glass case!'

'Did Amyas Crale mean so much to you?'

She nodded. It was a queer confiding little nod – oddly pathetic. She said:

'I think I've always had a single-track mind.' She mused sombrely. 'I suppose – really – one ought to put a knife into oneself – like Juliet. But – but to do that is to acknowledge that you're done for – that life's beaten you.'

'And instead?'

'There ought to be everything – just the same – once one has got over it. I *did* get over it. It didn't mean anything to me any more. I thought I'd go on to the next thing.'

Yes, the next thing. Poirot saw her plainly trying so hard to fulfil that crude determination. Saw her beautiful and rich, seductive to men, seeking with greedy predatory hands to fill up a life that was empty. Hero worship – a marriage to a famous aviator – then an explorer, that big giant of a man, Arnold Stevenson – possibly not unlike Amyas Crale physically – a reversion to the creative arts: Dittisham!

Elsa Dittisham said:

'I've never been a hypocrite! There's a Spanish proverb I've always liked. *Take what you want and pay for it, says God.* Well, I've done that. I've taken what I wanted – but I've always been willing to pay the price.'

Hercule Poirot said:

'What you do not understand is that there are things that cannot be bought.'

She stared at him. She said:

'I don't mean just money.'

Poirot said:

'No, no, I understand what you mean. But it is not everything in life that has its ticket, so much. There are things that are *not for sale.*'

'Nonsense!'

He smiled very faintly. In her voice was the arrogance of the successful mill hand who had risen to riches.

Hercule Poirot felt a sudden wave of pity. He looked at the ageless, smooth face, the weary eyes, and he remembered the girl whom Amyas Crale had painted . . .

Elsa Dittisham said:

'Tell me all about this book. What is the purpose of it? Whose idea is it?'

'Oh! my dear lady, what other purpose is there but to serve up yesterday's sensation with today's sauce.'

'But *you're* not a writer?'

'No, I am an expert on crime.'

'You mean they consult you on crime books?'

'Not always. In this case, I have a commission.'

'From whom?'

'I am – what do you say – vetting this publication on behalf of an interested party.'

'What party?'

'Miss Carla Lemarchant.'

'Who is she?'

'She is the daughter of Amyas and Caroline Crale.'

Elsa stared for a minute. Then she said:

'Oh, of course, there *was* a child. I remember. I suppose she's grown up now?'

'Yes, she is twenty-one.'

'What is she like?'

'She is tall and dark and, I think, beautiful. And she has courage and personality.'

Elsa said thoughtfully:

'I should like to see her.'

'She might not care to see you.'

Elsa looked surprised.

'Why? Oh, I see. But what nonsense! She can't possibly remember anything about it. She can't have been more than six.'

'She knows that her mother was tried for her father's murder.'

'And she thinks it's my fault?'

'It is a possible interpretation.'

Elsa shrugged her shoulders. She said:

'How stupid! If Caroline had behaved like a reasonable human being –'

'So you take no responsibility?'

'Why should I? *I've* nothing to be ashamed of. I loved him. I would have made him happy.' She looked across at Poirot. Her face broke up – suddenly, incredibly, he saw the girl of the picture. She said: 'If I could make you see. If you could see it from my side. If you knew –'

Poirot leaned forward.

'But that is what I want. See, Mr Philip Blake who was there at the time, he is writing me a meticulous account of everything that happened. Mr Meredith Blake the same. Now if you –'

Elsa Dittisham took a deep breath. She said contemptuously:

'Those two! Philip was always stupid. Meredith used to trot round after Caroline – but he was quite a dear. But you won't have *any* real idea from *their* accounts.'

He watched her, saw the animation rising in her eyes, saw a living woman take shape from a dead one. She said quickly and almost fiercely:

'Would you like the *truth*? Oh, not for publication. But just for yourself –'

'I will undertake not to publish without your consent.'

'I'd like to write down the truth . . .' She was silent a minute or two, thinking. He saw the smooth hardness of her cheeks falter and take on a younger curve, he saw life ebbing into her as the past claimed her again.

'To go back – to write it all down . . . To show you what she was –'

Her eyes flashed. Her breast heaved passionately.

'She killed him. She killed Amyas. Amyas who wanted to live – who enjoyed living. Hate oughtn't to be stronger than love – but her hate was. And my hate for her is – I hate her – I hate her – I hate her . . .'

She came across to him. She stooped, her hand clutched at his sleeve. She said urgently:

'You must understand – you *must* – how we felt about each other. Amyas and I, I mean. There's something – I'll show you.'

She whirled across the room. She was unlocking a little desk, pulling out a drawer concealed inside a pigeon hole.

Then she was back. In her hand was a creased letter, the ink faded. She thrust it on him and Poirot had a sudden poignant memory of a child he had known who had thrust on him one of her treasures – a special shell picked up on the seashore and zealously guarded. Just so had that child stood back and watched him. Proud, afraid, keenly critical of his reception of her treasure.

He unfolded the faded sheets.

Elsa – you wonderful child! There never was anything as beautiful. And yet I'm afraid – I'm too old – a middle-aged, ugly tempered devil with no stability in me. Don't trust me, don't believe in me – I'm no good – apart from my work. The best of me is in that. There, don't say you haven't been warned.

Hell, my lovely – I'm going to have you all the same. I'd go to the devil for you and you know it. And I'll paint a picture of you that will make the fat-headed world hold its sides and gasp! I'm crazy about you – I can't sleep – I can't eat. Elsa – Elsa – Elsa – I'm yours for ever – yours till death. Amyas.

Sixteen years ago. Faded ink, crumbling paper. But the words still alive – still vibrating . . .

He looked across at the woman to whom they had been written.

But it was no longer a woman at whom he looked.

It was a young girl in love.

He thought again of Juliet . . .

CHAPTER 9

THIS LITTLE PIG HAD NONE

'May I ask why, M. Poirot?'

Hercule Poirot considered his answer to the question. He was aware of a pair of very shrewd grey eyes watching him out of the small wizened face.

He had climbed to the top floor of the bare building and knocked on the door of No. 584 Gillespie Buildings, which had come into existence to provide what were called 'flatlets' for working women.

Here, in a small cubic space, existed Miss Cecilia Williams, in a room that was bedroom, sitting-room, dining-room, and, by judicious use of the gas ring, kitchen – a kind of cubby hole attached to it contained a quarter-length bath and the usual offices.

Meagre though these surroundings might be, Miss Williams had contrived to impress upon them her stamp of personality.

The walls were distempered an ascetic pale grey, and various reproductions hung upon them. Dante meeting Beatrice on a bridge – and that picture once described by a child as a 'blind girl sitting on an orange and called, I don't know why, "Hope".' There were also two water colours

of Venice and a sepia copy of Botticelli's 'Primavera'. On the top of
the low chest of drawers were a large quantity of faded photographs,
mostly, by their style of hairdressing, dating from twenty to thirty years
ago.

The square of carpet was threadbare, the furniture battered and of
poor quality. It was clear to Hercule Poirot that Cecilia Williams lived
very near the bone. There was no roast beef here. This was the little pig
that had none.

Clear, incisive and insistent, the voice of Miss Williams repeated its
demand.

'You want my recollections of the Crale case? May I ask why?'

It had been said of Hercule Poirot by some of his friends and associates,
at moments when he has maddened them most, that he prefers lies to truth
and will go out of his way to gain his ends by means of elaborate false
statements, rather than trust to the simple truth.

But in this case his decision was quickly made. Hercule Poirot did
not come of that class of Belgian or French children who have had an
English governess, but he reacted as simply and inevitably as various small
boys who had been asked in their time: 'Did you brush your teeth this
morning, Harold (or Richard or Anthony)?' They considered fleetingly
the possibility of a lie and instantly rejected it, replying miserably, 'No,
Miss Williams.'

For Miss Williams had what every successful child educator must have,
that mysterious quality – authority! When Miss Williams said 'Go up
and wash your hands, Joan,' or 'I expect you to read this chapter on
the Elizabethan poets and be able to answer my questions on it,' she
was invariably obeyed. It had never entered Miss Williams' head that she
would not be obeyed.

So in this case Hercule Poirot proffered no specious explanation of
a book to be written on bygone crimes. Instead he narrated simply the
circumstances in which Carla Lemarchant had sought him out.

The small, elderly lady in the neat shabby dress listened attentively.

She said:

'It interests me very much to have news of that child – to know how
she has turned out.'

'She is a very charming and attractive young woman, with plenty of
courage and a mind of her own.'

'Good,' said Miss Williams briefly.

'And she is, I may say, a very persistent person. She is not a person
whom it is easy to refuse or put off.'

The ex-governess nodded thoughtfully. She asked:

'Is she artistic?'

'I think not.'

Miss Williams said drily:

'That's one thing to be thankful for!'

The tone of the remark left Miss Williams' views as to artists in no doubt whatever.

She added:

'From your account of her I should imagine that she takes after her mother rather than after her father.'

'Very possibly. That you can tell me when you have seen her. You would like to see her?'

'I should like to see her very much indeed. It is always interesting to see how a child you have known has developed.'

'She was, I suppose, very young when you last saw her?'

'She was five and a half. A very charming child – a little over-quiet, perhaps. Thoughtful. Given to playing her own little games and not inviting outside co-operation. Natural and unspoilt.'

Poirot said:

'It was fortunate she was so young.'

'Yes, indeed. Had she been older the shock of the tragedy might have had a very bad effect.'

'Nevertheless,' said Poirot, 'one feels that there *was* a handicap – however little the child understood or was allowed to know, there would have been an atmosphere of mystery and evasion and an abrupt uprooting. These things are not good for a child.'

Miss Williams replied thoughtfully:

'They may have been less harmful than you think.'

Poirot said:

'Before we leave the subject of Carla Lemarchant – little Carla Crale that was, there is something I would like to ask you. If any one can explain it, I think you can.'

'Yes?'

Her voice was inquiring, non-committal.

Poirot waved his hands in an effort to express his meaning.

'There is a something – a *nuance* I cannot define – but it seems to me always that the child, when I mention her, is not given her full representational value. When I mention her, the response comes always with a vague surprise, as though the person to whom I speak had forgotten altogether that there *was* a child. Now surely, mademoiselle, that is

not natural? A child, under these circumstances, is a person of importance, not in herself, but as a pivotal point. Amyas Crale may have had
reasons for abandoning his wife – or for not abandoning her. But in the
usual break-up of a marriage the child forms a very important point.
But here the child seems to count for very little. That seems to me –
strange.'

Miss Williams said quickly:

'You have put your finger on a vital point, M. Poirot. You are quite
right. And that is partly why I said what I did just now – that Carla's
transportation to different surroundings might have been in some respects
a good thing for her. When she was older, you see, she might have suffered
from a certain lack in her home life.'

She leaned forward and spoke slowly and carefully.

'Naturally, in the course of my work, I have seen a good many aspects
of the parent and child problem. Many children, *most* children, I should
say, suffer from over-attention on the part of their parents. There is too
much love, too much watching over the child. It is uneasily conscious of
this brooding, and seeks to free itself, to get away and be unobserved.
With an only child that is particularly the case, and of course mothers are
the worst offenders. The result on the marriage is often unfortunate. The
husband resents coming second, seeks consolation – or rather flattery and
attention – elsewhere, and a divorce results sooner or later. The best thing
for a child, I am convinced, is to have what I should term healthy neglect
on the part of both its parents. This happens naturally enough in the case
of a large family of children and very little money. They are overlooked
because the mother has literally no time to occupy herself with them. They
realize quite well that she is fond of them, but they are not worried by too
many manifestations of the fact.

'But there is another aspect. One does occasionally find a husband and
wife who are so all-sufficient to each other, so wrapped up in each other,
that the child of the marriage hardly seems very real to either of them.
And in those circumstances I think a child comes to resent that fact, to
feel defrauded and left out in the cold. You understand that I am not
speaking of *neglect* in any way. Mrs Crale, for instance, was what is termed
an excellent mother, always careful of Carla's welfare, of her health –
playing with her at the right times and always kind and gay. But for all
that, Mrs Crale was really completely wrapped up in her husband. She
existed, one might say, only in him and for him.' Miss Williams paused
a minute and then said quietly: 'That, I think, is the justification for what
she eventually did.'

Hercule Poirot said:

'You mean that they were more like lovers than like husband and wife?'

Miss Williams, with a slight frown of distaste for foreign phraseology, said:

'You could certainly put it that way.'

'He was devoted to her as she was to him?'

'They were a devoted couple. But he, of course, was a man.'

Miss Williams contrived to put into that last word a wholly Victorian significance.

'Men –' said Miss Williams, and stopped.

As a rich property owner says 'Bolsheviks' – as an earnest Communist says 'Capitalists!' – as a good housewife says 'Blackbeetles' – so did Miss Williams say 'Men!'

From her spinster's, governess's life, there rose up a blast of fierce feminism. Nobody hearing her speak could doubt that to Miss Williams Men were the Enemy!

Poirot said: 'You hold no brief for men?'

She answered drily:

'Men have the best of this world. I hope that it will not always be so.'

Hercule Poirot eyed her speculatively. He could quite easily visualize Miss Williams methodically and efficiently padlocking herself to a railing, and later hunger-striking with resolute endurance. Leaving the general for the particular, he said:

'You did not like Amyas Crale?'

'I certainly did not like Mr Crale. Nor did I approve of him. If I were his wife I should have left him. There are things that no woman should put up with.'

'But Mrs Crale did put up with them?'

'Yes.'

'You thought she was wrong?'

'Yes, I do. A woman should have a certain respect for herself and not submit to humiliation.'

'Did you ever say anything of that kind to Mrs Crale?'

'Certainly not. It was not my place to do so. I was engaged to educate Angela, not to offer unasked advice to Mrs Crale. To do so would have been most impertinent.'

'You liked Mrs Crale?'

'I was very fond of Mrs Crale.' The efficient voice softened, held warmth and feeling. 'Very fond of her and very sorry for her.'

'And your pupil – Angela Warren?'

'She was a most interesting girl – one of the most interesting pupils I have had. A really good brain. Undisciplined, quick-tempered, most difficult to manage in many ways, but really a very fine character.'

She paused and then went on:

'I always hoped that she would accomplish something worth while. And she has! You have read her book – on the Sahara? And she excavated those very interesting tombs in the Fayum! Yes, I am proud of Angela. I was not at Alderbury very long – two years and a half – but I always cherish the belief that I helped to stimulate her mind and encourage her taste for archæology.'

Poirot murmured: 'I understand that it was decided to continue her education by sending her to school. You must have resented that decision.'

'Not at all, M. Poirot. I thoroughly concurred with it.'

She paused and went on:

'Let me make the matter clear to you. Angela was a dear girl – really a very dear girl – warm-hearted and impulsive – but she was also what I call a difficult girl. That is, she was at a difficult age. There is always a moment where a girl feels unsure of herself – neither child nor woman. At one minute Angela would be sensible and mature – quite grown up, in fact – but a minute later she would relapse into being a hoydenish child – playing mischievous tricks and being rude and losing her temper. Girls, you know, *feel* difficult at that age – they are terribly sensitive. Everything that is said to them they resent. They are annoyed at being treated like a child and then they suddenly feel shy at being treated like adults. Angela was in that state. She had fits of temper, would suddenly resent teasing and flare out – and then she would be sulky for days at a time, sitting about and frowning – then again she would be in wild spirits, climbing trees, rushing about with the garden boys, refusing to submit to any kind of authority.'

Miss Williams paused and went on:

'When a girl gets to that stage, school is very helpful. She needs the stimulation of other minds – that, and the wholesome discipline of a community, help her to become a reasonable member of society. Angela's home conditions were not what I would have called ideal. Mrs Crale spoiled her, for one thing. Angela had only to appeal to her and Mrs Crale always backed her up. The result was that Angela considered she had first claim upon her sister's time and attention, and it was in these moods of hers that she used to clash with Mr Crale. Mr Crale naturally thought that *he* should come first – and intended to do so. He was really very fond of the girl – they were good companions and used to spar together quite amiably, but there were times when Mr Crale used suddenly to resent Mrs Crale's preoccupation with Angela. Like all men, he was a spoilt child; he expected everybody to make a fuss of *him*. Then he and Angela used to have a real set-to – and very often Mrs Crale would take Angela's side. Then he would be furious. On the other hand, if *she* supported *him*, Angela would be furious. It was on these occasions that Angela used to revert to childish ways and play some spiteful trick on him. He had a habit of tossing off his drinks and she once put a lot of salt into his drink. The whole thing, of course, acted as an emetic, and he was inarticulate with fury. But what really brought things to a head was when she put a lot of slugs into his bed. He had a queer aversion for slugs. He lost his temper completely and said that the girl had got to be sent away to school. He wasn't going to put up with all this petty nonsense any more. Angela was terribly upset – though actually she had once or twice expressed a wish herself to go to a boarding school – but she chose to make a huge grievance of it. Mrs Crale didn't want her to go but allowed herself to be persuaded – largely owing, I think, to what I said to her on the subject. I pointed out to her that it would be greatly to Angela's advantage, and that I thought it would really be a great benefit to the girl. So it was settled that she should go to Helston – a very fine school on the south coast – in the autumn term. But Mrs Crale was still unhappy about it all those holidays. And Angela kept up a grudge against Mr Crale whenever she remembered. It wasn't really serious, you understand, M. Poirot, but it made a kind of undercurrent that summer to – well – to everything *else* that was going on.'

Poirot said: 'Meaning – Elsa Greer?'

Miss Williams said sharply:

'Exactly.' And shut her lips very tight after the word.

'What was your opinion of Elsa Greer?'

'I had no opinion of her at all. A thoroughly unprincipled young woman.'

'She was very young.'

'Old enough to know better. I can see no excuse for her – none at all.'

'She fell in love with him, I suppose –'

Miss Williams interrupted with a snort.

'Fell in love with him indeed. I should hope, M. Poirot, that whatever our feelings, we can keep them in decent control. And we can certainly control our actions. That girl had absolutely no morals of any kind. It meant nothing to her that Mr Crale was a married man. She was absolutely shameless about it all – cool and determined. Possibly she may have been badly brought up – but that's the only excuse I can find for her.'

'Mr Crale's death must have been a terrible shock to her.'

'Oh, it was. And she herself was entirely to blame for it. I don't go as far as condoning murder, but all the same, M. Poirot, if ever a woman was driven to breaking point, that woman was Caroline Crale. I tell you frankly, there were moments when I would have liked to murder them both myself. Flaunting the girl in his wife's face, listening to her having to put up with the girl's insolence – and she *was* insolent, M. Poirot. Oh no, Amyas Crale deserved what he got. No man should treat his wife as he did and not be punished for it. His death was a just retribution.'

Hercule Poirot said: 'You feel strongly . . .'

The small woman looked at him with those indomitable grey eyes. She said:

'I feel *very strongly* about the marriage tie. Unless it is respected and upheld, a country degenerates. Mrs Crale was a devoted and faithful wife. Her husband deliberately flouted her and introduced his mistress into her home. As I say, he deserved what he got. He goaded her past endurance and I, for one, do not blame her for what she did.'

Poirot said slowly: 'He acted very badly – that I admit – but he was a great artist, remember.'

Miss Williams gave a terrific snort.

'Oh yes, I know. That's always the excuse nowadays. An artist! An excuse for every kind of loose living, for drunkenness, for brawling, for infidelity. And what kind of an artist was Mr Crale, when all is said and done? It may be the fashion to admire his pictures for a few years. But they won't last. Why, he couldn't even draw! His perspective was terrible! Even his anatomy was quite incorrect. I know something of what I am talking about, M. Poirot. I studied painting for a time, as a girl, in Florence, and to any one who knows and appreciates the great masters, these daubs of Mr Crale's are really ludicrous. Just splashing a few colours about on the canvas – no construction – no careful drawing. No,' she shook her head, 'don't ask me to admire Mr Crale's painting.'

'Two of them are in the Tate Gallery,' Poirot reminded her.

Miss Williams sniffed.

'Possibly. So is one of Mr Epstein's statues, I believe.'

Poirot perceived that, according to Miss Williams, the last word had been said. He abandoned the subject of art.

He said:

'You were with Mrs Crale when she found the body?'

'Yes. She and I went down from the house together after lunch. Angela had left her pullover on the beach after bathing, or else in the boat. She was always very careless about her things. I parted from Mrs Crale at the door of the Battery garden, but she called me back almost at once. I believe Mr Crale had been dead over an hour. He was sprawled on the bench near his easel.'

'Was she terribly upset at the discovery?'

'What exactly do you mean by that, M. Poirot?'

'I am asking you what your impressions were at the time.'

'Oh, I see. Yes, she seemed to me quite dazed. She sent me off to telephone for the doctor. After all, we couldn't be absolutely sure he was dead – it might have been a cataleptic seizure.'

'Did she suggest such a possibility?'

'I don't remember.'

'And you went and telephoned?'

Miss Williams' tone was dry and brusque.

'I had gone half up the path when I met Mr Meredith Blake. I entrusted my errand to him and returned to Mrs Crale. I thought, you see, she might have collapsed – and men are no good in a matter of that kind.'

'And had she collapsed?'

Miss Williams said drily:

'Mrs Crale was quite in command of herself. She was quite different from Miss Greer, who made a hysterical and very unpleasant scene.'

'What kind of a scene?'

'She tried to attack Mrs Crale.'

'You mean she realized that Mrs Crale was responsible for Mr Crale's death?'

Miss Williams considered for a moment or two.

'No, she could hardly be sure of that. That – er – terrible suspicion had not yet arisen. Miss Greer just screamed out: "It's all your doing, Caroline. You killed him. It's all your fault." She did not actually say "You've poisoned him," but I think there is no doubt that she thought so.'

'And Mrs Crale?'

Miss Williams moved restlessly.

'Must we be hypocritical, M. Poirot? I cannot tell you what Mrs Crale really felt or thought at that moment. Whether it was horror at what she had done –'

'Did it seem like that?'

'N-no, n-no, I can't say it did. Stunned, yes – and, I think, frightened. Yes, I am sure, frightened. But that is natural enough.'

Hercule Poirot said in a dissatisfied tone:

'Yes, perhaps that is natural enough . . . What view did she adopt officially as to her husband's death?'

'Suicide. She said, very definitely from the first, that it must be suicide.'

'Did she say the same when she was talking to you privately, or did she put forward any other theory.'

'No. She – she – took pains to impress upon me that it must be suicide.'

Miss Williams sounded embarrassed.

'And what did you say to that?'

'Really, M. Poirot, does it matter *what* I said?'

'Yes, I think it does.'

'I don't see why –'

But as though his expectant silence hypnotized her, she said reluctantly:

'I think I said: "Certainly, Mrs Crale. It must have been suicide."'

'Did you believe your own words?'

Miss Williams raised her head. She said firmly:

'No, I did not. But please understand, M. Poirot, that I was entirely on Mrs Crale's side, if you like to put it that way. My sympathies were with her, not with the police.'

'You would have liked to have seen her acquitted?'

Miss Williams said defiantly:

'Yes, I would.'

Poirot said:

'Then you are in sympathy with her daughter's feelings?'

'I have every sympathy with Carla.'

'Would you have any objection to writing out for me a detailed account of the tragedy?'

'You mean for her to read?'

'Yes.'

Miss Williams said slowly:

'No, I have no objection. She is quite determined to go into the matter, is she?'

'Yes. I dare say it would have been preferable if the truth had been kept from her –'

Miss Williams interrupted him:

'No. It is always better to face the truth. It is no use evading unhappiness by tampering with facts. Carla has had a shock learning the truth – now she wants to know exactly how the tragedy came about. That seems to me the right attitude for a brave young woman to take. Once she knows all about it she will be able to forget it again and go on with the business of living her own life.'

'Perhaps you are right,' said Poirot.

'I'm quite sure I'm right.'

'But you see, there is more to it than that. She not only wants to know – she wants to prove her mother innocent.'

Miss Williams said: 'Poor child.'

'That is what you say, is it?'

Miss Williams said:

'I see now why you said that it might be better if she had never known. All the same, I think it is best as it is. To wish to find her mother innocent is a natural hope – and hard though the actual revelation may be, I think from what you say of her that Carla is brave enough to learn the truth and not flinch from it.'

'You are sure it *is* the truth?'

'I don't understand you?'

'You see no loophole for believing that Mrs Crale was innocent?'

'I don't think that possibility has ever been seriously considered.'

'And yet she herself clung to the theory of suicide?'

Miss Williams said drily:

'The poor woman had to say *something*.'

'Do you know that when Mrs Crale was dying she left a letter for her daughter in which she solemnly swears that she is innocent?'

Miss Williams stared.

'That was very wrong of her,' she said sharply.

'You think so?'

'Yes, I do. Oh, I dare say you are a sentimentalist like most men –'

Poirot interrupted indignantly:

'I am *not* a sentimentalist.'

'But there is such a thing as false sentiment. Why write that, a lie, at such a solemn moment? To spare your child pain? Yes, many women would do that. But I should not have thought it of Mrs Crale. She was a brave woman and a truthful woman. I should have thought it far more like her to have told her daughter not to judge.'

Poirot said with slight exasperation:

'You will not even consider then the possibility that what Caroline Crale wrote was the truth?'

'Certainly not!'

'And yet you profess to have loved her?'

'I did love her. I had a great affection and deep sympathy for her.'

'Well, then –'

Miss Williams looked at him in a very odd way.

'You don't understand, M. Poirot. It doesn't matter my saying this now – so long afterwards. You see, I happen to *know* that Caroline Crale was guilty!'

'*What?*'

'It's true. Whether I did right in withholding what I knew at the time I cannot be sure – but I *did* withhold it. But you must take it from me, quite definitely, that I *know* Caroline Crale was guilty . . .'

CHAPTER 10

THIS LITTLE PIG CRIED 'WEE WEE WEE'

Angela Warren's flat overlooked Regent's Park. Here, on this spring day, a soft air wafted in through the open window and one might have had the illusion that one was in the country if it had not been for the steady menacing roar of the traffic passing below.

Poirot turned from the window as the door opened and Angela Warren came into the room.

It was not the first time he had seen her. He had availed himself of the opportunity to attend a lecture she had given at the Royal Geographical. It had been, he considered, an excellent lecture. Dry, perhaps, from the view of popular appeal. Miss Warren had an excellent delivery, she neither paused nor hesitated for a word. She did not repeat herself. The tones of her voice were clear and not unmelodious. She made no concessions to romantic appeal or love of adventure. There was very little human interest in the lecture. It was an admirable recital of concise facts, adequately illustrated by excellent slides, and with intelligent deductions from the facts recited. Dry, precise, clear, lucid, highly technical.

The soul of Hercule Poirot approved. Here, he considered, was an orderly mind.

Now that he saw her at close quarters he realized that Angela Warren might easily have been a very handsome woman. Her features were regular, though severe. She had finely marked dark brows, clear intelligent brown eyes, a fine pale skin. She had very square shoulders and a slightly mannish walk.

There was certainly about her no suggestion of the little pig who cries 'Wee Wee.' But on the right cheek, disfiguring and puckering the skin, was that healed scar. The right eye was slightly distorted, the corner pulled downwards by it but no one would have realized that the sight of that eye was destroyed. It seemed to Hercule Poirot almost certain that she had lived with her disability so long that she was now completely unconscious of it. And it occurred to him that of the five people in whom he had become interested as a result of his investigations, those who might have been said to start with the fullest advantages were not those who had actually wrested the most success and happiness from life. Elsa, who might have been said to start with all advantages – youth, beauty, riches – had done worst. She was like a flower overtaken by untimely frost – still in bud – but without life. Cecilia Williams, to outward appearances, had no assets of which to boast. Nevertheless, to Poirot's eye, there was no despondency there and no sense of failure. Miss Williams's life had been interesting to her – she was still interested in people and events. She had that enormous mental and moral advantage of a strict Victorian upbringing denied to us in these days – she had done her duty in that station of life to which it had pleased God to call her, and that assurance encased her in an armour impregnable to the slings and darts of envy, discontent and regret. She had her memories, her small pleasures, made possible by stringent economies, and sufficient health and vigour to enable her still to be interested in life.

Now, in Angela Warren – that young creature handicapped by disfigurement and its consequent humiliation, Poirot believed he saw a spirit strengthened by its necessary fight for confidence and assurance. The undisciplined schoolgirl had given place to a vital and forceful woman, a woman of considerable mental power and gifted with abundant energy to accomplish ambitious purposes. She was a woman, Poirot felt sure, both happy and successful. Her life was full and vivid and eminently enjoyable.

She was not, incidentally, the type of woman that Poirot really liked. Though admiring the clear-cut precision of her mind, she had just a sufficient *nuance* of the *femme formidable* about her to alarm him as a mere man. His taste had always been for the flamboyant and extravagant.

With Angela Warren it was easy to come to the point of his visit. There was no subterfuge. He merely recounted Carla Lemarchant's interview with him.

Angela Warren's severe face lighted up appreciatively.

'Little Carla? She is over here? I would like to see her so much.'

'You have not kept in touch with her?'

'Hardly as much as I should have done. I was a schoolgirl at the time she went to Canada, and I realized, of course, that in a year or two she would have forgotten us. Of late years, an occasional present at Christmas has been the only link between us. I imagined that she would, by now, be completely immersed in the Canadian atmosphere and that her future would lie over there. Better so, in the circumstances.'

Poirot said: 'One might think so, certainly. A change of name – a change of scene. A new life. But it was not to be so easy as that.'

And he then told of Carla's engagement, the discovery she had made upon coming of age and her motives in coming to England.

Angela Warren listened quietly, her disfigured cheek resting on one hand. She betrayed no emotion during the recital, but as Poirot finished, she said quietly:

'Good for Carla.'

Poirot was startled. It was the first time that he had met with this reaction. He said:

'You approve, Miss Warren?'

'Certainly. I wish her every success. Anything I can do to help, I will. I feel guilty, you know, that I haven't attempted anything myself.'

'Then you think that there is a possibility that she is right in her views.'

Angela Warren said sharply:

'Of course she's right. Caroline didn't do it. I've always known that.'

Hercule Poirot murmured:

'You surprise me very much indeed, mademoiselle. Everybody else I have spoken to –'

She cut in sharply:

'You mustn't go by that. I've no doubt that the circumstantial evidence is overwhelming. My own conviction is based on knowledge – knowledge of my sister. I just know quite simply and definitely that Caro *couldn't* have killed any one.'

'Can one say that with certainty of any human creature?'

'Probably not in most cases. I agree that the human animal is full of curious surprises. But in Caroline's case there were special reasons – reasons which I have a better chance of appreciating than any one else could.'

She touched her damaged cheek.

'You see this? You've probably heard about it?' Poirot nodded. 'Caroline did that. That's why I'm sure – I *know* – that she didn't do murder.'

'It would not be a convincing argument to most people.'

'No, it would be the opposite. It was actually used in that way, I believe. As evidence that Caroline had a violent and ungovernable temper! Because she had injured me as a baby, learned men argued that she would be equally capable of poisoning an unfaithful husband.'

Poirot said:

'I, at least, appreciated the difference. A sudden fit of ungovernable rage does not lead you to first abstract a poison and then use it deliberately on the following day.'

Angela Warren waved an impatient hand.

'That's not what I mean at all. I must try and make it plain to you. Supposing that you are a person normally affectionate and of kindly disposition – but that you are also liable to intense jealousy. And supposing that during the years of your life when control is most difficult, you do, in a fit of rage, come near to committing what is, in effect, murder. Think of the awful shock, the horror, the remorse that seizes upon you. To a sensitive person, like Caroline, that horror and remorse will never quite leave you. It never left her. I don't suppose I was consciously aware of it at the time, but looking back I recognize it perfectly. Caro was haunted, continually haunted, by the fact that she had injured me. That knowledge never left her in peace. It coloured all her actions. It explained her attitude to me. Nothing was too good for me. In her eyes, I must always come first. Half the quarrels she had with Amyas were on my account. I was inclined to be jealous of him and played all kinds of tricks on him. I pinched cat stuff to put in his drink, and once I put a hedgehog in his bed. But Caroline was always on my side.'

Miss Warren paused, then she went on:

'It was very bad for me, of course. I got horribly spoilt. But that's neither here nor there. We're discussing the effect on Caroline. The result of that impulse to violence was a life-long abhorrence of any further act of the same kind. Caro was always watching herself, always in fear that something of that kind might happen again. And she took her own ways of guarding against it. One of these ways was a great extravagance of language. She felt (and I think, psychologically quite truly) that if she were violent enough in speech she would have no temptation to violence in action. She found by experience that the method worked. That's why I've heard Caro say things like "I'd like to cut so and so in pieces and boil him slowly in oil." And she'd say to me, or to Amyas, "If you go on annoying me I shall murder you." In the same way she quarrelled easily and violently. She recognized, I think, the impulse to violence that there was in her nature, and she deliberately gave it an outlet that way. She and Amyas used to have the most fantastic and lurid quarrels.'

Hercule Poirot nodded.

'Yes, there was evidence of that. They quarrelled like cat and dog, it was said.'

Angela Warren said:

'Exactly. That's what is so stupid and misleading about evidence. Of course Caro and Amyas quarrelled! Of course they said bitter and outrageous and cruel things to each other! What nobody appreciates is that they *enjoyed* quarrelling. But they did! Amyas enjoyed it too. They were that kind of couple. They both of them liked drama and emotional scenes. Most men don't. They like peace. But Amyas was an artist. He liked shouting and threatening and generally being outrageous. It was like letting off steam to him. He was the kind of man who when he loses his collar stud bellows the house down. It sounds very odd, I know, but living that way with continual rows and makings-up was Amyas's and Caroline's idea of fun!'

She made an impatient gesture.

'If they'd only not hustled me away and let me give evidence, I'd have told them that.' Then she shrugged her shoulders. 'But I don't suppose they would have believed me. And anyway then it wouldn't have been as clear in my mind as it is now. It was the kind of thing I knew but hadn't thought about and certainly had never dreamed of putting into words.'

She looked across at Poirot.

'You do see what I mean?'

He nodded vigorously.

'I see perfectly – and I realize the absolute rightness of what you have said. There are people to whom agreement is monotony. They require the stimulant of dissension to create drama in their lives.'

'Exactly.'

'May I ask you, Miss Warren, what were your own feelings at the time?'

Angela Warren sighed.

'Mostly bewilderment and helplessness, I think. It seemed a fantastic nightmare. Caroline was arrested very soon – about three days afterwards, I think. I can still remember my indignation, my dumb fury – and, of course, my childish faith that it was just a silly mistake, that it would be all right. Caro was chiefly perturbed about *me* – she wanted me kept right away from it all as far as possible. She got Miss Williams to take me away to some relations almost at once. The police had no objection. And then, when it was decided that my evidence would not be needed, arrangements were made for me to go to school abroad.

'I hated going, of course. But it was explained to me that Caro had me terribly on her mind and that the only way I could help her was by going.'

She paused. Then she said:

'So I went to Munich. I was there when – when the verdict was given. They never let me go to see Caro. Caro wouldn't have it. That's the only time, I think, when she failed in understanding.'

'You cannot be sure of that, Miss Warren. To visit someone dearly loved in a prison might make a terrible impression on a young sensitive girl.'

'Possibly.'

Angela Warren got up. She said:

'After the verdict, when she had been condemned, my sister wrote me a letter. I have never shown it to any one. I think I ought to show it to you now. It may help you to understand the kind of person Caroline was. If you like you may take it to show to Carla also.'

She went to the door, then turning back she said:

'Come with me. There is a portrait of Caroline in my room.'

For a second time, Poirot stood gazing up at a portrait.

As a painting, Caroline Crale's portrait was mediocre. But Poirot looked at it with interest – it was not its artistic value that interested him.

He saw a long oval face, a gracious line of jaw and a sweet, slightly timid expression. It was a face uncertain of itself, emotional, with a withdrawn hidden beauty. It lacked the forcefulness and vitality of her daughter's face – that energy and joy of life Carla Lemarchant had doubtless inherited from her father. This was a less positive creature. Yet, looking at the painted face, Hercule Poirot understood why an imaginative man like Quentin Fogg had not been able to forget her.

Angela Warren stood at his side again – a letter in her hand.

She said quietly:

'Now that you have seen what she was like – read her letter.'

He unfolded it carefully and read what Caroline Crale had written sixteen years ago.

My darling little Angela,

You will hear bad news and you will grieve, but what I want to impress upon you is that it is all all right. I have never told you lies and I don't now when I say that I am actually happy – that I feel an essential rightness and a peace that I have never known before. It's all

right, darling, it's all right. Don't look back and regret and grieve for
me – go on with your life and succeed. You can, I know. It's all, all
right, darling, and I'm going to Amyas. I haven't the least doubt that
we shall be together. I couldn't have lived without him . . . Do this one
thing for me – be happy. I've told you – I'm happy. One has to pay
one's debts. It's lovely to feel peaceful.
   Your loving sister,
   Caro

Hercule Poirot read it through twice. Then he handed it back. He said:

'That is a very beautiful letter, mademoiselle – and a very remarkable one. A *very* remarkable one.'

'Caroline,' said Angela Warren, 'was a very remarkable person.'

'Yes, an unusual mind . . . You take it that this letter indicates innocence?'

'Of course it does!'

'It does not say so explicitly.'

'Because Caro would know that I'd never dream of her being guilty!'

'Perhaps – perhaps . . . But it might be taken another way. In the sense that she was guilty and that in expiating her crime she will find peace.'

It fitted in, he thought, with the description of her in court. And he experienced in this moment the strongest doubts he had yet felt of the course to which he had committed himself. Everything so far had pointed unswervingly to Caroline Crale's guilt. Now, even her own words testified against her.

On the other side was only the unshaken conviction of Angela Warren. Angela had known her well, undoubtedly, but might not her certainty be the fanatical loyalty of an adolescent girl, up in arms for a dearly loved sister?

As though she had read his thoughts Angela Warren said:

'No, M. Poirot – I *know* Caroline wasn't guilty.'

Poirot said briskly:

'The Bon Dieu knows I do not want to shake you on that point. But let us be practical. You say your sister was not guilty. Very well, then, *what really happened?*'

Angela nodded thoughtfully. She said:

'That is difficult, I agree. I suppose that, as Caroline said, Amyas committed suicide.'

'Is that likely from what you know of his character?'

'Very unlikely.'

'But you do not say, as in the first case, that you *know* it is impossible?'

'No, because, as I said just now, most people *do* do impossible things – that is to say things that seem out of character. But I presume, if you know them intimately, it wouldn't be out of character.'

'You knew your brother-in-law well?'

'Yes, but not like I knew Caro. It seems to me quite fantastic that Amyas should have killed himself – but I suppose he *could* have done so. In fact, he *must* have done so.'

'You cannot see any other explanation?'

Angela accepted the suggestion calmly, but not without a certain stirring of interest.

'Oh, I see what you mean. . . . I've never really considered that possibility. You mean one of the other people killed him? That it was a deliberate cold-blooded murder . . .'

'It might have been, might it not?'

'Yes, it might have been . . . But it certainly seems very unlikely.'

'More unlikely than suicide?'

'That's difficult to say . . . On the face of it, there was no reason for suspecting anybody else. There isn't now when I look back . . .'

'All the same, let us consider the possibility. Who of those intimately concerned would you say was – shall we say – the most likely person?'

'Let me think. Well, I didn't kill him. And the Elsa creature certainly didn't. She was mad with rage when he died. Who else was there? Meredith Blake? He was always very devoted to Caroline, quite a tame cat about the house. I suppose that *might* give him a motive in a way. In a book he might have wanted to get Amyas out of the way so that he himself could marry Caroline. But he could have achieved that just as well by letting Amyas go off with Elsa and then in due time consoling Caroline. Besides I really can't *see* Meredith as a murderer. Too mild and too cautious. Who else was there?'

Poirot suggested: 'Miss Williams? Philip Blake?'

Angela's grave face relaxed into a smile for a minute.

'Miss Williams? One can't really make oneself believe that one's governess could commit a murder! Miss Williams was always so unyielding and so full of rectitude.'

She paused a minute and then went on:

'She was devoted to Caroline, of course. Would have done anything for her. And she hated Amyas. She was a great feminist and disliked men. Is that enough for murder? Surely not.'

'It would hardly seem so,' agreed Poirot.

Angela went on:

'Philip Blake?' She was silent for some few moments. Then she said quietly: 'I think, you know, if we're just talking of *likelihoods*, *he's* the most likely person.'

Poirot said:

'You interest me very much, Miss Warren. May I ask why you say that?'

'Nothing at all definite. But from what I remember of him, I should say he was a person of rather limited imagination.'

'And a limited imagination predisposes you to murder?'

'It might lead you to take a crude way of settling your difficulties. Men of that type get a certain satisfaction from action of some kind or other. Murder is a very crude business, don't you think so?'

'Yes – I think you are right . . . It is definitely a point of view, that. But all the same, Miss Warren, there must be more to it than that. What motive could Philip Blake possibly have had?'

Angela Warren did not answer at once. She stood frowning down at the floor.

Hercule Poirot said:

'He was Amyas Crale's best friend, was he not?'

She nodded.

'But there is something in your mind, Miss Warren. Something that you have not yet told me. Were the two men rivals, perhaps, over the girl – over Elsa?'

Angela Warren shook her head.

'Oh, no, not Philip.'

'What is there then?'

Angela Warren said slowly:

'Do you know the way that things suddenly come back to you – after years perhaps. I'll explain what I mean. Somebody told me a story once, when I was eleven. I saw no point in that story whatsoever. It didn't worry me – it just passed straight over my head. I don't believe I ever, as they say, thought of it again. But about two years ago, sitting in the stalls at a revue, that story came back to me, and I was so surprised that I actually said aloud, "Oh, *now* I see the point of that silly story about the rice pudding." And yet there had been no direct allusion on the same lines – only some fun sailing rather near the wind.'

Poirot said: 'I understand what you mean, mademoiselle.'

'Then you will understand what I am going to tell you. I was once staying at a hotel. As I walked along a passage, one of the bedroom doors opened and a woman I knew came out. It was not her bedroom – and she registered the fact plainly on her face when she saw me.

'*And I knew then the meaning of the expression I had once seen on Caroline's face when at Alderbury she came out of Philip Blake's room one night.*'

She leant forward, stopping Poirot's words.

'I had no idea at the *time*, you understand. I *knew* things – girls of the age I was usually do – but I didn't connect them with reality. Caroline coming out of Philip Blake's bedroom was just Caroline coming out of Philip Blake's bedroom to me. It might have been Miss Williams' room or my room. But what I *did* notice was the expression on her face – a queer expression that I didn't know and couldn't understand. I didn't understand it until, as I have told you, the night in Paris when I saw that same expression on another woman's face.'

Poirot said slowly:

'But what you tell me, Miss Warren, is sufficiently astonishing. From Philip Blake himself I got the impression that he disliked your sister and always had done so.'

Angela said:

'I know. I can't explain it but there it is.'

Poirot nodded slowly. Already, in his interview with Philip Blake, he had felt vaguely that something did not ring true. That overdone animosity against Caroline – it had not, somehow, been natural.

And the words and phrases from his conversation with Meredith Blake came back to him. 'Very upset when Amyas married – did not go near them for over a year . . .'

Had Philip, then, always been in love with Caroline? And had his love, when she chose Amyas, turned to bitterness and hate?

Yes, Philip had been too vehement – too biased. Poirot visualized him thoughtfully – the cheerful prosperous man with his golf and his comfortable house. What had Philip Blake really felt sixteen years ago.

Angela Warren was speaking.

'I don't understand it. You see, I've no experience in love affairs – they haven't come my way. I've told you this for what it's worth in case – in case it might have a bearing on what happened.'

BOOK II

NARRATIVE OF PHILIP BLAKE

(Covering letter received with manuscript)

Dear M. Poirot,
   I am fulfilling my promise and herewith find enclosed an account
of the events relating to the death of Amyas Crale. After such a
lapse of time I am bound to point out that my memories may not be
strictly accurate, but I have put down what occurred to the best of my
recollection.
   Yours truly,
   Philip Blake

Notes on Progress of Events Leading
up to Murder of Amyas Crale on Sept., 19 . . .

My friendship with deceased dates back to a very early period. His home
and mine were next door to each other in the country, and our families
were friends. Amyas Crale was a little over two years older than I was.
We played together as boys, in the holidays, though we were not at the
same school.

From the point of view of my long knowledge of the man I feel myself
particularly qualified to testify as to his character and general outlook on
life. And I will say this straight away – to any one who knew Amyas Crale
well – the notion of his committing suicide is quite ridiculous. Crale would
never have taken his own life. He was far too fond of living! The contention
of the defence at the trial that Crale was obsessed by conscience, and took
poison in a fit of remorse, is utterly absurd to any one who knew the man.
Crale, I should say, had very little conscience, and certainly not a morbid
one. Moreover, he and his wife were on bad terms, and I don't think he
would have had any scruples about breaking up what was, to him, a very
unsatisfactory married life. He was prepared to look after her financial
welfare and that of the child of the marriage, and I am sure would have

done so generously. He was a very generous man – and altogether a warm-hearted and lovable person. Not only was he a great painter, but he was a man whose friends were devoted to him. As far as I know he had no enemies.

I had also known Caroline Crale for many years. I knew her before her marriage, when she used to come and stay at Alderbury. She was then a somewhat neurotic girl, subject to uncontrollable outbursts of temper, not without attraction, but unquestionably a difficult person to live with.

She showed her devotion to Amyas almost immediately. He, I do not think, was really very much in love with her. But they were frequently thrown together – she was, as I say, attractive, and they eventually became engaged. Amyas Crale's best friends were rather apprehensive about the marriage, as they felt that Caroline was quite unsuited to him.

This caused a certain amount of strain in the first few years between Crale's wife and Crale's friends, but Amyas was a loyal friend and was not disposed to give up his old friends at the bidding of his wife. After a few years, he and I were on the same old terms and I was a frequent visitor at Alderbury. I may add that I stood godfather to the little girl, Carla. This proves, I think, that Amyas considered me his best friend, and it gives me authority to speak for a man who can no longer speak for himself.

To come to the actual events of which I have been asked to write, I arrived down at Alderbury (so I see by an old diary) five days before the crime. That is, on Sept. 13th. I was conscious at once of a certain tension in the atmosphere. There was also staying in the house Miss Elsa Greer whom Amyas was painting at the time.

It was the first time I had seen Miss Greer in the flesh, but I had been aware of her existence for some time. Amyas had raved about her to me a month previously. He had met, he said, a marvellous girl. He talked about her so enthusiastically that I said to him jokingly: 'Be careful, old boy, or you'll be losing your head again.' He told me not to be a bloody fool. He was painting the girl; he'd no personal interest in her. I said: 'Tell that to the marines! I've heard you say that before.' He said: 'This time it's different'; to which I answered somewhat cynically: 'It always is!' Amyas then looked quite worried and anxious. He said: 'You don't understand. She's just a girl. Not much more than a child.' He added that she had very modern views and was absolutely free from old-fashioned prejudices. He said: 'She's honest and natural and absolutely fearless!'

I thought to myself, though I didn't say so, that Amyas had certainly got it badly this time. A few weeks later I heard comments from other people. It was said that the 'Greer girl was absolutely infatuated.' Somebody else said that it was a bit thick of Amyas considering how young the girl was, whereupon somebody else sniggered and said that Elsa Greer knew her way about all right. Further remarks were that the girl was rolling in money and had always got everything she wanted, and also that 'she was the one who was making most of the running.' There was a question as to what Crale's wife thought about it – and the significant reply that she must be used to that sort of thing by now, to which someone demurred by saying they'd heard that she was jealous as hell and led Crale such an impossible life that any man would be justified in having a fling from time to time.

I mention all this because I think it is important that the state of affairs before I got down there should be fully realized.

I was interested to see the girl – she was remarkably good-looking and very attractive – and I was, I must admit, maliciously amused to note that Caroline was cutting up very rough indeed.

Amyas Crale himself was less light-hearted than usual. Though to any one who did not know him well, his manner would have appeared much as usual, I who knew him so intimately noted at once various signs of strain, uncertain temper, fits of moody abstraction, general irritability of manner.

Although he was always inclined to be moody when painting, the picture he was at work upon did not account entirely for the strain he showed. He was pleased to see me and said as soon as we were alone: 'Thank goodness you've turned up, Phil. Living in a house with four women is enough to send any man clean off his chump. Between them all they'll send me into a lunatic asylum.'

It was certainly an uncomfortable atmosphere. Caroline, as I said, was obviously cutting up rough about the whole thing. In a polite, well-bred way, she was ruder to Elsa than one would believe possible – without a single actually offensive word. Elsa herself was openly and flagrantly rude to Caroline. She was top dog and she knew it – and no scruples of good breeding restrained her from overt bad manners. The result was that Crale spent most of his time scrapping with the girl Angela when he wasn't painting. They were usually on affectionate terms, though they teased and fought a good deal. But on this occasion there was an edge in everything Amyas said or did, and the two of them really lost their tempers with each other. The fourth member of the party was the governess. 'A sour-faced hag,' Amyas called her. 'She hates me like poison. Sits there with her lips set together, disapproving of me without stopping.'

It was then that he said:

'God damn all women! If a man is to have any peace he must steer clear of women!'

'You oughtn't to have married,' I said. 'You're the sort of man who ought to have kept clear of domestic ties.'

He replied that it was too late to talk about that now. He added that no doubt Caroline would be only too glad to get rid of him. That was the first indication I had that something unusual was in the wind.

I said: 'What's all this? Is this business with the lovely Elsa serious then?' He said with a sort of groan:

'She *is* lovely, isn't she? Sometimes I wish I'd never seen her.'

I said: 'Look here, old boy, you must take a hold on yourself. You don't want to get tied up with any more women.' He looked at me and laughed. He said: 'It's all very well for you to talk. I can't let women alone – simply can't do it – and if I could, they wouldn't let me alone!' Then he shrugged those great shoulders of his, grinned at me and said: 'Oh well, it will all pan out in the end, I expect. And you must admit the picture is good?'

He was referring to the portrait he was doing of Elsa, and although I had very little technical knowledge of painting, even I could see that it was going to be a work of especial power.

Whilst he was painting, Amyas was a different man. Although he would growl, groan, frown, swear extravagantly, and sometimes hurl his brushes away, he was really intensely happy.

It was only when he came back to the house for meals that the hostile atmosphere between the women got him down. That hostility came to a head on Sept. 17th. We had had an embarrassing lunch. Elsa had been particularly – really, I think *insolent* is the only word for it! She had ignored Caroline pointedly, persistently addressing the conversation to Amyas as though he and she were alone in the room. Caroline had talked lightly and gaily to the rest of us, cleverly contriving so that several perfectly innocent-sounding remarks should have a sting. She hadn't got Elsa Greer's scornful honesty – with Caroline every thing was oblique, suggested rather than said.

Things came to a head after lunch in the drawing-room just as we were finishing coffee. I had commented on a carved head in highly polished beechwood – a very curious thing, and Caroline said: 'That is the work of a young Norwegian sculptor. Amyas and I admire his work very much. We hope to go and see him next summer.' That calm assumption of possession was too much for Elsa. She was never one to let a challenge pass. She waited a minute or two and then she spoke in her clear, rather over-emphasized voice. She said: 'This would be a lovely room if it was properly fixed. It's got far too much furniture in it. When I'm living here I shall take all the rubbish out and just leave one or two good pieces. And I shall have copper-coloured curtains, I think – so that the setting sun will just catch them through that big western window.' She turned to me and said: 'Don't you think that would be rather lovely?'

I didn't have time to answer. Caroline spoke, and her voice was soft and silky and what I can only describe as dangerous. She said:

'Are you thinking of buying this place, Elsa?'

Elsa said: 'It won't be necessary for me to buy it.'

Caroline said: 'What do you mean?' And there was no softness in her voice now. It was hard and metallic. Elsa laughed. She said: 'Must we pretend? Come now, Caroline, you know very well what I mean!'

Caroline said: 'I've no idea.'

Elsa said to that: 'Don't be such an ostrich. It's no good pretending you don't see and know all about it. Amyas and I care for each other. This isn't your home. It's his. And after we're married I shall live here with him!'

Caroline said: 'I think you're crazy.'

Elsa said: 'Oh no, I'm not, my dear, and you know it. It would be much simpler if we were honest with each other. Amyas and I love each other – you've seen that clearly enough. There's only one decent thing for you to do. You've got to give him his freedom.'

Caroline said: 'I don't believe a word of what you are saying.'

But her voice was unconvincing. Elsa had got under her guard all right.

And at that minute Amyas Crale came into the room and Elsa said with a laugh:

'If you don't believe me, ask him.'

And Caroline said: 'I will.'

She didn't pause at all. She said:

'Amyas, Elsa says you want to marry her. Is this true?'

Poor Amyas. I felt sorry for him. It makes a man feel a fool to have a scene of that kind forced upon him. He went crimson and started blustering. He turned on Elsa and asked her why the devil she couldn't have held her tongue?

Caroline said: 'Then it *is* true?'

He didn't say anything, just stood there passing his finger round inside the neck of his shirt. He used to do that as a kid when he got into a jam of any kind. He said – and he tried to make the words sound dignified and authoritative – and of course couldn't manage it, poor devil:

'I don't want to discuss it.'

Caroline said: 'But we're going to discuss it!'

Elsa chipped in and said:

'I think it's only fair to Caroline that she should be told.'

Caroline said, very quietly:

'Is it true, Amyas?'

He looked a bit ashamed of himself. Men do when women pin them down in a corner.

She said:

'Answer me, please. I've got to know.'

He flung up his head then – rather the way a bull does in the bull-ring. He snapped out:

'It's true enough – but I don't want to discuss it now.'

And he turned and strode out of the room. I went after him. I didn't want to be left with the women. I caught up with him on the terrace. He was swearing. I never knew a man swear more heartily. Then he raved:

'Why couldn't she hold her tongue? Why the devil couldn't she hold her tongue? Now the fat's in the fire. And I've got to finish that picture – do you hear, Phil? It's the best thing I've done. The best thing I've ever done in my *life*. And a couple of damn' fool women want to muck it up between them!'

Then he calmed down a little and said women had no sense of proportion.

I couldn't help smiling a little. I said:

'Well, dash it all, old boy, you have brought this on yourself.'

'Don't I know it,' he said, and groaned. Then he added: 'But you must admit, Phil, that a man couldn't be blamed for losing his head about her. Even Caroline ought to understand that.'

I asked him what would happen if Caroline got her back up and refused to give him a divorce.

But by now he had gone off into a fit of abstraction. I repeated the remark and he said absently:

'Caroline would never be vindictive. You don't understand, old boy.'

'There's the child,' I pointed out.

He took me by the arm.

'Phil, old boy, you mean well – but don't go on croaking like a raven. I can manage my affairs. Everything will turn out all right. You'll see if it doesn't.'

That was Amyas all over – an absolutely unjustified optimist. He said now, cheerfully:

'To hell with the whole pack of them!'

I don't know whether we would have said anything more, but a few minutes later Caroline swept out on the terrace. She'd got a hat on, a queer, flopping, dark-brown hat, rather attractive.

She said in an absolutely ordinary, every-day voice:

'Take off that paint-stained coat, Amyas. We're going over to Meredith's to tea – don't you remember?'

He stared, stammered a bit as he said:

'Oh, I'd forgotten. Yes, of c-c-course we are.'

She said:

'Then go and try and make yourself look less like a rag-and-bone man.'

Although her voice was quite natural, she didn't look at him. She moved over towards a bed of dahlias and began picking off some of the overblown flowers.

Amyas turned round slowly and went into the house.

Caroline talked to me. She talked a good deal. About the chances of the weather lasting. And whether there might be mackerel about, and if so Amyas and Angela and I might like to go fishing. She was really amazing. I've got to hand it to her.

But I think, myself, that that showed the sort of woman she was. She had enormous strength of will and complete command over herself. I don't know whether she'd made up her mind to kill him then – but I shouldn't be surprised. And she was capable of making her plans carefully and unemotionally, with an absolutely clear and ruthless mind.

Caroline Crale was a very dangerous woman. I ought to have realized then that she wasn't prepared to take this thing lying down. But like a fool I thought that she had made up her mind to accept the inevitable – or else possibly she thought that if she carried on exactly as usual Amyas might change his mind.

Presently the others came out. Elsa looking defiant – but at the same time triumphant. Caroline took no notice of her. Angela really saved the situation. She came out arguing with Miss Williams that she wasn't going to change her skirt for any one. It was quite all right – good enough for darling old Meredith anyway – *he* never noticed anything.

We got off at last. Caroline walked with Angela. And I walked with Amyas. And Elsa walked by herself – smiling.

I didn't admire her myself – too violent a type – but I have to admit that she looked incredibly beautiful that afternoon. Women do when they've got what they want.

I can't remember the events of that afternoon clearly at all. It's all blurred. I remember old Merry coming out to meet us. I think we walked round the garden first. I remember having a long discussion with Angela about the training of terriers for ratting. She ate an incredible lot of apples, and tried to persuade me to do so too.

When we got back to the house, tea was going on under the big cedar tree. Merry, I remember, was looking very upset. I suppose either Caroline or Amyas had told him something. He was looking doubtfully at Caroline, and then he stared at Elsa. The old boy looked thoroughly worried. Of course Caroline liked to have Meredith on a string more or less, the devoted, platonic friend who would never, never go too far. She was that kind of woman.

After tea Meredith had a hurried word with me. He said:

'Look here, Phil, Amyas *can't* do this thing!'

I said:

'Make no mistake, he's going to do it.'

'He can't leave his wife and child and go off with this girl. He's years older than she is. She can't be more than eighteen.'

I said to him that Miss Greer was a fully sophisticated twenty.

He said: 'Anyway, that's under age. She can't know what she's doing.'

Poor old Meredith. Always the chivalrous pukka sahib. I said:

'Don't worry, old boy. *She* knows what she's doing, *and* she likes it!'

That's all we had the chance of saying. I thought to myself that probably Merry felt disturbed at the thought of Caroline being a deserted wife. Once the divorce was through she might expect her faithful Dobbin to marry her. I had an idea that hopeless devotion was really far more in his line. I must confess that that side of it amused me.

Curiously enough I remember very little about our visit to Meredith's stink room. He enjoyed showing people his hobby. Personally I always found it very boring. I suppose I was in there with the rest of them when he gave a dissertation on the efficacy of coniine, but I don't remember it. And I didn't see Caroline pinch the stuff. As I've said, she was a very adroit woman. I do remember Meredith reading aloud the passage from Plato describing Socrates' death. Very boring I thought it. Classics always did bore me.

There's nothing much more I can remember about that day. Amyas and Angela had a first-class row, I know, and the rest of us rather welcomed it. It avoided other difficulties. Angela rushed off to bed with a final vituperative outburst. She said A, she'd pay him out. B, she wished he were dead. C, she hoped he'd die of leprosy, it would serve him right. D, she wished a sausage would stick to his nose, like in the fairy story, and never come off. When she'd gone we all laughed, we couldn't help it, it was such a funny mixture.

Caroline went up to bed immediately afterwards. Miss Williams disappeared after her pupil. Amyas and Elsa went off together into the garden. It was clear that I wasn't wanted. I went for a stroll by myself. It was a lovely night.

I came down late the following morning. There was no one in the dining-room. Funny the things you do remember. I remember the taste of the kidneys and bacon I ate quite well. They were very good kidneys. Devilled.

Afterwards I wandered out looking for everybody. I went outside, didn't see anybody, smoked a cigarette, encountered Miss Williams running about looking for Angela, who had played truant as usual when she ought to have been mending a torn frock. I went back into the hall and realized that Amyas and Caroline were having a set-to in the library. They were talking very loud. I heard her say:

'You and your women! I'd like to kill you. Some day I will kill you.' Amyas said: 'Don't be a fool, Caroline.' And she said: 'I mean it, Amyas.'

Well, I didn't want to overhear any more. I went out again. I wandered along the terrace the other way and came across Elsa.

She was sitting on one of the long seats. The seat was directly under the library window, and the window was open. I should imagine that there wasn't much she had missed of what was going on inside. When she saw me she got up as cool as a cucumber and came towards me. She was smiling. She took my arm and said:

'Isn't it a lovely morning?'

It was a lovely morning for her all right! Rather a cruel girl. No, I think merely honest and lacking in imagination. What she wanted herself was the only thing that she could see.

We'd been standing on the terrace talking for about five minutes, when I heard the library door bang and Amyas Crale came out. He was very red in the face.

He caught hold of Elsa unceremoniously by the shoulder.

He said: 'Come on, time for you to sit. I want to get on with that picture.'

She said: 'All right. I'll just go up and get a pullover. There's a chilly wind.'

She went into the house.

I wondered if Amyas would say anything to me, but he didn't say much. Just: 'These women!'

I said: 'Cheer up, old boy.'

Then we neither of us said anything till Elsa came out of the house again.

They went off together down to the Battery garden. I went into the house. Caroline was standing in the hall. I don't think she even noticed me. It was a way of hers at times. She'd seem to go right away – to get inside herself as it were. She just murmured something. Not to me – to herself. I just caught the words:

'It's too cruel . . .'

That's what she said. Then she walked past me and upstairs, still without seeming to see me – just like a person intent on some inner vision. I think myself (I've no authority for saying this, you understand) that she went up to get the stuff, and that it was then she decided to do what she did do.

And just at that moment the telephone rang. In some houses one would wait for the servants to answer it, but I was so often at Alderbury that I acted more or less as one of the family. I picked up the receiver.

It was my brother Meredith's voice that answered. He was very upset. He explained that he had been into his laboratory and that the coniine bottle was half-empty.

I don't need to go again over all the things I know now I ought to have done. The thing was so startling and I was foolish enough to be taken aback. Meredith was dithering a good bit at the other end. I heard someone on the stairs, and I just told him sharply to come over at once.

I myself went down to meet him. In case you don't know the lay of the land, the shortest way from one estate to the other was by rowing across a small creek. I went down the path to where the boats were kept by a small jetty. To do so I passed under the wall of the Battery garden. I could hear Elsa and Amyas talking as he painted. They sounded very cheerful and carefree. Amyas said it was an amazingly hot day (so it was, very hot for September), and Elsa said that sitting where she was, poised on the battlements, there was a cold wind blowing in from the sea. And then she said: 'I'm horribly stiff from posing. Can't I have a rest, darling?' And I heard Amyas cry out: 'Not on your life. Stick it. You're a tough girl. And this is going good, I tell you.' I heard Elsa say, 'Brute' and laugh, as I went out of earshot.

Meredith was just rowing himself across from the other side. I waited for him. He tied up the boat and came up the steps. He was looking very white and worried. He said to me:

'Your head's better than mine, Philip. What ought I to do? That stuff's dangerous.'

I said: 'Are you absolutely sure about this?' Meredith, you see, was always a rather vague kind of chap. Perhaps that's why I didn't take it as seriously as I ought to have done. And he said he was quite sure. The bottle had been full yesterday afternoon.

I said: 'And you've absolutely *no* idea who pinched it?'

He said none whatever and asked me what *I* thought. Could it have been one of the servants? I said I supposed it might have been, but it seemed unlikely to me. He always kept the door locked, didn't he? Always, he said, and then began a rigmarole about having found the window a few inches open at the bottom. Someone might have got in that way.

'A chance burglar?' I asked sceptically. 'It seems to me, Meredith, that there are some very nasty possibilities.'

He said what did I really think? And I said, if he was sure he wasn't making a mistake, that probably Caroline had taken it to poison Elsa with – or that alternatively Elsa had taken it to get Caroline out of the way and straighten the path of true love.

Meredith twittered a bit. He said it was absurd and melodramatic and couldn't be true. I said: 'Well, the stuff's gone. What's *your* explanation?' He hadn't any, of course. Actually thought just as I did, but didn't want to face the fact.

He said again: 'What are we to do?'

I said, damned fool that I was: 'We must think it over carefully. Either you'd better announce your loss, straight out when everybody's there, or else you'd better get Caroline alone and tax her with it. If you're convinced *she's* nothing to do with it, adopt the same tactics for Elsa.' He said: 'A girl like that! She couldn't have taken it.' I said I wouldn't put it past her.

We were walking up to the house as we talked. After that last remark of mine neither of us spoke for some few seconds. We were rounding the Battery garden again and I heard Caroline's voice.

I thought perhaps a three-handed row was going on, but actually it was Angela that they were discussing. Caroline was protesting. She said: 'It's very hard on the girl.' And Amyas made some impatient rejoinder. Then the door to the garden opened just as we came abreast of it. Amyas looked a little taken aback at seeing us. Caroline was just coming out. She said: 'Hallo, Meredith. We've been discussing the question of Angela's going to school. I'm not at all sure it's the right thing for her.' Amyas said: 'Don't fuss about the girl. She'll be all right. Good riddance.'

Just then Elsa came running down the path from the house. She had some sort of scarlet jumper in her hand. Amyas growled:

'Come along. Get back into the pose. I don't want to waste time.'

He went back to where his easel was standing. I noticed that he staggered a bit and I wondered if he had been drinking. A man might easily be excused for doing so with all the fuss and the scenes.

He grumbled.

'The beer here is red hot. Why can't we keep some ice down here?'

And Caroline Crale said:

'I'll send you down some beer just off the ice.'

Amyas grunted out:

'Thanks.'

Then Caroline shut the door of the Battery garden and came up with us to the house. We sat down on the terrace and she went into the house. About five minutes later Angela came along with a couple of bottles of beer and some glasses. It was a hot day and we were glad to see it. As we were drinking it Caroline passed us. She was carrying another bottle and said she would take it down to Amyas. Meredith said he'd go, but she was quite firm that she'd go herself. I thought – fool that I was – that it was just her jealousy. She couldn't stand those two being alone down there. That was what had taken her down there once already with the weak pretext of arguing about Angela's departure.

She went off down that zigzag path – and Meredith and I watched her go. We'd still not decided anything, and now Angela clamoured that I should come bathing with her. It seemed impossible to get Meredith alone. I just said to him: 'After lunch.' And he nodded.

Then I went off bathing with Angela. We had a good swim – across the creek and back, and then we lay out on the rocks sunbathing. Angela was a bit taciturn and that suited me. I made up my mind that directly after lunch I'd take Caroline aside and accuse her point-blank of having stolen the stuff. No use letting Meredith do it – he'd be too weak. No, I'd tax her with it outright. After that she'd have to give it back, or even if she didn't she wouldn't dare use it. I was pretty sure it must be her on thinking things over. Elsa was far too sensible and hard-boiled a young woman to risk tampering with poisons. She had a hard head and would take care of her own skin. Caroline was made of more dangerous stuff – unbalanced, carried away by impulses and definitely neurotic. And still, you know, at the back of my mind was the feeling that Meredith *might* have made a mistake. Or some servant might have been poking about in there and spilt the stuff and then not dared to own up. You see, poison seems such a melodramatic thing – you can't believe in it.

Not till it happens.

It was quite late when I looked at my watch, and Angela and I fairly raced up to lunch. They were just sitting down – all but Amyas, who had remained down in the Battery painting. Quite a normal thing for him to do – and privately I thought him very wise to elect to do it today. Lunch was likely to have been an awkward meal.

We had coffee on the terrace. I wish I could remember better how Caroline looked and acted. She didn't seem excited in any way. Quiet and rather sad is my impression. What a devil that woman was!

For it is a devilish thing to do, to poison a man in cold blood. If there had been a revolver about and she caught it up and shot him – well, that might have been understandable. But this cold, deliberate, vindictive poisoning . . . And so calm and collected.

She got up and said she'd take his coffee to him in the most natural way possible. And yet she knew – she must have known – that by now she'd find him dead. Miss Williams went with her. I don't remember if that was at Caroline's suggestion or not. I rather think it was.

The two women went off together. Meredith strolled away shortly afterwards. I was just making an excuse to go after him, when he came running up the path again. His face was grey. He gasped out:

'We must get a doctor – quick – Amyas –'

I sprang up.

'Is he ill – dying?'

Meredith said:

'I'm afraid he's dead . . .'

We'd forgotten Elsa for the minute. But she let out a sudden cry. It was like the wail of a banshee.

She cried:

'Dead? Dead? . . .' And then she ran. I didn't know any one could move like that – like a deer – like a stricken thing. And like an avenging Fury, too.

Meredith panted out:

'Go after her. I'll telephone. Go after her. You don't know what she'll do.'

I did go after her – and it's as well I did. She might quite easily have killed Caroline. I've never seen such grief and such frenzied hate. All the veneer of refinement and education was stripped off. You could see her father and her father's mother and father had been millhands. Deprived of her lover, she was just elemental woman. She'd have clawed Caroline's face, torn her hair, hurled her over the parapet if she could. She thought for some reason or other that Caroline had knifed him. She'd got it all wrong – naturally.

I held her off, and then Miss Williams took charge. She was good, I must say. She got Elsa to control herself in under a minute – told her she'd got to be quiet and that we couldn't have this noise and violence going on. She was a tartar, that woman. But she did the trick. Elsa was quiet – just stood there gasping and trembling.

As for Caroline, so far as I am concerned, the mask was right off. She stood there perfectly quiet – you might have said dazed. But she wasn't dazed. It was her eyes gave her away. They were watchful – fully aware and quietly watchful. She'd begun, I suppose, to be afraid . . .

I went up to her and spoke to her. I said it quite low. I don't think either of the two women overheard.

I said:

'You damned murderess, you've killed my best friend.'

She shrank back. She said:

'No – oh no – he – he did it himself . . .'

I looked her full in the eyes. I said:

'You can tell that story – to the police.'

She did – and they didn't believe her.

End of Philip Blake's Statement.

....

NARRATIVE OF MEREDITH BLAKE

Dear M. Poirot,

As I promised you, I have set down in writing an account of all I can remember relating to the tragic events that happened sixteen years ago. First of all I would like to say that I have thought over carefully all you said to me at our recent meeting. And on reflection I am more convinced than I was before that it is in the highest degree unlikely that Caroline Crale poisoned her husband. It always seemed incongruous, but the absence of any other explanation and her own attitude led me to follow, sheep-like, the opinion of other people and to say with them – that if she didn't do it, what explanation could there be?

Since seeing you I have reflected very carefully on the alternative solution presented at the time and brought forward by the defence at the trial. That is, that Amyas Crale took his own life. Although from what I knew of him that solution seemed quite fantastic at the time, I now see fit to modify my opinion. To begin with, and highly significant, is the fact that Caroline believed it. If we are now to take it that that charming and gentle lady was unjustly convicted, then her own frequently reiterated belief must carry great weight. She knew Amyas better than anyone else. If *she* thought suicide possible, then suicide *must* have been possible in spite of the scepticism of his friends.

I will advance the theory, therefore, that there was in Amyas Crale some core of conscience, some undercurrent of remorse and even despair at the excesses to which his temperament led him, of which only his wife was aware. This, I think, is a not impossible supposition. He may have shown that side of himself only to her. Though it is inconsistent with anything I ever heard him say, yet it is nevertheless a truth that in most men there is some unsuspected and inconsistent streak which often comes as a surprise to people who have known them intimately. A respected and austere man is discovered to have had a coarser side to his life hidden. A vulgar money-maker has, perhaps, a secret appreciation of some delicate work of art. Hard and ruthless people have been convicted of unsuspected hidden kindnesses. Generous and jovial men have been shown to have a mean and cruel side to them.

So it may be that in Amyas Crale there ran a strain of morbid self-accusation, and that the more he blustered out his egoism and his right to do as he pleased, the more strongly that secret conscience of his worked. It is improbable, on the face of it, but I now believe that it must have been so. And I repeat again, Caroline herself held steadfastly to that view. That, I repeat, is significant!

And now to examine *facts*, or rather my memory of facts, in the light of that new belief.

I think that I might with relevance include here a conversation I held with Caroline some weeks before the actual tragedy. It was during Elsa Greer's first visit to Alderbury.

Caroline, as I have told you, was aware of my deep affection and friendship for her. I was, therefore, the person in whom she could most easily confide. She had not been looking very happy. Nevertheless I was surprised when she suddenly asked me one day whether I thought Amyas really cared very much for this girl he had brought down.

I said: 'He's interested in painting her. You know what Amyas is.'

She shook her head and said:

'No, he's in love with her.'

'Well – perhaps a little.'

'A great deal, I think.'

I said: 'She is unusually attractive, I admit. And we both know that Amyas is susceptible. But you must know by now, my dear, that Amyas really only cares for one person – and that is you. He has these infatuations – but they don't last. You are the one person to him, and though he behaves badly, it does not really affect his feeling for you.'

Caroline said: 'That is what I always used to think.'

'Believe me, Caro,' I said. 'It is so.'

She said: 'But this time, Merry, I'm afraid. That girl is so – so terribly sincere. She's so young – and so intense. I've a feeling that this time – it's serious.'

I said: 'But the very fact that she is so young and, as you say, so sincere, will protect her. On the whole, women are fair game to Amyas, but in the case of a girl like this it will be different.'

She said: 'Yes, that's what I'm afraid of – it will be different.'

And she went on. 'I'm thirty-four, you know, Merry. And we've been married ten years. In looks I can't hold a candle to this Elsa child, and I know it.'

I said: 'But you know, Caroline, you *know* – that Amyas is really devoted to you?'

She said to that: 'Does one ever know with men?' And then she laughed a little ruefully and said: 'I'm a very primitive woman, Merry. I'd like to take a hatchet to that girl.'

I told her that the child probably didn't understand in the least what she was doing. She had a great admiration and hero-worship for Amyas, and she probably didn't realize at all that Amyas was falling in love with her.

Caroline just said to me:

'Dear Merry!' and began to talk about the garden. I hoped that she was not going to worry any more about the matter.

Shortly afterwards, Elsa went back to London. Amyas was away too for several weeks. I had really forgotten all about the business. And then I heard that Elsa was back again at Alderbury in order that Amyas might finish the picture.

I was a little disturbed by the news. But Caroline, when I saw her, was not in a communicative mood. She seemed quite her usual self – not worried or upset in any way. I imagined that everything was all right.

That's why it was such a shock to me to learn how far the thing had gone.

I have told you of my conversations with Crale and with Elsa. I had no opportunity of talking to Caroline. We were only able to exchange those few words about which I have already told you.

I can see her face now, the wide dark eyes and the restrained emotion. I can still hear her voice as she said:

'*Everything's finished . . .*'

I can't describe to you the infinite desolation she conveyed in those words. They were a literal statement of truth. With Amyas's defection, everything was finished for her. That, I am convinced, was why she took the coniine. It was a way out. A way suggested to her by my stupid dissertation on the drug. And the passage I read from the Phædo gives a gracious picture of death.

Here is my present belief. She took the coniine, resolved to end her own life when Amyas left her. He may have seen her take it – or he may have discovered that she had it later.

That discovery acted upon him with terrific force. He was horrified at what his actions had led her to contemplate. But notwithstanding his horror and remorse, he still felt himself incapable of giving up Elsa. I can understand that. Any one who had fallen in love with her would find it almost impossible to tear himself away.

He could not envisage life without Elsa. He realized that Caroline could not live without *him*. He decided there was only one way out – to use the coniine himself.

And the manner in which he did it might be characteristic of the man, I think. His painting was the dearest thing in life to him. He chose to die literally with his brush in his hand. And the last thing his eyes would see was the face of the girl he loved so desperately. He might have thought, too, that his death would be the best thing for her . . .

I admit that this theory leaves certain curious facts unexplained. Why, for instance, were only Caroline's fingerprints found on the empty coniine bottle. I suggest that after Amyas had handled it, all prints got smudged or rubbed off by the soft piles of stuffs that were lying over the bottle and that, after his death, Caroline handled it to see if any one had touched it. Surely that is possible and plausible? As to the evidence about the fingerprints on the beer bottle, the witnesses for the defence were of opinion that a man's hand *might* be distorted after taking poison and so could manage to grasp a beer bottle in a wholly unnatural way.

One other thing remains to be explained. Caroline's own attitude throughout the trial. But I think I have now seen the cause for that. It was *she who actually took the poison from my laboratory*. It was *her* determination to do away with herself that impelled her husband to take his own life instead. Surely it is not unreasonable to suppose that in a morbid excess of responsibility she considered herself responsible for his death – that she persuaded herself that she *was* guilty of murder – though not the kind of murder of which she was being accused?

I think all that could be so. And if that is the case, then surely it will be easy for you to persuade little Carla of the fact? And she can marry her young man and rest contented that the only thing of which her mother was guilty was an impulse (no more) to take her own life.

All this, alas, is not what you asked me for – which was an account of the happenings as I remember them. Let me now repair that omission. I have already told you fully what happened on the day preceding Amyas's death. We now come to the day itself.

I had slept very badly – worried by the disastrous turn of events for my friends. After a long wakeful period whilst I vainly tried to think of something helpful I could do to avert the catastrophe, I fell into a heavy sleep about six a.m. The bringing of my early tea did not awaken me, and I finally woke up heavy-headed and unrefreshed about half-past nine. It was shortly after that that I thought I heard movements in the room below me, which was the room I used as a laboratory.

I may say here that actually the sounds were probably caused by a cat getting in. I found the window-sash raised a little way as it had carelessly been left from the day before. It was just wide enough to admit the passage of a cat. I merely mention the sounds to explain how I came to enter the laboratory.

I went in there as soon as I had dressed, and looking along the shelves I noticed that the bottle containing the preparation of coniine was slightly out of line with the rest. Having had my eye drawn to it in this way, I was startled to see that a considerable quantity of it had gone. The bottle had been nearly full the day before – now it was nearly empty.

I shut and locked the window and went out, locking the door behind me. I was considerably upset and also bewildered. When startled, my mental processes are, I am afraid, somewhat slow.

I was first disturbed, then apprehensive, and finally definitely alarmed. I questioned the household, and they all denied having entered the laboratory at all. I thought things over a little while longer, and then decided to ring up my brother and get his advice.

Philip was quicker than I was. He saw the seriousness of my discovery, and urged me to come over at once and consult with him.

I went out, encountering Miss Williams, who had come across from the other side to look for a truant pupil. I assured her that I had not seen Angela and that she had not been to the house.

I think that Miss Williams noticed there was something amiss. She looked at me rather curiously. I had no intention, however, of telling her what had happened. I suggested she should try the kitchen garden – Angela had a favourite apple tree there – and I myself hurried down to the shore and rowed myself across to the Alderbury side.

My brother was already there waiting for me.

We walked up to the house together by the way you and I went the other day. Having seen the topography you can understand that in passing underneath the wall of the Battery garden we were bound to overhear anything being said inside it.

Beyond the fact that Caroline and Amyas were engaged in a disagreement of some kind, I did not pay much attention to what was said.

Certainly I overheard no threat of any kind uttered by Caroline. The subject of discussion was Angela, and I presume Caroline was pleading for a respite from the fiat of school. Amyas, however, was adamant, shouting out irritably that it was all settled, he'd see to her packing.

The door of the Battery opened just as we drew abreast of it, and Caroline came out. She looked disturbed – but not unduly so. She smiled rather absently at me, and said they had been discussing Angela. Elsa came down the path at that minute, and as Amyas clearly wanted to get on with the sitting without interruption from us, we went on up the path.

Philip blamed himself severely afterwards for the fact that we did not take immediate action. But I myself cannot see it the same way. We had no earthly right to assume that such a thing as murder was being contemplated. (Moreover I now believe that it was *not* contemplated.) It was clear that we should have to adopt *some* course of action, but I still maintain that we were right to talk the matter over carefully first. It was necessary to find the right thing to do – and once or twice I found myself wondering if I had not after all made a mistake. Had the bottle really been full the day before as I thought? I am not one of those people (like my brother Philip) who can be cock-sure of everything. One's memory does play tricks on one. How often, for instance, one is convinced one has put an article in a certain place, later to find that you have put it somewhere quite different. The more I tried to recall the state of the bottle on the preceding afternoon, the more uncertain and doubtful I became. This was very annoying to Philip, who began completely to lose patience with me.

We were not able to continue our discussion at the time, and tacitly agreed to postpone it until after lunch. (I may say that I was always free to drop in for lunch at Alderbury if I chose.)

Later, Angela and Caroline brought us beer. I asked Angela what she had been up to playing truant, and told her Miss Williams was on the warpath, and she said she had been bathing – and added that she didn't see why she should have to mend her horrible old skirt when she was going to have all new things to go to school with.

Since there seemed no chance of further talk with Philip alone, and since I was really anxious to think things out by myself, I wandered off down the path towards the Battery. Just above the Battery, as I showed you, there is a clearing in the trees where there used to be an old bench. I sat there smoking and thinking, and watching Elsa as she sat posing for Amyas.

I shall always think of her as she was that day. Rigid in the pose, with her yellow shirt and dark-blue trousers and a red pullover slung round her shoulders for warmth.

Her face was so alight with life and health and radiance. And that gay voice of hers reciting plans for the future.

This sounds as though I was eavesdropping, but that is not so. I was perfectly visible to Elsa. Both she and Amyas knew I was there. She waved her hand at me and called up that Amyas was a perfect bear that morning – he wouldn't let her rest. She was stiff and aching all over.

Amyas growled out that she wasn't as stiff as he was. He was stiff all over – muscular rheumatism. Elsa said mockingly: 'Poor old man!' And he said she'd be taking on a creaking invalid.

It shocked me, you know, their lighthearted acquiescence in their future together whilst they were causing so much suffering. And yet I couldn't hold it against her. She was so young, so confident, so very much in love. And she didn't really know what she was doing. She didn't understand suffering. She just assumed with the naïve confidence of a child that Caroline would be 'all right', that 'she'd soon get over it.' She saw nothing, you see, but herself and Amyas – happy together. She'd already told me my point of view was old-fashioned. She had no doubts, no qualms – no pity either. But can one expect pity from radiant youth? It is an older, wiser emotion.

They didn't talk very much, of course. No painter wants to be chattering when he is working. Perhaps every ten minutes or so Elsa would make an observation and Amyas would grunt a reply. Once she said:

'I think you're right about Spain. That's the first place we'll go to. And you must take me to see a bullfight. It must be wonderful. Only I'd like the bull to kill the man – not the other way about. I understand how Roman women felt when they saw a man die. Men aren't much, but animals are splendid.'

I suppose she was rather like an animal herself – young and primitive and with nothing yet of man's sad experience and doubtful wisdom. I don't believe Elsa had begun to *think* – she only *felt*. But she was very much alive – more alive than any person I have ever known . . .

That was the last time I saw her radiant and assured – on top of the world. Fey is the word for it, isn't it?

The bell sounded for lunch, and I got up and went down the path and in at the Battery door, and Elsa joined me. It was dazzlingly bright there coming in out of the shady trees. I could hardly see. Amyas was sprawled back on the seat, his arms flung out. He was staring at the picture. I've so often seen him like that. How was I to know that already the poison was working, stiffening him as he sat?

He so hated and resented illness. He would never own to it. I dare say he thought he had got a touch of the sun – the symptoms are much the same – but he'd be the last person to complain about it.

Elsa said:

'He won't come up to lunch.'

Privately I thought he was wise. I said:

'So long, then.'

He moved his eyes from the picture until they rested on me. There was a queer – how shall I describe it – it looked like malevolence. A kind of malevolent glare.

Naturally I didn't understand it then – if his picture wasn't going as he liked he often looked quite murderous. I thought *that* was what it was. He made a sort of grunting sound.

Neither Elsa nor I saw anything unusual in him – just artistic temperament.

So we left him there and she and I went up to the house laughing and talking. If she'd known, poor child, that she'd never see him alive again . . . Oh, well, thank God she didn't. She was able to be happy a little longer.

Caroline was quite normal at lunch – a little preoccupied; nothing more. And doesn't that show that she had nothing to do with it? She *couldn't* have been such an actress.

She and the governess went down afterwards and found him. I met Miss Williams as she came up. She told me to telephone a doctor and went back to Caroline.

That poor child – Elsa, I mean! She had that frantic unrestrained grief that a child has. They can't believe that life can do these things to them. Caroline was quite calm. Yes, she was quite calm. She was able, of course, to control herself better than Elsa. She didn't seem remorseful – then. Just said he must have done it himself. And we couldn't believe that. Elsa burst out and accused her to her face.

Of course she may have realized, already, that she herself would be suspected. Yes, that probably explains her manner.

Philip was quite convinced that she *had* done it.

The governess was a great help and standby. She made Elsa lie down and gave her a sedative, and she kept Angela out of the way when the police came. Yes, she was a tower of strength, that woman.

The whole thing became a nightmare. The police searching the house and asking questions, and then the reporters, swarming about the place like flies and clicking cameras and wanting interviews with members of the family.

A nightmare, the whole thing . . .

It's a nightmare, after all these years. Please God, once you've convinced little Carla what really happened, we can forget it all and never remember it again.

Amyas *must* have committed suicide – however unlikely it seems.

End of Meredith Blake's Narrative.

NARRATIVE OF LADY DITTISHAM

I have set down here the full story of my meeting with Amyas Crale, up to the time of his tragic death.

I saw him first at a studio party. He was standing, I remember, by a window, and I saw him as I came in at the door. I asked who he was. Someone said: 'That's Crale, the painter.' I said at once that I'd like to meet him.

We talked on that occasion for perhaps ten minutes. When any one makes the impression on you that Amyas Crale made on me, it's hopeless to attempt to describe them. If I say that when I saw Amyas Crale, everybody else seemed to grow very small and fade away, that expresses it as well as anything can.

Immediately after that meeting I went to look at as many of his pictures as I could. He had a show on in Bond Street at the moment, and there was one of his pictures in Manchester and one in Leeds and two in public galleries in London. I went to see them all. Then I met him again. I said: 'I've been to see all your pictures. I think they're wonderful.'

He just looked amused. He said:

'Who said you were any judge of painting? I don't believe you know anything about it.'

I said: 'Perhaps not. But they are marvellous, all the same.'

He grinned at me and said: 'Don't be a gushing little fool.'

I said: 'I'm not. I want you to paint me.'

Crale said: 'If you've any sense at all, you'll realize that I don't paint portraits of pretty women.'

I said: 'It needn't be a portrait and I'm not a pretty woman.'

He looked at me then as though he'd begun to see me. He said: 'No, perhaps you're not.'

I said: 'Will you paint me then?'

He studied me for some time with his head on one side. Then he said: 'You're a strange child, aren't you?'

I said: 'I'm quite rich, you know. I can afford to pay well for it.'

He said: 'Why are you so anxious for me to paint you?'

I said: 'Because I want it!'

He said: 'Is that a reason?'

And I said: 'Yes, I always get what I want.'

He said then: 'Oh, my poor child, how young you are!'

I said: 'Will you paint me?'

He took me by the shoulders and turned me towards the light and looked me over. Then he stood away from me a little. I stood quite still, waiting.

He said: 'I've sometimes wanted to paint a flight of impossibly-coloured Australian Maccaws alighting on St Paul's Cathedral. If I painted you against a nice traditional bit of outdoor landscape, I believe I'd get exactly the same result.'

I said: 'Then you will paint me?'

He said: 'You're one of the loveliest, crudest, most flamboyant bits of exotic colouring I've ever seen. I'll paint you!'

I said: 'Then that's settled.'

He went on: 'But I'll warn you, Elsa Greer. If I do paint you, I shall probably make love to you.'

I said: 'I hope you will . . .'

I said it quite steadily and quietly. I heard him catch his breath, and I saw the look that came into his eyes.

You see, it was as sudden as all that.

A day or two later we met again. He told me that he wanted me to come down to Devonshire – he'd got the very place there that he wanted for a background. He said:

'I'm married, you know. And I'm very fond of my wife.'

I said if he was fond of her she must be very nice.

He said she was extremely nice. 'In fact,' he said, 'she's quite adorable – and I adore her. So put that in your pipe, young Elsa, and smoke it.'

I told him that I quite understood.

He began the picture a week later. Caroline Crale welcomed me very pleasantly. She didn't like me much – but, after all, why should she? Amyas was very circumspect. He never said a word to me that his wife couldn't have overheard, and I was quite polite and formal to him. Underneath, though, we both knew.

After ten days he told me I was to go back to London.

I said: 'The picture isn't finished.'

He said: 'It's barely begun. The truth is, I can't paint you, Elsa.'

I said: 'Why?'

He said: 'You know well enough why, Elsa. And that's why you've got to clear out. I can't think about the painting – I can't think about anything but you.'

We were in the Battery garden. It was a hot sunny day. There were birds and humming bees. It ought to have been very happy and peaceful. But it didn't feel like that. It felt – somehow – tragic. As though – as though what was going to happen was already mirrored there.

I knew it would be no good my going back to London, but I said: 'Very well, I'll go if you say so.'

Amyas said: 'Good girl.'

So I went. I didn't write to him.

He held out for ten days and then he came. He was so thin and haggard and miserable that it shocked me.

He said: 'I warned you, Elsa. Don't say I didn't warn you.'

I said: 'I've been waiting for you. I knew you'd come.'

He gave a sort of groan and said: 'There are things that are too strong for any man. I can't eat or sleep or rest for wanting you.'

I said I knew that and that it was the same with me, and had been from the first moment I'd seen him. It was Fate and it was no use struggling against it.

He said: 'You haven't struggled much, have you, Elsa?' And I said I hadn't struggled at all.

He said he wished I wasn't so young, and I said that didn't matter. I suppose I might say that for the next few weeks we were very happy. But happiness isn't quite the word. It was something deeper and more frightening than that.

We were made for each other and we'd found each other – and we both knew we'd got to be together always.

But something else happened, too. The unfinished picture began to haunt Amyas. He said to me: 'Damned funny, I couldn't paint you before – you yourself got in the way of it. But I *want* to paint you, Elsa. I want to paint you so that that picture will be the finest thing I've ever done. I'm itching and aching now to get at my brushes to see you sitting there on that hoary old chestnut of a battlement wall with the conventional blue sea and the decorous English trees – and you – you – sitting there like a discordant shriek of triumph.'

He said: 'And I've got to paint you that way! And I can't be fussed and bothered while I'm doing it. When the picture's finished I'll tell Caroline the truth and we'll get the whole messy business cleared up.'

I said: 'Will Caroline make a fuss about divorcing you?'

He said he didn't think so. But you never knew with women.

I said I was sorry if she was going to be upset, but after all, I said, these things did happen.

He said: 'Very nice and reasonable, Elsa. But Caroline isn't reasonable, never has been reasonable, and certainly isn't going to feel reasonable. She loves me, you know.'

I said I understood that, but if she loved him, she'd put his happiness first, and at any rate she wouldn't want to keep him if he wanted to be free.

He said: 'Life can't really be solved by admirable maxims out of modern literature. Nature's red in tooth and claw, remember.'

I said: 'Surely we are all civilized people nowadays?' and Amyas laughed. He said: 'Civilized people my foot! Caroline would probably like to take a hatchet to you. She might do it too. Don't you realize, Elsa, that she's going to suffer – *suffer*? Don't you know what suffering means?'

I said: 'Then don't tell her.'

He said: 'No. The break's got to come. You've got to belong to me properly, Elsa. Before all the world. Openly mine.'

I said: 'Suppose she won't divorce you?'

He said: 'I'm not afraid of that.'

I said: 'What are you afraid of then?'

And then he said slowly: 'I don't know . . .'

You see, he knew Caroline. I didn't.

If I'd had any idea . . .

We went down again to Alderbury. Things were difficult this time. Caroline had got suspicious. I didn't like it – I didn't like it – I didn't like it a bit. I've always hated deceit and concealment. I thought we ought to tell her. Amyas wouldn't hear of it.

The funny part of it was that he didn't really care at all. In spite of being fond of Caroline and not wanting to hurt her, he just didn't care about the honesty or dishonesty of it all. He was painting with a kind of frenzy, and nothing else mattered. I hadn't seen him in one of his working spells before. I realized now what a really great genius he was. It was natural for him to be so carried away that all the ordinary decencies didn't matter. But it was different for me. I was in a horrible position. Caroline resented me – and quite rightly. The only thing to put the position quite straight was to be honest and tell her the truth.

But all Amyas would say was that he wasn't going to be bothered with scenes and fusses until he'd finished the picture. I said there probably wouldn't be a scene. Caroline would have too much dignity and pride for that.

I said: 'I want to be honest about it all. We've *got* to be honest!'

Amyas said: 'To hell with honesty. I'm painting a picture, damn it.'

I did see his point of view, but he wouldn't see mine.

And in the end I broke down. Caroline had been talking of some plan she and Amyas were going to carry out next autumn. She talked about it quite confidently. And I suddenly felt it was too abominable, what we were doing – letting her go on like this – and perhaps, too, I was angry, because she was really being very unpleasant to me in a clever sort of way that one couldn't take hold of.

And so I came out with the truth. In a way, I still think I was right. Though, of course, I wouldn't have done it if I'd had the faintest idea what was to come of it.

The clash came right away. Amyas was furious with me, but he had to admit that what I had said was true.

I didn't understand Caroline at all. We all went over to Meredith Blake's to tea, and Caroline played up marvellously – talking and laughing. Like a fool, I thought she was taking it well. It was awkward my not being able to leave the house, but Amyas would have gone up in smoke if I had. I thought perhaps Caroline would go. It would have made it much easier for us if she had.

I didn't see her take the coniine. I want to be honest so I think that it's just possible that she may have taken it as she said she did, with the idea of suicide in her mind.

But I don't *really* think so. I think she was one of those intensely jealous and possessive women who won't let go of anything that they think belongs to them. Amyas was her property. I think she was quite prepared to kill him rather than to let him go – completely and finally – to another woman. I think she made up her mind, right away, to kill him. And I think that Meredith's happening to discuss coniine so freely just gave her the means to do what she'd already made up her mind to do. She was a very bitter and revengeful woman – vindictive. Amyas knew all along that she was dangerous. I didn't.

The next morning she had a final showdown with Amyas. I heard most of it from the outside on the terrace. He was splendid – very patient and calm. He implored her to be reasonable. He said he was very fond of her and the child and always would be. He'd do everything he could do to assure their future. Then he hardened up and said: 'But understand this. I'm damned well going to marry Elsa – and nothing shall stop me. You and I always agreed to leave each other free. These things happen.'

Caroline said to him: 'Do as you please. I've warned you.'

Her voice was very quiet, but there was a queer note in it.

Amyas said: 'What do you mean, Caroline?'

She said: 'You're mine and *I don't mean to let you go*. Sooner than let you go to that girl *I'll kill you* . . .'

Just at that minute, Philip Blake came along the terrace. I got up and went to meet him. I didn't want him to overhear.

Presently Amyas came out and said it was time to get on with the picture. We went down together to the Battery. He didn't say much. Just said that Caroline was cutting up rough – but for God's sake not to talk about it. He wanted to concentrate on what he was doing. Another day, he said, would about finish the picture.

He said: 'And it'll be the best thing I've ever done, Elsa, even if it is paid for in blood and tears.'

A little later I went up to the house to get a pullover. There was a chilly wind blowing. When I came back again Caroline was there. I suppose she had come down to make one last appeal. Philip and Meredith Blake were there too.

It was then that Amyas said he was thirsty and wanted a drink. He said there was beer but it wasn't iced.

Caroline said she'd send him down some iced beer. She said it quite naturally in an almost friendly tone. She was an actress, that woman. She must have known then what she meant to do.

She brought it down about ten minutes later. Amyas was painting. She poured it out and set the glass down beside him. Neither of us were watching her. Amyas was intent on what he was doing and I had to keep the pose.

Amyas drank it down the way he always drank beer, just pouring it down his throat in one draught. Then he made a face and said it tasted foul – but at any rate it was cold.

And even then, when he said that, no suspicion entered my head, I just laughed and said: 'Liver.'

When she'd seen him drink it Caroline went away.

It must have been about forty minutes later that Amyas complained of stiffness and pains. He said he thought he must have got a touch of muscular rheumatism. Amyas was always intolerant of any ailment and he didn't like being fussed over. After saying that he turned it off with a light: 'Old age, I suppose. You've taken on a creaking old man, Elsa.' I played up to him. But I noticed that his legs moved stiffly and queerly and that he grimaced once or twice. I never dreamt that it wasn't rheumatism. Presently he drew the bench along and sat sprawled on that, occasionally stretching up to put a touch of paint here and there on the canvas. He used to do that sometimes when he was painting. Just sit staring at me and then the canvas. Sometimes he'd do it for half an hour at a time. So I didn't think it specially queer.

We heard the bell go for lunch, and he said he wasn't coming up. He'd stay where he was and he didn't want anything. That wasn't unusual either, and it would be easier for him than facing Caroline at the table.

He was talking in rather a queer way – grunting out his words. But he sometimes did that when he was dissatisfied with the progress of the picture.

Meredith Blake came in to fetch me. He spoke to Amyas, but Amyas only grunted at him.

We went up to the house together and left him there. We left him there – to die alone. I'd never seen much illness – I didn't know much about it – I thought Amyas was just in a painter's mood. If I'd known – if I'd realized – perhaps a doctor could have saved him . . . Oh God, why didn't I – it's no good thinking of that now. I was a blind fool. A blind, stupid fool.

There isn't much more to tell.

Caroline and the governess went down there after lunch. Meredith followed them. Presently he came running up. He told us Amyas was dead.

Then I knew! Knew, I mean, that it was Caroline. I still didn't think of poison. I thought she'd gone down that minute and either shot him or stabbed him.

I wanted to get at her – to kill her . . .

How *could* she do it? How *could* she? He was so alive, so full of life and vigour. To put all that out – to make him limp and cold. Just so that I shouldn't have him.

Horrible woman . . .

Horrible, scornful, cruel, vindictive woman . . .

I hate her. I still hate her.

They didn't even hang her.

They ought to have hanged her . . .

Even hanging was too good for her . . .

I hate her . . . I hate her . . . I hate her . . .

End of Lady Dittisham's Narrative.

....

NARRATIVE OF CECILIA WILLIAMS

Dear M. Poirot,

I am sending you an account of those events in September, 19 . . . actually witnessed by myself.

I have been absolutely frank and have kept nothing back. You may show it to Carla Crale. It may pain her, but I have always been a believer in truth. Palliatives are harmful. One must have the courage to face reality. Without that courage, life is meaningless. The people who do us most harm are the people who shield us from reality.

Believe me, yours sincerely,

Cecilia Williams

My name is Cecilia Williams. I was engaged by Mrs Crale as governess to her half-sister Angela Warren, in 19 . . . I was then forty-eight.

I took up my duties at Alderbury, a very beautiful estate in south Devon which had belonged to Mr Crale's family for many generations. I knew that Mr Crale was a well-known painter, but I did not meet him until I took up residence at Alderbury.

The household consisted of Mr and Mrs Crale, Angela Warren (then a girl of thirteen), and three servants, all of whom had been with the family many years.

I found my pupil an interesting and promising character. She had very marked abilities and it was a pleasure to teach her. She was somewhat wild and undisciplined, but these faults arose mainly through high spirits, and I have always preferred my girls to show spirit. An excess of vitality can be trained and guided into paths of real usefulness and achievement.

On the whole, I found Angela amenable to discipline. She had been somewhat spoiled – mainly by Mrs Crale, who was far too indulgent where she was concerned. Mr Crale's influence was, I considered, unwise. He indulged her absurdly one day, and was unnecessarily peremptory on another occasion. He was very much a man of moods – possibly owing to what is styled the artistic temperament.

I have never seen, myself, why the possession of artistic ability should be supposed to excuse a man from a decent exercise of self-control. I did not myself admire Mr Crale's paintings. The drawing seemed to me faulty and the colouring exaggerated, but naturally I was not called upon to express any opinion on these matters.

I soon formed a deep attachment to Mrs Crale. I admired her character and her fortitude in the difficulties of her life. Mr Crale was not a faithful husband, and I think that that fact was the source of much pain to her. A stronger-minded woman would have left him, but Mrs Crale never seemed to contemplate such a course. She endured his infidelities and forgave him for them – but I may say that she did not take them meekly. She remonstrated – and with spirit!

It was said at the trial that they led a cat and dog life. I would not go as far as that – Mrs Crale had too much dignity for that term to apply, but they *did* have quarrels. And I consider that that was only natural under the circumstances.

I had been with Mrs Crale just over two years when Miss Elsa Greer appeared upon the scene. She arrived down at Alderbury in the summer of 19 . . . Mrs Crale had not met her previously. She was Mr Crale's friend, and she was said to be there for the purpose of having her portrait painted.

It was apparent at once that Mr Crale was infatuated with this girl and that the girl herself was doing nothing to discourage him. She behaved, in my opinion, quite outrageously, being abominably rude to Mrs Crale, and openly flirting with Mr Crale.

Naturally Mrs Crale said nothing to me, but I could see that she was disturbed and unhappy, and I did everything in my power to distract her mind and lighten her burden. Miss Greer sat every day to Mr Crale, but I noticed that the picture was not getting on very fast. They had, no doubt, other things to talk about!

My pupil, I am thankful to say, noticed very little of what was going on. Angela was in some ways young for her age. Though her intellect was well developed, she was not at all what I may term precocious. She seemed to have no wish to read undesirable books, and showed no signs of morbid curiosity such as girls often do at her age.

She, therefore, saw nothing undesirable in the friendship between Mr Crale and Miss Greer. Nevertheless she disliked Miss Greer and thought her stupid. Here she was quite right. Miss Greer had had, I presume, a proper education, but she never opened a book and was quite unfamiliar with current literary allusions. Moreover she could not sustain a discussion on any intellectual subject.

She was entirely taken up with her personal appearance, her clothes, and men.

Angela, I think, did not even realize that her sister was unhappy. She was not at that time a very perceptive person. She spent a lot of time in hoydenish pastimes, such as tree climbing and wild feats of bicycling. She was also a passionate reader and showed excellent taste in what she liked and disliked.

Mrs Crale was always careful to conceal any signs of unhappiness from Angela, and exerted herself to appear bright and cheerful when the girl was about.

Miss Greer went back to London – at which, I can tell you, we were all very pleased! The servants disliked her as much as I did. She was the kind of person who gives a lot of unnecessary trouble and forgets to say thank you.

Mr Crale went away shortly afterwards, and of course I knew that he had gone after the girl. I was very sorry for Mrs Crale. She felt these things very keenly. I felt extremely bitter towards Mr Crale. When a man has a charming, gracious, intelligent wife, he's no business to treat her badly.

However, she and I both hoped the affair would soon be over. Not that we mentioned the subject to each other – we did not – but she knew quite well how I felt about it.

Unfortunately, after some weeks, the pair of them reappeared. It seemed the sittings were to be resumed.

Mr Crale was now painting with absolute frenzy. He seemed less preoccupied with the girl than with his picture of her. Nevertheless I realized that this was not the usual kind of thing we had gone through before. This girl had got her claws into him and she meant business. He was just like wax in her hands.

The thing came to a head on the day before he died – that is on Sept. 17. Miss Greer's manner had been unbearably insolent the last few days. She was feeling sure of herself and she wanted to assert her importance. Mrs Crale behaved like a true gentlewoman. She was icily polite, but she showed the other clearly what she thought of her.

On this day, Sept. 17, as we were sitting in the drawing-room after lunch, Miss Greer came out with an amazing remark as to how she was going to redecorate the room when she was living at Alderbury.

Naturally Mrs Crale couldn't let that pass. She challenged her, and Miss Greer had the impudence to say, before us all, that she was going to marry Mr Crale. She actually talked about marrying a married man – and she said it to his wife!

I was very, very angry with Mr Crale. How dared he let this girl insult his wife in her own drawing-room? If he wanted to run away with the girl, he should have gone off with her, not brought her into his wife's house and backed her up in her insolence.

In spite of what she must have felt, Mrs Crale did not lose her dignity. Her husband came in just then, and she immediately demanded confirmation from him.

He was, not unnaturally, annoyed with Miss Greer for her unconsidered forcing of the situation. Apart from anything else, it made *him* appear at a disadvantage, and men do not like appearing at a disadvantage. It upsets their vanity.

He stood there, a great giant of a man, looking as sheepish and foolish as a naughty schoolboy. It was his wife who carried off the honours of the situation. He had to mutter foolishly that it was true, but that he hadn't meant her to learn it like this.

I have never seen anything like the look of scorn she gave him. She went out of the room with her head held high. She was a beautiful woman – much more beautiful than that flamboyant girl – and she walked like an Empress.

I hoped, with all my heart, that Amyas Crale would be punished for the cruelty he had displayed and for the indignity he had put upon a long-suffering and noble woman.

For the first time, I tried to say something of what I felt to Mrs Crale, but she stopped me.

She said:

'We must try and behave as usual. It's the best way. We're all going over to Meredith Blake's to tea.'

I said to her then:

'I think you are wonderful, Mrs Crale.'

She said:

'You don't know . . .'

Then, as she was going out of the room, she came back and kissed me. She said:

'You're such a comfort to me.'

She went to her room then and I think she cried. I saw her when they all started off. She was wearing a big-brimmed hat that shaded her face – a hat she very seldom wore.

Mr Crale was uneasy, but was trying to brazen things out. Mr Philip Blake was trying to behave as usual. That Miss Greer was looking like a cat who has got at the cream-jug. All self-satisfaction and purrs!

They all started off. They got back about six. I did not see Mrs Crale again alone that evening. She was very quiet and composed at dinner, and she went to bed early. I don't think that any one knew how she was suffering.

The evening was taken up with a kind of running quarrel between Mr Crale and Angela. They brought up the old school question again. He was irritable and on edge, and she was unusually trying. The whole matter was settled and her outfit had been bought, and there was no sense in starting up an argument again, but she suddenly chose to make a grievance of it. I have no doubt she sensed the tension in the air and that it reacted on her as much as on everybody else. I am afraid I was too preoccupied with my own thoughts to try and check her as I should have done. It all ended with her flinging a paperweight at Mr Crale and dashing out of the room.

I went after her and told her sharply that I was ashamed of her behaving like a baby, but she was still very uncontrolled, and I thought it best to leave her alone.

I hesitated as to whether to go to Mrs Crale's room, but I decided in the end that it would, perhaps, annoy her. I wish since that I had overcome my diffidence and insisted on her talking to me. If she had done so, it might possibly have made a difference. She had no one, you see, in whom she could confide. Although I admire self-control, I must regretfully admit that sometimes it can be carried too far. A natural outlet to the feelings is better.

I met Mr Crale as I went along to my room. He said goodnight, but I did not answer.

The next morning was, I remember, a beautiful day. One felt when waking that surely with such peace all around even a man must come to his senses.

I went into Angela's room before going down to breakfast, but she was already up and out. I picked up a torn skirt which she had left lying on the floor and took it down with me for her to mend after breakfast.

She had, however, obtained bread and marmalade from the kitchen and gone out. After I had had my own breakfast I went in search of her. I mention this to explain why I was not more with Mrs Crale on that morning as perhaps I should have been. At the time, however, I felt it was my duty to look for Angela. She was very naughty and obstinate about mending her clothes, and I had no intention of allowing her to defy me in the matter.

Her bathing-dress was missing and I accordingly went down to the beach. There was no sign of her in the water or on the rocks, so I conceived it possible that she had gone over to Mr Meredith Blake's. She and he were great friends. I accordingly rowed myself across and resumed my search. I did not find her and eventually returned. Mrs Crale, Mr Blake and Mr Philip Blake were on the terrace.

It was very hot that morning if one was out of the wind, and the house and terrace were sheltered. Mrs Crale suggested they might like some iced beer.

There was a little conservatory which had been built on to the house in Victorian days. Mrs Crale disliked it, and it was not used for plants, but it had been made into a kind of bar, with various bottles of gin, vermouth, lemonade, ginger-beer, etc., on shelves, and a small refrigerator which was filled with ice every morning and in which some beer and ginger-beer was always kept.

Mrs Crale went there to get the beer and I went with her. Angela was at the refrigerator and was just taking out a bottle of beer.

Mrs Crale went in ahead of me. She said:

'I want a bottle of beer to take down to Amyas.'

It is so difficult now to know whether I ought to have suspected anything. Her voice, I feel almost convinced, was perfectly normal. But I must admit that at that moment I was intent, not on her, but on Angela. Angela was by the refrigerator and I was glad to see that she looked red and rather guilty.

I was rather sharp with her, and to my surprise she was quite meek. I asked her where she had been, and she said she had been bathing. I said: 'I didn't see you on the beach.' And she laughed. Then I asked her where her jersey was, and she said she must have left it down on the beach.

I mention these details to explain why I let Mrs Crale take the beer down to the Battery garden.

The rest of the morning is quite blank in my mind. Angela fetched her needle-book and mended her skirt without any more fuss. I rather think that I mended some of the household linen. Mr Crale did not come up for lunch. I was glad that he had at least *that* much decency.

After lunch, Mrs Crale said she was going down to the Battery. I wanted to retrieve Angela's jersey from the beach. We started down together. She went into the Battery – I was going on when her cry called me back. As I told you when you came to see me, she asked me to go up and telephone. On the way up I met Mr Meredith Blake and then went back to Mrs Crale.

That was my story as I told it at the inquest and later at the trial.

What I am about to write down I have never told to any living soul. I was not asked any question to which I returned an untrue answer. Nevertheless I *was* guilty of withholding certain facts – I do not repent of that. I would do it again. I am fully aware that in revealing this I may be laying myself open to censure, but I do not think that after this lapse of time any one will take the matter very seriously – especially since Caroline Crale was convicted without my evidence.

This, then, is what happened.

I met Mr Meredith Blake as I said, and I ran down the path again as quickly as I could. I was wearing sandshoes and I have always been light on my feet. I came to the open Battery door, and this is what I saw.

Mrs Crale was busily polishing the beer bottle on the table with her handkerchief. Having done so, she took her dead husband's hand and pressed the fingers of it on the beer bottle. All the time she was listening and on the alert. It was the fear I saw on her face that told me the truth.

I knew then, beyond any possible doubt, that Caroline Crale had poisoned her husband. And I, for one, do not blame her. He drove her to a point beyond human endurance, and he brought his fate upon himself.

I never mentioned the incident to Mrs Crale and she never knew that I had seen it.

Caroline Crale's daughter must not bolster up her life with a lie. However much it may pain her to know the truth, truth is the only thing that matters.

Tell her, from me, that her mother is not to be judged. She was driven beyond what a loving woman can endure. It is for her daughter to understand and forgive.

End of Cecilia Williams's Narrative.

....

NARRATIVE OF ANGELA WARREN

Dear M. Poirot,

I am keeping my promise to you and have written down all I can remember of that terrible time sixteen years ago. But it was not until I started that I realized how very little I *did* remember. Until the thing actually happened, you see, there is nothing to fix anything by.

I've just a vague memory of summer days – and isolated incidents, but I couldn't say for certain what summer they happened even! Amyas's death was just a thunderclap coming out of the blue. I'd had no warning of it, and I seem to have missed everything that led up to it.

I've been trying to think whether that was to be expected or not. Are most girls of fifteen as blind and deaf and obtuse as I seem to have been? Perhaps they are. I was quick, I think, to gauge people's moods, but I never bothered my head about what *caused* those moods.

Besides, just at that time, I'd suddenly begun to discover the intoxication of words. Things that I read, straps of poetry – of Shakespeare – would echo in my head. I remember now walking along the kitchen garden path repeating to myself in a kind of ecstatic delirium 'under the glassy green translucent wave' . . . It was just so lovely I had to say it over and over again.

And mixed up with these new discoveries and excitements there were all the things I'd liked doing ever since I could remember. Swimming and climbing trees and eating fruit and playing tricks on the stable boy and feeding the horses.

Caroline and Amyas I took for granted. They were the central figures in my world, but I never *thought* about them or about their affairs or what they thought and felt.

I didn't notice Elsa Greer's coming particularly. I thought she was stupid and I didn't even think she was good-looking. I accepted her as someone rich but tiresome, whom Amyas was painting.

Actually, the very first intimation I had of the whole thing was what I overheard from the terrace where I had escaped after lunch one day – Elsa said she was going to marry Amyas! It struck me as just ridiculous. I remember tackling Amyas about it. In the garden at Handcross it was. I said to him:

'Why does Elsa say she's going to marry you? She couldn't. People can't have two wives – it's bigamy and they go to prison.'

Amyas got very angry and said: 'How the devil did you hear that?'

I said I'd heard it through the library window.

He was angrier than ever then, and said it was high time I went to school and got out of the habit of eavesdropping.

I still remember the resentment I felt when he said that. Because it was so *unfair*. Absolutely and utterly unfair.

I stammered out angrily that I hadn't been listening – and anyhow, I said, why did Elsa say a silly thing like that?

Amyas said it was just a joke.

That ought to have satisfied me. It did – almost. But not quite.

I said to Elsa when we were on the way back: 'I asked Amyas what you meant when you said you were going to marry him, and he said it was just a joke.'

I felt that ought to snub her. But she only smiled.

I didn't like that smile of hers. I went up to Caroline's room. It was when she was dressing for dinner. I asked her then outright if it were possible for Amyas to marry Elsa.

I remember Caroline's answer as though I heard it now. She must have spoken with great emphasis.

'Amyas will only marry Elsa after I am dead,' she said.

That reassured me completely. Death seemed ages away from us all. Nevertheless, I was still very sore with Amyas about what he had said in the afternoon, and I went for him violently all through dinner, and I remember we had a real flaming row, and I rushed out of the room and went up to bed and howled myself to sleep.

I don't remember much about the afternoon at Meredith Blake's, although I *do* remember his reading aloud the passage from the Phædo describing Socrates' death. I had never heard it before. I thought it was the loveliest, most beautiful thing I had ever heard. I remember that – but I don't remember when it was. As far as I can recall now, it might have been any time that summer.

I don't remember anything that happened the next morning either, though I have thought and thought. I've a vague feeling that I must have bathed, and I think I remember being made to mend something.

But it's all very vague and dim till the time when Meredith came panting up the path from the terrace, and his face was all grey and queer. I remember a coffee cup falling off the table and being broken – Elsa did that. And I remember her running – suddenly running for all she was worth down the path – and the awful look there was on her face.

I kept saying to myself: 'Amyas is dead.' But it just didn't seem real.

I remember Dr Faussett coming and his grave face. Miss Williams was busy looking after Caroline. I wandered about rather forlornly, getting in people's way. I had a nasty sick feeling. They wouldn't let me go down and see Amyas. But by and by the police came and wrote down things in notebooks, and presently they brought his body up on a stretcher covered with a cloth.

Miss Williams took me into Caroline's room later. Caroline was on the sofa. She looked very white and ill.

She kissed me and said she wanted me to go away as soon as I could, and it was all horrible, but I wasn't to worry or think about it any more than I could help. I was to join Carla at Lady Tressillian's because this house was to be kept as empty as possible.

I clung to Caroline and said I didn't want to go away. I wanted to stay with her. She said she knew I did, but it was better for me to go away and would take a lot of worry off her mind. And Miss Williams chipped in and said:

'The best way you can help your sister, Angela, is to do what she wants you to do without making a fuss about it.'

So I said I would do whatever Caroline wished. And Caroline said: 'That's my darling Angela.' And she hugged me and said there was nothing to worry about, and to talk about it and think about it all as little as possible.

I had to go down and talk to a Police Superintendent. He was very kind, asked me when I had last seen Amyas and a lot of other questions which seemed to me quite pointless at the time, but which, of course, I see the point of now. He satisfied himself that there was nothing that I could tell him which he hadn't already heard from the others. So he told Miss Williams that he saw no objection to my going over to Ferriby Grange to Lady Tressillian's.

I went there, and Lady Tressillian was very kind to me. But of course I soon had to know the truth. They arrested Caroline almost at once. I was so horrified and dumb-founded that I became quite ill.

I heard afterwards that Caroline was terribly worried about me. It was at her insistence that I was sent out of England before the trial came on. But that I have told you already.

As you see, what I have to put down is pitiably meagre. Since talking to you I have gone over the little I remember painstakingly, racking my memory for details of this or that person's expression or reaction. I can remember nothing consistent with guilt. Elsa's frenzy. Meredith's grey worried face. Philip's grief and fury – they all seem natural enough. I suppose, though, someone *could* have been playing a part?

I only know this, *Caroline did not do it.*

I am quite certain on this point, and always shall be, but I have no evidence to offer except my own intimate knowledge of her character.

End of Angela Warren's Narrative.

BOOK III

CONCLUSIONS

Carla Lemarchant looked up. Her eyes were full of fatigue and pain. She pushed back the hair from her forehead in a tired gesture.

She said:

'It's so bewildering all this.' She touched the pile of manuscripts. 'Because the angle's different every time! Everybody sees my mother differently. But the facts are the same. Everyone agrees on the facts.'

'It has discouraged you, reading them?'

'Yes. Hasn't it discouraged you?'

'No, I have found those documents very valuable – very informative.' Poirot spoke slowly and reflectively.

Carla said:

'I wish I'd never read them!'

Poirot looked across at her.

'Ah – so it makes you feel that way?'

Carla said bitterly:

'They all think she did it – all of them except Aunt Angela and what she thinks doesn't count. She hasn't got any reason for it. She's just one of those loyal people who'll stick to a thing through thick and thin. She just goes on saying: 'Caroline couldn't have done it.''

'It strikes you like that?'

'How else should it strike me? I've realized, you know, that if my mother didn't do it, then one of these five people must have done it. I've even had theories as to why.'

'Ah! That is interesting. Tell me.'

'Oh, they were only theories. Philip Blake, for instance. He's a stockbroker, he was my father's best friend – probably my father trusted him. And artists are usually careless about money matters. Perhaps Philip Blake was in a jam and used my father's money. He may have got my father to sign something. Then the whole thing may have been on the point of coming out – and only my father's death could have saved him. That's one of the things I thought of.'

'Not badly imagined at all. What else?'

'Well, there's Elsa. Philip Blake says here she had her head screwed on too well to meddle with poison, but I don't think that's true at all. Supposing my mother had gone to her and told her that she wouldn't divorce my father – that nothing would induce her to divorce him. You may say what you like, but I think Elsa had a bourgeois mind – she wanted to be respectably married. I think that then Elsa would have been perfectly capable of pinching the stuff – she had just as good a chance that afternoon – and might have tried to get my mother out of the way by poisoning her. I think that would be quite *like* Elsa. And then, possibly, by some awful accident, Amyas got the stuff instead of Caroline.'

'Again it is not badly imagined. What else?'

Carla said slowly:

'Well, I thought – perhaps – *Meredith*!'

'Ah – Meredith Blake?'

'Yes. You see, he sounds to me just the sort of person who would do a murder. I mean, he was the slow dithering one the others laughed at, and underneath, perhaps, he resented that. Then my father married the girl he wanted to marry. And my father was successful and rich. And he did make all those poisons! Perhaps he really made them because he liked the idea of being able to kill someone one day. He had to call attention to the stuff being taken, so as to divert suspicion from himself. But he himself was far the most likely person to have taken it. He might, even, have liked getting Caroline hanged – because she turned him down long ago. I think, you know, it's rather fishy what he says in his account of it all – how people do things that aren't characteristic of them. Supposing he meant *himself* when he wrote that?'

Hercule Poirot said:

'You are at least right in this – not to take what has been written down as necessarily a true narrative. What has been written may have been written deliberately to mislead.'

'Oh, I know. I've kept that in mind.'

'Any other ideas?'

Carla said slowly:

'I wondered – before I'd read this – about Miss Williams. She lost her job, you see, when Angela went to school. And if Amyas had died suddenly, Angela probably wouldn't have gone after all. I mean if it passed off as a natural death – which it easily might have done, I suppose, if Meredith hadn't missed the coniine. I read up coniine, and it hasn't got any distinctive post-mortem appearances. It might have been thought to be sunstroke. I know that just losing a job doesn't sound a very adequate motive for murder. But murders have been committed again and again for what seem ridiculously inadequate motives. Tiny sums of money sometimes. And a middle-aged, perhaps rather incompetent governess might have got the wind up and just seen no future ahead of her.

'As I say, that's what I thought before I read this. But Miss Williams doesn't sound like that at all. She doesn't sound in the least incompetent –'

'Not at all. She is still a very efficient and intelligent woman.'

'I know. One can see that. And she sounds absolutely trustworthy too. That's what has upset me really. Oh, *you* know – *you* understand. You don't mind, of course. All along you've made it clear it was the truth you wanted. I suppose now we've *got* the truth! Miss Williams is quite right. One must accept truth. It's no good basing your life on a lie because it's what you want to believe. All right then – I can take it! My mother wasn't innocent! She wrote me that letter because she was weak and unhappy and wanted to spare me. I don't judge her. Perhaps I should feel like that too. I don't know what prison does to you. And I don't blame her either – if she felt so desperately about my father, I suppose she couldn't help herself. But I don't blame my father altogether either. I understand – just a little – how *he* felt. So alive – and so full of wanting everything . . . He couldn't help it – he was made that way. And he was a great painter. I think that excuses a lot.'

She turned her flushed excited face to Hercule Poirot with her chin raised defiantly.

Hercule Poirot said:

'So – you are satisfied?'

'Satisfied?' said Carla Lemarchant. Her voice broke on the word.

Poirot leant forward and patted her paternally on the shoulder.

'Listen,' he said. 'You give up the fight at the moment when it is most worth fighting. At the moment when I, Hercule Poirot, have a very good idea of what really happened.'

Carla stared at him. She said:

'Miss Williams loved my mother. She saw her – with her own eyes – faking that suicide evidence. If you believe what she says –'

Hercule Poirot got up. He said:

'Mademoiselle, because Cecilia Williams says she saw your mother faking Amyas Crale's fingerprints on the beer bottle – on the beer *bottle*, mind – that is the only thing I need to tell me definitely, once for all, that your mother did not kill your father.'

He nodded his head several times and went out of the room, leaving Carla staring after him.

CHAPTER 2

POIROT ASKS FIVE QUESTIONS

'Well, M. Poirot?'

Philip Blake's tone was impatient.

Poirot said:

'I have to thank you for your admirable and lucid account of the Crale tragedy.'

Philip Blake looked rather self-conscious.

'Very kind of you,' he murmured. 'Really surprising how much I remembered when I got down to it.'

Poirot said:

'It was an admirably clear narrative, but there were certain omissions, were there not?'

'Omissions?' Philip Blake frowned.

Hercule Poirot said:

'Your narrative, shall we say, was not entirely frank.' His tone hardened. 'I have been informed, Mr Blake, that on at least one night during the summer, Mrs Crale was seen coming out of your room at a somewhat compromising hour.'

There was a silence broken only by Philip Blake's heavy breathing. He said at last: 'Who told you that?'

Hercule Poirot shook his head.

'It is no matter who told me. That I *know*, that is the point.'

Again there was a silence; then Philip Blake made up his mind. He said:

'By accident, it seems, you have stumbled upon a purely private matter. I admit that it does not square with what I have written down. Nevertheless, it squares better than you might think. I am forced now to tell you the truth.

'I *did* entertain a feeling of animosity towards Caroline Crale. At the same time I was always strongly attracted by her. Perhaps the latter fact induced the former. I resented the power she had over me and tried to stifle the attraction she had for me by constantly dwelling on her worst points. I never *liked* her, if you understand. But it would have been easy at any moment for me to make love to her. I had been in love with her as a boy and she had taken no notice of me. I did not find that easy to forgive.

'My opportunity came when Amyas lost his head so completely over the Greer girl. Quite without meaning to I found myself telling Caroline I loved her. She said quite calmly: "Yes, I have always known that." The insolence of the woman!

'Of course I knew that she didn't love me, but I saw that she was disturbed and disillusioned by Amyas's present infatuation. That is a mood when a woman can very easily be won. She agreed to come to me that night. And she came.'

Blake paused. He found now a difficulty in getting the words out.

'She came to my room. And then, with my arms round her, she told me quite coolly that it was no good! After all, she said, she was a one-man woman. She was Amyas Crale's, for better or worse. She agreed that she had treated me very badly, but said she couldn't help it. She asked me to forgive her.

'And she left me. *She left me!* Do you wonder, M. Poirot, that my hatred of her was heightened a hundredfold? Do you wonder that I have never forgiven her? For the insult she did me – as well as for the fact that she killed the friend I loved better than any one in the world!'

Trembling violently, Philip Blake exclaimed:

'*I don't want to speak of it,* do you hear? You've got your answer. Now go! And never mention the matter to me again!'

'I want to know, Mr Blake, the order in which your guests left the laboratory that day?'

Meredith Blake protested.

'But, my dear M. Poirot. After sixteen years! How can I possibly remember? I've told you that Caroline came out last.'

'You are *sure* of that?'

'Yes – at least – I think so . . .'

'Let us go there now. We must be *quite* sure, you see.'

Still protesting, Meredith Blake led the way. He unlocked the door and swung back the shutters. Poirot spoke to him authoritatively.

'Now then, my friend. You have showed your visitors your interesting preparations of herbs. Shut your eyes now and think –'

Meredith Blake did so obediently. Poirot drew a handkerchief from his pocket and gently passed it to and fro. Blake murmured, his nostrils twitching slightly:

'Yes, yes – extraordinary how things come back to one. Caroline, I remember, had on a pale coffee-coloured dress. Phil was looking bored . . . He always thought my hobby was quite idiotic.'

Poirot said:

'Reflect now, you are about to leave the room. You are going to the library where you are going to read the passage about the death of Socrates. Who leaves the room first – do you?'

'Elsa and I – yes. She passed through the door first. I was close behind her. We were talking. I stood there waiting for the others to come so that I could lock the door again. Philip – yes, Philip came out next. And Angela – she was asking him what bulls and bears were. They went on through the hall. Amyas followed them. I stood there waiting still – for Caroline, of course.'

'So you are quite sure Caroline stayed behind. Did you see what she was doing?'

Blake shook his head.

'No, I had my back to the room, you see. I was talking to Elsa – boring her, I expect – telling her how certain plants must be gathered at the full of the moon according to old superstition. And then Caroline came out – hurrying a little – and I locked the door.'

He stopped and looked at Poirot, who was replacing a handkerchief in his pocket. Meredith Blake sniffled disgustedly and thought: 'Why, the fellow actually uses *scent*!'

Aloud he said:

'I am quite sure of it. That was the order. Elsa, myself, Philip, Angela and Caroline. Does that help you at all?'

Poirot said:

'It all fits in. Listen. I want to arrange a meeting here. It will not, I think, be difficult . . .'

'Well?'

Elsa Dittisham said it almost eagerly – like a child.

'I want to ask you a question, madame.'

'Yes?'

Poirot said:

'After it was all over – the trial, I mean – did Meredith Blake ask you to marry him?'

Elsa stared. She looked contemptuous – almost bored.

'Yes – he did. Why?'

'Were you surprised?'

'Was I? I don't remember.'

'What did you say?'

Elsa laughed. She said:

'What do you think I said? After *Amyas* – Meredith? It would have been ridiculous! It was stupid of him. He always was rather stupid.'

She smiled suddenly.

'He wanted, you know, to protect me – to "look after me" – that's how he put it! He thought like everybody else that the Assizes had been a terrible ordeal for me. And the reporters! And the booing crowds! And all the mud that was slung at me.'

She brooded a minute. Then said:

'Poor old Meredith! Such an ass!' And laughed again.

Once again Hercule Poirot encountered the shrewd penetrating glance of Miss Williams, and once again felt the years falling away and himself a meek and apprehensive little boy.

There was, he explained, a question he wished to ask.

Miss Williams intimated her willingness to hear what the question was.

Poirot said slowly, picking his words carefully:

'Angela Warren was injured as a very young child. In my notes I find two references to that fact. In one of them it is stated that Mrs Crale threw a paperweight at the child. In the other that she attacked the baby with a crowbar. Which of those versions is the right one?'

Miss Williams replied briskly:

'I never heard anything about a crowbar. The paperweight is the correct story.'

'Who was your own informant?'

'Angela herself. She volunteered the information quite early.'

'What did she say exactly?'

'She touched her cheek and said: "Caroline did this when I was a baby. She threw a paperweight at me. Never refer to it, will you, because it upsets her dreadfully."'

'Did Mrs Crale herself ever mention the matter to you?'

'Only obliquely. She assumed that I knew the story. I remember her saying once: "I know you think I spoil Angela, but you see, I always feel there is nothing I can do to make up to her for what I did." And on another occasion she said: "To know you have permanently injured another human being is the heaviest burden any one could have to bear."'

'Thank you, Miss Williams. That is all I wanted to know.'

Cecilia Williams said sharply:

'I don't understand you, M. Poirot. You showed Carla my account of the tragedy?'

Poirot nodded.

'And yet you are still –' She stopped.

Poirot said:

'Reflect a minute. If you were to pass a fishmonger's and saw twelve fish laid out on his slab, you would think they were all real fish, would you not? But one of them might be stuffed fish.'

Miss Williams replied with spirit:

'Most unlikely and anyway –'

'Ah, unlikely, yes, but not impossible – because a friend of mine once took down a stuffed fish (it was his trade, you comprehend) to compare it with the real thing! And if you saw a bowl of zinnias in a drawing-room in December you would say that they were false – but they might be real ones flown home from Baghdad.'

'What is the meaning of all this nonsense?' demanded Miss Williams.

'It is to show you that it is the eyes of the mind with which one really sees . . .'

Poirot slowed up a little as he approached the big block of flats overlooking Regent's Park.

Really, when he came to think of it, he did not want to ask Angela Warren any questions at all. The only question he did want to ask her could wait . . .

No, it was really only his insatiable passion for symmetry that was bringing him here. Five people – there should be five questions! It was neater so. It rounded off the thing better.

Ah well – he would think of something.

Angela Warren greeted him with something closely approaching eagerness. She said:

'Have you found out anything? Have you got anywhere?'

Slowly Poirot nodded his head in his best China mandarin manner. He said:

'At last I make progress.'

'Philip Blake?' It was halfway between statement and a question.

'Mademoiselle, I do not wish to say anything at present. The moment has not yet come. What I will ask of you is to be so good as to come down to Handcross Manor. The others have consented.'

She said with a slight frown:

'What do you propose to do? Reconstruct something that happened sixteen years ago?'

'See it, perhaps, from a clearer angle. You will come?'

Angela Warren said slowly:

'Oh, yes, I'll come. It will be interesting to see all those people again. I shall see *them* now, perhaps, from a clearer angle (as you put it) than I did then.'

'And you will bring with you the letter that you showed me?'

Angela Warren frowned.

'That letter is my own. I showed it to you for a good and sufficient reason, but I have no intention of allowing it to be read by strange and unsympathetic persons.'

'But you will allow yourself to be guided by me in this matter?'

'I will do nothing of the kind. I will bring the letter with me, but I shall use my own judgement which I venture to think is quite as good as yours.'

Poirot spread out his hands in a gesture of resignation. He got up to go. He said:

'You permit that I ask one little question?'

'What is it?'

'At the time of the tragedy, you had lately read, had you not, Somerset Maugham's *The Moon and Sixpence*?'

Angela stared at him. Then she said:

'I believe – why, yes, that is quite true.' She looked at him with frank curiosity. 'How did you know?'

'I want to show you, mademoiselle, that even in a small unimportant matter, I am something of a magician. There are things I know without having to be told.'

CHAPTER 3

RECONSTRUCTION

The afternoon sun shone into the laboratory at Handcross Manor. Some easy chairs and a settee had been brought into the room, but they served more to emphasize its forlorn aspect than to furnish it.

Slightly embarrassed, pulling at his moustache, Meredith Blake talked to Carla in a desultory way. He broke off once to say: 'My dear, you are very like your mother – and yet unlike her, too.'

Carla asked: 'How am I like her and how unlike?'

'You have her colouring and her way of moving, but you are – how shall I put it – more *positive* than she ever was.'

Philip Blake, a scowl creasing over his forehead, looked out of the window and drummed impatiently on the pane. He said:

'What's the sense of all this? A perfectly fine Saturday afternoon –'

Hercule Poirot hastened to pour oil on troubled waters.

'Ah, I apologize – it is, I know, unpardonable to disarrange the golf. *Mais voyons*, M. Blake, this is the daughter of your best friend. You will stretch a point for her, will you not?'

The butler announced: 'Miss Warren.'

Meredith went to welcome her. He said: 'It's good of you to spare the time, Angela. You're busy, I know.'

He led her over to the window.

Carla said: 'Hallo, Aunt Angela. I read your article in *The Times* this morning. It's nice to have a distinguished relative.' She indicated the tall, square-jawed young man with the steady grey eyes. 'This is John Rattery. He and I – hope – to be married.'

Angela Warren said: 'Oh! – I didn't know . . .'

Meredith went to greet the next arrival.

'Well, Miss Williams, it's a good many years since we met.'

Thin, frail and indomitable, the elderly governess advanced up the room. Her eyes rested thoughtfully on Poirot for a minute, then they went to the tall, square-shouldered figure in the well-cut tweeds.

Angela Warren came forward to meet her and said with a smile: 'I feel like a schoolgirl again.'

'I'm very proud of you, my dear,' said Miss Williams. 'You've done me credit. This is Carla, I suppose? She won't remember me. She was too young . . .'

Philip Blake said fretfully: 'What *is* all this? Nobody told me –'

Hercule Poirot said: 'I call it – me – an excursion into the past. Shall we not all sit down? Then we shall be ready when the last guest arrives. And when she is here we can proceed to our business – to lay the ghosts.'

Philip Blake exclaimed: 'What tomfoolery is this? You're not going to hold a *séance*, are you?'

'No, no. We are only going to discuss some events that happened long ago – to discuss them and, perhaps, to see more clearly the course of them. As to the ghosts, they will not materialize, but who is to say they are not here, in this room, although we cannot see them. Who is to say that Amyas and Caroline Crale are not here – listening?'

Philip Blake said: 'Absurd nonsense –' and broke off as the door opened again and the butler announced Lady Dittisham.

Elsa Dittisham came in with that faint, bored insolence that was a characteristic of her. She gave Meredith a slight smile, stared coldly at Angela and Philip, and went over to a chair by the window a little apart from the others. She loosened the rich pale furs round her neck and let them fall back. She looked for a minute or two about the room, then at Carla, and the girl stared back, thoughtfully appraising the woman who had wrought the havoc in her parents' lives. There was no animosity in her young earnest face, only curiosity.

Elsa said: 'I am sorry if I am late, M. Poirot.'

'It was very good of you to come, madame.'

Cecilia Williams snorted ever so slightly. Elsa met the animosity in her eyes with a complete lack of interest. She said:

'I wouldn't have known *you*, Angela. How long is it? Sixteen years?'

Hercule Poirot seized his opportunity.

'Yes, it is sixteen years since the events of which we are to speak, but let me first tell you why we are here.'

And in a few simple words he outlined Carla's appeal to him and his acceptance of the task.

He went on quickly, ignoring the gathering storm visible on Philip's face, and the shocked distaste on Meredith's.

'I accepted that commission – I set to work to find out – the truth.'

Carla Lemarchant, in the big grandfather chair, heard Poirot's words dimly, from a distance.

With her hand shielding her eyes she studied five faces, surreptitiously. Could she see any of these people committing murder? The exotic Elsa, the red-faced Philip, dear, nice, kind Mr Meredith Blake, that grim tartar of a governess, the cool, competent Angela Warren?

Could she – if she tried hard – visualize one of them killing someone?

Yes, perhaps – but it wouldn't be the right kind of murder. She could picture Philip Blake, in an outburst of fury, strangling some woman – yes, she *could* picture that . . . And she could picture Meredith Blake, threatening a burglar with a revolver – and letting it off by accident . . . And she could picture Angela Warren, also firing a revolver, but not by accident. With no personal feeling in the matter – the safety of the expedition depended on it! And Elsa, in some fantastic castle, saying from her couch of oriental silks: 'Throw the wretch over the battlements!' All wild fancies – and not even in the wildest flight of fancy could she imagine little Miss Williams killing anybody at all! Another fantastic picture: 'Did you ever kill anybody, Miss Williams?' 'Go on with your arithmetic, Carla, and don't ask silly questions. To kill anybody is very wicked.'

Carla thought: 'I must be ill – and I must stop this. Listen, you fool, listen to that little man who says he knows.'

Hercule Poirot was talking.

'That was my task – to put myself in reverse gear, as it were, and go back through the years and discover what really happened.'

Philip Blake said: 'We all know what happened. To pretend anything else is a swindle – that's what it is, a bare-faced swindle. You're getting money out of this girl on false pretences.'

Poirot did not allow himself to be angered. He said:

'You say, *we all know what happened.* You speak without reflection. The accepted version of certain facts is not necessarily the true one. On the face of it, for instance, you, Mr Blake, disliked Caroline Crale. That is the accepted version of your attitude. But anyone with the least flair for psychology can perceive at once that the exact opposite was the truth. You were always violently attracted towards Caroline Crale. You resented the fact, and tried to conquer it by steadfastly telling yourself her defects and reiterating your dislike. In the same way, Mr Meredith Blake had a tradition of devotion to Caroline Crale lasting over many years. In his story of the tragedy he represents himself as resenting Amyas Crale's conduct on *her* account, but you have only to read carefully between the lines and you will see that the devotion of a lifetime had worn itself thin and that it was the young, beautiful Elsa Greer that was occupying *his* mind and thoughts.'

There was a splutter from Meredith, and Lady Dittisham smiled.

Poirot went on.

'I mention these matters only as illustrations, though they have their bearing on what happened. Very well, then, I start on my backward journey – to learn everything I can about the tragedy. I will tell you how

I set about it. I talked to the Counsel who defended Caroline Crale, to the Junior Counsel for the Crown, to the old solicitor who had known the Crale family intimately, to the lawyer's clerk who had been in court during the trial, to the police officer in charge of the case – and I came finally to the five eye-witnesses who had been upon the scene. And from all of these I put together a picture – a composite picture of a woman. And I learned these facts:

'*That at no time did Caroline Crale protest her innocence* (except in that one letter written to her daughter).

'That Caroline Crale showed no fear in the dock, that she showed, in fact, hardly any interest, that she adopted throughout a thoroughly defeatist attitude. That in prison she was quiet and serene. That in a letter she wrote to her sister immediately after the verdict, she expressed herself as acquiescent in the fate that had overtaken her. And in the opinion of everyone I talked to (with one notable exception) *Caroline Crale was guilty.*'

Philip Blake nodded his head. 'Of course she was!'

Hercule Poirot said:

'But it was not my part to accept the verdict of *others*. I had to examine the evidence for *myself*. To examine the facts and to satisfy myself that the psychology of the case accorded itself with them. To do this I went over the police files carefully, and I also succeeded in getting five people who were on the spot to write me out their own accounts of the tragedy. These accounts were very valuable for they contained certain matter which the police files could not give me – that is to say: A, certain conversations and incidents which, from the police point of view, were not relevant; B, the opinions of the people themselves as to what Caroline Crale was thinking and feeling (not admissible legally as evidence); C, certain facts which had been deliberately withheld from the police.

'I was in a position now to judge the case for *myself*. There seems no doubt whatever that Caroline Crale had ample motive for the crime. She loved her husband, he had publicly admitted that he was about to leave her for another woman, and by her own admission she was a jealous woman.

'To come from motives to means, an empty scent bottle that had contained coniine was found in her bureau drawer. There were no fingerprints upon it but hers. When asked about it by the police, she admitted taking it from this room we are in now. The coniine bottle here also had her fingerprints upon it. I questioned Mr Meredith Blake as to the order in which the five people left this room on that day – for it seemed to me hardly conceivable that *any one* should be able to help themselves to the poison whilst five people were in the room. The people left the room in this order – Elsa Greer, Meredith Blake, Angela Warren and Philip Blake, Amyas Crale, and lastly Caroline Crale. Moreover, Mr Meredith Blake had his back to the room whilst he was waiting for Mrs Crale to come out, so that it was impossible for him to see what she was doing. She had, that is to say, the opportunity. I am therefore satisfied that she did take the coniine. There is indirect confirmation of it. Mr Meredith Blake said to me the other day: 'I can remember standing here and smelling the jasmine through the open window.' But the month was September, and the jasmine creeper outside that window would have finished flowering. It is the ordinary jasmine which blooms in June and July. But the scent bottle found in her room and which contained the dregs of coniine had originally contained jasmine scent. I take it as certain, then, that Mrs Crale decided to steal the coniine, and surreptitiously emptied out the scent from a bottle she had in her bag.

'I tested that a second time the other day when I asked Mr Blake to shut his eyes and try and remember the order of leaving the room. A whiff of jasmine scent stimulated his memory immediately. We are all more influenced by smell than we know.

'So we come to the morning of the fatal day. So far the facts are not in dispute. Miss Greer's sudden revealing of the fact that she and Mr Crale contemplate marriage, Amyas Crale's confirmation of that, and Caroline Crale's deep distress. None of these things depend on the evidence of one witness only.

'On the following morning there is a scene between husband and wife in the library. The first thing that is overheard is Caroline Crale saying: "You and your women!" in a bitter voice, and finally going on to say, "Some day I'll kill you." Philip Blake overheard this from the hall. And Miss Greer overheard it from the terrace outside.

'She then heard Mr Crale ask his wife to be reasonable. And she heard Mrs Crale say: "Sooner than let you go to that girl – I'll kill you." Soon after this Amyas Crale comes out and brusquely tells Elsa Greer to come down and pose for him. She gets a pullover and accompanies him.

'There is nothing so far that seems psychologically incorrect. Every one has behaved as they might be expected to behave. But we come now to something that *is* incongruous.

'Meredith Blake discovers his loss, telephones his brother; they meet down at the landing stage and they come up past the Battery garden, where Caroline Crale is having a discussion with her husband on the subject of Angela's going to school. Now that does strike me as very odd. Husband and wife have a terrific scene, ending in a distinct threat on Caroline's part, and yet, twenty minutes or so later, she goes down and starts a trivial domestic argument.'

Poirot turned to Meredith Blake.

'You speak in your narrative of certain words you overheard Crale say. These were: "It's all settled – I'll see to her packing." That is right?'

Meredith Blake said: 'It was something like that – yes.'

Poirot turned to Philip Blake.

'Is your recollection the same?'

The latter frowned.

'I didn't remember it till you say so – but I do remember now. Something *was* said about packing!'

'Said by Mr Crale – not Mrs Crale?'

'Amyas said it. All I heard Caroline say was something about its being very hard on the girl. Anyway, what does all this matter? We all know Angela was off to school in a day or two.'

Poirot said: 'You do not see the force of my objection. Why should *Amyas Crale* pack for the girl? It is absurd, that! There was Mrs Crale, there was Miss Williams, there was a housemaid. It is a woman's job to pack – not a man's.'

Philip Blake said impatiently:

'What does it matter? It's nothing to do with the crime.'

'You think not? For me, it was the first point that struck me as suggestive. And it is immediately followed by another. Mrs Crale, a desperate woman, broken-hearted, who has threatened her husband a short while before and who is certainly contemplating either suicide or murder, now offers in the most amicable manner to bring her husband down some iced beer.'

Meredith Blake said slowly: 'That isn't odd if she was contemplating murder. Then, surely, it is just what she *would* do. Dissimulate!'

'You think so? She has decided to poison her husband, she has already got the poison. Her husband keeps a supply of beer down in the Battery garden. Surely if she has any intelligence at all, she will put the poison in one of *those* bottles at a moment when there is no one about.'

Meredith Blake objected.

'She couldn't have done that. Somebody else might have drunk it.'

'Yes, Elsa Greer. Do you tell me that having made up her mind to murder her husband, Caroline Crale would have scruples against killing the girl too?

'But let us not argue the point. Let us confine ourselves to facts. Caroline Crale says she will send her husband down some iced beer. She goes up to the house, fetches a bottle from the conservatory where it was kept and takes it down to him. She pours it out and gives it to him.

'Amyas Crale drinks it off and says: "Everything tastes foul today."

'Mrs Crale goes up again to the house. She has lunch and appears much as usual. It has been said of her that she looks a little worried and preoccupied. That does not help us – for there is no criterion of behaviour for a murderer. There are calm murderers and excited murderers.

'After lunch she goes down again to the Battery. She discovers her husband dead and does, shall we say, the obviously expected things. She registers emotion and she sends the governess to telephone for a doctor. We now come to a fact which has previously not been known.' He looked at Miss Williams. 'You do not object?'

Miss Williams was rather pale. She said: 'I did not pledge you to secrecy.'

Quietly, but with telling effect, Poirot recounted what the governess had seen.

Elsa Dittisham moved her position. She stared at the drab little woman in the big chair. She said incredibly:

'You actually saw her do *that*?'

Philip Blake sprang up.

'But that settles it!' he shouted. 'That settles it once and for all.'

Hercule Poirot looked at him mildly. He said: 'Not necessarily.'

Angela Warren said sharply: 'I don't believe it.' There was a quick hostile glint in the glance she shot at the little governess.

Meredith Blake was pulling at his moustache, his face dismayed. Alone, Miss Williams remained undisturbed. She sat very upright and there was a spot of colour in each cheek.

She said: 'That is what I saw.'

Poirot said slowly: 'There is, of course, only your word for it . . .'

'There is only my word for it.' The indomitable grey eyes met his. 'I am not accustomed, M. Poirot, to having my word doubted.'

Hercule Poirot bowed his head. He said:

'I do not doubt your word, Miss Williams. What you saw took place exactly as you say it did – and because of what you saw I realized that Caroline Crale was not guilty – could not possibly be guilty.'

For the first time, that tall, anxious-faced young man, John Rattery, spoke. He said: 'I'd be interested to know *why* you say that, M. Poirot.'

Poirot turned to him.

'Certainly. I will tell you. What did Miss Williams see – she saw Caroline Crale very carefully and anxiously wiping off fingerprints and subsequently imposing her dead husband's fingerprints on the beer bottle. On the beer *bottle*, mark. But the coniine was in the glass – not in the bottle. The police found no traces of coniine in the bottle. There had never been any coniine in the bottle. *And Caroline Crale didn't know that.*

'She who is supposed to have poisoned her husband didn't know *how* he had been poisoned. She thought the poison was in the bottle.'

Meredith objected: 'But why –'

Poirot interrupted him in a flash.

'Yes – *why*? Why did Caroline Crale try so desperately to establish the theory of suicide? The answer is – must be – quite simple. Because she knew who *had* poisoned him and she was willing to do anything – endure anything – rather than let that person be suspected.

'There is not far to go now. Who could that person be? Would she have shielded Philip Blake? Or Meredith? Or Elsa Greer? Or Cecilia Williams? No, there is only one person whom she would be willing to protect at all costs.'

He paused: 'Miss Warren, if you have brought your sister's last letter with you, I should like to read it aloud.'

Angela Warren said: 'No.'

'But, Miss Warren –'

Angela got up. Her voice rang out, cold as steel.

'I realize very well what you are suggesting. You are saying, are you not, that I killed Amyas Crale and that my sister knew it. I deny that allegation utterly.'

Poirot said: 'The letter . . .'

'That letter was meant for my eyes alone.'

Poirot looked to where the two youngest people in the room stood together.

Carla Lemarchant said: 'Please, Aunt Angela, won't you do as M. Poirot asks?'

Angela Warren said bitterly: 'Really, Carla! Have you no sense of decency? She was your mother – you –'

Carla's voice rang out clear and fierce.

'Yes, she was my mother. That's why I've a right to ask you. I'm speaking for *her*. I *want* that letter read.'

Slowly, Angela Warren took out the letter from her bag and handed it to Poirot. She said bitterly:

'I wish I had never shown it to you.'

Turning away from them she stood looking out of the window.

As Hercule Poirot read aloud Caroline Crale's last letter, the shadows were deepening in the corners of the room. Carla had a sudden feeling of someone in the room, gathering shape, listening, breathing, waiting. She thought: '*She's* here – my mother's here. Caroline – Caroline Crale is *here* in this room!'

Hercule Poirot's voice ceased. He said:

'You will all agree, I think, that that is a very remarkable letter. A beautiful letter, too, but certainly remarkable. For there is one striking omission in it – it contains no protestation of innocence.'

Angela Warren said without turning her head: 'That was unnecessary.'

'Yes, Miss Warren, it was unnecessary. Caroline Crale had no need to tell her sister that she was innocent – because she thought her sister knew that fact already – knew it for the best of all reasons. All Caroline Crale was concerned about was to comfort and reassure and to avert the possibility of a confession from Angela. She reiterates again and again – *It's all right, darling, it's all right.*'

Angela Warren said: 'Can't you understand? She wanted me to be happy, that's all.'

'Yes, she wanted you to be happy, that is abundantly clear. It is her one preoccupation. She has a child, but it is not that child of whom she is thinking – that is to come later. No, it is her sister who occupies her mind to the exclusion of everything else. Her sister must be reassured, must be encouraged to live her life, to be happy and successful. And so that the burden of acceptance may not be too great, Caroline includes that one very significant phrase: "*One must pay one's debts.*"

'That one phrase explains everything. It refers explicitly to the burden that Caroline has carried for so many years ever since, in a fit of uncontrolled adolescent rage, she hurled a paperweight at her baby sister and injured that sister for life. Now, at last, she has the opportunity to pay the debt she owes. And if it is any consolation, I will say to you all that I earnestly believe that in the payment of that debt, Caroline Crale did achieve a peace and serenity greater than any she had ever known. Because of her belief that she was paying that debt, the ordeal of trial and condemnation could not touch her. It is a strange thing to say of a condemned murderess – but she had everything to make her happy. Yes, more than you imagine, as I will show you presently.

'See how, by this explanation, everything falls into its place where Caroline's own reactions are concerned. Look at the series of events from her point of view. To begin with, on the preceding evening, an event occurs which reminds her forcibly of her own undisciplined girlhood. Angela throws a *paperweight* at Amyas Crale. That, remember, is what she herself did many years ago. Angela shouts out that she wishes Amyas was dead. Then, on the next morning, Caroline comes into the little conservatory and finds Angela tampering with the beer. Remember Miss Williams's words: "Angela was there. She looked guilty . . ." Guilty of playing truant, was what Miss Williams meant, but to Caroline, Angela's guilty face, as she was caught unawares, would have a different meaning. Remember that on at least one occasion before Angela had put things in Amyas's drink. It was an idea which might readily occur to her.

'Caroline takes the bottle *that Angela gives her* and goes down with it to the Battery. And there she pours it out and gives it to Amyas, and he makes a face as he tosses it off and utters those significant words: "Everything tastes foul today."

'Caroline has no suspicions then – but after lunch she goes down to the Battery and finds her husband dead – and she has no doubt at all but that he has been poisoned. *She* had not done it? Who, then, has? And the whole thing comes over her with a rush – Angela's threats, Angela's face stooping over the beer and caught unawares – guilty – guilty – guilty. Why has the child done it? As a revenge on Amyas, perhaps not meaning to kill, just to make him ill or sick? Or has she done it for her, Caroline's sake? Has she realized and resented Amyas's desertion of her sister? Caroline remembers – oh, so well – her own undisciplined violent emotions at Angela's age. And only one thought springs to her mind. How can she protect Angela? Angela handled that bottle – Angela's fingerprints will be on it. She quickly wipes it and polishes it. If only everybody can be got to believe it is suicide. If Amyas's fingerprints are the only ones found. She tries to fit his dead fingers round the bottle – working desperately – listening for someone to come . . .

'Once take that assumption as true, and everything from then on fits in. Her anxiety about Angela all along, her insistence on getting her away, keeping her out of touch with what was going on. Her fear of Angela's being questioned unduly by the police. Finally, her overwhelming anxiety to get Angela out of England before the trial comes on. Because she is always terrified that Angela might break down and confess.'

CHAPTER 4

TRUTH

Slowly, Angela Warren swung round. Her eyes, hard and contemptuous, ranged over the faces turned towards her.

She said:

'You're blind fools – all of you. Don't you know that if I had done it I *would* have confessed! I'd never have let Caroline suffer for what I'd done. Never!'

Poirot said:

'But you did tamper with the beer.'

'I? Tamper with the beer?'

Poirot turned to Meredith Blake.

'Listen, monsieur. In your account here of what happened, you describe having heard sounds in this room, which is below your bedroom, on the morning of the crime.'

Blake nodded.

'But it was only a cat.'

'How do you know it was a cat?'

'I – I can't remember. But it was a cat. I am quite sure it was a cat. The window was open just wide enough for a cat to get through.'

'But it was not fixed in that position. The sash moves freely. It could have been pushed up and a human being could have got in and out.'

'Yes, but I know it was a cat.'

'You did not *see* a cat?'

Blake said perplexedly and slowly:

'No, I did not see it –' He paused, frowning. 'And yet I know.'

'I will tell you *why* you know presently. In the meantime I put this point to you. Someone could have come up to the house that morning, have got into your laboratory, taken something from the shelf and gone again without your seeing them. Now if that someone had come over from Alderbury it could not have been Philip Blake, nor Elsa Greer, nor Amyas Crale nor Caroline Crale. We know quite well what all those four were doing. That leaves Angela Warren and Miss Williams. Miss Williams was over here – you actually met her as you went out. She told you then that she was looking for Angela. Angela had gone bathing early, but Miss Williams did not see her in the water, nor anywhere on the rocks. She could swim across to this side easily – in fact she did so later in the morning when she was bathing with Philip Blake. I suggest that she swam across here, came up to the house, got in through the window, and took something from the shelf.'

Angela Warren said: 'I did nothing of the kind – not – at least –'

'Ah!' Poirot gave a yelp of triumph. '*You have remembered.* You told me, did you not, that to play a malicious joke on Amyas Crale you pinched some of what you called "the cat stuff" – that is how you put it –'

Meredith Blake said sharply:

'Valerian! Of course.'

'Exactly. *That* is what made you sure in your mind that it was a cat who had been in the room. Your nose is very sensitive. You smelled the faint, unpleasant odour of valerian without knowing, perhaps, that you did so – but it suggested to your subconscious mind "Cat". Cats love valerian and will go anywhere for it. Valerian is particularly nasty to taste, and it was your account of it the day before which made mischievous Miss Angela plan to put some in her brother-in-law's beer, which she knew he always tossed down his throat in a draught.'

Angela Warren said wonderingly: 'Was it really that day? I remember taking it perfectly. Yes, and I remember getting out the beer and Caroline coming in and nearly catching me! Of course I remember . . . But I've never connected it with that particular day.'

'Of course not – because there was no connection *in your mind.* The two events were entirely dissimilar to you. One was on a par with other mischievous pranks – the other was a bombshell of tragedy arriving without warning and succeeding in banishing all lesser incidents from your mind. But me, I noticed when you spoke of it that you said: "I pinched, etc., etc., *to put it* in Amyas's drink." You did not say you had actually *done* so.'

'No, because I never did. Caroline came in just when I was unscrewing the bottle. Oh!' It was a cry. 'And Caroline thought – she thought it was *me* –!'

She stopped. She looked round. She said quietly in her usual cool tones: 'I suppose you all think so, too.'

She paused and then said: '*I didn't kill Amyas.* Not as the result of a malicious joke nor in any other way. If I had I would never have kept silence.'

Miss Williams said sharply:

'Of course you wouldn't, my dear.' She looked at Hercule Poirot. 'Nobody but a *fool* would think so.'

Hercule Poirot said mildly:

'I am not a fool and I do not think so. *I know quite well who killed Amyas Crale.*'

He paused.

'There is always a danger of accepting facts as proved which are really nothing of the kind. Let us take the situation at Alderbury. A very old situation. Two women and one man. We have taken it for granted that Amyas Crale proposed to leave his wife for the other woman. But I suggest to you now *that he never intended to do anything of the kind.*

'He had had infatuations for women before. They obsessed him while they lasted, but they were soon over. The women he had fallen in love with were usually women of a certain experience – they did not expect too much of him. But this time the woman did. She was not, you see, a woman at all. She was a girl, and in Caroline Crale's words, she was terribly sincere . . . She may have been hard-boiled and sophisticated in speech, but in love she was frighteningly single-minded. *Because* she herself had a deep and overmastering passion for Amyas Crale she assumed that he had the same for her. She assumed without any question that their passion was for life. She assumed without asking him that he was going to leave his wife.

'But why, you will say, did Amyas Crale not undeceive her? And my answer is – the picture. He wanted to finish his picture.

'To some people that sounds incredible – but not to anybody who knows about artists. And we have already accepted that explanation in principle. That conversation between Crale and Meredith Blake is more intelligible now. Crale is embarrassed – pats Blake on the back, assures him optimistically the whole thing is going to pan out all right. To Amyas Crale, you see, everything is simple. He is painting a picture, slightly encumbered by what he describes as a couple of jealous, neurotic women – but neither of them is going to be allowed to interfere with what to him is the most important thing in life.

'If he were to tell Elsa the truth it would be all up with the picture. Perhaps in the first flush of his feelings for her he did talk about leaving Caroline. Men do say these things when they are in love. Perhaps he merely let it be assumed, as he is letting it be assumed now. He doesn't care what Elsa assumes. Let her think what she likes. Anything to keep her quiet for another day or two.

'Then – he will tell her the truth – that things between them are over. He has never been a man to be troubled with scruples.

'He did, I think, make an effort not to get embroiled with Elsa to begin with. He warned her what kind of a man he was – but she would not take warning. She rushed on her Fate. And to a man like Crale women were fair game. If you had asked him he would have said easily that Elsa was young – she'd soon get over it. That was the way Amyas Crale's mind worked.

'His wife was actually the only person he cared about at all. He wasn't worrying much about her. She'd only got to put up with things for a few days longer. He was furious with Elsa for blurting out things to Caroline, but he still optimistically thought it would be "all right". Caroline would forgive him as she had done so often before, and Elsa – Elsa would just have to "lump it". So simple are the problems of life to a man like Amyas Crale.

'But I think that that last evening he became really worried. About Caroline, not about Elsa. Perhaps he went to her room and she refused to speak with him. At any rate, after a restless night, he took her aside after breakfast and blurted out the truth. He had been infatuated with Elsa, but it was all over. Once he'd finished the picture he'd never see her again.

'And it was in answer to that that Caroline Crale cried out indignantly: "You and your women!" That phrase, you see, put Elsa in a class with others – those others who had gone their way. And she added indignantly: "Some day I'll kill you."

'She was angry, revolted by his callousness and by his cruelty to the girl. When Philip Blake saw her in the hall and heard her murmur to herself, "It's too cruel!" it was of Elsa she was thinking.

'As for Crale, he came out of the library, found Elsa with Philip Blake, and brusquely ordered her down to go on with the sitting. What he did not know was that Elsa Greer had been sitting just outside the library window and had overheard everything. And the account she gave later of that conversation was not the true one. There is only her word for it, remember.

'Imagine the shock it must have been to her to hear the truth, brutally spoken!

'On the previous afternoon Meredith Blake has told us that whilst he was waiting for Caroline to leave this room he was standing in the doorway with his back to the room. He was talking to Elsa Greer. That means that she would have been *facing* him and that *she* could see exactly what Caroline was doing over his shoulder – and that she *was the only person who could do so.*

'She saw Caroline take that poison. She said nothing, but she remembered it as she sat outside the library window.

'When Amyas Crale came out she made the excuse of wanting a pullover, and went up to Caroline Crale's room to look for that poison. Women know where other women are likely to hide things. She found it, and being careful not to obliterate any fingerprints or to leave her own, she drew off the fluid into a fountain-pen filler.

'Then she came down again and went off with Crale to the Battery garden. And presently, no doubt, she poured him out some beer and he tossed it down in his usual way.

'Meanwhile, Caroline Crale was seriously disturbed. When she saw Elsa come up to the house (this time really to fetch a pullover), Caroline slipped quickly down to the Battery garden and tackled her husband. What he is doing is shameful! She won't stand for it! It's unbelievably cruel and hard on the girl! Amyas, irritable at being interrupted, says it's all settled – when the picture is done he'll send the girl packing! "*It's all settled – I'll send her packing. I tell you.*"

'And then they hear the footsteps of the two Blakes, and Caroline comes out and, slightly embarrassed, murmurs something about Angela and school and having a lot to do, and by a natural association of ideas the two men judge the conversation they have overheard refers to *Angela*, and "I'll send her packing" becomes "I'll see to her packing."

'And Elsa, pullover in hand, comes down the path, cool and smiling, and takes up the pose once more.

'She has counted, no doubt, upon Caroline's being suspected and the coniine bottle being found in her room. But Caroline now plays into her hands completely. She brings down some iced beer and pours it out for her husband.

'Amyas tosses it off, making a face and says: "Everything tastes foul today."

'Do you not see how significant that remark is? *Everything* tastes foul? Then there has been something else *before* that beer that has tasted unpleasant and the taste of which is *still in his mouth*. And one other point. Philip Blake speaks of Crale's staggering a little and wonders "if he has been drinking." But that slight stagger was the *first sign of the coniine working*, and that means *that it had already been administered to him some time before Caroline brought him the iced bottle of beer.*

'And so Elsa Greer sat on the grey wall and posed and, since she must keep him from suspecting until it was too late, she talked to Amyas Crale brightly and naturally. Presently she saw Meredith on the bench above and waved her hand to him and acted her part even more thoroughly for his behalf.

'And Amyas Crale, a man who detested illness and refused to give in to it, painted doggedly on till his limbs failed and his speech thickened, and he sprawled there on that bench, helpless, but with his mind still clear.

'The bell sounded from the house and Meredith left the bench to come down to the Battery. I think in that brief moment Elsa left her place and ran across to the table and dropped the last few drops of the poison into the beer glass that held that last innocent drink. (She got rid of the dropper on the path up to the house – crushing it to powder.) Then she met Meredith in the doorway.

'There is a glare there coming in out of the shadows. Meredith did not see very clearly – only his friend sprawled in a familiar position and saw his eyes turn from the picture in what he described as a malevolent glare.

'How much did Amyas know or guess? How much his conscious mind knew we cannot tell, but his hand and his eye were faithful.'

Hercule Poirot gestured towards the picture on the wall.

'I should have known when I first saw that picture. For it is a very remarkable picture. It is the picture of a murderess painted by her victim – it is the picture of a girl watching her lover die . . .'

CHAPTER 5

AFTERMATH

In the silence that followed – a horrified, appalled silence, the sunset slowly flickered away, the last gleam left the window where it had rested on the dark head and pale furs of the woman sitting there.

Elsa Dittisham moved and spoke. She said:

'Take them away, Meredith. Leave me with M. Poirot.'

She sat there motionless until the door shut behind them. Then she said: 'You are very clever, aren't you?'

Poirot did not answer.

She said: 'What do you expect me to do? Confess?'

He shook his head.

Elsa said:

'Because I shall do nothing of the kind! And I shall admit nothing. But what we say here, together, does not matter. Because it is only a question of your word against mine.'

'Exactly.'

'I want to know what you are going to do?'

Hercule Poirot said:

'I shall do everything I can to induce the authorities to grant a posthumous free pardon to Caroline Crale.'

Elsa laughed. She said: 'How absurd! To be given a free pardon for something you didn't do.' Then she said: 'What about me?'

'I shall lay my conclusion before the necessary people. If they decide there is the possibility of making out a case against you then they may act. I will tell you in my opinion there is not sufficient evidence – there are only inferences, not facts. Moreover, they will not be anxious to proceed against any one in your position unless there is ample justification for such a course.'

Elsa said:

'I shouldn't care. If I were standing in the dock, fighting for my life – there might be something in that – something alive – exciting. I might – enjoy it.'

'Your husband would not.'

She stared at him.

'Do you think I care in the least what my husband would feel?'

'No, I do not. I do not think you have ever in your life cared about what any other person would feel. If you had, you might be happier.'

She said sharply:

'Why are you sorry for me?'

'Because, my child, you have so much to learn.'

'What have I got to learn?'

'All the grown-up emotions – pity, sympathy, understanding. The only things you know – have ever known – are love and hate.'

Elsa said:

'I saw Caroline take the coniine. I thought she meant to kill herself. That would have simplified things. And then, the next morning, I found out. He told her that he didn't care a button about me – he *had* cared, but it was all over. Once he'd finished the picture he'd send me packing. She'd nothing to worry about, he said.

'And she – was sorry for me . . . Do you understand what that did to me? I found the stuff and I gave it to him and I sat there watching him die. I've never felt so alive, so exultant, so full of power. I watched him die . . .'

She flung out her hands.

'I didn't understand that I was killing *myself* – not him. Afterwards I saw her caught in a trap – and that was no good either. I couldn't hurt her – she didn't care – she escaped from it all – half the time she wasn't there. She and Amyas both escaped – they went somewhere where I couldn't get at them. But they didn't die. *I* died.'

Elsa Dittisham got up. She went across to the door. She said again:

'*I died . . .*'

In the hall she passed two young people whose life together was just beginning.

The chauffeur held open the door of the car. Lady Dittisham got in and the chauffeur wrapped the fur rug round her knees.